Sigrid Undset (1882–1949) was the daughter of a well-known Norwegian archaeologist, whose death when she was only eleven years old so reduced the family circumstances that her education was curtailed. When she was sixteen, she went to work in an office. The experience thus gained was to provide her with the material for her first novels. In 1920–22, after a somewhat unproductive period during the First World War, she produced her masterpiece, the historical trilogy *Kristin Lavransdatter*. She received the Nobel Prize in 1948.

Sigrid Undset's combination of historical grasp and vividness of style makes her work uniquely attractive and impressive. She and Knut Hamsun are the two great Norwegian novelists of this century.

Sigrid Undset

KRISTIN LAVRANSDATTER

Translated from the Norwegian by
Charles Archer and J. S. Scott

published by Pan Books

The title of this volume is
the same as that of the Norwegian original;
but the original titles of the three books of
which it is composed were:

I *Kransen* (THE GARLAND)
II *Husfrue* (THE MISTRESS OF HUSABY)
III *Korset* (THE CROSS)

This translation first published in Great Britain
1930 by Cassell & Company, Limited
This Picador edition published 1977 by Pan Books Ltd,
Cavaye Place, London sw10 9pg
2nd printing 1980
© The literary Estate of the late Sigrid Undset 1969
ISBN 0 330 25202 X
Printed and bound in Great Britain by
Richard Clay (The Chaucer Press) Ltd, Bungay, Suffolk

TRANSLATORS' FOREWORD

F o r the comfort of those readers of this volume who like to know, approximately, how the names of new acquaintance, whether places or people, are pronounced, it may be well to say that in Norwegian *aa* = broad *o*, while the rest of the vowels, including final *e*, may for practical purposes be sounded much as in German; that *j* always = *y*, and that final *d* is usually silent. Thus Jörundgaard = Yörungoar, Arne = Arnë, Aashild = Oas-hil.

Oslo was the ancient city occupying the eastern portion of the site of the modern capital; Nidaros the old northern capital, now called Trondhjem, the modern name having originally been that of the surrounding district (Trondheim in this book).

The main route from Oslo to Nidaros ran past the great lake, Mjösen, and up Gudbrandsdal to Dovre Church; proceeding thence either (1) down Romsdal to Næs on the Romsdalsfjord, and thence by sea to Nidaros, or (2) over the Dovrefjeld and down Opdal and Suldal.

A few notes have been appended in explanation of words or passages in the text, which seem to require elucidation to make them fully intelligible to English readers.

The plates attached show (1) plans of a typical manor farm of the period, and of the "aarestue" or "hearth-room house," which was the usual form of dwelling-house before wall fireplaces were introduced; and (2) a sketch of a typical "stavkirke" or "stave-church."

At the period of this book, and, indeed, for long after it, surnames were little used in Norway; men and women being called by their Christian names, with the addition of a patronymic formed by adding the suffix "sön" (son), or "datter" (daughter) to the father's Christian name; *e.g.* Simon Andressön (Simon Andrew's son), Kristin Lavransdatter (= Kristin Laurence's daughter). Rudimentary surnames, however, had already begun to appear. Thus the heroine's mother, though always spoken of as Ragnfrid Ivarsdatter, belongs to a family known as the Gjeslings; while Simon Andressön is sometimes called Darre, from the nickname given to the founder of his family several generations back.

CONTENTS

THE GARLAND

THE MISTRESS OF HUSABY

THE CROSS

THE GARLAND

Part One
JÖRUNDGAARD

W H E N the lands and goods of Ivar Gjesling the younger, of Sundbu, were divided after his death in 1306, his lands in Sil of Gudbrandsdal fell to his daughter Ragnfrid and her husband Lavrans Björgulfsön. Up to then they had lived on Lavrans' manor of Skog at Follo, near Oslo; but now they moved up to Jörundgaard * at the top of the open lands of Sil.

Lavrans was of the stock that was known in this country as the Lagmandssons. It had come here from Sweden with that Laurentius, Lagmand † of East Gothland, who took the Belbo Jarl's sister, the Lady Bengta, out of Vreta convent, and carried her off to Norway. Sir Laurentius lived at the Court of King Haakon ‡ the Old, and won great favour with the King, who gave him the Skog manor. But when he had been in this country about eight years he died in his bed, and his widow, who belonged to the Folkunga kindred, and had the name of a King's daughter among the Norwegians, went home and made matters up with her relations. Afterwards she made a rich marriage in another land. She and Sir Laurentius had no children, so the heritage of Skog fell to Laurentius' brother, Ketil. He was father's father to Lavrans Björgulfsön.

Lavrans was married very young; he was three years younger than his wife, and was only twenty-eight when he came to Sil. As a youth he had been in the King's bodyguard, and had enjoyed a good up-bringing; but after his marriage he lived a quiet life on his estate, for Ragnfrid was something strange and heavy of mood, and seemed not at home among the people of the south. After she had had the ill-hap to lose three little sons, one after the other, in the cradle, she grew yet more shy of people. Thus it was in part to bring his wife nearer to her kinsfolk and old acquaintance that Lavrans moved to Gud-brandsdalen. When they came there, they brought with them the one child that was left, a little maid called Kristin.

But when they had settled at Jörundgaard they lived for the most part just as quietly there, keeping very much to themselves; it seemed as though Ragnfrid did not care much for her kindred, for she saw them no oftener than seemly use and wont required. This was in part because Lavrans and Ragnfrid were more than commonly pious and God-fearing folk, diligent in churchgoing, and always pleased to give harbour to God's servants, to messengers sent on the Church's errands, or to pilgrims on their way up the valley to Nidaros; and showing the

* Jörundgaard, see Note 2.   † Lagmand, see Note 3.
‡ King Haakon, see Note 4.

greatest honour to their parish priest—who was also their nearest neighbour, living at Romundgaard. Other folk in the valley were rather given to think that the Church cost them quite dear enough in tithes and in goods and money; and that there was no need to fast and pray so hard besides, or to bring priests and monks into their houses, unless at times when they were really needed.

Otherwise the Jörundgaard folk were much looked up to, and well-liked too; most of all Lavrans, for he was known as a strong man and a bold, but peace-loving, quiet and upright, plain in his living, but courteous and seemly in his ways, a rarely good husbandman and a mighty hunter—'twas wolves and bears and all kinds of harmful beasts he hunted most keenly. In a few years he had bought much land into his hands; but he was a good and helpful landlord to his tenants.

Folk saw so little of Ragnfrid that they soon gave up talking much about her. In the first time after she came back to the valley many people had wondered, for they remembered her as she had been at her home at Sundbu in her youth. Beautiful she had never been, but she had looked kind and happy; now she had fallen off so that you might well believe she was ten years older than her husband, and not only three. Most folk deemed she took the loss of her children harder than was reason, for but for this she was better off in every way than most wives—she lived in great plenty and in high esteem, and things were well between her and her husband, so far as people could see; Lavrans did not go after other women, he took counsel with her in all affairs, and, sober or drunk, he never said a harsh word to her. Besides she was not so old but she might yet bear many children, if it were God's pleasure.

It was somewhat hard for them to get young folks to take service at Jörundgaard, the mistress being thus heavy of mood and all the fasts so strictly kept. Otherwise it was a good house to serve in; hard words and punishments were little in use; and both Lavrans and Ragnfrid took the lead in all the work. The master, indeed, was glad of mood in his own way, and would join in a dance or lead the singing when the young folk held their games on the church-green on vigil nights. But still it was mostly older folks who came and took service at Jörundgaard; these like the place well, and stayed there long.

When the child Kristin was seven years old, it so fell out one time that she got leave to go with her father up to their mountain sæter.

It was a fine morning, a little way on in the summer. Kristin was in the loft-room, where they were sleeping now summer had come; she saw the sun shining outside and heard her father and his men talking in the courtyard below, and she was so joyful that she could not stand still while her mother put on her clothes, but hopped and jumped about as each piece of clothing was put on her. She had never been up in the mountains before; only across the pass to Vaage, when she was taken to visit her mother's kinsfolk at Sundbu, and sometimes to the woods near by the manor with her mother and the housefolk, when they went out to pluck berries for Ragnfrid to mix with the small beer, or to make into the sour paste of cranberries and cowberries that she ate on her bread in Lent instead of butter.

The mother twisted up Kristin's long yellow hair and tied it into her old blue cap, then kissed her daughter on the cheek, and Kristin sprang away and down to her father. Lavrans was in the saddle already; he lifted her up behind him and seated her on his cloak, which he had folded up and placed on the horse's loins for a pillion. Kristin had to sit there astride and hold on to his belt. They called out "Good-bye" to Ragnfrid; but she came running down from the balcony with Kristin's hooded cape—she handed it to Lavrans and bade him look well to the child.

The sun shone, but it had rained much in the night, so that everywhere the becks came rushing and singing down the grassy slopes, and wreaths of mist clung and drifted under the mountain-sides. But over the hill-crest white fair-weather clouds were swelling up in the blue air, and Lavrans and his men said among themselves that it was like to be hot as the day went on. Lavrans had four men with him, and they were all well armed; for at this time there were many kinds of outlandish people lying up among the mountains—though a strong party like this, going but a short way, was not like to see or hear aught of such folk. Kristin was fond of all the men; three of them were men past youth, but the fourth, Arne Gyrdsön, from Finsbrekken, was a half-grown boy, and he was Kristin's best friend; he rode next after Lavrans and her, for it was he that was to tell her about all they saw on their road.

They passed between the Romundgaard houses, and changed greetings with Eirik priest.* He was standing outside, and chiding his daughter—she kept house for him—about a web of new-dyed cloth that she had hung out and forgotten the day before; it was all spoilt now with the night's rain.

On the hill behind the parsonage lay the church; it was not large, but fair and pleasant, well kept and newly tarred. By the cross outside the churchyard gate Lavrans and his men took off their hats and bowed their heads; then the father turned in the saddle, and he and Kristin waved to Ragnfrid, whom they could see down below at home standing out on the sward by the houses; she waved back to them with the fall of her linen headdress.

* Priests, see Note 5.

Up here on the church-green and in the churchyard Kristin was used to come and play near every day, but to-day, when she was setting out to go so far, the sight she knew so well—home and all the parish round it—seemed new and strange to the child. The clusters of houses at Jörundgaard looked, as it were, smaller and greyer, lying there down on the flats, courtyard and farmyard. The river wound shining on its way, the valley spread far with broad green meadows and marshes in its bottom, and farms with ploughland and pasture stretched up the hillsides under the grey and headlong mountain walls.

Far below, where the mountains came together and closed the valley, Kristin knew that Loptsgaard lay. There lived Sigurd and Jon, two old men with white beards; they were always for playing and making merry with her when they came to Jörundgaard. She was fond of Jon, for he would carve out the fairest beasts in wood for her, and once she had had a gold finger-ring of him; nay, the last time he came to them, at Whitsuntide, he had brought her a knight so sweetly carved and coloured so fairly that Kristin thought she had never had so fine a gift. She must needs take the knight to bed with her every single night; but when she woke in the morning he was always standing on the step in front of the bed she lay in with her father and mother. Her father said the knight jumped up at the first cockcrow; but Kristin knew well enough that, after she had fallen asleep, her mother took him away, for she had heard her say that he was so hard, and hurt so if he got underneath them in the night. Sigurd of Loptsgaard Kristin was afraid of, and she did not like him to take her on his knee; for he used to say that when she grew up he meant to sleep in her arms. He had outlived two wives, and he said himself he was sure to outlive the third, and then Kristin could be the fourth. But when she began to cry at this, Lavrans laughed and said he had no fear that Margit would give up the ghost so speedily; but if the worst came to pass and Sigurd should come a-wooing, let Kristin have no fear—he should have No for his answer.

A bowshot or so north of the church there lay by the roadside a great block of stone, and around it a thick, small grove of birch and aspen. Here the children were wont to play at church, and Tomas, the youngest son of Eirik priest's daughter, stood up in the person of his grandfather and said mass, sprinkled holy water, and even baptized, when there was rain-water in the hollows of the rock. But once, the autumn before, this game had fallen out but sadly for them. For first Tomas had married Kristin and Arne—Arne was not so old but he would go off and play with the children when he saw a chance. Then Arne caught a baby pig that was going by, and they brought it into church to be baptized. Tomas anointed it with mud, dipped it into a pool of water, and, copying his grandfather, said mass in Latin and chid them for the smallness of their offerings—and at this the children laughed, for they had heard their elders talk of Eirik's exceeding greed of money. But the more they laughed the worse Tomas got in the things he hit on: for next he said that this child had been gotten in Lent, and they must pay penalty for their sin to the priest and the Church. The great boys shouted with laughter at this; but Kristin was so ashamed that she was all but weeping, as she stood there with the little pig in her arms. And just as this was going on who must chance to come that way but Eirik himself, riding home from a sick visit. When he understood what the young folks were about, he sprang from his horse, and handed the holy vessels to Bentein, his eldest grandson, who was with him, so suddenly that Bentein nearly dropped the silver dove with God's body in it on the hillside, while the priest rushed in among the children belabouring all he could reach. Kristin let slip the little pig, and it rushed shrieking down the road with the christening robe trailing after it, while Eirik's horses reared and plunged with terror; the priest pushed her, too, so that she fell down, and he knocked against her with his foot so hard that she felt the pain in her hip for many days after. Lavrans had thought when he heard of this that Eirik had been too hard with Kristin, seeing she was but a little child. He said he would speak to the priest of it, but Ragnfrid begged him not to do so, for the child had gotten but what she deserved, for joining in such a blasphemous game. So Lavrans said no more of the matter; but he gave Arne the worst beating the boy had ever had.

So now, as they rode by the stone, Arne plucked Kristin by the sleeve. He dared not say aught for fear of Lavrans, but he made a face, then smiled and clapped his hand to his back. But Kristin bowed her head shamefacedly.

Their way led on into thick woods. They rode along under Hammer-hill; the valley grew narrow and dark here, and the roar of the river sounded louder and more harsh—when they caught a glimpse of the Laagen it ran ice-green and white with foam between walls of rock. The mountains on either side of the valley were black with forest; it was dark and narrow and ugly in the gorge, and there came cold gusts of wind. They rode across the Rostaa stream by the log-bridge, and soon could see the bridge over the great river down in the valley. A little below the bridge was a pool where a kelpie lived. Arne began to tell Kristin about it, but Lavrans sternly told the boy to hold his peace in the woods about such things. And when they came to the bridge he leaped off his horse and led it across by the bridle, while he held the child round the waist with his other arm.

On the other side of the river was a bridle-path leading steeply up the hillside, so the men got off their horses and went on foot; but her father lifted Kristin forward into the saddle, so that she could hold on to the saddle-bow, and let her ride Guldsveinen all alone.

New greystone peaks and blue domes flecked with snow rose above the mountain ridges as they climbed higher up; and now Kristin saw through the trees glimpses of the parish north of the gorge, and Arne pointed and told her the names of the farms that they could make out down there.

High up the mountain-side they came to a little croft. They stopped by the stick fence; Lavrans shouted, and his voice came back again and again from the mountains round. Two men came running down, between the small tilled patches. These were both sons of the house; they were good men at the tar-burning, and Lavrans was for hiring them to burn some tar for him. Their mother came after them with a great bowl of cooled milk, for the day was now grown hot, as the men had foretold.

"I saw you had your daughter with you," she said, when she had greeted them, "and methought I must needs have a sight of her. But you must take the cap from her head; they say she hath such bonny hair."

Lavrans did as the woman asked him, and Kristin's hair fell over her shoulders and hung down right to the saddle. It was thick and yellow like ripe wheat. The woman, Isrid, took some of it in her hand, and said:

"Ay, now I see the word that has gone about concerning this little maid of yours was nowise too great—a lily-rose she is, and looks as should the child of a knightly man. Mild eyes hath she too—she favours you and not the Gjeslings. God grant you joy of her, Lavrans Björgulfsön! And you're riding on Guldsveinen, as stiff and straight as a courtier," she said laughingly, as she held the bowl for Kristin to drink.

The child grew red with pleasure, for she knew well that her father was held to be the comeliest man far around; he looked like a knight, standing there among his men, though his dress was much of the farmer fashion, such as he wore at home for daily use. He wore a coat of green-dyed wadmal, somewhat wide and short, open at the throat, so that the shirt showed beneath. For the rest, his hose and shoes were of undyed leather, and on his head he had a broad-brimmed woollen hat of the ancient fashion. For ornaments he had only a smooth silver buckle to his belt, and a little silver brooch in his shirt-band; but some links of a golden neck-chain showed against his neck. Lavrans always wore this chain, and on it there hung a golden cross set with great rock-crystals; it was made to open, and inside there were shreds of the hair and the shroud of the holy Lady Elin of Skövde, for the Lagmandssons counted their descent from one of that blessed lady's daughters. But when Lavrans was in the woods or out at his work he was used to thrust the cross in next his bare breast, so that he might not lose it.

Yet did he look in his coarse homely clothing more high-born than many a knight of the King's household in his finest banqueting attire. He was stalwart of growth, tall, broad-shouldered, and small waisted; his head was small and sat fairly on his neck, and he had comely features, somewhat long—cheeks of a seemly fullness, chin fairly rounded and mouth well shaped. His skin was light and his face fresh of hue; he had grey eyes and thick, smooth, silky-yellow hair.

He stood there and talked with Isrid of her affairs; and asked about Tordis too, a kinswoman of Isrid's that was tending the Jörundgaard sæter this summer. Tordis had just had a child; Isrid was only waiting for the chance of a safe escort through the woods before taking the boy down to have him christened. Lavrans said that she had best come with them up to the sæter; he was coming down again the next evening, and 'twould be safer and better for her to have many men to go along with her and the heathen child.

Isrid thanked him. "To say truth, 'twas even this I was waiting for. We know well, we poor folk under the uplands here, that you will ever do us a kind turn if you can, when you come hither." She ran up to the hut to fetch a bundle and a cloak.

It was indeed so that Lavrans liked well to come among these small folk who lived on clearings and leaseholdings high up on the outskirts of the parish; amongst them he was always glad and merry. He talked with them of the ways of the forest beasts and the reindeer of the upland wastes, and of all the uncanny things that are stirring in such places. And he stood by them and helped them with word and deed; saw to their sick cattle, helped them with their errands to the smith or to the carpenter; nay, would sometimes take hold himself and bend his great strength to the work, when the worst stones or roots were to be broken out of the earth. Therefore were these people ever glad to greet Lavrans Björgulfsön and Guldsveinen, the great red stallion that he rode upon. 'Twas a comely beast with a shining skin, white mane and tail and light eyes—strong and fiery, so that his fame was spread through all the country round; but with his master he was gentle as a lamb, and Lavrans used to say that the horse was dear to him as a younger brother.

Lavrans' first errand was to see to the beacon on Heimhaugen. For in the hard and troubled times a hundred years or more gone by, the yeoman of the dales had built beacons here and there high up on the fells above them, like the seamarks in the roadsteads upon the coast. But these beacons in the uplands were not in the ward of the King's levies, but were cared for by the yeoman guilds,* and the guild brothers took turns at their tending.

When they were come to the first sæter, Lavrans turned out all but the pack-horse to graze there; and now they took a steep footpath upwards. Before long the trees grew thin and scattered. Great firs stood dead and white as bones upon the marshy grounds—and now Kristin saw bare greystone peaks rising to the sky on all hands. They climbed long stretches amid loose stones, and at times the becks ran in the track, so that her father must carry her. The wind blew strong and fresh up here, and the ground was black with berries amidst the heather, but Lavrans said they could not stop now to gather them. Arne sprang now in front and now behind, plucked berries for her, and told her whose the sæters were that they saw below them in the forest—for there was forest over the whole of Hövringsvangen in those days.

And now they were close below the highest round bare top and saw the great pile of timber against the sky, with the watch-house under the lee of a crag.

As they came up over the brow the wind rushed against them and buffeted their clothing—it seemed to Kristin as though something living, that dwelt up here, met and greeted them. It blew gustily around her and Arne as they went forward over the mosses, till they sat them down far out on a jutting point, and Kristin gazed with great eyes—never before had she dreamed that the world was so big and wide.

Forest-shagged ranges lay below her on all sides; the valley was but a cleft betwixt the huge fells, and the side-glens still lesser clefts; there were many such, yet was there little of dale and much of fell. All around grey peaks, flaming with golden lichen, rose above the sea of forest, and far off, on the very brink of heaven, stood blue crests flashing here and there with snow, and melting, before their eyes, into the grey-blue and pure white summer-clouds. But north-eastwards, nearer by—just beyond the sæter woods—lay a cluster of mighty slate-coloured domes with streaks of new-fallen snow down their slopes. These Kristin guessed to be the Boar Fells she had heard tell of, for they were indeed like naught but a herd of heavy boar wending inland that had just turned their backs upon the parish. Yet Arne told her 'twas a half-day's ride to get even so far.

Kristin had ever thought that could she but win over the top of the home-fells she would look down upon another parish like their own, with tilled farms and dwellings, and 'twas great wonder to her now to see how far it was betwixt the places where folks dwelt. She saw the small yellow and green flecks down below in the dale-bottom, and the tiny clearings with their grey dots of houses amid the hill forests; she

* Peasant Guilds, see Note 6.

began to take tale of them, but when she had reckoned three times twelve, she could keep count of them no longer. Yet the human dwelling-places were as nothing in that waste.

She knew that in the wild woods wolves and bears lorded it, and that under every stone there dwelt trolls and goblins and elfin-folk, and she was afraid, for no one knew the number of them, but there must be many times more of them than of Christian men and women. Then she called aloud on her father, but he could not hear for the blowing of the wind—he and his men were busy rolling heavy stones up the bare mountain-top to pile round the timbers of the beacon.

But Isrid came to the children and showed Kristin where the fell west of Vaage lay. And Arne pointed out the Grayfell, where folk from the parish took reindeer in pits, and where the King's falcon-catchers lay in stone huts. That was a trade Arne thought to take to some day—but if he did he would learn as well to train the birds for the chase—and he held his arms aloft as though to cast a hawk.

Isrid shook her head.

"'Tis a hard and evil life, that, Arne Gyrdsön. 'Twould be a heavy sorrow for your mother, boy, should you ever come to be a falcon-catcher. None may earn his bread in those wild hills except he join in fellowship with the worst of men—ay, and with them that are worse still."

Lavrans had come toward them and had heard this last word. "Ay," says he, "there's more than one hide of land in there that pays neither tax nor tithe——"

"Yes; many a thing must you have seen," said Isrid coaxingly, "you who fare so far afield——"

"Ay, ay," said Lavrans slowly. "Maybe—but methinks 'tis well not to speak of such things overmuch. One should not, I say, grudge folks who have lost their peace in the parish, whatever peace they can find among the fells. Yet have I seen yellow fields and brave meadows where few folk know that such things be; and herds have I seen of cattle and small stock, but of these I know not whether they belonged to mankind or to other folk——"

"Oh, ay!" says Isrid. "Bears and wolves get the blame for the beasts that are missed from the sæters here, but there are worse thieves among the fells than they."

"Do you call them worse?" asked Lavrans thoughtfully, stroking his daughter's cap. "In the hills to the south under the Boar Fells I once saw three little lads, and the greatest was even as Kristin here—yellow hair they had, and coats of skin. They gnashed their teeth at me like wolf-cubs before they ran to hide. 'Twere little wonder if the poor man who owned them were fain to lift a cow or two——"

"Oh, both wolves and bears have young!" says Isrid testily; "and you spare not them, Lavrans, neither them nor their young. Yet they have no lore of law nor of Christendom, as have these evil-doers you wish so well to——"

"Think you I wish them too well, because I wish them a little better than the worst?" said Lavrans, smiling a little. "But come now, let us see what cheer Ragnfrid has sent with us to-day." He took Kristin by the hand and led her with him. And as they went he bent and said softly, "I thought of your three small brothers, little Kristin."

They peeped into the watch-house, but it was close in there and smelt of mould. Kristin took a look around, but there were only some earthen benches about the walls, a hearth-stone in the middle of the floor, and some barrels of tar and faggots of pine-roots and birch-bark. Lavrans thought 'twould be best they should eat without doors, and a little way down among the birches they found a fine piece of green sward.

The pack-horse was unloaded, and they stretched themselves upon the grass. In the wallets Ragnfrid had given them was plenty food of the best—soft bread and bannocks, butter and cheese, pork and wind-dried reindeer meat, lard, boiled brisket of beef, two kegs with German beer, and of mead a little jar. The carving of the meat and portioning it round went quickly, while Halvdan, the oldest of the men, struck fire and made a blaze—it was safer to have a good fire out here in the woods.

Isrid and Arne gathered heather and dwarf-birch and cast it on the blaze. It crackled as the fire tore the fresh green from the twigs, and small white flakes flew high upon the wisps of red flame; the smoke whirled thick and black toward the clear sky. Kristin sat and watched; it seemed to her the fire was glad that it was out there, and free, and could play and frisk. 'Twas otherwise than when, at home, it sat upon the hearth and must work at cooking food and giving light to the folks in the room.

She sat nestled by her father with one arm upon his knee; he gave her all she would have of the best, and bade her drink her fill of the beer and taste well of the mead.

"She will be so tipsy she'll never get down to the sæter on her feet," said Halvdan, laughing; but Lavrans stroked her round cheeks:

"Then here are folk enough who can bear her—it will do her good— drink you too, Arne; God's gifts do good, not harm, to you that are yet growing—make sweet, red blood, and give deep sleep, and rouse not madness and folly——"

The men, too, drank often and deep; neither was Isrid backward. And soon their voices and the roar and crackle of the fire were but a far-off hubbub in Kristin's ears, and she began to grow heavy of head. She was still aware how they questioned Lavrans and would have him tell of the strange things he had met with when out a-hunting. But much he would not say; and this seemed to her so good and so safe—and then she had eaten so well.

Her father had a slice of soft barley-bread in his hand; he pinched small bits of it between his fingers into shapes of horses, and, cutting shreds of meat, he set these astride the steeds and made them ride over his thigh and into Kristin's mouth. But soon she was so weary she could neither open her mouth nor chew—and so she sank back upon the ground and slept.

When she came to herself again she was lying in a warm darkness within her father's arm—he had wrapped his cloak about them both. Kristin sat up, wiped the moisture from her face, and unloosed her cap that the air might dry her damp locks.

The day was surely far spent, for the sunlight was golden, and the shadows had lengthened and fell now toward the south-east. No breath of wind was stirring, and gnats and flies buzzed and swarmed about the group of sleeping men. Kristin sat stock still, scratched her gnat-bitten hands and gazed about her. The mountain-top above them shone white with moss and golden with lichen in the sunshine, and the pile of weather-beaten timber stood against the sky like the skeleton of some wondrous beast.

She grew ill at ease—it was so strange to see them all sleeping there in the naked daylight. At home if by hap she woke at night, she lay snug in the dark with her mother on the one side, and on the other the tapestry stretched upon the wall. And then she knew that the chamber with its smoke-vent was shut and barred against the night and the weather without, and sounds of slumber came from the folk who lay soft and safe on the pillows 'twixt the skins. But all these bodies, lying twisted and bent on the hillside, about the little heap of black and white ashes, might well be dead—some lay upon their faces, some upon their backs with knees updrawn, and the noises that came from them scared her. Her father snored deeply, but when Halvdan drew a breath, it piped and whistled in his nose. And Arne lay upon his side, his face hidden on his arm, and his glossy, light brown hair spread out amongst the heather; he lay so still Kristin grew afraid lest he be dead. She had to bend forward and touch him, and on this he turned a little in his sleep.

Kristin suddenly bethought her, maybe they had slept through the night and this was the next day—and this frightened her so that she shook her father; but he only grunted and slept on. Kristin herself was still heavy of head, but she dared not lie down to sleep again. And so she crept forward to the fire and raked in it with a stick—there were still some embers aglow beneath. She threw upon it heather and small twigs which she broke off round about her—she dared not pass the ring of sleepers to find bigger branches.

There came a rattling and crashing in the woods near by, and Kristin's heart sank and she went cold with fear. But then she spied a red shape amidst the trees, and Guldsveinen broke out of the thicket. He stood there and gazed upon her with his clear, bright eyes. She was so glad to see him, she leapt to her feet and ran to the stallion. And there, too, was the brown horse Arne had ridden, and the pack-horse as well. Now she felt safe and happy again; she went and patted them all three upon their flanks, but Guldsveinen bent his head so that she could reach up to fondle his cheeks, and pull his yellow-white forelock, while he nosed round her hands with his soft muzzle.

The horses wandered, feeding, down the birch-grown slope, and Kristin went with them—she felt there was naught to fear so long as she kept close to Guldsveinen—he had driven off a bear before now, she knew. And the bilberries grew so thick in here, and the child was thirsty now, with a bad taste in her mouth; the beer was not to her liking any more, but the sweet, juicy berries were good as wine. Away, on a scree, she saw raspberries growing too, so she grasped Guldsveinen by the mane, and sweetly bade him go there with her, and the stallion followed willingly with the little maid. Thus, as she wandered farther and farther down the hillside, he followed her when she called, and the other two horses followed Guldsveinen.

Somewhere near at hand she heard the gurgling and trickling of a beck; she followed the sound till she found it, and then lay out upon a great slab and washed her hot, gnat-bitten face and hands. Below the slab the water stood, a still, black pool, for over against it there rose a wall of rock behind some small birches and willows. It made the finest of mirrors, and Kristin leaned over and looked at herself in the water, for she wished to see whether 'twas true, as Isrid said, that she bore a likeness to her father.

She smiled and nodded and bent forward till her hair met the bright hair about the round, great-eyed child-face she saw in the beck.

Round about grew a great plenty of those gay, pink flower clusters they name valerian—redder far and finer here by the fell-beck than at home by the river. Of these Kristin plucked, and bound them about with grass, till she had woven herself the finest, thickest wreath of rose-pink. The child pressed it down on her head and ran to the pool to see how she looked now she was decked out like a grown maid who goes a-dancing.

She stooped over the water and saw her own dark image rise from the bottom and grow clearer as it came to meet her—and then in the mirror of the pool she saw another figure standing among the birches opposite and bending toward her. In haste she got upon her knees and gazed across. At first she thought it was but the rock and the bushes clinging round its foot. But all at once she was aware of a face amid the leaves—there stood a lady, pale, with waving, flaxen hair—the great, light-grey eyes and wide, pink nostrils were like Guldsveinen's. She was clad in something light, leaf-green, and branches and twigs hid her up to the broad breasts, which were covered over with brooches and sparkling chains.

The little girl gazed upon the figure, and as she gazed the lady raised a hand and showed her a wreath of golden flowers—she beckoned with it.

Behind her Kristin heard Guldsveinen neigh loud in fear. She turned her head—the stallion reared, screaming till the echoes rang, then flung around and fled up the hill with a thunder of hoofs. The other horses followed—straight up the scree, while stones came rumbling down and boughs and roots broke and rattled.

Then Kristin screamed aloud. "Father!" she shrieked, "father!" She gained her feet, tore after the horses and dared not look behind. She clambered up the scree, trod on the hem of her dress and slipped back downwards; climbed again, catching at the stones with bleeding hands, creeping on sore bruised knees, and crying now to Guldsveinen, now to her father—sweat started from every pore of her body and ran like water into her eyes, and her heart beat as though 'twould break against her ribs, while sobs of terror choked her throat:

"Oh, father! oh, father!"

Then his voice sounded somewhere above: she saw him come with great bounds down the scree—the bright, sunlit scree; birch and aspen stood along it and blinked from their small silvered leaves—the hillside was so quiet, so bright, while her father came leaping, calling her by name; and Kristin sank down and knew that now she was saved.

"Sancta Maria!" Lavrans knelt and clasped his daughter. He was pale and strange about the mouth, so that Kristin grew yet more afraid; 'twas as though only now in his face she read how great had been her peril.

"Child, child——" He lifted her bleeding hands, looked at them, saw the wreath upon her bare head, and touched it. "What is it—how came you hither, my little Kristin——?"

"I went with Guldsveinen," she sobbed upon his breast. "I got so afraid seeing you all asleep, but then Guldsveinen came, and then there was some one by the beck down yonder that beckoned me——"

"Who beckoned—was it a man?"

"No, 'twas a lady—she beckoned with a wreath of gold—I think 'twas the dwarf-maiden,* father——"

* Elf or dwarf-maiden, see Note 7.

"Jesus Kristus!" said Lavrans softly, and crossed himself and the child.

He helped her up the scree till they came to a grassy slope; then he lifted and bore her. She clung about his neck and sobbed—could not stop for all his soothing.

Soon they met the men and Isrid. The woman smote her hands together, when she heard what had befallen:

"Ay, 'twas the elf-maiden* sure enough—she would have lured the fair child into the mountain, trust you me."

"Hold your peace!" bade Lavrans sternly. "Never should we have talked of such things here in the woods as we did—one knows not what may lie beneath the rocks and hearken to each word."

He drew the golden chain from out his shirt and hung it and the relic-holding cross about Kristin's neck and thrust them in upon her bare body.

"But see to it, all of you," he said, "that you watch well your mouths, so Ragnfrid may never know the child has been in such peril."

Then they caught the three horses, which had made off into the woods, and went quickly down to the pasture where the other horses were grazing. There they all mounted and rode to the Jörundgaard sæter; it was no great way.

The sun was near setting when they came thither; the cattle were in the pens, and Tordis and the herds were busy at the milking. Within the hut porridge stood cooked awaiting them, for the sæter-folk had spied them by the beacon earlier in the day, and they were looked for.

Now, at length, was Kristin's weeping stilled. She sat upon her father's knee and ate porridge and cream from out the same spoon as he.

Lavrans was to go next day to a lake farther in the mountains, where lay some of his herdsmen with the bulls. Kristin was to have gone with him, but now he said she must stay in the hut while he was gone. "And you must take heed, both Tordis and Isrid, to keep the door barred and the smokehole closed till we come back, both for Kristin's sake and for the poor unchristened babe's here in the cradle."

Tordis was so frighted now that she dared no longer stay with the little one up here, for she was still unchurched since her lying-in—rather would she go down at once and bide in the parish. Lavrans said this seemed to him but wise; she could go down with them the next evening; he thought he could get an older widow woman, serving at Jörundgaard, up hither in her stead.

Tordis had spread sweet, fresh mountain grass under the skins on the benches; it smelt so strong and good, and Kristin was near asleep while her father said Our Father and Ave Maria over her.

* Elf or dwarf-maiden, see Note 7.

"Ay, 'twill be a long day before I take you with me to the fells again," said Lavrans, patting her cheek.

Kristin woke up with a start:

"Father, mayn't I go with you either when you go southwards at harvest, as you promised——"

"We must see about that," said Lavrans, and straightway Kristin fell asleep between the sheepskins.

II

E A C H summer it was Lavrans Björgulfsön's wont to ride southward and see to his manor in Follo. These journeys of her father were landmarks of each year in Kristin's life—the long weeks while he was gone, and the joy of his homecoming with brave gifts: fine outlandish stuffs for her bride-chest, figs, raisins and honey-bread from Oslo—and many strange things to tell her.

But this year Kristin marked that there was something more than common afoot toward the time of her father's going. 'Twas put off and off; the old men from Loptsgaard rode over at odd times and sat about the board with her father and mother; spoke of heritage, and freehold and redemption rights, and hindrances to working the estate from so far off, and the Bishop's seat and the King's palace in Oslo, which took so much labour from the farms round about the town. They scarce ever had time to play with her, and she was sent out to the kitchen-house to the maids. Her mother's brother, Trond Ivarsön, of Sundbu, came over to them more often than was his wont—but *he* had never been used to play with Kristin or pet her.

Little by little she came to have some inkling of what it was all about. Ever since he was come to Sil, Lavrans had sought to gather to himself land here in the parish, and now had Sir Andres Gudmundsön tendered him Formo in Sil, which was Sir Andres' heritage from his mother, in change for Skog, which lay more fittingly for him, since he was with the King's bodyguard and rarely came hither to the Dale. Lavrans was loth to part with Skog, which was his freehold heritage, and had come to his forbears by royal gift; and yet the bargain would be for his gain in many ways. But Lavrans' brother, Aasmund Björgulfsön, too, would gladly have Skog—he dwelt now in Hadeland, where he had wedded an estate—and 'twas not sure that Aasmund would waive the right his kinship gave him.

But one day Lavrans told Ragnfrid that this year he would have Kristin with him to Skog. She should see the manor where she was born, and which was his fathers' home, now that it was like to pass from their hands. Ragnfrid deemed this but right, though she feared not a little to send so young a child on such a long journey, where she herself could not be by.

For a time after Kristin had seen the elf-maid she was so fearful that she kept much within doors by her mother—she was afraid even when she saw the folk who had been with them on the fells and knew what had befallen her, and she was glad her father had forbidden all talk of that sight of hers.

But when some little time was gone by, she began to think she would like to speak of it. In her thoughts she told the story to some one—she knew not whom—and, 'twas strange, the more time went by, the better it seemed she remembered it, and the clearer and clearer grew the memory of the fair lady.

But, strangest of all, each time she thought of the elf-maid there came upon her such a longing for the journey to Skog, and more and more fear that her father would not take her with him.

At last she woke one morning in the loft-room and saw her mother and old Gunhild sitting on the threshold looking over a heap of Lavrans' squirrel-skins. Gunhild was a widow who went the round of the farms and sewed fur-lining into cloaks and the like. And Kristin guessed from their talk that now it was she should have a new cloak, lined with squirrel-skin and edged with marten. And then she knew she was to go with her father, and she sprang up in bed and shrieked with gladness.

Her mother came over to her and stroked her cheek:

"Are you so glad, then, my daughter, you are going so far from me?"

Ragnfrid said the same that morning they were to set out. They were up at cock-crow; it was dark without, with thick mist between the houses, as Kristin peeped out of the door at the weather. The mist billowed like grey smoke round the lanterns, and out by the open house-doors. Folk ran 'twixt stables and outhouses, and women came from the kitchen with steaming porridge-pots and trenchers of meat and pork— they were to have a plenty of good, strong food before they rode out into the morning cold.

Indoors, saddle-bags were shut and opened, and forgotten things packed inside. Ragnfrid called to her husband's mind all the errands he must do for her, and spoke of kin and friends upon the way—he must greet this one and not forget to ask for that one.

Kristin ran out and in; she said farewell many times to all in the house, and could not hold still a moment in any place.

"Are you so glad, then, Kristin, you are going from me so far and for so long?" asked her mother. Kristin was abashed and uneasy, and wished her mother had not said this. But she answered as best she could:

"No, dear my mother, but I am glad that I am to go with father."

"Ay, that you are indeed," said Ragnfrid, sighing. Then she kissed the child and put the last touches to her dress.

At last they were in the saddle, the whole train—Kristin rode on Morvin, who ere now had been her father's saddle-horse—he was old, wise and steady. Ragnfrid held up the silver stoup with the stirrup-cup to her husband, and laid a hand upon her daughter's knee and bade her bear in mind all her mother had taught her.

And so they rode out of the courtyard in the grey light. The fog lay white as milk upon the parish. But in a while it began to grow thinner and the sunlight sifted through. And, dripping with dew, there shone through the white haze hillsides green with the aftermath, and pale stubble fields, and yellow trees, and rowans bright with red berries. Glimpses of blue mountain-sides seemed rising through the steamy haze —then the mist broke and drove in wreaths across the slopes, and they rode down the Dale in the most glorious sunshine, Kristin in front of the troop at her father's side.

They came to Hamar one dark and rainy evening, with Kristin sitting in front on her father's saddle-bow, for she was so weary that all things swam before her eyes—the lake that gleamed wanly on their right, the gloomy trees which dripped wet upon them as they rode beneath, and the dark, leaden clusters of houses on the hueless, sodden fields by the wayside.

She had stopped counting the days—it seemed as though she had been an endless time on the journey. They had visited kindred and friends all down the Dale; she had made acquaintance with children on the great manors and had played in strange houses and barns and court-yards, and had worn many times her red dress with the silk sleeves. They had rested by the roadside by day when the weather was fair; Arne had gathered nuts for her and she had slept after meals upon the saddle-bags wherein were their clothes. At one great house they had silk-covered pillows in their beds; but one night they lay at an inn, and in one of the other beds was a woman who lay and wept softly and bitterly each time Kristin was awake. But every night she had slumbered safely behind her father's broad, warm back.

Kristin awoke with a start—she knew not where she was, but the wondrous ringing and booming sound she had heard in her dream went on. She was lying alone in a bed, and on the hearth of the room a fire was burning.

She called upon her father, and he rose from the hearth where he had been sitting, and came to her along with a stout woman.

"Where are we?" she asked; and Lavrans laughed, and said:

"We're in Hamar now, and here is Margret, the wife of Fartein the shoemaker. You must greet her prettily now, for you slept when we came hither. But now Margret will help you to your clothes."

"Is it morning, then?" said Kristin. "I thought you were even now coming to bed. Oh! do *you* help me," she begged; but Lavrans said, something sternly, that she should rather be thankful to kind Margret for helping her.

"And see what she has for you for a gift!"

'Twas a pair of red shoes with silken latchets. The woman smiled at Kristin's glad face, and drew on her shift and hose up on the bed, that she should not need to tread barefoot upon the clay floor.

"What is it makes such a noise," asked Kristin, "like a church bell, but many bells?"

"Ay, those are our bells," laughed Margret. "Have you not heard of the great minster here in the town?—'tis there you are going now. There goes the great bell! And now 'tis ringing in the cloister and in the church of Holy Cross as well."

Margret spread the butter thick upon Kristin's bread and gave her honey in her milk, that the food she took might stand in more stead— she had scant time to eat.

Out of doors it was still dark and the weather had fallen frosty. The fog was biting cold. The footprints of folk and of cattle and horses were hard as though cast in iron, so that Kristin bruised her feet in the thin, new shoes, and once she trod through the ice on the gutter in the middle of the street and her legs got wet and cold. Then Lavrans took her on his back and carried her.

She strained her eyes in the gloom, but there was not much she could see of the town—she caught a glimpse of black house-gables and trees through the grey air. Then they came out upon a little meadow that shone with rime, and upon the farther side of the meadow she dimly saw a pale grey building, big as a fell. Great stone houses stood about, and at points lights glimmered from window-holes in the walls. The bells, which had been silent for a time, took to ringing again, and now it was with a sound so strong that a cold shiver ran down her back.

'Twas like going into the mountain-side, thought Kristin, when they mounted into the church forehall; it struck chill and dark in tnere. They went through a door, and were met by the stale, cold smell of incense and candles. Now Kristin was in a dark and vastly lofty place. She could not see where it ended, neither above nor to the sides, but lights burned upon an altar far in front. There stood a priest, and the echoes of his voice stole strangely round the great place, like breathings and whisperings. Her father signed the cross with holy water upon himself and the child, and so they went forward; though he stepped warily, his spurs rang loudly on the stone floor. They passed by giant pillars, and betwixt the pillars it was like looking into coal-black holes.

Forward, nigh to the altar, the father bent his knee, and Kristin knelt beside him. She began to be able to make things out in the gloom—gold and silver glittered on altars in between the pillars, but upon that before them shone tapers which stood and burned on gilt candlesticks, while the light streamed back from the holy vessels and the big beautiful picture-panel behind. Kristin was brought again to think of the mountain-folk's hall—even so had she dreamed it must be, splendid like this, but maybe with yet more lights. And the dwarf-maid's face came up before her—but then she raised her eyes and spied upon the wall above the altar Christ Himself, great and stern, lifted high upon the Cross. Fear came upon her—He did not look mild and sorrowful as at home in their own snug timber-brown church, where He hung heavily, with pierced feet and hands, and bowed His blood-besprinkled head beneath the crown of thorns. Here He stood upon a footboard with stiff, outstretched arms and upright head; His gilded hair glittered; He was crowned with a crown of gold, and His face was upturned and harsh.

Then she tried to follow the priest's words as he read and chanted, but his speech was too hurried and unclear. At home she was wont to understand each word, for Sira Eirik had the clearest speech, and had taught her what the holy words betokened in Norse, that she might the better keep her thoughts with God while she was in church.

But she could not do that here, for every moment she grew ware of something new in the darkness. There were windows high up in the walls, and these began to shimmer with the day. And near by where they knelt there was raised a wondrous scaffolding of timber, but beyond lay blocks of light-coloured stone; and there stood mortar-troughs and tools—and she heard folks coming tiptoeing about in there. But then again her eyes fell upon the stern Lord Christ upon the wall, and she strove to keep her thoughts fixed upon the service. The icy cold from the stone floor stiffened her legs right up to the thighs, and her knees gave her pain. At length everything began to sway about her, so weary was she.

Then her father rose; the mass was at an end. The priest came forward and greeted her father. While they spoke, Kristin sate herself down upon a step, for she saw the choir-boy had done the like. He yawned—and so she too fell a-yawning. When he marked that she looked at him, he set his tongue in his cheek and twisted his eyes at her. Thereupon he dug up a pouch from under his clothing and emptied upon the flags all that was in it—fish-hooks, lumps of lead, leather thongs and a pair of dice, and all the while he made signs to her. Kristin wondered mightily.

But now the priest and her father looked at the children. The priest laughed, and bade the boy be gone back to school, but Lavrans frowned and took Kristin by the hand.

It began to grow lighter in the church now. Kristin clung sleepily to Lavrans' hand, while he and the priest walked beneath the pile of timber and talked of Bishop Ingjald's building-work.

They wandered all about the church, and in the end went out into the forehall. Thence a stone stairway led to the western tower. Kristin tumbled wearily up the steps. The priest opened a door to a fair chapel, and her father said that Kristin should set herself without upon the steps and wait while he went to shrift; and thereafter she could come in and kiss St. Thomas's shrine.

At that there came an old monk in an ash-brown frock from out the chapel. He stopped a moment, smiled at the child, and drew forth some sacks and wadmal cloths which had been stuck into a hole in the wall. These he spread upon the landing.

"Sit you here, and you will not be so cold," said he, and passed down the steps upon his naked feet.

Kristin was sleeping when Canon Martein, as the priest was called, came out and wakened her with a touch. Up from the church sounded the sweetest of song, and in the chapel candles burned upon the altar. The priest made sign that she should kneel by her father's side, and then he took down a little golden shrine which stood above the communion-table. He whispered to her that in it was a piece of St. Thomas of Canterbury's bloody garments, and he pointed at the saint's figure on the shrine that Kristin might press her lips to his feet.

The lovely tones still streamed from the church as they came down the steps; Canon Martein said 'twas the organist practising his art and the schoolboys singing; but they had not the time to stay and listen, for her father was hungry—he had come fasting for confession—and they were now bound for the guest-room of the canons' close to take their food.

The morning sun without was gilding the steep shores on the farther side of the great lake, and all the groves of yellowing leaf-trees shone like gold-dust amid the dark-blue pine-woods. The lake ran in waves with small dancing white caps of foam to their heads. The wind blew cold and fresh, and the many-hued leaves drifted down upon the rimy hillsides.

A band of riders came forth from between the Bishop's palace and the house of the Brothers of Holy Cross. Lavrans stepped aside and bowed with a hand upon his breast, while he all but swept the sward with his hat, so Kristin could guess the nobleman in the fur cloak must be the Bishop himself, and she curtsied to the ground.

The Bishop reined in his horse, and gave back the greeting; he beckoned Lavrans to him and spoke with him a while. In a short space Lavrans came back to the priest and child, and said:

"Now am I bidden to eat at the Bishop's palace—think you, Canon Martein, that one of the serving-men of the canonry could go with this little maid of mine home to Fartein the shoemaker's, and bid my men send Halvdan to meet me here with Guldsveinen at the hour of nones."

The priest answered, doubtless what he asked could be done. But on this the bare-footed monk who had spoken to Kristin on the tower stairs came forward and saluted them:

"There is a man here in our guest-house who has an errand of his own to the shoemaker's; he can bear your bidding thither, Lavrans Björgulfsön, and your daughter can go with him or bide at the cloister with me till you yourself are for home. I shall see to it that she has her food there."

Lavrans thanked him, but said, "'Twere shame you should be troubled with the child, brother Edvin——"

"Brother Edvin draws to himself all the children he can lay hands upon," said Canon Martein, and laughed. "'Tis in this wise he gets some one to preach to——"

"Ay, before you learned lords here in Hamar I dare not proffer my poor discourses," said the monk without anger, and smiling. "All I am fit for is to talk to children and peasants, but even so 'tis not well, we know, to muzzle the ox that treadeth out the corn."

Kristin looked up at her father beseechingly; she thought there was nothing she would like more than to go with Brother Edvin. So Lavrans gave thanks again, and while her father and the priest went after the Bishop's train, Kristin laid her hand in the monk's, and they went down towards the cloister, a cluster of wooden houses and a light-hued stone church far down by the lake-side.

Brother Edvin gave her hand a little squeeze, and as they looked at one another they had both to laugh. The monk was thin and tall, but very stoop-backed; the child thought him like an old crane in the head, for 'twas little, with a small, shining, bald pate above a shaggy, white rim of hair, and set upon a long, thin, wrinkled neck. His nose was large too, and pointed like a beak. But 'twas something which made her light of heart and glad, only to look up into the long, narrow, deep-lined face. The old, sea-blue eyes were red-rimmed and the lids brown and thin as flakes. A thousand wrinkles spread out from them; the wizened cheeks with the reddish network of veins were scored with furrows which ran down towards the thin-lipped mouth, but 'twas as though Brother Edvin had grown thus wrinkled only through smiling at mankind. Kristin thought she had never seen any one so blithe and gentle; it seemed he bore some bright and privy gladness within which she would get to know of when he began to speak.

They followed the fence of an apple-orchard where there still hung upon the trees a few red and golden fruit. Two Preaching Brothers in black-and-white gowns were raking together withered beanshaws in the garden.

The cloister was not much unlike any other farm steading, and the guest-house whither the monk led Kristin was most like a poor peasant's house, though there were many bedsteads in it. In one of the beds lay an old man, and by the hearth sat a woman swathing a little child; two bigger children, boy and girl, stood beside her.

They murmured, both the man and the woman, that they had not been given their breakfast yet: "None will be at the pains to bear in food to us twice in the day, so we must e'en starve while you run about the town, Brother Edvin! "

"Nay, be not peevish, Steinulv," said the monk. "Come hither and make your greetings, Kristin—see this bonny, sweet little maid who is to stay and eat with us to-day."

He told how Steinulv had fallen sick on the way home from a fair, and had got leave to lie here in the cloister guest-house, for he had a kinswoman dwelling in the spital, and she was so cursed he could not endure to be there with her.

"But I see well enough, they will soon be weary of having me here," said the peasant. "When you set forth again, Brother Edvin, there will be none here that has time to tend me, and they will surely have me to the spital again."

"Oh, you will be well and strong long before I am done with my work in the church," said Brother Edvin. "Then your son will come and fetch you——" He took up a kettle of hot water from the hearth and let Kristin hold it while he tended Steinulv. Thereupon the old man grew somewhat easier, and soon after there came in a monk with food and drink for them.

Brother Edvin said grace over the meat, and set himself on the edge of the bed by Steinulv that he might help him to take his food. Kristin went and sat by the woman and gave the boy to eat, for he was so little he could not well reach up to the porridge-dish, and he spilled upon himself when he tried to dip into the beer-bowl. The woman was from Hadeland, and she was come hither with her man and her children to see her brother who was a monk here in the cloister. But he was away wandering among the country parishes, and she grumbled much that they must lie here and waste their time.

Brother Edvin spoke the woman fair: she must not say she wasted time when she was here in Bishopshamar. Here were all the brave churches, and the monks and canons held masses and sang the livelong day and night—and the city was fine, finer than Oslo even, though 'twas somewhat less; but here were gardens to almost every dwelling-place: "You should have seen it when I came hither in the spring—'twas white with blossom over all the town. And after, when the sweetbriar burst forth——"

"Ay, and much good is that to me now," said the woman sourly. "And here are more of holy places than of holiness, methinks——"

The monk laughed a little and shook his head. Then he routed amidst the straw of his bed and brought forth a great handful of apples and pears which he shared amongst the children. Kristin had never tasted such good fruit. The juice ran out from the corners of her mouth every bite she took.

But now Brother Edvin must go to the church, he said, and Kristin should go with him. Their path went slantwise across the close, and, by a little side wicket, they passed into the choir.

They were still building at this church as well, so that here, too, there stood a tall scaffolding in the cross where nave and transepts met. Bishop Ingjald was bettering and adorning the choir, said Brother Edvin. The Bishop had great wealth, and all his riches he used for the adornment of the churches here in the town; he was a noble bishop and a good man. The Preaching Friars in St. Olav's cloister were good men too, clean-living, learned and humble. 'Twas a poor cloister, but they had made him most welcome—Brother Edvin had his home in the Minorite cloister at Oslo, but he had leave to spend a term here in Hamar diocese.

"But now come hither," said he, and led Kristin forward to the foot of the scaffolding. First he climbed up a ladder and laid some boards straight up there, and then he came down again and helped the child up with him.

Upon the greystone wall above her Kristin saw wondrous fluttering flecks of light; red as blood and yellow as beer, blue and brown and green. She would have turned to look behind her, but the monk whispered, "Turn not about." But when they stood together high upon the planking, he turned her gently round, and Kristin saw a sight so fair she almost lost her breath.

Right over against her on the nave's south wall stood a picture, and shone as if it were made of naught but gleaming precious stones. The many-hued flecks of light upon the wall came from rays which stood out from that picture; she herself and the monk stood in the midst of the glory; her hands were red as though dipped in wine; the monk's visage seemed all golden, and his dark frock threw the picture's colours softly back. She looked up at him questioningly, but he only nodded and smiled.

'Twas like standing far off and looking into the heavenly kingdom. Behind a network of black streaks, she made out little by little the Lord Christ Himself in the most precious of red robes, the Virgin Mary in raiment blue as heaven, holy men and maidens in shining yellow and green and violet array. They stood below arches and pillars of glimmering houses, wound about with branches and twigs of strange bright leafage.

The monk drew her a little farther out upon the staging.

"Stand here," he whispered, "and 'twill shine right upon you from Christ's own robe."

From the church beneath there rose to them a faint odour of incense and the smell of cold stone. It was dim below, but the sun's rays slanted in through a row of window-bays in the nave's south wall. Kristin began to understand that the heavenly picture must be a sort of window-pane, for it filled just such an opening. The others were empty or filled with panes of horn set in wooden frames. A bird came, set itself upon a window-sill, twittered a little and flew away, and outside the wall of the choir they heard the clank of metal on stone. All else was still; only the wind came in small puffs, sighed a little round about the church walls and died away.

"Ay, ay," said Brother Edvin, and sighed. "No one here in the land can make the like—they paint on glass, 'tis true, in Nidaros, but not like this. But away in the lands of the south, Kristin, in the great minsters, there they have such picture-panes, big as the doors of the church here——"

Kristin thought of the pictures in the church at home. There was St. Olav's altar, and St. Thomas of Canterbury's altar, with pictures on their front panels and on the tabernacles behind; but those pictures seemed to her dull and lustreless as she thought of them now.

They went down the ladder and up into the choir. There stood the altar-table, naked and bare, and on the stone slab were set many small boxes and cups of metal and wood and earthenware; strange little knives and irons, pens and brushes lay about. Brother Edvin said these were his gear; he plied the crafts of painting pictures and carving altar-tabernacles, and the fine panels which stood yonder by the choir-stalls were his work. They were for the altar-pieces here in the Preaching Friars' church.

Kristin watched how he mixed up coloured powders and stirred them into little cups of stoneware, and he let her help him bear the things away to a bench by the wall. While the monk went from one panel to another and painted fine red lines in the bright hair of the holy men and women so that one could see it curl and crinkle, Kristin kept close at his heels and gazed and questioned, and he explained to her what it was that he had limned.

On the one panel sat Christ in a chair of gold, and St. Nicholas and St. Clement stood beneath a roof by His side. And at the sides was painted St. Nicholas' life and works. In one place he sat as a suckling child upon his mother's knee; he turned away from the breast she reached him, for he was so holy that from the very cradle he would not suck more than once on Fridays. Alongside of that was a picture of him as he laid the money-purses before the door of the house where dwelt the three maids who were so poor they could not find husbands. She saw how he healed the Roman knight's child, and saw the knight sailing in a boat with the false chalice in his hands. He had vowed the holy bishop a chalice of gold which had been in his house a thousand years, as guerdon for bringing his son back to health again. But he was minded to trick St. Nicholas, and gave him a false chalice instead; therefore the boy fell into the sea with the true beaker in his hands. But St. Nicholas led the child unhurt underneath the water and up on to the shore, just as his father stood in St. Nicholas' church and offered the false vessel. It all stood painted upon the panels in gold and the fairest colours.

On another panel sat the Virgin Mary with the Christ-child on her knee; He pressed His mother's chin with the one hand, and held an apple in the other. Beside them stood St. Sunniva* and St. Christina. They bowed in lovely wise from their waists, their faces were the fairest red and white, and they had golden hair and golden crowns.

Brother Edvin steadied himself with the left hand on the right wrist, and painted leaves and roses on the crowns.

"The dragon is all too small, methinks," said Kristin, looking at her holy namesake's picture. "It looks not as though it could swallow up the maiden."

"And that it could not either," said Brother Edvin. "It was not bigger. Dragons and all such-like that serve the devil, seem great only so long as fear is in ourselves. But if a man seek God fervently and with all his soul, so that his longing wins into his strength, then does the devil's power suffer at once such great downfall that his tools become small and powerless—dragons and evil spirits sink down and become no bigger than sprites and cats and crows. You see that the whole mountain St. Sunniva was in is no larger than that she can wrap it within the skirt of her gown."

"But were they not in the caves, then," asked Kristin, "St. Sunniva and the Selje-men? Is not that true?"

* St. Sunniva, see Note 8.

The monk twinkled at her, and smiled again:

"'Tis both true and untrue. It seemed so to the folk who found the holy bodies. And true it is that it seemed so to Sunniva and the Selje-men, for they were humble and thought only that the world is stronger than all sinful mankind, and they thought not that they themselves were stronger than the world, because they loved it not. But had they but known it, they could have taken all the hills and slung them forth into the sea like so many pebbles. No one, nor anything, can harm us, child, save what we fear or love."

"But if a body doth not fear nor love God?" asked Kristin, affrighted.

The monk took her yellow hair in his hand, bent Kristin's head back gently, and looked down into her face; his eyes were wide open and blue.

"There is no man nor woman, Kristin, who does not love and fear God, but 'tis because our hearts are divided twixt love of God and fear of the devil and fondness for the world and the flesh, that we are un-happy in life and death. For if a man had not any yearning after God and God's being, then should he thrive in hell, and 'twould be we alone who would not understand that there he had gotten what his heart desired. For there the fire would not burn him if he did not long for coolness, nor would he feel the torment of the serpents' bite, if he knew not the yearning after peace."

Kristin looked up in his face; she understood none of all this. Brother Edvin went on:

"'Twas God's loving-kindness towards us that, seeing how our hearts are drawn asunder, He came down and dwelt among us, that He might taste in the flesh the lures of the devil when He decoys us with power and splendour, as well as the menace of the world when it offers us blows and scorn and sharp nails in hands and feet. In such wise did He show us the way and make manifest His love——"

He looked down upon the child's grave, set face—then he laughed a little, and said with quite another voice:

"Do you know who 'twas that first knew our Lord had caused Him-self to be born? 'Twas the cock; he saw the star, and so he said—all the beasts could talk Latin in those days; he cried: 'Christus natus est!' "

He crowed these last words so like a cock that Kristin fell to laughing heartily. And it did her good to laugh, for all the strange things Brother Edvin had just been saying had laid a burden of awe on her heart.

The monk laughed himself:

"Ay, and when the ox heard that, he began to low: 'Ubi, ubi, ubi.'

"But the goat bleated, and said: 'Betlem, Betlem, Betlem!'

"And the sheep longed so to see Our Lady and her Son that she baa-ed out at once: 'Eamus, eamus!'

"And the new-born calf that lay in the straw, raised itself and stood upon its feet. 'Volo, volo, volo!' it said.

"You never heard that before? No, I can believe it; I know that he is a worthy priest, that Sira Eirik that you have up in your parts, and learned; but he knows not this, I warrant; for a man does not learn it except he journey to Paris——"

"Have *you* been to Paris, then?" asked the child.

"God bless you, little Kristin, I have been in Paris and have travelled round elsewhere in the world as well; and you must not believe aught else than that I am afraid of the devil, and love and covet like any other fool. But I hold fast to the Cross with all my might—one must cling to it like a kitten to a lath when it has fallen in the sea.

"And you, Kristin—how would you like to offer up this bonny hair and serve Our Lady like these brides I have figured here?"

"We have no child at home but me," answered Kristin. "So 'tis like that I must marry. And I trow mother has chests and lockers with my bridal gear standing ready even now."

"Ay, ay," said Brother Edvin, and stroked her forehead. "'Tis thus that folk deal with their children now. To God they give the daughters who are lame or purblind or ugly, or blemished, or they let Him have back the children when they deem Him to have given them more than they need. And then they wonder that all who dwell in the cloisters are not holy men and maids——"

Brother Edvin took her into the sacristy and showed her the cloister books which stood there in a book-case; there were the fairest pictures in them. But when one of the monks came in, Brother Edvin made as though he were but seeking an ass's head to copy. Afterwards he shook his head at himself:

"Ay, there you see what fear does, Kristin—but they're so fearful about their books in the house here. Had I the true faith and love, I would not stand here as I do, and lie to Brother Aasulv——. But then I could take these old fur mittens here and hang them upon yonder sunbeam——"

She was with the monk to dinner over in the guest-house, but for the rest she sat in the church the whole day and watched his work and chatted with him. And first when Lavrans came to fetch her, did either she or the monk remember the message that should have been sent to the shoemaker.

Afterwards Kristin remembered these days in Hamar better than all else that befell her on the long journey. Oslo, indeed, was a greater town than Hamar, but now that she had seen a market-town, it did not seem to her so notable. Nor did she deem it as fair at Skog as at

Jörundgaard, though the houses were grander—but she was glad she was not to dwell there. The manor lay upon a hillside; below was the Botnfjord, grey, and sad with dark forest; and on the farther shore and behind the houses the forest stood with the sky right down upon the tree-tops. There were no high, steep fells as at home, to hold the heavens high above one, and to keep the sight sheltered and in bounds so that the world might seem neither too big nor too little.

The journey home was cold; it was nigh upon Advent; but, when they were come a little way up the Dale, snow was lying, and so they borrowed sleighs and drove most of the way.

With the affair of the estates it fell out so that Lavrans made Skog over to his brother Aasmund, keeping the right of redemption for himself and his heirs.

III

T H E spring after Kristin's long journey, Ragnfrid bore her husband another daughter. Both father and mother had wished indeed that it might be a son, but they soon took comfort, and were filled with the tenderest love for little Ulvhild. She was a most fair child, healthy, good, happy and quiet. Ragnfrid doted so on this new baby that she went on suckling it during the second year of its life; wherefore, on Sira Eirik's counsel, she left off somewhat her strict fasts and religious exercises while she had the child at the breast. On this account and by reason of her joy in Ulvhild, her bloom came back to her, and Lavrans thought he had never seen his wife so happy or so fair and kindly in all the years he had been wed.

Kristin, too, felt that great happiness had come to them with this tender little sister. That her mother's heavy mood made a stillness about her home had never come into her thought; she had deemed it was but as it should be that her mother should correct and chide her, while her father played and jested with her. But Ragnfrid was much gentler with her now and gave her more freedom; petted her more, too; and so Kristin little heeded that her mother had much less time to tend her. She loved Ulvhild as much as the others, and was joyful when they let her carry or rock her sister, and in time there was still more sport with the little one when she began to creep and walk and talk and Kristin could play with her.

Thus there went by three good years for the Jörundgaard folk. They had fortune with them in many ways, and Lavrans built and bettered round about on the manor, for the buildings and cattle-sheds were old and small when he came thither—the Gjeslings had had the place leased but for more lifetimes than one.

Now it fell out at Whitsuntide in the third year that Trond Ivarsön, from Sundbu, with his wife Gudrid and his three small sons, were come to Jörundgaard to visit them. One morning the older folk were sitting talking in the balcony of the loft-room, while the children played about in the courtyard below. In the yard Lavrans had begun a new dwelling-house, and the children were climbing and creeping about on the timber brought together for the building. One of the Gjesling boys had struck at Ulvhild and made her weep; and at that Trond came down and gave his son a buffet, and took Ulvhild up into his arms. She was the fairest and sweetest child a man's eyes could see, and her uncle had much love for her, though else he cared not for children.

Just then there came a man across the court from the cattle-yard, dragging at a great black bull; but the bull was savage and unmanage-able and broke away from the man. Trond sprang up upon the pile of timber, driving the bigger children up before him, but he had Ulvhild in his arms and his youngest son by the hand. Then a beam turned under his feet and Ulvhild slipped from his grasp and fell to the ground. The beam slipped after, rolled over on the child and lay across her back.

Lavrans was down from the balcony in the same instant; he ran up and was in act to lift the beam when the bull rushed at him. He tried to seize it by the horns, but was flung down and gored. But getting then a grip of its nostrils, he half raised himself from the ground and managed to hold the brute till Trond came to himself from his bewilderment, and the farm servants, running from the houses, cast thongs about the beast and held it fast.

Ragnfrid was on her knees trying to lift the beam; and now Lavrans was able to ease it so far that she could draw the child from under and into her lap. The little one wailed piteously when they touched her, but her mother sobbed aloud: " She lives, thank God, she lives—— !"

It was great wonder the child had not been quite crushed; but the log had chanced to fall so that it rested with one end upon a stone in the grass. When Lavrans stood up again, blood was running from the corners of his mouth, and his clothes were all torn at the breast by the bull's horns.

Tordis came running with a skin coverlet; warily she and Ragnfrid moved the child on to it, but it seemed as though she suffered unbearable pain at the lightest touch. Her mother and Tordis bore her into the winter-room.

Kristin stood upon the timber-pile, white and stock-still, while the little boys clung round her weeping. All the house and farm folk were now huddled together in the courtyard, the women weeping and wail-ing. Lavrans bade them saddle Guldsveinen and another horse as well; but when Arne came with the horses, Lavrans fell to the ground when he tried to climb to the saddle. So he bade Arne ride for the priest, while Halvdan went southward for a leech-woman who dwelt by the meeting of the rivers.

Kristin saw that her father was ashy white in the face, and that he had bled till his light blue garments were covered all over with red-brown stains. All at once he stood upright, snatched an axe from one of the men and went forward where some of the folk stood holding on to the bull. He smote the beast between the horns with the back of the axe—it dropped forward on its knees; but Lavrans ceased not striking till its blood and brains were scattered all about. Then a fit of coughing took him and he sank backwards on the ground. Trond and another man came to him and bore him within the house.

At that Kristin thought her father was surely dead; she screamed loudly and ran after, calling to him as if her heart were breaking.

In the winter-room Ulvhild had been laid on the great bed—all the pillows were thrown out upon the floor, so that the child lay flat. 'Twas as though already she lay stretched upon the dead-straw. But she wailed loudly and without cease, and her mother lay bent over her, soothing and patting the child, wild with grief that she could do naught to help her.

Lavrans lay upon the other bed: he rose and staggered across the floor that he might comfort his wife. At that she started up, and shrieked:

"Touch me not, touch me not! Jesus, Jesus—'twere liker you should strike me dead—never will it end, the ill-fortune I bring upon you——"

"You! Dear my wife, 'tis not you that have brought this on us," said Lavrans, and laid a hand upon her shoulder. She shuddered at that, and her light grey eyes shone in her lean, sallow face.

"Doubtless she means that 'twas my doing," said Trond Ivarsön roughly. His sister looked at him with hate in her eyes, and answered:

"Trond knows what I mean."

Kristin ran forward to her parents, but both thrust her away from them; and Tordis, coming in with a kettle of hot water, took her gently by the shoulder, and said, " Go—go over to our house, Kristin; you are in the way here."

Tordis was for seeing to Lavrans' hurt—he had set himself down on the step before the bed—but he said there was little amiss with him:

"But is there naught you can do to ease Ulvhild's pain a little—God help us! her crying would move the very stones in the mountain-side!"

"Nay; we dare not touch her ere the priest or Ingegjerd, the leech-wife, comes," said Tordis.

Arne came just then with word that Sira Eirik was not at home. Ragnfrid stood a while wringing her hands. Then she said:

"Send to Lady Aashild of Haugen! Naught matters now, if only Ulvhild may be saved——"

No one gave heed to Kristin. She crept on to the bench behind the bed's head, crouched down and laid her head upon her knees.

It seemed to her now as if stony hands were pressing on her heart. Lady Aashild was to be fetched! Her mother would not have them send for Lady Aashild, even when she herself was near death's door at Ulvhild's birth, nor yet when Kristin was so sick of the fever. She was a witch-wife, folk said—the Bishop of Oslo and the chapter had held session on her; and she must have been put to death or even burned, had it not been that she was of such high birth and had been like a sister to Queen Ingebjörg—but folk said she had given her first husband poison, and him she now had, Sir Björn, she had drawn to her by witchcraft; he was young enough to be her son. She had children too, but they came never to see their mother, and these two highborn folk, Björn and Aashild, lived upon a petty farm in Dovre, and had lost all their wealth. None of the great folk in the Dale would have to do with them; but, privily, folk sought her counsel—nay, poor folk went openly to her with their troubles and hurts; they said she was kind, but they feared her too.

Kristin thought her mother, who else was wont to pray so much, should rather have called on God and the Virgin now. She tried to pray herself—to St. Olav most of all, for she knew he was so good and helped so many who suffered from sickness and wounds or broken bones. But she could not keep her thoughts together.

Her father and mother were alone in the room now. Lavrans had laid himself upon his bed again, and Ragnfrid sat bent over the sick child, passing, from time to time, a damp cloth over her forehead and hands, and wetting her lips with wine.

A long time went by. Tordis looked in between whiles, and would fain have helped, but Ragnfrid sent her out each time. Kristin wept silently and prayed to herself, but all the while she thought of the witch-wife and waited eagerly to see her come in.

Suddenly Ragnfrid asked in the silence:

"Are you sleeping, Lavrans?"

"No," answered her husband. "I am listening to Ulvhild. God will surely help His innocent lamb, wife—we dare not doubt it. But 'tis weary lying here waiting——"

" God," said Ragnfrid hopelessly, "hates me for my sins. 'Tis well with my children, where they are, I doubt not that; and now 'tis like Ulvhild's hour has come, too—but me He has cast off, for my heart is a viper's nest, full of sin and sorrow——"

Then some one lifted the latch—Sira Eirik stepped in, straightened his huge frame where he stood, and said in his clear, deep voice: "God help all in this house!"

The priest put the box with his medicines on the step before the bed, and went to the open hearth and poured warm water over his hands. Then he took a cross from his bosom, struck out with it to all four corners of the room and mumbled something in Latin. Thereupon he opened the smoke-vent, so that the light might stream into the room, and went and looked at Ulvhild.

Kristin grew afraid he might find her and send her out—not often did Sira Eirik s eyes let much escape them. But the priest did not look round. He took a flask from the box, poured somewhat upon a wad of finely carded wool and laid it over Ulvhild's mouth and nose.

"Now she will soon suffer less," said the priest. He went to Lavrans and tended his wounds, while they told him how the mishap had come to pass. Lavrans had two ribs broken and had a wound in the lungs; but the priest thought that for him there was no great fear.

"And Ulvhild?" asked the father fearfully.

"I will tell you when I have looked at her more nearly," answered the priest; "but you must lie in the loft-room, so that there may be more quiet and room here for those who must tend her." He laid Lavrans' arm about his own shoulder, took firm hold under the man, and bore him out. Kristin would fain have gone with her father now, but she dared not show herself.

When Sira Eirik came back, he did not speak to Ragnfrid, but first cut the clothes off Ulvhild, who now moaned less and seemed half asleep. Then carefully he felt with his hands over the child's body and limbs.

" Is it so ill with my child, Eirik, that you know not how to save her, since you say naught?" asked Ragnfrid under her breath.

The priest answered low:

" It seems as though her back were badly hurt, Ragnfrid; I see no better way than to leave all in God's hands and St. Olav's—much there is not that I can do."

" Then must we pray!" cried the mother passionately. "You know well that Lavrans and I will give you all you ask and spare nothing, if so be your prayers can win God to grant that Ulvhild may live."

" 'Twould seem to me a miracle," said the priest, " were she to live and have her health again."

"And is't not of miracles that you preach late and early—believe you not that a miracle can happen with my child?" she said, as wildly as before.

"'Tis true," replied the priest, "that miracles happen; but God does not grant the prayers of all—we know not His secret counsel. And think you not, it would be worst of all should this fair little maid grow up marred or crippled?"

Ragnfrid shook her head. She wailed softly:

" I have lost so many, priest; I cannot lose her too !"

"I will do all that I may," answered the priest, "and pray with all my power. But you must strive, Ragnfrid, to bear the cross God lays upon you."

The mother moaned low:

"None of my children have I loved like this little one—if she too be taken from me, full sure I am my heart will break."

"God help you, Ragnfrid Ivarsdatter," said Sira Eirik, and shook his head. "In all your praying and fasting, you have thought only to force your will upon God. Can you wonder that it has helped but little?"

Ragnfrid looked defiantly at the priest, and spoke:

"I have sent for the Lady Aashild even now."

"Ay, you know her; I know her not," replied the priest.

"I cannot live without Ulvhild," said Ragnfrid as before. "If so be God will not help her, I will seek counsel of Lady Aashild, or e'en give myself to the devil if he will help !"

The priest looked as though he would answer sharply, but checked himself again. He bent and felt the limbs of the little sick girl once more.

"Her hands and feet are cold," he said. "We must lay jars of hot water about her—and then you must touch her no more till Lady Aashild comes."

Kristin let herself sink back noiselessly on the bench and lay as if asleep. Her heart beat hard with fear—she had understood but little of the talk between Sira Eirik and her mother, but it had frighted her terribly, and the child knew well that it had not been for her ears.

Her mother rose up to go for the hot-water jars, and suddenly she burst out sobbing: "But yet pray for us, Sira Eirik !"

Soon after she came back with Tordis. Then the priest and the women busied themselves with Ulvhild, and soon Kristin was found and sent away.

The light dazzled the child as she stood without in the courtyard. She had thought that most of the day must have gone by while she sat in the dark winter-room, and yet the houses stood there light-grey, and the grass was shining like silk in the white midday sunshine. The river gleamed behind the dun and golden trellis-work of the alder-brakes—it filled the air with its gladsome rushing sound, for here by Jörundgaard it ran swiftly over a flat bed strewn with boulders. The mountain walls rose into the thin blue haze, and the becks sprang down their sides through the melting snows. The sweet, strong springtide out of doors brought tears to her eyes, for sorrow at the helplessness she felt all about her.

There was no one in the courtyard, but she heard voices in the house-carls' cottage. Fresh earth had been strewn over the spot where her father had killed the bull. She knew not what to do with herself, so she crept behind the wall of the new house—two log-courses had already been laid. Inside lay Ulvhild's playthings and her own; she put them all together and laid them in a hole between the lowest log and the foundation wall. Of late Ulvhild had wanted all her toys; this had vexed her sometimes. Now she thought, if her sister got well, she would give her all she had. And this thought comforted her a little.

She thought of the monk in Hamar—*he* was sure that miracles could happen for every one. But Sira Eirik was not so sure about it, nor parents either—and she was used to think as they did. A heavy weight fell upon her as it came to her for the first time that folk could think so unlike about so many things—not only bad, ungodly men and good men, but such men as Brother Edvin and Sira Eirik—even her mother and her father: she felt all at once that they too thought not alike about many things. . . .

Tordis found her there in the corner, asleep, late in the day, and took her to her own house; the child had eaten nothing since the morning. Tordis watched with Ragnfrid over Ulvhild through the night, and Kristin lay in Tordis' bed with Jon, Tordis' husband, and Eivind and Orm, their little boys. The smell of their bodies, the man's snoring and the children's even breathing made Kristin weep silently. It was no longer ago than last evening that she had lain down, as each night of her life before, by her own father and mother and little Ulvhild—it was as though a nest had been riven asunder and scattered and she herself lay cast out from the shelter of the wings which had always kept her warm. At last she cried herself to sleep, alone and unhappy among these strange folk.

Next morning as soon as she was up, she heard that her mother's brother and all his party had left the place—in anger; Trond had called his sister a foolish, crazy woman, and his brother-in-law a soft simpleton who had never known how to rule his wife. Kristin grew hot with wrath, but she was ashamed too—she understood well enough that a most unseemly thing had befallen in that her mother had driven her nearest kin from the house. And for the first time she dimly felt that there was something about her mother that was not as it should be—that she was not the same as other women.

While she stood brooding on this, a serving-maid came and said she was to go up to the loft-room to her father.

But when she was come into the room Kristin forgot to look at him, for right opposite the open door, with the light full upon her face, sat a little woman who she guessed must be the witch-wife. And yet Kristin had never thought that she would look like this.

She seemed small as a child and slightly made, as she sat in the great high-backed arm-chair which had been brought up thither. A table had been set before her too, covered with Ragnfrid's finest, fringed, linen tablecloth. Bacon and fowl were set out upon the silver platter; there was wine in a mazer bowl, and she had Lavrans' own silver goblet to drink from. She had finished eating and was busy drying her small and slender hands on one of Ragnfrid's best hand-towels. Ragnfrid herself stood in front of her and held for her a brass basin with water.

Lady Aashild let the hand-towel sink into her lap; she smiled to the child, and said in a clear and lovely voice:

"Come hither to me, child!" Then to her mother: "Fair children are these you have, Ragnfrid."

Her face was greatly wrinkled, but as clear white and pink as a child's, and it looked as though her skin must be just as soft and fine to the touch. Her mouth was as red and fresh as a young woman's, and her large, hazel eyes shone bright. A fine, white, linen headdress lay close about her face and was fastened under her chin with a golden clasp; over it she had a veil of soft, dark-blue wool; it fell over her shoulders and far down upon her dark, well-fitting dress. She was upright as a wand, and Kristin felt more than thought that she had never seen a woman so fair and so mannerly as was this old witch-wife, with whom the great folk of the valley would have naught to do.

Lady Aashild held Kristin's hand in her old, soft one, and spoke to her with kindly jesting; but Kristin could not answer a word. Then said Lady Aashild with a little laugh:

"Is she afraid of me, think you?"

"Nay, nay," Kristin all but shouted. And then Lady Aashild laughed still more, and said to the mother:

"She has wise eyes, this daughter of yours, and good strong hands, nor is she used to be idle, I can see. You will need one by and by to help you tend Ulvhild, when I am gone. 'Twere well, therefore, you let Kristin be by me and help while yet I am here . . . she is old enough for that; eleven years is she not?"

Thereupon the Lady Aashild went out, and Kristin would have followed her, but Lavrans called to her from his bed. He lay flat upon his back with the pillows stuffed beneath his up-drawn knees; Lady Aashild had bidden that he should lie so, that the hurt in his breast might sooner heal.

"Now surely you will soon be well, sir father, will you not?" asked
Kristin.

Lavrans looked up at her—the child had never said "sir" to him
before. Then he said gravely:

"For me there is naught to fear; 'tis worse with your sister."

"Ay," said Kristin, and sighed.

She stood yet a little while by his bed. Her father said no more, and
Kristin found naught to say. And when Lavrans after a while said she
should go down to her mother and Lady Aashild, Kristin hastened out
and ran across the courtyard down into the winter-room.

IV

LADY AASHILD stayed on at Jörundgaard most of the summer.
Thus it fell out that folk came thither seeking her counsel. . . . Kristin
heard Sira Eirik fling at this now and then, and it came into her mind
that her father and mother, too, were not pleased. But she put all
thoughts of such things from her, nor did she ponder over what she
thought of Lady Aashild, but was with her ever, and tired not of
listening to the lady and of watching her.

Ulvhild still lay stretched upon her back in the great bed. Her little
face was white to the lips, and dark rings had come about her eyes. Her
lovely yellow hair had a stale smell, it had been unwashed for so long,
and it had grown dark and lost all gloss and curl, so that it looked like
old, burnt-up hay. She looked tired and suffering and patient; but she
smiled faintly and wanly at her sister when Kristin sat down on the
bedside by her and chattered and showed the child all the fine gifts
there were for her from her father and mother and from their friends
and kinsfolk from far around. There were dolls and wooden birds and
beasts, and a little draught-board, trinkets and velvet caps and coloured
ribbons; Kristin kept them all together in a box for her—and Ulvhild
looked at them all with her grave eyes, and, sighing, dropped the
treasures from her weary hands.

But when Lady Aashild came nigh, Ulvhild's face lit up with gladness. Eagerly she drank the quenching and sleepy drinks Lady Aashild
brewed for her; when Aashild tended her hurts she made no plaint, and
lay happy listening when the lady played on Lavrans' harp and sang—
she had great store of ballads strange to the folk of the Dale.

Often she sang to Kristin when Ulvhild lay asleep. And then at
times she would tell of her youth, when she dwelt in the South at the
courts of King Magnus and King Eirik and their Queens.

Once as they sat thus and Lady Aashild told of these things, there
slipped from Kristin's lips a thought she had often had in mind:

"Methinks it is strange you can be so glad at all times, you who have been used to——" She broke off and grew red.

Lady Aashild looked down at the child with a smile:

"Mean you because I am parted from all that now?" She laughed quietly, and said: "I have had my happy time, Kristin, and I am not so foolish as to murmur, if now, since I have drunk up my wine and beer, I have to put up with skimmed milk and sour. Good days may last long if one lives wisely, and deals warily with what one has; all wise folk know that, and 'tis therefore, I trow, that wise folk must rest content with good days—for the best days of all cost very dear. In this world they call him a fool who wastes his heritage that he may make merry in the days of his youth. As to that, each man may deem as he lists. But that man only do I call a fool and a very dolt who rues his bargain after it is made; and twice a simpleton and a fool of fools is he who thinks to see more of his boon-companions after his heritage is gone . . ."

". . . Is there aught amiss with Ulvhild?" she called gently across to Ragnfrid, who had made a sharp movement where she sat by the child's bed.

"Nay, she sleeps well," said the child's mother, and came over to Lady Aashild and Kristin at the hearth. Her hands on the pole of the smoke-vent, she stood and looked down into Lady Aashild's face.

"Kristin doth not understand such things," she said.

"No," answered the lady. "But she learned her prayers, too, I doubt not, before she understood them. The times when we need prayers or counsel, we are little like to be in a mood to learn, nor yet to understand."

Ragnfrid drew her dark eyebrows together thoughtfully. At such times her bright, deep-set eyes looked like tarns below a dark-wooded hillside, so Kristin had often thought when she was little—or so she had heard others say. Lady Aashild looked at Ragnfrid with her little half-smile, and the mother seated herself upon the edge of the hearth, and, taking a twig, stuck it into the embers.

"But he who has wasted his heritage upon the sorriest goods—and thereafter beholds a treasure he would gladly give his life to own—think you not he must rue bitterly his own folly?"

"No doing without some rueing, Ragnfrid," said Lady Aashild. "And he who is willing to give his life should make a venture and see what he can win——"

Ragnfrid plucked the burning twig from the fire, blew out the flame and bent her hand about the glowing end, so that it shone out blood-red from between her fingers.

"Oh! these are words, words, and only words, Lady Aashild."

"Well," said the other, "truly Ragnfrid, there is not much that's worth buying so dear as with one's life."

"Nay, but there is," said Ragnfrid passionately; and she whispered so it could scarce be heard: "My husband."

"Ragnfrid," said Lady Aashild, in a low voice, "so hath many a maid thought when she strove to bind a man to her and gave her maidenhood to do it. But have you not read of men and maids who gave to God all they owned, went into a cloister or naked into the wilds, and repented after. Ay, they are called fools in the godly books. And 'twould sure be sinful to think God cheated *them* over their bargain."

Ragnfrid sat quite still a while. Then Lady Aashild said:

"You must come now, Kristin; 'tis time we went and gathered dew for Ulvhild's morning wash."

Outside the courtyard lay all black and white in the moonlight. Ragnfrid went with them, through the farmyard, down to the gate of the cabbage garden. Kristin saw her mother's thin dark figure leaning there, while she was shaking the dew from the big, icy-cold cabbage leaves, and the folds of the lady's-mantles, into her father's silver goblet.

Lady Aashild walked silent at Kristin's side. She was there only to watch over her, for it was not well to let a child go out alone on such a night. But the dew had more virtue if gathered by an innocent maid.

When they came back to the gate Ragnfrid was gone. Kristin was shaking with the cold as she gave the icy silver cup into Lady Aashild's hands. She ran in her wet shoes over toward the loft-room, where she slept now with her father. She had her foot upon the first step when Ragnfrid stepped out of the shadow of the balcony. In her hands she bore a steaming bowl.

"Here, I have warmed some beer for you, daughter," said the mother.

Kristin thanked her mother gladly, and put the bowl to her lips. Then Ragnfrid asked:

" Kristin—the prayers and all the other things that Lady Aashild teaches you—you are sure there is naught sinful or ungodly in them?"

"That I can never believe," answered the child. "There is Jesus' name and the Virgin Mary's, and the names of the Saints in them all——"

"What is it she teaches you?" asked her mother again.

"Oh!—about herbs—and charms to stop running blood and cure warts and sore eyes—and moth in clothes and mice in the store-room. And what herbs one should pluck in sunshine, and which have virtue in the rain. . . . But the prayers I must not tell to any one, for then they lose their power," said she quickly.

Her mother took the empty bowl and put it upon the step. Then suddenly she threw her arms around her daughter, and pressed her tightly to her and kissed her. . . . Kristin felt that her mother's cheeks were wet and hot:

"May God and Our Lady guard and shield you from all evil—we have naught else but you, your father and I, that has not been touched by our ill-fortune. Darling, darling—never forget that you are your father's dearest joy——"

Ragnfrid went back to the winter-room, undressed and crept into bed beside Ulvhild. She put an arm about the child and laid her cheek close to the little one's, so that she felt the warmth of Ulvhild's body and smelt the keen odour of her damp hair. Ulvhild slept heavily and soundly, as she ever did after Lady Aashild's evening draught. The lady's bedstraw, spread beneath the bedding, gave out a drowsy scent. None the less did Ragnfrid lie long sleepless, gazing at the little spot of light in the roof where the moon shone upon the smoke-hole's pane of horn.

Over in the other bed lay Lady Aashild, but Ragnfrid never knew whether she slept or waked. The lady never spoke of their having known each other in former days—this frightened Ragnfrid. And it seemed to her she had never known such bitter sorrow and such haunting dread as now—even though she knew that Lavrans would have his full health again—and that Ulvhild would live.

It seemed as though Lady Aashild took pleasure in talking to Kristin, and with each day that passed the maid became better friends with her. One day, when they had gone to gather herbs, they sat together high up the hillside on a little green, close under the scree. They could look down into the farm-place at Formo and see Arne Gyrdsön's red jerkin: he had ridden down the valley with them, and was to look after their horses while they were up the hillside seeking herbs.

As they sat, Kristin told Lady Aashild of her meeting with the dwarf-maiden. She had not thought of it for many years, but now it rose before her. And while she spoke, the thought came to her strangely that there was some likeness betwixt Lady Aashild and the dwarf-lady—though she knew well all the time they were not really like. But when she had told all, Lady Aashild sat still a while and looked out down the Dale; at length she said:

"You were wise to fly, since you were only a child then. But have you never heard of folk who took the gold the dwarfs offered, and after bound the troll in stone?"

"I have heard such tales," said Kristin, "but I would never dare to do it. And methinks it is not a fair deed."

"'Tis well when one dares not do what one doth not think a fair deed," said Lady Aashild, laughing a little. "But it is not so well when one thinks a thing to be no fair deed because one dares not do it. . . . You have grown much this summer," the lady said of a sudden. "Do you know yourself, I wonder, that you are like to be fair?"

"Ay," said Kristin. "They say I am like my father."

Lady Aashild laughed quietly.

"Ay, 'twould be best for you if you took after Lavrans, both in mind and body, too. Yet 'twould be pity were they to wed you up here in the Dale. Plainness and country ways let no man scorn; but they think themselves, these big folk up here, they are so fine that their like is not to be found in Norway's land. They wonder much, belike, that I can live and thrive, though they bar their doors against me. But they are lazy and proud and will not learn new ways—and they put the blame on the old strife with the King in Sverre's days. 'Tis all lies; your mother's forefather made friends with King Sverre and received gifts from him; but were your mother's brother to become one of our King's men and wait upon his Court, he would have to trim himself up both without and within, and that Trond would not be at the pains to do. But you, Kristin,—you should be wedded to a man bred in knightly ways and *curteisie*——"

Kristin sat looking down into the Formo yard, at Arne's red back. She scarce knew it herself, but when Lady Aashild talked of the world she had once moved in, Kristin ever thought of the knights and earls in Arne's likeness. Before, when she was little, she had always seen them in her father's shape.

"My sister's son, Erlend Nikulaussön of Husaby, *he* might have been a fitting bridegroom for you—he has grown comely, has the boy. My sister Magnhild looked in on me last year as she passed through the Dale, and he with her. Ay, 'tis not like you could get him, but I had gladly spread the coverlid over you two in the bridal bed—he is as dark-haired as you are fair, and he has goodly eyes. . . . But if I know my brother-in-law aright, he has bethought him already for sure of a better match for Erlend than you."

"Am I not a good match, then?" asked Kristin, wondering. She never thought of being hurt by anything Lady Aashild said, but she felt humbled and sad that the lady should be in some way better than her own folks.

"Ay, you are a good match," said the other. "Yet you could scarce look to come into my kindred. Your forefather in this land was an outlaw and a stranger, and the Gjeslings have sat and grown moulded on their farms so long that soon they'll be forgotten outside the Dale. But I and my sister had for husbands the nephews of Queen Margaret Skulesdatter."

Kristin could not even pluck up heart to say it was not her forefather, but his brother, who had come to the land an outlaw. She sat and gazed at the dark hillsides across the Dale, and she thought of the day many years gone by, when she had been up on the upland wastes and seen how many fells there were 'twixt her own valley and the outer world. Then Lady Aashild said they must go home now, and bade her call on Arne. So Kristin put her hands to her mouth, and hallooed and waved her kerchief, till she saw the red spot in the farm-place move and wave back.

Not long after this Lady Aashild went home; but through the autumn and the first part of the winter she came often to Jörundgaard to spend some days with Ulvhild. The child was taken out of bed in the day-time now, and they tried to get her to stand, but her legs gave way beneath her when she put her feet to the ground. She was fretful, white and weary, and the laced jacket of horsehide and thin withes which Lady Aashild had made for her plagued her sorely, so that she would rather lie still in her mother's lap. Ragnfrid had her sick daughter for ever in her arms, so that Tordis had the whole care of the house now; and, at her mother's bidding, Kristin went with Tordis to learn and to help.

Kristin longed for Lady Aashild between whiles, and sometimes the lady would chat much with her, but at other times the child would wait in vain for a word beyond the other's greeting when she came and when she went. Lady Aashild sat and talked with the grown-up folk only. That was always the way when she had her husband with her, for it happened now at times that Björn Gunnarsön came with his wife. Lavrans had ridden to Haugen one day in the autumn to take the lady her leech's fee—it was the very best silver tankard they had in the house, with a plate to match. He had slept there the night, and ever since he praised the farm mightily; it was fair and well ordered, and not so small as folks would have it, he said. And within the house all spoke of well-being, and the customs of the house were seemly, following the ways of great folks' houses in the South. What he thought of Björn, Lavrans said not, but he welcomed him fairly at all times when he came with his wife to Jörundgaard. But the Lady Aashild Lavrans liked exceeding well, and he said he deemed most of the tales that had been told of her were lies. He said, too, 'twas most sure that twenty years since she could have had small need of witchcraft to bind a man to her—she was near the sixties now, yet she still looked young and had a most fair and winning bearing.

Kristin saw well that her mother liked all this but little. Of Lady Aashild, it is true, Ragnfrid said naught; but once she likened Björn to the yellow, flattened grass one sometimes finds growing under big stones, and Kristin thought this fitted him well. Björn looked strangely faded; he was somewhat fat, pale and sluggish, and a little bald, although he was not much older than Lavrans. Yet one saw he had once been a very comely man. Kristin never came to speech with him—he spoke little, and was wont to sit in the same place where he first settled down, from the time he stepped into the room till he went to bed. He drank hugely, but one marked it but little on him; he ate scarce any food, but gazed now and again at one or another in the room with a fixed, brooding look in his strange, pale eyes.

They had seen naught of their kinsfolk at Sundbu since the mishap befell, though Lavrans had been over at Vaage more times than one. But Sira Eirik came to Jörundgaard as before; and there he often met Lady Aashild, and they were good friends. Folk thought this was good of the priest, for he was himself a very skilful leech. That, too, was doubtless one cause why the folk of the great estates had not sought Lady Aashild's counsel, at least not openly, as they held the priest to be skilful enough, nor was it easy for them to know how they should bear themselves toward two folks who had been cast off, in a manner, by their own kin and fellows. Sira Eirik said himself they did not graze on one another's meadows, and as to her witchcraft, he was not her parish priest—it might well be the lady knew more than was good for her soul's health —yet one must not forget ignorant folk were all too ready to talk of witchcraft as soon as a woman was a bit wiser than her neighbours. Lady Aashild, on her side, praised the priest much, and was diligent at church if it chanced she was at Jörundgaard on a holy day.

Yuletide was sorrowful that year; Ulvhild could not yet put her feet to the ground, and they neither heard not saw aught of the Sundbu folk. Kristin knew that it was talked of in the parish and that her father took it to heart. But her mother seemed to care naught; and Kristin thought this wrong of her.

But one evening, toward the end of Yuletide, came Sira Sigurd, Trond Gjesling's house-priest, driving in a great sledge, and his chief errand was to bid them all to a feast at Sundbu.

Sira Sigurd was ill-liked in the parishes about, for it was he who really managed Trond's estates; or, at the least, he got the blame for Trond's hard and unjust dealings, and there was no denying Trond was something of a plague to his tenants. His priest was most learned in writing and reckoning, versed in the law, and a skilful leech—if not quite so skilful as he deemed himself. But from his ways, no one would have thought him overwise; he often said foolish things. Ragnfrid and Lavrans had never liked him, but the Sundbu folk, as was but reason, set great store by their priest, and both they and he felt very bitter that he had not been called in to Ulvhild.

Now by ill-fortune it fell out that when Sira Sigurd came to Jörundgaard, Lady Aashild and Sir Björn were there already, besides Sira Eirik, Gyrd and Inga of Finsbrekken, Arne's parents, old Jon from Loptsgaard, and a Preaching Friar from Hamar, Brother Aasgaut.

While Ragnfrid had the tables spread anew with Christmas fare, and Lavrans looked into the letters brought by Sira Sigurd, the priest wished to look at Ulvhild. She was already abed for the night and sleeping, but Sira Sigurd woke her, felt her back and limbs, and asked her many questions, at first gently enough, but then roughly and impatiently as the child grew frightened. Sigurd was a little man, all but a dwarf, with a great, flaming, red face. As he made to lift her out upon the floor to test her feet, she began screaming loudly. On this Lady Aashild rose, went to the bed, and covered Ulvhild with the skins, saying the child was so sleepy she could not have stood upon the floor even had her legs been strong,

The priest began then to speak loudly; he too was reckoned to know somewhat of leech-craft. But Lady Aashild took him by the hand, brought him forward to the high-seat and fell to telling him what she had done for Ulvhild, and asking his judgment on each and every matter. On this he grew somewhat milder of mood, and ate and drank of Ragnfrid's good cheer.

But as the beer and wine began to mount to his head, Sira Sigurd's humour changed again and he grew quarrelsome and hot-headed—he knew well enough there was no one in the room who liked him. First he turned on Gyrd—he was the bishop of Hamar's bailiff in Vaage and Sil, and there had been many quarrels 'twixt the Bishop's see and Trond Ivarsön. Gyrd said not much, but Inga was a fiery woman, and then Brother Aasgaut joined in, and spoke:

"You should not forget, Sira Sigurd, our reverend Father Ingjald is your overlord, too—we know enough of you in Hamar. You wallow in all good things at Sundbu, never thinking that you are vowed to other work than to do Trond eye-service, helping him in all wrong and injustice, to the peril of his soul and the minishing of the rights of Holy Church. Have you never heard how it fares with the false and unruly priests who hatch out devices against their spiritual fathers and those in authority? Wot you not of that time when the angels took St. Thomas of Canterbury to the door of hell and let him peep in? He wondered much that he saw none of the priests who had set themselves up against him, as you have set yourself against your bishop. He was about to praise God's mercy, for the holy man begrudged not salvation to all sinners—but at that the angel bade the devil lift his tail a little, and out there came, with a great bang and a foul smell of sulphur, all the priests

and learned men who had wrought against the good of the Church.
Thus did he come to know whither *they* had gone."

"*There* you lie, monk," said the priest. "I have heard that tale too;
only they were not priests, but beggar-monks, who came from the rear
of the devil like wasps out of a wasp-nest."

Old Jon laughed louder than all the serving-folk, and roared:

"There were both sorts, I'll be bound——"

"Then the devil must have a fine broad tail," said Björn Gunnarsön;
and Lady Aashild smiled, and said:

"Ay, have you not heard that all evil drags a long tail behind it?"

"Be still, Lady Aashild," cried Sira Sigurd: "do not you talk of the
long tail evil drags after it. You sit here as though *you* were mistress in
the house, and not Ragnfrid. But 'tis strange you could not help her
child—have you no more of that strong water you dealt in once, which
could make whole the sheep already boiling in the pot, and turn women
to maids in the bridal-bed? Think you I know not of the wedding in
this very parish where you made a bath for the bride that was no
maid——"

Sira Eirik sprang up, gripped the other priest by the shoulder and
thigh, and flung him right over the table, so that the jugs and tankards
were overturned and food and drink ran upon the cloths and floor, while
Sira Sigurd lay his length upon the ground with torn garments. Eirik
leaped over the board, and would have struck him again, roaring above
the tumult:

"Hold your filthy mouth, priest of hell that you are——"

Lavrans strove to part them, but Ragnfrid stood, white as death, by
the board, and wrung her hands. Then Lady Aashild ran and helped
Sira Sigurd to his feet, and wiped the blood from his face. She poured
a beaker of mead down his throat, saying:

"You must not be so strict, Sira Eirik, that you cannot bear to listen
to jesting so far on in a drinking bout. Seat yourselves now and you
shall hear of that wedding. 'Twas not here in the Dale at all, nor had
I the good fortune to be the one that knew of that water—could I have
brewed it, I trow we would not be sitting now on a hill-croft in the
wilds. I might have been a rich woman and had lands in the great, rich
parishes—nigh to town and cloisters and bishop and chapter," and she
smiled at the three churchmen.

"But 'tis said, sure enough, that the art was known in the olden days."

And the lady told a merry tale of a misadventure that befell in King
Inga's time, when the magic wash was used by mistake by the wrong
woman, and of what followed thereon.

Great was the laughter in the room, and both Gyrd and Jon shouted
for more such tales from Lady Aashild. But the lady said: "No! Here

sit two priests and Brother Aasgaut, and young lads and serving-maids; 'tis best we cease before the talk grows unseemly and gross; let us bear in mind 'tis a holy day."

The men made an outcry, but the women held with Lady Aashild. No one saw that Ragnfrid had left the room. Soon after, it was time that Kristin, who sat lowest on the women's bench among the serving-maids, should go to bed—she was sleeping in Tordis' house, there were so many guests at the manor.

It was biting cold, and the northern lights flamed and flickered over the brows of the fells to the north. The snow crackled under Kristin's feet as she ran over the courtyard shivering, her arms crossed on her breast.

Then she was aware of a woman in the shadow of the old loft walking hurriedly to and fro in the snow, throwing her arms about, wringing her hands, and wailing aloud. Kristin saw it was her mother, and ran to her affrighted, asking if she were ill.

"No, no," burst out Ragnfrid. "But I could not stay within—go you to bed, child."

As Kristin turned away, her mother called her softly:

"Go back to the room and lie beside your father and Ulvhild—take her in your arms so that he may not roll upon her by mischance; he sleeps so heavily when he has drunk deep. I am going up to sleep in the old loft-room to-night."

"Jesus, mother," says Kristin, "you will freeze to death if you lie there —alone, too. And what think you father will say if you come not to bed to-night?"

"He will not mark it," answered her mother, "he was all but asleep when I left, and to-morrow he will waken late. Go and do as I have said."

"'Twill be so cold for you," said Kristin, whimpering; but her mother sent her away, a little more kindly, and shut herself into the loft-room.

Within it was as cold as without, and it was pitch dark. Ragnfrid groped her way to the bed, pulled off her headdress, undid her shoes, and crept in among the skins. They chilled her to the bone; it was like sinking into a snowdrift. She pulled the skins over her head, and drew her knees up to her chin, and thrust her hands into her bosom—so she lay and wept; now quite low, with flowing tears; now crying aloud and grinding her teeth. But in time she had warmed the bed around her so much that she grew drowsy, and at last wept herself to sleep.

V

T H E year that Kristin was fifteen in the spring, Lavrans Björgulfsön and Sir Andres Gudmundsön of Dyfrin made tryst at the Holledis Thing. There 'twas agreed between them that Andres' second son, Simon, should wed Kristin Lavransdatter and should have Formo, Sir Andres' mother's udal estate. This the two men shook hands upon; yet it was not put in writing, for Sir Andres had first to settle with his other children about their heritage. And for this reason no betrothal feast was held; but Sir Andres and Simon came to Jörundgaard to see the bride, and Lavrans gave them a great banquet.

By this time Lavrans had ready his new dwelling-house of two storeys, with corner fireplaces of masonry both in the living-room and the loft-room above; richly furnished and adorned with fair wood-carvings. He had rebuilt the old loft-room too, and bettered the other houses in many ways, so that he was now housed as befitted an esquire bearing arms. He was very wealthy now, for he had had good fortune in his undertakings and was a shrewd and careful husband of his goods; above all was he known as a breeder of the finest horses and the goodliest cattle of all kinds. And now he had been able so to order things that his daughter was to wed into the Dyfrin kindred and the Formo estate, all folks deemed he had brought to a happy end his purpose to be the foremost man in the countryside. He, and Ragnfrid too, were well pleased with the betrothal, as were Sir Andres and Simon.

Kristin was a little cast down when she first saw Simon Andressön; for she had heard great talk of his good looks and seemly bearing, so that she had outrun all measure in her hopes of what her bridegroom would be.

Truly Simon was well favoured, but he was something fat to be only twenty years of age; he was short of neck and had a face as round and shining as the moon. He had goodly hair, brown and curly, and his eyes were grey and clear, but lay deep and as it were shut in, the lids were so fat; his nose was over small and his mouth was small too, and pouting, but not unsightly. In spite of his stoutness he was light, and quick, and nimble in all his ways, and was skilled in all sports. He was something too brisk and forward in his speech, but Lavrans held he showed both good wit and learning when he talked with older men.

Ragnfrid soon came to like him, and Ulvhild was taken at once with the greatest love for him—he was more gentle and kind with the little sick maid than with any other. And when Kristin had grown used a little to his round face and his way of speech, she grew to be well content with her betrothed, and happy in the way her father had ordered things for her.

Lady Aashild was at the feast. Since Jörundgaard had opened its doors to her, the great folk in the parishes round about had begun to call to mind her high birth and to think less of her doubtful fame, so that the lady came much out among people. She said when she had seen Simon:

"'Tis a good match, Kristin; this Simon will go forward in the world —you will be spared many cares, and he will be good to live with. But to my mind he seems something too fat and too cheerful——. Were it now in Norway as it was in days gone by, and as it is still in other lands— that folk were not more hard to sinners than is God Himself, I would say you should find yourself a friend who is lean and sorrowful—one you could have to sit and hold converse with. Then would I say, you could not fare better than you would with Simon."

Kristin grew red, though she understood not well what the lady's words might mean. But as time went on and her bridal chests filled, and she evermore heard talk of her wedding, and of what she was to take into the new household, she began to long that the betrothal-knot should be tied once for all, and that Simon should come north; thus she thought much about him in the end, and was glad at the thought of meeting him again.

Kristin was full-grown now and very fair to look upon. She was most like her father and had grown tall; she was small waisted, with slender, fine limbs and joints, yet round and plump withal. Her face was somewhat short and round, her forehead low and broad and white as milk; her eyes large, grey and soft, under fairly drawn eyebrows. Her mouth was something large, but it had full bright red lips, and her chin was round as an apple and well shaped. She had goodly long, thick hair; but 'twas something dark in hue, almost as much brown as yellow, and quite straight. Lavrans liked nothing better than to hear Sira Eirik boast of Kristin—the priest had seen the maid grow up, had taught her her books and writing, and loved her much. But the father was not so pleased when the priest sometimes likened his daughter to an unblemished, silken-coated filly.

Yet all men said that had not that sorrowful mishap befallen, Ulvhild had been many times more comely than her sister. She had the fairest and sweetest face, white and red as lilies and roses; and light yellow hair, soft as silk, which waved and clung about her slender throat and small shoulders. Her eyes were like those of her Gjesling kin; they were deep set, under straight, dark brows, and were clear as water and grey-blue; but her glance was mild, not sharp like theirs. Then, too, the child's voice was so clear and lovely that it was a joy to hearken to her, whether she spoke or sang. She was most apt at book-learning and all kinds of string-instruments and draughts, but had little mind to work with her hands, for her back soon grew weary.

There seemed little hope, indeed, this fair child should ever have full use of her limbs. It is true she had mended a little after her father and mother had been to Nidaros with her to St. Olav's shrine. Lavrans and Ragnfrid had gone thither on foot, without man or serving-maid to attend them; they bore the child between them on a litter the whole way. After the journey Ulvhild grew so far well that she could walk a little with a crutch. But they could not hope that she should grow well enough to be wedded, and so it was like that, when the time came, she must be given to a cloister with all the wealth that should fall to her.

They never spoke of this, and Ulvhild herself scarce knew how much unlike she was to other children. She was very fond of finery and pretty clothes, and her father and mother had not the heart to deny her anything; so Rangfrid stitched and sewed for her, and decked her out like any king's child. Once some pedlars passing through the parish lay overnight at Laugarbru; and Ulvhild got a sight of their wares there. They had some amber-coloured silk-stuff, and she set her heart on having a shift of it. Lavrans was not wont to deal with such folk, who went around against the law, selling wares from the market-towns in the country parishes; but now he bought the whole bale at once. He gave Kristin some of the stuff, too, for a bridal shift, and she was sewing on it this summer. Until now all the shifts she owned had been of wool, or of linen for best wear. But now Ulvhild had a shift of silk for feast days and a Sunday shift of linen with silk let in above.

Lavrans Björgulfsön owned Laugarbru too now, and Tordis and Jon were in charge there. With them was Lavrans' and Ragnfrid's youngest daughter, Ramborg, whom Tordis had nursed. Ragnfrid would scarce look at the child for some time after it was born, for, she said, she brought her children ill-fortune. Yet she loved the little maid much and was ever sending gifts to her and Tordis; and later she went often over to Laugarbru and saw Ramborg, but she liked best to come after the child was asleep and sit by her. Lavrans and the two older daughters were often at Laugarbru to play with the little one; she was a strong and healthy child, but not so fair as her sisters.

This was the last summer Arne Gyrdsön was on Jörundgaard. The Bishop had promised Gyrd to help the youth on in the world, and in the autumn Arne was to set out for Hamar.

Kristin knew well enough that she was dear to Arne, but she was in many ways still a child in mind, and she thought little about it, but bore herself to him as she had always done from the time they were children; was with him as often as she could, and always stood up with him when there was dancing at home or upon the church-green. That her mother did not like this, seemed to her something of a jest. But she never spoke to Arne of Simon or of her wedding, for she marked that he grew heavy-hearted when there was talk of it.

Arne was a very handy man, and was now making Kristin a sewing-chair * as a keepsake. He had covered both the box and the frame of the chair with fair, rich carving, and was now busy in the smithy on iron bands and a lock for it. On a fine evening well on in summer Kristin had gone down to him. She had taken with her a jacket of her father's she had to mend, and sat upon the stone threshold sewing while she chatted with the youth in the smithy. Ulvhild was with her; she hopped about upon her crutch, eating the raspberries which grew among the heaps of stone around the field.

After a while Arne came to the smithy door to cool himself. He made as though to seat himself beside Kristin, but she moved a little away and bade him have a care not to dirty the sewing she had upon her knee.

"Is it come to this between us," said Arne, "that you dare not let me sit by you for fear the peasant boy should soil you?"

Kristin looked at him in wonder, and answered:

"You know well enough what I meant. But take your apron off, wash the charcoal from your hands and sit down a little and rest you here by me——" And she made room for him.

But Arne laid himself in the grass in front of her; then she said again:

"Nay, be not angry, my Arne. Can you think I could be unthankful for the brave gift you are making me, or ever forget you have been my best friend at home here all my days?"

"Have I been that?" he asked.

"You know it well," said Kristin. "And never will I forget you. But you, who are to go out into the world—maybe you will gain wealth and honour or ever you think—you will like enough forget me, long before I forget you——"

"You will never forget me?" said Arne, smiling. "And I will forget you ere you forget me?—you are naught but a child, Kristin."

"*You* are not so old either," she replied.

" I am as old as Simon Darre," said he again. "And we bear helm and shield as well as the Dyfrin folk; but my folks have not had fortune with them——"

He had dried his hands on the grass tufts; and now he took Kristin's ankle and pressed his cheek to the foot which showed from under her dress. She would have drawn away her foot, but Arne said:

"Your mother is at Laugarbu, and Lavrans has ridden forth—from

* Sewing-chair, see Note 9.

the houses none can see us where we sit. Surely you can let me speak this once of what is in my heart."

Kristin answered:

"We have known all our days, both you and I, that 'twas bootless for us to set our hearts on each other."

"May I lay my head in your lap?" said Arne, and as she did not answer, he laid his head down and twined an arm about her waist. With his other hand he pulled at the plaits of her hair.

"How will you like it," he asked in a little, "when Simon lies in your lap thus, and plays with your hair?"

Kristin did not answer. It seemed as though a heaviness fell upon her of a sudden—Arne's words and Arne's head on her knee—it seemed to her as though a door opened into a room, where many dark passages led into a greater darkness; sad, and heavy at heart, she faltered and would not look inside.

"Wedded folk do not use to do so," said she of a sudden, quickly, as if eased of a weight. She tried to see Simon's fat, round face looking up into hers as Arne was looking now; she heard his voice—and she could not keep from laughing:

"I trow Simon will never lie on the ground to play with my shoes—not he!"

"No, for he can play with you in his bed," said Arne. His voice made her feel sick and powerless all at once. She tried to push his head from off her lap, but he pressed it against her knees, and said softly:

"But _I_ would play with your shoes and your hair and your fingers, and follow you out and in the livelong day, Kristin, were you ever so much my wife and slept in my arms each single night."

He half sat up, put his arm round her shoulder and gazed into her eyes.

"'Tis not well done of you to talk thus to me," said Kristin bashfully, in a low voice.

"No," said Arne. He rose and stood before her. "But tell me one thing—would you not rather it were I——?"

"Oh! I would rather"—she sat still awhile—"I would rather not have any man—not yet——"

Arne did not move, but said:

"Would you rather be given to the cloister then, as 'tis to be with Ulvhild, and be a maid all your days?"

Kristin pressed her folded hands down into her lap. A strange, sweet trembling seized her—and with a sudden shudder she seemed to understand how much her little sister was to be pitied—her eyes filled with tears of sorrow for Ulvhild's sake.

"Kristin!" said Arne, in a low voice.

At that moment a loud scream came from Ulvhild. Her crutch had caught between the stones, and she had fallen. Arne and Kristin ran to her, and Arne lifted her up into her sister's arms. She had cut her mouth, and much blood was flowing from the hurt.

Kristin sat down with her in the smithy door, and Arne fetched water in a wooden bowl. Together they set to washing and wiping her face. She had rubbed the skin off her knees, too. Kristin bent tenderly over the small, thin legs.

Ulvhild's wailing soon grew less, but she wept silently and bitterly as children do who are used to suffering pain. Kristin held her head to her bosom and rocked her gently.

Then the bell began to ring for vespers up at Olav's Church.

Arne spoke to Kristin, but she sat bent over her sister as though she neither heard nor marked him, so that at last he grew afraid and asked if she thought there was danger in the hurt. Kristin shook her head, but looked not at him.

Soon after she got up and went towards the farmstead, bearing Ulvhild in her arms. Arne followed, silent and troubled—Kristin seemed so deep in thought, and her face was set and hard. As she walked, the bell went on ringing out over the meadows and the dale; it was still ringing as she went into the house.

She laid Ulvhild in the bed which the sisters had shared ever since Kristin had grown too big to sleep by her father and mother. She slipped her shoes off and lay down beside the little one—lay and listened for the ringing of the bell long after it was hushed and the child slept.

It had come to her as the bell began to ring, while she sat with Ulvhild's little bleeding face in her hands, that maybe it was a sign to her. If she should go to the convent in her sister's stead—if she should vow herself to the service of God and the Virgin Mary—might not God give the child health and strength again?

She thought of Brother Edvin's word: that nowadays 'twas only marred and crippled children and those for whom good husbands could not be found that their fathers and mothers gave to God. She knew her father and mother were godly folks—yet had she never heard aught else but that she should wed—but when they understood that Ulvhild would be sickly all her days, they planned for her straightway that she should go to the cloister. . . .

And she had no mind to go herself—she strove against the thought that God would do a miracle for Ulvhild if she herself turned nun. She hung on Sira Eirik's word that in these days not many miracles come to pass. And yet she felt this evening it was as Brother Edvin said: had a man but faith enough, his faith might work miracles. But she had no mind to have that faith herself, she did not love God and His Mother, and the Saints *so* much, did not even wish to love them so—she loved the world and longed for the world.

Kristin pressed her lips down into Ulvhild's soft, silken hair. The child slept soundly, and the elder sister sat up restlessly, but lay down again. Her heart bled with sorrow and shame, but she knew she did not wish to believe in signs and wonders, for she would not give up her heritage of health and beauty and love.

So she tried to comfort herself with the thought, that her father and mother would not be willing she should do such a thing. Nor would they think it could avail. Then, too, she was promised already, and she was sure they would not give up Simon, of whom they were so fond. She felt it a betrayal of herself that they were so proud of this son-in-law; of a sudden she thought with dislike of Simon's round, red face and small laughing eyes—of his jaunty gait—he bounced like a ball, it came to her all at once; of his bantering talk, that made her feel awkward and foolish. 'Twas no such glory either to get him, and move with him just down to Formo. Still she would rather have him than be sent to a convent. But, ah! the world beyond the hills, the King's palace and the earls and knights Lady Aashild talked of—and a comely man with sorrowful eyes who would follow her in and out and never grow weary. She thought of Arne that summer day when he lay on his side and slept with his brown, glossy hair outspread among the heather—she had loved him then as though he were her brother. It was not well done of him to have spoken to her so, when he knew they could never belong to one another. . . .

Word came from Laugarbru that her mother would stay there over-night. Kristin got up to undress and go to rest. She began to unlace her dress—then she put her shoes on again, threw her cloak about her and went out.

The night sky stretched clear and green above the hill-crests. It was near time for the moon to rise, and where it was yet hid behind the fell, sailed some small clouds their lower edges shining like silver; the sky grew brighter and brighter, like metal under gathering drops of dew.

She ran up between the fences, over the road, and up the slope toward the church. It stood there, as though asleep, dark and shut, but she went up to the cross which stood near by to mark the place where St. Olav once rested as he fled before his enemies.

Kristin knelt down upon the stone and laid her folded hands upon the base of the cross: "Holy Cross, strongest of masts, fairest of trees, bridge for the sick to the fair shores of health——"

At the words of the prayer, it was as if her longing widened out and faded little by little like rings on a pool. The single thoughts that troubled her smoothed themselves out one after the other, her mind grew calmer, more tender, and there came upon her a gentle, vague sadness in place of her distress.

She lay kneeling there and drank in all the sounds of the night. The wind sighed strangely, the rushing sound of the river came from beyond the wood by the church, the beck ran near by right across the road—and all about, far and near, in the dark, she half saw and heard small rills of running and dripping water. The river gleamed white down below in the valley. The moon crept up in a little nick in the hills—the dewy leaves and stones sparkled faintly, and the newly tarred timber of the belfry shone dull and dark by the churchyard gate. Then the moon was hid once more where the mountain ridge rose higher, and now many more white and shining clouds floated in the sky.

She heard a horse coming at a slow pace from higher up the road, and the sound of men's voices speaking low and even. She had no fear of folk here close at home where she knew every one—so she felt quite safe.

Her father's dogs rushed at her turned and dashed back into the wood, then turned back and leaped upon her again. Her father shouted a greeting as he came out from among the birches. He was leading Guldsveinen by the bridle; a brace or two of birds hung dangling from the saddle, and Lavrans bore a hooded hawk upon his left wrist. He had with him a tall, bent man in a monk's frock, and even before Kristin had seen his face she knew it was Brother Edvin. She went to meet them, wondering no more than if it had been a dream—she only smiled when Lavrans asked whether she knew their guest again.

Lavrans had chanced upon him up by the Rost bridge, and had coaxed him home with him to spend the night. But Brother Edvin would have it, they must let him lie in an outhouse: "For I'm grown so lousy," said he, "you cannot put me in the good beds."

And for all Lavrans talked and begged, the monk held out; nay, at first he would have it they should give him his food out in the courtyard. But at last they got him into the hall with them, and Kristin made up the fire in the fireplace in the corner and set candles on the board, while a serving-maid brought in meat and drink.

The monk seated himself on the beggars' bench by the door, and would have naught but cold porridge and water for his supper. Neither would he have aught of Lavrans' proffer to have a bath made ready for him, and have his clothes well washed.

Brother Edvin fidgeted and scratched himself, and laughed all over his lean, old face.

"Nay, nay," said he, "these things bite into my proud hide better than either whips or the Gardian's words. I have been sitting under a rock up here among the fells all summer—they gave me leave to go out into the wilderness to fast and pray, and there I sat and thought: now was I like a holy hermit indeed; and the poor folk away in Setnadal came up with food for me, and thought here they saw, in very truth, a godly and clean-living monk. Brother Edvin, they said, were there many such monks as you, we would be better men fast enough; but when we see priests and bishops and monks biting and fighting like young swine in a trough. . . . Ay, I told them it was unchristian-like to talk so—but I liked to hear it well enough, and I sang and I prayed till the mountain rang again. Now will it be wholesome for me to feel the lice biting and fighting upon my skin, and to hear the good housewives, who would have all clean and seemly in their houses, cry out: 'That dirty pig of a monk can lie out in the barn well enough now 'tis summer.' I am for northwards now to Nidaros for St. Olav's vigil, and 'twill be well for me to mark that folk are none too fain to come nigh me——"

Ulvhild woke, and Lavrans went and lifted her up and wrapped her in his cloak:

"Here is the child I spoke of, dear Father. Lay your hands upon her and pray to God for her as you prayed for the boy away north in Meldal who we heard got his health again——"

The monk lifted Ulvhild's chin gently and looked into her face. And then he raised one of her hands and kissed it.

"Pray rather, you and your wife, Lavarans Björgulfsön, that you be not tempted to try and bend God's will concerning this child. Our Lord Jesus Himself has set these small feet upon the path which will lead her most surely to the home of peace—I see it by your eyes, you blessed Ulvhild, you have your intercessors in our second home."

"The boy in Meldal got well, I have heard," said Lavrans, in a low voice.

"He was a poor widow's only child, and there was none but the parish to feed or clothe him when his mother should be gone. And yet the woman prayed only that God might give her a fearless heart so that she might have faith He would bring that to pass which would be best for the lad. Naught else did I do but join in that prayer of hers."

"'Tis hard for her mother and for me to rest content with this," answered Lavrans heavily. "The more that she is so fair and so good."

"Have you seen the child at Lidstad, south in the Dale?" asked the monk. "Would you rather your daughter had been like that?"

Lavrans shuddered and pressed the child close to him.

"Think you not," said Brother Edvin again, "that in God's eyes we are all children He has cause to grieve for, crippled as we are with sin? And yet we deem not we are so badly off in this world."

He went to the picture of the Virgin Mary upon the wall, and all knelt down while he said the evening prayer. It seemed to them that Brother Edvin had given them good comfort.

But, none the less, after he had gone from the room to seek his place of rest, Astrid, the head serving-wench, swept with care all parts of the floor where the monk had stood, and cast the sweepings at once into the fire.

Next morning Kristin rose early, took milk-porridge and wheat-cakes in a goodly dish of flame-grained birchwood—for she knew that the monk never touched meat—and herself bore the food out to him. But few of the folk were yet about in the houses.

Brother Edvin stood upon the bridge of the cow-house, ready for the road with staff and scrip; with a smile he thanked Kristin for her pains, and sat himself down on the grass and ate, while Kristin sat at his feet.

Her little white dog came running up, the little bells on his collar tinkling. She took him into her lap, and Brother Edvin snapped his fingers at him, threw small bits of wheat-cake into his mouth, and praised him mightily the while.

"'Tis a breed Queen Euphemia brought to the country," said he. "You are passing fine here on Jörundgaard now, both in great things and small."

Kristin flushed with pleasure. She knew already the dog was of a fine breed, and she was proud of having it; no one else in the parish had a lapdog. But she had not known it was of the same kind as the Queen's pet dogs.

"Simon Andressön sent him to me," said she, and pressed it to her, while it licked her face. "His name is Kortelin."

She had thought to speak to the monk about her trouble, and to pray for his counsel. But she had no longer any wish to let her mind dwell on the thoughts of the past evening. Brother Edvin was sure God would turn all things to the best for Ulvhild. And it was good of Simon to send her such a gift before even their betrothal was fixed. Arne she would not think of—he had not borne himself as he should towards her, she thought.

Brother Edvin took his staff and scrip, and bade Kristin greet those within the house—he would not stay till folk were up, but go while the day was yet cool. She went with him up past the church and a little way into the wood.

When they parted he wished her God's peace, and blessed her.

"Give me a word, like the word you gave to Ulvhild, dear Father," begged Kristin, as she stood with his hand in hers.

The monk rubbed his naked foot, knotted with gout, in the wet grass:

"Then would I bid you, daughter, that you lay to heart how God cares for folks' good here in the Dale. Little rain falls here, but He has

given you water from the fells, and the dew freshens meadow and field
each night. Thank God for the good gifts He has given you, and murmur
not if you seem to miss aught you think might well be added to you.
You have bonny yellow hair; see you fret not because it does not curl.
Have you not heard of the old wife who sat and wept for that she had
only a small bite of swine's flesh to give to her seven little ones for Christmas cheer? Pat at the moment St. Olav came riding by, and he
stretched out his hand over the meat and prayed that God might give
the poor little ravens their fill. But when the woman saw a whole pig's
carcase lying upon the board, she wept that she had not pots and
platters enow!"

Kristin ran homewards, with Kortelin dancing at her heels, snapping
at the hem of her dress, and barking and ringing all his little silver bells.

VI

ARNE stayed at home at Finsbrekken the last days before he was to set
out for Hamar; his mother and sisters were making ready his clothes.

The day before he was to ride southward, he came to Jörundgaard to
bid farewell. And he made a chance to whisper to Kristin: would she
meet him on the road south of Laugarbru next evening?

"I would so fain we two should be alone the last time we are together,"
said he. "Does it seem such a great thing that I ask?—after all, we were
brought up together like brother and sister," he said, when Kristin hung
doubtful a little before making reply.

So she promised to come, if she could slip away from home.

It snowed next morning, but through the day it turned to rain, and
soon roads and fields were a sea of grey mud. Wreaths of mist hung and
drifted along the lower hillsides; now and then they sank yet lower and
gathered into white rollers along the roots of the hills; and then the
thick rain-clouds closed in again.

Sira Eirik came over to help Lavrans draw up some deeds. They went
down to the hearth-room, for in such weather it was pleasanter there
than in the great hall, where the fireplace filled the room with smoke.
Ragnfrid was at Laugrabru, where Ramborg was now getting better of a
fever she had caught early in the autumn.

Thus it was not hard for Kristin to slip away unseen, but she dared
not take a horse, so she went on foot. The road was a quagmire of snow-
slush and withered leaves; there was a saddening breath of death and
decay in the raw, chill air, and now and again there came a gust of wind
driving the rain into her face. She drew her hood well down over her
head and, holding her cloak about her with both hands, went quickly
forward. She was a little afraid—the roar of the river sounded so hollow

in the heavy air, and the clouds drove dark and ragged over the hill-crests. Now and again she halted and listened for Arne's coming.

After a time she heard the splashing of hoofs upon the slushy road behind her, and she stopped then where she was, for this was a somewhat lonely spot and she thought 'twas a good place for them to say their farewells in quiet. Almost at once, she saw the horseman coming, and Arne sprang from his horse and led it as he came to meet her.

"'Twas kindly done of you to come," said he, "in this ugly weather."

"'Tis worse for you who have so far to ride—and how is it you set out so late?" she asked.

"Jon has bidden me to lie the night at Loptsgaard," answered Arne. "I thought 'twas easier for you to meet me at this time of day."

They stood silent for a time. Kristin thought she had never seen before how fair a youth Arne was. He had on a smooth steel cap, and under that a brown woollen hood that sat tight about his face and spread out over his shoulders; under it, his narrow face showed bright and comely. His leather jerkin was old, spotted with rust and rubbed by the coat of mail which had been worn above it—Arne had taken it over from his father—but it fitted closely to his slim, lithe, and powerful body, and he had a sword at his side and in his hand a spear—his other weapons hung from his saddle. He was full-grown now and bore himself manfully.

She laid her hand upon his shoulder, and said:

"Mind you, Arne, you asked me once if I thought you as good a man as Simon Andressön? Now will I tell you one thing, before we part; 'tis that you seem to me as much above him in looks and bearing as he is reckoned above you in birth and riches by those who look most to such things."

"Why do you tell me this?" asked Arne breathlessly.

"Because Brother Edvin told me to lay to heart, that we should thank God for His good gifts, and not be like the woman when St. Olav added to her meat, and she wept because she had not trenchers to put it in—so you should not grieve that He has not given you as much of riches as of bodily gifts——"

"Was it *that* you meant," said Arne. And then, as she was silent, he said:

"I wondered if you meant that you would rather be wedded to me than to the other——"

"That I would, truly," said she, in a low voice. " . . . I know you better——"

Arne threw his arms around her so that her feet were lifted from the ground. He kissed her face many times, and then set her down again:

"God help us, Kristin, what a child you are!"

She stood and hung her head, but left her hands upon his shoulders. He caught her wrists and held them tight:

"I see how 'tis with you, my sweeting: you little know how sore I am at heart to lose you. Kristin, you know we have grown up together like two apples on one branch; I loved you long before I began to understand that one day another would come and break you from me. As sure as God suffered death for us all—I know not how I can ever be happy in this world again after to-day——"

Kristin wept bitterly and lifted her face, so that he might kiss her.

"Do not talk so, my Arne," she begged, and patted him on the shoulder.

"Kristin," said Arne in a low voice, and took her into his arms again, "think you not that if you begged your father—Lavrans is so good a man, he would not force you against your will—if you begged them but to let you wait a few years—no one knows how fortune may turn for me —we are both of us so young——"

"Oh, I fear I must do as they wish at home," she wept.

And now weeping came upon Arne too.

"You know not, Kristin, how dear you are to me. He hid his face upon her shoulder. "If you did, and if you cared for me, for sure you would go to Lavrans and beg hard——"

"I cannot do it," she sobbed. "I could never come to love any man so much as to go against my father and mother for his sake." She groped with her hands for his face under the hood and the heavy steel cap. "Do not cry so, Arne, my dearest friend——"

"You must take this at least," said he after a time, giving her a little brooch; "and think of me sometimes, for I shall never forget you nor my grief——"

It was all but dark when Kristin and Arne had said their last farewell. She stood and looked after him when at length he rode away. A streak of yellow light shone through a rift in the clouds, and was reflected in the footprints, where they had walked and stood in the slush on the road —it all looked so cold and sorrowful, she thought. She drew up her linen neckerchief and dried her tear-stained face, then turned and went homeward.

She was wet and cold, and walked quickly. After a time she heard some one coming along the road behind her. She was a little frightened; even on such a night as this there might be strange folk journeying on the highway, and she had a lonely stretch before her. A great black scree rose right up on one side, and on the other the ground fell steeply and there was fir-forest all the way down to the leaden-hued river in the bottom of the Dale. So she was glad when the man behind her called to her by name; and she stood still and waited.

The newcomer was a tall, thin man in a dark surcoat with lighter sleeves; as he came nearer she saw he was dressed as a priest and carried an empty wallet on his back. And now she knew him to be Bentein Priestson, as they called him—Sira Eirik's daughter's son. She saw at once that he was far gone in drink.

"Ay, one goes and another comes," said he, laughing, when they had greeted one another. "I met Arne of Brekken even now—I see you are weeping. You might as well smile a little now I am come home—we have been friends, too, ever since we were children, have we not?"

"'Tis an ill exchange, methinks, getting you into the parish in his stead," said Kristin bluntly. She had never liked Bentein. "And so, I fear, will many think. Your grandfather here has been so glad you were in Oslo making such a fair beginning."

"Oh, ay," said Bentein, with a nickering laugh. "So 'twas a fair beginning I was making, you think? I was even like a pig in a wheat-field, Kristin—and the end was the same, I was hunted out with cudgels and the hue and cry. Ay, ay! ay, ay! 'Tis no great thing, the gladness my grandfather gets from his offspring. But what a mighty hurry you are in!"

"I am cold," said Kristin curtly.

"Not colder than I," said the priest. "I have no more clothes on me than you see here—my cloak I had to sell for food and beer in little Hamar. Now, you should still have some heat in your body from making your farewells with Arne—methinks you should let me get under your fur with you——" and he caught her cloak, pulled it over his shoulders and gripped her round the waist with his wet arm.

Kristin was so amazed with his boldness it was a moment before she could gather her wits—then she strove to tear herself away, but he had a hold of her cloak, and it was fastened together by a strong silver clasp, Bentein got his arms about her again, and made to kiss her, his mouth nearly touching her chin. She tried to strike, but he held her fast by the upper arm.

"I trow you have lost your wits," she hissed, as she struggled, "dare you to lay hands on me as I were a . . . dearly shall you rue this to-morrow, dastard that you are——"

"Nay, to-morrow you will not be so foolish," says Bentein, putting his leg in front of her so that she half fell into the mud, and pressing one hand over her mouth.

Yet she had no thought of crying out. Now for the first time it flashed on her mind what he dared to want with her, but rage came upon her so wild and furious she had scarce a thought of fear: she snarled like an animal at grips with another, and fought furiously with the man as he tried to hold her down, while the ice-cold snow-water soaked through her clothes on to her burning skin.

"To-morrow you will have wit enough to hold your tongue," said Bentein, ". . . and if it cannot be hidden, you can put the blame on Arne—'twill be believed the sooner——"

Just then one of his fingers got into her mouth, and at once she bit it with all her might, so that Bentein shrieked and let go his hold. Quick as lightning Kristin got one hand free, seized his face with it, and pressed her thumb with all her might against the ball of one of his eyes: he roared out and rose to his knees; like a cat she slipped from his grasp, threw herself upon him so that he fell upon his back, and, turning, rushed along the road with the mud splashing over her at every bound.

She ran and ran without looking back. She heard Bentein coming after, and she ran till her heart thumped in her throat, while she moaned softly and strained her eyes forward—should she never reach Laugarbru? At last she was out on the road where it passed through the fields; she saw the group of houses down on the hill-slope, and at the same moment she bethought her that she durst not run in there, where her mother was—in the state she was now in, plastered with clay and withered leaves from head to foot, and with her clothing torn to rags.

She marked that Bentein was gaining upon her; and on that she bent down and took up two great stones. She threw them when he came near enough; one struck him with such force it felled him to the ground. Then she ran on again and stayed not before she stood upon the bridge.

All trembling, she stood and clutched the railing of the bridge; a darkness came before her eyes, and she feared she would drop down in a swoon—but then she thought of Bentein; what if he should come and find her. Shaken with rage and shame she went onwards, though her legs would scarce bear her, and now she felt her face smart where finger-nails had scarred it, and felt too she had hurts upon both back and arms. Her tears came hot as fire.

She wished Bentein might have been killed by the stone she had thrown; she wished she had gone back and made an end of him; she felt for her knife, but found that she must have lost it.

Then again came the thought, she must not be seen at home as she was; and so it came into her mind that she would go to Romundgaard. She would complain to Sira Eirik.

But the priest had not come back yet from Jörundgaard. In the kitchen-house she found Gunhild, Bentein's mother; the woman was alone, and Kristin told her how her son had dealt with her. But that she had gone out to meet Arne she did not tell her. When she saw that Gunhild thought she had been at Laugarbru, she left her to think so.

Gunhild said little, but wept a great deal while she washed the mud off Kristin's clothes and sewed up the worst rents. And the girl was so shaken she paid no need to the covert glances Gunhild cast on her now and then.

When Kristin went, Gunhild took her cloak and went out with her, but took the way to the stables. Kristin asked her whither she was going.

"Surely I may have leave to ride down and look after my son," answered the woman. "See whether you have killed him with that stone of yours, or how it fares with him."

There seemed to be naught Kristin could answer to this, so she said only that Gunhild should see to it Bentein got out of the parish as soon as might be, and kept out of her sight, ". . . or I will speak of this to Lavrans, and you can guess, I trow, what would happen then."

And indeed, Bentein went southward not more than a week later; he carried letters from Sira Eirik to the Bishop of Hamar, begging the Bishop to find work for him or otherwise to help him.

VII

O N E day at Yuletide Simon Andressön came riding to Jörundgaard, a quite unlooked-for guest. He craved pardon for coming thus, unbidden and alone, without his kinsfolk. But Sir Andres was in Sweden on the King's business; he himself had been home at Dyfrin for a time, but only his young sisters and his mother, who lay ill abed, were there; so time had hung on his hands, and a great longing had taken him to look in upon them up here.

Ragnfrid and Lavrans thanked him much for having made this long journey in the depth of winter. The more they saw of Simon the more they liked him. He knew of all that had passed between Andres and Lavrans, and it was now fixed that his and Kristin's betrothal ale should be drunk before the beginning of Lent if Sir Andres could be home by that time, but, if not, then as soon as Easter was past.

Kristin was quiet and downcast when with her betrothed; she found not much to talk of with him. One evening when they had all been sitting drinking, he asked her to go out with him a little into the cool. Then, as they stood on the balcony in front of the upper hall, he put his arm round her waist and kissed her. After that he did the same often when they were alone. It gave her no gladness, but she suffered him to do it, since she knew the betrothal was a thing that must come. She thought of her wedding now only as something which she must go through with, not as something she wished for. None the less she liked

Simon well enough—most, though, when he talked with others and did not touch or talk to her.

She had been so unhappy through this whole autumn. It was of no use, however often she told herself Bentein had been able to do her no harm; none the less she felt herself soiled and shamed.

Nothing could be the same as it had been before, since a man had dared try to wreak such a will on her. She lay awake of nights and burned with shame and could not stop thinking of it. She felt Bentein's body close against hers as when they fought, his hot, beery breath—she could not help thinking of what might have happened—and she thought, with a shudder through all her body, of what he had said: how Arne would get the blame if it could not be hidden. There rushed through her mind all that would have followed if such a calamity had befallen and then folk had heard of her meeting with Arne—what if her father and mother had believed such a thing of Arne—and Arne himself. . . . She saw him as she had seen him that last evening, and she felt as though she sank crushed before him at the very thought that she might have dragged him down with her into sorrow and disgrace. And then she had such ugly dreams. She had heard tell in church and in holy stories of fleshly lusts and the temptations of the body, but they had meant naught to her. Now it was become real to her that she herself and all mankind had a sinful, carnal body which enmeshed the soul and ate into it with hard bonds.

Then she would think out for herself how she might have killed or blinded Bentein. It was the only solace she could find—to sate herself with dreams of revenge upon the dark, hateful man who stood always in the way of her thoughts. But this did not help for long; she lay by Ulvhild's side of nights and wept bitter tears at the thought of all this that had been brought upon her by brute force. Bentein had not failed altogether—he had wrought scathe to the maidenhood of her spirit.

The first work-day after Christmas all the women on Jörundgaard were busy in the kitchen-house; Ragnfrid and Kristin had been there, too, for most of the day. Late in the evening, while some of the women were clearing up after the baking, and others making ready the supper, the dairymaid came rushing in, shrieking and wringing her hands:

"Jesus, Jesus—did ever any hear such a dreadful thing—they are bringing Arne Gyrdsön home dead on a sleigh—God help Gyrd and Inga in this misery——"

A man who dwelt in a cottage a little way down the road came in with Halvdan. It was these two who had met the bier.

The women crowded round them. Outside the circle stood Kristin, white and shaking. Halvdan, Lavrans' own body-servant, who had known Arne from his boyhood, wept aloud as he told the story:

It was Bentein Priestson who had killed Arne. On New Year's eve the men of the Bishop's household were sitting and drinking in the men's hall, and Bentein had come in—he had been given a clerkship now with the Corpus Christi prebendary. The men did not want him amongst them at first, but he had put Arne in mind that they were both from the same parish, and Arne had let him sit by him, and they had drunk together. But presently they had quarrelled and fought, and Arne had fallen on so fiercely that Bentein had snatched a knife from the table and stabbed him in the throat and then more than once in the breast. Arne had died almost at once.

The Bishop had taken this mischance much to heart; he himself had cared for the laying-out of the corpse, and had it brought all the long way home by his own folk. Bentein he had thrown into irons, cast him out from the church, and if he were not already hanged, he was going to be.

Halvdan had to tell all this over again many times as fresh people streamed in. Lavrans and Simon came over to the kitchen too, when they marked all the stir and commotion about the place. Lavrans was much moved; he bade them saddle his horse, he would ride over to Brekken at once. As he was about to go, his eyes fell on Kristin's white face.

"Maybe *you* would like to go with me?" he asked. Kristin faltered a little; she shuddered—but then she nodded, for she could not utter one word.

"Is't not too cold for her?" said Ragnfrid. "Doubtless they will have the wake to-morrow, and then 'tis like we shall all go together——"

Lavrans looked at his wife; he marked Simon's face too; and then he went and laid his arm round Kristin's shoulders.

"She is his foster-sister, you must bear in mind," said he. "Maybe, she would like to help Inga with the laying-out the body."

And though Kristin's heart was benumbed with despair and fear, she felt a glow of thankfulness to her father for his words.

Ragnfrid said then, that if Kristin was to go, they must eat their evening porridge before they started. She wished, too, to send gifts to Inga by them—a new linen sheet, wax-candles and fresh-baked bread; and she bade them say she would come up herself and help to prepare for the burial.

There was little eating, but much talking in the room while the food was on the table. One reminded the other of the trials that God had laid upon Gyrd and Inga. Their farm had been laid waste by stone-slips and floods; more than one of their elder children were dead, so that all Arne's brothers and sisters were still but little ones. They had had fortune with them now for some years, since the Bishop placed Gyrd at Finsbrekken as his bailiff; and the children who were left to them were fair and full of promise. But his mother loved Arne more than all the rest. . . .

They pitied Sira Eirik too. The priest was beloved and well respected, and the folk of the parish were proud of him; he was learned and skilled in his office, and in all the years he had had their church he had never let a holy-day or a mass or a service pass that he was in duty bound to hold. In his youth he had been man-at-arms under Count Alv of Tornberg, but he had had the misfortune to kill a man of very high birth, and so had taken refuge with the Bishop of Oslo; when the Bishop saw what a turn Eirik had for book-learning, he had him trained for a priest. And had it not been that he still had enemies by reason of that slaying of long ago, it was like Sira Eirik would not have stayed here in this little charge. True enough, he was very greedy of pence, both for his own purse and for the church, but then, was not his church richly fitted out with plate and vestments and books? and he himself had these children—and he had had naught but sorrow and trouble with his family. In these far-away country parishes folk held it was not reason that priests should live like monks, for they must at the least have women to help on their farms, and they might well need a woman to look after things for them, seeing what long and toilsome journeys they must make round the parishes, and that too in all kinds of weather; besides folk had not forgotten that it was not so very long since priests in Norway had been wedded men. Thus, no one had blamed Sira Eirik overmuch that he had had three children by the woman who tended his house, while he was yet young. But, this evening they said, it looked, indeed, as though 'twas God's will to punish Eirik for his loose living, so much evil had his children and his children's children brought upon him. And some thought there was good reason, too, that a priest should have neither wife nor children—for after this it was much to be feared that bitterness and enmity would arise between the priest and the folk on Finsbrekken, who until now had been the best of friends.

Simon Andressön knew much of Bentein's doings in Oslo; and he told of them. Bentein had been clerk to the Dean of the Church of the Holy Virgin, and he had the name of being a quick-witted youth. There were many women, too, who liked him well—he had roving eyes, and a glib tongue. Some held him a comely man—these were for the most part such women as thought they had a bad bargain in their husbands, And then young maids, the sort that liked well that men should be somewhat free with them. Simon laughed—ay, they understood? Well, Bentein was so sly, he never went too far with that kind of woman; he was all talk with them, and so he got a name for clean-living. But the thing was that King Haakon, as they knew, was a good and pious man himself, and fain would keep order among his men, and hold them to a seemly walk and conversation—the young ones at least; the others were apt to be too much for him. And it came about that whatever pranks the youngsters managed to slip out and take part in—drinking bouts, gambling and beer-drinking and such-like—the priest of the King's household always got to hear of, and the madcaps had to confess and pay scot and suffer hard reproof; ay, two or three of the wildest youths of all were hunted away. But at last it came out, it was this fox, Bentein secretarius—unknown to any one he had been made free of all the beer-houses and worse places still; he confessed the serving-wenches and gave them absolution. . . .

Kristin sat at her mother's side; she tried to eat so that no one should mark how it was with her, though her hand shook so that she spilled the milk porridge at each spoonful, and her tongue felt so thick and dry in her mouth that she could not swallow the morsels of bread. But when Simon began to tell of Bentein, she had to give up making believe to eat; she held on to the bench beneath her—terror and loathing seized her, so that she felt dizzy and sick. It was he who had wanted to. . . . Bentein and Arne, Bentein and Arne. . . . Beside herself with impatience, she waited for them to be finished. She longed to see Arne, Arne's comely face, to throw herself down beside him and mourn and forget all else.

As her mother helped her with her outer wrappings, she kissed her daughter on the cheek. Kristin was so little used to endearments from her mother now, it comforted her much—she laid her head upon Ragn-frid's shoulder a moment, but she could not weep.

When they came out into the courtyard, she saw that others were going with them—Halvdan, Jon from Laugarbru, and Simon and his man. It gave her a pang, she knew not why, that the two strangers should be coming with them.

It was a bitter cold evening, and the snow crackled underfoot; in the black sky the stars crowded thick, glittering like rime. When they had ridden a little way, they heard yells and howls and furious hoof-beats from the flats to the south—a little farther up the road a whole troop of horsemen came tearing up behind and swept past them with a ringing of metal, leaving behind a vapour of reeking, rime-covered horse-flesh, which reached them even where they stood aside in the deep snow. Halvdan hailed the wild crew—they were youths from the farms in the south of the parish; they were still keeping Yuletide and were out trying their horses. Some, who were too drunk to understand, thundered on at a gallop, roaring at the top of their voices and hammering on their shields. But a few grasped the tidings which Halvdan shouted to them; they fell out of the troop, grew silent, joined Lavrans' company and talked in whispers to those in the rear.

At last they came in sight of Finsbrekken, on the hillside beyond the Sil river. There were lights about the houses—in the middle of the courtyard pine-root torches had been planted in a heap of snow, and their glare lay red over the white slopes, but the black houses looked as though smeared with clotted blood. One of Arne's little sisters stood outside and stamped her feet; she hugged her hands beneath her cloak. Kristin kissed the tear-stained, half-frozen child. Her heart was heavy as stone, and it seemed as though she had lead in her limbs, as she climbed the stairs to the loft-room where they had laid him.

The sound of singing and the glitter of many lighted candles met them in the doorway. In the middle of the room stood the coffin he had been brought home in, covered with a sheet; boards had been laid on trestles and the coffin placed upon them. At the head of the bier a young priest stood with a book in his hands, chanting; round about knelt the mourners with their faces hidden in their heavy cloaks.

Lavrans lit his candle at one of those already burning, set it firmly upon one of the boards of the bier and knelt down. Kristin tried to do the like, but could not get her candle to stand; so Simon took it and helped her. As long as the priest went on chanting, all stayed upon their knees and repeated his words in whispers, their breath hanging like steam about their mouths in the bitter cold air of the room.

When the priest shut his book and the folk rose—there were many gathered in the death-chamber already—Lavrans went forward to Inga. She stared at Kristin, and seemed scarce to hear what Lavrans said; she stood holding the gifts he had handed to her, as though she knew not she had aught in her hand.

"Are *you* come, too, Kristin," she said in a strange, choking voice. "Maybe you would see my son, so as he is come back to me?"

She pushed some of the candles aside, seized Kristin's arm with a shaking hand, and with the other swept the napkin from the face of the dead.

It was greyish-yellow like clay, and the lips had the hue of lead; they had parted a little, so that the small, even, bone-white teeth showed through as in a mocking smile. Under the long eyelashes there was a gleam of the glassy eyes, and there were some livid stains below the temples, either marks of blows or the death-spots.

"Maybe you would kiss him?" asked Inga, as before; and Kristin bent forward at her bidding and pressed her lips upon the dead man's cheek. It was clammy as with dew, and she thought she could feel the least breath of decay; the body had begun to thaw perhaps with the heat from all the tapers round.

Kristin stayed still, lying with her hands on the bier, for she could not rise. Inga drew the shroud farther aside, so that the great gash above the collar-bone came to sight. Then she turned towards the people and said with a shaking voice:

"They lie, I see, who say a dead man's wounds will bleed when he is touched by him who wrought his death. He is colder now, my boy, and less comely, than when you met him last down there upon the road. You care not much to kiss him now, I see—but I have heard you scorned not his lips then."

"Inga," said Lavrans, coming forward, "have you lost your wits—are you raving——"

"Oh, ay, you are all so fine, down at Jörundgaard—you were far too rich a man, you Lavrans Björgulfsön, for my son to dare think of courting your daughter with honour—and Kristin, too, she thought herself too good. But she was not too good to run after him on the highway at night and play with him in the thickets the night he left—ask her yourself and we will see if she dare deny it here, with Arne lying dead—and all through her lightness——"

Lavrans did not ask; he turned to Gyrd:

"Curb your wife, man—you see she has clean lost her wits——"

But Kristin lifted her white face and looked desperately about her:

"I went and met Arne the last evening because he begged me to. But naught of wrong passed between us." And then, as she seemed to come to herself and to understand all, she cried out: "I know not what you mean, Inga—would you slander Arne and he lying here—never did he tempt me nor lure me astray——"

But Inga laughed aloud:

"Nay, not Arne! but Bentein Priest—he did not let you play with him so—ask Gunhild, Lavrans, that washed the dirt off your daughter's back; and ask each man who was in the Bishop's henchmen's hall on New Year's Eve, when Bentein flouted Arne for that he had let her go, and leave him standing like a fool. She let Bentein walk homward with her under her cloak, and would have played the same game with him——"

Lavrans took her by the shoulder and laid his hand over her mouth:

"Take her away, Gyrd. Shameful it is that you should speak such words by this good youth's body—but if all your children lay here dead, I would not stand and hear you lie about mine—you, Gyrd, must answer for what this mad-woman says——"

Gyrd took hold of his wife and tried to lead her away, but he said to Lavrans:

"'Tis true, though, 'twas of Kristin they talked, Arne and Bentein, when my son lost his life. Like enough you have not heard it, but there hath been talk in the parish here, too, this autumn——"

Simon struck a blow with his sword upon the clothes-chest beside him:

"Nay, good folk, now must you find somewhat else to talk of in this death-chamber than my betrothed. . . . Priest, can you not rule these folk and keep seemly order here——?"

The priest—Kristin saw now he was the youngest son from Ulvsvolden, who had been at home for Yule—opened his book and stood up beside the bier. But Lavrans shouted that those who had talked about his daughter, let them be who they might, should be made to swallow their words; and Inga shrieked:

"Ay, take my life then, Lavrans, since she has taken all my comfort and joy—and make her wedding with this knight's son; but yet do all folk know that she was wed with Bentein upon the highway. . . . Here . . ." and she cast the sheet Lavrans had given her right across the bier to Kristin, " I need not Ragnfrid's linen to lay my Arne in the grave—make head-cloths of it, you, or keep it to swaddle your roadside brat—and go down and help Gunhild to moan for the man that's hanged——"

Lavrans, Gyrd and the priest took hold of Inga. Simon tried to lift Kristin, who was lying over the bier. But she thrust his arm fiercely aside, drew herself up straight upon her knees, and cried aloud :

"So God my Saviour help me, it is false!" and, stretching out one hand, she held it over the nearest candle on the bier.

It seemed as if the flame bent and waved aside—Kristin felt all eyes fixed upon her—what seemed to her a long time went by. And then all at once she grew ware of a burning pain in her palm, and with a piercing cry she fell back upon the floor.

She thought herself she had swooned—but she was aware that Simon and the priest raised her. Inga shrieked out something; she saw her father's horror-stricken face, and heard the priest shout that no one must take account of this ordeal—not thus might one call God to witness,—and then Simon bore her from the room and down the stairs. Simon's man ran to the stable, and soon after Kristin was sitting, still half senseless, in front of Simon on his saddle, wrapped in his cloak, and he was riding toward Jörundgaard as fast as his horse could gallop.

They were nigh to Jörundgaard when Lavrans came up with them. The rest of their company came thundering along the road far behind.

"Say naught to your mother," said Simon, as he set her down at the door of the house. "We have heard all too much wild talk to-night; 'tis no wonder you lost your wits yourself at the last."

Ragnfrid was lying awake when they came in, and she asked how things had been in the wake-chamber. Simon took it upon himself to answer for all. Ay, there had been many candles and many folk; ay, there had been a priest—Tormod from Ulsvolden—Sira Eirik he heard had ridden off to Hamar this very evening, so there would be no trouble about the burial.

"We must have a mass said over the lad," said Ragnfrid. "God strengthen Inga; the good, worthy woman is sorely tried."

Lavrans sang the same tune as Simon, and in a little Simon said that now they must all go to rest, "for Kristin is both weary and sorrowful."

After a time, when Ragnfrid slept, Lavrans threw on a few clothes, and went and seated himself on the edge of his daughters' bed. He found Kristin's hand in the dark, and said very gently:

"Now must you tell me, child, what is true and what is false in all this talk Inga is spreading."

Sobbing, Kristin told him all that had befallen the evening Arne set out for Hamar. Lavrans said but little. Kristin crept toward him in her bed, threw her arms round his neck and wailed softly:

"It *is* my fault that Arne is dead—'tis but too true, what Inga said——"

"'Twas Arne himself that begged you to go and meet him," said Lavrans, pulling the coverlid up over his daughter's bare shoulders. "I trow it was heedless in me to let you two go about together, but I thought the lad would have known better. . . . I will not blame you two—I know these things are heavy for you to bear. Yet did I never think that daughter of mine would fall into ill-fame in this parish of ours—and 'twill go hard with your mother when she hears these tidings. . . . But that you went to Gunhild with this and not to me, 'twas so witless a thing—I understand not how you could behave so foolishly——"

"I cannot bear to stay here in the Dale any more," sobbed Kristin. "Not a soul would I dare look in the face—and all I have brought upon them—the folks at Romundgaard and at Finsbrekken——"

"Ay, they will have to see to it, both Gyrd and Sira Eirik," said Lavrans, "that these lies about you are buried with Arne. For the rest, 'tis Simon Andressön can best defend you in this business," said he, and patted her in the dark. "Think you not he took the matter well and wisely——"

"Father"—and Kristin clung close to him and begged piteously and fervently—"send me to the convent, father. Ay, listen to me—I have thought of this for long; maybe Ulvhild will grow well if I go in her stead. You know the shoes with beads upon them that I sewed for her in the autumn—I pricked my fingers sorely, and my hands bled from the sharp gold-thread—yet I sat and sewed on them, for I thought it was wicked of me not to love my sister so that I would be a nun to help her—Arne once asked if I would not. Had I but said 'Ay' then, all this would not have befallen——"

Lavrans shook his head:

"Lie down now," he bade. "You know not yourself what you say, poor child. Now you must try if you can sleep——"

But Kristin lay and felt the smart in her burnt hand, and despair and bitterness over her fate raged in her heart. No worse could have befallen her had she been the most sinful of women; every one would believe—no, she could not, could not bear to stay on here in the Dale. Horror after horror rose before her—when her mother came to know of this—and now there was blood between them and their parish priest, ill-will betwixt all who had been friends around her the whole of her life. But the worst, the most crushing fear of all fell upon her when she thought of Simon and of how he had taken her and carried her away and stood forth for her at home, and borne himself as though she were his own possession—her father and mother had fallen aside before him as though she belonged already more to him than to them . . .

Then she thought of Arne's face in the coffin, cold and cruel. She remembered the last time she was at church, she had seen, as she left, an open grave that stood waiting for a dead man. The upthrown clods of earth lay upon the snow, hard and cold and grey like iron—to this had she brought Arne . . .

All at once the thought came to her of a summer evening many years before. She was standing on the balcony of the loft-room at Finsbrekken, the same room where she had been struck down that night. Arne was playing ball with some boys in the courtyard below, and the ball was hit up to her in the balcony. She had held it behind her back, and would not give it up when Arne came after it; then he had tried to wrest it from her by strength—and they had fought for it, in the balcony, in the room amid the chests, with the leather sacks, which hung there full of clothes, bumping their heads as they knocked against them in their frolic; they had laughed and struggled over that ball . . .

And then, at last, the truth seemed to come home to her: he was dead and gone, and she should never again see his comely, fearless face nor feel the touch of his warm, living hands. And she had been so childish and so heartless as never to give a thought to what it must be for him to lose her. . . . She wept bitter tears, and felt she had earned all her unhappiness. But then the thought came back of all that still awaited her, and she wept anew, for, after all, it seemed to her too hard a punishment . . .

It was Simon who told Ragnfrid of what had happened in the corpse-chamber at Brekken the night before. He did not make more of it than he needs must. But Kristin was so mazed with sorrow and night-waking that she felt a senseless anger against him because he talked as if it were not so dreadful a thing after all. Besides it vexed her sorely that her father and mother let Simon behave as though he were master in the house.

"And you, Simon—surely you believe not aught of this?" asked Ragnfrid fearfully.

"No," replied Simon. "Nor do I deem there is any one who believes it—they know you and her and this Bentein; but so little befalls for folk to talk of in these outparishes, 'tis but reason they should fall to on such a fat titbit. 'Tis for us to teach them Kristin's good name is too fine fare for such clowns as they. But pity it was she let herself be so frighted by his grossness that she went not forthwith to you or to Sira Eirik with the tale—methinks this bordel-priest would but too gladly have avowed he meant naught worse than harmless jesting, had you, Lavrans, got a word with him."

Both Kristin's parents said that Simon was right in this. But she cried out, stamping her foot:

"But he threw me down on the ground, I say—I scarce know myself what he did or did not do—I was beside myself; I can remember naught—for all I know it may be as Inga says—I have not been well nor happy a single day since——"

Ragnfrid shrieked and clasped her hands together; Lavrans started up—even Simon's face fell. He looked at her sharply, then went up to her and took her by the chin. Then he laughed:

"God bless you, Kristin—you had remembered but too well if he had done you any harm. No marvel if she has been sad and ill since that unhappy evening she had such an ugly fright—she who had never known aught but kindness and goodwill before," said he to the others. "Any but the evil-minded, who would fain think ill rather than good, can see by her eyes that she is a maid, and no woman."

Kristin looked up into her betrothed's small, steady eyes. She half lifted her hands—as if to throw them round his neck—when he went on:

"You must not think, Kristin, that you will not forget this. 'Tis not in my mind that we should settle down at Formo as soon as we are wed, so that you would never leave the Dale. No one has the same hue of hair or mind in both rain and sunshine, said old King Sverre, when they blamed his Birch-legs* for being overbearing in good-fortune——"

Lavrans and Ragnfrid smiled—it was pleasant enough to hear the young man discourse with the air of a wise old bishop. Simon went on:

"'Twould ill beseem me to seek to teach you, who are to be my father-in-law; but so much, maybe, I may make bold to say, that we, my brothers and sisters and I, were brought up more strictly; we were not let run about so freely with the house folk as I have seen that Kristin is used to. My mother often said that if one played with the cottar-carls' brats, 'twas like one would get a louse or two in one's hair in the end—and there's somewhat in that saying."

Lavrans and Ragnfrid held their peace; but Kristin turned away, and the wish she had felt but a moment before, to clasp Simon round the neck, had quite left her.

Towards noon, Lavrans and Simon took their ski and went out to see to some snares up on the mountain ridges. The weather was fine outside—sunshine, and the cold not so great. Both men were glad to slip away from all the sadness and weeping at home, and so they went far—right up among the bare hilltops.

They lay in the sun under a crag and drank and ate; Lavrans spoke a little of Arne—he had loved the boy well. Simon chimed in, praised the dead lad, and said he thought it not strange that Kristin grieved for her foster-brother. Then Lavrans said: maybe they should not press her much, but should give her a little time to get back her peace of mind before they drank the betrothal ale. She had said somewhat of wishing to go into a convent for a time.

Simon sat bolt upright and gave a long whistle.

"You like not the thought?" asked Lavrans.

"Nay, but I do, I do," said the other hastily. "Methinks it is the best way, dear father-in-law. Send her to the Sisters in Oslo for a year—there will she learn how folk talk one of the other out in the world. I know a little of some of the maidens who are there," he said, laughing. "*They* would not throw themselves down and die of grief if two mad yonkers tore each other to pieces for their sakes. Not that I would have such an one for wife—but methinks Kristin will be none the worse for meeting new folks."

Lavrans put the rest of the food into the wallet, and said, without looking at the youth:

"Methinks you love Kristin——?"

Simon laughed a little and did not look at Lavrans.

"Be sure, I know her worth—and yours, too," he said quickly and

* Birch-legs, see Note 10.

shamefacedly, as he got up and took his ski. "None that I have ever met would I sooner wed with——"

A little before Easter, when there was still snow enough for sleighing down the Dale and the ice still bore on Mjösen, Kristin journeyed southward for the second time. Simon came up to bear her company—so now she journeyed driving in a sleigh, well wrapped in furs and with father and betrothed beside her; and after them followed her father's men, and sledges with her clothes and gifts of food and furs for the Abbess and the Sisters of Nonneseter.

Part Two

THE GARLAND

I

A A S M U N D B J Ö R G U L F S Ö N ' S church-boat stood in round the point of Hovedö* early one Sunday at the end of April, while the bells were ringing in the cloister-church and were answered from across the bay by the chime of bells from the town, now louder and now fainter as the breeze rose or fell.

Light, fluted clouds were floating over the high, pale-blue heavens, and the sun was glittering on the dancing ripples of the water. It was quite spring-like along the shores; the fields lay almost bare of snow, and over the leaf-tree thickets the light had a yellow shimmer and the shadows were blue. But in the pine-forests up on the high ridges, which framed in the settled lands of Akersbygd, there were glimpses of snow, and on the far blue fells to the westward, beyond the fjord, there still showed many flashes of white.

Kristin was standing in the bow of the boat with her father, and Gyrid, Aasmund's wife. She gazed at the town, with all the light-hued churches and stone buildings that rose above the swarm of grey-brown wooden houses and bare tree-tops. The wind ruffled the skirts of her cloak and snatched at her hair beneath her hood.

They had let the cattle out at Skog the day before, and a great longing had come on her to be at Jörundgaard. It would be a long time still before they could let the cattle out there—she longed with tender pity for the lean, winter-worn cows in the dark byres; they would have to wait and suffer a long while yet. Her mother, Ulhvild, who had slept in her arms each night all these years, little Ramborg—she yearned so much for them; she longed for all the folk at home, and the horses and the dogs, for Kortelin, whom Ulvhild was to have while she was gone, and for her father's hawks as they sat there on their perches with their hoods over their heads. She saw the horse-hide gloves that hung beside them to wear when you took them on to your wrist, and the ivory staves to scratch them with.

It was as if all the woe of the last winter had gone far away from her, and she only saw her home as it used to be. They had told her, too, that none thought ill of her in the parish—Sira Eirik did not believe that story; he was angry and grieved at what Bentein had done. Bentein had fled from Hamar; 'twas said he had gone to Sweden. So things were not so bad between them and their neighbour as she had feared.

On the journey down to Oslo they had stayed as guests at Simon's home, and she had come to know his mother and sisters—Sir Andres

* Hovedö, see Note 11.

was in Sweden still. She had not felt at ease there, and her dislike of the Dyfrin folk was all the stronger that she could think of no good ground for it. All the way thither, she had said to herself that they had no cause to be proud or to think themselves better than her kin—no man knew aught of Reidar Darre, the Birch-leg, before King Sverre got him the widow of the Dyfrin Baron* to wife. But lo! they were not proud at all; and when Simon himself spoke one night of his forefather: "I have found out now for sure—he was a comb-maker—so 'tis as though you were to come into a kingly stock—almost, Kristin," said he. "Take heed to your tongue, boy," said his mother, but they all laughed together. It vexed her strangely when she thought of her father; he laughed much, if Simon gave him the least cause—a thought came to her dimly that maybe her father would gladly have had more laughter in his life. But 'twas not to her mind that he should like Simon so much.

They had all been at Skog over Easter. She had found that her uncle was a hard master to his farmers and serving-folk—she had met one and another who asked after her mother and spoke lovingly of Lavrans; they had better times when he lived here. Aasmund's mother, Lavrans' stepmother, lived on the manor in a house by herself; she was not so very old, but sickly and failing. Lavrans had but seldom spoke of her at home. Once when Kristin asked him if he had had a hard stepmother, her father answered: "She never did much to me of either good or ill."

Kristin felt for her father's hand, and he pressed hers:

"You will be happy soon enough, my daughter, with the good Sisters —you will have other things to think of besides longing to be home with us——"

They sailed so near by the town that the smell of tar and salt fish was borne out to them from the wharves. Gyrid named all the churches, the traders' quarters, and the open places which run up from the water's edge—Kristin remembered nothing from the time she was here before but the great heavy towers of St. Halvard's Church. They sailed westward past the whole town and laid to at the convent pier.

Kristin walked between her father and her uncle through a cluster of warehouses, and came out upon a road which led up through the fields. Simon came after, leading Gyrid by the hand. The serving-folk stayed behind to help some men from the convent load the baggage upon a cart.

Nonneseter and the whole Leiran quarter lay within the boundaries of the town grazing-grounds, but there were but a few clusters of houses here and there along the roadside. The larks were trilling over their heads in the pale-blue sky, and the small yellow flowers of the coltsfoot

* Baron, see Note 12.

were thickly sprinkled over the wan clay slopes, but along by the fences the roots of the grass were green.

When they were through the gate and were come into the cloister, all the nuns came marching two by two towards them from the church, while song and music streamed out after them through the open door.

Ill at ease, Kristin watched the many black-robed women with white linen wimples about their faces. She curtsied low, and the men bowed with their hats held close to their breasts. After the nuns came a flock of young maidens—some of them but children—in gowns of undyed wadmal, their waists bound with belts of twined black and white, and their hair braided tightly back from their faces with cords of the same black and white. Without thinking, Kristin put on a bold and forward look as the young maids passed, for she felt bashful, and was afraid they must think she looked countrified and foolish.

The convent was so glorious that she was quite overcome. All the buildings round the inner court were of grey stone; on the north side the main wall of the church stood up high above the other houses; it had two tiers of roofs and towers at the west end. The court itself was laid with stone flags, and round the whole there ran a covered way, whose roof was borne on pillars fairly wrought. In the midst of the court stood a stone statue of the Mater Misericordiæ, spreading her cloak over some kneeling figures.

Then a lay-sister came and prayed them to go with her to the Abbess' parlour. The Lady Groa Guttormsdatter was a tall and stoutly made old woman—she would have been comely had she not had so many hairs about her mouth. Her voice was deep like a man's. But her bearing was gentle and kindly—she called to mind that she had known Lavrans' father and mother, and asked after his wife and his other children. Last she spoke to Kristin in friendly wise:

"I have heard good report of you, and you look to be wise and well nurtured—sure I am you will give us no cause for miscontent. I have heard that you are plighted to this good and well-born man, Simon Andressön, whom I see here—it seems to us that 'twas wise counsel of your father and your husband to be, to grant you leave to live here awhile in the Virgin Mary's house, that you may learn to obey and serve before you are called to rule and to command. Now would I have you lay to heart this counsel: that you learn to find joy in prayer and the worship of God, that you may use yourself in all your doings to remember your Creator, God's gentle Mother, and all the Saints who have given us the best patterns of strength, uprightness, faithfulness and all the virtues you must show forth in guiding your people and your goods and nurturing your children. And you will learn in this house, too, to take good heed of time, for here every hour has its use and its task also.

Many young maids and women love all too well to lie abed late of a
morning, and sit long at table of an evening in idle talk—yet look not
you as you were one of these. Yet may you learn much in the year you
are here that may profit you both here on earth and in our heavenly
home."

Kristin curtsied and kissed her hand. After that Lady Groa bade
Kristin go with a monstrously fat old nun, whom she called Sister
Potentia, over to the nuns' refectory. The men and Gyrid she asked
to dine with her in another house.

The refectory was a great and fair room with a stone floor and pointed
windows with glass panes. There was a doorway into another room,
where, Kristin could see, there must be glass windows too, for the sun
shone in.

The Sisters were already seated at the table waiting for their food—
the elder nuns upon a cushioned stone-bench along the wall under the
windows; the younger Sisters and the bareheaded maidens in light-
hued wadmal dresses sat upon a wooden bench on the outer side of the
board. In the next room a board was laid too; this was for the commoners* and the lay-servants; there were a few old men among them.
These folk did not wear the convent habit, but were none the less clad
soberly in dark raiment.

Sister Potentia showed Kristin to a seat on the outer bench, but went
and placed herself near to the Abbess' high-seat at the end of the board
—the high-seat was empty to-day.

All rose, both in this room and in the side-room, while the Sisters said
grace. After that a fair, young nun went and stood at a lectern placed
in the doorway between the two chambers. And while the lay-sisters
in the greater room, and two of the youngest nuns in the side-room,
bore in food and drink, the nun read in a high and sweet voice, and
without stopping or tripping at a single word, the story of St. Theodora
and St. Didymus.

At first Kristin was thinking most of minding her table-manners, for
she saw all the Sisters and the young maids bore them as seemly and ate
as nicely as though they had been sitting at the finest feast. There was
abundance of the best food and drink, but all helped themselves
modestly, and dipped but the very tips of their fingers into the dishes;
no one spilled the broth either upon the cloths or upon their garments,
and all cut up the meat so small that they did not soil their mouths, and
ate with so much care that not a sound was to be heard.

Kristin grew hot with fear that she might not seem as well behaved as
the others; she was feeling ill at ease, too, in her bright dress in the midst
of all these women in black and white—she fancied they were all looking

* Commoners, see Note 13.

at her. So when she had to eat a fat piece of breast of mutton, and was holding it by the bone with two fingers, while cutting morsels off with her right hand, and taking care to handle the knife lightly and neatly— suddenly the whole slipped from her fingers; her slice of bread and the meat flew on to the cloth, and the knife fell clattering on the stone flags.

The noise sounded fearfully in the quiet room. Kristin flushed red as fire and would have bent to pick up the knife, but a lay-sister came noiselessly in her sandals and gathered up the things.

But Kristin could eat no more. She found, too, that she had cut one of her fingers, and she was afraid of bleeding upon the cloth; so she sat with her hand wrapped in a corner of her skirt, and thought of how she was staining the goodly light blue dress she had gotten for the journey to Oslo, and she did not dare to raise her eyes from her lap.

Howbeit, in a little she began to listen more to what the nun was reading. When the ruler found he could not shake the steadfastness of the maid, Theodora—she would neither make offerings to the false gods nor let herself be given in marriage—he bade them lead her to a brothel. Yet while on the way thither he exhorted her to think of her freeborn kindred and her honoured father and mother, upon whom everlasting shame must now be brought, and gave his word she should be let live in peace and stay a maid, if she would but join the service of a heathen goddess, whom they called Diana.

Theodora answered fearlessly: "Chastity is like a lamp, but love of God is the flame; were I to serve the devil-woman whom you call Diana, my chastity were no more worth than a rusty lamp without flame or oil. Thou callest me freeborn, but we are all born bondsmen, since our first parents sold us to the devil; Christ has bought me free, and I am bound to serve Him, so that I cannot wed me with His foes. He will guard His dove; but should He even suffer you to break my body, that is the temple of His Holy Spirit, it shall not be counted to me for shame, if so be that I consent not to betray what is His into the hands of His enemies."

Kristin's heart began to throb, for this in some way reminded her of her meeting with Bentein—she was smitten by the thought that this perhaps was her sin—she had not for a moment thought of God nor prayed for His help. And now Sister Cecilia read further of St. Didymus. He was a Christian knight, but heretofore he had kept his faith hidden from all save a few friends. He went now to the house where the maid was; he gave money to the woman who owned the house, and thus was the first to be let in to Theodora. She fled into a corner like a frightened hare, but Didymus hailed her as his sister and as his Lord's bride, and said he was come to save her. Then he spake with her awhile, saying: Was it not meet that a brother should wage his life for his sister's honour? And at last she did as he bade her, changed clothes with him, and let herself be clad in Didymus' coat of mail; he pulled the hat down over her eyes and drew the cape up about her chin, and bade her go out with her face hidden, like a youth who is abashed at having been in such a place.

Kristin thought of Arne, and was scarce able to hold back her tears. She gazed straight before her with wet eyes while the nun was reading to the end—how Didymus was led to the place of execution, and how Theodora came hastening down from the mountains, cast herself at the headsman's feet and begged that she might die in his stead. And now the holy man and maid strove together who should first win the crown; and both were beheaded on the one day. This was the eighth-and-twentieth day of April in the year 304 after the birth of Christ, in Antioch, as was written by St. Ambrosius.

When they rose from the table, Sister Potentia came and patted Kristin kindly on the cheek: "Ay, you are longing for your mother, I can well believe." And on that Kristin's tears began to fall. But the nun made as though she did not see them, and led Kristin to the hostel where she was to dwell.

It was in one of the stone houses by the cloisters; a goodly room with glass windows and a big fireplace in the short wall at the far end. Along one main wall stood six bedsteads, and along the other all the maidens' chests.

Kristin wished they would let her sleep with one of the little girls, but Sister Potentia called a fat, fair-haired, grown maiden: "Here is Ingebjörg Filippusdatter, who is to be your bed-fellow—you must see now and learn to know each other." And with that she went out.

Ingebjörg took Kristin at once by the hand and began to talk. She was not very tall, and was much too fat, above all in the face—her cheeks were so plump that her eyes looked quite small. But her skin was clear, red and white, and her hair was yellow as gold, and so curly that her thick plaits twisted and twined together like strands of rope, and small locks kept ever slipping from under her snood.

She began straightway to question Kristin about many things, but never waited for an answer; instead she talked about herself, reckoned out the whole of her kindred in all its branches—they were naught but fine and exceeding rich folk. She was betrothed, too, to a rich and mighty man, Einar Einarssön of Aganæs—but he was far too old, and twice widowed; this was her greatest sorrow, she said. Yet could Kristin not mark that she took it much to heart. Then she talked a little of Simon Darre—'twas a marvel how closely she had looked him over in the short moment when they were passing in the cloisters. After that she had a mind to look into Kristin's chest—but first she opened her own and brought forth all her clothes. While they were ransacking their chests, Sister Cecilia came in—she rebuked them and said that this was no seemly Sunday pastime. This made Kristin unhappy again— she had never been taken to task by any but her own mother, and that was not the same as being chid by a stranger.

Ingebjörg was not abashed. After they were come to bed in the evening, she lay chattering until Kristin fell asleep. Two elder lay-sisters slept in a corner of the room; they were to see that the maidens did not take their shifts off at night—for it was against the rules for the girls to undress entirely—and to see that they were up in time for matins in the church. But else they did not trouble themselves to keep order in the hostel, and made as though they marked it not when the maids were lying talking, or eating the dainties which they had hidden in their chests.

When Kristin was awakened next morning, Ingebjörg was in the midst of a long tale already, so that Kristin almost wondered whether the other had been talking the whole night through.

II

THE foreign merchants who lay in Oslo during the summer and trafficked there, came to the town in the spring about Holy Rood Day, which is ten days before the Halvards-wake Fair.* To this folk streamed in from all the parishes between Mjösen and the Swedish marches, so that the town swarmed with people in the first weeks of May. This was the best time to buy from the strangers, before they had sold too many of their wares.

Sister Potentia had the care of the marketing for Nonneseter, and she had promised Ingebjörg and Kristin that they should go with her down to the town the day before the Halvards-wake. But about midday some of Sister Potentia's kin came to the convent to see her; and so she could not go that day. Then Ingebjörg begged and prayed till at last she let them go alone—although it was against the rules. An old peasant who was a commoner of the convent was sent with them as escort—Haakon was his name.

Kristin had been three weeks now at Nonneseter, and in all that time she had not set foot outside the convent grounds and gardens. She wondered to see how spring-like it was outside. The little woods out in the fields were pale-green; the wood anemones grew thick as a carpet round the light-coloured tree stems; white fair-weather clouds came sailing up over the islands in the fjord, and the water lay fresh and blue, slightly ruffled here and there by the light flaws of wind.

* Saints' Days and Festivals, see Note 14.

Ingebjörg skipped about, plucked bunches of leaves from the trees and smelt them, and peeped round after the folk they met; till Haakon chid her—were these seemly goings-on for a well-born maid, and in the convent habit too? The maidens were made to walk just behind him, hand in hand, quietly and seemly; but Ingebjörg used her eyes and her tongue all the same—Haakon was somewhat deaf. Kristin, too, was wearing the novices' garb now—an undyed, light-grey wadmal dress, woollen belt and head-band, and a plain, dark blue cloak over all, with a hood turned up so that the plaited hair was quite hid. Haakon strode in front with a stout brass-knobbed staff in his hand. He was dressed in a long black gown, had a leaden Agnus Dei hanging on his breast and an image of St. Christopher in his hat—his white hair and beard were so well brushed that they shone like silver in the sunshine.

The upper part of the town between the Nunsbeck and the bishop's palace was a quiet neighbourhood; there were here neither shops nor taverns; most of the dwelling-places belonged to great folk from the parishes around, and the houses turned dark, windowless, timber gables to the street. But on this day whole crowds of people were roaming about the roads even up here, and the serving-folk stood loitering about the courtyard gates gossiping with the passers-by.

When they were come out near the bishop's palace, there was a great crush upon the place in front of Halvard's Church and the Olav-cloister—booths had been set up on the grassy slopes, and there were showmen making trained dogs jump through barrel-hoops. But Haakon would not have the maids stand and look at these things, and he would not let Kristin go into the church—he said 'twould be better worth her seeing on the great Feast-day itself.

As they came down over the open space by St. Clement's Church, Haakon took them by the hands, for here was the greatest press of folk coming from the wharves or out from the alleys between the traders' yards.* The maidens were bound for the Mickle Yard, where the shoe-makers plied their trade. For Ingebjörg had found the clothes Kristin had brought from home very good and sightly, but she said the shoes she had with her from the Dale were not fit to wear for best. And when Kristin had seen the shoes from the outland Ingebjörg had in her chest —more pairs than one—she felt she could not rest until she too had bought some like them.

The Mickle Yard was one of the largest in Oslo; it stretched from the wharves up to the Souters' Alley, with more than forty houses round two great courts. And now they had set up booths with wadmal roofs in the courts as well. Above the roofs of these tents there rose a statue of St. Crispinus. Within the courts was a great throng of folk buying and

* Town Yards, see Note 15.

selling, women running between the kitchens with pots and pails, children getting in the way of folks' feet, horses being led in and out of the stables, and serving-men carrying packages to and from the warehouses. From the balconies of the lofts above, where the finest wares were sold, shoemakers and their apprentices shouted to the two maids and dangled small gaily-coloured or gold-embroidered shoes before them.

But Ingebjörg made her way toward the loft where Didrek the shoemaker sat; he was a German, but had a Norse wife and owned a house in the Mickle Yard.

The old man was standing bargaining with an esquire wearing a traveller's cloak, and a sword at his belt; but Ingebjörg went forward unabashed, bowed, and said:

"Good sir, will you not suffer us of your courtesy to have speech with Didrek first? We must be home in our convent by vespers; you, perchance, have no such great haste? "

The esquire bowed and stepped aside. Didrek nudged Ingebjörg with his elbow and asked, laughing, whether they danced so much in the convent that she had worn out already all the shoon she had of him the year before. Ingebjörg nudged him again and said they were still unworn, thank Heaven, but here was this other maid—and she pulled Kristin forward. Then Didrek and his lad bore forth a box into the balcony; and out of it he brought forth shoes, each pair finer than the last. They had Kristin sit down upon a chest that he might try them on her—there were white shoes and brown and red and green and blue, shoes with painted wooden heels and shoes without heels, shoes with buckles and shoes with silken laces in them, shoes in leather of two or of three hues. Kristin felt she would fain have had them all. But they cost so dear she was quite dismayed—not one pair cost less than a cow at home. Her father had given her a purse with a mark of silver in counted money* when he left—that was for pocket money, and Kristin had deemed it great riches. But she soon saw that Ingebjörg thought it no great store to go a marketing with.

Ingebjörg, too, must try on some shoes for the jest of it; that cost no money, said Didrek laughing. She did buy one pair of leaf-green shoes with red heels—she said she must have them on trust, but then Didrek knew her and her folks.

Kristin thought, indeed, that Didrek liked this none too well, and that he was vexed too, that the tall esquire in the travelling cloak had left the loft—much time had been taken up with the trying-on. So she chose for herself a pair of heelless shoes of thin purple-blue leather, broidered with silver and with rose-red stones. But she liked not the

* Currency, see Note 16.

green silk laces in them. Didrek said he could change these, and took the maids with him into a room at the back of the loft. Here he had coffers full of silk ribbons and small silver buckles—'twas against the law, strictly, for shoemakers to trade in these things—and the ribbons, too, were many of them too broad and the buckles too big for footgear.

They felt they had to buy one or two of the smaller things, and when they had drunk a cup of sweet wine with Didrek and he had packed the things they had bought into a wadmal cloth, the hour was grown somewhat late, and Kristin's purse much lighter.

When they were come to the Ostre Stræte again the sunlight was turned golden, and, by reason of the traffic in the town, the dust hung over the street in a bright haze. The evening was warm and fair, and folk were coming down from Eikaberg with great armfuls of young green branches wherewith to deck their houses for the holy-day. And now the whim took Ingebjörg that they should go out to the Gjeita bridge—at fair-times there was wont to be so much merry-making in the fields on the farther side of the river, both jugglers and fiddlers—nay, Ingebjörg had heard there was come a whole shipful of outlandish beasts that were being shown in booths down by the waterside.

Haakon had had a pot or two of German beer at the Mickle Yard, and was now easy and mild of mood; so when the maidens took him by the arm and begged him sweetly, he gave way at last, and the three went out towards Eikaberg.

Beyond the stream there were but a few small dwelling-places scattered about the green slopes between the river and the steep hillside. They went past the Minorite monastery, and Kristin's heart sank with shame as she bethought her how she had meant to give most of her silver for the good of Arne's soul. But she had had no mind to speak of it to the priest at Nonneseter; she feared to be asked questions—she had thought that she could maybe come out to the barefoot friars and find if by chance Brother Edvin were in the cloister now. She was fain to meet him again—but she knew not, either, what would be the most seemly way to get speech with one of the monks and tell him her desire. And now she had so little money she knew not whether she could buy a mass—maybe she must be content to offer a thick wax-candle.

Of a sudden they heard a fearful yell from countless throats down by the shore—a storm seemed to sweep over the press of human beings down there—and now the whole mass rushed towards them, shrieking and shouting. All seemed wild with terror, and some of the runners-by cried out to Haakon and the maids that the pards were loose. . . .

They set out running back to the bridge, and heard folk shout to one another that a booth had fallen down and two pards had broken loose—some spoke of a serpent, too. The nearer they came to the bridge the worse became the crush. Just in front of them a woman dropped a little child out of her arms—Haakon stood astride the little one to shield it—soon after they caught sight of him far away with the child in his arms, and then they lost him.

At the narrow bridge the press of people was so great that the maids were pushed right out into a field. They saw folks run down to the river-bank; young men jumped in and swam, but elder folk sprang into boats that lay there, and these were overladen in a trice.

Kristin tried to make Ingebjörg hear—she cried out to her that they should run up to the Minorite cloister—they could see the Grey Friars come running out from it, striving to gather in the terrified people. Kristin was not so frightened as the other girl—they saw nothing, either, of the wild beasts—but Ingebjörg had quite lost her wits. And now, when there was a fresh uproar in the throng, and it was driven back by a whole troop of men from the nearest dwellings, who had armed themselves and forced their way back over the bridge, some riding and some running, and Ingebjörg was nigh coming under the feet of a horse—she gave a scream and set off running for the woods. Kristin had never thought the girl could have run so fast—it made her think of a hunted pig. She ran after her, so that they two, at least, should not be parted.

They were deep in the woods before Kristin could get Ingebjörg to stop—they were on a little path which seemed to lead down toward the road to Trælaborg. They stood still for a little to get their breath again; Ingebjörg was snivelling and weeping, and said she dared not go back alone through the town and all the way out to the convent.

Nor did Kristin deem that this would be well, with the streets in such commotion; she thought they must try to find a house where they might hire a lad to take them home. Ingebjörg thought there was a bridle-path to Trælaborg farther down by the shore, and along it there lay some houses she knew. So they followed the path downward, away from the town.

Fearful and uneasy as they both were, it seemed to them they had gone far ere at last they came to a farmstead lying off in a field. In the courtyard there they found a band of men sitting drinking at a board under some ash trees, while a woman came and went, bearing out tankards to them. She looked wonderingly and sourly at the two maids in convent habit, and none of the men seemed to have a mind to go with them when Kristin told their need. At last, though, two young men stood up and said they would bring the girls to Nonneseter, if Kristin would give them a silver ducat.

She heard by their speech that they were not Norse, but she thought they seemed honest folk enough. 'Twas a shameless sum they asked, she thought, but Ingebjörg was beside herself with fright and she saw not how they could go home alone so late; and so she struck the bargain.

No sooner were they come to the forest-path than the men drew closer to them and began to talk. Kristin liked this but ill, but she would not show she was afraid; so she answered them quietly, told oi the pards and asked the men where they were from. She spied about her, too, and made as though she looked each moment to meet the serving-men they had had with them—she talked as though there had been a whole band. As they went on the men spoke less and less—nor did she understand much of their speech.

After a while she became aware that they were not going the same way she had come with Ingebjörg—the course their path took was not the same; 'twas more northerly—and she deemed they had already gone much too far.

Deep within her there smouldered a fear she dared not let herself think upon—but it strengthened her strangely to have Ingebjörg with her, for the girl was so foolish that Kristin knew she must trust in herself alone to find a way out for them both. Under her cloak, she managed by stealth to pull out the cross with the holy relic she had had of her father; she clasped it in her hand, praying fervently in her heart that they might soon meet some one, and in all ways sought to gather all her courage and to make no sign.

Just after this she saw that the path came out on to a road and there was a clearing in the forest. The town and the bay lay far below. The men had led them astray, whether wilfully or because they knew not the paths—they were high up on the mountain-side and far north o. Gjeita bridge, which she could see below; the road they had now met seemed to lead thither.

Thereupon she stopped, drew forth her purse and made to count out ten silver pennies into her hand.

"Now, good fellows," said she, "we need you not any more to guide us; for we know the way from here. We thank you for your pains, and here is the wage we bargained for. God be with you, good friends."

The men looked at one another so foolishly, that Kristin was near smiling. Then one said with an ugly grin that the road down to the bridge was exceeding lonely; 'twas not wise for them to go alone.

"None, surely, are such nithings or such fools that they would seek to stop two maids, and they in the convent habit," answered Kristin. "We would fain go our own way alone now——" and she held out the money.

The man caught her by the wrist, thrust his face close up to hers, and said somewhat of "kuss" and "beutel"—Kristin made out he was saying they might go in peace if she but gave him a kiss and her purse.

She remembered Bentein's face close to hers like this, and such a fear came on her for a moment that she grew faint and sick. But she pressed her lips together, and called in her heart upon God and the Virgin Mary—and in the same instant she thought she heard hoof-falls on the path from the north.

She struck the man in the face with her purse so that he staggered—and then she pushed him in the breast with all her strength so that he tumbled off the path and down into the wood. The other German gripped her from behind, tore the purse from her hand and her chain from her neck so that it broke—she was near falling, but clutched the man and tried to get her cross from him again. He struggled to get free—the robbers, too, had now heard folk coming—Ingebjörg screamed with all her might, and the riders on the path came galloping forward at full speed. They burst out of the thicket—three of them—and Ingebjörg ran shrieking to meet them as they sprang from their horses. Kristin knew one for the esquire of Didrek's loft; he drew his sword, seized the German she was struggling with by the back of the neck, and thrashed him with the flat of his blade. His men ran after the other, caught him and beat him to their heart's content.

Kristin leaned against the face of the rock; she was trembling now that all was over, but what she felt most was marvel that her prayer had brought such speedy help. Then she caught sight of Ingebjörg, who had thrown back her hood, hung her cape loosely over her shoulders and was in the act of bringing her heavy, shining plaits of hair forward into sight upon her breast. At this sight Kristin burst out a-laughing—her strength left her and she had to hold on to a tree to keep her feet, for 'twas as though the marrow of her bones was turned to water, she felt so weak; and so she trembled and laughed and cried.

The esquire came forward and laid a hand warily upon her shoulder: "You were more frightened, I see, than you would show," said he, and his voice was kindly and gentle. "But now you must take a hold on yourself—you bore you so bravely while yet there was peril——"

Kristin could only look up at him and nod. He had fine, bright eyes set in a narrow, pale-brown face, and coal-black hair clipped somewhat short over the forehead and behind the ears.

Ingebjörd had her hair in order now; she came and thanked the stranger with many fair words. He stood there still with a hand on Kristin's shoulder while he answered her comrade.

"We must take these birds along," said he to his men, who stood holding the two Germans—they were from a Rostock ship, they said—"we must have them along with us to the town that they may be sent to the black hole. But first must we take these two maids home to the convent. You can find some thongs, I trow, to bind them with——"

"Mean you the maids, Erlend?" asked one of the men. They were young, stout, well-appointed yeomen, and were in high feather from the tussle.

Their master frowned and seemed about to answer sharply, but Kristin laid her hand upon his sleeve:

"Let them go, dear sir!" She shuddered a little. "Loth would we be, in truth, both my sister and I, this matter should be talked of."

The stranger looked down at her—he bit his lip and nodded, as though he understood her. Then he gave each of the captives a blow on the nape with the flat of his sword which sent them sprawling forwards. "Run for it, then," he said, kicking them, and both scrambled up and took to their heels as fast as they could. Then he turned again to the maidens and asked if they would please to ride.

Ingebjörg let herself be lifted into Erlend's saddle, but it was soon plain that she could not keep her seat—she slid down again at once. He looked at Kristin doubtfully, and she said that she was used to ride on a man's saddle.

He took hold of her below the knees and lifted her up. A sweet and happy thrill ran through her to feel how carefully he held her from him, as though afraid to come near her—at home, no one ever minded how tight they held her when they helped her on to a horse. She felt marvellously honoured and uplifted.

The knight—as Ingebjörg called him, though he had but silver spurs —now offered that maiden his hand, and his men sprang to their saddles. Ingebjörg would have it that they should ride round the town to the northward below the Ryenberg and Martestokke, and not through the streets. First, she gave as a reason that Sir Erlend and his men were fully armed—were they not? The knight answered gravely that the ban on carrying arms was not over strict at any time—for travellers at least—and now every one in the town was out on a wild beast hunt. Then she said she was fearful of the pards. Kristin saw full well that Ingebjörg was fain to go by the longest and loneliest road, that she might have the more talk with Erlend.

"This is the second time this evening that we hinder you, good sir," said she, and Erlend answered soberly:

"'Tis no matter, I am bound no farther than to Gerdarud to-night— and 'tis light the whole night long."

It liked Kristin well that he jested not, nor bantered them, but talked to her as though she were his like or even more than his like. She thought of Simon; she had not met other young men of courtly breeding. But 'twas true, this man seemed older than Simon.

They rode down into the valley below the Ryenberg hills and up along the beck. The path was narrow, and the young bushes swung wet, heavily scented branches against her—it was a little darker down here, and the air was cool and the leaves all dewy along the beck-path.

They went slowly, and the horses' hoofs sounded muffled on the damp, grass-grown path. She rocked gently in the saddle; behind her she heard Ingebjörg's chatter, and the stranger's deep, quiet voice. He said little, and answered as if his mind wandered—it sounded almost as if his mood were like her own, she thought—she felt strangely drowsy, yet safe and content now that all the day's chances were safely over.

It was like waking to come out of the woods on to the green slopes under the Martestokke hills. The sun was gone down, and the town and the bay lay below them in a clear, pale light—above the Aker ridges there was a light-yellow strip edging the pale-blue sky. In the evening hush, sounds were borne to them from far off, as they came out of the cool depths of the wood—a cart-wheel creaked somewhere upon a road, dogs on the farms bayed at each other across the valley. And from the woods behind them birds trilled and sang full-throated, now the sun was down.

Smoke was in the air from the fires on lands under clearance, and out in a field there was the red flare of a bonfire; against the great ruddy flame the clearness of the night seemed a kind of darkness.

They were riding between the fences of the convent-fields when the stranger spoke to her again. He asked her what she thought best; should he go with her to the gate and ask for speech of the Lady Groa, so that he might tell her how this thing had come about. But Ingebjörg would have it that they should steal in through the church; then maybe they might slip into the convent without any one knowing they had been away so much too long—it might be her kinsfolks' visit had made Sister Potentia forget them.

The open place before the west door of the church was empty and still, and it came not into Kristin's thoughts to wonder at this, though there was wont to be much life there of an evening, with folks from the neighbourhood who came to the nuns' church, and from the houses round about wherein lay-servants and commoners dwelt. They said farewell to Erlend here. Kristin stood and stroked his horse; it was black, and had a comely head and soft eyes—she thought it like Morvin, whom she had been wont to ride at home when she was a child.

"What is your horse's name, sir?" she asked, as it turned its head from her and snuffed at its master's breast.

"Bayard," said he, looking at her over the horse's neck. "You ask my horse's name, but not mine?"

"I would be fain to know your name, sir," she replied, and bent her head a little.

"I am called Erlend Nikulaussön," said he.

"Then, Erlend Nikulaussön, have thanks for your good service this night," said Kristin, and proffered him her hand.

Of a sudden she flushed red, and half withdrew her hand from his. "Lady Aashild Gautesdatter of Dovre, is she your kinswoman?" she asked.

To her wonder she saw that he, too, blushed—he dropped her hand suddenly, and answered:

"She is my mother's sister. And I am Erlend Nikulaussön of Husaby." He looked at her so strangely that she became still more abashed, but she mastered herself, and said:

"'Tis true I should have thanked you with better words, Erland Nikulaussön; but I know not what I can say to you."

He bowed before her, and she felt that now she must bid him good-bye, though she would fain have spoken more with him. In the church door she turned, and as she saw that Erlend still stood beside his horse, she waved her hand to him in farewell.

The convent was in a hubbub, and all within in great dismay. Haakon had sent word home by a horseman, while he, himself, went seeking the maids in the town; and folks had been sent from the convent to help him. The nuns had heard the wild beasts had killed and eaten up two children down in the town. This, to be sure, was a lie, and the pard—there was only one—had been caught before vespers by some men from the King's palace.

Kristin stood with bent head and kept silence, while the Abbess and Sister Potentia poured out their wrath upon the two maidens. She felt as though something were asleep within her. Ingebjörg wept and began to make excuse—they had gone out with Sister Potentia's leave, with fitting attendance, and, sure, they were not to blame for what had happened after.

But Lady Groa said they might now stay in the church till the hour of midnight struck, that they might strive to turn their thoughts to the things of the spirit, and might thank God who had saved their lives and honour. "God hath now manifested clearly to you the truth about the world," said she; "wild beasts and the servants of the devil threaten his children there at every footstep, and there is no salvation except ye hold fast to Him with prayer and supplication."

She gave them each a lighted candle and bade them go with Sister Cecilia Baardsdatter, who was often alone in the church praying the whole night long.

Kristin put her candle upon St. Lawrence's altar and knelt on the praying-stool. She fixed her gaze on the flame while she said over the

Paternoster and the Ave Maria softly. The sheen of the candle seemed little by little to enfold her and to shut out all that was outside her and the light. She felt her heart open and overflow with thankfulness and praise and love of God and His gentle Mother—they came so near to her. She had always known they saw her, but to-night she *felt* that it was so. She saw the world as in a vision; a great dark room whereinto fell a sunbeam; the motes were dancing in and out between the darkness and the light, and she felt that now she had at last slipped into the sunbeam.

She felt she would gladly have stayed for ever in this dark, still church —with the few small spots of light like golden stars in the night, the sweet stale scent of incense, and the warm smell of the burning wax. And she at rest within her own star.

It was as if some great joy were at an end, when Sister Cecilia came gliding to her and touched her shoulder. Bending before the altars, the three women went out of the little south door into the convent close.

Ingebjörg was so sleepy that she went to bed without a word. Kristin was glad—she had been loth to have her good thoughts broken in on. And she was glad, too, that they must keep on their shifts at night—Ingebjörg was so fat and had been so over-hot.

She lay awake long, but the deep flood of sweetness that she had felt lifting her up as she knelt in the church would not come again. Yet she felt the warmth of it within her still; she thanked God with all her heart, and thought she felt her spirit strengthened while she prayed for her father and mother and sisters, and for Arne Gyrdsön's soul.

Father, she thought—she longed so much for him, for all they had been to one another before Simon Darre came into their lives. There welled up in her a new tenderness for him—there was, as it were, a fore-taste of mother's love and care in her love for her father this night; dimly she felt that there was so much in life that he had missed. She called to mind the old, black wooden church at Gerdarud—she had seen there this last Easter the graves of her three little brothers and of her grandmother, her father's own mother, Kristin Sigurdsdatter, who died when she brought him into the world.

What could Erlend Nikulaussön have to do at Gerdarud—she could not think.

She had no knowledge that she had thought much of him that evening, but the whole time the thought of his dark, narrow face and his quiet voice had hung somewhere in the dusk outside the glow of light that enfolded her spirit.

When she awoke the next morning, the sun was shining into the dormitory, and Ingebjörg told her how Lady Groa herself had bidden the lay-sisters not to wake them for matins. She had said that when they woke, they might go over to the kitchen-house and get some food. Kristin grew warm with gladness at the Abbess' kindness—it seemed as if the whole world had been good to her.

III

T H E farmers' guild* of Aker had St. Margaret for their patroness, and they began their festival each year on the twentieth of July, the day of St. Margaret's Mass. On that day the guild brothers and sisters, with their children, their guests and their serving-folk, gathered at Aker's church and heard mass at St. Margaret's altar there; after that they wended their way to the hall of the guild, which lay near the Hofvin Hospital—there they were wont to hold a drinking-feast lasting five days.

But since both Aker's church and the Hofvin spital belonged to Nonneseter, and as, besides, many of the Aker farmers were tenants of the convent, it had come to be the custom that the Abbess and some of the elder Sisters should honour the guild by coming to the feasting on the first day. And those of the young maids who were at the convent only to learn, and were not to take the veil, had leave to go with them and to dance in the evening; therefore at this feast they wore their own clothes and not the convent habit.

And so there was great stir and bustle in the novices' sleeping rooms on the eve of St. Margaret's Mass; the maids who were to go to the guild feast ransacking their chests and making ready their finery, while the others, less fortunate, went about something moodily and looked on. Some had set small pots in the fireplace and were boiling water to make their skin white and soft; others were making a brew to be smeared on their hair—then they parted the hair into strands and twisted them tightly round strips of leather, and this gave them curling, wavy tresses.

Ingebjörg brought out all the finery she had, but could not think what she should wear—come what might, not her best, leaf-green velvet dress; that was too good and too costly for such a peasant rout. But a little, thin sister who was not to go with them—Helga was her name; she had been vowed to the convent by her father and mother while still a child—took Kristin aside and whispered: she was sure Ingebjörg would wear the green dress and her pink silk shift too.

"You have ever been kind to me, Kristin," said Helga. "It beseems me little to meddle in such doings—but I will tell you none the less. The knight who brought you home that evening in the spring—I have seen and heard Ingebjörg talking with him since—they spoke together in the church, and he has tarried for her up in the hollow when she hath gone to Ingunn at the commoners' house. But 'tis you he asks for,

* Farmers' Guilds, see Note 17.

and Ingebjörg has promised him to bring you there along with her. But I wager you have not heard aught of this before!"

"True it is that Ingebjörg has said naught of this," said Kristin. She pursed up her mouth that the other might not see the smile that would come out. So this was Ingebjörg's way. "'Tis like she knows I am not of such as run to trysts with strange men round house-corners and behind fences," said she proudly.

"Then I might have spared myself the pains of bringing you tidings whereof 'twould have been but seemly I should say no word," said Helga, wounded, and they parted.

But the whole evening Kristin was put to it not to smile when any one was looking at her.

Next morning, Ingebjörg went dallying about in her shift, till Kristin saw she meant not to dress before she herself was ready.

Kristin said naught, but laughed as she went to her chest and took out her golden-yellow silken shift. She had never worn it before, and it felt so soft and cool as it slipped down over her body. It was broidered with goodly work, in silver and blue and brown silk, about the neck and down upon the breast, as much as should be seen above the low-cut gown. There were sleeves to match, too. She drew on her linen hose, and laced up the small, purple-blue shoes which Haakon, by good luck, had saved that day of commotion. Ingebjörg gazed at her—then Kristin said laughing:

"My father ever taught me never to show disdain of those beneath us —but 'tis like you are too grand to deck yourself in your best for poor tenants and peasant-folk——"

Red as a berry, Ingebjörg slipped her woollen smock down over her white hips and hurried on the pink silk shift. Kristin threw over her own head her best velvet gown—it was violet-blue, deeply cut out at the bosom, with long slashed sleeves flowing well-nigh to the ground. She fastened the gilt belt about her waist, and hung her grey squirrel cape over her shoulders. Then she spread her masses of yellow hair out over her shoulders and back, and fitted the golden fillet, chased with small roses, upon her brow.

She saw that Helga stood watching them. Then she took from her chest a great silver clasp. It was that she had on her cloak the night Bentein met her on the highway, and she had never cared to wear it since. She went to Helga, and said in a low voice:

"I know 'twas your wish to show me goodwill last night; think me not unthankful——" and with that she gave her the clasp.

Ingebjörg was a fine sight, too, when she stood fully decked in her green gown, with a red silk cloak over her shoulders and her fair, curly hair waving behind her. They had ended by striving to outdress each other, thought Kristin, and she laughed.

The morning was cool and fresh with dew as the procession went forth from Nonneseter and wound its way westward toward Frysja. The hay-making was near at an end here on the lowlands, but along the fences grew blue-bells and yellow crowsfoot in clumps; in the fields the barley was in ear, and bent its heads in pale silvery waves just tinged with pink. Here and there, where the path was narrow and led through the fields, the corn all but met about folks' knees.

Haakon walked at the head, bearing the convent's banner with the Virgin Mary's picture upon the blue silken cloth. After him walked the servants and the commoners, and then came the Lady Groa and four old Sisters on horseback, while behind these came the young maidens on foot; their many-hued holiday attire flaunted and shone in the sunlight. Some of the commoners' women-folk and a few armed serving-men closed the train.

They sang as they went over the bright fields, and the folk they met at the byways stood aside and gave them reverent greeting. All round, out on the fields, they could see small groups of men coming walking and riding, for folks were drawing toward the church from every house and every farm. Soon they heard behind them the sound of hymns chanted in men's deep voices, and the banner of the Hovedö monastery rose above a hillock—the red silk shone in the sun, swaying and bending to the step of the bearer.

The mighty, metal voice of the bells rang out above the neighing and screaming of stallions as the procession climbed the last slope to the church. Kristin had never seen so many horses at one time—a heaving, restless sea of horses' backs round about the green before the church door. Upon the sward stood and sat lay folk dressed in all their best—but all rose in reverence as the Virgin's flag from Nonneseter was borne in amongst them, and all bowed deeply before the Lady Groa.

It seemed as though more folk had come than the church could hold, but for those from the convent room had been kept in front near the altar. Straightway after them the Cistercian monks from Hovedö marched in and went up into the choir—and forthwith song burst from the throats of men and boys and filled the church.

Soon after the mass had begun, when the service brought all to their feet, Kristin caught sight of Erlend Nikulaussön. He was tall, and his head rose above those about him—she saw his face from the side. He had a high, steep, and narrow forehead, and a large, straight nose—it jutted, triangle-like, from his face, and was strangely thin about the fine, quivering nostrils—something about it reminded Kristin of a rest-less, high-strung stallion. His face was not as comely as she had thought it—the long-drawn lines running down to his small, weak, yet well-formed mouth gave it as 'twere a touch of joylessness—ay, but yet he *was* comely.

He turned his head and saw her. She knew not how long they stood thus, looking into each other's eyes. From that time she thought of naught but the end of the mass; she waited, intent on what would then befall.

There was some pressing and thronging as the folks made their way out from the overcrowded church. Ingebjörg held Kristin back till they were at the rear of the throng; she gained her point—they were quite cut off from the nuns, who went out first—the two girls were among the last in coming to the offertory-box and out of the church.

Erlend stood without, just by the door, beside the priest from Ger-darud and a stoutish, red-faced man, splendid in blue velvet. Erlend himself was clad in silk, but of a sober hue—a long coat of brown, figured with black, and a black cloak with a pattern of small yellow hawks inwoven.

They greeted each other and crossed the green together to where the men's horses stood tethered. While they spoke of the fine weather, the goodly mass and the great crowd of folk that were mustered, the fat, ruddy knight—he bore golden spurs and was named Sir Munan Baard-sön—took Ingebjörg by the hand; 'twas plain he was mightily taken with the maid. Erlend and Kristin fell behind—they were silent as they walked.

There was a great to-do upon the church-green as folk began to ride away—horses jostled one another, people shouted—some angry, others laughing. Many sat in pairs upon the horses; men had their wives behind them, or their children in front upon the saddle; youths swung themselves up beside a friend. They could see the church banners, the nuns and the priests far down the hill already.

Sir Munan rode by; Ingebjörg sat in front of him, his arm about her. Both of them called out and waved. Then Erlend said:

"My serving-men are both with me—they could ride one horse and you have Haftor's—if you would rather have it so?"

Kristin flushed as she replied: "We are so far behind the others already—I see not your serving-men hereabouts, and——" Then she broke into a laugh, and Erlend smiled.

He sprang to the saddle and helped her to a seat behind him. At home Kristin had often sat thus sidewise behind her father, after she had grown too big to ride astride the horse. Still, she felt a little bashful and none too safe as she laid a hand upon Erlend's shoulder; the other she put on the horse's back to steady herself. They rode slowly down towards the bridge.

In a while Kristin thought she must speak, since he was silent, so she said:

"We looked not, sir, to meet you here to-day."

"Looked you not to meet me?" asked Erlend, turning his head. "Did not Ingebjörg Filippusdatter bear you my greeting, then?"

"No," said Kristin. "I heard naught of any greeting—she hath not named you once since you came to our help last May," said she guilefully. She was not sorry that Ingebjörg's falseness should come to light.

Erlend did not look back again, but she could hear by his voice that he was smiling when he asked again:

"But the little dark one—the novice—I mind not her name—her I even fee'd to bear you my greeting."

Kristin blushed, but she had to laugh too: "Ay, 'tis but Helga's due I should say that she earned her fee," she said.

Erlend moved his head a little—his neck almost touched her hand. Kristin shifted her hand at once farther out on his shoulder. Somewhat uneasily she thought, maybe she had been more bold than was fitting, seeing she had come to this feast after a man had, in a manner, made tryst with her there.

Soon after Erlend asked:

"Will you dance with me to-night, Kristin?"

"I know not, sir," answered the maid.

"You think, mayhap, 'tis not seemly?" he asked, and, as she did not answer, he said again: "It may well be it is not so. But I thought now maybe you might deem you would be none the worse if you took my hand in the dance to-night. But, indeed, 'tis eight years since I stood up to dance."

"How may that be, sir?" asked Kristin. "Mayhap you are wedded?" But then it came into her head that had he been a wedded man, to have made tryst with her thus would have been no fair deed of him. On that she tried to mend her speech, saying: "Maybe you have lost your betrothed maid or your wife?"

Erlend turned quickly and looked on her with strange eyes.

"Hath not Lady Aashild . . .? Why grew you so red when you heard who I was that evening?" he asked a little after.

Kristin flushed red once more, but did not answer; then Erlend asked again:

"I would fain know what my mother's sister said to you of me."

"Naught else," said Kristin quickly, "but in your praise. She said you were so comely and so great of kin that—she said that beside such as you and her kin we were of no such great account—my folk and I——"

"Doth she still talk thus, living the life she lives," said Erlend, and laughed bitterly. "Ay, ay—if it comfort her. . . . Said she naught else of me?"

"What should she have said?" asked Kristin; she knew not why she was grown so strangely heavy-hearted.

"Oh, she might have said——" he spoke in a low tone, looking down, "she might have said that I had been under the Church's ban, and had to pay dear for peace and atonement——"

Kristin was silent a long time. Then she said softly:

"There is many a man who is not master of his own fortunes—so have I heard said. 'Tis little I have seen of the world—but I will never believe of you, Erland, that 'twas for any—dishonourable—deed."

"May God reward you for those words, Kristin," said Erlend, and bent his head and kissed her wrist so vehemently that the horse gave a bound beneath them. When Erlend had it in hand again, he said earnestly: "Dance with me to-night then, Kristin. Afterward I will tell how things are with me—will tell you all—but to-night we will be happy together?"

Kristin answered: "Ay," and they rode a while in silence.

But ere long Erlend began to ask of Lady Aashild, and Kristin told all she knew of her; she praised her much.

"Then all doors are not barred against Björn and Aashild?" asked Erlend.

Kristin said they were thought much of, and that her father and many with him deemed that most of the tales about these two were untrue.

"How liked you my kinsman, Munan Baardsön?" asked Erlend, laughing slily.

"I looked not much upon him," said Kristin, "and methought, too, he was not much to look on."

"Knew you not," asked Erlend, "that he is her son?"

"Son to Lady Aashild!" said Kristin, in great wonder.

"Ay, her children could not take their mother's fair looks, though they took all else," said Erlend.

"I have never known her first husband's name," said Kristin.

"They were two brothers who wedded two sisters," said Erlend. "Baard and Nikulaus Munansön. My father was the elder, my mother was his second wife, but he had no children by his first. Baard, whom Aashild wedded, was not young either, nor, I trow, did they ever live happily together—ay, I was a little child when all this befell, they hid from me as much as they could. . . . But she fled the land with Sir Björn and married him against the will of her kin—when Baard was dead. Then folk would have had the wedding set aside—they made out that Björn had sought her bed while her first husband was still living, and that they had plotted together to put away my father's brother. 'Tis clear they could not bring this home to them, since they had to leave them together in wedlock. But to make amends, they had to forfeit all their estate—Björn had killed their sister's son, too—my mother's and Aashild's, I mean——"

Kristin's heart beat hard. At home her father and mother had kept strict watch that no unclean talk should come to the ears of their children or of young folk—but still, things had happened in their own parish and Kristin had heard of them—a man had lived in adultery with a wedded woman. That was whoredom, one of the worst of sins; 'twas said they plotted the husband's death, and that brought with it outlawry and the Church's ban. Lavrans had said no woman was bound to stay with her husband, if he had had to do with another's wife; the state of a child gotten in adultery could never be mended, not even though its father and mother were free to wed afterward. A man might bring into his family and make his heir his child by any wanton or strolling beggar-woman, but not the child of his adultery—not if its mother came to be a knight's lady. She thought of the misliking she had ever felt for Sir Björn, with his bleached face and fat, yet shrunken body. She could not think how Lady Aashild could be so good and yielding at all times to the man who had led her away into such shame; how such a gracious woman could have let herself be beguiled by him. He was not even good to her; he let her toil and moil with all the farmwork; Björn did naught but drink beer. Yet Aashild was ever mild and gentle when she spoke with her husband. Kristin wondered if her father could know all this, since he had asked Sir Björn to their home. Now she came to think, too, it seemed strange Erlend should think fit to tell such tales of his near kin. But like enough he deemed she knew of it already.

"I would like well," said Erlend in a while, "to visit her, Moster* Aashild, some day—when I journey northwards. Is he comely still, Björn, my kinsman?"

"No," said Kristin. "He looks like hay that has lain the winter through upon the fields."

"Ay, ay, it tells upon a man, I trow," said Erlend, with the same bitter smile. "Never have I seen so fair a man—'tis twenty years since, I was but a lad then—but his like have I never seen——"

A little after they came to the hospital. It was an exceeding great and fine place, with many houses both of stone and of wood—houses for the sick, almshouses, hostels for travellers, a chapel and a house for the priest. There was great bustle in the courtyard, for food was being

* Moster = mother's sister.

made ready in the kitchen of the hospital for the guild feast, and the poor and sick too, that were dwelling in the place, were to be feasted on the best this day.

The hall of the guild was beyond the garden of the hospital, and folks took their way thither through the herb-garden, for this was of great renown. Lady Groa had had brought hither plants that no one had heard of in Norway before, and, moreover, all plants that else folks were used to grow in gardens, throve better in her herbaries, both flowers and pot-herbs and healing herbs. She was a most learned woman in all such matters, and had herself put into the Norse tongue the herbals of the Salernitan school. . . . Lady Groa had been more than ever kind to Kristin since she had marked that the maid knew somewhat of herb-lore, and was fain to know yet more of it.

So Kristin named for Erland what grew in the beds on either side the grassy path they walked on. In the midday sun there was a warm and spicy scent of dill and celery, garlic and roses, southernwood and wallflower. Beyond the shadeless, baking herb-garden, the fruit orchards looked cool and enticing—red cherries gleamed amid the dark leafy tops, and the apple trees drooped their branches heavy with green fruit.

About the garden was a hedge of sweet briar. There were some flowers on it still—they looked the same as other briar roses, but in the sun the leaves smelt of wine and apples. Folk plucked sprays to deck themselves as they went past. Kristin, too, took some roses and hung them on her temples, fixed under her golden fillet. One she kept in her hand. . . . After a time Erland took it, saying no word. A while he bore it in his hand as they walked, then fastened it with the brooch upon his breast—he looked awkward and bashful as he did it, and was so clumsy that he pricked his fingers till they bled.

Broad tables were spread in the loft-room of the guild's hall—two by the main walls, for the men and the women; and two smaller boards out on the floor, where children and young folk sat side by side.

At the women's board Lady Groa was in the high-seat, the nuns and the chief of the married women sat on the inner bench along the wall, and the unwedded women on the outer benches, the maids from Nonneseter at the upper end. Kristin knew that Erland was watching her, but she durst not turn her head even once, either when they rose or when they sat down. Only when they got up at last to hear the priest read the names of the dead guild-brothers and sisters, she stole a hasty glance at the men's table—she caught a glimpse of him where he stood by the wall, behind the candles burning on the board. He was looking at her.

The meal lasted long, with all the toasts in honour of God, the Virgin Mary, and St. Margaret and St. Olav and St. Halvard, and prayers and song between.

Kristin saw through the open door that the sun was gone; sounds of fiddling and song came in from the green without, and all the young folks had left the tables already when Lady Groa said to the convent maidens that they might go now and play themselves for a time if they listed.

Three red bonfires were burning upon the green; around them moved the many-coloured chains of dancers. The fiddlers sat aloft on heaped-up chests and scraped their fiddles—they played and sang a different tune in every ring; there were too many folk for *one* dance. It was nearly dark already—northward the wooded ridge stood out coal-black against the yellow-green sky.

Under the loft-balcony folk were sitting drinking. Some men sprang forward, as soon as the six maids from Nonneseter came down the steps. Munan Baardsön flew to meet Ingebjörg and went off with her, and Kristin was caught by the wrist—Erlend, she knew his hand already. He pressed her hand in his so that their rings grated on one another and bruised the flesh.

He drew her with him to the outermost bonfire. Many children were dancing there; Kristin gave her other hand to a twelve-year-old lad, and Erlend had a little, half-grown maid on his other side.

No one was singing in the ring just then—they were swaying in and out to the tune of the fiddle as they moved round. Then some one shouted that Sivord the Dane should sing them a new dance. A tall, fair-haired man with huge fists stepped out in front of the chain and struck up his ballad:

> Fair goes the dance at Munkolm
>   On silver sand.
> There danceth Ivar Sir Alfsön—
>   Holds the Queen's own hand.
>   *Know ye not Ivar Sir Alfsön?*

The fiddlers knew not the tune, they thrummed their strings a little, and the Dane sang alone—he had a strong, tuneful voice:

> "Mind you, Queen of the Danemen,
>   That summer fair,
> They led you out of Sweden,
>   To Denmark here?
>
> They led you out of Sweden,
>   To Denmark here,
> All with a crown of the red gold
>   And many a tear.

> All with a crown of the red gold
> And tear-filled eyne—
> —Mind you, Queen of the Danemen
> You first were mine?"

The fiddles struck in again, the dancers hummed the new-learned tune and joined in the burden:

> "And are you, Ivar Sir Alfsön,
> Sworn man to me,
> Then shall you hang to-morrow
> On the gallows tree!"

> But 'twas Ivar Sir Alfsön,
> All unafraid
> He leaped into the gold-bark
> In harness clad.

> "God send you, oh Dane-Queen,
> So many a good night,
> As in the high heavens
> Are stars alight.

> God send you, oh Dane-King,
> So many ill years
> As be leaves on the linden—
> Or the hind hath hairs."
> *Know ye not Ivar Sir Alfsön?*

It was far on in the night, and the fires were but heaps of embers growing more and more black. Kristin and Erlend stood hand in hand under the trees by the garden fence. Behind them the noise of the revellers was hushed—a few young lads were hopping round the glowing mounds singing softly, but the fiddlers had sought their resting-places, and most of the people were gone. One or two wives went round seeking their husbands, who were lying somewhere out of doors overcome by the beer.

"Where think you I can have laid my cloak?" whispered Kristin. Erlend put his arm about her waist and drew his mantle round them both. Close pressed to one another they went into the herb-garden.

A lingering breath of the day's warm spicy scents, deadened and damp with the chill of the dew, met them in there. The night was very dark, the sky overcast, with murky grey clouds close down upon the tree-tops. But they could tell that there were other folks in the garden. Once Erlend pressed the maiden close to him and asked in a whisper:

"Are you not afraid, Kristin?"

In her mind she caught a faint glimpse of the world outside this night —and knew that this was madness. But a blessed strengthlessness was upon her. She only leaned closer to the man and whispered softly— she herself knew not what.

They came to the end of the path; a stone wall divided them from the woods. Erlend helped her up. As she jumped down on the other side, he caught her and held her lifted in his arms a moment before he set her on the grass.

She stood with upturned face to take his kiss. He held her head between his hands—it was so sweet to her to feel his fingers sink into her hair—she felt she must repay him, and so she clasped his head and sought to kiss him, as he had kissed her.

When he put his hands upon her breast, she felt as though he drew her heart from out her bosom; he parted the folds of silk ever so little and laid a kiss betwixt them—it sent a glow into her inmost soul.

"You I could never harm," whispered Erlend. "You should never shed a tear through fault of mine. Never had I dreamed a maid might be so good as you, my Kristin——"

He drew her down into the grass beneath the bushes; they sat with their backs against the wall. Kristin said naught, but when he ceased from caressing her, she put up her hand and touched his face.

In a while Erlend asked: "Are you not weary, my dear one?" And when Kristin nestled in to his breast, he folded his arms around her, and whispered: "Sleep, sleep, Kristin, here in my arms——"

She slipped deeper and deeper into darkness and warmth and happiness upon his breast.

When she came to herself again, she was lying outstretched in the grass with her cheek upon the soft brown silk above his knees. Erlend was sitting as before with his back to the stone wall, his face looked grey in the grey twilight, but his wide opened eyes were marvellously clear and fair. She saw he had wrapped his cloak all about her—her feet were so warm and snug with the fur lining around them.

"Now have you slept in my lap," said he, smiling faintly. "May God bless you, Kristin—you slept as safe as a child in its mother's arms——"

"Have *you* not slept, Sir Erlend?" asked Kristin; and he smiled down into her fresh opened eyes:

"Maybe the night will come when you and I may lie down to sleep together—I know not what you will think when you have weighed all things. I have watched by you to-night—there is still so much betwixt us two that 'tis more than if there had lain a naked sword between you and me. Tell me if you will hold me dear, when this night is past?"

"I will hold you dear, Sir Erlend," said Kristin. "I will hold you dear, so long as you will—and thereafter I will love none other."

"Then," said Erlend slowly, "may God forsake me if any maid or woman come to my arms ere I may make you mine in law and honour. Say you this, too," he prayed. Kristin said:

"May God forsake me if I take any other man to my arms so long as I live on earth."

"We must go now," said Erlend, a little after, "before folk waken." They passed along without the wall among the bushes.

"Have you bethought you," asked Erlend, "what further must be done in this?"

"'Tis for you to say what we must do, Erlend," answered Kristin.

"Your father," he asked in a little, "they say at Gerdarud he is a mild and a righteous man. Think you he will be so exceeding loth to go back from what he hath agreed with Andres Darre?"

"Father has said so often, he would never force us, his daughters," said Kristin. "The chief thing is that our lands and Simon's lie so fitly together. But I trow father would not that I should miss all my gladness in this world for the sake of that." A fear stirred within her that so simple as this perhaps it might not prove to be—but she fought it down.

"Then maybe 'twill be less hard than I deemed in the night," said Erlend. "God help me, Kristin—methinks I *cannot* lose you now—unless I win you now, never can I be glad again."

They parted among the trees, and in the dawning light Kristin found her way to the guest-chamber where the women from Nonneseter were to lie. All the beds were full, but she threw a cloak upon some straw on the floor and laid her down in all her clothes.

When she awoke, it was far on in the day. Ingebjörg Filippusdatter was sitting on a bench near by, stitching down an edge of fur that had been torn loose on her cloak. She was full of talk as ever.

"Were you with Erlend Nikulaussön the whole night?" she asked. "'Twere well you went warily with that lad, Kristin—how think you Simon Andressön would like it if you came to be dear friends with him?"

Kristin found a hand-basin and began to wash herself.

"And your betrothed—think you he would like that you danced with Dumpy Munan last night? Surely we must dance with him who chooses us out on such a night of merry-making—and Lady Groa had given us leave."

Ingebjörg pshawed:

"Einar Einarssön and Sir Munan are friends—and, besides, he is wedded and old. Ugly he is to boot for that matter—but likeable and hath becoming ways—see what he gave me for a remembrance of last night," and she held forth a gold clasp which Kristin had seen in Sir Munan's hat the day before. "But this Erlend—'tis true he was freed of the ban at Easter last year, but they say Eline Ormsdatter has been with him at Husaby since—Sir Munan says Erlend hath fled to Sira

Jon at Gerdarud, and he deems 'tis because he cannot trust himself not to fall back into sin, if he meet her again——"

Kristin crossed over to the other—her face was white.

"Knew you not this?" said Ingebjörg. "That he lured a woman from her husband somewhere in Haalogaland in the North—and held her with him at his manor in despite of the King's command and the Archbishop's ban—they had two children together—and he was driven to fly to Sweden, and hath been forced to pay in forfeit so much of his lands and goods, Sir Munan says he will be a poor man in the end unless he mend his ways the sooner."

"Think not but that I know all this," said Kristin, with a set face. "But 'tis known the matter is ended now."

"Ay, but as to that Sir Munan said there had been an end between them so many times before," said Ingebjörg pensively. "But all these things can be nothing to you—you that are to wed Simon Darre. But a comely man is Erlend Nikulaussön, sure enough."

The company from Nonneseter was to set out for home that same day after nones. Kristin had promised Erlend to meet him by the wall where they had sat the night before, if she could but find a way to come.

He was lying face downwards in the grass with his head upon his hands. As soon as he saw her, he sprang to his feet and held out both his hands, as she was about jumping from the wall.

Kristin took them, and the two stood a little, hand in hand. Then said Kristin:

"Why told you me that of Sir Björn and Lady Aashild yesterday?"

"I can see you know it all," said Erlend, and let go her hands suddenly. "What think you of me now, Kristin?

"I was eighteen then," he went on vehemently, "'tis ten years since that the King, my kinsman, sent me with the mission to Vargöyhus,* and we stayed the winter at Steigen. . . . She was wife to the Lagmand, Sigurd Saksulvsön. . . . I thought pity of her, for he was old and ugly beyond belief. I know not how it came to pass—ay, but I loved her too. I bade Sigurd crave what amends he would; I would fain have done right by him—he is a good and doughty man in many ways—but he would have it that all must go by law; he took the matter to the Thing—I was to be branded for whoredom with the wife of him whose guest I had been, you understand . . .

"Then it came to my father's ears, and then to King Haakon's . . . he—he drove me from his court. And if you must know the whole—there is naught more now betwixt Eline and me save the children, and she cares not much for them. They are in Osterdal, upon a farm I owned there; I have given it to Orm, the boy—but she will not stay

* Mission to Vargöyhus, see Note 18.

with them. Doubtless she reckons that Sigurd cannot live for ever—but I know not what she would be at.

"Sigurd took her back again—but she says she fared like a dog and a bondwoman in his house—so she set a tryst with me at Nidaros. 'Twas little better for me at Husaby with my father. I sold all I could lay hands on, and fled with her to Holland—Count Jacob stood my friend. Could I do aught else?—she was great with my child. I knew many a man had lived even so with another's wife and had got off cheap enough —if he were rich, that is. But so it is with King Haakon, he is hardest upon his own kin. We were away from one another for a year, but then my father died and then she came back. Then there were other troubles. My tenants denied me rent and would have no speech with my bailiffs because I lay under ban—I, on my side, dealt harshly with them, and so they brought suit against me for robbery; but I had not the money to pay my household withal; and you can see I was too young to meet these troubles wisely, and my kinsfolk would not help me—save Munan —he did all his wife would let him. . . .

"Ay, now you know it, Kristin: I have lost much both of lands and goods and of honour. True it is; you would be better served if you held fast to Simon Andressön."

Kristin put her arms about his neck.

"We will abide by what we swore to each other yesternight, Erlend— if so be you think as I do."

Erlend drew her close to him, kissed her and said:

"You will see too, trust me, that all things will be changed with me now—for none in the world has power on me now but you. Oh, my thoughts were many last night, as you slept upon my lap, my fairest one. So much power the devil cannot have over a man that I should ever work you care and woe—you, my dearest life. . . ."

IV

At the time he dwelt at Skog, Lavrans Björgulfsön had made gifts of land to Gerdarud church, that masses for the souls of his father and mother might be said on their death-days. Björgulf Ketilsön's day was the thirteenth of August, and Lavrans had settled with his brother that this year Aasmund should bring Kristin out to Skog that she might be at the mass.

She went in fear that something should come in the way, so that her uncle would not keep his promise—she thought she had marked that Aasmund did not care overmuch about her. But the day before the mass was to be, Aasmund Björgulfsön came to the convent to fetch his brother's daughter. Kristin was told to clothe herself in lay garb, but simply and in dark garments. There had been some carping at the Sisters of Nonneseter for going about too much without the convent walls; therefore the Bishop had given order that the maidens who were not to take the veil must wear naught like to the habit of the order when they went visiting their kinsfolk—so that laymen could not mistake them for novices or nuns.

Kristin's heart was full of gladness as she rode along the highway with her uncle, and Aasmund grew more friendly and merry with her when he saw the maid was not so tongue-tied after all with folk. Otherwise Aasmund was somewhat moody and downcast; he said it looked as though there would be a call to arms in the autumn, and that the King would lead an army into Sweden to avenge the slaying of his son-in-law and the husband of his niece. Kristin had heard of the murder of the Swedish Dukes, and thought it a most foul deed—yet all these questions of state seemed far away from her. No one spoke much of such things at home in the Dale; she remembered, too, that her father had been to the war against Duke Eirik at Ragnhildarholm and Konungahella. Then Aasmund told her of all that had come and gone between the King and the Dukes. Kristin understood but little of this, but she gave careful heed to all her uncle told of the making and breaking of the betrothals of the King's daughters. It gave her comfort to think 'twas not everywhere as it was at home in her countryside, that a betrothal once fixed by word of mouth was held to bind nigh as fast as a wedding. Then she took courage to tell of her adventure on the evening before Halvard-wake, and asked her uncle if he knew Erlend of Husaby. Aasmund spoke well of Erlend—said he had guided his affairs unwisely, but his father and the King were most to blame; they had borne themselves as though the young lad were a very limb of the devil only because he had fallen into this misfortune. The King was over-pious in such matters, and Sir Nikulaus was angry because Erlend had lost much good land, so they had thundered about whoredom and hell fire —"and there must be a bit of the dare-devil in every likely lad," said Aasmund Björgulfsön. "And the woman was most fair. But you have no call now to look Erlend's way, so trouble yourself no more about his doings."

Erlend came not to the mass, as he had promised Kristin he would, and she thought about this more than of God's word. She felt no sorrow that this was so—she had only that strange new feeling that she was cut off from all the ties that she had felt binding on her before.

She tried to take comfort—like enough Erlend deemed it wisest that no one in whose charge she was should come to know of their friendship at this time. She could understand herself that 'twas wise. But her heart had longed so for him, and she wept when she had gone to rest in the loft-room where she was to sleep with Aasmund's little daughters.

The day after, she went up into the wood with the youngest of her uncle's children, a little maid of six years. When they were come to the pastures among the woods a little way off, Erlend came running after them. Kristin knew it was he before she had seen who was coming.

"I have sat up here on the hill spying down into the courtyard the whole day," said he. "I thought surely you would find a chance to come out——"

"Think you I came out to meet you then?" said Kristin, laughing. "And are you not afraid to beat about my uncle's woods with dogs and bow?"

"Your uncle gave me leave to take my pastime hunting here," said Erlend. "And the dogs are Aasmund's—they found me out this morning." He patted them and lifted the little girl up in his arms.

"*You* know me, Ragndid? But say not you have spoken with me, and you can have this"—and he took out a bunch of raisins and gave them to the child. "I had brought them for you," he said to Kristin. "Think you this child can hold her tongue?"

They talked fast and laughed together. Erlend was dressed in a short close-fitting brown jacket and had a small red silk cap pulled down over his black hair—he looked so young; he laughed and played with the child; but sometimes he would take Kristin's hand, and press it till it hurt her.

He spoke of the rumours of war and was glad: "'Twill be easier for me to win back the King's friendship," said he, "and then will all things be easy," he said vehemently.

At last they sat down in a meadow up among the woods. Erlend had the child on his lap; Kristin sat by his side; under cover of the grass he played with her fingers. He pressed into her hand three gold rings bound together by a cord:

"By and by," he whispered, "you shall have as many as will go on your fingers. . . ."

"I shall wait for you here on this field each day about this time, as long as you are at Skog," he said, as they parted. "And you must come if you can."

The next day Aasmund Björgulfsön set out with his wife and children to the manor of Gyrid's kin in Hadeland. They had been scared by the talk of war; the folk about Oslo still went in terror since Duke Eirik's harrying of that countryside some years before. Aasmund's old mother was so fearful, she was minded to seek shelter in Nonneseter—besides, she was too weak to travel with the others. So Kristin was to stay at

Skog with the old woman—she called her grandmother—till Aasmund came back from Hadeland.

About the midday hour, when the folk on the farm were resting, Kristin went to the loft-room where she slept. She had brought some clothes with her in a sheepskin bag, and now she changed her garments, humming to herself the while.

Her father had given her a dress of thick cotton stuff from the East, sky-blue with a close pattern of red flowers; this she put on. She brushed and combed out her hair and bound it back from her face with a red silk ribbon, wound a red silk belt tightly about her waist, and put Erlend's rings upon her fingers; all the time she wondered if he would think her fair.

The two dogs that had been with Erlend in the forest had slept in the loft-room over-night—she called them to go with her now. She stole out round the houses and took the same path as the day before up through the hill-pastures.

The field amid the forest lay lonely and silent in the burning midday sun; the pine woods that shut it in on all sides gave out a hot, strong scent. The sun stung, and the blue sky seemed strangely near and close down upon the tree-tops.

Kristin sat down in the shade in the borders of the wood. She was not vexed that Erlend was not there; she was sure he would come, and it gave her an odd gladness to sit there alone a little and to be the first.

She listened to the low hum of tiny life above the yellow, scorched grass, pulled a few dry, spicy-scented flowers that she could reach without moving more than her hand, and rolled them between her fingers and smelt them—she sat with wide-open eyes sunk in a kind of drowse.

She did not move when she heard a horse in the woods. The dogs growled, and the hair on their necks bristled—then they bounded up over the meadow, barking and wagging their tails. Erlend sprang from his horse at the edge of the forest, let it go with a clap on its flank, and ran down towards her with the dogs jumping about him. He caught their muzzles in his hands and came to her leading the two elk-grey, wolf-like beasts. Kristin smiled and held out her hand without getting up.

Once, while she was looking at the dark head that lay in her lap, between her hands, something bygone flashed on her mind. It stood out, clear yet distant, as a homestead far away on a mountain slope may start to sight of a sudden, from out dark clouds, when a sunbeam strikes it on a stormy day. And it was as though there welled up in her

heart all the tenderness Arne Gyrdsön had once begged for, while, as
yet, she did not understand his words. With timid passion, she drew
the man up to her and laid his head upon her breast, kissing him as if
afraid he should be taken from her. And when she saw his head upon
her arm, she felt as though she clasped a child—she hid his eyes with
one of her hands, and showered little kisses upon his mouth and
cheek.

The sunshine had gone from the meadow—the leaden colour above
the tree-tops had thickened to dark-blue, and spread over the whole
sky; little, coppery flashes like fire-tinged smoke flickered within the
clouds. Bayard came down to them, neighed loudly once, and then
stood stock-still, staring before him. Soon after came the first flash of
lightning, and the thunder followed close, not far away.

Erlend got up and took hold of the horse. An old barn stood at the
lowest end of the meadow; they went thither, and he tied Bayard to
some woodwork just inside the door. At the back of the barn lay some
hay; Erlend spread his cloak out, and they seated themselves with the
dogs at their feet.

And now the rain came down like a sheet before the doorway. It
hissed in the trees and lashed the ground—soon they had to move farther
in, away from the drips from the roof. Each time it lightened and
thundered, Erlend whispered:

"Are you not afraid, Kristin——?"

"A little——" she whispered back, and drew closer to him.

They knew not how long they had sat—the storm had soon passed
over—it thundered far away, but the sun shone on the wet grass outside
the door, and the sparkling drops fell more and more rarely from the
roof. The sweet smell of the hay in the barn grew stronger.

"Now must I go," said Kristin; and Erlend answered: "Ay, 'tis like
you must." He took her foot in his hand: "You will be wet—you must
ride and I must walk—out of the woods . . ." and he looked at her so
strangely.

Kristin shook—it must be because her heart beat so, she thought—
her hands were cold and clammy. As he kissed her vehemently she
weakly tried to push him from her. Erlend lifted his face a moment—
she thought of a man who had been given food at the convent one day
—he had kissed the bread they gave him. She sank back upon the
hay. . . .

She sat upright when Erlend lifted his head from her arms. He
raised himself suddenly upon his elbow:

"Look not so—Kristin!"

His voice sent a new, wild pang into Kristin's soul—he was not glad —*he* was unhappy too——!

"Kristin, Kristin! Think you I lured you out here to me in the woods meaning this—to make you mine by force——?" he asked in a little.

She stroked his hair and did not look at him.

"'Twas not force, I trow—you had let me go as I came, had I begged you——" said she, in a low voice.

"I know not," he answered, and hid his face in her lap. . . .

"Think you that I would betray you?" asked he vehemently. "Kristin—I swear to you by my Christian faith—may God forsake me in my last hour, if I keep not faith with you till the day of my death——"

She could say naught, she only stroked his hair again and again.

"'Tis time I went home, is it not?" she asked at length, and she seemed to wait in deadly terror for his answer.

"Maybe so," he answered dully. He got up quickly, went to the horse, and began to loosen the reins.

Then she, too, got up. Slowly, wearily, and with crushing pain it came home to her—she knew not what she had hoped he might do— set her upon his horse, maybe, and carry her off with him so she might be spared from going back amongst other people. It was as though her whole body ached with wonder—that this ill thing was what was sung in all the songs. And since Erlend had wrought her this, she felt herself grown so wholly his, she knew not how she should live away from him any more. She was to go from him now, but she could not understand that it should be so.

Down through the woods he went on foot, leading the horse. He held her hand in his, but they found no words to say.

When they were come so far that they could see the houses at Skog, he bade her farewell.

"Kristin—be not so sorrowful—the day will come or ever you know it, when you will be my wedded wife——"

But her heart sank as he spoke.

"Must you go away, then?" she asked, dismayed.

"As soon as you are gone from Skog," said he, and his voice already rang more bright. "If there be no war, I will speak to Munan—he has long urged me that I should wed—he will go with me and speak for me to your father."

Kristin bent her head—at each word he said, she felt the time that lay before grow longer and more hard to think of—the convent, Jörund-gaard—she seemed to float upon a stream which bore her far from it all.

"Sleep you alone in the loft-room, now your kinsfolk are gone?" asked

Erlend. "Then will I come and speak with you to-night—will you let me in?"

"Ay," said Kristin low. And so they parted.

The rest of the day she sat with her father's mother, and after supper she took the old lady to her bed. Then she went up to the loft-room, where she was to lie. There was a little window in the room; Kristin sate herself down on the chest that stood below it—she had no mind to go to bed.

She had long to wait. It was quite dark without when she heard the soft steps upon the balcony. He knocked upon the door with his cloak about his knuckles, and Kristin got up, drew the bolt, and let Erlend in.

She marked how glad he was, when she flung her arms about his neck and clung to him.

"I have been fearing you would be angry with me," he said.

"You must not grieve for our sin," he said, sometime after. "'Tis not a deadly sin. God's law is not like to the law of the land in this. . . . Gunnulv, my brother, once made this matter plain to me—if two vow to have and hold each other fast for all time, and thereafter lie together, then they are wedded before God and may not break their troths without great sin. I can give you the words in Latin when they come to my mind—I knew them once. . . ."

Kristin wondered a little why Erlend's brother should have said this —but she thrust from her the hateful fear that it might have been said of Erlend and another—and sought to find comfort in his words.

They sat together on the chest, he with his arm about her, and now Kristin felt that 'twas well with her once more and she was safe—beside him was the only spot now where she could feel safe and sheltered.

At times Erlend spoke much and cheerfully—then he would be silent for long, while he sat caressing her. Without knowing it, Kristin gathered up out of all he said each little thing that could make him fairer and dearer to her, and lessen his blame in all she knew of him that was not good.

Erlend's father, Sir Nikulaus, had been so old before he had children, he had not patience enough nor strength enough left to rear them up himself; both the sons had grown up in the house of Sir Baard Petersön at Hestnæs. Erlend had no sisters and no brother save Gunnulv; he was one year younger and was a priest at Christ's Church in Nidaros. "He is dearest to me of all mankind, save only you."

Kristin asked if Gunnulv were like him, but Erlend laughed and said they were much unlike, both in mind and body. Now Gunnulv was in foreign lands studying—he had been away these three years, but had sent letters home twice, the last a year ago, when he thought to go from

St. Geneviève's in Paris and make his way to Rome. "He will be glad, Gunnulv, when he comes home and finds me wed," said Erlend.

Then he spoke of the great heritage he had had from his father and mother—Kristin saw he scarce knew himself how things stood with him now. She knew somewhat of her father's dealings in lands. . . . Erlend had dealt in his the other way about, sold and scattered and wasted and pawned, worst of all in the last years, when he had been striving to free him of his paramour, thinking that, this done, his sinful life might in time be forgotten and his kin stand by him once more; he had thought he might some day come to be Warden* of half the Orkdöla country, as his father had been before him.

"But now do I scarce know what the end will be," said he. "Maybe I shall sit at last on a mountain croft like Björn Gunnarsön, and bear out the dung on my back as did the thralls of old, because I have no horse."

"God help you," said Kristin, laughing. "Then I must come to you for sure—I trow I know more of farm-work and country ways than you."

"I can scarce think you have borne out the dung-basket," said he, laughing too.

"No; but I have seen how they spread the dung out—and sown corn have I, well-nigh every year at home. 'Twas my father's wont to plough himself the fields nearest the farm, and he let me sow the first piece that I might bring good fortune." The thought sent a pang through her heart, so she said quickly: "And a woman you must have to bake, and brew the small beer, and wash your one shirt, and milk—and you must hire a cow or two from the rich farmer near by——"

"Oh, God be thanked that I hear you laugh a little once more!" said Erlend, and caught her up so that she lay on his arms like a child.

Each of the six nights which passed ere Aasmund Björgulfsön came home, Erlend was in the loft-room with Kristin.

The last night he seemed as unhappy as she; he said many times they must not be parted from one another a day longer than needful. At last he said very low:

"Now should things go so ill that I cannot come back hither to Oslo before winter—and if it so falls out you need help of friends—fear not to turn to Sira Jon here at Gerdarud; we are friends from childhood up; and Munan Baardsön, too, you may safely trust."

Kristin could only nod. She knew he spoke of what she had thought on each single day; but Erlend said no more of it. So she, too, said naught, and would not show how heavy of heart she was.

On the other nights he had gone from her when the night grew late,

* Wardens, see Note 19.

but this last evening he begged hard that he might lie and sleep by her an hour. Kristin was fearful, but Erlend said haughtily, "Be sure that were I found here in your bower, I am well able to answer for myself." She herself, too, was fain to keep him by her yet a little while, and she had not strength enough to deny him aught.

But she feared that they might sleep too long. So most of the night she sat leaning against the head of the bed, dozing a little at times, and scarce knowing herself when he caressed her and when she only dreamed it. Her one hand she held upon his breast, where she could feel the beating of his heart beneath, and her face was turned to the window that she might see the dawn without.

At length she had to wake him. She threw on some clothes and went out with him upon the balcony. He clambered over the railing on the side that faced on to another house near by. Now he was gone from her sight—the corner hid him. Kristin went in again and crept into her bed; and now she quite gave way and fell to weeping for the first time since Erlend had made her all his own.

v

A t Nonneseter the days went by as before. Kristin's time was passed between the dormitory and the church, the weaving-room, the book-hall and the refectory. The nuns and the convent-folk gathered in the pot-herbs and the fruits from the herb-garden and the orchard; Holy-cross Day came in the autumn with its procession, then there was the fast before Michaelmas. Kristin wondered—none seemed to mark any change in her. But she had ever been quiet when amongst strangers, and Ingebjörg Filippusdatter, who was by her night and day, was well able to chatter for them both.

Thus no one marked that her thoughts were far away from all around her. Erlend's paramour—she said to herself, she was Erlend's paramour now. It seemed now as though she had dreamed it all—the eve of St. Margaret's Mass, that hour in the barn, the nights in her bower at Skog —either she had dreamed it, or else all about her now was a dream. But one day she must waken, one day it must all come out. Not for a moment did she think aught else than that she bore Erlend's child within her.

But what would happen to her when this came to light, she could not well think. Would she be put into the black hole, or be sent home? She saw dim pictures of her father and mother far away. Then she shut her eyes, dizzy and sick, bowed in fancy beneath the coming storm and tried to harden herself to bear it, since she thought it must end by sweeping her for ever into Erlend's arms—the only place where now she felt she had a home.

Thus was there in this strained waiting as much of hope as terror, as much of sweetness as of torment. She was unhappy—but she felt her love for Erlend as it were a flower planted within her—and, spite of her unhappiness, it put forth fresher and richer blooms each day. That last night when he had slept by her side she had felt, as a faint and fleeting bliss, that there awaited her a joy and happiness in his arms such as she had not yet known—she thrilled now at the thought of it; it came to her like warm, spicy breaths from sun-heated gardens. Wayside brat—Inga had flung the word at her—she opened her arms to it and pressed it to her bosom. Wayside brat was the name they gave to the child begotten in secret in woods or fields. She felt the sunshine, and the smell of the pines in the forest pasture. Each new, creeping tremor, each sudden pulse-beat in her body she took as a reminder from the unborn babe that now she was come out into new paths—and were they never so hard to follow to the end, she was sure they must lead to Erlend at the last.

She sat betwixt Ingebjörg and Sister Astrid and sewed at the great tapestry of knights and birds amidst leafy tendrils. And as she sewed she thought of how she should fly when the time was come, and it could no longer be hidden. She saw herself walking along the highways, clothed like a poor woman; all she owned of gold and silver she bore within a bundle in her hand. She bought herself shelter on a farm somewhere in a far-away countryside—she went as a serving-wench, bore the water-carrier's yoke upon her neck, worked in the byres, baked and washed, and was cursed because she would not tell who was the child's father. Then Erlend came and found her.

Sometimes she dreamed that he came too late. She lay snow-white and fair in the poor peasant's bed. Erlend stooped as he came in at the door; he had on the long black cloak he had used to wear when he came to her by night at Skog. The woman led him forward to where she lay, he sank down and took her cold hands, his eyes were sad as death—Dost thou lie here, my one delight . . .? Bent with sorrow he went out with his tender son clasped to his breast, in the folds of his cloak—nay, she thought not in good sooth that it would so fall out; she had no mind to die, Erlend should have no such sorrow. . . . But her heart was so heavy it did her good to dream these dreams. . . .

Then for a moment it stood out cold and clear as ice before her—the child, that was no dream, that must be faced; she must answer one day for what she had done—and it seemed as if her heart stood still with terror.

But after a little time had gone by, she came to think 'twas not so sure after all she was with child. She understood not herself why she was not glad—it was as though she had lain and wept beneath a warm covering, and now must get up in the cold. A month went by—then two; now she was sure that she had been spared this ill-hap—and, empty and chill of soul, she felt yet unhappier than before. In her heart there dawned a little bitterness toward Erlend. Advent drew near, and she had heard neither from or of him; she knew not where he was.

And now she felt she could not bear this fear and doubt—it was as though a bond betwixt them had snapped; now she was afraid indeed—might it not so befall that she should never see him more? All she had been safely linked to once, she was parted from now—and the new tie that bound her to her lover was such a frail one. She never thought that he would mean to play her false—but there was so much that might happen. . . . She knew not how she could go on any longer day after day, suffering the tormenting doubt of this time of waiting.

Now and then she thought of her father and mother and sisters—she longed for them, but as for something she had lost for ever.

And sometimes in church, and elsewhere too, she would feel a great yearning to take part in all that this meant, the communion of mankind with God. It had ever been a part of her life; now she stood outside with her unconfessed sin.

She told herself that this cutting adrift from home and kin and Church was but for a time. Erlend must take her by the hand and lead her back into it all. When her father had given consent to their love, she could go to him as of yore; when she and Erlend were wed, they could confess and do penance for their transgression.

She began to seek for tokens that other folk were not without sin any more than they. She hearkened more to tale-bearing, and marked all the little things about her which showed that not even the Sisters in the convent here were altogether godly and unworldly. These were only little things—under Lady Groa's rule Nonneseter to the world was a pattern of what a godly sisterhood should be. Zealous in their devotions, diligent, full of care for the poor and sick, were the nuns. Their aloofness from the world was not so strict but that the Sisters both had visits from their friends and kin in the parlour, and themselves were given leave to visit these in the town when aught was afoot; but no nun had brought shame upon the house by her life all the years of Lady Groa's rule.

But Kristin had now an ear alive to all the little jars within the convent walls—little wranglings and spites and vanities. Save in the nursing of the sick, none of the Sisters would help with the rough housework —all were minded to be women of learning or skilled in some craft; the one strove to outdo the other, and the Sisters who had no turn for learning or the nobler crafts, lost heart and mooned through the hours as though but half awake.

Lady Groa herself was wise as well as learned; she kept a wakeful eye on her spiritual daughters' way of life and their diligence, but she troubled herself little about their souls' health. She had been kind and friendly to Kristin at all times—she seemed to like her better than the other young girls, but that was because Kristin was apt at books and needlework, diligent and sparing of words. Lady Groa never looked for an answer from any of the Sisters; but, on the other hand, she was ever glad to speak with men. They came and went in her parlour—tenant farmers and bailiffs of the convent, Preaching Friars from the Bishop, stewards of estates on Hovedö with whom she was at law. She had her hands full with the oversight of the convent's great estates, with the keeping of accounts, sending out church vestments, and taking in books to be copied and sending them away again. Not the most evil-minded of men could find aught unseemly in Lady Groa's way of life. But she liked only to talk of such things as women seldom know about.

The prior, who dwelt in a house by himself, northward of the church, seemed to have no more will of his own than the Abbess' writing-reed or her scourge. Sister Potentia looked after most things within the house; and she thought most of keeping such order as she had seen in the far-famed German convent where she had passed her noviciate. She had been called Sigrid Ragnvaldsdatter before, but had taken a new name when she took the habit of the order, for this was much the use in other lands; it was she, too, who had thought of making the maidens, who were at Nonneseter as pupils, and for a time only, wear novice's dress.

Sister Cecilia Baardsdatter was not as the other nuns. She went about quietly, with downcast eyes, answered always gently and humbly, was serving-maid to all, did for choice all the roughest work, fasted much more than she need—as much as Lady Groa would let her—and knelt by the hour in the church after evensong or went thither before matins.

But one evening, after she had been all day at the beck with two lay-sisters washing clothes, she suddenly burst into a loud sobbing at the supper-table. She cast herself upon the stone floor, crept among the Sisters on hands and knees, beat her breast, and with burning cheeks and streaming tears begged them all to forgive her. She was the worst sinner of them all—she had been hard as stone with pride all her days; pride, and not meekness or thankfulness for Jesus' redeeming death, had held her up, when she had been tempted in the world; she had fled thither not because she loved a man's soul, but because she loved her own vainglory. She had served her sisters out of pride, vanity had she drunken from her water-cup, self-righteousness had she spread thick upon her dry bread, while the other Sisters were drinking their beer and eating their bread-slices with butter.

Of all this Kristin understood no more than that not even Cecilia
Baardsdatter was truly godly at heart. An unlit tallow candle that has
hung from the roof and grown foul with soot and cobweb—to this she
herself likened her unloving chastity.

Lady Groa went herself and lifted up the sobbing woman. Sternly she
said, that for this disorder Cecilia should as a punishment move from
the Sisters' dormitory into the Abbess's own bed, and lie there till she
was free of this fever.

"And thereafter, Sister Cecilia, shall you sit in my seat for the space of
a week; we will seek counsel of you in spiritual things and give you such
honour for your godly life, that you may have your fill of the homage
of sinful mankind. Thus may you judge if it be worth so much striving,
and thereafter choose whether you will live by the rules, as do we others,
or keep on in exercises that no one demands of you. Then can you
ponder whether you will do for love of God, that He may look down upon you in His mercy, all those things which you say you have done that
we should look up to you."

And so it was done. Sister Cecilia lay in the Abbess's room for fourteen days; she had a high fever, and Lady Groa herself tended her.
When she got up again, she had to sit for a week at the side of the
Abbess in the high-seat, both in the church and in the convent, and all
waited on her—she wept all the time as though she were being beaten
with whips. But afterwards she was much calmer and happier. She
lived much as before, but she blushed like a bride if any one looked at
her, whether she was sweeping the floor or going alone to the church.

None the less did this matter of Sister Cecilia awake in Kristin a great
longing for peace and atonement with all wherefrom she had come to feel
herself cast out. She thought of Brother Edvin, and one day she took
courage and begged leave of Lady Groa to go out to the barefoot friars
and visit a friend she knew there.

She marked that Lady Groa misliked this—there was scant friendship
between the Minorites and the other cloisters in the bishopric. And the
Abbess was no better pleased when she heard who was Kristin's friend.
She said this Brother Edvin was an unstable man of God—he was ever
wandering about the country and seeking leave to pay begging visits to
strange bishoprics. The common folk in many places held him to be a
holy man, but he did not seem to understand that a Franciscan's first
duty was obedience to those set over him. He had shriven freebooters
and outlaws, baptized their children and chanted them to their graves,
without asking leave—yet, doubtless, he had sinned as much through
ignorance as in despite, and he had borne meekly the penances laid upon
him on account of these things. He was borne with, too, because he was

skilled in his handicraft—but even in working at this, he had fallen out
with his craft-fellows; the master-limners of the Bishop of Bergen would
not suffer him to come and work in the bishopric there.

Kristin made bold to ask where he had come from, this monk with the
un-Norse name. Lady Groa was in the mood for talking; she told how
he had been born here in Oslo, but his father was an Englishman,
Rikard Platemaster, who had wedded a farmer's daughter from the
Skogheim Hundred, and had taken up his abode in the town—two of
Edvin's brothers were armourers of good repute in Oslo. But this eldest
of the Platemaster's sons had been a restless spirit all his days. 'Twas
true he had felt a call to the life of the cloister from childhood up; he had
joined the Cistercians at Hovedö as soon as he was old enough. They
sent him to a monastery in France to be trained—for his gifts were good;
while still there he had managed to get leave to pass from the Cistercian
into the Minorite Order. And at the time the unruly friars began building their church eastward in the fields in despite of the Bishop's command, Brother Edvin had been one of the worst and most stiffnecked of
them all—nay, he had half killed with his hammer one of the men the
Bishop sent to stop the work.

It was a long time now since any one had spoken so much with
Kristin at one time, so when Lady Groa said that now she might go,
the young girl bent and kissed the Abbess's hand, fervently and reverently;
and as she did so, tears came into her eyes. And Lady Groa, who saw
she was weeping, thought it was from sorrow—and so she said: maybe
she might, after all, let her go out one day to see Brother Edvin.

And a few days later she was told some of the convent folk had an
errand to the King's palace, and they could take her out along with
them to the Brothers in the fields.

Brother Edvin was at home. Kristin had not thought she could have
been so glad to see any one, except it had been Erlend. The old man sat
and stroked her hand while they talked together, in thanks for her coming. No, he had not been in her part of the country since the night he lay
at Jörundgaard, but he had heard she was to wed, and he wished her all
good fortune. Then Kristin begged that he would go over to the church
with her.

They had to go out of the monastery and round to the main door;
Brother Edvin durst not take her through the courtyard. He seemed
altogether exceeding downcast, and fearful of doing aught that might
offend. He had grown very old, thought Kristin.

And when she had laid upon the altar her offering for the officiant
monk who was in the church, and afterward asked Edvin if he would
confess her, he grew very frightened. He dared not, he said; he had been
strictly forbidden to hear confession.

"Ay, maybe you have heard of it," said he. "So it was that I felt I could not deny to those poor unfortunates the gifts which God had given me of His free grace. But, 'tis true, I should have enjoined on them to seek forgiveness in the right place—ay, ay. . . . . And you, Kristin, you are in duty bound to confess to your own prior."

"Nay, but this is a thing I cannot confess to the prior of the convent," said Kristin.

"Think you it can profit you aught to confess to me what you would hide from your true father confessor," said the monk more severely.

"If so be you cannot confess me," said Kristin, "at least you can let me speak with you and ask your counsel about what lies upon my soul."

The monk looked about him. The church was empty at the moment. Then he sate himself down on a chest which stood in a corner: "You must remember that I cannot absolve you, but I will counsel you, and keep silence as though you had told me in confession."

Kristin stood up before him, and said:

"It is this: I cannot be Simon Darre's wife."

"Therein you know well that I can counsel no otherwise than would your own prior," said Brother Edvin. "To undutiful children God gives no happiness, and your father has looked only to your welfare— that you know full well."

" I know not what your counsel will be, when you have heard me to the end," answered Kristin. "Thus stands it now with us: Simon is too good to gnaw the bare branch from which another man has broken the blossom."

She looked the monk straight in the face. But when she met his eyes and marked how the dry, wrinkled old face changed, grew full of sorrow and dismay—something seemed to snap within her, tears started to her eyes, and she would have cast herself upon her knees. But Edvin stopped her hurriedly:

"Nay, nay, sit here upon the chest by me—confess you I cannot." He drew aside and made room for her.

She went on weeping; he stroked her hand, and said gently:

"Mind you that morning, Kristin, I first saw you there on the stairway in the Hamar church . . .? I heard a tale once, when I was in foreign lands, of a monk who could not believe that God loved all us wretched sinners. . . . Then came an angel and touched his eyes, and he beheld a stone in the bottom of the sea, and under the stone there lived a blind, white, naked creature; and he gazed at it until he came to love it, for it was so frail and weak. When I saw you sitting there, so little and so frail, within the great stone house, methought it was but reason that God should love such as you. Fair and pure you were, and yet did you need a helper and a protector. Methought I saw the whole church, with you in it, lying in the hollow of God's hand."

Kristin said low:

"We have bound ourselves one to the other with the dearest oaths—and I have heard that, in the eyes of God, such a pact hallows our coming together as much as if our fathers and mothers had given us one to the other."

The monk answered sadly:

" I see well, Kristin, some one who knew it not to the full has spoken to you of the canonical law. You could not bind yourself by oath to this man without sinning against your father and mother: them had God set over you before you met him. And is it not a sorrow and a shame for his kin, too, if they learn that he has lured astray the daughter of a man who has borne his shield with honour at all seasons—betrothed, too, to another? I hear by your words, you deem you have not sinned so greatly—yet dare you not confess this thing to your appointed priest. And if so be you think you are as good as wed to this man, wherefore set you not on your head the linen coif of wedlock, but go still with flowing hair amidst the young maids with whom you can have no great fellowship any more—for now must the chief of your thoughts be with other things than they have in mind?"

" I know not what they have in their minds," said Kristin wearily. "True it is that all my thoughts are with the man I long for. Were it not for my father and mother, I would gladly bind up my hair this day—little would I care if I were called wanton, if only I might be called his."

" Know you if this man means so to deal toward you, that you may be called his with honour some day?" asked Brother Edvin.

Then Kristin told of all that had passed between Erlend Nickulaussön and herself. And while she spoke, she seemed not even to call to mind that she had ever doubted the outcome of it all.

" See you not, Brother Edvin," she began again, "we could not help ourselves. God help me, if I were to meet him without here, when I go from you, and should he pray me to go with him, I would go. I wot well, too, I have seen now there be other folk who have sinned as well as we. . . . When I was a girl at home 'twas past my understanding how aught could win such power over the souls of men that they could forget the fear of sin; but so much have I learnt now: if the wrongs men do through lust and anger cannot be atoned for, then must heaven be an empty place. They tell of you, even, that you, too, once struck a man in wrath——"

"'Tis true," said the monk. "God's mercy alone have I to thank that I am not called manslayer. 'Tis many years agone—I was a young man then, and methought I could not endure the wrong the Bishop would have put upon us poor friars. King Haakon—he was Duke then—had given us the ground for our house, but we were so poor we had to work upon our church ourselves—with some few workmen who gave their help more for heavenly reward than for what we could pay them. Maybe 'twas sinful pride in us beggar-monks to wish to build our church so fair and goodly—but we were happy as children in the fields, and sang songs of praise while we hewed and built and toiled. Brother Ranulv—God rest his soul—was master-builder—he was a right skilful stonecutter; nay, I trow the man had been granted skill in all knowledge and all arts by God Himself. I was a carver of stone panels in those days; I had but just finished one of St. Clara, whom the angels were bearing to the church of St. Francis in the dawn of Christmas Day—a most fair panel it had proved, and all of us joyed in it greatly—then the hellish miscreants tore down the walls, and a stone fell and crushed my panels—I struck at a man with my hammer, I could not contain me. . . .

"Ay, now you smile, my Kristin. But see you not that 'tis not well with you now, since you would rather hear such tales of other folks' frailties than of the life and deeds of good men, who might serve you as a pattern . . .?

"'Tis no easy matter to give you counsel," he said, when it was time for her to go. "For were you to do what were most right, you would bring sorrow to your father and mother and shame to all your kin. But you must see to it that you free yourself from the troth you plighted to Simon Andressön—and then must you wait in patience for the lot God may send you, make in your heart what amends you can—and let not this Erlend tempt you to sin again, but pray him lovingly to seek atonement with your kin and with God.

"From your sin I cannot free you," said Brother Edvin, as they parted, "but pray for you I will with all my might . . ."

He laid his thin, old hands upon her head and prayed, in farewell, that God might bless her and give her peace.

VI

AFTERWARD, there was much in what Brother Edvin had said to her that Kristin could not call to mind. But she left him with a mind strangely clear and peaceful.

Hitherto she had striven with a dull, secret fear and tried to brave it out; telling herself she had not sinned so deeply. Now she felt Edvin had shown her plainly and clearly that she had sinned indeed; such and such was her sin, and she must take it upon her and try to bear it meekly and well. She strove to think of Erlend without impatience—either because he did not send word of himself, or because she must want his caresses. She would only be faithful and full of love for him.

She thought of her father and mother, and vowed to herself that she would requite them for all their love, once they had got over the sorrow she must bring upon them by breaking with the Dyfrin folk. And well-nigh most of all, she thought of Brother Edvin's words of how she must not seek comfort in looking on others' faults; she felt she grew humble and kind, and now she saw at once how easy it was for her to win folks' friendship. Then was she comforted by the thought that after all 'twas not so hard to come to a good understanding with people—and so it seemed to her it surely could not be so hard for her and Erlend either.

Until the day she gave her word to Erlend, she had always striven earnestly to do what was right and good—but she had done all at the bidding of others. Now she felt she had grown from maid to woman. 'Twas not only by reason of the fervent secret caresses she had taken and given, not only that she had passed from her father's ward and was now under Erlend's will. For Edvin had laid upon her the burden of answering for her own life, ay, and for Erlend's too. And she was willing to bear it well and bravely. Thus she went about among the nuns at Yuletide; and throughout the goodly rites and the joy and peace of the holy time, though she felt herself unworthy, yet she took comfort in thinking that the time would soon come when she could set herself right again.

But the second day of the new year, Sir Andres Darre with his wife and all five children came, all unlooked for, to the convent. They were come to keep the last days of Yule-tide with their friends and kindred in the town, and they asked that Kristin might have leave to be with them in their lodging for a short space.

"For methought, my daughter," said Lady Angerd, "you would scarce be loth to see a few new faces for a time."

The Dyfrin folk dwelt in a goodly house that stood in a dwelling-place* near the Bishop's palace—Sir Andres' cousin owned it. There was a great hall where the serving-folk slept, and a fine loft-room with a fireplace of masonry and three good beds; in the one Sir Andres and Lady Angerd slept with their youngest son, Gudmund, who was yet a child; in another slept Kristin and their two daughters, Astrid and Sigrid, and in the third Simon and his eldest brother Gyrd Andressön.

All Sir Andres' children were comely; Simon the least so, yet he too was reckoned to be well-favoured. And Kristin marked still more than when she was at Dyfrin the year before, that both his father and mother and his four brothers and sisters hearkened most to Simon, and did all

* Town dwelling-places, see Note 15.

he would have them. They all loved each other dearly, but all agreed, without grudging or envy, in setting Simon foremost amongst them.

Here these good folk lived a merry, care-free life. They visited the churches and made their offerings every day, came together with their friends and drank in their company each evening, while the young folk had full leave to play and dance. All showed Kristin the greatest kindness, and none seemed to mark how little glad she was.

Of an evening, when the light had been put out in the loft-room, and all had sought their beds, Simon was wont to get up and go to where the maidens lay. He would sit a while on the edge of the bed; his talk was mostly to his sisters, but in the dark he would let his hand rest on Kristin's bosom—while she lay there hot with wrath.

Now that her sense of such things was keener, she understood well that there were many things Simon was both too proud and too shy to say to her, since he saw she had no mind to such talk from him. And she felt strangely bitter and angry with him, for it seemed to her as though he would fain be a better man than he who had made her his own—even though Simon knew not there was such a one.

But one night, when they had been dancing at another house, Astrid and Sigrid were left behind there to sleep with a playmate. When, late at night, the Dyfrin folk had gone to rest in their loft-room, Simon came to Kristin's bed and climbed up into it; he laid himself down above the fur cover.

Kristin pulled the coverlid up to her chin and crossed her arms firmly upon her breast. In a little Simon tried to put his hand upon her bosom. She felt the silken broidery on his wristband, and knew he had not taken off any of his clothes.

"You are just as bashful in the dark as in the light, Kristin," said Simon, laughing a little. "Surely you can at least let me have one hand to hold," he said, and Kristin gave him the tips of her fingers.

"Think you not we should have somewhat to talk of, when it so falls out that we can be alone a little while," said he; and Kristin thought, now was the time for her to speak. So she answered "Yes." But after that she could not utter a word.

"May I come under the fur?" be begged again. "'Tis cold in the room now——" And he slipped in between the fur coverlid and the woollen blanket she had next her. He bent one arm round the bed head, but so that he did not touch her. Thus they lay awhile.

"You are not over-easy to woo, i' faith," said Simon soon after, with a resigned laugh. "Now I pledge you my word, I will not so much as kiss you, if you would not I should. But surely you can speak to me at least?"

Kristin wet her lips with the tip of her tongue, but still she was silent.

"Nay, if you are not lying there trembling!" went on Simon. "Surely it cannot be that you have aught against me, Kristin?"

She felt she could not lie to Simon, so she said "No,"—but nothing more.

Simon lay a while longer; he tried to get her into talk with him. But at last he laughed again, and said:

"I see well you think I should be content with hearing that you have naught against me—for to-night—and be glad to boot. 'Tis a parlous thing, so proud as you are—yet one kiss must you give me; then will I go my way and not plague you any more——"

He took the kiss, then sat up and put his feet to the floor. Kristin thought, now must she say to him what she had to say—but he was away already by his own bed, and she heard him undress.

The day after Lady Angerd was not so friendly to Kristin as was her wont. The girl saw that the lady must have heard somewhat the night before, and that she deemed her son's betrothed had not borne her toward him as she held was fitting.

Late that afternoon Simon spoke of a friend's horse he was minded to take in barter for one of his own. He asked Kristin if she would go with him to look at it. She was nothing loth; and they went out into the town together.

The weather was fresh and fair. It had snowed a little over-night, but now the sun was shining, and it was freezing so that the snow crackled under their feet. Kristin felt 'twas good to be out and walk in the cold air, and when Simon brought out the horse to show her, she talked of it with him gaily enough; she knew something of horses, she had been so much with her father. And this was a comely beast—a mouse-grey stallion with a black stripe down the back and a clipped mane, well-shapen and lively, but something small and slightly built.

"He would scarce hold out under a full-armed man for long," said Kristin.

"Indeed, no; nor did I mean him for such a rider," said Simon.

He led the horse out into the home-field behind the house, made it trot and walk, mounted to try its paces, and would have Kristin ride it too. Thus they stayed together a good while out on the snowy field.

At last, as Kristin stood giving the horse bread out of her hand, while Simon leant with his arm over its back, he said all at once:

"Methinks, Kristin, you and my mother are none too loving one with another."

"I have not meant to be unloving to your mother," said she, "but I find not much to say to Lady Angerd."

"Nor seems it you find much to say to me either," said Simon. "I would not force myself upon you, Kristin, before the time comes—but things cannot go on as now, when I can never come to speech with you."

"I have never been one for much speaking," said Kristin. "I know it myself; and I look not you should think it so great a loss, if what is betwixt us two should come to naught."

"You know well what my thoughts are in that matter," said Simon, looking at her.

Kristin flushed red as blood. And it gave her a pang that she could not mislike the fashion of Simon Darre's wooing. After a while he said:

"Is it Arne Gyrdsön, Kristin, you feel you cannot forget?" Kristin but gazed at him; Simon went on, and his voice was gentle and kind: "Never would I blame you for that—you had grown up like brother and sister, and scarce a year is gone by. But be well assured, for your comfort, that I have your good at heart——"

Kristin's face had grown deathly white. Neither of them spoke again as they went back through the town in the twilight. At the end of the street, in the blue-green sky, rode the new moon's sickle with a bright star within its horn.

A year, thought Kristin; and she could not think when she had last given a thought to Arne. She grew afraid—maybe she was a wanton, wicked woman—but one year since she had seen him on his bier in the wake-room, and had thought she should never be glad again in this life —she moaned within herself for terror of her own heart's inconstancy, and of the fleeting changefulness of all things. Erlend! Erlend!—could he forget her—and yet it seemed to her 'twould be worse, if at any time she should forget him.

Sir Andres went with his children to the great Yule-tide feast at the King's palace. Kristin saw all the pomp and show of the festival—they came, too, into the hall where sat King Haakon and the Lady Isabel Bruce, King Eirik's widow. Sir Andres went forward and did homage to the King, while his children and Kristin stood somewhat behind. She thought of all Lady Aashild had told her; she called to mind that the King was near of kin to Erlend, their fathers' mothers were sisters—and she was Erlend's light-o'-love, she had no right to stand here, least of all amid these good and worthy folk, Sir Andres' children.

Then all at once she saw Erlend Nikulaussön—he had stepped forward in front of Queen Isabel, and stood with bowed head, and with his hand upon his breast, while she spoke a few words to him; he had on the brown silk clothes that he had worn at the guild feast. Kristin stepped behind Sir Andres' daughters.

When, some time after, Lady Angerd led her daughters up before the Queen, Kristin could not see him anywhere, but indeed she dared not lift her eyes from the floor. She wondered whether he was standing somewhere in the hall, she thought she could feel his eyes upon her— but she thought, too, that all folks looked at her as though they must know she was a liar, standing there with the golden garland on her outspread hair.

He was not in the hall where the young folk were feasted, and where they danced when the tables had been taken away; this evening it was Simon with whom Kristin must dance.

Along one of the longer walls stood a fixed table, and thither the King's men bore ale and mead and wine the whole night long. Once when Simon drew her thither and drank to her, she saw Erlend standing near, behind Simon's back. He looked at her, and Kristin's hand shook when she took the beaker from Simon's hand and set it to her lips. Erlend whispered vehemently to the man who was with him—a tall, comely man, well on in years and somewhat stout, who shook his head impatiently and looked as he were vexed. Soon after Simon led her back to the dance.

She knew not how long this dancing lasted—the music seemed as though 'twould never end, and each moment was long and evil to her with longing and unrest. At last it was over, and Simon drew her to the drinking-board again.

A friend came forward to speak to him, and led him away a few steps, to a group of young men. And Erlend stood before her.

"I have so much I would fain say to you," he whispered. "I know not what to say first—in Jesus' name, Kristin, what ails you?" he asked quickly, for he saw her face grow white as chalk.

She could not see him clearly; it seemed as though there were running water between their two faces. He took a goblet from the table, drank from it and handed it to her.   Kristin felt as though 'twas all too heavy for her, or as though her arm had been cut off at the shoulder; do as she would, she could not lift the cup to her mouth.

"Is it so, then, that you will drink with your betrothed, but not with me?" asked Erlend softly; but Kristin dropped the goblet from her hand and sank forward into his arms.

When she awoke she was lying on a bench with her head in a strange maiden's lap—some one was standing by her side, striking the palms of her hands, and she had water on her face.

She sat up. Somewhere in the ring about her she saw Erlend's face, white and drawn. Her own body felt weak, as though all her bones had melted away, and her head seemed as it were large and hollow; but somewhere within it shone one clear, desperate thought—she must speak with Erlend.

She said to Simon Darre—he stood near by:

"'Twas too hot for me, I trow—so many tapers are burning here—and I am little used to drink so much wine——"

"Are you well again now?" asked Simon. "You frightened folks. Mayhap you would have me take you home now?"

"We must wait, surely, till your father and mother go," said Kristin calmly. "But sit down here—I can dance no more." She touched the cushion at her side—then she held out her other hand to Erland:

"Sit you here, Erlend Nikulaussön; I had no time to speak my greetings to an end. 'Twas but of late Ingebjörg said she deemed you had clean forgotten her."

She saw it was far harder for him to keep calm than for her—and it was all she could do to keep back the little tender smile, which would gather round her lips.

"You must bear the maid my thanks for thinking of me still," he stammered. "Almost I was afraid she had forgotten me."

Kristin paused a little. She knew not what she should say, which might seem to come from the flighty Ingebjörg and yet might tell Erland her meaning. Then there welled up in her the bitterness of all these months of helpless waiting, and she said:

"Dear Erlend, can you think that we maidens could forget the man who defended our honour so gallantly——"

She saw his face change as though she had struck him—and at once she was sorry; then Simon asked what this was they spoke of. Kristin told him of Ingebjörg's and her adventure in the Eikaberg woods. She marked that Simon liked the tale but little. Then she begged him to go and ask of Lady Angerd, whether they should not soon go home; 'twas true that she was weary. When he was gone, she looked at Erland.

"'Tis strange," said he in a low voice, "you are so quick-witted—I had scarce believed it of you."

"Think you not I have had to learn to hide and be secret?" said she gloomily.

Erland's breath came heavily; he was still very pale.

"'Tis so then?" he whispered. "Yet did you promise me to turn to my friends if this should come to pass. God knows, I have thought of you each day, in dread that the worst might have befallen——"

"I know well what you mean by the worst," said Kristin shortly. "*That* you have no need to fear. To me what seemed the worst was that you would not send me one word of greeting—can you not understand that I am living there amongst the nuns—like a stranger bird——?" She stopped—for she felt that the tears were coming.

"Is it therefore you are with the Dyfrin folk now?" he asked. Then such grief came upon her that she could make no answer.

She saw Lady Angerd and Simon come through the doorway. Erlend's hand lay upon his knee, near her, and she could not take it.

"I must have speech with you," said he eagerly, "we have not said a word to one another we should have said——"

"Come to mass in the Maria Church at Epiphany," said Kristin quickly, as she rose and went to meet the others.

Lady Angerd showed herself most loving and careful of Kristin on the way home, and herself helped her to bed. With Simon she had no talk until the day after. Then he said:

"How comes it that you bear messages betwixt this Erlend and Ingebjörg Filippusdatter? 'Tis not fit you should meddle in the matter, if there be hidden dealings between them!"

"Most like there is naught in it," said Kristin. "She is but a chatterer."

"Methinks too," said Simon, "you should have taken warning by what's past, and not trusted yourself out in the wild-wood paths alone with that magpie." But Kristin reminded him hotly, that it was not their fault they had strayed and lost themselves. Simon said no more.

The next day the Dyfrin folks took her back to the convent, before they themselves left for home.

Erlend came to evensong in the convent church every evening for a week without Kristin getting a chance to change a word with him. She felt as she thought a hawk must feel sitting chained to its perch with its hood over its eyes. Every word that had passed between them at their last meeting made her unhappy too—it should never have been like that. It was of no use to say to herself: it had come upon them so suddenly, they had hardly known what they said.

But one afternoon in the twilight there came to the parlour a comely woman, who looked like a townsman's wife. She asked for Kristin Lavransdatter, and said she was the wife of a mercer and her husband had come from Denmark of late with some fine cloaks; Aasmund Björgulfsön had a mind to give one to his brother's daughter, and the maid was to go with her and choose for herself.

Kristin was given leave to go with the woman. She thought it was unlike her uncle to wish to give her a costly gift, and strange that he should send an unknown woman to fetch her. The woman was sparing of her words at first, and said little in answer to Kristin's questions, but when they were come down to the town, she said of a sudden:

"I will not play you false, fair child that you are—I will tell you all this thing as it is, and you must do as you deem best. 'Twas not your uncle who sent me, but a man—maybe you can guess his name, and if you cannot, then you shall not come with me. I have no husband—I make a living for myself and mine by keeping a house of call and selling beer; for such a one it boots not to be too much afraid either of sin or of the watchmen—but I will not lend my house for you to be betrayed inside my doors."

Kristin stood still, flushing red. She was strangely sore and ashamed for Erlend's sake. The woman said:

"I will go back with you to the convent, Kristin; but you must give me somewhat for my trouble—the knight promised me a great reward; but I, too, was fair once, and I, too, was betrayed. And 'twould not be amiss if you should name me in your prayers to-night—they call me Brynhild Fluga."

Kristin drew a ring off her finger and gave it to the woman:

"'Tis fairly done of you, Brynhild—but if the man be my kinsman Erlend Nikulaussön, then have I naught to fear; he would have me make peace betwixt him and my uncle. You may set your mind at ease; but I thank you none the less that you would have warned me."

Brynhild Fluga turned away to hide a smile.

She led Kristin by the alleys behind St. Clement's Church, northward towards the river. Here a few small dwelling-places stood by themselves along the river-bank. They went towards one of them, along a path between fences, and here Erlend came to meet them. He looked about him on all sides, then took off his cloak, wrapped it about Kristin, and pulled the hood over her face.

"What think you of this device?" he asked, quickly and low. "Think you 'tis a great wrong I do?—yet needs must I speak with you."

"It boots but little now, I trow, to think what is right and what is wrong," said Kristin.

"Speak not so," begged Erlend. "I bear the blame. . . . Kristin, every day and every night have I longed for you," he whispered close to her.

A shudder passed through her as she met his eyes for a moment. She felt it as guilt in her, when he looked so at her, that she had thought of anything but her love for him.

Brynhild Fluga had gone on before. Erlend asked, when they were come into the courtyard:

"Would you that we should go into the living-room, or shall we talk up in the loft-room?"

"As you will," answered Kristin; and they mounted to the loft-room.

The moment he had barred the door behind them she was in his arms. . . .

She knew not how long she had lain folded thus in his arms, when Erlend said:

"Now must we say what has to be said, my Kristin—I scarce dare let you stay here longer."

"I dare stay here all night long if you would have me stay," whispered she.

Erlend pressed his cheek to hers.

"Then were I not your friend.   'Tis bad enough as it is, but you shall not lose your good name for my sake."

Kristin did not answer—but a soreness stirred within her; how could he speak thus—he who had lured her here to Brynhild Fluga's house; she knew not why, but she felt it was no honest place. And he had looked that all should go as it had gone, of that she was sure.

" I have thought at times," said Erlend again, "that if there be no other way, I must bear you off by force—into Sweden. Lady Ingebjörg welcomed me kindly in the autumn and was mindful of our kinship. But now do I suffer for my sins—I have fled the land before, as you know—and I would not they should name you as the like of that other.'

"Take me home with you to Husaby," said Kristin low. "I cannot bear to be parted from you, and to live on among the maids at the convent. Both your kin and mine would surely hearken to reason, and let us come together and be reconciled with them——"

Erlend clasped her to him, and groaned:

"I cannot bring you to Husaby, Kristin."

"Why can you not?" she asked softly.

"Eline came thither in the autumn," said he after a moment. "I cannot move her to leave the place," he went on hotly, " not unless I bear her to the sledge by force and drive away with her. And that methought I could not do—she has brought both our children home with her."

Kristin felt herself sinking, sinking. In a voice breaking with fear, she said:

"I deemed you were parted from her."

"So deemed I, too," answered Erlend shortly. "But she must have heard in Österdal, where she was, that I had thoughts of marriage. You saw the man with me at the Yuletide feast—'twas my foster-father, Baard Petersön of Hestnæs. I went to him when I came from Sweden; I went to my kinsman, Heming Alvsön in Saltviken, too; I talked with both about my wish to wed, and begged their help. Eline must have come to hear of it. . . .

"I bade her ask what she would for herself and the children—but Sigurd, her husband—they look not that he should live the winter out—and then none could deny us if we would live together. . . .

"I lay in the stable with Haftor and Ulv, and Eline lay in the hall in my bed. I trow my men had a rare jest to laugh at behind my back."

Kristin could not say a word. A little after, Erlend spoke again:

"See you, the day we pledge each other at our espousals, she must understand that all is over between her and me—she has no power over me any more. . . .

"But 'tis hard for the children. I had not seen them for a year—they are fair children—and little can I do to give them a happy lot. 'Twould not have helped them greatly had I been able to wed their mother."

Tears began to roll down over Kristin's cheeks. Then Erlend said :

"Heard you what I said but now, that I had talked with my kinsfolk? Ay, they were glad enough that I was minded to wed. Then I said 'twas you I would have and none other."

"And they liked not that?" asked Kristin at length, forlornly.

"See you not," said Erlend gloomily, "they could say but one thing— they cannot and they will not ride with me to your father, until this bargain 'twixt you and Simon Andressön is undone again. It has made it none the easier for us, Kristin, that you have spent your Yuletide with the Dyfrin folk."

Kristin gave way altogether and wept noiselessly. She had felt ever that there was something of wrong and dishonour in her love, and now she knew the fault was hers.

She shook with the cold when she got up soon after, and Erlend wrapped her in both the cloaks. It was quite dark now without, and Erlend went with her as far as St. Clement's Church; then Brynhild brought her the rest of the way to Nonneseter

VII

A week later Brynhild Fluga came with word that the cloak was ready, and Kristin went with her and met Erlend in the loft-room as before.

When they parted, he gave her a cloak: "So that you may have something to show in the convent," said he. It was of blue velvet with red silk inwoven, and Erlend bade her mark that 'twas of the same hues as the dress she had worn that day in the woods. Kristin wondered it should make her so glad that he said this—she thought he had never given her greater happiness than when he said these words.

But now they could no longer make use of this way of meeting, and it was not easy to find a new one. But Erlend came often to vespers at the convent church, and sometimes Kristin would make herself an errand after the service, up to the commoners' houses; and then they would snatch a few words together by stealth up by the fences in the murk of the winter evening.

Then Kristin thought of asking leave of Sister Potentia to visit some old, crippled women, alms-folk of the convent, who dwelt in a cottage standing in one of the fields. Behind the cottage was an outhouse where the women kept a cow; Kristin offered to tend it for them; and while she was there Erlend would join her and she would let him in.

She wondered a little to mark that, glad as Erlend was to be with her, it seemed to rankle in his mind that she could devise such a plan.

"'Twas no good day for you when you came to know me," said he one evening. "Now have you learnt to follow the ways of deceit."

"*You* ought not to blame me," answered Kristin sadly.

"'Tis not you I blame," said Erlend quickly, with a shamed look.

"I had not thought myself," went on Kristin, "that 'twould come so easy to me to lie. But one *can* do what one *must* do."

"Nay, 'tis not so at all times," said Erlend as before. "Mind you not last winter, when you could not bring yourself to tell your betrothed that you would not have him?"

To this Kristin answered naught, but only stroked his face.

She never felt so strongly how dear Erlend was to her, as when he said things like this, that made her grieve or wonder. She was glad when she could take upon herself the blame for all that was shameful and wrong in their love. Had she found courage to speak to Simon as she should have done, they might have been a long way now on the road to have all put in order. Erlend had done all he could when he had spoken of their wedding to his kinsmen. She said this to herself, when the days in the convent grew long and evil—Erlend had wished to make all things right and good again. With little tender smiles she thought of him as he drew a picture of their wedding for her—she should ride to church in silks and velvet, she should be led to the bridal-bed with the high golden crown on her flowing hair—your lovely, lovely hair, he said, drawing her plaits through his hand.

"Yet can it not be the same to you as though I had never been yours," said Kristin musingly, once when he talked thus.

Then he clasped her to him wildly:

"Can I call to mind the first time I drank in Yuletide, think you, or the first time I saw the hills at home turn green when winter was gone? Ay, well do I mind the first time you were mine, and each time since—but to have you for my own is like keeping Yule and hunting birds on green hillsides for ever——"

Happily she nestled to him. Not that she ever thought for a moment it would turn out as Erlend was so sure it would—Kristin felt that before long a day of judgment must come upon them. It could not be that things should go well for them in the end. . . . But she was not so much afraid—she was much more afraid Erlend might have to go northward before it all came to light, and she be left behind, parted from him. He was over at the castle at Akersnes now; Munan Baardsön was posted there while the bodyguard was at Tunsberg, where the King lay grievously sick. But sometime Erlend must go home and see to his possessions. That she was afraid of his going home to Husaby because Eline sat there waiting for him, she would not own even to herself; and neither would she own that she was less afraid to be taken in sin along with Erlend, than of standing forth alone and telling Simon and her father what was in her heart.

Almost she could have wished for punishment to come upon her, and that soon. For now she had no other thought than of Erlend; she longed for him in the day and dreamed of him at night; she could not feel remorse, but she took comfort in thinking the day would come when she would have to pay dear for all they had snatched by stealth. And in the short evening hours she could be with Erlend in the alms-women's cowshed, she threw herself into his arms with as much passion as if she knew she had paid with her soul already that she might be his.

But time went on, and it seemed as though Erlend might have the good fortune he had counted on. Kristin never marked that any in the convent mistrusted her. Ingebjörg, indeed, had found out that she met Erlend, but Kristin saw the other never dreamed 'twas aught else than a little passing sport. That a maid of good kindred, promised in marriage, should dare wish to break the bargain her kinsfolk had made, such a thought would never come to Ingebjörg, Kristin saw. And once more a pang of terror shot through her—it might be 'twas a quite unheard-of thing, this she had taken in hand. And at this thought she wished again that discovery might come, and all be at an end.

Easter came. Kristin knew not how the winter had gone; every day she had not seen Erlend had been long as an evil year, and the long evil days had linked themselves together into weeks without end; but now it was spring and Easter was come, she felt 'twas no time since the Yuletide feast. She begged Erlend not to seek her till the Holy Week was gone by; and he yielded to her in this, as he did to all her wishes, thought Kristin. It was as much her own blame as his that they had sinned together in not keeping the Lenten fast. But Easter she was resolved they should keep. Yet it was misery not to see him. Maybe he would have to go soon; he had said naught of it, but she knew that now the King lay dying, and mayhap this might bring some turn in Erlend's fortunes, she thought.

Thus things stood with her, when one of the first days after Easter word was brought her to go down to the parlour to her betrothed.

As soon as he came toward her and held out his hand, she felt there was somewhat amiss—his face was not as it was wont to be; his small, grey eyes did not laugh, they did not smile when he smiled. And Kristin could not help seeing it became him well to be a little less merry. He looked well, too, in a kind of travelling dress—a long blue, close-fitting outer-garment men called *kothardi*, and a brown shoulder-cape with a hood, which was thrown back now; the cold air had given his light-brown hair a yet stronger curl.

They sat and talked for a while. Simon had been at Formo through Lent, and had gone over to Jörundgaard almost daily. They were well there; Ulvhild as well as they dared look that she should be; Ramborg was at home now, she was a fair child and lively.

"'Twill be over one of these days—the year you were to be here at Nonneseter," said Simon. "By this the folks at your home will have begun to make ready for our betrothal-feast—yours and mine."

Kristin said naught, and Simon went on:

"I said to Lavrans, I would ride hither to Oslo and speak to you of this."

Kristin looked down and said low:

"I, too, would fain speak with you of that matter, Simon—alone."

"I saw well myself that we must speak of it alone," answered Simon; "and I was about to ask even now that you would pray Lady Groa to let us go together into the garden for a little."

Kristin rose quickly and slipped from the room without a sound. Soon after she came back followed by one of the nuns with a key.

There was a door leading from the parlour out into an herb-garden that lay behind the most westerly of the convent buildings. The nun unlocked the door and they stepped out into a mist so thick they could see but a few paces in among the trees. The nearest stems were coal-black; the moisture stood in beads on every twig and bough. A little fresh snow lay melting upon the wet mould, but under the bushes some white and yellow lily plants were blooming already, and a fresh, cool smell rose from the violet leaves.

Simon led her to the nearest bench. He sat a little bent forward, with his elbows resting upon his knees. Then he looked up at her with a strange little smile:

"Almost I think I know what you would say to me," said he. "There is another man, who is more to you than I——"

"It is so," answered Kristin faintly.

"Methinks I know his name, too," said Simon, in a harder tone. "It is Erlend Nikulaussön of Husaby?"

After a while Kristin asked in a low voice:

"It has come to your ears, then?"

Simon was a little slow in answering:

"You can scarce think I could be so dull as not to see somewhat when we were together at Yule? I could say naught then, for my father and mother were with us. But this it is that has brought me hither alone this time. I know not whether it be wise of me to touch upon it—but methought we must talk of these things before we are given to one another.

". . . . But so it is now, that when I came hither yesterday—I met my kinsman, Master Öistein. And he spoke of you. He said you two had passed across the churchyard of St. Clement's one evening, and with you was a woman they call Brynhild Fluga. I swore a great oath that he must have seen amiss! And if you say it is untrue, I shall believe your word."

"The priest saw aright," answered Kristin defiantly. "You forswore yourself, Simon."

He sat still a little ere he asked:

"Know you who this Brynhild Fluga is, Kristin?" As she shook her head, he said: "Munan Baardsön set her up in a house here in the town, when he wedded—she carries on unlawful dealings in wine—and other things——"

"You know her?" asked Kristin mockingly.

"I was never meant to be a monk or a priest," said Simon, reddening. "But I can say at least that I have wronged no maid and no man's wedded wife. See you not yourself that 'tis no honourable man's deed to bring you out to go about at night in such company——?"

"Erlend did not draw me on," said Kristin, red with anger, "nor has he promised me aught. I set my heart on him without his doing aught to tempt me—from the first time I saw him, he was dearer to me than all other men."

Simon sat playing with his dagger, throwing it from one hand to the other.

"These are strange words to hear from a man's betrothed maiden," said he. "Things promise well for us two now, Kristin."

Kristin drew a deep breath:

"You would be ill served should you take me for your wife now, Simon."

"Ay, God Almighty knows that so it seems indeed," said Simon Andressön.

"Then I dare hope," said Kristin meekly and timidly, "that you will uphold me, so that Sir Andres and my father may let this bargain about us be undone."

"Do you so?" said Simon. He was silent for a little. "God knows whether you rightly understand what you say."

"That do I," said Kristin. "I know the law is such that none may

force a maid to marriage against her will; else can she take her plea
before the Thing——"

"I trow 'tis before the Bishop," said Simon, with something of a grim
smile. "True it is, I have had no cause to search out how the law
stands in such things. And I wot well you believe not either that 'twill
come to that pass. You know well enough that I will not hold you to
your word, if your heart is too much set against it. But can you not
understand—'tis two years now since our marriage was agreed, and
you have said no word against it till now, when all is ready for the
betrothal and the wedding. Have you thought what it will mean, if
you come forth now and seek to break the bond, Kristin?"

"But you want not me either," said Kristin.

"Ay, but I do," answered Simon curtly. "If you think otherwise,
you must even think better of it——"

"Erlend Nikulaussön and I have vowed to each other by our Christian faith," said she, trembling, "that if we cannot come together in
wedlock, then neither of us will have wife or husband all our days——"

Simon was silent a good while. Then he said with effort:

"Then I know not, Kristin, what you meant when you said Erlend
had neither drawn you on nor promised you aught—he has lured you
to set yourself against the counsel of all your kin. Have you thought
what kind of husband you will get, if you wed a man who took another's
wife to be his paramour—and now would take for wife another man's
betrothed maiden——?"

Kristin gulped down her tears; she whispered thickly:

"This you say but to hurt me."

"Think you I would wish to hurt you?" asked Simon, in a low voice.

"'Tis not as it would have been, had you . . ." said Kristin falteringly. "You were not asked either, Simon—'twas your father and my
father who made the pact. It had been otherwise had you chosen me
yourself——"

Simon struck his dagger into the bench so that it stood upright. A
little after he drew it out again, and tried to slip it back into its sheath,
but it would not go down, the point was bent. Then he sat passing it
from hand to hand as before.

"You know yourself," said he, in a low tone and with a shaking
voice, "you know that you lie, if you would have it that I did not——.
You know well enough what I would have spoken of with you—many
times—when you met me so that I had not been a man, had I been
able to say it—after that—not if they had tried to drag it out of me
with red-hot pincers. . . .

"First I thought 'twas yonder dead lad. I thought I must leave you
in peace awhile—you knew me not—I deemed 'twould have been a

wrong to trouble you so soon after. Now I see you did not need so long a time to forget—now—now—now——"

"No," said Kristin quietly. "I know it, Simon. Now I cannot look that you should be my friend any longer."

"*Friend . . .!*" Simon gave a short, strange laugh. "Do you need my friendship now, then?"

Kristin grew red.

"You are a man," said she softly. "And old enough now—you can choose yourself whom you will wed."

Simon looked at her sharply. Then he laughed as before.

"I understand. You would have me say 'tis I who——. I am to take the blame for the breaking of our bond?

"If so be that your mind is fixed—if you have the will and the boldness to try to carry through your purpose—then I will do it," he said low. " At home, with all my own folks, and before all your kin—save one. To your father you must tell the truth, even as it is. If you would have it so, I will bear your message to him, and spare you, in giving it, in so far as I can—but Lavrans Björgulfsön shall know that never, with my will, would I go back from one word that I have spoken to him."

Kristin clutched the edge of the bench with both hands; this was harder for her to bear than all else that Simon Darre had said. Pale and fearful, she stole a glance at him.

Simon rose.

"Now must we go in," said he. "Methinks we are nigh frozen, both of us, and the sister is sitting waiting with the key. I will give you a week to think upon the matter—I have business in the town here. I shall come hither and speak with you when I am ready to go, but you will scarce care to see aught of me meanwhile."

VIII

KRISTIN said to herself: now that, at least, is over. But she felt broken with weariness and sick for Erlend's arms.

She lay awake most of the night, and she resolved to do what she had never dared think of before—send word to Erlend. It was not easy to find any one who could go such an errand for her. The lay-sisters never went out alone, nor did she know of any of them she thought would be willing; the men who did the farm-work were elder folk and but seldom came near the dwellings of the nuns, save to speak with the Abbess herself. There was only Olav. He was a half-grown lad who worked in the gardens; he had been Lady Groa's foster-son from the time when he was found, a new-born babe, upon the church steps one morning. Folk said one of the lay-sisters was his mother; she was to have been a nun; but after she had been kept in the dark cell for six months—for grave disobedience, as 'twas said—and it was about that time the child was found—she had been given the lay-sisters' habit and had worked in the farmyard ever since. Kristin had often thought of Sister Ingrid's fate throughout these months, but she had had few chances to speak with her. It was venturesome to trust to Olav—he was but a child, and Lady Groa and all the nuns were wont to chat and jest with him, when they saw the boy. But Kristin deemed it mattered little what risks she took now. And a day or two later, when Olav was for the town one morning, Kristin sent word by him to Akersnes, that Erlend must find some way whereby they might meet alone.

That same afternoon Erlend's own man, Ulv, came to the grille. He said he was Aasmund Björgulfsön's man, and was to pray, on his master's behalf, that his brother's daughter might go down to the town for a little, for Aasmund had not time to come to Nonneseter. Kristin thought this device must surely fail—but when Sister Potentia asked if she knew the bearer of the message, she said, "Yes." So she went with Ulv to Brynhild Fluga's house.

Erlend awaited her in the loft-room—he was uneasy and anxious, and she knew at once, 'twas that he was afraid again of what he seemed to fear the most.

Always it cut her to the soul he should feel such a haunting dread that she might be with child—when yet they could not keep apart. Harassed as she was this evening, she said this to him—hotly enough. Erlend's face flushed darkly, and he laid his head down upon her shoulder.

"You are right," said he. "I must try to let you be, Kristin—not to put your happiness in such jeopardy. If you will——"

She threw her arms around him and laughed, but he caught her round the waist, forced her down upon a bench, and seated himself on the farther side of the board. When she stretched her hand over to him, he covered the palm with vehement kisses.

"I have tried more than you," said he with passion. "You know not how much I deem it means for both of us, that we should be wed with all honour."

"Then you should not have made me yours," said Kristin.

Erlend hid his face in his hands.

"Ay, would to God I had not done you that wrong," he said.

"Neither you nor I wish that," said Kristin, laughing boldly. "And if I may but be forgiven and make my peace at last with my kindred and with God, then shall I not sorrow overmuch though I must wear the woman's hood when I am wed. Ay, and often it seems to me. I could do without peace even, if only I may be with you."

"You shall bring honour with you into my house once more," said Erlend, "not I drag *you* down into dishonour."

Kristin shook her head. Then she said:

"'Tis like you will be glad then, when you hear that I have talked with Simon Andressön—and he will not hold me to the pact that was made for us by our fathers before I met you."

At once Erlend was wild with joy, and Kristin was made to tell him all. Yet she told not of the scornful words Simon had spoken of Erlend, though she said that before Lavrans he would not take the blame upon himself.

"'Tis but reason," said Erlend shortly. "They like each other well, your father and he? Ay, me he will like less, I trow—Lavrans."

Kristin took these words as a sign that Erlend felt with her she had still a hard road to travel ere yet they reached their journey's end; and she was thankful to him for it. But he did not come back to this matter; he was glad above measure, saying he had feared so that she would not have courage to speak with Simon.

"You like him after a fashion, I mark well," said he.

"Can it be aught to you," asked Kristin, " . . . after all that has come and gone between you and me, that I can see that Simon is an honest man and a stout?"

"Had you never met me," said Erlend, "you might well have had good days with him, Kristin. Why laugh you?"

"Oh, I did but call to mind somewhat Lady Aashild said once," answered Kristin. "I was but a child then—but 'twas somewhat about good days falling to wise folk, but the best days of all to those who dare be unwise."

"God bless my kinswoman, if she taught you that," said Erlend, and took her upon his knee. "'Tis strange, Kristin, never have I marked that you were afraid."

"Have you never marked it?" she asked, as she nestled close to him.

He seated her on the bedside and drew off her shoes, but then drew her back again to the table.

"Oh, my Kristin—now at last it looks as if bright days might come for us two. Methinks I had never dealt with you as I have done," he said, stroking and stroking her hair, "had it not been that each time I saw you, I thought ever 'twas not reason that they should give so fine and fair a wife to *me*. . . . Sit you down here and drink to me," he begged.

A moment after came a knock on the door—it sounded like the stroke of a sword hilt.

"Open, Erlend Nikulaussön, if you are within!"

"'Tis Simon Darre," said Kristin, in a low voice.

"Open, man, in the devil's name—if you be a man!" shouted Simon, and beat on the door again.

Erlend went to the bed and took his sword down from the peg in the wall. He looked round, at a loss what to do: "There is nowhere here you can hide——"

"'Twould scarce make things better if I hid," said Kristin. She had risen to her feet; she spoke very quietly, but Erlend saw that she was trembling. "You must open," she said, in the same tone. Simon hammered on the door again.

Erlend went and drew the bolt. Simon stepped in; he had a drawn sword in his hand, but he thrust it back into its sheath at once.

For a while the three stood in silence. Kristin trembled; but yet, in this first moment, she felt a strange, sweet thrill—from deep within her something rose, scenting the combat between two men—she drew a deep breath; here was an end to these endless months of dumb waiting and longing and dread. She looked from one to the other, pale and with shining eyes—then the strain within her broke in a chill, unfathomable despair. There was more of cold scorn than of rage or jealousy in Simon Darre's eyes, and she saw that Erlend, behind his defiant bearing, burned with shame. It dawned upon her, how other men would think of him, who had let her come to him in such a place, and she saw 'twas as though he had had to suffer a blow in the face; she knew he burned to draw his sword and fall upon Simon.

"Why have you come hither, Simon?" she cried aloud in dread.

Both men turned towards her.

"To fetch you home," said Simon. "Here you cannot be——"

"'Tis not for you, any more, to lay commands on Kristin Lavransdatter," said Erlend fiercely, "she is mine now——"

"I doubt not she is," said Simon savagely, "and a fair bridal bower have you brought her to——" He stood a little, panting; then he mastered his voice and spoke quietly: "But so it is that I am her betrothed still—till her father can come for her. And for so long I mean to guard with edge and point so much of her honour as can be saved—in others' eyes——"

"What need of *you* to guard her; I can——" he flushed red as blood under Simon's eyes. Then, flying out: "Think you I will suffer threats from a boy like you," he cried, laying his hand on his sword-hilt.

Simon clapped both hands behind him.

"I am not such a coward as to be afraid you should deem me afraid," said he as before. "I will fight you, Erlend Nikulaussön, you may stake your soul upon that, if, within due time, you have not made suit for Kristin to her father——"

"That will I never do at your bidding, Simon Andressön," said Erlend angrily; the blood rushed into his face again.

"Nay—do you it to set right the wrong you have done so young a maid," answered Simon, unmoved, "'twill be better so for Kristin."

Kristin gave a loud cry, in pain at Erlend's pain. She stamped upon the floor:

"Go, then, Simon, go—what have you to do with our affairs?"

"I told you but now," said Simon. "You must bear with me till your father has loosed you and me from each other."

Kristin broke down utterly.

"Go, go, I will follow straightway. . . . Jesus! why do you torture me so, Simon? . . . you know you deem not yourself I am worthy that you should trouble about me——"

"'Tis not for your sake I do it," answered Simon. "Erlend—will you not tell her to go with me?"

Erlend's face quivered. He touched her on the shoulder:

"You must go, Kristin. Simon Darre and I will speak of this at another time——"

Kristin got up obediently, and fastened her cloak about her. Her shoes stood by the bedside. . . . She remembered them, but she could not put them on under Simon's eyes.

Outside, the fog had come down again. Kristin flew along, with head bent and hands clutched tight in the folds of her cloak. Her throat was bursting with tears—wildly she longed for some place where she could be alone, and sob and sob. The worst, the worst was still before her; but she had proved a new thing this evening, and she writhed under it—she had proved how it felt to see the man to whom she had given herself humbled.

Simon was at her elbow as she hurried through the lanes, over the common lands and across the open places, where the houses had vanished and there was naught but fog to be seen. Once when she stumbled over something, he caught her arm and kept her from falling.

"No need to run so fast," said he. "Folk are staring after us. . . . How you are trembling!" he said more gently. Kristin held her peace and walked on.

She slipped in the mud of the street, her feet were wet through and icy cold—the hose she had on were of leather, but they were thin; she felt they were giving way, and the mud was oozing through to her naked feet.

They came to the bridge over the convent beck, and went more slowly up the slopes on the other side.

"Kristin," said Simon of a sudden, "your father must never come to know of this."

"How knew you that I was—there?" asked Kristin.

"I came to speak with you," answered Simon shortly. "Then they told me of this man of your uncle's coming. I knew Aasmund was in Hadeland. You two are not over cunning at making up tales.—Heard you what I said but now?"

"Ay," said Kristin. "It was I who sent word to Erlend that we should meet at Fluga's house; I knew the woman——"

"Then shame upon you! But, oh, you could not know what she is—and he. . . . Do you hear," said Simon harshly, "if so be it *can* be hidden, you must hide from Lavrans what you have thrown away. And if you cannot hide it, then you must strive to spare him the worst of the shame."

"You are ever so marvellous careful for my father," said Kristin, trembling. She strove to speak defiantly, but her voice was ready to break with sobs.

Simon walked on a little. Then he stopped—she caught a glimpse of his face, as they stood there alone together in the midst of the fog. He had never looked like this before.

"I have seen it well, each time I was at your home," said he, "how little you understood, you his womenfolk, what a man Lavrans is. Knows not how to rule you, says yonder Trond Gjesling—and 'twere like he should trouble himself with such work—he who was born to rule over *men*. He was made for a leader, ay, and one whom men would have followed—gladly. These are no times for such men as he—my father knew him at Baagahus. . . . But, as things are, he has lived his life up there in the Dale, as he were little else but a farmer. . . . He was married off all too young—and your mother, with her heavy mood, was not the one to make it lighter for him to live that life. So it is that he has many friends—but think you there is *one* who is his fellow? His sons were taken from him—'twas you, his daughters, who were to build up his race after him—must he live now to see the day when one is without health and the other without honour——?"

Kristin pressed her hands tightly over her heart—she felt she must hold it in to make herself as hard as she had need to be.

"Why say you this?" she whispered after a time. "It cannot be that you would ever wish to wed me now——"

"That—would I—not," said Simon unsteadily. "God help me, Kristin—I think of you that evening in the loft-room at Finnsbrekken.—

But may the foul fiend fly away with me living the day I trust a maiden's eyes again!

". . . . Promise me, that you will not see Erlend before your father comes," said he, when they stood at the gate.

"That will I not promise," answered Kristin.

"Then *he* shall promise," said Simon.

"I will not see him," said Kristin quickly.

"The little dog I sent you once," said Simon before they parted, "him you can let your sisters have—they are grown so fond of him—if you mislike not too much to see him in the house.

". . . . I ride north to-morrow early," said he, and then he took her hand in farewell, while the sister who kept the door looked on.

Simon Darre walked downward towards the town. He flung out a clenched fist as he strode along, talked half aloud, and swòre out into the fog. He swore to himself that he grieved not over *her*. Kristin—'twas as though he had deemed a thing pure gold—and when he saw it close at hand, it was naught but brass and tin. White as a snowflake had she knelt and thrust her hand into the flame—that was last year; this year she was drinking wine with an outcast ribald in Fluga's loft-room. The devil, no! 'Twas for Lavrans Björgulfsön he grieved, sitting up there on Jörundgaard believing—full surely never had it come into Lavrans' mind that he could be so betrayed by his own. And now he himself was to bear the tidings, and help to lie to *that* man—it was for this that his heart burned with sorrow and wrath.

Kristin had not meant to keep her promise to Simon Darre, but, as it befell, she spoke but a few words with Erlend—one evening up on the road.

She stood and held his hand, strangely meek, while he spoke of what had befallen in Brynhild's loft-room at their last meeting. With Simon Andressön he would talk another time. "Had we fought there, 'twould have been all over the town," said Erlend hotly. "And that he too knew full well—this Simon."

Kristin saw how this thing had galled him. She, too, had thought of it unceasingly ever since—there was no hiding the truth, Erlend came out of this business with even less honour than she herself. And she felt that now indeed they were one flesh—that she must answer for all he did, even though she might mislike his deeds, and that she would feel it in her own flesh when so much as Erlend's skin was scratched.

Three weeks later Lavrans Björgulfsön came to Oslo to fetch his daughter.

Kristin was afraid, and she was sore of heart as she went to the par-

lour to meet her father. What first struck her, when she saw him standing there speaking to Sister Potentia, was that he did not look as she
remembered him. Maybe he was but little changed since they parted a
year ago—but she had seen him all her years at home as the young,
lusty, comely man she had been so proud to have for father when she
was little. Each winter, and each summer that passed over their heads
up there at home, had doubtless marked him with the marks of growing
age, as they had unfolded her into a full-grown young woman—but she
had not seen it. She had not seen that his hair was fading here and
there and had taken on a tinge of rusty red near the temples—as yellow
hair does when 'tis turning grey. His cheeks had shrunken and grown
longer so that the muscles ran in harder lines down to the mouth; his
youthful white and red had faded to one weather-beaten shade. His
back was not bowed—but yet his shoulder-blades had an unaccustomed
curve beneath his cloak. His step was light and firm, as he came
toward her with outstretched hand, but yet 'twas not the old brisk and
supple motion. Doubtless, all these things had been there last year,
only she had not seen them. Perhaps there had been added a little
touch—of sadness—which made her see them now. She burst into
weeping.

Lavrans put his arm about her shoulder and laid his hand against
her cheek.

"Come, come, be still now, child," he said gently.

"Are you angry with me, father?" she asked low.

"Surely you must know that I am," he answered—but he went on
stroking her cheek. "Yet so much, too, you sure must know, that you
have no need to be afraid of me," said he sadly. "Nay, now must you
be still, Kristin; are you not ashamed to bear you in such childish
wise." For she was weeping so that she had to seat herself upon the
bench. "We will not speak of these things here, where folk go out and
in," said he, and he sat himself down by her side and took her hand.
"Will you not ask after your mother then—and your sisters . . .?"

"What does my mother say of this?" asked his daughter.

"Oh, that you can have no need to ask—but we will not talk of it
now," he said again. "Else she is well——" and he set to telling this
and that of the happenings at home on the farm, till Kristin grew
quieter little by little.

But it seemed to her that the strain did but grow worse because her
father said naught of her breach of troth. He gave her money to deal
out among the poor of the convent and to make gifts to her fellow-
pupils. He himself gave rich gifts to the cloister and the Sisters; and
no one in Nonneseter knew aught else than that Kristin was now to
go home for her betrothal and her wedding. They both ate the last

meal at Lady Groa's board in the Abbess' room, and the Lady spoke of Kristin with high praise.

But all this came to an end at last. She had said her last farewell to the Sisters and her friends at the convent gate; Lavrans led her to her horse and lifted her into the saddle. 'Twas so strange to ride with her father and the men from Jörundgaard down to the bridge, along this road, down which she had stolen in the dark; wonderful, too, it seemed to ride through the streets of Oslo freely and in honour. She thought of their splendid wedding train, that Erlend had talked of so often— her heart grew heavy; 'twould have been easier had he carried her away with him. There was yet such a long time before her in which she must live one life in secret and another openly before folks. But then her eye fell on her father's grave, ageing face, and she tried to think that, after all, Erlend was right.

There were a few other travellers in the inn. At eventide they all supped together in a little hearth-room, where there were two beds only; Lavrans and Kristin were to sleep there, for they were the first in rank among the guests. Therefore, when the night drew on a little, the others bade them a friendly good-night as they broke up and went to seek their sleeping-places. Kristin thought how it was she who had stolen to Brynhild Fluga's loft-room to Erlend's arms—sick with sorrow and with fear that she might never more be his, she thought, no, there was no place for her any more amongst these others.

Her father was sitting on the farther bench looking at her.

"We are not to go to Skog this time?" asked Kristin, to break the silence.

"No," answered Lavrans. "I have had enough for some time with what your mother's brother made me listen to—because I would not constrain you," he added, as she looked up at him questioningly.

"And, truly, I would have made you keep your word," said he a little after, "had it not been that Simon said he would not have an unwilling wife."

"*I* have never given my word to Simon," said Kristin quickly. "You have ever said before, that you would never force me into wedlock——"

"'Twould not have been force if I had held you to a bargain that had been published long since and was known to all men," answered Lavrans. "These two winters past you two have borne the name of handfasted folk, and you have said naught against it, nor shown yourself unwilling, till now your wedding-day was fixed. If you would plead that the business was put off last year, so that you have not yet given Simon your troth, then that I call not upright dealing."

Kristin stood gazing down into the fire.

"I know not which will seem the worse," went on her father, "that it be said that you have cast off Simon, or that he has cast off you. Sir Andres sent me a word," Lavrans flushed red as he said it, "he was wroth with the lad, and bade me crave such amends as I should think fit. I had to say what was true—I know not if aught else had been better—that, should there be amends to make, 'twas rather for us to make them. We are shamed either way."

"I cannot think there is such great shame," said Kristin low. "Since Simon and I are of one mind."

"Of one mind?" repeated Lavrans. "He did not hide from me that he was unhappy, but he said, after you had spoken together, he deemed naught but misfortune could come of it if he held you to the pact. . . . But now must you tell me how this has come over you."

"Has Simon said naught?" asked Kristin.

"It seemed as though he thought," said her father, "that you have given your love to another man. Now must you tell me how this is, Kristin."

Kristin thought for a little.

"God knows," said she, in a low voice, "I see well, Simon might be good enough for me, and maybe too good. But 'tis true that I came to know another man; and then I knew I would never have one happy hour more in all my life were I to live it out with Simon—not if all the gold in England were his to give—I would rather have the other if he owned no more than a single cow."

"You look not that I should give you to a serving-man, I trow?" said her father.

"He is as well born as I, and better," answered Kristin. "I meant but this—he has enough both of lands and goods, but I would rather sleep with him on the bare straw than with another man in a silken bed——"

Her father was silent a while.

"'Tis one thing, Kristin, that I will not force you to take a man that likes you not—though God and St. Olav alone know what you can have against the man I had promised you to. But 'tis another thing whether the man you have set your heart upon is such as I can wed you to. You are young yet, and not over-wise—and to cast his eyes upon a maid who is promised to another—'tis not the wont of an upright man——"

"No man can rule himself in that matter," broke in Kristin.

"Ay, but he can. But so much you can understand, I trow: I will not do such offence to the Dyfrin folk as to betroth you to another the moment you have turned your back on Simon—and least of all to a man who might be more high in rank or richer.—You must say who this man is," he said after a little.

Kristin pressed her hands together and breathed deeply. Then she said very slowly:

"I cannot, father. Thus it stands, that should I not get this man, then you can take me back to the convent and never take me from it again. . . . I shall not live long there, I trow. But 'twould not be seemly that I should name his name, ere yet I know he bears as good a will toward me as I have to him. You—you must not force me to say who he is, before—before 'tis seen whether—whether he is minded to make suit for me through his kin."

Lavrans was a long time silent. He could not but be pleased that his daughter took the matter thus; he said at length:

"So be it, then. 'Tis but reason that you would fain keep back his name, if you know not more of his purposes."

"Now must you to bed, Kristin," he said a little after. He came and kissed her.

"You have wrought sorrow and pain to many by this waywardness of yours, my daughter—but this you know, that your good lies next my heart. . . . God help me, 'twould be so, I fear me, whatever you might do—He and His gentle Mother will surely help us, so that this may be turned to the best. . . . Go now, and see that you sleep well."

After he had lain down, Lavrans thought he heard a little sound of weeping from the bed by the other wall, where his daughter lay. But he made as though he slept. He had not the heart to say to her that he feared the old talk about her and Arne and Bentein would be brought up again now, but it weighed heavily upon him that 'twas but little he could do to save the child's good name from being besmirched behind his back. And the worst was that he must deem much of the mischief had been wrought by her own thoughtlessness.

Part Three

LAVRANS BJÖRGULFSÖN

K R I S T I N came home when the spring was at fairest. The Laagen rushed headlong round its bend, past the farmstead and the fields; through the tender leaves of the alder-thickets its current glittered and sparkled with flashes of silver. 'Twas as though the gleams of light had a voice of their own, and joined in the river's song, for when the evening twilight fell, the waters seemed to go by with a duller roar. But day and night the air above Jörundgaard was filled with the rushing sound, till Kristin thought she could feel the very timbers of the houses quivering like the sound-box of a cithern.

Small threads of water shone high up on the fell-sides, that stood wrapped in blue haze day after day. The heat brooded and quivered over the fields; the brown earth of the plough-lands was nigh hidden by the spears of corn; the meadows grew deep with grass, and shimmered like silk where the breaths of wind passed over. Groves and hill-sward smelt sweet; and as soon as the sun was down, there streamed out all around the strong, cool, sourish breath of sap and growing things—it was as though the earth gave out a long, lightened sigh. Kristin thought, trembling, of the moment when Erlend's arms released her. Each evening she lay down, sick with longing, and in the mornings she awoke, damp with sweat and tired out with her dreams.

'Twas more than she could understand how the folks at home could forbear to speak ever a word of the one thing that was in her thoughts. But week went by after week, and naught was said of Simon and her broken faith, and none asked what was in her heart. Her father lay much out in the woods, now he had the spring ploughing and sowing off his hands—he went to see to his tar-burners' work, and he took hawks and hounds with him, and was away many days together. When he was at home, he spoke to his daughter kindly as ever—but it was as though he had little to say to her, and never did he ask her to go with him when he rode out.

Kristin had dreaded to go home to her mother's chidings; but Ragn-frid said never a word—and this seemed even worse.

Every year when he feasted his friends at St. John's Mass, it was Lavrans Björgulfsön's wont to give out among the poor folks of the parish the meat and all sorts of food that had been saved in his house-hold in the last week of the Fast. Those who lived nighest to Jörund-gaard would come themselves to fetch away the alms; these poor folks were ever welcomed and feasted, and Lavrans and his guests, and all the house-servants, would gather round them; for some of them were old men who had by heart many sagas and lays. They sat in the hearth-room and whiled the time away with the ale-cup and friendly talk; and in the evening they danced in the courtyard.

This year the Eve of St. John was cloudy and cold; but none was sorry that it was so, for by now the farmers of the Dale had begun to fear a drought. No rain had fallen since St. Halvard's Wake, and there had been little snow in the mountains; not for thirteen years could folk remember to have seen the river so low at midsummer.

So Lavrans and his guests were of good cheer when they went down to greet the almsmen in the hearth-room. The poor folks sat round the board eating milk-porridge and washing it down with strong ale; and Kristin stood by the table, and waited on the old folk and the sick.

Lavrans greeted his poor guests, and asked if they were content with their fare. Then he went about the board to bid welcome to an old bedesman, who had been brought thither that day for his term at Jörundgaard. The man's name was Haakon; he had fought under King Haakon the Old, and had been with the King when he took the field for the last time in Scotland. He was the poorest of the poor now, and was all but blind; the farmers of the Dale had offered to set him up in a cottage of his own, but he chose rather to be handed on as bedesman from farm to farm, for everywhere folk welcomed him more like an honoured guest, since he had seen much of the world, and had laid up great store of knowledge.

Lavrans stood by with a hand on his brother's shoulder; for Aasmund Björgulfsön had come to Jörundgaard on a visit. He asked Haakon, too, how the food liked him.

"The ale is good, Lavrans Björgulfsön," said Haakon. "But methinks a jade has cooked our porridge for us to-day. 'While the cook cuddles, the porridge burns,' says the byword; and this porridge is singed."

"An ill thing indeed," said Lavrans, "that I should give you singed porridge. But I wot well the old byword doth not always say true, for 'tis my daughter, herself, who cooked the porridge for you." He laughed, and bade Kristin and Tordis make haste to bring in the trenchers of meat.

Kristin slipped quickly out and made across to the kitchen. Her heart was beating hard—she had caught a glimpse of Aasmund's face when Haakon was speaking.

That evening she saw her father and his brother walking and talking together in the courtyard, long and late. She was dizzy with fear; and it was no better with her the next day, when she marked that her father was silent and joyless. But he said no word.

Nor did he say aught after his brother was gone. But Kristin marked well that he spoke less with Haakon than was his wont, and, when their turn for harbouring the old warrior was over, Lavrans made no sign towards keeping him a while longer, but let him move on to the next farm.

For the rest, Lavrans Björgulfsön had reason enough this summer to be moody and downcast, for now all tokens showed that the year would be an exceeding bad one in all the country round; and the farmers were coming together time and again to take counsel how they should meet the coming winter. As the late summer drew on, it was plain to most, that they must slaughter great part of their cattle or drive them south for sale, and buy corn to feed their people through the winter. The year before had been no good corn year, so that the stocks of old corn were but scanty.

One morning in early autumn Ragnfrid went out with all her three daughters to see to some linen she had lying out on the bleachfield. Kristin praised much her mother's weaving. Then the mother stroked little Ramborg's hair, and said:

"We must save this for your bride-chest, little one."

"Then, mother," said Ulvhild, "shall I not have any bride-chest when I go to the nunnery?"

"You know well," said Ragnfrid, "your dowry will be nowise less than your sisters'. But 'twill not be such things as they need that you will need. And then you know full well, too, that you are to bide with your father and me as long as we live—if so be you will."

"And when you come to the nunnery," said Kristin unsteadily, "it may be, Ulvhild, that I shall have been a nun there for many years."

She looked across at her mother, but Ragnfrid held her peace.

"Had I been such an one that I could marry," said Ulvhild, "never would I have turned away from Simon—he was so kind, and he was so sorrowful when he said farewell to us all."

"You know your father bade us not speak of this," said Ragnfrid; but Kristin broke in defiantly:

"Ay; well I know that 'twas far more sorrow for him parting from you than from me."

Her mother spoke in anger:

"And little must his pride have been, I wot, had he shown his sorrow before you—you dealt not well and fairly by Simon Andressön, my daughter. Yet did he beg us to use neither threats nor curses with you——"

"Nay," said Kristin as before, "he thought, maybe, he had cursed me himself so much, there was no need for any other to tell me how vile I was. But I marked not ever that Simon had much care for me, till he saw that I loved another more than him."

"Go home, children," said Ragnfrid to the two little ones. She sat herself down on a log that lay by the green, and drew Kristin down beside her.

"You know, surely," said she then, "that it has ever been held seemly and honourable, that a man should not talk overmuch of love to his betrothed maiden—nor sit with her much alone, nor woo too hotly——"

"Oh!" said Kristin, "much I wonder whether young folk that love one another bear ever in mind what old folk count for seemly, and forget not one time or another all such things."

"Be you ware, Kristin," said her mother, "that you forget them not." She sat a little while in silence: "What I see but too well now is that your father goes in fear that you have set your heart on a man he can never gladly give you to."

"What did my uncle say?" asked Kristin in a little while.

"Naught said he," answered her mother, "but that Erlend of Husaby is better of name than of fame. Ay, for he spoke to Aasmund, it seems, to say a good word for him to Lavrans. Small joy was it to your father when he heard this."

But Kristin sat beaming with gladness. Erlend had spoken to her father's brother. And she had been vexing her heart because he made no sign!

Then her mother spoke again:

"Yet another thing is: that Aasmund said somewhat of a waif word that went about in Oslo, that folk had seen this Erlend hang about in the byways near by the convent, and that you had gone out and spoken with him by the fences there."

"What then?" asked Kristin.

"Aasmund counselled us, you understand, to take this proffer," said Ragnfrid. "But at that Lavrans grew more wroth than I can call to mind I saw him ever before. He said that a wooer who tried to come to his daughter by that road should find him in his path sword in hand. 'Twas little honour enough to us to have dealt as we had with the Dyfrin folk; but were it so that Erlend had lured you out to gad about the ways in the darkness with him, and that while you were dwelling in a cloister of holy nuns, 'twas a full good token you would be better served by far by missing such a husband."

Kristin crushed her hands together in her lap—the colour came and went in her face. Her mother put an arm about her waist—but the girl shrank away from her, beside herself with the passion of her mood, and cried:

"Let me be, mother! Would you feel, maybe, if my waist hath grown——"

The next moment she was standing up, holding her hand to her cheek—she looked down bewildered at her mother's flashing eyes. None had ever struck her before since she was a little child.

"Sit down," said Ragnfrid. "Sit down," she said again, and the girl was fain to obey. The mother sat awhile silent; when she spoke, her voice was shaking:

"I have seen it full well, Kristin—much have you never loved me. I told myself, maybe 'twas that you thought I loved not you so much—not as your father loves you. I bided my time—I thought when the time came that you had borne a child yourself, you would surely understand. . . . .

"While yet I was suckling you, even then was it so, that when Lavrans came near us two, you would let go my breast and stretch out towards him, and laugh so that my milk ran out over your lips. Lavrans thought 'twas good sport—and God knows I was well content for his sake. I was well content, too, for your sake, that your father laughed and was merry each time he laid eyes on you. I thought my own self 'twas pity of you, you little being, that I could not have done with all that much weeping. I was ever thinking more whether I was to lose you too, than joying that I had you. But God and His holy Mother know that I loved you no whit less than Lavrans loved."

The tears were running down over Ragnfrid's cheeks, but her face was quite calm now, and so too was her voice:

"God knows I never bore him or you a grudge for the love that was between you. Methought 'twas little enough joy I had brought him in the years we had lived together; I was glad that he had joy in you. I thought, too, that had my father, Ivar, been such a father to me . . .

"There are many things, Kristin, that a mother should have taught her daughter to beware of. But methought there was little need of this with you, who have followed about with your father all these years—you should know, if any know, what right and honour are. That word you spoke but now—think you I could believe you would have the heart to bring on Lavrans such a sorrow . . .?

"I would say but this to you—my wish is that you may win for husband a man you can love well. But that this may be, you must bear you wisely—let not Lavrans have cause to think that he you have chosen is a breeder of trouble, and one that regards not the peace of women, nor their honour. For to such an one he will never give you—not if it were to save you from open shame. Rather would Lavrans let the steel do judgment between him and the man who had marred your life. . . ."

And with this the mother rose and went from her.

11

A T the Haugathing held on the day of Bartholomew's Mass, the 24th
of August, the daughter's son of King Haakon of happy memory was
hailed as King. Among the men sent thither from Northern Gudbrandsdal was Lavrans Björgulfsön. He had had the name of kingsman
since his youth, but in all these years he had but seldom gone nigh the
Household, and the good name he had won in the war against Duke
Eirik he had never sought to turn to account. Nor had he now much
mind to this journey to the homaging, but he could not deny himself to
the call. Besides, he and the other Thing-men from the upper valley
were charged to try and buy corn in the south and send it round by
ship to Romsdal.

The folk of the parishes round about were heartless now, and went
in dread of the winter that was at hand. An ill thing, too, the farmers
deemed it that once again a child would be King in Norway. Old folks
called to mind the time when King Magnus was dead and his sons
were little children, and Sira Eirik said:

" *Væ terræ, ubi puer rex est.*   Which in the Norse tongue is: 'No resting
o' nights for rats in the house where the cat's a kitten.' "

Ragnfrid Ivarsdatter managed all things on the manor while her
husband was gone, and it was good both for Kristin and for her that
they had their heads and hands full of household cares and work. All
over the parish the folks were busy gathering in moss from the hills and
stripping bark from the trees, for the hay-crop had been but light, and
of straw there was next to none; and even the leaves gathered after St.
John's Eve were yellow and sapless. On Holy Cross Day, when Sira
Eirik bore the crucifix about the fields, there were many in the procession who wept and prayed aloud to God to have mercy on the
people and the dumb beasts.

A week after Holy Cross, Lavrans Björgulfsön came home from the
Thing.

It was long past the house-folks' bedtime, but Ragnfrid still sat in
the weaving-house. She had so much to see to in the daytime now,
that she often worked on late into the night at weaving and sewing.
Ragnfrid liked the house well, too. It had the name of being the
oldest on the farm; it was called the Mound-house, and folk said it
had stood there ever since the old heathen ages. Kristin and the girl
called Astrid were with Ragnfrid; they were sitting spinning by the
hearth.

They had been sitting for a while sleepy and silent, when they heard
the hoof-beats of a single horse—a man came riding at a gallop into

the wet farm-place. Astrid went to the outer room to look out—in a moment she came in again, followed by Lavrans Björgulfsön.

Both his wife and his daughter saw at once that he had been drinking more than a little. He reeled in his walk, and held to the pole of the smoke-vent while Ragnfrid took from him his dripping wet cloak and hat and unbuckled his sword-belt.

"What have you done with Halvdan and Kolbein?" she said, in some fear; "have you left them behind on the road?"

"No, I left them behind at Loptsgaard," he said, with a little laugh. "I had such a mind to come home again—there was no rest for me till I did—the men went to bed down at Loptsgaard, but I took Guldsveinen and galloped home. . . .

"You must find me a little food, Astrid," he said to the servant. "Bring it in here, girl; then you need not go so far in the rain. But be quick, for I have eaten no food since early morning——"

"Had you no food at Loptsgaard, then?" asked his wife in wonder.

Lavrans sat rocking from side to side on the bench, laughing a little.

"Food there was, be sure—but I had no stomach to it when I was there. I drank a while with Sigurd—but—methought then 'twas as well I should come home at once as wait till to-morrow——"

Astrid came back bearing food and ale; she brought with her, too, a pair of dry shoes for her master.

Lavrans fumbled with his spur-buckles to unloose them; but came near to falling on his face.

"Come hither, Kristin, my girl," he said, "and help your father. I know you will do it from a loving heart—ay, a loving heart—to-day."

Kristin kneeled down to obey. Then he took her head between his two hands and turned her face up:

"One thing I trow you know, my daughter—I wish for naught but your good. Never would I give you sorrow, except I see that thereby I save you from many sorrows to come. You are full young yet, Kristin—'twas but seventeen years old you were this year—three days after Halvard's Mass—but seventeen years old——"

Kristin had done with her service now. She was a little pale as she rose from her knees and sat down again on her stool by the hearth.

Lavrans' head seemed to grow somewhat clearer as he ate and was filled. He answered his wife's questions and the servant-maid's about the Haugathing. . . . Ay, 'twas a fair gathering. They had managed to buy corn, and some flour and malt, part at Oslo and part at Tunsberg; the wares were from abroad—they might have been better, but they might have been worse, too. Ay, he had met many, both kinsfolk and friends, and they had sent their greetings home with him. . . . But the answers dropped from him, one by one, as he sat there.

"I spoke with Sir Andres Gudmundsön," he said, when Astrid was gone out. "Simon marries the young widow at Manvik; he has held his betrothal feast. The wedding will be at Dyfrin at St. Andrew's Mass. He has chosen for himself this time, has the boy. I held aloof from Sir Andres at Tunsberg, but he sought me out—'twas to tell me he knew for sure that Simon saw Lady Halfrid for the first time this midsummer. He feared that I should think Simon had this rich marriage in mind when he broke with us." Lavrans paused a little and laughed joylessly. "You understand—that good and worthy man feared much that we should believe such a thing of his son."

Kristin breathed more freely. She thought it must be this that had troubled her father so sorely. Maybe he had been hoping all this time that it might come to pass after all, her marriage with Simon Andressön. At first she had been in dread lest he had heard some tidings of her doings in the south at Oslo.

She rose up and said good-night; but her father bade her stay yet a little.

"I have one more thing to tell," said Lavrans. "I might have held my peace about it before you—but 'tis better you should know it. This it is, Kristin—the man you have set your heart on, him must you strive to forget."

Kristin had been standing with arms hanging down and bent head. She looked up now into her father's face. She moved her lips, but no sound came forth that could be heard.

Lavrans looked away from his daughter's eyes; he struck out sideways with his hand:

"I wot well you know that never would I set myself against it, could I anyways believe 'twould be for your good."

"What are the tidings that have been told you on this journey, father?" said Kristin, in a clear voice.

"Erlend Nikulaussön and his kinsman, Sir Munan Baardsön, came to me at Tunsberg," answered Lavrans. "Sir Munan asked for you for Erlend, and I answered him: No."

Kristin stood awhile, breathing heavily.

"Why will you not give me to Erlend Nikulaussön?" she asked.

"I know not how much you know of the man you would have for husband," said Lavrans. "If you cannot guess the reason for yourself, 'twill be no pleasing thing for you to hear from my lips."

"Is it because he has been outlawed, and banned by the Church?" asked Kristin as before.

"Know you what was the cause that King Haakon banished his near kinsman from his Court—and how at last he fell under the Church's ban for defying the Archbishop's bidding—and that when he fled the land 'twas not alone?"

"Ay," said Kristin. Her voice grew unsteady: "I know, too, that he was but eighteen years old when he first knew her—his paramour."

"No older was I when I was wed," answered Lavrans. "We reckoned, when I was young, that at eighteen years a man was of age to answer for himself, and care for others' welfare and his own."

Kristin stood silent.

"You called her his paramour, the woman he has lived with for ten years, and who has borne him children," said Lavrans after awhile. "Little joy would be mine the day I sent my daughter from her home with a husband who had lived openly with a paramour year out, year in, before ever he was wed. But you know that 'twas not loose life only, 'twas life in adultery."

Kristin spoke low:

"You judged not so hardly of Lady Aashild and Sir Björn."

"Yet can I not say I would be fain we should wed into their kindred," answered Lavrans.

"Father," said Kristin, "have you been so free from sin all your life, that you can judge Erlend so hardly——?"

"God knows," said Lavrans sternly, "I judge no man to be a greater sinner before Him than I am myself. But 'tis no just reckoning that I should give away my daughter to any man that pleases to ask for her, only because we all need God's forgiveness."

"You know I meant it not so," said Kristin hotly. "Father—mother —you have been young yourselves—have you not your youth *so* much in mind that you know 'tis hard to keep oneself from the sin that comes of love——?"

Lavrans grew red as blood:

"No," he said curtly.

"Then you know not what you do," cried Kristin wildly, "if you part Erlend Nikulaussön and me."

Lavrans sate himself down again on the bench.

"You are but seventeen, Kristin," he began again. "It may be so that you and he—that you have come to be more dear to each other than I thought could be. But he is not so young a man but he should have known—had he been a good man, he had never come near a young, unripe child like you, with words of love. . . . That you were promised to another seemed to him, mayhap, but a small thing.

"But I wed not my daughter to a man who has two children by another's wedded wife. You know that he has children?

"You are too young to understand that such a wrong breeds enmity in a kindred—and hatred without end. The man cannot desert his own offspring, and he cannot do them right—hardly will he find a way to bring his son forth among good folk, or to get his daughter married with any but a serving-man or a cottar. They were not flesh and blood, those children, if they hated not you and your children with a deadly hate. . . .

"See you not, Kristin—such sins as these—it may be that God may forgive such sins more easily than many others—but they lay waste a kindred in such wise that it can never be made whole again. I thought of Björn and Lady Aashild too—there stood this Munan, her son; he was blazing with gold; he sits in the Council of the King's Counsellors; they hold their mother's heritage, he and his brothers; and he hath not come once to greet his mother in her poverty in all these years. Ay, and 'twas this man your lover had chosen to be his spokesman.

"No, I say—no! Into that kindred you shall never come, while my head is above the ground."

Kristin buried her face in her hands and broke into weeping:

"Then will I pray God night and day, night and day, that if you change not your will, He may take me away from this earth."

"It boots not to speak more of this to-night," said her father, with anguish in his voice. "You believe it not now, maybe; but I must needs guide your life so as I may hope to answer it hereafter. Go now, child, and rest."

He held out his hand toward her; but she would not see it, and went sobbing from the room.

The father and mother sat on a while. Then Lavrans said to his wife:

"Would you fetch me in a draught of ale?—no, bring in a little wine," he asked. "I am weary——"

Ragnfrid did as he asked. When she came back with the tall wine stoup, her husband was sitting with his face hidden in his hands. He looked up, and passed his hand over her headdress and her sleeves:

"Poor wife, now you are wet. . . . Come, drink to me, Ragnfrid."

She barely touched the cup with her lips.

"Nay, now drink with me," said Lavrans vehemently, and tried to draw her down on his knees. Unwillingly the woman did as he bade. Lavrans said: "You will stand by me in this thing, wife of mine, will you not? Surely 'twill be best for Kristin herself that she understand from the very outset she must drive this man from her thoughts."

"'Twill be hard for the child," said the mother.

"Ay; well do I see it will," said Lavrans.

They sat silent awhile, then Ragnfrid asked:

"How looks he, this Erlend of Husaby?"

"Oh," said Lavrans slowly, "a proper fellow enough—after a fashion. But he looks not a man that is fit for much but to beguile women."

They were silent again for awhile; then Lavrans said:

"The great heritage that came to him from Sir Nikulaus—with that I trow he has dealt so that it is much dwindled. 'Tis not for such a son-in-law that I have toiled and striven to make my children's lives sure."

The mother wandered restlessly up and down the room. Lavrans went on:

"Least of all did it like me that he sought to tempt Kolbein with silver—to bear a secret letter to Kristin."

"Looked you what was in the letter?" asked Ragnfrid.

"No, I did not choose," said Lavrans curtly. "I handed it back to Sir Munan, and told him what I thought of such doings. Erlend had hung his seal to it too—I know not what a man should say of such child's tricks. Sir Munan would have me see the device of the seal; that 'twas King Skule's privy seal, come to Erlend through his father. His thought was, I trow, that I might bethink me how great an honour they did me to sue for my daughter. But 'tis in my mind that Sir Munan had scarce pressed on this matter for Erlend so warmly, were it not that in this man's hands 'tis downhill with the might and honour of the Husaby kindred, that it won in Sir Nikulaus' and Sir Baard's days. . . . No longer can Erlend look to make such a match as befitted his birth."

Ragnfrid stopped before her husband:

"Now I know not, husband, if you are right in this matter. First must it be said that, as times are now, many men round about us on the great estates have had to be content with less of power and honour than their fathers had before them. And you, yourself, best know that 'tis less easy now for a man to win riches either from land or from merchantry than it was in the old world——"

"I know, I know," broke in Lavrans impatiently. "All the more does it behove a man to guide warily the goods that have come down to him——"

But his wife went on:

"And this, too, is to be said: I see not that Kristin can be an uneven match for Erlend. In Sweden your kin sit among the best, and your father, and his father before him, bore the name of knights in this land of Norway. My forefathers were Barons * of shires, son after father, many hundred years, down to Ivar the Old; my father and my father's father were Wardens.* True it is, neither you nor Trond have held

* Barons and Wardens, see Note 19.

titles or lands under the Crown. But, as for that, methinks it may be said that 'tis no otherwise with Erlend Nikulaussön than with you."

"'Tis not the same," said Lavrans hotly. "Power and the knightly name lay ready to Erlend's hand, and he turned his back on them to go a-whoring. But I see, now, you are against me, too. Maybe you think, like Aasmund and Trond, 'tis an honour for me that these great folks would have my daughter for one of their kinsmen——"

Ragnfrid spoke in some heat: "I have told you, I see not that you need be so over-nice as to fear that Erlend's kinsmen should think they stoop in these dealings. But see you not what all things betoken—a gentle and a biddable child to find courage to set herself up against us and turn away Simon Darre—have you not seen that Kristin is nowise herself since she came back from Oslo—see you not she goes around like one bewitched. . . . Will you not understand, she loves this man so sorely, that, if you yield not, a great misfortune may befall?"

"What mean you by that?" asked the father, looking up sharply.

"Many a man greets his son-in-law and knows not of it," said Ragnfrid.

The man seemed to stiffen where he sat; his face grew slowly white: "You that are her mother!" he said hoarsely. "Have you—have you seen—such sure tokens—that you dare charge your own daughter——"

"No, no," said Ragnfrid quickly. "I meant it not as you think. But when things are thus, who can tell what has befallen, or what may befall? I have seen her heart; not one thought hath she left but her love for this man—'twere no marvel if one day she showed us that he is dearer to her than her honour—or her life."

Lavrans sprang up:

"Oh, you are mad! Can you think such things of our fair, good child? No harm, surely, can have come to her where she was—with the holy nuns. I wot well she is no byre-wench to go clipping behind walls and fences. Think but of it: 'tis not possible she can have seen this man or talked with him so many times—be sure it will pass away; it cannot be aught but a young maid's fancy. God knows, 'tis a heavy sight enough for me to see her sorrow so; but be sure it must pass by in time.

"Life, you say, and honour. . . . At home here by my own hearth-stone 'twill go hard if I cannot guard my own maiden. Nor do I deem that any maid come of good people and bred up Christianly in shame-fastness will be so quick to throw away her honour—nor yet her life. Ay, such things are told of in songs and ballads, sure enough—but methinks 'tis so that when a man or a maid is tempted to do such a deed, they make up a song about it, and ease their hearts thereby—but the deed itself they forbear to do——.

"You yourself," he said, stopping before his wife: "there was another man you would fain have wed, in those days when we were brought together. How think you it would have gone with you, had your father let you have your will on that score?"

It was Ragnfrid now that was grown deadly pale:

"Jesus, Maria! Who hath told——"

"Sigurd of Loptsgaard said somewhat . . . 'twas when we were just come hither to the Dale," said Lavrans. "But answer me what I asked. . . . Think you your life had been gladder had Ivar given you to that man?"

His wife stood with head bowed low:

"That man," she said—he could scarce hear the words: "'twas *he* would not have *me*." A throb seemed to pass through her body—she struck out before her with her clenched hand.

The husband laid his hands softly on her shoulders:

"Is it *that*," he asked as if overcome, and a deep and sorrowful wonder sounded in his voice; ". . . is it *that*—through all these years—have you been sorrowing for *him*—Ragnfrid?"

She trembled much, but she said nothing.

"Ragnfrid?" he asked again. "Ay, but afterward—when Björgulf was dead—and afterward—when you—when you would have had me be to you as—as I could not be. Were you thinking then of that other?" He spoke low, in fear and bewilderment and pain.

"How can you have such thoughts?" she whispered, on the verge of weeping.

Lavrans pressed his forehead against hers and moved his head gently from side to side.

"I know not. You are so strange—and all you have said to-night. I was afraid, Ragnfrid. Like enough I understand not the hearts of women——"

Ragnfrid smiled palely and laid her arms about his neck.

"God knows, Lavrans—I was a beggar to you, because I loved you more than 'tis good that a human soul should love. . . . And I hated that other so that I felt the devil joyed in my hate."

"I have held you dear, my wife," said Lavrans, kissing her, "ay, with all my heart have I held you dear. You know that, surely? Methought always that we two were happy together—Ragnfrid?"

"You were the best husband to me," said she with a little sob, and clung close to him.

He pressed her to him strongly:

"To-night I would fain sleep with you, Ragnfrid. And if you

would be to me as you were in old days, I should not be—such a fool——"

The woman seemed to stiffen in his arms—she drew away a little: "'Tis Fast-time." She spoke low—in a strange, hard voice.

"It is so." He laughed a little. "You and I, Ragnfrid—we have kept all the fasts, and striven to do God's bidding in all things. And now almost I could think—maybe we had been happier had we more to repent——"

"Oh, speak not so—*you*," she begged wildly, pressing her thin hands to his temples. "You know well I would not you should do aught but what you feel yourself is the right."

He drew her to him closely once more—and groaned aloud: "God help her! God help us all, my Ragnfrid——"

Then: "I am weary," he said, and let her go. "And 'tis time, too, for you to go to rest."

He stood by the door waiting, while she quenched the embers on the hearth, blew out the little iron lamp by the loom, and pinched out the glowing wick. Together they went across through the rain to the hall.

Lavrans had set foot already on the loft-room stair, when he turned to his wife, who was still standing in the entry-door.

He crushed her in his arms again, for the last time, and kissed her in the dark. Then he made the sign of the cross over his wife's face, and went up the stair.

Ragnfrid flung off her clothes and crept into bed. Awhile she lay and listened to her husband's steps in the loft-room above; then she heard the bed creak, and all was still. Ragnfrid crossed her thin arms over her withered breasts.

Ay, God help her! What kind of woman was she, what kind of mother? She would soon be old now. Yet was she the same; though she no longer begged stormily for love, as when they were young and her passion had made this man shrink and grow cold when she would have had him be lover and not only husband. So had it been—and so, time after time, when she was with child, had she been humbled, beside herself with shame, that she had not been content with his lukewarm husband-love. And then, when things were so with her, and she needed goodness and tenderness—then he had so much to give; the man's tireless, gentle thought for her, when she was sick and tormented, had fallen on her soul like dew. Gladly did he take up all she laid on him and bear it—but there was ever something of his own he would not give. She had loved her children, so that each time she lost one, 'twas as though the heart was torn from her. God! God! what woman was she then, that even then, in the midst of her torments, she could feel it as a drop of sweetness that he took her sorrow into his heart and laid it close beside his own.

Kristin—gladly would she have passed through the fire for her daughter; they believed it not, neither Lavrans nor the child—but 'twas so. Yet did she feel toward her now an anger that was near to hate—'twas to forget his sorrow for the child's sorrow that he had wished to-night that he could give himself up to his wife. . . .

Ragnfrid dared not rise, for she knew not but that Kristin might be lying awake in the other bed. But she raised herself noiselessly to her knees, and with forehead bent against the footboard of the bed she strove to pray. For her daughter, for her husband and for herself. While her body, little by little, grew stiff with the cold, she set out once more on one of the night-wanderings she knew so well, striving to break her way through to a home of peace for her heart.

III

H A U G E N lay high up in the hills on the west side of the valley. This moonlight night the whole world was white. Billow after billow, the white fells lay domed under the pale blue heavens with their thin-strewn stars. Even the shadows that peaks and domes stretched forth over the snow-slopes seemed strangely thin and light, the moon was sailing so high.

Downward, toward the valley, the woods stood fleecy-white with snow and rime, round the white fields of crofts scrolled over with tiny huts and fences. But far down in the valley-bottom the shadows thickened into darkness.

Lady Aashild came out of the byre, shut the door after her, and stood awhile in the snow. White—the whole world; yet was it more than three weeks still to Advent. Clementsmass cold—'twas like winter had come in earnest already. Ay, ay; in bad years it was often so.

The old woman sighed heavily in the desolate air. Winter again, and cold and loneliness. . . . Then she took up the milk-pail and went towards the dwelling-house. She looked once again down over the valley.

Four black dots came out of the woods half-way up the hillside. Four men on horseback—and the moonlight glanced from a spear-head. They were ploughing heavily upward—none had come that way since the snowfall. Were they coming hither?

Four armed men. . . . 'Twas not like that any who had a lawful errand here would come so many in company. She thought of the cehst with her goods and Björn's in it. Should she hide in the outhouse?

She looked out again over the wintry waste about her. Then she went into the living-house. The two old hounds that lay before the smoky fireplace smote the floor-boards with their tails. The young dogs Björn had with him in the hills.

Aashild blew the embers of the fire into flame, and laid more wood on them; filled the iron pot with snow and set it on the fire; then poured the milk into a wooden bowl and bore it to the closet beside the outer room.

Then she doffed her dirty, undyed, wadmal gown, that smelt of the byre and of sweat, put on a dark-blue garment, and changed her tow-linen hood for a coif of fine white linen, which she smoothed down fairly round her head and neck. Her shaggy boots of skin she drew off, and put on silver-buckled shoes. Then she fell to setting her room in order—smoothed the pillows and the skin in the bed where Björn had lain that day, wiped the long-board clean, and laid the bench-cushions straight.

When the dogs set up their warning barking, she was standing by the fireplace, stirring the supper-porridge. She heard horses in the yard, and the tread of men in the outer room; some one knocked on the door with a spear-butt. Lady Aashild lifted the pot from the fire, settled her dress about her, and, with the dogs at her side, went forward to the door and opened.

Out in the moonlit yard were three young men holding four horses white with rime. A man that stood before her in the porch cried out joyfully:

"Moster * Aashild! come you yourself to open to us? Nay, then must I say *Ben trouvè!*"

"Sister's son, is it you indeed? Then the same say I to you! Go into the room, while I show your men the stable."

"Are you all alone on the farm?" asked Erlend. He followed her while she showed the men where to go.

"Ay; Sir Björn and our man are gone into the hills with the sleigh—they are to see and bring home some fodder we have stacked up there," said Lady Aashild. "And serving-woman I have none," she said, laughing

A little while after, the four young men were sitting on the outer bench with their backs to the board, looking at the old lady, as, busily but quietly, she went about making ready their supper. She laid a cloth on the board, and set on it a lighted candle; then brought forth butter, cheese, a bear-ham and a high pile of thin slices of fine bread. She fetched ale and mead up from the cellar below the room, and then poured out the porridge into a dish of fine wood, and bade them sit in to the board and fall to.

* Moster=mother's sister.

"'Tis but little for you young folk," she said, laughing. "I must boil another pot of porridge. To-morrow you shall fare better—but I shut up the kitchen-house in the winter, save when I bake or brew. We are few folks on the farm, and I begin to grow old, kinsman."

Erlend laughed and shook his head. He had marked that his men behaved before the old woman seemly and modestly as he had scarce ever seen them bear themselves before.

"You are a strange woman, Moster. Mother was ten years younger than you, and she looked older when last we were in your house than you look to-day."

"Ay, Magnhild's youth left her full early," said Lady Aashild softly. "Where are you come from, now?" she asked after a while.

"I have been for a season at a farmstead up north in Lesja," said Erlend. "I had hired me lodging there. I know not if you can guess what errand has brought me to this countryside?"

"You would ask: know I that you have had suit made to Lavrans Björgulfsön of Jörundgaard for his daughter?"

"Ay," said Erlend. "I made suit for her in seemly and honourable wise, and Lavrans Björgulfsön answered with a churlish: No. Now I see no better way, since Kristin and I will not be forced apart, than that I bear her off by the strong hand. I have—I have had a spy in this countryside, and I know that her mother was to be at Sundbu at Clementsmass and for a while after, and Lavrans is gone to Romsdal with the other men to fetch across the winter stores to Sil."

Lady Aashild sat silent awhile.

"That counsel, Erlend, you had best let be," said she. "I deem not either that the maid will go with you willingly; and I trow you would not use force?"

"Ay, but she will. We have spoken of it many times—she has prayed me herself many times to bear her away."

"Kristin has——?" said Lady Aashild. Then she laughed. "None the less I would not have you make too sure that the maid will follow when you come to take her at her word."

"Ay, but she will," said Erlend. "And, Moster, my thought was this: that you send word to Jörundgaard and bid Kristin come and be your guest—a week or so, while her father and mother are from home. Then could we be at Hamar before any knew she was gone," he added.

Lady Aashild answered, still smiling:

"And had you thought as well what we should answer, Sir Björn and I, when Lavrans comes and calls us to account for his daughter?"

"Ay," said Erlend. "We were four well-armed men, and the maid was willing."

"I will not help you in this," said the lady hotly. "Lavrans has been a trusty man to us for many a year—he and his wife are honourable folk, and I will not be art or part in deceiving them or beshaming their child. Leave the maid in peace, Erlend. 'Twill soon be high time, too, that your kin should hear of other deeds of yours than running in and out of the land with stolen women."

"I must speak with you alone, lady," said Erlend shortly.

Lady Aashild took a candle, led him to the closet, and shut the door behind them. She sate herself down on a corn-bin; Erlend stood with his hands thrust into his belt, looking down at her.

"You may say this, too, to Lavrans Björgulfsön: that Sira John of Gerdarud joined us in wedlock ere we went on our way to Lady Ingebjörg Haakonsdatter in Sweden."

"Say you so?" said Lady Aashild. "Are you well assured that Lady Ingebjörg will welcome you, when you are come thither?"

"I spoke with her at Tunsberg," said Erlend. "She greeted me as her dear kinsman and thanked me when I proffered her my service either here or in Sweden. And Munan hath promised me letters to her."

"And know you not," said Aashild, "that even should you find a priest that will wed you, yet will Kristin have cast away all right to the heritage of her father's lands and goods? Nor can her children be your lawful heirs. Much I doubt if she will be counted as your lawfully wedded wife."

"Not in this land, maybe. 'Tis therefore we fly to Sweden. Her forefather, Laurentius Lagmand, was never wed to the Lady Bengta in any other sort—they could never win her brother's consent. Yet was she counted as a wedded lady——"

"There were no children," said Lady Aashild. "Think you my sons will hold their hands from your heritage if Kristin be left a widow with children and their lawful birth can be cast in dispute?"

"You do Munan wrong," said Erlend. "I know but little of your other children—I know indeed that you have little cause to judge them kindly. But Munan has ever been my trusty kinsman. He is fain to have me wed; 'twas he went to Lavrans with my wooing. . . . Besides, afterwards, by course of law, I can assure our children their heritage and rights."

"Ay, and thereby mark their mother as your concubine," said Lady Aashild. "But 'tis past my understanding how that meek and holy man, Jon Helgesön, will dare to brave his Bishop by wedding you against the law."

"I confessed—*all*—to him last summer," said Erlend, in a low voice "He promised then to wed us, if all other ways should fail."

"Is it even so?" said Lady Aashild slowly. . . ."A heavy sin have you laid upon your soul, Erlend Nikulaussön. 'Twas well with Kristin at home with her father and mother—a good marriage was agreed for her with a comely and honourable man of good kindred——"

"Kristin hath told me herself how you said once that she and I would match well together. And that Simon Andressön was no husband for her——"

"Oh—I have said, and I have said!" Aashild broke in. "I have said so many things in my time. . . . Neither can I understand at all that you can have gained your will with Kristin so lightly. So many times you cannot have met together. And never could I have thought that maid had been so light to win——"

"We met at Oslo," said Erlend. "Afterward she was dwelling out at Gerdarud with her father's brother. She came out and met me in the woods." He looked down and spoke very low: "I had her alone to myself out there——"

Lady Aashild started up. Erlend bent his head yet lower.

"And after that . . . she still was friends with you?" she asked unbelievingly.

"Ay." Erlend smiled a weak, wavering smile. "We were friends still. And 'twas not so bitterly against her—but no blame lies on her. 'Twas then she would have had me take her away—she was loth to go back to her kin——"

"But you would not?"

"No. I was minded to try to win her for my wife with her father's will."

"Is it long since?" asked Lady Aashild.

"'Twas a year last Lawrence-mass," answered Erlend.

"You have not hasted overmuch with your wooing," said the other.

"She was not free before from her first betrothal."

"And since then you have not come nigh her?" asked Aashild.

"We managed so that we met once and again." Once more the wavering smile flitted over the man's face. "In a house in the town."

"In God's name!" said Lady Aashild. "I will help you and her as best I may. I can see it well: not long could Kristin bear to live there with her father and mother, hiding such a thing as this. . . . Is there yet more?" she asked of a sudden.

"Not that I have heard," said Erlend shortly.

"Have you bethought you," asked the lady in a while, "that Kristin has friends and kinsmen dwelling all down the Dale?"

"We must journey as secretly as we can," said Erlend. " And therefore it behoves us to make no delay in setting out, that we may be well on the way before her father comes home. You must lend us your sleigh, Moster."

Aashild shrugged her shoulders.

"Then is there her uncle at Skog—what if he hear that you are holding your wedding with his brother's daughter at Gerdarud?"

"Aasmund has spoken for me to Lavrans," said Erlend. "He would not be privy to our counsels, but 'tis like he will wink an eye—we must come to the priest by night, and journey onward by night. And afterward, I trow well Aasmund will put it to Lavrans that it befits not a God-fearing man like him to part them that a priest has wedded—and that 'twill be best for him to give his consent, that we may be lawful wedded man and wife. And you must say the like to the man, Moster. He may set what terms he will for atonement between us, and ask all such amends as he deems just."

"I trow Lavrans Björgulfsön will be no easy man to guide in this matter," said Lady Aashild. "And God and St. Olav know, sister's son, I like this business but ill. But I see well 'tis the last way left you to make good the harm you have wrought Kristin. To-morrow will I ride myself to Jörundgaard, if so be you will lend me one of your men, and I get Ingrid of the croft above us here to see to my cattle."

Lady Aashild came to Jörundgaard next evening just as the moonlight was struggling with the last gleams of day. She saw how pale and hollow-cheeked Kristin was, when the girl came out into the courtyard to meet her guest.

The lady sat by the fireplace playing with the two children. Now and then she stole keen glances at Kristin, as she went about and set the supper-board. Thin she was truly, and still in her bearing. She had ever been still, but it was a stillness of another kind that was on the girl now. Lady Aashild guessed at all the straining and the stubborn defiance that lay behind.

"'Tis like you have heard," said Kristin, coming over to her, "what befell here this last autumn."

"Ay—that my sister's son has made suit for you."

"Mind you," asked Kristin, "how you said once he and I would match well together? Only that he was too rich and great of kin for me?"

"I hear that Lavrans is of another mind," said the lady drily.

There was a gleam in Kristin's eyes, and she smiled a little. She will do, no question, thought Lady Aashild. Little as she liked it, she must hearken to Erlend, and give the helping hand he had asked.

Kristin made ready her parents' bed for the guest, and Lady Aashild asked that the girl should sleep with her. After they had lain down and the house was silent, Lady Aashild brought forth her errand.

She grew strangely heavy at heart as she saw that this child seemed to think not at all on the sorrow she would bring on her father and mother. Yet *I* lived with Baard for more than twenty years in sorrow and torment, she thought. Well, maybe 'tis so with all of us. It seemed Kristin had not even seen how Ulvhild had fallen away this autumn—'tis little like, thought Aashild, that she will see her little sister any more. But she said naught of this—the longer Kristin could hold to this mood of wild and reckless gladness, the better would it be, no doubt.

Kristin rose up in the dark, and gathered together her ornaments in a little box which she took with her into the bed. Then Lady Aashild could not keep herself from saying:

"Yet methinks, Kristin, the best way of all would be that Erlend ride hither, when your father comes home—that he confess openly he hath done you a great wrong—and put himself in Lavrans' hands."

"I trow that, then, father would kill Erlend," said Kristin.

"That would not Lavrans, if Erlend refuse to draw steel against his love's father."

"I have no mind that Erlend should be humbled in such wise," said Kristin. "And I would not father should know that Erlend had touched me before he asked for me in seemliness and honour."

"Think you Lavrans will be less wroth," asked Aashild, "when he hears that you have fled from his house with Erlend; and think you 'twill be a lighter sorrow for him to bear? So long as you live with Erlend, and your father has not given you to him, you can be naught but his paramour before the law."

"'Tis another thing," said Kristin, "if I be Erlend's paramour after he has tried in vain to win me for his lawful wife."

Lady Aashild was silent. She thought of her meeting with Lavrans Björgulfsön when he came home and learnt that his daughter had been stolen away.

Then Kristin said:

"I see well, Lady Aashild, I seem to you an evil, thankless child. But so has it been in this house ever since father came from the Haugathing, that every day has been a torment to him and to me. 'Tis best for all that there be an end of this matter."

They rode from Jörundgaard betimes the next day, and came to Haugen a little after nones. Erlend met them in the courtyard, and Kristin threw herself into his arms, paying no heed to the man who was with her and Lady Aashild.

In the house she greeted Björn Gunnarsön; and then greeted Erlend's two men, as though she knew them well already. Lady Aashild could see no sign in her of bashfulness or fear. And after, when they sat at the board, and Erlend set forth his plan, Kristin put her word in with the others and gave counsel about the journey: that they should ride forth from Haugen next evening so late that they should come to the gorge when the moon was setting, and should pass in the dark through Sil to beyond Loptsgaard, thence up along the Otta stream to the bridge, and from thence along the west side of the Otta and the Laagen over bypaths through the waste as far as the horses could bear them. They must lie resting through the day at one of the empty spring sæters on the hillside there; "for till we are out of the Holledis country there is ever fear that we may come upon folk that know me."

"Have you thought of fodder for the horses?" said Aashild. "You cannot rob folk's sæters in a year like this—even if so be there is fodder there—and you know none in all the Dale has fodder to sell this year."

"I have thought of that," answered Kristin. "You must lend us three days' food and fodder. 'Tis a reason the more why we must not journey in so strong a troop. Erlend must send Jon back to Husaby. The year has been better on the Trondheim side, and surely some loads can be got across the hills before the Yuletide snows. There are some poor folk dwelling southward in the parish, Lady Aashild, that I would fain you should help with a gift of fodder from Erlend and me."

Björn set up an uncanny, mirthless horse-laugh. Lady Aashild shook her head. But Erlend's man Ulv lifted his keen, swarthy visage and looked at Kristin with his bold smile:

"At Husaby there is never abundance, Kristin Lavransdatter, neither in good years nor in bad. But maybe things will be changed when you come to be mistress there. By your speech a man would deem you are the housewife that Erlend needs."

Kristin nodded to the man calmly, and went on. They must keep clear of the high-road as far as might be. And she deemed it not wise to take the way that led through Hamar. But, Erlend put in, Munan was there—and the letter to the Duchess they must have.

"Then Ulv must part from us at Fagaberg and ride to Sir Munan, while we hold on west of Mjösen and make our way by land and the byroads through Hadeland down to Hakedal. Thence there goes a waste way south to Margretadal, I have heard my uncle say. 'Twere not wise for us to pass through Raumarike in these days, when a great wedding-feast is toward at Dyfrin," she said with a smile.

Erlend went round and laid his arm about her shoulders, and she leaned back to him, paying no heed to the others who sat by looking on. Lady Aashild said angrily:

"None would believe aught else than that you are well-used to running away;" and Sir Björn broke again into his horse-laugh.

In a little while Lady Aashild stood up to go to the kitchen-house and see to the food. She had made up the kitchen fire so that Erlend's men could sleep there at night. She bade Kristin go with her: "For I must be able to swear to Lavrans Björgulfsön that you were never a moment alone together in my house," she said wrathfully.

Kristin laughed and went with the lady. Soon after, Erlend came strolling in after them, drew a stool forward to the hearth, and sat there, hindering the women in their work. He caught hold of Kristin every time she came nigh him, as she hurried about her work. At last he drew her down on his knee:

"'Tis even as Ulv said, I trow; you are the housewife I need."

"Ay, ay," said Aashild, with a vexed laugh. "She will serve your turn well enough. 'Tis she that stakes all in this adventure—you hazard not much."

"You speak truth," said Erlend. "But I wot well I have shown I had the will to come to her by the right road. Be not so angry, Moster Aashild."

"I do well to be angry," said the lady. "Scarce have you set your house in order, but you must needs guide things so that you have to run from it all again with a woman."

"You must bear in mind, kinswoman—so hath it ever been, that 'twas not the worst men who fell into trouble for a woman's sake—all sagas tell us that."

"Oh, God help us all!" said Aashild. Her face grew young and soft. "That tale have I heard before, Erlend." She laid her hand on his head and gave his hair a little tug.

At that moment Ulv Haldorsön tore open the door, and shut it quickly behind him:

"Here is come yet another guest, Erlend—the one you are least fain to see, I trow."

"Is it Lavrans Björgulfsön?" said Erlend, starting up.

"Well if it were," said the man. "'Tis Eline Ormsdatter.'

The door was opened from without; the woman who came in thrust Ulv aside and came forward into the light. Kristin looked at Erlend; at first he seemed to shrivel and shrink together; then he drew himself up, with a dark flush on his face:

"In the devil's name, where come you from—what would you here?"

Lady Aashild stepped forward and spoke:

"You must come with us to the hall, Eline Ormsdatter. So much manners at least we have in this house, that we welcome not our guests in the kitchen."

"I look not, Lady Aashild," said the other, "to be welcomed as a guest by Erlend's kinsfolk.—Asked you from whence I came?—I come from Husaby, as you might know. I bear you greetings from Orm and Margret; they are well."

Erlend made no answer.

"When I heard that you had had Gissur Arnfinsön raise money for you, and that you were for the south again," she went on, "I thought 'twas like you would bide awhile this time with your kinsfolk in Gud-brandsdal. I knew that you had made suit for the daughter of a neighbour of theirs."

She looked across at Kristin for the first time, and met the girl's eyes. Kristin was very pale, but she looked calmly and keenly at the other.

She was stony-calm. She had known it from the moment she heard who was come—this was the thought she had been fleeing from always; this thought it was she had tried to smother under impatience, restless-ness and defiance; the whole time she had been striving not to think whether Erlend had freed himself wholly and fully from his former paramour. Now she was overtaken—useless to struggle any more. But she begged not nor beseeched for herself.

She saw that Eline Ormsdatter was fair. She was young no longer; but she was fair—once she must have been exceeding fair. She had thrown back her hood; her head was round as a ball, and hard; the cheek-bones stood out—but none the less it was plain to see, once she had been very fair. Her coif covered but the back part of her head; while she was speaking, her hands kept smoothing the waving, bright-gold front-hair beneath the linen. Kristin had never seen a woman with such great eyes; they were dark brown, round and hard; but under the narrow coal-black eyebrows and the long lashes they were strangely beautiful against her golden hair. The skin of her cheeks and lips was chafed and raw from her ride in the cold, but it could not spoil her much; she was too fair for that. The heavy riding-dress covered up her form, but she bore herself in it as does only a woman most proud and secure in the glory of a fair body. She was scarce as tall as Kristin; but she held herself so well that she seemed yet taller than the slender, spare-limbed girl.

"Hath she been with you at Husaby the whole time?" asked Kristin, in a low voice.

"I have not been at Husaby," said Erlend curtly, flushing red again. "I have dwelt at Hestnæs the most of the summer."

"Here now are the tidings I came to bring you, Erlend," said Eline. "You need not any longer take shelter with your kinsfolk and try their hospitality for that I am keeping your house. Since this autumn I have been a widow."

Erlend stood motionless.

"It was not I that bade you come to Husaby last year, to keep my house," said he with effort.

"I heard that all things were going to waste there," said Eline. "I had so much kindness left for you from old days, Erlend, that me-thought I should lend a hand to help you—although God knows you have not dealt well with our children or with me."

"For the children I have done what I could," said Erlend. "And well you know, 'twas for their sake I suffered you to live on at Husaby. That you profited them or me by it you scarce can think yourself, I trow," he added, smiling scornfully. "Gissur could guide things well enough without your help."

"Ay, you have ever had such mighty trust in Gissur," said Eline, laughing softly. "But now the thing is this, Erlend—now I am free. And if so be you will, you can keep the promise now you made me once."

Erlend stood silent.

"Mind you," asked Eline, "the night I bore your son? You promised then that you would wed me when Sigurd died."

Erlend passed his hand up under his hair, that hung damp with sweat.

"Ay,—I remember," he said.

"Will you keep that promise now?" asked Eline.

"No," said Erlend.

Eline Ormsdatter looked across at Kristin—then smiled a little and nodded. Then she looked again at Erlend.

"It is ten years since, Eline," said the man. "And since that time you and I have lived together year in year out like two damned souls in hell."

"But not only so, I trow!" said she, with the same smile.

"It is years and years since aught else has been," said Erlend dully. "The children would be none the better off. And you know—you know I can scarce bear to be in a room with you any more!" he almost screamed.

"I marked naught of that when you were at home in the summer," said Eline, with a meaning smile. "Then we were not unfriends—always."

"If you deem that we were friends, have it as you will, for me," said Erlend wearily.

"Will you stand here without end?" broke in Lady Aashild. She poured the porridge from the pot into two great wooden dishes and gave one to Kristin. The girl took it. "Bear it to the hall—and you, Ulv, take the other—and set them on the board; supper we must have, whether it be so, or so."

Kristin and the man went out with the dishes. Lady Aashild said to the two others:

"Come now, you two; what boots it that you stand here barking at each other?"

"'Tis best that Eline and I have our talk out together now," said Erlend.

Lady Aashild said no more, but went out and left them.

In the hall Kristin had laid the table and fetched ale from the cellar. She sat on the outer bench, straight as a wand and calm of face, but she ate nothing. Nor had the others much stomach to their food, neither Björn nor Erlend's men. Only the man that had come with Eline and Björn's hired man ate greedily. Lady Aashild sat herself down and ate a little of the porridge. No óne spoke a word.

At length Eline Ormsdatter came in alone. Lady Aashild bade her sit between Kristin and herself; Eline sat down and ate a little. Now and again a gleam as of a hidden smile flitted across her face, and she stole a glance at Kristin.

Awhile after, Lady Aashild went out to the kitchen-house.

The fire on the hearth was almost burnt out. Erlend sat by it on his stool, crouched together, his head down between his arms.

Lady Aashild went to him and laid her hand on his shoulder.

"God forgive you, Erlend, that you have brought things to this pass."

Erlend turned up to her a face besmeared with wretchedness.

"She is with child," he said, and shut his eyes.

Lady Aashild's face flamed up, she gripped his shoulder hard.

"Which of them?" she asked, roughly and scornfully.

"My child it is not," said Erlend, in the same dead voice. "But like enough you will not believe me—none will believe me——" He sank together again.

Lady Aashild sat down in front of him on the edge of the hearth.

"Now must you try to play the man, Erlend. 'Tis not so easy to believe you in this matter. Do you swear it is not yours?"

Erlend lifted his ravaged face.

"As surely as I need God's mercy—as surely as I hope—that God in heaven has comforted mother for all she suffered here—I have not touched Eline since first I saw Kristin!" He cried out the words, so that Lady Aashild had to hush him.

"Then I see not that this is so great a misfortune. You must find out who the father is, and make it worth his while to wed her."

"'Tis in my mind that it is Gissur Arnfinsön—my steward at Husaby," said Erlend wearily. "We talked together last year—and since then too—Sigurd's death has been looked for this long time past. He was willing to wed her, when she was a widow, if I would give her a fitting portion——"

"Well?" said Lady Aashild. Erlend went on:

"She swears with great oaths she will have none of him. She will name me as the father. And if I swear I am not—think you any will believe aught but that I am forsworn?"

"You must sure be able to turn her purpose," said Lady Aashild. "There is no other way now but that you go home with her to Husaby no later than to-morrow. And there must you harden your heart and stand firm till you have this marriage fixed between your steward and Eline."

"Ay," said Erlend. Then he threw himself forward again and groaned aloud:

"Can you not see—Moster—what think you Kristin will believe——?"

At night Erlend lay in the kitchen-house with the men. In the hall Kristin slept with Lady Aashild in the lady's bed, and Eline Ormsdatter in the other bed that was there. Björn went out and lay down in the stable.

The next morning Kristin went out with Lady Aashild to the byre. While the lady went to to the kitchen to make ready the breakfast, Kristin bore the milk up to the hall.

A candle stood burning on the table. Eline was sitting dressed on the edge of her bed. Kristin greeted her silently, then fetched a milk-pan and poured the milk into it.

"Will you give me a drink of milk?" asked Eline. Kristin took a wooden ladle, filled it and handed it to the other; she drank eagerly, looking at Kristin over the rim of the cup.

"So you are that Kristin Lavransdatter, that hath stolen from me Erlend's love," she said, as she gave back the ladle.

"You should know best if there was any love to steal," said the girl. Eline bit her lip.

"What will *you* do," she said, "if Erlend one day grow weary of you, and offer to wed you to his serving-man? Will you do his will in that as well?"

Kristin made no answer. Then the other laughed, and said:

"You do his will in all things now, I well believe. What think you, Kristin—shall we throw dice for our man, we two paramours of Erlend Nikulaussön?" When no answer came, she laughed again and said: "Are you so simple, that you deny not you are his paramour?"

"To you I care not to lie," said Kristin.

"'Twould profit you but little if you did," answered Eline, still laughing. "I know the boy too well. He flew at you like a black-cock, I trow, the second time you were together. 'Tis pity of you too, fair child that you are."

Kristin's cheeks grew white. Sick with loathing, she said low:

"I will not speak with you——"

"Think you he is like to deal with you better than with me?" went on Eline. Then Kristin answered sharply:

"No blame will I ever cast on Erlend, whatever he may do. I went astray of my own will—I shall not whimper or wail if the path lead out on to the rocks——"

Eline was silent for a while. Then she said unsteadily, flushing red:

"*I* was a maid too, when he came to me, Kristin—even though I had been wife in name to the old man for seven years. But like enough you could never understand what the misery of that life was."

Kristin began to tremble violently. Eline looked at her. Then from her travelling-case that stood by her on the step of the bed she took a little horn. She broke the seal that was on its mouth and said softly:

"You are young and I am old, Kristin. I know well it boots not for me to strive against you—your time is now. Will you drink with me, Kristin?"

Kristin did not move. Then the other raised the horn to her own lips; but Kristin marked that she did not drink. Eline said:

"So much honour you sure can do me, to drink to me—and promise you will not be a hard stepmother to my children?"

Kristin took the horn. At that moment Erlend opened the door. He stood a moment, looking from one to the other of the women.

"What is this?" he asked.

Kristin answered, and her voice was wild and piercing:

"We are drinking to each other—we—your paramours——"

He gripped her wrist and took the horn from her.

"Be still," he said harshly. "You shall not drink with her."

"Why not?" cried Kristin as before. "She was pure as I was, when you tempted her——"

"That hath she said so often, that I trow she is come to believe it herself," said Erlend. "Mind you, Eline, when you made me go to Sigurd with that tale, and he brought forth witness that he had caught you before with another man?"

White with loathing, Kristin turned away. Eline had flushed darkly —now she said defiantly:

"Yet will it scarce bring leprosy on the girl, if she drink with me!"

Erlend turned on Eline in wrath—then of a sudden his face seemed to grow long and hard as stone, and he gasped with horror:

"Jesus!" he said below his breath. He gripped Eline by the arm.

"Drink to *her*, then," he said, in a harsh and quivering voice. "Drink you first; then she shall drink to you."

Eline wrenched herself away with a groan. She fled backwards through the room, the man after her. "Drink," he said. He snatched the dagger from his belt and held it as he followed. "Drink out the drink you have brewed for Kristin!" He seized Eline's arm again and dragged her to the table, then forced her head forward toward the horn.

Eline shrieked once and buried her face on her arm. Erlend released her and stood trembling.

"A hell was mine with Sigurd," shrieked Eline. "You—you promised—but you have been worst to me of all, Erlend!"

Then came Kristin forward and grasped the horn:

"One of us two must drink—both of us you cannot keep——"

Erlend wrenched the horn away and flung her from him so that she reeled and fell near by Lady Aashild's bed. Again he pushed the horn against Eline Ormsdatter's mouth—with one knee on the bench he stood by her side, and with a hand round her head tried to force the drink between her teeth.

She reached out under his arm, snatched his dagger from the table, and struck hard at the man. The blow did but scratch his flesh through the clothes. Then she turned the point against her own breast, and the instant after sank sidelong down into his arms.

Kristin rose and came to them. Erlend was holding Eline, her head hanging back over his arm. The rattle came in her throat almost at once—blood welled up and ran out of her mouth. She spat some of it out and said:

"'Twas for you I meant—that drink—for all the times—you deceived me——"

"Bring Lady Aashild hither," said Erlend, in a low voice. Kristin stood immovable.

"She is dying," said Erlend as before.

"Then is she better served than we," said Kristin. Erlend looked at her—the despair in his eyes softened her. She left the room.

"What is it?" asked Lady Aashild, when Kristin called her out from the kitchen.

"We have killed Eline Ormsdatter," said Kristin. "She is dying——"

Lady Aashild set off running to the hall. But Eline breathed her last as the lady crossed the threshold.

Lady Aashild had laid out the dead woman on the bench, wiped the blood from her face and covered it with the linen of her coif. Erlend stood leaning against the wall, behind the body.

"Know you," said Aashild, "that this was the worst thing that could befall?"

She had filled the fireplace with twigs and firewood; now she thrust the horn into the midst of them and blew them into a blaze.

"Can you trust your men?" asked the lady again.

"Ulv and Haftor are trusty, methinks—of Jon and the man with Eline I know but little."

"You know, belike," said the lady, "should it come out that Kristin and you were together here, and that you two were alone with her when she died, 'twere as well for Kristin you had let her drink of Eline's brew. . . . And should there be talk of poison, all men will call to mind what once was laid to *my* charge. . . . Had she any kindred or friends?"

"No," said Erlend, in a low voice. "She had none but me."

"Yet," said Lady Aashild again, "it may well be a hard matter to cover up this thing and hide the body away, without the ugliest of mis-thought falling on you."

"She shall rest in hallowed ground," said Erlend, "if it cost me Husaby. What say you, Kristin?"

Kristin nodded.

Lady Aashild sat silent. The more she thought, the more hopeless it seemed to her to find any way out. In the kitchen-house were four men—even if Erlend could bribe them all to keep silence, even if some of them, if Eline's man, could be bribed to leave the country—still, sure they could never be. And 'twas known at Jörundgaard that Kristin had been here—if Lavrans heard of this, she feared to think what he would do. And how to bear the dead woman hence. The mountain-path to the west was not to be thought of now—there was the road to Romsdal, or over the hills to Trondheim, or south down the Dale. And should the truth come out, it would never be believed—even if folk let it pass for true.

"I must take counsel with Björn in this matter," she said, and rose and went out to call him.

Björn Gunnarsön listened to his wife's story without moving a muscle and without withdrawing his eyes from Erlend's face.

"Björn," said Aashild desperately. "There is naught for it but that one must swear he saw her lay hands upon herself."

Björn's dead eyes grew slowly dark, as life came into them; he looked at his wife, and his mouth drew aside into a crooked smile:

"And you mean that I should be the one?"

Lady Aashild crushed her hands together and lifted them towards him:

"Björn, you know well what it means for these two——"

"And you think that, whether or no, 'tis all over with me?" he said slowly. "Or think you there is so much left of the man I once was that I dare be forsworn to save that boy there from going down to ruin? I that was dragged down myself—all those years ago. Dragged down, I say," he repeated.

"You say it because I am old now," whispered Aashild.

Kristin burst out into such weeping that the piercing sound filled the room. She had sat in the corner by Aashild's bed, stark and silent. Now she began weeping wildly and loud. It was as though Lady Aashild's voice had torn her heart open. The voice had been heavy with the memories of the sweetness of love; it was as though its sound had made her understand for the first time what her love and Erlend's had been. The memory of hot and passionate happiness swept over all else—swept away the hard despair and hatred of last night. All she knew of now was her love and her will to hold out.

They looked at her—all three. Then Sir Björn went across and lifted her chin with his hand and looked at her:

"Say you, Kristin, she did it herself?"

"Every word you have heard is true," said Kristin firmly. "We threatened her till she did it."

"She had meant Kristin should suffer a worse fate," said Aashild.

Sir Björn let go the girl. He went over to the body, lifted it up into the bed where Eline had lain the night before, and laid it close to the wall, drawing up the coverings well over it:

"Jon and the man you do not know you must send home to Husaby, with word that Eline is journeying south with you. Let them ride at midday. Say that the women are asleep in the hall; they must take their food in the kitchen. Afterward you must speak with Ulv and Haftor. Hath she threatened before to do this? So that you can bring witness to it, if such question should be asked?"

"Every soul that was at Husaby the last years we lived together there," said Erlend wearily, "can witness that she threatened to take her own life—and mine too sometimes—when I spoke of parting from her."

Björn laughed harshly:

"I thought as much. To-night we must clothe her in her riding-coats and set her in the sleigh. You must sit beside her——"

Erlend swayed on his feet where he stood:

"I cannot!"

"God knows how much manhood will be left in you when you have gone your own gait twenty years more," said Björn. "Think you, then, you can drive the sleigh? For then will I sit beside her. We must travel by night and by lonely paths, till we are come down to Fron. In this cold none can know how long she has been dead. We will drive in to the monks' hospice at Roaldstad. There will you and I bear witness that you two were together in the sleigh, and it came to bitter words betwixt you. There is witness enough that you would not live with her since the ban was taken off you, and that you have made suit for a maiden of birth that fits your own. Ulv and Haftor must hold themselves aloof the whole way, so they can swear, if need be, she was alive when last they saw her. You can bring them to do so much, I trow? At the monastery you can have the monks lay her in her coffin—and afterward you must bargain with the priests for grave-peace for her and soul's peace for yourself. . . .

". . . Ay, a fair deed it is not. But so as you have guided things, no fairer can it be. Stand not there like a breeding woman ready to swoon away. God help you, boy, a man can see *you* have not proved before what 'tis to feel the knife-edge at your throat."

A biting blast came rushing down from the mountains, driving a fine silvery smoke from the snow-wreaths up into the moon-blue air, as the men made ready to drive away.

Two horses were harnessed, one in front of the other. Erlend sat in the front of the sleigh. Kristin went up to him:

"This time, Erlend, you must try to send me word how this journey goes, and what becomes of you after."

He crushed her hand till she thought the blood must be driven out from under the nails.

"Dare you still hold fast to me, Kristin?"

"Ay, still," she said; and after a moment: "Of this deed we are both guilty—I egged you on—for I willed her death."

Lady Aashild and Kristin stood and looked after the sleigh, as it rose and dipped over the snow-drifts. It went down from sight into a hollow—then came forth again farther down on a snow-slope. And then the men passed into the shadow of a fell, and were gone from sight for good.

The two women sat by the fireplace, their backs to the empty bed, from which Aashild had borne away all the bedding and straw. Both could feel it standing there empty and gaping behind them.

"Would you rather that we should sleep in the kitchen-house to-night?" asked Lady Aashild at length.

"'Tis like it will be the same where we lie," said Kristin.

Lady Aashild went out to look at the weather.

"Ay, should the wind get up or a thaw come on, they will not journey far before it comes out," said Kristin.

"Here at Haugen it blows ever," answered Lady Aashild. "'Tis no sign of a change of weather."

They sat on as before.

"You should not forget," said the lady at last, "what fate she had meant for you two."

Kristin answered low:

"I was thinking, maybe in her place I had willed the same."

"Never would you have willed that another should be a leper," said Aashild vehemently.

"Mind you, Moster, you said to me once that 'tis well when we dare not do a thing we think is not good and fair, but not so well when we think a thing not good and fair because we dare not do it?"

"You had not dared to do it, because 'twas sin," said Lady Aashild.

"No, I believe not so," said Kristin. "Much have I done already that I deemed once I dared not do because 'twas sin. But I saw not till now what sin brings with it—that we must tread others underfoot."

"Erlend would fain have made an end of his ill life long before he met you," said Aashild eagerly. "All was over between those two."

"I know it," said Kristin. "But I trow she had never cause to deem Erlend's purposes so firm that she could not shake them."

"Kristin," begged the lady fearfully, "surely you would not give up Erlend now? You cannot be saved now except you save each other."

"So would a priest scarce counsel," said Kristin, smiling coldly. "But well I know that never can I give up Erlend now—not if I should tread my own father underfoot."

Lady Aashild rose:

"We had as well put our hands to some work as sit here thus," she said. "Like enough 'twould be vain for us to try to sleep."

She fetched the butter-churn from the closet, then bore in some pans of milk, filled the churn and made ready to begin churning.

"Let me do it," Kristin asked. "My back is younger."

They worked without speaking; Kristin stood by the closet-door churning, while Aashild carded wool by the hearth. At last, when Kristin had emptied the churn and was kneading the butter, the girl asked of a sudden:

"Moster Aashild—are you never afraid of the day when you must stand before God's judgment?"

Lady Aashild rose, and came and stood before Kristin in the light:

"It may be I shall find courage to ask Him that hath made me as I am, if He will have mercy on me in His own good time. For I have never begged for His mercy when I broke His commands. And never have I begged God or man to forgive me a farthing of the price I have paid here in this mountain hut."

A little while after she said softly:

"Munan, my eldest son, was twenty years old. He was not such an one then, as I know he is now. They were not such ones then, my children——"

Kristin answered low:

"But yet have you had Sir Björn by your side each day and each night in all these years."

"Ay—that too have I had," said Aashild.

In a little while after, Kristin was done with the butter-making. Lady Aashild said then that they must lie down and try to sleep a little.

Inside, in the dark bed, she laid her arm round Kristin's shoulders, and drew the young head in to her breast. And it was not long before she heard by her even and gentle breathing that Kristin was fallen asleep.

IV

T H E frost held on. In every byre in the parish the half-starved beasts bellowed dolefully with hunger and cold. Already the farmers were skimping and saving on their fodder, every straw they could.

There was little visiting round at Yule this year; folks stayed quiet in their own homes.

During Yuletide the cold grew greater—it was as though each day was colder than the last. Scarce any one could call to mind so hard a winter—there came no more snow, not even up in the mountains; but the snow that had fallen at Clementsmass froze hard as a stone. The sun shone from a clear sky, now the days began to grow lighter. At night the northern lights flickered and flamed above the range to the north—they flamed over half the heaven, but they brought no change of weather; now and again would come a cloudy day, and a little dry snow would sprinkle down—and then came clear weather again and biting cold. The Laagen muttered and gurgled sluggishly under its ice-bridges.

Kristin thought each morning that she could bear no more, that she could never hold out to the day's end. For each day she felt was as a duel between her and her father. And *could* they be against each other so, when every living being in the parish, man and beast, was suffering under one common trial? . . . But still, when the evening came, she had held out one day more.

It was not that her father was unfriendly. They spoke no word of what was between them, but she felt, behind all that he did not say, his firm unbending will to hold fast to his denial.

And her heart ached within her for the lack of his friendship. The

ache was so dreadful in its keenness, because she knew how much else
her father had on his shoulders—and had things been as before, he
would have talked with her of it all. . . . It was indeed so, that at
Jörundgaard they were in better case than most other places; but here,
too, they felt the pinch of the year each day and each hour. Other
years it had been Lavrans' wont in the winters to handle and break in
his young colts; but this year he had sent them all south in the autumn
and sold them. And his daughter missed the sound of his voice out in
the courtyard, and the sight of him struggling with the slender, ragged
two-year-olds in the game he loved so well. Storehouses and barns and
bins at Jörundgaard were not bare yet—there was store left from the
harvest of the year before—but many folk came to ask for help—to
buy, or to beg for gifts—and none ever asked in vain.

Late one evening came a huge old skin-clad man on ski. Lavrans
talked with him out in the courtyard, and Halvdan bore food across
to the hearth-room for him. None on the place who had seen him
knew who he was—he might well be one of those wild folk who lived
far in among the fells; like enough Lavrans had come upon him there.
But Lavrans said naught of the visitor, nor Halvdan either.

But one evening came a man whom Lavrans Björgulfsön had been
at odds with for many years. Lavrans went to the storeroom with him.
When he came back to the hall again he said:

"They come to me for help, every man of them. But here in my
own house you are all against me. You, too, wife," he said hotly.

The mother flamed up at Kristin:

"Hear you what your father says to me! No, I am not against you,
Lavrans. I know—and I wot well you know it too, Kristin—what
befell away south at Roaldstad late in the autumn, when he journeyed
down the Dale with that other adulterer, his kinsman of Haugen—she
took her own life, the unhappy woman he had lured away from all
her kin."

Kristin stood with a hard, frozen face:

"I see that 'tis all one—you blame him as much for the years he has
striven to free himself from sin, as for the years he lived in it."

"Jesus, Maria!" cried Ragnhild, clasping her hands together:
"What is come to you! Has even this not availed to change your
heart?"

"No," said Kristin. "I have not changed."

Then Lavrans looked up from the bench where he sat by Ulvhild:
"Neither have I changed, Kristin," he said, in a low voice.

But Kristin felt within her that in a manner she was changed, in
thoughts if not in heart. She had had tidings of how it had fared with

them on that dreadful journey. As things fell out it had gone off more easily than they looked it should. Whether the cold had got into the hurt or whatever the cause might be, the knife-wound in Erlend's breast had festered, and constrained him to lie sick some while in the hospice at Roaldstad, Sir Björn tending him. But that Erlend was wounded made it easier to win belief for their tale of how that other things had befallen.

When he was fit to journey on, he had taken the dead woman with him in a coffin all the way to Oslo. There, by Sira Jon's help, he had won for her Christian burial in the churchyard of the old church of St. Nikolaus that had been pulled down. Then had he made confession to the Bishop of Oslo himself, and the Bishop had laid on him as penance to go on pilgrimage to the Holy Blood at Schwerin.* Now was he gone out of the land.

She could not make pilgrimage to any place on earth, and find absolution. For her there was naught but to sit here and wait and think, and strive to hold out in the struggle with her father and mother. A strange wintry-cold light fell on all her memories of meetings with Erlend. She thought of his vehemency—in love and in grief—and it was borne in on her that had she been able, like him, to take up all things of a sudden, and straightway rush forward with them headlong, afterwards maybe they might have seemed less fearful and heavy to bear. At times, too, she would think: maybe Erlend will give me up. It seemed to her she must always have had a little lurking fear that if things grew too hard for them he would fail her. But she would never give *him* up, unless he himself loosed her from all vows.

So the winter dragged on toward its end. And Kristin could not cheat herself any more; she had to see that the hardest trial of all lay before them—that Ulvhild had not long to live. And in the midst of her bitter sorrow for her sister she saw with horror that truly her own soul was wildered and eaten away with sin. For, with the dying child and the parents' unspeakable sorrow before her eyes, she was still brooding on this one thing—if Ulvhild dies, how can I bear to look at my father and not throw myself at his feet and confess all and beseech him to forgive me—and command me . . .

They were come far on in the long fast. Folks had begun slaughtering the small stock they had hoped to save alive, for fear they should die of themselves. And the people themselves sickened and pined from living on fish, with naught besides but a little wretched meal and flour.

* The Holy Blood at Schwerin, see Note 20.

Sira Eirik gave leave to the whole parish to eat milk food if they would. But few of the folk could come by a drop of milk.

Ulvhild lay in bed. She lay alone in the sisters' bed, and some one watched by her each night. It chanced sometimes that both Kristin and her father would be sitting by her. On such a night Lavrans said to his daughter:

"Mind you what Brother Edvin said that time about Ulvhild's lot? Even then the thought came to me that maybe he meant this. But I thrust it from me then."

Sometimes in these nights he would speak of this thing and that from the time when the children were small. Kristin sat there, white and desperate—she knew that behind the words her father was beseeching her.

One day Lavrans had gone with Kolbein to hunt out a bear's winter lair in the wooded hills to the north. They came home with a she-bear on a sledge, and Lavrans brought with him a living bear-cub in the bosom of his coat. Ulvhild brightened a little when he showed it to her. But Ragnfrid said that was surely no time to rear up such a beast—what would he do with it at a time like this?

"I will rear it up and bind it before my daughters' bower," said Lavrans, laughing harshly.

But they could not get for the cub the rich milk it needed, and Lavrans had to kill it a few days after.

The sun had gained so much strength now that sometimes, at midday, the roofs would drip a little. The titmice clambered about, clinging on the sunny side of the timber walls, and pecked till the wood rang, digging for the flies sleeping in the cracks. Over the rolling fields around, the snow shone hard and bright as silver.

At last one evening clouds began to draw together over the moon. And the next morning the folk at Jörundgaard woke in the midst of a whirling world of snow that shut in their sight on every hand.

That day they knew that Ulvhild was dying.

All the house-folk were indoors, and Sira Eirik came over to them. Many candles were burning in the hall. Early in the evening Ulvhild passed away quietly and peacefully, in her mother's arms.

Ragnfrid bore it better than any had thought possible. The father and mother sat together; both were weeping very quietly. All in the room were weeping. When Kristin went across to her father, he laid his arm round her shoulders. He felt how she shook and trembled, and he drew her close in to him. But to her it seemed that he must feel as if she were farther from him far than the dead child in the bed.

She understood not how it was that she still held out. She scarce remembered herself what it was she held out for; but, dulled and dumb with grief as she was, she held herself up and did not yield. . . .

. . . A few planks were torn up from the church floor in front of St. Thomas's shrine, and a grave was hewn in the stone-hard ground beneath for Ulvhild Lavransdatter.

It was snowing thick and silently all through those days, while the child lay in the dead-straw; it was snowing still when she was borne to the grave; and it went on snowing, almost without cease, till a whole month was out.

To the folk of the Dale, waiting and waiting for the spring to deliver them, it seemed as though it would never come. The days grew long and light, and the steam-cloud from the melting snow lay on all the valley as long as the sun shone. But the cold still held the air, and there was no strength in the heat to overcome it. By night it froze hard—there was loud cracking from the ice, there were booming sounds from the distant fells; and the wolves howled and the fox barked down among the farms as at midwinter. Men stripped the bark from the trees for their cattle, but they dropped down dead in their stalls by scores. None could tell how all this was to end.

Kristin went out on such a day, when water was trickling in the ruts, and the snow on the fields around glistened like silver. The snow-wreaths had been eaten away hollow on the side toward the sun, so that the fine ice-trellis of the snow-crust edges broke with a silver tinkle when her foot touched them. But everywhere, where the smallest shadow fell, the sharp cold held the air and the snow was hard.

She went upward towards the church—she knew not herself what she went to do, but something drew her there. Her father was there—some of the free-holders, guild-brothers, were to meet in the cloister-way, she knew.

Half-way up the hill she met the troop of farmers, coming down. Sira Eirik was with them. The men were all on foot; they walked stoopingly in a dark, shaggy knot, and spoke no word together. They gave back her greeting sullenly as she went by them.

Kristin thought how far away the time was when every soul in the parish had been her friend. Like enough all men knew now that she was a bad daughter. Perhaps they knew yet more about her. It might well be that all believed now there had been some truth in the old talk about her and Arne and Bentein. It might be that she had fallen into the worst ill-fame. She held her head high and passed on toward the church.

The door stood ajar. It was cold in the church, yet was it as though a mild warmth streamed into her heart from the brown dusky hall with the high, upspringing pillars holding up the darkness under the roof-beams. There was no light on the altars, but a ray of sun shone in through the chink of the door and gleamed faintly back from the pictures and the holy vessels.

Far in before the altar of St. Thomas she saw her father kneeling with head bent forward on his folded hands, which held his cap crushed to his breast.

Shrinking back in fear and sadness, Kristin stole out and stood in the cloister-way, with her hands about two of its small pillars. Framed in the arch between them she saw Jörundgaard lying below, and behind her home the pale blue haze that filled the valley. Where the river lay stretched through the countryside its ice and water sent out white sparkles in the sunshine. But the alder thickets along its bed were yellow-brown with blossom, even the pine-wood up by the church was tinged with spring green, and there was a piping and twittering and whistling of little birds in the grove near by. Ay, there had been bird-song like this each evening after the sun was down.

And she felt that the longing she thought must have been racked out of her long since, the longing in her body and her blood, was stirring now again, faintly and feebly, as about to waken from a winter sleep.

Lavrans Björgulfsön came out and locked the church door behind him. He came and stood by his daughter, looking out through the arch next to her. She saw how the winter gone by had harrowed her father's face. She understood not herself how she could touch now on what was between them, but the words seemed to rush out of themselves:

"Is it true what mother told me the other day—that you said to her: had it been Arne Gyrdsön you would have given me my will?"

"Ay," said Lavrans, not looking at her.

"You said not so while yet Arne lived," said Kristin.

"It never came in question. I saw well enough that the boy held you dear—but he said nothing—and he was young—and I marked not ever that you had such thoughts towards him. You could scarce think I would *proffer* my daughter to a man of no estate?" He smiled slightly. "But I loved the boy," he said, in a low voice; "and had I seen you pining for love of him——"

They stood still, gazing. Kristin felt that her father was looking at her—she strove hard to be calm of face, but she felt herself grow deadly white. Then her father came towards her, put both his arms around her and pressed her strongly to him. He bent her head backwards, looked down into his daughter's face, and then hid it again on his shoulder.

"Jesus Kristus, little Kristin, are you *so* unhappy——?"

"I think I shall die of it, father," she said, her face pressed to him.

She burst into weeping. But she wept because she had felt in his caress and seen in his eyes that now he was so worn out with pain that he could not hold out against her any more. She had overcome him.

Far on in the night she was wakened in the dark by her father's touch on her shoulder.

"Get up," he said softly. "Do you hear——?"

She heard the singing of the wind round the house-corners—the deep, full note of the south wind, heavy with wetness. Streams were pouring from the roof; there was the whisper of rain falling on soft, melting snow.

Kristin flung her dress on her back and went after her father to the outer door. They stood together looking out into the twilight of the May night. Warm wind and rain smote against them; the heavens were a welter of tangled drifting rain-clouds, the woods roared, the wind whistled between the houses, and from far up in the fells they heard the dull boom of snow-masses falling.

Kristin felt for her father's hand and held it. He had called her that he might show her this. So had it been between them before, that he would have done this; and so it was now again.

When they went in to go to bed again, Lavrans said:

"The stranger serving-man that came last week brought me letters from Sir Munan Baardsön. He is minded to come up the Dale to our parts next summer to see his mother; and he asked if he might meet me and have speech with me."

"What will you answer him, my father? she whispered.

"That can I not tell you now," said Lavrans. "But I will speak with him; and then must I order this matter so as I may deem I can answer it to God, my daughter."

Kristin crept in again beside Ramborg, and Lavrans went and lay down by the side of his sleeping wife. He lay thinking that if the flood came over-sudden and strong there were few places in the parish that lay so much in its path as Jörundgaard. Folk said there was a prophecy that some day the river would carry it away.

V

S p r i n g came at a single bound. Only a few days after the sudden thaw the whole parish lay dark brown under the flooding rain. The waters rushed foaming down the hillsides, the river swelled up and lay in the valley-bottom, like a great leaden-grey lake, with lines of tree-tops floating on its waters and a treacherous bubbling furrow where the current ran. At Jörundgaard the water stood far up over the fields. But everywhere the mischief done was less than folks had feared.

Of necessity the spring work was thrown late, and the people sowed their scanty corn with prayers to God that He would save it from the night-frosts in autumn. And it looked as though He would hearken to them and a little ease their burdens. June came in with mild, growing weather, the summer was good, and folk set their faces forward in hope that the marks of the evil year might be wiped out in time.

The hay harvest had been got in, when one evening four men rode up to Jörundgaard. First came two knights, and behind them their serving-men; and the knights were Sir Munan Baardsön and Sir Baard Petersön of Hestnæs.

Ragnfrid and Lavrans had the board spread in the upper hall, and beds made ready in the guest-room over the store-house. But Lavrans begged the knights to tarry with their errand till the next day, when they should be rested from their journey.

Sir Munan led the talk throughout the meal; he turned much to Kristin in talking, and spoke as if he and she were well acquainted. She saw that this was not to her father's liking. Sir Munan was square built, red-faced, ugly, talkative, and something of a buffoon in his bearing. People called him Dumpy Munan or Dance Munan. But for all his flighty bearing, Lady Aashild's son was a man of understanding and parts, who had been used by the Crown more than once in matters of trust, and was known to have a word in the counsels of them that guided the affairs of the kingdom. He held his mother's heritage in the Skogheim Hundred; was exceeding rich, and had made a rich marriage. Lady Katrin, his wife, was hard-featured beyond the common, and seldom opened her mouth; but her husband ever spoke of her as if she were the wisest of dames, so that she was known in jest as Lady Katrin the Ready-witted, or the Silver-tongued. They seemed to live with each other well and lovingly, though Sir Munan was known all too well for the looseness of his life both before and after his marriage.

Sir Baard Petersön was a comely and a stately old man, even though now somewhat ample of girth and heavy-limbed. His hair and beard were faded now, but their hue was still as much yellow as 'twas white. Since King Magnus Haakonsön's death he had lived retired, managing his great possessions in Nordmöre. He was a widower for the second time, and had many children, who, it was said, were all comely, well-nurtured and well-to-do.

The next day Lavrans and his guests went up to the upper hall for their parley. Lavrans would have had his wife be present with them, but she would not.

"This matter must be in your hands wholly. You know well 'twill be the heaviest of sorrows for our daughter if it should come to naught; but I see well that there are but too many things that may make against this marriage."

Sir Munan brought forth a letter from Erlend Nikulaussön. Erlend's proffer was that Lavrans should fix, himself, each and all of the conditions,* if he would betroth his daughter Kristin to him. Erlend was willing to have all his possessions valued and his incomings appraised by impartial men, and to grant to Kristin such extra-gift and morning-gift, that she would possess a third of all his estate besides her own dowry and all such heritage as might come to her from her kin, should she be left a widow without living children. Further, his proffer was to grant Kristin full power to deal at her pleasure with her share of the common estate, both what she had of her own kindred and what came to her from her husband. But if Lavrans wished for other terms of settlement, Erlend was most willing to hear his wishes and to follow them in all things. To one thing only he asked that Kristin's kindred, on their side, should bind themselves: that, should the guardianship of his children and Kristin's ever come to them, they would never try to set aside the gifts he had made to his children by Eline Ormsdatter, but would let all such gifts hold good, as having passed from his estate before his entry into wedlock with Kristin Lavransdatter. At the end of all Erlend made proffer to hold the wedding in all seemly state at Husaby.

Lavrans spoke in reply:

"This is a fair proffer. I see by it that your kinsman has it much at heart to come to terms with me. All the more is this plain to me by reason that he has moved you, Sir Munan, to come for the second time on such an errand to a man like me, who am of little weight beyond my own countryside; and that a knight like you, Sir Baard, hath been at the pains of making such a journey to further his cause. But concerning Erlend's proffer I would say this: my daughter has not been bred up to deal herself with the ordering of goods and gear, but I have

* Marriage Settlements, see Note 21.

ever hoped to give her to such a man as that I could lay the maid's welfare in his hands with an easy mind. I know not, indeed, whether Kristin be fit to be set in such authority, but I can scarce believe that 'twould be for her good. She is mild of mood and biddable—and 'twas one of the reasons I have had in mind in setting myself against this marriage, that 'tis known Erlend has shown want of understanding in more matters than one. Had she been a power-loving, bold and head-strong woman, then indeed the matter had taken on another face."

Sir Munan burst out laughing:

"Dear Lavrans, lament you that the maid is not headstrong enough?" and Sir Baard said with a little smile:

"Methinks your daughter has shown that she lacks not a will of her own—for two years now she has held to Erlend clean against your will."

Lavrans said:

"I have not forgotten it; yet do I know well what I say. She has suffered sorely herself all this time she has stood against me; nor will she long be glad with a husband who cannot rule her."

"Nay, then the devil's in it!" said Sir Munan. "Then must your daughter be far unlike all the women I have known; for I have never seen *one* that was not fain to rule herself—and her man to boot!"

Lavrans shrugged his shoulders and made no answer.

Then said Baard Petersön:

"I can well believe, Lavrans Björgulfsön, that you have found this marriage between your daughter and my foster-son no more to your liking, since the woman who had lived with him came to the end we know of last year. But you must know it has come out now that the unhappy woman had let herself be led astray by another man, Erlend's steward at Husaby. Erlend knew of this when he went with her down the Dale; he had proffered to portion her fittingly, if the man would wed her."

"Are you well assured that this is so?" asked Lavrans. "And yet I know not," he said again, "if the thing is anyway bettered thereby. Hard must it be for a woman come of good kindred to go into a house hand in hand with the master, and be led out by the serving-man."

Munan Baardsön took the word:

"'Tis plain to me, Lavrans Björgulfsön, that what goes against my cousin most with you, is that he has had these hapless dealings with Sigurd Saksulvsön's wife. And true it is that 'twas not well done of him. But in God's name, man, you must remember this—here was this young boy dwelling in one house with a young and fair woman, and she had an old, cold, strengthless husband—and the night is a half-year long up there: methinks a man could scarce look for aught else to happen, unless Erlend had been a very saint. There is no denying it: Erlend had made at all times but a sorry monk; but methinks your young, fair daughter would give you little thanks, should you give her a monkish husband. True it is that Erlend bore himself like a fool then, and a yet greater fool since. . . . But the thing should not stand against him for ever—we his kinsmen have striven to help the boy to his feet again; the woman is dead; and Erlend has done all in his power to care for her body and her soul; the Bishop of Oslo himself hath absolved him of his sin, and now is he come home again made clean by the Holy Blood at Schwerin—would you be stricter than the Bishop of Oslo, and the Archbishop at Schwerin—or whoever it may be that hath charge of that precious blood . . .?

"Dear Lavrans, true it is that chastity is a fair thing indeed; but 'tis verily hard for a grown man to attain to it without a special gift of grace from God. By St. Olav . . . Ay, and you should remember too that the holy King himself was not granted that gift till his life here below was drawing to an end—very like 'twas God's will that he should first beget that doughty youth King Magnus, who smote down the heathen when they raged against the Nordlands. I wot well King Olav had that son by another than his Queen—yet doth he sit amidst the highest saints in the host of heaven. Ay, I can see in your face that you deem this unseemly talk——"

Sir Baard broke in:

"Lavrans Björgulfsön, I liked this matter no better than you, when first Erlend came to me and said he had set his heart on a maid that was handfast to another. But since then I have come to know that there is so great kindness between these two young folk, that 'twould be great pity to part their loves. Erlend was with me at the last Yuletide feasting King Haakon held for his men—they met together there, and scarce had they seen each other when your daughter swooned away and lay a long while as one dead—and I saw in my foster-son's face that he would rather lose his life than lose her."

Lavrans sat still awhile before answering:

"Ay; all such things sound fair and fine when a man hears them told in a knightly saga of the southlands. But we are not in Bretland here, and 'tis like you too would ask more in the man you would choose for son-in-law than that he had brought your daughter to swoon away for love in all folks' sight——"

The two others were silent, and Lavrans went on:

"'Tis in my mind, good sirs, that had Erlend Nikulaussön not made great waste both of his goods and of his fame, you would scarce be sitting here pleading so strongly with a man of my estate that I should give my daughter to him. But I would be loth it should be said of

Kristin that 'twas an honour for her to wed a great estate and a man from amongst the highest in the land—after the man had so beshamed himself, that he could not look to make a better match, or keep undiminished the honour of his house."

He rose in heat, and began walking to and fro.

But Sir Munan started up:

"Now, before God, Lavrans, if the talk is of shame, I would have you know you are over-proud in——"

Sir Baard broke in quickly, going up to Lavrans:

"Proud you are, Lavrans—you are like those udal farmers we have heard of in olden times, who would have naught to do with the titles the Kings would have given them, because their pride could not brook that folk should say they owed thanks to any but themselves. I tell you, that were Erlend still master of all the honour and riches the boy was born to, yet would I never deem that I demeaned him or myself in asking a well-born and wealthy man to give his daughter to my foster-son, if I knew that the two young creatures might break their hearts if they were parted. And the rather," he said in a low voice, laying his hand on Lavrans' shoulder, "if so it were that 'twould be best for the souls of both they should wed each other."

Lavrans drew away from the other's hand; his face grew set and cold:

"I scarce believe I understand your meaning, Sir Knight?"

The two men looked at each other for a space; then Sir Baard said:

"I mean that Erlend has told me, they two have sworn troth to each other with the dearest oaths. Maybe you would say that you have power to loose your child from her oath, since she swore without your will. But Erlend you cannot loose. . . . And for aught I can see what most stands in the road is your pride—and the hate you bear to sin. But in that 'tis to me as though you were minded to be stricter than God Himself, Lavrans Björgulfsön."

Lavrans answered somewhat uncertainly:

"It may be there is truth in this that you say to me, Sir Baard. But what most has set me against this match is that I have deemed Erlend to be so unsure a man that I could not trust my daughter to his hands."

"Methinks I can answer for my foster-son now," said Baard quietly. "Kristin is so dear to him that I know, if you will give her to him, he will prove in the event such a son-in-law that you shall have no cause of grief."

Lavrans did not answer at once. Then Sir Baard said earnestly, holding out his hand:

"In God's name, Lavrans Björgulfsön, give your consent!"

Lavrans laid his hand in Sir Baard's:
"In God's name!"

Ragnfrid and Kristin were called to the upper hall, and Lavrans told them his will. Sir Baard greeted the two women in fair and courtly fashion; Sir Munan took Ragnfrid by the hand and spoke to her in seemly wise, but Kristin he greeted in the foreign fashion with a kiss, and he took time over his greeting. Kristin felt that her father looked at her while this was doing.

"How like you your new kinsman, Sir Munan?" he asked jestingly, when he was alone with her for a moment late that evening.

Kristin looked beseechingly at him. Then he stroked her face a little and said no more.

When Sir Baard and Sir Munan went to their room, Munan broke out:

"Not a little would I give to see this Lavrans Björgulfsön's face, should he come to know the truth about this precious daughter of his. Here have you and I had to beg on our knees to win for Erlend a woman he has had with him in Brynhild's house many times——"

"Hold your peace—no word of that," answered Sir Baard in wrath. "'Twas the worst deed Erlend ever did, to lure that child to such places—and see that Lavrans never hear aught of it; the best that can happen now for all, is that those two should be friends."

The feast for the drinking of the betrothal ale was appointed to be held that same autumn. Lavrans said he could not make the feast very great, the year before had been such a bad one in the Dale; but to make up he would bear the cost of the wedding himself, and hold it at Jörundgaard in all seemly state. He named the bad year again as the cause why he required that the time of betrothal should last a year.

VI

F o r more reasons than one the betrothal feast was put off; it was not held till the New Year; but Lavrans agreed that the bridal need not therefore be delayed; it was to be just after Michaelmas, as was fixed at first.

So Kristin sat now at Jörundgaard as Erlend's betrothed in all men's sight. Along with her mother she looked over all the goods and gear that had been gathered and saved up for her portion, and strove to add still more to the great piles of bedding and clothes; for when once

Lavrans had given his daughter to the master of Husaby, it was his will that naught should be spared.

Kristin wondered herself at times that she did not feel more glad. But, in spite of all the busyness, there was no true gladness at Jörundgaard.

Her father and mother missed Ulvhild sorely, that she saw. But she understood too that 'twas not that alone which made them so silent and so joyless. They were kind to her, but when they talked with her of her betrothed, she saw that they did but force themselves to it to please her and show her kindness; 'twas not that they themselves had a mind to speak of Erlend. They had not learned to take more joy in the marriage she was making, now they had come to know the man. Erlend, too, had kept himself quiet and withdrawn the short time he had been at Jörundgaard for the betrothal—and like enough this could not have been otherwise, thought Kristin; for he knew it was with no goodwill her father had given his consent.

She herself and Erlend had scarce had the chance to speak ten words alone together. And it had brought a strange unwonted feeling, to sit together thus in all folks' sight; at such times they had little to say, by reason of the many things between them that could not be said. There arose in her a doubtful fear, vague and dim, but always present—perhaps 'twould make it hard for them in some way after they were wedded, that they had come all too near to each other at the first, and after had lived so long quite parted.

But she tried to thrust the fear away. It was meant that Erlend should visit them at Whitsuntide; he had asked Lavrans and Ragnfrid if they had aught against his coming, and Lavrans had laughed a little, and answered that Erlend might be sure his daughter's bridegroom would be welcome.

At Whitsuntide they would be able to go out together; they would have a chance to speak together as in the old days, and then surely it would fade away, the shadow that had come between them in this long time apart, when each had gone about alone bearing a burden the other could not share.

At Easter Simon Andressön and his wife came to Formo. Kristin saw them in the church. Simon's wife was standing not far off from her.

She must be much older than he, thought Kristin—nigh thirty years old. Lady Halfrid was little and slender and thin, but she had an exceeding gracious visage. The very hue of her pale brown hair as it flowed in waves from under her linen coif, seemed, as it were, so gentle, and her eyes too were full of gentleness; they were great grey eyes flecked with tiny golden specks. Every feature of her face was fine and pure—but her skin was something dull and grey, and when she opened her mouth one saw that her teeth were not good. She looked not as though she were strong, folks said indeed that she was sickly—she had miscarried more than once already, Kristin had heard. She wondered how it would fare with Simon with this wife.

The Jörundgaard folk and they of Formo had greeted each other across the church-green more than once, but had not spoken. But on Easter-day Simon was in the church without his wife. He went across to Lavrans, and they spoke together awhile. Kristin heard Ulvhild's name spoken. Afterward he spoke with Ragnfrid. Ramborg, who was standing by her mother, called out aloud: "I mind you quite well—*I* know who you are." Simon lifted the child up a little and twirled her round: "'Tis well done of you, Ramborg, not to have forgotten me." Kristin he only greeted from some way off; and her father and mother said no word afterward of the meeting.

But Kristin pondered much upon it. For all that had come and gone, it had been strange to see Simon Darre again as a wedded man. So much that was past came to life again at the sight; she remembered her own blind and all-yielding love for Erlend in those days. Now, she felt, there was some change in it. The thought came to her: how if Simon had told his wife how they had come to part, he and she—but she knew he had kept silence—"for my father's sake," she thought scoffingly. 'Twas a poor showing, and strange, that she should be still living here unwed, in her parents' house. But at least they were betrothed; Simon could see that they had had their way in spite of all. Whatever else Erlend might have done, to *her* he had held faithfully, and she had not been loose or wanton.

One evening in early spring Ragnfrid had to send down the valley to old Gunhild, the widow who sewed furs. The evening was so fair that Kristin asked if she might not go; at last they gave her leave, since all the men were busy.

It was after sunset, and a fine white frost-haze was rising toward the gold-green sky. Kristin heard at each hoof-stroke the brittle sound of the evening's ice as it broke and flew outwards in tinkling splinters. But from all the roadside brakes there was a happy noise of birds singing, softly but full-throated with spring, into the twilight.

Kristin rode sharply downwards; she thought not much of anything, but felt only it was good to be abroad alone once more. She rode with her eyes fixed on the new moon sinking down toward the mountain ridge on the far side of the Dale; and she had near fallen from her horse when he suddenly swerved aside and reared.

She saw a dark body lying huddled together at the roadside—and at first she was afraid. The hateful fear that had passed into her blood—the fear of meeting people alone by the way—she could never quite be rid of. But she thought 'twas maybe a wayfaring man who had fallen sick; so when she had mastered her horse again, she turned and rode back, calling out to know who it was.

The bundle stirred a little, and a voice said:

"Methinks 'tis you yourself, Kristin Lavransdatter——"

"Brother Edvin?" she asked softly. She came near to thinking this was some phantom or some deviltry sent to trick her. But she went nigh to him; it was the old monk himself, and he could not raise himself from the ground without help.

"Dear my Father—are you out wandering at this time of the year?" she said in wonder.

"Praise be to God, who sent you this way to-night," said the monk. Kristin saw that his whole body was shaking. "I was coming north to you folks, but my legs would carry me no farther this night. Almost I deemed 'twas God's will that I should lie down and die on the roads I have been wandering about on all my life. But I was fain to see you once again, my daughter——"

Kristin helped the monk up on her horse; then led it homeward by the bridle, holding him on. And all the time he was lamenting that now she would get her feet wet in the icy slush, she could hear him moaning softly with pain.

He told her that he had been at Eyabu since Yule. Some rich farmers of the parish had vowed in the bad year to beautify their church with new adornments. But the work had gone slowly; he had been sick the last of the winter—the evil was in his stomach—it could bear no food, and he vomited blood. He believed himself he had not long to live, and he longed now to be home in his cloister, for he was fain to die there among his own brethren. But he had a mind first to come north up the Dale one last time, and so he had set out, along with the monk who came from Hamar to be the new prior of the pilgrim hospice at Roaldstad. From Fron he had come on alone.

"I heard that you were betrothed," he said, "to that man—and then such a longing came on me to see you. It seemed to me a sore thing that that should be our last meeting, that time in our church at Oslo. It has been a heavy burden on my heart, Kristin, that you had strayed away into the path where is no peace——"

Kristin kissed the monk's hand.

"Truly I know not, Father, what I have done, or how deserved, that you show me such great love."

The monk answered in a low voice:

"I have thought many a time, Kristin, that had it so befallen we had met more often, then might you have come to be as my daughter in the spirit."

"Mean you that you would have brought me to turn my heart to the holy life of the cloister?" asked Kristin. Then, a little after, she said: "Sira Eirik laid a command on me that, should I not win my father's consent and be wed with Erlend, then must I join with a godly sisterhood and make atonement for my sins——"

"I have prayed many a time that the longing for the holy life might come to you," said Brother Edvin. "But not since you told me that you wot of—I would have had you come to God, wearing your garland, Kristin——"

When they came to Jörundgaard Brother Edvin had to be lifted down and borne in to his bed. They laid him in the old winter-house, in the hearth-room, and cared for him most tenderly. He was very sick, and Sira Eirik came and tended him with medicines for the body and the soul. But the priest said the old man's sickness was cancer, and it could not be that he had long to live. Brother Edvin himself said that when he had gained a little strength he would journey south again and try to come home to his own cloister. But Sira Eirik told the others he could not believe this was to be thought of.

It seemed to all at Jörundgaard that a great peace and gladness had come to them with the monk. Folks came and went in the hearth-room all day long, and there was never any lack of watchers to sit at nights by the sick man. As many as had time flocked in to listen, when Sira Eirik came over and read to the dying man from godly books, and they talked much with Brother Edvin of spiritual things. And though much of what he said was dark and veiled, even as his speech was wont to be, it seemed to these folks that he strengthened and comforted their souls, because each and all could see that Brother Edvin was wholly filled with the love of God.

But the monk was fain to hear, too, of all kind of other things—asked the news of the parishes round, and had Lavrans tell him all the story of the evil year of drought. There were some folk who had betaken them to evil courses in that tribulation, turning to such helpers as Christian men should most abhor. Some way in over the ridges west of the Dale was a place in the mountains where were certain great white stones, of obscene shapes, and some men had fallen so low as to sacrifice boars and gib-cats before these abominations. So Sira Eirik moved some of the boldest, most God-fearing farmers to come with him one night and break the stones in pieces. Lavrans had been with them, and could bear witness that the stones were all besmeared with blood, and there lay bones and other refuse all around them. 'Twas said that up in Heidal the people had had an old crone sit out on a great earthfast rock three Thursday nights, chanting ancient spells.

One night Kristin sat alone by Brother Edvin. At midnight he woke up, and seemed to be suffering great pain. Then he bade Kristin take the book of the Miracles of the Virgin Mary, which Sira Eirik had lent to Brother Edvin, and read to him.

Kristin was little used to read aloud, but she set herself down on the step of the bed and placed the candle by her side; she laid the book on her lap and read as well as she could.

In a little while she saw that the sick man was lying with teeth set tight, clenching his wasted hands as the fits of agony took him.

"You are suffering much, dear Father," said Kristin sorrowfully.

"It seems so to me, now. But I know 'tis but that God has made me a little child again, and is tossing me about, up and down. . . .

"I mind me one time when I was little—four winters old I was then —I had run away from home into the woods. I lost myself, and wandered about many days and nights. My mother was with the folks that found me, and when she caught me up in her arms, I mind me well, she bit me in my neck. I thought it was that she was angry with me—but afterward I knew better. . . .

"I long, myself, now, to be home out of this forest. It is written: 'Forsake ye all things and follow Me'—but there has been all too much in this world that I had no mind to forsake——"

"*You*, Father?" said Kristin. "Ever have I heard all men say that you have been a pattern for pure life and poverty and humbleness——"

The monk laughed slily.

"Ay, a young child like you thinks, maybe, there are no other lures in the world than pleasure and riches and power. But I say to you, these are small things men find by the wayside; and I—I have loved the ways themselves—not the small things of the world did I love, but the *whole* world. God gave me grace to love Lady Poverty and Lady Chastity from my youth up, and thus methought with these play-fellows it was safe to wander, and so I have roved and wandered, and would have been fain to roam over all the ways of the earth. And my heart and my thoughts have roamed and wandered too—I fear me I have often gone astray in my thoughts on the most hidden things. But now 'tis all over, little Kristin; I will home now to my house and lay aside all my own thoughts, and hearken to the clear words of the Gardian telling what I should believe and think concerning my sin and the mercy of God——"

A little while after, he dropped asleep. Kristin went and sat by the hearth, tending the fire. But well on in the morning, when she was nigh dozing off herself, of a sudden Brother Edvin spoke from the bed:

"Glad am I, Kristin, that this matter of you and Erlend Nikulaussön is brought to a good end."

Kristin burst out weeping:

"We have done so much wrong before we came so far. And what gnaws at my heart most is that I have brought my father so much sorrow. He has no joy in this wedding either. And even so he knows not; did he know all, I trow he would take his kindness quite from me."

"Kristin," said Brother Edvin gently, "see you not, child, that 'tis therefore you must keep it from him, and 'tis therefore you must give him no more cause of sorrow—because he never will call on you to pay the penalty. Nothing you could do could turn your father's heart from you."

A few days later Brother Edvin was grown so much better that he would fain set out on his journey southward. Since his heart was set on this, Lavrans had a kind of litter made, to be slung between two horses, and on this he brought the sick man as far south as to Lidstad; there they gave him fresh horses and men to tend him on his way, and in this wise was he brought as far as Hamar. There he died in the cloister of the Preaching Friars, and was buried in their church. Afterward the Barefoot Friars claimed that his body should be delivered to them; for that many folks all about in the parishes held him to be a holy man, and spoke of him by the name of Saint Evan. The peasants of the Uplands and the Dales, all the way north to Trondheim, prayed to him as a saint. So it came about that there was a long dispute between the two Orders about his body.

Kristin heard naught of this till long after. But she grieved sorely at parting from the monk. It seemed to her that he alone knew all her life—he had known the innocent child as she was in her father's keeping, and he had known her secret life with Erlend; so that he was, as it were, a link binding together all that had first been dear to her with all that now filled her heart and mind. Now was she quite cut off from herself as she had been in the time when she was yet a maid.

VII

"A y," said Ragnfrid, feeling with her hand the lukewarm brew in the vats, "methinks 'tis cool enough now to mix in the barm."

Kristin had been sitting in the brew-house doorway spinning, while she waited for the brew to cool. She laid down the spindle on the threshold, unwrapped the rug from the pail of risen yeast, and began measuring out.

"Shut the door first," bade her mother, "so the draught may not come in—you seem walking in your sleep, Kristin," she said testily.

Kristin poured the yeast into the vats, while Ragnfrid stirred.

. . . Geirhild Drivsdatter called on Hatt,* but he was Odin. So he came and helped her with the brewing; and he craved for his wage that which was between the vat and her. . . . 'Twas a saga that Lavrans had once told when she was little.

. . . That which was between the vat and her. . . .

Kristin felt dizzy and sick with the heat and the sweet, spicy-smelling steam that filled the dark close-shut brew-house.

Out in the farm-place Ramborg and a band of children were dancing in a ring, singing:

> "The eagle sits on the topmost hill-crag
> Crooking his golden claws——"

Kristin followed her mother through the little outer room where lay empty ale-kegs and all kinds of brewing gear. A door led from it out to a strip of ground between the back wall of the brew-house and the fence round the barley-field. A herd of pigs jostled each other, and bit and squealed as they fought over the lukewarm grains thrown out to them.

Kristin shaded her eyes against the blinding midday sunlight. The mother looked at the pigs, and said:

"With less than eighteen reindeer we shall never win through."

"Think you we shall need so many?" said her daughter absently.

"Ay, for we must have game to serve up with the pork each day," answered Ragnfrid. "And of wild-fowl and hare we shall scarce have more than will serve for the table in the upper hall. Remember, 'twill be well on toward two hundred people we shall have on the place—counting serving-folk and children—and the poor that have to be fed. And even should you and Erlend set forth on the fifth day, some of the guests, I trow, will stay out the week—at the least."

"You must stay here and look to the ale, Kristin," she went on. "'Tis time for me to get dinner for your father and the reapers."

Kristin fetched her spinning gear and sat herself down there in the back doorway. She put the distaff with the bunch of wool up under her arm-pit, but her hands, with the spindle in them, sank into her lap.

Beyond the fence the ears of barley gleamed silvery and silken in the

* Hatt, see Note 22.

sunshine. Above the song of the river she heard now and again from the meadows on the river-island the ring of a scythe—sometimes the iron would strike upon a stone. Her father and the house-folk were hard at work on the hay-making, to get it off their hands. For there was much to get through and to make ready against her wedding.

The scent of the lukewarm grains, and the rank smell of the swine—she grew qualmish again. And the midday heat made her so dizzy and faint. White and stiffly upright she sat and waited for it to pass over—she *would* not be sick again. . .

Never before had she felt what now she felt. 'Twas of no avail to try to tell herself for comfort; it was not certain yet—she might be wrong. . . . That which was between the vat and her. . . .

Eighteen reindeer. Well on toward two hundred wedding guests. . . . Folk would have a rare jest to laugh at when 'twas known that all this hubbub had but been about a breeding woman they had to see and get married before . . .

Oh no! She threw her spinning from her and started up as the sickness overcame her again. . . . Oh no! it was sure enough! . . .

They were to be wedded the second Sunday after Michaelmas, and the bridal was to last for five days. There were more than two months still to wait; they would be sure to see it on her—her mother and the other housewives of the parish. They were ever so wise in such things —knew them months before Kristin could understand how they saw them. "Poor thing, she grows so pale. . . ." Impatiently Kristin rubbed her hands against her cheeks; she felt that they were white and blood-less.

Before, she had so often thought: this must happen soon or late. And she had not feared it so terribly. But 'twould not have been the same then, when they could not—were forbidden to come together in lawful wise. It was counted—ay, a shame in a manner, and a sin too —but if 'twere two young things who *would not* let themselves be forced apart, folk remembered that 'twas so, and spoke of them with forbear-ance. *She* would not have been ashamed. But when such things hap-pened between a betrothed pair—there was naught for them but laughter and gross jesting. She saw it herself—one could not but laugh: here was brewing and mixing of wine, slaughtering and baking and cooking for a wedding that should be noised far abroad in the land—and she, the bride, grew qualmish if she but smelt food, and crept in a cold sweat behind the outhouses to be sick.

Erlend! She set her teeth hard in anger. He should have spared her this. For she had not been willing. He should have remembered that before, when all had been so unsure for her, when she had had naught to trust to but his love, she had ever, ever gladly been his. He should have let her be now, when she tried to deny him because she thought 'twas not well of them to take aught by stealth, after her father had joined their hands together in the sight of Erlend's kinsmen and hers. But he had taken her to him, half by force, with laughter and caresses; so that she had not had strength enough to show him she was in earnest in her denial.

She went in and saw to the beer in the vats, then came back again and stood leaning on the fence. The standing grain moved gently in shining ripples before a breath of wind. She could not remember any year when she had seen the corn-fields bear such thick and abundant growth. . . . The river glittered far off, and she heard her father's voice shouting—she could not catch the words, but she could hear the reapers on the island laughing.

. . . Should she go to her father and tell him : 'Twould be best to let be all this weary bustle and let Erlend and her come together quietly without church-wedding or splendid feasts—now that the one thing needful was that she should bear the name of wife before 'twas plain to all men that she bore Erlend's child under her heart already?

He would be a laughing-stock, Erlend too, as much as she—or even more, for he was no green boy any longer. But it was he who would have this wedding; he had set his heart on seeing her stand as his bride in silk and velvets and tall golden crown—*that* was his will, and it had been his will, too, to possess her in those sweet secret hours of last spring. She had yielded to him in that. And she must do his will too in this other thing.

But in the end 'twas like he would be forced to see—no one could have it both ways in such things. He had talked so much of the great Yuletide feast he would hold at Husaby the first year she sat there as mistress of his house—how he would show forth to all his kinsmen and friends and all the folks from far around the fair wife he had won. Kristin smiled scornfully. A seemly thing 'twould be this Yuletide, such a home-coming feast!

Her time would be at St. Gregory's Mass or thereabout. Thoughts seemed to swarm and jostle in her mind when she said to herself that at Gregory's Mass she was to bear a child. There was some fear among the thoughts—she remembered how her mother's cries had rung all round the farm-place for two whole days, the time that Ulvhild was born. At Ulvsvold two young wives had died in childbirth, one after the other—and Sigurd of Loptsgaard's first wives too. And her own father's mother, whose name she bore. . . .

But fear was not uppermost in her mind. She had often thought, when after that first time she saw no sign that she was with child— maybe this was to be their punishment—hers and Erlend's. She would

always be barren. They would wait and wait in vain for what they
had feared before, would hope as vainly as of old they had feared needlessly—till at last they would know that one day they should be borne
forth from the home of his fathers, and be as though they had never
been—for his brother was a priest, and the children he had could
inherit naught from him. Dumpy Munan and his sons would come in
and sit in their seats, and Erlend would be blotted out from the line ot
his kindred.

She pressed her hand hard to her body. It was there—between the
fence and her—between the vat and her. 'Twas between her and all
the world—Erlend's own son. She had made the trial already that she
had once heard Lady Aashild speak of; with blood from her right arm
and her left. 'Twas a son that was coming to her—whatever fate he
was to bring. . . . She remembered her dead little brothers, her parents'
sorrowful faces when they spoke of them; she remembered all the
times she had seen them both in despair for Ulvhild's sake—and the
night when Ulvhild died. And she thought of all the sorrow she herself had brought them, of her father's grief-worn face—and the end
was not yet of the sorrows she was to bring on her father and mother.

And yet—and yet. Kristin laid her head on the arm that rested on
the fence; the other hand she still held to her body. Even if it brought
her new sorrows, even if it led her feet down to death—she would
rather die in bearing Erlend a son than that they should both die one
day, and leave their houses standing empty, and the corn on their
lands should wave for strangers. . . .

She heard a footstep in the room behind her. The ale! thought
Kristin—I should have seen to it long ago. She stood up and turned
—and Erlend came stooping through the doorway and stepped out
into the sunlight—his face shining with gladness.

"Is this where you are?" he asked. "And not a step will you come
to meet me, even?" he said; and came and threw his arms about her.

"Dearest; are you come hither?" she said in wonder.

It was plain he was just alighted from his horse—his cloak still hung
from his shoulder, and his sword at his side—he was unshaven, travel-
soiled and covered with dust. He was clad in a red surcoat that hung
in folds from its collar and was open up the sides almost to the arm-
pits. As they passed through the brew-house and across the courtyard,
the coat swung and flapped about him so that his thighs showed right
up to the waist. His legs bent a little outwards when he walked—it
was strange she had never marked it before—she had only seen that
he had long slender legs, with fine ankles and small well-shaped feet.

Erlend had come well attended—with five men and four led horses.
He told Ragnfrid that he was come to fetch Kristin's goods—'twould

be more homely for her, he thought, to find the things awaiting her at Husaby when she came thither. And so late in the autumn as the wedding was to be, it might be harder then to have the goods brought across the hills—besides they might easily be spoiled by the sea-water on shipboard. Now the Abbot of Nidarholm had proffered to give him leave to send them by the Laurentius galleass—'twas meant she would sail from Veöy about Assumption Day. So he was come to have the goods carted over to Romsdal and down to Næs.

He sat in the doorway of the kitchen-house, drinking ale and talking while Ragnfrid and Kristin plucked the wild-duck Lavrans had brought home the day before. Mother and daughter were alone on the place; all the women were busy raking in the meadows. He looked so glad and happy—he was pleased with himself for coming on such a wise and prudent errand.

Ragnfrid went out, and Kristin stayed minding the spit with the roasting birds. Through the open door she could catch a glimpse of Erlend's men lying in the shadow on the other side of the courtyard, with the ale-bowl circling among them. Erlend himself sat on the threshold, chatting and laughing—the sun shone right down on his uncovered coal-black hair; she spied some white threads in it. Ay, he must be near thirty-two years old—but he bore himself like a mischievous boy. She knew she would not be able to tell him of her trouble—time enough when he saw it for himself. Laughing tenderness streamed through her heart, over the hard little spot of anger at its core, like a glittering river flowing over stones.

She loved him above all on earth—her soul was filled with her love, though all the time she saw and remembered all those other things. How ill this gallant in the fine red surcoat, with silver spurs on heel and belt adorned with gold, suited with the busy harvest-time at Jörundgaard. . . . She marked well, too, that her father came not up to the farm, though her mother had sent Ramborg down to the river to bear him word of the guest that was come.

Erlend stood beside her and passed his arm around her shoulders: "Can you believe it!" he said joyfully. "Seems it not marvellous to you—that 'tis for our wedding, all this toil and bustle?"

Kristin gave him a kiss and thrust him aside—then turned to basting the birds and bade him stand out of the way. No, she would not say it. . . .

It was not till supper-time that Lavrans came back to the farm— along with the other harvesters. He was clad much like his workmen in an undyed wadmal coat cut off at the knees and loose breeches reaching to the ankles; he walked barefoot, with his scythe over his shoulder. There was naught in his dress to mark him off from the serving-men, save the leathern shoulder-piece that made a perch for the hawk he bore on his left shoulder. He led Ramborg by the hand.

He greeted his son-in-law heartily enough, begging him to forgive that he had not come before—'twas that they must push on with the farmwork as hard as they could, for he himself had a journey to make to the market-town between the hay and the corn harvests. But when Erlend told the errand he had come on, as they sat at the supper-board, Lavrans grew something out of humour.

'Twas impossible he should spare carts and horses for such work at this time. Erlend answered: he had brought four pack-horses with him. But Lavrans said there would be three cartloads at the least. Besides, the maid must have her wearing apparel with her here. And the bed-furniture that Kristin was to have with her they would need here too for the wedding, so many guests as they would have in the house.

Well, well, said Erlend. Doubtless some way could be found to have the goods sent through in the autumn. But he had been glad, and had thought it seemed a wise counsel, when the Abbot had proffered to have the goods brought in the church galleass. The Abbot had reminded him of their kinship. "They are all ready now to remember that," said Erlend, smiling. His father-in-law's displeasure seemed not to trouble him in the least.

But in the end it was agreed that Erlend should be given the loan of a cart, and should take away a cartload of the things Kristin would need most when first she came to her new home.

The day after they were busy with the packing. The big and the little loom the mother thought might go at once—Kristin would scarce have time for weaving much more before the wedding. Ragnfrid and her daughter cut off the web that was on the loom. It was undyed wadmal, but of the finest, softest wool, with inwoven tufts of black sheep's wool that made a pattern of spots. Kristin and her mother rolled up the stuff and laid it in the leather sack. Kristin thought: 'twould make good warm swaddling cloths—and right fair ones, too, with blue or red bands wrapped round them.

The sewing-chair, too, that Arne had once made her, was to be sent. Kristin took out of the box-seat all the things Erlend had given her from time to time. She showed her mother the blue velvet cloak patterned in red that she was to wear at the bridal, on the ride to church. The mother turned it about and about, and felt the stuff and the fur lining.

"A costly cloak, indeed," said Ragnfrid. "When was it Erlend gave you this?"

"He gave it me when I was at Nonneseter," said her daughter.

Kristin's bride-chest, that held all the goods her mother had gathered together and saved up for her since she was a little child, was emptied and packed anew. Its sides and cover were all carved in squares, with a leaping beast or a bird amidst leaves in each square. The wedding-dress Ragnfrid laid away in one of her own chests. It was not quite ready yet, though they had sewed on it all winter. It was of scarlet silk, cut to sit very close to the body. Kristin thought, 'twould be all too tight across the breast now.

Toward evening the whole load stood ready, firmly bound under the wagon-tilt. Erlend was to set forth early the next morning.

He stood with Kristin leaning over the courtyard gate, looking northward to where a blue-black storm-cloud filled the Dale. Thunder was rolling far off in the mountains—but southward the green fields and the river lay in yellow, burning sunshine.

"Mind you the storm that day in the woods at Gerdarud?" he asked softly, playing with her fingers.

Kristin nodded and tried to smile. The air was so heavy and close —her head ached, and at every breath she took her skin grew damp with sweat.

Lavrans came across to the two as they stood by the gate, and spoke of the storm. 'Twas but rarely it did much harm down here in the parish—but God knew if they should not hear of cattle and horses killed up in the mountains.

It was black as night above the church up on the hillside. A lightning-flash showed them a troop of horses standing uneasily huddled together on the green-sward outside the church gate. Lavrans thought they could scarce belong here in the parish—rather must they be horses from Dovre that had been running loose up on the hills below Jetta; but yet he had a mind to go up and look at them, he shouted through a peal of thunder—there might be some of his among them. . . .

A fearful lightning-flash tore the darkness above the church—the thunder crashed and bellowed so as to deafen them to all other sounds. The cluster of horses burst asunder, scattering over the hill-slopes beneath the mountain-ridge. All three of them crossed themselves. . . .

Then came another flash; it was as though the heavens split asunder right above them, a mighty snow-white flame swooped down upon them—the three were thrown against each other, and stood with shut, blinded eyes, and a smell in their nostrils as of burning stone—while the crashing thunder rent their ears.

"Saint Olav, help us!" said Lavrans, in a low voice.

"Look! the birch—the birch!" shouted Erlend; the great birch-tree in the field near by seemed to totter, and a huge bough parted from the tree and sank to the ground, leaving a great gash in the trunk.

"Think you 'twill catch fire—Jesus Kristus! The church-roof is alight!" shouted Lavrans.

They stood and gazed—no—yes! Red flames were darting out among the shingles beneath the ridge-turret.

Both men rushed back across the courtyard. Lavrans tore open the doors of all the houses he came to, and shouted to those inside; the house-folk came swarming out.

"Bring axes, bring axes—timber axes," he cried, "and bill-hooks." He ran on to the stables. In a moment he came out leading Gulds-veinen by the mane; he sprang on the horse's bare back and dashed off up the hill, with the great broad-axe in his hand. Erlend rode close behind him—all the men followed; some were a-horseback, but some could not master the terrified beasts, and, giving up, ran off afoot. Last came Ragnfrid and all the women on the place with pails and buckets.

None seemed to heed the storm any longer. By the light of the flashes they could see folk streaming out of the houses farther down the valley. Sira Eirik was far up the hill already, running with his house-folk behind him. There was a thunder of horses' hoofs on the bridge below—some men galloped past, turning white, appalled faces toward their burning church.*

It was blowing a little from the south-east. The fire had a strong hold on the north wall; on the west the entrance door was blocked already. But it had not caught yet on the south side nor on the apse.

Kristin and the women from Jörundgaard came into the graveyard south of the church at a place where the fence was broken.

The huge red glare lighted up the grove of trees north of the church, and the green by it where there were bars to tie the horses to. None could come thither for the glowing heat—the great cross stood alone out there, bathed in the light of the flames. It looked as though it lived and moved.

Through the hissing and roar of the flames sounded the thudding of axes against the staves of the south wall. There were men in the cloister-way hewing and hammering at the wall, while others tried to tear down the cloister itself. Some one called out to the Jörundgaard women that Lavrans and a few other men had followed Sira Eirik into the church, and now 'twas high time to cut a passage through the south wall—small tongues of flame were peeping out among the shingles here too; and should the wind go round or die down, the fire would take hold on the whole church.

* Stave churches, see Note 23.

To think of putting out the fire was vain; there was no time to make a chain down to the river; but at Ragnfrid's bidding the women made a line and passed water along from the little beck that ran by the roadside—it was but little to throw on the south wall and over the men working there. Many of the women sobbed and wept the while, in terror for the men who had made their way into the burning building, and in sorrow for their church.

Kristin stood foremost in the line of women handing along the pails. She gazed breathless at the burning church; they were both there, inside—her father, and surely Erlend too.

The torn-down pillars of the cloister-way lay in a tangled mass of timber and shingles from its roof. The men were attacking the inner wall of staves now with all their might—a group of them had lifted up a great log and were battering the wall with it.

Erlend and one of his men came out of the little door in the south wall of the choir, carrying between them the great chest from the sacristy—the chest Eirik was used to sit on when he heard confession. Erlend and the man flung the chest out into the churchyard.

He shouted out something, but Kristin could not hear; he dashed on at once into the cloister-way. Nimble as a cat he seemed as he ran —he had thrown off his outer garments and had naught on him but shirt, breeches and hose.

The others took up his shout—the choir and the sacristy were burning; none could pass from the nave to the south door any longer—the fire had blocked both ways of escape. Some of the staves in the wall had been splintered by the ram. Erlend had seized a fire-hook, and with it he tugged and wrenched at the wreckage of the staves; he and those with him tore a hole in the side of the church, while other folks cried to take care, for the roof might fall and shut in the men inside; the shingle roof on this side too was burning hard now, and the heat had grown till 'twas scarce to be borne.

Erlend burst through the hole and helped out Sira Eirik. The priest came bearing the holy vessels from the altars in the skirt of his gown.

A young boy followed, with one hand over his face and the other holding the tall processional cross lance-wise in front of him. Lavrans came next. He kept his eyes shut against the smoke—he staggered under the weight of the great crucifix, which he bore in his arms; it was much taller than the man himself.

Folk ran forward and helped them out and into the churchyard. Sira Eirik stumbled and fell on his knees, and the altar vessels rolled out down the slope. The silver dove flew open and the Host fell out; the priest took it up, brushed the soil off it and kissed it, sobbing aloud; he kissed the gilded head, too, that had stood on the altar with shreds of the nails and hair of St. Olav in it.

Lavrans Björgulfsön still stood holding up the Holy Rood. His arm lay along the arms of the cross; his head was bowed against the shoulder of the Christ-figure; it seemed as though the Redeemer bent His fair, sorrowful face over the man to pity and to comfort.

The roof on the north side of the church had begun to fall in by bits —a burning piece from a falling beam was hurled outwards and struck the great bell in the belfry by the churchyard gate. The bell gave out a deep sobbing note, which died in a long wail that was drowned in the roaring of the flames.

None had paid heed to the weather all this time—the whole had lasted indeed no long time, but whether short or long scarce any could have told. The thunder and lightning had passed now far down the Dale; the rain, that had begun some time back, fell ever the more heavily, and the wind had died down.

But of a sudden it was as though a sheet of flame shot up from the groundsill of the building—a moment, and with a mounting roar the fire had swallowed up the church from end to end.

The people scattered, rushing away to escape the devouring heat. Erlend was at Kristin's side on the instant, dragging her away down the hill. The whole man smelt of burning—when she stroked his head and face her hand came away full of burnt hair.

They could not hear each other's voices for the roaring of the fire. But she saw that his eyebrows were burnt off to the roots; he had burns on his face, and great holes were burnt in his shirt. He laughed as he dragged her along with him after the others.

All the folk followed the old priest as he went weeping, with Lavrans Björgulfsön bearing the crucifix.

At the foot of the churchyard Lavrans set the Rood from him up against a tree, and sank down to a seat on the wreckage of the fence. Sira Eirik was sitting there already; he stretched out his arms toward the burning church:

"Farewell, farewell, thou Olav's Church; God bless thee, thou my Olav's Church; God bless thee for every hour I have chanted in thee and said mass in thee—thou Olav's Church, good-night, good-night——"

The church-folk wept aloud with their priest. The rain streamed down on the groups of people, but none thought of seeking shelter. Nor did it seem to check the fierce burning of the tarred woodwork— brands and glowing shingles were tossed out on every side. Then, suddenly, the ridge-turret crashed down into the fiery furnace, sending a great shower of sparks high into the air.

Lavrans sat with one hand over his face; the other arm lay in his lap, and Kristin saw that the sleeve was all bloody from the shoulder down, and blood ran down over his fingers. She went to him and touched his arm.

"Not much is amiss, methinks—there fell somewhat on my shoulder," he said, looking up. He was white to the lips. "Ulvhild," he murmured in anguish, gazing into the burning pile.

Sira Eirik heard the word, and laid a hand on his shoulder.

"'Twill not wake your child, Lavrans—she will sleep none the less sound for the burning above her bed. *She* hath not lost her soul's home, as we others have lost ours this night."

Kristin hid her face on Erlend's breast, and stood there feeling the grasp of his arm round her shoulders. Then she heard her father asking for his wife.

Some one answered that a woman had fallen in labour from the right; they had borne her down to the parsonage, and Ragnfrid had gone with her there.

Then Kristin called to mind again what she had clean forgotten ever since they saw that the church was afire. She should not have looked on this. There lived a man in the south of the parish who had a red stain over half his face; 'twas said he was thus because his mother had looked at a burning house while she was big with him. "Dear, holy Virgin Mother," she prayed in her heart, "let not my child have been marred by this!"

The day after, the whole parish was called to meet on the church-green to take counsel how best to build up the church anew.

Kristin sought out Sira Eirik at Romundgaard before the time set for the meeting. She asked the priest if he deemed she should take this as a sign. Maybe 'twas God's will that she should say to her father she was unworthy to wear the bridal crown; that it were more seemly she should be given in marriage to Erlend Nikulaussön without feasting or bridal honours.

But Sira Eirik flew up at her with eyes glistening with wrath:

"Think you that God cares so much how you sluts may fly about and cast yourselves away, that He would burn up a fair, venerable church for your sake? Leave you your sinful pride, and bring not on your mother and Lavrans such a sorrow as they would scarce win through for many a day. If you wear not the crown with honour on your honourable day—the worse for you; but the more need have you and Erlend of all the rites of the Church when ye are brought together. Each and all of us have sins to answer for; 'tis therefore, I trow, that this visitation is come upon us all. See you to it that you mend your life, and that you help to build up our church again, both you and Erlend.''

It was in Kristin's mind that he knew not all, for that yet she had not told him of this last thing that was come upon her—but she rested content and said no more.

She went with the men to the meeting. Lavrans came with his arm in a sling, and Erlend had many burns on his face; he was ill to look upon, but he laughed it off. None of the wounds were large, and he said he hoped they would not spoil his face too much when he came to be a bridegroom. He stood up after Lavrans and promised four marks of silver as an offering to the church, and, for his betrothed, with Lavrans' assent, land* worth sixty cows from her holdings in the parish.

It was found needful for Erlend to stay a week at Jörundgaard by reason of his burns. Kristin saw that 'twas as though Lavrans had come to like his son-in-law better since the night of the fire; the men seemed now to be good friends enough. She thought, maybe her father might grow to like Erlend Nikulaussön so well that he would not judge them too strictly, and would not take the matter so hardly as she had feared when the time came when he must know that they had transgressed against him.

VIII

T H E year proved a rarely good one over all the north part of the Dale. The hay crop was heavy, and it was got in dry; the folk came home from the sæters in autumn with great store of dairy stuff and full and fat flocks and herds—they had been mercifully spared from wild beasts, too, this year. The corn stood tall and thick as few folks could call to mind having seen it before—it grew full-eared and ripened well, and the weather was fair as heart could wish. Between St. Bartholomew's and the Virgin's Birthfeast, the time when night-frosts were most to be feared, it rained a little and was mild and cloudy, but thereafter the time of harvest went by with sun and wind and mild, misty nights. The week after Michaelmas most of the corn had been garnered all over the parish.

At Jörundgaard all folks were toiling and moiling, making ready for the great wedding. The last two months Kristin had been so busy from morning to night that she had but little time to trouble over aught but her work. She saw that her bosom had filled out; the small pink nipples were grown brown, and they were tender as smarting hurts

* Land measurement, see Note 24.

when she had to get out of bed in the cold—but it passed over when she had worked herself warm, and after that she had no thought but of all she must get done before evening. When now and again she was forced to straighten up her back and stand and rest a little, she felt that the burden she bore was growing heavy—but to look on she was still slim and slender as she had ever been. She passed her hands down her long, shapely thighs. No, she would not grieve over it now. Sometimes a faint creeping longing would come over her with the thought: like enough in a month or so she might feel the child quick within her. . . . By that time she would be at Husaby. . . . Maybe Erlend would be glad. . . . She shut her eyes and fixed her teeth on her betrothal ring —then she saw before her Erlend's face, pale and moved, as he stood in the hall here in the winter and said the words of espousal with a loud clear voice:

"So be God my witness and these men standing here, that I Erlend Nikulaussön do espouse Kristin Lavransdatter according to the laws of God and men, on such conditions as here have been spoken before these witnesses standing hereby. That I shall have thee to my wife and thou shalt have me to thy husband, so long as we two do live, to dwell together in wedlock, with all such fellowship as God's law and the law of the land do appoint."

As she ran on errands from house to house across the farm-place, she stayed a moment—the rowan trees were so thick with berries this year— 'twould be a snowy winter. The sun shone over the pale stubble-fields where the corn sheaves stood piled on their stakes. If this weather might only hold over the wedding!

Lavrans stood firmly to it that his daughter should be wedded in church. It was fixed, therefore, that the wedding should be in the chapel at Sundbu. On the Saturday the bridal train was to ride over the hills to Vaage; they were to lie for the night at Sundbu and the neighbouring farms, and ride back on Sunday after the wedding mass. The same evening after vespers, when the holy-day was ended, the wedding feast was to be held, and Lavrans was to give his daughter away to Erlend. And after midnight the bride and bridegroom were to be put to bed.

On Friday afternoon, Kristin stood in the upper hall balcony, watching the bridal train come riding from the north, past the charred ruins of the church on the hillside. It was Erlend coming with all his grooms-men; she strained her eyes to pick him out among the others. They must not see each other—no man must see her now before she was led forth to-morrow in her bridal dress.

Where the ways divided, a few women left the throng and took the road to Jörundgaard. The men rode on toward Laugarbru; they were to sleep there that night.

Kristin went down to meet the comers. She felt wearied after the bath, and the skin of her head was sore from the strong lye her mother had used to wash her hair, that it might shine fair and bright on the morrow.

Lady Aashild slipped down from her saddle into Lavrans' arms. How can she keep so light and young? thought Kristin. Her son Sir Munan's wife, Lady Katrin, might have passed for older than she; a big, plump dame, with dull and hueless skin and eyes. Strange, thought Kristin; she is ill-favoured and he is unfaithful, and yet folks say they live well and kindly together. Then there were two daughters of Sir Baard Petersön, one married and one unmarried. They were neither comely nor ill-favoured; they looked honest and kind, but held themselves something stiffly in the strange company. Lavrans thanked them courteously that they had been pleased to honour this wedding at the cost of so far a journey so late in the year.

"Erlend was bred up in our father's house, when he was a boy," said the elder, moving forward to greet Kristin.

But now two youths came riding into the farm-place at a sharp trot— they leaped from their horses and rushed laughing after Kristin, who ran indoors and hid herself. They were Trond Gjesling's two young sons, fair and likely lads. They had brought the bridal crown with them from Sundbu in a casket. Trond and his wife were not to come till Sunday, when they would join the bridal train after the mass.

Kristin fled into the hearth-room; and Lady Aashild, coming after, laid her hands on the girl's shoulders, and drew down her face to hers to kiss it.

"Glad am I that I live to see this day," said Lady Aashild.

She saw how thin they were grown, Kristin's hands, that she held in hers. She saw that all else about her was grown thin, but that her bosom was high and full. All the features of the face were grown smaller and finer than before; the temples seemed as though sunken in the shadow of the heavy damp hair. The girl's cheeks were round no longer, and her fresh hue was faded. But her eyes were grown much larger and darker.

Lady Aashild kissed her again:

"I see well you have had much to strive against, Kristin," she said. "To-night will I give you a sleepy drink, that you may be rested and fresh to-morrow."

Kristin's lips began to quiver.

"Hush," said Lady Aashild, patting her hand. "I joy already that I shall deck you out to-morrow—none hath seen a fairer bride, I trow, than you shall be to-morrow."

Lavrans rode over to Laugarbru to feast with his guests who were housed there.

The men could not praise the food enough—better Friday food than this a man could scarce find in the richest monastery. There was rye-meal porridge, boiled beans and white bread—for fish they had only trout, salted and fresh, and fat dried halibut.

As time went on and the men drank deeper, they grew ever more wanton of mood, and the jests broken on the bridegroom's head ever more gross. All Erlend's groomsmen were much younger than he—his equals in age and his friends were all long since wedded men. The darling jest among the groomsmen now was that he was so aged a man and yet was to mount the bridal-bed for the first time. Some of Erlend's older kinsmen, who kept their wits, sat in dread, at each new sally, that the talk would come in upon matters it were best not to touch. Sir Baard of Hestnæs kept an eye on Lavrans. The host drank deep, but it seemed not that the ale made him more joyful—he sat in the high-seat, his face growing more and more strained, even as his eyes grew more fixed. But Erlend, who sat on his father-in-law's right hand, answered in kind the wanton jests flung at him, and laughed much; his face was flushed red and his eyes sparkled.

Of a sudden Lavrans flew out:

"That cart, son-in-law—while I remember—what have you done with the cart you had of me on loan in the summer?"

"Cart——?" said Erlend.

"Have you forgot already that you had a cart on loan from me in the summer. . . . God knows 'twas so good a cart I look not ever to see a better, for I saw to it myself when 'twas making in my own smithy on the farm. You promised and you swore—I take God to witness, and my house-folk know it besides—you gave your word to bring it back to me—but that word you have not kept——"

Some of the guests called out that this was no matter to talk of now, but Lavrans smote the board with his fist and swore that he would know what Erlend had done with his cart.

"Oh, like enough it lies still at the farm at Næs, where we took boat out to Vöey," said Erlend lightly. "I thought not 'twas meant so nicely. See you, father-in-law, thus it was—'twas a long and a toilsome journey with a heavy-laden cart over the hills, and when we were come down to the fjord, none of my men had a mind to bring the cart all the way back here, and then journey north again over the hills to Trondheim. So we thought we might let it be there for a time——"

"Now, may the devil fly off with me from where I sit this very hour, if I have ever heard of your like," Lavrans burst out. "Is this how things are ordered in your house—doth the word lie with you or with your men, where they are to go or not to go——?"

Erlend shrugged his shoulders:

"True it is, much hath been as it should not have been in my household. . . . But now will I have the cart sent south to you again, when Kristin and I are come thither. . . . Dear my father-in-law," said he, smiling and holding out his hand, "be assured, 'twill be changed times with all things, and with me too, when once I have brought Kristin home to be mistress of my house. 'Twas an ill thing, this of the cart. But I promise you, this shall be the last time you have cause of grief against me."

"Dear Lavrans," said Baard Petersön, "forgive him in this small matter——"

"Small matter or great——" began Lavrans, but checked himself, and took Erlend's hand.

Soon after he made the sign for the feast to break up, and the guests sought their sleeping-places.

On the Saturday before noon all the women and girls were busy in the old storehouse loft-room, some making ready the bridal bed, some dressing and adorning the bride.

Ragnfrid had chosen this house for the bride-house, in part for its having the smallest loft-room—they could make room for many more guests in the new storehouse loft, the one they had used themselves in summer-time to sleep in when Kristin was a little child, before Lavrans had set up the great new dwelling-house, where they lived now both summer and winter. But besides this, there was no fairer house on the farm than the old storehouse, since Lavrans had had it mended and set in order—it had been nigh falling to the ground when they moved in to Jörundgaard. It was adorned with the finest wood-carving both outside and in, and if the loft-room were not great, 'twas the easier to hang it richly with rugs and tapestries and skins.

The bridal bed stood ready made, with silk-covered pillows; fine hangings made as it were a tent about it; over the skins and rugs on the bed was spread a broidered silken coverlid. Ragnfrid and some other women were busy now hanging tapestries on the timber walls and laying cushions in order on the benches.

Kristin sat in a great arm-chair that had been brought up thither. She was clad in her scarlet bridal robe. Great silver brooches held it together over her bosom, and fastened the yellow silk shift showing in the neck-opening; golden armlets glittered on the yellow silken sleeves.

A silver-gilt belt was passed thrice around her waist, and on her neck and bosom lay neck-chain over neck-chain, the uppermost her father's old gold chain with the great reliquary cross. Her hands, lying in her lap, were heavy with rings.

Lady Aashild stood behind her chair, brushing her heavy, gold-brown hair out to all sides.

"To-morrow shall you spread it loose for the last time," she said, smiling, as she wound the red and green silk cords that were to hold up the crown, around Kristin's head. Then the women came thronging round the bride.

Ragnfrid and Gyrid of Skog took the great bridal crown of the Gjesling kin from the board. It was gilt all over, the points ended in alternate crosses and clover-leaves, and the circlet was set with great rock-crystals.

They pressed it down on the bride's head. Ragnfrid was pale, and her hands were shaking, as she did it.

Kristin rose slowly to her feet. Jesus! how heavy 'twas to bear up all this gold and silver. . . . Then Lady Aashild took her by the hand and led her forward to a great tub of water—while the bridesmaids flung open the door to the outer sunlight, so that the light in the room should be bright.

"Look now at yourself in the water, Kristin," said Lady Aashild, and Kristin bent over the tub. She caught a glimpse of her own face rising up white through the water; it came so near that she saw the golden crown above it. Round about, many shadows, bright and dark, were stirring in the mirror—there was somewhat she was on the brink of remembering—then 'twas as though she was swooning away—she caught at the rim of the tub before her. At that moment Lady Aashild laid her hand on hers, and drove her nails so hard into the flesh, that Kristin came to herself with the pain.

Blasts of a great horn were heard from down by the bridge. Folk shouted up from the courtyard that the bridegroom was coming with his train. The women led Kristin out on to the balcony.

In the courtyard was a tossing mass of horses in state trappings and people in festival apparel, all shining and glittering in the sun. Kristin looked out beyond it all, far out into the Dale. The valley of her home lay bright and still beneath a thin misty-blue haze; up above the haze rose the mountains, grey with screes and black with forest, and the sun poured down its light into the great bowl of the valley from a cloudless sky.

She had not marked it before, but the trees had shed all their leaves—the groves around shone naked and silver-grey. Only the alder-thickets along the river had a little faded green on their topmost branches, and here and there a birch had a few yellow-white leaves clinging to its outermost twigs. But, for the most, the trees were almost bare—all but the rowans; they were still bright with red-brown leaves around the clusters of their blood-red berries. In the still, warm day a faint mouldering smell of autumn rose from the ashen covering of fallen leaves that strewed the ground all about.

Had it not been for the rowans, it might have been early spring. And the stillness too—but this was an autumn stillness, deathly still. When the horn-blasts died away, no other sound was heard in all the valley but the tinkling of bells from the stubble fields and fallows where the beasts wandered, grazing.

The river was shrunken small, its roar sunk to a murmur; it was but a few strands of water running amidst banks of sand and great stretches of white round boulders. No noise of becks from the hillsides—the autumn had been so dry. The fields all around still gleamed wet—but 'twas but the wetness that oozes up from the earth in autumn, howsoever warm the days may be, and however clear the air.

The crowd that filled the farm-place fell apart to make way for the bridegroom's train. Straightway the young groomsmen came riding forward—there went a stir among the women in the balcony.

Lady Aashild was standing by the bride.

"Bear you well now, Kristin," said she, "'twill not be long now till you are safe under the linen coif." *

Kristin nodded helplessly. She felt how deathly white her face must be.

"Methinks I am all too pale a bride," she said, in a low voice.

"You are the fairest bride," said Lady Aashild; "and there comes Erlend, riding—fairer pair than you twain would be far to seek."

Now Erlend himself rode forward under the balcony. He sprang lightly from his horse, unhindered by his heavy, flowing garments. He seemed to Kristin so fair that 'twas pain to look on him.

He was in dark raiment, clad in a slashed silken coat falling to the feet, leaf-brown of hue and inwoven with black and white. About his waist he had a gold-bossed belt, and at his left thigh hung a sword with gold on hilt and sheath. Back over his shoulders fell a heavy dark-blue velvet cloak, and pressed down on his coal-black hair he wore a black French cap of silk that stood out at both sides in puckered wings and ended in two long streamers, whereof one was thrown from his left shoulder right across his breast and out behind over the other arm.

Erlend bowed low before his bride as she stood above; then went up

* Linen coif, see Note 25.

to her horse and stood by it with his hand on the saddle-bow, while Lavrans went up the stairs. A strange dizzy feeling came over Kristin at the sight of all this splendour—in this solemn garment of green velvet, falling to his feet, her father might have been some stranger. And her mother's face, under the linen coif, showed ashy-grey against the red of her silken dress. Ragnfrid came forward and laid the cloak about her daughter's shoulders.

Then Lavrans took the bride's hand and led her down to Erlend. The bridegroom lifted her to the saddle, and himself mounted. They stayed their horses, side by side, these two, beneath the bridal balcony, while the train began to form and ride out through the courtyard gate. First the priests: Sira Eirik, Sira Tormod from Ulvsvolden, and a Brother of the Holy Cross from Hamar, a friend of Lavrans. Then came the groomsmen and the bridesmaids, pair by pair. And now 'twas for Erlend and her to ride forth. After them came the bride's parents, the kinsmen, friends and guests, in a long line down betwixt the fences to the highway. Their road for a long way onward was strewn with clusters of rowan-berries, branchlets of pine, and the last white dog-fennel of autumn, and folk stood thick along the waysides where the train passed by, greeting them with a great shouting.

On the Sunday, just after sunset, the bridal train rode back to Jörund-gaard. Through the first falling folds of darkness the bonfires shone out red from the courtyard of the bridal house. Minstrels and fiddlers were singing and making drums and fiddles speak as the crowd of riders drew near to the warm red glare of the fires.

Kristin came near to falling her length on the ground when Erlend lifted her from her horse beneath the balcony of the upper hall.

"'Twas so cold upon the hills," she whispered. "I am so weary——" She stood for a moment, and when she climbed the stairs to the loft-room, she swayed and tottered at each step.

Up in the hall the half-frozen wedding guests were soon warmed up again. The many candles burning in the room gave out heat; smoking hot dishes of food were borne around, and wine, mead and strong ale circled about. The loud hum of voices and the noise of many eating sounded like a far-off roaring in Kristin's ears.

It seemed as she sat there she would never be warm through again. In a while her cheeks began to burn, but her feet were still unthawed, and shudders of cold ran down her back. All the heavy gold that was on her head and body forced her to lean forward as she sat in the high-seat by Erlend's side.

Every time her bridegroom drank to her, she could not keep her eyes from the red stains and patches that stood out on his face so sharply as he began to grow warm after his ride in the cold. They were the marks left by the burns of last summer.

The horror had come upon her last evening, when they sat over the supper-board at Sundbu, and she met Björn Gunnarsön's lightless eyes fixed on her and Erlend—unwinking, unwavering, eyes. They had dressed up Sir Björn in knightly raiment—he looked like a dead man brought to life by an evil spell.

At night she had lain with Lady Aashild, the bridegroom's nearest kinswoman in the wedding company.

"What is amiss with you, Kristin?" said Lady Aashild, a little sharply. "Now is the time for you to bear up stiffly to the end—not give way thus."

"I am thinking," said Kristin, cold with dread, "on all them we have brought to sorrow that we might see this day."

"'Tis not joy alone, I trow, that you two have had," said Lady Aashild. "Not Erlend at the least. And methinks it has been worse still for you."

"I am thinking on his helpless children," said the bride again. "I am wondering if they know their father is drinking to-day at his wedding-feast——"

"Think on your own child," said the lady. "Be glad that you are drinking at your wedding with him who is its father."

Kristin lay awhile, weak and giddy. 'Twas so strange to hear that named that had filled her heart and mind each day for three months and more, and whereof yet she had not dared speak a word to a living soul. It was but for a little, though, that this helped her.

"I am thinking on her who had to pay with her life, because she held Erlend dear," she whispered, shivering.

"Well if you come not to pay with your life yourself, ere you are half a year older," said Lady Aashild harshly. "Be glad while you may——"

"What shall I say to you, Kristin?" said the old woman in a while, despairingly. "Have you clean lost courage this day of all days? Soon enough will it be required of you twain that you shall pay for all you have done amiss—have no fear that it will not be so."

But Kristin felt as though all things in her soul were slipping, slipping—as though all were toppling down that she had built up since that day of horror at Haugen, in that first time when, wild and blind with fear, she had thought but of holding out one day more, and one day more. And she had held out till her load grew lighter—and at last grew even light, when she had thrown off all thought but this one thought: that now their wedding-day was coming at last, Erlend's wedding-day at last.

But when she and Erlend knelt together in the wedding-mass, all around her seemed but some trickery of the sight—the tapers, the pictures, the glittering vessels, the priests in their copes and white gowns. All those who had known her where she had lived before—they seemed like visions of a dream, standing there, close-packed in the church in their unwonted garments. But Sir Björn stood against a pillar, looking at those two with his dead eyes, and it seemed to her that that other who was dead must needs have come back with him, on his arm.

She tried to look up at Saint Olav's picture—he stood there red and white and comely, leaning on his axe, treading his own sinful human nature underfoot—but her glance would ever go back to Sir Björn; and nigh to him she saw Eline Ormsdatter's dead face, looking unmoved upon her and Erlend. They had trampled her underfoot that they might come hither—and she grudged it not to them.

The dead woman had arisen and flung off her all the great stones that Kristin had striven to heap up above her: Erlend's wasted youth, his honour and his welfare, his friends' good graces, his soul's health. The dead woman had shaken herself free of them all. He would have me and I would have him; you would have him and he would have you, said Eline. I have paid—and he must pay and you must pay when your time comes. When the time of sin is fulfilled it brings forth death. . . .

It seemed to her she was kneeling with Erlend on a cold stone. He knelt there with the red, burnt patches on his pale face; she knelt under the heavy bridal crown, and felt the dull, crushing weight within her—the burden of sin that she bore. She had played and wantoned with her sin, had measured it as in a childish game. Holy Virgin—now the time was nigh when it should lie full-born before her, look at her with living eyes; show her on itself the brands of sin, the hideous deformity of sin; strike in hate with misshapen hands at its mother's breast. When she had borne her child, when she saw the marks of her sin upon it and yet loved it as she had loved her sin, then would the game be played to an end.

Kristin thought: what if she shrieked aloud now, a shriek that would cut through the song and the deep voices intoning the mass, and echo out over the people's heads? Would she be rid then of Eline's face— would there come life into the dead man's eyes? But she clenched her teeth together.

. . . Holy King Olav, I cry upon thee. Above all in heaven I pray for help to thee, for I know thou didst love God's justice above all things. I call upon thee, that thou hold thy hand over the innocent that is in my womb. Turn away God's wrath from the innocent; turn it upon me. Amen, in the precious name of the Lord. . . .

My children, said Eline's voice, are *they* not guiltless? Yet is there no place for them in the lands where Christians dwell. Your child is begotten outside the law, even as were my children. No rights can you claim for it in the land you have strayed away from, any more than I for mine. . . .

Holy Olav! Yet do I pray for grace. Pray thou for mercy for my son; take him beneath thy guard; so shall I bear him to thy church on my naked feet, so shall I bear my golden garland of maidenhood in to thee and lay it down upon thy altar, if thou wilt but help me. Amen.

Her face was set hard as stone in her struggle to be still and calm; but her whole body throbbed and quivered as she knelt there through the holy mass that wedded her to Erlend.

And now, as she sat beside him in the high-seat at home, all things around her were but as shadows in a fevered dream.

There were minstrels playing on harps and fiddles in the loft-room; and the sound of music and song rose from the hall below and the courtyard outside. There was a red glare of fire from without, when the door was opened for the dishes and tankards to be borne in and out.

Those around the board were standing now; she was standing up between her father and Erlend. Her father made known with a loud voice that he had given Erlend Nikulaussön his daughter Kristin to wife. Erlend thanked his father-in-law, and he thanked all good folk who had come together there to honour him and his wife.

She was to sit down, they said—and now Erlend laid his bridal gifts in her lap. Sira Eirik and Sir Munan Baardsön unrolled deeds and read aloud from them concerning the jointures and settlements of the wedded pair; while the groomsmen stood around, with spears in their hands, and now and again during the reading, or when gifts and bags of money were laid on the table, smote with the butts upon the floor.

The tables were cleared away; Erlend led her forth upon the floor, and they danced together. Kristin thought: our groomsmen and our bridesmaids—they are all too young for us—all they that were young with us are gone from these places; how is it we are come back hither?

"You are so strange, Kristin," whispered Erlend, as they danced. "I am afraid of you, Kristin—are you not happy——?"

They went from house to house and greeted their guests. There were many lights in all the rooms, and everywhere crowds of people drinking and singing and dancing. It seemed to Kristin she scarce knew her home again—and she had lost all knowledge of time—hours and the pictures of her brain seemed strangely to float about loosely, mingled with each other.

The autumn night was mild; there were minstrels in the courtyard too, and people dancing round the bonfire. They cried out that the bride and bridegroom must honour them too—and then she was dancing with Erlend on the cold, dewy sward. She seemed to wake a little then, and her head grew more clear.

Far out in the darkness a band of white mist floated above the murmur of the river. The mountains stood around coal-black against the star-sprinkled sky.

Erlend led her out of the ring of dancers, and crushed her to him in the darkness under the balcony.

"Not once have I had the chance to tell you—you are so fair—so fair and so sweet. Your cheeks are red as flames——" He pressed his cheek to hers as he spoke. "Kristin, what is it ails you?"

"I am so weary, so weary," she whispered back.

"Soon now will we go and sleep," answered her bridegroom, looking up at the sky. The Milky Way had wheeled, and now lay all but north and south. "Mind you that we have not once slept together since that one only night I was with you in your bower at Skog?"

Soon after, Sira Eirik shouted with a loud voice out over the farmstead that now it was Monday. The women came to lead the bride to bed. Kristin was so weary that she was scarce able to struggle and hold back as 'twas fit and seemly she should do. She let herself be seized and led out of the loft-room by Lady Aashild and Gyrid of Skog. The groomsmen stood at the foot of the stair with burning torches and naked swords; they formed a ring round the troop of women and attended Kristin across the farm-place, and up into the old loft-room.

The women took off her bridal finery, piece by piece, and laid it away. Kristin saw that over the bed-foot hung the violet velvet robe she was to wear on the morrow, and upon it lay a long, snow-white, finely-pleated linen cloth. It was the wife's linen coif. Erlend had brought it for her; to-morrow she was to bind up her hair in a knot and fasten the head-linen over it. It looked to her so fresh and cool and restful.

At last she was standing before the bridal bed, on her naked feet, bare-armed, clad only in the long golden-yellow silken shift. They had set the crown on her head again; the bridegroom was to take it off, when they two were left alone.

Ragnfrid laid her hands on her daughter's shoulders, and kissed her on the cheek—the mother's face and hands were strangely cold, but it was as though sobs were struggling deep in her breast. Then she drew back the coverings of the bed, and bade the bride seat herself in it. Kristin obeyed, and leaned back on the pillows heaped up against the bed-head—she had to bend her head a little forward to keep on the crown. Lady Aashild drew the coverings up to the bride's waist, and laid her hands before her on the silken coverlid; then took her shining hair and drew it forward over her bosom and the slender bare upper arms.

Next the men led the bridegroom into the loft-room. Munan Baardsön unclasped the golden belt and sword from Erlend's waist; when he leaned over to hang it on the wall above the bed, he whispered something to the bride—Kristin knew not what he said, but she did her best to smile.

The groomsmen unlaced Erlend's silken robe and lifted off the long heavy garment over his head. He sate him down in the great chair and they helped him off with his spurs and boots.

Once, and once only, the bride found courage to look up and meet his eyes.

Then began the good-nights. Before long all the wedding-guests were gone from the loft. Last of all, Lavrans Björgulfsön went out and shut the door of the bride-house.

Erlend stood up, stripped off his underclothing, and flung it on the benches. He stood by the bed, took the crown and the silken cords from off her hair, and laid them away on the table. Then he came back and mounted into the bed. Kneeling by her side he clasped her round the head, and pressed it in against his hot, naked breast, while he kissed her forehead all along the red streak the crown had left on it.

She threw her arms about his shoulders and sobbed aloud—she had a sweet, wild feeling that now the horror, the phantom visions, were fading into air—now, now once again naught was left but he and she. He lifted up her face a moment, looked down into it, and drew his hand down over her face and body, with a strange haste and roughness, as though he tore away a covering.

"Forget," he begged, in a fiery whisper, "forget all, my Kristin—all but this, that you are my own wife, and I am your own husband. . . ."

With his hand he quenched the flame of the last candle, then threw himself down beside her in the dark—he too was sobbing now:

"Never have I believed it, never in all these years, that we should see this day. . . ."

Without, in the courtyard, the noise died down little by little. Wearied with the long day's ride, and dizzy with much strong drink, the guests made a decent show of merry-making a little while yet, but

more and ever more of them stole away and sought out the places
where they were to sleep.

Ragnfrid showed all the guests of honour to their places, and bade
them good-night. Her husband, who should have helped her in this,
was nowhere to be seen.

The dark courtyard was empty, save for a few small groups of young
folks—servants most of them—when at last she stole out to find her husband and bring him with her to his bed. She had seen as the night
wore on that he had grown very drunken.

She stumbled over him at last, as she crept along in her search outside the cattle-yard—he was lying in the grass behind the bath-house
on his face.

Groping in the darkness, she touched him with her hand—ay, it was
he. She thought he was asleep, and took him by the shoulder—she
must get him up off the icy-cold ground. But he was not asleep, at
least not wholly.

"What would you?" he asked, in a thick voice.

"You cannot lie here," said his wife. She held him up, as he stood
swaying. With one hand she brushed the soil off his velvet robe. "'Tis
time we too went to rest, husband." She took him by the arm, and
drew him, reeling, up towards the farmyard buildings.

"*You* looked not up, Ragnfrid, when you sat in the bridal bed beneath the crown," he said in the same voice. "Our daughter—*she* was
not so shamefast—her eyes were not shamefast when she looked upon
her bridegroom."

"She has waited for him seven half-years," said the mother in a low
voice. "No marvel if she found courage to look up——"

"Nay, devil damn me if they have waited!" screamed the man, as
his wife strove fearfully to hush him.

They were in the narrow passage between the back of the privy and
a fence. Lavrans smote with his clenched fist on the beam across the
cess-pit.

"I set thee here for a scorn and for a mockery, thou beam. I set thee
here that filth might eat thee up. I set thee here in punishment for
striking down that tender little maid of mine.—I should have set thee
high above my hall-room door, and honoured thee and thanked thee
with fairest carven ornament; because thou didst save her from shame
and from sorrow—because 'twas thy work that my Ulvhild died a sinless child. . . ."

He turned about, reeled toward the fence and fell forward upon it,
and with his head between his arms fell into an unquenchable passion
of weeping, broken by long, deep groans.

His wife took him by the shoulder.

"Lavrans, Lavrans!" But she could not stay his weeping. "Husband!"

"Oh, never, never, never should I have given her to that man! God help me—I must have known it all the time—he had broken down her youth and her fairest honour. I believed it not—nay, could I believe the like of Kristin?—but still I knew it. And yet is she too good for this weakling boy, that hath made waste of himself and her—had he lured her astray ten times over, I should never have given her to him, that he may spill yet more of her life and her happiness——"

"But what other way was there?" said the mother despairingly. "You know now, as well as I—she was his already——"

"Ay, small need was there for me to make such a mighty to-do in giving Erlend what he had taken for himself already," said Lavrans. "'Tis a gallant husband she has won—my Kristin——" He tore at the fence; then fell again a-weeping. He had seemed to Ragnfrid as though sobered a little, but now the fit overcame him again.

She deemed she could not bring him, drunken and beside himself with despair as he was, to the bed in the hearth-room where they should have slept—for the room was full of guests. She looked about her—close by stood a little barn where they kept the best hay to feed to the horses at the spring ploughing. She went and peered in—no one was there; she took her husband's hand, led him inside the barn, and shut the door behind them.

She piled up hay over herself and him and laid their cloaks above it to keep them warm. Lavrans fell a-weeping now and again, and said somewhat—but his speech was so broken she could find no meaning in it. In a little while she lifted up his head on to her lap.

"Dear my husband—since now so great a love is between them, maybe 'twill all go better than we think——"

Lavrans spoke by fits and starts—his mind seemed growing clearer:

"See you not—he has her now wholly in his power—he that has never been man enough to rule himself. . . . 'Twill go hard with her before she finds courage to set herself against aught her husband wills—and should she one day be forced to it, 'twill be bitter grief to her—my own gentle child——

". . . Now am I come so far I scarce can understand why God hath laid so many and such heavy sorrows upon me—for I have striven faithfully to do His will. Why hath He taken our children from us, Ragnfrid, one by one—first our sons—then little Ulvhild—and now have I given her that I loved dearest, honourless, to an untrusty and a witless man. Now is there none left to us but the little one—and unwise must I deem it to take joy in her, before I see how it will go with her—with Ramborg."

Ragnfrid shook like a leaf. Then the man laid his arm about her shoulders:

"Lie down," he said, "and let us sleep——" He lay for a while with his head against his wife's arm, sighing now and then, but at last he fell asleep.

It was still pitch dark in the barn when Ragnfrid stirred—she wondered to find that she had slept. She felt about with her hand; Lavrans was sitting up, with knees updrawn and his arms around them.

"Are *you* awake already?" she asked in wonder. "Are you cold?"

"No," said he, in a hoarse voice; "but I cannot go to sleep again."

"Is it Kristin you are thinking on?" asked the mother. "Like enough 'twill go better than we think, Lavrans," she said again.

"Ay, 'tis of that I was thinking," said the man. "Ay, ay—maid or woman, at least she is come to the bride-bed with the man she loves. And 'twas not so with either you or me, my poor Ragnfrid."

His wife gave a deep, dull moan, and threw herself down on her side amongst the hay. Lavrans put out a hand and laid it on her shoulder.

"But 'twas that I *could* not," said he, with passion and pain. "No, I *could* not—be as you would have had me—when we were young. I am not such a one——"

In a while Ragnfrid said softly through her weeping:

"Yet 'twas well with us in our life together, Lavrans—was it not?— all these years?"

"So thought I myself," answered he gloomily.

Thoughts crowded and tossed to and fro within him. That single unveiled glance in which the hearts of bridegroom and bride had leapt together—the two young faces flushing up redly—to him it seemed a very shamelessness. It had been agony, a scorching pain to him, that this was his daughter. But the sight of those eyes would not leave him; and wildly and blindly he strove against the tearing away of the veil from something in his own heart, something that he had never owned was there, that he had guarded against his own wife when she sought for it.

'Twas that he *could* not, he said again stubbornly, to himself. In the devil's name—he had been married off as a boy; he had not chosen for himself; she was older than he—he had not desired her; he had had no will to learn this of her—to love. He grew hot with shame even now when he thought of it—that she would have had him love her, when he had no will to have such love from her. That she had proffered him all this that he had never prayed for.

He had been a good husband to her—so he had ever thought. He had shown her all the honour he could, given her full power in her own affairs, and asked her counsel in all things; he had been true to her—and they had had six children together. All he had asked had been that he might live with her, without her for ever grasping at this thing in his heart that he would not lay bare. . . .

To none had he ever borne love. . . . Ingunn, Karl Steinsön's wife, at Bru? Lavrans flushed red in the pitch darkness. He had been their guest ever, as often as he journeyed down the Dale. He could not call to mind that he had spoken with the housewife *once* alone. But when he saw her—if he but thought of her, a sense came over him as of the first breath of the plough-lands in spring, when the snows are but now melted and gone. He knew it now—it might have befallen him too—he, too, could have loved.

But he had been wedded so young, and he had grown shy of love. And so it had come about that he throve best in the wild woods—or out on the waste uplands—where all things that live must have wide spaces around them—room to flee through—fearfully they look on any stranger that would steal upon them. . . .

One time in the year there was, when all the beasts in the woods and on the mountains forgot their shyness—when they rushed to their mates. But his had been given him unsought. And she had proffered him all he had not wooed her for.

But the young ones in the nest—they had been the little warm green spot in the wilderness—the inmost, sweetest joy of his life. Those little girl-heads under his hand. . . .

Marriage—they had wedded him, almost unasked. Friends—he had many, and he had none. War—it had brought him gladness, but there had been no more war—his armour hung there in the loft-room, little used. He had turned farmer. . . . But he had had his daughters—all his living and striving had grown dear to him, because by it he cherished them and made them safe, those soft, tender little beings he had held in his hands. He remembered Kristin's little two-year-old body on his shoulder, her flaxen, silky hair against his cheek; her small hands holding to his belt, while she butted her round, hard child's forehead against his shoulder-blades, when he rode out with her behind him on his horse.

And now had she that same glow in her eyes—and she had won what was hers. She sat there in the half-shadow against the silken pillows of the bed. In the candle-light she was all golden—golden crown and golden shift and golden hair spread over the naked golden arms. Her eyes were shy no longer——

Her father winced with shame.

And yet it was as though his heart was bleeding within him, for what he himself had never won; and for his wife, there by his side, whom he had never given what should have been hers.

Weak with pity, he felt in the darkness for Ragnfrid's hand:

"Ay, methought it was well with us in our life together," he said. "Methought 'twas but that you sorrowed for our children—ay, and that you were born heavy of mood. Never did it come to my mind, it might be that I was no good husband to you——"

Ragnfrid trembled fitfully:

"You were ever a good husband, Lavrans."

"H'm!" Lavrans sat with his chin resting on his knees. "Yet had it mayhap been better with you, if you had been wedded even as our daughter was to-day——"

Ragnfrid started up with a low, piercing cry:

"You know! How did you know it—how long have you known——?"

"I know not what 'tis you speak of," said Lavrans after a while, in a strange, deadened voice.

"This do I speak of—that I was no maid, when I came to be your wife," said Ragnfrid, and her voice rang clear in her despair.

In a little while Lavrans answered, as before:

"That have I never known, till now."

Ragnfrid laid her down among the hay, shaken with weeping. When the fit was over she lifted her head a little. A faint grey light was beginning to creep in through the window-hole in the wall. She could dimly see her husband, sitting with his arms thrown round his knees, motionless as stone.

"Lavrans—speak to me——" she wailed.

"What would you I should say?" asked he, without stirring.

"Oh—I know not—curse me—strike me——"

"'Twould be something late now," answered the man; there seemed to be the shade of a scornful smile in his voice.

Ragnfrid wept again: "Ay—I heeded not then that I was betraying you. So betrayed and so dishonoured, methought, had I been myself. There was none had spared me. They came and brought you—you know yourself, I saw you but three times before we were wed. . . . Methought you were but a boy, white and red—so young and child-ish——"

"I was so," said Lavrans, and a faint ring of life came to his voice. "And therefore a man might deem that you, who were a woman—you might have been more afraid to—to deceive one who was so young that he knew naught——"

"So did I think after," said Ragnfrid, weeping. "When I had come to know you. Soon came the time, when I would have given my soul twenty times over, to be guiltless of sin against you."

Lavrans sat silent and motionless; then said his wife:

"You ask not anything?"

"What use to ask? It was he that . . . we met his burial-train at Feginsbrekka, as we bore Ulvhild in to Nidaros——"

"Ay," said Ragnfrid. "We had to leave the way—go aside into a meadow. I saw them bear him by on his bier—with priests and monks and armed yeomen. I heard he had made a good end—had made his peace with God. I prayed as we stood there with Ulvhild's litter between us—I prayed that my sin and my sorrow might be laid at his feet on the Last Day——"

"Ay, like enough you did," said Lavrans, and there was the same shade of scorn in his quiet voice.

"You know not all," said Ragnfrid, cold with despair. "Mind you that he came out to us at Skog the first winter we were wedded——?"

"Ay," answered the man.

"When Björgulv was dying. . . . Oh, no one, no one had spared me. . . . He was drunk when he did it—afterwards he said he had never cared for me, he would not have me—he bade me forget it. My father knew it not; *he* did not betray you—never think that. But Trond —we were the dearest of friends to each other then—I made my moan to him. He tried to force the man to wed me; but he was but a boy; he was beaten. . . . Afterwards he counselled me to hold my peace, and to take you——"

She sat a while in silence.

"Then *he* came out to Skog—a year was gone by; I thought not on it so much any more. But he came out thither—he said that he repented, he would have had me now, had I been unwedded—he loved me. He said so. God knows if he said true. When he was gone—I dared not go out on the fjord, dared not for my sin, not with the child. And I had begun—I had begun to love you so!" She cried out, a single cry of the wildest pain. The man turned his head quickly towards her.

"When Björgulv was born—oh, I thought he was dearer to me than my life. When he lay in the death-throes—I thought, if he died, I must die too. But I prayed *not* God to spare my boy's life——"

Lavrans sat a long time silent—then he asked in a dead, heavy voice:

"Was it because I was not his father?"

"I knew not if you were," said Ragnfrid, growing stiff and stark where she sat.

Long they sat there in a deathly stillness. Then the man asked vehemently of a sudden:

"In Jesu name, Ragnfrid—why tell you me all this—now?"

"Oh, I know not!" She wrung her hands till the joints cracked. "That you may avenge you on me—drive me from your house——"

"Think you that would help me——" His voice shook with scorn.

"And then there are our daughters," he said quietly. "Kristin—and the little one."

Ragnfrid sat still awhile.

"I mind me how you judged of Erlend Nikulaussön," she said softly. "How judge you of me, then——?"

A long shudder of cold passed over the man's body—yet a little of the stiffness seemed to leave him.

"You have—we have lived together now for seven and twenty years—almost. 'Tis not the same as with a stranger. I see this, too—worse than misery has it been for you."

Ragnfrid sank together sobbing at his words. She plucked up heart to put her hand on one of his. He moved not at all—sat as still as a dead man. Her weeping grew louder and louder—but her husband still sat motionless, looking at the faint grey light creeping in around the door. At last she lay as if all her tears were spent. Then he stroked her arm lightly downward—and she fell to weeping again.

"Mind you," she said through her tears, "that man who came to us one time, when we dwelt at Skog? He that knew all the ancient lays? Mind you the lay of a dead man that was come back from the world of torment, and told his son the story of all that he had seen? There was heard a groaning from hell's deepest ground, the querns of untrue women grinding mould for their husbands' meat. Bloody were the stones they dragged at—bloody hung the hearts from out their breasts——"

Lavrans was silent.

"All these years have I thought upon those words," said Ragnfrid. "Every day 'twas as though my heart was bleeding, for every day methought I ground you mould for meat——"

Lavrans knew not himself why he answered as he did. It seemed to him his breast was empty and hollow, like the breast of a man that has had the blood-eagle* carven through his back. But he laid his hand heavily and wearily on his wife's head, and spoke:

"Mayhap mould must needs be ground, my Ragnfrid, before the meat can grow."

When she tried to take his hand and kiss it, he snatched it away. But then he looked down at his wife, took one of her hands and laid it on his knee, and bowed his cold, stiffened face down upon it. And so they sat on, motionless, speaking no word more.

* Blood-eagle, see Note 26.

THE MISTRESS OF HUSABY

Part One

THE FRUIT OF SIN

I

T H E evening before Simon's Mass,* Baard Peterssön's galleass lay in
to the landing-place at Birgsi. Abbot Olav of Nidarholm had himself
ridden down to the strand to greet his kinsman, Erlend Nikulaussön,
and bid welcome to the young wife he was bringing with him home.
The pair were to be the Abbot's guests, and to sleep at Vigg that night.

It was a deathly pale, woebegone young wife that Erlend led shore-
ward from the pier. The Abbot spoke jestingly of the pains of the sea-
voyage; Erlend laughed and said he well believed his wife longed for
nothing so much as to lie once more in a bed well fixed into a house-
wall. And Kristin strove to smile; but within herself she thought that
never, so long as she lived, would she willingly set foot on shipboard
again. She turned sick if Erlend so much as came near her, he smelt
so of the ship and of the sea—his hair was all matted and sticky with
sea-water. He had been crazy with joy all the time on board—and
Sir Baard had laughed: at his home in Möre, where Erlend had grown
up, the boys had been out in the boats sailing or rowing late and early.
'Twas true they had been a little sorry for her, Erlend and Sir Baard,
but not so sorry, Kristin thought, as her wretchedness deserved. They
kept on saying the sea-sickness would pass when she grew used to being
aboard ship. But from first to last her misery had not abated.

Even the next morning she felt as if she were still sailing, as she rode
up through the settled lands. Uphill and downhill, their road led over
great, steep clay ridges, and when she tried to fix her eyes on some
spot on the hills far ahead, it was as though the whole country-side
were dipping, then rising, in waves cast up against the shining, blue-
white winter-morning sky.

A whole troop of Erlend's friends and neighbours had come to Vigg
in the early morning to attend the bridal pair, so that they rode in a
great company. The ground sounded hollow under the horses' hoofs,
for the earth was as hard as iron with the black frost. The air was full
of steam from the men and horses; the bodies of the beasts and the
men's hair and furs were white with rime. Erlend seemed as white-
haired as the Abbot; his face glowed from his morning draught and
the biting wind. He wore his bridegroom's dress to-day; youth and
gladness seemed to shine out of him, and joy and wantonness welled
out in the tones of his mellow, supple voice as he rode, shouting and
laughing, amidst his guests.

Kristin's heart began to tremble strangely—with sorrow, with tenderness and with fear. She was still sick from the voyage; she had the

* 28th October.

burning pain at her breast that came now whenever she had eaten or drunk never so little; she was bitterly cold; and deep down in her mind was a dull, dumb spot of anger with Erlend, that he could be so gay and care-free. . . . And yet, now that she saw his childlike pride and sparkling happiness in bringing her home as his wife, a bitter regret welled up in her; her breast ached with pity for him. She wished now that she had not hearkened to the counsel of her own self-will, but had let Erlend know when he was at her home last summer —let him know what made it most unfit that their wedding should be held with too great pomp. She saw now that she had wished he should be made to feel—he too—that they could not escape unhumbled from what they had done.

——And she had been afraid of her father, too. And she had thought in her mind: when once their bride-ale had been drunk, they were to journey so far off; 'twas like she would not see her home-country again for a long, long time—not till all talk about her had had good time to die away. . . .

Now she saw that things here would be much worse than she had deemed. True, Erlend had spoken of the great house-warming he would hold at Husaby, but she had not thought it would be like a second wedding-feast. And the guests here were the folk that Erlend and she were to live among—it was their respect and friendship they had need to win. It was these folk that had had Erlend's folly and evil fortunes before their eyes all these years. Now he himself believed that he had redeemed himself in their judgment, that now he could take the place among his fellows that was due to his birth and fortune. And now 'twas like he would be a laughing-stock through this whole country-side when it came out that he had done amiss with his own betrothed bride.

The Abbot leant over towards her from his horse:

"You look so sad, Kristin Lavransdatter; are you not quit of your sea-sickness yet? Or is it, perhaps, that you are home-sick for your mother?"

"Even so, sir," said Kristin softly; "'tis of my mother I am thinking."

They had come up into Skaun, and were riding high on a hill-side. Below them in the valley bottom the woods stood white and shaggy with rime; everywhere the sunlight glittered, and a small lake in the midst flashed blue. Then all at once the troop passed out from a little pinewood, and Erlend pointed ahead:

"There lies Husaby,* Kristin. God grant you many happy days there, my own wife!" he said, with a thrill in his voice.

Before them stretched broad plough-lands, white with rime. The

* See Note 1.

manor stood, as it were, on a broad shelf midway on the hill-side—nearest them lay a small church of light-coloured stone, and just south of it were the clustered houses; they were many and great; the smoke whirled up from their smoke-vents. Bells began ringing from the church, and many folk came streaming from the courtyard to meet them, with shouts of greeting. The young men in the bridal trains clashed their weapons one on another—and with a great clattering and the thunder of hoofs and joyous uproar the troop swept forward towards the new-married man's abode.

They stopped before the church. Erlend lifted his bride from her horse, and led her forward to the church-door, where a little crowd of priests and clerks stood waiting to welcome them. Within, it was bitterly cold, and the daylight, sifting in through the small round-arched windows of the nave, dulled the shine of the tapers burning in the choir.

Kristin felt lost and afraid when Erlend loosed her hand and went over to the men's side, while she herself took her place among the throng of strange women, all in festal dress. The service was most goodly. But Kristin was very cold, and it seemed as though her prayers were blown back upon her when she tried to free her heart and lift it upwards. She thought maybe it was no good omen that this should be St. Simon's day—the guardian saint of the man by whom she had done so ill.

From the church all the people went in procession down to the manor, the priests first, then Kristin and Erlend hand in hand, then their guests pair by pair. Kristin was not enough herself to see much of the manor buildings. The courtyard was long and narrow; the houses lay in two rows, south and north of it. They were big and built close together; but they looked old and ill-tended.

The procession halted at the door of the hall-house, and the priests blessed it with holy water. Then Erlend led her through a dark outer room. On her right a door was thrown open, letting out a flood of light. She bent, passing through the doorway, and stood with Erlend in his hall.

It was the greatest room* she had ever seen in any man's dwelling-house. There was a hearth-place in the midst of the floor, and it was so long that there were two fires on it, one at each end; and the room was so broad that the cross-beams were borne up on carven pillars—it seemed to her more like the body of a church or a king's hall than a room in a manor-house. Up by the eastern gable-end, where the high seat stood in the middle of the wall-bench, closed box-beds were built in between the timber pillars.

* See Note 2.

And what a mass of lights were burning in the hall—on the tables, that groaned with costly cups and vessels, and on sconces fastened to the walls! After the fashion of the old age, weapons and shields hung amidst the stretched-out tapestries. Behind the high seat the wall was covered with a velvet hanging, and against it a man was even now fastening up Erlend's gold-mounted sword and his white shield with the red lion salient.

Serving-men and women had taken the guests' outer garments from them. Erlend took his wife by the hand and led her forward to the hearth, the guests standing in a half-ring just behind them. A fat lady with a gentle face came forward and shook out Kristin's head-linen, where it had been crumpled by the hood of her cloak. As she stepped back into her place, she nodded to the young couple and smiled; Erlend nodded and smiled back to her, and looked down at his wife —his face, as he looked, was beautiful. And again Kristin felt her heart sink—with pity for him. She knew what he was thinking now, as he saw her standing there in his hall with the long snow-white linen coif over her scarlet bridal dress. And this morning she had had to wind a long woven belt tight around her waist under her clothes before she could get the dress to fit upon her, and she had rubbed upon her cheeks some of a red salve that Lady Aashild had given her; and while she thus bedecked herself, she had thought in sorrow and bitterness that Erlend must look but little upon her, now that he had her safely his own—since he still saw and knew nothing. Bitterly she repented now that she had not told him.

While the married pair stood thus, hand in hand, the priests were walking the round of the hall, blessing house and hearth and bed and board.

Next a serving-woman bore forth the keys of the house to Erlend. He hooked the heavy bunch on Kristin's belt—and looked, as he did so, as though he had been fain to kiss her where she stood. A man brought a great horn ringed about with golden rings—Erlend set it to his lips and drank to her:

"Hail, and welcome to thy house, Lady of Husaby!"

And the guests shouted and laughed while she drank with her husband and poured out the rest of the wine on the hearth-fire.

Then the minstrels struck up their music, as Erlend Nikulaussön led his wedded wife to the high-seat, and the wedding guests took their seats at the board.

On the third day the guests began to break up, and by the hour of nones on the fifth day the last of them were gone, and Kristin was alone with her husband at Husaby.

The first thing she did was to bid the serving-folk take all the bed-gear out of the bed, wash it and the walls round about it with lye, and carry out and burn up the straw. Then she had the bedstead filled with fresh straw, and above it made up the bed with bed-clothes from the store she had brought with her. It was late in the night before this work was at an end. But Kristin gave order that the same should be done with all the beds on the place, and that the skin rugs should be well baked in the bath-house—the maids must set to the work in the morning the first thing, and get as much done towards it as they could before the Sunday holiday. Erlend shook his head and laughed—she was a housewife indeed! But he was not a little ashamed.

For Kristin had not had much sleep the first night, even though the priests had blessed her bed. 'Twas spread above with silken pillows, with sheets of linen and the bravest rugs and furs; but beneath was dirty, mouldy straw, and there were lice in the bed-clothes and in the splendid black bearskin that was spread over all.

Many things had she seen already in these few days. Behind the costly tapestry hangings, the unwashed walls were black with dirt and soot. At the feast there had been masses of food, but much of it spoilt with ill dressing and ill service. And to make up the fires they had had naught but green and wet logs, that would scarce catch fire, and that filled the hall with smoke.

Everywhere she had seen ill husbandry when on the second day she went round with Erlend and looked over the manor and farm. By the time the feasting was over, little would be left in barn and store-house; the corn-bins were all but swept clean. And she could not understand how Erlend could think to keep all the horses and so many cattle through the winter on the little hay and straw that was in the barns —of leaf-fodder there was not enough even for the sheep and goats.

But there was a loft half full of flax that had been left lying unused —there must have been the greatest part of many years' harvest. And then a storehouse full of old, old unwashed and stinking wool, some in sacks and some lying loose in heaps. When Kristin took up a handfull, a shower of little brown eggs fell from it—moth and maggots had got into it.

The cattle were wretched, lean, galled and scabby; and never had she seen so many aged beasts together, in one place. Only the horses were comely and well-tended. But, even so, there was no one of them that was the equal of Guldsveinen or of Ringdrotten, the stallion her father had now. Slöngvanbauge, the horse he had given her to take along with her from home, was the fairest beast in the Husaby stables. When she came to him, she had to go and throw her arms round his neck and press her face against his cheek.

She thought on her father's face, when the time came for her to ride away with Erlend and he lifted her to the saddle. He had put on an air of gladness, for many folk were standing round them; but she had seen his eyes. He stroked her arm downwards, and held her hand in his for farewell. At the moment, it might be, she had thought most how glad she was that she was to get away at last. But now it seemed to her that as long as she lived her soul would be wrung with pain when she remembered her father's eyes at that hour.

And so Kristin Lavransdatter began to guide and order all things in her house. She was up at cock-crow every morning, though Erlend raised his voice against it, and made as though he would keep her in bed by force—surely no one expected a newly-married wife to rush about from house to house long before 'twas daylight.

When she saw in what an ill way all things were here, and how much there was for her to set her hand to, a thought shot through her clear and hard; if she had burdened her soul with sin that she might come hither, let it even be so—but 'twas no less sin to deal with God's gifts as they had been dealt with here. Shame upon the folk that had had the guidance of things here, and on all them that had let Erlend's goods go so to waste! There had been no fit steward at Husaby for the last two years; Erlend himself had been much away from home in that time, and besides, he understood but little of the management of the estate. 'Twas no more than was to be looked for, then, that his bailiffs in the outlying parishes should cheat him, as she was sure they did, and that the serving-folk at Husaby should work only as much as they pleased, and when and how it chanced to suit them. 'Twould be no light task for her to put things right again.

One day she talked of these things with Ulf Haldorssön, Erlend's own henchman. They ought to have had the threshing done by now, at least of the corn from the home farm—and there was none too much of it either—before the time came to slaughter for winter meat. Ulf said:

"You know, Kristin, that I am not a farm-hand. It has been our place to be Erlend's arms-bearers—Haftor's and mine—and I have no skill in husbandry any longer."

"I know it," said the mistress of the house. "But so it is, Ulf, that 'twill be no easy task for me to guide things here this winter, a new-comer as I am here north of Dovre, and with no knowledge of our folks. 'Twould be a friend's turn of you if you would help and counsel me."

"I can well believe it, Kristin—that you will have no easy task this winter," said the man, looking at her with a little smile—the strange

smile that was always on his face when he spoke with her or with
Erlend. It was bold and mocking, and yet there were both kindness
and a sort of respect for her in his bearing. Nor, it seemed to her, had
she a right to take offence that Ulf should bear himself more forwardly
towards her than might have been seemly otherwise. She herself and
Erlend had made this serving-man a party to their wanton and deceitful doings; and she could see that he knew, too, how things stood with
her now. She must let this pass—and indeed she saw that Erlend put
up with anything Ulf might say or do, and that the man showed but
little reverence for his master. True, they had been friends from childhood; Ulf came from Möre, and was son to a small farmer that lived
near Baard Petersson's manor. He called Erlend by his name; and
her, too, now—it was true that this way of speech was commoner here
north of Dovre than in her own country.

Ulf Haldorssön was a proper man, tall and dark, with sightly eyes;
but his mouth was ugly and coarse. Kristin had heard ugly tales of
him from the maids on the place—when he was in at the city he drank
beyond measure and spent his time in revel and roistering in the lowest
houses of call—but at home at Husaby he was the best man to have at
one's beck, the fittest, the hardest worker, and the shrewdest. Kristin
had come to like him well.

"'Twere no easy thing for any woman," he went on, "to come hither
to this house—after all that has come and gone. And yet, Mistress
Kristin, I deem that you will win through it better than most could
have done. You are not the woman to sit down and moan and whimper; but you will set your thoughts on saving your children's inheritance yourself, since none else here takes thought for such things. And
methinks you know that you can trust me, and that I will help you as
far as in me lies. You must bear in mind that I am unused to farm
work. But if you will take counsel with me and let me come to you
for counsel, I trow we will tide over this winter none so ill."

Kristin thanked Ulf, and went into the house.

She was heavy at heart with unrest and fear, but she tried to forget
it in work. One thing was that she understood not Erlend—even now
he seemed to suspect nothing. But another and a worse trouble was
that she could feel no life in the child she bore within her. At twenty
weeks it should quicken, she knew—and now more than three weeks
over the twenty had gone by. She lay awake at night and felt the
burden within her that grew greater and heavier, but was still as dull
and lifeless as ever. And there floated through her mind all she had
heard of children that were born crippled, with sinews stiff as stone,
of births that had come to the light without limbs—with scarce a

semblance of human shape. Before her tight-shut eyes would pass pictures of little infants, dreadfully misshapen; one shape of horror melting into another still worse. Southward in the dale at home, at Lidstad, the folks had a child—nay, it must be grown up now. Her father had seen it, but would never speak of it; she had marked that he grew ill at ease if anyone but named aught of it. What did it look like?—Oh, no! Holy Saint Olav, pray for me!—She must needs trust firmly on the holy King's tender mercy; had she not placed her child under His ward? She would suffer for her sins in meekness, and with her whole heart have faith that there would be help and mercy for the child. It must be the Enemy himself that tempted her with these ugly visions, to drive her to despair. But her nights were evil. . . . If a child had no limbs, if it were palsied, like enough the mother would feel no sign of life within her. . . . Erlend, half waking, marked that his wife was restless, drew her closer into his arms, and laid his face against the hollow of her throat.

But by day she showed no sign of trouble. And every morning she dressed her body with care so as to hide from the house-folk yet a little longer that she bore another life about with her.

It was the custom at Husaby that after the evening meal the serving-folk went off to the houses where they slept; so that she and Erlend were left alone in the hall. Altogether the ways of this manor were more as they had been in the ancient days, when folks kept thralls and bondswomen for the household work. There was no fixed table in the hall, but morning and evening the meals were spread on a great board that was laid on trestles, and after the meal it was hung up again on the wall. At the other meals folks took their food over to the benches and sat and ate it there. Kristin knew such had been the custom in former times. But nowadays, when 'twas hard to find men to serve at table, and all folks had to content them with maids for indoor work, it fitted the times no longer—the women were loath to break their backs lifting the heavy tables. Kristin remembered her mother telling how at Sundbu they had put a fixed table into the hall when she was but eight winters old, and that the women thought it in every way the greatest boon—they need no longer take all their sewing out to the women's house, but could sit in the hall and clip and cut out—and it made such a goodly show to have candlesticks and a few costly vessels standing out in view. Kristin thought: next summer she would pray Erlend to have a fixed table set up along the northern wall.

So it was at her home, and there her father had his high seat at the board's end—but then the beds there were by the entrance wall. At home her mother sat highest up on the outer bench, so that she could go to and fro and keep an eye on the service of the food. Only when there was a feast did Ragnfrid sit by her husband's side. But here the high seat stood in the middle of the eastern gable-end, and Erlend would have her always sit in it with him. At home her father always placed God's servants in the high seat, if any such were guests at the manor, and he himself and Ragnfrid served them while they ate and drank. But Erlend would have none of this, unless they were high of station. He was no great lover of priests and monks—they were costly friends, he was used to say. Kristin could not but think of what her father and Sira Eirik alway: said, when folk complained of the church-men's greed of money: men forgot the sinful joys they had snatched for themselves when the time came to pay for them.

She questioned Erlend about the life here at Husaby in ancient days. But he knew strangely little. Things were thus and thus, he had heard; but he could not remember so nicely. King Skule had owned the manor and built on it—'twas said he had meant to make Husaby his dwelling-place, when he gave away Rein for a nunnery. Erlend was right proud of his descent from the Duke, whom he always called King, and from Bishop Nikulaus; the Bishop was the father of his grandfather, Munan Bishopsson. But it seemed to Kristin that he knew no more of these men than she herself knew already from her father's tales. At home it was otherwise. Neither her father nor her mother was overproud of the power of their forbears and the high esteem they had enjoyed. But they spoke often of them; held up the good that they knew of them as a pattern, and told of their faults and the evil that had come of them as a warning. And they had little tales of mirth too—of Ivar Gjesling the Old and his quarrel with King Sverre; of Ivar Provst's quick and witty sallies; of Haavard Gjesling's huge bulk; and of Ivar Gjesling the Young's wonderful luck in the chase. Lavrans told of his grand-father's brother that carried off the Folkunga maid from Vreta cloister; of his grandfather's mother Ramborg Sunesdatter, who longed always for her home in Wester Gothland and at last went through the ice and was lost, when driving on Lake Vener one time she was staying with her brother at Solberga. He told of his father's prowess in arms, and of his unspeakable sorrow over his young first wife, Kristin Sigurds-datter, that died in childbirth when Lavrans was born. And he read, from a book, of his ancestress the holy Lady Elin of Skövde, who was given grace to be one of God's blood-witnesses. Her father had often spoken of making a pilgrimage with Kristin to the grave of this holy widow. But it had never come to pass.

In her fear and distress, Kristin tried to pray to this saint that she herself was linked to by the tie of blood. She prayed to St. Elin for her child, kissing the reliquary that she had had of her father; in it was a shred of the holy lady's shroud. But Kristin was afraid of St. Elin, now when she had brought such shame on her race. When she prayed to St. Olav and St. Thomas for their intercession, she often felt that her complaints found a way to living ears and merciful hearts. These two martyrs for righteousness her father loved above all other saints; above even St. Laurentius himself, though this was the saint he was called after, and in honour of whose day in the late summer he always held a great drinking-feast and gave richly in alms. St. Thomas her father had himself seen in his dreams one night when he lay wounded outside Baagahus. No tongue could tell how lovely and venerable he was to look on, and Lavrans himself had been able to say naught but "Lord! Lord!" But the radiant figure in the Bishop's raiment had gently touched his wounds and promised that he should have his life and the use of his limbs, so that he should see again his wife and his daughter, according to his prayer. But at that time no man had believed that Lavrans Björgulfsön could live the night through.

Aye, said Erlend. One heard of such things. Naught of the kind had ever befallen him, and to be sure 'twas not like that it should— for he had never been a pious man, such as Lavrans was.

Then Kristin asked of all the folk who had been at their home-coming feast. Erlend had not much to say of them either. It seemed to Kristin that her husband was not much like the folks of this country-side. They were comely folk, many of them, fair and ruddy of hue, with round hard heads and bodies strong and heavily built—many of the older folks were hugely fat. Erlend looked like a strange bird among his guests. He was a head taller than most of the men, slim and lean, with slender limbs and fine joints. And he had black silky hair and was pale brown of hue—but with light-blue eyes under coal-black brows and long black eyelashes. His forehead was high and narrow, the temples hollow, the nose somewhat too great and the mouth something too small and weak for a man—but he was comely none the less; she had seen no man that was half so fair as Erlend. Even his mellow, quiet voice was unlike the others' thick full-fed utterance.

Erlend laughed and said his forbears were not of these parts either —only his grandfather's mother, Ragnfrid Skulesdatter. Folks said he was much like his mother's father, Gaute Erlendssön of Skogheim. Kristin asked what he knew about this grandfather. But it proved to be almost nothing.

One night Erlend and Kristin were undressing in the hall. Erlend could not get his shoe-latchet unloosed; as he cut it, the knife slipped and gashed his hand. He bled much and swore savagely. Kristin fetched a piece of linen from her chest. She was in her shift. As she was binding up his hand, Erlend passed his other arm around her waist.

Of a sudden he looked down into her face with fear and confusion in his eyes, and his face grew red as fire. Kristin bowed her head. Erlend took away his arm, saying nothing—then Kristin went off in silence and crept into the bed. Her heart beat with hard dull strokes against her ribs. Now and again she looked over at her husband. He had turned his back to her, and was slowly drawing off one garment after another. At last he came to the bed and lay down.

Kristin waited for him to speak. She waited so, that at times 'twas as though her heart no longer beat, but only stood still and quivered in her breast.

But Erlend said no word. Nor did he take her in his arms. At last, falteringly, he laid a hand across her breast and pressed his chin down on her shoulder so strongly that the stubble of his beard pricked her skin. As he still spoke not a word, Kristin turned to the wall.

It was as though she were sinking, sinking. Not a word could he find to give her—now when he knew that she had borne his child within her all this long weary time. She clenched her teeth hard in the dark. Never would she beg and beseech—if he chose to be silent, she would be silent too, even, if need be, till the day she bore his child. Bitterness surged through her heart; but she lay stock-still against the wall. And Erlend too lay still in the dark. Hour after hour they lay thus, and each knew that the other was not sleeping. At last she heard by his even breathing that he had fallen asleep; and then she let the tears flow as they would, in sorrow and bitterness and shame. Never, it seemed to her, could she forgive him this.

For three days Erlend and Kristin went about thus—he like a wet dog, the young wife thought. She was hot and hard with wrath—she grew wild with rage when she marked that he would look searchingly at her and then hastily look away again if she turned her eyes towards him.

On the morning of the fourth day, as she sat in the hall, Erlend came in through the doorway, dressed for riding. He said he was going westward to Medalby; maybe she would come with him and see the place; it was one of the farms that fell under her morning-gift. Kristin said yes; and Erlend helped her himself to put on her long shaggy boots and the black sleeve-cloak with the silver clasps.

In the courtyard were four horses ready saddled, but Erlend said now that Haftor and Egil might stay at home and help with the thresh-ing. Then he helped his wife up into the saddle. Kristin felt that 'twas in Erlend's mind to speak now of what lay between them unuttered. Yet he said naught as they rode slowly southward towards the woods.

It was far on now in the early winter, but no snow had yet fallen in this country-side. The day was fresh and fair, the sun just risen, and the white rime glittered in silver and gold everywhere, on the fields and on the trees. They were riding over the Husaby lands. Kristin saw that there was little sown or stubble land, but mostly fallows left for grass, and old meadow-land, uneven, moss-grown and choked with alder-shoots. She spoke of this.

Her husband answered jauntily:

"Know you not, Kristin, you that have such skill in guiding goods and gear, that it profits not to raise corn so near to a great market?— a man does better by bartering his wool and butter for the outland merchants' corn and flour——"

"Then should you have bartered away all that wool that lies now in your lofts and is long since spoiled," said Kristin. "But so much I know, that the law says every man that leases land shall sow corn on three parts of it, and let the fourth part lie fallow for grass. And 'tis not fit that the landlord's manor should be worse cared for than the tenants' farms—so my father always said."

Erlend laughed a little, and answered:

"I have never searched out the law in that matter—so long as I have my dues, my tenants can till their farms as likes them best, and, for Husaby, I manage it as seems to me best and fittest."

"Would you be wiser, then," asked Kristin, "than our fathers that went before us, and St. Olav and King Magnus that made these laws?"

Erlend laughed again and said:

"'Tis a matter I have never thought on—but the devil and all must be in it, Kristin, that you have the laws of the land so at your finger-ends——"

"I know a little of these things," said Kristin, "because my father often prayed Sigurd of Loptsgaard to say over the laws to us when he came to visit us and we sat at home of an evening. Father deemed it profitable for the servants and the young folk to learn somewhat of such things; and so Sigurd would repeat one passage or another."

"Sigurd——" said Erlend. "Aye, now I remember seeing him at our wedding. He was that long-nosed toothless old fellow that wept and drivelled and patted you on the breast—he was drunk as an owl even the next morning, when the folks came up to see me set the linen coif on your head——"

"He has known me from before I can remember," said Kristin angrily. "He used to take me on his lap and play with me when I was a little maid——"

Erlend laughed again:

"Well, 'twas a strange pastime enough—for you all to sit there and listen to that old fellow chanting out the laws, part by part. Sure Lavrans is in all ways unlike other men—others are used to say that if the peasant knew the laws of the land in full, and the stallion knew his strength, 'twould take the devil to be a knight."

Suddenly, with a cry, Kristin struck her horse on the quarter and dashed on, leaving Erlend gazing after his wife in wonderment and anger.

Of a sudden he put spurs to his horse. Christ—the ford—there was no crossing over it now—the clay bank had slipped in the autumn. Slöngvanbauge stretched himself to gallop the harder when he heard the other horse behind him. Erlend was in deadly fear—how she was dashing down the steep hill-sides too! At last he tore past her through the undergrowth, then swung into the road where it ran level for a little way, and stood so that she must needs stop. When he came along-side her, he saw that she seemed a little frightened herself now.

Erlend leant forward towards his wife and struck her a ringing blow under the ear—so that Slöngvanbauge leapt aside and reared in fright.

"Aye, and you deserved it," said Erlend in a shaken voice, when the horses had quieted down and they were riding side by side again. "To carry on so—clean crazy with rage. You frighted me——"

Kristin held her head so that he could not see her face. Erlend was wishing that he had not struck her. But he said again:

"You made me afraid, Kristin—to behave so! And of all times, now——" he added in a low voice.

Kristin neither answered nor looked at him. But Erlend could feel that she was less angry now than before, when he had mocked at her home. He wondered much at this—but he saw that so it was.

They came to Medalby, and Erlend's tenant came out and would have them into the dwelling-house. But Erlend said 'twere well they should look round the farm-buildings first—and Kristin must come with them. "The farm is hers now—and she understands these things better than I, Stein," he said, laughing. There were some other farmers there, come to act as witnesses—some of them too were Erlend's tenants.

Stein had come to the farm last term-day, and ever since he had been praying that the landlord would come up and see the state of the houses when he took them over, or would send men to act for him. The other farmers bore witness that not one of the houses had been weather-tight, and that those which now were tumble-down had been no better when Stein came. Kristin saw that it was a good farm, but that it had been ill cared for. She could see that this Stein was a hard-working man. Erlend, too, was reasonable and promised him some relief in his rents, till such time as he had got the houses mended.

Then they went into the hall, and found the board set out with good food and strong ale. The farmer's wife begged Kristin to forgive that she had not come out to meet her. She said her husband would not suffer her to go out under open sky till she had been churched after her childbed. Kristin greeted the woman kindly, and had her take her over to the cradle to look at the child. It was these people's first-born: a son twelve days old, and big and sturdy.

Next Erlend and Kristin were led to the high-seat, and all the folks sat down, and ate and drank a good while. Kristin was the one that talked most during the meal; Erlend said little, and the peasants not much; but Kristin thought she could mark that they liked her well.

Then the child awoke, and began first to whimper, and then to shriek so fearfully that the mother had to fetch it and give it the breast to stop its cries. Kristin looked more than once across at the two, and when the boy was full-fed and quiet, she took him from the woman and laid him on her arm.

"Look, husband!" she said. "Is not this a fair and lusty knave?"

"Doubtless it is," said her husband, not looking towards them.

Kristin sat holding the child a little before she gave it back to the mother.

"I will send over a gift for this little son of yours, Arndis," she said, "for that he is the first child I have held in my arms since I came hither north of Dovre."

Hot and defiant, with a little smile, she looked at her husband and then along the row of peasants on the bench. There was the least little twitching at the corners of the mouths of one or two of them; but immediately they stared before them, stiff with solemnity. Then stood up a very old fellow who had drunk well already. He took the ladle out of the ale-bowl, laid it on the table and lifted the heavy vessel aloft:

"Then will we pledge you, mistress, on a wish: that the next child you hold in your arms may be the new master of Husaby!"

Kristin rose up and took the heavy bowl. First she held it out to her husband. Erlend but touched it with his lips, but Kristin drank deep and long.

"Thanks for that good wish, Jon o' the Woods," she said, nodding to him, her face shining and gleeful. Then she passed on the bowl.

Erlend sat there darkly flushed and, Kristin could see, in great wrath. She herself felt naught now but an unthinking need to laugh and be glad. Some time after, Erlend gave the sign for breaking up, and they set out on their homeward way.

They had ridden a good way in silence, when Erlend broke out of a sudden:

"Think you it was needful to let our very peasants know you were with child when you were wedded? You may stake your soul that 'twill be no time now ere the tale about us two is all over every parish by the Trondheim Fjord. . . ."

Kristin made no answer at first. She looked straight forth over her horse's head, and her face grew so white that Erlend was afraid.

"As long as I live, I shall not forget," she said at last, without looking at him, "that this was your first greeting to your young son that is beneath my girdle."

"Kristin!" said Erlend beseechingly. "My Kristin," he implored, when she answered not, nor looked at him. "Kristin!"

"Sir?" she said in cold, measured tones, without turning her head.

Erlend swore furiously, set spurs to his horse and dashed forward along the road. But, a little after, he came riding back to meet her.

"Now had you vexed me so sorely," he said, "that *I* was nigh riding off and leaving *you*."

"And if you had," answered Kristin quietly, "it might have been that you had had long and long to wait ere I came after you to Husaby."

"How you talk!" said the man despairingly.

Again they rode for a space without speaking. In a while they came to a place where a bridle-path led off over a ridge. Erlend said to his wife:

"I had meant that we should ride home by this way over the hill— 'tis a little farther, but I had a mind to take you up here with me some time."

Kristin nodded listlessly.

In a little, Erlend said it would be better they should go on foot. He tied their horses to a tree.

"Gunnulf and I had a fort on the hill-top here," he said. "I would like well to see if any of our castle is left——"

He took her hand. She let him hold it, but walked with her eyes cast down, looking to her footing. It was not long before they reached the top. Over the rime-covered woods in the gorge of the little stream they saw Husaby on the hill-side right over against them, lying wide-stretched and brave, with its stone church and the many great houses, wide plough-lands around it and dark pine-clad ridges behind.

"Mother," said Erlend in a low voice, "she would come with us up here—often. But always she sat gazing south, up towards the Dovref-jeld. I trow she longed both early and late to be gone from Husaby. Or sometimes she would turn to the north and look towards the hill-glen where you see the far-off blue—the hills beyond the fjord. Never did she look across at Husaby."

His voice was soft and beseeching. But Kristin neither spoke nor looked at him. Soon he went off and began kicking the frozen heather: "No, I can see there's naught left here of Gunnulf's and my stronghold. True enough, 'tis many a long day since we played about here, Gunnulf and I——"

There was no answer.—Right below where they stood lay a little frozen pool—Erlend took up a stone and threw it down on to the ice. The pool was frozen to the bottom, so the stone did but make a small white star on the black mirror. Erlend took another stone and threw harder—then another and yet another, till at last he was showering down stones furiously, bent on splintering the ice to shards. Then he caught sight of his wife's face—she stood there with eyes dark with scorn, smiling disdainfully at his childishness.

Erlend turned sharp round—but at the same moment Kristin grew deadly pale, and her eyelids closed. She stood clutching in the air with her hands, swaying as if about to fall—then caught the trunk of a tree and held to it.

"Kristin—what is it?" he asked fearfully.

She made no answer, but stood as if she were listening for something. Her eyes were far away and strange.

Now she felt it again. Deep down within her she felt as though a fish moved its tail. And again it was as if the whole earth swayed around her, and she grew dizzy and weak, but less now than at first.

"What is amiss with you?" said Erlend once again.

She had waited so for this—hardly daring to acknowledge to herself the anguish of her waiting. She could not speak of it—now, when they had been unfriends this whole day. But then *he* said it:

"Was it the child that grew quick within you?" he asked in a low voice, touching her shoulder.

At that she cast from her all her wrath against him, and clung to her child's father and hid her face in his breast.

Soon after, they went down again to the place where their horses were tied. The short day was nearly done; behind them in the southwest the sun went down behind the tree-tops, a blurred red ball in the frost-haze.

Erlend tried his wife's saddle-girths and buckles with care before he lifted her up to the saddle. Then he went and untied his own horse. He felt under his belt for his gloves, which he had stuck in there, and found but one. He began to look about on the hill-side.

Kristin could not forbear saying:

"'Tis of no use seeking here for your glove, Erlend."

"You might as lief have told me, if you saw me lose it—though you were never so wroth with me," he said. The gloves were those Kristin had sewn for him and given him with her betrothal-gifts.

"It fell from your belt when you struck me," said Kristin very low, and with downcast eyes.

Erlend stood by his horse's shoulder, with his hand on the saddle-bow. He looked abashed and unhappy; but of a sudden he burst out laughing:

"Never had I deemed, Kristin—in those days when I was wooing you, running around beseeching my kinsmen to speak for me, and making me so supple-jointed and so humble to win you—that you could ever be such a troll!"

Then Kristin, too, laughed:

"No—for if you had, doubtless you had given up that quest long before—and doubtless that had been best for you."

Erlend took a couple of strides across to her and laid his hand upon her knee:

"Jesus help us, Kristin—when have you ever heard tell of me that I did the thing that was best for me——?"

He laid his head down on her lap and looked with shining eyes up in his wife's face. Flushed and happy, Kristin bent her head and tried to hide from him her smile and her eyes.

He took her horse by the bit and let his own follow after them; so he led her till they were come down from the hill-side. Every time he looked at her, he laughed; and she turned away her head from him to hide that she was laughing too.

"Now," he said gaily when they were down again on the road, "now will we ride home to Husaby, my Kristin, and be as happy as two thieves!"

II

ON Yule Eve it blew and rained in torrents. 'Twas no fit weather for sleighing, so Kristin had to stay at home when Erlend and the house-folk rode off to midnight mass at Birgsi church.

She stood in the doorway of the hall and looked after them. The fir-root torches they bore shone red on the murky old house-walls, and were mirrored in the watery glaze of the courtyard. The wind took the flames and blew them flat out sidewise. Kristin stood till the noise of their going died away in the night.

Within, in the hall, tapers burned on the board. It was littered with the leavings of the supper—slabs of porridge in platters, half-eaten bread-slices and fishbones in puddles of spilt ale. The serving-maids who were to stay at home had lain down already in their resting-places on the floor-straw. Kristin was alone on the manor with them and one old man that they called Aan. He had served at Husaby since the days of Erlend's grandfather; he lived now in a little hut down by the lake, but often came up to the manor in the day-time, and went pottering about, doing, as he thought, a deal of work. Aan had fallen asleep at the board to-night, and Erlend and Ulf had borne him off to a corner, laughing, and laid him there, covered with a rug.

By now, the floor would be strewn thick with rushes at home at Jörundgaard; for all the house-folk slept in the hall together the holy nights of Yule-tide. Ere they set forth to the church, it was their use to clear away the broken food of the fast supper, and her mother and the wenches set out the board as fairly as they could, with butter and cheeses, piles of thin, light-brown bread-slices, shining white bacon and the thickest of smoked knuckles of mutton. The silver flagons and mead-horns stood shining on the board; and her father had himself put the ale-cask up on the bench.

Kristin turned her chair round to the hearth—she would look no longer at the sluttish table. One of the girls was snoring—the sound was horrible to hear.

'Twas one of the things she could not like in Erlend—at home in his own house he ate in such a slovenly fashion, raked about in the dishes for tit-bits, and would scarce so much as wash his hands before he went to meat. And then he would let his dogs get up on his lap and snatch at bits of food while people were eating. So 'twas only what might have been looked for that the serving-folk had no manners at the board. . . .

At home she had been taught to eat daintily—and slowly. For 'twas not seemly, her mother said, that the folk of the house should sit waiting while the servants ate—and those who swinked and toiled must be given time to eat well and be filled.

"Gunna," Kristin called softly to the great yellow bitch that lay with a whole litter of whelps up against the stone border of the hearth. She was so snappish that Erlend had called her after the ill-tempered old lady of the house at Raasvold.

"Poor old barebones!" whispered Kristin, patting the beast, as it came and laid its head on her knee. She was sharp as a scythe along the backbone, and her dugs almost swept the floor. The whelps were eating their mother quite up. "So, so, my poor old barebones!"

Kristin laid her head back against the chair and looked up at the sooty rafters. She was weary. . . .

Oh, no—no easy time had she had, these months she had been at Husaby. She had had some talk with Erlend in the evening of the day they had been at Medalby; and had seen that he believed she was bitter against him because he had brought this upon her.

"I mind me well," he said in a whisper, "that day in the spring when we went in the woods north of the church. I mind well you prayed me to let you be——"

Kristin was glad because he said this. For at other times she had often wondered to see how many things Erlend seemed to have forgotten. But now he said:

"Yet had I not believed of you, Kristin, that you could go about thus, bearing a hidden grudge against me, and yet seeming kind and joyous as ever. For you must have known long since how things were with you. I had thought you were as clear and open as the sun in heaven——"

"Ah, Erlend," she said sadly, "you should know best of any in this world that I have followed secret ways and been false to them that trusted me most." But she was fain that he should understand. "I know not if you remember now, my dearest, that, long before that, your deeds towards me had been such as none would call fair. And yet God and Mary Virgin know that I bore you no grudge, nor loved you any less——"

Erlend's face grew tender.

"So thought I," he said low. "But this too I trow you know—through all those years I strove to set up again what I had broken down. I took comfort in the thought that things would go in the end so that I could reward you for being so long-suffering and so true."

Then she had asked him:

"You have heard of my grandfather's brother and the Lady Bengta, who fled together from Sweden against the will of her kin. God punished them by giving them no child. Have you never been afraid, in these last years, that He would punish us in like wise——?"

And she had said to him, softly and trembling:

"You may well believe, my Erlend, that small joy was mine last summer, when first I grew aware of this. And yet methought—methought if you should die and leave me before we were wedded, I had liefer you left me with a child of yours than all alone. And I thought, if *I* should die in bearing you a child—'twould yet be better than that you should have no true-born son to mount into the high-seat in your place when you have to part from this earthly home."

Erlend answered hotly:

"For me, I would deem my son all too dear bought if he should cost you your life. Speak not so, Kristin. . . . So dear to me Husaby is not," he said in a while. "And least of all since I have been sure that Orm can never inherit after me——"

"Care you more for *her* son than for mine?" asked Kristin then.

"*Your* son——" Erlend laughed a little. "Of him, see you, I know but this, that he comes hither a half-year or so too soon. Orm I have loved for twelve years——"

A while after, Kristin asked:

"These children of yours—you miss them sometimes?"

"Aye," said the man. "Before, I would often go inland to Österdal, where they are, to see them."

"You could go there this Advent," said Kristin in a low voice.

"Would it not mislike you if I went?" asked Erlend eagerly.

Kristin had answered that she would think it but right. Then he had asked whether 'twould be against her liking if he brought the children home with him for Yule. "Soon or late, look you, you must see them." And again she had answered that this seemed to her but right.

While Erlend was gone to Österdal, Kristin had worked hard making things ready for Yule. It irked her much to go about now amidst these strange henchmen and serving-women—she had much ado to force herself to dress and undress in the presence of the two maids, who Erlend had said were to sleep near her in the hall. She had to remind herself that she could never have borne to lie alone in that great house—where another before her had slept with Erlend.

The serving-women of the manor were no better than one might have looked they should be. Such peasants as took good heed of their daughters had had no mind to send them to service in a house where the master lived in open adultery with a wedded woman, and had set her to rule his house. The maids were idle and unused to obey a mistress. But some of them soon began to like the new order that Kristin brought in, and that she took a hand herself in their tasks. They grew full of talk and cheer, since the mistress hearkened to them and answered them kindly and cheerily. And Kristin showed the house-folk daily a calm and gentle face. She rebuked none harshly, but if any serving-maid should gainsay her bidding, the mistress seemed to think the girl knew not what to do, and quietly showed her how she would have the work done. It was thus Kristin had seen her father take things with new serving-men who grumbled—and no man at Jörundgaard had ever offered to gainsay Lavrans a second time.

Thus they might get through this winter well enough. Later she must contrive to get rid of the women that she could not come to like, or that she could not bring into shape.

One piece of work there was that 'twas beyond her to take in hand, except when she was free from the eyes of these strangers. But in the mornings when she sat alone in the hall, she sewed on clothes for her child—swaddling-clothes of soft wadmal, bands of bought stuff, red and green, and white linen for the christening-gown. While she sat sewing on her seam, her mind was tossed about between fear and trust in the holy friends of mankind she had prayed to intercede for her. True, the child lived and moved within her now, so that she had no rest night or day. But she had heard of children born with a belly where their face should have been, or with heads turned backwards, or toes where the heels should be. And she could see before her eyes Svein, who was bluish-red over half his face, because his mother had taken fright at a fire. . . .

Then she would throw down her seam, go and bend the knee before the picture of the Virgin Mary, and say seven Aves. Brother Edvin had said that God's Mother was filled with exceeding great joy each time she heard the Angel's greeting, even if it were in the mouth of the vilest sinner. And 'twas the words *Dominus tecum* that most rejoiced Mary's heart; therefore must she ever say them three times over.

It helped her always for a while.

One evening when she was sitting at the table with the house-folk, one of the women, a young maid that helped in the indoor work, had said:

"Methinks, mistress, 'twere better we should begin sewing swaddling-bands and baby-clothes now, before we set up this web you speak of——"

Kristin made as though she had not heard, and went on speaking of the dyeing of the web. Then the girl began again:

"But maybe you brought baby-clothes with you from home?"

Kristin smiled a little and turned again towards the others. When, a little while after, she glanced round, the wench was sitting, fiery-red in the face, peeping fearfully across at her mistress. Kristin smiled again and began speaking to Ulf across the table. Then of a sudden the girl burst out crying. Kristin laughed a little, and the girl wept more and more, till she was snivelling and sobbing.

"Nay, Frida—let us have no more of this," said Kristin at last, quietly. "You came hither as a grown serving-maid; try now not to behave like a baby girl."

The maid whimpered—she had not meant to be saucy—Kristin must not be wroth.

"No," said Kristin, still smiling. "Eat your supper now and weep no more. We have none of us more wit than God hath been pleased to grant us."

Frida jumped up and ran out, sobbing bitterly.

Afterwards, when Ulf Haldorssön stood talking with Kristin of the work to be done next day, he said with a laugh:

"Erlend should have betrothed him to you ten years agone, Kristin. Then had things stood better with him now in every wise."

"Think you so?" said she, smiling as before. "In those days I was but nine winters old. Think you Erlend was the man to go around waiting long years for a child-bride?"

Ulf laughed and went out.

But that night Kristin lay awake, weeping tears of loneliness and shame.

Then Erlend had come home, the week before Yule, with Orm, his son, riding at his father's side. A stab of pain went through Kristin's heart when he led the boy up to her and bade him greet his step-mother.

He was a most comely child. 'Twas thus she had thought *he* might look, the son she was to bear. Sometimes when she dared to be glad, to trust that her child would be born sound and shapely, to dream ahead of the boy that should grow up by her knee, it was thus he looked in her dream—so like his father.

He was, maybe, somewhat small of his age, and slight, but well-shaped, fine-limbed and fair of face, dark of skin and hair, but with great blue eyes and red, soft mouth. He greeted his stepmother in seemly wise, but his face was hard and cold. Kristin had had no chance to speak much with the boy. But she felt his eyes upon her, wherever she went, and she felt as though she grew yet more heavy and awkward of body and gait when she knew that the lad was gazing at her.

She saw not that Erlend spoke much with his son, but she could see that of the two it was the boy that held back. Kristin spoke to her husband of Orm, saying that he was a comely lad and seemed of a good wit. His daughter Erlend had not brought with him; he deemed Margret was too small to make such a long journey in winter-time. She was fairer still than her brother, he said proudly when Kristin asked of the little maid—and much quicker of wit; she could turn her foster-father and mother round her little finger. She had gold-yellow, curling locks and brown eyes.

Then must she be like her mother, thought Kristin. In spite of herself, jealousy gnawed her heart. Did Erlend love this daughter of his as her father had loved her? His voice had been so soft and warm when he spoke of Margret.

Kristin stood up now and went to the outer doorway. It was so dark without and so heavy with rain that neither moon nor stars were seen. She thought, though, it must be nigh on midnight now. She brought in the lantern from the outer room and lighted it. Then she threw her cloak around her and went out into the rain.

"In Jesu name," she whispered, crossing herself thrice, as she stepped out into the night.

At the top of the courtyard stood the priest's house. It was empty now. Though Erlend had long since been freed from the ban, no priest had yet come to dwell at Husaby; now and then one of the chaplains from Orkedal would come over and say mass; but the new priest appointed to the church was in foreign parts with Master Gunnulf; it seemed they had been school-friends. They had been looked for home the last summer—but now Erlend said they could scarce be there before the late spring. Gunnulf had had the lung-sickness in his youth —he would scarce travel in the winter-time.

Kristin let herself into the cold, empty house, and found the church-key. Then she paused awhile. The ground was a slippery glaze— there was pitch-darkness, and wind, and rain. 'Twas a parlous thing for her, as she was now, to go out at night-time, and most of all on Yule Eve, when all evil spirits are in the air. But she could not give it up—she must come into the church.

"In the name of God the Almighty I go forth here," she whispered out into the storm. Lighting herself with the lantern, she set her feet with care where grass-tufts and stones showed above the ice-crust. In the dark the road to the church seemed long; but at last she stood on the threshold-stone.

Inside, it was bitter cold, much colder than outside in the rain. Kristin went forward to the chancel and knelt down before the crucifix, which gleamed dimly in the darkness above her.

When she had said her prayers and risen up, she stood still a little. It was as though she had looked that something should befall her. But there happened nothing. She was cold and afraid in the dark, desolate church.

She crept up to the altar and turned her light on the pictures. They were old, harsh and ugly. The altar-table was of naked stone—altar-cloths, books and vessels she knew were locked away in a chest.

In the nave was a bench running along the wall. Kristin went down and sat on it, placing her lantern on the floor. Her cloak was wet, and her feet were wet and cold. She tried to draw up one foot under her, but it hurt her to sit so. So she wrapped her cloak well about her, and strove to gather and fix her thoughts on this one thing, that now was come again the holy midnight hour, when Christ had Himself born of Mary Virgin in Bethlehem.

Verbum caro factum est et habitavit in nobis. *

She remembered Sira Eirik's deep, clear voice. And Audun, the old deacon, that was never to be aught but deacon. And their church at home where she had stood by her mother's side and heard the Christmas mass. Every single year she had heard it. She tried to remember more

* St. John's Gospel, i. 14.

of the holy words, but she could think of naught but the church and all the well-known faces. Farthest in front, on the men's side, stood her father and gazed with far-off eyes into the blaze of light from the choir.

'Twas so unbelievable that their church was no more. It was burnt down. She burst into tears at the thought. And here was she sitting all alone this night, when all Christian folk were gathered together in joy and gladness in God's house. But 'twas like this was as it should be—that she was barred out to-night from the rejoicings for the birth of God's Son by a pure and stainless maid.—Her father and mother were surely at Sundbu this Christmas. But there would be no mass to-night in the chapel there; she knew on Yule Eve the Sundbu folk ever rode over to mass in the head church at Ladalm.

It was the first time, as far back as she could remember, that she had not been at Christ's Mass. She must have been quite small the first time her father and mother took her with them. For she could remember that they had stuffed her into a sheepskin bag with the wool inside, and her father had borne her in his arms. It was a night of fearful cold, and they rode through a forest—the light of the fir-root torches gleamed on snow-laden pines. Her father's face was purple-red in the glare, and the furred rim of his hood was snowy-white with rime. Now and again he bent his head a little and bit the tip of her nose, asking her if she felt the bite; then called laughing over his shoulder to her mother that Kristin's nose was not frozen off yet. It must have been while they still dwelt at Skog—belike when she was three winters old. In those days her father and mother were quite young folk. She remembered now her mother's voice that night—high and glad and full of laughter as she called out to her husband and asked about the child. Aye, her mother's voice had been young and fresh then. . . .

——Bethlehem—it betokens in Norse the place of heavy bread. For there was given to men the bread that nourisheth unto life everlasting. . . .

'Twas at the day mass that Sira Eirik stepped up into the lectern and set forth the evangel in the people's own tongue.

Between the masses the folks sat in the guest-shed northward of the church. They had drink with them and the cups went round. Betweenwhiles the men would go out to the stalls and see to the horses. But on vigil nights in the summer-time the congregation sat out on the church-green, and between the services the young folks danced.

——And the blessed maid, Mary, herself wrapped her son in the swaddling-clothes. And she laid him in the manger from which oxen and asses were wont to eat. . . .

Kristin pressed her hands strongly against her sides.

Little son, sweetest son, son of mine, God will have mercy on us for His blessed Mother's sake. Blessed Mary, thou brightest star of the sea, thou dawn of life eternal, who didst bring forth the sun of all the world —help us! Little child, what ails thee to-night, that thou art so unquiet —canst thou feel, even beneath my heart, that I am so bitter cold——?

On Childermas Day last Yule-tide Sira Eirik had set forth the gospel concerning the innocent children whom the cruel soldiers slaughtered in their mothers' arms. But so it was, he said, that God had chosen out these young children to enter into the hall of heaven before all the other blood-witnesses. And this was for a sign that the Kingdom of Heaven is of such as these. And He took a little lad and set him in the midst of them. Except ye make yourselves over in the likeness of these, dear brothers and sisters, ye cannot enter into the halls of the heavenly kingdom. And let this be for a comfort for everyone, man or woman, who mourneth the death of a young child. . . . At that Kristin had seen her father's and mother's eyes meet across the church; and she looked away quickly, for she knew that in this she had no part. . . .

This had been last year. The first Yule-tide after Ulvhild's death. Oh—but not *my* child! Jesus, Mary! Let me keep my son!

Her father had been loath to go for the St. Stephen's riding last year—but all the men had begged and prayed him till at last he joined them. The ride set out from the church-green at home and galloped down to the riversmeet by Loptsgaard; there they met the men from Ottadal. She remembered her father dashing past on his golden-chestnut stallion—he stood in his stirrups and leaned forward along his horse's neck, whooping and cheering on the beast, the whole ride thundering after.

But last year he had been home early, and he came quite sober. Other years the men were used to come home late that day, and beyond measure drunken. For they had to call in at all the farm-yards by the way and drink the healths brought out to them, to Christ and to St. Stephen, who was the first to see the Star in the East as he was riding King Herod's colts to water them in Jordan river. The horses, too, were given ale to drink that day, to make them wild and fiery. On Stephen's day it was ever so that the farmers must be busy with horsegames even till the time of evensong—scarce could the men be got to think of aught or speak of aught but horses. . . .

She could remember one Yule-tide when they had had the great common drinking-feast at Jörundgaard, and her father had promised a priest that was among the guests that he should have a young chestnut colt, a son of Guldsveinen, if he could catch it and back it, as it ran, loose and bare-backed, in the courtyard.

'Twas a long time since—before the mishap to Ulvhild. Their mother stood before the house-door with the little sister on her arm, and Kristin stood holding to her skirt—a little afraid.

The priest ran after the horse, seized the halter, leapt from the ground so that his long gown flew out on all sides; but had to loose the rearing fiery beast again. "So—coltie, coltie—heia, coltie, heia, sonny!" he sang out, hopping and dancing like a billy-goat. Her father and an old farmer that was there stood helpless, holding each other up, their features all drawn awry with laughter and strong drink.

Either the priest must have earned and won the colt, or Lavrans must have given it him unearned, for Kristin remembered that he was riding it when he left the manor. Then were they all sober enough; as he mounted, Lavrans held the stirrup for him with great reverence, and he blessed them with three fingers as he said farewell. 'Twas like he had been a priest of some dignity. . . .

Aye, her home was often right merry at Yule-tide. There was the coming of the guisers, too. Her father tossed her up on to his back, and she felt his coat all icy and his hair wet. To clear their heads before they went to Vespers, the men went off to the well and poured icy water over each other. They laughed when the woman scolded about this. Her father took her little cold hands and pressed them against his forehead, which was red and burning-hot still. This was out in the courtyard, in the evening—a young white sliver of moon hung over the mountain ridge in the sea-green sky. When he was bearing her into the hall, he hit her head by mischance against the door-lintel, so that a great bump rose up on her forehead. Afterwards she sat on his lap at the board. He held the hilt of his dagger against the bump, and fed her with tit-bits, and let her drink mead from his beaker. And, sitting there, she felt no fear of the noisy guisers that were ramping about the hall.

——O father, O father—my kind, dear father!

Sobbing aloud, Kristin hid her face in her hands. Oh, if her father knew how things were with her this Christmas Eve!

As she went back to the hall, she saw sparks flying up above the kitchen-house roof. The maids were getting ready food for the church-goers.

It was dark in the hall. The candles on the table were burnt out, and the hearth was almost black. Kristin laid on more wood, and blew up the embers. Then she saw that Orm was sitting in her chair. He rose up as soon as she caught sight of him.

"Orm!" said Kristin. "Went you not to the mass with your father and the others?"

Orm swallowed once or twice:

"He must have forgot to wake me, methinks. He bade me lie down awhile on the south bed. He said he would wake me——"

"'Twas pity, Orm," said Kristin.

The boy made no answer. In a little while he said:

"I thought you were gone with them after all—I woke up all alone in the hall."

"I was over awhile in the church," said Kristin.

"Dare you go out on Yule night, then?" asked the lad. "Know you not that the Asgards-ride might have come by and taken you——?"

"I trow 'tis not only the evil spirits that are abroad this night," she answered. "On Yule night they say all spirits—— I knew a monk once, that is now dead—I trust well he stands before God's face, for there was naught in him but good. He told me once—heard you ever of the beasts in their stalls, how they spoke together on Christmas night? They could talk Latin in those days. So the cock crowed: *Christus natus est*—nay, I remember not the whole. But the other beasts asked: Where? and the goat bleated: *Betlem, Betlem*—and the sheep said: *Eamus, eamus*——"

Orm smiled scornfully:

"Think you I am such a babe you can comfort me with nurses' tales——? Why offer you not to take me in your lap and give me suck——?"

"Methinks I said it most to comfort my own self, Orm," said Kristin, quietly. "I too had been fain to go with them to the mass."

She felt now that she could not bear to look at the dirty, littered table any longer. She went over, swept all the leavings on to a platter, and set it on the floor for the dogs. Then she took the mop of sedge-grass from beneath the bench and wiped the table-top dry with it.

"Will you come with me to the west storehouse, Orm, to fetch bread and salt meat?" asked Kristin. "Then will we set out the table for Christmas morning."

"Why bid you not your serving-women to do all this?" asked the boy.

"'Twas taught me at home in my father's and mother's house," said the young wife, "that at Yule-tide none should ask another for aught, but each should strive to do the most. He was most blest that most could serve the others throughout the holy days."

"Yet you ask me," said Orm.

"'Tis another thing to ask you—that are the son of the house."

Orm took the lantern, and they went together across the courtyard. In the storehouse Kristin filled two great platters with Christmas fare. She took, too, a bundle of great tallow candles. While they were about this, the boy said:

"I trow 'tis farmer's fashion that you spoke of but now. For I have heard he is but a wadmal-farmer, Lavrans Björgulfsön."

"Of whom have you heard this?" asked Kristin.

"Of mother," said Orm. "Many a time I heard her say to father, when we lived at Husaby before, that he might see now, not even a grey-clad farmer would give his daughter to him in marriage."

"A pleasant home was Husaby in those days," said Kristin, shortly. The boy made no answer. His mouth quivered a little.

Kristin and Orm bore the laden platters back to the hall, and she set the table for the meal. But some things were still lacking, to be fetched from the storehouse. Orm took a platter and said, a little bashfully:

"I will go for you, Kristin; 'tis so slippery in the yard."

She stood outside the door, and waited till he came back.

Afterward they sat them down by the hearth—she in the arm-chair and the boy on a joint-stool near her. In a while Orm Erlendssön said in a low voice:

"Tell me something more, while we sit waiting here, stepmother."

"Tell you——?" asked Kristin in the same tone.

"Aye—a story or the like—something fitting for Christmas night," said the boy, shyly.

Kristin leaned back in her chair, grasping in her thin hands the carven beasts' heads at the arm-ends.

"That monk I named but now, he had been in England, too. And he used to tell that there is a place there where grow thorn-bushes that bloom with white blossoms each Christmas night. St. Joseph of Arimathea came to land in that country-side, when he fled before the heathen, and there he thrust his staff into the earth, and it took root and blossomed—he was the first that brought the Christian faith to Bretland. Glastonborg that place is called—I mind me now. Brother Edvin had seen those bushes himself. . . . 'Twas there in Glastonborg that he was buried, along with his Queen, that King Arthur that you will have heard tell of—he that was one of the Seven Champions of Christendom.

"They say in England that Christ's Cross was made of alder-wood. But we at home used to burn ash in the holy days; for 'twas ash-wood he made up the fire with, St. Joseph, Christ's stepfather, when he was to light a fire to comfort Mary Virgin and the new-born Son of God. Father heard that too of Brother Edvin——"

"But there's little ash grows here north of Dovre," said the boy. "They used it up in the old times for spear-shafts, you know. I know not of one other ash on all the lands of Husaby but the one that stands by the eastern yard-gate, and that one father cannot cut, for the

Brownie of the Yard dwells under it.—But, Kristin, I wot they have the Holy Rood itself at Romaborg; surely they can find out if 'tis true that it is made of alder-wood——"

"Aye," said Kristin, "I know not if it be true. For you know 'tis said that the Cross was made of a shoot from the Tree of Life, that Seth was given grace to fetch from the Garden of Eden and bear home to Adam before he died——"

"Aye," said Orm. "But tell it to me."

A while after, Kristin said to the boy:

"'Twere well you lay down now, kinsman, and slept awhile. It will be long yet till the church-folk are back."

Orm stood up.

"We have not pledged each other yet as kin, Kristin Lavransdatter." He went and brought over a drinking-horn from the table, drank to his stepmother, and handed her the horn.

She felt as though an icy stream ran down her back. She could not but remember that hour when Orm's mother would have drunk with her. And the child in her womb moved unquietly. How is it with him to-night? thought the mother. It was as though the unborn babe felt all that she felt, was cold when she was cold, shrank in fear when she was afraid. But since 'tis so, I must not be so weak, thought Kristin. She took the horn and drank to her stepson.

As she gave it back to Orm, she passed her hand lightly over his black mane of hair. No, she thought, to thee I shall be no hard step-dame, be sure—thou fair, fair young son of Erlend's. . . .

She had fallen asleep in her chair when Erlend came in and flung his frozen mittens on the table.

"Are you come back already?" asked Kristin, wondering. "I deemed you would have stayed for the morning mass."

"Oh, two masses will serve my turn for a long time," said Erlend. The cloak that Kristin took from him was heavy with ice. "Aye, now 'tis clear again, and freezing hard——"

"'Twas pity you should have forgot to wake Orm," said his wife.

"Was he vexed about it?" asked the father. "'Twas not that I forgot, either," he said in a low voice. "But he was sleeping so sound that I thought—— You may be sure the good folk gaped at me enough in church, for that I came there without you—— I had no mind, on the top of that, to go forward with the boy at my side."

Kristin said naught; but the words hurt her. She could not think this well done of Erlend.

III

T H E Y saw not much of outside folk at Husaby that Yule-tide. Erlend would not go abroad to any place where he was bidden, but stayed at home on the manor, in no pleasant mood.

The thing was that this misadventure galled him more nearly than his wife could know. He had boasted not a little of his betrothed ever since his kinsmen had gone to Jörundgaard and won her father's consent. It was the last thing he had wished, that any should believe he held her or her kin of less account that his own kindred. No—all men should know that he held himself honoured and uplifted again to worship by Lavrans Björgulfssön's betrothing his daughter to him. Now would all folks say he could scarce have held the maid much better than a peasant's child, since he had dared to do her father such despite as to sleep with his daughter before she was given him in wedlock. At his wedding Erlend had pressed his bride's parents strongly to come to Husaby the next summer and see how things were with him there. Not alone was he fain to show them it was no mean condition he had brought their daughter to; but he had been glad, too, at the thought of going about and showing himself in the company of these comely and stately new kinsfolk, for he knew that Lavrans and Ragnfrid could hold their own with the foremost, wherever they might come. And he had deemed, since the time he was at Jörundgaard when the church burned down, that, in spite of all, Lavrans liked him none so ill. But now there was small reason to think that the next meeting between him and his wife's kin would bring joy to either part.

It vexed Kristin that Erlend vented his ill-humour so often upon Orm. The boy had no playfellows of his own age, and so it came that he was often troublesome and in the way. He did his share of mischief, too. One day he had taken his father's French cross-bow without leave, and had broken something in the lock. Erlend was in great wrath; he struck Orm a box on the ear, and swore that the boy should never more touch a bow at Husaby.

"'Twas not Orm's fault," said Kristin without turning. She was sitting sewing with her back to the two. "The spring was out of gear when he took the bow, and he tried to put it right. You should not be so unfair as to deny a great boy like your son the use of one from among all the bows you have in this house. Rather give him one of the bows that are up in the armoury."

"You can give him a bow yourself, if you have a mind," said Erlend, wrathfully.

"That will I gladly," answered Kristin as before. "I will speak of it to Ulf, next time he goes in to the city."

"You must go and thank your kind stepmother, Orm," said Erlend, in a voice of anger and scorn.

Orm did as he was bid, and then flew out of the room as swiftly as he might. Erlend stood still awhile.

"'Twas most to vex me you did this, Kristin," he said.

"Aye, I know I am a troll. You have told me that already," she replied.

"But mind you too, my sweet," said Erlend sorrowfully, "that I spoke not in earnest when I said that word?"

Kristin made no answer, nor looked up from her seam. Soon he went out, and when he was gone she sat there weeping. She had come to care for Orm, and she deemed that Erlend was often unjust to his son. But then, too, her husband's silence and unjoyous looks were tormenting her so that she lay weeping half the night; and then her head would ache all the day after. Her hands were grown so thin now that she had to thrust on some small silver rings she had had since childhood above her betrothal ring and her wedding-ring, to keep them from falling off while she slept.

The Sunday before the beginning of the fast, late in the afternoon, Sir Baard Peterssön with his daughter, the widow, and Sir Munan Baardssön with his lady came to Husaby as unlooked-for guests. Erlend and Kristin went out into the courtyard to bid the strangers welcome.

The moment Sir Munan set eyes on Kristin, he clapped his hand on Erlend's shoulder:

"I see well, kinsman, you have known how to care so for your wife that she hath thriven in your house. You are nowise so thin and peaked, now, Kristin, as you were at your wedding—and far fresher of hue are you too," said he, laughing, for Kristin had flushed red as a berry.

Erlend made no answer. Sir Baard's face was clouded; but the two ladies seemed neither to hear nor see aught; they greeted their hosts seemly and quietly.

Kristin had ale and mead brought forth to them by the hearth while they waited for the meal. Munan Baardssön talked without cease. He had letters with him for Erlend from the Duchess—she had asked what was become of him and his bride; and was the maid he had wedded now the same that he would have carried off to Sweden? 'Twas the devil's own journey in midwinter that he had made—up through the dales and by ship to Nidaros. But he journeyed on the King's errand, and it booted not to murmur. He had looked in on his mother at Haugen, and he brought her greetings.

"Were you at Jörundgaard?" asked Kristin, in a low voice.

No; for he had come to know they were gone from home to the grave-ale at Blakarsarv. There had been a grievous mischance. The mistress of the house, Tora, Ragnfrid's cousin—she had fallen down from the storehouse balcony and broken her back—and 'twas her husband coming against her unawares that had pushed her over—it was one of those old storehouses where there was no right balcony, but only a few boards laid on the beam-ends of the upper story. He heard they had had to bind Rolf and watch him night and day since the mishap befell—to keep him from laying hands on himself.

The listeners sat very still, shuddering. Kristin knew but little of these kinsfolk, but they had been at her wedding. Suddenly she felt strange and faint—there was a blackness before her eyes. Munan, who sat over against her, leapt up and came to her. When he stood by her with his arm around her shoulders, he looked kind—Kristin thought, 'twas maybe not so strange that this cousin of Erlend's was dear to him.

"I knew him, Rolf, when we were young," he said now. "Folk were used to pity Tora Guttormsdatter—they said he was wild and hard-hearted. Yet one can see now that he held her dear. Aye, aye—many a man blusters and talks big about how glad he would be to be quit of his wedlock, but most men know well that a wife is the worst loss they can have——"

Baard Peterssön rose suddenly and went over to the bench by the wall.

"Beshrew my mouth," said Sir Munan softly. "To think I can never remember to watch my tongue——"

Kristin understood not what was amiss. The dizziness had passed now, but she had a feeling of discomfort—they seemed all so strange. She was glad when the serving-folk brought in the meal.

Munan looked at the table and rubbed his hands:

"Sure I was that we should do well to look in on you, Kristin, before we settle down to munching Lenten fare. Where have you gotten savoury dishes like these from in such a little while? A man might go nigh to think you had learned witchcraft of my mother. But I see well you are quick to bring forth all things that a housewife should gladden her husband withal."

They sat down to the table. Velvet cushions had been laid for the guests on the wall-bench on either side of the high seat. The serving-folk sat on the outer bench, Ulf Haldorssön in the midst, over against his master.

Kristin talked a little, quietly, with the strange ladies, striving to hide how ill at ease she was. Time and again Munan Baardssön broke in with would-be playful words, ever harping on Kristin's state. She made as though she did not hear.

Munan was a man fatter than the common. His small well-formed ears were sunk right into the flesh of his thick red neck, and his belly got in his way when sitting down to table.

"Aye, often have I wondered about that matter of the resurrection of the body," he said; "whether I shall be raised up with all this blubber I have laid on around my bones, when that day comes. *You* will soon enough be slim-waisted again now, Kristin—but with me 'tis no such easy matter. You will scarce believe it, but my belt was no wider than Erlend's there when I was twenty winters old——"

"Be still now, Munan," Erlend begged, in a low voice. "You are plaguing Kristin——"

"I shall be so, since so you say," the other took him up. "You are a proud man now, I dare swear—sitting at your own table with your wedded wife by you in the high-seat. Aye, and God that's over all knows that 'twas none too soon either—you are old enough, boy! Surely I will hold my tongue, since you bid me. But never did any tell you when you should speak or be silent, in days gone by when *you* sat at *my* table. Often and long were you my guest, and I deem not you marked at any time that you were not welcome.

"But much I wonder whether indeed it likes Kristin so ill that I jest a little with her—what say you, fair wife of my kinsman?—you were not wont to be so startlish in days gone by. I have known Erlend since he was as high as my knee, and methinks I can say I have wished the boy well all his days. Mettlesome and manful are you, Erlend, with a sword in your hand, either a-horseback or a-shipboard. But I will pray to St. Olav to cleave me in two halves with his axe the day I see you stand up on those long legs of yours, look man or woman straight in the face, and answer for the mischief you have wrought in your light-mindedness. No, dear kinsman of mine, then do you hang your head like a bird in the snare, and wait upon God and your kindred to help you out of the pinch. Aye, and so clear-witted a woman are you, Kristin, that I trow you know this—and methinks you may well have need to laugh a little now; for I wager you have seen enough this winter past of shamefaced looks and sorrow and repentance——"

Kristin sat with face darkly flushed. Her hands were shaking, and she dared not look towards Erlend. Anger seethed within her—here sat the strange ladies and Orm and her serving-folk. So these were the courtly ways of Erlend's rich kinsmen. . . .

Then said Sir Baard, in a low voice that only those who sat next him were meant to hear:

"I see not that 'tis aught to jest abou —that Erlend should have behaved him thus before his wedding. I pledged my word for you, Erlend, with Lavrans Björgulfsön."

"Aye, devil knows 'twas unwisely done of you, foster-father," said

Erlend, loud and hotly. "And I marvel how you could be so foolish. For you—I trow you know me too——"

But now was there no checking Munan any longer:

"Aye, but now will I say why this seems to me a merry jest. Mind you what answer you made me, Baard, when I came to you and said we must needs help Erlend to make this marriage—nay, now I *will* tell of it; Erlend shall know what you believed of me—thus and thus it stands between them, said I, and if he wins not Kristin Lavransdatter to wife, God and Mary Virgin alone know what mad doings we shall next hear of. Then it was you asked me, was I so fain have him wedded to the maid he had betrayed because I thought belike she was barren, since after so long she had yet shown no sign? But I trow you know me, you others—you know me for a trusty kinsman to my kin——" Quite overcome, he burst out weeping. "God and all holy men be my witness—never have I coveted your goods, kinsman—and then, to be sure, there is Gunnulf besides between me and Husaby. And I answered you, Baard, well you know it—the first son that Kristin bore, I would give him my gold-mounted dagger with the ivory sheath—and you can have it now!" he shouted through his tears, throwing the costly weapon along the table to her. "If it be not a son this time, 'tis like there will come one next year——"

Tears of shame and wrath rolled down on Kristin's cheeks. She had a hard struggle not to give way altogether. But the two stranger ladies sat eating as calmly as if they were well used to such scenes. And Erlend whispered to her to take the dagger: "Or Munan will keep on with this all night."

"Aye, and I deny not, Kristin," went on Munan, "that I am not so ill pleased your father should be made to see he was too rash when he answered for your mind. So haughty was Lavrans—we were not good enough for him, forsooth—and you were all too fine and pure to suffer a man like Erlend for your bedfellow. He spoke as if he deemed you could not bear to do aught of nights but sing in a nunnery choir. I said to him: 'Dear Lavrans,' I said, 'your daughter is a fair and fresh and sprightly young maid, and the winter nights are long and cold in this our land——"

Kristin drew the linen of her coif across her face. She sobbed aloud, and would have risen, but Erlend drew her down again into her seat.

"Be still," he said vehemently. "Pay no heed to Munan—surely you can see he is raving drunk——?"

She felt that Lady Katrin and Lady Vilborg deemed that 'twas poor-spirited of her not to be better mistress of herself. But she could not stay her weeping.

Baard Peterssön said in fury:

"Hold your rotten tongue. A swine have you been all your days—
yet might you well leave a sick woman in peace from your filthy
talk——"

"Said you 'swine'——? Aye, true it is, I have more bastards than
you. But one thing have I never done—nor Erlend either—bought
another man to be called our child's father in our place——"

"Munan!" shouted Erlend, springing up. "Now call I for peace in
my hall!"

"Oh, call for peace in your tail!—*Our* children call father him that
got them—in swinish living, as you call it!" Munan smote the board
so that cups and platters leapt in the air. "*Our* sons dwell not as serving-men in the house of their kindred. But here sits son of yours at the
board with you, and he sits on the varlets' bench. Now should I deem
that the worst shame of all——"

Baard sprang up and drove a flagon into the other's face. The two
men grappled, half upsetting the table-top, so that food and vessels
went sliding down into the laps of those on the outer bench.

Kristin sat deadly white, with mouth half opened. Once she glanced
across at Ulf—the man was laughing aloud, with a coarse, evil laughter.
Then, taking hold of the table-top, he heaved it into place and thrust
it against the two struggling men.

Erlend leapt on to the table. Kneeling on it amid the litter of the
feast, he caught Munan round the arms below his shoulders and
dragged him bodily up beside himself—his own face purpling with the
strain. Munan kicked out at the old man, drawing blood from his
mouth, but the next moment Erlend had flung him clean across the
table on to the open floor. He himself leapt after him—and stood
panting like a bellows.

Munan scrambled to his feet and rushed at Erlend, who slipped clear
of his grasp once or twice, then suddenly leapt upon him and held him
tightly grappled with his long sinewy legs and arms. Erlend was lithe
as a cat, but Munan, solid and heavy, kept his footing and would not
be thrown. They swayed struggling about the hall, while the serving-
women shrieked and screamed, and none of the men moved a hand to
part them.

Then Lady Katrin, fat, heavy and slow-moving as ever, arose from
her seat and stepped over the table as calmly as though she were
mounting her storehouse-steps.

"Have done, now," she said in her thick, dragging voice. "Loose
him, Erlend! This was ill done of you, husband—to speak thus to an
old man and a near kinsman——"

The men obeyed her. Munan stood meekly and let his wife stanch
the blood from his nose with the hem of her coif. She bade him go to

bed, and he followed obediently when she led him over to the southern box-bed. His wife and one of his men pulled the clothes off him, rolled him into the bed, and shut the bed-doors on him.

Erlend had gone over to the table. He leant across it beside Ulf, who had not stirred from his place.

"Foster-father!" he said in an unhappy voice. He seemed quite to have forgotten his wife. Sir Baard sat rocking with his head, the tears trickling down his cheeks.

"There had been no need, either, for Ulf to serve," he brought out, through the weeping that made him gasp and sob. "You could have had the farm when Haldor died—you know well 'twas my intent you should."

"The farm you gave to Haldor was none so brave—you bought a husband for your wife's maid good cheap," said Ulf. "He cleared and tilled and bettered it—methought, for one thing, it was but reason that my brothers should have it after their father. And besides, little was I minded to sit down and be a farmer—and least of all up on yonder hill-side, gaping down into the Hestnes courtyard—meseemed I could hear every day up there the voices of Paal and Vilborg, cursing that you had given all too rich a gift to your bastard son——"

"I proffered you help, Ulf," said Baard, still weeping, "when you were bent on faring forth with Erlend. I told you all the truth of this matter, as soon as you were of age to understand. I prayed you to turn to your father——"

"I call him my father who fostered me when I was a child. And that man's name was Haldor. He was good to mother and to me. He taught me to ride a horse and to handle a sword—as a churl doth his cudgel, I mind me Paal once said."

Ulf hurled from him the knife he had in his hand, so that it flew ringing across the table. He rose and picked it up again, wiped it on the back of his thigh, and stuck it in its sheath. Then he turned to Erlend:

"Make an end now with this feast of yours, and send your people to bed! See you not your wife is unused as yet to the fair fashions of our kindred in their feasting?"

And with that he was gone from the hall.

Sir Baard looked after him—he seemed of a sudden wretchedly old and feeble, as he sat there, huddled together among the velvet cushions. His daughter, Vilborg, and one of his men helped him to his feet and led him out.

Kristin sat alone on the high-seat, weeping and weeping. When Erlend tried to take hold on her, she struck his hand aside vehemently. She swayed about on her feet once or twice when she walked across the floor; but she answered curtly: "No," when her husband asked if she were sick.

She liked not these shut-up box-beds. At home the beds were only curtained off from the hall by hangings, so that the air inside was less hot and stifling. And to-night it was worse in there than ever—for at best she could scarce draw breath. The hard lump she felt pressing right up under her breast-bone she thought must be the child's head— she fancied that it lay with its little head bored in amongst the roots of her heart—it choked her breathing as Erlend had done in old days, when he pressed his dark-haired head against her breast. But to-night there was no sweetness in the thought. . . .

"Will you never make an end of weeping?" asked her husband, trying to pass his arm beneath her shoulders.

He was quite sober. He could bear much liquor, and for the most part he drank but little. Kristin was thinking—never in the world could aught like this have befallen in her home. Never had she heard folk there revile each other, or rake up in their talk things that were best left unnamed. Often as she had seen her father reeling in drunken- ness, and the hall full of drunken guests, not once had it befallen even then that he had not been fit to keep order in his house—peace and goodwill had ever ruled, even till the folks dropped off the benches to the floor, and fell asleep together in joy and harmony.

"Dearest one, take not this so hardly," Erlend begged.

"And Sir Baard," she broke out through her tears. "Fie on such doings—he that talked to my father as if he bore a message from God himself—aye, Munan told me of it at our betrothal-feast——"

Erlend answered softly:

"Well enough I know it, Kristin, that I have cause to cast down my eyes before your father. He is a good man—but my foster-father is no worse than he. Inga—Paal and Vilborg's mother—she lay crippled and sick for six years before she died. 'Twas before I came to Hestnes, but I have heard all the story, and never has a husband cherished a sick wife more truly and lovingly. But 'twas at that time Ulf was born——"

"All the more the shame, then—with his sick wife's maid——"

"You show you so childish sometimes, a man can scarce talk with you," said Erlend in despair. "God help us, Kristin, you will be twenty come next spring—and more winters than one are gone by since you must needs be accounted a grown woman——"

"Aye, 'tis true *you* have the right to scorn me for it——"

Erlend groaned aloud:

"You know yourself that I meant it not so.—But you have lived there at Jörundgaard and hearkened to Lavrans—and for all he is a

bold man and a manful, he talks oft-times as if he had been a monk
and not a whole grown man——"

"Heard you ever of any monk that had six children?" she said
angrily.

"I have heard of one, Skurda-Grim, that had seven," said Erlend,
desperately. "The Abbot of Holm that was—— Nay, Kristin, Kristin,
weep not so, in God's name! Methinks you have lost your wits——"

Munan was passing meek the next morning. "I could never have
thought you would take my drunken pratings so much to heart, Kristin,
girl," he said gravely, patting her cheek. "Else had I kept a better
watch on my tongue, be sure."

He spoke to Erlend of Orm, saying it must be irksome for Kristin
now to see this boy about. 'Twould be best to send him out of the way
at this time—he offered to take the boy for a while. Erlend liked the
proffer well—and Orm was glad to go with Munan. But Kristin missed
the child much—she had come to hold her stepson dear.

Again now in the evenings she was left alone with Erlend, and he
was no great company for her. He sat by the hearth, said a word now
and then, or took a draught from the ale-bowl, and played a little with
his dogs. Then he would go and stretch himself on the bench—then
go to bed—would ask once or twice if she should not go to rest soon,
and then fall asleep.

Kristin sat and sewed. Her breaths came short and so heavy they
could be heard. But there was not long to wait now. She could scarce
remember, it seemed, what 'twas like to be free and supple in the waist,
to be able to tie her shoe without pain and labour.

Now that Erlend slept, she need not even try to keep back the tears.
There was no sound in the hall, save when a crumbling brand would
drop on the hearth, or a dog would move in its sleep. Sometimes she
would wonder—what had they spoken of in the days that were gone—
Erlend and she? Like enough they had not spoken much—they had
had other pastime in their short, stolen trysts. . . .

This was the time of year when her mother and the serving-maids
were wont to sit of evenings in the weaving-house. And her father and
the men too would come in and sit down by the women with their
own tasks—mending leather gear and farm tools, and carving in wood.
The little house was filled full of folk, and talk ran on quietly and easily
amongst them. When one had gone over to get him a drink from the
ale-tub, he asked ever, before he hung up the ladle again, if any other
had a mind to drink—'twas a firm, fixed rule.

Then would there be someone who could say forth a snatch of some
saga—of champions in the old age that had fought with mound-

dwellers and giantesses of the hills. Or her father would tell them, as he sat at his wood-carving, tales of knighthood, such as he had heard read aloud in his Lord's hall, when he was a page to Duke Haakon in his youth. Fair outlandish names—King Osantrix, Sir Titurel the knight—and Sisibe, Guniver, Gloriana and Isood were the Queens' names. . . . But other evenings they would tell cock-and-bull stories and merry tales, till the menfolk guffawed with laughter, and her mother and the maids shook their heads and tittered.

Ulvhild and Astrid would sing. Her mother had the sweetest voice of all, but it took much praying before they could bring her to sing to them. Her father was not so backward—and he could play so tunably on his harp.

Then Ulvhild would lay from her wheel and spindle and press her hands to her back.

"Is your back weary now, little Ulvhild?" her father would ask, and would take her up in his lap. Someone would bring the draughtboard, and father and Ulvhild would play till bedtime came. She remembered her little sister's yellow locks flowing down over her father's greenish-brown wadmal sleeve. He held up the weak little back so tenderly with the circle of his arm.

Father's long slender hands, with a heavy gold ring on each little finger. The rings had been his mother's. The one with the red stone, her bridal-ring, he had said that Kristin should have after him. But the one on his right hand, with a stone that was half blue and half white like the device of his shield, that had Sir Björgulf had made for his wife when she went with child of Lavrans—she was to be given it when she had borne him a son. Three nights had Kristin Sigurdsdatter worn the ring; then she tied it round her boy's neck; and Lavrans said he would take it with him to his grave.

Oh, what would her father say when he heard this of her? When 'twas noised abroad all over the country-side at home, and he could not but know, wherever he might fare, to church, to Thing, or to meetings, that all men were laughing at him behind his back, that he had let him be so fooled. At Jörundgaard they had decked out a wanton with the Sundbu bridal crown above the flowing hair of maidenhood——

"Folk say of me, I know well, that I cannot rule my children." She remembered her father's look when he said it—he would fain have been sad and stern of face, but his eyes were merry. She had done amiss in some little matter—spoken to him, unspoken to, before strangers, or the like. "Aye, Kristin, sooth it is you go not much in fear of your father." Then a laugh broke out, and she laughed too. "Aye, but 'tis an ill thing, Kristin." And neither of them knew what it was that was so ill a thing—that she stood not in seemly awe of him; or that he could in no wise keep a sad brow when he had to chide her.

It was as though the unbearable dread that there should be somewhat amiss with the child grew fainter and farther off as Kristin's pains and bodily trouble grew. She tried to send her thoughts forward—in a month—she would have had her boy for a while then already. But she could not make it seem true. She could only long and long for her home.

Once Erlend had asked if she would he should send for her mother. But she said: No—she deemed not her mother was fit to journey so far in winter-time. Now she repented this. And she repented that she had said: No, to Tordis of Laugarbru, who had been so fain to come north with her and help her through her first winter as the mistress of a house. But she had thought shame to have Tordis by. Tordis had been Ragnfrid's maid at her home at Sundbu, and had followed her mistress to Skog and back again to the Dale. When she married, Lavrans had made her husband steward at Jörundgaard, since Ragnfrid could not bear to be parted from her dear hand-maiden. Kristin had no mind to have with her any woman from her home.

But now it seemed to her a fearful thing that she should not have a single known face to look upon when her time came to lie in the straw. She was afraid—she knew so little of the bringing to bed of women. Her mother had never spoken to her of it, and would never have young maids with her when she helped women in their labour—it would but frighten the young things, she said. But Kristin knew it must sometimes be fearful—she remembered the time Ulvhild was born. That, though, Ragnfrid had said was because she had forgot herself and crept under a fence-rail—her other children she had borne easily. But Kristin remembered now that she herself had been thoughtless, and passed under a rope on the ship. . . .

Yet this did not always bring heavy labour—she had heard her mother and other women talk of such things. Ragnfrid had the name in their country-side of the best midwife far around, and never would she deny her help, not if it was to a beggar woman or the poorest man's daughter that had fallen in trouble, nor if the weather was such that three men must go with her on ski and take turns at bearing her on their backs. . . .

But surely, it came to Kristin in a flash, 'twas not to be believed that a woman of such skill in these things as her mother had, should not have seen what was amiss with her last summer, when she was so ailing. But then—sure it was that her mother would come, even though they had not sent to call her. Ragnfrid would never suffer that her daughters should go through that struggle in a stranger's arms. Her mother would come—surely she was even now on her way hither. . . . Oh, and then she could pray her mother's forgiveness for all that she had sinned against her—her own mother would hold her up, she would kneel at her mother's knee when she bore her child. Mother comes, mother comes. . . . Kristin sobbed behind her hands from a lightened heart. O mother—forgive me, mother.

The thought that her mother was on her way up to her grew so fixed in Kristin that one day she deemed she could feel within herself: Mother will come to-day. And on in the morning she took her cloak about her and went out to meet her on the road that leads from Gauldal over to Skaun. None marked her as she left the manor.

Erlend had had timber driven down from the woods for the mending and bettering of the houses, so that the road was well trodden; but 'twas heavy going for her none the less—she lost her breath, her heart beat hard, and sharp pain came in her sides—it felt as though the over-stretched flesh would break asunder when she had walked a little while. And most of the way was through thick forest. She was afraid indeed—but there had been no word of wolves in the country-side this winter. And surely God would guard her that went forth to meet her mother, fall at her feet, and pray her for forgiveness—and she could not but go on and on.

She came by and by to a little lake, where there lay some small farmsteads. Where the road led on to the ice, she sat down upon a log—and sometimes sitting, sometimes walking to keep warm, stayed waiting there many hours. But at last she must needs turn home again.

The day after, she strayed out again by the same road. But as she crossed the yard of one of the small farms by the lake, the woman of the house came running after her.

"In God's name, mistress, what is this you do?"

No sooner had she spoke than Kristin herself grew so afraid that she could not move from the spot—trembling, with eyes wild with fear, she gazed at the peasant woman.

"Through the woods—think but if the wolf got scent of you! And other ill things too might well come upon you—how can you bear you so witlessly?"

The goodwife threw her arms around the young lady of the manor to hold her up—and looked into her thin face, all yellowish-white and flecked with brown:

"You must come into our house and rest awhile—and then we will take you home—someone from here," she said, as she led Kristin away with her.

It was a little and a poor house, and within all was in much disorder, for there were many small children playing on the floor. The mother sent them out to the kitchen-house, took her guest's cloak, led her to a seat on the bench, and drew off her snowy shoes. Then she wrapped a sheepskin round her feet.

For all Kristin prayed the other not to put herself about, her hostess was not to be hindered from serving her with food and with ale from the Yule-cask. And she was thinking the while—a rare rule must they keep at Husaby! She herself was but a poor man's wife; little help had they had on their farm, and often none at all; but never would Öistein suffer her to go alone without the farm-yard fence when she was with child—nay, if she but went across to the byre after dark had fallen, someone must ever keep an eye on her. But the richest lady in all the country-side might stray out and run the risk of the most dreadful death, and not a Christian soul to take care of her—though the serving-folk at Husaby were tumbling over each other and doing naught. 'Twas like, then, the folks said sooth that said Erlend Nikulaussön was weary of his marriage already, and cared not for his wife. . . .

But she chatted away to Kristin all the time, and forced her to eat and drink. And Kristin was much ashamed—but she had such a stomach to her meat as she had not felt—not since the last spring; the kind woman's food tasted so good. And the woman laughed and said 'twas like great folks' womenkind were made no otherwise than poor. 'Twas often so that when a body could not bear to look at food at home, one would be right greedy for strangers' fare even if 'twere coarse and poor.

Her name was Audfinna Andunsdatter, and she was from Updal, she said. When she marked that it cheered her guest, she took to telling of her home and her country. And before Kristin was aware, *her* tongue too was loosed—and she was talking of *her* home and her parents and her own country-side. Audfinna saw well that the young wife's heart was near breaking with home-sickness—so she tempted and beguiled Kristin into going on. And Kristin, hot and dizzy with the strong ale, went on talking till she was laughing and crying in the same breath. All that she had tried in vain to sob away from her heart in the lonesome evening hours at Husaby, seemed to melt now little by little as she told her tale to this kind peasant wife.

It was quite dark now above the smoke-vent, but Audfinna would have Kristin stay till Öistein or their sons came home from the wood and could take her home. Kristin grew silent and drowsy, but she sat smiling, with shining eyes—so happy she had not felt since she came to Husaby.

Suddenly the door was flung open, and a man shouted in to ask if they had seen aught of the mistress—then caught sight of her sitting there and rushed out again. A minute after, Erlend's long shape came stooping low through the doorway. He set from him the axe he bore, and staggered back against the wall—he had to prop himself with hands thrust behind him, and he could not speak.

"You have been afraid for your lady?" asked Audfinna, going over to him.

"Aye—I take no shame to say it." He passed his hand up under his hair. "So frighted has man scarce ever been, I trow, as I have been this night. When I heard she had gone off into the woods——"

Audfinna told how it was Kristin had come thither. Erlend took the woman's hand.

"Never will I forget what I owe you and your husband for this," he said.

Then he went across to where his wife sat, and, standing beside her, laid a hand upon her neck. He spoke not a word to her, but stood still thus as long as they were in the house.

Now came crowding in henchmen from Husaby and men from the nearest farms. All looked as though they needed a heartening draught, so Audfinna bore round the ale-bowl before they set forth again.

The men went off on ski across the fields, but Erlend had given his to one of his followers; he walked down the hill holding Kristin inside his cloak. It was quite dark now, and the stars shone bright.

Then came a sound from the woods behind them—a long-drawn howl that mounted higher and higher in the night. It was wolves—and there were many. Erlend stopped short, shivering, loosed his hold on her, and Kristin knew that he crossed himself, while he gripped the axe in his other hand. "Had you now been—oh, no——" He crushed her to him so fiercely that she moaned with pain.

The ski-runners in the fields turned sharp about, and toiled back to the pair as fast as they could climb. Then they flung the ski over their shoulders, and made a close ring around her with their spears and axes. The wolves followed them all the way to Husaby—so near that now and then they could see a glimpse of them through the darkness.

When they came into the lighted hall, many of the men's faces showed grey and white. One said: "This was the grimmest——" and straightway fell a-vomiting into the hearth-fire. The frightened maids brought their mistress to her bed. Eat she could not. But now that the sick, awful dread was overpast, it yet seemed to her comforting after a fashion to see that all had been so affrighted for her sake.

When they were left alone in the hall, Erlend came across and sat himself down on the edge of her bed.

"Why did you this?" he whispered. And when she made no answer, he said, yet lower:

"Is it such grief to you that you have come into my house——?"

It was a little while before she understood what he meant:

"Jesus, Maria! How can you think such a thought?"

"What had you in mind that time you said—when we had been at Medalby, when I would have ridden from you—that I might have had long to wait ere you came after me to Husaby?" he asked in the same low tone.

"Oh, I spoke but in wrath," said Kristin, bashfully, in a low voice. And she told him now what it was that had taken her out these days. Erlend sat very still and listened.

"Much do I wonder when the day will come when my house of Husaby will seem home to you," said he, bending over her in the dark.

"Oh—in not much more than a week now, maybe," whispered Kristin, with a wavering laugh. When he laid his face down against hers, she threw her arms round his neck and gave back his kiss eagerly.

"'Tis the first time you have laid your arms about my neck of your own accord since I struck you," said Erlend in a low voice. "You are slow to forgive, my Kristin——"

It came into her mind that this was the first time since the night when he had learned she was with child, that she had had courage to offer him a caress unasked.

But after this day Erlend showed such kindness towards her that Kristin repented each hour she had felt anger against him.

IV

GREGORY'S Mass * came and went by. Kristin had believed so surely that her time must come then, at the latest. But now it would soon be Mary's Mass in Lent,† and still she was about on her feet.

Erlend was forced to go to Nidaros for the mid-fast Thing; he said he would surely be home Monday night, but now it was Wednesday morning and he was not yet come. Kristin sat in the hall, scarce knowing what to be about—it was as though she had no power to begin upon any work.

The sunlight streamed in through the smoke-vent—she felt that without it must be like spring to-day. She rose up and threw a cloak about her.

One of the maids had told her that folk said if a woman went beyond her due time, a good way was for her to let the horse she rode at her bridal eat corn from her lap. Kristin stood a little while in the halldoor—in the blinding sunlight the yard lay all brown, but glittering rills of water ran in bright frozen runnels through the horse-dung and

* 13th February.   † 25th March.

litter. The skies were spread bright and silky-blue above the old houses—on the two figure-heads fixed to the beams of the east store-house, the traces of their old-time gilding shone out to-day in the clear air. Water dribbled and ran from the roofs, and the smoke whirled and danced in little mild puffs of wind.

She went to the stables and in, and filled the lap of her skirt with oats from the corn-bin. The stable smell, and the sound of the horses stirring in there in the dark, did her good. But some of the folks were in the stable; and she was ashamed to do what she had come to do.

She went out and threw the grain to the hens that were scratching around and sunning themselves in the yard. Her thoughts far off, she looked at Tore, the stable-man, currying and brushing down the grey gelding—it was fast shedding its winter coat. Now and then she shut her eyes, and turned her face, faded and pale with the indoor air, up to the sunshine.

So she was standing when three men rode into the court-yard. The foremost of them was a young priest whom she did not know. As soon as he was aware of her, he leapt from his horse and came straight up to her with outstretched hand.

"You had not meant me this great honour, I trow—that you, the lady of the house, should come forth to welcome me," said he, smiling. "But I must thank you for it, none the less. For I wot well you must be my brother's wife, Kristin Lavransdatter?"

"Then must you bé Master Gunnulf, my brother-in-law," she answered, flushing red. "Well met, sir! And welcome home to Husaby!"

"Thanks for a fair welcome," said the priest; and he stooped and kissed her cheek, after the fashion she knew was used in foreign lands, when kinsfolk met. "Happy be your coming hither, Erlend's wife!"

Ulf Haldorssön came out, and bade a groom take the strangers' horses. Gunnulf greeted Ulf right heartily:

"Are you here, kinsman?—I had looked to hear that you were a wedded man and a householder by now."

"Nay, no wedding for me, till I must choose between a wife and the gallows," said Ulf, with a laugh; and the priest laughed too. "I have pledged me to the devil to live unwed as firmly as you have promised it to God."

"Aye, then should you be scatheless whichever way you turn you, Ulf," answered Master Gunnulf, laughing. "For you will do well the day you break your promise to yonder man; and yet 'tis said also that a man should keep his word, were it to the fiend himself. . . . Is Erlend not at home?" he asked in wonder. He proffered Kristin his hand, as they turned to go into the hall.

To hide her bashfulness, Kristin moved about among the serving-women, and saw to the spreading of the board. She bade Erlend's learned brother sit in the high-seat, but, when she would not sit there with him, he moved down to the bench beside her.

Now she was sitting at his side, she saw that Master Gunnulf must be shorter than Erlend by half a head at the least—but he seemed to bulk larger. He was stronger-built and more thickset in body and limbs, and his broad shoulders were quite straight—Erlend's slouched a little. He was clad in dark raiment, most seemly for a priest, but the long cassock, reaching to his feet, and upward almost to the band of his linen shirt, was fastened with buttons of enamel, and from his woven belt his eating-gear hung in a silver sheath.

She looked up into the priest's countenance. He had a round strong head and a round but thin face, with broad low forehead, cheek-bones a little large, and a fine rounded chin. The nose was straight and the ears small and comely, but his mouth was wide and thin-lipped, and the upper lip came forward never so little and overshadowed the lower lip's little splash of red. Only his hair was like Erlend's—the close-cropped ring round the priest's tonsure was black, with a dry, sooty gleam, and looked as though 'twere as silky-soft as Erlend's mane. For the rest he was not unlike his cousin Munan Baardssön—she could see now it might be true that Munan had been comely in his youth. Nay, 'twas Aashild, his mother's sister, that he favoured—now she saw that he had the same eyes as Lady Aashild—amber-yellow eyes, shining under narrow straight black brows.

At first Kristin was a little shy of this brother-in-law of hers that had laid up such store of learning at the great schools in Paris and Valland.* But little by little she forgot her bashfulness. It was so easy to talk to Master Gunnulf. It seemed not as though he talked of himself—far less that he was fain to flaunt his learning. But when she had time to bethink herself a little, she found he had told her so much that Kristin thought she never had known before how great a world there was outside Norway. She forgot herself and all her affairs, as she sat looking up in the priest's round large-boned face, with its subtile sprightly smile. He had laid one leg over the knee of the other under his cassock, and sat with his white sinewy hands clasped round his ankle.

When, late in the afternoon, he joined her in the hall, he asked if they should play draughts. Kristin could but answer that she thought not there was any draught-board in the house.

"Is there not?" asked the priest in wonder. He went over to Ulf:

"Know you, Ulf, what Erlend has done with mother's gilded draught-set?—The things for pastime that she left behind her here—surely he has not let any other have them?"

* A general name for the Latin countries.

"They are in a chest above in the armoury," said Ulf. "'Twas in his mind, methinks, that they should not come into the hands of others—that were on the manor heretofore," he added low. "Would you have me fetch the chest, Gunnulf?"

"Aye—Erlend cannot, surely, have aught against it now," said the priest.

A little after, the two came back bearing a great carven chest. The key was in it, and Gunnulf opened it. On top lay a cithern and another stringed instrument whose like Kristin had never seen before. Gunnulf called it a salterion—he let his fingers stray over the strings, but it was untuned. There were rolls of ribands, reels of silk, broidered gloves, and silken hoods, and three books with clasps. At length the priest found the draught-board; the squares were in white and gold, and the men were of narwhal ivory, white and golden.

Kristin had to own now to her brother-in-law that she was slow-witted at the draughts and had no great skill of stringed music. But the books she was eager to look into.

"Aye—belike you have learnt to read in books, Kristin?" the priest asked; and now she could answer, a little proudly, that so much she had indeed learned while she was yet a child. And in the cloister she had been praised for her skill in reading and writing.

The priest stood over her with a smile on his face while she turned the leaves of the books. One was a knightly saga of Tristan and Isolde, and the other held histories of holy men—she opened it at St. Martin's saga. The third book was in Latin, and was in a passing fair script with great capital letters painted in many hues.

"This one belonged to our ancestor, Bishop Nikulaus," said Gunnulf. Kristin read, half aloud:

> *Averte faciam tuam a peccatis meis—*
> *et omnes iniquitates meas dele.*
> *Cor mundum crea in me, Deus—*
> *et spiritum rectum innova in visceribus meis.*
> *Ne projicias me a facie tua—*
> *et Spiritum Sanctum tuum ne auferas a me.**

"Understand you this?" asked Gunnulf, and Kristin nodded and said she understood a little. She knew enough of the words' meaning to be strangely moved that her eyes should fall on them just now. Her face quivered a little, and she could not keep back her tears. Then Gunnulf took the psaltery on his lap, and said he would try if he could not mend it.

While they sat thus, they heard the trampling of horses in the court-yard—and straightway after Erlend burst into the hall, beaming with

* Psalm li. 9-11.

gladness—he had heard who it was that was come. The brothers stood with their hands on each other's shoulders, Erlend asking questions and waiting for the answers. Gunnulf had been in Nidaros two days, so it was pure chance that they had not met there.

"'Tis strange too," said Erlend. "Methought that all the priesthood of Christ's Church would have gone forth in procession to meet you, when you came home—so wise and stuffed with learning as you must be now——"

"And know you so surely that they did not?" asked his brother, laughing. "You come not over nigh to Christ's Church when you are in the city, I have heard tell."

"True, boy—I draw not nigh to my Lord Archbishop when I can steer clear of him—he hath singed my hide for me once already," Erlend laughed unrepentantly. "How like you your brother-in-law, my sweet?—I see you have made friends with Kristin already, brother —she cares not much for our other kindred. . . ."

It was not till they were sitting down to the supper-board that Erlend marked that he still had his fur cap and his cloak on and the sword at his belt.

It was the merriest evening Kristin had yet had at Husaby. Erlend forced his brother to sit with her in the high-seat; he himself carved for him and filled his cup. The first time he drank to Gunnulf, he kneeled down on one knee, and made as though to kiss his brother's hand.

"All hail, Lord! We must use us, Kristin, to show the Archbishop all seemly honour—nay, for Archbishop you surely will be one day, Gunnulf!"

It was late before the house-folk left the hall, but the two brothers and Kristin sat on over their drink. Erlend had set himself on the table facing his brother.

"Aye, this gear I had thought on at our bridal," said he, pointing to his mother's chest, "and thought that Kristin should have it. But 'tis so easy for me to forget; and you, brother—you forget nothing. But the ring my mother left hath found its way on to a fair hand, me-thinks?" He laid Kristin's hand on his knee and turned round her betrothal-ring.

Gunnulf nodded. He laid the psaltery in Erlend's lap:

"Sing now, brother; you were wont to sing so sweetly and play so well in old days——"

"'Tis many years since," said Erlend, more gravely. Then he ran his fingers over the strings:

> Good King Olav, Harald's son,
>   Rode in the thick woods' shade;
> Found in the earth a footprint small,
>   —Here be tidings great!

Out spoke he then, Finn Arnessön,
—Rode of the meiny foremost:
"Fair would show such a little foot,
All in scarlet hosen. . . ."

Erlend smiled as he sang, and Kristin looked up at the priest a little timidly—not knowing but he might mislike this ditty of St. Olav and Alvhild. But Gunnulf sat smiling—yet she felt sure, of a sudden, that 'twas not at the song, but at Erlend.

"Kristin need not sing to-night. I trow you are short of breath now, my dearest," said Erlend, stroking her cheek. "But now 'tis your turn——" He gave the psaltery to his brother.

One could tell from the priest's playing and singing that he had been well schooled:

The King rode northward into the hills—

He heard a dove that made her moan,
Lamenting that her mate was gone:

Lully, lulley! lully lulley!
The falcon hath borne my mate away!

After the hawk he is fain to ride;
It flies through the wild hills far and wide.

It led him up, it led him down,
It led him into an orchard brown.

In that orchard there was an hall
That was hangèd with purple and pall.

There lieth a fair knight in his blood—
He is the Lord so brave and good.

At his bed's head there standeth a stone,
Corpus Domini written thereon.

Lully lulley! lully lulley!
The falcon hath borne my mate away! *

"Where learned you that song?" asked Erlend.

"Oh—some boys sang it outside the hostel where I lodged in Kanterborg," said Gunnulf. "And methought I would try to turn it into our Norse tongue. But it goes not so well in Norse." He sat playing snatches of the tune on the strings.

"Well, brother—'tis long past midnight. Like enough, Kristin needs to come to her bed now—are you weary, my wife?"

Kristin looked up at the men in fear; she was very pale:

"I know not. . . . Methinks 'twere best now I should not lie in the bed in here——"

"Are you sick?" they both asked, bending over her.

"I know not," she said as before. She pressed her hands behind her hips. "My back feels so strange——"

* See Note 3.

Erlend sprang up and went towards the door. Gunnulf followed him:

"'Tis an ill chance that you brought them not here before this, the ladies that are to help her," he said. "Is it come much before she looked for it——?"

Erlend flushed a burning red.

"Kristin deemed she would need none other but her own maids—they have borne children themselves, some of them——" He tried to laugh.

"Are you beside yourself!" Gunnulf gazed at him. "Hath not every cottar's wife skilled women and neighbours' wives * to help her when she is brought to bed—and shall your wife creep off and hide herself in a hole, like a tib-cat kittening? Nay, brother—so much of a man I would have you be as to fetch the foremost ladies of the country-side to Kristin——"

Erlend bent his face, flushed with shame:

"You say truly, brother. I will ride myself to Raasvold—I must send men to the other manors. And do you bide here with Kristin!"

"Are you going forth?" asked Kristin fearfully, when she saw Erlend put on his riding-cloak.

He came across and threw his arms around her.

"I go to fetch the best women in the country-side for you, my Kristin. Gunnulf will stay by you, while the maids make ready for you in the little hall," he said, kissing her.

"Could you not send one to Audfinna Andunsdatter?" she begged. "But not before daylight—I would not have her waked from sleep for my sake—she has so much on her hands, I know——"

Gunnulf asked his brother who Audfinna was.

"It seems not to me over-seemly," said the priest. "The wife of one of your tenants——"

"Kristin shall have it as she will," said Erlend. And as the priest went out with him and he stood waiting for his horse, he told the other how Kristin had come to know the farmer's wife. Gunnulf bit his lip and stood deep in thought.

There was noise and commotion now throughout the manor; men rode away into the night, and serving-women came running in to ask how it fared with their mistress. Kristin said there was not much amiss as yet, but they must make all things ready for her in the little hall. She would send word when she would be brought in there.

Then she was left alone again with the priest. She strove to speak evenly and cheerily with him as before.

"*You* are not afraid," he said with a little smile.

"Nay, but I *am* afraid!" She looked up into his eyes—her own were

* See Note 4.

dark and frightened. "Know you, brother-in-law—were they born here at Husaby, Erlend's other children?"

"No," said the priest, quickly. "The boy was born at Hunehals, and the little maid up in Strind—on a farm he once owned there.—Is it," he asked in a little, "that it has troubled you to remember that this other woman lived here with Erlend before?"

"Aye," said Kristin.

"'Tis hard for you to judge justly of Erlend's doings in this matter of Eline," said the priest gravely. "It was no easy thing for Erlend to rule himself—never has it been easy for Erlend to know what right was. For, ever since we were little children, so has it been, that whatever Erlend did, mother thought it was well done, and father that it was ill. Aye, he has told you, doubtless, so much of our mother, that you know of all this——"

"For all I can remember, he has named her but twice or thrice," said Kristin. "But I have seen well enough that he loved her."

Gunnulf said softly:

"Surely there has never been such love between a mother and her son. Mother was much younger than my father. Then there befell this mischance of her sister, Aashild—Baard, our father's brother, died, and 'twas said—aye, doubtless you know of that? Father believed the worst, and he said to mother—— Erlend flung his knife at father once, when he was yet a boy—he flew at father's throat more than once for mother's sake, when he was half-grown. . . .

"When mother fell sick, he parted him from Eline Ormsdatter. Mother fell sick with sores and scabs on her flesh, and father said 'twas leprosy. He sent her from him—would have forced her to dwell as a commoner * with the Sisters at the spital. Then Erlend fetched mother away and bore her with him to Oslo—they went, on the way, to Aashild, who is skilled in leechcraft, and she, and the King's French leech too, said that she was no leper. King Haakon welcomed Erlend kindly then, and bade him try the virtue of the holy Erik Valdemarssön's grave—the King's mother's father. Many had there found healing for skin-sicknesses.

"Erlend set forth for Denmark with mother, but she died aboard his ship, south of Stad. When Erlend came home with her—aye, you must bear in mind that father was stricken in years, and Erlend had been an unruly son all his days—when Erlend came to Nidaros with mother's body—father was in our town dwelling then, and he would not take Erlend in—before he saw whether the boy had taken the sickness, he said. Erlend took horse and rode off, and rested not till he came to the farm where Eline was with her son. And after that he held fast to her,

* See Note 13 to *The Bridal Wreath* (*The Garland*).

in despite of all, despite that he himself was weary of her; and so it came about that he brought her to Husaby and set her to rule his house, when he was once master here. She had this hold on him, that she said if he failed her after this, he were worthy to be smitten down himself with leprosy.—But now 'tis time, I trow, for your women to see you, Kristin——" he said, looking down at her young face, grown grey and stiff with horror and torment. But when he would have gone to the door, she cried aloud after him:

"No, no, go not from me——"

"'Twill be all the sooner over," the priest said to comfort her, "since you are so sick already."

"'Tis not that!" She gripped his arm hard. "Gunnulf——" It seemed to him he had never seen such terror in a human face.

"Kristin—remember—you must remember, this is no worse for you than for other women!"

"Yes. Yes." She pressed her face down on the priest's arm. "For now I know that Eline and her children should be sitting in my place. For he had pledged her his faith and wedded troth, ere ever I came to be his paramour——"

"Know you that?" said Gunnulf calmly. "Erlend knew no better himself then. But you know that that word of his he could not keep—never had the Archbishop given his leave that they two should wed. Think not it can be that your marriage holds not good. You are Erlend's true wife——"

"Oh, I had thrown away all right to tread the earth long before he wed me. And 'twas yet worse than I knew—oh, would I might die, and this child never be born—I dare not see what 'tis I have borne within me——"

"God forgive you, Kristin—you know not what you say! Would you wish that your child die unborn and unchristened——?"

"Aye, for, whatever befall, what I bear beneath my heart must be the devil's. It cannot be saved. Oh, had I but drunk the draught Eline proffered me—it had mayhap been some atonement for all we had sinned, Erlend and I.—Then had this child never been gotten—oh, Gunnulf, all the time have I known it—that when I should see the thing I had nourished within me, then would I know full well it had been better for me to drink the draught of leprosy that she proffered me, than to drive her to death, to whom Erlend had first bound himself——"

"Kristin," said the priest, "you speak you know not what. 'Twas not you that drove that hapless woman to her death. Erlend *could* not keep the word he had pledged her when he was young and knew little of law or of right. Never could he have lived with her but in sin. And she had let herself be led astray by another too, and Erlend would have wed her to that other when he heard it. 'Twas not your doing that she took her life——"

"Would you know how it came to pass that she took her life?" Kristin was so hopeless now that she spoke quite calmly. "We were at Haugen together, Erlend and I, and she came thither. She had a horn with her, she would have had me drink with her—'twas for Erlend she had meant it, I can see now, but when she found me there with him, she would have had me—I knew that there was treachery—I saw that she drank no drop herself when she set her lips to the horn. But I would as lief have drunk—I cared not whether I lived or died, since I had come to know he had had her with him at Husaby all the time. Then came Erlend in—he threatened her with his knife, to make her drink first. She begged and prayed, and he would have let her go. Then the devil took hold on me—I took the horn.—'One of us two, your paramours,' said I—I egged Erlend on—'you cannot keep us both,' said I. So it was that she slew herself with Erlend's knife—but Björn and Aashild found a device to hide how it had come about——"

"So, Moster * Aashild was of this counsel!" said Gunnulf grimly. "I understand—she had beguiled you into Erlend's hands——"

"No," said Kristin vehemently. "Lady Aashild prayed us—she prayed Erlend and she prayed me, in such wise that I know not how I could hold out against her—that we should deal honourably, so far as that yet might be—fall at my father's feet and pray him to forgive us our misdeeds. But I dared not. I made pretence that I was fearful lest father should slay Erlend—oh, though I knew well father would never have harmed a man who yielded himself and his cause into his hands. I made pretence that I feared to bring on him such sorrow that he could never hold up his head again. Oh, but I have shown since, I feared not so much to bring my father sorrow—— You cannot believe, Gunnulf, how good a man my father is—none could know, that knows not my father, how good he has been to me all my days. Ever has father loved me so. 'Twas that I could not bear he should know I had borne me so shamelessly, that while he deemed I was sitting among the Sisters at Oslo, learning all that was good and right—aye, for I bore the novices' weed while I was lying with Erlend in barns and in lofts down in the city——"

She looked up at Gunnulf. His face was white and hard as stone.

"See you now why I am afraid? She that took him to her, when he cametainted with leprosy——"

"Would *you* not have done it?" asked the priest, in a still voice.

"Yes, yes, yes." A shadow of the wild smile of former days flew over the woman's ravaged face.

* Moster = mother's sister.

"And, besides, Erlend was not tainted," said Gunnulf. "None but father ever believed that mother died of leprosy."

"But surely *I* must be as a leper in the sight of God," said Kristin. She laid her face down on the priest's arm, to which she was clinging. "Such as I am now, tainted with all sin——"

"My sister," said the priest softly, laying his other hand on her linen coif, "so sinful sure you cannot be, you young child, that you have forgotten that as sure as God can cleanse a man in the flesh from leprosy, so surely can He cleanse your soul from sin——"

"Oh, I know not," she sobbed, her face still hidden in his arm. "I know not—and I repent not either, Gunnulf. Frighted am I, but yet—frighted was I when I stood before the church-door with Erlend and the priest joined us together—frighted was I when I went with him in to the bride's mass—with golden crown on flowing hair, for I dared not speak of my shame to my father—with all my sins unatoned, aye, I dared not confess the truth to my own parish priest. But when I went about here at Husaby in the winter, and saw myself grow fouler with each day that passed—then was I yet more afraid, because Erlend was not towards me as he once had been—I thought of the time when he came to me in my bower at Skog of nights——"

"Kristin——" The priest tried to lift up her face. "You dare not think of such things now! Think but that God sees now your sorrow and your repentance. Turn you to the merciful maid, Mary, that hath compassion on all that are sorrowful——"

"But understand you not?—I have driven another to cast away her own life——"

"Kristin," said the priest sternly, "dare you think in your wicked pride that sin of yours can be so great that God's loving-kindness is not greater?"

He stroked and stroked her linen hood.

"Mind you not, my sister, how it was when the devil would have tempted St. Martin? Did not the fiend ask if St. Martin dared believe fully his own word when he promised all the sinners he shrove God's mercy? But the Bishop answered: 'To thee also I dare to promise God's forgiveness, in the hour that thou prayest for it—wouldst thou but cast away thy pride and believe that His love is greater than thy hate——'"

Gunnulf stood for a little space, still patting the weeping woman's head. And he thought the while—his mouth white-lipped and hard-set—was it *so* that Erlend had dealt with his young bride!

Audfinna Andunsdatter was the first woman to come. She found the lying-in woman in the little hall; Gunnulf sat by her, and a couple of maids were busy in the room.

Audfinna greeted the priest with reverence, but Kristin rose up and went toward her with outstretched hand:

"Have thanks, Audfinna, for your coming—I know 'tis no light thing for your folks at home to do without you——?"

Gunnulf had looked searchingly at the woman. Now he too rose:

"'Twas bravely done of you to come so quick; there is need that my brother's wife should have one with her she can trust—she is strange to this country-side, young and unaccustomed——"

"Jesus, she is white as her coif!" whispered Audfinna. "Think you, sir, I might give her a little sleeping-draught?—methinks she had need to win some rest before it comes on her more sorely."

She set about making ready busily but quietly; felt the couch that the serving-women had made up on the floor, and bade them bring more cushions and more straw. Next she placed small stone pots with herbs in them against the fire. Thereafter she set about loosing all bands and knots in Kristin's dress, and last of all drew out all the pins from the sick woman's hair.

"Never did I see fairer," said she, when the whole flood of gold-brown silky locks rolled down around the white visage. She could not forbear to laugh a little: "Methinks it can scarce have lost much either of strength or brightness, even if so be that you bore it uncovered a little longer than was right——"

She got Kristin softly bedded among the cushions on the floor and covered her well with rugs:

"Drink this now; then will you not feel the pains so sorely; and try to get a little sleep between-times."

It was time for Gunnulf to go. He went across and bent over Kristin.

"You will pray for me, Gunnulf," she asked, beseechingly.

"I will pray for you even till I see you with your child upon your arm—and after too," he said, and laid her hand back again under the coverlid.

Kristin lay and dozed. She felt almost well. The shooting pains across her loins came and went and came again—but it was so unlike all she had felt before, that each time they had passed she wondered almost if it were not but her fancy. After the torment and horror of the early morning hours she felt as though she were already happily over the worst dread and anguish. Audfinna went about so softly, hanging up child's clothing, rugs and furs to warm at the hearth—and stirring her pots a little, so that a spicy smell stole out into the room. At length Kristin fell half asleep between the fits of pain, and dreamed she was at home in the brewhouse at Jörundgaard, and was helping her mother with the dyeing of a great web of cloth—doubtless 'twas the steam from the ash-bark and nettles.

Then came the lady-midwives, one after another—ladies from the manors of their parish and of Birgsi. Audfinna drew back among the serving-women. And when evening was drawing on, Kristin felt the pains grew sore. The ladies said she should walk about the room as long as she could bear to do so. It was torture to her—the room was chock-full of women now, and she must pace about like a mare put up for sale. Between-whiles, too, she must let the strange ladies press and feel round about her body with their hands; and then they would talk together. At length Lady Gunna of Raasvold, who was to have the ordering of all things in the room, said that now she might lie down upon the floor. The lady divided the women in two parts, one to sleep while the other waked and watched: "Aye, 'twill not be quickly over, this—but scream all you will, Kristin, when you feel the pains sore—take no heed of the sleepers. We are all here for naught but to help you, poor child!" she said gently and kindly, patting the girl's cheek.

But Kristin lay gnawing her lips and crushing the edges of the coverlid in her sweat-bathed hands. It was stiflingly hot—but they said that so it should be. After every fit of pain the sweat poured from her.

Between-times she would lie thinking of the food for all these women. She was so fain they should deem that she had her house in good order. She had bidden Torbjörg, the cook, pour buttermilk into the water the fresh fish were boiled in. If only Gunnulf would not deem it a breach of the fast. Sira Eirik had said 'twas no breach, for buttermilk is not milk food, and, besides, the fish-broth is thrown away. The dried fish that Erlend had gotten for the house last autumn, they must nowise be let touch—spoiled and full of maggots as it was.

Mary, Blessed Lady of mine—will it be long, think you, till you will help me?—oh—now 'tis so hard, so hard—so hard——

She must try to hold out a little longer yet, before she gave way and screamed. . . .

Audfinna sat over by the hearth, tending the pots of hot water. Kristin wished so that she dared pray her to come to her and hold her hand. She knew not what she would have given now for the clasp of a friendly hand that she knew. But she was ashamed to ask it. . . .

All through the next forenoon a sort of bewildered stillness lay over Husaby. It was the eve of Mary's Mass, and all the work of the place should have been out of hand by the hour of nones; but the men were bemused and cast down, and the scared serving-wenches scrambled through the house-work in slovenly wise. The house-folk had grown fond of their young mistress—and things were going none too well with her, 'twas said.

Erlend stood out in the courtyard talking with his smith. He tried to keep his thoughts on what the man was saying. Then Lady Gunna came towards him swiftly:

"We can come no way with your wife, Erlend—now have we tried all shifts. You must come down—maybe 'twill help if she be set in your lap. Go in and put on you a short coat—but be hasty; she is hard bested, the poor young thing."

Erlend had grown red as blood. He remembered, he had heard—if a woman could no otherwise be delivered of a child she had conceived in secret, 'twas said it might help if she were set on the father's knee.

Kristin lay on the floor under some rugs; two women sat by her. As Erlend came in, he saw that she shrank together, bored her head into the lap of one of the women, and rolled it about here and there—but not a moan came from her.

When the fit was over, she looked up with wild, terrified eyes; the brown, cracked lips gasped open. Every trace of youth and comeliness was gone from the swollen, red, flaming face—even the hair was tangled up into a dirty mat, with bits of straw and wool from the sheepskins. She looked at Erlend as if she knew him not at first. But when she understood why the women had sent for him, she shook her head vehemently:

"'Tis not our use, where I come from—that men should be by when a woman bears a child——"

"They use it sometimes here north of Dovre," said Erlend softly. "If it might shorten the pain for you a little, my Kristin, you must suffer it——"

"Oh——!" As he knelt beside her, she threw her arms about his waist and crushed herself against him. Crouched together and shaking, she fought through the fit without a cry.

"Can I speak two words with my husband alone?" she said, swiftly, breathlessly, when it was past. The women drew back.

"Was it when she was in labour that you promised her what she said—that you would wed her when she was a widow—that night when Orm was born?" whispered Kristin.

Erlend gasped for breath, as though he had been struck a blow above the heart. Then he shook his head vehemently:

"I was at the castle that night—'twas my troop that had the watch. 'Twas when I came home to our lodging in the morning and they laid the boy in my arms—— Have you been lying here thinking of this, Kristin?"

"Aye——" Again she clung tight to him, while a wave of pain swept over her. Erlend dried away the sweat that poured down over her face.

"Now you know this," he asked when she was still again, "would you not I should bide with you as Lady Gunna says?"

But Kristin shook her head again. And at last the women were forced to let Erlend go.

But with that it seemed as if her strength to hold out were broken. She shrieked aloud in wild terror of the pangs she felt coming, and wailed out prayers for help. Yet when the women talked of fetching the husband in again, she screamed out: no—she had rather be tortured to death——

Gunnulf and the clerk that was with him went to the church to hold evensong. Every soul on the manor who was not with the lying-in woman went with them. But Erlend stole out of the church before the service was over, and went southward toward the houses.

In the west over the hill-tops on the farther side of the Dale the sky was yellowish red—dusk was beginning to fall in the clear mild spring evening. A star came forth here and there, white in the light-hued sky. A little flake of mist was drifting over the wood down by the lake—there were bare patches where the fields faced sunwards, and the smell of mould and melting snow was in the air.

The little hall lay westmost of the houses, out towards where the ground dipped to the valley. Erlend went over to it and stood awhile behind its wall. The timbers were still warm with the sun, when he leaned against them. Oh, her cries——! He had heard a heifer once bellowing in the grip of a bear—it was up at their sæter, when he was a half-grown lad. Arnbjörn, the cowherd, and himself had run south through the woods. He remembered the shaggy mass that stood up and turned into a bear with hot red open maw. Arnbjörn's spear broke off in the bear's paws—then the man snatched Erlend's from him, for he stood palsied with horror. The heifer lay there still living, but udder and things were eaten away——

Kristin mine—oh, Kristin mine——! Lord, for Thy blessed Mother's sake, have mercy——

He fled back to the church.

The maids came into the hall with the supper—the board was not set up, but they put down the food by the hearth. The men took bread and fish for themselves over to the benches, and sat in their places silent; they ate a little, but none seemed to have a stomach to his food. No one came to take away the dishes after the meal, and none of the men got up to go to rest. They sat on, gazing into the hearth-fire, and spoke not to each other.

Erlend had hidden himself in the corner by the bed—he could not bear that any should see his face.

Master Gunnulf had lit a little hand-lamp and set it on an arm of the high-seat. He set himself on the bench below it with a book in his hands—and sat there, his lips just moving, soundlessly and without cease.

Once Ulf Haldorssön rose up, went over to the hearth and took a slice of soft bread, then searched a little among the sticks of firewood and picked out one. Then he went down the hall, to the corner near the entrance-door, where old Aan sat. The two busied themselves with the bread, hidden behind Ulf's cloak; and Aan cut and carved at the stick. The other men glanced across at them now and then. In a while Ulf and Aan stood up and left the hall.

Gunnulf looked after the two, but said no word. He went on again with his prayers.

Once a young lad fell off the bench in his sleep and rolled out on the floor. He rose up and looked about him bewildered. Then he sighed a little and sat down again on the bench.

Ulf Haldorssön and Aan came in again quietly and went to the places where they had sat before. The men looked over at them, but none spoke.

Of a sudden Erlend sprang up. He went across the hall to his housefolk. His face was grey as clay, and his eyes hollow.

"Is there none of you that knows a way?" said he. "You, Aan?" he whispered.

"It availed not," Ulf whispered back.

"Methinks 'tis written that she shall not have this child," said Aan, wiping his nose, "and then neither runs nor offerings avail. 'Tis pity of you, Erlend—to lose this kind young wife so soon——"

"Oh, speak not as though she were dead already," said Erlend, broken and despairing. He went back to his corner and threw himself down with his head within the bed-end.

Once a man went out and came in again. "The moon is up," he said. "'Twill soon be morning."

A little while after, Lady Gunna came into the hall. She sank down on the beggars' bench by the door—her grey hair bunched out on all sides; her head-dress had slipped back on her shoulders.

The men rose—drew near to her slowly.

"One of you must come down there and hold her," she said, weeping. "We cannot, any more. You must go to her, Gunnulf—none can tell how it may end——"

Gunnulf stood up and thrust the prayer-book into the pouch at his belt.

"*You* must come too, Erlend," said the Lady.

The rough, hoarse crying met him in the doorway—Erlend stopped, trembling. He caught a glimpse of Kristin's distorted unknowable face in the midst of a group of weeping women—she was on her knees, they holding her up.

Near by the door some serving-women had flung themselves down with their faces hidden on the benches; they were praying aloud, unceasingly. He threw himself down beside them and hid his head in his arms. Shriek after shriek came from her, and each time it was as though an icy pang of unbelieving horror went through him. This thing *could* not be. . . .

Once he plucked up heart and looked across. Gunnulf was sitting now in front of her on a stool, holding her under the arms. Lady Gunna knelt by her side, and had her arms round Kristin's waist, but Kristin was struggling, in deadly terror, to thrust the other away.

"Oh, no—oh, no—loose me—I cannot bear—God, God, help me——"

"God will help you soon now, Kristin," said the priest each time. A woman stood by, holding a basin of water, and after every spasm she took a wet cloth and wiped the sick woman's face—the sweat from under her hair-roots and the slime from between her lips.

Then her head fell forward between Gunnulf's arms, and she slept for a moment—but the torments dragged her out of her sleep again, at once. And the priest went on saying:

"Now, Kristin, will you soon be helped——"

None thought any more what time of the night it might be. But through the smoke-vent already the dawn grinned greyly down.

Then, after a long frantic shriek of anguish, there came a sudden utter stillness. Erlend heard the women bustling about—he would have looked up; but he heard someone weeping aloud, and he shrank down again—he dared not know——

Then Kristin screamed again—a high wild scream of lamentation, unlike the mad inhuman animal cries that had gone before. Erlend started up.

Gunnulf stood bending over, holding Kristin, who still knelt. She was looking in deadly horror at something Lady Gunna was holding in a sheepskin—a raw, dark-red mass, like naught but the entrails of a slaughtered beast.

The priest drew her close to him:

"Kristin mine—you have borne as fine and fair a son as ever mother had need to thank God for—and he breathes!" he said vehemently to the weeping women. "He breathes—God will not be so cruel as not to hear us——"

Even while the priest was speaking, it came to pass. Through the mother's weary, bewildered head there flitted, half remembered, the vision of a bud she had once seen in the convent garden—something from out of which broke red crinkled silken petals—and spread themselves out into a flower.

The shapeless lump of flesh moved—sounds came from it—it stretched itself out and turned into a quite small wine-red child in human likeness—it had arms and legs and hands and feet, with full-formed fingers and toes on them—it struggled and wheezed a little. . . .

"So little, so little, so little he is——" she cried aloud in a thin hoarse voice, and sank down, helpless between laughter and weeping. The women round about burst into laughter and dried their tears, and Gunnulf passed her over into their arms.

"Roll him in a trough, that he may scream the better," said the priest, following the women who bore the new-born boy away to the hearth-place.

When Kristin waked from her long swoon, she was lying in her bed. Someone had taken off the dreadful sweat-drenched clothes, and a blessed sense of warmth and healing was streaming into her body—they had laid small bags of hot nettle-porridge upon her, and packed her in with heated rugs and skins.

One bade her hush when she would have spoken. There was a great stillness in the room. And through the stillness came a voice that she could scarce call to mind:

"——Nikulaus, in the name of the Father, the Son and the Holy Ghost——"

There was a trickling of water.

Kristin rose a little on her elbow and looked out. Out there by the hearth stood a priest in white vestments, and Ulf Haldorssön lifted a red, sprawling naked child up out of the great brazen cauldron, gave it to the godmother, and took from her the lighted taper.

She had her child—it was he that was shrieking now so as almost to drown the priest's words. But she was so weary—she cared but little, and only wished to sleep——

Then she heard Erlend's voice, saying hastily and in fear:

"His head—his head is so strange."

"'Tis swollen up," said a woman calmly. "That is nothing strange—he has had to fight hard, this lad, for his life."

Kristin cried out something. It was as though she grew awake right into her inmost heart—this was her son, and he had striven for his life even as had she.

Gunnulf turned quickly, laughing—caught the little bundle of swaddling-clothes from Lady Gunna's lap and bore it over to the bed. He laid the boy in his mother's arms. Sick with tenderness and joy, she rubbed her face against the little glimpse of a red silky-soft face within the linen cloths.

She looked up at Erlend. She knew that once before she had seen him with a grey, ravaged face like this—she could not remember when, she was so strange and dizzy in the head—but she knew that it was well that she need not remember. And it was good to see him stand thus by his brother—the priest had laid a hand upon his shoulder. A sense of measureless peace and safety came upon her, as she looked up at the tall man in alb and stole; the round, lean face under the black ring of hair was so strong, but his smile was comely and kind.

Erlend drove his dagger deep into the timber wall-post behind the mother and child.

"'Tis needless now," said the priest, laughing, "for the boy is baptised."

Kristin came to think of somewhat Brother Edvin had once said. A new-christened child, he said, was as holy as the holy angels in heaven. 'Twas washed clean from the sins of its parents, and as yet it had done no sin itself. Timidly and warily she kissed the little face.

Lady Gunna came over to them. She was worn out and weary, and wroth with the father, who had not had wit enough to say a word of thanks to the lady helpers. And the priest had taken the child from her and borne it to the mother—she should have done that, for she had delivered the woman, and, besides that, she was godmother to the boy.

"You have not greeted your son yet, Erlend, or taken him in your arms," she said angrily.

Erlend lifted the babe out of its mother's arms, and laid his face against it for a moment.

"I doubt I shall scarce come to like you from my heart, Naakkve, till I have forgotten that you tormented your mother so cruelly," he said, and laid the boy down again by Kristin.

"Aye, blame *him* for it, do," said the old lady wrathfully. Master Gunnulf laughed, and then Lady Gunna laughed too. She would have taken the child and laid it in the cradle, but Kristin begged hard to keep him with her a little longer. Soon after, she fell asleep, with her son close in by her—knew dimly that Erlend touched her, warily, as if he feared to hurt her by a touch, and then slept again.

v

THE tenth day after the child's birth, Master Gunnulf said to his brother, when they were alone in the hall in the morning:

"Methinks 'tis full time now, Erlend, that you send word to your wife's kin of how things stand with her."

"I see not that there is such haste," answered Erlend. "They will scarce be overjoyful at Jörundgaard when they hear that there is a son in our house already."

"Can you believe," said Gunnulf, "that Kristin's mother knew not in the autumn that her daughter was ailing? And if she knew, then must she now be going in fear——"

Erlend made no answer.

But a little later in the day, as Gunnulf sat in the little hall talking with Kristin, Erlend came in. He had a skin-cap on his head, a short and thick outer coat of wadmal, long breeches and shaggy boots. He bent over his wife and patted her cheek:

"Tell me, Kristin mine—would you have me bear any greeting from you to Jörundgaard?—for now am I bound southward to tell them of our son."

Kristin flushed deeply—she looked both affrighted and glad.

"'Tis no more than your father has a right to crave of me," said Erlend gravely, "that I come myself with these tidings."

Kristin lay still a little.

"Tell them at home," she said softly, "that I have longed every day, since I left my home, to fall at my father's and mother's feet and pray them for forgiveness."

Soon after, Erlend left her. Kristin did not think to ask him how he was journeying. But Gunnulf went with his brother out into the courtyard. Outside the hall-door stood Erlend's ski and a spear-headed staff.

"You go on ski?" said Gunnulf. "Who goes with you?"

"None," said Erlend, laughing. "You should know best, Gunnulf, that 'tis no easy thing for any to bear me company on ski."

"Methinks 'tis folly and rashness," said the priest. "There are many wolves in the Höiland woods this year, they say——"

Erlend only laughed and began to fasten on his ski.

"I shall be up by the Gjeitskar sæters, I trow, before 'tis dark. There is long light already. By evening the third day I should be at Jörundgaard——"

"'Tis ill going from Gjeitskar on to the beaten road—and there are bad fog-pockets to pass through. And you know that those sæters are ill places in winter-time."

"You can give me your flint and steel," said the other, still laughing, "lest by chance I should have to cast away my own—at some elf-woman if she should crave such *kurteisi* of me as beseems not a wedded man. Come, brother; now am I to do as you would have me—betake me to Kristin's father and bid him crave such amends from me as he deems fair and right—so far you can sure let me guide myself, as to choose how I shall journey."

With this Master Gunnulf was forced to be content. But he warned the house-folk strictly to keep it hidden from Kristin that Erlend had gone forth alone.

The southern sky stretched pale-yellow over the deepening blue of the mountain snowfields, the evening that Erlend rushed down past the Sil churchyard, the snow-crust hissing and crunching under his ski. High up rode a half-moon, shining misty-white in the evening twilight.

At Jörundgaard dark smoke was whirling up from the vent-holes towards the pale clear sky. The strokes of an axe rang out, measured and cold through the stillness.

From the gateway a pack of farm-dogs rushed out barking at the new-comer. Inside the courtyard a flock of shaggy goats were picking their way about, dark in the clear dusk—they were tugging at a heap of pine-branches in the midst of the yard. Three little children in thick winter clothes ran about amongst them.

The homely peace of this place took hold on Erlend strangely. He stood uneasily and waited for Lavrans, who came out to meet the stranger—he had been standing down by the woodshed talking to a man who was splitting fence-staves. He stopped short when he saw it was his son-in-law—thrust the spear he bore in his hand hard down into the snow.

"Is it *you?*" he asked in a low voice. "Alone——? Is there—is aught——? How is it that you come in this wise?" he added in a moment.

"Thus it is." Erlend pulled himself together and looked his father-in-law in the face. "Methought that less I could not do than come myself to bear you these tidings: Kristin bore a son on Mary's Mass in the morning.—Aye, she does well now," he added quickly.

Lavrans stood still awhile. He set his teeth hard in his under lip—his chin shook and quivered a little.

"These were tidings!" he said at last.

Little Ramborg had come up, and stood at her father's side. She looked up, her face glowing red.

"Be still," said Lavrans harshly, though the little maid had not said a word, but only blushed. "Stand not here—begone——"

He said no more. Erlend stood, bent forward, leaning on the staff clenched in his left hand. He looked down at the snow. His right hand was thrust into his breast. Lavrans pointed:

" Are you hurt? "

"A little," said Erlend. "I came over some bare rocks last night in the dark."

Lavrans took hold of the wrist and felt it warily: "No bone is broke methinks," he said.—"You must tell her mother yourself——" He went off towards the hall as Ragnfrid came into the yard. She looked in wonderment after her husband—then she knew Erlend and went swiftly towards him.

She hearkened without a word, while Erlend for the second time had to bring forth his tidings. But her eyes shone with moisture when he said at the end:

"Methought that you had maybe seen somewhat before she left you last autumn—and that you might be fearful now for her——"

"'Twas kindly done of you, Erlend," said she, in a voice that shook, "to think of this. True it is that I have been afraid for her every day since you took her from us."

Lavrans came back:

"Here is fox's fat—I see your cheek is frozen, son-in-law. You must bide awhile in the outer room while Ragnfrid dresses it with this and gets you thawed—how stands it with your feet?—you must take off your boots that we may see——"

When the house-folk came in to supper, Lavrans told them the tidings, and bade that strong ale be brought in for them to make merry on. But there was no right merriment over the ale-drinking—the master himself sat there with a cup of water. He prayed Erlend to forgive this—'twas a vow he had made while yet a boy, to drink naught but water in fast-time. And so the folks sat somewhat soberly, and the talk went but tardily over the good ale. The children would come round to Lavrans now and then—he put an arm round them when they came close to his knee, but he answered absently when they spoke to him. Ramborg answered short and sharply when Erlend tried to jest with her—bent, it seemed, on showing that she misliked this brother-in-law of hers. She was in her eighth winter now; lively and comely, but bearing no likeness to her sisters.

Erlend asked who the other children might be. Lavrans answered that the boy was Haavard Trondssön, the youngest of the Sundbu children. 'Twas dull for him there amid his grown-up brothers and sisters; and last Yule he had set his heart on coming home with Ragnfrid, his father's sister. The little maid was Helga Rolfsdatter of Blakarsarv—there had been naught for it but for the kinsfolk to take the children away home with them after the grave-ale there—'twere pity they should see their father as he was now. For Ramborg it was a happy thing to have this foster-brother and sister. "We begin to grow old now, Ragnfrid and I," said Lavrans, "and this little one is more frolicsome and fond of play than Kristin was"—he stroked his daughter's curly hair.

Erlend went and sat by his mother-in-law, and she asked him of Kristin's childbed. He saw that Lavrans was listening to what they said. But soon he stood up, crossed the room, and put on hat and cloak. He had a mind to go over to the parsonage, he said—he would pray Sira Eirik to come and drink with them.

Lavrans went by the well-trodden path over the fields to Romund-gaard. The moon was dipping behind the hills now—but thousands of stars glittered above the white mountains.—He hoped that the priest might be at home—he could bear no longer to sit alone with the others.

But when he was come in between the fences near the farm, he saw a little taper coming towards him. Old Audun was bearing it—when he marked that there was someone on his path, he rang his little silver bell. Lavrans Björgulfsön threw himself on his knees in the snow-drift by the path.

Audun went by bearing the taper, and the bell that still tinkled gently. Behind him came Sira Eirik a-horseback. He lifted the pyx high in his hands when he came by the kneeling man—looked not to right or left, but rode calmly past, while Lavrans bowed himself down and stretched his two hands up in greeting towards his Saviour.

——'Twas Einar Hnufa's son, the man that was with the priest—so 'twas drawing to an end with the old man now——! Aye, aye. Lavrans said the prayers for the dying before he rose from the snow and went homewards. Even so, this meeting with God in the night had strengthened and comforted him much.

When they had gone to rest, he asked his wife:

"Knew you aught of this—that 'twas *so* with Kristin?"

"Did you not know?" said Ragnfrid.

"No," answered her husband, so shortly that she understood it must none the less have been in his thought at times.

"'Tis true I was afraid one while this last summer," said the mother, haltingly. "I saw that she had no joy in her food. But as time wore on, I deemed I must have been deceived. She seemed so joyous all the time we were making ready for the wedding——"

"Aye, for *that* she had good reason," said the father somewhat grimly. "But that she said naught to you—you that are her mother——"

"Aye, you can remember that, now she has done amiss," answered Ragnfrid bitterly. "You know full well, never has Kristin been used to turn to me——"

Lavrans said no more. In a little while he gently bade his wife sleep well, and lay quiet beside her. He felt that sleep would scarce come to him for a long time yet.

Kristin—Kristin—his little maid——

——Never had he touched with a single word on what Ragnfrid had confessed to him that night of the bridal. And she could not with reason think that he had let her feel he thought of it. He had not changed in his bearing towards her—rather had he striven to show her yet more friendliness and love. But 'twas not the first time this winter that he had marked this bitterness in Ragnfrid, or seen her search for some hidden offence in innocent words of his. He understood it not, and he knew of no remedy—he must let it be.

Our Father which art in heaven—— He prayed for Kristin and her child. Then he prayed for his wife and himself. Last of all he prayed for strength to bear with Erlend Nikulaussön in patience of spirit, for so long as he needs must have his son-in-law dwelling on this, his manor.

Lavrans would not have his daughter's husband set forth for home till it was seen what turn things would take with his wrist. And he would not hear of Erlend's going back alone.

"Kristin would be joyful if you bore me company," said Erlend, one day.

Lavrans was silent awhile. Then he brought forward many lets and hindrances. Ragnfrid would like little to be left alone here on the manor. And should he fare so far north, he could scarce hope to be back for the spring sowings. But the end was that he set out with Erlend. He took no man with him—he would come back by ship to Raumsdal; he could hire horses to bring him thence down the Dale—he had acquaintance everywhere along that road.

They spoke not much together on their way, but they journeyed in good accord. It tasked Lavrans' strength to keep up with Erlend, for he would not own that the other went too fast for him. But Erlend soon marked this, and suited his pace to his father-in-law's. He gave himself great pains to please his wife's father—and he had this quiet compliant way with him when he wished to win the friendship of any.

The third night they took shelter in a stone hut. They had had foul weather, with mist, but Erlend seemed to find the way as surely as ever. Lavrans had marked that Erlend had a marvellous sure eye for all signs and marks in the air and on the earth, and for the nature and ways of beasts—and he ever knew where he was. All that he himself, used as he was to the hills, had taught himself by looking and marking and remembering, the other seemed to know blindly. Erlend laughed himself about it—he did but feel it all within him.

They found the hut in the pitch-darkness, at the very hour Erlend had foretold. Lavrans thought to himself of a night like this when he had made a bed for himself in the snow but a bowshot from his own horse-camp. The snow was drifted high around the hut, so that they had to break in through the smoke-hole. Erlend covered over the opening with a horse-hide that was lying in the hut, and fastened it with slats of wood which he pressed in under the rafters. He scraped away with a ski the snow that had sifted in, and managed to make up a fire in the fire-place with the frozen wood that lay there. He drew out three or four ptarmigan from under the bench—he had hid them away there on his way south—plastered them round with clay from the floor by the fire-place where it had thawed, and threw the lumps into the glowing embers.

Lavrans lay on the earthen bench, where Erlend had made a couch for him as well as he could with their wallets and cloaks.

"'Tis the fashion the soldiers use with stolen fowls, Erlend," said he, laughing.

"Aye, for I learned one thing and another when I was serving the Count," said Erlend, in the same tone.

He was as brisk now and full of life as he had been quiet and almost sluggish at most times his father-in-law had seen him. He began to tell tales, as he sat on the ground in front of the other, of the years when he had served Count Jacob of Halland. He had been troop-leader in the Castle, and he had cruised about with three small ships to guard the coast. Erlend's eyes were like a child's now—he did not brag, he but let his tongue run on. Lavrans lay looking down at him. . . .

He had prayed God to grant him patience with this husband of his daughter—and now he was well-nigh angry with himself that he liked Erlend so much better than he had a mind to. He remembered, too, that that night when their church burned down he had liked his son-in-law well. 'Twas not in that long carcass of his that Erlend lacked manhood. A stab of pain went through the father's heart—'twas pity of Erlend, he might have been fit for better things than beguiling of women. But, as things were, little more had come of all the rest of him than boyish pranks. Had the times been such that a chieftain could have taken this man in hand and used him—but as the world now was, when each man must trust to his own judgment in many things—and a man in Erlend's place had in his hands not his own welfare only, but so many others'—— And this was Kristin's husband. . . .

Erlend looked up at his father-in-law. He too grew grave. Then he said:

"One thing would I pray you, Lavrans—before we come home to my house—that you would say to me what you must needs have on your heart."

Lavrans was silent.

"You know well," said Erlend, as before, "that I will willingly submit me to you in any fashion you may wish, and make such amends as you deem may be a fitting punishment for me."

Lavrans looked down into the young man's face—then he smiled strangely:

"That might be a hard matter, Erlend—for me to say and for you to do.—But at the least you must give fitting gifts to the church at Sundbu and to the priests whom you two fooled as well as other folk," he said vehemently. "I will speak of it no more. You cannot blame it on your youth either. More honour had it been to you, Erlend, had you confessed and made submission before I made your bridal——"

"Aye," said Erlend. "But I knew not then that things stood so that the wrong I had done you must come to light."

Lavrans sat up.

"Knew you not, when you were wedded, that Kristin——?"

"No," said Erlend, with a crestfallen look. "We had been wedded nigh on two months before I knew it."

Lavrans looked at him with some wonder, but he said naught. Then Erlend went on, haltingly and weakly:

"Glad am I that you came with me, father-in-law. Kristin has been all this winter so heavy of mood—she has scarce cared to speak a word to me. Many a time has it seemed to me as though she found but little happiness either at Husaby or with me."

Lavrans answered somewhat coldly:

"'Tis the same, I trow, with all young wives. Now she is well once more, doubtless you will soon be as good friends again as you were before," he added, smiling a little mockingly.

But Erlend sat gazing into the heap of embers. It came over him so surely, of a sudden—though truly he had felt it ever since he first saw the little red baby face against Kristin's white shoulder—things would nevermore be between them as once they had been.

When her father came into the little hall where Kristin lay, she sat up in bed and stretched out towards him. She threw her arms around him, and wept and wept so sorely that Lavrans was afraid.

She had been up for a time, but then she came to know that Erlend had gone south over the hills alone, and when time dragged on and he returned not, she grew so fearful that fever came on her and she must needs lie abed again.

It was plain to see that she was weak still—weeping came on her for never so little things.—The new chaplain, Sira Eiliv Serkssön, had come to the manor while Erlend was away. He had taken it on him to go now and then to sit by the lady of the house and read to her—but she wept at the least thing so causelessly that he scarce knew what he dared let her hear.

One day when her father sat with her, Kristin had set her heart on swaddling the child herself, so that he might see rightly how fair and well-shaped the boy was. As he lay sprawling amidst his swaddling-clothes on the coverlid in front of his mother:

"What is yonder mark he has on his breast?" asked Lavrans.

Right over his heart the boy had some small blood-red spots—it looked as though a bloody hand had touched him there. Kristin had herself been troubled when first she saw this mark. But she had tried to comfort herself with the reason she now gave:

"'Tis but a fire-mark, belike—I caught at my breast when I saw the church burning."

Her father started. Aye—true it was that he knew not how long—or how much—she had kept hidden. And he could not understand how it had been possible for her—his own child—from him. . . .

"Methinks you have no right liking for my son," Kristin said to her father many times; and Lavrans laughed and said: nay, that he liked him right well. He had brought rich gifts, too, to lay both in the cradle and in the lying-in woman's bed. But Kristin deemed that no one truly thought enough of her son—Erlend least of all. "Look on him, Father," she begged; "see you, he is laughing—did you ever see so fair a babe as Naakkve, Father?"

She asked this, time and again. Once Lavrans said, as though in thought:

"Haavard, your brother—our second son—was a passing fair child." In a little Kristin asked, in a weak voice:

"'Twas he that lived the longest of my brothers? "

"Aye, he lived to be two winters old. . . . Nay, now, my Kristin, you must not weep again," he prayed her gently.

Neither Lavrans nor Gunnulf Nikulaussön liked the boy to be called Naakkve; he was christened Nikulaus. Erlend would have it that 'twas the same name; but Gunnulf said: no; sagas told of men called Naakkve back in heathen times. But naught could bring Erlend to use the name his father had borne; and Kristin ever called the boy the name by which Erlend had first greeted their son.

So to Kristin's mind there was but one at Husaby besides herself who fully understood how noble and hopeful a child Naakkve was. This was

he new priest, Sira Eiliv.—In this matter his judgment was scarce less
ound than the mother's own.

Sira Eiliv was a short spare-limbed man with a little round belly, and
his gave him a somewhat laughable look. His presence was unremark-
ble—folks who had spoken with him more than once still found it
ard to know the priest again, so common was his face. His hair and
kin were of the same hue—like reddish-yellow sand—and his round
vatery-blue eyes were flat with his head. In his bearing he was quiet and
etiring; but Master Gunnulf said that Sira Eiliv was so learned that he,
oo, could have passed through all the degrees, had he but had more
orwardness. But much more than by learning was he adorned with
urity of life, humility and devout love towards Christ and His
Church.

He was of low kindred, and though he was but little older than
Gunnulf Nikulaussön, he seemed already not far from an old man.
Gunnulf had known him since they went to school together at Nidaros,
nd he spoke always with great love of Eiliv Serkssön. Erlend deemed
twas no great matter of a priest they had gotten for Husaby, but
Kristin soon looked on him with trust and love.

Kristin still lived down in the little hall with the child, even after she
ad been churched. 'Twas a heavy day for Kristin that—Sira Eiliv
ed her within the church-door, but he dared not give her the Lord's
ody. She had confessed herself to him, but for the sin she had com-
nitted, as partner in the guilt of another's unblessed death, she must
eek absolution from the Archbishop. That morning when Gunnulf had
at with her in her soul's agony, he had strictly charged her that, as soon
s she was free from danger of bodily death, she must haste to seek
ealing for her soul. So soon as health and strength enough were hers,
he must fulfil her vow to St. Olav. Now that he by his intercession had
aved her son and brought him alive and whole to the light and to
leansing baptism, she must walk barefoot to his grave and lay down
pon it the golden garland of maidenhood, which she had guarded so
l and borne so wrongfully. And Gunnulf counselled her to prepare
erself for this pilgrimage by solitary life, prayers, reading and medi-
ation, also by fasting, but this with due measure, for the sake of the
hild at her breast.

The evening of her churching, when she was sitting sorrowful, Gun-
ulf had come to her and given her a rosary. He said that in foreign
ands 'twas not only cloister-folk and priests that used such bead-rolls
or a help in their pious exercises. This rosary was a most fair one; the
eads were of a sort of yellow wood that came from India, and smelt so
weet and delicate that they were well fitted to bring to mind that which
good prayer should be—the heart's sacrifice and yearning for help to

live righteously before God. Some among the beads were of amber and
gold, and the cross was of a fair enamel.

This spring Erlend Nikulaussön busied himself much with setting his
estate in order. This year all fences were mended and gates set up in
due time, the ploughing and spring-sowing well and early gotten out
of hand, and Erlend bought some right good horned cattle. He had had
to slaughter many at the new year, and 'twas no great loss, so many old
and wretched beasts as there had been in his herd. He got together folk
for tar-burning and birch-bark-peeling, and the houses of the manor
were timbered up and their roofs repaired. There had not been such
order at Husaby, folks said, since old Sir Nikulaus was in his full
strength. Aye, and 'twas known, too, that the master sought counsel
and help from his wife's father. With him and with his brother, the
priest, Erlend went about and visited friends and kinsfolk in the country
round when he had leisure from his work. But now he went around in
seemly wise, with a few brisk and likely serving-men. In former days
Erlend had used to ride about with a whole troop of unruly hotheads.
And so the talk of the countryside, which so long had seethed with
wrath over Erlend Nikulaussön's shameless evil life and shiftless and
ruinous husbandry at Husaby, died away now into good-humoured
jesting. Folks smiled and said that the young housewife Erlend had
gotten had brought much to pass in six months.

A while before Botolph's Mass, Lavrans Björgulfsön set forth for
Nidaros in Master Gunnulf's company. He was to be the priest's guest
for some days, while he sought out the shrine of St. Olav and the other
churches in the city, before he journeyed south to his home again. He
parted from his daughter and her husband in all love and kindness.

VI

K R I S T I N was to set out on her walk to Nidaros three days after the
mass of the Seljemen *—later on in the month the city would be full of
bustle and commotion making ready for the Olav's Mass † festival
and earlier the Archbishop would not be in the town.

The evening before, Master Gunnulf had come to Husaby, and early
in the morning he went with Sira Eiliv to the church to sing Matins.
The grass was as a grey fur coverlid with the heavy dew, as Kristin
walked to the church; but the sunlight was golden on the woods that
topped the ridge, and the cuckoo called from the hill-side—it looked as
though she would have fair weather for her pilgrimage.

There was none in the church save Erlend and his wife, and the two

* 8th July.   † 29th July.

priests in the lighted choir. Erlend looked across at Kristin's naked feet. Ice-cold must it be for her, standing on the stone floor. She was to walk the twenty miles with no other company than their prayers. He strove to lift up his heart to God, so as he had not striven for many a year.

She was clad in an ashen-grey kirtle, and had a rope about her waist. Underneath, he knew, she wore a shift of sackcloth. A tightly bound wadmal cloth hid her hair.

When they stepped from the church out into the morning sunshine, a maid met them with the child. Kristin set herself down on some logs of wood. With her back to her husband she sat and let the boy suck his fill, that he might be full-fed when she set out. Erlend stood, unmoving, a little space away from her—he was white and cold in the face with the strain.

The priests came out a little later—they had taken off their vestments in the sacristy. They stopped by Kristin. Then Sira Eiliv went on down towards the manor, but Gunnulf stayed and helped her to get the child securely bound on her back. In a bag that hung from her neck she had the golden garland, money and a little bread and salt. She took her staff in her hand, bowed deeply before the priest, and began to walk quietly northwards up the path that led to the woods.

Erlend was left standing—deadly white of face. Of a sudden he began to run. North of the church were some small hillocks covered with scanty grass and close-cropped juniper and birch—goats were used to graze there. Erlend ran up them—from there he could see her yet a little way on—till she was swallowed up in the woods.

Gunnulf walked slowly up after his brother. The priest looked tall and dark in the bright morning light. He, too, was very pale.

Erlend stood with mouth half open, the tears running down over his white cheeks. Of a sudden he fell on his knees—then threw himself forward headlong on the short grass, and lay, sobbing, sobbing, and tearing at the heather with his long brown fingers.

Gunnulf stood motionless. He looked down at the weeping man—then out towards the woods where the woman had vanished.

Erlend lifted his head a little.

"Gunnulf, was it needful that you should lay this upon her?—Was it needful?" he asked again. "Could not *you* have absolved her?"

The other made no answer; and he went on again:

"Had not I confessed and done penance?" He sat up. "I bought *her* thirty days' masses and vigils and a yearly mass on her death-day for ever and a grave in hallowed ground—I confessed the sin to Bishop Helge, and made pilgrimage to the Holy Blood at Schwerin—could not all this help a little for Kristin——?"

"If you have done this," said the priest quietly, "laid before God a contrite heart and won His full forgiveness—you sure must know tha the marks left by your sin here on earth you must yet strive, year in year out, to wipe away. What you brought on her that is now your wife when you first dragged her down into unclean living and after into manslaughter—that cannot you amend for her, but only God. Pray that He may hold His hand over her on this journey, where you canno bear her company and guard her. And forget not, brother, so long a you two live, that you saw your wife go forth from your house in thi wise—by reason of your sins, more than of her own."

Erlend said in a little:

"I had sworn by God and my Christian faith, before I took her honour, that I would never have another to wife; and she promised tha never would she have another to husband, so long as we lived on th earth. You have said yourself, Gunnulf, that they that vow thus are bound in wedlock before God; any of them who thereafter wedded another would be living in adultery in His eyes. But if so it be, then was it not unclean living, I trow, for Kristin to be mine——"

"The sin was not in that you lived with her," said the priest in a while, "had that been possible without your transgressing other laws— but you had led this child away into sinful revolt against all whom God had set over her—and at last you brought blood-guiltiness upon her. told you this also, that time when we spoke of the matter: therefore hath the Church ordained laws concerning marriage, that banns be pub lished forth to the world, and that we priests shall not wed man and maid against the will of the kindred." He sat down, clasped one knee with his hands, and gazed out over the country-side bright with summer with the little lake gleaming blue in the valley-bottom. "You must have known it yourself, Erlend—a thicket of briers and thorns and nettle had you sowed around you—how could you draw a young maid in to your side and she not be torn and wounded and bleeding——"

"You stood my friend more than once, brother, in the days when it wa Eline and I," said Erlend, low. "I have ever been thankful for it——"

"I scarce deem that I had done it," said Gunnulf in a voice tha shook, "could I have believed of you that you had the heart to deal a you have done with a fine and pure young maid—a child in year beside you."

Erlend made no answer. Gunnulf asked in a low voice:

"That time in Oslo—thought you never of how it would have gon with Kristin, if she had been found with child—while dwelling in a cloister of nuns?—and was the betrothed of another—her father a prou man, jealous of his honour—all her kindred high-born folk, unused t suffer shame——"

"You may well believe I thought of it——" Erlend had turned his head aside. "I had Munan's word to stand by her—I told her, too, of this——"

"Munan! Could you find in your heart to talk to a man like Munan of Kristin's honour?"

"He is not what you think him," said Erlend, shortly.

"And how of his wife, our kinswoman, Lady Katrin? For 'twas not your meaning, I trow, that he should carry her to one of those other places of his where he keeps his paramours——?"

Erlend smote the ground with his fist till the knuckles grew bloody:

"Aye, 'tis the devil's own business for a man, when his wife goes to shrift with his brother!"

"She hath not confessed her to me," said the priest. "And I am not her parish priest. She made her moan to me in her bitter agony and fear—and I strove to help her and to give her such counsel and such comfort as seemed best."

"Well," Erlend threw back his head and looked at his brother, "I know it myself—I should not have done it—have had her come to me in Brynhild's house——"

The priest sat speechless a moment.

"In Brynhild Fluga's——?"

"Aye; told she not of that, when she told the rest——?"

"'Twould be hard enough, methinks, for Kristin to tell such things of her own husband in confession," said the priest in a while. "I think that she would rather die than tell them any other place." He sat awhile, and then said with a harsh vehemency:

"If so it were, Erlend, that you deemed you were her husband before God, he that should protect and guard her—then do your doings seem yet worse to me. You tempted her astray in groves and hay-lofts, you led her over a harlot's threshold—and, last of all, you brought her to Björn Gunnarssön and Lady Aashild. . . ."

"You shall not speak so of Moster Aashild," said Erlend softly.

"You have said yourself, before now, that you believed her guilty of our uncle's death—she and this man Björn——"

"I care naught for that," said Erlend vehemently. "Moster Aashild is dear to me——"

"Aye, I understood as much," said the priest. His mouth twisted into a little crooked scornful smile. "Since you grudged it not to her that she should meet Lavrans Björgulfsön after you had borne away his daughter. 'Twould seem, indeed, Erlend, that you deem your friendship can scarce be bought too dear——"

"Jesus!" Erlend hid his face in his hands. But the priest went on:

"Had you seen your wife's anguish of soul, as she shuddered with horror of her sins, unshriven and helpless—and she sat there and was to bear your child, and death stood at her door—so young a child herself, and so unhappy——"

"I know, I know!" Erlend trembled. "I know that she lay thinking of it, in her torment. For Jesu sake, Gunnulf, be still now—I am your brother after all!"

But the priest went on without mercy:

"Had I been a man like you and not a priest—and had I led so young and good a maid astray—I had freed me from the other—God help me, rather would I have done as Moster Aashild did with her husband and burned in hell for it world without end, than I would have borne that she should suffer such things as you have brought down on the head of your innocent love——"

Erlend sat awhile, trembling

"You call yourself a priest," he said in a low voice. "Are you *so* good a priest that you have never sinned—with a woman?"

Gunnulf looked not at his brother. A wave of red flooded his face:

"You have no right to ask such things—but yet I will answer you. He knows that died for us upon the Cross what bitter need I have of His mercy. But I say to you, Erlend—had He on all the earth's round not one single servant that was pure and unstained by sin, and were there not in His holy Church one single priest more faithful and worthy than I, wretched traitor to my Lord that I am—yet is it the Lord's laws and commandments that are taught in it. Never can His Word be polluted by the mouth of an unclean priest, it will but burn and consume our lips—but this, maybe, you cannot understand. Yet this you know as well as I and every other filthy thrall of Satan whom He hath bought with His blood—God's law cannot be shaken nor His honour diminished. As surely as His sun is alike mighty, whether it shine upon the barren sea and waste grey mountain or upon these fair and fertile lands——"

Erlend had hidden his face in his hands. He sat long silent, and when he spoke his voice was dry and hard:

"Priest or no priest—since you are not so absolute in saintly living— understand you not——? Could you do to a woman who had slept in your arms—borne you two children—could you do to her as Aashild did to her husband?"

The priest was silent a little. Then he said, a little mockingly:

"You were not wont to judge Moster Aashild so hardly——"

"It cannot be the same for a man, I trow, as for a woman. I mind me the last time they were here at Husaby, and Sir Björn was with them. We were sitting by the hearth, mother and Aashild, and Sir Björn was playing his harp and singing to them—I was standing by his knee. Then

Baard called her—he was in bed, and he would have her go to rest at once—he used words so shameless and immodest—Moster Aashild rose, and Sir Björn too; he left the hall, but first they looked at each other—— Aye, afterwards I thought, when I grew old enough to understand—it may well be it is true—— I had begged leave to light Sir Björn across to the house he was to sleep in, but I dared not, and I dared not lie in the hall. I ran out and laid me down by the men in the servants' house. By Jesus, Gunnulf—for a man it can never be as it was for Aashild that night——

"No, Gunnulf—kill a woman that—except I took her with another——"

Yet had he done that very thing. But *this* Gunnulf could not say to his brother. So he asked coldly:

"Was it not true, then, either, that Eline had been untrue to you?"

"Untrue?" Erlend turned on his brother, suddenly afire. "Mean you that I should have laid it to her charge that she had given herself to Gissur—after I had made plain to her again and yet again that betwixt us all must be at an end?"

Gunnulf bowed his head.

"No, like enough you are right," he said wearily, in a low voice. But under this little breath of approval Erlend flamed up—he threw back his head and looked at the priest.

"You are so tender of Kristin, Gunnulf. Strange how you have hung over her all the spring—almost more than is seemly for a brother and a priest. Almost it might seem you grudged her to me—— Were it not that things were with her as they were when you first saw her, folks might deem——"

Gunnulf looked at him. Beside himself under his brother's look, Erlend sprang up—and Gunnulf, too, rose. He did not withdraw his look, and Erlend struck out at him with his clenched fist. The priest caught and gripped his wrist. Erlend tried to close with his brother, but Gunnulf stood immovable, holding him off.

Erlend grew quiet straightway. "I should have remembered you were a priest," he said low.

"You see that on that score you have no need to repent," said Gunnulf, with a little smile.—Erlend stood chafing his wrist.

"Aye, you ever had the devil's own strength in your hands——"

"This is like the days when we were boys." Gunnulf's voice had grown strangely soft and mild. "I have thought of it often all these years I have been from home—the times when we were boys. Often were we unfriends then, but never did it last long, Erlend."

"But now, Gunnulf," said the other sorrowfully, "it can nevermore be as when we were boys."

"No," answered the priest quietly, "'tis like it cannot——"

They stood still a long time. At last Gunnulf said:

"I leave you now, Erlend. I will go now down to Eiliv, and bid him farewell, and then I shall set out. Aye, 'tis to the priest in Orkedal that I go; I shall not come to Nidaros while *she* is there." He smiled a little.

"Gunnulf! I meant it not so—go not from me like this——"

Gunnulf stood still. He drew one or two deep breaths, then said:

"One thing I would have you know of me, Erlend—since you know that I have knowledge of all this concerning you.—Sit down."

The priest sat himself down as before. Erlend stretched himself on the ground before him, and, hand under chin, looked up into his brother's strangely stiff and strained face. Then he smiled a little:

"What is it, Gunnulf—would you make confession to me?"

"Aye," said his brother, softly. Yet then he sat a long time silent. Erlend saw his lips move once, and he clenched his folded hands tightly round his knee.

"What is it?" A smile flickered over Erlend's face. "Sure it cannot be so—that some fair lady, far off in southern lands——"

"No," said the priest. His voice grew rough and hoarse. "'Tis not of love——

"Know you, Erlend, how it came about that I was vowed to be a priest?"

"Aye. When our brothers died, and they feared they would lose us too——"

"No," said Gunnulf. "Munan they thought was well again, and Gaute had not taken the sickness—'twas not till the winter after that he died. But you were lying, choking to death, and mother vowed me to the service of St. Olav if he would save your life——"

"Who has told you this?" asked Erlend in a while.

"Ingrid, my foster-mother."

"Aye, 'tis true, indeed, that *I* had been a strange gift to give St. Olav," said Erlend, laughing a little. "He had been ill-served with me.—But you have said yourself, Gunnulf, you were well content that you had been called to the priesthood from childhood up——"

"Aye," said the priest. "But 'twas not always so. I mind me well the day you rode from Husaby with Munan Baardssön, to fare to the King, our kinsman, and become his man. Your horse danced under you; your new arms glittered and shone. *I* was never to bear arms.—Fair were you, my brother—you were but sixteen winters old; and already I had seen, for many a day past, that you were well loved of dames and damsels——"

"That glory endured not long," said Erlend. "I learned to cut my nails straight across, swear by Jesus at each second word, and use my dagger to ward with while I struck with my sword. Then was I sent north, and met *her*—and was hunted from the body-guard with shame, and my father shut his doors against me——"

"And you fled forth from the land with a fair lady," said Gunnulf, quietly as before. "And we heard at home that you were Captain of Count Jacob's castle."

"Aye, that was no such great matter as it sounded here at home," said Erlend, laughing.

"Father and you were not friends—me he thought not enough of to care to be unfriends with me. Mother held me dear, I know—but how little she deemed me worth, weighed against you—that marked I best when you had fled from the land. You, brother, were the only one that loved me truly. And God knows that you were my dearest friend on earth. But in those days when I was young and witless, times have been when I deemed you had been given all too much more than I. This it was that I would have told you, Erlend."

Erlend lay face downwards on the hill-side.

"Leave us not, Gunnulf," he begged.

"Yes," said the priest, "I go. Too much have we said now one to the other. God and Mary Virgin grant that we may meet again in a better hour. Farewell, Erlend——"

"Farewell," said Erlend, not looking up.

When Gunnulf, some hours after, came forth from the priest's house, ready for his journey, he saw a man riding over the fields towards the southern woods. He had a bow slung across his back, and three hounds ran by his horse's side. It was Erlend.

Meanwhile Kristin was walking swiftly on her way, by the forest path that led over the hills. The sun stood high in the heavens now, and the pine-tops shone against the summer sky, but within the woods was still the cool and freshness of morning. The air was full of the balmy scent of pine-needles and peaty soil, and of the twinflower that sprinkled all the knolls with its small pink bells; and the grassy pathway was damp and soft and comforting to her feet. Kristin walked, saying over her prayers, and now and then she looked up at the little white fair-weather clouds that swam in the blue above the tree-tops.

All the time she could not but think of Brother Edvin. So had he walked and walked, year in, year out, from early spring to deepest winter. Over the mountain paths, under black scaurs and white snow-fields. He had rested him at the sæters, drunk of the beck, and eaten of the bread that sæter-girls and horse-herds bore out to him—then had he bidden farewell and called down God's peace and benison on fold and cattle. Down through the sighing woods of the hill-sides he had passed, down into the Dale; tall and stoop-shouldered, with head bent forward, he had wandered along the high-road past the well-tilled farms and the dwelling-places—and everywhere, wheresoever he passed, his loving intercessions for all men left, as it were, fair weather in his track.

She met not a living thing, save now and then a few cattle—there were sæters on these hill-tops. But the path was well-trodden, and over the marshy grounds were cordwood bridgeways. Kristin was unafraid—she felt as though the monk walked invisibly by her side. Brother Edvin, if in truth thou art a holy saint, if thou standest before the face of God, pray for me now!

Lord Jesus Christ, holy Mary, St. Olav—— She longed to reach the goal of her pilgrimage—she longed to cast from her the burden of the hidden sins of years, the weight of masses and offices that she had filched unlawfully while yet unshriven and unrepentant—she longed to be free and cleansed, yet more keenly than she had yearned to be delivered of her burden in the spring before the boy was born. . . .

He slept so soundly and securely on his mother's back. He waked not till she had passed through the woods and come down to the Snow-bird farms, and could look out over Budvik and the Saltnes arm of the fjord. She sat down in a pasture off the path, slung the bundle with the babe in it round into her lap, and opened the breast of her kirtle. It was sweet to feel him against her breast; sweet to be able to sit awhile; a blessed sweetness through all her body to feel the stone-hard, milk-swollen breasts grow soft as he sucked.

The country-side lay still below her, baking in the sunshine—with green meadows and bright cornfields amid dark woods. Here and there a little smoke went up above the house-roofs. In some places the hay-harvest had begun.

She had leave to cross from Saltnes-sand over to Steine by boat. Once across, she had come to a quite unknown country. The road she must follow across the Bynes led up for a while among farms, then she came into woods again, but here she never had to go for long out of sight of human dwellings. She was passing weary. But she thought of her parents—had they not walked barefoot all the way from Jörund-gaard in Sil, over Dovre and down to Nidaros, bearing Ulvhild between them on a litter? She must not think how heavy Naakkve was upon her back.

——Worse was the dreadful itching in her head from the thick sweat-drenched wadmal hood. And round her waist, where the rope pressed her garments against her body, her shift had gnawed at the flesh till there must be raw places on it.

Other wayfarers began to pass her on the road. Now and again folk would ride by her, going one way or the other. She overtook a peasant cart bound for the city with wares—the heavy solid wheels bumped and jolted over roots and stones, creaking and squeaking. Two men were dragging along a beast for the slaughter-house. They looked a little at the young pilgrim woman, for her comeliness' sake—but such wayfarers were a common sight in this country-side. At one place some men were busy putting up a house a little off the road; they called out to her, and an oldish man came running up and proffered her a drink of ale. Kristin curtsied, drank, and gave thanks in words such as poor folks were wont to say to her when she gave alms.

Soon after she must needs rest again. She found a little green slope near by the road, with a stream running by it. Kristin laid her child in the grass; he wakened and began to shriek piteously, so that she hastened with a wandering mind through the prayers she should have said. Then she took Naakkve in her lap and unwound his swaddling-clothes. He had fouled his cloths, and she had but little with her to put in their stead; so she washed out the cloths and laid them on a warm smooth rock to dry in the sun. The outer clothes she wrapped loosely round the boy. He liked this well, for he could kick and sprawl now, as he drank from his mother's breast. Kristin looked with joy at his fine rosy-white limbs, and pressed down one of his hands between her breasts as she suckled him.

Two horsemen rode by at a sharp trot. Kristin glanced up—'twas a master and his man; but suddenly the master reined up his horse, sprang from the saddle, and came back on foot to where she sat. It was Simon Andressön.

"Maybe you had liefer I should not greet you?" he asked. He stood holding his horse and looking down at her. He was clad as for a journey, in a sleeveless leather jerkin over a light-blue linen coat—a silk cap was on his head, and his face was red and shone with sweat. "'Tis strange to see you—but maybe you have no mind to talk with me——?"

"Surely you must know—how is it with you, Simon?" Kristin drew up her bare feet under her skirt, and tried to take the child away from her breast. But the boy screamed and gulped and groped about so that she was forced to lay him to it again. She gathered her kirtle over the breast as well as she could, and sat with eyes downcast.

"Is it yours?" asked Simon, pointing to the child. "Nay, that was a foolish question!" he said, laughing. "'Tis a son, I warrant? Erlend Nikulaussön has fortune with him." He had bound his horse to a tree, and now he sat down on a stone a little way from Kristin. He brought his sword forward between his knees, and sat with his hands on the hilt, turning up the earth with the scabbard-end.

"I looked not to meet you here, north of Dovre, Simon," said Kristin, that she might say something

"No," said Simon. "I have had no errands in this part of the land before."

Kristin called to mind that she had heard somewhat—at her home-coming feast—of the youngest son of Arne Gjavvaldssön of Ranheim being to wed Andres Darre's youngest daughter.—Had he been at Ranheim, she asked.

"You know of it?" said Simon. "Aye, it has got about already in this country-side, I can well believe."

"It is so, then," said Kristin, "that Gjavvald is to wed Sigrid?"

Simon looked up sharply, pressing his lips together:

"I see you know *not* of it yet."

"I have not set foot outside Husaby courtyard all the winter," said Kristin. "And few folks have I seen. I heard there was talk of this wedding——"

"Aye—as well that you hear it from my lips, I trow—it must needs get abroad up here." He sat silent a little. "Gjavvald died three days before winter-night*—he fell with his horse and broke his back. Mind you, just before you come to Dyfrin, where the road runs east of the river, and the ground falls sheer—oh, no, you would scarce remember. We were on our way to their betrothal-ale; Arne and his sons had come by sea to Oslo——" Simon stopped short.

"Maybe she loved Gjavvald—Sigrid—and had been joyful that she was to wed him?" asked Kristin, shyly and fearfully.

"Aye," said Simon. "And she bore a son to him—at Apostles' Mass last spring——"

"Oh, Simon!"

Sigrid Andresdatter, with the brown curls about her little round face. When she laughed there came deep pits in her cheeks. Dimples and little childish white teeth—Simon had these too. Kristin remembered that when she was in her less gentle moods towards her betrothed, this had seemed to her unmanly—most of all after she had come to know Erlend. They were much alike, Sigrid and Simon; but that she was so plump and laughing made *her* but the fairer. She was fourteen winters old then.—Such joyful laughter as Sigrid's Kristin had never heard. Simon was ever teasing and jesting with his youngest sister—Kristin had felt that he held her dearest of them all.

"You know that father was fondest of Sigrid," said Simon. "So he was fain that she and Gjavvald should see if they could like one another, before he clinched the bargain with Arne. And they did—methought a little more than seemed good—they must ever be flinging at each other

* Winter-night = 14th October, the beginning of the winter half-year.

when they met and glancing and laughing—this was last summer at
Dyfrin. But they were so young—none could have thought of this. And
Astrid—you know she was betrothed when you and I—— Aye, she said
naught against it; and Torgrim, you know, has great wealth, and is
kind, too, after a fashion—but nothing, nor no one, can please him, and
he thinks ever he has all the hurts and ailments that folks ever heard
tell of. So we were glad, all of us, that Sigrid was so joyful in the match
that had been made for her. . . .

"And when we brought Gjavvald home like this—Halfrid, my wife,
managed things so that she went home with us to Mandvik. And
then, afterward, it came to light that Gjavvald had not left her—
alone——"

They were silent awhile. Then Kristin said, softly:

"This has been no joyous journey for you, then, Simon?"

"Oh, no." Then he laughed a little. "But soon I shall be used now
to riding on woeful errands, Kristin. And for this one, you see, I was
the properest—father had not the strength, and 'tis with me at Mandvik
that Sigrid and the boy are. Now have we ordered things so that he will
take his father's place among the Ranheim kindred, and I could see on
them all, I trow, that unwelcome he will not be, the poor little lad, when
presently he is sent thither——"

"And your sister," asked Kristin, catching her breath, "where will
she be?"

Simon looked down at the ground.

"Father will have her home to Dyfrin now," he said in a low
voice.

"Simon! Oh, have you the heart to let this be——?"

"You sure can see," he answered, without looking up, "how great a
gain it is for the boy to be taken into his father's kindred from the very
first. Halfrid and I would gladly have them both with us. No sister
could have been more faithful and loving towards another than Halfrid
was to Sigrid. None of her kindred have been hard to her—believe not
that of us. Not even father—though this thing has made of him a broken
man. But see you not?—unrighteous had it been if any of us had set
ourselves against that which gives the innocent boy his father's name
and heritage."

Kristin's babe let go the breast. The mother drew the clothes quickly
over her bosom, and pressed the little one to her, trembling. He gulped
contentedly a couple of times, and slobbered over himself and his
mother's hands.

Simon glanced over at the two, and said with a sort of smile:

"You had better fortune, Kristin, than befell my sister."

"Aye—surely it must seem to you no righteous fate," said Kristin softly, "that I am called wife and my son is true-born. For had I been left with a fatherless bastard, I had been rightly served——"

"I had deemed that the worst tidings I could hear," said Simon. "I wish you naught but good, Kristin," he said in a lower voice.

Soon after, he asked her of the road. Northward he had journeyed by ship from Tunsberg, he said, "I must ride on now and see to it that I overtake my man——"

"Is it Finn that you have with you?" asked Kristin.

"No, Finn is wedded now; he is with me no longer. Do you remember him still?" asked Simon, with a little gladness in his voice.

"Is he a fair child, Sigrid's boy?" asked Kristin, looking at Naakkve.

"I hear them say so. To me one babe in arms looks much like all others," answered Simon.

"Then I trow you have no children yourself," said Kristin, and could not forbear to smile.

"No," he answered shortly. And thereupon he bade farewell and rode away.

When Kristin set out again, she had the child on her back no longer. She bore it in her arms, pressing its face into the hollow of her neck. She could think of naught else but Sigrid Andresdatter.

But *her* father could never have done it. Lavrans Björgulfsön ride out to beg for his daughter's base-born child part and lot with its father's kindred!—never could he have done it. And never, never would he have had the heart to take her babe from her—tear a little being out of his mother's arms, tear him from her breast, with her milk still on his innocent lips. My Naakkve, no, *he* would never have had the heart—if 'twas righteous ten times over, my father would never have done it. . . .

But she could not drive a picture from her mind. A troop of riders vanishing northward through the gorge, where the Dale grows narrow and the mountains crowd together, black with pine-woods. Cold gusts come from the river that rushes thundering over the great rocks, ice-green, foaming, with here and there black pools. He that should fall over there would be hurled from rock to rock and crushed straightway— Jesus, Maria——

Then she saw the fields at home at Jörundgaard of a clear summer night—saw herself running down the path to the little green clearing in the alder-brake by the river—where they were used to wash clothes. The river ran with a changeless harsh roar among the great stones of its shelving bed—Lord Christ, I cannot do aught else——

Oh, but father had never had the heart to do it. Not if it were never so right. When I prayed, prayed on my bare bended knees: Father, you must not take my child from me——

Kristin stood on Feginsbrekka and saw the city lying below her in the golden sunlight. Beyond the river's broad shining curves lay brown houses with green turfed roofs, dark domes of leaves in the gardens, light-hued stone houses with pointed gables, churches that heaved up black shingled backs, and churches with dully gleaming leaden roofs. But above the green land, above the fair city, rose Christ's church,* so mighty, so gloriously shining, 'twas as though all things else lay prostrate at its feet. With the evening sun blazing full upon its breast and on the shining glass of its windows, with towers and giddy spires and golden vanes, it stood pointing up into the bright summer heavens.

Around lay a country-side green with summer, bearing worshipful great manors on its slopes. Outside again the fjord stretched wide and bright, with shadows drifting upon it from the great summer clouds that rose over the shining blue hills beyond. The cloister-holm, low among plashing wavelets, lay like a green garland, white-flowered with its stone houses. So many ships' masts out in the roadstead, so many fairest houses——

Quite overcome, sobbing, the young woman flung herself down before the cross by the wayside, where thousands of pilgrims had lain before her, thanking God for that helping hands were stretched out towards human souls on their journey through this fair and perilous world.

The bells were ringing to Vespers in churches and cloisters when Kristin came into Christ's churchyard. She dared to glance for a moment up at the church's west front—then, blinded, she cast down her eyes.

Human beings had never compassed this work of their own strength —God's spirit had worked in holy Öistein, and the builders of this house that came after him. Thy Kingdom come, Thy will be done on earth as it is in heaven—now she understood the words. A reflection of the glory of God's kingdom witnessed in these stones that His will was all that was fair. Kristin trembled. Aye, well might God turn in wrath from all that was foul—from sin and shame and uncleanness.

In the galleries of the heavenly dwelling stood holy men and women, so fair that she dared not look upon them. Lovely unwithering tendrils of eternity wound silently upwards—broke into leaf on tower and spire, and blossomed in stone monstrances. Over the midmost door hung Christ upon His cross, Mary and John the Evangelist stood by His side.

* See Note 5.

and they were white as though fashioned out of snow, and gold glinted on the white.

Three times she walked around the church, praying. The mighty wall-masses with bewildering riches of pillars and arches and windows, the glimpses of the huge slopes of the roof, the tower, the gold of the spire far up in the skyey spaces—Kristin sank under her load of sin.

She trembled when she kissed the hewn stone of the portal. In a lightning flash she saw the dark carven wood round the church-door at home—that she had kissed with childish lips after her father and mother. . . .

She sprinkled holy water over the child and herself—and thought of the time her father used to do this, when she was small. With the child pressed tight in her arms, she went forward up the church.

She went as through a forest—the columns were furrowed like ancient trees, and in through the forest flowed the light, many-hued and clear as song, from the pictured windows. High up above her, beasts and men sported among the stone leafage, and angels played—and yet far, dizzily far higher, the vaulting soared, lifting the church towards God. In a hall that lay to one side, worship was being held at an altar. Kristin sank down on her knees by a pillar. The singing cut into her like a too strong light. Now she saw how low she lay in the dust. . . .

Pater noster. Credo in unum Deum. Ave Maria, gratia plena. She had learnt her prayers by saying them after her father and mother before she understood a word—longer since than she could remember. Lord Jesus Christ! Was there ever woman so sinful as she——?

High under the triumphal arch, uplifted over the people, hung Christ the Crucified. The stainless Virgin that was His mother stood gazing in deathly anguish up at her innocent Son, suffering a death of torment like an evil-doer.

And here knelt she, with the fruit of sin in her arms. She pressed the child to her—he was fresh as an apple, red and white as a rose—he was awake now, and lay looking up at her with his clear sweet eyes. . . .

Conceived in sin. Borne under her hard evil heart. Drawn from her sin-polluted body, so fair, so whole, so unspeakably lovely and fresh and pure. The undeserved mercy broke her heart asunder; she knelt, crushed with penitence, and the weeping welled up out of her soul as blood flows from a death-wound.

Naakkve, Naakkve, child of mine—God visiteth the sins of the fathers upon the children. Knew I not that?—Ah, yes, I knew it. But I had no mercy in my heart for the innocent life that might be wakened in my womb—to be accursed and condemned to torment for my sin——

Repented I my sin, when I bore you within me, my beloved, beloved son? Oh, no, 'twas not repentance.—My heart was hard with anger and evil thoughts in the hour when I first felt thee move, so little and so defenceless.—*Magnificat anima mea Dominum. Et exaltavit spiritus meus in Deo salutari meo*—thus she sang, the gentle Queen of all women, when she was chosen out to bear Him that was to die for our sins.—I called not to mind Him that had power to take away the burden of my sin and my child's sin—oh, no, 'twas not repentance, I but feigned me lowly and wretched, and begged and begged that the commands of righteousness be broken; for that I could not bear it if God upheld His law and chastened me according to the Word that I had known all my days——

Oh, aye, now she knew it. She had thought that God was such an one as her own father, that St. Olav was as her father. She had thought all the time, deep in her heart, that when her punishment grew to be heavier than she could bear, then would she meet, not with justice, but with compassion. . . .

She was weeping so that she could not rise when the people stood up during the worship. She lay on, crouched in a heap over her child. Near her there were other folk that did not rise—two well-dressed peasant women with a young boy between them.

She looked up towards the choir. Behind the golden grated doors St. Olav's shrine gleamed in the darkness, towering high behind the altar. An icy-cold shuddering ran through her. There lay his holy body awaiting the day of resurrection. Then would the lid fly open, and he would arise. With his axe in hand he would stride down this mighty church; and up from the paven floor, up from the earth outside, up from every graveyard in Norway's land would the dead yellow skeletons arise.—They would be clothed upon with flesh and would muster themselves round their King. They that had striven to tread in his blood-marked footsteps, and they that had only sought him that he might help them with the burdens of sin and sorrow and sickness that here in life they had bound on themselves and their children. Now they throng around their lord and pray him to lay their needs before God. Lord, hearken to my prayer for this folk, which I held so dear that I would rather suffer outlawry and need and hatred and death, than that man or maid should grow up in Norway and not know that Thou diedst to save all sinners. Lord, Thou who didst bid us go out and make all the peoples Thy disciples—with my blood did I, Olav Haraldssön, write Thy Evangel in the Norse tongue, for these my poor freedmen. . . .

Kristin shut her eyes, sick and dizzy. The King's countenance was before her—his flaming eyes saw to the bottom of her soul—she trembled under St. Olav's glance.

Understand you now, Kristin, that you need help?

Aye, Lord King, now I understand it. Sore need is mine that thou

support me, that I may not turn me from God again. Be with me, thou
Chief of His people, when I bear forth my prayers, and pray thou that
I be granted mercy. Holy Olav, pray for me!

Cor mundum crea in me, Deus, et spiritum rectum innova in visceribus meis.
Ne projicias me a facie tua—
Libera me de sanguinibus, Deus, Deus salutis meæ——

The worship was at an end. Folks were leaving the church. The two
peasant women, who had knelt near Kristin, rose up. But the boy
between them did not rise; he began to move over the pavement by
pressing the knuckles of his clenched hands on the flags and jerking himself along like a young unfledged crow. He had tiny legs, twisted up
close under his body. The women walked so as to hide him as well as
they could with their garments.

When they were out of sight, Kristin threw herself down and kissed
the church-floor where they had passed by her.

Somewhat doubtful and at a loss, she stood by the entrance to the
choir, when a young priest came out of the grated door. He stopped
before the red-eyed young woman, and Kristin told him her errand, as
well as she might. At first he scarce understood. She brought out the
golden garland and held it toward him.

"Oh, are you Kristin Lavransdatter, Erlend's wife, of Husaby——?"
He looked at her with a little wonder; her face was all swollen with
weeping. "Aye, aye, your brother-in-law, Master Gunnulf, spoke of this,
aye——"

He led her out into the sacristy, took the wreath, and unwrapped the
linen cloth from around it and looked at it; then he smiled a little.

"Aye, you will understand, I trow—there must be witnesses and such-
like by—you cannot give away such a precious thing, mistress, as though
'twere a piece of buttered bread—but I can take it in charge, meanwhile—'tis like you would not choose to bear it about with you in the
city.—Oh, pray Canon Arne to be so good as to come hither," he said
to a church-servant.

"Your husband should be with you too, I trow, rightly. But it may be
Gunnulf has some letter from him. . . .

"You are to be brought before the Archbishop himself—was it not so?
Else 'tis Hauk Tomassön who is Pœnitentiarius—I know not whether
Gunnulf has talked with Lord Eiliv—but you must come hither to
matins to-morrow, and you can ask for me after lauds; I am called Paal
Aslakssön. Him"—he pointed to the child—"you must leave in the
hostel. You are to sleep in the Sisters' hostel at Bakke, I mind me your
brother-in-law said."

Another priest came in, and the two spoke together awhile. The first opened a little locker in the wall, took out a pair of scales, and weighed the wreath, while the other wrote in a book. Then they laid the wreath away in the press and locked it.

Canon Paal was about to lead her out—but he asked first if she wished he should lift her son up to St. Olav's shrine.

He took the boy with the sure, somewhat careless deftness of a priest used to holding babies at baptism. Kristin went with him into the church, and he asked if she, too, would not fain kiss the shrine.

I dare not, thought Kristin; but she followed the priest up the steps to the high platform whereon the shrine was set. There came, as it were, a great blinding white light before her eyes when she approached her lips to the golden tabernacle.

The priest looked at her a moment, fearing she might fall down in a swoon. But she rose again to her feet. Then he let the child's forehead touch the sacred shrine.

Canon Paal went with her to the church-door and asked if she were sure she could find her way to the ferry. Then he bade her good-night —he had spoken all the time in smooth, dry fashion, like any other mannerly young courtier.

——It had begun to rain a little, and a breathing of sweet scents came balmily from the gardens and from the street, which was fresh and green like a country courtyard, save for the strips worn bare by the coming and going of people and carts.

Kristin sheltered the boy from the rain as best she could; he was so heavy now, so heavy that her arms were numb and dead from bearing him. And he whimpered and cried unceasingly—like enough he was hungry again.

His mother was deadly tired—from the day-long walking, and from all the weeping and the vehemency of her emotion in the church. She was cold—and the rain grew heavier; the leaves of the trees glanced and shivered under the spattering drops. She threaded her way through the lanes and came out on an open place, where she could see ahead to where the river ran broad and grey, its surface pitted like a sieve by the falling drops.

There was no ferry-boat. Kristin spoke to two men who had taken shelter under the floor of a warehouse that stood on piles at the water's edge. They said she must go out to the landing-place—the nuns had a house there, and there was a ferry-man.

Kristin dragged herself up again across the open place, footsore and wet and weary. She came to a little grey stone church—behind it lay some houses inside a fence. Naakkve was shrieking wildly, so that she could not go into the church. But the sound of singing came to her through the unglazed window-openings, and she knew the antiphon:

Lætare Regina Cæli—Rejoice, thou Queen of Heaven—for He whom thou wert chosen to bear—is arisen even as He said. Alleluja!

It was the song the Minorites sang after compline. Brother Edvin had taught her this hymn to the Lord's Mother when she watched by his bed those nights when he lay in mortal sickness at home with them at Jörundgaard.—She stole into the churchyard, and, standing by the wall with her child upon her arm, she said it softly over to herself.

——Nothing, Kristin, that you could do could turn your father's heart from you. 'Tis therefore you must give him no more cause for sorrow. . . .

——Even as Thy nail-pierced hands were outstretched upon the Cross, O dear Lord of heaven—howsoever far away a soul had strayed from the straight path, yet were the nail-pierced hands stretched out towards it yearningly. Naught was needful save this one thing: that the sinful souls should turn them to those open arms, freely, as a child goes to its father, not like thralls hunted home to their cruel master. Now she understood how hateful sin was. Again there came that pain in her breast; as though her heart would break asunder in penitence and in shame at her unworthiness of the mercy shown her. . . .

Close in to the church-wall there was a little shelter from the rain. She sat down upon a grave-stone and began to still the child's hunger. Now and then she bent forward and kissed the little down-covered head.

She must have fallen asleep. Someone touched her shoulder. A monk in orders and an old lay brother with a sexton's spade in his hand stood before her. The barefoot friar asked if she sought lodging for the night.

It flashed across her—she would far rather abide here to-night with the Minorites, Brother Edvin's brethren. And it was so far to Bakke—and she was sinking with weariness. Then the monk bade the lay brother bring this woman to the women's hostel—"and give her a little calamus-wash for her feet—she is footsore, I see."

It was close and dark in the women's hostel—it stood without the fence, out by the lane. The lay brother brought her water to wash with and a little food, and she sat by the hearth and tried to quiet the child. 'Twas plain that Naakkve felt it in his food that his mother was worn out and had fasted that day; he wept and whimpered between-times while sucking at her exhausted breasts. Kristin took mouthfuls of the milk the lay brother had brought her; she tried to spirt it from her mouth into the child's—but the little knave clamoured loudly against this new fashion of taking in food, and the old man laughed and shook his head. She must drink it herself, he said, then the boy would soon get the good of it. . . .

At last he went away. Kristin crept up into one of the uppermost box-beds, close under the roof. From it she could reach up to open a trap in the roof—and there was need, for there was a sickening smell in the hostel. Kristin opened the trap—the rain-washed air of the bright cool summer night streamed in about her. She sat in the short bed with her head and neck propped against the wall-timbers—there were so few pillows in the bed. The boy slept on her lap. She had meant to shut the trap again in a while, but she fell asleep unawares.

Far on in the night she awoke. The summer moon shone in, pale and honey-yellow, across the child and her, and lit up the wall over against them. And she was ware of a figure in the midst of the stream of moon-light, hovering between floor and roof-tree.

He was clad in an ashen-grey frock—he was tall and stoop-backed. Now he turned his old, old furrowed face towards her. It was Brother Edvin. He smiled, and his smile was unspeakably tender—a little roguishly merry, just as when he lived on earth.

Kristin wondered not at all. Humble, happy, full of hope and trust, she looked at him, awaiting that which he might say or do.

The monk laughed and held up an old, heavy fur mitten towards her —then he hung it on the moonbeam and left it hanging there. And then he smiled still more, nodded to her, and melted away.

Part Two

HUSABY

O n a day early in the new year, there came to Husaby some unlooked-for guests. They were Lavrans Björgulfsön and old Smid Gudleiksön from Dovre, and with them were two gentlemen whom Kristin knew not. And Erlend wondered much to see his father-in-law come in their company—they were Sir Erling Vidkunssön of Giske and Haftor Graut of Godöy—he had not deemed that Lavrans knew these men. But Sir Erling made things clear, telling how they had met together at Nes of Raumsdal, where he had sat with Lavrans and Smid on the Court of Six* that had at last set at rest the dispute between Sir Jon Haukssön's distant heirs. Lavrans and he had fallen into talk of Erlend, and the thought came to Sir Erlin that, since he had an errand to Nidaros, he would like well to wait upon the folks at Husaby, if Lavrans would join him and sail north with him. Smid Gudleiksön said, laughing, that he had all but bidden himself to come along with them:

"For I was fain to see our Kristin again—the fairest rose of the Norddal. And then, methought my kinswoman, Ragnfrid, would be beholden to me if I kept an eye on her husband, to mark what weighty counsels he may be hatching with wise and mighty men like these. Aye, your father has other gear to guide this winter, my Kristin, than making the rounds of the manors with us, drinking out Yule till the Fast comes in. Now have we sat at home on our lands in peace and quiet all these years, and looked, each man of us, to his own affairs. But now would Lavrans have all us King's-men of the Dale ride in a troop to Oslo at hardest midwinter—now are we to counsel the great lords of the King's council in the King's behoof—they are ruling things so ill for the poor boy in his nonage, says Lavrans——"*

Sir Erling looked somewhat ill at ease. Erlend raised his eyebrows.

"Are you of these counsels, father-in-law—the calling of the great meeting of King's-men?"

"No, no," said Lavrans. "I but ride to the meeting like the other King's-men in the Dale, since we have been summoned thither——"

But Smid Gudleiksön took up his tale again: 'Twas Lavrans that had talked him over—and Herstein of Kruke, and Trond Gjesling and Guttorm Sneis and others that had had no mind to go. . . .

"Nay but—is it not your wont in these parts to bid stranger folk step into the house?" asked Lavrans. "Let us try now whether Kristin brews as good ale as her mother!" . . .

Erlend looked doubtfully, and Kristin wondered greatly.

* See Note 6.   † See Note 7.

"What is this, father?" she asked a little later, when he was with her in the little hall, whither she had brought the child to be out of the strangers' way.

Lavrans sat dancing his grandson on his knee. Naakkve was ten months old now, a great child and comely. Already, at Yule-tide, he had been put into short coats and hose.

"Never before, father, have I known you put in your word in matters such as this," went on his daughter. "I have ever heard you say that for the welfare of the land in peace and war and of his subjects 'twas best the King should take order, and the men whom he called to his side. Erlend says that this venture is the work of the nobles in the south—they would set aside Lady Ingebjörg and the men her father gave her for councillors—and seize again for themselves such power as they had when King Haakon and his brother were children. But you yourself were used to say that the kingdom suffered great scathe from their rule——"

Lavrans whispered to her to send away the child's nurse. When they were alone, he asked:

"Whence came these tidings to Erlend—was it from Munan?"

Kristin told him that Orm had brought with him a letter from Sir Munan when he came home in the autumn. She did not tell that she herself had read it to Erlend—he had no great skill in making out writing. But in the letter Munan had made bitter complaint that every man in Norway that bore arms on his shield deemed now that he understood the governing of the realm better than the men who had stood at King Haakon's side when he lived; and they held that they knew better what was for the young King's welfare than the high-born lady, his own mother. He had warned Erlend that should there be signs that the Norwegian nobles had a mind to copy what the Swedes had done at Skara in the summer—hatch plots against Lady Ingebjörg and her old and tried councillors—the lady's kinsmen must hold them ready, and Erlend should come south and meet Munan at Hamar.

"Said he not, too," said Lavrans, pushing his finger in under Naakkve's fat chin, "that I was one of the men that set their faces against the unlawful call to arms that Munan brought with him up the Dale —in our King's name?"

"You!" said Kristin. "Met *you* Munan Baardssön in the autumn?"

"I did so," answered Lavrans. "And we agreed not over-well together."

"Spoke you of me?" asked Kristin, quickly.

"No, little Kristin," said her father, laughing a little. "I cannot call to mind that at that meeting your name came up between us.—Know you if it is so that your husband has a mind to fare south and seek out Munan Baardssön?"

"I believe it," said Kristin. "Sira Eiliv drew up a letter for Erlend not long since—and he spoke of having soon to journey south."

Lavrans sat silent a little, looking at the child groping with its fingers about his dagger-hilt and trying to bite the rock-crystal set in it.

"Is it true that they would take away the rule of the realm from Lady Ingebjörg?" asked Kristin.

"The lady is as old as you, or thereabouts," answered her father, still smiling a little. "None would take from the King's mother the honour or the power whereto she is born. But the Archbishop, and certain of the friends and kinsmen of our King that is gone, have called a meeting to take counsel how the lady's power and honour and the good of the people of the land can best be guarded."

Kristin said low:

"I can see well, father, that you are not come to Husaby this time only to see Naakkve and me."

"Not only for that," said Lavrans. Then he laughed: "And I can see, my daughter, that this likes you but little!"

He laid one of his hands over her face and stroked it up and down. 'Twas so he had been used to do, ever since she was a little girl, whenever he had been scolding or teasing her.

Meantime Sir Erling and Erlend sat up in the armoury—so was called the great storehouse that lay north-east of the courtyard, near by the main gate. It was high as a tower, having three stories; in the uppermost was a chamber with loopholed walls, and there were kept all the arms that were not in daily use on the manor. King Skule had built this house.

Sir Erling and Erlend had fur cloaks on, for it was bitter cold in the room. The guest walked about, looking at the many fair weapons and suits of armour that Erlend had inherited from his mother's father, Gaute Erlendssön.

Erling Vidkunssön was a somewhat short man, slightly built, though a little plump, but he bore himself lightly and with grace. Fair of face he was not, though his features were well formed—but his hair was of a light reddish hue, and his eyelashes and brows were white—the eyes themselves, too, were of the palest blue. That Sir Erling was deemed, none the less, to be a well-looking man may have been because all knew he was the richest knight in Norway. But 'twas true he had a rarely winning, quiet way with him. He was of excellent understanding, well-taught and rich in knowledge, and since he never strove to show off his learning, but always was found ready to hearken to others,

KRISTIN LAVRANSDATTER

he had gotten him the name of one of the wisest men in the land. He was much of the same age as Erlend Nikulaussön, and they were of kin to each other, though far off, through their kinship to the Stovreim house. They had known each other long, but there had been no close friendship between the two men.

Erlend sat on a great chest, talking of the ship he had built him last summer; 'twas a thirty-two-oar ship, and he deemed that she would prove a rarely swift sailer and easy steerer. He had had two ship-wrights down from the Nordland, and had himself overseen the work along with them.

"Ships are among the few things whereof I know a little, Erling," said he; "and you shall see, 'twill be a fair sight to watch *Margygren* cleave the sea-surges——"

"*Margygren**—'tis a fearsome, heathenish name you have given your ship, kinsman," said Sir Erling, laughing a little. "You mean to sail south in her, then?"

"You are as holy as my wife, I see—she too says 'tis a heathenish name. Aye, she likes not the ship either; but she is inland-bred—she cannot endure the sea."

"Aye, she seems right holy and fine and gracious, your lady," said Sir Erling, courteously. "As one might look she should be, seeing the kindred she comes of."

"Aye——" Erlend laughed a little. "There goes by no day when she hears not mass. And Sira Eiliv, our priest whom you saw, reads aloud for us from godly books—'tis what he likes best, next to ale and dainty dishes, to read aloud. And poor folk come hither to Kristin for counsel and help—they would be fain to kiss the hem of her garment, I well believe—my men I scarce know again any more. She is likest one of the ladies of whom there is record in the holy sagas that King Haakon forced us to sit and hear the priest read aloud—mind you?— when we were pages together. Much is changed at Husaby since last you were my guest, Erling.—I marvel, indeed, that you would come to me as things were then," he said, a little after.

"You spoke of the time when we were pages together," said Erling Vidkunssön, with a smile that became him well. "We were friends then, were we not? In those days all of us, Erlend, deemed that you would go far in this land of ours——"

But Erlend only laughed: "Aye, so did I deem too."

"Can you not sail southward along with me, Erlend?" asked Sir Erling.

"My purpose is to journey by land," answered the other.

"A toilsome journey for you—over the mountains in midwinter,"

* *Margygren* = the *Sea-Ogres*.

said Sir Erling. "'Twould be pleasant if you would bear Haftor and me company."

"I have given my promise to certain other folks to go with them," answered Erlend.

"Doubtless you go along with your father-in-law—aye—that is but reason."

"No, not so—I know so little of these men from the Dale he is to ride with." Erlend sat silent a little. "No, I have promised to look in on Munan at Stange," he brought out hurriedly.

"You can spare yourself the pains," answered the other. "Munan is gone down to his estates in Hising, and it may well be that 'twill be long ere he come north again. Is it long since you heard from him?"

"'Twas at Michaelmastide—he wrote to me from Ringabu."

"Aye—but you know what befell in the Dale this last autumn?" asked Erling. "You know it not? Sure you must know that he rode round himself to the Wardens, all about Mjös and up the Dale, with letters, bearing that the farmers should bring forth full levies of horses and supplies—one horse to every six farmers—and the nobles and free-holders should send horses, but might stay at home themselves? *Have* you not heard of this? And that the men of the northern Dale denied to furnish this levy when Munan came with Eirik Topp to the Thing at Vaage? Moreover, 'twas Lavrans Björgulfsön that led the opposers —he challenged Eirik, if there were aught outstanding from the lawful levies, to gather it in in lawful wise; but he called it high-handed oppression on the people to crave war-taxes from the farmers only to help a Danish man to wage war on the Danish King. And, should our King call for service from his King's-men, said Lavrans, he should find them ready enough to come to tryst with good weapons and horses and men-at-arms—but *he* sent not from Jörundgaard so much as a he-goat in a hempen halter, except the King craved he should ride it himself to the muster. Nay, now, know you not this? Smid Gud-leiksson says that Lavrans had promised his farmers he would pay their levy-fines* for them, if need should be——"

Erlend sat in wonderment:

"Did Lavrans so? Never have I heard before that my wife's father meddled in aught but what might touch his own estates, or his friends'——"

"'Tis not often he does so, like enough," said Sir Erling. "But so much I could see, when I was in at Nes with him, that when Lavrans Björgulfsön speaks his mind in a matter, he lacks not followers in plenty—for he speaks not except he know the business so well that his word can hardly be overthrown. Now, touching these supplies, 'tis

* See Note 8.

said he has changed letters with his kin in Sweden—as you know, Lady Ramborg, his father's mother, and Sir Erngisle's grandfather were cousins, so that his kinsfolk there are many and worshipful. Quiet a man as he is, your father-in-law, he has no little power in the country-side where folks know him—though he use it not often."

"Aye, then do I understand why you seek his company, Erling," said Erlend, laughing. "I marvelled that you were grown such hot friends."

"Marvel you at that?" answered Erling, unmoved. "A strange man must be he that would not be fain to call Lavrans of Jörundgaard his friend. You, kinsman, would serve your turn better by hearkening to him than to Munan."

"Munan has been like an elder brother to me ever since the day I first went forth from my home," said Erlend, a little hotly. "Never did he fail me when the pinch came. And if, now, a pinch be come for him——"

"Munan will be safe enough," said Erling Vidkunssön, calmly as before. "The letters he bore around were sealed with the Great Seal of Norway—unlawfully, but that touches not him. True, there is more —that which he was privy to, and attested with his seal, when he was witness to the Lady Eufemia's betrothal—but that can scarce be brought to light without touching one whom we would not—— Truth to tell, Erlend—I trow Munan can save his own skin without your help —but you may harm yourself——"

"'Tis the Lady Ingebjörg you aim at, I see well," said Erlend. "I have promised our kinswoman to serve her both here and in foreign lands——"

"And even so have I promised," answered Erling. "And I mean to keep that promise—and so, I trow, does every Norseman that served and loved our lord and kinsman, King Haakon. And the best service that can be shown her is to part her from those councillors who counsel so young a lady to her own hurt and her son's."

"Believe you," asked Erlend in a low voice, "that you can compass *that?*"

"Aye," said Erling Vidkunssön firmly. "I believe it. And I trow all believe it who hearken not to"—he shrugged his shoulders—"evil-minded—and loose—talk. And that should we, the lady's kinsmen, be the last of all to do."

A serving-maid lifted the trap-door in the floor, and asked if it would suit them now that the mistress have the supper borne into the hall. . . .

While the house-folk were still at the board, the talk ever and anon kept glancing towards these weighty matters that were in question.

Kristin marked that both her fathe, and Sir Erling tried to hinder this; they turned the talk with news of wedding-bargains and deaths, strife among heirs, and dealings in farms. She was uneasy, though she scarce herself knew why. They had some errand of weight to Erlend, she could see. And though she would not own it to herself, she knew her husband so well now as to feel that, headstrong as he was, he might mayhap easily enough be turned aside by one who had a firm hand in a soft glove, as the saying went.

After the meal, the men moved over to the hearth and sat there drinking. Kristin settled down on the bench, took her broidery frame into her lap, and began plaiting the fringes. Soon after, Haftor Graut came across to her, laid a cushion on the floor, and sat on it at her feet. He had found Erlend's cithern, and he held it on his knee and sat thrumming on it and prattling. Haftor was a quite young man with yellow ringleted hair; most comely of face, but freckled beyond measure. Kristin soon marked that he was a most heedless talker. He had but just wedded richly; but he had grown weary at home on his estates, he said; 'twas therefore that he was going now to the meeting of the King's-men.

"But 'tis no more than reason that Erlend Nikulaussön bide at home," he said, and laid his head back on Kristin's lap. She drew a little aside, laughed, and said, if she mistook not, her husband too was minded to journey south—"whatever the cause may be"—she said, with an air of innocence. "There is so much unrest in the land these days; 'tis no easy thing for a simple woman to judge of such things."

"Yet 'tis a woman's simplicity that is most to blame for it," answered Haftor, laughing, and shifting nearer again. "Aye, so at least say Erling and Lavrans Björgulfsön—I would be fain to know what they mean by it. What think you, Mistress Kristin? Lady Ingebjörg is a good, simple woman—maybe she is sitting now, even as you are, plaiting silk with her snow-white fingers, and thinking: hard-hearted would it be to deny her departed husband's trusty vassal a little matter of help towards bettering his fortunes——"

Erlend came over and sat by his wife; Haftor had to move a little to make room.

"'Tis such trumpery tales the dames hatch out in their lodging when their husbands are fools enough to take them with them to the assemblies——"

"Folks say, where I am from," said Haftor, "that there is no smoke without fire——"

"Aye, we have that byword too," said Lavrans—he and Erling had joined them—"yet was I cheated, Haftor, last winter—when I would have lit my lantern with a piece of fresh horse-dung." He sat himself down on the edge of the table. Straightway Sir Erling fetched Lavrans' beaker across and proffered it to him with a bow, then sat down near him on the bench.

"'Tis not possible, Haftor," said Erlend, "that you can know, away north in Haalogaland, what Lady Ingebjörg and her councillors know of the purposes and undertakings of the Danes. I know not if you were not short-sighted when you set you up against the King's call for help. Sir Knut—aye, we may as lief call him by his name, 'tis he we all have in our thoughts—he seemed not to me to be the man to let himself be caught dozing on his perch. You folk dwell too far away from the great cauldrons to smell what is cooking in them. And, better timely ware than after yare, say I——"

"Aye," said Sir Erling. "Almost a man might say, they cook for us now in our neighbour's manor—soon will we Norsemen be most like folk living on a pittance from their heirs; they send us in at the door the porridge they have cooked in Sweden—eat it, if you would have meat! I deem that 'twas an error of our Lord, King Haakon—that, as it were, he moved the kitchen to an outskirt of the farm, when he made Oslo the first city of the land. Before, it lay midway of the farm-place, if we may keep to this way of speech—Björgvin* or Nidaros—but now there is none to rule in these parts but the Archbishop and chapter.—Aye, what say you, Erlend—you that are a Trönder, with all your goods and all your lordship in Trondheim here——"

"Aye, God's blood, Erling—if 'tis that you would be at—carry home the pot and hang it up at the right hearth-stone once again——"

"Aye," said Haftor. "All too long have we here in the north had to be content with a smell of singeing and a gulp of cold broth——"

Lavrans broke in:

"Thus it stands, Erlend—I had not taken it on me to be spokesman for the folk of our country-side at home, but that I had in my keeping letters from my kinsman, Sir Erngisle. So I knew none of the men who bear rightful rule either in the Dane-King's or in our King's realms have any thought of breaking the peace and friendship between our lands."

"If you know who bears rule in Denmark now, father-in-law, I wot you know more than do most other men," said Erlend.

"One thing I know. There is *one* man whom none would see bear rule, neither here nor in Sweden, nor in Denmark. And that was the drift of the Swedes' doings at Skara last summer, and that is the drift of the meeting we would now hold at Oslo—to make clear to all who have not yet understood it, that on this all prudent men are at one."

* Bergen.

By now they had all drunk so much that they were grown somewhat loud-voiced—all but old Smid Gudleikssön, who sat nodding in his chair by the hearth. Erlend cried out:

"Aye, you folks are so prudent that the devil himself cannot trick you! 'Tis no marvel you should be afeard of Knut Porse. You cannot understand him, you good gentry—he is not the man to be content to sit mumchance watching the days slip by and the grass grow as God wills it. Fain would I be to meet that knight again; I knew him when I was in Halland. And naught would I have against it if I stood in Knut Porse's shoes."

"So much dared not I have said where my wife could hear me," said Haftor Graut.

But Erling Vidkunssön, too, was now well on in drink. He tried to keep a hold on his courtly ways, but they slipped from his grasp:

"You!" said he, bursting into a great laughter. "You, kinsman!— Nay, Erlend!" He slapped the other on the shoulder and laughed and laughed.

"Nay, Erlend," said Lavrans, bluntly; "there needs more for that than beguiling of fair ladies. Were there no more in Knut Porse than that he can play the fox in the goose-pen, I trow we gentlefolk of Norway were all too slothful to turn out of our houses to hunt him off —even were the goose our King's mother. But whomsoever Sir Knut can beguile to play the fool for his sake, he himself plays no tricks that have not a meaning in them. *He* has his goal, and be sure that he takes not his eyes from it——"

There was a pause in the talk. Then Erlend said, his eyes glittering: "Then I would that Sir Knut were a Norseman."

The others sat silent a little. Sir Erling took a draught from his goblet, then said:

"God forbid—had we such a man among us here in Norway, I fear me there would quickly be an end of peace in the land."

"Peace in the land!" said Erlend scornfully.

"Aye, peace in the land," answered Erling Vidkunssön. "Bear in mind, Erlend—'tis not we of the knighthood alone that own this land and live in it. To you 'twould mayhap seem sport if there should arise here a man greedy of adventure and of power like Knut Porse. So it was in bygone days that when a man raised revolt in this our land, 'twas ever easy for him to find followers from among the nobles. Either they would gain the upper hand and win titles and fiefs, or their kinsmen won and they were given grace for life and goods—aye, the record tells who lost their lives, but the more part saved their skins, whether things went so or so—the more part of *our* fathers, mark you. But the mass of the common farmers and the townsmen, Erlend—the working-folk that many a time had their dues wrung from them twice over in one year, and might be joyful, moreover, each time a troop had passed through the country-side without burning their farms and slaughtering their cattle—the common folk that had to suffer such unbearable burdens and oppressions—*they*, I trow, thank God and St. Olav for old King Haakon and King Magnus and his sons, who strengthened the laws and made the peace sure." . . .

"Aye, I well believe that you believe 'tis so."—Erlend threw back his head. Lavrans sat looking at the younger man—he was wide awake enough now, was Erlend. His dark vehement countenance was flushed red, his throat seemed to swell into an arch in the slender brown neck. Then Lavrans looked at his daughter. Kristin had let her work fall on her lap and was following the men's talk intently.

"Are you so sure that the peasants and the common folk think thus and praise so much the new order of things? 'Tis true they had hard times often—in the old days when kings and rival kings warred with each other through all the land. I know that they remember still the time when they must often take to the hills with cattle and wives and children, while their farms went up in flames all down the valleys. I have heard them speak of it. But I know that they remember somewhat else as well—that their own fathers were in the armies; not we alone played for power, Erling, the peasants' sons played too—and time and again they won our lands from us. 'Tis not when law rules in a land that the son of a Skidan* trull, that knows not his own father's name, wins a Baron's widow with her lands and goods, as did Reidar Darre—you deemed a son of his house a good enough match for your daughter, Lavrans, and now hath he wedded your lady's niece, Erling! But now law and justice rule; and—I know not how it comes, but I know that 'tis so—the peasants' land comes into our hands more and more, and that *with* the law—the more law and right rule, the quicker it goes, the quicker their power in the kingdom's affairs and their own slips from their hands. And, Erling, the common farmers know it too! Oh, no! be not too sure, good sirs, that the common folk have no yearnings back to that time when they might lose their farms by fire and by rapine—but they might also win by arms more than they can win by law."

Lavrans nodded:

"There is some truth in what Erlend says," he said in a low voice.

But Erling Vidkunssön rose:

"I can well believe it—that the common folk remember better the

* The modern Skien.

few men that rose from nothing and came to might and mastery in the time of the sword, than the numberless men that went under in black poverty and misery. And yet none were harder masters to the small folks than these first—I trow 'tis of them the byword was first made: none more unkind than kin. If a man be not born to mastery, he is ever a hard master—but if he have grown up in childhood amid serving-men and serving-women, 'tis far easier for him to understand that without the common folk we are in many a wise as helpless as children all our days, and that, not only for the love of God, but quite as much for our own sake, we should serve them on our part with our knowledge and guard them with our knighthood. Never yet has a kingdom stood except there were in it great men with the strength and the will to use their power to make sure the lesser folk's rights——"

"You could preach against my brother for a wager, Erling," said Erlend, laughing. "But my belief is that these stubborn Trönders liked us great folk better in the old days when we led their sons to battle and foray, let our blood flow out over the deck-planks mixed with theirs, and hewed rings in sunder and shared the booty with our house-carls. —Aye, you see, Kristin, sometimes I sleep with one ear open when Sira Eiliv reads from his great books."

"Goods that are won by unright come not down to the third heir," said Lavrans Björgulfsön. "Have you not heard this, Erlend?"

"Surely have I heard it!" Erlend laughed aloud. "But seen it I have not——"

Erling Vidkunssön said:

"So it is, Erlend, that few are born to be masters, but all are born to serve; the right lord is the servant of his servants——"

Erlend clasped his hands together behind his neck and stretched himself, smiling:

"Thereon have I never thought. And I deem not that my tenants have any service to thank me for. And yet, strange though it be, I trow they like me well."—He rubbed his cheek against Kristin's black kitten, which had sprung up on his shoulder, and now, arching its back, was walking, purring, around his neck. "But my wife here— she is the most serviceable of ladies to all—though in faith you have no cause to believe it—for our cans and flagons are empty, Kristin mine!"

Orm, who had sat silent, following the men's talk, got up at once and went out.

"The lady grew so weary she fell asleep," said Haftor smiling, "and the fault is yours—'twere liker you had left her in peace to speak with me that have the wit to know how to talk to ladies."

"Aye, this talk has run on too long for you, I fear, mistress," began Sir Erling, in excuse; but Kristin answered with a smile:

"So indeed it is, sir, that I have not understood all that has been said here to-night; but I bear it well in mind, and I shall have good time to think over it hereafter." . . .

Orm came back with some maids bearing in more liquor. He went round filling the cups. Lavrans looked sorrowfully at the comely boy. He had tried to have some speech with Orm Erlendssön, but the boy was of few words, though his bearing was mannerly and courteous.

One of the maids whispered to Kristin that Naakkve was awake down in the little hall and was screaming terribly. On this the lady of the house bade her guests good-night, and left the hall with her maids.

The men turned to the ale-cup again. Sir Erling and Lavrans changed glances now and again, and at last the knight said:

"There is a matter, Erlend, that I had a mind to speak of with you. 'Tis sure that a levy of ships will be called out from the lands around the fjord here and from Möre—folks in the north dread that the Russians will come again in strength in the summer and that without help they will not be strong enough to guard the land. This Russian feud is the first profit we have drawn from our sharing a King with Sweden—'twould not be just that the Haalogalanders should be left to enjoy it all alone. Now, it so falls out that Arne Gjavvaldssön is too old and sickly—and there has been talk of naming you as chief of all the ships from this side of the fjord. How would that like you——?"

Erlend smote one fist into the palm of the other hand—his whole face shone: "How would it like me——!"

"'Twill scarce be possible to raise any great force," said Erling, as though to sober him. "But we thought that, if you will, 'twere well you should set things in train with the wardens round about.—You know all this country well—and 'twas said among the Lords of the Council that mayhap you were the man best fitted to make somewhat of this matter. There are they that still remember that you won no small honour when you were warden of the Halland coast under Count Jacob—I mind myself that I heard him say to King Haakon he had been unwise to deal so harshly with a likely young fellow; he said there was the stuff in you for a trusty servant to your King——"

Erlend snapped his fingers. "Nay, now, never tell me *you* are to be our King, Erling Vidkunssön! Is this the plot you are hatching," he said, laughing loudly, "to make Erling King?"

Erling said, testily:

"Nay, Erlend, see you not that I speak now in all sadness——"

"God help us—were you jesting before, then? Methought you had spoken in sadness enough all the night.—Aye, aye, let us speak in sadness, then, kinsman—tell me all concerning this affair."

Kristin lay sleeping with the child by her breast when Erlend came down to the little hall. He lit a fir-root brand at the embers on the hearth, and looked at the two for a little while by its light.

So fair she was—and a fair child was he, too, their son. She was always so sleepy in the evenings now, Kristin—the moment she had laid her down and drawn her child close to her, both of them fell asleep. Erlend laughed a little and threw the stick back on to the hearth. Slowly he drew off his garments.

Northward in the spring with *Margygren* and three or four war-ships. Haftor Graut with three ships from Haalogaland—but Haftor was new and untried in such work, him 'twas like he could manage as seemed good to him. Aye, he saw well he could have things as he would, up there; for this Haftor looked not as though he were a coward or half-hearted. Erlend stretched himself out and smiled in the dark. He had thought to raise a crew for *Margygren* from Möre, outside the fjord. But both this country-side and Birgsi swarmed with stout bold young fellows—the finest choice of men was his. . . .

Not much more than a year since he was wedded. Child-bearing, penance and fasting, and now the boy first and the boy last, both day and night. Yet—she was the same young sweet Kristin—when he could get her to forget the prating priests and her greedy suckling for a little while. . . .

He kissed her shoulder, but she marked it not. Poor child, let her sleep—he had so much to think on to-night. Erlend turned him away from her and gazed out into the room at the little glowing spark on the hearth. Aye, maybe he should get up and cover up the embers—but he had no mind to. . . .

Memories of his youth came in shreds and snatches. A quivering ship's-stem standing as 'twere waiting a second for the oncoming wave —and the sea that came washing inboard. The mighty clamour of storm and waves. The whole vessel groaned in the press of the seas—the mast-head cut its wild curve on the flying clouds. 'Twas somewhere off the Halland coast.—Erlend lay overwhelmed—feeling the tears fill his eyes. He had not known, himself, how these years of idleness had irked him.

The next morning Lavrans Björgulfsön and Sir Erling stood at the upper end of the courtyard, looking at some of Erlend's horses that ran loose without the fence.

"——Methinks," said Lavrans, "should Erlend appear in this

assembly, such rank and birth are his—since he is kinsman to the King and the King's mother—that he must needs come forth among the foremost. Now I know not, Sir Erling, whether you deem you can be sure that his judgment in these affairs will not rather lead him to the other side. If Ivar Ogmundssön should try a countermove—Erlend has near ties, too, with the men who will follow Sir Ivar——"

"I have little thought that Sir Ivar will do aught," said Erling Vidkussön. "And Munan"—his lip curled a little—"*he* will be wise enough, I trow, to stay away—he knows that else it might well be made clear to all men how much or how little Munan Baardssön counts for." They both laughed. "And there is this to be thought on—aye, you know yet better than I, Lavrans Lagmandssön,* you who have kith and kin there, that the Swedish lords are loath to count our knighthood as the equals of theirs. It might seem needful, then, that we should let no man be lacking from among those we have richest and of highest birth—we can ill afford to let a man like Erlend have leave to sit at home, dallying with his wife and tending his farms—tend he them well or ill," he added, as he saw Lavrans' look.

Lavrans smiled slightly.

"But should you deem it unwise to press Erlend to come with us, I will let it be."

"Methinks, dear sir," said Lavrans, "that Erlend would do better service here, in his own country. As you said yourself—we look for no goodwill towards this levy in the parishes south of Namdalseid—whose folk deem they have naught to fear from the Russians. It might be that Erlend would be the very man to change folks' thoughts of the matter in some measure——"

"He hath such a cursed loose tongue," Sir Erling burst out.

Lavrans answered with a little smile:

"Maybe his kind of talk will be understood by many better than—more clear-headed people's speech——" They looked at each other again, and both laughed. "Howsoever that may be—he could sure do greater hurt should he go to the meeting and talk too loudly there."

"Aye, if so be that you cannot stay him."

"That can I at no rate do, when once he meets with birds of the flock he has been wont to fly with—my son-in-law and I are too unlike."

Erlend came up to them:

"Have you had so much profit of the mass that you have no need of breakfast?"

"I heard not aught of breakfast—I am hollow as a wolf—and thirsty—— Lavrans caressed a dirty white horse he had been handling

* See *The Bridal Wreath* (*The Garland*), p. 13.

as he stood there. "The man that tends your farm-horses, son-in-law, I would drive off the place before I sat down to table, were he *my* man."

"I dare not, for fear of Kristin," said Erlend. "One of her maids is with child by him——"

"Nay, but count you that so great a deed in this country-side," said Lavrans, raising his eyebrows a little, "that you deem, because of it, you cannot be lacking him——?"

"No, but see you," said Erlend, laughing, "Kristin and the priest will have them wed—and they will have me put him in the way of earning a living for himself and her. The girl would not, and her guardian would not, and Tore himself is none too willing—but they will not let me turn him out; she fears he would fly the parish. Then, too, there is Ulf Haldorssön to oversee him—when Ulf is at home——"

Erling Vidkunssön went to meet Smid Gudleiksson. Lavrans said to his son-in-law:

"Methinks Kristin looks somewhat pale in the day-time——"

"Aye," said Erlend, eagerly. "Can you not speak to her, father-in-law?—that boy of hers is sucking the very marrow out of her. I trow she will keep him at the breast till the third fast comes round, like any cottar woman——"

"Aye, she loves her son much," said Lavrans, with a little smile.

"Aye," Erlend shook his head. "They will sit for three hours—she and Sira Eiliv—and talk of it, should a little rash show on him here or there; and for every tooth he cuts, it seems to them a great miracle has come to pass. I have never known aught else but that children were apt to cut teeth; and methinks it had been a greater marvel if our Naakkve had had none."

II

THE year after, one evening at the end of the Yule-tide festival, Kristin Lavransdatter and Orm Erlendssön came, quite unlooked-for guests, to Master Gunnulf's house in the city.

It had blown and sleeted the whole day since before noon, and now in the late evening a heavy snowstorm had come on. The two were thick with snow when they came into the room where the priest sat at the supper-board with his household.

Gunnulf asked, in some fear, whether there was aught amiss at home on the manor. But Kristin shook her head. Erlend was away from home, at a feast in Gelmin, she answered when the priest questioned; but she had been so tired, she could not go with him.

The priest thought how she had now ridden all the way into the city—her horse and Orm's were quite worn out, the last of the way they had scarce had strength to struggle through the snow-drifts. Gunnulf sent the two women of his household with Kristin—they were to get dry garments for her. They were his foster-mother and her sister—other women there were none in the priest's house. He himself cared for his brother's son. Meantime Orm was speaking:

"Kristin is sick, I trow. I said it to father, but he grew angry——"

She had been quite unlike herself in these last days, said the boy. He knew not what it was. He could not remember whether 'twas she or himself that had first thought of coming hither—oh, yes, 'twas she that had first spoken of how much she longed to come in to Christ's Church, and he had said that if that were so, he would go with her. So this morning, straightway after his father had ridden off, Kristin had said that now they would go. Orm had let her have her way, though he saw the weather was threatening—but he liked not the look in her eyes.

Gunnulf thought that neither did he like it, when Kristin now came in. Sorely thin she looked in Ingrid's black habit; her face was wan as bast, and the eyes were sunken, with blue-black rings beneath them —their glance was dark and strange.

It was more than three months since he had seen her—when he was at Husaby for the christening-feast. She had looked well then, as she lay in state in her bed, and she had said that she felt strong—it had been an easy delivery. So he had spoken against it when Ragnfrid Ivarsdatter and Erlend would have the child given to a foster-mother—while Kristin wept and begged that she might nurse Björgulf herself—the second son was called after Lavrans' father.

The priest asked, therefore, first after Björgulf—for he knew too that Kristin had not liked the nurse they gave the child to. But she said that he was thriving well and Frida was fond of him, and tended him much better than any could have deemed she would. And Nikulaus? asked the uncle; was he as bonny as ever? A little smile came to the mother's face. Naakkve grew comelier and comelier every day. No, he spoke not much; but else he was ahead of his age in every wise, and so big—no one would believe he was but in his second winter—Lady Gunna said so too.

Then she sat lost again. Master Gunnulf looked at the two, his brother's wife and his brother's son, sitting one on each side of him. They looked so weary and sorrowful, he grew sad at heart to see them.

Orm, indeed, seemed ever heavy of mood. The boy was fifteen years old now; he would have been the comeliest of youths, had he not looked so weak and ailing. He was well-nigh as tall as his father, but his form was all too slender and narrow of shoulder. In face, too, he favoured Erlend, but his eyes were a much darker blue, and the mouth under its first short black down was yet smaller and softer than his father's, and ever, when it was closed, a sad little furrow showed at its corners. Even Orm's narrow brown neck under his black curled hair looked strangely unhappy as he sat, stooping a little over his food.

Kristin had not sat at the board with her brother-in-law before in his own hall. The year before, she had been with Erlend in the city at the spring-tide Thing,* and then they lodged in this house, which Gunnulf had from his father—but the priest himself had lived then in the house of the Crossed Friars, as vicar for one of the canons. Now was Master Gunnulf parish priest of Steine; but he kept a chaplain in his charge, and himself oversaw the work of engrossing books for the churches of the Archbishopric, while the precentor, Eirik Finssön, was sick. Thus he lived for the time in his own house.

The hall was unlike the rooms Kristin was used to see. 'Twas a timber house, but in the midst of the eastern gable-wall Gunnulf had had built a great stone fire-place, such as he had seen in the south-lands; a log fire burned between cast-iron dogs. The table stood along one of the long walls, and by the wall over against it were benches with writing-desks; before a picture of Mary Virgin burned a lamp of yellow metal, and near by stood frames filled with books.

Strange seemed the room to her and strange her brother-in-law, now she saw him sitting here at his board with his household, clerks and serving-men with a strange half-priestly look. There were some poor folk too—old men and a young boy with film-like thin red eyelids clinging tightly over the empty sockets. On the women's bench with the two old women-servants sat a girl with a two years' child in her lap; she swallowed down the meat hungrily, and stuffed the child's mouth till its cheeks seemed like to burst.

So it was that all the priests of Christ's Church fed the poor at even-tide. But Kristin had heard that to Gunnulf Nikulaussön came fewer beggars than to the other priests, although—or because—he made them sit with him in his own hall and welcomed every beggar man as an honoured guest. They were given food from his own dish and drink from the priest's own casks. Therefore they came hither when they felt the need of a meat-meal—but else they would liefer go to the other priests, where they were given porridge and small ale in the kitchen.

And as soon as the scribe had said grace after meat, the poor folk made ready to depart. Gunnulf talked kindly to each one, asked if they would not lodge here for the night, or whether there were aught else they desired; but only the blind boy stayed. The girl with the child in special the priest asked to stay, and not take the little one out into the

* See Note 9.

night; but she muttered an excuse and hastened out. Gunnulf bade a serving-man see to it that blind Arnstein was given ale and a good bed in the guest-house. Then he rose and cast a hooded cloak about him: "You are weary, I trow, Orm and Kristin, and would go to rest. Audhild will see to you—belike you will be asleep when I come from the church."

But Kristin begged that she might go with him. "'Tis for that I am come hither," she said, fixing desperate eyes on Gunnulf. He bade Ingrid lend her a dry cloak, and she and Orm went with the little company that followed him from the house.

The ringing of the bells sounded as though they were right above their heads in the black night sky—the church was not many paces off. They dragged heavily through deep wet new-fallen snow. The weather was still now—now and then single flakelets of snow still floated down, shining faintly in the dark.

In deadly weariness Kristin tried to lean against the pillar she stood by; but the stone chilled her through. She stood in the dark church and looked up towards the lights of the choir. She could not see Gunnulf up there. But she knew he sat there amidst the priests, with his taper by his book—no, after all she was sure she could not speak to him. . . .

To-night it seemed as though there could be no help found for her anywhere. Sira Eiliv at home reproved her, that she took her everyday sins so hardly—he said 'twas the lure of spiritual pride: let her but be diligent in prayer and good works, and she would have no time to brood so much over such things. "The devil is no such fool as not to see then that your soul must needs escape him at last, and he will no longer care to tempt you so much——"

Oh, no! 'Twas like the devil was none so sure that he must lose her soul—— But when she had lain here before, crushed by sorrow for her sins, for the hardness of her heart, her unclean life and her soul's blindness—then had she felt that the sainted King had taken her in beneath the sheltering hem of his cloak. She had felt the clasp of his strong warm hand on hers, he had pointed out to her the light that is the source of all strength and holiness. St. Olav had turned her eyes toward Christ upon His Cross—see, Kristin, God's loving-kindness.—Aye, she had begun to understand God's long-suffering love.—But since then she had turned her again from the light, and shut her heart against it, and now was there naught else in her soul but disquiet and wrath and fear.

Wretched, wretched was she. She had seen it for herself: such a woman as she was had need of hard trials ere she could be healed of her unloving spirit. And yet so rebellious was she that it seemed her heart must break under the trials that had been laid upon her. They were but small trials—but they were so many—and she so rebellious.

——She had a glimpse of her stepson's tall slender form over on the men's side——

She *could* not help herself. Orm she loved like a child of her own; but 'twas not possible for her to grow to love Margret. She had striven and striven, and tried to force herself to like the child, ever since the day last winter when Ulf Haldorssön had brought her home to Husaby. She deemed herself it was a fearful thing—could she feel such misliking and wrath towards a little maid of nine years old! And well she knew that in part it was that the child was so strangely like her mother—she understood not Erlend, he showed naught but pride that his little brown-eyed daughter was so fair; never did the child seem to wake discomforting memories in her father. 'Twas as though Erlend had forgotten all that concerned these children's mother.—But it was not *only* because Margret favoured her mother that Kristin misliked her. Margret would not endure to be taught by any; she was haughty and harsh to the serving-folk; untruthful was she too, and, with her father, a flatterer. She loved him not, as did Orm—it was ever to gain something that she clung to Erlend with kisses and caresses. And Erlend poured out gifts upon her and humoured all the little maid's whims. Orm liked not his sister either, she had seen that. . . .

It was pain to her to feel herself so hard and cruel that she could not look on at Margret's doings without anger and harsh judgment. But 'twas much more pain to see and hear the endless bickerings between Erlend and his eldest son. The pain was the keener because she saw that Erlend in his inmost heart had a boundless love for the boy—and he was unjust and rough towards Orm because he was at his wit's end to know what he should do with his son or how he could make his future sure. He had given his bastard children lands and goods—but it seemed unthinkable that Orm could ever make a farmer. And Erlend grew desperate when he saw how weak and sinewless Orm was —he would call his son rotten; strive fiercely to harden him; practise him, hour after hour, in use of heavy weapons that 'twas impossible the boy could wield; force him to drink himself sick in the evenings, and bring him back half dead from perilous and toilsome huntings. Beneath all this Kristin could see the anguish of Erlend's heart—he was wild with sorrow often, she saw, that this fine-grained and comely son of his was fit but for one place—and from that his birth barred him out. And thus had Kristin come to understand how little patience Erlend had when he must fear for one that was dear to him or feel pity for him.

She saw that Orm understood it too. And she saw that the youth's heart was torn between love of his father and pride in him—and scorn for the man's unreason when Erlend made his child suffer because troubles lay before them for which he and not the boy was to blame. But Orm had drawn close to his young stepmother—it was as though with her he breathed freely and felt lighter of mood. When he was alone with her, he would jest and laugh by times—in his still fashion. But Erlend liked not this—'twas as though he misdoubted that these two might sit in judgment on his doings.

Oh, no; 'twas no easy lot for Erlend—no marvel that he was sore and hasty in all that touched the two children. And yet——

She winced with pain still when she thought on it.

They had had the manor full of guests the week before. Now when Margret came home, Erlend had had the loft at the lower end of the hall, over the outer room and the closet, set in order for a sleeping-room—it should be her maiden bower, he said—and there she slept, with the maid whom her father had set to tend and serve her; Frida slept there too, with Björgulf. But now, in this press of Yule-tide guests, Kristin had made this loft a sleeping-room for the young men, and the two maids and the babe must sleep in the serving-women's house. But since she had thought Erlend would maybe not like that she should send Margret to sleep with the serving-folk, she had made up a bed for her on one of the benches in the hall, where the ladies and maidens were sleeping. Margret was ever loath to rise in the mornings; that morning Kristin had waked her many times, but she had turned over again, and still lay sleeping after all the others were up. Kristin must needs have the hall cleared and made ready—the guests must have their morning meal—and at length she quite lost patience. She pulled the down pillows from under Margret's head, and took away the coverings from above her. But when she saw the child lying there naked on the fur rug, she threw over her the cloak from her own shoulders. It was a piece of plain undyed wadmal—she wore it only when she went to and from the kitchen and storehouses to see to the service of the food.

Erlend came in at that moment—he had slept in one of the store-house lofts with some other men, for Lady Gunna lay with Kristin in the great bed. When he saw what was towards he had fallen into a fury. He had grasped Kristin by the arm so hard that the marks of his fingers still showed on her flesh.

"Think you it is fit that this daughter of mine lie in straw and wad-mal? Margit is mine, see you, even though she be not yours—what is not too good for your own children is none too good for her. But since you have held up the innocent little maid to scorn before these women,

you must even make it good again before their eyes—spread over
Margit again what you took off her——!"

True it was that Erlend had drunk heavily the night before, and
when that was so he was ever fretful next morning. And he might well
have thought that there was talk among the women when they saw
Eline's children. And he was thin-skinned and sore in all that touched
the esteem they were held in.—And yet——

She had tried to speak of it with Sira Eiliv. But here he could not
help her. Gunnulf had said the sins she had confessed and done
penance for, before Eiliv Serkssön came to be her father confessor, she
need not name to him unless she saw that he must know them in order
that he might judge and counsel in her concerns. So there was much
that she had never told him, though she felt herself that thus she had
come to seem in Sira Eiliv's eyes a better woman than she was. But
yet 'twas so comforting for her to have the friendship of this good and
pure-hearted man. Erlend mocked—but she had so much comfort
from Sira Eiliv. With him she could talk as much as she would of her
children; all the little things that she wearied Erlend to death with,
the priest was ready to talk over with her. He had a way with little
children, and good skill in their little troubles and sicknesses. Erlend
laughed at her when she went herself to the kitchen and cooked dainty
dishes to send to the priest's house—for Sira Eiliv was fond of good food
and drink, and it pleased her to busy herself with such things and try
her hand with what she had learnt from her mother or seen in the
cloister. Erlend cared not what he ate, if one but let him have flesh-
meat at all times, when 'twas not a fast. But Sira Eiliv came and talked
and thanked her and praised her skill when she had sent him a spitful
of young ptarmigans in wrappings of fine bacon, or a dish of reindeer's
tongues in French wine and honey. And he counselled her with her
garden, and from Olav's Cloister, where the prior was his good friend.
And then he read to her, and he could tell her so many fair things of
the life out in the great world.

But for the very reason that he was so good and so simple-hearted a
man, 'twas often hard to speak to him of the evil she saw in her own
heart. When she confessed to him how wroth she had been with Erlend
for his behaviour in this matter of Margret, he had enjoined on her
her duty to bear with her husband. But he seemed to deem that 'twas
Erlend alone that had offended in speaking so unjustly to his wife—
and that in the hearing of strangers. And Kristin, indeed, thought the
like. But in her inmost heart she felt that she shared in the guilt; she
could not make it clear, but it troubled her heart sorely.

Kristin looked up at the shrine, gleaming faintly golden up in the
twilight behind the high altar. She had looked so surely that when she

stood here once more, something should again befall her—some deliverance of her spirit. Again would a living spring well up in her heart and wash away all the unrest and fear and bitterness and doubt that filled it.

But to-night there was none that had patience with her. Have you not learnt it once already, Kristin—to bring your self-righteousness forth into the light of God's righteousness, to hold up your heathenish and selfish desire in the light of love? 'Tis that you *will* not learn it, Kristin. . . .

But when last she knelt there, she had had Naakkve in her arms. His little mouth against her breast sent such warmth into her heart that it grew even as soft wax, easy for the heavenly love to refashion. And still she *had* Naakkve—he ran about the hall at home, so fair and so sweet that her breast ached if she but thought of him. His soft curly hair began to darken now—he would be black-haired like his father. And he was so bursting with life and naughtiness.—She made beasts for him out of old bits of fur rug, and he threw them away and ran after them, racing the young hounds. And 'twould often end with the bear falling into the hearth-fire, and burning up with much smoke and an evil smell, while Naakkve stood howling and jumping and stamping, and then buried his head in her lap—all his adventures ended there as yet. The maids fought for his favour, the men caught hold of him and threw him up to the roof, whenever they came into the hall. Did the boy see Ulf Haldorssön, he ran at once and clung to the man's leg— Ulf had taken him out into the farm-place now and then. Erlend snapped his fingers to his son and set him on his shoulder for a moment —but his father was the one at Husaby that paid least heed to the boy. Though he *was* fond of Naakkve. Erlend *was* glad that he had two trueborn sons now.

The mother's heart turned in her:

Björgulf they had taken from her. He whimpered now when she would have held him; and Frida put him straightway to her breast— the foster-mother watched over the boy jealously. But the new child she would never give away from her. They had said, her mother and Erlend, that she must spare her strength now, and so they took her new-born son and gave him to another woman. 'Twas as though she had felt a sort of vengeful joy at the thought that all that had come of this was that now she looked to have yet a third child before Björgulf was full eleven months old.

She dared not speak of it with Sira Eiliv, he would maybe only think that she was vexed that already she must go through all this again. But it was not that. . . .

From her pilgrimage she had come home with a deep awe in her soul—nevermore should this madness overmaster her. All summer through she had sat alone with her child down in the old hall, weighed in her mind the Archbishop's words and Gunnulf's sayings, been vigilant in prayer and penance, diligent in working to restore the neglected manor and to win her house-folk by kindness and thought for their welfare, eager to help and serve all around her so far as her hands and her power might reach. There had sunk over her a calm delicious peace. She upheld herself with thoughts of her father, with prayers to the holy men and women Sira Eiliv read of, and meditation on their courage and steadfastness. And with a heart tender with happiness and thankfulness she remembered Brother Edvin, as he had appeared to her in the moonlight that night. She had understood full well his message, when he smiled so gently and hung his mitten on the beam of moonlight. Had she but faith enough, she could grow to be a good woman.

When the first year of marriage was at an end, she had to remove back to her husband. She comforted herself, when she felt herself unsure—the Archbishop himself had enjoined upon her that in the life in common with her husband she should show her new heart. And indeed she strove with an eager care for his welfare and his honour. Erlend himself had said it: "It has come to pass, after all, Kristin—you have brought back honour to Husaby." Folks showed her so much kindness and respect—all seemed willing to forget that she had begun her wedded life a little over-hastily. Where housewives came together, she was taken into council; they praised her ordering of her home; she was fetched to be brideswoman and to be helper at births on the great manors, none made her feel that she was young and unskilled, and a new-comer to the country. The serving-folk sat on in the hall through the evening, even as at Jörundgaard—all had somewhat to ask their mistress of. It came over her, in a glow of joy, how kind folks were to her and that Erlend was proud of her. . . .

Then Erlend had gone to work to take order for the ship-levy from the harbours south of the fjord. He journeyed about the country, riding or sailing, and was busy with folk who came to him, and letters that were to be sent off. He was so young and glad and comely—the sluggish unjoyous air she had often seen upon him in former days seemed blown clean away from the man. He glittered new-wakened like the morning. He had little time to spare for her now—but she grew dizzy and wild again when he came near her with his smiling face and his venture-loving eyes.

She had laughed with him over the letter that had come from Munan Baardssön. The knight had not been at the meeting of the King's-men himself, but he scoffed at the whole affair, and most of all at Erling

Vidkunssön's being made Regent. It seemed, said Munan, his first task was to give himself new titles—he would have folk call him High Steward now, 'twas said. Munan wrote of her father, too:

"The hill-wolf from Sil crept under a rock and sat mum. That is to say, your father-in-law took lodging with the priests of St. Laurentius Church and raised not his honeyed voice in the parleys. There in his keeping had he letters under the seals of Sir Erngisle and Sir Karl Turessön; if they be not yet worn to shreds, then must the parchment be tougher than the devil's shoe-soles. This also you must know: that Lavrans gave eight marks, pure silver, to Nonneseter. Like enough the man hath got it in his head that Kristin had not so wearisome a life there as of rights she should——"

She had, indeed, felt a pang of shame and pain, but yet she could not help laughing with Erlend. The winter and spring had passed over her in a whirl of mirth and gladness. Now and then a storm on Orm's account—Erlend knew not if he should take the boy north with him. It ended with an outburst at Easter-tide—that night Erlend wept in her arms; he dared not take his son aboard with him; he feared that Orm must needs come short in war. She had comforted him and herself—and the lad—maybe the boy would grow stronger as he grew in years.

The day she rode down with Erlend to the haven at Birgsi, she could not feel aught of fear or sorrow at his going. She was drunken, as it were, with him and his overflowing gladness.

She had not known herself then that already she was with child again. She had thought when she felt sick, 'twas but with the bustle over Erlend's going, with the unquiet times and drinking-feasts at home, and that she was worn out with suckling Naakkve. When she felt new life quicken within her, she had been—— She had so looked forward to the winter, to going about in city and country-side with her fair and gallant husband—while yet she, too, was fair and young. She was so sure that in his Russian warfare Erlend would show he was fit for other things than wasting his name and fame and goods. She had thought to wean the boy in autumn—'twas troublesome to take him and his nurse with her wherever she might go.—And now—no, she had not been glad, and she had told this to Sira Eiliv. Then had the priest rebuked her most sharply for her unloving and worldly spirit. And the whole summer she had passed striving to be glad and to thank God for the new child she was to bear, and for the good tidings that came to her of Erlend's worthy deeds in the north.

Then he came home just before Michaelmas. She had seen well that *he* was not overglad when he saw what was at hand. And that night he said it:

"Methought that when once you were mine—'twould be like drinking Yule-tide every day. But it looks as though most of the time would be long fasts."

Each time she remembered it, a wave of blood flooded her face, as hotly as that evening when she had turned her from him, darkly flushed and tearless. Erlend had tried to make amends with love and kindness. But she could not forget it. The fire in her that not all her tears of penitence had had power to quench, nor her anguish for her sin to choke—'twas as though Erlend had trod it out with his foot when he said those words.

Late at night, the service over, they sat before the chimney-place in Gunnulf's hall, he and Kristin and Orm. A flagon of wine, with some small goblets, stood on the edge of the fire-place. Master Gunnulf had asked more than once if his guests would not to rest now. But Kristin begged that she might sit on.

"Mind you, brother-in-law," she asked, "I told you once that our priest at home counselled me to give myself to a cloister, should father not consent that Erlend and I should wed."

Gunnulf glanced swiftly across at Orm. But Kristin said with a little sick smile:

"Think you this grown youth knows not that I am a weak and sinful woman?"

Master Gunnulf answered softly:

"Had you a call to the life of the cloister, then, Kristin?"

"God might sure have opened my eyes, when once I was come into His service."

"Mayhap He deemed your eyes had need to be opened to understand that you should be in His service wheresoever you may be. Husband, children, house-folk at Husaby have surely need that a trusty and patient serving-woman of God go about among them and care for their welfare. . . .

"Surely that maid weds best who chooses Christ to her bridegroom and gives herself not into the power of any sinful man. But a child that hath already sinned——"

" 'I would have had you come to God, wearing your garland,' " whispered Kristin. "So said he to me, Brother Edvin Rikardssön, of whom I have often told you. Think you the same——?"

Gunnulf Nikulaussön nodded:

"——Though many a woman has raised herself up out of a life of sin with such strength and steadfastness that we now may safely pray for her intercession. But this befell more often in the days gone by, when she was threatened with torture and the stake and red-hot pincers, if she avowed herself a Christian. I have oft-times thought, Kristin, that 'twas easier then to tear oneself free from the bonds of sin, when it could be done thus by might and main at a single wrench. Even though mankind is so corrupted—yet does courage still dwell by nature in many a breast—and 'tis courage that oftest drives on a soul to seek out God. And so 'tis like the tortures spurred on as many souls to steadfastness as they terrified to apostasy. But a young wildered child that is torn from the lusts of the flesh ere yet she has learned to understand what they bring upon her soul, is brought into sisterhood with holy maids who have given themselves up to watch and pray for them that sleep without in the world. . . .

"Would it might soon be summer!" he said of a sudden, rising up. The two others looked up at him in wonder.

"Aye—it came into my mind, the cuckoo's call from the hill-sides at Husaby of a morning. Always we heard it first from the eastward in the hills behind the houses, and then an answer came from far off in the woods round By—it sounded so sweet across the lake in the morning stillness. Think you not 'tis fair at Husaby, Kristin?"

"East-cuckoo is grief-cuckoo," said Orm Erlendssön in a low voice. "Methinks Husaby is the fairest place in all the world."

The priest laid his hands on his nephew's narrow shoulders for a moment:

"So thought I too, kinsman. 'Twas *my* father's home, too. The youngest son stands no nearer the heritage than do you, my Orm."

"When father lived with my mother, you were nearest heir," said the youth, softly as before.

"We cannot help it, I and my children, Orm," said Kristin, sorrowfully.

"I trow you will have marked, too, that I bear you no grudge," he answered quietly.

"'Tis such a wide, open country-side," said Kristin in a little. "One sees so far around from Husaby—and the heaven is so—so wide. Where I am from, it lies like a roof right down upon the hill-tops. The Dale lies low in shelter, so hollow and green and fresh. The world is of so fit a size—not too great and not too narrow." She sighed and moved her hands in her lap.

"His home was there, the man your father would have wed you to?" asked the priest, and the woman nodded.

"Have you ever repented that you took him not?" he asked again, and she shook her head.

Gunnulf crossed the room and took a book from the case. He sat down again by the fire with it, opened its clasps, and turned over the leaves. He did not read from it, but sat with the book open in his lap.

"When Adam and his wife had defied the will of God, then felt they in their own flesh a power that defied their wills. God had created them, man and woman, young and fair, for that they should live in wedlock, and bring forth co-heirs with themselves of His bounteous gifts, the loveliness of the Garden of Paradise, the fruit of the tree of life and bliss everlasting. They needed not to feel shame of their bodies, for, as long as they obeyed God, their whole body and all their limbs were in the power of their will, even as are hand and foot."

Flushing red as blood, Kristin pressed her hands cross-wise under her breast. The priest bent towards her a little; she felt his strong yellow eyes on her bowed visage.

"Eve made spoil of that which belonged to God, and her husband received it, when she gave him that which by right was the possession of their Father and Creator. They would fain have made themselves His like—now they marked that they were like unto Him first in this: as they had betrayed His lordship in the great world, so now was their lordship over the little world, the soul's house of flesh, betrayed. As they had played false to the Lord their God, so now would the body play false to its lord, the soul.

"Then did these bodies seem to them so ugly and hateful that they made them garments to hide them. First but a short apron of fig-leaves. But as they came to know more and more the inwardness of their own fleshy nature, they drew the garments up higher and higher, over the place of their hearts and over their backs so unwilling to bow. Until these last days when men clothe themselves in steel to the outermost joints of fingers and toes, and hide their faces behind the bars of the helm—so are strife and treachery spread abroad in the world."

"Help me, Gunnulf," prayed Kristin. She was white to the lips. "I—I know not my own will."

"Say then: 'Thy will be done,'" answered the priest softly. "You know that His will is that you should open your heart to His love, and that then must you love Him again with all your soul's might."

Kristin turned suddenly towards her brother-in-law:

"You know not—you—how dearly I loved Erlend. And my children——"

"My sister—all other love is but as an image of heaven in the water-puddles of a muddy road. Bemired must you needs be if you will dabble in them. But if you bear ever in mind that 'tis a mirroring of the light from yonder other home, then will you rejoice in its fairness, and will take good heed not to destroy it by stirring up the mud beneath——"

"Aye. But you, Gunnulf, are a priest—you have vowed to God to fly these—lures——"

"That have you too, Kristin—when you promised to forsake the devil and all his works. The devil's work is that which begins in sweet desire, and ends in them that work it stinging and biting each other like toad and asp. 'Twas that Eve learnt—that when she would have given her husband and her offspring that which was God's possession, then brought she them naught but outlawry and blood-guiltiness and death, that came into the world when brother slew brother on that first small field where thorns and thistles grew on the stone-heaps between the little plots——"

"Aye. But *you* are a priest," she said, as before. "You have not to strive every day to agree with another in your will"—she burst into tears—"to be patient——"

The priest said with a little smile:

"In that matter there is strife between soul and body in each mother's son. Therefore are bride-mass and wedlock appointed, that man and woman shall find help to live, wedded pair and parents and children and housemates, as trusty and helpful travelling companions on the journey towards the home of peace."

Kristin said low:

"Methinks it must be easier to watch and pray for them that sleep without in the world, than to strive against one's own sins——"

"It is so," said the priest sharply. "But think you, Kristin, there has lived one holy man that hath not had to defend *himself* against the enemy, at the same time as he strove to guard the lambs against the wolf——?"

Kristin said, low and timidly:

"I had thought—they that move from holy place to holy place and have command of all prayers and words of power——"

Gunnulf leaned forward, mended the fire, and remained sitting with his elbows on his knees:

"'Twas six years ago, about this time of year, that we came to Rome, Eiliv and I and two Scots priests that we had come to know in Avignon. We had gone afoot the whole way. . . . .

"We came to the city just before the Fast. At that time the folk in the south-lands hold great feastings and banquets—they call it *carnevale*. Then does wine, both red and white, run like rivers in the tavern-houses, and folks dance at nights without doors, and have torches and bonfires in the open places. It is spring in Italia then, and the flowers are blooming in meadows and gardens, and the women deck themselves with these, and throw roses and violets to the passers-by in the streets—they sit up in the windows, and they have carpets of silk and gold brocade hanging from the sills down over the wallstones. For all the houses are of stone down there, and the knights have their castles and strong places in the midst of the cities. Belike there is no town-law or market-peace in that city—for they and their serving-men fight in the streets till the blood runs down——

"There stood such a castle in the street where we dwelt, and the lord who ruled there was named Ermes Malavolti. It shadowed all the narrow lane where we lodged, and our chamber was as dark and cold as a dungeon in a stone fortress. Often when we went out, we must needs press close to the wall while he rode by, with silver bells on his garments and a whole troop of armed followers, while filth and rotten-ness splashed up from under the horses' hoofs—for in that land the people do but cast all filth and sweepings without doors. The streets are cold and dark and strait as rock-cliffs—little like the green road-ways of our towns. In those streets they hold races when the time of *carnevale* comes—send out wild Arab horses to race against each other——"

The priest paused a little, then he went on:

"This Sir Ermes had a kinswoman dwelling in his house. Isota was her name, and she might well have been Isold the Fair herself. Her skin and hair were of the hue of honey, but her eyes, I trow, were black. I saw her time and again at a window——

"But outside the city the land is more waste than the most desolate uplands in our land, where nothing haunts but wolf and reindeer, and the eagle screams. Yet are there towns and castles in the mountains round about, and out on the green uplands a man can see everywhere marks of folk who must have dwelt there in days gone by; and great flocks of sheep and herds of white oxen are grazing. Herdsmen armed with long spears follow them about a-horseback, and these are perilous folk for wayfarers to meet, for they murder and rob them and cast the bodies into holes in the earth——

"But out upon these green plains lie the churches of pilgrimage."

Master Gunnulf was silent for a while:

"Maybe that land seems so unspeakably desolate because the city lies in the midst of it, she that was queen over all the heathen world and was chosen to be the bride of Christ. For now the watchmen have forsaken the city, and in the whirl of feasting and riot the town seems like a forsaken spouse. Ribalds have set up their abode in the castle, where the husband is not at home, and they have lured the lady on to wanton with them in their lust and strife and bloodshed.* . . .

"But under the earth are treasures, dearer than all the treasures the sun shines upon. There are the graves of the holy martyrs, hewn out of the living rock beneath—and there are so many that a man grows dizzy but to think of it. When one calls to mind how many they are, the torture-witnesses that here have suffered death for the cause of

* See Note 10.

Christ, one might deem that each grain of dust that whirls up from the hoofs of the ribalds' horses must be holy and worthy of worship." . . .

The priest drew a thin chain out from under his clothing, and opened the little silver cross that hung from it. Within was something black that looked like tinder, and a little green bone.

"Once we had been down in these passages all the day, and we had said our prayers in caves and oratories, where the first disciples of St. Peter and St. Paul had met together to hold mass. Then the monks, who owned the church where we went down, gave us these holy relics. 'Tis a little piece of such a sponge as the holy maids used to wipe up the blood of the martyrs withal, that it might not be lost; and a knuckle of a finger-joint of a holy man whose name God alone knows. Then did we four promise one another that we would every day call upon this holy one whose honour is unknown to men, and we took this nameless martyr to witness that we should never forget how quite unworthy we were to be rewarded of God and honoured of men, and ever remember that naught in the world is worthy to be desired save only His mercy." . . .

Kristin kissed the cross reverently and gave it to Orm, who did the like. Then Gunnulf said suddenly:

"I will give you this holy relic, kinsman."

Orm knelt on one knee and kissed his uncle's hand. Gunnulf hung the cross around the youth's neck.

"Would you not be fain to see these places, Orm?"

The boy's face lighted up in a smile:

"Yes—and I know now that some day I shall come thither."

"Have you never had a mind to be a priest?" asked Gunnulf.

"Yes," answered the boy. "When father has cursed these weak arms of mine. But I know not if he would like that I should be a priest. And then there is that you wot of," he said softly.

"For your birth a dispensation could be had, I trow," said the priest quietly. "Maybe, Orm, some day we might journey southward together, you and I——"

"Tell us more, uncle," prayed Orm softly.

"Aye, that will I." Gunnulf clasped the arms of the chair with his hands and looked into the fire.

"While I wandered there, seeing naught else but memorials of the blood-witnesses, and remembered the unbearable torments they had endured for Jesu name's sake, there came upon me a sore temptation. I thought of how the Lord had hung nailed to the Cross those six hours. But His witnesses had been tormented with unutterable tortures for many days—women saw their children tortured to death before their eyes, young tender maids had their flesh torn from their bones with iron combs, young boys were driven on the claws of wild beasts and the horns of mad oxen. . . . Then seemed it to me as though many of these had borne more than Christ Himself. . . .

"I brooded over this till I thought that my heart and my brain must break in sunder. But at last the light I had begged and prayed for came to me. And I understood that as these had suffered, so ought we all to have strength to suffer. Who would be so foolish that he would not willingly endure pains and torment, when this was the path that led to a faithful and steadfast bridegroom, who waiteth with arms stretched out and breast bloody and burning with love?

"For He loved mankind. And therefore did He die, as the bridegroom who hath gone forth to save his bride from the hands of robbers. And they bind him and torment him unto death, while he sees his dearest love sit feasting with his slayers, jesting with them and mocking his torments and his faithful love——"

Gunnulf Nikulaussön buried his face in his hands:

"Then did I understand that this mighty love upholdeth all things in the world—even the fires of hell. For if God would, He could take the soul by force—we should be strengthless motes in His hand. But He loves us as the bridegroom loves his bride, who will not force her, but if she yield not to him willingly, must suffer that she flee him and shun him. But I have thought, too, that mayhap no soul can yet be lost to all eternity. For every soul must desire this love, methinks, but it seems so dear a purchase to give up all other delights for its sake. But when the fire hath burnt away all stiff-necked and rebellious will, then at last shall the will to God, were it no greater in a man than a single nail in a whole house, remain in the soul unconsumed, as the iron nail is left in the ashes of a house burned down——"

"Gunnulf"—Kristin half rose—"I am afraid——"

Gunnulf looked up, with white face and flaming eyes:

"I too was afraid. For I understood that this torment of God's love can have no end so long as man and maid are born upon this earth and He must be fearful that He may lose their souls—so long as He daily and hourly giveth His body and His blood on a thousand altars—and there are men who scorn the offering. . . .

"And I was afraid to think of myself, that unclean had served at His altar, said mass with unclean lips and lifted Him with unclean hands—and methought I was even as the man who had brought his beloved to a house of shame and betrayed her——"

He caught Kristin in his arms as she sank down, and he and Orm bore the swooning woman over to the bed.

In a little she opened her eyes—sat upright and covered her face with her hands. She burst into a wild, wailing weeping:

"I cannot, I cannot—Gunnulf, when you speak, I see that I can never——"

Gunnulf took her hand; but she turned her face away from the man's wild pale visage:

"Kristin, never can you content you with any lesser love than the love that is between God and the soul——

"Kristin, look about you—see what the world is. You who have borne two children—have you never thought on this: that every child that is born is baptised in blood, and that every human being born into this world draws in with his first breath the scent of blood? Think you not that you, who are a mother, should fix all your intent on this: that your sons fall not back to that first baptismal pact with the world, but hold fast to the other pact they made with God when made clean by the waters of the font——?"

She sobbed and sobbed.

"I am afraid of you," she said again. "Gunnulf, when you speak thus, I see well that never can I find my way onward to peace."

"God will find you," said the priest softly. "Be still, and fly not from Him who hath sought after you before you were conceived in your mother's womb."

He sat awhile there by the bedside. Then he asked quietly and calmly if he might wake Ingrid and ask the woman to come and help her to undress. Kristin shook her head.

Then he made the sign of the cross over her thrice, and, bidding Orm good-night, went into the closet where he slept.

Orm and Kristin drew off their clothes. The boy seemed sunk in fathomless thoughts. When Kristin had lain down, he came across to her. He looked at her grey-flecked face and asked if she would have him sit by her till she slept.

"Oh, aye—oh, no, Orm; you must be weary, you that are young. The night must be far spent——"

Orm stood yet a little while.

"Seems it not strange to you?" he said of a sudden; "father and my Uncle Gunnulf—unlike as they are to each other—yet they are like, too, after a fashion——"

Kristin lay a little, thinking:

"Aye, maybe so—they are unlike other men."

Soon after, she fell asleep and Orm went over to the other bed. He stripped and crept in. There was a linen sheet below, and linen covers on the pillows. The boy stretched himself out at ease on the smooth cool couch. His heart beat, thrilled with the thought of these new adventures whereto his uncle's words had shown the way. Prayers, fasts, all the observances he had practised because he had been taught

to—all grew new of a sudden—weapons in a goodly warfare that he
longed for. Maybe he would be a monk—or a priest—if he could win
dispensation for his birth in adultery.

Gunnulf's couch was a wooden bench with a sheet of skin spread over
a little straw, and a single small pillow—so that he was forced to lie
stretched straight out. The priest took off his frock, lay down in his
underclothes, and drew the thin coverlid of wadmal over him. The
little lighted wick, twined round an iron rod, he left burning.

His own words had left him crushed with unrest and fear. He was
faint with yearning for that time gone by—would he never again find
that bridal gladness of heart that had filled his whole being that spring
in Rome?

It was when he had come back to Norway that strong disquietude
took hold upon him.

There was so much to disquiet him. There were his riches. The great
inheritance from his fathers—and the rich benefice. There was the
path that he could see lying before him. His place in the Cathedral
chapter—he knew that it was meant for him. If he forsook not all his
possessions, to go into the cloister of the Preaching Friars, take the
vows, and bow himself under the rule—this was the life he desired—
with but half a heart.

——And then when he was old enough and hardened to the fight——
There were men in Norway's realm that lived and died in utter
heathendom, or led astray by the false doctrines that the Russians put
forth under the name of Christendom. The Lapps and the other half-
wild folks that he could never cease to think on—was it not as though
God had wakened in him this longing to fare forth to their land,
bringing the Word and the Light——?

——But he thrust the thought of this mission from him, on the plea
that he must obey the Archbishop. Lord Eiliv counselled him against
it. Lord Eiliv had hearkened to him and spoken with him, showing
him clearly that he spoke as to the son of his old friend, Sir Nikulaus
of Husaby: "But you can never keep you within measure, you that
come of the line of old Skogheim-Gaute's daughters, whether 'tis good
or ill you have set your heart upon." The Lapp-folks' salvation he
had much at heart himself, he said—but they had no need of a teacher
that wrote and spoke Latin as well as his mother-tongue, and was
learned in the Law no less than in Arithmetica and Algorismus. Sure
it was that he had been given learning that he might use it. "And to
my mind 'tis uncertain whether you have been granted the gift of
speaking to the poor and simple peoples up north."

Ah, but in that sweet spring his learning had seemed to him no more to be held in reverence than the learning every little maid gets from her mother—to spin and brew and bake and milk—the teaching every child needs that it may do its work in the world.

Gunnulf stood up. On one end-wall of the closet hung a great crucifix, and in front of it was a great flat stone upon the floor.

He knelt down upon the stone and stretched his arms out sidewise. He had used his body to endure this posture, so that he could kneel thus by the hour, still as stone. With eyes fastened on the crucifix he awaited the comfort that came to him when he could lose himself wholly in contemplation of the Cross.

But the first thought that came into his mind now was this: had he the will to part with this crucifix? St. Franciscus and his brethren had crosses that they joined together themselves out of branches of trees. He should give away this fair Rood—to the church at Husaby he might give it. Peasants, children and women that came thither to mass—they might well be strengthened by feeding their eyes with such a visible picture of the Saviour's lovely mildness in His Passion. Simple souls like Kristin—— For himself it should not be needful.

Night after night he had knelt with close-shut senses and limbs benumbed, till he saw the vision. The hill with the three crosses against the sky. Yonder cross in the midst, which was destined to bear the Lord of earth and heaven, trembled and shook, it bent like a tree before the storm, affrighted that it should bear that all too precious burden, the sacrifice for the sins of all the world. The Lord of the Tents of Storm held it in, as the knight curbs his charger, the Chief of the Castle of Heaven it bore to battle. Then was made manifest the wonder that was the key to deeper and ever deeper wonders. The blood that ran down the Cross for the remission of all sins and the boot of all sorrows, that was the visible miracle. By this first wonder the soul's eye could be opened to behold the yet darker mysteries—God that descended unto earth, and became the Son of a Virgin and Brother to mankind, that harried hell, and stormed with his booty of souls set free up to the blinding sea of light, wherefrom the world hath issued and whereby the world is upholden. And towards those bottomless and eternal deeps of light his thoughts were drawn up, and there they passed into the light and vanished, as a flight of birds passes away into the glory of the evening sky.

Gunnulf did not move until the church-bell rang for matins. All was still when he passed through the hall—they slept, Kristin and Orm.

Out in the pitch-dark yard the priest tarried a little. But none of his house-folk came to go with him into the church. He required not that they should go to worship more than twice in the day's round; but Ingrid, his foster-mother, well-nigh always bore him company to matins. This morning it seemed she, too, slept. Aye, she had been late up the night before——

All that day the three kinsfolk spoke but little together, and of naught but small matters. Gunnulf looked weary, but he talked jestingly of this and that. "Foolish were we yester-evening—we sat there as sorrowful as three fatherless children," he said once; and told of some of the many merry little haps that befell here in Nidaros—with the pilgrims and such folk—which the priests jested over among themselves. An old man from Herjedal had had errands here for all the folks of his parish, and got the prayers all mingled together—things would have looked but ill in the parish, it came into his head after, if St. Olav had taken him at his word!

Late in the evening Erlend came in, dripping wet—he had sailed in to the city and it was blowing hard again. He was raging, and fell upon Orm at once with furious words. Gunnulf listened awhile in silence; then:

"When you speak so to Orm, Erlend, you are like our father—as he used to be when he spoke to you——"

Erlend went silent at once. Then he flung round:

"Well I wot, so witlessly did I never bear myself when I was a boy— make off from the manor, a sick woman and a whelp of a boy, in a snowstorm! Else 'tis not much to brag of, Orm's manfulness, but you see that at least he fears not his father!"

"You feared not your father either," said his brother, smiling.

Orm stood up before his father, saying naught and striving to seem careless.

"Aye, you can go," said Erlend. And then: "I am nigh sick of the whole affair at Husaby. But one thing I know—this summer shall Orm fare with me northward—then I trow we will lick this pet lamb of Kristin's into shape.—He is not a bungler, either," he went on eagerly to his brother. "He shoots with a sure aim—and a coward he is not— but ever is he cross-grained and mopish, and 'tis as though he had no marrow to his bones——"

"Nay, if you berate your son often as you did but now, 'tis no marvel if he mope," said the priest.

Erlend changed his tone, laughing as he said:

"For that matter, I had often to suffer worse things from father—and God knows that I moped not much for that. But let that be—now I am come hither, let us even be merry for Yule, since Yule it is. Where is Kristin?—What was it she had to speak of to you now, again?"

"I believe not that she had aught to speak of with me," said the priest. "She had set her heart on hearing mass here at Yule."

"She might well make shift with those she hears at home, methinks," said Erlend. "But 'tis pity of her—as things are going, all youth is being worn away from her." He struck one hand against the other. "I see not how the Lord can think we have need of a new son every year——"

Gunnulf looked up at his brother:

"What——! Nay, I know not what our Lord may deem that you two need. But what Kristin needs most, I trow, is that you be kind to her now——"

"Aye, like enough she does," said Erlend in a low voice.

The next morning Erlend went to the day-mass with his wife. They were bound for St. Gregory's Church—Erlend heard mass there always when he was in the city. The two walked alone; and down the street, where the snow lay swept up into drifts, heavy and wet, Erlend led his wife by the hand fairly and courteously. He had not said a word to her of her flight from home, and he had been friendly to Orm after the first storm.

Kristin walked quiet and pale, with head a little bent; the long black fur cloak with the silver clasps seemed to weigh down her slight thin body.

"Would you that I should ride with you homeward—and let Orm sail with the boat?" said the man, to say somewhat. "Maybe you would scarce care to cross the fjord?"

"No—you know that I like not to go on boats——"

It was calm now, and the weather mild—every moment a load of heavy, wet snow would fall from the trees. The skies hung low and dark-grey above the white town. There was a greenish-grey watery tinge on the snow, and the houses' timber walls and the fences and tree-trunks showed black in the damp air. Never, Kristin thought, had she seen the world look so cold and wan and faded. . . .

III

K R I S T I N sat with Gaute on her lap, gazing from the little hill north of the manor. The evening was so fair. The lake lay below her bright and still, mirroring the hills and the farms of By, and the golden clouds in the sky. It had rained earlier in the day, and the smell of leaves and earth rose strongly up. The grass on the meadows below must be knee-deep already, and the fields were hidden with the spears of corn.

Sounds came from far to-night. Now the pipes and drums and fiddles struck up again, down on the green at Vinjar—up here the sounds came so sweetly to the ear.

The cuckoo would fall into long spells of silence, and then send forth its call once and again from far off in the southern woods. And in all the groves round about the manor the birds whistled and sang—but in scattered notes and softly, for the sun was still high.

The home cattle came tinkling and lowing out of the pasture above the courtyard gate.

"See, see—my Gaute will get his milk soon," she babbled to the child, lifting him up. The boy, as was his wont, laid his heavy head down on his mother's shoulder. Now and then he clung closer to her—and Kristin took it for a sign that he *did* take in somewhat of her petting and her prattle.

She walked down to the houses. Before the door of the hall, Naakkve and Björgulf were running about, and trying to coax back the cat, which had fled from them up on to the roof. But in a moment they set to work again with the broken dagger they owned in common, digging deeper the hole they had made in the earthen floor of the outer room.

Dagrun came into the hall with goat's milk in a wooden pail, and the mistress gave Gaute ladleful after ladleful of the warm drink. The boy grunted angrily when the serving-woman spoke to him, and struck out at her and hid himself against his mother's breast when the woman would have taken hold of him.

"Yet methinks he comes on better," said the byre-woman.

Kristin lifted the little face in her hand—it was yellow-white like tallow, and the eyes were always weary. Gaute had a great, heavy head and thin, strengthless limbs. He would be two years old a week after Lawrence Mass, but as yet he could not set foot to ground, and he had but five teeth and could not speak a word.

Sira Eiliv said 'twas not rickets; for neither the alb nor the altar-books had availed. High and low, wherever he came, the priest sought for some remedy for this sickness that was come upon Gaute. She knew he remembered the child in all his prayers. But to her he could but say that she must bow in patience before the will of God. And she must give him plenty of warm goat's milk to drink. . . .

Poor, poor little boy of hers! Kristin hugged and kissed him when the woman was gone. So fair, so fair he was! She thought she saw he favoured her father's kindred—his eyes were dark grey and his hair flaxen white, thick, and soft as silk.

Now he began to whimper again. Kristin got up and walked about the room with him. Little and thin as he was, he grew heavy after a while—but Gaute would be content nowhere but in his mother's arms. So she bore him up and down the murky hall, crooning to him as she walked.

Someone rode into the courtyard, and Ulf Haldorssön's voice echoed loudly from the house-walls. Kristin came out to the doorway of the outer room, with the child in her arms.

"You must unsaddle your own horse to-night, Ulf, I fear—they are at the dancing—all the men. Shame it is you should be troubled, but you must forgive it——"

Ulf muttered testily as he unsaddled his horse. Naakkve and Björgulf pressed about him the while, and begged for a ride on the horse up to the garden-close.

"Nay, you must bide here with Gaute, my Naakkve—play with your brother and let him not cry while I am away in the kitchen——"

The boy looked glum. But in a moment he was down on all-fours, butting and lowing at the little one, whom Kristin had set down on a cushion at the door. The mother bent down and stroked Naakkve's hair. He was so good to his little brothers.

When Kristin came back to the hall bearing the great platter on her arms, Ulf Haldorssön sat on the bench playing with the children. Gaute was happy with Ulf, if his mother were but out of sight—but now he whimpered at once and reached out after her. Kristin set down the platter and took Gaute in her arms.

Ulf blew the froth off the newly-drawn ale, drank, and began eating from the small dishes on the platter.

"Are they out, all your maids, to-night?"

Kristin said:

"There are both fiddles and drums, and pipes too—a troupe of glee-men—come over from Orkdal from the bridal there. You may well believe, when they heard of it—they are but young girls after all——"

"You let them gad and frisk about their fill, Kristin. A man might think you were afraid 'twould be hard to find a wet-nurse here this autumn——"

Without thinking, Kristin smoothed her kirtle down over her slender waist. She had flushed darkly red at the man's words. Ulf laughed short and harshly:

"But if you will go about ever dragging Gaute with you, 'twill go with you as it went last year, I trow. . . . Come hither to your foster-father, boy, and you shall eat out of one dish with me." . . .

Kristin made no answer. She set her three small sons in a row on the bench by the other wall, and fetched a bowl of milk-porridge, and, for herself, a little stool. There she sat and fed them, though Naakkve and

Björgulf grumbled—they would have had spoons to eat with themselves. One was four years old now, and the other nigh three.

"Where is Erlend?" asked Ulf.

"Margret had a mind to go to the dancing, so he went with her."

"'Tis well at least he hath wit enough to watch his own maid," said Ulf.

Again the wife said nothing. She undressed the children and put them to bed, Gaute in the cradle and the two others in her own bed. Erlend had resigned himself to have them there, since she had grown well of her great sickness the year before.

When Ulf was done, he stretched himself out on the bench. Kristin dragged the block-chair over to the cradle, fetched a basket of woollen yarns, and began winding balls of wool for her weaving, while she gently and softly rocked the cradle with her foot.

"Will you not go to rest?" she asked once without turning her head. "You must be weary, Ulf?"

The man rose, put some fuel on the fire, and came across to his mistress. He sat down on the bench over against her. Kristin saw he was not so worn out with hard living as he was wont to be when he had been some days in Nidaros.

"You ask not even what the tidings are from the city, Kristin," he said, leaning forward, elbows on knees, and gazing on her.

Her heart began to beat with fear—she understood from the man's looks and bearing that there must again be tidings that were not good. But she answered with a calm and gentle smile:

"You must tell me, Ulf; have you heard aught?"

"Oh, aye——" But first he brought his wallet and took out from it the things he had fetched for her from the town. Kristin thanked him.

"I see you have heard news in the city?" she asked a little after.

Ulf looked at his young mistress—then he turned his eyes to the pale child, asleep in the cradle.

"Does he always sweat so much in the head?" he asked, low, touching the hair gently where it was dark with damp. "Kristin, when you were wed to Erlend—the letter that was drawn out concerning the settlement of your goods—stood it not so that you should deal yourself at your will with the lands of his extra-gift and your morning-gift?"

Kristin's heart beat harder, but she spoke calmly:

"Aye, and so it is, Ulf, that Erlend has ever asked my counsel and sought my consent in all dealings with these lands. Speak you of the parcels of farms in Verdalen that he has sold to Vigleik of Lyng?"

"Aye," said Ulf. "Now has he bought Hugrekken* from Vigleik, so he will keep up two ships now, it seems. . . . And what are you to have, Kristin? "

"Erlend's part of Skjervastad, half a hide† in Ulfkelstad, and what he owns of Aarhammar," said she. "You sure did not believe that Erland had sold those lands without my will and without making good their worth to me?"

"Hm." Ulf sat silent a little. "Yet will your incomings be less, Kristin. Skjervastad—'twas there Erlend got hay last winter and released the rent to the farmer for three years——"

"'Twas not Erlend's fault that we got no dry hay last year—I know, Ulf, you did all you could—but with all the misery there was here last summer——"

"Of Aarhammar he sold more than half to the Sisters of Rein convent, that time when he made ready to flee the land with you"—Ulf laughed a little—"or pledged it—'tis the same thing with Erlend. Free from the King's levy—the whole of that is on Audun's shoulders, who holds the farm that now is to be called yours!"

"Can he not rent the land that is come under the convent?" asked Kristin.

"The Sisters' tenant on the neighbour farm hath rented it," said Ulf. "'Tis a hard and an unsure task for tenants to make ends meet when the farms are split up as Erlend is busy doing."

Kristin was silent. She knew well enough it was true.

"'Tis ever quick work with Erlend," spoke out Ulf again. "His goods wane as swiftly as his household waxes."

As the woman made no answer, he spoke again:

"You will soon have many children, Kristin Lavransdatter."

"Yet none that I can spare," she answered in a voice that shook a little.

"Be not so afraid for Gaute—he will grow strong, I warrant him," said Ulf, in a low voice.

"It must be as God will—but 'tis long waiting."

He heard the hidden suffering in the mother's voice—a strange look of helplessness seemed to come upon the dark, heavy man.

"It avails so little, Kristin—much have you brought to pass here at Husaby, but if Erlend is to take the sea again with two ships——I believe not overmuch in peace coming in the north, and your husband is so little crafty that he knows not how to turn to his profit what he has won in these two years. Ill years have they been—and all through them you have been a sick woman. Should things go on in this wise, 'twill break your courage at last, young wife that you are. I have helped you

* Hugrekken = *The Valiant*.   † See Note 11.

all I could on the manor here—but this other thing—Erlend's un-wisdom——"

"Aye," she broke in, "that God knows you have—you have been the staunchest kinsman to us, friend Ulf, and never can I thank you enough or repay you——"

Ulf stood up, lit a candle at the hearth, set it on the taper-holder on the table, and stood there with his back turned to his mistress. Kristin had let her hands sink into her lap—now she began again winding wool and rocking the cradle.

"Can you not send word home to your folks," asked Ulf softly, "so that Lavrans might come up too this autumn when your mother comes to you?"

" I had not meant to trouble my mother this autumn. She begins to grow old—and it befalls so often that I must lie in the straw that I can scarce ask her to come to me every time——" She forced a smile.

"But do it this time," answered Ulf. "And pray your father to bear her company—so that you may ask his counsel in these matters——"

"In this matter I will not ask my father's counsel," she said quietly and firmly.

"But Gunnulf, then?" asked Ulf in a little. "Can you not speak with him?"

"'Twould not be seemly to trouble him with such things now," said Kristin as before.

"Mean you because he has withdrawn him into a cloister?" Ulf laughed mockingly. "Never did I mark that monks knew less of guiding goods and gear than other folks.

"If so be you will not take counsel of any, Kristin, then must you speak yourself with Erlend," he said, when she made no answer. "Think on your sons, Kristin!"

Kristin sat long in silence.

"You that are so good to our children, Ulf," she said at last, "me-thinks 'twere liker you should wed and have your own folk to care for than that you should go on here—plaguing yourself with Erlend's—and my—troubles."

Ulf turned towards the woman. He stood with his hands grasping the table-edge behind him and looked at Kristin Lavransdatter. Still was she as straight and slim and fair as ever, as she sat there. Her dress was of dark home-dyed woollen stuff, but the linen coif that lay around her still, pale face was fine and soft. The belt from which hung her bunch of keys was set with little silver roses. On her breast glittered two chains bearing crosses; the great one with gilded links hung down well-nigh to her waist—'twas it she had had of her father. Above lay the thin silver chain with the little cross that Orm had prayed them to give to his stepmother and say that she should wear it always.

As yet she had arisen from each child-bearing fair as ever—only a little stiller, with the weight on her young shoulders a little heavier. A little thinner in the cheeks, the eyes a little darker and more sad under the broad white forehead, the mouth a little less full and red. But 'twas like her comeliness would be worn away ere she was many years older, if things went on as they were going. . . .

"Think you not, Ulf, it were happier for you if you settled down on your own farm?" she went on again. "You have bought twenty marks' worth more of Skjoldvirkstad land, Erlend said—you own nigh half the farm now. And Isak has but the one child—Aase is both comely and kindly, and a notable woman—and she seems to like you——"

"Yet will I not have her, if I must marry her," the man said gruffly, with a harsh laugh. "And Aase Isaksdatter is too good for——" His voice changed. "I never knew other father than a foster-father, Kristin—and I trow 'tis my lot that I shall have no children either but foster-children."

"Nay, I will pray Mary Virgin that you may have better fortune, kinsman."

"I am not so young, either. Five-and-thirty winters, Kristin," he laughed. "There wants not much but that I might be your father——"

"Nay, but then must you have sinned full early," answered Kristin, striving to speak lightly and laughingly.

"Would you not go to bed now?" asked Ulf soon after.

"Yes, in a little—but *you* must be weary, Ulf—you should go to rest." The man bade her good-night quietly and went out.

Kristin took the candle from the board, and looked in by its light at the two boys sleeping in the box-bed. There was no matter on Björgulf's eyelashes—God be thanked for that. There had been fair weather for a while past. As soon as the wind came a little keen, or the weather was so rough that the children must play within by the hearth-fire, his eyes grew sore. She stood long looking at the two. Then she bent over Gaute in the cradle.

They had been as fresh and healthy as little birds, all her three young sons—until the sickness came to the country-side last summer. Folk called it the scarlet fever—it carried off children from the homes all around the fjord, so that 'twas a piteous thing to see or hear tell of. She had been granted grace to keep all hers—all her own. . . .

For five days and nights had she sat by the southern bed, where they lay, all three, with red spots over all their skin, and sick eyes that shunned the light—the little bodies fiery-hot. She sat with her hand under the coverlid patting the soles of Björgulf's feet, and sang and sang, till her slender voice was sunken to a hoarse whisper :

> Shoe, shoe, guardsman's steed—
> How can we shoe him best at need?
> Iron shoes are fitting for the guardsman's steed.

> Shoe, shoe, Earlie's steed—
> How can we shoe him best at need?
> Silver shoes are fitting for the Earlie's steed.

> Shoe, shoe, King's own steed—
> How can we shoe him best at need?
> Gold shoes are fitting for the King's own steed.

Björgulf was the least sick and the most restless. If she stopped singing but a moment, he would cast the coverlid off him at once. Gaute was only ten months old—he was so deathly sick, she deemed he could not live. He lay at her breast, wrapped in rugs and furs, and had no strength to suck. She held him in one arm and patted Björgulf's foot-soles with the other hand.

From time to time, when it chanced that all three slept for a little space, she would lay herself down on the front of the bed beside them, fully clothed. Erlend came and went, looking helplessly at his three sons. He tried to sing for them, but they cared naught for their father's mellow voice—'twas their mother they would have sing, though she had no singing-voice.

The serving-women hovered round and would have had their mistress spare herself; the men came and asked tidings; Orm tried to make sport for his little brothers. Margret Erland they sent away to Österdal, by Kristin's counsel ; but Orm was set upon staying—besides, he was grown up now. Sira Eiliv sat by the children's bed when he was not out visiting his sick. Much toil and sorrow stripped the priest of all the fat he had laid on at Husaby—it went hard with him to see so many fair young children die. And some grown folks died too.

The sixth evening all the children were so much better that Kristin promised her husband that to-night she would take her clothes off and go to bed—Erlend proffered to watch along with the maids and call her if there were need. But at the supper-board she saw that Orm's face was a fiery red—and his eyes shining with fever. He said 'twas nothing—but suddenly he started from the table and out. When Erlend and Kristin followed, they found him vomiting in the courtyard.

Erlend threw his arms about him :

" Orm—my son—are you sick——?"

"My head is aching so," moaned the boy, and let it sink heavily on his father's shoulder.

And so that night they sat watching Orm. For the most part he lay muttering in brain-sickness—he would shriek aloud and fight the air with his long arms—it seemed as though he had ugly visions. What he said they could not understand.

And in the morning Kristin broke down. It proved that she had been with child again; now she miscarried, and afterward she lay sunk in a drowse, as though half dead, and then fell into a high fever. Orm had lain in his grave more than two weeks before she knew of her stepson's death.

She was so weak then that she scarce had strength to feel sorrow. She was so bloodless and faint that naught could come home to her keenly —it seemed to her that it was well with her now, as she lay there but half alive. There had been a dreadful time, when the women hardly dared touch her or do what was needed for cleanliness—but it all seemed part of her fevered wanderings. Now it was good to lie and be tended. Round her bed hung so many sweet-scented wreaths of mountain flowers to keep the flies away—folk had sent them down from the sæters, and they smelt so sweet, most of all when there was rain in the air. Erlend brought their children in to her one day—she saw that they were wasted by the sickness, and that Gaute knew her not again, but even that did not hurt her yet. She only felt that Erlend seemed ever to be by her.

He went to mass every day, and he knelt long praying by Orm's grave. The churchyard was by the parish church at Vinjar, but some of the little children of the house had been given burial in the chapel of ease at Husaby—Erlend's two brothers and a little daughter of Munan Bishopssön. Kristin had often felt pity for these little ones, lying all alone under the stone flags. Now had Orm Erlendssön found his last resting-place amongst these children.

It was while the others still feared for Kristin's life that the companies of beggars, which made into Nidaros as Olav's Wake drew nigh, came through the parish. 'Twas mostly the same mumpers, men and women, that came thither each year—the pilgrims were always open-handed to them, for it was held that the intercession of the poor availed much. And they had grown used to come round through Skaun in these years of Kristin's rule at Husaby, for they knew that there they would be given lodging for the night, food in plenty, and alms before they passed on their way. This time the serving-folk would have turned them away, since the mistress lay sick. But when Erlend, who had been away in the north the last two summers, heard that his wife had been wont to deal so lovingly with the beggars, he bade that they should be given lodging and entertainment even as they had had them of her. And in the morning he went himself among the beggars, helped to pour their liquor and bear round food for them, and gave them the almspennies himself, while he meekly begged them for their prayers for his wife. Many of the beggars wept when they heard that the gentle young woman lay at death's door.

Sira Eiliv had told her all this when she grew better. It was not till nigh on Yule-tide that she was strong enough to take up her keys again herself.

Erlend had sent word to her parents as soon as she fell sick, but then they were gone south to the wedding at Skog. Later they came to Husaby; she was better then, but so weary she was not fit to talk much with them. She was best pleased to have none but Erlend by her bedside.

Weak and chilly and bloodless, she crept for shelter into his health and strength. The old fire in her blood was gone, so utterly gone that she could not call to mind any more what it was like to love in such wise; but with it was gone the unrest and bitterness of the last years. It seemed to her that she was happy now—even though grief for Orm lay heavy on them both, and though Erlend knew not how afraid she was for little Gaute, yet was she happy with him now. She had understood how sorely he had feared to lose her. . . .

'Twas a nice and a hard matter, then, to have to speak to him now—to touch on things that might break the peace and the content that were between them.

She stood without before the door of the hall in the shining summer night when the house-folk came back from the dancing. Margret hung on her father's arm. She was clad and adorned more fittingly for a bridal feast than for a dance on the church-green, where all kind of folk come together. But the stepmother had quite given over making or meddling in the maid's upbringing. Erlend must guide his own daughter as he would.

They were thirsty, Erlend and Margret, and Kristin went to fetch ale for them. The girl sat awhile prattling—she and her stepmother were good friends, now that Kristin no longer tried to teach her. Erlend laughed at all his daughter's chatter of the dancing. But at last Margret and her maid went up to their loft to go to rest.

The man went on wandering up and down the hall—stretched himself and yawned, but said he was not weary. He ran his fingers through his long black hair:

"There was not time for it, when we came from the bath-house—because of this dancing—I trow you must set to and cut my hair, Kristin—I cannot go about in this wise in the holy-days——"

Kristin made answer that it was dark—but Erlend laughed and pointed up at the smoke-vent—'twas daylight again already. So she lit the candle again, bade him sit down, and spread a cloth over his shoulders. While she clipped, he shifted about ticklishly, and laughed when the scissors came near his neck.

She gathered the shorn hair carefully together and burnt it in the hearth-fire, and shook the cloth, too, over the fire. Then she combed Erlend's hair down smooth from the crown, and snipped with the scissors here and there where the edge was not quite even.

Erlend caught her hands as she stood behind him, held them together round his throat, and looked up at her with smiling face thrown backward.

"You are tired," he said then, letting go her hands and rising with a little sigh.

Erlend sailed to Björgvin when midsummer was but just past. He complained much because this time again his wife was unfit to bear him company—she smiled wearily; howsoever things had been, she said, she had not been able to leave Gaute.

Thus it came that Kristin was alone at Husaby again this summer. At least it was well that this year she looked not that the child should come till Matthews Mass;* 'twas doubly hard for both herself and for the ladies who came to tend her when it came at the busy harvest season.

She wondered whether things would go on thus ever. Times were not now as they had been when she was a girl. The Danish war she had heard her father tell of, and she remembered when he was from home on the war against Duke Eirik. 'Twas from that he had brought back the great scars on his body. But, all the same, at home in the Dales they seemed, as it were, so far from war—thither it would come nevermore— so, she felt, did all men think. Most of her memories were of peace, of her father dwelling at home, guiding his possessions, caring and taking thought for all of them.

Now all the time there was unrest—all men spoke of contention and warlike levies and the government of the realm. In Kristin's mind it all went together with the picture of the sea and the coast, as she had seen them that single time when first she came hither to the north. Along the coast they came sailing, men that had their heads full of counsels and plans and counter-plans and deliberations, spiritual lords and laymen. Among these did Erlend belong, by his high birth and his riches. But she felt that he stood but half within their circle.

She pondered much on why it was that he stood thus, half without. What were his fellows' real thoughts of him?

When he was but the man she loved, she had never asked such questions. She had seen, indeed, that he was sudden and vehement, un-

* 21st September.

thinking and ever apt to bear him unwisely. But then she had found excuses for all—had never troubled to think what his humour might bring down upon them both. When once they two had got leave to wed, all would be changed—so she had comforted herself. Sometimes she dimly felt that 'twas not till the hour when she knew they two had given life to a child that she had begun to think—what manner of man was Erlend, he whom folk called light-minded and unwise, a man in whom none could trust. . . .

She had trusted in him. She remembered Brynhild's loft; she remembered how the bond between him and that other had been cut asunder in the end. She remembered his dealings, after she was his lawfully betrothed bride. But he had held fast to her in despite of all rebuffs and abasements; and she had seen that, now too, he would not lose her for all the gold on earth. . . .

She could not but think of Haftor of Godöy. Ever, when they had met, he had been dangling about her with toying gallantry; but she had never troubled her for this. She deemed it was but his fashion of jesting. She could scarce believe aught else even now; she had liked the comely gamesome young man—aye, she liked him still. But that anyone could deem such things to be but a jest—no, that she could not understand.

She had met Haftor Graut again at the royal banquets at Nidaros, and he hung about her there too, after his wont. One evening he got her to go with him into a loft-room, and she lay down with him on a made-up bed that was there. At home in the Dales she could never have thought of doing aught of the kind—there 'twas no custom at the feasts for men and women to steal aside, thus alone, two and two together. But here all were used to it, and it seemed not that any found it unseemly—'twas said it was a fashion of the knights and ladies in foreign lands. When first they came in, Lady Elin, Sir Erling's wife, lay on the other bed with a Swedish knight; she would hear that they were talking of the King's ear-ache—— The Swede looked pleased when Lady Elin made a motion to get up and go back to the hall.

When she understood that Haftor meant in sober sadness what he prayed her for as they lay there talking, she had been so amazed that she seemed unable to be either afraid or greatly angered. Were they not, both of them, wedded, and had not both children by their wedded spouses? She felt she never could have fully believed before that such things happened. Even after all she herself had done and gone through —no; this she must have believed could not befall. Laughing and gay and coaxing had Haftor been with her—she could not bring herself to say he had tried to lure her astray; for that he had not been earnest enough. And yet it seemed he would have had her do the deadliest sin. . . .

He stepped down from the bed the moment she bade him begone—he had grown meek enough, but he seemed more amazed than beshamed. And he asked in sheer unbelief—did she truly dream that married folk were never unfaithful——? Sure, she must know that few men could swear they had kept no paramours. Women, maybe, were somewhat better, but truly——

"Believed you then, too, when you were a young maid, all the priests preach of sin and suchlike?" he asked. "But then I understand not, Kristin Lavransdatter, how it could come to pass that Erlend had his will with you."

He had looked up into her face—and her eyes must have spoken, though not for much gold would she have talked with Haftor of this. For 'twas in a high singing voice of wonderment that he said:

"The like of this I had deemed was but a thing they told of—in songs and ballads——"

She had told no one of this; not even Erlend. He liked Haftor well. And truly it was fearful that there could be any folk as light-minded as Haftor Graut—but 'twas as though she could not feel that it touched her at all. Nor had he ever tried to be too free with her since—he but sat and stared when they met, his sea-blue eyes wide with wonderment.

No, if Erlend were light-minded, at least it was not in that way. And, she thought, *was* he so unwise? She saw that folk startled at things he said, and afterward laid their heads together over them. There was often much right and reason in what Erlend Nikulaussön put forth. 'Twas but that he never saw what the other great folk never lost from sight—the cautious heedfulness with which they kept watch on each other. Trickery, Erlend called it, and laughed his reckless laugh, which nettled folks somewhat but disarmed them in the long run. They then, too, would laugh, and slap him on the shoulder, saying he might be sharp-witted enough, but short-witted he was for sure.

Then would he undo the work of his own words with wanton and malapert jesting. And folk would suffer much of that from Erlend. Dimly his wife felt—and was humbled by the feeling—why all men bore with his flippant tongue. Erlend would flinch and give way the moment he met a man who stood firmly by his own judgment—even if, to Erlend, that judgment seemed folly, he would yet give up his own, whatever the matter might be, but would cover his retreat with fleering talk about the man. And folk were well content to know that Erlend had this timorousness of mind—reckless as he was of his own welfare, hungry for adventure, desperately in love with every peril that could be met by force of arms. After all, they felt, they need not be too much disquieted by Erlend Nikulaussön.

The year before, when the winter was well-nigh gone, the High Steward had been in Nidaros, and he had brought the little King with him. Kristin had been in the city for the great banquet in the palace. Still and stately she had sat in her silken coif, bearing her red bridal dress with all her richest adornments, amidst the most high-born ladies of the court. With watchful eyes she had followed her husband's doings among the men, watched and listened and pondered—even as she watched and listened and pondered wherever she went with Erlend, or whenever she marked that folk spoke of him.

One thing and another she had understood. Sir Erling Vidkunssön was willing to stake all on upholding the rule of Norway northward toward the Icy Sea, on guarding and securing Haalogaland. But the Council and the Knighthood were against him, and were loath to agree to any undertaking great enough to serve this purpose. The Archbishop himself and the priesthood of thé archdiocese were not unwilling to stand by him with money help—this she knew from Gunnulf—but else all churchmen throughout the land were set against him, even though 'twas a war against God's enemies, heretics and heathens. And the great laymen worked against the High Steward, here in Trondheim at least. They had grown used to paying small regard to the words of the law-books and the rights of the Crown, and it liked them but little that Sir Erling stood so sharply in these matters for the spirit of his kinsman, King Haakon of happy memory. But it was not on this account that Erlend would not let himself be used, as she now understood the High Steward had meant to use her husband. With Erlend it was but that the other's grave and stately bearing wearied him—and he avenged himself by scoffing a little at his powerful kinsman.

Kristin thought she understood Erlend's footing with Sir Erling now. One thing was that the knight had had a sort of kindness for Erlend from their youth up; and then he had doubtless thought that, could he win over the high-born and valiant master of Husaby, who had gained some skill too in the craft of war from his service with Count Jacob—who at least knew more of war than most of his fellows, that had done naught but sit at home—he might thereby serve both his own plans and Erlend's welfare. But it had not fallen out as he planned.

Two summers had Erlend kept the sea till late autumn, wallowing in the seas that wash the long northern coast, and hunting the robbers' barks with the four small ships that followed his banner. He had come in for fresh meat to a new Norse settlement far north in Tana, just as the Karelians were hard at work plundering it—and, with the handful of men he had with him ashore, he had caught eighteen of the robbers and hung them to the roof-tree of the half-burnt barn. He had cut to pieces a band of Russians that was flying to the hills, and had burnt some enemy ships amid the outer skerries and destroyed their crews. The fame of his swiftness and daring had spread wide in the north; his Trönder and men of Möre loved their leader for his hardihood's sake and for his will to share all toil and all hardness with his men. He made friends both among the small folk and among the young sons of the great manors north in Haalogaland, where before the people had well-nigh grown used to thinking they must guard their coasts unaided.

Yet could not Erlend be of service to the High Steward in his plans for a great northern crusade. True, the folk of Trondheim bragged of his deeds against the Russians—if the talk turned on them, they let no one forget he was of their country-side. Aye, 'twas proven clearly enough that there was plenty of the good old mettle in the young fellows round about the fjord here. But what Erlend of Husaby said and what he did were not things that counted with full-grown and prudent men.

She saw that Erlend was still reckoned as one of the young men— though he was a year older than the High Steward. She understood that it suited many folk well that such he should be held to be, so that his words and his deeds could be belittled as being but the deeds and counsels of a hot-headed young man. Thus was he liked, spoiled and bragged of—but not accounted as a man come to man's estate. And she saw how willing he seemed to fall in with this and be what his fellows would have him be.

He spoke up for the Russian war; he spoke of the Swedes who owned half our King, and yet would not reckon the Norse gentry and knights as nobles, the equals of their own. Or had the like ever been heard of in any land, he asked, as long as the world had stood, that anyone had craved war-levies from noblemen in other wise than that they should ride their own horses and bear their own shields to the field?—Kristin knew that this was much what her father had said at the Thing in Vaage some years back, and he had pressed it on Erlend when his son-in-law had been loath to part company with Munan Baardssön and his counsels. No, said Erlend now—and he named his father-in-law's powerful kinsmen in Sweden—he knew well enough what account these Swedish gentry made of us. If we show not what we can do, we shall soon be fit but to be reckoned as pensioners of the Swedes. . . .

Aye, folk would say, there was somewhat in all this. But then they would talk again of the High Steward. Sir Erling had his own pot to boil in the north there; the Karelians had burned Bjarkö over his steward's head one year, and harried his farmers. And then Erlend changed his note and grew merry over the knight: Erling Vidkunssön thought not on his own concerns, of that he was sure. He was so noble and fine and stately a knight—no more worshipful man could they have found to be the corner-stone of their affairs. By God's Cross, Erling was as worshipful and as venerable as the bravest golden capital letter in the Book of the Laws. Folk laughed, and bore in mind not so much Erlend's praise of the High Steward's honour as that he had likened him to a gilded letter in a book.

No, they took not Erlend in earnest—not even now, when he was honoured after a fashion. But in those days when, young and headstrong and desperate, he had lived in whoredom with a woman, and would not put her away in despite of King's command and Church's ban—then they had taken him sadly enough, turning their backs on him in furious wrath over his godless and shameless life. Now was all this forgotten and forgiven—and Kristin understood that there was something of thankfulness for this in her husband's willingness to yield, and be what folk would have him to be—he had suffered bitterly, she knew, in the days when he lived an outcast from among his fellows here in his home.

There was but one thing—she must needs think of her father when he forgave some good-for-naught his rent or his debt—with the slightest shrug of his shoulders. 'Twas our Christian duty to bear with them that could not play a man's part. Was it thus that Erlend had gained forgiveness for his sins of youth——?

But Erlend *had* paid for those deeds of his when he lived with Eline. He had answered for his sin till the day when he had met *her* and she had followed him, nothing loath, into new sins. Was it she, then, who——?

No. She grew afraid now of her own thoughts.

And she tried to shut out from her mind all care for things wherein she could take no hand. She would only think of those matters in which she could do some good by her carefulness. All the rest she must leave in God's hand. God had helped her in all things wherein her own toil and pains could avail. The home-farm at Husaby had now been worked up again into a good farm as of yore—in despite of the bad years. Three healthy comely sons had He vouchsafed her to bear—every year had He granted her life anew when she must face death in child-bearing; He had let her arise in full health after each childbed. All her sweet little ones had she been given grace to keep last year when the sickness bore away so many fair little children in the country round. And Gaute—Gaute *would* grow strong, that she believed full surely.

Doubtless it must be as Erlend said—he must needs spend freely as he did and have all things costly about him. Else could he never play his part amongst his peers or win his way to such rights and rewards under the King as were his due by birth. She must believe that he understood such things better than she.

'Twas witless to think things could have been better with him in any wise in those days when he lived as in bonds of sin with that other—and with herself. Glimpse after glimpse came before her eyes of his face as it was in those days, ravaged with sorrow, drawn with passion. No, no, 'twas well as now it was. He was but somewhat too careless and unthinking.

Erlend came home at Michaelmas-tide. He had hoped to find Kristin in bed; but she was still up and about, and she came to meet him a little way. She was piteously heavy-footed this time—but she bore Gaute on her arm, as ever; the two bigger boys ran before her.

Erlend leapt from his horse and set the two boys up on it. Then he took the little one from his wife and would have borne him. Kristin's white, worn face lighted up when Gaute showed no fear of his father—it must sure be that he knew him again. She asked not aught of her husband's doings; she talked only of the four little teeth Gaute had gotten. He had been so sick when he cut them.

Then the boy burst out screaming—he had scratched his cheek on his father's neck-brooch. He fought to go back to his mother again, and she would take him, in despite of all that Erlend could say.

It was not till the evening, when they sat in the hall and the children slept, that Kristin asked her husband of his sojourn in Björgvin—as though it were a thing she had but now remembered.

Erlend stole a glance at his wife. Poor love—she looked so wretched. So first he brought forth odds and ends of news. Erling had prayed him to greet her and give her this—'twas a bronze dagger, green and eaten up with copper rust. They had found it in a stone-heap out at Giske—they said such things would be good to lay in the cradle, if 'twere rickets that ailed Gaute.

Kristin wrapped the cloth about the dagger again, rose toilsomely from her chair, and went across to the cradle. She put the little bundle in amongst all the other things that already lay there under the coverings—a flint axe found in the earth, some beaver-grease, a little cross of mezereon, heirloom silver, a fire-steel, roots of purples and fingerfern.

"Lie down now, my Kristin," he begged lovingly. He came over and drew off her shoes and hose—and he told his tidings the while.

Haakon Ogmundssön was come back, and peace with the Russians and Karelians was made and sealed. He himself would have to journey north again now, this autumn. For 'twas nowise sure that things would calm down so quickly, and there was need that Vargöy* should be held by a man who knew the land and people. Aye, he would have full power as the King's Governor there—the fortress needed strengthening

* The modern Vardö.

so that the King's peace might be upheld in the lands within the new boundary marks.

Erlend looked in suspense up at his wife's face. She seemed a little affrighted—but she asked not many questions, and it was clear that she understood not much of the full meaning of his tidings. He saw how weary she was—so he spoke no more of these things, but stayed by her awhile, sitting on the bed's edge.

He knew himself what he had undertaken. Erlend laughed quietly to himself as he lingered over his undressing. 'Twould be no sitting with silver-belted belly, giving ale-feasts to friends and kinsmen, and trimming your nails fine and even, while you sent your sheriffs and lieutenants hither and thither on your errands—after the fashion of the King's Governors in the castles down here in the south. For the castle of Vargöy—'twas a stronghold of another kidney.

Lapps, Russians, Karelians, and the mixed spawn of all the races—troll-pack, wizards, heathen hounds, the foul fiend's own pet lambs—had to be taught to pay their dues again to the Norse commissaries, and to leave in peace the Norse homes lying scattered, with as far between them as from here out to Möre maybe. Peace—maybe the land up there would be at peace some time—in his time 'twould be but the peace there is while the devil is at mass. And then there would be his own dare-devils to keep in check. As they would be towards spring, when they began to grow brain-sick with the dark and the storms and the cold and the hellish noise of the sea—and meal and butter and drink began to run low, and they fought about their womenfolk, and life on the island was more than flesh and blood could bear. He had seen somewhat of it when he was there with Gissur Galle as a young lad; ho, ho—'twould be no bed of roses.

Ingolf Peit, the man there now, was a good man enough. But Erling was right. A man from among the knighthood must take things up there in hand—till this was done, none would understand that 'twas the Norse King's firm intent to uphold his rule over the land. Ho, ho—in that land would he be stuck like a needle in a blanket. The nearest Norse parish down at Malang, the devil knows how far.

Ingolf was a worthy fellow—when he had someone over him. He would give Ingolf the command of *Hugrekken*. *Margygren* was the finest ship of them all, he had proved that now. Erlend laughed softly and happily. He had said it to Kristin so often—that was a woman-follower she must needs suffer him to cleave to.

He was waked by the noise of a child crying in the dark. Over in the bed by the other wall he heard Kristin moving and speaking coaxingly in a low voice—it was Björgulf that was crying. Sometimes the boy would wake in the night and could not open his eyes for the matter on the lashes—and then the mother would wet them with her tongue. It had ever seemed to him ugly to look on.

Kristin lulled the child softly. The thin small tones of her voice irked him.

Erlend remembered what he had dreamed. He was walking somewhere on a rocky strand—it was ebb-tide, and he leapt from stone to stone. The sea lay pale and bright, licking at the tangle far outside—'twas like a still, clouded summer night, no sun. Against the silvery light at the fjord-mouth he saw his ship lying at anchor, black and slender, rocking gently, gently on the swell. There was an unearthly sweet smell of sea and sea-weed. . . .

His heart within him grew sick with longing. Now, in the darkness of the night, lying here in the guest-bed with the long-drawn tones of the nurses' lullaby chafing at his ears—now he felt how great his longing was. Away from his home and the children that the house overflowed with, away from talk of husbandry and housefolk and tenants and young ones—and from heart-heaviness for her who was ever sick and ailing, and whom he must for ever pity. . . .

Erlend pressed his clenched hands over his heart. 'Twas as though it had ceased beating and did but lie shaking with fear in his breast. He longed to leave her! When he thought on what she was to go through, weak and strengthless as she now was—it might come at any moment, he knew—'twas as though he strangled with fear. Should he lose Kristin—he saw not how he could endure to live without her. But neither could he endure to live with her—not now; he must needs come away from it all, and take breath again—'twas as though *his* life were at stake too.

Jesus, my Saviour—oh, what sort of man was he! Now, to-night, he saw it clearly—Kristin, his sweet, his dearest love—true, deep-hearted joy he had never known with her, save in those days when he was leading her astray in sin.

And he had believed so surely that the day when he won Kristin to have and to hold her before God and man—that day all evil would be wiped away from his life so wholly that he would forget it had ever been.

He must be such an one that he could not suffer aught that was truly good and pure near him. For Kristin—aye, since she was escaped from the sin and uncleanness he had led her into, she had been as an angel from God's heaven. Mild and trusty, gentle, diligent, worthy of honour. She had brought honour to Husaby once more. She was become again what she had been on yonder summer night when the pure young maiden soul nestled in under his cloak out there in the cloister garden

and he had thought, as he felt the slender young body against his side—
the devil himself could not find in his heart to hurt this child or cause
her sorrow. . . .

The tears ran down over Erlend's face.

——Then belike it was true, what they had told him, the priests, that
sin ate up a man's soul like rust—for no rest, no peace was his, here with
his own sweet love—he but longed to be gone from her and all that was
hers. . . .

He had wept himself into a half-slumber, when he marked that she
was up, and walking about the room lulling and crooning to the child.

Erlend leapt out of bed, stumbling in the dark over some children's
shoes on the floor, came to his wife, and took Gaute from her. The boy
shrieked aloud and Kristin said plaintively:

"I had almost gotten him to sleep."

The father shook the screaming child, gave him some slaps behind—
and as the boy shrieked still louder bade him hush in such a harsh voice
that Gaute suddenly stopped in terror. No such thing had ever befallen
him before in his life. . . .

"Now, for God's sake, use any wits that you have left, Kristin." His
vehemency seemed to strip him of all strength as he stood there in the
pitch-dark room, naked, shivering and half awake, with a sobbing child
in his arms. "An end of this there must be, I tell you—what have you
nursemaids for?—the young ones must sleep with them. You cannot go
on thus."

"Can you not suffer me to have my children with me in the time that
is left to me?" answered his wife in a low, wailing voice.

Erlend *would* not understand what she meant.

"In the time that is left, what you need is *rest*. Lay you down now,
Kristin," he begged, more mildly.

He took Gaute with him to his own bed—lulled the child a little and
groped in the darkness till he found his belt on the bed-step. The small
silver scales it was set with chinked and tinkled as the boy played
with it.

"The dagger is not in it?" asked Kristin fearfully from her bed; and
Gaute set up a fresh howl when he heard his mother's voice. Erlend
hushed him again and tinkled the belt—and at last the child gave way
and grew quiet.

Poor miserable little soul, maybe one should scarce wish he might
grow up—'twas unsure if Gaute had all his wits.

Oh, no, oh, no—most blessed maid Mary—he meant it not—he
wished not that his own little son should lose his life. No, no—Erlend
took the child close within his arms and laid his face down on the warm
downy hair.

Their fair sons—— But he grew so weary of hearing of them early and late; of stumbling over them wherever he went at home here. That three small young ones could be in all places at once on a great manor like this passed his understanding. But he remembered his burning wrath with Eline because she had troubled herself little about their children. An unjust man he must surely be—for he was vexed now because he never saw Kristin anywhere without children hanging about her.

Never had he known, when he took his true-born sons in his embrace, the like of what he had felt the first time they laid Orm in his arms. Oh, Orm, Orm, my son—— He had been so weary of Eline even then—sickened with her self-will and her rages and her ungovernable love. He had seen that she was too old for him. And he had begun to understand what this madness was like to cost him. But he had thought: give her up he could not—since she had lost all for his sake. The boy's birth had given him, he thought, a cause the more to bear with the mother. He had been so young when he became Orm's father that he had not fully understood what the child's standing would be—with a mother that was another's wedded wife.

Weeping came over him again, and he drew Gaute closer to him. Orm—none of his children had he loved as he loved that boy; he missed him so, and he repented so bitterly every hard and hasty word he had said to him. It could not be that Orm had known how his father loved him. It had all come from his bitterness and despair, as he came to see clearly that never could Orm be counted for his true-born son, never could he bear his father's arms. And from jealousy, too, as he saw his son draw closer to his stepmother than to him; and this, too, that Kristin's even, gentle kindness to the youth seemed to him like a reproach.

And then came the days he could not endure to remember. Orm lay in the loft-room in the dead-straw, and the women came and told him they thought not that Kristin could live through her sickness. They dug Orm's grave over in the chapel, and asked if Kristin were to lie there or were to be taken in to St. Gregory's and buried where his father and mother lay.

Oh, but—and at this he held his breath in fear. Behind him lay all his life, filled with memories he fled from, because he could not endure to think of them. Now, to-night, he saw it—— He could forget, after a sort, in the daily fellowship with his kind. But he could not so guard himself that it rose not up in some hour such as this—and then 'twas as though an evil spell had robbed him of all courage.

Those days at Haugen—at most times he had well-nigh managed to forget them. He had not been at Haugen since yonder night he and

Björn had driven away from it; and he had not seen Björn and Aashild since his wedding-day. It was Sir Björn he had been afraid to meet. And now—— He thought of what Munan had told him—'twas said they walked there; Haugen was so felly haunted that the houses stood empty; none would live there now, not if they were given the farm free.

Björn Gunnarssön had had a kind of hardihood that Erlend knew he could never attain to. He had been steady of hand when he stabbed his wife—right in the heart, Munan said.

'Twould be two years next winter since Björn and Lady Aashild died. No smoke had been seen from the houses at Haugen for a week; and at last some men plucked up heart and went thither. Sir Björn lay in the bed with his throat cut across; he held his wife's body in his arms. Before the bed, on the floor, lay his bloody dagger.

None had doubted how this had come to pass. . . . Yet did Munan Baardssön and his brother so order things that the two were buried in hallowed ground.—'Twas put about that it might well have been robbers; though the chest with Björn and Aashild's goods was untouched. The bodies were untouched by rats or mice—the truth was such vermin were not to be found at Haugen—and folk took this for a sure sign of the lady's skill in witchcraft.

Munan Baardssön was fearfully shaken by his mother's end. He had set forth straightway on pilgrimage to St. James of Compostella.

Erlend remembered the morning after the night his own mother died. They lay at anchor inside Moldöy Sound, but the white fog was so thick that 'twas but in short moments now and then they caught a glimpse of the cliff-wall they lay close under. Yet did it give back a muffled echo of the hollow sounds as the boat rowed landwards with the priest. He stood in the fore-part and watched them row away from the ship. All things he came near were wet with the fog; the wet stood in beads on his hair and his clothes, and the stranger priest and his acolyte sat in the boat's bow crouched with updrawn shoulders over the sacred elements in their lap. They looked like hawks in rainy weather. The oar-strokes and the creaking of the rowlocks and the echoes from the cliff sounded on faintly long after the boat was blotted out in the fog.

Then he too had vowed a pilgrimage. He had had but *one* thought then—that he must see again his mother's sweet and lovely face as it had been of old—with the soft smooth skin of palest brown. Now she lay dead below there, with face ravaged by the fearful sores, that cracked and oozed small clear drops of moisture when she had tried to smile to him. . . .

Was it his fault that his father had met his return in such a fashion? Or that he had turned him then to one who was outcast like himself——? And after that he had thrust all thought of pilgrimage from his mind, and had not troubled to think of his mother any more. Ill as things had gone with her on earth 'twas like that now she was come where there was peace—and but little peace had fallen to *his* lot after he had sought Eline again. . . .

Peace—but once in his life, it seemed now, had he known it—that night when he sat behind the stone wall out towards the woods by Hofvin, and held Kristin in his lap, sleeping her soft, secure, unbroken, childlike sleep. Not for long had he been able to refrain him from breaking that calm. And 'twas not peace that he had found with her since—that he found with her now. Though he saw that all others in his home found peace with his young wife.

And now his one longing was to be gone to strife again. He longed wildly for that outermost barren rock, for the sea thundering round the northern forelands, for the endless coast, and the mighty fjords where all manner of snares and pitfalls might await him, for the folks whose tongues he knew but by bits and scraps, for their sorceries and fickleness and slippery wiles, for war and the sea, and the song of his men's weapons and his own——

He fell asleep at last, but wakened again—what was it he had just been dreaming? Aye, black Lapp girls—something half forgotten that had befallen when he was in the north with Gissur—a wild night when they had all been crazed with drink.

And here lay he with his little sick son in his arms and dreamed such dreams.—He grew so frighted of himself that he dared not try to sleep any more. And he could not endure to lie awake. Aye, truly he must be an unhappy wretch.—Stiff with dread, he lay unmoving and felt the heart tolling in his breast, while he longed for the dawn to release him.

He talked Kristin over into keeping her bed the next day; for he felt he could not bear to see her go dragging herself about the house—in such wretchedness. He sat by her and played with her hand. She had had the comeliest arms—slim, but so round that the fine small bones in the slender joints were not seen. Now they stood out like knots on the gaunt arms whose skin on the underside was more blue than white.

Without, it blew, and rained till the water came streaming from the hill-sides. Once, well on in the day, as he came down from the armoury, he heard Gaute screaming somewhere in the courtyard. In the narrow passage between two houses he found his three small sons, sitting in the midst of the runnels splashing from the roofs. Naakkye held the little one tight, while Björgulf tried to force a living earthworm into his mouth—he had his hand quite full of writhing pink worms.

The boys stood with injured looks when their father seized and scolded them. 'Twas old Aan, they said, that had told them of it——

Gaute would get his teeth without pain or trouble if they could but get him to take a bite or two of living earthworms.

All three were dripping wet from top to toe. Erlend roared out for the children's nurses—they came rushing, one from the wright's shop and one from the stable. Their master cursed them heartily, then thrust Gaute under his arm like a sucking-pig, and drove the others before him into the hall.

Soon after, the three were sitting dry and happy in their blue holy-day kirtles on the step before their mother's bed. Their father had drawn up a stool for himself, and he chattered and romped, and, laughing, hugged the young ones to him, to deaden in his own mind the memory of last night's fear. But the mother smiled happily to see Erlend playing with their children. Erlend kept a Lapland witch, he said; she was two hundred winters old, and dried up till she was no bigger than *that*. He kept her in a skin bag in the great chest that stood in his ship-house. Food? Aye—she got food—every Yule night the thigh of a Christian man—she got through a whole year on that. And if they were not good and quiet and ceased not plaguing their mother, that was so sick, they should go into the skin bag too. . . .

"Mother is to have our little sister—that is why she is sick," said Naakkve, proud of having the clue to the riddle. Erlend pulled the boy by the ears on to his knee:

"Aye—and when she is born, this sister of yours, I will have my old Lapp hag throw a spell over you three, and you shall turn into white bears and root about in the wild woods; but my daughter shall inherit all my goods and gear."

The children shrieked, and clambered up to their mother in her bed —Gaute understood not what was amiss, but he shrieked and crawled up to keep his brothers company. Kristin chid her husband—such jesting was too uncanny. But Naakkve tumbled out again—in a rapture of laughter and fear he rushed at his father, hung on to his belt, and snapped at Erlend's hands, with mingled shrieks and shouts of joy.

Erlend did not get the daughter he would so fain have had this time either. Kristin bore him two great and comely sons, but they had well-nigh cost her life.

Erlend had them baptised, one after Ivar Gjesling and the other after King Skule. Skule's name had not been kept up among their kindred— Lady Ragnfrid had said that her father was an ill-omened man, and it was best therefore that his name be let drop. But Erlend swore that none of his sons bore a prouder name than this, his youngest.

The autumn was so far spent that Erlend must needs set forth for the north as soon as Kristin was through the worst of the danger. And he thought in his heart 'twas as well he should be gone before she came upon her feet again. Five sons in five years—'twas enough for any man; and he was loath to have cause to dread that she might die in childbed while he was tied up there at Vargöy.

He saw that Kristin, too, thought somewhat of the kind. She murmured no longer that he was to leave her alone. She had taken each child as it came, as a precious gift of God, and the troubles it brought as things she must bear without repining. But this time it had gone so fearfully hard with her that Erlend saw 'twas as though all heart had been wrung out of her. She lay there, her face yellow as clay, and looked on the two small bundles of swaddling-clothes by her side, and her eyes were not so happy as when she had gazed first on the others.

Erlend went through the whole journey north in his thoughts as he sat beside her. A hard voyage 'twould be, belike, so late in autumn— and strange to come up there into the long night. But he yearned to be gone, unspeakably. This last terror for his wife had broken down all resistance in his soul—will-lessly he gave himself up to his longing to flee away from home.

IV

ERLEND NIKULAUSSÖN held the post of Captain of the Vargöy stronghold and keeper of the Northern Marches for well-nigh two years. In all that time he came not further south than to Bjarköy, and that but once, when he and Sir Erling Vidkunssön had made tryst there. The second summer Erlend was in the north, Heming Alfssön died at last, and Erlend was made Warden* of Orkdöla County in his stead. Haftor Graut went north to take his place at Vargöy.

Erlend was a glad man when he sailed for the south, some days after Mary's Mass in autumn. It was the cure for his honour that he had wished for all these years—to be given the Wardenship his father once held. Not that this had been a goal he had ever wittingly worked to reach. But it had ever seemed to him that 'twas this he needed, so that he might come into the place where he rightfully belonged—both in his own and in his fellows' eyes. Now 'twas no matter if men still deemed him to be somewhat unlike the other, the home-keeping nobles —there was no disgrace in the unlikeness any more.

And he longed to be home. Things had been more peaceful in Finmarken than he had looked for. Even the first winter had worn on him—he sat there idle in the castle, and could do naught at that season towards the mending and bettering of the works. They had been put in good order seventeen years before, but now were quite fallen in ruin.

Then came the spring and summer, with life and bustle—meetings

* See Note 12.

here and there in the fjords with the Norse and half-Norse tax-gatherers and the spokesmen from the tribes of the uplands. Erlend roved the seas and fjords with his two ships and amused himself royally. On the island the houses were mended, and the works strengthened. But the next year there was but little doing.

Haftor would see to it, doubtless, that the quiet did not last long. Erlend laughed. They had sailed together eastward well-nigh as far as Trianema, and there had Haftor taken a Russian Lapp woman and had brought her back with him. Erlend had talked to him gravely: he must remember, 'twas above all needful that the heathen should understand always that we were the masters—and to that end, seeing one had but a handful of men, one must bear one so as not to stir up trouble needlessly. No making or meddling should the Lapps fight and slay each other; that pleasure one must let them enjoy in peace. But be ever ready to pounce like a hawk on Russians and Kolbjags and whatever else the pack might call themselves. And leave the womenfolk in peace—for one thing, they were witches, every one—and, for another, there were enough to proffer themselves.—But the Godöy lad must steer his course as he would; he would learn in time. Haftor was joyful at getting free from his farms and his wife, and now Erlend was fain to come home to his. He had a right blissful longing now for Kristin and Husaby and his own country-side and all his children—for all things at his home where Kristin was.

In Lyngsfjord he heard tidings of a ship with some monks aboard; 'twas said they were Preaching Friars from Nidaros, who were journeying north, bent on planting the true faith amidst the heathen and heretics of the marches.

Erlend felt sure within him that Gunnulf was of the company. And, true enough, three nights later he sat alone with his brother in an earthen hut on a little Norse farm that lay by the strand where they had met.

Erlend was strangely moved. He had heard mass and taken the sacrament with his crew—the only time since he came here to the north, save that once when he had been at Bjarköy. The church at Vargöy was without a priest; a deacon had been left in the fort, and he had striven to keep count of the holy-days for them, but else had there been but scurvy provision for the souls of the Norsemen in these northern lands. They must even comfort themselves with the thought that it was a crusade of a kind they were on, and 'twas like they would not be held to such strict account for their sins.

He sat speaking to Gunnulf of this, and his brother listened with a far-off, strange smile on his wide thin lips. It looked as if he ever sucked in the under-lip a little, as a man may often do when he is thinking hard of some matter, and is nigh to understanding, but has not yet come to full clearness in his thoughts.

The night was far spent already. All other folks on the farm were sleeping up in the shed; the brothers knew that they alone were waking. And they were both stirred by the strangeness of their sitting here —they two alone.

The roaring of the sea and of the storm came to them lulled and deadened by the turf-walls. Now and then a puff of wind would force its way in, blowing up the embers in the fire-place, and flapping the flame of the train-oil lamp a little. There were no furnishings in the hut; the brothers sat on the low earthen bench that ran round three sides of the room, and between them lay Gunnulf's writing-board, with ink-horn, feather pen and a roll of parchment. Gunnulf had been writing down one thing and another his brother had told him of trysting-places and settled farms, of sailing-marks and weather signs and words in the Lapp's tongues—just as the things chanced to come into Erlend's mind. Gunnulf commanded the ship—she was named the *Sunniva*, for the Preaching Brothers had chosen St. Sunniva as guardian saint for their mission.

" Aye, if only you come not to the same end as the Seljemen,"* said Erlend, and again Gunnulf smiled a little.

"You tell me I am restless, Gunnulf," Erlend went on. "What should a man call you, then? First you go wandering about in the south-lands all those years, and no sooner are you come home but you must needs turn your back on living and prebends and be off to preach to the devil and all his imps away north in Velli-aa. You know not their tongue and they understand not yours. Methinks you are yet more unstable than I."

"I have neither goods nor kin to answer for," said the monk. "I have loosed me now from all bonds; but you have bound you, brother."

"Oh, aye. He is the free man that owns naught."

Gunnulf answered;

"All things that a man owns hold him far more than he holds them."

"Hm. Nay, by God, 'tis not ever so. Grant that Kristin holds me— but I have no mind that my lands and my children should own me."

"Think not so, brother," said Gunnulf, low. "For then may it easily come to pass that you lose them."

"Nay, no mind have I to grow like to all those other goodmen—sticking up to their ears in the mud of their lands," said Erlend, laughing, and again his brother smiled a little.

"Fairer children than Ivar and Skule have I never seen," he spoke.

* For St. Sunniva and the Seljemen, see *The Bridal Wreath* (*The Garland*), Note 8.

"Methinks 'twas so you must have looked at their age—no marvel that our mother loved you so much."

Each brother rested a hand on the writing-board that lay between them. Even in the faint light of the train-oil lamp it could be seen how unlike these two men's hands were. The monk's, bare of rings and all adornments, white and sinewy, smaller and much more closely set than the other's, looked also much stronger—though Erlend's fist was as hard as horn in the palm, and the bluish-white scar of an arrow-wound furrowed the dark flesh from the wrist up under the sleeve. But the fingers of his narrow brown-tanned hand, dry and knotted at the joints like the twigs of trees, were covered with golden and jewelled rings.

Erlend would fain have taken his brother's hand, but he was ashamed —so he but drank, pulling a wry face over the bad beer.

"She seemed to you to be well and hearty again, Kristin?" Erlend asked in a while.

"Aye, she blossomed like a rose when I was at Husaby in the summer," said the monk, smiling a little. He waited awhile and then said gravely: "One thing I would pray you, brother—to think somewhat more of Kristin's and the children's welfare than till now you have done. And be counselled by her and clinch the bargains that she and Sira Eiliv have agreed for; they wait but for your assent to close them."

"I like not much these plans of hers you speak of," said Erlend haltingly. "——And now too, my standing will be other than it has been——"

"Your lands will be of more worth when you bring your holdings close together," answered the monk. "Methought Kristin's counsels were wise when she told me of the matter."

"I warrant there is scarce a woman in Norway's land that is freer than she to guide things as she will," said Erlend.

"In the end 'tis you that guide things," answered the monk. "And you—you guide Kristin, too, as you will," he added in a low voice.

Erlend laughed softly, low in his throat, stretched himself, and yawned. Then of a sudden he said soberly:

"You have guided her, too, at times, my brother. And I marvel if sometimes your counsels have not come nigh to parting our friendship."

"Mean you the friendship that has been betwixt you and your wife, or the friendship between us two brothers?" said the monk slowly.

"Both," said Erlend, as if it was a thought that but now came to him. "So holy there is sure no need for a lay-woman to be," he said more lightly.

"I have counselled her as I deemed to be best. As *is* best," he corrected himself.

Erlend looked at the monk in the Preaching Brothers' coarse grey-white frock, with the black cowl thrown back, so that it lay in thick folds round the neck and over the shoulders. The crown of the head was shaven now so that there was but a narrow fringe of hair about the round, lean, pallid face—but the hair was thick and black as in Gunnulf's earliest youth.

"Aye, you are no brother of mine now, I trow, any more than you are brother to all mankind," said Erlend, and wondered at the deep bitterness in his own voice.

"So is it not—though so it should be."

"So help me God—almost I believe 'tis therefore you would go to dwell among the Lapps," said Erlend.

Gunnulf bent his head. There was a glow in his yellow-brown eyes. "Therefore it is—in some measure," he said low and quickly.

They spread out the skins and rugs they had brought with them. It was too cold and raw in the hut for them to take off aught, so they bade each other good-night and lay down on the earthen bench, which, to escape the smoke that hung above, was but little raised above the floor.

Erlend lay thinking of the tidings that had come to him from home. 'Twas not much he had heard in these two years—two letters from his wife had come to his hands, but they had been old already when they reached him. Sira Eiliv had written them for her—she could print herself, fair and plain, but she was ever loath to write, since it seemed to her scarce seemly for an unlearned woman.

Doubtless she would be yet holier now they had a new shrine in their neighbour parish, and that sacred to a man whom she had herself known in his life—and now had Gaute found healing for his sickness there, and she herself won her full health again, after being sickly ever since the birth of the twins. Gunnulf had told him that the Preaching Brothers at Hamar had at last been forced to give back Edvin Rikardssön's body to his brethren at Oslo, and these were now having full record made of all things concerning Brother Edvin's life, and the miracles 'twas said he had wrought both in life and after he was dead. It was their intent to send this writing to the Pope, and try to have the monk beatified. Some peasants from Gaudall and Medaldal had gone south and borne witness to wonders that Brother Edvin had wrought in their parishes by his intercession, and by means of a crucifix that he had carved out, and that now was at Medalhus. They had vowed to build a little church on Vatsfjeld, where he had lived some summers as a hermit, and where was a healing spring that owed to him its virtue. So they were given a hand from his body to enshrine in the church.

Kristin had made offering of two silver cups and of the great clasp set with blue stones that had come to her from her mother's mother, Ulvhild Haavardsdatter, and had had Tiedeken Paus, the goldsmith in the

city, make of them a silver hand to hold the bones of Brother Edvin's
hand and fingers. And she had been at the Vatsfjeld with Sira Eiliv and
her children and a great following, when the Archbishop hallowed the
church at St. John's Mass tide the year after Erlend had gone northward.

After this Gaute had gained health swiftly, and had learnt to walk and
talk—he was now like other children of his age. Erlend stretched himself—sure it was the greatest joy that could have befallen them that
Gaute was grown whole and well. He would give some land to that
church. Gaute was fair, Gunnulf said, and comely of face like his
mother. Pity that he had not been a little maid—then should he have
been called Magnhild. Aye—he was fain now to see all these fair sons
of his too. . . .

Gunnulf Nikulaussön lay thinking of the spring day, three years back,
when he had ridden up toward Husaby. On the road he met a man
from the manor—the mistress was not at home, he said—she was with a
sick woman.

He rode along a narrow grassy path between old stick-fences; there
were young leaf-trees covering the steep clay banks, both above him,
and down towards the river, that ran below in the bottom, loud with
the spring freshets. He rode towards the sun, and the tender green
leaves glanced like golden flames on the twigs, but farther in the wood
the shade lay cool and deep already on the grassy sward.

He rode on till he caught a glimpse of the lake, lying below him and
mirroring darkly the farther shore, with the heavens all blue and the
picture of the great summer clouds ruffled and broken by the current
ripples. Deep down below the bridle-path lay a little farm on the green,
flower-sprinkled slopes. A group of white-coifed housewives stood out
in the courtyard—but Kristin was not amongst them.

A little farther on he saw her horse; it was loose in the close along
with some others. The path dipped down in front of him, into a hollow
filled with green shadow, and where it wound up over the next billow
of the clay banks she was standing by the fence under the leaves listening to the birds' song. He saw her slender black-clad shape bent over
the fence in towards the wood; only the coif and an arm showed white.
He reined in his horse and rode on towards her at a foot-pace; but when
he came near he saw that 'twas the trunk of an old birch tree that stood
there.

The next evening, when his serving-folk sailed him in to the city, the
priest himself was at the helm. He felt his heart firm and, as it were,
new-born in his breast. Nothing now could shake his purpose.

He knew then that what had held him back, had kept him in the
world, was the unquenchable longing he had borne within him from his

boyhood up—the longing to win the love of men. That he might be beloved he had been generous, mild and mirthful with small folk; he had
let his light of learning shine, but with all modesty and humility, among
the priests in the city, so that they might like him; he had been compliant
with Lord Eiliv Kortin, since the Archbishop had been a friend of his
father's, and he knew how Lord Eiliv liked those around him to behave. He had been kindly and gentle with Orm, to win a little of the
boy's love away from his fitful father. And he had been stern and un-
sparing with Kristin, because he knew that she had needed to meet with
somewhat that did not give way when she grasped at it for support;
something that led her not astray when she came forward, ready to
follow.

But that evening he had understood—he had sought to win her trust
in himself far more than to strengthen her trust on God. . . .

Erlend had found the word to-night. Not my brother more than all
men's brother. That was the way he must go, before his brotherly love
could profit *any*.

Two weeks later he had parted all his goods between his kin and the
Church, and taken on the habit of a professed Preaching Brother. And
last spring, when all souls were deeply shaken by the fearful calamity
that had fallen on the land—the lightning had struck Christ's church in
Nidaros and half consumed St. Olav's house—Gunnulf had won the
Archbishop's support for his old plan. Along with Brother Olav Jonssön, who was a consecrated priest like himself, and three younger
monks, one from Nidaros and two from the Preachers' Convent in
Björgvin, he was now journeying northward to bring the light of the
Word to the unhappy heathen who lived and died in gross darkness
within the boundaries of a Christian land.

Christ, Thou Crucified One, now have I given from me all that could
bind me. Myself have I given into Thy hands, if Thou wilt deign with
my life to buy Satan's household free. Take me, in such wise that I feel
I am Thy thrall, for so shall I also possess Thee.—And so should his
heart, maybe, one day sing and shout in his breast as it had sung and
exulted when he walked the green plains by Romaborg, from pilgrims'
church to pilgrims' church—"I am my Beloved's and to Him is my
desire——"

The brothers lay, each on his bench in the little hut, thinking and
thinking until they slept. A live ember on the hearth between them
glowed faintly. Their thoughts drew them farther and farther away one
from the other. And the next day the one set forth for the north and the
other southward.

Erland had promised Haftor Graut to sail round by Godöy, and take

Haftor's sister with him southward. She was wed to Thorolf Aasulfssön of Lensvik—he, too, was a kinsman of Erlend's, but far off.

The first morning, when *Margygren* stood out of Godöy Sound, her sail bellying against the background of blue mountains in the fine breeze, Erlend stood on the after-deck and Ulf Haldorssön was at the helm. Lady Sunniva came up on deck. She had thrown back the hood of her cloak, and the wind blew the linen of her coif backwards, uncovering her curly sun-bright yellow hair. She had the same sea-blue glittering eyes as her brother, and, like him, she was fair of face, but thickly freckled, both on her face and her small plump hands.

From the first evening he saw her at Godöy—their eyes had met, and then they had looked aside, a secret smile on each face—Erlend had been assured that she knew him—and he knew her. Sunniva Olavsdatter—he could take her with his bare hands; and she looked for him to do it.

Now, as he stood with her hand in his—he had helped her up—he chanced to look at Ulf's rough, dark face. Ulf knew it too, he could see. He was strangely abashed at the man's look. He remembered in a flash all this kinsman and henchman of his had been privy to in his life—every coil his folly had snared him in from earliest youth up. Ulf had no need to look so scornfully at him—he comforted himself—as though he had meant to be more free with the lady than right and honour would allow. He was old enough now, and wise enough from much burning of his fingers, to be let loose in Haalogaland without tangling him up in witless folly with the wife of another. He had a wife himself now—he had been true to Kristin from the first day he had seen her till now—one or two matters that had befallen away in the north, no reasonable man would bring into the account. Else had he not once looked at a woman —in such wise. He knew it himself—with a Norse woman—and their equal in birth to boot—no, he would never have an hour's peace of mind if he was false to Kristin in such wise.—But this voyage southward with her on board—it might well be perilous.

It was some help to him that they met with rough weather along the coast, so that he had somewhat else to do than to dally with the lady. At Dynöy they had to take shelter, and tarry there in harbour some days. And while they lay there a thing befell which made Lady Sunniva seem much less alluring.

Erlend, with Ulf and one or two other men, slept in the same shed where she and her women lay. One morning he was alone in there and the lady was not yet risen. She called him to her—said she had lost a finger-ring in the bed. He had to come and help her to search—she was creeping about on the bed. They turned towards each other now and then in their search, and each time they had that lurking smile in their eyes.—But when she took hold of him—— Aye, *he* had maybe not borne him in over-seemly wise—time and place were against it—but she was so bold and shameless·that now of a sudden he grew hard and cold. Red with shame, he looked away from her face of laughter and wantonness; freed himself with scant excuse, then went out and sent in the lady's serving-women to her.

No, devil take it, he was not so young a bird as to be caught with chaff. 'Twas one thing to beguile—quite another thing to be beguiled. But he could not but laugh—here stood he, and he had just fled away from a fair dame, like yonder Hebrew, Joseph! Aye, strange things befall both by sea and land

Nay—Lady Sunniva—— Ah, he could not but remember *one*—one whom he knew. She had gone to tryst with him in a house of call for ribald men-at-arms—and she had come shamefast and worshipful as a young maid of kingly birth might go to mass. In woods and barns had she met him—God forgive him, he had forgotten her birth and her honour; and she had forgotten them for his sake, but she had not been able to fling them from her. Her blood rose up and spoke in her, even when she thought not on it.

God bless thee, my Kristin—so help me God, my faith that I pledged thee in secret and before the altar, that will I keep or nevermore be called a man. So be it.

He landed Lady Sunniva soon after at Yrjar, where she had kinsfolk. The best of the matter was that she seemed not too angry either when they parted. He had had no need to hang his head and mope like a monk—they had had much frolic and dalliance on the way. At parting he gave the lady some costly pelts for a cloak, and she promised he should see her in the cloak. They would surely meet now and then.— Poor woman, her husband was sickly and no longer young.

But he was happy that he was coming home to his wife and had naught on his mind that he need hide from her; and he was proud of his well-proved steadfastness. And he was dizzy and mad with longing for Kristin—she was the sweetest and loveliest of roses and lilies after all —and she was his.

Kristin was at the landing-place to meet him when Erlend came in to Birgsi. Fishers had brought word to Vigg that *Margygren* had been seen out at Yrjar. She had her two eldest sons and Margret with her, and at home at Husaby all was making ready for a great banquet to friends and kinsmen for Erlend's welcome home.

She was grown so fair that Erlend caught his breath when he saw her. But 'twas true she was changed. The girlish look that had still come back to her after she had come through each childbed—the tender, frail, nun-like look under the matron's coif—was gone. She was a young, blooming wife and mother. Her cheeks were round and freshly red between the white lappets of her coif; her bosom full and firm for chains and brooches to glitter on. Her thighs were rounder and fuller under the key-belt and the gilded case that held knife and scissors. Yes, yes—she had but grown more fair—she looked not now as though they could blow her away from him to heaven so lightly as before. Even the long narrow hands were grown fuller and more white.

They tarried at Vigg for the night, in the Abbot's house there. And it was a young, rosy and joyful Kristin, mild and beaming with happiness, that went with him this time to the feast at Husaby, when they rode homeward next day.

There were many grave matters she should have spoken of to her husband when he came home. There were a thousand things about their children; misgivings for Margret; and there were her plans for putting the estates on their feet again. But all was swallowed up in the whirl of festivity.

They passed around from one banquet to another, and she bore the Warden company on his progresses. Erlend kept now yet more men at Husaby, for messages and letters were ever passing betwixt him and his sheriffs and deputies. All the time Erlend was joyous and reckless as ever—how should he not be the very man for Warden, he asked, he that had run his head against well-nigh every rule in the law of the land and the Church's law? Hardly learned was well remembered!— The man was of a quick and ready wit, he had been well taught in boyhood, and this now stood him in stead. He used himself to read his own letters, and took an Icelander into service as scribe. Till now he had been wont to set his seal to whatever others read out to him, and was ever loath to look on a line of writing—Kristin had seen much of the fruits of this in these two years, in which she had made acquaintance with all the papers in his muniment-chests.

But now there came on Kristin a recklessness the like of which she had never known. She grew livelier and less still in her mien when she was out among strangers—for she felt herself very fair, and she was healthful and fresh for the first time since she had been wed. And at nights when Erlend and she lay in a strange bed in a loft on one of the great folks' manors or in the hall of a farm, they laughed and whispered and made sport of the folk they had met, and jested over tidings they had heard. Erlend's tongue was more devil-may-care than ever, and folk seemed to like him better than ever before.

She saw it in their own children—they were almost spellbound with delight when their father would now and again take notice of them.

Naakkve and Björgulf did naught now but play with bows and spears and axes and such gear. And it might chance, now and then, that their father would stop in crossing the courtyard, look at their games, and put them right: "Not like that, my son—hold it in this wise—"he changed the grip of the little fist and placed the fingers as they should be. When this chanced, they were beside themselves with eagerness.

The two eldest sons were not to be parted. Björgulf was the biggest and strongest of the children, as tall as Naakkve, who was three half-years older, and stouter than he. He had tight-curled raven-black hair; his little face was broad but comely; the eyes dark blue. One day Erlend asked their mother somewhat fearfully if she knew that Björgulf had not good sight in one eye—and that he had the slightest squint, too. Kristin said she believed not there was much amiss; 'twas like he would grow out of it. Things had so fallen out that she had always made least ado with this child—he had been born when she was worn out with nursing Naakkve, and Gaute had followed so close on his heels. He was the strongest of the children, and, it seemed, the quickest-witted, but he was most silent. Erlend was fondest of this son.

Though he did not make it clear to himself, he had a little grudge against Naakkve, because the boy had come at an untoward time, and because he had to be called after his grandfather. And Gaute was not as he had looked to find him.—The boy had a great head, as was but reason, since for two years 'twas the only part of him that had grown— now his body and limbs were making up their growth. His wits were good enough, but he talked right slowly, for if he spoke fast he began to lisp or stammer, and then Margret mocked at him. Kristin was most fond of this boy—though Erlend could see that, in a manner, the eldest was still dearest to her—but Gaute had been so ailing, and he favoured her father somewhat, with his flaxen hair and dark-grey eyes—and he was ever at his mother's skirts. He was a little lonely, between the two elder boys, who held together always, and the twins, who were still so small that they were ever with their foster-mothers.

Kristin had less time now to care for her children, and she was forced to do more as other ladies did and let the serving-women mind them— but the two eldest ran about, for choice, among the men on the farm. She no longer brooded over them with the old overwrought tenderness —but she laughed and played with them more, when she had time to gather them about her.

At the New Year there came to Husaby a letter under Lavrans Björgulfsön's seal. It was written with his own hand and had been sent by the priest of Orkedal who had been south—so 'twas two months old. The weightiest news it brought was that he had betrothed Ramborg to

Simon Andressön of Formo. The wedding was appointed for the spring, at the time of the Feast of Holy Cross.

Kristin was amazed beyond measure, but Erlend said he had deemed things might go thus—ever since he had heard that Simon Darre was left a widower, and had come to live on his manor in Sil after old Sir Andres Gudmundssön's death.

V

SIMON DARRE had taken it as a thing that was as it should be, when his father had agreed with Lavrans Björgulfsön on his match with Lavrans' daughter. In his kindred it had ever been the custom that all such matters were in the parents' hands. He had been glad when he saw that his bride was so fair and gracious. He had, indeed, never looked for aught else than that he should be good friends with the wife his father chose for him. Kristin and he suited each other well in age and birth and fortune—if Lavrans were of a somewhat higher kin, his father, on his side, was a knight and had been much about King Haakon, while the other had always lived retired on his estates. And Simon had never marked aught else than that wedded folk agreed well together when they were an equal match.

Then came that night in the loft at Finsbrekken—when evil tongues would have undone the innocent young child. From that hour he had known well enough that his betrothed was dearer to him than if he had but loved her as in duty bound. He thought not much on the matter— but he was glad; he saw that the maid was bashful and coy, but he thought not much on that, either. Then came the time in Oslo, when he was forced to think things over—and then the evening in Fluga's loft.

He had come against something here that he had not thought could hap in this world—amongst honourable folk of a good kindred and in these times. Blinded and stunned, he had flung himself free of his ties— though in bearing he had been cool and calm and steady in talking of the matter with his father and hers.

Thus had he departed from the customs of his house; and next he had done another thing unheard of in his kindred: without even taking counsel with his father, he had wooed the rich young widow at Mandvik. He was dazzled when he saw that Lady Halfrid liked him—she was much more rich and high-born than Kristin, being son's daughter to Baron Tore Haakonssön of Tunsberg, and widow of Sir Finn Aslakssön —and she was comely, and had so fine and noble a bearing that, likened with her, all the women he was used to seemed to him but as farmers' wives. In the devil's name, he would show them all that he could win the noblest wife; in riches and all else she bore the bell from this Trönder that Kristin had let herself be smirched by. And a widow —that, too, was well—plain and above-board—the devil might trust in maids any more, for him.

He had been made to learn 'twas not such a plain straightforward thing to live in the world as he had deemed it when at home at Dyfrin. There his father had ruled all things, and his judgments were right. True, Simon had been with the body-guard and served as page for a time, and he had gained a little learning from his father's house-priest at home—it might chance now and again that he deemed his father's wisdom a little behind the time. He would venture to gainsay him too, now and then—but it was but as in jest, and it was taken as a jest—a quick-witted lad, Simon, laughed his father and mother, and so said his brothers and sisters, who would never gainsay Sir Andres. But all things were done as his father willed—Simon himself deemed this but reason.

In the years when he was wedded to Halfrid Erlingsdatter and dwelt at Mandvik, he learnt each day more thoroughly that life might be more cross-grained and crooked than Sir Andres Gudmundssön had ever dreamt.

That he should not be able to be happy with such a wife as he had won—such a thought could never have come to him. Deep down in his mind lurked a rueful wonder when he looked at his wife as she moved about the house all day long—so comely was she, with her gentle eyes and the mouth that was so sweet when the lips were shut—no woman had he ever seen wear her robes and her adornments with so much grace. And in the black darkness of the night distaste for her wore all youth and freshness out of him—she was sickly, her breath unhealthful, her caresses tortured him. She was so good that it filled him with a desperate shame—but he could not overcome his misliking.

And then 'twas not long after they were wed before he saw that she could never bear him a living, healthful child. He saw that she sorrowed over it herself even more than he—it cut him to the heart when he thought of *her* fate in that matter. One thing and another he had heard—'twas so with her because Sir Finn had struck and kicked her more than once while she was wed with him, so that she had miscarried. He had been mad with jealousy of his young fair lady. Her kinsmen would have taken her from him, but Halfrid deemed that it behoved a Christian wife to cleave to her wedded husband, were he good or evil.

But should he not have children of her, then must he ever feel, as now he did, that it was *her* lands they dwelt on, *her* riches that he dealt with and controlled. He dealt with them heedfully and wisely. But all through these years there grew up in his mind a longing for Formo, the manor that was Sir Andres' mother's heritage, which it had always been meant he should take over after his father. He came at last to deem that his home was away yonder north in Gudbrandsdal, almost more than in Romerike.

Folks still went on calling his wife Lady Halfrid, as in the time of her first husband, the knight. And this made Simon feel all the more as if he were but her steward at Mandvik.

It chanced one day that they sat alone in the hall, Simon and his wife. One of the serving-women had come into the hall on some errand. Halfrid looked after her as she left.

"I wonder——" said she. "I fear me Jorunn is with child this summer."

Simon sat with a bow in his lap, mending its lock. He changed the tap-bolt, gazed down into the spring-box, and said, without looking up:

"Aye. And the child is mine."

His wife was silent. When at last he looked up at her, she sat sewing, as intent on her work as he had been on his.

Simon was sick at heart. Sickened because he had so affronted his wife, and sickened at his folly in having to do with the girl, and vexed that he had taken the fatherhood on his shoulders. He was in no wise sure himself. Jorunn was a light piece of goods, he knew. In truth, he had never much liked her; she was ugly, but had a sharp tongue in her head, and was merry to talk with; and it had been she who sat up for him ever when he had come home late during the last winter. He had answered over-hastily, fearing that his wife might complain and blame him. 'Twas a clownish fear; he should have known Halfrid would never stoop to such complaints. But now 'twas done—go back from his own word he would not. He must even put up with being held for the father of his serving-woman's child, whether he were so or not.

Halfrid spoke not again of the matter till a year after; then, one day, she asked if he knew that Jorunn was to be wed over at Borg. Simon knew it well enough, for he had given her dowry himself. Where was the child to be? asked his wife. With its mother's parents, where it was now, answered Simon. Then said she:

"Methinks it would be more seemly that your daughter should grow up here in your manor."

"In your manor, mean you?" asked Simon.

A little tremor passed over the lady's face.

"You know well, my husband, that as long as we both live, you are master here at Mandvik," said she.

Simon went and laid his hands on his wife's shoulders:

"If, indeed, Halfrid, you deem you can bear to see the child here in our home, great thanks shall I owe you for your high-heartedness."

He liked it not. He had seen the young one more than once—'twas not a comely child, and he could not see that it favoured him or any of his folks. Less than ever did he believe that he was the father. And he had been sorely angered when he heard that Jorunn had had the child christened Arngjerd, after his mother, without leave asked of him. But he must let Halfrid have her way.

She fetched the child to Mandvik, found a foster-mother for it, and saw to it herself that the little one lacked naught. If her eyes chanced to fall upon the child, she often took it on her lap and ten*ied* it kindly and lovingly. And by little and little, as Simon saw more of it, he grew fond of the little maid—he had a great love of children. Now, too, he thought he could see a likeness in Arngjerd to his father. It was like that Jorunn had been wise enough to be on her good behaviour after the master had gone too far with her.—So it might well be that Arngjerd was his daughter, and what he had done at Halfrid's asking was the best and most honourable way.

When they had been five years wedded, Halfrid bore her husband a son, a full-formed man-child. She was transfigured with joy, but after her delivery she fell so sick that it was soon plain to all that she must die. Yet was she of good cheer, the last time when for a while she was herself. "Now shall you live on here as master, Simon, and hand on Mandvik and all our lands to your children and mine," she said to her husband.

After this the fever mounted so high that she knew no more, and she had not the grief, while yet on earth, of hearing that her boy had died a day before his mother. And in the other home, Simon thought, 'twas most like she felt no sorrow for such things, but was glad that she had their Erling with her.

Simon remembered afterward that, the night the two bodies lay up in the loft-room, he had stood leaning over the fence of a field that lay down by the sea-shore. It was just before St. John's Mass, and the night was so bright that the full moon's light was well-nigh blotted out. The water lay there palely shining, and plashed and gurgled a little on the strand. Simon had hardly slept more than an hour at a time, ever since the night the boy had been born—it seemed to him now very long ago— and he was so weary that he could scarce feel grief.

He was seven-and-twenty years old at this time.

Well on in the summer, when the estate was settled, Simon made over Mandvik to Stig Haakonssön, Halfrid's uncle's son. He moved to Dyfrin and stayed there the winter.

Old Sir Andres was bedridden, with dropsy and many other ills and aches; he was nearing his end now, and he bemoaned him much—life had not been so plain and simple for him either in these latter days. Things had not gone so with his fair and likely children as he had wished and looked that they should. Simon sat by his father and tried hard to get back to the easy jesting note of old—but the old man bemoaned himself without cease; Helga Saksesdatter, whom Gyrd had wedded, was so fine that she knew not what follies she should hit upon next— Gyrd dared not belch in his own house without asking his wife's leave. And this Torgrim, ever and always in a pother about his belly—never should Torgrim have had daughter of his, had he known that the man was such a poor wretch he could neither live nor die. Astrid could have no joy of her youth or her wealth so long as her husband lived. And here was Sigrid, broken and grieving—smiles and song had quite gone from her, his good child. That she should have had that child—and Simon no children! Sir Andres wept, an old, unhappy, sick man. Gudmund had set himself against every match his father had spoken of for him, and he was so old and useless now he had let the lad run wild altogether. . . .

——But all the ill fortune had begun when Simon and that maid from the Dale set themselves up against their parents. And 'twas Lavrans' blame—for, bold a man as he was among men, he was chicken-hearted with his womenkind. The girl had snivelled and screeched, no doubt—and straightway he gave in and sent for that gilded whore-monger from Trondheim that could not so much as wait till he had been given his bride in wedlock. But if Lavrans had but been master in his own house, he, Andres Darre, would soon have shown that he could put sense in the head of a beardless whelp of a son. Kristin Lavrans-datter—*she* bore children a-plenty—a strapping son every eleventh month, he had heard. . . .

"Aye, but that comes dear, father," said Simon, laughing. "The heritage comes to be split up sadly." He took Arngjerd up and set her on his lap—she had just come trotting into the room.

"Aye, 'twill not be through *her* that your heritage will be split up too small—whoever else it be that shall divide it," said Sir Andres testily. He was fond of his grandchild in a fashion, but it angered him that Simon had a base-born child. "Have you thought upon any new match, Simon?"

"Nay, you must let Halfrid grow cold in her grave first, father," said Simon, stroking the child's pale hair. "I shall wed again in good time— but sure there is no such haste——"

He took his bow and his ski and set forth for the woods, where he could breathe more freely. With his dogs he tracked the elk on the snow-crust, and he shot the capercailzie drowsing in the tree-tops. At night he slept in the Dyfrin forest sæter, and felt that 'twas good to be alone.

There was a scraping of ski outside on the hard snow; his dogs flew up barking, and other dogs answered from without. Simon opened the door upon a night blue with moonlight, and his elder brother Gyrd came in, tall and slender and comely and quiet. He looked younger now than Simon, who had ever been somewhat stout, and had grown a deal heavier in his years at Mandvik.

The brothers sat with the food-wallet between them, eating and drinking, and gazing into the hearth-fire.

"You must have seen," said Gyrd, "that Torgrim means to set us all by the ears when father is gone—and he has gotten Gudmund on his side. And Helga. They would fain keep Sigrid out of her full sister's share——"

"I have seen it. Her full share she shall have—you and I, brother, can sure make that good in despite of them."

"The best, mayhap, would be that father should take order in this before he dies," said Gyrd.

"Nay, let father die in peace," said Simon. "You and I between us should be able to guard our sister and see that they strip her not because she has fallen into such mischance."

Thus it came about that on Sir Andres Darre's death his heirs parted in bitter unkindness. Gyrd was the only one to whom Simon said farewell when he set out from home—and he knew that the life Gyrd's wife was leading him in these days was a none too happy one. Sigrid he took with him to Formo—she was to manage his house and he to see to her lands and goods.

He rode into his manor on a grey-blue day of melting snows, when the alder thickets by the Laagen were brown with blossom. When he had alighted and was entering the hall, with Arngjerd on his arm, Sigrid Andresdatter asked:

"Why smiled you, Simon?"

"Smiled——?"

He had been thinking how far unlike was this home-coming to what he had looked for once—when the day came when he should take up his abode here on the manor of his father's mother's kin. A sister dishonoured, and a bastard child, these were his belongings now.

The first summer he saw but little of the Jörundgaard folks—he took much pains to shun them.

But the Sunday after the second Mary's Mass in the autumn, it chanced that he stood by Lavrans Björgulfsön's side in the church, so that 'twas they two that had to give each other the kiss of peace when Sira Eirik had prayed that the peace of Holy Church might be increased in us. And when he felt the elder man's thin, dry lips against his cheek,

and heard him murmur the prayer for peace upon him, he was strangely
moved. He saw that Lavrans meant more by it than but to follow a
usage of the Church.

He hastened out when the mass was over; but at the standing for the
horses he came on Lavrans, who prayed him to come with him to
Jörundgaard and dine. Simon answered that his daughter was sick and
his sister sitting by her. Lavrans then prayed that God might heal the
child, and shook hands for farewell.

One evening some days after, they had been hard at work at Formo
getting in the harvest, for the weather looked doubtful. The most of the
corn was housed by the evening, when the first shower came down.
Simon ran across the courtyard in pouring rain, while a stream of
yellow sunlight from between the clouds shone on the hall-house and
the mountain wall behind it—and there he was ware of a little maid
standing at the door in sun and rain. She had his favourite dog with
her—it broke loose and leaped upon the man, dragging after it a
woman's woven belt tied to its collar.

He saw that the girl was the child of a good house—she was cloakless
and bare-headed, but her wine-red frock was of city-bought cloth,
broidered, and made fast on the breast with a silver-gilt brooch. A silk
cord held back the ringleted hair, now dark with the wet, from her
forehead. She had a lively little face with broad forehead and pointed
chin and great shining eyes, and her cheeks were flaming red, as though
she had been running hard.

Simon saw who the maid must be, and greeted her by name,
Ramborg.

"How comes it that you do me so much honour as to come hither
to us?"

'Twas the dog, she said, as she went with him into the house out of
the rain. It had a trick of running off to Jörundgaard; now had she
brought it back. Aye, she knew it was his dog; she had seen it running
after him as he rode by.

Simon rebuked her a little for having come hither on foot quite
alone; he said he would have horses saddled and take her home himself.
But first, to be sure, she must have some food. Ramborg ran across at
once to the bed where little Arngjerd lay ailing, and both the child and
Sigrid were much pleased with the guest, for Ramborg was quick and
lively. She was not like her sisters, Simon thought.

He rode with Ramborg as far as the by-road to the manor, and
would then have turned about; but there he met Lavrans, who had just
learned that the child was not with her playmates at Laugarbru, and
was setting forth with his people to search—he was much alarmed.
Simon was made to come in, and when he had once taken his seat up in

the hall his shyness fell from him and he felt quickly at home again with Ragnfrid and Lavrans. They sat late over their drink, and as it was now set in foul weather, he was thankful to stay the night.

There were two beds in the hall. Ragnfrid made up one of them fairly for the guest, and now someone asked where Ramborg was to sleep—with her parents, or in another house.

"Nay, for I will be in my own bed," said the child. "Can I not sleep with you, Simon?" she begged.

Her father said their guest must not be plagued with children in his bed; but Ramborg went on clamouring that she *would* sleep along with Simon. At last Lavrans said sternly that she was too old to share a bed with a strange man.

"No, father, that am I not," she said stubbornly. "I am not too big, am I, Simon?"

"You are too little," said Simon, laughing. "Ask me in five years, Ramborg, and be sure I shall not say you nay. But I warrant that then you will have another sort of man, little Ramborg, than a fat and ugly old widower."

It seemed that Lavrans liked not the jest; he told the girl sharply to hold her tongue and go lie down in her parents' bed. But Ramborg cried out once more:

"Now have you asked for me, Simon Darre, and in my father's hearing."

"So have I, indeed," answered Simon, laughing. "But I fear me, Ramborg, he will answer no."

After this day the Jörundgaard folks and those of Formo were much together. Ramborg was over at the neighbour manor whenever a chance served; she played with Arngjerd as if the child had been her doll, ran about with Sigrid helping in the housekeeping, and would sit in Simon's lap when they were in the hall. He fell again into the habit of petting and romping with the maid, as he had been used to do in old days, when she and Ulvhild had been as little sisters to him.

Simon had dwelt two years in the Dale, when Geirmund Hersteinssön of Kruke made suit for Sigrid Andresdatter. The Kruke kindred were of old yeoman stock, but though one and another of the men had served the Kings in the body-guard, they had never won any name beyond their own country-side. Yet was it as good a match as Sigrid could look to make, and she herself was willing to be wed with Geirmund. So her brother closed the bargain, and Simon held his sister's wedding at his house.

One evening just before, while the hurry and bustle of making ready for the feast were at their worst, Simon said in jest that he knew not what would become of his house when Sigrid had left him. Then said Ramborg:

"You must do the best you can for two years, Simon. At fourteen years a maid is fit to wed, and then you can bring me home."

"Nay, *you* will I not have," said Simon, laughing. "I dare not undertake to bridle so wild a maid as you."

"'Tis the stillest tarns that run the deepest, says my father!" Ramborg cried. "*I* am the wild kind, I. My sister, she was meek and mild. Have you forgotten Kristin now, Simon Andressön?"

Simon leapt up from the bench, lifted the maid up against his breast, and kissed her throat so hard that the skin was flecked with red. Aghast and amazed at himself, he loosed her, caught up Arngjerd, and threw her up and crushed her to him in the same way to hide his disorder. He went on romping with the two, the little and the half-grown maid, and chasing them about, while they fled from him up on tables and benches; at last he set them up on the cross-beam next the door, and ran out.

——Kristin's name was scarce ever named at Jörundgaard—in his hearing.

Ramborg Lavransdatter grew comely as she grew in years. The talk of the country-side grew busy making matches for her. At one time it was Eindride Haakonssön of the Valders Gjeslings. They were kin in the fourth degree, but Lavrans and Haakon were both so rich they could well afford to send letters to the Pope in Valland and get dispensation. The match would put an end to some of the old suits-at-law that had gone on ever since the old Gjeslings went out with Duke Skule, and King Haakon took the Vaage lands from them and gave them to Sigurd Eldjarn. Ivar Gjesling the Young had won back Sundbu by weddings and exchanges, but these matters had led to endless jars and dissensions. Lavrans laughed at it all himself; the part of the spoil he could claim in his wife's right was not worth the calfskin and wax he had used up in the suit—to say naught of the trouble and the journeys. But seeing he had been in the broil ever since he was a wedded man, he must hold out to the end. . . .

But Eindride Gjesling took another maid to wife, and the Jörundgaard folks seemed not overmuch cast down. They were at the bride-ale, and Ramborg told her friends proudly, when she came home, that four men had come forward to sound Lavrans about her, either for themselves or for kinsmen. Lavrans had answered that he would not make any bargain for his daughter's hand till she was old enough to say a word in the matter herself.

So things went on till the spring of the year when Ramborg was fourteen winters old. One evening that spring she was in the byre at Formo with Simon, looking at a calf that had been born. It was white with a brown patch, and the patch seemed to Ramborg to be the very shape of a church. Simon sat on the edge of the corn-bin, while the girl leaned across his knees, and he pulled at her plaits:

"Then I wager 'tis a token that you will soon ride to church, a bride, Ramborg."

"Aye, you know well enough my father will not answer no the day you ask for me," she said. "I am so grown up now, I might well wed this year."

Simon was a little taken aback, but he tried to laugh:

"Are you there again with that foolish old jest?"

"You know well that 'tis no jest," said the girl, looking up at him with her great eyes. "I have known it long—that 'tis to you here, at Formo, I would most fain come. Why have you kissed me and set me in your lap many a time and often, if you would not have me?"

"Right fain would I be to have you, my Ramborg. But I had never thought that so fair and young a maid could be meant for me. I am seventeen years older than you—you have not thought, I trow, how you would like to have an old blear-eyed, big-bellied husband when you were a woman in your best years——"

"*These* are my best years," said she, beaming, "and not yet are you so old and tottering, Simon!"

"But ugly I am—soon would you be sick of kissing *me*."

"That have you no cause to believe," she answered, laughing as before, and held up her mouth to be kissed. But he did not kiss her.

"I will not profit by your simpleness, my sweet. Lavrans will take you with him to the south this summer. Should you not have changed your thoughts ere you come back, then will I thank God and Our Lady for better fortune than I had looked for—but bind you I will not, fair Ramborg."

He called his dogs, took his spear and bow, and went up on the hills that same evening. There was much snow in on the uplands still; he struck off to his sæter and got him a pair of ski, then lay out for a week by the tarn south of the Boar Fells and hunted reindeer. But the evening he set off down towards home he grew uneasy and fearful again. 'Twould be like Ramborg if she had spoken of it to her father in spite of all. When he came over the hill-crest by the Jörundgaard sæter, he saw smoke and sparks going up from the roof. He thought maybe 'twas Lavrans himself that was there, and he went up to the huts.

He thought he could see from the other's bearing that he had guessed right. But they sat there talking of the bad summer last year and of when it would likely be best to move up the cattle this year, of the hunting, and of Lavrans' new hawk, which sat on the floor, flapping its wings over the pluck of the birds that were roasting on a spit over the fire. Lavrans had come up but to see to his horse-shelter in Ilmandsdal —some folks from Alvdal that had come by it that day had told him it was fallen down. So passed the most of the evening. At last Simon spoke up:

"I know not if—has Ramborg said aught to you of a matter she and I spoke of one night?"

Lavrans said slowly:

"Methinks it had been well you had spoken to me first, Simon—you might have known what answer you would have had of me. Aye, aye— I understand how it may have chanced that you named it first to the maid—and it shall make no odds. I am glad that things are so that I can bestow the child in a good man's hands."

After this there was not much more to be said, thought Simon. Strange enough, all the same—here sat he who had never dreamed of making too free with an honest maid or a wife, and he was bound in honour to wed one whom he would liefer not have had. But he made one trial:

"Yet neither is it so, Lavrans, that I have gone wooing your daughter behind your back—I thought I was so old that she would not take it for more than brotherly kindness from old days that I spoke so much with her. And if you deem I am too old for her, I should not marvel at it, nor let it part the friendship betwixt us."

"Few men have I met whom I would rather have in a son's stead than you, Simon," said Lavrans. "And I would fain give Ramborg away myself. You know who will be her guardian when I am gone." It was the first time aught had been said between these two of Erlend Niku-laussön. "In many ways my son-in-law is a better man than I took him to be, when first I knew him. But I know not if he is the man to deal wisely with the giving of a young maid in marriage. And I mark well that Ramborg herself is willing."

"So thinks she now," said Simon. "But she is scarce out of her child-hood. Therefore have I no wish to press the matter on you now, if you deem it should stand over yet awhile."

"And I," said Lavrans, frowning a little, "have no wish to force my daughter upon you—believe not that."

"*You* must believe," said Simon quickly, "there is no maid in Nor-way's land that I would rather have than Ramborg. So it is, Lavrans, that I deemed it all too great good fortune for me if I should get me so fair and young and good a bride, rich, and come on both sides of the highest kin. And you for father-in-law," he said a little sheepishly.

A slight laugh came from Lavrans:

"Oh, you know well what I think of you. And I know you will so deal with my child and her heritage that we never shall have cause to repent this bargain, her mother and I——"

"That will I, God and all holy men helping me," said Simon.

On that they shook hands. Simon remembered the first time he had clasped hands with Lavrans on such a bargain; and his heart grew little and sore in his breast.

But Ramborg *was* a better match than he could have looked for. There were only the two daughters to divide between them what Lavrans left. And he would be as a son to the man whom, of all men he knew, he had ever honoured and loved the most. And Ramborg was young and fresh and sweet. . . .

And surely by this time he should be a grown man with a grown man's wit. Had he been waiting here thinking that he might wed as a widow her whom he could not win as a maid—after yon other had enjoyed her youth—and a dozen of stepsons of that breed—nay, then he would be rightly served if his brothers had him adjudged incapable and set him aside from managing his own affairs. Erlend would live to be as old as the hills—such fellows as he always did. . . .

Aye, so now they were to be brothers-in-law. They had not seen each other since that night in yonder house at Oslo. Well, it must be yet less joyful for the other to remember than for him.

He would be a good husband to Ramborg, without falsehood or guile. Though it might almost be said the child had beguiled *him* into a snare——

"You are laughing?" asked Lavrans.

"Did I laugh? 'Twas but a thought that came into my head."

"You must tell me what it was, Simon—so that I may have a laugh too."

Simon Andressön fastened his little, sharp eyes on the other.

"I was thinking of—women. I marvel if any woman regards men's faith and men's laws as we do amongst ourselves—when she or hers can gain by setting them at naught. Halfrid, my first wife—aye, this have I never told to any Christian soul before you, Lavrans Björgulfsön, and to none other will I ever tell it—she was so good and holy and upright a woman that methinks her like has scarce ever lived—I have told you how she took the matter of Arngjerd's birth. But that time when we saw how things were with Sigrid—aye—she would have had me hide away my sister and that *she* should feign to be with child, and should pass off Sigrid's child for hers. For thus had we had an heir, and the child had been well provided, and Sigrid could dwell with us and need not be parted from it. I verily believe she understood not it would have been treachery against her own kinsmen——"

Lavrans said, after a pause:

"Then you could have kept Mandvik, Simon——"

"Aye." Simon Darre laughed harshly. "And mayhap with as good a right as many another man to the land he calls the heritage of his fathers. Since we have naught to trust to in such matters but the honour of women."

Lavrans slipped the hood over his falcon's head, and lifted the bird upon his wrist.

"This is strange talk for a man thinking of marriage," he said low. There was something like distaste in his voice.

"Of *your* daughters I trow none thinks such things," answered Simon.

Lavrans looked down at the falcon and scratched its feathers with a stick.

"Not of Kristin either?" he asked yet lower.

"No," said Simon firmly. "She behaved not well towards me, but never did I find that she dealt in falsehood. She told me plainly and honestly that she had met a man whom she loved more than me."

"When you gave her up so willingly," asked the father in a low voice, "was it not because you had heard some—some rumours—about her?"

"No," said Simon as before. "I had never heard rumours about Kristin."

It was fixed that the betrothal-ale should be drunk that same summer, and the wedding be held after Easter the next year, when Ramborg would be full fifteen years old.

Kristin had not seen her home since the day she had ridden away from it as a bride—'twas now eight winters since. Now she came back with a great company—her husband, Margret, five sons, nurse-girls, handmaids, men and pack-horses with baggage. Lavrans rode out to join them, and met them at Dovre. Kristin no longer wept so lightly as in her youth, but when she saw her father come riding to meet her, her eyes filled with tears. She stopped her horse, slipped down from the saddle, and ran to meet him, and when they met she took his hand and kissed it humbly. Lavrans leapt from his horse at once, and lifted his daughter up in his arms. Then he shook hands with Erlend, who had also alighted, and now came to meet his father-in-law with a reverent greeting.

The next day Simon came over to Jörundgaard to greet his new kins-folk. Gyrd Darre and Geirmund of Kruke were with him, but their wives they had left at Formo. Simon had chosen to hold his wedding at home, so the women there were in a great bustle.

As to the manner of the meeting—Simon and Erlend greeted each other freely and without constraint. Simon was master of himself, and Erlend was so gay and cheerful that Simon thought he must have forgotten where they had last seen each other. Then Simon gave Kristin his hand. They were less sure of themselves, and their eyes met but for an instant.

Kristin thought to herself that he had fallen off greatly. In youth he had been comely enough, although even then too thickset and short-necked. His steel-grey eyes had looked little under the full eyelids; his mouth had been too small, and the dimples in his round boyish face too large. But he had had a fresh-hued visage, and a broad milk-white forehead beneath goodly light-brown curly hair. The curly hair he had still, as thick and nut brown as before, but his face was now an even red-brown all over, wrinkled under the eyes, and with heavy cheeks and a double chin. His body, too, was grown heavy—and he had something of a paunch. He looked not now like a man who would care to lie at night on the edge of a bed for the sake of whispering with his betrothed maid. Kristin felt pity for her young sister; she was so fresh and gracious and so childishly joyful that she was to be wed. The very first day she had shown Kristin the chests filled with her bridal gear and Simon's betrothal-gifts—and she had told how she had heard from Sigrid Andresdatter of a gilded casket that stood in the bridal-loft at Formo; there were twelve costly linen coifs in it, and they were to be a gift to her from her husband the first morning. Poor little soul, how could she understand what marriage was? 'Twas pity that she knew so little of this young sister—Ramborg had been at Husaby twice, but there she had ever been sullen and unfriendly—she could not get to like Erlend, nor yet Margret, who was of her own age.

Simon thought that he had looked—perhaps hoped—that Kristin should seem somewhat worn, seeing she had had so many children. But she bloomed with youth and health, and she bore her as proudly straight as ever, and walked as graciously, though it might be she trod the earth now a little more firmly than of old. She was the comeliest mother, with her five fair little sons around her.

She was clad in a dress of home-made rusty-brown woollen with dark-blue birds woven into it—he remembered standing about and leaning up against her loom while she sat weaving on the stuff.

There was a little trouble when they came to sit down to table in the upper hall. Skule and Ivar began shrieking, for they were bent on sitting between their mother and their foster-mother as they were used to do. Lavrans thought it not seemly that Ramborg should sit below her sister's serving-woman and small children—so he bade his younger daughter sit in the high-seat beside him, since she was so soon to be parted from her home.

The little lads from Husaby were restless, and seemed not to know much of behaviour at the board. The meal had not gone far, when the little fair-haired boy slid down under the table and came up by the wall-bench beside Simon's knee.

"May I look at that strange sheath you have there in your belt, kinsman Simon?" he said; he spoke slowly and gravely. It was the great silver-mounted sheath to hold a spoon and two knives he had caught sight of.

"You may so, kinsman. What is your name, cousin?"

"Gaute Erlendssön is my name, cousin."

He put down the piece of bacon he was holding on the lap of Simon's festal doublet of silver-grey Flemish cloth, drew the knife from the sheath, and looked closely at it. Then he took the knife Simon was eating with, and the spoon, and put them all in their places, so that he could see how it looked when all the things were in the sheath. He was exceeding grave and exceeding greasy on fingers and face. Simon smiled as he looked at the little visage, so comely and so intent.

Soon after, the two eldest also made their way across to the men's bench; and the twins slipped down under the table and began crawling about there under folk's feet—then out and away to the dogs by the fireplace. There was little chance for the grown-up folk to eat in peace. The children's mother and father spoke to them, indeed, and bade them sit down prettily and be quiet; but the children paid no heed; and the parents, on their side, laughed at them the whole time and seemed to think their ill behaviour no great matter—not even when Lavrans, somewhat sharply, bade one of the serving-men take the dogs down into the room below, so that folks might be able to hear themselves speak in the upper hall.

Ramborg left the hall with her betrothed and went with him through the spring night a little way up between the fences. Gyrd and Geirmund had ridden on ahead, and Simon stopped to say good-night. He had his foot in the stirrup already—when he turned again, took her in his arms, and crushed the slender child to him so tightly that she moaned softly and happily.

"God bless you, my Ramborg—so fine and fair as you are—all too fine and fair for me," he murmured into her tangled curls.

Ramborg stood looking after him as he rode off in the misty moonlight. She rubbed her upper arm—he had grasped it so hard that it hurt her. Dizzy with joy, she thought: in three days more she would be wed to him.

Lavrans stood with Kristin before the children's bed, and watched her tucking the small bodies into their places. The eldest were big boys already, with thin bodies and slender bony limbs; but the two little ones were plump and rosy, with creases in their flesh and dimples at the joints. A fair sight they seemed to him, lying there red and warm, their thick-growing hair damp with sweat, breathing evenly in their sleep. They were healthy, comely children—but never had he seen young ones so ill brought up as these grandsons of his. 'Twas well, indeed, that Simon's sister and brother's wife had not been there that night. But maybe 'twas not for him to talk about breaking in children—— Lavrans sighed a little, and made the sign of the cross above the small heads.

So Simon Andressön drank the bride-ale with Ramborg Lavransdatter, and the wedding was in all ways fair and sumptuous. Bride and bridegroom looked joyous, and many deemed that Ramborg was lovelier on her day of honour than her sister had been—not dazzling fair, like Kristin, but far gentler and more glad; all could see in the clear innocent eyes of this bride that she bore the golden crown of the house of Gjesling with full honour this day.

And glad and proud she sat in the arm-chair before her bride-bed with hair bound up when the guests next morning came up to greet the young folk. With laughter and free jesting they looked on while Simon laid the housewife's head-dress over his young wife's head. Shouts of greeting and the clashing of arms made the rafters ring, as Ramborg rose and took her husband's hand, upright and red-cheeked under the white coif.

It was not so often that two children of great houses of the one parish were wedded—when the kindred was gone through in all its branches, the kinship would most often be found too near. So all accounted this wedding a rare and joyous festival.

VI

ONE of the first things Kristin had marked at her old home was that all the old heads of men, that had stood where the vergeboards crossed at the house-gables, were gone now. Instead there had been set up spires with carven birds and foliage-work, and the new storehouse had a gilded weather-vane. The old posts of the high seat in the hearth-room house, too, had been changed for new. The old ones had been carved in the likeness of two men; ugly enough—but 'twas thought they had been

there ever since the house was built, and the custom had been to smear
them with fat and bathe them with ale at festivals. On the new posts her
father had carved out two men with helms and shields marked with the
Cross. 'Twas not St. Olav himself, said he, for it seemed to him unmeet that a sinful man should have images of the holy ones in his house,
except to pray before them—but they might, he thought, be two
warriors of Olav's guard. All the old carvings Lavrans had himself cut
up and burnt—the serving-men dared not touch them. It was with
some doubt he still let them bear out food to the great stone at Jörund's
grave-mound on holy eves—but yet he deemed 'twere sin and shame
to deny to the tenant of the mound what he had been used to be given
ever since folk had dwelt upon the place. He had died long before
Christendom had come to Norway, so it was not his fault that he was a
heathen.

Folks liked these new-fangled doings of Lavrans' but little. 'Twas
well enough for him, who could afford to buy himself protection in other
quarters. What he got seemed, indeed, to have all the virtue needed, for
he had the same good fortune in husbandry as before. But there were
those who asked whether yonder folk would not avenge themselves
when there came a master to the manor who was less pious and not so
open-handed towards the Church and all her belongings. And for small
folk 'twas cheaper to give the old ones what they were used to have,
rather than make foes of them and trust wholly to the priests.

Besides, it was none too sure, folk deemed, how 'twould go with the
friendship between Jörundgaard and the parsonage when Sira Eirik
should pass away. The priest was grown old and weakly now, so that
he had need of a chaplain to help him. He had first spoken to the Bishop
of his daughter's son Bentein Jonssön—but Lavrans, too, spoke to the
Bishop, who was a friend of his of old. Folks deemed this misjudged.
Truly it might well be that the young priest had been too forward with
Kristin Lavransdatter that evening and maybe frighted the girl—but
none could know that she might not herself have given some cause for
the fellow's boldness. It had come out plainly enough since that she
was none so coy as she had seemed. But the truth was, Lavrans had
ever put too much faith in that daughter of his, adoring her almost as if
she had been a sacred thing.

Afterwards there had been coldness for a time between Sira Eirik and
Lavrans. But then came this Sira Solmund as chaplain, and he straightway fell at loggerheads with his parish priest over some lands, whether
they belonged to the glebe or were Sira Eirik's own. Lavrans knew more
than all other men in the parish of all sales of land and the like from the
earliest days, and it was on his witness that the case was adjudged.
Since then he and Sira Solmund had not been friends; but Sira Eirik

and Audun, the old deacon, now lived at Jörundgaard, one might say; for they went thither daily and sat with Lavrans, bemoaned the wrongs and vexations they had to suffer at the hands of the new priest, and were waited on as they had been two bishops.

Kristin had already heard somewhat of all this from Borgar Trondssön of Sundbu; he had wedded a wife from the Trondheim country, and had been a guest at Husaby more than once. Trond Gjesling was dead some years ago; none deemed him much loss, for he had been a cankered shoot of the old tree, churlish, cross-grained and sickly. Lavrans was the only one who had put up with Trond; he pitied his brother-in-law, and yet more Gudrid, his wife. Now they were gone, all their four sons lived together on the manor; they were comely, bold and likely men, so folk deemed it a good exchange. There was close friendship between them and their uncle at Jörundgaard—he rode over to Sundby a couple of times each year and went a-hunting with them in the West Hills. But Borgar had told Kristin 'twas beyond all reason, the way Lavrans and Ragnfrid tormented themselves now with penances and godliness. "He swills down water as hard as ever on fast-days; but he communes not with the ale-cup, your father, with the good old heartiness that he used," said Borgar. None could understand the man—'twas not to be believed that Lavrans had any secret sin to atone for; so far as folks knew, he must sure have lived as Christianly as any son of Adam, saving the holy saints.

Deep down in Kristin's heart there stirred a dim surmise why her father strove thus to come near and ever nearer to his God. But she dared not think it clearly out.

She would not own to herself that she saw how changed her father was. 'Twas not that he was so greatly aged; he had kept his shapely form and his upright and gracious bearing. He was greying fast, but folk marked it not much, because his hair had always been so light in hue. And yet—her remembrance was ever haunted by the picture of the young, fair-shining man—the fresh rounding of the cheeks in the long narrow face, the clear red of the skin under the sunburn, the red full mouth with deep-cut corners. Now was the well-rounded muscular body shrunk into naught but bone and sinew, the face brown and sharp, as though carven in wood, the cheeks were flat and lean, the mouth had a knot of muscle at each corner. Aye, but then he was no young man any more—though neither, after all, was he so old.

Quiet, sedate and thoughtful he had always been, and she knew that from childhood up he had followed the commands of Christ with a rare zeal, had loved masses and prayers in the Roman tongue, and ever sought the church as the place where he found his best solace. But all had felt that a full, gentle tide of courage and joy in life flowed through the quiet man's soul. Now 'twas as though something had ebbed away from him.

She had not seen him drunken more than a single time since she came home—it was one evening of the wedding-feast at Formo. He had staggered somewhat then and been thick of speech, but he had not been out of the way merry. She remembered him as he had been in her childhood at the great ale-drinkings in festival seasons and at banquets— laughing his great laughter and slapping his thighs at each jest; offering to fight and wrestle with any man there who had a name for strength; trying horses; leaping about in the dance, and the first to laugh when his feet failed him; strewing around gifts and overflowing with goodwill and loving-kindness toward all mankind. She understood that her father had need of these great outbursts of revelry, in the midst of his steadfast labours, his strenuous fastings and his quiet home life with his own folks, who saw in him their best friend and surest stay.

She felt, too, that if her husband never had this need to drink himself drunken, 'twas because he kept so little check on himself even if he were never so sober, but ever followed his own devices without much pondering over right and wrong or what folk accounted seemly and wise behaviour. Erlend was the most sober man as to strong drink that she had known—he drank to quench his thirst and for the sake of good-fellowship, without caring much about the matter.

But now Lavrans Björgulfsön had lost his good old heartiness over the ale-cup. No longer had he that within him which needed to be given vent in revelry. It had never come into his mind to drown his cares with hard drinking, and it came not now into his mind—to him it had ever seemed that a man should take his joy to the drinking-feast.

With his sorrows he had gone elsewhere. There was a picture which always hung dim and half-remembered in his daughter's mind—her father on that night when the church was burned. He stood beneath the crucifix that he had saved from the flames, bearing the cross and staying himself by it. Without thinking it clearly out, Kristin felt in her heart that it was in part fear for her and her children's future with the man she had chosen, and the feeling of his own helplessness in this matter, that had changed Lavrans.

This knowledge gnawed secretly at her heart. And, as it was, she had come to Jörundgaard weary of the restless winter they had spent, and of her own weakness in making no stand against Erlend's heedlessness. She knew that he was, and would ever be, a spendthrift; that he had no wit in guiding goods and gear—they dwindled under his hands slowly but ceaselessly. One thing and another she had got him to set in order as she and Sira Eiliv had counselled—but she could not evermore be speaking to him of such things; and it was tempting, too, now to give herself up to gladness with him. She was so weary of striving and struggling with all things both without her and in her own soul. And yet was she such an one that careless pleasure, too, made her careworn and fearful.

Here at home she had looked to find again the peace she had felt in her childhood under her father's safe-keeping.

But no—she felt so unsafe. Erlend had good incomings from his Wardenship, but he was living now with yet more pomp, with a greater household and the following of a great chief. And he had begun to keep her quite outside all things in his life that touched not their most private life together. She understood that he would not have her heedful eyes watching his doings. With men he would talk willingly enough of all he had seen and gone through in the north—but to her he never named it. And there were other things. He had met Lady Ingebjörg, the King's mother, and Sir Knut Porse more than once in these years; it had never so chanced at these times that she could be with him. Sir Knut was now a Duke in Denmark, and King Haakon's daughter had bound her to him in wedlock. The marriage had waked bitter wrath in many Norsemen's minds; and steps—Kristin understood not what they were—had been taken against the lady. But the Bishop of Björgvin had sent certain chests to Husaby; they were now on board *Margygren*, and the ship lay out at Ness. Erlend had been given letters and was to sail for Denmark later in the summer. He pressed her to go with him— but she set herself against it. She knew that Erlend moved among these great folk as their equal and dear kinsman, and she feared what might come of it; 'twas unsafe with so rash a man as Erlend. But she could not pluck up heart to go with him—never could she get him to hearken to counsel there, and she was loath to adventure herself in company with folks among whom she, a plain housewife, could scarce hold her own. And then there was the terror of the sea—sea-sickness to her was a thing worse than the hardest childbed.

Thus, as she went about in her old home, her heart was tremulous and ill at ease.

One day she had gone with her father down to Skjenne. And she had seen again the precious rarity which the folk of that manor had in their keeping. 'Twas a spur of the purest gold, huge and in shape old-fashioned, with strange chasings. Like every child in the country-side, she knew where it had come from.

'Twas in the first times after St. Olav had christened the Dale that Audhild the Fair of Skjenne was spirited away into the mountain-side. They dragged the church-bell up on to the mountain and rang for the maid—and the third evening she came walking over the pastures, so decked out with gold that she shone like a star. Then the rope broke, the bell rolled down the scree, and Audhild must turn back again into the hillside.

But many years after there came one night twelve warriors to the priest—he was the first priest that ever was in Sil. They had golden helms and silver corselets, and they rode on dark-brown stallions. 'Twas Audhild's sons by the Mountain-king, and they prayed that their mother might be given burial as a Christian woman and a grave in hallowed earth. She had striven to hold fast her faith and to keep the Church's holy days in the mountain, and she had prayed so sorely for this grace. But the priest denied it to her—folk said because of this he himself had found no rest in his grave, but in autumn nights he could be heard walking in the grove north of the church, weeping and bemoaning his harshness. The same night Audhild's sons had appeared at Skjenne, bearing their mother's greeting to her old parents. And in the morning they found the golden spur in the courtyard. And 'twas clear that yonder folk still accounted the men of Skjenne as kin, for they had ever rare good fortune in the mountains.

Lavrans said to his daughter, as they rode homeward in the summer night:

"These Audhildssons said over the Christian prayers they had learnt of their mother. God's name and Jesu name they could not name; but they said the Lord's Prayer, and the Credo in this wise: I believe on yonder Almighty One, I believe on the only-begotten Son, I believe on the most mighty Spirit. And then they said: Hail thou Lady that art the blessed one among women—and blessed is the fruit of thy womb, the Comfort of all the world——"

Kristin looked timidly up in her father's lean weather-beaten face. In the light summer night it looked so ravaged with sorrows and broodings as never before she had seen it.

"This you had never told me before," she said in a low voice.

"Had I not? Oh, no; I may have deemed it might give you heavier thoughts than your years gave you strength to bear. Sira Eirik says it is written in the books of St. Paul the Apostle: not Manhome alone groaneth in travail——"

One day Kristin sat sewing on the topmost step of the stair to the upper hall, when Simon came riding into the courtyard and stopped just below her, but saw her not. Her parents both came out to him. No, Simon would not alight; Ramborg had but bidden him ask, as he was passing by here—the sheep that had been her pet lamb, they would scarce have sent it to the hills; she would fain have it with her now.

Kristin heard her father smite his hand to his head. Aye, Ramborg's sheep—— He gave an angry laugh. An ill thing, this—he had hoped she had forgotten it. For he had given his two eldest grandsons a little hatchet each; and the first thing they had used them for was to slaughter Ramborg's sheep.

Simon laughed a little:

"Aye, the Husaby boys—a rascal crew they are——!"

Kristin ran down the stairway, loosing her silver scissors from its belt-chain:

"Give Ramborg this in amends for my sons' killing her sheep—I know she has wanted this ever since she was small. None shall say that my sons——" She had spoken hotly, and now she fell suddenly silent. She had seen her father's and mother's faces—they looked on her gravely and wonderingly.

Simon made no motion to take the scissors; he seemed somewhat abashed. Then he caught sight of Björgulf and, riding across to him, leaned over and lifted the boy to the saddle-bow in front of him: "So —you're a Viking harrying our coasts? Well, now are you my prisoner, and to-morrow your parents can come over to me and we will bargain about your ransom——"

Therewith he waved laughingly to the others and rode off, with the boy struggling and laughing in his arms. Simon had come to be right good friends with Erlend's sons; Kristin remembered that he had ever had a way with children; her little sisters had loved him. It vexed her strangely that he should be so fond of children and have such a turn for playing with them, when her husband was ever so loath to hearken to children's talk.

The day after, though, when they were at Formo, she could see well that Simon's wife had given him small thanks for bringing this guest home with him.

"No one could look that Ramborg should greatly care for children now," said Ragnfrid. "She is scarce out of childhood yet, herself. She will change, I warrant, as she grows older."

"Doubtless she will." Simon and his mother-in-law exchanged a glance and the slightest of smiles. Ah, thought Kristin—aye, 'twas nigh on two months from the wedding now. . . .

In the trouble and unease of mind that Kristin now suffered, she was apt to vent her disquiet on Erlend. He took this sojourn on the manor of his wife's father contentedly and happily, like a man with conscience at ease. He was good friends with Ragnfrid, and made no secret of his hearty love for his wife's father. Lavrans, too, seemed fond of his son-in-law. But so sore and watchful was Kristin now grown that she felt that in Lavrans' kindness for Erlend there was much of that pitying tenderness that Lavrans had always had for every living thing that seemed to him in some measure unfit to stand on its own feet. His love for his other daughter's husband was not of this kind—Simon could meet him as a friend and comrade.

Simon and Erlend, too, were good friends when they met, but they sought not each other's company. Kristin still felt a secret shrinking from Simon Darre—both by reason of what he knew of her, and still more because she knew that from that day at Oslo he had come off with honour and Erlend with shame. She raged at the thought that even this Erlend should be able to forget. Thus she was not ever good-humoured with her husband. And if Erlend chanced to be in the mood to bear her testiness good-humouredly and with meekness, it vexed her that he took her words so little to heart. Another day it might chance that his temper was short, and then he would grow hot, and she would answer him coldly and bitterly.

One evening they sat in the hearth-room house at Jörundgaard. Lavrans still felt most at home in this house, most of all in rainy weather when the air was heavy, as to-day, for in the great hall the roof was flat, and the smoke from the fire-place was a plague; but in the hearth-room the smoke rose up and hung under the roof-tree even when they had to shut the vent-hole against the weather.

Kristin sat by the hearth, sewing; she was moody and dull. Over against her, Margret was half asleep over her seam, and yawned now and then; the children were romping noisily in the room. Ragnfrid was at Formo, and the most of the serving-folk were gone out. Lavrans sat in his high-seat, and Erlend at the upper end of the outer bench; they had the chess-board between them, and moved the pieces in silence and after much pondering. Once when Ivar and Skule seemed set on pulling a puppy into two pieces betwixt them, Lavrans rose and took the shrieking little beast from them; he said nothing, but sat down again to the game holding the puppy in his lap.

Kristin went over to them and stood with a hand on her husband's shoulder, watching the game. Erlend had much less skill as a chess-player than his father-in-law, and most often lost when they played in the evenings; but he took such things with careless good-humour. This evening he played yet worse than was his wont. Kristin chid him for it once or twice—not too mildly and sweetly. Then Lavrans said at last, somewhat testily:

"How should Erlend keep his thoughts on the game while you stand thus disturbing him? What would you here, Kristin? You have never had any skill of these games."

"No; I trow you folks think I have no understanding of aught——"

"Of one thing I see you have no understanding," said her father sharply, "and that is how it beseems a wife to speak to her husband. Better were it you should go and keep your young ones in bounds—the din they make is worse than the Wild Hunt."

Kristin went and set up her children in a row on the bench and sat down beside them.

"Be still now, my sons," she said. "Your grandfather likes not that you should romp and play in here."

Lavrans looked at his daughter, but said no word. Soon after, the foster-mothers came in, and Kristin, the maids and Margret went out with the children to put them to bed. Erlend said, when he was alone with his father-in-law:

"I could have wished, father-in-law, that you had not chidden Kristin as you did. If it comfort her to pick at me when she is in ill humour, why—it boots not to speak to her, and she will not suffer any to say a word about her children——"

"And you," asked Lavrans, "mean you to suffer your sons to grow up so uncorrected? Where are they got to, the maids that should keep the children by them and see to them——?"

"To your serving-men's quarters, I warrant," said Erlend, laughing and stretching himself. "But I dare not say a word to Kristin about her serving-maids—she grows wroth in earnest then, and casts it in my teeth that she and I have scarce been a pattern for others."

The day after, as Kristin went plucking strawberries along a meadow south of the manor, her father called to her from the smithy-door, and bade her come to him.

Kristin went, somewhat against the grain. 'Twas Naakkve again, likely—this morning he had left a gate open and the home cattle had gotten into the barley-field.

Her father took a red-hot iron from the forge and laid it on the anvil. The daughter sat and waited, and for long there was no sound but the strokes of the hammer, as they beat the sparking iron into a pot-hook, and the answering clang of the anvil. At last Kristin asked what he would with her.

The iron was cold now. Lavrans put from him tongs and sledge-hammer and came to her. With the soot on his face and hair, his clothes and hands black, and the great leathern apron in front of him, he looked sterner than was his wont.

"I called you to me, my daughter, to say to you this: Here in my house you must show your wedded husband such reverence as beseems a wife. I will not hear my daughter speak to her master as you answered and spoke to Erlend yesterday."

"'Tis somewhat new, father, that you should deem Erlend to be a man to whom folks should show reverence."

"He is *your* man," said Lavrans. "I put not force upon you either to bring about your match with him. That you should bear in mind."

"You two are such warm friends," answered Kristin. "Had you known him then as you know him now, doubtless you would have been fain to put force on me."

Her father looked down at her, gravely and sadly:

"Now do you speak over-hastily, Kristin, and say that which you know is untrue. I tried not to put force upon you, even when you were bent on throwing off your lawful betrothed husband, though you know that I loved Simon heartily——"

"No—but since Simon too would have none of *me*——"

"Nay. He was too high-minded to stand stiffly on his rights, seeing you were unwilling. But I know not if in his heart 'twould have gone so much against him had I done as Andres Darre would have had me—paid no heed to the wilfulness of you two young folks. And I could well-nigh doubt whether Sir Andres was not right—now when I see that you cannot live in seemly wise with the husband you set all at naught to win——"

Kristin laughed aloud, an ugly laugh:

"Simon! Never would you have forced Simon to take for wife the woman whom he had found with another man in such a house——"

Lavrans caught his breath. "House?" he gasped out.

"Aye—a house such as you men call a bordel. She that owned it—she had been Munan's paramour—she warned me herself that I should not go thither. I said I went to meet my kinsman—I knew not that he was *her* kinsman——" She laughed again, a wild, cruel laugh.

"Be silent!" said the father.

He stood still a moment. A shiver passed over his face—a smile that seemed to blanch it. There came to her the thought of a wooded hill-side—how it whitens when a storm-gust turns over all its leaves in a wave of palely glittering light:

"He learns much that questions not——"

Kristin huddled down where she sat on the bench, leaning on one elbow, and hiding her eyes with the other hand. For the first time in her life she was in fear of her father—in deadly fear.

He turned him from her, went and took up the sledge, and put it in its place amongst the other hammers. Then he gathered together files and other small tools, and set himself to placing them in order on the cross-beam between the walls. He stood with his back to her; his hands shook violently.

"Have you never thought, Kristin—that Erlend kept silence about this?" He stood before her, looking down into her white frighted face. "I gave him no for an answer, curtly enough, when he came to me at Tunsberg with his rich kinsmen and made suit for you—I knew not then that I should have been but too thankful that he was willing to restore my daughter's honour.—Many men would have let me know it then. . . .

"*He* came again and made suit for you in full honour. Not all men would have been so steadfast in striving to win to wife one who was already—was already—what you then were."

"*That* I trow no man had dared to tell to you——"

"'Tis not of cold steel that Erlend has ever been afraid——" Lavrans' face had grown unspeakably weary; his voice had gone hollow and dead. But soon he spoke again quietly and firmly:

"Ill as all this has been, Kristin—methinks 'tis worst of all that you should tell it, now he is your husband and the father of your sons——

"If it be as you say, you knew the worst of him before you braved all things that you might wed him. And he was willing to buy you at as great a price as though you had been an honest maid. Much freedom to rule your life and manage your affairs has he given you—therefore should you make amends for your sin by managing with understanding, and making up for what Erlend lacks in prudence—so much do you owe to God and your children.

"I have said myself—and others have said the same—that Erlend seemed not to be fit for aught else than to beguile women. You are answerable in part for such things being said—to that you have now yourself borne witness. Since then, he has shown that after all he *was* fit for somewhat else—your husband has won himself a good name for a bold and swift leader in war. 'Tis no small gain for your sons that their father has won fame for boldness and skill in arms. That he was—unwise —*you* should have known best of all of us. Best may you make amends for your shame by honouring and helping the husband yourself have chosen——"

Kristin had bent forward over her lap, her head in her hands. Now she looked up, wildly and despairingly:

"Cruel was it of me to tell you this. Oh—Simon begged me—'twas the only thing he begged of me—that I should spare you the knowledge of the worst——"

"Simon bade you spare me——?" She heard the suffering in his voice. And she knew this, too, was cruel of her, to tell him that a stranger had seen she needed to be bidden spare her father.

Then Lavrans sat down by her, took one of her hands between both of his, and laid them on his knee.

"Cruel it was, my Kristin," he said gently and sadly. "Kind are you to all, my child, my treasure, but—I have seen it before this too—you can be cruel to them you love too dear. For Jesu sake, Kristin, spare me from the need of going in such fear for you—fear that this wild heart of yours will yet bring more sorrow over you and yours. You tug and strain like a young horse when 'tis first tied up to the stake, wherever you are tied by your heart-strings."

Sobbing, she sank against him, and her father drew her into his arms and held her close and firmly. They sat thus a long while, but Lavrans said no more. At last he lifted up her head.

"Now you are all black," he said with a little smile. "There is a cloth in yonder corner—but 'tis like it would but make you blacker. You must go home and make you clean again—anyone can see you have been sitting in the smith's lap——"

He pushed her gently out of the door, closed it behind her, and stood still a space. Then he staggered the few steps across to the bench, sank down on it and sat with head thrown back against the log wall and up-turned, distorted face. With all his force he pressed one hand against his heart.

Well that it never lasted long. The breathlessness, the black dizzi-ness, the pain shooting out through the limbs from the heart that struggled and shook, gave one or two heavy thuds, and then stood quivering still again. The blood hammering in the neck-veins.

'Twould pass in a little while. It passed always when he had sat still a little. But it came again, more and more often.

Erlend had trysted his ship's crew to meet at Veöy* on the eve of St. James' Mass, but he tarried at Jörundgaard a little longer to go with Simon and hunt down a big bear that had been harrying the sæter cattle. When he came home from the hunt, he found word awaiting him that his men had fought with the townsmen and he must hasten thither to bail them out. Lavrans had an errand in those parts, so he rode along with his son-in-law.

It was nigh the end of the Olav's Mass feast when they came out to the island. Erlend Vidkunssön's ship lay there, and at evensong in Peter's Church they met the High Steward. He came with them to the monastery where Lavrans had taken lodging, ate supper with them there, and sent his men down to the ship to fetch some rarely good French wine he had gotten at Nidaros.

But the talk went but haltingly over the wine. Erlend sat wrapped in his own thoughts, his eyes bright and eager, as ever when a new venture was before him, but unheedful of the others' speech.

* See Note 13.

Lavrans but sipped the wine, and Sir Erling was quiet and said little.

"You look weary, kinsman," said Erlend to him.

Aye, they had had heavy weather crossing Husastadviken the night before; he had been up——·

"And you must ride hard if you would be at Tunsberg by Lawrence Mass day. And much rest or solace you will scarce find there either. Is Master Paal with the King now——?"

"Aye. Do you touch at Tunsberg on your way?"

"To ask if the King would have me bear his loving and duteous greetings to his mother?" Erlend laughed. "Of if Bishop Audfinn would send word by me to the Lady——?"

"Many wonder that you should be journeying to Denmark, now that the chief men of the kingdom are gathering to the meeting at Tunsberg," said Sir Erling.

"Aye, is it not strange that folk must ever be wondering at me? Surely 'tis no marvel if I have a mind to see a little of such manners and breeding as I have not seen since I was last in Denmark—to ride in a tourney once again—and since our kinswoman has bidden us to come. You know well that none other of her kindred in this land will avow her now, save only Munan and I."

"Munan——" Erling frowned, and then laughed. "Is there so much life left in the old boar, I had well-nigh asked, that he can still move his brawn about?—So Duke Knut is to hold a tourney. Doubtless, then, Munan is to ride in the jousting?"

"Aye—'tis pity of you, Erling, that you cannot bear us company and see that sight." Erling, too, laughed. "I mark well that you fear Lady Ingebjörg has bidden us to this christening-ale so that we may brew the ale for another feast and bid her to it. Nay, you should know best that I am too heavy-handed and too light at heart to be of use in hatching plots. And you have drawn every tooth in Munan's head——"

"Oh, no, we are not so fearful either of plots from that quarter. Methinks it must be clear as day to Ingebjörg Haakonsdatter now that she made forfeit of all rights in her own land when she wedded with the Porse. 'Twill be a hard matter for her to get a foot inside our doors, now she has laid her hand in that man's whose least finger we will never suffer in our affairs."

"Aye, 'twas wisely done of you, indeed, to part the boy from his mother," said Erlend darkly. "He is but a child yet—and already have we Norsemen cause to hold our heads high when we think of the King we have sworn fealty to——"

"Be still!" said Erling Vidkunssön, low and vehemently. "It—for sure it is untrue——"

Erlend said:

"'Tis whispered in every manor and in every cabin in our north country that Christ's Church burned because our King is unworthy to sit in St. Olav's seat——"

"In God's name, Erlend—I say 'tis unsure whether it be true. And if it were, a child, like King Magnus, we must sure believe is without sin in God's eyes—he can redeem himself—— Say you that *we* have parted him from his mother? I say, God punish that mother who betrays her son as Ingebjörg betrayed hers—and put not your trust in such an one, Erlend —bear in mind that they are faithless folk you journey now to meet!"

"Methinks they have kept faith with each other fairly enough.—But, as for you, you talk as if letters from Heaven dropped every day into your lap—'tis that, maybe, makes you so bold to fight with the Lords of the Church."

"Nay, let us have an end of this, Erlend. Talk of things you have wit to understand, boy, and else be silent."—Sir Erling had risen, and he and Erlend stood face to face, red with anger.

"Oh, take heed to your tongue, Erlend," he went on in a little. "Think twice before you speak, where you are going. And think, and think again twenty times, before you do aught——"

"If 'tis so that *you* do, you who rule the roost here, then I marvel not that all things move but haltingly. But you need not be afraid," he yawned. "I—shall do naught, I trow. But 'tis grown a rare land to live in now, this of ours——

"Aye—you are setting forth early to-morrow. And my father-in-law is weary——"

The two others sat on in silence, after he had bidden them good-night. —Erlend was sleeping aboard his ship.—Erling Vidkunssön sat turning his goblet between his fingers.

"You are coughing?" he said, that he might say somewhat.

"Old men grow full of rheum so easily. We have many plagues, you see, my lord, that you young folk know naught of," said Lavrans smiling.

Again they were silent, till Erling Vidkunssön said, as though half to himself:

"Aye—so think all men—that this land is ill guided. Six years ago at Oslo I deemed I had seen clearly that there was a firm intent to uphold the kingly power—among the men of the houses to whom that duty falls by birth. I—built upon that."

"I believe you saw rightly, my lord. But you said yourself—we are used to rally round our King—and now our King is a child—and half the time in a foreign land——"

"Aye. There be times when I think—nothing is so ill but it is in some ways good. In the old times, when our Kings bore them like wild stallions—there was store of brave foals to rear; our folk needed but to choose the one that was the best fighter——"

Lavrans laughed a little: "Oh, aye——"

"We talked together three years ago, Lavrans Lagmandssön, when you came back from pilgrimage to Skövde and had seen your kinsfolk in Gautland——"

"I remember, my lord, you did me the honour to seek me out."

"Nay, nay, Lavrans, no need for so much *kurteisi*." He struck out a little impatiently with his hand. "'Tis even as I said then," he went on gloomily. "None now can bring together the nobles of this land. *They* push to the front that are most fain to fill their bellies—there is yet some meat left in the trough. But they that might aspire to win might and riches by such service as was held in honour in our fathers' days, they come not forth!"

"So would it seem. True it is that honour follows the banner of the chief."

"Then men must deem, I trow, that with my banner there follows little honour," said Erling dryly. "You, too, have held aloof from all that might have made you a name, Lavrans Lagmandssön."

"So have I done ever since I have been a wedded man, my lord. I was wedded early—my wife was sickly, her health could not bear much going about in company. And it seems as if our stock doth not thrive here in Norway. My sons died early, and only one of my brother's sons lived to a man's age."

They sat again in silence awhile.

"Such men as Erlend," said the High Steward low—"they are the most dangerous. They that have thoughts that go a little farther than their own concerns—but not far enough. Aye, is he not like an idle child, this Erlend——?" He shoved his wine-cup round about on the table in his vexation. "He is no dullard! And he has birth and valour. But never doth he trouble to hear so much of any matter as to understand it through and through.—And should he ever care to hear a man out, he had forgot the beginning, like enough, before one got to the end——"

Lavrans looked across at the other. Sir Erling had aged much since last he had seen him. He looked worn and weary—seemed not to fill his seat so fully as before. He had fine, clear-cut features, but they were a little too small, and his hue was, as it were, a little faded—had been so always. Lavrans felt that this man—though he was an upright, knightly man, prudent, and willing to serve faithfully and unflinchingly—yet, however measured, was somewhat too small to be the first man in the realm. Had he been a head taller, 'twas like he would more easily have found full following.

Lavrans said low:

"Sir Knut, too, be sure, is wise enough to see this—if they are hatching aught down there—that in any secret counsels he would find Erlend of small use——"

"You like this son-in-law of yours in a fashion, Lavrans," said the other, almost testily. "Though, truth to tell, cause to love him you have not——"

Lavrans sat drawing with his finger on the table in some spilled wine. Sir Erling marked how loosely the rings sat on his fingers now.

"Have *you* cause?" Lavrans looked up with his faint smile. "And yet I trow that you like him too."

"Oh, aye. God knows——

"But you may make your oath, Lavrans, many things are running in Sir Knut's head now—he is father of a son that is King Haakon's grandson."

"Aye, but even Erlend must sure understand that that child's father has all too broad a back for the little lordling ever to be able to get around it. And the mother has our whole country against her because of this marriage."

A little while after, Erling Vidkunssön stood up and buckled on his sword; Lavrans had courteously taken his guest's cloak from the hook where it hung, and stood with it in his hands—then of a sudden he swayed and would have fallen to the ground, had not Sir Erling caught him in his arms. With much pains and labour he managed to bear the other, a big, tall man, over to the bed. A stroke it was not—but Lavrans lay there, his lips blue and white, with slack, strengthless limbs. Sir Erling ran across the yard and waked up the hospice-father.

Lavrans seemed much abashed when he came to himself. Aye, it was a weakness that took hold on him now and then—'twas from an elk-hunt he had been on two winters back—he had lost his way in a snowstorm. Maybe something like this was ever needed to teach a man his youth is gone from him—he smiled in excuse.

Sir Erling tarried till the monk had bled the sick man, though Lavrans prayed him not to trouble himself, seeing that he was to set forth at daybreak. . . .

The moon shone bright, riding high above the hills of the mainland, and the water lay black in their shadow, but out on the fjord the light floated in flakes of silver. No smoke from any vent-hole—the grass on the house-roofs glittered with dew in the moonlight. Not a human soul in the one short street of the little town, as Sir Erling walked swiftly the short space, but a few steps, to the King's mansion, where he slept. He looked strangely slim and small in the moonlight—with the black cloak gathered closely about him—shivering a little. A pair of sleepy serving-men, who had sat up for him, came tumbling out into the courtyard with a lanthorn. The High Steward took the lanthorn and sent the men to bed—he shivered a little again as he climbed the staircase to the store-house-loft, where he was to sleep.

VII

A LITTLE after Bartholomew Mass, Kristin set out on her homeward journey, with her great company of children and serving-folk, and all their baggage. Lavrans rode with her to Hjerdkinn.

They walked up and down the courtyard in talk, he and his daughter, the morning he was to set forth down the Dale again. The hill country round them lay in sparkling sunshine—the mosses were red already, and the knolls yellow as gold with the birch copses; out on the upland wastes, tarns glittered and grew dark again, as the shadows of the great shining fair-weather clouds floated across them. They kept rolling up unceasingly, and sank down over the distant clefts and glens, amidst all the grey-stone peaks, and blue mountains with combs of new snow, and old snow-fields, which lay around as far as the eye could reach. The little grey-green patches of corn belonging to the rest-house stood out strangely against the autumn hues of this shining mountain world.

The wind blew fresh and sharp—Lavrans drew up the hood of Kristin's cloak, which had blown back upon her shoulders, and smoothed with his fingers the strip of linen coif that showed beneath it.

"Methinks you have grown pale and thin-cheeked in my house," said he. "Have we not taken good care of you at home, Kristin?"

"That you have. 'Tis not that——"

"Truly, too, this is a toilsome journey for you, with all these children," said her father.

"Oh, aye. Though 'tis not because of these five that my cheeks are pale——" A smile flitted over her face, and when her father looked at her questioningly, in alarm, she nodded and smiled a little again. The father looked away from her, but in a little while he asked:

"Since this is so, then maybe 'twill not be so soon that you can come home to us in the Dale again?"

"At least I hope 'twill not be eight years this time," she said in the same tone. Then she caught a glimpse of the man's face: "Father! Oh—father!"

"Hush, hush, my daughter——" Unwittingly he caught her by the upper arm and stopped her as she would have flung herself upon him. "Nay, Kristin——"

He took her hand firmly in his, and began walking again beside her. They had come away from the houses; they were following now a little path in among the yellow birch thickets—they marked not where they were going. Lavrans jumped over a little rill that crossed the path, turned towards his daughter, and gave her his hand over.

She saw, even in this little movement, he was no longer springy and nimble as of old. She had seen before without marking it—he no longer leapt into the saddle as lightly as he had done; he ran no longer up a loft-stairway; he lifted not a heavy thing easily as he was wont to do. He bore his body more stiffly and carefully—as if he had a slumbering pain within him and went softly so as not to wake it. The blood could be seen beating in his neck-veins when he came in from riding. Sometimes she had seen what seemed swellings or pouches under his eyes—and she remembered that one morning when she came into the hall he lay half dressed in the bed with his naked legs over the bed-foot, and her mother was crouched in front of him, chafing his ankle-joints.

"Should you sorrow for every man that old age strikes down, child, much will be your mourning," he said, evenly and quietly. "You have great sons yourself now, Kristin; sure it cannot come on you unlooked for that you see your father will soon be an old fellow. When we parted in old days while I was yet young—we could not know any more then than we know now, whether 'twas to be our lot to meet again on this earth. I may yet live long—'twill be as God wills, Kristin."

"Are you sick, father?" she asked, tonelessly.

"Some ailments come with the years," answered her father, lightly.

"You are not old, father. You are but two and fifty years——"

"My father never was so old. Come and sit here by me."

There was a low grass-grown shelf under a rocky wall that leaned over the beck. Lavrans unclasped his cloak, folded it together, and, sitting on it, drew her down beside him. In front of them the beck clucked and rippled over the little stones in its bed, swaying a branch of willow that lay in the water. The father sat with his eyes fixed on the blue and white mountains far off behind the warm-hued autumn uplands.

"You are cold, father," said Kristin; "take my cloak——" She unfastened it; and he drew the skirt of it round his shoulders, so that they both sat in its shelter. Under it he put one arm about her waist.

"You know it well, my Kristin: unwise is he that mourns a man's going hence—let Christ have thee, rather than I—'tis like you have heard the saying. I trust firmly in God's mercy. 'Tis not so long, the time for which friends are parted. Maybe 'twill seem so to you sometimes, while yet you are young; but you have your children and your husband. When you come to my years you will deem 'tis no time since you saw us who are gone away, and you will wonder, when you reckon up the winters that have passed, that they are so many. . . . To me it seems now 'tis not long since I myself was a boy—and yet is it many years since you were the little light-haired maid that ran about after me, wherever I might stand or go—you followed your father so lovingly—God reward you, my Kristin, for the joy I had of you——"

"Aye—if He reward me as I rewarded you——" She sank on her knees before him, caught his wrists, and kissed the palms of his hands as she hid her weeping face in them. "Oh, father, my dear father—no sooner was I a grown maid than I paid you for your love with the bitterest sorrow——"

"Nay, nay, child; weep not so." He drew his hands loose, and lifted her up beside him, and they sat as before.

"Much joy have I had of you, in these years too, Kristin. Fair and hopeful children have I seen growing up by your knee, a notable and understanding woman are you grown—and I have seen that more and more you have used yourself to seek help where it may best be had, when you were in any trouble. Kristin, my most precious gold, weep not so sorely. You may hurt him you bear under your belt," he whispered. "Nay, sorrow not so."

But he could not check her weeping. Then he lifted his daughter up into his lap and sat her on his knee; now he had her even as when she was a little one—her arms around his neck and her face pressed to his shoulder.

"There is a thing I have never told to any mother's child but to my priest—now will I tell it you. In the days when I was growing up—at home at Skog, and when first I was with the body-guard—I had a mind to take the vows, as soon as I were old enough. Nay, I made no promise, not even in my own heart. There was much that drew me the other way, too.—But when I lay out fishing in the Botn Fjord and heard the bells ring from the cloister on Hovedö—it seemed that drew me most of all.— Then, when I was sixteen years old, father had made for me that habergeon of mine of Spanish steel plates soldered with silver—Rikard the Englishman at Oslo welded it together; and I got my sword too—the one I use always, and my horse-armour. 'Twas not so peaceful in the land then as in your young years—there was war with the Danes—and I knew I was like soon to have the chance to use my fair weapons. And I could not lay them from me.—I comforted me with the thought that my father would mislike it if his eldest son turned monk, and that I should not cross my parents.

"But 'twas I myself that made choice of the world, and I have striven to think when the world went against me: unmanful would it be to murmur at the lot I had chosen myself. For I have seen it more and more with each year I have lived—no worthier work can there be for a human soul that has found grace to conceive somewhat of God's loving-kindness, than to serve Him and watch and pray for those men whose sight is still darkened by the shadow of the things of this world. Yet must I needs say, my Kristin—hard would it be for me to give up for God's sake the life I have lived on my farms and lands, with cares for earthly things and with worldly cheer—with your mother by my side, and with you my children. Therefore must a man suffer in patience, when he has begotten offspring of his body, that it scorch his heart if he lose them or the world go badly with them. God, who gave them souls, owned them, and not I——"

Kristin's body was still shaken with weeping; and her father began rocking her in his arms like a little child.

"Many things there are that I understood not when I was young. Father held Aasmund dear too, but not so as he loved me. 'Twas for my mother's sake, you see—her he never forgot, though he took Inga because 'twas his father's will. Now would I wish that I could have met my stepmother again in this earthly home and prayed her to forgive that I set no store by her kindness——"

"But you have said often, father, that your stepmother did you neither good nor evil," said Kristin, through her weeping.

"Aye, God help me—'twas my lack of understanding. Now does it seem a great thing to me that she hated me not, and never gave me an angry word. How would you like it, Kristin, if so it were that you saw a stepson put before your own son, at all times and in all things?"

Kristin was grown somewhat quieter. She lay now with her face turned outwards looking towards the mountain range. A great grey-blue pile of cloud was passing over the sun, darkening the air—some yellow beams stabbed through it, and a sharp glitter was thrown up from the water of the beck.

Then her tears broke out anew:

"Oh, no—father, my father—should I nevermore see you in life——"

"God guard you, Kristin, my child, so that we may find each other again on yonder day, all we who were friends in life—and every human soul.—Christ and Mary Virgin and St. Olav and St. Thomas will keep you all your days." He took her face between his hands and kissed her on the mouth. "God be gracious to you—God give you light in this world's light and in that great light hereafter——"

Some hours later, when Lavrans Björgulfsön rode off from Hjerdkinn, his daughter went with him some way, walking by his horse's side. Lavrans' man had ridden a long way ahead, but he still kept on at a foot's pace. It was grievous to look on her despairing face, all marred by weeping. So had she sat in the guest-shed too, all the time, while he ate and talked to the children, jested with them, and took them in his lap, one by one.

Lavrans said softly:

"Grieve no more for what you have to repent toward *me*, Kristin. But remember it, when your children grow big, and you may deem that they bear them not towards you or towards their father as you might think was right. And remember then, too, what I said to you of my youth. Faithful is your love to them, I know it well; but you are hardest where you love most, and I have marked that in these boys of yours dwells self-will enow," he said with a little smile.

At last Lavrans bade her turn and go back: "I would not have you go alone any farther from the houses." They were come into a hollow between little hills with birch trees round their foot and stone screes higher up their sides.

Kristin pressed herself against her father's foot in its stirrup. She groped with her fingers over his clothes and his hand and the saddle and the horse's neck and quarters, rocked her head from side to side, and wept with such a deep lamentable sobbing that her father thought his heart must break to see her plunged in such great sorrow.

He sprang from his horse and took his daughter in his arms, holding her in his embrace for the last time. Again and again he made the sign of the cross over her and commended her to the keeping of God and the holy saints. At last he said that now she must let him go.

So they parted. But when he was gone a little way, Kristin saw that her father slackened his horse's pace, and she knew that he was weeping as he rode away from her.

She ran into the birch-wood, hastened through it, and began climbing up over the golden lichen-covered stones of the scree on the nearest knoll. But the stones were big, and hard to climb over, and the little hill was higher than she had thought. At last she was at the top, but by that time he was gone from sight among the low hills. She laid her down in the moss and bear-berry heath that grew on the top of the knoll, and there lay long weeping, with her face hidden in her arms.

Lavrans Björgulfsön came home to Jörundgaard of an evening late. A cheering little warmth passed over him when he saw folks were still up in the hearth-room house—there was a faint flicker of firelight behind the tiny pane of glass in the pent-house wall. He had always felt that in this house was most of home.

Ragnfrid sat alone in the room with a great seam of work before her on the table—a tallow candle on a brass holder stood by her. She rose to her feet at once, bade him good-evening, put more wood on the hearth-fire, and went herself to fetch food and drink. No—she had sent the maids to bed long ago—they had had a hard day; but now, at any rate, they had barley-bread ready baked to last till Yule. Paal and Gun-

stein had gone to the hills to gather moss. Speaking of moss—would
Lavrans have his winter clothes made from the litmus-dyed web of cloth
or from the heather-green? Orm of Moar had been there that morning asking to buy some leather rope. She had taken out the ropes that
hung next the door in the shed, and said he could have them as a gift.
Aye—his daughter was going on a little better now—the wound on her
leg was healing up well. . . .

Lavrans answered or nodded, as he and his man ate and drank. But
the master was soon done eating. He stood up, dried his knife on the
back of his thigh, and took up a bobbin that lay by Ragnfrid's place.
The thread was wound on a pin that was carven into a bird at each end
—one of these had had a piece of its tail broken off. Lavrans rounded off
the break, and carved a little on it, making the bird dock-tailed. At one
time, long ago, he had made a great many such bobbin-pins for his
wife.

"Must you mend these yourself?" he asked, looking at her work. It
was a pair of his leather hose; Ragnfrid was sewing patches on the inside
of the thighs, where they had been worn by the saddle. "'Tis stiff work
for your fingers, Ragnfrid."

"Oh——" His wife laid the pieces of leather edge on edge and bored
holes in them with her awl.

The servant bade good-night and went out. Man and wife were a-
lone. He stood by the hearth warming himself, with one foot on the
hearth-rim and a hand on the pole of the smoke-vent. Ragnfrid looked
across at him. And she grew aware that the little ring with the rubies
—his brother's betrothal-ring—was gone from his hand. He saw that she
had marked it.

"Aye—I gave it to Kristin," said he. "It has ever been meant for her
—methought 'twas as well she should have it now."

At times thereafter one of them would say to the other—maybe 'twas
time they went to bed. But he stood up where he was, and she sat on at
her work. They spoke some words about Kristin's journey; about work
that was towards on the farm, about Ramborg and Simon. Then they
said somewhat again about its being, perhaps, well to go to rest—but
neither of them moved.

Then Lavrans took the gold ring with the blue and white stone from
off his right hand, and went across with it to his wife. Shyly and awk-
wardly he took her hand and slipped the ring on to it—he had to change
it once or twice before he found the finger it fitted. It came to rest on
the middle finger, above her wedding-ring.

"I would have you take this now," he said, low, without looking at
her.

Ragnfrid sat still as a stone—her cheeks blood-red.

"Why do you this?" she whispered at last. "Think you I grudge our daughter her ring?"

Lavrans shook his head and smiled a little:

"Oh, methinks you know why I do it."

"You said before, this ring you would take with you to the grave," she said in the same whisper. "None was to bear it after you were gone——"

"Therefore must you never take it from off your hand, Ragnfrid—promise me that. I would not have any bear it after you——"

"Why do you this?" she asked again, holding her breath.

The man looked down into her face.

"Last spring 'twas four and thirty years since we were wedded to each other. I was not yet a full-grown man—and all through my manhood you were at my side, both when sorrow came and when things went well with me. God help us—all too little did I understand how heavy was the burden you bore, while we lived together. But methinks now that it ever seemed good to me that you were there. . . .

"I know not whether 'tis so that you have deemed I held Kristin dearer than you. True it is that she was my greatest joy and that she brought me my worst sorrow.—But you were mother to them all. It seems now to me that the worst of all will be to leave you, when I go hence. . . .

"Therefore must you never give my ring to any—not to either of our daughters even—but say that they must leave it on your hand.

"Maybe you deem, wife, you have had more sorrow with me than joy —and in a way things went wrong between us; but yet methinks through all we have been faithful friends. And I have thought that hereafter we shall find each other again in such wise that the wrong will not part us any more, but the love that was between us God will build up again, better than before——"

The wife lifted her pale, furrowed face—her great sunken eyes burned as she looked up at her husband. He held her hand still; she looked at it as it lay in his, lifted a little. The three rings gleamed, one above the other—lowest down the betrothal-ring, then the wedding-ring, and above it this one.

It came over her so strangely. She remembered when he had put the first on her hand—by the hearth in the hall of her Sundbu home, their fathers standing by them. He was white and red, round-cheeked, scarce out of his boyhood—a little bashful as he stepped forward from Sir Björgulf's side.

The other he had set on her finger before the church-door at Gerdarud, in God's triune name, under the priest's hand.

She felt it—with this last ring he had wedded her again. When, in a little while, she sat over his lifeless body, he willed that she should know that with this ring he had espoused to her the strong and living force that had dwelt in that dust and ashes.

She felt as though her heart was cloven in her breast, and bled and bled, wildly as in youth—for sorrow for the warm and living love she still secretly bemoaned that she had missed, for fearful joy in this pale, shining love that drew her with it towards the uttermost bounds of the earthly life. Through the pitchy darkness that was coming she saw the glimmer of another, milder sun, she smelt the scent of the herbs in the garden at the world's end. . . .

Lavrans laid his wife's hand back in her lap, and sat down on the bench, a little way from her, with his back to the board, and one arm upon it. He looked not at her, but gazed into the hearth-fire.

When she spoke again, her voice was calm and quiet:

"I had not thought, my husband, that I had been so dear to you."

"Aye, but you were;" he spoke as evenly as she.

They sat silent awhile. Ragnfrid moved her sewing from her lap to the bench beside her. In a while she asked in a low voice:

"The thing I told you that night—have you forgotten it?"

"Such things a man cannot forget in this earthly home. And so it is, I have felt myself, that things grew not better between us after I had come to know it. Though God knows, Ragnfrid, I strove hard that you might never mark I thought so much of it——"

"I knew not that you thought so much of it."

He turned sharply towards his wife and looked at her. Then said Ragnfrid:

"'Twas my fault that things grew worse between us, Lavrans. Methought that since you could be to me in all ways as you were before—after that night—then must you have cared about me even less than I had believed. Had you grown to be a hard husband to me—had you struck me, if only once and when you were drunken—then could I have better borne my sorrow and my remorse. But that you took it so lightly——!"

"Did you deem that I took it lightly?"

The faint tremble in his voice made her wild with longing. She longed to plunge herself within him, to sound the unquiet depths from which his voice came forth strained and labouring. She flamed up:

"Aye, had you taken me in your arms one single time, not for that I was your Christian wedded wife that they had laid at your side, but that I was the wife you had longed for and fought to win—never then could you have been to me as though those words had been unspoken."

Lavrans thought a space:

"No. It—may be I could not. No."

"Had you joyed in the betrothed that was given you, as Simon joyed in our Kristin——"

Lavrans made no answer. In a little he said softly, as though against his will and in fear:

"Why named you—*Simon?*"

"Nay, it could not come to my mind to liken you with the other," answered the wife, herself somewhat confused and fearful, but trying to smile: "You and he are too unlike."

Lavrans rose to his feet and walked a few steps, restlessly—then he said yet lower:

"God will not forsake Simon."

"Seemed it never to you," asked his wife, "as though God had forsaken *you?*"

"No."

"What were your thoughts on that night we sat there in the barn—when you learned in *one* hour that we whom you had held dearest and loved most faithfully, we had both been false to you as we could be——"

"I thought not much, I trow," said the man.

"And since," his wife went on, "when you thought upon it always—as you say you did——"

Lavrans turned away from her. She saw a flush spread over his sunburned neck.

"I thought on all the times I had been false to Christ," he said very low.

Ragnfrid rose—she stood still a moment before she ventured to go to her husband and lay her hands on his shoulders. When he put his arms around her, she bowed her forehead against his breast; he felt that she was weeping. He drew her close in to him and pressed his face down on her head.

"Now, Ragnfrid, we will go to rest," he said in a little.

Together they went over to the crucifix, bowed before it, and crossed themselves. Lavrans said over the evening prayers; he spoke, low and clearly, in the Church's tongue, and his wife spoke the words after him.

They took off their clothes. Ragnfrid lay down on the inner side of the bed—the pillows were made up now much lower than of old, because her husband in these latter days had been often troubled with dizziness. Lavrans bolted and barred the room-door, scraped ashes over the fire on the hearth, blew out the light, and lay down beside her. They lay in the darkness, their arms touching. In a little the fingers of their hands twined together.

Ragnfrid Ivarsdatter thought—'twas like a new bridal night, and a strange bridal night. Happiness and unhappiness flowed together and lifted her up on waves so mighty that she felt within her now the first loosening of the roots of her soul—now had death's hand given her, too, a wrench—the first time.

"Speak to me, Lavrans," she prayed him softly. "I am so weary——"

The man whispered:

"*Venite ad me, omnes qui laboratis et onerati estis. Ego reficiam vos,** hath the Lord said."

He passed an arm around her shoulders and drew her in to his side. They lay a little, cheek against cheek. Then she said softly:

"Now have I prayed God's Mother to make for me this prayer, that I may not outlive you, my husband, many days."

His lips and eyelashes touched her cheek in the darkness as lightly as the touch of butterflies' wings.

"My Ragnfrid, my Ragnfrid——"

VIII

K R I S T I N stayed at home at Husaby this autumn and winter and would go nowhither—she gave for a reason that she was ailing. But she was only tired. So tired she had never been before in her life—tired of being merry and tired of sorrowing, and tired, most of all, of brooding.

It would be better when this new child had come, she thought—she longed much for it; it was as though it was to be the saving of her. If it were a son, and her father died before its birth, it should bear his name. And she thought how she would love this child, and nurse it at her own breast—it was so long since she had nursed a child that she could weep with longing when she thought that now she should soon have a suckling in her arms again.

She gathered her sons about her knee again as she had been used to do in early days, and strove to make their upbringing somewhat more orderly and mannerly. She felt that in this she was obeying her father's wish, and this brought some peace into her soul. Sira Eiliv had begun now to teach Naakkve and Björgulf their letters and the Latin tongue, and Kristin often sat over in the priest's house when the children were there at their book. But as scholars they showed not much thirst for knowledge, and all the children were wild and unruly, save Gaute alone, so that he still was his mother's poppet, as Erlend called it.

Erlend came back from Denmark about All Saints' tide, in high feather. He had been entertained with the greatest honour by the Duke and his kinswoman Lady Ingebjörg; they had thanked him right heartily for his gifts of silver and furs; he had ridden in the jousts, and chased the hart and the hind; and when they parted, Sir Knut had

* Matthew xi. 28.

bestowed on him a coal-black Spanish stallion, while the Lady had sent loving greetings and two silver-grey greyhounds to his wife. Kristin deemed that these outlandish hounds looked faithless and treacherous, and she was afraid they might do her children hurt. And the folk all through the country-side talked much of the Castilian steed. 'Twas true, Erlend looked well on the long-legged, light-built horse; but such beasts suited not this northern land, and God only knew how the stallion would get about on the hill-paths. Howbeit, Erlend bought up now, wherever he went about in his charge, the bravest black mares, till he had made him a stud that was fair to look on at the least. In other days Erlend Nikulaussön had used to give his riding-horses fine outlandish names: Belkolor and Bayard and suchlike; but this horse, he said, was so rare a beast that he needed no such adornment—plain Soten * should be his name.

Erlend chafed much that his wife would not go about with him anywhither. Sick he could not mark that she was—she neither swooned away nor vomited this time—no sign was to be seen upon her yet—and most like her paleness and weariness were from evermore sitting indoors brooding and pondering over his misdeeds. Yule-tide came round—and hot quarrels arose between them. And now Erlend no longer came afterward to beg forgiveness for his hot temper, as he had ever used to do before. Till now he had thought always, when there was strife between them, that 'twas he was at fault. Kristin was good; she was ever in the right; and if he wearied and was ill at ease in his home, it was but that his nature was such that he grew weary of what was good and right when he had too much of it. But last summer he had marked more than once that his father-in-law held with him, and seemed to deem that Kristin was lacking in wifely gentleness and forbearance. And then it came into his thought that she took things to heart in a petty way and was hardly brought to forgive him small misdeeds that had not been so ill meant on his part. Always had he prayed her for forgiveness when he had had time to think—and she had said that she forgave, but afterward he had been made to see that 'twas hidden away, but not forgotten.

So he was much from home, and now he often took his daughter Margret with him. The maid's upbringing had ever been one of the things that set them at odds. Kristin had never said aught of it, but Erlend knew well what she—and others—thought. He had dealt with Margret in all ways as she had been his true-born child, and folk made her welcome as though she were such when she went about with her father and stepmother. At Ramborg's wedding she had been one of the bridesmaids, and had borne a golden garland on her flowing hair.

* Soten = Soot.

Many of the women liked this but ill, but Lavrans had talked them round, and Simon, too, had said that none must say aught against it to Erlend or speak of it to the maid herself—'twas not the fair child's fault that she was so luckless in her birth. But Kristin saw that Erlend had planned to wed Margret to an esquire bearing arms, and that he believed, with the standing he now had, he would be able to bring this about, although the maid was begotten in adultery, and 'twould be a hard matter to win for her a safe, firm footing amongst good folk. It might, perchance, have been done if folk had felt any right faith that Erlend had it in him to keep up and increase the might and riches of his house. But though Erlend was liked and honoured after a fashion, 'twas as though no one had full faith that the fair fortunes of Husaby would endure. Thus Kristin feared he would be hard put to it to bring his plans for Margret to a good end. And though she liked not Margret overmuch, yet she pitied the maid, and dreaded the day when, maybe, her pride must be broken—if she must be content with a much humbler match than her father had taught her to look for, and quite another way of life than the one he had nurtured her in.

Thus things were, when just after Candlemas three men from Formo came to Husaby; they had come across the hills on ski in haste, bringing Erlend letters from Simon Andressön. Simon wrote that their father-in-law had now fallen so sick that 'twas not to be looked for that he could live long; and that Lavrans had bade him pray that Erlend would come to Sil if 'twere possible for him; he was fain to have speech with his two sons-in-law of how all things should be ordered when he was gone.

Erlend went about casting stolen glances at his wife. She was far gone with child now, pale and thin-faced—and she looked so sorrowful—every moment the tears would be welling up. He began to repent his behaviour to her in the winter—her father's sickness had not come on her unlooked for, and if so it was that she had had to bear about this secret sorrow, he could better forgive her unreasonable ways.

Alone he could have made the journey to Sil and back swiftly enough, going on ski across the mountains. But if he took his wife with him, 'twould be a slow and toilsome business. And then he would need to tarry till after the wapinschaws * in Lent, and set trysts there with his sheriffs; and there were some meetings, too, so that he must attend himself. Before they could set forth, 'twould be perilously near the time she looked to be delivered—and Kristin, too, who could nowise endure the sea even when she was well! But he was loath to think of her not seeing her father before he died. In the evening, when they had lain down, he asked her if she dared make the journey.

* Wapinschaw = Arms-muster.

It seemed to him he was well repaid when she threw herself weeping in his arms, full of thankfulness, and of penitence for her unfriendliness towards him in the winter. Erlend grew soft and tender, as he ever was when he had brought grief to a woman and had to see her sorrow it out before his eyes; and he bore well enough afterward with Kristin's fantasies. He had said from the first, the children he would not have with them. But the mother would have it that Naakkve was so great a boy now, 'twould be well for him to see his grandfather's going hence. Erlend said: No. Then she was sure that Ivar and Skule were too small to be left behind in the serving-women's charge. No, said their father. And then Lavrans had been so fond of Gaute. No, said Erlend—'twas hard enough as it was—things being as they were with her—for Ragnfrid to have a childbirth in the house, while her husband lay on his sickbed—and for themselves on the journey homeward with a new-born babe. Either must she give the child out to nurse on one of Lavrans' farms, or she must tarry at Jörundgaard till 'twas summer—but then he must come home before her. He had to put all this to her, over and over again; but he strove to speak calmly and reasonably.

Then he bethought him that he should take from Nidaros one thing and another that his mother-in-law might need for the grave-ale—wine and wax, wheat flour and millet and the like. But at length they were ready to set forth, and they came to Jörundgaard the day before Gertrude's Mass.

But Kristin found 'twas far otherwise than she had thought to be at home at this time.

She should have rejoiced with all her heart that it had been given her to see her father once again. And when she remembered his joy at her coming and how he had thanked Erlend for it, she was indeed glad. But she felt that she was shut out now from so much that passed, and this hurt her.

It was but a short month before her time; and Lavrans utterly forbade that she should have the least hand in nursing or tending him; they would not let her watch by him at night in turn with the others, nor would her mother suffer her to move a finger towards helping in all the press of work. She sat by her father all day, but 'twas seldom that they were alone at any time. Almost daily there came guests to the house—friends come to see Lavrans Björgulfsön once again in life. These visits pleased her father, though they made him exceeding weary. He talked heartily and cheerfully with all, men and women, rich and poor, young and old—thanked them for their friendship, asked their prayers for his soul—and God grant that we may meet on the day of bliss! At night, when only his own folk were with him, Kristin lay above in the upper hall, staring into the dark, and could not sleep for thinking on her father's going and on her own heart's folly and wickedness.

Lavrans' end was swiftly drawing nigh. He had kept himself up and about till Ramborg had borne her child, and there was no more need for Ragnfrid to be so much at Formo; he had had himself driven down there one day and seen his daughter and granddaughter; Ulvhild the little maid had been called. But after that he took to bed, and it was not likely he would ever rise again.

He lay in the great room under the upper hall. They had made a kind of bed for him there on the bench of the high seat, for he could not endure to have his head pillowed high—when it was so, he grew dizzy at once and had swooning-fits and heart-spasms. They dared not let him blood any more; they had had to do it so often all through the autumn and winter that now he was quite drained of blood; and he could eat and drink but little.

Her father's fine and comely features were sharp now, and the brownness was faded from his face that had weathered before to so fresh a hue; it was yellow now as bone, and the lips and corners of the eyes pale and bloodless. The thick hair, flaxen but powdered with white, lay unclipped, withered and strengthless over the blue-patterned pillow-cover, but what changed him most was the coarse grey stubble growing now on the lower face and on the long wide throat, where the sinews stood out like strong cords. Lavrans had always been so nice in shaving himself before each holy day. His body was wasted till it was but little more than a skeleton. But he said that he was easy so long as he lay stretched out and moved but little. And he was cheerful and glad at all times.

They slaughtered and brewed and baked for the grave-ale; had out bed-gear for all the beds and went through it with care—all that could be got out of hand now was done, so that all might be still and quiet when the last struggle came. It cheered Lavrans greatly to hear of all that was making ready—his last feast would not be the least of all the festivals that had been held at Jörundgaard; in honour and worship would he depart from the governance of his lands and his people. One day he had a mind to see the two cows that were to follow in his funeral train, as gifts for Sira Eirik and Sira Solmund; and they were led into the hall. They had been given double feed all the winter, and they were, in sooth, as fine and fat as sæter cattle at Olav's Mass, though it was now the midst of the spring dearth. He was the one that laughed most when one of them dropped somewhat on the hall-floor.—But he was fearful that his wife would be altogether worn out. Kristin had thought she herself was a notable housewife—she had the name of one at home in Skaun; but it seemed to her now that beside her mother she was naught. None could understand how Ragnfrid was able to compass all she did—and yet she seemed never to be long away from her husband; and she took her share of watching every night.

"Never trouble about me, husband," she said, laying her hand in his. "When you are dead, you know that I shall rest altogether from all such cares."

Lavrans Björgulfsön had bought him some years back a resting-place in the church of the Preaching Friars at Hamar, and Ragnfrid Ivarsdatter was set on going thither with his corpse and dwelling there near by it; she was to be a commoner in a hospice the monks owned in the town. But first the coffin was to be taken into the Olav's Church here at home, with great gifts to the Church and the priests; his stallion was to be led after with his armour and weapons, and these were to be redeemed by Erlend for five-and-forty marks of silver. One of his and Kristin's sons would most like be given these things—for choice the child she was soon to bear, if 'twere a son—perhaps he might some day be Lavrans of Jörundgaard, said the sick man with a smile. On the way down through Gudbrandsdal, too, the body was to be taken into certain churches over-night—and these were all remembered in Lavrans' testament with money-gifts and wax tapers.

Kristin felt sick, but it was with sorrow and disquiet of soul. For she could not hide from herself—it hurt her the more, the longer she was at home. Such was her heart that it hurt her to see that, now her father was drawing nigh to death, 'twas his wife that was nearest to him of all.

Ever had she heard her parents' life together held up as a pattern of seemly and worthy wedlock in unity, troth and loving-kindness. But she had felt, though without thinking upon it, that none the less there was somewhat that stood between them—an uncertain shadow, but it dulled the life in their house, though they lived together in peace and kindness. Now was there no shadow any more between her parents. They talked evenly and quietly together, mostly of the little things of every day; but Kristin felt that there was something new in their eyes and in the tone of their voices. She saw that her father missed his wife always when she was not by his side. When he had himself talked her over into going to seek a little rest, he would lie as if waiting somewhat restlessly; and when she came in, 'twas as though peace and gladness came with her to the sick man. One day she heard them speaking of their dead children; yet did they look happily. When Sira Eirik came over and read to Lavrans, Ragnfrid sat ever beside them, and then he would often take his wife's hand, and lie playing with her fingers and turning the rings on them.

She knew that her father loved her not less than before. But she had not seen clearly before now that he loved her mother. And she under-stood how unlike must be the man's love for his wife, who had lived with him a long life in evil days and good, to his love for the child who had but shared his joys and taken to herself his inmost heart's tenderness. And she wept and prayed God and St. Olav for help—for she remem-bered that tearful and tender farewell last autumn on the hills, but it *could* not be true that she wished now that farewell had been the last!

On the day that begins the summer half-year * Kristin bore her sixth son, and already, the fifth day after, she was up and had gone across to the hall to sit with her father. Lavrans misliked this—it had never been the use in his house for a lying-in woman to come into the open air before the day she went to be churched. At least, he said, she must never cross the courtyard except when the sun was in the heavens. Ragnfrid was listening when he spoke of this.

"I was thinking but now, husband," she said, "that from us, your womenkind, you have never had great obedience, but we have most often done as we ourselves would."

"Knew you not that before?" asked her husband, laughing. "'Tis not your brother Trond's fault, then—mind you not that he would rail at me always for an old woman because I let you women have the upper hand?"

Sira Eirik came over daily to the dying man. The old parish priest's sight was nearly gone, but the story of the creation in the Norse tongue, and the evangels and psalter in Latin, he read as plainly and flowingly as ever, for he knew the books so well. But Lavrans had gotten a great book some years before down at Saastad, and he was most fain to be read to from it—but Sira Eirik could not manage to read in it, by reason of his bad eyes. So her father prayed Kristin to try if she could read it. And when she was grown a little used to the book, she found, sure enough, that she could read from it fairly and well, and it was a great joy to her that now there was somewhat that she could do for her father.

In this book were such things as debates between Fear and Courage, between Faith and Doubt, Body and Soul. There were likewise some sagas of holy men, and more than one account of men who, while yet alive, had been rapt away in the spirit and had seen the pains of the place of torment, the tribulations of purgatory fire, and the bliss of the heavenly kingdom. Lavrans spoke much now of purgatory fire, which he looked soon to enter; but he was quite without fear. He hoped for great solacement from his friends' and the priests' intercessions, and

* Summer day = 14th April.

trusted firmly that St. Olav and St. Thomas would give him strength in this his last trial, as he had so often felt that they had strengthened him in this life. He had ever heard that he that was firm in the faith would never for a single moment lose from before his eyes the bliss to which the soul was going through the scorching fires. Kristin deemed that her father thought with gladness of what was coming, as of a trial of his manhood. She remembered dimly from her childhood that time when the King's sworn men from the Dale set out for the war against Duke Eirik—it seemed to her that now her father looked forward to his death as he had looked forward then to adventures and battles.

One day she said to him she deemed he had had so many trials in this life that 'twas like he would come off lightly from those of the life to come. Lavrans answered: it seemed not so to him now; he had been a rich man; he had been born of a noble house; friends had he had and good advancement in the world. "My heaviest sorrows were that I never saw my mother's face, and that I lost my children—but soon these will be sorrows no longer. And so it is with other things that have weighed on me while I lived—they are no longer sorrows."

Her mother was often with them while Kristin read; strangers, too; and Erlend now was glad to sit and listen. All these folks had delight of the reading, but she herself was shaken and made hopeless by it—she thought on her own heart that knew so well what good and right were, and yet was ever intent on unrighteousness. And she feared for her little child—scarce dared sleep at night for fear it might die a heathen. She had two women ever to sit up and watch, and yet was she afraid to fall asleep herself. Her other children had all been baptised before they were three days old; but they had put off this one's christening, since it was a big, strong child, and they would fain name it after Lavrans—and in the Dale here folk held stiffly to the custom that children must not be named after living men.

One day when she sat by her father and had the child in her lap, he prayed her to unwrap its swaddling-clothes; for as yet he had seen no more than the little lad's face. She did so and laid the boy on her father's arm. Lavrans stroked the little rounded breast and took one of the small tight-clenched hands in his:

"Strange it is, kinsman, that you are to bear my breastplate—now would you fill no more room in it than a worm in a hollow nut, and this hand has a great way to grow before it can grasp my sword-hilt round. When a man sees such things as this little knave, he well-nigh comes to understand that God's will with us was not that we should bear arms. But not much greater shall you be, you little one, before you long to take them up. 'Tis but the fewest men born of women that bear so great love towards God that they will forswear the bearing of arms. I had not such love."

He lay a little, looking at the babe.

"You bear your children under a loving heart, my Kristin—the boy is great and fat, but you are pale and thin as a wand, and so, your mother says, it was with them all when you were delivered of them. Ramborg's daughter was little and thin," he said, laughing, "but Ramborg blooms like a rose."

"Yet seems it to me strange that she would not suckle her child herself," said Kristin.

"Simon would not have it either—he says he will not repay her for the gift by letting her wear herself away. Bear in mind, Ramborg was not full sixteen years—she had scarce worn out her own childish footgear when she had this daughter—and never had she felt an hour's sickness before—'twas no marvel that her patience was short. You were a grown woman when you were wedded, my Kristin."

Of a sudden Kristin fell into a wild weeping—she scarce knew herself what she wept for so. But it was so true—she had loved her children from the first hour that she knew she bore them in her womb; she had loved them while they plagued her with unrest, weighed her down and made her uncomely. She had loved their little faces from the first moment she saw them, and had loved them every hour as they grew and changed. But none had rightly loved them with her, and joyed with her in them—'twas not Erlend's way—he was fond of them enough; but Naakkve he deemed had come too early, and as each of the others came, he had ever thought him one too many. She dimly remembered what she had thought of the fruit of sin the first winter she was at Husaby—she knew that she had been forced to taste its bitterness, though in other wise than she had feared. Something had gone awry between her and Erlend in those first days, and 'twas like it could never be made straight again.

"What is it now, Kristin?" asked her father quietly, in a while. She could not tell him all this. So she said, as soon as she could speak for weeping:

"Should not I sorrow, father, when you lie here——?"

At length, when Lavrans pressed her, she spoke of her fear for the unchristened child. On this he gave order straightway that the child should be brought to church the next holy-day—he said he believed not that this would slay him before God's good time.

"Besides, I have lain here long enough now," he said, laughing. "Sad work there is over our coming and our going, Kristin—in sickness are we born and in sickness do we die, he that dies not on a sudden. To me when I was young the best death seemed to be slain on the battle-field.

But a sinful man may well have need of the sick-bed—though now I cannot feel that my soul is like to grow stronger through my lying on here——"

So the boy was christened the next Sunday, and was given his mother's father's name. Kristin and Erlend were much blamed for this in the country-side, though Lavrans Björgulfsön said to all who came to see him that 'twas done at his desire: he would not have a heathen in his house when death came to the door.

Lavrans began now to grow fearful lest his death should fall in the midst of the spring sowing, thereby putting to great hardship the many folk who would be fain to honour his funeral by following in its train. But one morning, fourteen days after the christening, Erlend came to Kristin in the old weaving-house, where she had lain since the boy's birth. It was well on in the morning, past the dinner-time; but she was still abed, for the boy had been restless. Erlend was much moved; he said to her, quietly and lovingly, that she must get up now and come to her father. Lavrans had had some fearful heart-spasms at daybreak, and since had lain long swooning. Sira Eirik was with him now and had just heard his confession.

It was the fifth day after Halvard's Mass. Rain was falling gently and steadily. When Kristin came out into the courtyard, there came to her on the soft breath of air from the south the smell of fields new-ploughed and dressed. The country-side lay brown under the spring rain, the air was blue between the high mountains, and the mists drifted along half-way up the hill-sides. A tinkling of little bells came from the thickets along the brimming grey river—the flocks of goats had been let loose, and were nibbling at the blossoming twigs. 'Twas the weather that had ever rejoiced her father's heart, the end of winter and cold for folk and for cattle, the beasts all set free from narrow dark byres and scanty forage.

She saw at once in her father's face that now death was very near. About his nostrils the skin was snow-white, his lips and the circles round his great eyes were bluish, the hair had fallen apart, and lay in damp strands over the broad dewy forehead. But he was in his full senses now, and spoke clearly, though slowly and in a weak voice.

The house-folk went forward to his bed, one by one, and Lavrans took each of them by the hand, thanked them for their service, bade them farewell, and prayed them to forgive him if he had ever wronged them in any wise; he prayed them, too, to think of him with a prayer for his soul. Then he said farewell to his kindred. He bade his daughters bend down so that he might kiss them, and he called down the blessing of God and of all the saints upon them. Both wept bitterly, and young Ramborg threw herself into her sister's arms; then, with arms twined round each other, Lavrans' two daughters went to their place at their father's bed-foot, the younger one still weeping on Kristin's breast.

Erlend's face quivered, and tears ran down over his cheeks when he lifted Lavrans' hand and kissed it, while he prayed his wife's father in a low voice to forgive him all his sins against him at all times. Lavrans said he did so with all his heart, and he prayed that God might be with him all his days. There was a strange pale light over Erlend's comely face when he came softly round and stood at his wife's side, hand in hand with her.

Simon Darre wept not, but he knelt down when he took his father-in-law's hand to kiss, and he stayed kneeling a little while holding it fast. "Warm and good is your hand, son-in-law," said Lavrans with a faint smile. Ramborg turned her to her husband when he came to her side, and Simon threw his arm about her slender girlish shoulders.

Last of all, Lavrans bade farewell to his wife. They whispered some words to each other that none could hear, and exchanged a kiss in the sight of all, as was fitting and seemly, since death was in the room. After this, Ragnfrid kneeled down in front of her husband's couch, with her face turned towards his; she was white and calm and still.

Sira Eirik tarried on after he had anointed the dying man with the sacred oil and given him the viaticum. He sat by the bed-head, saying over prayers; Ragnfrid was sitting now on the bed's edge. Some hours went by. Lavrans lay with half-shut eyes. Now and again he moved his head restlessly on the pillow, groped a little with his hands on the cover-lid, and breathed heavily and moaningly once or twice. They deemed that he had lost power of speech, but there were no death-throes.

It grew dusk early, and the priest lit a candle. The folk sat still, looking at the dying man and listening to the dripping and trickling of the rain without the house. Then an unrest seemed to come upon the sick man, his body shook, a blue shade came upon his face, and he seemed to struggle for breath. Sira Eirik passed his arm behind his shoulders and lifted him up to a sitting posture, while he stayed his head on his own breast and held the cross up before his face.

Lavrans opened his eyes, fixed them on the crucifix in the priest's hand, and spoke softly, but so clearly that most in the room heard the words:

"*Exsurrexi, et adhuc sum tecum.*" *

Once more some tremors passed over the body, and his hands groped on the coverlid. Sira Eirik went on holding him close for a little while. Then he warely laid his friend's body back on the pillows, kissed the

* Psalm cxxxix. 13.

forehead and smoothed the hair about it, before he pressed the eyelids and nostrils shut, then rose to his feet and began to pray.

Kristin was given leave to take her turn in watching the body at night. They had laid out Lavrans on straw in the upper hall; for there was most room there, and they looked to have a great gathering of folk for the wake.

Her father seemed to her unspeakably beautiful as he lay there in the tapers' light with his pale-golden visage bared. They had turned down the napkin from his face so that it might not be soiled by the hands of the many folk that came to see the corpse. Sira Eirik and the parish priest from Kvam chanted over him—the Kvam priest had come up in the evening to bid Lavrans a last farewell, but had been too late.

But already next day the guests began to come riding to the manor, and now it behoved Kristin, for seemliness' sake, to betake her to bed again, since she had not yet been to church. Now it was her turn to have her bed decked out with silken coverings and the finest cushions the house could furnish. The Gjesling cradle was brought back from Formo on loan; Lavrans the younger was laid in it, and every day people came in and out to see her and the child.

Her father's body kept fresh and sweet, she heard—it was but grown somewhat more yellow. And none had seen before so many candles brought to set about a dead man's bier.

On the fifth day began the grave-ale—and 'twas stately beyond measure in every wise—there were more than a hundred strange horses on the manor and at Laugarbru, and, besides, some guests had to lie at Formo. On the seventh day the heirs divided the lands and goods in all friendliness and concord—Lavrans had taken order for all things himself before he died, and all followed his wishes faithfully.

The next day the body, which lay now in the Olav's church, was to be brought forth to begin the journey to Hamar.

The evening before—rather 'twas far on in the night—Ragnfrid came into the hearth-room house, where her daughter lay with her child. The mistress of the house was exceeding weary, but her face was clear and calm. She bade the serving-women go out:

"Every house on the place is full, but I trow you will find a corner somewhere; I have a mind to watch over my daughter myself, on this my last night in my home."

She took the child from Kristin's arms, bore it across to the hearth, and made it ready for the night.

"Strange must it be for you, mother, to flit away from this place where you have lived with my father all these years," said Kristin. "I scarce understand how you can bear it."

"Much less could I bear it, methinks," said Ragnfrid, rocking little Lavrans in her lap, "to live here and not see your father going about among the houses.

"You have never heard how it came about that we flitted hither to the Dale and made our home here," she began again in a while. "The time word came that they looked my father, Ivar, should soon breathe his last, I was unfit to take the road; Lavrans had to journey north alone. I mind well 'twas such fair weather the evening he set forth—already in those days he had come to like riding late, in the cool; so he was to ride to Oslo that night; 'twas just before midsummer. I went with him to where the road from the manor cuts the church road—mind you? there are some great bare rocks there and barren soil round about—the worst lands on all Skog, they ever feel the drought first—but that year the corn grew well and fairly on those fields, and we spoke of it. Lavrans walked, leading his horse; and I had you by the hand—you were four winters old——

"When we came to where the roads joined, I told you to run home to the houses. You were loath to go, but then your father said that you should see if you could find five white stones and set them in a cross in the beck below the spring—'twas to guard him from the trolls of the Mjörsa Wood when he sailed by there. Then you set off running——"

"Is that a thing that folks there tell?" asked Kristin.

"I have never heard it, either before or since. Your father must have made it up, methinks, there and then. Mind you not, he made up so many tales when he played with you?"

"Yes, I remember."

"I went with him through the wood, all the way to the dwarf-stone. Then he bade me turn back, and he, too, went back with me to the cross-roads again—he laughed and said I might have known he would not let me walk alone through the wood, and when the sun was gone down, too. As we stood there at the cross-roads, I put my arms round his neck; I was so cast down because I could not come back home—I never could thrive rightly at Skog, and I longed ever to be back north in the Dale. Lavrans comforted me, and at last he said: 'When I come back, if I find you with my son in your arms, then you may ask me for what you will, and if 'tis in the power of man to give it, you shall not have asked in vain.' I answered: then would I pray that we might flit up hither and dwell on the lands of my heritage. Your father liked this but little, and he said: 'Could you not have found a greater thing to pray for?'—he laughed a little, and I thought: he will never do this—and it seemed to me, too, but reason that he should not. Afterward you know how things went with me—Sigurd, your youngest brother, lived not an hour—Halvdan christened him and he died straightway after. . . .

"Your father came home one morning early—he had heard at Oslo, the night before, how things stood at home, and had ridden straight on without tarrying. I was still in bed; I was so sorrowful I had not the heart to rise—it seemed to me I would liefest never have risen again. God forgive me, when they brought you in to me, I turned my face to the wall, and would not look on you, my little child. But then said Lavrans, as he sat on my bedside, with his cloak and sword still on him, that now must we try whether things would go better for us if we lived here at Jörundgaard—and 'twas thus we came to make our flitting from Skog. But since it was so, you may think that I have no mind to dwell here, now Lavrans is gone."

Ragnfrid came over with the child and laid it to its mother's breast. She took the silk coverlid that had been spread over Kristin's bed in the day-time, folded it up, and laid it aside. Then she stood a while looking at her daughter, and touched the thick yellow-brown plait that lay between her white breasts:

"Your father asked me so often if your hair were as thick and fair as ever. 'Twas a great joy to him that you lost not your loveliness through bearing so many children. He rejoiced much over you in these last years, that you had grown to be so notable a woman and still stood fresh and fair with all your fair little sons about you."

Kristin gulped down her tears once or twice.

"To me, mother, he would often speak of how you had been the best of wives—he said I should tell you——" She stopped abashed, and Ragnfrid laughed softly.

"Lavrans might have known that he needed not to have any bear me word of his loving-kindness towards me." She stroked the child's head and her daughter's hand, which was round the little one. "But maybe he would have—— It is not so, my Kristin, that on any day I have envied you your father's love. 'Twas but right and reason that you have loved him more than me. You were so sweet and lovely a little maid— I was not grateful enough that God had let me keep you. But I ever thought more on what I had lost than on what I possessed."

Ragnfrid sat down on the bedside:

"They had other ways at Skog than our ways at home here. I cannot call to mind that my father ever kissed me—he kissed my mother when she was laid in the dead-straw. Mother kissed Gudrun at mass, for she stood nearest her, and then sister kissed me—but else we never used to kiss. . . .

"At Skog there was a custom that when we came from church after having taken the sacrament, and we alighted from our horses in the courtyard, Sir Björgulf kissed his sons and me on the cheek, and we kissed his hand. Afterward all married pairs kissed each other, and then we shook hands with all the serving-folk that had been at the service, and wished each other all good of the sacred food. And it was much their use, Lavrans' and Aasmund's, to kiss their father's hand when he made them gifts and at suchlike times. When he or Inga came in, the sons rose always to their feet and stood till they were bidden to sit down. At first these all seemed to me foolish, outlandish ways. . . .

"Afterward, in the years I lived with your father, when we lost our sons, and through all those years when we suffered such great fear and sorrow for our Ulvhild—it was well for me then that Lavrans had been nurtured so—to follow gentler and more loving ways."

In a while Kristin said, low:

"Father never saw Sigurd, then?"

"No," said Ragnfrid in the same low tones. "I saw him not either while he lived."

Kristin lay silent awhile; then she said:

"None the less, mother, so it seems to me, you have yet had much good in your life——"

Tears began to drip down over Ragnfrid Ivarsdatter's white face:

"Aye, God help me. To me, too, it seems so now."

Soon after, she took the babe, which was sleeping now, from its mother's breast, and laid it in the cradle. She fastened up Kristin's shift with its little brooch, stroked her daughter's cheek, and bade her sleep now. Kristin lifted a hand.

"Mother——" she said beseechingly.

Ragnfrid bent down, drew her daughter close in her arms, and kissed her many times. She had not done this before in all the years since Ulvhild died.

Next day 'twas the fairest spring weather, as Kristin stood behind the corner of the hall-house and looked over at the hill-sides beyond the river. The smell of growth was everywhere, and the song of becks set free; there was a tinge of green on all the woods and meadows. Where the road ran along the mountain-side above Laugarbru, a patch of winter rye shone out fresh and bright—Jon had burnt the undergrowth there last year and sowed rye in the burned path.

She would see the funeral train best when it passed by there. . . .

And there it was, moving slowly along, below the hill-side scree, and above the fresh new rye-field.

She could make out all the priests riding ahead of all; there were acolytes, too, in the first troop, bearing crosses and tapers. She could not see the flames in the bright daylight, but she saw the tapers themselves as slender white streaks. Then came two horses bearing between them her father's coffin on a litter; and then she could pick out Erlen on his black horse, her mother, Simon and Ramborg, and many of her kinsfolk and friends in the long funeral train.

For a while she could clearly hear the priests' chant above the roar of the Laagen, but then the sound of the hymn died away, lost in the noise of the river and the humming of the becks on the hill-sides. Kristin stood still, gazing, long after the last pack-horse with baggage was lost from sight in the wayside woods.

Part Three

ERLEND NIKULAUSSÖN

I

R AGNFRID I VARSDATTER lived not full two years after her
husband's death; she died early in the winter of 1332. It is far from
Hamar to Skaun, so that they heard not aught of her death at Husaby
till she had lain in her grave more than a month. But at Whitsuntide
the next year Simon Andressön came to them; there was one thing
and another to be talked over between the kinsfolk concerning
Ragnfrid's inheritance. Kristin Lavransdatter owned Jörundgaard
now, and it was settled that Simon should hold the charge of her
lands and goods, and draw her farmers to account; he had managed
his mother-in-law's estates in the Dale while she had dwelled at
Hamar.

Just at this time Erlend had much trouble and vexation over certain
cases that had come up in his Wardenship. The autumn before, Huntjov, the farmer of Forbregd in Updal, had slain a neighbour of his for
calling his wife a troll-woman. The parish folk brought the slayer bound
to the Warden, and Erlend had him shut up in a loft. But when the cold
grew fierce in the winter-time, he let the man go about loose among his
followers. Huntjov had been with Erlend in *Margygren* in the north, and
had done manful service there. So when Erlend sent in letters touching
Huntjov's case, praying that he be given grace * to abide at home till
his case was judged, he set the man in the fairest light; and, as Ulf
Haldorssön went surety that Huntjov would present him in due time at
the Orkedal Thing, Erlend let the man go home for the Yule holy-days.
But from home he and his wife set out to visit the rest-house keeper in
Drivdal—he was a kinsman of theirs—and on that journey they disappeared. Erlend believed that they had lost their lives in the great
storm that had raged about that time; but many folk said they had run
away—the Warden's people might whistle for them now. And then new
matters were brought up against the runaways—that Huntjov had killed
a man some years before away in the hills and buried his body in a scree
—a man that he thought had slashed his mare on the rump. And it
came out clearly that the wife had dealt in witchcraft.

Next the Updal priest and the Archbishop's commissary set to work
to search and sift all these rumours of witchcraft. And this led to sorry
things coming out about the way folks held by their Christian faith in
many parts of the Orkdöla County. 'Twas most in the outlying parishes,
like Rennabu and Updalsskog; but the case of one old man from
Budvik, too, was brought before the Archbishop's Court at Nidaros.
And in this Erlend showed so little zeal that there was much talk of it.

* See Note 14.

It was the old carl Aan, who had lived down by the lake below Husaby, and must well-nigh be reckoned as one of Erlend's house-folk. He had dealt in runes and spells, and there was talk of some images in his hut, which folk said he had used to sacrifice to. But naught of this kind was found after his death. Erlend himself and Ulf Haldorssön had been with him, 'twas known, when he died—and doubtless they had made away with both one thing and another before the priest came, people said. Aye, and when folk came to think of it, had not Erlend's own mother's sister been charged with witchcraft, whoredom and husband-murder? —though Lady Aashild Gautesdatter was too crafty and slippery, and no doubt besides had had too many mighty friends, for aught to be proved against her. And at the same time people called to mind that Erlend in his youth had lived in sadly unchristian fashion, and had set at naught the ban of the Church.

The end of all this was that the Archbishop summoned Erlend Nikulaussön to come and confer with him at Nidaros. Simon went with his brother-in-law into the city; he was to fetch his sister's son from Ranheim, for it was meant that the boy should go back with him to the Dale, and be with his mother for a while.

It was but a week from the time set for the Frostathing, and the city was full of people. When the brothers-in-law came to the Archbishop's palace and were shown into the hall of audience, a number of Crossed Friars were there, and some laymen of standing—among them, the Lagmand of the Frostathing, Harald Nikulaussön; Olav Hermanssön, Lagmand of Nidaros; Sir Guttorm Helgessön, Warden of Jemtland; and also Arne Gjavvaldssön, who at once came up to Simon Darre and greeted him heartily. Arne drew Simon apart with him into a window-nook and they sat down there.

Simon was somewhat ill at ease. He had not met the other since he had been at Ranheim ten years before, and, though the Ranheim folk had then welcomed him most fairly, his visit there on such an errand had left a sore spot in his mind.

Whilst Arne was bragging of young Gjavvald, Simon sat watching his brother-in-law. Erlend stood talking with the Treasurer,* whose name was Sir Baard Peterssön, but who was not of kin to the Hestnæs house. One could not have said that Erlend's bearing lacked due courtesy; yet he was exceeding free and unabashed as he stood there talking with the old nobleman—swaying a little back and forth, with his hands laid together behind his back. As was mostly his use, he was clad in dark colours, but most richly: violet *kothardi* sitting close to his body and slashed up the sides, black tippet, with hood thrown back to show the grey silk lining, silver-mounted belt, and long red boots that were laced

* See Note 15.

tight round the calves and set off the man's slender, shapely legs and feet.

In the sharp light from the glass windows of the hall, 'twas plain enough to see that the hair at Erlend Nikulaussön's temples was not a little sprinkled with grey. Round his mouth and beneath the eyes the fine sunburned skin was scratched, as it were, with fine wrinkles, and cross-furrows had appeared in the long, fairly arched neck. Yet he seemed full young amongst the others there—though he was in no wise the youngest man in the room. 'Twas that he was slender and lithe as ever, bore his body in the same supple, somewhat careless fashion as in his youth, and walked no less lightly and springily, as now, after the Treasurer had left him, he began to stroll up and down the room, still with his hands clasped behind him. All the other men were seated; they talked a little among themselves in low, dry voices. Erlend's light step and the jingle of his small silver spurs were too clearly heard.

At length one of the younger men testily bade him sit down, "and be a little quieter, man!"

Erlend stopped short and knit his brows, then turned to the man who had spoken.

"Where were you drinking yestereven, kinsman Jon, that your head is so sore to-day?" he said with a laugh, sitting down. When Harald Lagmand came across to him, he rose, indeed, and stood till the other had sat down, but then he dropped down by the Lagmand's side, crossed one leg over the other, and sat with his hands clasped over his knee, while Harald was speaking.

Erlend had told Simon frankly of all the trouble he had fallen into by reason of the manslayer and the witch-woman having slipped through his fingers. But no man could have seemed more care-free than Erlend, as he sat talking the matter over with the Lagmand.

Now the Archbishop entered. He was led to his high seat by two men, who propped him up with pillows. Simon had never before seen Lord Eiliv Kortin. He looked old and feeble, and seemed to be cold, though he was clad in a fur cloak and wore a fur-lined cap. When their turn came, Erlend led his brother-in-law up to him, and Simon knelt on one knee while he kissed Lord Eiliv's ring. Erlend, too, kissed the ring reverently.

He bore him most seemly and reverently, too, when at last he stood forth before the Archbishop, after the churchman had spoken a good while with the others on divers matters. But he answered somewhat lightly the questions one of the Canons put to him, and his mien was that of a man confident in his innocence.

Yes, he had heard the common talk of witchcraft for many years. But, so long as no one had come to him for guidance, surely he could in no wise be bound to search out the truth of all the talk that went on among the womenfolk in a parish. Surely 'twas the priest's affair to make inquiry, if there were grounds for making out a case against any.

Then he was asked of the old man who had dwelt at Husaby, and who folks said was a wizard.

Erlend smiled a little; yes, Aan had bragged of it himself, but no proof of his mystery had Erlend ever seen. From his childhood up he had heard Aan talk of some women he called Hæn and Skögul and Snotra, but he had never taken all this to be aught else but toys and nursery-tales. "My brother Gunnulf and our priest, Sira Eiliv, cross-questioned him once or twice, I know, but I trow they cannot have found aught against him, since they did nothing. The man came to the church each mass-day, and knew his Christian prayers." Great faith in Aan's sorceries he had never had, and since he had seen somewhat in the north of Lapp magic and spells, he had seen full well that the magic Aan dealt in was but foolery.

Then the priest asked if 'twas true that Erlend himself had once been given a thing by Aan—something that was to bring him fortune in *amor?*

Aye, answered Erlend quickly and clearly, with a smile. 'Twas when he was about fifteen, he thought—eight-and-twenty years ago or so. A skin pouch with a little white stone in it, and some dried-up things—bits of some beast, he believed. But he had not had much faith in such things in those days either—he had given it away the next year, the first year he was at the palace. It was in a bath-house up in the town—in a rash, jesting moment he had shown the charm to some other young lads—and afterwards one of the gentlemen of the guard had come to him wanting to buy it. Erlend had given it him in barter for a razor of fine steel.

It was asked who this gentleman might be.

At first Erlend would not come out with it. But the Archbishop himself bade him speak. Then Erlend looked up with a gleam of mischief in his blue eyes. "'Twas Sir Ivar Ogmundssön."

There came a somewhat strained look into the men's faces. Strange snorting sounds came from old Sir Guttorm Helgessön. Lord Eiliv himself had some ado not to smile. Then Erlend, growing venturesome, went on, with eyes cast down and biting his under lip a little:

"My Lord, I trust you will not trouble the good knight with this ancient matter. As I have said to you, I believed not much in the thing myself, and I have never marked that it made any odds to either of us, my giving him this treasure——"

Sir Guttorm doubled up in a roar, and the other men had to give in, one after the other, and laugh aloud. The Archbishop tittered a little, coughing and shaking his head. It was well known that Sir Ivar's will had ever been better than his fortune in certain matters.

In a while, however, one of the Crossed Friars grew sober again and reminded the company they were come together to speak of grave matters. Erlend asked a little sharply if a charge had been laid against him from any quarter, and if he were on his trial—he had not supposed aught else than that he had been sent for to a friendly conference. The talk then went on as before, but some disorder was caused by Guttorm Helgessön bursting out every now and then into little snickers of laughter.

The day after, when the brothers-in-law rode home from Ranheim, Simon brought up the matter of this meeting. It seemed to Simon that Erlend took the thing over-lightly—he thought he had marked clearly that more than one of the great folk there would be fain to do him an ill turn if they could.

Erlend said he knew well enough they would, if they had the power. For here in the north most men leaned to the Chancellor's party not the Archbishop, though: in him Erlend had a trusty friend. But Erlend's dealings in all things were conformable to the law—he took counsel in all cases with his clerk, Klöng Aressön, who was most skilful in such matters. Erlend spoke gravely now, but he smiled slightly as he said that he deemed none had looked that he should be as well skilled in the matters of his charge as he was—neither his dear friends in this countryside nor the lords of the Council. For the rest, he was not sure that he cared to keep the Wardenship if 'twas to be on other terms than those he had while Erling Vidkunssön was at the helm. His affairs were now in such a posture—the more so since his wife's parents' death—that he had no need to bargain for the favour of the men that had come to power when the King was declared of age.

Aye, that rotten boy they might just as well call of age now as later; 'twas unlike he would grow more of a man by keeping. One would come to know all the sooner what he was planning—he or the Swedish lords that pulled the strings. Folk would soon own that Erling had been clear-sighted after all. It would cost us dear if King Magnus tried to bring Skaane under the Swedish crown, and 'twould mean war with the Danes the moment *one* man, be he Danish or German, came to power in Denmark. And the peace in the north that was to last ten years—half the time was gone by now, and 'twas unsure whether the Russians would hold to the pact even for the five years left. Erlend had little faith in them, nor had Erling either, for that matter. Aye, Chancellor Paal was doubtless a learned man, long-headed too, in many ways, perhaps. But these gentry of the Council who had taken him for their leader— Soten here had more wit than the whole of them put together. Well, now they had got quit of Erling—for the time. And for the time, Erlend, too, had just as lief step aside. But Erling and his friends would doubt-less rather that Erlend kept a hold on his powers and fortunes in the north here—so he had not made up his mind.

"Methinks you have learned now to sing Sir Erling's tune," Simon Darre could not help saying.

Erlend answered : aye, it was so. He had dwelt in Sir Erling's house last summer, when he was at Björgvin, and he had learned to understand the man better now. So it was that Sir Erling wished above all things to uphold the King's peace in the land. But he wished, too, that Norway's realm should have the lion's peace—that none should have leave to break a tooth or clip a claw of their kinsman King Haakon's lion—and that it should not be turned, either, into a trained hunting-dog for the people of another land. For the rest, Erling had it much at heart now to bring to an end the old quarrels between Norsemen and Lady Inge-björg. Now that she had been left a widow by Sir Knut, one could not but wish that she should get some power over her son again. True it was that she bore such exceeding great love to the children she had borne to Knut Porse that it seemed she had in some measure forgotten her eldest son, but doubtless all this would be changed when she came to meet with him again.

Simon deemed that all this sounded as though Erlend were well-informed of what was afoot. But he wondered at Erling Vidkunssön—did the fallen High Steward believe that Erlend Nikulaussön had the wit to form a judgment in such things, or was it that Erling was catch-ing now at any straw within reach? Like enough, the Knight of Giske was loath to loose his grasp on power. None could ever have said of him that he used it for his own profit, but then, with his riches and his standing, he had no need to do so. And all said that as the years of his Stewardship went on he had grown more and more self-willed and wise in his own conceit, and as the other lords of the Council began more and more to withstand him, he had at last grown so masterful that he would scarce deign to listen to a word from any man.

It was like Erlend that he had now, so to speak, gotten aboard Erling Vidkunssön's ship with both feet—just as it had met with head winds and it seemed most unsure whether his throwing himself with all his heart on his rich kinsman's side would profit either Sir Erling or Erlend himself. Yet Simon could not but confess to himself that, rashly as Erlend talked both of people and of affairs, there seemed to be a kernel of good sense in what he said.

But that night he was in a wild and reckless mood. He was dwelling now in Sir Nikulaus' mansion, which his brother had given to Erlend when he took the cowl. Kristin was with him, with three of their chil-dren, the two eldest and the youngest, and his daughter Margret.

Late in the evening many folk looked in on them, amongst them some of the men who had been at the meeting at the Archbishop's the morning before. As they sat drinking at the board after supper, Erlend overflowed with noise and laughter. He had taken an apple from a dish upon the table, and he cut scrolls and scratches on it with his knife—and then rolled it across the board into the lap of Lady Sunniva Olavsdatter, who sat over against him.

The lady who sat by Sunniva's side wanted to see the apple, and snatched at it; the other would not give it up, and the two women pushed and struggled with each other, with laughter and little shrieks. But Erlend shouted out that Lady Eyvor should have an apple all to herself. Before long he had thrown apples to all the women in the company, and there were love-runes carved on them all, he said.

"You'll be ruined, lad, should you redeem all these pledges!" cried out a man.

"Then will I let them go unredeemed—'tis not the first time I have had to," Erlend answered back; and again there was much laughter.

But Klöng, the Icelander, had looked at one of the apples and he cried out that these were not runes, but only meaningless scrolls. He would show them, he said, how runes should rightly be cut. But Erlend cried out he must do no such thing:

"For then 'tis like they would bid me lay you by the heels, Klöng—and I cannot get on without you."

In the midst of all this turmoil, Erlend and Kristin's youngest son had come toddling into the hall. Lavrans Erlendssön was a little over two years old now, and was as comely a child as one could see, fair and fat, with silky-fine yellow curly hair. And so all the women on the outer bench were at once set on getting hold of the child—they passed him from lap to lap, and caressed him, not too gently, for they were now all heated and in wild mirth. Kristin, who sat with her husband in the high-seat against the wall, begged to have the child brought round to her, and the little one whimpered and tried to come at her, but 'twas of no avail.

Of a sudden, Erlend leapt across the table and took the child, which was shrieking now, because Lady Sunniva and Lady Eyvor were dragging at him and struggling over him. The father took the boy up in his arms, coaxing him, and as the little one still went on crying, he began hushing and lulling him, walking up and down with him out in the hall in the half-darkness. It seemed now as though Erlend had quite forgotten his guests. The child's little bright head lay on its father's shoulder under the man's black hair, and now and then Erlend would caress, with lips half opened, the little hand that rested on his breast in front. So he walked up and down till the maid came in that should have looked to the child and put him to bed long before.

Some of the guests called out now that Erlend should sing for them to dance to—he had such a fine strong voice. At first he was unwilling, but then he went over to where his young daughter sat on the women's bench. He put his arm around Margret and drew her out on to the floor.

"You must come along, then, my Margret, and dance with your father."

A young man came forward and took the maid's hand—"Margret has promised to dance with me to-night"—but Erlend lifted his daughter in his arms and set her down on his other side:

"Dance you with your wife, Haakon—never did I dance with others when I was as newly wed as you are."

"Ingebjörg says she cannot dance to-night—and I have promised Haakon to dance with him, father," said Margret.

Simon Darre had no mind to dance. He stood awhile with an old lady, looking on—now and then his glance rested a moment on Kristin. While her serving-maids were clearing the board and wiping it dry and bearing in more drink and dishes of walnuts, she stood up at the end of the table. After, she sat down by the fire-place and talked with a priest who was among the guests. In a while Simon sat down beside the two.

When they had danced one or two dances, Erlend came over to his wife.

"Come and dance with us, Kristin," he said beseechingly, holding out his hand.

"I am tired," she said, looking up for an instant.

"Do you ask her, Simon—she cannot deny you a dance."

Simon half rose from his seat and reached out his hand, but Kristin shook her head: "Ask me not, Simon—I am so weary——"

Erlend stood there a little; he looked as though he were sorely vexed at this. Then he went back to Lady Sunniva and took her hand in the chain of dancers, while he called out that now Margret should sing for them.

"Who is he that is dancing next your stepdaughter?" asked Simon. He thought in his mind that he liked the man's looks but little—though he was a fine manful-looking young fellow with a fresh brown skin, good teeth and shining eyes—but the eyes were set close in to the bridge of the nose, and, though he had a big strong mouth and chin, his forehead and upper head were narrow. Kristin said 'twas Haakon Eindridessön of Gimsar, grandson of Tore Eindridessön, the Warden of Gauldöla County. Haakon had but just been wedded to the comely little woman that sat there in Olav Lagmand's lap—Olav was her godfather. Simon had marked this woman, for she somewhat favoured his first wife, though she was not so fair. As he found out now that there was a distant kinship, too, he went over and greeted Ingebjörg and sat down and talked with her.

The ring of dancers broke up in a while. The elders betook them to the drinking-board; but the young folks went on singing and disporting themselves out in the hall. Erlend came over to the fire-place along with some of the older men, but he still held Lady Sunniva's hand and led her with him, as if without thinking. The men sat down near the fire; there was no seat for the lady, but she stood before Erlend, eating walnuts, which he cracked for her with his fingers.

"An uncourteous man you are, Erlend, for sure," she said, suddenly. "There you sit, and I have to stand in front of you."

"Nay, do you sit too," said Erlend, laughing, and pulled her down into his lap. She struggled, laughing, and called out to the mistress of the house, asking if she saw how her husband was behaving to her.

"'Tis but the kindness of Erlend's heart," answered Kristin, laughing. "Never does my cat rub herself against his legs but he must needs take her up and lay her in his lap."

Erlend and the lady sat on as before, making no sign, but both had grown very red. He held one arm loosely about her, as if he hardly marked that she sat there, whilst he and the other men talked of the feud between Erling Vidkunssön and Chancellor Paal, which was so much in folks' thoughts just then.

"What are you thinking on now, Kristin?" Simon asked in a while— she was sitting quite still and straight, with her hands folded in her lap. She answered:

"I was thinking now of Margret."

Later in the night, when Erlend and Simon had an errand out in the courtyard, they frighted away from each other a couple that was standing behind the house-corner. The night was clear as day, and Simon knew them for Haakon of Gimsar and Margret Erlendsdatter. Erlend looked after them—he was sober enough—and Simon saw that he misliked this; but he said, as though in excuse, that those two had known each other from childhood and were for ever teasing and jesting with each other. Simon thought that even if there were no other harm, 'twas pity of the young wife, Ingebjörg.

But the day after, when young Haakon came to the house on some errand and asked after Margit, Erlend flamed out at him:

"My daughter is not *Margit* to you. And if so be you left your talk unfinished yesterday, you had best keep awhile what you have to say to her——"

Haakon shrugged his shoulders and, when he left, begged them to greet *Margareta* from him.

The Husaby folk stayed in Nidaros till the Thing was over, but Simon felt none too happy or at home among them. Erlend was apt to fall into fretful moods when in his town-house, because Gunnulf had given the hospital, which lay on the other side of the orchard, the right to use some of the houses that opened from the orchard, and also some rights in the garden. Erlend had set his mind on buying out these rights; he liked not to see the sick folk in the garden and in the courtyard—many of them, indeed, were an ill-favoured sight—and he was fearful lest his children might take some sickness. But he could not come to agreement with the monks who managed the hospital.

Then there was Margret Erlendsdatter. Simon understood that there was much talk about her, and that Kristin was disquieted by it; but the girl's father seemed not to care—it seemed that he felt sure he could guard his own maid and that there was naught to dread. Yet he named one day to Simon that he thought Klöng Aressön had a mind to wed his daughter, and he knew not rightly what to do in the matter. He had naught else against the Icelander than that he was the son of a priest— he was loath it should be said of Margret's children that there was a stain on both their parents' birth. Else was Klöng a man that all liked, cheerful, keen-witted and most learned. His father, Sira Are, had brought him up and taught him himself; he had meant his son to be a priest, and 'twas said he had even taken steps to get a dispensation for him, but Klöng had drawn back and would not take the frock. It seemed as though Erlend was minded to let the matter rest awhile—if no better match offered, he could always give the maid to Klöng Aressön.

Yet was it known that Erlend had already had such a good offer for his daughter that folk had had much to say of his pride and folly in letting the bargain slip. It was from a grandson of Baron Sigvat of Leirhóle— Sigmund Finssön was the man's name; he was not rich, for Finn Sigvatssön had had eleven children who all lived; and he could not be called young—he was about Erlend's age—but he was a man in good esteem and of a good understanding. And with the lands that Erlend had given his daughter when he wedded Kristin Lavransdatter, and with all the jewellery and costly gifts he had given the child from time to time, and with the dowry he had agreed with Sigmund to give with her, Margret would have been more than well-to-do. Erlend, indeed, had been glad enough to find such a suitor for his base-born daughter. But when he came home to his daughter with the bridegroom, the maid took a whimsy that she would not have him because Sigmund had some warts on the edge of one of his eyelids, and she said this gave her such a loathing of him. Erlend gave in to the girl; and when Sigmund grew angry and talked of breach of troth, Erlend, too, grew hot, and said that the other must surely understand that all betrothal-pacts were made on condition that the maid was willing—his daughter should not be forced into her bride-bed. Kristin thought with her husband in so far as that he should not force the girl, but 'twas known that she had deemed Erlend should have spoken in sober sadness to his daughter and made her understand that Sigmund Finssön was so good a match as, seeing how things stood with her birth, she could not hope to find a better. But Erlend had been wroth with his wife for venturing to speak thus, though she said it to him only. These things Simon had heard at Ranheim. The folk there foretold that all this must needs end badly; 'twas true Erlend was a man of weight now, and the maid was a passing fair maid, but yet 'twas impossible it could be for her good that her father had spoiled her all these years and fed the flames of her pride and self-will.

After the Frosta Thing, Erlend went home to Husaby with his wife and children, and with them went Simon Darre.

Now, when the eldest sons were big enough to ride abroad with Erlend, he had begun to take more heed of the boys. Simon marked that Kristin was not wholly glad of this—she deemed that 'twas not only good they got by going amongst their father's men. And it was about the children that unfriendly words most often passed between this wedded pair—even if they did not quarrel outright, they often came more nigh to it than Simon deemed fitting. And it seemed to him that Kristin was the most at fault. Erlend was quick-tempered and hasty, but she often spoke as though from a deep-hidden grudge. So it was one day when she made some complaint about Naakkve. Erlend answered that he would speak strictly to the boy, but, on his wife's saying something more, he broke out testily, saying he could not well thrash a big boy like him, because of the house-folk.

"No, 'tis too late now; had you done it while he was younger, he might have hearkened to you now. But in those days you never so much as looked his way."

"Oh, but I did. Though it was but reason surely that I should let him go about with you when he was little—and 'tis no work for a man, I trow, to beat little breechless brats."

"You thought not so last week," said Kristin, scornfully and bitterly.

Erlend made no answer, but rose to his feet and went out. And to Simon this seemed an ill speech of Erlend's wife. She was recalling a thing that had befallen the week before; as Erlend and Simon came riding into the courtyard, little Lavrans had come running towards them with a wooden sword, and as he ran by his father's horse, he struck it, in mischievous play, on the leg with his sword. The horse reared—and next moment the boy had fallen to the ground beneath its feet. Erlend jerked back and flung the horse to one side, then leapt down, throwing the rein to Simon; his face was white with fear when he lifted the boy up in his arms. But when he saw that the child was quite unhurt, he laid him over his left arm, took the wooden sword, and thrashed him with it on the bare bottom—the boy had not been breeched yet. In his flurry he knew not how hard he struck, and Lavrans was still going about black and blue. But since then Erlend had tried all the time to make friends again with the boy—while the little man sulked, held to his mother's skirts, and threatened and slapped at his father. And when Lavrans had been put to rest in the evening in his parents' bed, where he slept (for he was still nursed by his mother at night), Erlend sat over on the bedside the whole evening, looking down on the sleeping child and touching him. He said himself, to Simon, that this boy was the one of his sons that he loved best.

When Erlend set forth for the summer meetings in his charge, Simon took the road for home. He galloped south through Gauldal, so that the sparks flew from the stones under his horse's hoofs. Once, when they rode a little slower up a steep hill, his men asked, laughing, whether they were to ride three days' march in two. Simon laughed back, and said he had more than a mind they should—"for now am I fain to be back at Formo."

He ever longed to be back when he had been away from his manor awhile—he was a home-loving man, and rejoiced always when he turned his horse into the homeward road. But it seemed to him that so much as this time he had never before yearned to get back to the Dale, and his manor, and his little daughters—aye, and now he longed for Ramborg too. It seemed to him that he had no good reason for this great eagerness, but the life at Husaby had so weighed upon his mood that he deemed he knew now from himself how the cattle feel when a storm is gathering.

II

ALL the summer through, Kristin thought of little else than what Simon had told her of her mother's death.

Ragnfrid Ivarsdatter had died all alone—none had been near when she drew her last breath, saving a serving-woman, who slept. 'Twas not much comfort, what Simon said—that, though death came so suddenly, she was yet well prepared. It seemed like a special providence of God that, a few days before, she had felt in her such a hunger for her Redeemer's Body that she had confessed and taken the sacrament from the priest in the cloister who was her director. 'Twas certain she had made a good death—Simon had seen her body, and said it had seemed to him a marvellous sight. In death she had been so fair; she was, one knew, a woman nigh threescore years of age, and for many years her face had been much wrinkled and furrowed; but this was changed alto- gether: her face was grown young and smooth, so that she looked like naught else but a young woman fallen asleep. Now had she been laid to rest by her husband's side; thither, too, had they brought Ulvhild Lavransdatter's bones a short time after her father's death. Over the graves was laid a great stone slab, divided in two by a fairly carven cross, and on a winding scroll was written a long Latin verse that the Prior of the cloister had made; but Simon could not remember it rightly, for he knew but little of that tongue.

Ragnfrid had had a house to herself in the yard up in the town where the commoners of the cloister lived—a single room and above it a fair loft-room. There she dwelt alone with a poor peasant woman who had been taken in by the friars for small payment, in return for her helping one or other of the richer women-commoners. But for the last half-year at least it had rather been Ragnfrid who helped the other, for the widow —Torgunna was her name—had been ailing, and Ragnfrid tended her with great kindness and care.

The last evening of her life she had been at evensong in the cloister- church, and went afterwards into the kitchen of the commoners' yard. There she cooked a good bowl of soup with strengthening herbs in it, and said to the other women who were there that she would give this to Torgunna, and she hoped the woman would be well enough in the morning to come with her to matins. This was the last time any saw the Jörundgaard widow alive. They came not to matins—neither she nor the peasant woman—nor yet to prime. When some of the monks in the choir marked that Ragnfrid was not in the church for the day-mass either, they began to wonder—she had never before missed three ser- vices in a day. They sent word up to the town to ask if Lavrans Björ- gulfsön's widow were sick. When the folk came into the loft, they found the bowl of soup standing untouched on the board; in the bed Tor- gunna was sleeping sweetly by the wall, but Ragnfrid Ivarsdatter lay on the outside of the bed with her hands crossed on her breast, dead, and well-nigh cold already. Simon and Ramborg had come down to her burial, and it was a most fair one.

Now that the household at Husaby was grown so great and Kristin had six sons, she could no longer take a hand herself in all parts of the housekeeping. She was obliged to have a housekeeper under her, and so it came about that most of the time the mistress of the house sat in the hall sewing; there was ever someone wanting clothes—Erlend, Margret or the boys.

The last she had seen of her mother was riding after her husband's bier—that bright spring day when she had stood in the meadow at Jörundgaard and seen her father's funeral train pass the green patch of winter rye beneath the scree.

Kristin's needle flew and flew, and she thought on her parents and their home at Jörundgaard. Now, when all was memory, she seemed to herself to grow ware of much that she had not seen when she lived in the midst of it, and took as things of course her father's tender guardianship and her silent, sad-faced mother's quiet, constant work and care. She thought on her own children—they were dearer to her than her own heart's blood; they were not out of her mind one hour of her waking life. Yet was there much in her mind that she pondered over more—she loved her children without brooding on the matter. She had never thought aught else, when she was at home, but that her parents' whole life and all their doings and strivings were for herself and her sisters. Now she seemed to see that betwixt those two, who in their youth had been brought together by their fathers, well-nigh unasked, there had run strong swift currents both of sorrow and of joy—yet *she* knew naught of it save that they had passed now, hand in hand, out of her life. Now she understood that this man's and woman's lives had held much beside their love for their children—and yet that love had been strong and wide and unfathomably deep, while the love she gave them back had been weak and thoughtless and self-seeking, even when, in her childhood, those two had been her whole world. She seemed to see herself standing far, far away—so small, so small beyond that great stretch of time and distance; she stood in the beam of sunlight that streamed down through the smoke-vent in the old hearth-room house at home, the winter-house of her childhood. Her parents stood a little back, in the shadow—they bulked as great as they had seemed to her sight when she was small, and they smiled to her—the smile that she knew now comes to one's face when a little child comes and thrusts aside heavy and troublous thoughts.

"I thought, Kristin, when you had borne a child yourself, you would surely understand better."

She remembered when her mother had said these words. Sorrowfully she thought—it was not true, she feared, even now, that she understood her mother. But she began to understand how much there was she did not understand.

This autumn Archbishop Eiliv died. And about the same time King Magnus changed the terms of service of many of the Wardens, but not

Erlend Nikulaussön's. When Erlend was in Björgvin the last summer of the King's nonage, he had been given letters granting him the fourth part of all grace-payments,* fines and forfeitures in his Wardenship— the thing had made much talk, that he should have been given such a grant towards the close of a Regency. Since Erlend now owned much land in the country, and most often lived on his own farms when he moved round his Wardenship, and as he let his farmers redeem their land-dues, his incomings were large. True, this meant that the incomings from land-dues in kind were small; and he kept a great and costly train—besides his own manor-folk he had never fewer than twelve men-at-arms with him at Husaby; these were bravely mounted and exceeding well armed; and when he moved about his charge, his men lived like lords.

There was some talk of this one day when Lagmand Harald and Tore the old Warden of Gauldöla County were at Husaby. Erlend made answer that many of these men had been with him when he kept the marches in the north; "and there we shared alike in such cheer as was to be had—dried fish and sour small beer. Now the men I give food and clothes to know that I grudge them not white bread and strong ale; and if now and then, in a rage, I bid them to go to hell, they understand well enough that I mean not they should set forth before I lead the way myself."

Ulf Haldorssön, who was the headman of Erlend's guard now, said afterwards to his mistress that 'twas even so. Erlend's men loved him, and he had them wholly in his hand.

"You know yourself, Kristin, none should take much account of what Erlend says; 'tis what he does one must judge him by."

Another matter that made much talk was that, besides his house-carls, Erlend had men all about the country-side—and not in Orkdöla County only—that he had sworn to his service on his sword-hilt. Some time back he had received royal letters about this matter, but he had answered that these men had made up his ship's crew, and that he had taken oath from them the first spring when he was to sail for the north. Upon this it was enjoined upon him that he should loose these men from their oath at the next Thing he held to publish the judgments and decrees of the Lagthing, and that, to that end, he should summon thither the men from outside the county, bearing himself the costs of their journeys. And in truth he had sent for some of his old sailors from Möre to the Orkedal Thing; but no one heard aught of his having loosed them, or any other man who had ever been his follower, from their oaths. Howbeit the matter was not again opened; and so, as the autumn passed, the talk about it died down.

* See Note 14.

Late in the autumn Erlend journeyed south, and stayed over Yule-tide at King Magnus' Court, which was at Oslo that year. He was vexed that he could not bring his wife to go with him; but Kristin shrank from the toilsome winter journey, and stayed on at home at Husaby.

Erlend came back three weeks after Yule, bringing fair gifts to his wife and all the children. Kristin had given her a silver bell to ring for her maids; but to Margret he gave a clasp of pure gold, for she had naught of the sort before, though she had many ornaments of every kind of silver and silver kilt. But while the women were putting away these costly gifts in their jewel-chests, something in Margret's chest caught on her sleeve and hung from it. The girl covered it up swiftly with her hand, saying to her stepmother:

"'Twas my mother left me this, so father would not that I should show it to you."

Kristin had flushed much redder than the maid. Her heart beat hard with fear, but it seemed to her that she *must* speak a word to the young girl to warn her.

In a little she said in a low, faltering voice:

"'Tis like the gold buckle that Lady Helga of Gimsar used to wear at festivals."

"Aye—many gold things are alike," answered the girl, shortly.

Kristin locked her chest and stood still with her hands resting on it, so that Margret might not see how they shook.

"My Margret," she said softly and gently—she had to stop—but she gathered all her strength and went on:

"My Margret, bitterly have I repented—never could I joy fully in any gladness, though my father forgave me with all his heart for all that I had sinned against him—you know that I sinned against my parents for your father's sake. But the longer I live and the more I come to understand, the heavier it grows for me to remember that I repaid their goodness towards me by bringing them sorrow. My Margret, your father has been good to you all the days of your life——"

"You need not be afraid, mother," answered the girl. "I am not your own daughter; you need not be afraid that I shall ever wear out your dirty shift or stand in your shoes——"

Kristin turned a face flaming with wrath on her stepdaughter. Then she clutched the cross she wore about her neck tightly in her hand, and forced back the words that were on her lips.

She went to Sira Eiliv with this the same evening after Vespers, and she looked in vain in the priest's face for a sign—had the worst befallen already, and did he know it? She remembered her own wildered youth, and she remembered Sira Eirik's visage that betrayed nothing, while he lived day by day with her and her trusting parents, with her sinful secret locked in his bosom—and herself hard and dumb under his harsh threats and warnings. And she remembered the time after she had been lawfully betrothed to Erlend, when she herself showed her mother the gifts he had given her at Oslo. The mother's mien had been immovable in its calmness while she took things in her hand, one by one, looked at them, praised them, and laid them away.

She was in deadly, hopeless fear, and kept as wary a watch as she could on Margret. Erlend marked that there was something amiss with his wife, and one evening, when they had gone to rest, he asked if it was that she was with child again.

Kristin lay silent for a little before she answered that she believed it was so. And when her husband, on this, took her lovingly in his arms and asked no more, she could not bring herself to say that 'twas somewhat else that was weighing on her. But when Erlend whispered to her that this time she must do her devoir and give him a daughter, she had no power to answer, but lay there stiff with dread, thinking that Erlend might come to know all too soon what kind of joy a man has of his daughters.

Some nights after this the folk at Husaby had gone to bed somewhat in drink and heavy with much eating, for it was in the last days before the Fast began—and thus all slept heavily. But well on in the night little Lavrans woke in his parents' bed and, still half asleep, began to whimper and cry for his mother's breast. But the time had now come for him to be weaned. Erlend woke up, grunted angrily, but took the boy and gave him milk from a cup that stood on the bed-step, and laid him down then at his other side.

Kristin had sunk again in deep drowsiness, when, of a sudden, she felt Erlend sit upright in the bed. Half awake, she asked what it was—he bade her hush, in a voice she did not know. Without a sound he slipped out of the bed; she marked that he was putting on some pieces of clothing, but when she raised herself on her elbow, he pressed her down again on the cushions with one hand while he leant in above her and took his sword, which hung above the bed-head.

He moved as silently as a lynx; but she felt that he had gone off to the ladder that led up to Margret's bower above the outer room.

For a moment she lay palsied with dread; then she sat up, found her shift and skirt, and groped in the dark for her shoes on the floor by the bed.

At the same moment a woman's shriek rang out from the loft-room—it must have been heard over the whole manor. Erlend's voice shouted a word or two—then she heard the ring of clashing swords and the trampling of feet up above—then the noise of a weapon falling on the floor, and a shriek of terror from Margret.

Kristin knelt crouching by the hearth—raked away the hot ashes with her bare hands and blew on the embers. When she had gotten the fir-root torch alight and held it up in her shaking hands, she saw Erlend high up in the darkness—he leapt down without heeding the ladder, bearing his naked sword in his hands, and ran out of the outer door.

From every side, in the darkness, the boys' heads peeped out. She went to the northern bed, where the three eldest slept, bade them lie down, and shut the bed-door. Ivar and Skule, who sat up on the bench where their beds had been made, blinking in fear and bewilderment at the light, she made creep into her own bed and shut them, too, in. Then she lighted a candle and went out into the courtyard.

It was raining—for one moment, while the light of her candle was mirrored in the wet-shining ice-crust, she saw a crowd of folk outside the door of the nearest house—the servants' quarter where Erlend's house-carls slept. Then her light was blown out—for a moment 'twas pitch-black night—but then Ulf Haldorssön came from the servants' quarter, bearing a lantern.

He bent down over a dark body that lay in a huddled heap on the wet lumpy ice. Kristin knelt down and felt the man's body with her hands—'twas young Haakon of Gimsar—and he was swooning or dead. Straightway her hands were covered with blood. Helped by Ulf, she turned and straightened out the body. The blood was gushing from the right arm, from which the hand had been cut off.

Unawares she cast a glance upward to where the shutter of the window-hole of Margret's bower was clapping in the wind. She could not see any face up there—but 'twas exceeding dark.

While she knelt in the puddles pressing Haakon's wrist with all her might to stop the gush of blood, she was dimly aware of Erlend's men standing around, half clad. Then she saw Erlend's grey, writhen face—with the skirt of his mantle he was wiping his bloody sword—he was naked beneath and his feet were bare.

"One of you, find me a band," she said, "and you, Björn, go up and wake Sira Eiliv—we must bear him up to the priest's house."

She took the leather strap that someone reached her and wound it tight around the stump of the arm. Of a sudden Erlend said, in a wild, hard voice:

"Let none touch him! Let the man lie where himself has laid him——"

"You know well, husband," said Kristin calmly, though her heart was beating till 'twas like to choke her, "that that cannot be."

Erlend thrust the sword-point hard against the ground.

"Aye—your flesh and blood it is not—that have I been made to feel each day in all these years."

Kristin rose and spoke softly, close in to him:

"Yet would I be fain for her sake that this should be hid—if hid it can be. You men"—she turned to the men that stood about—"are true enough to your master, I trow, not to speak of this till he has told you all of how this strife between Haakon and him came about?"

All the men answered, yes. One ventured forward—they had been wakened, he said, by hearing a woman shriek as though one were ravishing her—then straightway someone had leapt down on the roof of their house, but he must have slipped on the ice-crust, for they heard something sliding down and then a heavy fall in the courtyard. But Kristin bade the man be silent. Now came Sira Eiliv running.

When Erlend turned and went in, his wife ran after him, trying to thrust past him. When he made for the loft-ladder, she got before him and caught him around the arms.

"Erlend—what would you do with the child?" she gasped out into his grey, wild face.

He made no answer—he tried to fling her aside, but she held fast to him.

"Stay, Erlend, stay—your child! You know not—the man was fully clad," she cried despairingly.

He gave a loud hoarse cry before answering—and she grew deathly white with horror—his words were so gross and his voice so changed by his wild agony.

Again she wrestled dumbly with the raging man that growled and gnashed his teeth together. At last she caught his eyes in the half-light:

"Erlend—let me go to her first. I have not forgotten the day when I was no better than Margret——"

Then he loosed her and, staggering back against the closet-wall, stood there quivering like a dying beast. Kristin went and lit a candle, then came back and went past him up to Margret in her bower.

The first thing the light fell on was a sword that lay on the floor not far from the bed, and, close by, a man's severed hand. Kristin tore off her head-dress, which, hardly knowing it, she had flung loosely round her flowing hair before she went out to the men. Now she threw it over those things lying on the floor.

Margret sat huddled together on the pillows of the bed-head gazing at Kristin's light with great wide-open eyes. She held the bed-clothes up about her, but her naked shoulders shone white through the golden locks of her hair. There was much blood all about the room.

The strain of Kristin's spirit burst in a vehement fit of weeping—'twas so miserable a sight to see the fair child amidst all this horror. Then Margret shrieked aloud:

"Mother—what will father do with me?"

Kristin could not help it—in the midst of her deep pity for the girl, her heart seemed to grow small and hard in her breast. Margret asked not what her father had done with Haakon. In a flash it came before her— Erlend lying on the ground, her father standing over him with a bloody sword, and she herself—— But Margret had not moved from the spot. She could not hinder the old scornful dislike for Eline's daughter from coming up in her again, as Margret clung to her, shaking, well-nigh crazy with fear, and she sat down on the bed's edge and strove to quiet the child a little.

So they sat when Erlend came up through the trap-door. He was fully clad now. Margret shrieked again, and hid in her stepmother's arms—Kristin looked up at her husband for a moment—he was calm now, but pale and strange of face. For the first time he looked as old as he was.

But when he said quietly: "You must go down, Kristin—I would speak with my daughter alone," she obeyed. She laid the girl down in the bed carefully, covered her up to the chin with the clothes, and then went down the ladder.

As Erlend had done, she dressed herself fully—'twas certain none at Husaby would sleep any more that night—and set herself to quiet the frightened children and serving-women.

The next morning, in a driving snowstorm, Margret's maid went weeping off the place with all her worldly goods in a sack on her back. Her master had driven her out with the direst words, and threats that she should be flayed alive because she had sold her mistress thus.

Then he put the rest of the serving-folk to the question—had not the maids suspected mischief when Ingeleiv in the autumn and winter had begun sleeping with them, instead of in Margret's bower? And how came it that the dogs had been locked inside their house? But they denied all, as 'twas like they would.

Last of all, he took his wife to task, they two alone. Heart-sick and weary, Kristin listened to him and strove to turn aside his injustice with soft answers. She denied not that she had been fearful, and she refrained her from saying that she had not spoken to him of her fear, because she had never reaped aught but unthankfulness from him when she had tried to counsel either him or Margret for the maid's good. But she swore by God and Mary Virgin that she had never known, nor could have thought, such a thing as that this man came to Margret in the loft at night.

"You!" said Erlend scornfully. "You say yourself you mind the time when you were no better than Margret—and the Lord God in heaven knows that you have let me mark, every day of the years we have lived together, that you remembered the wrong I did you—though your will was as good as mine, and your father and not I caused much of the trouble by denying to let you wed me—I was willing enough from the first hour to make amends for the sin. When you saw the Gimsar gold" —he gripped her hand tightly and held it up so that the two rings she had had of him at Gerdarud glittered in the light—"knew you not what it meant? You have worn every day in these years the rings I gave you when you gave me your honour——"

Kristin was ready to sink down with weariness and sorrow; she answered in a low voice:

"I marvel, Erlend, if you still remember the time you overcame my honour——"

He buried his head in his arms, and flung himself down on the bench, tossing and writhing. Kristin sat down a little way off—she wished she could help her husband. She understood that this calamity fell yet more hardly upon him because he himself had sinned against others in the same sort as now he had been sinned against. And he, who had never been willing to look his fault in the face in any trouble he himself had caused, could never bear to take the blame for this—and there was none else but she on whom he could fasten it. But she was not so much angered as sorrowful, and fearful of what now might come to pass.

Now and again she was above with Margret. The girl lay white and unmoving, staring before her. She had not yet asked what had befallen Haakon—Kristin knew not whether 'twas that she dared not, or that she was quite dulled by her own misery.

Well on in the afternoon Kristin saw Erlend and Klöng the Icelander going together through the thick-falling snow to the armoury. But a short time passed, and Erlend came back alone. Kristin looked up a moment as he came into the light and passed her by—afterward she did not dare to turn her eyes toward the corner of the hall where he hid himself away. She had seen that he was quite broken.

Soon after, when she had an errand over at the storehouse, Ivar and Skule came running and told their mother that Klöng the Icelander was going away that evening—the boys were sad about it, for the clerk was a good friend of theirs. He was packing his things now, and was to go down to Birgsi to-night——

She had guessed already what must have befallen. Erlend had offered his daughter to the clerk, and he had refused to have a fallen maid.

But what that parley must have meant to Erlend—she grew dizzy and sick and could not bear to think the thought out.

The day after, word came from the priest's house. Haakon Eindridessön prayed that he might have speech with Erlend. Erlend sent back in answer that he had naught more to say to Haakon. Sira Eiliv said to Kristin that if Haakon lived he would be crippled wholly—besides that he had lost his right hand, he had hurt his back and hips badly in falling from the roof of the servants' house. But he was set on coming home, even as he was, and the priest had promised to get him a sleigh. He repented his sin now with all his heart—he said that Margret's father had been within his rights, however the law might stand; but he was most fain that all should do their best to hush up the matter, so that his misdeed and Margret's shame should be hidden as much as might be. In the afternoon he was borne out to the sleigh, which Sira Eiliv had borrowed from Repstad, and the priest himself rode with him to Gauldal.

Thus the next day, which was Ash Wednesday, the Husaby folk had to go down to Vinjar to the parish church. But at the time of vespers Kristin had the acolyte let her into the chapel at home.

She could feel the ashes still on her forehead when she knelt down by her stepson's grave and said over the paternosters for his soul.

Not much but bones would be left of the boy now, down under his stone. Bones and the hair, and some shreds of the clothes they had been laid in. She had seen the bones of her little sister when they took her up that they might bring her to her father at Hamar. Dust and ashes—she thought of her father's comely visage, of her mother with the great eyes in the furrowed face, and the form that still kept so strangely young and slim and light, though her face grew old so early. There they lay under a stone, falling in sunder, as houses fall to ruin when the folks that lived there are gone. Pictures flitted and faded—the burned ruins of the church at home; a farm in Silsaadal that they used to ride by when they went to Vaage—the houses stood empty and were falling in pieces, the folk that tilled the lands dared not go nigh after the sun was down. She thought upon her beloved dead—their looks and their voices and smiles and ways and bearing—now that they themselves were gone away to yonder other country, to think on their shapes was sore; 'twas like remembering one's home when one knew that it stood desolate, and the rotting timbers were sinking into the soil.

She sat on the wall-bench in the empty church, and the smell of cold stale incense held her thoughts fast bound to pictures of death and the decay of all earthly things. And she was powerless to lift up her soul to see a glimpse of the land where her beloved were, whither all goodness and love and truth at last were taken away and there treasured up.

Every day when she prayed for the peace of their souls, it seemed to herself strange and unmeet that she should pray for them whose souls already on this earth had possessed a peace far deeper than she had ever known since she grew to be a woman. Sira Eiliv, indeed, said that prayer for the dead was good always—good for oneself, even if those others were already inheritors of God's peace.

But it helped not her. It seemed to her that when her weary body at last was rotting under a tombstone, her restless spirit would still be doomed to wander about somewhere near by, as an unhappy ghost wanders lamenting round the tumble-down houses of a ruined farm. For in her soul sin still had its being, as the root-tissue of the weeds is inwoven in the soil. It flowered and flamed and scented the air no longer, but 'twas still there in the soil, bleached, but strong and full of life. In despite of all the tenderness that welled up in her heart when she saw her husband's despair, she had not will or strength to stifle the voice in her that cried out, in bitterness and anger: Can you speak thus to *me*? have you forgotten the time when I gave you my troth and my honour? have you forgotten the time when I was your dearest love? And yet she knew that as long as this voice questioned thus within her, so long would she speak to him as though *she* had forgotten.

She flung herself in her thoughts before St. Olav's shrine; caught at the mouldering bones of Brother Edvin's hand far off in the church at Vatsfjeld; clenched her hands about the reliquaries with the shreds of a dead woman's shroud, and the splinters of the bones of an unknown blood-witness—caught for a safeguard at the small remains that through death and nothingness had kept a little of the virtue of the departed soul —like the magic power that clings about the rust-eaten swords dug up from ancient warriors' barrows.

The day after, Erlend rode into the city, taking with him only Ulf and one other man. All through the fast-time he came not home to Husaby, but Ulf came to fetch his body-guard and took them to meet him at the mid-fast Thing in Orkedal.

In talk with Kristin alone, Ulf told her that Erlend had agreed with Tiedeken Paus, the German goldsmith at Nidaros, that Margret should wed Tiedeken's son Gerlak as soon as Easter was past.

Erlend came home at Easter. He was quiet and calm now, but Kristin thought she could see that he would not be able to shake this off as he had shaken off so much else—whether 'twas because he was no longer so young, or because nothing before had ever humbled him so deeply. Margret seemed quite heedless how her father was ordering things for her.

But one evening when man and wife were alone, Erlend said:

"Had she been my true-born child—or her mother an unwed woman —never would I have given her to a stranger while things are so with her; I could have sheltered and guarded both her and hers. This is an ugly way out, but, seeing what her birth is, a wedded husband can best safeguard her."

While Kristin was making all ready for her step-daughter's going, Erlend said one day, curtly:

"Belike you are scarce well enough to go with us to the city?"

"If you wish it, you know that I will go," said Kristin.

"Why should I wish it? Since before you have never stood in a mother's stead to her, there is no need you should do so now—and a joyous wedding 'twill scarce be. Lady Gunna of Raasvold and her son's wife have promised to come for our kinship's sake."

So Kristin stayed at Husaby, while at Nidaros Erlend gave his daughter to Gerlak Tiedekenssön.

III

T H A T summer, just before St. John's Mass, Gunnulf Nikulaussön came back to his cloister. Erlend was in the city then for the Frosta Thing; he sent word to his wife asking her if she deemed she was able to come in thither to meet her brother-in-law. Kristin was none too well, but yet she came. When she met Erlend, he told her that his brother's health seemed to him quite broken down. They had made but little speed with their undertaking in the north, the Friars of Munkefjord. The church they had built they could never get consecrated, for the Archbishop could not journey so far north in these unquiet times; they had had to say mass the whole time at their travelling-altar. At length they came to lack both bread and wine and candles and oil for the services; and when Brother Gunnulf and Brother Aslak set sail for Vargöy to fetch these things, the Lapps had cast a spell on them, so that they capsized and had to sit for three days and nights on a rocky islet—after this they both fell sick, and Brother Aslak died some time after. They had suffered much from scurvy in the Long Fast, for they lacked both meal and herbs to eat with the dry fish. Therefore had Bishop Haakon of Björgvin and Master Arne (who were at the head of the Cathedral Chapter at Nidaros while the new Archbishop, Sir Paal, was gone to the Curia to be consecrated) ordered the monks who yet lived to come back home, and that the priests of Vargöy should tend the flock at Munkefjord till further order.

But though she was thus not unprepared, yet was Kristin dismayed when she saw Gunnulf Nikulaussön once more. She went with Erlend to the cloister the next day, and they were led into the parlour. The monk came in—his form was bent and crooked, the ring of hair was grown quite grey, under the sunken eyes the skin was wrinkled and dark-brown, but on the smooth white skin of the face were lead-coloured spots, and his hand showed like patches when he drew it out of the sleeve of his gown and held it out towards her. He smiled—and she saw that many of his teeth were gone.

They sat down and talked awhile, but it was as though Gunnulf had forgotten how to speak. He said as much himself before the others left him.

"But you, Erlend, are still the same—you seem not to have grown older," he said with a little smile.

Kristin knew well enough that she herself looked wretchedly just now. And Erlend was a comely sight, as he stood there tall and slender and dark and richly clad. And yet Kristin thought that he, too, had changed much—'twas strange that Gunnulf saw it not—he had used to be so sharp-sighted.

One day of late summer Kristin was in the clothes-loft, and Lady Gunna of Raasvold was with her—she had come to Husaby to help Kristin, now her lying-in was at hand. Standing there, they heard Naakkve and Björgulf singing out in the courtyard, while they sharpened their knives, a coarse ribald song which they were bawling at the top of their voices.

Their mother was beside herself with anger—she went down to the boys and chid them with the harshest words. And then she said she must know whom they learnt such things from—most like 'twas in the servants' house, but which of the men was it that taught children such things? The boys would not answer. Then Skule came out from under the loft-stairway, and said mother had best be still, for they had learnt the song from hearing father sing it.

Lady Gunna spoke up then; had they so little fear of God that they could sing such things—and now, when they could not know, any night when they lay down to rest, that they might not be motherless before cock-crow? Kristin said no more, but went quietly into the house.

After, when she had lain down for a little on her bed, Naakkve came in and went over to her. He took his mother's hand, but said nothing, and then he began to cry quite quietly. She spoke to him then mildly and jestingly, telling him not to weep or wail; she had won through this trouble six times, and surely she would win through the seventh time too. But the boy wept more and more. At last she had to let him creep in between her and the wall, and there he lay weeping with his arms around her neck and his head against her breast; but she could not make him say for what he sorrowed so, though he lay there by her until the serving-woman bore in the supper.

Naakkve was now in his twelfth year; he was a great boy for his age, and was most fain to bear himself grown-up and manly; but he had a soft heart, and the mother could see sometimes that he was still most childlike. He was old enough to have been able to understand his half-sister's mischance; the mother wondered if he understood, too, how much since then his father was changed.

Erlend had always been a man who could say the worst of things when he was enraged—but before this he had never given hard words to any save in wrath; and he had been quick to make all good when he himself was cool again. But now he could say hard and ugly things in cold blood. He had been a terrible man for cursing and swearing; yet had he, in some measure, left off this evil habit, because he saw it hurt his wife and gave offence to Sira Eiliv, for whom he had grown, little by little, to feel much respect. But never had he been foul-mouthed or unseemly in his talk—in that matter he had been much more modest than many a man who had led a purer life. Sorely as it hurt Kristin to hear such words on her young sons' boyish lips, most of all in the state she was in, and to hear that they had learnt them of their father, there was yet another thing which left the bitterest taste of all in her mouth: she saw that Erlend was still childish enough to deem he could brave out the shame of his daughter's fall by taking impure and unseemly words on his lips.

Fru Gunna had told her that Margret had had a still-born son a while before Olav's Mass. The lady had come to know, she said too, that Margret was already not so ill-content—she agreed well with Gerlak and he was kind to her. Erlend went to see his daughter when he was in the city, and Gerlak made a great to-do of his wife's father, though Erlend was none too forward to own the other as kinsman. Erlend himself had not named his daughter's name since she left Husaby.

Kristin bore yet another son; and he was christened Munan after Erlend's father's father. In all the time he lay in the little hall, Naakkve came daily in to his mother with berries and nuts he had plucked in the woods, or wreaths of healing herbs that he had plaited. Erlend came home when the new son was three weeks old; he sat much with his wife, and strove to be kind and loving—and this time he made no complaint because the new-born child was not a little maid, or because it was weakly and throve but ill. But Kristin made not much answer to his kind words; she was quiet and sadly brooding—and this time her strength came back to her exceeding slowly.

All through the winter Kristin was ailing, and the child seemed little like to live and thrive. Thus its mother had little thought to spare for aught else than the poor little being, and she heard with but half an ear all the talk of the great tidings that were stirring this winter. King Magnus had fallen into the greatest straits for money by reason of his endeavours to win the lordship over Skaane, and he had called for succours from Norway. Some of the lords of the Council were willing to stand by him in this matter. But when his messengers came to Tunsberg, the Treasurer had gone away, and Stig Haakonssön, who was Governor in Tunsberghus, shut the gates of the castle against the King's men, and made ready to hold the place by force of arms. He had but few folk with him, but Erling Vidkunssön, who was his uncle by marriage, and was then at his manor in Aker, sent forty of his men-at-arms to strengthen the fortress, while he himself sailed westwards. Much about the same time the King's cousins, Jon and Sigurd Haftorssön, rose against the King, on account of a judgment that had been passed against some of their men. Erlend laughed at this, and said the Haftorssöns had shown themselves raw and foolish. There was great discontent now with King Magnus throughout the land. The nobles demanded that a High Steward should be put at the head of the affairs of the realm and the great seal placed in the hands of a Norseman, since the King, for the sake of his affairs in Skaane, seemed minded to spend most of his time in Sweden. The townsmen and the clergy in the cities had been frighted by the rumours of the King's borrowings from the German cities. The haughtiness of the Germans and their flouting of the laws and customs of the land were already greater than could be borne, and now 'twas said that the King had promised them yet greater rights and franchises in Norwegian cities, so that the state of things would become quite unbearable for the Norse traders, who were already hard put to it. Among the commons the rumours concerning King Magnus' secret sin were still widespread, and many of the parish priests and of the wandering monks were at one in this, if in nothing else, that they believed this was the cause why the Olav's Church in Trondheim had burned down. And so the farmers, too, sought in this the reasons for the many mischances that in these last years had visited now one and now another country-side— plagues among the cattle, blight in the corn, causing sickness and disease to man and beast, and bad harvests of corn and hay. So Erlend said if only the Haftorssöns had had wit enough to hold still awhile yet and win themselves a name for open-handedness and chieftainly dealings, for sure folk would soon have called to mind that they were King Haakon's grandsons too.

These disorders quieted down, but their upshot was that the King made Ivar Ogmundssön High Steward in Norway. Erling Vidkunssön, Stig Haakonssön, the Haftorssöns and all their following were threatened with attainder of high treason. On this they yielded, came in, and made their peace with the King. There was a powerful man of the Uplands named Ulf Saksessön, who had joined in the Haftorssöns' rising; and he did not go with the others to make his peace, but came to Nidaros after Yule. He was much with Erlend in the city, and from him the folk north of Dovre had accounts of all these affairs, in the light he saw them in. Kristin greatly mistrusted this man; she knew him not, but she knew his sister, Helga Saksesdatter, who was wed with Gyrd Darre of Dyfrin. She was fair, but exceeding proud and haughty, and Simon liked her not, though Ramborg agreed well with her. Soon after the Fast was begun, letters came to the Wardens ordering that Ulf Saksessön be proclaimed an outlaw at the Things, but by that time he had left the land, having sailed in the depth of winter.

That spring Erlend and Kristin were at their town-house for Easter, and they had their youngest child, Munan, with them, for there was a sister at Bakke Cloister who was so skilled in leech-craft that all the sick children who were put in her hands got well, if so be it were not the will of God that they should die.

One day just after the holy-day, Kristin came home from the cloister with the little one. The serving-man and the maid who had been with her came with her into the hall. Erlend was alone there, lying on one of the benches. After the man was gone out and the woman had laid by their cloaks—Kristin had sat down by the fire with the child, and the maid was warming some oil they had gotten from the nun—Erlend began asking, from where he lay, what Sister Ragnhild had said of the child. Kristin gave short answers, as she sat unwrapping the child's swaddling-clothes; and at last she made no answer at all.

"Are things so ill with the child, Kristin, that you have no mind to speak of it?" he asked with a little impatience in his voice.

"You have asked this before, Erlend," answered his wife coldly, "and I have told you all there is to tell many times. But since you care not enough for the boy to remember it from one day to another——"

"It has chanced to me, too, Kristin," said Erlend, rising and coming over to her, "that I have had to answer you two and three times about things you yourself had asked of me, because you cared not to remember what I said."

"They were not things of such import as the children's health, I trow," she said in the same tone.

"They were not trifles, either—this last winter; I, at least, had them much at heart."

"'Tis not true, Erlend. 'Tis many a long day since you talked to me of the things you have most at heart."

"Go out, Signe," said Erlend to the maid. He had flushed to the forehead—now he turned to his wife. "I understand what you would speak of. Of that matter I would not speak to you in your serving-maid's hearing—even if you are such good friends with her that you count it for nothing she should be by when you pick a quarrel with your husband, and tell me I speak untrue——"

"'Tis the last thing a man sees, the beam in his own eye," said Kristin shortly.

"I understand not well what you mean. Never have I spoken ungently to you in strangers' hearing, or forgot to show you all honour and worship before our serving-folk."

Kristin burst into a strange, heart-sick, unsteady laugh.

"You are good at forgetting, Erlend! Through all these years has Ulf Haldorssön lived with us. Mind you when you sent him and Haftor to bring me to you in the sleeping-loft of Brynhild's house at Oslo?"

Erlend sank down on the bench, gazing at his wife, with parted lips. But she went on:

"Not much has befallen at Husaby—or elsewhere—of unseemly or dishonourable that you have taken thought to hide from your serving-folk—whether 'twere yourself or your wife it put to shame——"

Erlend sat still, looking at her in dismay.

"Mind you the first winter we were wed? I was with child of Naakkve, things were so that 'twas hard enough for me to win obedience and honour from my household. Mind you how you helped and stayed me? Mind you when your foster-father came to be our guest with strange ladies and maids and men, and our own folk sat at the board with us—mind you that Munan dragged off from me every rag I might have hid me with, and you sat mute and dared not stop his mouth——?"

"Jesus! Have you stored this up against me for fifteen years!" He looked up at her—his eyes, in that glance, seemed strangely light-blue, and his voice was weak and helpless. "Yet, my Kristin—methinks 'tis worse than this that we two should say unfriendly and bitter words to each other——"

"Aye," said Kristin, "worse indeed did it cut into my heart that time at our Yule-tide feast when you chid and rated me because I had thrown my cloak over Margret—and ladies from three counties were standing by and listening——"

Erlend made no answer.

"And now you blame me because things went with Margret as they did—when each time I tried to correct her with a word she would run to you, and you would bid me, in unfriendly words, to let the maid be—for she was yours and not mine——"

"Blamed you—I have not!" answered Erlend in a laboured voice, striving hard to speak calmly. "Had one of our children been a daughter, it had mayhap been easier for you to understand how such things as this that befell my daughter—how they pierce a father to the marrow——"

"I deemed I had shown you last year that I understood," said his wife in a low voice. "I needed but to think of my own father——"

"For all that," said Erlend, speaking quietly as before, "this was a worse thing. I was an unwed man. This man—was—wedded. I was not bound—I was not so bound," he corrected himself, "that I could never be set free——"

"And yet you did not free yourself," said Kristin. "Mind you how it came to pass that you were set free——?"

Erlend sprang up and struck her in the face. Afterward he stood gazing, aghast—a red mark came out on her white cheek. But she sat stiff and silent, with hard eyes. The child had begun to cry with fear—she rocked it a little in her lap and hushed it.

"'Twas—'twas cruelly spoken, Kristin," said the man, in a shaken voice.

"Last time you struck me," she said softly, "I bore your child beneath my heart. Now have you struck me whilst I sat with your son upon my lap—"

"Aye, these children—we are never without them——" he cried impatiently.

They fell silent. Erlend began walking swiftly up and down the hall. She bore the child into the closet and laid it on the bed; when she came out through the closet-door, he stopped in front of her:

"I—I should not have struck you, my Kristin. I wish with my heart I had not done it—I shall repent it, I trow, for as long as I repented the last time. But you—you have taunted me because you deem I forget too lightly. But you forget naught—no single wrong that I ever did you. Yet I have tried—I have tried to be a good husband to you; but that, I trow, you deem not worth remembrance. You—you are fair, Kristin——" He looked after her as she went past him.

Aye, the housewife's still and stately bearing was as beautiful as had been the young maid's supple loveliness; her bosom and hips were grown broader, but she was taller, too; she held herself upright, and the neck bore up the little round head proudly and graciously as ever. The pale, close-shut face with its great dark-grey eyes stirred and kindled him even as the round, rosy child-face had stirred and kindled his restless soul by its mysterious calm. He went over and took her hand:

"For me, Kristin, you are and ever will be the fairest of all women, and the dearest——"

She let him hold her hand, but gave not back the pressure of his. Then he flung it from him, as his bitterness overcame him again.

"Forgotten, say you I have? I trow 'tis not ever the worst of sins—to forget. I have never set up to be a pious man; but I remember what I learned of Sira Jon when a child, and God's ministers have reminded me of it since. 'Tis sin to brood and call back to mind the sins we have confessed to the priest and done penance for before God, and been granted His forgiveness for through the priest's hand and mouth. And 'tis not from holiness, Kristin, that you are ever tearing open these old sins of ours, but 'tis to have a weapon against me each time I go against you in aught——"

He walked away from her, and then came back.

"Greedy to rule—God knows that I love you, Kristin—yet do I see that you are greedy to rule, and never have you forgiven me that I did you wrong and tempted you to wrong. Much have I borne from you, Kristin, but I will no longer bear never to be left in peace for these old mischances, nor to have you speak to me as though I were your thrall——"

Kristin was shaking with passion as she answered:

"Never have I spoken to you as though you were a thrall. Have you *once* heard me speak harshly or angrily to any human being that could be counted as lesser than I—if it were the worst and most worthless of our servant-folk? I know myself free before God from the sin of having offended His poor in word or deed. But you should be my *master;* you should I obey and honour, bow myself before and stay myself on, next to God—according to God's law, Erlend. And if so be I have lost patience, and have spoken to you in such wise as it befits not a wife to speak to her husband—I trow it has been because you have many a time made it hard for me to bow my simplicity before your better understanding, to honour and obey my husband and lord so much as I fain would have done—and maybe I looked that you—maybe I deemed I might spur you on to show that you were a man, and I but a poor simple woman——

"But také comfort, Erlend. I shall not offend you with my words any more, for after this day never shall I forget to speak to you as gently as though, in truth, you were born of thralls——"

Erlend's face flushed darkly red—he lifted his clenched fist—then turned sharp about on his heel, seized his cloak and sword from the bench by the door, and rushed out.

Without there was sunshine and a sharp wind—it was cold, but the bright sparkles that besprinkled him from house-eaves and from wind-swept trees were drops of water thawed out and frozen again in the air. The snow on the house-tops shone like silver, and behind the dark-green tree-clad hills around the town the mountains glittered cold blue and shining white in the bitter, bright, wintry spring day.

Erlend passed through streets and lanes—swiftly, at haphazard. He was boiling inwardly—*she* had been wrong, 'twas as clear as day she had been wrong from the first, and he had been right; and he had played the fool and struck her and made him seem less right—but the wrong *was* with her. What he should do with himself now, he knew not. He had no mind to go to any acquaintance' house, and home he would not go.

There was some hurry and bustle in the city. A big trader from Iceland—the first of the year—had come in to the wharves in the morning. Erlend wandered westward through the lanes, came out by St. Martin's Church, and went down toward the water-side alleys. Though 'twas early in the afternoon, already there was noise and yelling in the alehouses and from the taverns. In his youth he had been able to go into such houses himself, with his friends and fellows. But now all the folks would stare the eyes out of their heads, and talk themselves hoarse afterwards, if the Warden of Orkdöla County, with his great house in the city, with ale and mead and wine at home to his heart's desire, should come into an ale-house and ask for a drink of their bad small beer. Yet truly this was what he had a mind to do—to sit and drink with small farmers in town for the day and serving-men and seamen. There was no to-do when those fellows caught their woman a buffet on the ear; and after that all was well again—hell and furies! how should a man rule a woman when he cannot thrash her soundly, by reason of her birth and his own honour?—at bandying words the devil himself could be no match for them. Troll she was—and so fair, too—if only he could beat her till she grew good again. . . .

The bells began ringing from all the city churches to call folks together to Vespers—the spring wind mingled all the notes together in the unquiet air above his head. 'Twas like she was going to Christ's Church now, the holy troll—to bemoan her to God and Mary Virgin and holy Olav that her husband had hit her a buffet on the ear. Erlend sent up towards his wife's guardian saints a greeting of sinful thoughts, while the bells clashed and clanged and resounded. He made his way towards St. Gregory's Church.

His father and mother's graves were before St. Anne's altar in the northern aisle. Whilst he said over his prayers, he caught sight of Lady Sunniva Olavsdatter and her maid coming in at the church-door. When he had done praying, he went across and greeted her.

It had been the way of these two, ever since he had come to know the lady, that whenever they met they fell to somewhat free toying and jesting. And this evening as they sat on the wall-bench waiting for evensong to begin, he was so forward that she had more times than one to remind him that they were in church and that folk kept coming by them.

"Aye, aye," said Erlend, "but you are so fair to-night, Sunniva! 'Tis so good to jest with a lady that has such gentle eyes——"

"Little do you deserve, Erlend Nikulaussön, that I should look at you with gentle eyes," said she, laughing.

"Then will I come and jest with you when 'tis dark," said Erlend, laughing too. "When evensong is over, I will go home with you——"

Then the priests came into the choir, and Erlend went across to the southern aisle to take his place among the men.

When the service was at an end, he went out at the great door. He saw Lady Sunniva and her maid a little way down the street, and thought he had best not go with her, but go home straightway. At that moment a band of Icelanders from the trader came up the street; they staggered along, holding on to each other, and seemed as they would block the two women's passage. Erlend ran after the lady. As soon as the sailors saw a gentleman with a sword at his belt come toward them, they swerved aside and made room for the women to pass.

"I trow I had best go home with you, after all," said Erlend. "The city is none too quiet to-night."

"Can you believe it, Erlend?—old a woman as I am, maybe I like it not ill that some men think I am yet so fair, 'tis worth while blocking my way——"

There was but one answer that a courteous man could make to this.

He came home to his own house the next morning in the grey of dawn, and stood a little outside the locked door of the hall, frozen, dead-weary, heart-sore and sickened. Rouse the household with his knocking; go in and creep into bed beside Kristin lying with the child at her breast— no! He had on him the key of the eastern storehouse loft; there were some goods stored there that he was answerable for. He let himself in, pulled off his boots, and got together some webs of wadmal and some empty sacks and spread them on straw in the bedstead. He wrapped his cloak about him, crept under the sacks, and, tired out and harassed as he was, was able at last to forget everything in sleep.

Kristin was pale and weary with waking when she sat down to the morning meal with her house-folk. One of the men told her that he had prayed the master to come to breakfast—he was sleeping up in the east storehouse loft, he said—but Erlend had bidden him go to the devil.

Erlend had a tryst out at Elgesæter after the day-mass; he had to witness some dealings in land. But he managed to slip away from the feast that followed in the refectory, and from Arne Gjavvaldssön, who, like himself, could not stay and drink with the Brothers, but was set on having Erlend go with him to Ranheim.

Afterwards he repented that he had parted company with the others
—dismay came over him as he went back alone to the town—now must
he needs think over what he had done. For a moment he had a mind to
go straightway to St. Gregory's Church—he had leave to confess to one
of the priests there, when he was in Nidaros. But if he did this again,
after he had confessed, the sin would be much greater. 'Twere better to
wait awhile——

She must think now, Sunniva, that he was a chicken she had caught
with her bare hands. But devil take him if he had ever thought a woman had been able to teach him so much that was new—here was he
going about yawning still from the adventure. He had flattered himself
he was not unskilled in *ars amoris*, or whatever the learned men called it.
Had he been young and green, like enough he had been proud of himself and deemed it fine and brave. But he liked not the woman—the
mad creature—he was sick of her; he was sick of *all* women save his wife
—and he was sick of her too! By the Cross itself—he had been so wedded
to her that he had grown most holy himself—for he had believed in her
holiness—but 'twas a fair reward he had had from his holy wife for his
faithfulness and love—troll that she was! He remembered her scorching
venomous words of the day before—so she deemed he bore himself as
though he were born of thralls!—— And the other, Sunniva, she
thought, doubtless, he was naught but a raw weakling, since he had let
himself be taken by surprise and had shown some dismay at her way of
love-making. He would show her now that he was no more of a holy
man than she was a woman. He had promised her to come down to
Thorolf's town-house that night, and he might e'en as well go; the sin
was sinned: why not enjoy any disport it might bring with it?"

Since he had broken his troth to Kristin already—and she herself had
brought it about, by her hateful and unjust ways towards him——

He went home, and wandered about the stables and outhouses seeking for somewhat to find fault with; he had words with the priest's serving-maid from the hospital because she had brought malt into his dry-
ing-house, though he knew well that his house-folk would have no use
for the house this time while they were in the town. He wished he had
had his boys here—they would have been some company—he wished
he could set forth back to Husaby at once. But he must needs wait in the
city for letters from the south—'twas too venturesome to have such things
come to hand at one's home in the country.

The mistress of the house came not in to supper—she was lying down
on the bed in the closet, said Signe, her maid, looking at her master re-
proachfully. Erlend answered harshly that he had not asked after her
mistress. When the house-folk had left the hall, he went into the closet.
It was pitch-dark in there. Erlend bent over the bed.

"Are you weeping?" he asked very low, her breath came so strangely. But she answered in a thick, husky voice that she was not weeping.

"Are you weary? Aye—I will go to rest too, now," he said in the same low voice.

Kristin's voice quivered as she said:

"Then I had liefer, Erlend, that you should go and lie to-night where you lay last night."

Erlend made no answer. He went out and fetched the candle from the hall into the closet, and opened his chest of clothing. He was well clad enough already to go wherever he listed, for he still bore the violet *kothardi* he had worn at Elgesæter in the morning. But now he changed his clothes slowly and deliberately—put on a red silk shirt and a mouse-grey knee-long velvet coat with little silver bells on the sleeve-points, brushed his hair, and washed his hands. Time and again he looked over towards his wife—she lay silent and motionless. Then he went out without bidding good night. Next day he came home openly at the breakfast-hour.

So things went on for a week. Then Erlend came home one evening from Hangrar where he had been on an errand and learnt that Kristin had ridden off that morning home to Husaby.

It had grown clear to him already that never had any man had less joy from a sin than he from these dealings of his with Sunniva Olavs-datter. In his heart he was so deadly weary of the crazy creature—sick of her even while he caressed and toyed with her. 'Twas a mad and reckless thing, too—like enough it was all over the town and the country-side by now, that he had his nightly resort in Thorolf's house—and to smirch his name for Sunniva's sake! Now and then he had thought, too, that the thing might raise some trouble—the woman had a husband such as he was, old and sickly—'twas pity of Thorolf that he should be wed to such a wild and witless woman—most like *he* was not the first that had made free with the husband's honour. And Haftor—he had clean forgotten, when he had to do with Sunniva, that she was Haf-tor's sister—he remembered it only when it was too late. All was as bad as it could be—and now he could see that Kristin knew it.

She surely could not take it in her head to bring suit against him before the Archbishop—crave leave to depart from him. She had Jörund-gaard to take refuge in—but it was impossible to travel thither over the mountains at this time of year, quite impossible if she would take the small children with her—and Kristin would not leave *them*. No—he thought, to comfort himself—and she could not go by sea either, with Munan and Lavrans, so early in the spring. Oh, but 'twould be unlike Kristin to crave the Archbishop's help against him—though she had good reason for it—but he would keep away from her bed of his own accord—till she saw that he repented from his heart. Kristin could never wish to have this thing publicly brought to question. But he knew in his heart that 'twas long since he had rightly known what his wife could or could not do.

He lay at night in his own bed, letting his thoughts go hither and thither. It dawned upon him that he had behaved yet more witlessly than he had understood at first, to let himself be tangled in this wretched adventure, now, when he was in the thick of the greatest plans of State.

He cursed himself that he was still such a fool about his wife that she had been able to drive him to this. He cursed both Kristin and Sunniva. In the devil's name, sure he was no fonder on women than other men—rather he had had to do with fewer of them than most others that he knew of. But 'twas as though the foul fiend himself had the ordering of things for him—he could not come near a woman without finding himself up to the neck in a bog. . . .

There should be an end of it now. God be thanked and praised that he had other things on hand. Soon, soon, for sure, would he have Lady Ingebjörg's letters. Aye, in that matter, too, he had to reckon with women's whims; belike that was God's punishment for the sins of his youth. Erlend laughed to himself in the dark. The lady must see that things were as they had so clearly set them forth to her. The question was whether it should be one of her sons or the sons of her base-born sister that the Norsemen set up against King Magnus. And she loved her children by Knut Porse as she had never loved her other children.

Soon, soon, 'twould be the sharp wind and the salt sea breakers that should fill his embrace. God in heaven! it would be good to be drenched by the waves once again and have the wind blow freshness to his very marrow—be quit of all womankind for a long, delicious time.

Sunniva—she might think what she would. Thither he would go no more. And Kristin might fare to Jörundgaard if she would, for him. 'Twould mayhap be best and safest for her and the children if they were well out of the way in Gudbrandsdal this summer. Afterward there was no fear but he could make friends with her again. . . .

Next morning he rode up into Skaun. Say what he would, he could not rest till he had made sure what his wife meant to do.

She met him with gentle, cold courtesy when he reached Husaby late in the day. She spoke not a word to him of her own accord, nor any unfriendly word; and she said naught against it when, in the evening, as if feeling his way, he came over and lay down in their bed. When they had lain awhile, he tried, falteringly, to lay a hand on her shoulder.

Kristin's voice shook, but Erlend could not tell whether it were in sorrow or from anger, as she whispered:

"So base a man I trow you are not, Erlend, that you would make this worse for me than need be. I cannot strive with you, with our children sleeping around us. And since I have seven sons by you, I would be loath that our house-folk should see that I know I am a wronged wife——"

Erlend lay long and silent before he ventured to answer:

"Aye. God have mercy on me, Kristin, I have wronged you. I had not—had not done it if I could have taken more lightly the cruel words you said to me that day at Nidaros. It is not so that I am come home to beg you for forgiveness; for I know well that that would be a great thing to ask you now——"

"I see that Munan Baardssön spoke true," answered his wife; "the day will never come when you will stand up and take the blame on yourself for what you have done amiss. 'Twere best you turned you to God and sought to make your peace with Him—you have less need to ask my forgiveness than His——"

"Aye, so much I can see," said Erlend bitterly. After this they spoke no more. And the next morning he rode back to Nidaros.

He had been in the city some days when Lady Sunniva's woman came to him one evening in St. Gregory's Church. It seemed to Erlend that after all it were well he should speak with the lady one last time; and he bade the girl keep watch that night—he would come by the same way as before.

He had had to creep and clamber about like a poultry-thief to come up into the loft where they had their meetings. It made him sick with shame now to think he had been such a fool—a man of his age and his place. But at first he had deemed it sport to play such youthful pranks.

The lady was in bed when he came in.

"Come you at long last and so late?" she laughed, and yawned. "Quick now, love, and come to bed; and we can talk afterward about where you have been so long——"

Erlend knew not rightly what to do, or how to tell her what he had at heart. Without thinking, he began to loose the fastenings of his dress.

" Foolhardy is it, this that we have done, Sunniva—I trow it were not well that I should stay here to-night. Thorolf must be looked for home ere long?" he said.

"Are you frighted at my husband?" asked Sunniva teasingly. "You saw yourself Thorolf never so much as pricked up an ear when we toyed and jested before his very eyes. Should he hear that you have been coming about the house, I warrant I make him believe that it is but the old foolery. He trusts me all too well——"

"Aye, it seems indeed that he trusts you all too well," laughed Erlend, burying his fingers in the bright hair on her firm white shoulders.

"Say you so?" She caught him round the wrist. "Yet you trust your wife too. And *I* was yet modest and shamefast when Baard wedded me——"

"*My* wife we will leave outside of this matter," said Erlend sharply, letting go his hold.

" Why so——? Think you 'tis more unseemly that we should speak of Kristin Lavransdatter than of Sir Thorolf, my husband?"

Erlend set his teeth hard and made no answer.

"Methinks you are one of those men, Erlend," said Sunniva mockingly, "that think you are so winning and fair that it can scarce be reckoned a fault in a woman that her virtue was as frail as glass against you—she may be staunch as steel against all others."

"Of you I have never thought so," answered Erlend coarsely.

Sunniva's eyes gleamed :

"What would you with me, then, Erlend—since you were so happily wedded?"

"I have said, you shall not name my wife——"

"Your wife or my husband——"

"'Twas ever you that began to speak of Thorolf; and 'twas you that scoffed at him worst," said Erlend bitterly. "And if you had not flouted him in words—'twas plain enough how dear you held his honour, when you took another man to you in your husband's place. *She*—is not brought low by my misdoing."

"Is this what you would say to me—that you love Kristin, though you like me well enough to play with me——"

"I know not how well I like you—you showed that you liked me——"

"And Kristin sets not your love at its true worth?" she scoffed. "I have seen well enough how gently she is used to look on you, Erlend."

"Hold your tongue, now !" shouted the man. "Maybe she knew what I deserved !" he said harshly and savagely. "You and I may well be each other's like——"

"Is it so," asked Sunniva threateningly, "that I was to be but a whip for you to lash your wife with?"

Erlend stood breathing hard :

"Call it so, if you will. But you laid yourself ready to my hand."

"Beware," said Sunniva, "that that whip smite not yourself——"

She sat up in the bed and waited. But Erlend offered not to gainsay her or to seek to make up the quarrel. He re-dressed fully and left her without a word.

He was not greatly pleased with himself, or with the fashion in which he had parted from Sunniva. There was small honour in it for him. But it could not be helped—and at least he was quit of her now.

I V

T H I S spring and summer not much was seen of the master at Husaby. At such times as he was at the manor, he and his wife met each other with courtesy and friendliness. Erlend in no way tried to break down the wall she now built up between them, though he would often look after her searchingly. For the rest, he seemed to have much to think on outside his home. Touching the management of the estate he never asked a single word.

It was this matter of the estates his wife brought forward when, just after the spring Holy Cross day, he would have had her go with him to Raumsdal. He had business in the Uplands—would she not take the children with her, stay awhile at Jörundgaard, and see her kinsfolk and friends in the Dale? But Kristin would on no account agree to this.

He was in Nidaros at the time of the Lagthing, and afterward out in Orkedal; then he came home to Husaby, but at once busied himself making ready for a journey to Björgvin. *Margygren* was lying out at Nidarholm, and he but waited for Haftor Graut, who was to sail along with him.

Three days before Margaret's Mass * they began the hay-harvest at Husaby. It was the fairest weather, and when the haymakers went back to the meadows after the midday rest, Olav, the foreman, got leave for the children to go with them.

Kristin was in the clothing storehouse that was in the second story of the armoury building. The house was so built that an outer stairway led up to this room, which had a balcony before it; the third story —the armoury itself—stood out above the balcony, and it could be reached only by a loose ladder from the clothing loft leading to a trap-door on the floor. The trap-door was open, for Erlend was up in the armoury.

Kristin bore out the fur cloak that Erlend was to take with him for the sea-voyage, and shook it out in the balcony. Then she was ware of the noise of a great company of horsemen, and at the same moment she saw folks come riding out of the woods on the Gauldal road. The next moment Erlend stood by her side.

"Was it so, did you say, Kristin, that the fire in the kitchen was put out this morning?"

* 10th June.

"Aye—Gudrid upset the broth-cauldron. We must borrow a light from Sira Eiliv——"

Erlend looked across at the priest's house.

"No; he must not be mixed in this. Gaute," he called softly to the boy, who was loitering under the balcony, lifting one rake after another, unwilling to set out to the haymaking. "Come up hither, up the stairs —no farther, or they might see you."

Kristin gazed at her husband. Like this she had never seen him before—the strained, alert calm in his voice, in his face, as he spied out southward along the road—in the whole of his tall supple form as he ran into the loft and came back at once with a flat packet, sewn up in linen cloth. He gave it to the boy:

"Hide this in your breast—and mark well what I say to you. You must save these letters—more is at stake than you can understand, my Gaute. Put your rake over your shoulder and go quietly down across the fields till you come to the alder-thickets. Keep well among the bushes till you get down to the wood—you know all the paths there, I know—and creep through the thickest brush all the way across to Skjoldvirkstad. When you get there, make sure first that all is quiet on the farm. Should you see signs of aught amiss or of strangers about, then hide you. But should you be sure all is safe, go down to the farm and give this to Ulf, if he be at home. But if you cannot give the letters into his hands while you are sure that none is near, burn them the moment you can come by the wherewithal to do it. But be sure that both writing and seals are altogether burnt up, and that they come not into any man's hands but Ulf's. God help us, my son—these be great matters to put in the hands of a boy of ten winters—the lives and welfare of many good men—understand you that much is at stake, Gaute?"

"Aye, father. I have understood all that you have said to me." Gaute looked up from the stairway, his little fair face full of earnestness.

"Say to Isak, if Ulf is not at home, that he must ride straight out to Havne and on all night—and tell them he wots of, that a head wind has sprung up, and I fear me evil spells have spoiled my journey. Do you understand?"

"Aye, father. I mind well all you have said to me."

"Go, then. God keep you, my son."

Erlend ran up into the armoury, and would have closed the trapdoor, but Kristin was already half-way through the opening. He waited till she was up, then shut the trap, ran over to a chest, and took out some written parchments. He tore the seals off and trampled them to pieces on the floor, tore the parchments into rags and wrapped them together round the key of the chest and dropped the little bundle from the window-hole into the midst of the nettles that grew high behind the storehouse. With his hands on the window-frame, he stood gazing after the little boy walking along the edge of the cornfield down towards the meadow, where the mowers were moving forward in a line, plying their scythes and rakes. When Gaute disappeared into the little copse between the corn-field and the meadow, he closed the shutter. The noise of hoofs came loudly now and from near by.

Erlend turned towards his wife:

"Can you have what I threw out but now made away with?—send Skule, he has his wits about him—tell him to fling it down into the pit behind the byre. Like enough they will keep an eye on you, and mayhap on the big boys too. But they will scarce search you——" He put the fragments of the seals down inside the bosom of her dress. "None could make them out, methinks; but yet——"

"Are you in peril, Erlend?" she asked quietly. When he had looked into her face, he drew her outspread arms around him. For a moment he pressed her to him:

"I know not, Kristin. We shall see soon, I trow. Tore Eindridessön rides at the head of the men, and Sir Baard is with them, if I saw aright. I can scarce deem that Tore comes hither for any good——"

The horsemen were in the courtyard now. Erlend stood still a moment. Then he kissed his wife vehemently, opened the trap-door, and ran down. When Kristin came out into the balcony, she saw Erlend in the courtyard helping the Treasurer, who was an old man and a heavy, to dismount from his horse. There were thirty men-at-arms, at least, with Sir Baard and the Warden of Gauldöla County. As Kristin crossed the yard, she heard the Warden say:

"I bring you greetings from your cousins, Erlend. Borgar and Guttorm Trondssöns are the King's honoured guests at Veöy, and I trow Haftor Toressön will have paid a friendly visit by this time to Ivar and the young lad at their home at Sundbu. Sir Baard took the Graut into keeping in the city yestermorn."

"And now I see you are come hither to bid me to this same meeting of the guardsmen," said Erlend, smiling.

"So it is, Erlend."

"And doubtless you would search my manor here too? Oh, I have done my part in such affairs so often that I ought to know the way 'tis done."

"Such great affairs as a high treason cause you have scarce had in your hands," said Tore.

"No, not before now," said Erlend. "And it looks as though I were playing with the black men, Tore, and you had mated me—is it not so, kinsman?"

"We must find forth the letters you have had from Lady Ingebjörg Haakonsdatter," said Tore Eindridessön.

"They are in the chest covered with red leather up in the armoury—but there is not much in them save such greetings as dear kinsfolk use to send to each other—and they are all old. Stein here can take you up."

The stranger horsemen had dismounted now, and the house-folk were coming crowding into the courtyard.

"There was more in the one we took from Borgar Trondssön," said Tore. Erlend whistled softly.

"We had best go into the hall," he said; "it begins to grow crowded here."

Kristin followed the men into the hall. At a sign from Tore, two of the stranger men-at-arms came with them.

"You must give up your sword, Erlend," said Tore of Gimsar, when they stood within, "for a sign that you are our prisoner."

Erlend smote his thighs to show that he wore no other weapon than the dagger in his belt. But Tore said again:

"You must reach us your sword for a token——"

"Aye, aye, if all is to be done to such a nicety——" said Erlend, laughing a little. He went over and took his sword from its peg, and holding the scabbard, held out the hilt to Tore Eindridessön with a little bow.

The old man of Gimsar loosened the fastenings, drew the blade right out, and ran his fingers along its groove.

"Was it this sword, Erlend, that you——?"

Erlend's blue eyes glittered like steel, his mouth grew narrow and straight-lipped:

"Aye. 'Twas with this sword I chastised your grandson when I found him with my daughter."

Tore stood holding the sword; he looked down at it and spoke threateningly:

"You that should uphold the law, Erlend—you must sure have known that that time you went a little farther than the law would follow you——"

Erlend threw back his head, flushing, and said hotly:

"There is a law, Tore, that cannot be set aside by Kings or Thingmen—his women's honour a man may guard with the sword——"

"Well for you, Erlend Nikulaussön, that no man has put that law to use against you," answered Tore of Gimsar malignantly. "Else had you need of as many lives as a cat——"

Erlend said with stinging slowness of speech:

"Think you not this matter is so grave that 'tis untimely to mix up with it old stories from my youth?"

"I know not if Thorolf of Lensvik deems those matters are so old."

Erlend flamed up and would have answered; but Tore shouted:

"You should try first, Erlend, whether your mistresses have skill to read writing, before you run about to nightly trysts with secret letters in your waist-band! Ask you of Baard there who it was that warned us that you were hatching traitorous counsels against your King that you have sworn troth to, and hold your place in fee from——"

Unwittingly Erlend raised a hand to his breast—he glanced for a moment at his wife, and his face flushed darkly. Then Kristin ran forward and threw her arms about his neck. Erlend looked down into her face—he saw naught in it but love:

"Erlend—husband."

The Treasurer had scarce spoken a word hitherto. Now he went over to the pair and said softly:

"Dear lady—mayhap it would be best that you take the children and your serving-women with you into the women's house, and stay there as long as we are on the manor."

Erlend loosed his wife, with a last pressure of his arm about her shoulders.

"It is best so, my own Kristin—do you as Sir Baard counsels."

Kristin lifted herself on tiptoe and offered him her mouth to kiss. Then she went out into the courtyard. And out of the confused throng of folks she gathered together her children and serving-women, and carried them with her into the little hall—other women's house there was not at Husaby.

For some hours they sat there, and the mistress' calm and steadfastness kept the frightened little company's terror somewhat in check. Then Erlend came in, disarmed and clad as for a journey. Two stranger men-at-arms took post down by the door.

He took his eldest sons by the hand, and then lifted the little ones in his arms, while he asked where Gaute was—"but you must greet him from me, Naakkve. He is run off to the woods with his bow, I warrant, as his wont is. Tell him he can have my English long-bow after all—I denied it him when he asked for it on Sunday."

Kristin crushed him to her without a word

"When will you come back, Erlend dearest?" she whispered pleadingly.

"That must be as God will, my wife."

She drew back from him, struggling that she might not break down. He was never used to speak to her but by her christened name, and these last words of his shook her to the very heart. It was as if only now she understood to the full what it was that had befallen.

At the sunset hour Kristin sat up on the hill north of the houses.

She had never seen the sky so red and golden before. Above the hill right over against her lay a great cloud; it was shaped like a bird's wing, it glowed within like iron in the forge, it shone clear as amber. Little golden wisps like feathers loosed themselves from it and floated out into the sky. And deep below on the lake in the valley-bottom the sky was mirrored with the cloud and the hill-side above it—it seemed as though it were from down there in the depths that the burning glow streamed up to tinge all that lay before her.

The grass in the meadows was seeding, and its silken spikes shone darkling red in the red light from the sky; the barley was in ear, and caught the radiance on its young silky-bright beards. The turf house-roofs of the manor were thick with sorrel and buttercups, and the sun-light lay in broad rays across them; the blackish shingles of the church-roof glowed darkly, and the light stones of the walls were softly gilded.

The sun broke forth beneath the cloud, rested on the mountain-crest and sent his light out over range behind range of wooded hills. The evening was so clear—the light showed up to sight little clearings among the pine-covered hill-sides; she could see sæters and little farms in among the woods that she had never before known one could see from Husaby. Great hill masses, deep violet in hue, rose in the south, in toward Dovre, where else there were wont to be clouds or haze.

The least of the bells in the chapel below began to ring, and the church-bell at Vinjar answered. Kristin sat bowed over her folded hands till the last of the three triple strokes died away on the air.

Now the sun was below the mountain-top, the golden radiance grew paler and the red more rosy and soft. After the bells had fallen silent, the soughing of the woods seemed to grow again and spread abroad; the noise of the little beck that ran through the leafwoods down in the valley sounded louder on the ear. From the close near by came the well-known clinking from the bells of the home cattle; a flying beetle hummed half-way round about her, and was gone.

She sent a last sigh after her prayers—a prayer for forgiveness because her thoughts had been elsewhere while she prayed.

The great goodly manor lay below her on the hill-side, like a jewel on the hill's broad bosom. She looked out over all the lands that she had owned along with her husband. Thoughts of this estate, cares for it, had filled her mind to the brim. She had worked and striven—never till to-night had she known herself how she had striven to set this manor on its feet and keep it safe—nor all she had found strength to do and how much she had compassed.

She had taken it as her lot, to be borne patiently and unflinchingly, that all this rested on her shoulders. Even so she had striven to be patient and to hold her head high under the burden her life laid on her, each time she knew she had again a child to bear under her heart— again and again. With each son added to the flock, she had felt more strongly the duty of upholding the welfare and safety of the house— she saw to-night, too, that her power to overlook the whole, her watchfulness, had grown with each new child she had to watch and strive for. Never had she seen so clearly as this evening what fate had craved of her and what it had granted her, in giving her these seven sons. Over again and over again had joy in them quickened the beating of her heart, fear for them pierced it—they were her children, these great lads with their lean angular boys' bodies, as they had been when they were so small and plump they could scarce hurt themselves when they tumbled in their journeys between the bench and her knee. They were hers, even as they had been when, as she would lift one of them from the cradle up to her breast for milk, she had to hold up its head, because it nodded on the slender neck as a bluebell nods on its stalk. Wherever they might wander out in the world, whithersoever they might fare, forgetful of their mother, she felt as though for her their life must still be an action of her life, they must still be as one with herself as they had been when she alone in all the world knew of the new life which lay hidden within and drank of her blood and made her cheeks pale. Over again and over again had she proved the sickening sweating terror when she felt: now her time was come again, now again was she to be dragged under in the breakers of travail—till she was borne up again with a new child in her arms; how much richer and stronger and braver with each child, never till to-night had she understood.

And yet she saw to-night that she was still the Kristin of Jörundgaard, who had never learned to endure an ungentle word, because she had been shielded all her days by so strong and tender a love. In Erlend's hands she was still the same. . . .

Aye. Aye. Aye. 'Twas true that she had gone on storing up, year in, year out, the memory of every wound he had dealt her—though she had known always that he had wounded her, not from ill will as a grown man wounds another, but as a child strikes his playfellow in their play. She had tended the memory of each time when he had offended her, as one tends a festering sore. And every abasement he had brought upon himself by following his own every whim struck her like a whip-stroke on the flesh, and left a running weal. 'Twas not so that she willingly and of purpose stored up grudges against her husband; she knew that towards others she was not petty-minded, but when he was concerned she grew so straightway. When Erlend was in question, she could forget nothing, and every least scratch on her soul went on smarting and bleeding and swelling and throbbing, when 'twas he that had dealt it her.

Towards him she never grew wiser, never stronger. She might strive to seem, in her life with him too, capable and brave and strong and pious, but 'twas not true that she was so. Ever, ever had longing gnawed within her—the longing to be again his Kristin of the woods of Gerdarud.

In those days she had been willing to do all that she knew was evil and sinful rather than lose him. To bind Erlend to her, she had given him all that was hers: her love and her body, her honour and her part in the salvation of her Lord. And she had given him what she could find to give that was not hers: her father's honour and his trust in his child; all that wise and prudent grown men had built up to safeguard a little maid in her nonage she had overturned; against their plans for the welfare and advancement of their race, against their hopes that their work would bear fruit when they themselves lay under the mould, she had set her love. Much more than her own life had she staked in the game, wherein the sole prize was Erlend Nikulaussön's love.

And she had won. She had known, from the time when he kissed her for the first time in the garden by Hofvin, even till to-day when he kissed her in the little hall before he was led away a prisoner from his home—Erlend loved her as his own life. And if he had not guided her life well, yet had she known well-nigh from the first hour she met him how he had guided his own. If he had not ever dealt well by her, yet had he dealt better by her than with himself.

Jesus, how she had won him! She confessed to herself this evening —she herself had driven him to breach of his marriage-vows by her coldness and by her venomous words. She confessed to herself now— even in these years when she had looked on, time and again, at his unseemly dalliance with this woman Sunniva, and had been angered by it, she had felt in the midst of her wrath a haughty and defiant joy— none knew of any open stain on Sunniva Olavsdatter's honour, yet Erlend talked and jested with her as a serving-man might with an ale-house wench. And of her he had known that she could lie and betray those that trusted her best, that she willingly let herself be lured to the most shameful places—yet had he trusted her, yet had he honoured her so far as in him lay. Easy as it was for him to forget all fear of sin, easy as it had been for him to break his promise made to God at the altar, yet had he sorrowed over his sins against her, and had struggled for years that he might be able to keep his promises to her.

She had chosen him herself. She had chosen him in a frenzy of love, and she had chosen anew each day of those hard years at home at Jörundgaard—chosen his wild reckless passion before her father's love that would not suffer the wind to blow ungently upon her. She had thrown away the lot her father had shaped for her, when he would have given her to the arms of a man who would surely have led her by the safest ways, and would have stooped down, to boot, to take away each little stone that she might have dashed her foot against. She had chosen to follow the other, who she knew was straying in perilous paths. Monks and priests had pointed the way of repentance and atonement to lead her home to peace—she had chosen turmoil rather than let slip her darling sin.

So there was but one way for her—not to murmur or cry out, whatever should befall her at this man's side. Dizzily far behind her it seemed now, the time when she had left her father. But she saw his beloved face, remembered his words that day in the smithy when she dealt his heart the last stab, remembered their talk together, up in the mountains in the hour when she saw that the door of death stood ajar waiting for him. Unworthy is it to murmur at the lot one has chosen for oneself.—Holy Olav, help me that now I may not show me altogether unworthy of my father's love!

Erlend, Erlend—— When she met him in her youth, life had become for her a swift river rushing over rocks and rapids. In these years at Husaby, life had spread out, lying wide and ample like a lake, mirroring all that surrounded her. She remembered, at home, when the Laagen overflowed in spring-time, and lay grey and mighty in the valley-bottom, bearing on its bosom the driftage that came floating, while the tops of the growing leaf-trees in its course swayed on the waters. Out in its midst showed little dark threatening eddies, where the current ran swift and wild and perilous under the shining surface. Now she knew that even so had her love for Erlend run like a swift and perilous current beneath the surface of her life through all these years. Now 'twas bearing forward—she knew not to what.

Erlend, beloved——!

Once more Kristin breathed an Ave out into the evening glow. Hail Mary, full of grace! I dare pray thee but for one mercy, that see I now: Save Erlend, save my husband's life——!

She looked down at Husaby and thought of her sons. Now when the manor lay there in the evening light like a dream vision that might melt away—now that fear for her children's doubtful fate shook her heart, it came to her mind: Never had she thanked God fully for the rich fruits her toil had borne in these years; and never had she thanked Him as she ought that seven times He had granted her a son.

Out of the dome of the evening heaven, from all the country-side beneath her eyes, came the murmured words of the mass that she had heard thousands of times, in her father's voice that had set forth the words for her when she was a little child at his knee: Thus sings Sira Eirik in the *Præfatio*, when he turns him to the altar, and thus it says in the Norse tongue:

It is truly meet and just, right and available to salvation, that we should always, and in all places, give thanks to Thee, O holy Lord, Father Almighty, eternal God.

When she lifted up her face from her hands, she saw Gaute coming up the hill. Kristin sat still and waited till the boy stood before her, then she stretched out her hand and took his. There was grassy sward a good way round the stone where she was sitting, with no place where any might hide.

"How did you do your father's errand, my son?" she asked softly.

"As he bade me, mother. I came to the farm so that none saw me. Ulf was not at home, so I burned what father had given me on the hearth-fire in the hall. I took it out of the cloth." He hesitated a little. "Mother—there were nine seals to it——"

"My Gaute." The mother moved her hands up till they rested on the boy's shoulders, and looked into his face. "Your father has had to lay great matters in your hands. If you deem that you cannot but speak of them to someone, then tell your mother what is weighing on you. But best of all would it like me if you could altogether be silent, my son."

The light-hued face under the smooth flaxen hair, the great eyes, the full, firm red mouth—how like he was to her father now! Gaute nodded. Then he laid an arm on his mother's shoulder.

Sweetly and sorrowfully it came on Kristin that now she could lean her head against the boy's spare little breast; he was so tall now that when he stood and she sat, her head reached to just above his heart. For the first time it was she that leaned against her child.

Gaute said:

"Isak was alone at home. I showed him not what I was bearing, but said only that I had somewhat I must burn. So he made up a big fire on the hearth before he went out to saddle his horse."

His mother nodded. Then he let go of her, turned towards her, and said, with childish awe and wonder in his voice:

"Mother, know you what they say? They say that father—would have been *King*——"

"It sounds not over-likely, boy——" she answered with a smile.

"But he is of kingly birth, my mother," said the boy earnestly and proudly. "And methinks father would be fitter to be a King than most men."

"Hush." She took his hand again. "My Gaute—you must understand, now that father has shown such trust in you—you and we all must say nor think nothing, but must watch our tongues well till we have learnt somewhat, so that we can judge whether and how we should speak. I ride to Nidaros to-morrow, and if I come to speech with your father alone at any time, I shall surely tell him that you have done his errand well——"

"Take me with you, mother!" begged the boy vehemently.

"We must not let any think, Gaute, that you are aught else than a thoughtless child. You must try, little son, to play about here at home and be as joyful as you can—so will you serve your father best."

Naakkve and Björgulf came slowly up the hill. They came up to their mother and stood there, their young faces strained with feeling. Kristin saw they were still so far children that they took refuge with their mother in this disquietude—and yet were come so far towards manhood that they would fain have comforted her and heartened her, if they could but find the way. She held out a hand to each of the boys. But not much was said between them.

Soon after, they all went down, Kristin with a hand on a shoulder of each of her two eldest sons.

"Why are you looking so at me, Naakkve?" But the boy grew red, turned away his head, and made no answer.

He had never before thought about his mother's looks. It was many a long day since he had begun to compare his father with other men —his father was the most comely of them all, and the most like a chieftain. His mother was the mother that had new children, who, as they grew from out the hands of the women, joined the little troop of brothers, to share its life in fellowship, its friendship and its strife; mother had open hands through which flowed all that they needed; mother knew what to do for well-nigh all ills; mother was like the fire on the hearth, she bore the life of the home as the lands round about Husaby bore the crops year by year; life and warmth streamed from her as from the cattle in the byre or the horses in the stalls. The boy had never thought of likening her to other women. . . .

This evening he saw all at once: she was a proud and fair lady. With the broad, white forehead under the linen coif, the steel-grey eyes' straight gaze under the calmly arched brows; with the heavy bosom and the long, shapely limbs. She bore her tall body straight as a lance. But he could not speak of this; he walked on flushed and silent with her hand upon his neck.

Gaute walked behind Björgulf and held by his mother's belt. The elder brother began grumbling because Gaute was treading on his heels —the two set to pushing and scuffling a little. The mother stopped the quarrel and bade them be quiet, and, so doing, her grave face softened into a smile. After all they were but children, her sons.

Kristin lay awake at night—Munan was sleeping at her breast, and Lavrans between her and the wall.

She tried to come to some judgment of her husband's case. She could not believe the peril could be so great. Erling Vidkunssön and the King's cousins at Sudrheim had been charged with disloyalty and treason; yet were they back at their homes now as safe and as rich as ever, though they stood not so high as before in the King's favour.

'Twas like that Erlend had engaged in some unlawful courses to serve Lady Ingebjörg. In all these years he had kept up the friendship with his noble kinswoman; she knew that he had given her some sort of unlawful aid that had to be kept secret, five winters ago when he was her guest in Denmark. Now that Erling Vidkunssön had taken up the lady's cause, and would have put her in possession of the estates she owned in Norway, it might well be that Erling had counselled her to go to Erlend, or that she had turned to her father's kinsman of her own accord, after Erling had made his peace with the King. And that Erlend had dealt foolhardily with the matter. . . .

But she could not well understand how her kinsfolk at Sundbu could be mixed up in this.

Yet 'twas impossible that the end of the matter could be aught else than that Erlend came to full atonement with the King, if all his offence was to have been too zealous in the King's mother's service.

High treason. She had heard of Audun Hestakorn's downfall—and his death on the gallows at Nordnes—it was in her father's youth that it befell. But frightful misdeeds had been charged against Sir Audun. No; she would not think on such things. 'Twas so little likely that Erlend's cause should have a worse outcome than—than Erling Vidkunssön's and the Haftorssöns', for example.

——Nikulaus Erlendssön of Husaby. Ah, now it seemed so to her too—Husaby was the fairest manor in Norway's land.

She would go to Sir Baard and find out all that could be known. The Treasurer had always been her friend. Olav Lagmand too—in former days. But Erlend had taken it in such bad part when the Lagmand's decree went against him in that suit about the town-house. And Olav had taken so much to heart the mischance that had befallen his god-daughter's husband.

Near kinsfolk they had none, neither Erlend nor she—widespread as their kindred was. Munan Baardssön scarce counted any more. He stood condemned for unlawful dealings when he held the Wardenship of Ringerike; he sought too eagerly to get his many children on in the world—four he had had in wedlock and five outside it. And 'twas said he had fallen away much since Lady Katrin's death. Inge of Ryfylke, Julitta and her husband, Ragnfrid, who was married in Sweden, knew but little of Erlend—these were the other children left by Lady Aashild. Between the Hestnes folk and Erlend there had been no friendship since Sir Baard Peterssön died; Tormod of Raasvold was in his second child-hood; his and Lady Gunna's children were dead, and their grand-children still in their nonage.

She herself had no other kin on her father's side in Norway than Ketil Aasmundssön of Skog, and Sigurd Kyrning, who was wedded to Aasmund's eldest daughter. The other daughter was a widow, and the third a nun. The men of Sundbu seemed to be all four mixed in the case.

The sick monk in the Preachers' Cloister was Erlend's only near kinsman. And the man who stood nearest to her in the world was Simon Darre, since he was wed with her only sister.

Munan awoke, whimpering. Kristin turned in her bed and laid the child to her breast on the other side. She could not take him with her to Nidaros, uncertain as all things were. Maybe this would be the last time this little one would drink from his own mother's breast. Maybe this would be the last time in this world that she should lie thus, holding a little child close to her, so blissfully, so blessedly. If Erlend's life were forfeit——! Blessed Mary, Mother of God, had she on any day or in any hour murmured by reason of the children God had granted her——? Would this be the last kiss she should ever have from such a little milky mouth as this——?

V

KRISTIN went to the palace the next evening as soon as she was come into the city. Where in all this great mansion have they put Erlend? she thought, as she looked round at the many stone houses. It seemed to her she thought more of how Erlend might be faring than of what she might have to learn. But she was told, on asking, that the Treasurer had left the town.

Her eyes smarted after the long boat-journey in the glittering sun-light, and her breasts, overfilled with milk, troubled her. When the serving-folk who lay in the room were gone to sleep, she got up and walked the floor all through the night.

Next day she sent Haldor, her own man, to the palace.—He came home, terrified and unhappy—Ulf Haldorssön, his father's brother, had been taken prisoner on the fjord, trying to come over to the cloister at Holm. The Treasurer was not yet come back.

This tidings put Kristin, too, in the greatest fear. Ulf had not dwelt at Husaby this last year, but had been working as one of the Warden's sheriffs, for the most part at Skjoldvirkstad, of which he now owned the greatest part. What kind of cause could this be, in which so many men were entangled? She could no longer keep at bay the worst fears, sick and worn with waking as she was now.

On the morning of the third day Sir Baard was still not come home. And a message that Kristin had tried to send to her husband did not reach him. She thought of seeking out Gunnulf in the cloister, but felt she could not. She walked and walked up and down the hall at home, with half-shut burning eyes. Sometimes 'twas as though she were walking half in her sleep; but as soon as she lay down, the fear and the pains came over her again so strongly that she was forced to rise again, broad awake, and walk, so as to endure them.

Just after nones Gunnulf Nikulaussön came in to her. Kristin went swiftly to meet the monk.

"Have you seen Erlend—Gunnulf, what is it they charge against him——?"

"There are heavy tidings, Kristin. No, they will not let any come near Erlend—least of all us cloister-folk. They believe that Abbot Olav has been privy to his plans. 'Tis true he borrowed money there, but the Brothers all swear that they knew naught of what he meant to do with it, when they put the Convent's seal to the deed. And the Abbot will give no account of his doings——"

"Aye. But what is it?—Is it the Duchess that has lured Erlend on to this——?"

Gunnulf answered:

"It seems rather as though they had to press her hard before she would join in their plans. The letter that—someone—has seen a draft of, which Erlend and his friends sent her last spring, they can scarce lay hands on, I trow, except they can force the lady to give it up to them. And they have found no draft. But by the answering letter and Sir Aage Laurissen's letter, which they took from Borgar Trondssön at Veöy, it seems sure enough that she has had such a writing from Erlend and the men who had bound them to stand by him in this plot. It seems to be clear that she was long afraid to send Prince Haakon to Norway —but that they urged upon her that, whatever the outcome of the matter might be, 'twas not possible that King Magnus should harm the child, his own brother. Should Haakon Knutssön not win the crown of Norway, he would not be much worse off than before—but these men were willing to venture their lives and all their goods to set him upon the throne."

For a long time Kristin sat quite still.

"I understand. These are greater matters than those that were between Sir Erling or the Haftorssöns and the King?"

"Aye," said Gunnulf in a low voice. "'Twas to be given out that Haftor Graut and Erlend sailed for Björgvin. But it was Kalundborg they were bound for, and they were to bring Prince Haakon back with them to Norway, while King Magnus was yet abroad about his wooing——"

A little after, the monk said, still low:

"'Tis more than—'tis well-nigh a hundred years now since any Norwegian noble has dared the like of this; tried to overthrow him who was King by inheritance, and set up a rival King——"

Kristin sat gazing before her. Gunnulf could not see her face.

"Aye," she said in a while, thoughtfully. "The last men who ventured on that game were your forbears and Erlend's—and that time, too, my dead and gone kinsmen of the Gjesling house stood by King Skule."

She met Gunnulf's questioning look, and burst out, hotly and vehemently:

"I am but a simple woman, Gunnulf—little heed did I pay when my husband spoke with other men of such things—and unwilling was I to listen when he would have spoken with me of them—God help me, such weighty matters were beyond my understanding. But, simple woman as I am, unskilled in aught but my household work and the nurture of my children—even I know that right and justice had too far to travel before any man's cause could win through to the King and back again whence it sprung; and I have understood, too, that the common folk of this land have less prosperity and harder times now than when I was a child and King Haakon of blessed memory was our overlord. My husband"—she breathed quickly and tremulously once or twice—"my husband, I see it now, had taken up a cause so great that none of the other chiefs of this land dared set a hand to it——"

"That had he." The monk clenched his hands tightly together; his voice sank to a whisper. "So great a cause that many will deem it an ill thing that he should himself have brought about its downfall—and in such wise——"

Kristin cried out and started up. The sudden violent motion made the pain in her breast and arms so sharp that her whole body was bathed in sweat. Wildly and feverishly she turned on the monk and cried loudly:

"'Twas not Erlend did it—it was doomed so to be—it was his evil chance——"

She flung herself forward on her knees, with her hands pressed against the bench, and lifted her flushed, despairing visage towards the monk:

"You and I, Gunnulf—you, his brother, and I, his wife for thirteen years—we should not throw blame on Erlend, now he is a poor prisoner, in peril of his life maybe——"

Gunnulf's face quivered. He looked down at the kneeling woman. "God requite it to you, Kristin, that you can take this matter so." Again he wrung his wasted hands together. "God—God grant Erlend life, and the power to repay you for your faithfulness. God turn away this evil from you and from your children, Kristin——"

"Speak not so!" She drew herself upright on her knees and looked up into the man's face. "No good has come of it, Gunnulf, when you have stepped in, in Erlend's affairs and mine. None has judged him so hardly as you—his brother and God's servant!"

"Never has it been my will to judge Erlend more harshly than—than I must." His white face had grown yet whiter. "None upon earth have I held so dear as my brother. It may well be, therefore—that it wrung my soul as it had been my own sin that I must myself atone for, when Erlend offended against you. And then there is Husaby—'twas for Erlend alone to carry onward the race that is mine as well as his. The greatest part of my heritage I gave into his hands. Your sons are the men that are nearest to me in blood——"

"Erlend has *not* offended against me! I was no better than he! Why speak you so to me, Gunnulf?—you have never been my confessor. Sira Eiliv did not blame my husband to me—he corrected *me* for my sins when I laid bare my troubles to him. He was a better priest than you—and he it is that God has set over me, that I should hearken to him—and he has never said that I suffered wrong. I will hearken to him!"

Gunnulf had risen when she stood up. He muttered, his face pale and troubled:

"You speak the truth. 'Tis Sira Eiliv you must hearken to——"

He turned to go, but she caught his hand impetuously:

"Nay, go not from me so! I remember, Gunnulf—I remember when I was your guest here in this house—'twas yours then; and you were good to me. I mind the first time I met you—I was plunged in fear and pain—I remember you spoke to me in Erlend's excuse—you could not know—— You prayed and prayed for my life and my child's life. I know that you wished us well, you held Erlend dear——

"Oh, speak not hardly of Erlend, Gunnulf—which of us is clean before God? My father grew to be fond of him; our children love their father. Remember, he found me weak and easy to lure astray, and he set me in a good and honourable place. Oh, aye, 'tis fair at Husaby—the last evening be!ore I left home it was so fair, the sunset that evening was so beautiful. We have lived many a good day there together, Erlend and I.—However it may go, however it may go, yet is he my husband, my husband whom I love——"

"Kristin—trust not to the sunset glow and to the—love—you remember now that you fear for his life.

"——I remember a thing when I was young—a subdeacon only. Gudbjörg, that was after wedded with Alf of Uvaasen, was a servant at Siheim then; she was charged with stealing a golden ring. It came out that she was guiltless; but the shame and fear had so shaken her soul that the enemy won power over her; she went down to the lake and would have thrown herself in. And she often bore witness for us afterwards that, as she went in, the world seemed to her so red and golden and fair, and the water shone bright and felt warm and comforting, but when she stood in it to her middle she was moved to name Jesu name and cross herself—and then did the whole world grow grey, and the waters cold, and she saw whither she had been bound——"

"Then will I not name it," Kristin spoke softly—she stood stiffly upright—"if I could believe that then I would be tempted to forsake my lord in his need. But methinks 'twould not be Christ's name, but rather the enemy's, that could do the like——"

"I meant not that; I meant—God strengthen you, Kristin, to bear your husband's faults with a loving spirit——"

"You see that I do so," said the wife in the same tone.

Gunnulf turned from her, white and trembling. He passed his hand over his face:

"I will go home. I can more easily—at home I can more easily gather my thoughts—that I may do all that lies in my power for Erlend and you. God—God and all holy men preserve my brother's life and freedom. Oh, Kristin—never believe that my brother is not dear to me——"

But after he was gone, Kristin deemed that all things were grown worse. She would not have the serving-folk in with her, but walked and walked, wringing her hands and moaning softly. The evening had grown late, when there came a noise of people riding into the courtyard. A moment after, the door was opened, and a tall, stout man in a riding-cloak, first dimly seen in the twilight, came quickly towards her with jingling spurs and trailing sword. When she knew him for Simon Andressön, she burst out into loud sobbing and ran towards him with outstretched arms, but she cried out in pain when he drew her to him. Simon loosed his hold. She stood with her hands on his shoulders and her forehead leaned upon his breast, sobbing helplessly. He put his arm lightly around her:

"In God's name, Kristin!"—It seemed as though there was rescue in the very tones of his dry, warm voice, in the living smell of man that came from him—mixed of sweat, dust of the high-road, horses and leather garments. "In God's name—'tis all too soon to lose hope and courage yet.—There must be some way out, be sure——"

In a little she had grown calm enough to beg him for pardon. She was quite sick and wretched, she said, for she had had to take her youngest child from the breast so suddenly.

Simon learned how she had fared these three days and nights. He called her serving-maid and asked angrily if there was not a single woman in the house that had wit enough to know what ailed their mistress. But the woman was a raw young maid, and the bailiff of Erlend's town-house was a widower with two unmarried daughters. Simon sent a man out into the town to fetch a leech-woman, and bade Kristin go to bed. When she had grown a little easier, he would come in and speak with her.

While they waited for the leech-woman, he and his man were served with food in the hall; and over his meal he talked with her as she undressed in the closet. Yes, he had ridden north as soon as he had heard what had befallen at Sundbu—he had come hither, and Ramborg gone thither to be with Ivar's and Borgar's wives. Ivar they had taken to Mjös Castle, but Haavard they had left at large, yet had he been made to promise not to leave the parish. 'Twas said that Borgar and Guttorm had been lucky enough to get clear away—Jon of Laugarbru had ridden out to Raumsdal for tidings, and was to send word hither. Simon had been at Husaby at midday, but had not tarried long. All was well with the boys, but Naakkve and Björgulf had begged and begged him to take them with him.

Kristin had got back her courage and calm when, late in the evening, Simon sat by her on the bed's edge. She lay, in the grateful weariness that comes after racking pains are gone, and looked at her brother-in-law's heavy sunburned face and small strong eyes. It stayed and comforted her that he had come. Simon grew most grave, indeed, when he heard more fully how the matter stood, but yet he spoke hearteningly.

Kristin lay looking at the elkskin belt round his bulky waist. The great flat buckle of copper thinly coated with silver, without other adornment than a pierced A and M, betokening Ave Maria; the long dagger with the silver-gilt mountings and great rock-crystals set in the hilt; the poor little table-knife with the handle of cracked horn mended with brass bands—all this she had known ever since she was a child as part of her father's everyday gear. She remembered when Simon had got these things—just before her father died, he had been minded to give Simon his gilded best belt, and silver to make plates enough to lengthen it to fit his son-in-law. But Simon begged he might be given this one—and when Lavrans said he was cheating himself, Simon would have it that the dagger, at least, was a costly piece. "Aye, and then the knife," said Ragnfrid with a little smile; and then the men laughed and said: "Aye, the knife, to be sure." For about this knife her father and mother had had so much debate. It was a daily and hourly vexation to Ragnfrid to see such an ugly, paltry thing at her husband's belt. But Lavrans swore she should never gain her end and part him from it. "Never have I drawn it against you, Ragnfrid; and 'tis as fine a knife as any in Norway's land to cut butter with— when 'tis hot enough."

She begged Simon to let her see the knife, and lay awhile with it in her hands.

"I could wish that I owned this knife," she said softly and beseechingly.

"Aye—that I can well believe—glad am I that I own it—I would not sell it for twenty marks." He caught her wrists laughingly, and took the knife back from her. Simon's small plump hands were always so good to touch, so warm and dry.

A little after, he bade her good-night, took the candle, and went into the hall. She heard him kneel before the crucifix in there, stand up again, throw off his boots on the floor, then in a little lie heavily down on the bed by the north wall. Then Kristin sank into a fathomless, sweet sleep.

She did not wake till far on in the next day. Simon Andressön had gone out long before, and the house-folk had orders to pray her from him that she stay quietly at home in the house.

It was well-nigh the time of nones before he came back; but he said at once:

"I bear you greetings from Erlend, Kristin—I came to speech with him."

He saw how young her face grew, how soft and anxiously tender. So he took her hand in his while he told his story. It was not much that he and Erlend had been able to say to each other, for the man that had brought Simon to the prisoner had stayed by them all the time. Olav Lagmand had got Simon leave for this visit, for the sake of the kinship that had been between them while Halfrid lived.— Erlend sent loving greeting to her and the children; he had asked much about them all, but most of all about Gaute. Simon thought that in some days Kristin might get leave to see her husband. Erlend had seemed calm and in good heart.

"Had I gone out with you to-day, I might have seen him too," said the wife softly.

Simon said no; he had got in because he came alone. "In many a wise, Kristin, it may be easier for you to make way when a man goes ahead of you."

Erlend was kept in a room in the East Tower, out towards the river— one of the gentlefolks' rooms, though a small one. Ulf, they said, was in the dungeon. Haftor in another cell.

Warily feeling his way, to make sure how much she could bear, Simon told her what he had heard in the town. When he saw that she already understood the case to the full, he hid not from her that he, too, thought it a perilous matter. But all those he had talked to said that 'twas not possible Erlend could have dared to plan such an undertaking, and to carry it forward as far as he had done, except he was sure that he had a great part of the knights and the nobles at his back And since the malcontent great folk were so strong in numbers, it was not like that the King would dare to deal too hardly with their leader; but rather that he must let Erlend make his peace with him in some fashion.

Kristin asked in a low voice:

"Where does Erling Vidkunssön stand in this matter?"

"*That* I can see many a man would give something to know," said Simon.

Though he said it not to Kristin, and had not said it to the men with whom he had talked of this, it seemed to him little likely that Erlend should have at his back any powerful band of men who had bound themselves to risk life and goods in such a perilous affair—had it been so, they would scarce have chosen him their chief, for that Erlend was rash and unstable all his fellows must know well. It was true that he was kinsman to Lady Ingebjörg and the young pretender; he had enjoyed much power and esteem in these latter years, he was not quite so unpractised in war as were most men of an age with him—was known as one that his men liked and followed—and though he had so often borne him witlessly, yet could he, when he would, speak well and to the point, so that it might well be thought that he had now at long last learnt prudence from his mischances. Simon thought 'twas most like there were some who had known of Erlend's undertaking and had pushed him forward; but he could scarce believe that they had bound them so strongly that they could not draw back now and leave Erlend to bear the brunt alone.

Simon deemed he had seen that Erlend himself looked for naught else, and that his mind seemed made up to having to pay dearly for his desperate venture. "When kine lie mired, 'tis for the owners to hang on to their tails," he said, laughing a little. But, to be sure, Erlend had not been able to say much, with a third man listening.

Simon marvelled that this meeting with his brother-in-law had moved him so much. But the narrow little turret-chamber, where Erlend had prayed him to take a seat on the bed—it went from wall to wall and filled half the room—Erlend's straight, slender form, as he stood by the little slit in the wall whence the light came—Erlend quite unafraid, clear-eyed, untroubled by either fear or hope—he was a fresh, cool, manful fellow, now all the clogging cobwebs of love-dalliance and foolery with women had been blown from off him. True, it was women and the commerce of love that had brought him hither, with all his daring plans that were ended ere yet he had brought them out into the light. But on that Erlend seemed not to think. He stood there like a man who had dared a desperate throw, had lost it, and knew how to suffer defeat well and manfully.

And his wondering and joyous thankfulness when he saw his brother-in-law sat well on him. Simon had said, when he saw it:

"Mind you not, kinsman, that night we watched together by our father-in-law? We gave one another our hands, and Lavrans laid his hand on ours—and we promised him and each other that we would stand together like brothers all our days."

"Aye." Erlend's face lit up with a smile. "Aye, and I trow Lavrans thought not that you would ever need *my* help."

"Nay," said Simon, unmoved, "'tis most like he deemed you, as you were placed, might well prove a stay to me, and not that you were like to need help from me."

Erlend smiled again:

"Lavrans was a wise man, Simon. And, strange as it may sound— I know that he liked me well."

Simon thought, aye, strange it was, God knew—yet even he himself—despite of all he knew of Erlend, and of all the other had done to him—even he could not help now feeling somewhat of a brother's tenderness towards Kristin's husband. Then Erlend asked of her.

Simon told him of how he had found her, sick and full of fear for her husband. Olav Hermanssön had promised to do his best to have her let in to see him, as soon as Sir Baard came home.

"Not before she is well!" said Erlend quickly. A strange flush, like a young girl's, passed over his brown unshaven face. "'Tis the one thing I dread, Simon—that I should not have strength to bear it well when I see her."

But in a little he said, as calmly as before:

"I know that you will stand by her faithfully, if she should be left a widow this year. Penniless they will not be, she and the children having her heritage from Lavrans. And she will have you near by, should she dwell at Jörundgaard."

The day after the Nativity of Mary,* the High Steward, Sir Ivar Ogmundssön, came to Nidaros. Twelve of the King's sworn liegemen from north of Dovre were named now as a Court to try Erlend Nikulaussön's cause. Sir Finn Ogmundssön, the High Steward's brother, had been chosen so set förth the charge against him.

Some time before this, in the summer, Haftor Olavssön of Godöy had slain himself with the little knife that each prisoner had been allowed to keep to cut his food with. Folk said that prison had so told on Haftor that he had not been in his right mind. Erlend said to Simon, when he heard of it, that now he need have no fear of Haftor's tongue. But yet he was much moved.

As time went on, it happened now and then that the guards would make themselves an errand without when Simon or Kristin was with Erlend. Both of these two saw—and spoke of it to each other—that Erlend's first and last thought was to come through this business without the names of those with him in the plot being discovered. To Simon one day he said so straight out. He had promised all who had joined in his counsels that he would hold the rope so that if it came to the worst, the blow should fall on his hands only, "and never yet have I betrayed any that put their trust in me." Simon looked at the man —Erlend's eyes were blue and clear; 'twas plain that he said this of himself in all good faith.

Nor had the King's agents yet been able to track down any other who had taken part in Erlend's treason, save the brothers Greip and Torvard Toressöns of Möre; and these would not confess that they had known the intent of Erlend's plan to be aught else than that he and other men had moved the Duchess to let Prince Haakon Knutssön be brought up in Norway. Afterwards it was meant that the chiefs should make prayer to King Magnus that 'twould be for the good of both his kingdoms if he gave his half-brother the name of King in Norway.

Borgar and Guttorm Trondssön had been lucky enough to escape from the palace at Veöy—none could say how, but folk guessed that Borgar had got help from some woman—he was a comely youth and something of a light liver. Ivar was still in prison in Mjös Castle; young Haavard his brothers seemed to have kept outside their counsels.

While the meeting of King's-men sat in the castle, the Archbishop held a concilium in his palace. Simon was a man with many friends

* 8th September.

and acquaintances; he could thus tell Kristin what was going forward. All deemed it likely that Erlend would be outlawed and banished and his lands and goods be forfeit to the King. Erlend, too, said 'twas like it would be so; he was in good heart—he meant to seek refuge in Denmark. As things stood in that land, the road to advancement was ever open to a man of mettle and skill in arms, and Lady Ingebjörg would surely welcome his wife as her kinswoman and keep her with her in all seemly honour. Simon would have to take the children, save the two eldest sons, whom Erlend was minded to have with him in Denmark.

Kristin had not been outside the city for a day in all this time, and had not seen her children, save Naakkve and Björgulf; they had come riding into the courtyard one evening alone. Their mother kept them with her for some days; but then she sent them to Raasvold, where Lady Gunna had taken the little ones to be with her.

Erlend wished it should be so. And Kristin was afraid of the thoughts that might arise in her if she were to see her sons about her, listen to their questions, and try to make things clear to them. She strove to thrust away from her all thoughts of her wedded years at Husaby. So rich had been those years that they seemed to her now to have been one great calm—even as there seems a sort of calm on a billowy sea when one stands high enough above it on a great cliff. The waves that chase each other seem everlasting and unchanging—even so had life billowed through her soul in those spacious years.

Now was it with her again as in her youth, when she had pitted her will to win Erlend against all things and all men. Now again was her life but a waiting from hour to hour, between the hours when she saw her husband, sat by his side on the bed in the turret-chamber of the castle, talked with him calmly and evenly—till by some chance they would be left alone for a moment, and would fall into each other's arms, with endless passionate kisses and wild embraces.

At other times she sat in Christ's Church, hours at a time. She kneeled, gazing up at St. Olav's golden shrine behind the grated lattice of the choir. Lord, I am his wife. Lord, I held fast to him when I was his in sin and unrighteousness. Through God's mercy were we two, all unworthy, joined together in holy wedlock. Seared with the brands of sin, weighed down with sin's burden, we came together to the threshold of God's house, and together received the body of our Redeemer from the priest's hands. Should I now murmur if God puts my faithfulness to the proof? Should I think of aught else than that I am his wife and he is my husband as long as we both live——?

The Thursday before Michaelmas, the meeting of the King's-men's

court was held and judgment given on Erlend Nikulaussön of Husaby.
He was found guilty of having plotted to despoil King Magnus of land
and lieges by treachery, to raise revolt against the King within the
land, and to lead into Norway forces hired from without. After having
made search into all such cases in former times, the judges decreed that
Erlend Nikulaussön had forfeited his life and all his goods into King
Magnus' hands.

Arne Gjavvaldssön came down to Simon Darre and Kristin Lavransdatter in the Nikulaus town-house. He had been at the meeting.

Erlend had not tried to deny what he had done. Clearly and firmly
he had acknowledged his purpose, by these measures to force King
Magnus to give his young half-brother, Prince Haakon Knutssön Porse,
the kingship of Norway. Arne had deemed that Erlend spoke exceeding well. He had pointed to the great hardships and troubles suffered
by the people of the land, by reason that the King, in these later years,
had scarce set foot on Norwegian soil, and had ever shown unwilling-
ness to appoint Stadtholders who could do justice and wield the kingly
powers. By reason of the King's undertakings in Skaane, and of the
wastefulness and the unwisdom in money matters that were shown by
the men he most hearkened to, the folk suffered oppression and im-
poverishment, and could never feel safe from new demands for help
and new-fangled taxes. Since the Norwegian knights and esquires
bearing arms had far fewer rights and liberties than the Swedish
knighthood, it was hard for them to contend with the Swedes on equal
terms, and it was but reason and nature that a man like Sir Magnus
Eirikssön, young and unskilled in affairs, should hearken more to
his Swedish lords and love them more, since they had greater riches
and therefore more power to support him with well-armed and well-
trained warriors.

He and his confederate friends had deemed they had such sure
knowledge of the minds of the greatest part of the folk, both nobles,
peasants and townsmen, in the north and west of Norway, that they had
doubted not at all they would find full following there, if they could
bring forward a Prince as nearly akin to their dear lord, King Haakon
of blessed memory, as he they had now. He had looked that then
the folk of the land would agree together that we should move King
Magnus to let his brother mount the throne here; while Prince Haakon
should swear to maintain peace and brotherhood with King Magnus,
to guard the realm of Norway in accordance with the ancient boundaries, to uphold the rights of God's Church, the laws and customs
of the land as handed down from of old, and the rights and liberties
of both country folk and townsmen; and to put a stop to foreigners'
forcing their way into the kingdom. This plan it had been his and his

friends' intent to put before King Magnus in friendly wise. Yet had it ever from of old been the right of the Norwegian farmers and chieftains to set aside a King who tried to rule unlawfully.

Of Ulf Saksesön's doings in England and Scotland, he said that Ulf's intent was but to win favour there for Prince Haakon, if so be God would grant that he became our lord. With him in this undertaking there had been no Norseman, saving Haftor Olavssön of Godöy (to whose soul God be merciful), his kinsmen Trond Gjesling's three sons of Sundbu, and Greip and Torvard Toressöns of the Hatteberg kindred.

Erlend's words had moved his hearers strongly, said Arne Gjavvaldssön. But at the end, when he spoke of the support they had looked for from the Church's men, he had recalled those old rumours of the time when King Magnus was not yet grown up, and that, Arne deemed, had been unwise. The Archbishop's officer had taken him sharply to task —Archbishop Paal Baardssön, as they knew, both while he was Chancellor and since, bore great love towards King Magnus, by reason of the King's godly turn of mind; and folk were fain now to forget that such rumours had ever been spread about their King; besides, he was even now about to wed a lady, the Count's daughter of Namur —had there ever been any truth in the matter, it must be deemed that now Magnus Eiriksson had altogether turned him from all such things.

——Arne Gjavvaldssön had shown Simon Andressön the greatest friendliness while Simon had been in Nidaros. It was Arne, too, who now reminded Simon that it must be open to Erlend to appeal from this judgment, as unlawfully come to. According to the words of the law, the charge against Erlend should have been brought forward by one of his peers; but Sir Finn of Hestbö was a knight, and Erlend but an esquire. It might well be, thought Arne, that a new court would find that a harder punishment than outlawry could not be awarded Erlend.

As for what Erlend had set forth, concerning the kind of kingly rule he deemed this land would best be served with, it had sounded fair and fine, truly. And all men knew where the man was to be found who would have been glad enough to take the helm and steer this course while the new King was in his nonage—Arne scratched the grey stubble on his chin, and glanced across at Simon.

"None has heard from him, or of him, this summer?" asked Simon in a low voice.

"No. He says, I did hear, that he is out of favour with the King and stands outside all such matters. 'Tis many a long day since he has been content to sit so long at home and listen to Lady Elin's talk. His daughters are as fair and as dull as their mother, folks say."

Erlend had heard the doom of the court with steadfast calm, and he had saluted the members of the court as mannerly, freely and fairly when he was led out as when he had come in. He was calm and cheerful when Kristin and Simon were granted speech with him next day. Arne Gjavvaldssön was with them, and Erlend said that he would follow Arne's counsel.

"Never could I bring Kristin here to come with me to Denmark in former days," he said, putting an arm about his wife's waist. "And I had ever such a mind to go forth into the world with her."

A kind of quiver passed over his face, and of a sudden he kissed her pale cheek vehemently, heedless of the two lookers-on.

Simon Andressön rode out to Husaby to take order for the moving of Kristin's goods to Jörundgaard. He counselled her to send the children, too, to Gudbrandsdal, at the same time. Kristin said:

"My sons shall not depart from their father's house till they are driven out."

"I would not wait for that, if I were in your place," said Simon. "They are so young, they can scarce rightly understand this matter. 'Twere better you let them leave Husaby believing that they are going but to visit their mother's sister, and to see to their mother's heritage in the Dale."

Erlend held with Simon in this. But the upshot was that only Ivar and Skule went south with their aunt's husband. Kristin could not send the two little ones so far away from her. When Lavrans and Munan were brought to her in the town-house, and she saw that her youngest son knew her not again, she quite broke down. Simon had not seen her shed a tear since the first evening he came to Nidaros; but now she wept and wept over Munan as he sprawled and struggled, close pressed in his mother's arms, striving to come to his foster-mother; and she wept over young Lavrans, who crept up into her lap and caught her round the neck, weeping because she wept. So she kept the two with her, and Gaute too—he was unwilling to go with Simon, and it seemed to her unwise to let this child, who was bearing a load all too heavy for his years, out of her sight.

Sira Eiliv had brought the children to the city. He had prayed the Archbishop to let him leave his church awhile and visit his brother at Tautra; and this was readily granted to Erlend Nikulaussön's house priest. And since it seemed to him that Kristin could scarce take care of so many children while staying alone in the city, he proffered to take Naakkve and Björgulf out with him to the cloister.

The last night before the priest and the boys were to set forth—Simon had left already with the twins—Kristin made confession to the holy and pure-hearted man who had been her spiritual father all these years. They sat together many hours, and Sira Eiliv was instant with her to be humble and obedient towards God, and patient, faithful and loving towards her wedded husband. She knelt by the bench where he sat; then Sira Eiliv rose up and knelt by her side, still bearing the red stole, the token of the yoke of Christ's love, and prayed long and fervently without words. But she knew that he prayed for the father and mother and the children and all the household, whose souls' health he had so faithfully striven to further all these years.

The day after, she stood on the shore at Bratören and watched the lay brothers from Tautra setting sail on the boat that was to bear away the priest and her two eldest sons. On the way home she went into the Minorites' Church, and tarried there till she deemed she was strong enough to venture back to her own house. And in the evening, when the two little ones were gone to sleep, she sat with her spinning and told Gaute stories till it was bedtime for him too.

VI

ERLEND was held prisoner in the castle till nigh upon Clement's Mass.* Then there came word and letters ordering that he should be taken south under safe-conduct,† to be brought before King Magnus. The King purposed to hold the Yule-tide feast at Baagahus‡ that year.

Kristin was thrown into deadly fear. With unspeakable struggles she had used herself to keep calm, with Erlend a prisoner under doom of death. Now was he to be taken far away to a doubtful fate; folk said all manner of things about the King, and in the band of men who were about him Erlend had no friends. Ivar Ogmundssön, who now was Governor of the castle at Baaghus, had spoken of Erlend's treason in the harshest words. And 'twas said he had been set against Erlend the more by being told of some malapert speech of Erlend's about him in former days.

But Erlend was glad of the tidings. Kristin saw, indeed, that he took not the parting now at hand lightly. But this long imprisonment had begun to wear so upon him that he grasped eagerly at the thought of the long sea journey, and seemed careless well-nigh of all else.

In three days all was ready, and Erlend set sail in Sir Finn's ship.—Simon had promised to come back to Nidaros before Advent, when he

* 23rd November.   † See Note 16.   ‡ See Note 17.

had cast about him a little and ordered his affairs at home; but if before that there were any new tidings, he had prayed Kristin to send him word, and he would come at once. Now it came to her that she would journey south to him, and from thence would she go on to where the King was, and would fall at his feet and pray for mercy for her husband —gladly would she offer all her possessions to redeem his life.

Erlend had sold or pledged his mansion in Nidaros to divers people; the Nidarholm cloister owned the hall-house now, but Abbot Olav had written lovingly to Kristin, praying her to use it as long as she had need. She was there alone with one serving-maid, Ulf Haldorssön (who had been set free, since they had not enough proof against him), and his nephew Haldor, Kristin's own man.

She took counsel with Ulf, and at first he showed himself somewhat doubtful—he deemed it would be too hard a journey for her across the Dovrefjeld; much snow had fallen in the hills already. But when he saw the woman's anguish of soul, he turned round and counselled that she should go. Lady Gunna took the two little children out to Raasvold; but Gaute would not be parted from his mother, and she felt, too, that she dared not well let the boy stay north of Dovre and out of her sight.

They met such hard weather when they came south on to the high mountains, that by Ulf's counsel they borrowed ski at Drivstuen and left their horses behind there, lest they should be forced to pass the next night in the open. Kristin had not had ski on her feet since she was a little maid, and it was hard for her to make headway on them, though the men upheld and helped her to the utmost. They could come no farther that day than midway in the hills between Drivstuen and Hjerdkinn; and when it grew dark, they had to seek shelter in a birch-wood and dig themselves down into the snow. At Toftar they were able to hire horses again; here they plunged into mists, and when they came a little down into the Dale, they found rainy weather. When, some hours after dark had fallen, they rode into the Formo courtyard, the wind howled about the house-corners, the river roared, and a rushing, soughing sound came from the hill-side woods. The courtyard was like a swamp, and deadened the sound of the horses' hoofs—in the Saturday evening holiday from work there was no sign of life on the great manor, and neither the folk nor the dogs seemed to be ware of their coming.

Ulf thundered on the door of the hall-house with his spear; a serving-man came and opened. A moment after, Simon himself stood in the outer-room door, broad and dark against the light behind, with a child on his arm; he drove the barking dogs behind him. He gave a cry when he saw his wife's sister, set down the child, and drew her and Gaute in, taking off their soaking outer garments himself.

It was goodly and warm in the hall, but the air was very thick, for it was a fire-place room with flat ceiling under the upper hall. And 'twas full of folk, and children and dogs seemed swarming out of every corner. Then Kristin made out her two little sons' faces, red, warm and joyous, in behind the table where a candle stood burning. They came forward now and greeted their mother and brother a little shyly. Kristin saw that she had broken in here into the midst of these good folks' comfort and cheer. For the rest, the whole room was in a litter, and at each step she took she trod on crunching nutshells—they were scattered all over the floor.

Simon sent the serving-men and women out on divers errands, and the most part of the dogs and children followed them, as well as the grown folks—these were neighbours with their following.—While he questioned and listened to her, he fastened up his shirt and coat, which had stood open, showing his naked, hairy chest. The children had made him in this plight, he said in excuse. He was indeed in sad disarray: his belt was twisted awry, his hands and clothes dirty, his face sooty, and his hair full of dust and straw.

Soon after came two serving-women and brought Kristin and Gaute over to Ramborg's ladies' hall. A fire had been lit there, and busy serving-maids lighted candles, made up the bed, and helped her and the boy into dry clothes, while others set the board with meat and drink. A half-grown maid with silk-bound plaits brought Kristin a foaming mug of ale. The girl was Simon's eldest daughter, Arngjerd.

Then he himself came in; he had made himself trim and was more as Kristin was used to see him—well and richly clad. He led his little daughter by the hand, and Ivar and Skule came with him.

Kristin asked after her sister, and Simon said Ramborg had gone with the ladies from Sundbu down to Ringheim; Jostein had come to fetch his daughter Helga, and he had wished to take Dagny and Ramborg with him too; he was a cheerful kindly old man, and he had promised to take the best care of the three young wives. So maybe Ramborg would stay there through the winter. She looked to have another child at St. Matthew's Mass or thereabout—and then Simon had thought that 'twas like he might have to be away from home this winter; so she would be better off with her young kinswomen. Oh, no—for the housekeeping here at Formo, it made no odds whether she were at home or away, laughed Simon—for he had never craved of a young child like Ramborg that she should wear herself out with the drudgery of a great household.

On hearing Kristin's plans, Simon said at once that he would go with her south. He had so many kinsfolk there, and so many old friends of his father's and his own, that he hoped he could be of more service to her there than in Trondheim. Whether it would be wise for her to seek the King herself, he could better judge when they came thither. He would be ready for the road in three or four days.

They went together to mass the next day, being Sunday, and afterward went to see Sira Eirik at Romungaard. The priest was old now; he welcomed Kristin lovingly, and seemed most sorrowful at her mischance. Then they went round by Jörundgaard.

The houses were the same, and in the rooms were the same beds and benches and tables. This was now her own manor, and it seemed most like that 'twas here her sons would grow up, and that here she herself would one day lay her down and close her eyes for ever. But never had she felt so clearly as in this hour that it was on her father and mother all the life of this home had rested. Whatever hidden troubles they might have had to struggle with, warmth and help, peace and safety had flowed out from them to all that lived about them.

Restless and heavy of heart as she was, it wearied her a little when Simon talked of his own affairs, his estates and the children. She saw herself that there was no reason in it; he was ready to help her with all his might; she saw that 'twas most good of him to be willing to leave his home at Yule-tide, and to be parted from his wife at a time like this—he surely was thinking much on whether he should soon have a son now— for he had only the one child by Ramborg as yet, though they would soon have been wedded six years. She could not look that he should take her mischance and Erlend's so much to heart as quite to forget all joy in his own happy lot; but it was strange to go about with him here, and see him so joyful and warm and secure in his own home.

Unwittingly Kristin had thought that Ulvhild Simonsdatter would be like her own little sister, whom she had been named after—would be fair-haired and slender and clear-skinned. But Simon's little daughter was round and fat, with cheeks like apples and a mouth like a red berry, quick grey eyes like her father's in his youth, and with his goodly brown curling hair. Simon loved the bonny, lively child much, and was proud of her quick-witted prattle.

"Though yet this little girl is so ugly and loathly and ill-favoured," he said, putting his hands on each side of her chest and twirling her while he lifted her into the air, "I deem 'tis a changeling that the trolls up in the fell here have brought for her mother and me and put into the cradle, such a grim and grum little thing is it"; then he set her down suddenly, and hastily made the sign of the cross over her three times, as though frighted by his own rash words.

His base-born daughter, Arngjerd, was not fair, but she looked good and understanding, and her father took her about with him as often as 'twas possible. He was full of praises of her handiness.—Kristin was made to look into Arngjerd's chest, and see all the things she had spun and woven and sewed already for her dowry.

"The day I lay the hand of this daughter of mine in a good true-hearted bridegroom's hand," said Simon, looking long after the girl, "will be one of the gladdest days I have known."

To save the cost and to get the journey over quickly, Kristin would not take with her any maid, nor any man other than Ulf Haldorssön. Fourteen days before Yule, then, she and he set forth from Formo, in company with Simon and his two stout young serving-men.

When they came to Oslo, Simon soon learnt that the King would not come to Norway—he was to hold the Yule-tide feast at Stockholm, it seemed. Erlend was in the castle at Akersnes; the Governor of the castle was away, so that in the meantime 'twas not possible for any of them to see the prisoner. But the Under-Treasurer, Olav Kyrning, promised to let Erlend know they were in the city. Olav showed much friendliness toward Simon and Kristin, for his brother was wedded to Ramborg Aasmundsdatter of Skog, so that he counted him a far-off kinsman of Lavrans' daughters.

Ketil of Skog came into the city and bade them out to Skog to drink Yule-tide with him; but Kristin would not keep the holy-days with feasting while things stood thus with Erlend. And Simon would not go alone, though she prayed him much to do so. Simon and Ketil knew somewhat of each other, but Kristin had seen her uncle's son but once since he was grown up.

Kristin and Simon took lodging in the same mansion where she had once been his parents' guest when they two were betrothed; but they dwelt in another house. There were two beds in the room; she slept in one, and Simon and Ulf in the other; the men lay in the stable.

On Christmas Eve, Kristin wished to go to the midnight mass in Non-neseter church—she said it was because the sisters sang so sweetly. So they all five went together. The night was clear starlight, mild and fair, and it had snowed a little in the evening, so that 'twas somewhat light. When the bells began ringing from the churches, folk streamed out of all the houses, and Simon had to lead Kristin by the hand. Now and then he stole a glance at her. She was grown greatly thinner this last autumn, but it was as though her tall, straight form had got back somewhat of the young maid's supple and tranquil grace. Over her pale face there was come again the look she had had in youth of calm and gentleness covering a deep and hidden, listening expectancy. She had taken on a strange ghostly likeness to the young Kristin of that Yule-tide long ago.—Simon pressed her hand, and knew not that he had done so till he felt an answering pressure. He looked up—she smiled and nodded, and he understood that she had taken his handclasp as a warning to her to be brave—and now she was striving to show him that indeed she was brave.

Toward the end of the holy-days, Sir Munan came to her—he had only now heard she was in the city, he said. He greeted her heartily, likewise Simon Andressön and Ulf, whom he spoke to at every second word as "kinsman" and "dear friend." It might be hard for them to gain sight of Erlend, he said; he was most strictly guarded—*he* had not been able to win in to see his cousin. But Ulf said, with a laugh, when the knight was gone, that he deemed not Munan had pressed so exceeding hard to gain entrance—he was in such deadly fear of being tangled in the affair that he could scarcely bear to hear it named. Munan had grown exceeding old, exceeding bald, and wasted in flesh; the skin hung loose on his bulky frame. He dwelt out at Skogheim, and had with him one of his base-born daughters who was a widow. The father would gladly have been quit of her, for none of his other children, neither those born in wedlock nor the others, would come near him so long as this half-sister ruled his house; she was an overbearing, greedy and shrewish woman. But Munan dared not bid her begone.

At length, some time on in the new year, Olav Kyrning got leave for Erlend's wife and Simon to see him. And now again it fell to Simon's lot to bear the sorrowful wife company at these heart-breaking meetings. Much stricter watch was kept here than at Nidaros to see that Erlend spoke with none, except the Governor's folk were by.

Erlend was calm as before, but Simon saw that this waiting was beginning to wear upon the man. He made no complaint at any time, and said that he suffered no ill-usage and that all was done for him that could be done; but he owned that he was much plagued with the cold—there was no fire-place in the cell. And 'twas not in his power to indulge himself overmuch in cleanliness—though, he laughed, had he not had the lice to fight with, like enough the time would have seemed yet longer out here.

Kristin, too, was calm—so calm that Simon waited in breathless fear for the day when she should break down altogether.

King Magnus made his royal progress in Sweden, and there seemed no likelihood that he would cross the boundary soon, or that any change in Erlend's state was at hand.

On the day of Gregory's Mass,* Kristin and Ulf Haldorssön had been at church at Nonneseter. When, on their way back, they had crossed the bridge over the Nonnebeck, she took not the way down towards her lodging, which lay near the Bishop's palace, but turned eastward to-

* 13th February.

wards the open place by Clement's Church, and into the narrow lanes between the church and the river.

The day was grey and thick—there had been soft weather for a time—and their footgear and the skirts of their cloaks quickly grew wet and heavy with the yellow clay of the riverside. They came out on the open lands towards the high bank of the river. Once their eyes met. Ulf laughed noiselessly, and his mouth twisted into a sort of grimace, but his eyes were sorrowful; Kristin smiled—a strange, sick smile.

Soon after they stood at the edge of the high ground; there had once been a landslip in the clay bank here, and Fluga's house lay right under it, so close up against the dirty yellow slope, where a few black stunted weeds were growing, that the stench of the pigsty, which they looked down on, came rankly up to them—two fat sows were snuffling about in the black mud. The river-bank was but a narrow strip here; the muddy grey river-current, with the jostling ice-flakes on it, came right up to the tumble-down houses with their bleached grey shingle roofs.

Whilst they stood there, a man and a woman came up to the fencing of the sty and looked at the pigs—the man leaned over and began scratching one of the sows with the shaft-end of the silver-mounted light axe he was using as a staff. It was Munan Baardssön himself, and the woman was Brynhild. He looked up and was ware of them—he stood gaping up at them, and Kristin called out a cheerful greeting.

Sir Munan fell a-laughing loudly.

"Come down and have a drink of warm ale to keep out this filthy weather," he called up.

As they went down to the gate of the houses, Ulf told Kristin that Brynhild Jonsdatter kept neither lodging-house nor ale-tap any more. She had been in trouble many times, and at last had been threatened with flogging, but Munan had got her out and gone surety for her that she would altogether cease her unlawful traffickings. Her sons, too, had now got so far on in the world that for their sake their mother was forced to think of bettering her ill repute. After his wife's death, Munan Baardssön had taken up with her again, and he was often to be found in her house.

He met them at the gate.

"Here we are—kinsfolk, all four of us, in a fashion," he snickered—he was a little in drink, but not much. "You are a good woman, Kristin Lavransdatter, pious but not proud.—Brynhild, too, is an honourable, worshipful woman now—and I was not yet a wedded man when I got the two sons I have by her—and they are much the best of all my children.—I have told you as much every day in all these years, Brynhild. Inge and Gudleik are dearest to me of all my children——"

Brynhild was comely still, but her skin was a pale yellow, and looked as if it must feel clammy, Kristin thought, as when one has stood all day over the fat-cauldrons. But her house was well kept, the food and drink that she put on the board were of the best, and the vessels fair and clean.

"Aye, I look in here when I have an errand in Oslo," said Munan. "You understand, the mother is fain to hear tidings of her sons. Inge writes to me from time to time, for he is a learned man, Inge; a Bishop's commissary must be so, you know—and I got him well wedded too, with Tora Bjarnesdatter of Grjote; think you many men have got such a wife for their bastard? So we sit here and talk about this, and Brynhild bears in the meat and ale to me, just as she used in days gone by, when she bore the keys of my house at Skogheim. 'Tis heavy work sitting out there now thinking of my wife that is gone.—So I ride in hither to find a little comfort—when it chances that Brynhild is in such mood that she grudges me not a little friendliness and comfort."

Ulf Haldorssön sat with his chin resting on his hand, looking at the lady of Husaby. Kristin sat and listened and answered quietly and gently and mannerly—as calm and courtly as if she had been a guest at one of the great folk's manors at home in Trondheim.

"Aye, you, Kristin Lavransdatter, you won a wife's name and came to honour," said Brynhild Fluga, "though you came willingly enough to meet Erlend in my loft. I have been called slut and loose woman all my days—my stepmother sold me into his hands, there—I bit and scratched, and left the marks of every one of my nails on his face before he had his will of me——"

"Must you speak of this ever?" grumbled Munan. "Be sure—I have told it you so often too—I had let you go in peace had you borne you like a human creature and bidden me spare you—but you flew at my face like a wildcat before I was well inside the door——"

Ulf Haldorssön laughed softly to himself.

"And I dealt well by you evermore thereafter," said Munan. "You had but to point to a thing and I gave it you—and our children—aye, for sure they are far better off and safer this day than Kristin's poor sons —God guard the poor young lads, so as Erlend has guided things for his children! Methinks that should mean more than the name of wife to a mother's heart—and you know that I wished often your birth had been such that I could have wedded you lawfully—no woman have I liked as well as you—though you were but seldom kind or good to me—and the wife I did get, God reward her——! I have set up an altar for my Katrin and myself out in our church at home, Kristin—I have thanked God and Our Lady every day for my wedded life—no man has had a better——" He whimpered and sniffed.

Soon after, Ulf Haldorssön said that they must go. He and Kristin exchanged not a word on the way back. But outside the door she reached out her hand to the man:

"Ulf—my kinsman and my friend."

"If it could help aught," he said in a low voice, "I would gladly go to the gallows in Erlend's stead—for his sake and for yours!"

That evening, a little before bedtime, Kristin sat alone in the hall with Simon. Of a sudden she began telling him where she had been that day. She told of the meeting at Brynhild Fluga's.

Simon sat on a stool not far from her. Leaning forward a little, with his arms resting on his thighs, and hands hanging down, he sat looking up at her with a strange, searching look in his small, sharp eyes. He spoke not a word, and not a muscle moved in his big, heavy face.

Then she let fall that she had told all to her father, and what he had said to her.

Simon sat as before, immovable. But in a while he said calmly:

"'Twas the one thing I ever prayed of you, in all the years we have known each other—if I mind aright—that you would not—but if you could not keep silence to spare Lavrans, why——"

Kristin's whole body trembled:

"Aye! But—oh, Erlend, Erlend, Erlend——"

At the wild cry the man leapt up—Kristin had thrown herself forward, with her head between her arms, and was rocking her body from side to side, still calling on Erlend, between quivering, moaning sobs that seemed to tear their way out of her body.

"Kristin—in Jesu name!"

When he seized her upper arm and tried to stay her sobbing, she flung herself on him with all the weight of her body, and caught him round the neck, while through her weeping she went on calling her husband's name.

"Kristin—be still——" He held her tight in his arms and saw that she marked it not—she was weeping so that she could not stand upright. Then he lifted her up in his arms—crushed her to him a moment, and then bore her over and laid her on the bed.

"Be still," he prayed her again, in a choking, almost a threatening voice—he laid his hands over her face, and she caught his wrists and arms and clung close to him.

"Simon—Simon—oh! he must be saved——"

"I do what I can, Kristin—but now you *shall* be still." He turned sharply, walked over to the door and out into the yard. He shouted, till the echoes rang back from the house-walls, for the maid whom Kristin had hired in Oslo. The girl came running, and Simon bade her go in to her mistress. In a moment she came out again—her mistress would be alone, she said affrightedly to Simon, who still stood on the same spot.

He nodded and walked over to the stables; and stayed there till Gunnar, his man, and Ulf Haldorssön came to give the beasts their evening feed. Simon talked with them awhile, and then went with Ulf back again to the hall.

Kristin saw not much of her brother-in-law the next day. But after nones, as she sat sewing on a garment she meant to take out to her husband, he came running in, said naught to her and looked not at her, but flung open the lid of his travelling-chest, filled his silver goblet with wine, and rushed out again. Kristin stood up and went after him. Before the door of the hall stood a strange man, still holding his horse—Simon drew a gold ring from his finger, dropped it into the goblet, and drank to the newcomer.

Kristin guessed what this must be, and cried out joyfully:

"You have a son, Simon!"

"Aye." He slapped the messenger on the shoulder, as the man, thanking him, put up the goblet and the ring safely inside his belt. Then Simon caught his wife's sister round the waist and whirled her round and round. He looked so glad that Kristin could not but put her two hands on his shoulders—and then he kissed her full on the mouth and laughed aloud.

"Then 'twill still be the Darre stock that will hold Formo when you are gone, Simon," she said joyfully.

"Aye, so will it be—if God will.—No, to-night I would go alone," he said, when Kristin asked if they should go together to evensong.

That night he said to Kristin that he had heard Sir Erling Vidkunssön was now at his manor of Aker near Tunsberg. And that morning he had hired him passage in a ship going down the fjord—he was minded to speak with Sir Erling of Erlend's case.

Kristin said not much in answer. They had barely touched on it before—had kept them from going much into the question—whether Sir Erling had been privy to Erlend's plans or not. Simon said now it would be well that he should ask Erling Vidkunssön's counsel as to Kristin's plan that Simon should go with her to Lavrans' powerful kinsfolk in Sweden to claim kinship and crave their help.

Then Kristin spoke her thought:

"But, now you have had these great tidings, brother-in-law, methinks that it were but reason you should put off this journey to Aker—and first ride up to Ringheim and see to Ramborg and your son."

He was forced to turn away, so overcome was he. He had waited so for this—whether Kristin would make any sign that she understood how he longed to see his son. But when he had mastered himself somewhat, he said, with some shyness in his voice:

"I have been thinking, Kristin—mayhap God will vouchsafe that the boy thrive and prosper the better if I can be patient and hold in check my longing to see him till I have managed to help you and Erlend a little forward in this matter."

The day after, he went out and bought rich and costly gifts for his wife and the boy—and for all the women, too, who had been with Ramborg when she bore the child. Kristin took out a fair silver spoon she had had from her mother's heritage—it was to be for Andres Simonssön —but to her sister she sent the heavy silver-gilt chain that Lavrans had given her in her childhood along with the reliquary cross. The cross she fastened now to the chain Erlend had given her as a betrothal-gift. The next day at midday Simon sailed.

In the evening the ship lay to under an island in the fjord. Simon stayed on board; he lay in a sleeping-bag of hide with some pieces of wadmal over him, looking up at the starry skies, where the constellations seemed to climb and dive again as the boat pitched on the sleepily gliding swell. The water plashed and the ice-flakes scraped and thumped softly against the vessel's sides. 'Twas almost comforting to feel the cold creeping farther and farther through his body. It deadened——

Yet now he was sure: so ill as things had been with him they could never be again. Now that he had a son. It was not that he thought he could be fonder of the boy than he was of his daughters. It was somewhat else. For all the heart's gladness that his little maids could give him, when they sought their father with their games and laughter and prattle—sweet as it was to hold them in his lap and feel their soft hair against his chin—yet in this wise a man could never take his place in the succession of the men of his house, if his lands and goods and the memory of his doings in the world must pass with a daughter's hand over into a strange kindred. But now, when he might hope, if God would but grant that this little son should grow to manhood, that at Formo son should come after father—Andres Gudmundssön, Simon Andressön, Andres Simonssön—now it must surely follow of itself that he must stand before Andres as his father had stood before himself, an honest man in his secret thoughts no less than in his open acts.

——Sometimes things had been so that he understood not how he could bear it any longer. Had he seen but *one* token that she understood aught! But she was to him as though they had been brother and sister by blood—careful for his well-being, kind and loving and gentle—— And he knew not how long this would last—how long they should live together in this wise in one house. Did the thought never come to her that he could not forget—that even though he was wedded with her sister, he could never quite forget that they two had been meant once to live together in wedlock?

But now he had this son. He had ever been ashamed to add in his own words aught of his wishes or his thanks when he said over his prayers. But he deemed that Christ and Mary Virgin knew well what it had meant that he had said double number of Paternosters and Aves each day in these last days. And he would keep on with this so long as he was from home. And in other wise, too, he would show his thankfulness in fitting and open-handed fashion. And thus maybe he would win help on this present journey too.

Though, indeed, he deemed himself there was little reason to look for much from this visit. Sir Erling was quite estranged now from the King. And however powerful and secure the former Regent of the realm might be, and however little he needed to fear the young King, who was much more ticklishly placed than was he—the richest and most high-born man in Norway—yet it could not be looked for that he should be willing to anger King Magnus yet more against himself by pleading Erlend Nikulaussön's cause, and bringing suspicion on himself of having been privy to Erlend's treason. Even if he had had a part in it—aye, even if he had been at the bottom of the whole plan, ready to step in and have himself placed at the head of affairs the moment a minor King was once more upon the throne—he would scarce feel himself bound to venture aught to help the man who had brought the whole plan to ruin for the sake of a shameful love-adventure. 'Twas as though Simon half forgot it when he was with Erlend and Kristin—for they, too, seemed scarce to remember it any more. But so it was that Erlend had himself wrought the mischief—that 'twas his doing that naught else had come of the whole undertaking than ruin for himself—and for the good men who had been betrayed by his wantonness and folly.

But he must try all shifts to help her and her husband. And now he began to hope; for mayhap God and Mary Virgin, or some of the saints whom he had used to honour with offerings and almsgivings, would vouchsafe their aid in this as well.

He came to Aker somewhat late the next evening. A steward met him, and sent off men, some with the horses, some with Simon's man to the serving-men's house; while Simon himself went to the loft-room where the knight was sitting drinking. Sir Erling himself came out into the balcony straightway, and stood there while Simon mounted the stair; then he greeted his guest courteously enough, and led him into the hall, where was Stig Haakonssön of Mandvik with Erling's only son, Bjarne Erlingssön, a quite young man.

He was welcomed fairly enough—the serving-folk took from him his outer garments and bore in meat and drink. But he guessed that the men guessed—at least Sir Erling and Stig—what he was come for, and he felt that they were holding back. So when Stig began saying how rarely he was to be seen in this part of the country now—how seldom he darkened the doors of his former kinsfolk—and asked if he had ever been further south than Dyfrin since Halfrid died—Simon answered: No, not before this winter. But now he had been in Oslo some months with his wife's sister, Kristin Lavransdatter, who was wed with Erlend Nikulaussön.

On this there was a short silence. Then Sir Erling asked courteously after Kristin and Simon's wife and his brothers and sisters; and Simon asked after Lady Elin and Erling's daughters, and how things were with Stig, and how his old neighbours at Mandvik were, and what were the tidings from there.

Stig Haakonssön was a stoutly made, dark-haired man, some year-older than Simon, son of Halfrid Erlingsdatter's half-brother, Sir Haakon Toressön, and brother's son of Erling Vidkunssön's lady, Elin Toresdatter. He had lost the Wardenship of Skidu and the Governorship of the Tunsberg castles two winters back, when he fell out with the King; but still was well enough off with his Mandvik estates. But he was a widower and childless. Simon knew him well, and had been good friends with him, as with all his first wife's kin—even if the friendship had not been over-hot. He knew exceeding well what they had all thought of Halfrid's second marriage—Sir Andres Gudmundssön's younger son was doubtless a man of substance and of good birth, but an even match for Halfrid Erlingsdatter he was not—besides that he was ten years younger; they could not understand why she had set her heart on this young man—but they must e'en let her do as she would, since she had suffered such unbearable misery with her first husband.

Erling Vidkunssön Simon had met but few times before; and then it had ever been in Lady Elin's company; and at such times no sound ever came from him—none needed say more than yes or no where she was in presence. Sir Erling had aged not a little since that time—he was grown somewhat stouter, but his form was still comely and noble, for he bore himself exceeding fairly, and it suited him well that his pale, reddish-yellow hair was now turned a shining silver-grey.

The young Bjarne Erlingssön Simon had not seen before. He had been brought up near Björgvin in the house of a cleric, a friend of Erling's—'twas said among the kindred that this was because his father would not have him live out at Giske in the midst of a pack of foolish women. Erling himself was there no more than he was forced to be, and he dared not take the boy with him on his constant journeys, for Bjarne had been weakly and ailing as a growing lad, and Erling had lost two other sons in their childhood.

The boy looked exceeding comely as he sat with the light behind him, showing his side-face. Black, tightly curling hair rolled forward over his forehead, his great eyes seemed black, his nose was large and strongly curved, the mouth full and firm and fine and the chin well formed. Withal he was tall, slender and broad-shouldered. But when Simon had to sit down to the table to eat, the serving-man moved the candle, and now he saw that the skin of Bjarne's neck was quite eaten up with the scars of scrofula—they stretched on both sides right up under the ears and forward beneath the chin, dead, dull-white patches and bluish-red stripes and swollen knots. And then Bjarne had a trick of time and again pulling up the hood of the round fur-edged velvet cape that he wore even here in the room—pulling it up half-way over his head. When, soon after, it grew too hot for him, he would turn it down, and then draw it up again—he seemed not to know that he did it. Simon felt his hands grow quite restless at length with but looking on at this— though he tried to keep from looking.

Sir Erling scarcely took his eyes from his son—but he, too, seemed not to know that he was gazing so intently at the boy. Erling Vidkunssön's face was set and unchanging and his pale-blue eyes showed his feeling but little—but beneath the somewhat vague and watery glance there seemed to lie the cares and thought and love of endless years.

So the three elder men exchanged mannerly, sluggish talk, while Simon ate, and the youth sat fiddle-faddling with his hood. Afterwards all four sat drinking for a fitting space of time, and then Sir Erling asked if Simon were not weary with his journey, and Stig asked if he would be pleased to sleep with him. Simon was glad to be able to put off speaking of his errand. This first evening at Aker had left him not a little cast down.

The next day, when he broached the matter, Sir Erling's answer was much what Simon had looked for. He said that King Magnus had never hearkened to him willingly, and he had seen, from the time Magnus Eirikssön was old enough to have a will of his own, that his will had been that Erling Vidkunssön should have naught to say in his affairs when once he was of age. And since the quarrel between him and his friends on the one side, and the King on the other, had been made up, he had heard, and tried to hear, naught of the King or the King's friends. If he pleaded Erlend's cause with King Magnus, it would scarce avail the man much. He knew well enough that many in this land believed that he had been in some wise at the bottom of Erlend's undertaking. But, whether Simon believed him or not, neither he nor his friends had known aught of what was hatching. Had this matter come to light in another fashion, or had these venturesome young dare-devils risked their throw and failed, then would he have stepped in and striven to make their peace. But as things had gone, he deemed not that any could justly crave of him that he should come forward and thereby strengthen all men's suspicion that he had played a double game.

But he counselled Simon to have recourse to the Haftorssöns. They were the King's cousins, and, when they chanced not to be at feud with him, they kept up between them a friendship of a kind. And, so far as Erling understood the matter, the men whom Erlend was shielding were rather to be found amongst the Haftorssöns' party, and among the youngest of the nobles.

Now, as Simon knew, the King was to hold his wedding in Norway this summer. And there might then be a fitting occasion for Magnus to show mildness and clemency to his enemies. And the King's mother and Lady Isabel would doubtless come to the wedding-feast. Since Simon's mother had been Queen Isabel's maid of honour in her youth, Simon might turn him to Lady Isabel, or Erlend's wife might throw herself before the King's bride and Lady Ingebjörg Haakonsdatter with prayers for their intercession.

Simon thought that the last shift of all to try would be for Kristin to kneel to Lady Ingebjörg. Had the Duchess understood what honour was, she had sure long since come forward and rescued Erlend from his straits. But when he had named this once to Erlend, he had but laughed and said, the lady had always so many ticklish matters of her own to see to; and doubtless she was angry, since it now seemed but little like that her dearest child should ever bear the name of King.

VII

S P R I N G was come when Simon Andressön journeyed north to Toten, to fetch his wife and his little son and take them home to Formo. Then he stayed there awhile to see a little to his own affairs.

Kristin would not remove from Oslo. And she dared not yield to her hungry, burning longing for her three sons who were up there in the Dale. That she might still hold out and endure the life she was now living from day to day, she must not think on her children. She held out, she seemed calm and brave; she spoke with strangers and listened to strangers, and bore with their counsels and comfort; but to do this she must hold fast to the thought of Erlend, of Erlend alone! In the stray moments when she failed to hold fast her thoughts in the grasp of her will, pictures and thoughts flashed through her mind: Ivar stood in the wood-shed at Formo with Simon, watching his uncle intently, as he searched out a piece of wood to helve the boy's hatchet, bending and testing the sticks with his hands. Gaute's fair boyish face set manfully as, bending forward, he struggled against the snowstorm that grey winter day in the mountains—his ski slipped back, he sank backward some way down the slope, and landed deep in a snow-drift—and for a moment his manful mien was all but gone, and he was an over-wearied, helpless child. Her thoughts would turn to the two little ones; 'twas like Munan could both walk and talk a little now—was he as lovely as the others had been at that age? Lavrans had perhaps forgotten her. And the two big ones out in the cloister at Tautra—Naakkve, Naakkve, her first-born—— How much did the two big ones understand, and what were their thoughts—how did Naakkve, child as he was, endure the thought that nothing in life now was like to be for him as she and he himself and all men had deemed that it would be?

Sira Eiliv had sent her a letter, and she had told Erlend what was written in it of their sons. Else they never spoke of their children. They spoke not any more either of the past or of the future. Kristin brought him a piece of clothing or a dish of food; he asked her how things had gone with her since he saw her last; they sat hand in hand on his bed. Then sometimes it might chance that they were left alone a moment in the small, cold, dirty, stinking room—and they clung together with dumb, burning caresses, hearing, without marking it, Kristin's woman laughing with the watchmen outside on the stair.

Time enough, when he had either been taken from her or given back to her, to face the thought of their troop of children and the change in their lot—of all else in her life save this man beside her. She could not bear to lose an hour of the time that was left them together, and she dared not think of the meeting again with the four children she had left in the north—so she was fain to assent when Simon Andressön proffered to go alone to Trondheim and, along with Arne Gjavvaldssön, watch over her interest in the settlement of the forfeited estates. Much richer King Magnus was not like to be for Erlend's possessions—the man was more heavily in debt than he himself had had any knowledge of, and he had raised moneys that had been sent off to Denmark and Scotland and England. Erlend shrugged his shoulders and said with a half-smile that he looked not now to reap any return from *them*.

Thus Erlend's case stood much as before when Simon came back to Oslo about Holy Cross day in the autumn.* But he was dismayed to see how worn out they looked, both Kristin and his brother-in-law, and he felt a strange, sinking qualm at his heart when they both had yet enough self-mastery to thank him for coming hither at this time of year, when he could least well be spared from his estates at home. But now were all

* 14th September.

folks' faces set towards Tunsberg, where King Magnus was come to await his bride.

A little on in the month, Simon managed to hire passage in a ship bound thither, with some merchants who were to sail in eight days time. Then one morning a strange serving-man came to pray Simon Andressön to be at the pains of coming at once to St. Halvard's Church—Olav Kyrning waited for him there.

The Under-Treasurer was vehemently stirred. He was holding charge at the castle, whilst the Treasurer was at Tunsberg. And, the evening before, there had come a company of gentlemen who showed him a letter under King Magnus' seal, signifying that they were to inquire into Erlend Nikulaussön's case; and he had had the prisoner brought in to them. Three of them were foreigners, Frenchmen doubtless—Olav had not understood their speech, but the chaplain had spoken with them in Latin this morning, and "'tis said they are kinsmen of the lady who is to be our Queen—a fair beginning!" They had put Erlend to the question by torture—they had with them a kind of ladder and some fellows used to work such things. To-day he had denied to bring Erlend out of his chamber, and had set a strong watch—for so much he was ready to answer, for these were lawless doings, such as never were heard tell of in Norway before!

Simon borrowed a horse from one of the priests of the church and rode with Olav straightway out to Akersnes.

Olav Kyrning looked a little fearfully at the other's grimly set face, over which stormy waves of red were beating. Now and again Simon made a wild, violent movement, as if knowing not what he did—and the strange horse leapt aside, reared and balked under his rider.

"One can see on you, Simon, that you are angered," said Olav Kyrning.

Simon scarce knew himself what was uppermost in his mind. He was so stirred to the depths that at times he felt qualms of sickness. The blind and wild feeling that struggled in him and goaded him to utmost fury was a kind of shame—a helpless man, without weapon or defence, forced to suffer strangers' fists in his clothes, strangers manhandling his body—it was like hearing of the outraging of women; he grew dizzy with thirst for revenge, with longing to see blood shed for it. No—such things had never been the use and wont of this land—would they accustom Norwegian nobles to suffer such things——? That should never be!

He was sick for horror of what he was to see—fear of the shame he must bring on another man by seeing him in such a pass overpowered him above all other feelings, when Olav Kyrning opened to him the door of Erlend's cell.

Erlend lay on the floor, stretched out aslant from one corner of the room to the other; he was so tall that only thus could he find room to stretch out at full length. Some straw and clothes had been laid under him on the thick layer of filth that covered the floor, and his body was covered over with his dark-blue fur-lined cloak right up to the chin, so that the soft grey-brown marten fur mingled with the curly, tufted black beard Erlend had grown while in his prison.

His mouth showed white through the beard; his face was snow-white. The great, straight-lined triangle of the nose stood out monstrously high above the sunken cheeks, the grizzled hair lay in clammy, separate wisps back from the high, narrow forehead—on each of the hollow temples was a great bluish-red mark, as though something had pressed on or gripped him there.

Slowly, with labour, he opened his great sea-blue eyes; essayed a sort of smile when he recognized the man; his voice sounded a little veiled and like a stranger's.

"Sit down, brother-in-law——" He moved his head slightly towards the empty bed. "Aye—now have I learned somewhat new—since we last met——"

Olav Kyrning bent over Erlend and asked if there was aught he would. There was no answer—doubtless because Erlend could not speak—and he took away the cloak from over him. Erlend had on him naught but a pair of linen drawers and a rag of shirt—and the sight of the swollen and discoloured limbs shook and maddened Simon like some loathsome horror. He wondered whether Erlend had a like feeling—a shade of red came over his face as Olav passed a wet cloth, which he dipped into a vessel of water, down over his arms and legs. And when he laid the cloak over again, Erlend pushed it into place with some small movements of his limbs and by drawing the hood up with his chin, till he was quite covered up.

"Aye," said Erlend—he was a little more like himself in voice now, and the smile on his pale mouth was a little plainer; "next time—will be worse! But I am not afraid—none need be afraid—they will break naught out of me—in this way——"

Simon felt within himself that the man spoke the truth. Torture would not force a word out of Erlend Nikulaussön. There was naught that he might not do, might not reveal, in anger or in recklessness—he would never be moved a hair's breadth by force. And Simon felt that the shame and insult that he himself suffered on another man's behalf, Erlend scarce felt at all—he was filled with an obstinate joy in defying his torturers and a contented trust in his hardihood. He, who ever broke down so pitifully when he came up against a firm will, who might himself doubtless have been cruel in a moment of fear, rose above himself now that in this cruelty he scented an opposer weaker than himself.

But Simon's answer, growled through his teeth, was:

"Next time—I trow there will be none! What say you, Olav?"

Olav shook his head, but Erlend said, with a shadow of his old reckless flippancy in his voice:

"Aye, if I could but—believe it—as firmly as you! But these gentry will scarce—be content with this——" He grew ware of the working of Simon's heavy, sinewy face: "Nay, Simon—kinsman!"—Erlend would have raised himself on his elbow; the pain forced from him a strange muffled groan, and he sank back in a swoon.

Olav and Simon ministered to him clumsily. When the swoon was over, Erlend lay a little with open eyes; he spoke then, more gravely:

"See you not—it means—much—for Magnus—to get on the track of —what men he would better not trust—farther than he can see them? So much unrest—and discontent—as there has been——" ·

"Aye—if he deems that this will quench the discontent——" said Olav Kyrning threateningly. Then said Erlend, in a low and clear voice:

"I have dealt so in this matter—that few will deem—it matters much how it goes with me—I know that myself——"

The other two men reddened. Simon had thought that Erlend saw not this himself—and never before had Lady Sunniva been so much as hinted at between them. Now Simon broke out desperately:

"How could you have borne yourself so recklessly—so madly?"

"Nay, I understand it not either—now," said Erlend simply. "But— in hell's name!—how could I have thought she could read writing? She seemed—most unlearned——"

His eyelids drooped and closed, he was nigh swooning once more. Olav Kyrning muttered about fetching something, and went out. Simon bent over Erlend, who now again lay with eyes half opened.

"Brother-in-law—was—was Erling Vidkunssön with you in this?"

Erlend shook his head a little, with a slow smile:

"By Jesus, no! We thought—either he would not be bold enough to join with us—or else he had kept all things in his own hands. But ask not, Simon—I will say naught—to any—so only am I sure not to let aught slip out——"

On a sudden Erlend whispered his wife's name. Simon bent over him again—he looked the other should ask him to bring Kristin to him now. But he said quickly, as if in a flicker of fever:

"She must not hear of this, Simon. Say order has come from the King that none is to come near me. Take her out to Munan—to Skogheim— hear you?—these French—or Moorish—new friends—of our King's— will not give up yet! Get her out of the city before it is noised about! Simon?"

"Aye." How he was to bring this about he knew not.

Erlend lay a little with his eyes shut. Then he said, with a kind of smile :

"I thought last night—of the time she bore our eldest son—she was in no better case than I—if a man may judge by her crying. And if she has been able to bear it—seven times—for the sake of our joys—I trow that I can——"

Simon was silent. The fearful shrinking he felt—from looking into life's deepest secrets of torment and of joy—Erlend seemed yet to have no touch of. He played with the worst and the loveliest things as simply as a guileless boy, whose friends have brought him with them to a bordel, drunken and curious. . . .

Erlend shook his head impatiently :

"These flies—are the worst—— Methinks they are the foul fiend himself——"

Simon took his cap, and smote high and low at the thick clusters of blue-black flies, so that they flew up in the air in buzzing noisy clouds— and trampled furiously into the mud of the floor those that fell stunned. It could not avail much, for the window-hole in the wall stood open— the winter before, it had been closed with a wooden shutter with a bladder-covered port-hole, but that had made the room too dark.

But he was still at this when Olav Kyrning came back with a priest bearing a drinking-cup. The priest lifted Erlend's head, and stayed it while he drank. A great deal of the liquor ran out into his beard and down his neck, and he lay quiet and untroubled as a child when the priest afterwards wiped it away with a cloth.

Simon felt his whole being in a ferment; the blood thumped and thumped in his neck below the ears, and his heart beat strangely and unsteadily. He stood a moment gazing back from the doorway at the long body outstretched beneath the cloak. The flush of fever came and went now in waves over Erlend's face; he lay with half-open glittering eyes, but he smiled to his brother-in-law, the shadow of his strangely boyish smile.

The next day, as Stig Haakonssön of Mandvik sat at the breakfast-board with his guests, Sir Erling Vidkunssön and his son Bjarne, the hoof-beats of a single horse were heard in the courtyard. The next moment the door of the hall was flung open, and Simon Andressön came swiftly towards them. He wiped his face with his sleeve as he came—he was splashed to the neck with mud from his ride.

The three men rose to meet the comer, with little outbursts, half of greeting, half of wonder. Simon answered not their greetings—he stood leaning on his sword, both hands upon the hilt, and said :

"Would you hear strange tidings? They have taken Erlend Nikulaussön and stretched him on a rack—some foreigners the King sent to put him to the question——"

With a cry the men gathered round Simon Andressön. Stig smote one hand into the other:

"What has he said——?"

At the same moment both he and Bjarne Erlingssön turned, as though unwittingly, towards Sir Erling. Simon burst out into laughter—he laughed and laughed.

He sank down on the chair that Bjarne Erlingssön had drawn forward for him, took the ale-bowl that the youth proffered him, and drank greedily.

"Why laugh you? " asked Sir Erling sternly.

"I laughed at Stig." He sat a little bent forward, with his hands resting on his muddy thighs—yet once or twice again little bursts of laughter came from him. "I thought—we are sons of nobles, all of us here— I had looked that you would be so wroth that one of our fellows should be so dealt with, that you would have asked first how such things can be. . . .

"I cannot say that I know to a hair how the law stands in such matters. Since my lord King Haakon died, it hath been enough for me that I owed him that came to his throne my service when he listed to call for it, in war and in peace—else have I dwelt in quiet upon my estates. But I cannot see aught else than that in this case against Erlend Nikulaussön there have been unlawful doings. His fellows had sifted his case and given judgment in it—with how much right they doomed him to death, I know not—then was he offered reprieve and safe-conduct till he could be brought to a meeting with the King, his kinsman—that perchance he might grant Erlend grace to make his peace with him. . . Since has the man lain in the tower of Akers Castle nigh on a year, and the King has been abroad well-nigh all that time—some letters have passed to and fro—naught has come of it. Then he sends hither some varlets— Norsemen they are not, nor of the King's guard—and tries to put Erlend to the question in such wise as none ever heard that a Norseman with a Guardsman's rights was dealt with before—this while there is peace in the land, and Erlend's fellows and his kinsmen are gathering at Tunsberg to honour the King's wedding. . . .

" What think you of this, Sir Erling?"

"I think——" Erling sat down on the bench over against him. "I deem that you have set the matter forth clearly and plainly, Simon Darre, as it stands. I see not that the King can do aught but one to three things: Either must he let Erlend pay the penalty according of the doom given at Nidaros—or he must choose out a new court of Guardsmen and have the case against Erlend set forth by a man who bears not the knightly name, and they must doom Erlend to outlawry with such respite as the law allows for him to remove himself from King Magnus' realm—or he must grant Erlend grace to make his peace with him. And that would be the wisest thing that he could do.

"This matter seems to me now so plain that whomsoever you will lay it before at Tunsberg will join with you and take up your cause. Jon Haftorssön and his brother are there. Erlend is their kinsman no less than the King's. And the Ogmundssön brothers must see that this is injustice and folly. 'Twere best you went first to the Lord Marshal—move him and Sir Paal Eiriksson to call a meeting of the sworn King's-men that are in the town now and that seem fittest to take the matter in hand——"

"Will not you and your kinsmen go with me, my lord?"

"We mean not to go to the wedding-feast," said Erling shortly.

"The Haftorssöns are young—and Sir Paal is old and ailing—and the others—— You know best yourself, my lord,—they doubtless have some small power, through the King's favour and suchlike, but—Erling Vidkunssön, what are they all beside you? You, sir, you have such power in this land as no other chief has had since—I know not when. Behind you, sir, are the old houses that folk in this land have known man by man, so far back as record goes of evil times and good times in these our country-sides. On the father's side—what is the birth of Magnus Eiriksson or Haftor of Sudrheim's sons beside yours—are their riches worth naming beside yours? These counsels you give me—all this will take time, and these Frenchmen are in Oslo, and you may stake your soul that they will not give over. . . . Olav Kyrning has sent letters, and all gentlemen he could find to join with him, the Bishop promised he would write—but all this unrest and strife, Erling Vidkunssön, you could end it, in the same hour you stepped forth before King Magnus. You stand foremost among the heirs of those that ruled this land in the old age—the King knows that you would have us all at your back." . . .

"I can scarce say that I marked as much some time back," said Erling bitterly. "You speak out warmly for your brother-in-law, Simon—but can you not understand? Now I cannot move. It would be said: the very moment they put such duress on Erlend that a man might fear he would not be able to keep his tongue between his teeth—that moment I came forward!"

There was silence for a while. Then Stig asked again:

"Has—Erlend spoken?"

"No," answered Simon impatiently. "He has held his tongue. And I trow he will go on holding it. Erling Vidkunssön," he said beseechingly, "he is your kinsman—you were friends——"

Erling breathed short and heavily once or twice.

"Aye.—Simon Andressön, have you fully understood *what* Erlend Nikulaussön had undertaken? To put an end to this sharing of our King with the Swedes—this way of rule that never has been tried before—that seems to bring more and more hardships and troubles on this land with each year that passes; to bring us back to the kingship that we knew of old, and that we know brings welfare and good fortune. See you not that this was a wise and a bold counsel—and see you not that this counsel can now hardly be taken up by others after him? He has ruined the cause of Knut Porse's sons—and other men of the kingly house there are none for the folk to rally round. You will say, mayhap, had Erlend carried through his intent and brought Prince Haakon to Norway, then had he played into *my* hands. Much further than the boy's landing had these—young boys—scarce been able to carry forward their plans without having need of prudent men to come forward and work out what remained to do. So it is—I dare avow it. Yet God knows that I gained nothing—rather had I to set aside the care of my own affairs, in those ten years when I lived in disquiet and toil and strife and troubles without end—some few men in this land have understood so much, and with that I must e'en be content." He struck his hand hard against the table. "See you not, Simon, that the man who had taken on his shoulders such mighty plans that none knows whether the welfare of us all in this land and of our children for long ages to come was not the stake in them— and flung it all from him with his breeches on a harlot's bedside!—God's blood!—he would be full well served with the measure that was dealt to Audun Hestakorn?"

He went on in a little more quietly:

"Yet would I be fain that Erlend should be saved; and believe not that I, too, am not angered at the tidings you have brought us. And I deem that, should you follow my counsel, you will find men and enough to join with you in this matter. But I believe not that my company would be of such great help to you that for the sake of it I should do well to come uncalled before the King."

Simon rose, stiffly and heavily. His face was streaked and grey with weariness. Stig Haakonssön went over and took him by the shoulders— now he would have some food brought; he had but bided till they had had their talk out before having serving-folk in. But now Simon must strengthen himself with meat and drink, and must sleep on top of it. Simon thanked him—he must ride on in a little while, if Stig could lend him a fresh horse. And would he give shelter to his man, Jon Daalk, to-night?—Simon had had to leave the man behind on the road, for his horse could not keep up with Digerbein.* Aye, he had ridden the most of the night—he had thought, for sure, that he knew

* Digerbein = Big-legs.

the road out hither well enough—but yet he had gone astray more than once.

Stig bade him stay till to-morrow, and he would ride with him himself—at the least a part of the way—aye, and he might as well go on to Tunsberg with him too. . . .

Simon said:

"Here is naught more for me to stay for. I would but go over to the Church—seeing that I am here once more, I would yet fain say a prayer where Halfrid lies——"

The blood rushed and tingled in his weary body; his heart beat deafeningly. It was as though he must drop down headlong; he was as one but half awake. But he heard his own voice say, calmly and evenly:

"Will not you bear me company, Sir Erling? I know she held you dearest of all her kinsmen."

He looked not at the other, but felt him stiffen. In a little he heard, through the rushing and singing of his own blood, Erling Vidkunssön's clear and courteous voice:

"That will I, willingly, Simon Darre.—It is rough weather," he said, as he buckled on his sword and threw a thick cloak about his shoulders. Simon stood still as a stone till the other was ready. Then they went out.

Without, the autumn rain poured down, and the mist drove in from the sea so thickly that they could scarce see more than a couple of horses' lengths over the fields and the yellow tree-clumps that bordered the path on each side. It was no long way to the church. Simon fetched the key from the chaplain's house near by—he was glad when he saw they were new folk, come since his time, since so he was spared much talk.

It was a little stone church with a single altar. Unheedingly Simon saw again the same pictures and ornaments he had seen so many hundred times, while he knelt by the white marble tomb a little way from Erling Vidkunssön, saying over his prayers, and crossing himself where 'twas fit—without knowing what he did.

He understood not himself that he had been able to try this. But now he was in the midst of it. Of what he should say, he had no guess—but, sick with horror and shame at himself as he was, he knew that he would make the trial at all costs.

He remembered the ageing woman's white, suffering face deep in the half-darkness of the bed, her lovely gentle voice—that afternoon when he sat on her bedside and she told him. It was a month before the child came—and she herself looked that it should cost her life—and she was willing and glad to buy their son so dear. The poor little soul that lay here beneath the great stone in a little coffin by his mother's side—— No, no man could do what he had meant to do. . . .

But Kristin's white face. She knew what had befallen, when he came home from Akersnes that day. Pale and calm she was as she spoke of it and questioned him—but he had seen her eyes in one short glimpse, and he had not dared to meet them after. Where she was now, or what she had done, he knew not—whether she had stayed in her lodging or was with her husband, or whether they had prevailed on her to go to Skogheim; he had left it in Olav Kyrning's and Sira Ingolf's hands—he could do no more, and he deemed that he must lose no time. . . .

Simon knew not that he had hidden his face in his hands. Halfrid—there is naught in it of shame or of sin, my Halfrid.—And yet—what she had said to him, her husband—of her sorrow, and of her love that had made her stay on under the old devil's roof. Once already had he killed his child under its mother's heart—and she had stayed on with him because she would not tempt her dearest love. . . .

Erling Vidkunssön knelt, his colourless, clear-cut face showing no sign. His hands he held close in to his breast, with the palms pressed together; from time to time he crossed himself with a quiet, supple, gracious gesture, then brought his finger-tips again together.

No, thought Simon. This was so hateful a thing that no man could do it. Not even for Kristin's sake could he do it.—They rose together, made obeisance to the altar, and went down the nave; Simon's spurs jingled a little at each step he took on the stone pavement. As yet they had spoken no word together since they had left the manor, and Simon knew not at all what would now come.

He locked the church-door; and Erling Vidkunssön walked ahead through the graveyard. Under the little roof of the lich-gate he stopped. Simon came up; they stood a little in the shelter before going out into the pouring rain.

Erling Vidkunssön spoke quietly and evenly, but Simon felt the dull, measureless rage muttering deep within the other—he dared not look up.

"In the devil's name, Simon Andressön, what mean you by—devising —this?"

Simon could not answer a word.

"Think you that you can threaten me—force me to do your will—because, maybe, you have heard some lying rumours of things that befell when you were scarce yet weaned from the breast——?" His rage growled nearer the surface now.

Simon shook his head:

"I thought, my lord, when you called to mind her who was better than the purest gold—mayhap you might take pity on Erlend's wife and children."

Sir Erling looked at him—he made no answer, but began stripping moss and lichen from the stones of the churchyard wall. Simon swallowed, and wet his lips with his tongue:

"I scarce know what I thought, Erling Vidkunssön—maybe that when you remembered her that suffered all those evil years—without other comfort or help than God alone—that then you would help so many unhappy beings—for you can!—since you could not help her. If you have repented at any time that you rode away from Mandvik yonder day and let Halfrid remain behind in Sir Finn's power——"

"But I have not!" Erling's voice was piercing now. "For I know that *she* never did—but this I trow *you* could not understand. For had you ever understood for one hour how proud she was, the lady you won to wife"—he laughed in his wrath—"then had you not done this. I know not how much you know—but you may as lief know this. They sent me —for Haakon lay sick then—to fetch her home to her kindred. Elin and she had grown up together as sisters—they were well-nigh of an age, though Elin was her father's sister;—we had—things had come about so that, had she come home from Mandvik, we had been forced to meet daily and hourly. We sat and talked, a whole night through, in the balcony of the dragon-house—every word that was spoken both she and I can answer for to God on the day of doom. And then let *Him* answer *us*, why it should have been so——"

"Though, indeed, God rewarded her holiness in the end. Gave her a good husband to comfort her for the one she had had before—a whelp of a boy like you—who lay with her serving-women in her own house— and had her bring up your bastards——" He flung away the ball of moss he had kneaded together.

Simon stood motionless and dumb. Erling peeled off a flake of moss again and flung it away:

"I did what *she* bade me. Have you heard enough? There was no other way. Wherever else in the world we might have met, we had— we had—— 'Adultery' is no fair word. 'Incest'—is yet uglier——"

Simon moved his head in a stiff little nod.

He felt it himself—it would be laughable to say what he thought. Erling Vidkunssön had been a man in the twenties, courtly and gallant. Halfrid had loved him so that she would fain have kissed his footprints in the dewy grass of the courtyard that morning in spring. *He* was an ageing, hulking, ugly farmer—and Kristin? Never, for sure, would the thought come in her head that there would be peril to the soul of either, should they live under one roof for twenty years. Surely he had learnt to understand that well enough. . . .

So he said in a low voice, almost humbly:

"She had not the heart to suffer the innocent child, even though 'twas her woman's child by her husband, to fare ill in the world. *She* it was that prayed me to do it right and justice so far as lay in my power. Oh, Erling Vidkunssön—for Erlend's poor innocent wife's sake—— She will grieve to death. Methought I could not leave any stone unturned in seeking help for her and all her children——"

Erling Vidkunssön stood leaning against the gate-post. His face was calm as it was wont to be, and his voice cool and courteous, when he spoke again:

"I liked her well, Kristin Lavransdatter, the little I have seen of her —a fair and stately woman she is—and I have told you already, Simon Andressön, I deem full surely that you will find help if you will follow my counsel. But I understand not rightly what you mean by this— strange device. You surely cannot think that because I had to suffer my father's brother to rule the matter of my wedding, being then in my nonage, and because the maid I liked best was betrothed elsewhere when we first met—— And so innocent as you say, I trow Erlend's wife is not, either. Aye, you are wedded to her sister, I know it; but you and not I have brought about this—strange parley—and so you must suffer that I name it. I mind me there was talk enough about it, the time Erlend was wed with her—'twas against Lavrans Björgulfsön's counsel and his will that that bargain came about; but the maid had thought more of having her own will than of obeying her father or guarding her honour. Aye, she may be a good wife none the less—but she *won* Erlend after all, and they have doubtless had their time of joy and mirth. I trow that Lavrans had never much joy of that son-in-law—*he* had chosen another man for his daughter ere she came to know Erlend—she was promised in marriage, I know——" He stopped short, looked at Simon a moment, and turned his head aside in some confusion.

Flushing red with shame, Simon bent his head on his breast, but he spoke, none the less, low but firmly:

"Aye; she was promised to me."

For a moment they stood, not venturing to look at each other. Then Erling Vidkunssön threw away the last ball of moss he had gathered, turned, and went out into the rain. Simon was left standing alone—but when the other was some way off in the mist, he stopped and beckoned impatiently.

Then they went back together, as silently as they had come. When they had well-nigh reached the manor, Sir Erling said:

"I will do it, Simon Andressön. You must wait until to-morrow; then we can ride in company, all four together."

Simon looked up at the other—with a face all drawn with pain and shame. He would have given thanks, but could not; he had to bite his lip hard, his lower jaw trembled so violently.

As they were passing through the door of the hall, Erling Vidkunssön touched Simon's shoulder, as it were by chance. But each knew that neither of them dared look at the other.

Next day, when they were making them ready for the journey, Stig Haakonssön pressed Simon to let him lend him clothes—Simon had brought no change of garments with him. Simon looked down at himself—his man had brushed and cleaned up his dress, but it had suffered past remedy in his long ride through foul weather. But he slapped himself on the thighs:

"I am too fat, Stig.—And I go not thither to be a guest at the feasting."

Erling Vidkunssön stood with one foot on the bench, while his son buckled the gilded spur on it—it seemed as though Sir Erling tried to keep his serving-folk at a distance to-day as much as might be. The knight laughed in an oddly vexed fashion:

"'Twill do no hurt, I trow, if it should show on Simon Darre that he has not spared himself in his kinsman's service, but bursts right in from the high-road with his bold and subtle speech. He is no tongue-tied loon, this one-time kinsman of ours, Stig. One thing only I fear—that he may not know himself when he should stop——"

Simon stood there, flushing darkly, but he said no word. In all that Erling Vidkunssön had said to him since the day before, he marked a grudging mockery—and a strange, unwilling kindness—and a firm will to see this matter through—since, once and for all, he had taken it up.

So they rode with him north from Mandvik, Sir Erling, his son and Stig, with, in all, ten fairly clad and well-armed yeomen. Simon with his single follower thought now he could have chosen to come to the meeting more fittingly attended and equipped—Simon Darre of Formo had no need to ride with his former kinsmen in the guise of a small franklin that had sought their aid in his helplessness. But he heeded not much. He was so weary and so broken with what he had gone through the day before, that almost it seemed to him now he cared not what the outcome of this journey might be.

Simon had ever averred that he put no faith in the ugly rumours about King Magnus. He was no such saint but that he could suffer a gross jest amongst grown-up men-folk. But when people stuck their heads together and muttered shudderingly of dark and secret sins, he ever grew ill at ease. And it seemed to him unseemly to believe or to hearken to aught of the kind about the King among whose sworn men he was counted.

Yet was he filled with wonder when he stood before the young King. He had not seen Magnus Eiriksson since the King was a child, and, in spite of his disbelief, he had looked to find something womanish, soft or

unhealthy about him—but this was one of the properest young men
Simon had set eyes on—and he looked manly and kingly too, despite of
his youth and slender fineness.

He wore a flowing robe of light blue shot with green, falling to his
feet, and girt about his slim waist with a gilded belt, and he bore his
tall, lean body with exceeding grace in the heavy dress. King Magnus
had light hair, which lay smoothly on his well-formed head, but was
cunningly curled at the ends, so that it seemed to toss and wave about
his neck's broad, free-standing pillar. His features were fine and boldly
cut, the hue of his skin fresh, with red cheeks and a yellowish tinge of
sunburn; he had clear eyes and an open look. He bore him fairly and
with winning gentleness as he greeted his liege men. Then in a while he
laid his hand on Erling Vidkunssön's sleeve and drew him some steps
apart from the others, while he thanked him for his coming.

They talked together awhile, and Erling let fall that there was a special
matter wherein he had to crave the King's grace and bounty. The royal
ushers then set a chair for the knight in front of the King's high seat,
showed the other three men to places somewhat further down the hall,
and then went out.

Without effort Simon seemed to have found again the mannerly and
courtly bearing he had learned in his youth, and, since he had yielded
and taken from Stig the loan of a long brown dress of state, in outward
looks, too, he differed in no wise from the other men. But as he sat there
he felt as though he were in the midst of a dream—he was and he was
not the same as yonder young Simon Darre, the quick-witted and *kurteis*
son of a noble knight, who had borne napkin and taper before King
Haakon in Oslo Palace an endless tale of winters agone—he was and he
was not Simon, the esquire of Formo, who had lived a life of freedom
and cheer away north in the Dale through all these years—free from
care, after a fashion, though he had known all his days that within him
lay this glowing ember—but he turned his thoughts away from it. A
dull and threatening humour of revolt rose up in the man—it was no
willed sin or fault of his that he knew of, but fate, that had blown the
embers into a blaze, so that he must strive and make no sign while
roasting over a slow fire.

He stood up when all the others did so—King Magnus had risen:

"Dear kinsman," came his young, fresh voice, "methinks the matter
stands thus. The Prince is my brother, but we have never tried to keep
court together with a common guard—the same men cannot serve us
both. Nor does it seem that Erlend had meant that things should con-
tinue in such wise—even though for a time he did hold his Wardenship
under my hand, while at the same time he was Haakon's sworn man.
But those of my men who would liefer follow my brother Haakon shall

have leave from my service and freedom to seek their fortune in his house. Who they may be—that I mean to learn from Erlend's mouth."

"Then must you, Sir King, try if you can come to agreement with Erlend Nikulaussön in this matter. You must keep the promise of safe-conduct that you have given, and grant your kinsman an audience——"

"Aye, he is my kinsman and your kinsman, and Sir Ivar moved me to promise him safe-conduct—but *he* kept not his oaths to me, and *he* remembered not the kinship betwixt us." King Magnus laughed a little and again laid his hand on Erling's arm. "My kinsmen seem to be faithful to the byword we have in this land : None so unkind as kin. Now is it my full will to show my kinsman Erlend of Husaby grace for the sake of God and Mary Virgin, and for my own lady's sake; life and goods and leave here to abide, if he will make his peace with me—lawful respite to remove him from my lands, if he would betake him to his new master, Prince Haakon.—The same grace will I grant to every man who has been leagued with him—but I will know who they are, and which of my men dwelling up and down this land of ours has been a false servant to his lord. What say you, Simon Andressön?—I know that your father was my grandfather's trusty henchman; you yourself served King Haakon with honour—think you not that I have the right to make inquiry in this matter?"

"I think, my lord King"—Simon stepped forward and again made obeisance—"that so long as your grace rules according to this land's law and custom, mercifully, you will surely never learn who the men may be that had planned to have recourse to lawlessness and treason. For as soon as the people of this land see that your Grace will hold fast to the right and justice that your forefathers have set up, of a surety no man in this realm will think of troubling the peace. And those will be silent and will bethink them again, to whom for a time it may have seemed hard to believe that you, my Lord, young as you are, could rule two great kingdoms with wisdom and strength."

"It is so, my lord King," put in Erling Vidkunssön. "No man in this land has thought of denying you obedience in aught that you may command rightfully——"

"Have they not? Then you deem, maybe, that Erlend has not been guilty of disloyalty and treason—when we look more closely into the case?"

For a moment Sir Erling seemed at fault for an answer, and Simon took the word :

"You, Sir, are our lord—to you each man looks to punish law-breaking by the law. But if you should follow where Erlend Nikulaussön has led the way, it might well befall that the men whose names you now so hotly seek to know should come forth and name them aloud, or other men who may begin to ponder over the rights and wrongs of this matter —for much talk will there come to be of it if your Grace should deal as you have threatened with a man so well-known and so high-born as Erlend Nikulaussön."

"What mean you, Simon Andressön?" said the King sharply—he grew red as he spoke.

"Simon means," Bjarne Erlingssön broke in, "that it might do your Grace an ill service if folk should begin to ask why Erlend must suffer such dishonour as the law warrants all men against, save thieves and nithings.* They might come then to think on King Haakon's other grandsons——"

Erling Vidkunssön turned sharply on his son—he looked angry—but the King only asked dryly:

"Count you not traitors and rebels as nithings?"

"None *call* them so, sir, if their plans speed well," answered Bjarne.

For a moment all stood silent. Then Erling Vidkunssön spoke: "Whatever Erlend should be called, my lord, it beseems not that you should override the law to come at him——"

"Then should the law be mended in this matter," said the King vehemently. "If 'tis so that I have no power to get me by all means the knowledge of how folk mean to keep faith with me——"

"Yet can you not act upon a mended law before it is changed," said Sir Erling doggedly, "without oppressing the folk of the land—and that folk has ever found it hard to use itself to oppression from its Kings."

"I have my knighthood and my sworn King's-men to back me," answered Magnus Eiriksson with a boyish laugh. "What say you, Simon?"

"I say, my lord—it might well prove that that was no such sure backing—to judge by the measure the knighthood and the nobles of Denmark and Sweden have dealt their Kings when the commons had no strength to back up the kingly power against them. But if your Grace be set upon such counsels, then would I pray that you will loose me from your service—for then would I liefer be found among the common folk."

Simon had spoken so calmly and soberly that it seemed as though the King at first understood not his meaning. Then he laughed:

"Is this a threat, Simon Andressön?—Is it so that you would throw down your glove to me?"

"That must be as you will, my lord," said Simon as evenly as before; but he took his gloves out of his belt and held them in his hand. Then young Bjarne bent forward and took them:

* See Note 18.

"These are not seemly wedding-gloves for your Grace to buy!" He held the thick, worn riding-gloves in the air and laughed. "If it should come out, Sir, that you are seeking for such gloves, you might well have proffered you all too many of them—and all too cheap."

Erling Vidkunssön uttered a cry. With a sharp movement he seemed to sweep the young King to one side, and the three men to another; and he drove the men down the hall toward the door:

"I must speak with the King alone."

"No, no! I would speak with Bjarne!" cried the King, running after. But Sir Erling pushed his son out with the others.

They loitered about awhile in the castle yard and on the hill outside—none of them spoke a word. Stig Haakonssön looked doubtfully, but held his tongue as he had done throughout; Bjarne Erlingssön went about all the time with a little, hidden smile. In a while Sir Erling's weapon-bearer came and prayed them from his master to wait for him at their lodging—their horses were in the castle yard.

Afterward they sat in the inn. They were shy of speech about what had just befallen—at last they fell into talk of their horses and hounds and hawks. The end of it was that Stig and Simon sat far on into the evening telling stories about women. Stig Haakonssön had always great store of such tales, but with Simon the worst was that most of those he called to mind Stig straightway began to tell, and 'twas ever so that either the thing had happened to himself, or it had befallen of late at some place near Mandvik—even if Simon remembered having heard the tale in his boyhood from the house-carls at home at Dyfrin.

But he chuckled and laughed as heartily as Stig. From time to time it was as though the bench rocked beneath him as he sat there—he was afraid of something, but dared not think what it was. Bjarne Erlingssön laughed quietly, drank wine and munched apples, fiddled with the hood of his cape, and told now and then a little snatch of a tale—they were the worst of all, but they were so cunningly veiled that Stig did not understand them. Bjarne had heard them from a priest in Björgvin, he said.

At last Erling came. His son went to meet him and take from him his outer garments. Erling turned angrily on the youth:

"You!" He flung his cloak into Bjarne's hands—and there flitted across his face, as though against his will, the shadow of a smile. He turned to Simon:

"Aye—now you must be content, Simon Andressön! I make no doubt that now you may safely hope the day is not far off when you shall sit in peace and comfort together on your neighbouring manors—you and Erlend—and his wife and all their sons."

Simon had grown a shade paler when he stood up and thanked Sir

Erling.—He knew now what the fear was that he had not dared to look in the face. But now there was no way out. . . .

About fourteen days after, Erlend Nikulaussön was set free. Simon, with his two men and Ulf Haldorssön, rode out to Akersnes and fetched him.

The trees were almost bare already, for it had blown hard the week before. A black frost had set in now—the earth rang hard under the horses' hoofs, and the fields were wan with rime, as they rode in towards the town. It looked as though snow were coming—the heavens were evenly overspread with cloud and the daylight was sullen and chilly grey.

Simon had seen that Erlend dragged one foot a little, as he came out into the castle yard, and he seemed somewhat stiff and unhandy in mounting. He was very pale, too. He had had his beard taken off and his hair cut and made trim—his upper face was now a dull yellow, and, below, the blue of his shaven beard showed against white cheeks and chin; there were hollows beneath his eyes. But he made a stately figure in his long dark-blue robe and cloak, and, as he said farewell to Olav Kyrning, and made gifts of money to the men who had guarded him and brought him food in prison, he bore him like a chieftain parting from the house-folk at a wedding-feast.

At first, as they rode, he seemed to feel cold; he shivered more than once. Then a little colour came into his cheeks—his face lighted up—it was as though sap and life were welling up in him. Simon thought: sure it was Erlend was no easier to break than a willow wand.

They came to the lodging, and Kristin went to meet her husband in the courtyard. Simon tried not to look thither, but he could not forbear.

They gave each other their hands and exchanged some words, in quiet, clear tones. They managed this meeting in the sight of all the people of the house in fair and seemly wise enough. Only that both flushed red, looked at each other a second, and then both dropped their eyes. Then Erlend proffered his hand again to his wife, and they went together towards the loft-room where they were to dwell whilst they were in the city.

Simon turned towards the room where he and Kristin had lived till now. Then Kristin turned at the lowest step of the stairway and called to him, in a wonderful ringing voice:

"Will you not come, brother-in-law?—get you some food first—and you, Ulf!"

She seemed so young and supple as she stood there, turned a little from the hips, and looked back over her shoulder. As soon as she came to Oslo, she had begun to fasten her head-gear in another fashion.

Here in the south it was only small farmers' wives who wore the linen head-dress in the old-world way she had used ever since she was wedded; tight round the face like a nun's coif, with the falls fastened cross-wise over the shoulders so that the neck was quite hid, and with many folds on the sides and over the knot of hair at the back of the head. In Trondheim it was accounted, so to speak, a token of piety to set up the coif in this fashion, which Archbishop Eiliv praised always as the most fitting and modest way for wedded women. But so as not to be too much marked out, she had taken up now with the fashion of these southern parts: the linen cloth laid smoothly over the crown of the head and hanging straight down behind, so that the front hair showed, and the neck and shoulders were free—and then it was the proper thing that the plaits should be but tied up so that they did not show under the edge of the coif, while the linen fitted close above, throwing out the form of the head. True, Simon had seen this before and deemed that it became her well—yet he had not seen before how young it made her look. And her eyes shone like stars.

Farther on in the day many folk appeared to greet Erlend—Ketil of Skog, Markus Torgeirssön, and later in the evening Olav Kyrning himself, Sira Ingolf and Canon Guttorm, a priest of St. Halvard's Church. When the two priests came it had begun to snow—a slight dry fine-grained drizzle—and they had missed the path and come in among some burdocks—their clothes were full of the burrs. Everyone set to work to pluck burrs off the priests and their followers—Erlend and Kristin rid Canon Guttorm of his—from time to time their faces flushed, and their voices were strangely unsteady, as they jested with the priest and laughed.

Simon drank much in the first part of the evening, but he grew not at all light-headed with the drink—only a little heavy in the body. He heard each word that was said with unnatural sharpness. The others soon grew free-spoken—none of them were friends to the King.

He was heartily sick of it all now 'twas all over. Foolish prate it was that they babbled forth as they sat there—loud-voiced and heated. Ketil Aasmundssön was somewhat simple, and his brother-in-law Markus was none too wise either; Olav Kyrning was a right-minded and sensible man, but short-sighted—neither did the two priests seem to Simon too clear-witted. They all sat there and listened to Erlend and chimed in with him, and he grew more and more like himself as he had ever been, wild and reckless. He had taken Kristin's hand now, and laid it over his knee, and sat playing with her fingers—they sat so that their shoulders touched. Now the deep flush showed clear through her skin, she could not take her eyes from him—when he stole an arm about her waist, her mouth trembled, so that she had much ado keeping her lips shut. . . .

Then the door opened and Munan Baardssön stepped in.

"Last came the great bull himself!" shouted Erlend, laughing, and leapt up to meet him.

"Help us God and Mary Virgin—I believe you care not a straw, Erlend," said Munan in vexation.

"Aye, deem you, then, it would help aught to whimper and sorrow now, kinsman?"

"Never have I seen the like of you—all your welfare have you cast away——"

"Aye—for I was never the kind to go unbreeched to hell, to save my breeches from the burning," said Erlend, and Kristin laughed softly and dizzily.

Simon laid him down over the table, his head between his arms. If only they might think he was so drunken already that he had fallen asleep!—he would fain be left in peace.

Nothing was otherwise than he had looked that it would be—should have looked it would be, at the least. Nothing—not even she. Here she sat, the only woman amongst all these men—as gentle and bashful and fearless and secure as ever. Even so had she been yonder other time— when she betrayed him—shameless or innocent, he knew not which. Oh, no, 'twas not so either; she had not been so secure, she had not been shameless—behind the calmness of her bearing she had not been calm.—But that man had bewitched her—for Erlend's sake she would gladly tread over red-hot stones—and she had trodden over him as though she knew not he was aught but a cold stone.

Oh, all this was folly—her mind was set on having her own way, and she heeded naught else. Let them have their joyance, he need not care a jot. What mattered it to him if they had seven sons more, so that there would be fourteen to part betwixt them the half of Lavrans Björgulf-söns' estate? It looked not as though *he* would need to be careful and troubled for his children—Ramborg was not so quick at bearing children as her sister—but as though in due time he would leave behind his children and children's children in riches and power. But 'twas all one to him—to-night. He would fain have drunk more—but he knew that to-night God's gifts would not cheer him—and then he would have had to raise his head and perhaps to join in the talk.

"Aye, you think, I trow, *you* were the man for Regent of the realm," said Munan scornfully.

"Nay, surely you must know we had meant that place for you," laughed Erlend.

"In God's name, heed your tongue, man——" The others laughed.

Erlend came over and touched Simon's shoulder:

"Are you asleep, brother-in-law?" Simon looked up. The other stood before him with a goblet in his hand. "Come, drink with me, Simon. You I have to thank most of all that I came off with my life—and, such as it is, 'tis dear to me, lad! You stood by me like a brother—had you not been my brother-in-law, I trow I had lost my head for sure.—And then could you have wed my widow——"

Simon sprang up. A moment the two stood looking at each other— Erlend grew white and sobered, his lips parted in a gasp.—With his clenched fist Simon struck the goblet out of the other's hand—the mead splashed on the floor. Then he turned and went out of the room.

Erlend stood there alone. Without knowing what he did, he dried his hand and wrist with the skirt of his coat, then looked behind him; the others had not marked aught. With his foot he thrust the goblet in under the bench—he stood still a moment—then went quietly out after his brother-in-law.

Simon Darre stood at the foot of the stairway—Jon Daalk was leading his horses out of the stable. He made no movement when Erlend came down to him:

"Simon! Simon—I knew not—I knew not what I said!"

"You know it now."

Simon's voice was toneless. He stood quite still, not looking at the other.

Erlend looked about him, as at his wit's end. The moon showed dimly, a pale patch, through the veil of cloud; small hard grains of snow showered down on them. Erlend made a shivering motion.

"Where—where are you bound?" he asked dully, looking at the man and the horses.

"To seek me another lodging," said Simon shortly. "Maybe you can understand that *here* I care not to be——"

"Simon!" Erlend burst out. " Oh, I know not what I would not give if it could be unsaid——!"

"Nor I either," answered the other as before.

The door of the upper room opened. Kristin came out on the balcony with a lanthorn in her hand; she bent over the railing and threw the light down on them.

"Why stand you there?" she asked in a clear voice. "What would you without the house?"

"I felt I must go out and see to my horses—as 'tis the courtly fashion to say," answered Simon, laughing up to her.

"But—you have taken your horses out," she said, in laughing wonder.

"Aye—a man will do strange things in his cups," said Simon in the same tone.

"Well, come back now," she broke in, brightly and gladly.

"Aye. In a moment." She went in, and Simon called out to Jon to take back the horses. He turned towards Erlend—the man was standing there, strangely helpless in looks and bearing. "I shall come in a little. We must—try to bear us as though this were unspoken, Erlend—for our wives' sake. But so much maybe·you too can understand—you were the last man on earth that I would—would have had know of—this. And forget not that I am not so forgetful as you!"

The door above was opened again; the guests came out in a troop; Kristin was with them, and her woman, bearing the lanthorn.

"Aye," tittered Munan Baardssön, "the night is well worn already—and these two good folks would fain to bed, I trow——"

"Erlend—Erlend—Erlend!" Kristin had thrown herself into his arms the moment they stood alone within the loft-room door. She clung close and tightly to him. "Erlend—you look so sorrowful——" she whispered in fear, with her half-open lips close to his mouth. "Erlend——" She pressed the palms of her hands to his temples.

He stood a little with his arms laid loosely around her. Then, with a soft moaning sound in his throat, he crushed her to him.

Simon went across to the stable—he would have said somewhat to Jon, but he forgot it on the way. For a while he stood in the stable-door, looking up at the light-haze of the moon and the tumbling snow—it had begun now to fall in great flakes. Jon and Ulf came out and shut the door behind them, and the three men went together across to the house where they were to sleep.

THE CROSS

Part One

KINSHIP'S DUES

I

T H E second year Erlend Nikulaussön and Kristin Lavransdatter dwelt on Jörundgaard, the mistress was minded to go herself and lie the summer over at the sæter.

She had thought upon this ever since the winter. At Skjenne it was the use from of old for the wife herself to pass the summer at the out-farm, for once a daughter of that house had been carried off by the mountain folk, and afterwards naught would serve the mother but she must herself lie on the mountain every summer. But in so many things they had their own ways down at Skjenne—and folk in the parish were used to this and thought it was but as it should be.

But elsewhere in the Dale 'twas not the use for the master's women-folk of the great manors to abide themselves at the sæters. Kristin knew that if she did it, there would be talk and wonderment among the folks.

——In God's name, then, they must even talk. Sure it was that they gossiped about her and hers whether or no.

——Audin Torbergssön had owned no more than his weapons and the clothes he stood up in when he was wed with Ingebjörg Nikulaus-datter of Loptsgaard. He had been henchman to the Bishop of Hamar; 'twas the time when the Bishop was in the north here to hallow the new church that Ingebjörg fell into trouble. Nikulaus Sigurdssön took it hardly at first, swore to God and all men that a horse-boy never should be son-in-law of his. But Ingebjörg was brought to bed of twins; and, said folks, laughing, Nikulaus maybe deemed their bringing up too hard a matter to tackle single-handed. However that might be, he gave Audin his daughter in marriage.

This had happed two years after Kristin's wedding. 'Twas not forgotten; folk still bore in mind that Audun was a stranger in the parish—he was a Hallander, of good kin, but his folk had fallen into great poverty. And the man himself was not over well liked in Sil; he was stiff-necked and hard, slow to forget either good or ill; yet was he a notable farmer, and had good knowledge of the laws—so in some ways Audun Torbergssön was a man of standing now in the parish, and a man that folk were little willing to fall at odds with.

Kristin thought of farmer Audun's broad, brown face set in its curly red hair and beard; of his sharp little blue eyes. He was like more men than one that she had seen—she had seen such faces amongst their serving-folk at Husaby—Erlend's house-carls and hip-folk.

The mistress sighed. It must be easier for such a man to hold his own, even though 'twas his wife's lands he lived on. *He* had never been master of aught before——

Throughout the winter and spring Kristin talked much with Frida Styrkaarsdatter, who had come with them from the Trondheim country and was the chief of her serving-women. Over and over again she would say to the girl that they were wont to have things so and so in the Dale here in summer, the harvest-folk were used to get this, and that was how they did in the fields in autumn—Frida must bear in mind how she, Kristin, had done last year. For it was her will that all things here on the farm should go as they had gone in Ragnfrid Ivarsdatter's time——

But to say outright that she herself would not be there on the farm that summer—this she found hard. She had lived at Jörundgaard two winters and a summer now as mistress, and she knew well that if she went to the sæter and abode there this year, 'twere much as though she ran away.

——She saw well that Erlend's lot was no easy one. From the time he sat upon his foster-mother's knee, he had known naught save that he was born to bid and rule over all and everything around him. And if so be he had let himself be ruled and bidden by others, at least the man himself had never known it.

'Twas impossible he could be within as outwardly he seemed. He must needs be unhappy here. She herself—— Her father's manor on the floor of the still, shut-in valley, the flat fields looped in by the river bends shining through the alder woods, the farmsteads on the low ploughed lands at the foot of the fells, and the headlong hill-sides above, with grey scaurs high up against the sky, pale-hued screes below, and pine woods and leaf woods scrambling up and over the slopes from the valley-bottom—no, this no longer seemed to her the fairest and safest home in the world. 'Twas so hemmed in. Surely this must seem to Erlend ugly and cramped and unkindly.

But none could mark aught on him but that he was well content——

At last, the day they let the cattle out on Jörundgaard, she got it said —in the evening, as they sat at supper. As she spoke, Erlend was groping in the fish-platter for a titbit—he sat stark still in wonderment, his fingers still in the dish, gazing at his wife. Then Kristin said quickly— 'twas most because of that throat evil that was ever about among the young children in the Dale; Munan was so weakly; she would take him and Lavrans with her up to the mountains.

Ay, said Erlend. Then 'twould mayhap be best that Ivar and Skule should go with her too.

The twins jumped with joy on their bench. Through the rest of the meal each tried to out-chatter the other. They would go with Erling, they said, who was to lie away to the north among the Graahö fells, with the sheep. Three years ago shepherds from Sil had chased a sheep-stealer and killed him by his own hut in among the Boar-fells—he was an outlaw from the Österdal. As soon as the house-folk had risen from the board, Ivar and Skule bore into the hall all the weapons they owned and set to work on them.

A little later in the evening Kristin went southward, with Simon Andressön's daughters and her sons Gaute and Lavrans. Arngjerd Simonsdatter had been at Jörundgaard the most of this winter. The maid was fifteen years old now; and one day in Yule, at Formo, Simon had said somewhat of how 'twas time that Arngjerd should learn something more than what she could pick up at her home; she knew already as much as the serving-women did. At that Kristin proffered to take the girl home with her and teach her as well as she could, for she knew that Simon held this daughter very dear and thought much on what was to come of her. And the child might well have need to learn other ways than those she saw at Formo. Now that his wife's father and mother were both dead, Simon Andressön was one of the richest men in the country-side. He guided his estates well and heedfully, and was a stirring and skilful farmer on his Formo lands. But within the house things went as best they might—the serving-women ruled and guided all things, and when Simon marked that disorder and waste went beyond all bounds, he would get him one or two serving-wenches more; but he never spoke of such things to his wife, and seemed not to look, nor yet to wish, that she should charge herself more with the house-mistress's work. Almost it was as though he did not deem her full-grown yet—but he was most kind and easy with Ramborg, and poured out gifts upon her and the children in season and out of season.

Kristin grew fond of Arngjerd when she came to know her. Fair the maid was not, but she was of a good wit, and was gentle, good-hearted, quick with her hands, and diligent. As the young girl went about with her in the house, or sat by her side in the weaving-house of an evening, Kristin often thought she could wish now that one of her children had been a daughter. A daughter must be with her mother more——

She was thinking the like this evening, as she walked, leading Lavrans by the hand, and looking on the two, Gaute and Arngjerd, who were on the path before her. Ulvhild Simonsdatter was running hither and thither, trampling to bits the brittle evening ice on the puddles—she was making believe she was a beast of some kind, and had put on her red cloak inside out, so that the white hare-skin was turned outward.

Down in the dale the shadows were thickening into dusk over the bare, brown fields. But the air of the spring evening seemed drenched with light. The first stars shone wet and white in the sky, high up where clear watery green shaded into blue-black night. But over the black edge of the fells on the further side of the dale there lingered yet a band of yellow light, and its sheen lit up the scree that overlay the steep hill-side above them. Highest up of all, where the drifts jutted over the mountain crests, there was the glimmer of snow and the glitter of the ice that hung beneath it, feeding the foaming becks that gushed down everywhere amidst the boulders. Above the valley the air was full of the noise of waters, and from below rose the river's hoarse roar. And there was the song of birds from all the groves and thickets, and from out the forest all around.

Once Ulvhild stopped, took up a stone, and threw it in where the birds were singing. But her big sister caught her by the arm. Then she went quietly for a while, but in a little she broke away and galloped down the slope—till Gaute called her back.

They were come close to where the way led into the fir woods; from among the trees ahead came the clang of a cross-bow. Snow was still lying in the woods; it smelt cold and fresh. A short way on, in a little opening, stood Erlend with Ivar and Skule.

Ivar had shot at a squirrel; the arrow was sticking in a pine branch high up, and he wanted now to get it down. He threw stone after stone; the thick, straight tree rang again when he hit the stem.

"Stay a little; let me try to shoot it down for you," said his father. He shook his cloak back over his shoulders, laid an arrow to his bow, and took aim, carelessly enough, in the deceitful light among the trees. The string twanged; the arrow sang through the air and buried itself in the pine branch close by the boy's shaft. Erlend took another arrow and shot again—one of the two arrows that had stuck in the tree slipped down clattering from branch to branch; the shaft of the other was splintered, but the head still stuck fast in the limb.

Skule ran into the snow to pick up the two arrows. Ivar stood gazing up into the tree-top.

"'Tis mine, father, the one that sticks fast! 'Tis in up to the socket— 'twas strongly shot, father!"—and he set about telling Gaute why it was he had not hit the squirrel——

Erlend laughed low and flung his cloak about him again:

"Will you turn back now, Kristin? I must be going homewards—we are off after capercailzie at daybreak, Naakkve and I——"

Kristin answered in haste, no, she would go on with the maids to the manor—she had somewhat to talk of with her sister this evening——

"Then Ivar and Skule can go with mother and be with her home—if I may go along with you, father?" said Gaute.

Erlend lifted Ulvhild Simonsdatter in his arms to bid her farewell. And bonny and fresh and rosy as she was, with her brown curls nestled in the white fur hood, he kissed her, ere he set her down, and turned and went homewards with Gaute.

Now that Erlend had naught else to take him up, he was ever about with some of his sons.——Ulvhild took her aunt's hand and walked a little—then she ran on again, bursting in between Ivar and Skule. Ay, she was a fair child—but wild and unruly. Had they had a daughter, no doubt but Erlend would have had her too ever with him for a plaything.

At Formo Simon was in the hall, alone with his little son, when they came in. He sat in the high-seat at the middle of the long board, and watched Andres; the child knelt on the outer bench playing with some old treenails, striving to make them stand upon their heads on the flat board-top. Soon as Ulvhild saw this, forgetting to greet her father, she rushed straight up on to the bench beside her brother, took him by the nape, and knocked his face against the board-top, shrieking out that they were *her* pegs; father had given them to her himself.

Simon got up to part the children, and in rising chanced to knock over a little dish of earthenware that stood by his elbow. It fell to the floor and was broken in pieces.

Arngjerd crept under the board and gathered up the bits. Simon took them from her and looked at them unhappily:

"I misdoubt me your mother will be vexed at this!" 'Twas a little dish of clear white ware, a fair pattern upon it, that Sir Andres Darre had brought home from France; 'twas left to Helga, but she had given it to Ramborg, said Simon; and the women deemed it of great price. At that minute he heard his wife in the outer room, and he hid his hands, with the shards in them, behind his back.

Ramborg came in and greeted her sister and her sister's sons. She took off Ulvhild's cloak, and the little maid ran to her father and clung about him.

"Are we so fine to-day, Ulvhild?—wearing our silver belt on a working day, I verily believe——" but he could not take hold of the child, with his hands full as they were.

Ulvhild cried out she had been to Moster Kristin's at Jörundgaard to-day, and that was why her mother had dressed her up this morning——

"Ay, your mother keeps you so brave and gay—they might well set you up in the shrine northward in the church, just as you stand," said Simon, smiling. The one work Ramborg busied herself with was sewing clothes for her daughter; Ulvhild went ever bravely decked out.

"Why stand you thus?" Ramborg asked her husband.

Simon showed forth the shards. "I know not what you will say to this——"

Ramborg took them from him: "No need to stand there and look so like a fool——"

Kristin grew ill at ease as she sat there. 'Twas true Simon had looked foolish enough as he stood hiding the shards behind him, and, as it were, playing the child. But there was sure no need for Ramborg to say so.

"I deemed it would vex you, that your bowl had been broken," said the man.

"Ay, you seem at all times so afraid aught may vex me—in small things like this," answered Ramborg—and now the other two saw she was on the brink of tears.

"You know well, Ramborg, 'tis not seeming only," said Simon. "And I trow 'tis not alone in small things either——"

"I know not," answered Ramborg as before. "'Tis never your wont, Simon, to speak to me of great matters——"

She turned sharply and went back to the outer room. Simon stood a little, looking after her. When he sat him down, the boy, Andres, came and tried to climb upon his father's knee. Simon lifted him up, and sat resting his chin on the top of the child's head, but seemed not to hear the little one's prattle.

After a while Kristin said, haltingly:

"Ramborg is not so young any more, Simon—your eldest child is seven winters old already——"

"What mean you?" asked Simon, more sharply than need was, she thought.

"I mean but that—maybe my sister deems you lay too little on her—could you not try to let her have things in her hands a little more, on the farm here—along with you?"

"My wife has all in her hands that she would have," answered Simon hotly. "I ask not that she should do more than she herself would, but never have I denied Ramborg the ruling of aught here on Formo. If you deem otherwise, 'tis that you do not know——"

"Nay, nay!" said Kristin. "But one time and another, brother-in-law, it has seemed to me you remember not that Ramborg is more grown-up now than in the days when you were wed. You should bear in mind, Simon——"

"Bear you in mind"—he set down the child and sprang up—"that Ramborg and I agreed together—and you and I could not——" Just then the mistress of the house stepped in, bearing a stoup of ale for the strangers; Simon went quickly to his wife and laid his hand upon her shoulder: "Heard you ever the like, Ramborg—here is your sister saying she deems not you are content with things as you have them here——" He laughed.

Ramborg looked up; there was a strange glitter in her great, dark eyes:

"How so? I got what I would have, I as well as you, Kristin—should we two sisters not be well content, I know not——" and she too laughed.

Kristin stood there red and wrathful; she took not the ale-bowl in her hands:

"Nay, 'tis late already—time we were going homeward——" and she looked about her for her sons.

"Nay, nay, Kristin." Simon took the bowl from his wife and drank to the other sister. "Be not angry now. 'Tis not well to weigh so nicely each word that falls 'twixt nearest kin—sit a little and rest your feet; content you again, and forget it, if I answered you in other wise than I ought——

"I am weary," said he, stretching and yawning a little. He asked how far they were got on with the spring work at Jörundgaard—here, now, they had ploughed up all the fields north of the manor road.

Kristin took her leave as soon as she deemed it seemly. Nay, Simon need not come with her, she said, as he took up his hooded cloak and axe—she had the great lads with her. But he would go—and he prayed Ramborg, too, to go with them, at least up through the home-fields. This, at most times, she had no mind to, but to-night she went with them right up to the road.

Without was black night, with clear, twinkling stars. A little warm springlike breath of new-dunged fields came through the frosty night air. The noise of water was about them everywhere in the darkness.

Simon and Kristin went northward, the three boys running before. She felt that the man walking by her would have said something, but she had no mind to help him to speech, for she was greatly vexed with him still. True it was she was fond of her brother-in-law—but there should be some bounds to what he deemed he might say and then turn it off—with a "'twas but among kinsfolk." He ought sure to understand —that he had stood by them so steadfastly in their pinch made it the less easy now for her to bear, when he grew hot and unmannerly—'twas hard for her to take him up. She thought of the first winter, when they were but newly come to the parish: Ramborg had sent for her, for that Simon lay abed with neck-boils, grievously sick. He was much plagued with this ill. But when she was come to Formo and went in to the man, he would not suffer her to touch him or even look at him; he was so unruly that Ramborg prayed her sister miserably to forgive her for having brought her thither. Simon had been no better with her, said she, when she would have tended him the first time he was sick after they were wed. When these throat boils came on him, he hid himself away in the old house they called the Sæmunds hall, and would suffer no one near him but a hideous, filthy, lousy old carl, Gunstein by name, that had served on Dyfrin before Simon was born.—True, Simon came to his sister-in-law afterwards and would have made things good again with her: he liked not, he said, that any should see him lying with such a sickness; it seemed to him such a pitiful ailment for a grown man. Kristin had answered, shortly enough, that she understood him not; 'twas sure neither sin nor shame to have a swollen throat.

He went with her now as far as to the bridge, and all the way they spoke of the weather and the farm work—saying over again things they had said in the hall. Simon bade her good-night—then, of a sudden, he asked:

"Know you, Kristin, what I have done to Gaute, that the boy is so wroth with me?"

"Gaute?" she asked, in wonder.

"Ay, have you not marked it? He shuns me—and if he must needs meet me, he will scarce open his mouth, when I speak with him——"

Kristin shook her head; no, she had marked naught of this—"but maybe you have said a word in jest, and he has taken it ill, like the child he is——"

He knew by her voice she was smiling; he laughed a little: "But I cannot remember aught of the kind——"

With that he bade good-night again and left her.

At Jörundgaard all was still; dark in the hall, and ashes raked over the fire. Björgulf was lying awake; he said his father and brothers were gone a good while since.

In the great bed Munan lay alone, sleeping—— His mother took him into her arms when she had lain down.

——'Twas hard to speak of it to Erlend, if he himself did not understand—that he ought not to take his great sons and go roaming the woods with them, when there was more than enough work to be done on the farm——

Truly, she had never looked that Erlend should go behind the plough himself. For that matter, he was scarce the man to cope with a good spell of work. And Ulf, like enough, would take it but ill if Erlend meddled with the farming. But her sons could not be suffered to grow to manhood as their father had done—learning but to handle arms, to hunt wild beasts and disport him with his horses—or hang over a draught-board with a priest whose task it was to coax into the knight's son some little lore of Latin and of writing, of singing and playing on strings. 'Twas therefore, in chief, that she had kept the manor short of working folk—her sons should learn, she thought, from childhood on, that they must use them to husbandry. There was small hope now for Erlend's sons in the knightly calling.

But of all the youths Gaute was the only one who had any turn for farming ways. Gaute was a worker—but he was scarce thirteen; naught else was to be looked for but that he would liefer be off with Erlend, when his father bade him come——

But 'twas hard to speak of this to Erlend. For she held fast to this—never from her should her husband hear one word he could take for blame of his deeds or lamentation over the fate he had brought upon himself and his sons. The harder was it for her to bring home to the father that his sons must needs use them to work themselves on their farm. If only Ulf would speak of it, she thought——

When the folk moved with the herds from the lower sæters up to Höv-ringen, Kristin went with them to the mountain. The twins she would not have with her. They were near eleven years old now, and were the most unruly and self-willed of all her children; 'twas all the harder for her to guide them since there were two of them, and they held together in all things. If it so happed that she could get Ivar alone, then was he good and biddable enough; but Skule was fiery and headstrong—and when the brothers were together, Ivar said and did whatsoever the other would.

II

ONE day in early autumn Kristin went out about the time of nones. The herd had said that, a little down the hill-side, if she followed the run of the river, she would find a forest clearing where were many Aaron's-rods growing.

Kristin found the spot: a steep hill-side with the sun beating straight upon it—'twas even now the best time to pick the flowers. They grew in masses all over the heaps of stones and round about the grey tree-stumps —tall, bright yellow stalks, set thick with little full-blown starlets.— Kristin set Munan to plucking raspberries amid some bushes he could not come away from without her help, and bade the dog stay and guard him. Then she drew her knife and set about cutting the flowers, while ever keeping an eye on the little child—— Lavrans kept by her side and helped her busily.

She was ever fearful for her two little ones up here. Otherwise she had no great dread of yonder folk any more. Already from many of the sæters the dairy-folks had gone down home, but she was minded to stay on over the second Maria Mass.* True, the nights were black now, and uncanny when it blew hard—uncanny for them when they must go out

* 8th September.

late. But for the most part the weather had been so fair up here—and down in the dale 'twas a year of drought and poor feed. Men had to bide up here both in the late fall and the winter-time—and her father had said he had never marked that there were any Dwellers in their sæter of winters——

Kristin came to a stand under a lone pine on the mid-hill-side; stood with her hands clasped about the heavy bunch of flower-stems resting upon her shoulder. From here one could see northwards, some way up into Dovre. The corn stood in stooks in many places out on the farm lands——

The sward was yellow and burnt-up there too. But truly green 'twas never here in the Dale, it seemed to her now—not green as in Trondheim——

Ay—her mind went back in longing to the home they had had there—the manor that lay so high and chieftainly forth on the broad-bosomed hill-side, fields and meadows spreading wide around and downward to the leaf woods in the glen that dipped to the lake in the dale bottom. The far outlook over low wooded ridges that rolled, wave behind wave, southwards to the Dovre-fjeld. And the grass-lands, so rank and deep in summer, red with ruddy flowers under the red of evening skies; and the aftermath, so green and sappy in the autumn——

Ay, there were times when longing came on her even for the fiord—— The strands at Birgsi, the wharves with boats and ships, the boat sheds, the smell of tar and fishing-gear, and of the sea—all those things she had liked so little when first she came to the north——

Erlend—he must long, surely, for that smell, and for the sea and the sea-winds——

She missed now all that once she had deemed did but weary her out—the great householding, the flocks of serving-folk, the din when Erlend's men rode into the courtyard with clashing arms and jingling gear—strangers coming and going, bearing great tidings from far in the land and gossip of folks in the country-side and the town—— She felt now how hushed her life had grown, when all this fell dumb——

The market town with its churches and cloisters and feasts in the great men's town houses—— She longed to pass along the streets, her own page and serving-maid behind her; to climb the stairs into the merchants' ware-rooms, to choose or throw aside; to be set aboard the trading-smacks on the river and to chaffer: English linen head-gear, fine veils, wooden horses, with knights astride of them, who could thrust with their lances when you pulled a string. She thought on the meadows outside the town, by Nidareid, where she would go with her children and watch the showmen's trained dogs and bears, and buy honey-bread and walnuts——

And at times she would be so fain to deck herself out once more——
Silken shifts and thin, fine head-linen. The sleeveless surcoat of light-
blue velvet that Erlend had bought for her the winter before mischance
fell on them. It had borders of ermine-skin about the deeply cut-out
bosom and round the long arm-slits, that reached right down to the hips
and showed the belt beneath——

And now and then she longed—oh no, 'twere witless not to be glad of
that, glad so long as she were spared the bearing of more children.
When she fell sick in the autumn, after the big slaughtering—'twas best
things fell out as they did. But she had wept a little over it, the first
nights after——

For it seemed to her a long, long time since she had held a little child.
Munan was but four winters old—but him she had had to give into
strangers' keeping ere yet he was full a year. And when she got him back
again, he could both walk and talk, and he knew her not——

Erlend! Oh, Erlend! She knew well that, in her inmost heart, she
knew he was not so—careless—as he seemed. He, that had been ever
restless—'twas as though now he was ever still: as a stream of water,
striking at last on a steep wall of rock, lets itself be turned aside, and
oozes through the peat to make a silent pool with marsh-land all
around. He passed his time on Jörundgaard, doing naught, and taking
now one and now another of his sons to keep him company in nothing-
doing. Or he went a-hunting with them. The whim might take him to
set to work, and tar and patch up one of the boats they kept on the tarns
for fishing. Or he would set about breaking one of the young colts. But
at that he never made any hand—he was all too hasty——

He kept to himself, and made at least as though he marked not that
none sought his company. The sons did as their father did. Liked they
were not, these strangers, whom ill-fortune had driven to the Dale, and
who went their ways now, proud and strange as ever, seeking not to
learn aught of the ways of the parish and of its folk. For Ulf Haldorssön
there was sheer ill-will—he scorned the Dalesmen openly, called them
thick-witted and old-fashioned; folk that were not bred by the sea-shore
were not folk——

And she herself—she knew she had not many friends either, here in
her own home country. Not now any more——

Kristin straightened herself in her moss-brown wadmal dress, and
shaded her eyes with her hand from the golden flood of afternoon sunlight——

Northward she caught a glimpse of the Dale along the river's white-
green riband, and then came the throng of mountain-hulks, one behind
the other, yellow-grey with scree and marsh, away to where, seen
through clefts and scaurs, snow-fields and clouds were one. Straight

before her Rostkampen bent forward a knee and hemmed the Dale, thrusting the Laagen aside in a great crook. A far-off thunder rose to her from the river, where it cut deep into the slate rocks below and fell, boiling and foaming, from shelf to shelf. On the moorish hills above Rostkampen's dome rose the rounded backs of the two great Blaahöer, that her father had likened to a woman's breasts——

Erlend must feel it cramped and ugly here—hard to draw breath in——

——A little to the south on this same hill-side, yonder, under the slopes near the sæter, was where she had seen the elf-maiden, when she was a little child——

A gentle, soft, fair, slender child with thick, silky hair about her round, red and white cheeks——Kristin shut her eyes, and turned her sunburnt face full to the flood of light. A young mother with milk-swollen breasts and a heart stirred and fruitful with childbearing like a new-ploughed field—ay. But for such an one as she was now there was no fear; her they would scarce try to draw into their clutches. Ill would the mountain-king deem a woman so worn and meagre would set off his bridal gold; the elf-wife would scarce be fain to put her child to such dried-up breasts. She felt herself hard and dry as the pine root beneath her foot, that crooked itself over the stones, and clawed itself fast. She struck her heel hard upon it with the thought.

The two little lads had come to her side; they made haste to do as their mother did, kicking the pine root with all their might, and then asking eagerly:

"Why did you so, mother?"

Kristin sat down, laid the Aaron's-rods in her lap, and began to strip off the full-blown blossoms into her basket.

"'Twas that my shoe pinched me on the toes," she answered, so long after that the boys minded not that they had asked. But they gave little heed to this—they were so used to have their mother seem not to hear when they spoke to her, or wake up and answer when they had forgot what 'twas they had asked.

Lavrans helped to strip off the blossoms; Munan would have helped too, but he only tore the tassels to shreds. So his mother took the flowers from him without a word, without anger, far away in her own thoughts. Soon the boys began to play and fight with the stripped stalks that she threw aside.

The game went on noisily before their mother's knees. Kristin looked on the two small, round, brown-haired child-heads. Much alike they were still: they had well-nigh the same light-brown hue of hair, but, by all kinds of small scarce-seen marks and signs that came and went in a flash, their mother could see they would grow to be most unlike. Mu-

nan would favour his father: he had his sea-blue eyes, and the silky hair
that clung, soft and close, in curls and little waves round the narrow
head; 'twould darken to sooty black with time. That little face of his,
that still was so round below the chin and on the cheeks, so that 'twas a
joy to lay a hand on its soft freshness, would narrow and lengthen out,
once he grew a little older; he, too, would one day show the high, narrow forehead sunken at the temples, and the straight, outstanding triangle of nose, sharp and narrow on the bridge, with thin, restless nostrils, that Naakkve had already and that the twins had plainly shown
they were to have.

Lavrans had had flaxen, silk-fine curls when he was little. Now his
hair had the hue of a hazel-nut, but it held golden gleams in the sunlight.
'Twas smooth, and soft enough, but yet much coarser and thicker; deep
masses you could bury your fingers in. Lavrans was like her; he had
grey eyes and a round face, broad of forehead and with softly rounded
chin; 'twas like he would keep the red and white of his cheeks well on
into manhood.

Gaute's skin too had this bright fresh hue; he was so like her father,
with his full oval face, iron-grey eyes, and light, light yellow hair.

Björgulf alone—she knew not whom he favoured. He was the tallest
of the sons, broad-shouldered, heavy and strong of limb. Untamed,
curly, coal-black hair grew low over the broad, white brow; his eyes
were blue-black, but strangely lustreless, and they blinked sorely when
he lifted them to the light. She knew not rightly when it had begun, for
it had chanced that this was the child she had always taken the least
heed of. They took him from her and gave him to a foster-mother soon
as he was born; eleven months afterward she bore Gaute, and Gaute
had been sickly the four first years he lived. After the twins' birth she
had come to her feet, sick still, with a hurt in the back, and yet must
take up the big boy again, carry him about and tend him, so that she
scarce had time to look on the new children save when Frida brought
Ivar thirsty and shrieking—and Gaute, too, lay and shrieked while she
sat and gave the little one the breast. She had not been able—holy
mother Mary, thou knowest I *could* not give more heed to Björgulf than I
did—— And from the first he was such an one as would rather go about
alone and fend for himself; strange and silent had he ever been, seemed
ever to mislike it when she would have fondled him. She had ever
deemed him the strongest of her brood; like a swart, headstrong little
bullcalf had Björgulf always seemed to her——

Little by little it had come home to her that there was somewhat amiss
with his sight. The monks had done something to his eyes when he and
Naakkve were at Tautra, but it seemed that had not helped——

He was still close and silent as ever; she made no way when now she tried to draw Björgulf to her. His father fared no better, she saw—Björgulf was the only one of their sons who did not warm to any heed from Erlend as a meadow takes the sunshine. Only with Naakkve was Björgulf otherwise—but when she would have talked with Naakkve of his brother, he turned the matter off. She knew not if Erlend fared any better in this—though greater love than Naakkve's for his father——!

——Oh no, with Erlend's offspring there could be no mistaking who their father was.—When she was last in Nidaros, she had seen that child from Lensvik. She met Sir Thorolf in Christ's Church yard; he came out with a train of men and women and serving-folk, a maid bearing the babe in its swaddling clothes. Thorolf Aasulfssön greeted her with a bow, quiet and courteous, as he went by. His wife was not there——

She had seen the child's face; in a single glance, but 'twas enough. It was like other children's faces that had lain at her own breast——

Arne Gjavvaldssön was with her, and he could not refrain him from talking—as his way ever was. Sir Thorolf's kinsmen that were his heirs were but ill pleased when the child saw the light last winter. But Thorolf had it christened Aasulf. Twixt Erlend Nikulaussön and Lady Sunniva there had never been more than the friendship all folk knew of—he made as though he never doubted this. Loose-tongued and rash as the man was, he had talked recklessly, without doubt, when bandying jests with her—and 'twas no more than the lady's duty to warn the king's wardens when she suspected mischief. But had they been *over*-good friends, Sunniva must sure have known that her own brother was privy to Erlend's plan. When Haftor Graut made forfeit of his life and his soul's salvation in the prison, she had gone clean from her wits—no one could pay heed to what she had laid to her own charge in that state. Sir Thorolf had laid his hand on his sword-hilt and looked around the company as he spoke of this, said Arne——

Arne had named the matter to Erlend too. One time when she was above in a loft-room, the two men had stood below under the balcony, knowing not that she could hear their words. The Lensvik knight was so o'erjoyed at the coming of the son his wife had borne last winter—'twas plain he had no doubt that he himself was the father.

"Ay, Thorolf himself must sure know best," Erlend had answered. She knew that tone in his voice—he was standing now with downcast eyes and the little smile at one corner of his mouth.

Sir Thorolf hated so those kinsmen of his who should have been his heirs if he died childless. But folk were talking, saying the thing was not as it should be—— "Oh, the man must sure know best himself," said Erlend as before——

"Ay, ay, Erlend! That one boy is heir to more than the seven sons you have by your wife——"

"For *my* seven sons shall I care myself, Arne——" But at that she went down; she would not suffer them to talk any more of this thing. Erlend looked a little out of countenance when he saw her. Then he came and took her hand, standing behind her so that her shoulder touched his body. She felt that, as he stood there looking down upon her, he was making over again, wordlessly, the promise he had just made—as it were to give her courage——

——Kristin grew ware now that Munan was gazing up into her face— somewhat fearful. She must have smiled—not a pleasant smile. But when his mother looked down at *him*, he smiled back to her straightway, doubtfully and provingly.

Vehemently she caught him up into her lap. He was little, little, little yet, her youngest—not too big yet to be kissed and fondled by his mother. She winked one eye at him. He did his best to wink back at her, but, try as he would, both eyes *would* shut together—his mother laughed aloud; Munan too went off into peals of laughter, while Kristin hugged and squeezed him in her arms——

Lavrans had been sitting with the dog in his lap. They both turned, listening, towards the woods below.

"'Tis father!" The dog first and the boy after him went leaping down the steep hill-side.

Kristin sat still awhile. Then she rose and went out on a jutting point. Now they were coming up the path from below: Erlend, Naakkve, Ivar, and Skule. They came along in wild glee, calling their greetings up to her.

Kristin greeted them again. Were they going up to fetch the horses? No, answered Erlend: Ulf, he thought, was sending Sveinbjörn up for them to-night. He and Naakkve were bound further afield after rein-deer, and the twins had had a mind to come along with them and see their mother——

She made no answer. She had known how 'twas ere she asked. Naak-kve had with him hounds in leash; he and his father were in wadmal jerkins of mingled grey and black, such as make little show against the screes. All four of them had bows.

Kristin asked the tidings from the manor, and Erlend talked as they climbed upward. Ulf was in full swing with the harvest work; he was not ill pleased, but the straw was cutting short; the corn had riped so quickly on the higher fields, the grain was dropping from the ears. And the oats were all but ready to cut—they must keep hard at it, Ulf said——

Kristin nodded as she walked, but said no word.

She went to the byre herself to help in the milking. It was ever pleas-ant to her, this hour when she sat in the dark close in to the swelling cow-flank, and felt the milk's sweet breath in her nostrils. Swish, swish, came the answer from the inner darkness, where the byre-woman and the herd were milking. 'Twas all so restful, the strong, warm smell in the byre, the sound of a withy-band creaking, of a horn knocking against wood, of a cow moving her feet in the miry earth floor of the stall, or whisking her tail at the flies.—The wagtails that nested in here in the summer were gone now——

The cows were restless to-night. Bluesides put her foot in the milk-pail—Kristin slapped at her and scolded her. The next cow turned rest-ive and ugly, as soon as Kristin sat in to her side. She had sores on her teats. Kristin pulled her wedding-ring from her finger and milked the first jet through it.

She heard Ivar and Skule down by the gate—they were shouting and throwing stones at the strange bull that followed her cattle home each evening. They had offered to help Finn to milk the goats in the pen, but they must have grown tired of that——

When she came by a little later, they were busy tormenting the pretty white bull-calf she had given Lavrans—the little boy stood by whimper-ing. His mother set down the pails, took the two by the shoulders, and pushed them aside—they must let their brother's calf be, when he bade them to——

Erlend and Naakkve were sitting on the doorstep; they had a fresh cheese between them; they were eating hunch upon hunch, and stuffing Munan, who stood betwixt Naakkve's knees. Naakkve had laid her strainer over the little one's head, saying that none could see Munan now—for this was no strainer, but a fairy hat. They were laughing, all three,—but no sooner did Naakkve see his mother than he handed her the strainer, stood up, and took the pails from her.

Kristin lingered in the dairy. The upper half of the door to the outer room stood ajar—she saw they had piled the hearth with fuel. Round the fire in the warm flickering glow they sat eating, Erlend, the children, the serving-wench, and the three herds.

When she came in, they had ended their meal. She saw that the two little ones had been put to bed upon the wall-bench; they seemed to be asleep already. Erlend lay huddled up in the bed. She stumbled over his jerkin and boots and, as she went by, picked them up and then went out.

The sky was bright still, with a red streak over the fells in the west; a few dark cloud-wisps swam in the clear heaven. It looked like good weather for to-morrow too, 'twas so still, and so nipping cold, now that night had well fallen—no wind, but an icy breath from the north-west, a steady air-drift from the naked grey-stone mountains. Over the low hills down to the south-east the moon was floating up, nigh the full, big and pale red yet in the thin haze that hung always over the marshes there.

The strange bull was bellowing mournfully somewhere away on the uplands. But for that, all was so still 'twas like an ache—naught but the rush of the river below their milking-place, the little beck tinkling down the grassy green, and a sleepy soughing off in the woods—an unrest among the pines, that stirred, settled for a space, and then stirred again——

She busied herself with some milk-pans and troughs that stood by the sæter wall. Naakkve and the twins came out—whither were they going? their mother asked.

They were going to lie in the barn—there was such a rank smell in the dairy from all the cheese and butter—and from the herds sleeping there.

Naakkve went not at once to the barn. His mother still saw his light-grey form faintly against the green darkness of the hay-field that bordered the woods. A little later the serving-wench came to the door—she started when she saw the mistress standing by the wall.

"Are you not for bed now, Astrid?—'tis late already——"

The wench mumbled—she was but going behind the byre. Kristin waited till she had seen her in again. Naakkve was in his sixteenth year. 'Twas some time now since his mother had begun to keep an eye upon the serving-women on the manor, when they grew merry with the comely and lively youth.

Kristin went down to the river and knelt upon the stone slab out over the water. Before her the river ran, well-nigh black, in a wide pool; only a few rings showed the current; but a little above, it foamed down, white in the darkness, with a drumming noise and cold puffs of air. The moon had risen so high now that its light was grown strong—here and there it glittered on a dewy leaf. Then a sparkle showed on a ripple on the stream——

Erlend spoke her name just behind her—she had not heard him coming down across the sward. Kristin sank her arm into the icy water and fished up a pair of milk-pans that lay at the bottom with stones on them, scouring in the river; she rose and followed her husband back with both hands full. They did not speak as they passed up the slope.

Once in the hut, Erlend stripped himself wholly and climbed into the bed:

"Will you not come to rest soon, Kristin?"

"I must get me a bite of food first——" She sat her down on her three-legged stool close by the hearth, with some bread and a slice of cheese in her lap, ate slowly, and gazed into the heap of embers that were dying out little by little in the stone-lined hole in the floor.

"Sleep you, Erlend?" she whispered, as she rose and shook her skirt.

"No——" Kristin went over and drank a dipperful of sour milk from the tub in the corner. Then she went back to the hearth, lifted a slab of stone and laid it on top, and spread the Aaron's-rod blossoms on it to dry.

But now there was no more she could think on to be done. She undressed in the dark and laid her down in the bed by Erlend. When he put his arms around her, she felt her weariness like a wave of cold sweeping through her whole body; her head grew hollow and heavy, as though all within it had settled down and made a lump of sheer pain where it joined her neck. But when he whispered to her, she dutifully put her arms about his neck.

She awoke in the night and knew not what time it was. But by the pane above the smoke-hole she could see the moon must be high.

The bed was narrow and short, so that they needs must lie close to one another. Erlend slept; he breathed quietly and evenly; his breast rose and fell gently in his sleep. At one time she had been wont to nestle close in to his warm, sound body when she woke of nights and grew fearful because he breathed so noiselessly—then it had seemed a sweet joy to feel his breast rise and fall in slumber against her side.

After a while she crept out of the bed, put on her clothes in the dark, and stole to the door.

The moon was sailing high over the whole world. Here and there was a glimmer from water in the mosses, or on cliffs over whose face it had trickled the day through and was freezing now to ice. The moon shone over the leaf woods and the pine woods. On the grass banks hoar-frost glittered. It was bitter cold—she crossed her arms upon her breast and stood a little.

Then she went up along the beck. It tinkled and gurgled, with little sounds of ice-needles breaking in sunder——

At the upper end of the fenced field lay a great deep-bedded boulder. No one went near it unless he must, and when he went, he crossed himself. They poured cream in under it when they came in the summer, and when they left again. True it was she had never known of any that had seen or heard aught there—but such had been the custom on the sæter from of old——

She knew not herself what had taken her, to leave the house in this wise, at dead of night. She came to a stand by the stone—set her foot in a notch in it. Her belly shrank, her body grew cold and numb with fear —but cross herself she *would* not. Then she crept up and sat her down upon the stone.

From here one saw far and wide around—away over the ugly grey-stone mountains in the moon-light. The big hump on Dovre rose mighty and pale against the pale sky, the snow-field glistened white in the scar on Graahö, the Boar-fells shone with blue clefts and new-fallen snow. In the moonlight the mountains were uglier than she had ever deemed they could be—hardly a single star or two shone here and there in the endless, icy-cold heavens. She was chilled through bone and marrow—terror and cold pressed in upon her from all sides. But she sat on defiant.

She *would* not go down and lay herself in the black darkness by her husband's warm, slumbering body. For her there was no sleep that night, she knew——

So sure as she was her father's daughter—her wedded husband should never hear her blame his deeds. For she remembered what she had sworn when she besought God Almighty and all the holy saints in heaven for Erlend's life——

So it was that she *must* go out into this ghostly night to take breath, when she felt nigh perishing——

She sat and let the bitter old thoughts come to her like old acquaintance. And met them with other old and well-known thoughts—in feigned excuse of Erlend——

True, he had not craved this of her. He had not laid upon her aught of the burden she had taken upon her shoulders. He had but begotten seven sons on her. "For my seven sons *I* shall care, Arne——" God alone might know what the man meant by those words. Like enough he had meant nothing—he had but said it——

Erlend had not begged her to set Husaby and his estates a-going again. He had not begged her fight for dear life to save him. Like a chieftain he had suffered—that his goods be wasted, that his life be set on the hazard, that all he owned be lost. Stripped and bare, he stood amidst mischance loftily unbowed and still; loftily still and unbowed he abode in her father's manor like some stranger guest——

But all that was hers was her sons' by right. By right they claimed her sweat and blood and all her strength. But, if so, the manor and she herself could lay rightful claim to them in return.

There had been no need for her to take the road to the sæter like any cottar's wife. But at home, as things were now, she felt herself crushed and hemmed in on every side—so that she seemed to fail for breath. Besides, she had needed to prove to herself that she *could* do a peasant woman's work. True, toil and struggle had been hers every hour since she rode, a bride, into Erlend Nikulaussön's manor—and saw that here *one* at least must fight to save the heritage of him she bore below her heart. If the father could not, then she must be the one. But now she must needs assure herself—that, if the pinch came, there was no piece of work she had set her maids and serving-women to in the old days that she could not do with her own hands. Up here 'twas a good day when she marked that she ached not across the loins when she had stood long a-churning. 'Twas good in the mornings to be along herself and help let out the cattle—they had grown fat and fair this summer—the weight on her heart lightened when she stood in the sunset, crying on the home-coming cows. She loved to see the food growing under her own hands—'twas as though she were reaching down to make firm the very ground-work on which her sons' fortunes were to be built up again.

Jörundgaard was a good estate, but 'twas not so good as she had deemed. And Ulf was a stranger here in the dale—he fell into mistakes and he lost patience. As folk reckoned in this country-side, they ever did well with their hay on Jörundgaard—they had water-meadows along the river and out on the holms—but 'twas not *the best* hay, nor such as Ulf was used to in the Trondheim country. He was unused to have to garner in so much moss and leaf fodder, so much heather and twigs, as was needful here——

Her father had known every inch of his land, had had all a farmer's lore: of the whims of seasons; of the way the divers fields took wet or dry years, windy summers or burning summers; of the strains of cattle that, generation after generation, he himself had coupled, fed and reared and sold from—all the knowledge that was needed for just this place. She knew not her manor so by heart. But she would yet—and her sons should——

But Erlend had never asked the like of her. He had not wed her to plunge her into toil and trouble; he had but wed her that she might sleep in his arms. And thus, ever, when her time was come, a child lay by her side, craved its place upon her arm, at her breast, in her cares——

Kristin moaned through her clenched teeth. She sat shivering with cold and wrath.

"*Pactum serva*—that is, in the Norse tongue, keep thy troth!"

'Twas in that time when Arne Gjavvaldssön and brother Leif of Holm had come to Husaby and fetched away her goods and her children's to Nidaros. That, too, had Erlend left her to deal with—he had taken lodging out at the Holm cloister. She sat in the town mansion—the monks owned it now—and Arne Gjavvaldssön was with her, helping her with rede and deed; Simon had sent letters praying for his help.

Arne could have been no more eager had it been for himself he was to save the goods and gear. The very evening he brought it to the town, he must needs have both her and Lady Gunna of Raasvold, who had come in with the two little ones, out to the stables. Seven picked horses—folk were minded to deal fairly towards Erlend Nikulaussön, and gave assent when Arne averred the five eldest sons each owned a riding-horse, and the lady of the house one for herself and one for her serving-man. As to the Castilian, Erlend's Spanish stallion, he could bring witness that him Erlend had made over in gift to his son Nikulaus—even though it might have been more jest than earnest. Not that Arne was much taken with the long-legged beast—but he knew Erlend loved the horse well——

'Twas an ill thing, said Arne, that he had to let the armour of state go, with the great helm and the gold-mounted sword—true, all this gear was fit for naught but the tournament; still 'twas worth a great sum. But he had got Erlend's body-shirt of black silk with the red lion broidered on it. And he had claimed the English battle-harness for Nikulaus. And that was so choicely wrought that Arne deemed there was not the like to be found in Norway's land—for them that had eyes to see. But 'twas much worn—ay, indeed, Erlend had worn his weapons more than most sons of nobles in these times—— Arne fondled each piece—helm, gorget, vambraces, greaves, gauntlets of the finest steel plates, corslet and hauberk of chain-mail, so light and easy-fitting and yet withal so strong. And then the sword—it had but a plain steel hilt, and the leather on the handle was chafed—but the like of such a blade one saw not every year——

Kristin sat and held the sword across her lap. She knew Erlend would take it to him like a much-loved bride—he had never used any other of all the swords he owned. It had been left to him when he was but a lad by Sigmund Torolfssön, who had been his bedfellow when first he joined the body-guard. Once only had he spoken of this friend to her: "Had God not been in such hot haste to take Sigmund from this world, 'tis like that much had gone otherwise with me. After his death I was ill at ease at the Court, and so with much begging I got me King Haakon's leave to go north with Gissur Galle that time.—Yet but for that I trow I had never won you, my sweeting—for belike I had been a wedded man long ere you were grown maid——"

From Munan Baardssön she had heard that Erlend had nursed his friend day and night, as a mother tends her babe, taking no sleep but a short doze now and then on the sick man's bed-side—that last winter, when Sigmund Torolfssön lay spitting out his lungs piecemeal, and his heart's blood. And when Sigmund had been brought to earth in Halvard's Church, Erlend had gone to his grave late and early, and lain flat on the gravestone sorrowing. But to her he had never spoken of him but that one time. In Halvard's Church, too, Erlend and she had had their trysts sometimes, that sinful winter in Oslo. But he had never named with a word that the dearest friend of his youth lay there.—'Twas thus he had mourned over his mother, she knew; and when Orm died he had been wild and ungoverned in his despair; yet them too he never named. She knew he had been in to the town and seen Margret—but he never spoke of his daughter.

——Right up under the hilt she saw some writing graven into the blade. 'Twas runes mostly, and she could not read them, nor Arne either; but the monk took the sword and looked on it a while. "*Pactum serva*," said he at last. "That means, in the Norse tongue, keep thy troth."

Arne and brother Leif spoke, too, of how a great part of her lands here, north of Dovre, Erlend's morning-gift to her, had been pledged and thrown away. Could not some device be found to save somewhat of this? But Kristin would not—'twas honour one must save first of all; she would not have any question raised whether her husband's dealings were lawful. And besides, she was well-nigh plagued to death by Arne's talk, well meant as it was. That night, when he and the monk had bidden good-night and gone to their lodging, she threw herself upon her knees before Lady Gunna and hid her face in her lap.

In a little the old woman lifted up the young one's head. Kristin looked up at the other—Lady Gunna's face was heavy, yellow, and fleshy, with three thick folds, as though moulded in wax, right across her brow, lightly freckled, with sharp, kind blue eyes and an indrawn, toothless mouth shaded by long, grey lip-hairs. Kristin had seen this face look down on her in so many an hour of torment—Lady Gunna had been with her each time she bore a child, save when Lavrans came, for then Kristin had been at home by her father's death-bed.

"Ay, ay, my daughter," said the lady, pressing a hand on her forehead. "I have stayed you more times than one now, when you needs must to your knees—ay. But in this trial, my Kristin, you must lay you down before God's mother Mary herself and pray her to help you through——"

—Ah, and she had done it too, Kristin thought. She said her prayers and somewhat of the psalter every sabbath eve; she kept the fasts Archibishop Eiliv had laid upon her when he gave her remission of her sins; she gave alms, and tended herself each wayfarer who begged night's lodging, looked he fair or foul. But she felt no longer now that the light shone within her when she did these things. That there *was* light without she knew, but it seemed as though mists shut in her soul. It must be what Gunnulf spoke of—the drought of the spirit. No soul should lose courage by reason of that, said Sira Eiliv; be steadfast in prayer and good deeds, as a farmer ploughs and dungs and sows—God will send the quickening rain in His own good time.—But then Sira Eiliv had never been a farmer——

Gunnulf she had not seen that time. He was making a term north in

Helgeland, preaching and gathering gifts for his cloister. Ay! there was
the one of the knights' sons of Husaby—and the other——

But Margret Erlendsdatter had come to her sometimes at the town
mansion. Two servants followed the merchant's wife; she was in goodly
clothing and shone with rich trinkets—her father-in-law was a goldsmith, so they had them handy in the house. She seemed happy and
content—albeit she had no children. She had got her dowry from her
father in good time. God only knew whether she ever gave a thought to
the poor cripple, Haakon, out at Gimsar—he could but just drag himself round the courtyard on two crutches, she had heard.——

But even then she had not thought on Erlend with bitterness, it
seemed to her. She must have felt that what waited Erlend, now he was
a free man again, was the worst of all for him. 'Twas therefore he hid
himself away out with Abbot Olav. Take order for the flitting, show
himself now in the town—it might well be too much for even Erlend
Nikulaussön to face——

And there was the day they sailed out over Trondheim's fjord—on the
Laurentius galleass, the selfsame bark by which Erlend had shipped
her bridal gear to the north when they first got leave to wed each
other——

A still day, well on in autumn—a pale, leaden glimmer upon the
fjord, the world about them cold, white-barred, unquiet—the first snow
drifted into ridges across the frozen lands, the cold-blue hills streaked
white with snow. The highest clouds, too, where the skies were blue,
seemed spread out thin as flour by a wind high up in the dome of heaven.
The ship drifted along slowly, sullenly, close under the land—the town
ness. Kristin stood looking at the white surf against the cliff—wondering
if she should be seasick when they got further out into the fjord.

Erlend stood by the rail, further forward near the bow, his two eldest
sons with him. The wind blew their hair and cloaks about.

Now they were looking up Kors fjord, toward Gaularos and the
landing at Birgsi. A gleam of sunshine lit up the brown and white hill-
side above the strand in there——

Erlend said somewhat to the lads. At that Björgulf turned sharply
round, left the bulwark, and came aft. With the spear he always bore
and used as a staff he groped his way among the empty rowing-benches;
he came past his mother—his curly black head thrust low down upon
his breast, his eyes blinking, well-nigh shut, his lips pressed close together. He went in under the poop——

The mother looked forward at the other two, Erlend and his eldest
son. Then she saw Nikulaus kneel down upon one knee, as a page does
homage to his lord, take his father's hand, and kiss it.

Erlend tore away his hand—Kristin had a glimpse of his face, deathly white, quivering, as he turned from the boy and went behind the sail away from view——

They put into a small haven down the Möre coast that night. More sea was running now—the galleass tugged at her land moorings, pitching and rolling. Kristin was down in the room below, where she was to sleep with Erlend and the two little children. She felt qualmish with sickness, could not keep her footing on the boards, which seemed to rise and sink beneath her feet; the lantern swung over her head, the tiny candle flickered—and she stood struggling with Munan, trying to get him to make water down between the planks. When he awoke, drugged with sleep, he would be sick or worse in their bed; and he raged and shrieked and would not suffer that the strange woman, his mother, should lay hands on him to help him and hold him over the side. Then Erland came down.

She could not see his face, as he asked, very low:

"Saw you Naakkve?—He was so like you in the eyes, Kristin." Erlend drew in his breath, short and hard. "'Twas so your eyes looked that morning by the wall of the nuns' garden—when you had heard the worst of me—and you plighted me your troth——"

It was then that she had felt the first drop of bitter gall well up in her heart. God shield the lad—may be never see the day when he must fix his faith on a hand that lets all slip through its fingers like cold water and dry sand——

A little while before, she had thought she heard the sound of hoofs from somewhere far south in the hill wastes. Now it came again, from nearer by: 'twas not the noise of stray horses, 'twas some rider; he rode sharply over the rock slabs below the hillock yonder.

Fear came over her, icy cold; who rides abroad so late? Dead men ride north under a waning moon—heard she not horsemen following the first, far behind——? Yet she sat on; she knew not herself whether 'twas that she was palsied, or that her heart to-night was so hardened——

He was bound hither, the rider—now he was crossing the stream below the home-pasture. She saw the glint of a spear-head above the willow bushes. Then she found strength to come down from the stone, and would have run back to the hut—but now the rider sprang from his horse, bound it to the wicket-spot, and threw his cloak over it for a covering. He came up the green; 'twas a big, broad man—and now she knew him—it was Simon.

When he saw her coming towards him in the moonlight, he seemed as affrighted as she had been before:

"Jesus, Kristin, is't you yourself or—how comes it you are out at dead of night——? Did you look for me to come?" he asked quickly, as in great dread; "have you had warning of my coming?"

Kristin shook her head:

"I could not sleep.—Brother-in-law, what ails you——?"

"Andres is so sick, Kristin—we are afeard for his life. And so we thought—we know you are the most skilful of women in such things—bear in mind he is your own sister's son. Will you do a good deed and go home with me to him?—You know well I would not come to you thus, but that I know full surely the boy's life is the stake," he said beseechingly.

Inside the hut he said the same to Erlend, who sat up in the bed, still half asleep, in silent wonderment. Then Erlend tried to comfort his brother-in-law, speaking as one with knowledge: such young children so easily went off into a high fever and wandered in their talk, even if they had only taken some little chill; mayhap there was not so much peril as there seemed. "You may well believe, Erlend, I had never come to fetch Kristin out at such hours of the night as this, had I not seen all too plain that the child is lying fighting with death——"

Kristin had blown up the embers and laid wood on the hearth; Simon sat staring into the fire; he drank eagerly of the milk she proffered him, but would have no food. He had a mind to set off down the hill as soon as the others came, "—if you are willing, Kristin?" One of his henchmen was bringing with him a widow that served at Formo, a notable woman, who could take the charge here for a time—Aasbjörg was a most handy woman, he said again.

When Simon had lifted Kristin to the saddle, he said:

"Fain am I that we should take the short cut southwards—if you have naught against it?"

Kristin had never been on that side of the fell, but she knew there was a path there going sheer down into the dale over the hill-side above Formo. She answered, ay—but then his man must ride the other way, round by Jörundgaard, to fetch her casket and the bags of roots and herbs. He must waken Gaute; the boy knew best about them.

By the edge of a wide moss they were able to ride side by side, and Kristin made Simon tell her again of the boy's sickness. The children at Formo had had the throat sickness about Olav's Mass, but had got over that lightly. This new sickness had taken hold on Andres quite of a sudden, when he seemed in the highest health—in the middle of the day three days ago. Simon had taken him out with him; he was to have a ride on the corn-sled down to the field—but he began to complain that he was cold, and, when Simon looked, the child was in a shivering fit, his teeth chattering in his head. Later came the hot fit and the cough; and he spat up an evil-looking brown slime, and had a sore pain in the breast—but, to be sure, he could not tell them much of where he felt worst, the poor little being——

Kristin spoke to Simon as cheerly as she could, and now she had to ride for a stretch behind him. Once he turned and asked if she were cold; he would have her to put on his mantle over her cloak——

Then he talked again of his son. 'Twas true, he had marked it—the boy was not strong. But Andres had grown much more hearty this summer and autumn—his foster-mother deemed so too Ay, the last days before he fell sick he had been a little strange and startlish—"frighted," he said when the dogs sprang up on him in play. And the day he took the fever Simon had come home at sunrise with some wild-ducks. Other days the boy would ever beg his father for the birds he brought home, to play with them awhile; but now Andres had shrieked out loud when his father had made as if to toss the leash of birds at him. He had indeed stolen across afterward and handled the ducks, but he got some blood upon him, and at that he grew quite wild with terror. And now to-night, as he lay moaning sore, getting no sleep nor rest—he had cried out somewhat of a hawk that was after him——

"——Mind you that day the tidings came to me at Oslo, and you said: 'Twill still be the Darre stock that will hold Formo when you are gone——'?"

"Talk not so, Simon—as though you deemed you would die sonless. God and his gentle mother can surely help—— 'Tis unlike you, brother-in-law, to be so faint of heart."

"Halfrid, my first wife, said the same to me when she had borne our son as you said at Oslo. Knew you, Kristin, that I had a son by her?"

"Ay—— But Andres is all but three years old—— 'Tis the first two years that are hardest to bring children through alive——" But even to herself it seemed that her words availed little here. And they rode, and they rode; the horses nodded as they mounted a rise, and tossed their heads so that the bits jingled; not a sound in the frosty night, save of their own riding, and at times the ripple of water as they crossed a beck; and the moon shone high and low; and scree and greystone crag glimmered grimly pale as death, where they rode on under the hill-sides.

At length they had come where they could look down upon the parish. Moonlight filled all the dale; the river and the marshes and the lake farther south shone like silver—fields and meadows were wan.

"Ay, to-night 'tis freezing in the lowlands too," said Simon.

He got down from his horse and led hers as they went down over the edge. The path was so steep in many places, Kristin felt she scarce dared look ahead. Simon steadied her with his back against her knee. and she held on with one hand behind the saddle. Now and then a stone rolled from under the horses' hoofs, trundled downward, stopped a little, then rolled again, loosening others and carrying them along——

At last they were down. They rode over the barley-fields north of the manor between the rime-covered corn-stooks. The aspens crackled and pattered eerily above their heads in the bright, still night.

"Said you sooth," asked Simon, wiping his face with his sleeve, "that you had had no warning——?"

Kristin answered that it was true. Then said he:

"I have heard tell that sometimes a forewarning goes forth when any one yearns sorely for another—— Ramborg and I said to each other more than once that had you been at home you might have known a way——"

"None of you have been in my thoughts all these days," said Kristin. "You must believe me, Simon." But she could not see that this comforted him.

In the courtyard a couple of house-carls sprang out at once and took the horses. "Ay, 'tis even as when you went, Simon; 'tis no worse," said one of them quickly; he had looked up at his master's face. Simon nodded; he went in front of Kristin towards the women's house.

Kristin saw clear enough that here was great peril of life. The little boy lay alone in the great, fine bed, moaning and gasping and tossing his head without cease to and fro on the pillows. He was burning hot, and dark red in the face; he lay with half-open, glistening eyes, fighting for breath. Simon stood, holding Ramborg's hand, and all the women of the manor, who were gathered in the room, pressed round Kristin while she handled the boy.

But she spoke as calmly as she could, and heartened the parents as best she was able. Sure enough 'twas the lung fever. But this night was now near an end without the evil having changed for the worse—and 'twas the way of this sickness to take a turn he third or seventh or ninth night, before cock-crow. She prayed Ramborg to send all the serving-women to bed save two, so that she might at all times have women, rested and fresh, to help her. And when the man came from Jörund-gaard with her leech-wife's gear, she brewed a sweating-drink for the boy and opened a vein in his foot to draw the humours somewhat away from his breast.

Ramborg's face blanched at the sight of her child's blood. Simon put an arm around her, but she pushed the man aside and sat down on a chair by the bed-foot; there she sat gazing at Kristin with big, black eyes, while her sister busied herself with the child.

On in the day, the boy seeming a little better, Kristin talked Ramborg over to lie down on the bench. She heaped cushions and coverings about the young wife; sat by her head, stroking her forehead gently. Ramborg took Kristin's hand:

"Surely now, you wish us naught else but good?" said she in a moaning breath.

"Could I wish you aught but well, sister—we two, sister, left here in the country of our home, alone of all our kindred——?"

Ramborg broke into sobs—a few half-choked sobs through lips pressed hard together. Kristin had but once seen her sister weep— the time they stood by their father's death-bed. Now a few small, hasty tears sprang to her eyes and trickled down her cheeks. She lifted Kristin's hand and looked upon it. It was long and slender, but red-brown now and rough——

"Even yet 'tis fairer than mine," she said. Ramborg's hands were small and white, but the fingers were short and the nails square.

"Yes," said she, almost angrily, as Kristin shook her head, smiling. "And you are even yet fairer than I have ever been. And our father and our mother held you dearer than me—all our days. You wrought them sorrow and shame; I was duteous and obedient and set my heart on the man they most fain would have me wed—yet withal 'twas you they loved much more——"

"Nay, sister. Be sure they held you every whit as dear. Be glad, Ramborg, to think you never gave them aught but joy—you know not how heavy the other thought is to bear. But you were younger the time when I was young; and therefore, maybe, they spoke more with me."

"Ay, I trow that all were younger that time when you were young," said Ramborg, sighing as before.

She slept soon after. Kristin sat and gazed at her. She had known her sister so little; Ramborg was yet a child when she herself was wed. And now it seemed to her that the other in some ways had never ceased to be a child. She had looked like a child as she sat by her sick boy—a pale, frighted child, striving to bear up against terror and unhappiness.

It befell at times that beasts stopped short in their growth if they bore young too early. Ramborg had not been full sixteen years when she bore her daughter, and since then it seemed as though she had never rightly taken up her growth again; she had stayed frail and small, without bloom or fruitfulness. She had had this one son since, and he was strangely ailing—comely of face, fine-featured and fair of hue, but piteously small and puny—he had been backward in walking, and he still spoke haltingly, so that only those about him daily understood aught of his prattle. He was so fearful and peevish with strangers, too, that he had scarce ever let his mother's sister touch him till now. Would God and Holy Olav but grant her grace to save this poor little being— oh! she would be thankful all her days. Such a child as this mother of his was, sure it was that she could never endure the loss of him. And she felt that for Simon Darre too 'twould be bitter hard to bear the blow well, if this only son were taken from him——

That she had grown to love her brother-in-law heartily she marked well, now that she understood how sorely he suffered in this sorrow and dread. She could well understand now her father's great love for Simon Andressön. And yet she wondered if he had not done Ramborg wrong in making such haste to bring about this match. For when she looked upon this little sister beside her, it came home to her that, after all said, Simon must be both too old and too sober and heavy to be husband to this young child.

III

T H E days went by and Andres lay sick; there was no great change either for the worse or for the better. The worst was he scarce got any sleep; the boy lay there with half-open eyes and seemed not to know any; cough and breathlessness wrung his wasted little frame, and the flickering fever rose and fell. One evening Kristin had given him a soothing drink—after it he sank into rest; but in a while she saw the child had gone a bluish-white, and his skin felt cold and clammy.

In all haste she got a draught of hot milk poured down his throat, and laid hot stones to the soles of his feet; but thereafter she no longer dared give him a sleeping potion.—She saw that he was too young to support it.

Sira Solmund came and brought him the Holy Elements from the church; Simon and Ramborg vowed perpetual prayer, fasts and alms, if God would hear them and grant their son his life.

Erlend came thither one day; he would not light from his horse and go within, but Kristin and Simon came out into the courtyard and spoke with him. He looked on them most sorrowfully. 'Twas strange that this look of his ever stirred in Kristin a vague dull anger. Certain 'twas that it gave him pain when he saw any sick or sorrowing, but he seemed most of all mazed and shamefaced—he ever looked so helpless when he was sorry for folk.

After that Naakkve or the twins came each day to Formo to ask for Andres.

The seventh night brought no turn in the sickness, but as the day drew on the boy seemed a little better—not so hot. Simon and Kristin were sitting alone by him towards midday.

The father pulled out a little gilded amulet he wore on a cord about his neck under his clothes. He bent down over the boy, dangled the amulet before his eyes, thrust it into the child's hand, and pressed the little fingers together around it—but Andres seemed not to heed.

This amulet Simon had had given him when a child, and he had borne it ever since—his father had brought it with him from France. It had been blessed in a cloister named St. Michael's Mount, and there was on it the likeness of St. Michael with great wings; this Andres liked right well to look upon, Simon told her, very low. But the little fellow deemed it was a cock; *he* called the chief of all the angels "the cock"—— At last he had got the boy taught to say "the angel." But one day they were standing in the courtyard Andres saw the cock pecking at one of his hens; "Angel angry now, father," said he.

Kristin looked up at the man beseechingly—it cut her to the heart to hear him, albeit Simon spoke so evenly and calmly. And she was so worn out by all these nights of watching; she felt she must break down if she began now to weep——

Simon thrust the charm into the bosom of his shirt again:

"Oh, ay. I shall give a three-year-old ox to the church on St. Michael's even, each autumn so long as I live, if he will but tarry a little ere he come to fetch this soul. Methinks too he would weigh in the balance no more than a plucked chicken—Andres—so little——" but when he tried to laugh, his voice broke a little.

"Simon, Simon!" the woman begged him.

"Ay, 'twill be as 'tis willed to be, Kristin. And 'tis God Himself that wills it; he must sure know best——" The father spoke no more, but stood looking down upon his son.

On the eighth night Simon and one of the serving-women watched, while Kristin slumbered a little over on the further bench. When she awoke, the girl was sleeping. Simon sat, as he had sat most nights, on the bench at the bed-head; he sat with his head bowed down over the bed and the child.

"Doth he sleep?" whispered Kristin, going forward to him.

Simon raised his head. He brushed his hand over his face; she saw that his cheeks were wet, but he answered low and calmly:

"I deem not, Kristin, that Andres will sleep any more till he lies beneath the turf in holy ground——"

Kristin stood—'twas as though she grew stark and stiff. Slowly she blanched beneath her sunburnt skin, grew white to the very lips.

Then she went to the corner and took her outdoor cloak.

"You must order it so—" she spoke as though her throat and mouth were dry—"that you are here alone when I come back. Stay you with him—and, when you see me enter, speak no word, and speak no word of this after, neither to me nor to any. Not even to your priest——"

Simon rose up—came slowly over to her. He too had grown pale.

"Nay—Kristin!" His voice could scarce be heard. "I—I dare not —have you go that road——"

She wrapped her cloak about her, took a cloth of linen from the chest in the corner, folded it together, and hid it in her bosom.

"I dare. You wot well not one must come nigh us after, before I call —no one must come nigh us after, nor speak to us, ere he wakes and himself has spoken——"

"What, trow you, would your father think of this?" he whispered, faintly as before. "Kristin—do it not——"

"I have done before now what my father deemed was wrong—then 'twas but to forward my own lusts—— Andres is *his* flesh and blood too —*my* own flesh, Simon—my only sister's son——"

Simon breathed hard, trembling; he stood looking down.

"But if you would not that I should make trial of this last shift of all——" He stood as before with bowed head, and made no answer. Thereon she said again—and knew not that a strange, nigh scornful half-smile had come about her white lips:

"Would you that I should not go?"

He turned his head aside, and she went by him, stepped through the door noiselessly, and closed it softly behind her.

Without was thick darkness, with little puffs of south wind, so that all the stars flickered and blinked unsteadily. She had come no farther than into the road between the fences, and yet it seemed as though she had passed out into the everlasting itself. An endless road behind her and before her. As though she would never come away from what she had stepped into when she set foot out into this night——

The darkness itself seemed a power that she pressed forward against. She was walking in deep mud—the way had been ploughed up by the dung-carts and was thawing in the south wind. At each step she must tear herself loose from the night and the raw cold that clung about her feet, sucked its way up, and clogged the hem of her skirts. Ever and anon a falling leaf brushed by her—as though a living thing in the dark touched her, softly, sure of its power: go back, go back!——

When she came out upon the highway, walking grew easier: it was grass-grown; her feet stuck in the mud no longer. She felt her face stiff as stone, her body strung and taut—each step bore her mercilessly towards the wood she must go through. An inner palsy seemed to mount up in her—'twas impossible she could dare go through that murky passage—yet she had no thought of turning. Terror had struck her body numb, yet she kept striding forward as though in sleep, stepping surely over stones and roots and puddles, all unaware—heedful not to stumble, not to drop her even gait and give her terror the mastery.

Now the firs sighed nearer and nearer in the night; she passed in among them, still calm, as if sleep-walking. She was ware of every sound, and scarce dared move an eyelid for the darkness. The thunder of the river, the heavy sighing in the trees, the tinkle over stones of a beck that she drew near to, passed, and left behind. Once, up on the scree, a stone rolled, as if some living thing stirred up there—sweat burst out over her whole body, but she dared neither slacken nor hasten her gait——

Kristin's eyes were now so used to the dark that, when she came out of the wood, she could see a little—there was a faint gleam upon the river, upon the waters of the marshes. The farm-lands showed now against the blackness; the clusters of houses looked like cores of blacker gloom upon them. The sky, too, was surely lightening high above her as she went—she felt it, but dared not look up the black hillsides that towered up to heaven. But she knew it must soon be time for the moon to rise——

She tried to remind herself—in four hours' time 'twill be day: folk will be setting about the day's work on all the farms—the air will be grey with dawn; 'twill grow light above the hills. The way will not be long then—in the light 'tis not far from Formo to the church. And long ere that she herself would be home and within-doors. But something told her that she must needs be another then than she was when she went forth——

She knew—had it been for one of her own children's lives, she had never dared to try this last shift of all. Turn God's hand aside, when He had stretched it forth to take a living soul! As she sat over her own sick little ones, when she was young and her heart bled with tenderness, she had tried to say, when ready to sink with dread and anguish: Lord, Thou lovest them better than I—Thy will be done——

Yet now went she here this night defying her own terror—— This child which was not hers—this child she *would* save, whatsoever she might save it for——

——For you too, Simon Darre, when the dearest thing you owned on earth was the stake, took at my hands more than a man may take with honour unabated——

"Would you that I should not go——?" And he had not been man enough to answer. In her heart of hearts she knew—were the child to die, that too Simon would somehow make shift to bear. But she had swooped down upon that single hour when she found him at the breaking-point—had seized the chance that moment gave her and gone her way. This secret now she would share with him—that he knew she too had seen *him* in an hour when he stood not firmly on his feet——

For he had come to know her too nearly. At the hands of the man she had thrown off she had taken help each time there was need, to save the man of her choice. The lover she had cast aside was the man she had turned to, each time she stood in need of a shield for her love. And she had never besought Simon in vain—time after time had he stepped forth to screen her with his kindness and his strength.

——So she walked this road through the night that she might lighten a little the load of debt whose crushing weight till that hour she had never felt to the full.

Simon had forced her to understand at the last that he was the strongest—stronger than she herself and stronger than the man she had chosen to give herself to. She must indeed have felt it from the very hour when they three had met face to face in that shameful den in Oslo —though she *would* not see it then—that this lumpish, round-checked, talking youth was stronger than——

So went she here, and dared not call upon a good and holy name, and took upon herself this sin, that she might win—she knew not what—was it revenge?—revenge for that she had been forced to see he was worthier than they two——?

But now you too know it, Simon—when 'tis for the life of him one loves more than one's own being—a poor human soul will grasp at aught, at aught——

The moon had risen over the edge of the hills as she went up the slope towards the church. Again 'twas as though she must ride over a fresh wave of terror—the moonlight lay like a thin cobweb layer over the tar-sprent mass; the church itself stood under the thin veil, awful and threateningly black. For the first time she saw the great cross on the green outside and dared not go thither to bow down before the holy tree. She crept across where she knew the churchyard wall of turf and stone was lowest and easiest to climb.

A gravestone here and there glistened like water in the long dewy grass. Kristin went straight across the churchyard, down to the poor folks' graves away by the south wall.

She went to the place where lay a poor new-comer to the parish. The man had frozen to death on the mountains one winter; his two mother-less daughters had been passed from house to house as bedesfolk, till Lavrans Björgulfsön had proffered to keep them for Christ's sake, and to give them nurture. They grew up and turned out well, and her father had himself sought out honest, hard-working men for them, and had given them away in wedlock, each with cow and calf and sheep; while Ragnfrid gave them beds and bedding and iron pots—now they were thriving housewives, well-to-do in their own way of life. One had been Ramborg's serving-maid, and Ramborg had borne children to baptism for her——

So now must you spare me a turf from your covering, Bjarne, for Ramborg's son. She knelt down and drew out her dagger.

The sweat burst out in ice-cold beads upon her brow and upper lip as she dug her fingers in under the dew-wet turf. Something held it from below—'twas but roots—she cut them with the dagger.

In guerdon the drow must have gold, or silver heired for three generations. She drew off the little gold ring with rubies that had been her grandmother's betrothal ring—the child is of my father's house. She thrust the ring down into the earth as deep as she could, wrapped the turf in the linen cloth, and covered the spot whence she had taken it with moss and leaves.

As she rose to her feet, her legs beneath her trembled—she had to stand a little ere she could turn. If she looked under her elbow now, she would see *them*——

And there was a dreadful dragging within her, as though they would force her to it—all the dead who had known her in days gone by. Is't you, Kristin Lavransdatter—come you hither thus?—Arne Gyrdssön in the grave without the western porch. Ay, Arne, well may you wonder —I was not such an one when you and I were friends——

Then she climbed over the wall again and went her way downward.

The moon shone now over the whole country-side. There lay Jörundgaard out on the river flat—dew glittered in the grass on all the roofs. She looked down yonder, well-nigh unmoved—— 'Twas as though she herself were dead to that home and all therein—the door barred for ever against her who went by that night on the high-road——

Nigh all her road back was shadowed by the hills. The wind blew stronger now—gust after gust pressed straight against her——Withered leaves blew against her and would have turned her thither whence she last came——

Nor seemed it to her that she walked alone. Of a sudden there would come a sound as of stealthy footsteps behind her. Is it you, Arne——? Look behind you, Kristin; look under your elbow, it whispered——

And yet 'twas as though she was rightly afraid no longer. Only cold and numb, sick with longing to give up and sink down to the ground. Surely after this night she could never know fear again in this world——

Simon sat in his wonted place at the head of the bed, bent over the child, when she opened the door and stepped in. For one short moment he looked up—Kristin wondered whether *she* had grown in this time to look as worn and marred and old. Then Simon bowed his face wholly down and hid it on his arm.

He reeled a little as he rose. He turned his head away from her as he went by towards the door, with stooping neck and shoulders.

Kristin lit two candles and set them on the board. The boy opened his eyes a little, looked up unseeingly, frowned a little, and tried to turn his head from the light. When Kristin laid the little body out straight, as one lays out a corpse, he tried not to change his posture—he seemed too weak to move.

Then she covered his face and breast with the linen cloth and laid the strip of turf across it.

With that the horror rushed upon her anew, like a breaking sea.

She must sit by the bed. The window was right over the short bench. She dared not sit there with her back to it—better to look them in the eyes, if any stood without looking in. She drew the high-backed chair up to the bed, and sat facing the pane—the night pressed in upon it, pitchy black; one of the candle flames was mirrored in the glass. Kristin stared hard at it, clenching her hands round the chair arms, so that the joints stood out white and her arms behind them trembled. Her legs had no feeling in them, so cold and wet were they—she sat with her teeth chattering from fear and cold, the icy sweat pouring down her face and back. She sat moveless—threw but now and then a lightning glance upon the linen cloth that rose and fell ever so little with the child's breathing.

At length the window-pane began to grey. Cocks crew shrilly. And then she heard men in the yard—they were going to the stables——

Limply she fell back against the back of the chair, shaking as in spasms, and tried to lie so as to still the twitching and jerking of her limbs.

Then beneath the linen cloth something moved strongly—Andres pulled it from his face, whimpering peevishly—he seemed to have his senses in a fashion, for he grunted crossly at her when she started up and bent over him——

She snatched up the cloth and the turf, ran to the fire-place, stuffed in twigs and wood and flung the demon-ware into the fresh, hissing new-lit fire. But then was she fain to stand a little, leaned against the wall—tears trickling down over her face.

She dipped milk from the little pot which stood by the hearth and took it to the child—Andres was asleep again already. It seemed now to be a healthy sleep——

She drank the milk herself. 'Twas so delicious that she was fain to swallow two or three dipperfuls of the warm drink.

She dared not speak yet—the boy had said no word that could be understood. But she fell upon her knees by the bed-foot and said over to herself, noiselessly :

Convertere, Domine, aliquantulum ; et deprecare super servos tuos. Ne ultra memineris iniquitatis nostræ: ecce respice; populus tuus omnes nos——*

——Ay, ay, ay, 'twas a fearful thing she had done——

But he was their only son. She, she had seven! Ought she not to venture *all* to save her sister's only son——?

All that in this night she had been thinking—'twas but a delusion of the night. Sure it was she had done it for naught else but that she could not bear to see the child die in her hands——

Simon—he that had never failed her. He, that had been faithful and kind to every mother's child she knew of—and best of all to her and hers. And this son that he loved more than the apples of his eyes—ought she not to make trial of all to save the boy's life—— Even if 'twere a sin——

Ay, 'twas sinful; but God, visit it on me. This little fair, innocent child of Simon and Ramborg—God would not let His wrath fall on Andres——

She crossed the room and bent over the bed—breathed down upon one of the little wax-white hands. Kiss it she dared not—he must not be waked——

Bright and sinless.—It was in those nights of horror, when they sat together alone at Haugen, that Lady Aashild had told her of this—told her of her faring to the graveyard in Konungahelle: "That, Kristin, be sure, is the heaviest task I ever took on my shoulders."—But Björn Gunnarssön was no innocent child when he lay at death's door, for that Aashild Gautesdatter's sister's sons had come over-nigh his heart with their swords. He had been the death of one of them ere he had fallen, and the other was never whole man again after the day he changed sword-strokes with Sir Björn——

Kristin stood by the window and looked out on the court-yard. Folk went thither and thither among the houses at their daily tasks. Some little heifer calves wandered about in the yard—so comely as they were——

All manner of thoughts spring up in the dark—like to those filmy plants that grow in the sea and wave and rock themselves, strangely, weirdly fair—awesome and enticing, they draw us with a strange dark lure while yet they grow within their own living, wavering dusk. But plucked up by the children and pulled into a boat, and they are naught but a brown, slimy clot. In the night many and strange are the thoughts that spring up to lure and affright. Surely 'twas brother Edvin that had said once, the damned in hell would not themselves be parted from their torment—hate and sorrow were their delight—therefore it was that

---

* Psalm xc. 13. Return, O Lord, how long? and let it repent thee concerning thy servants.
    Isaiah lxiv. 9. [Be not wroth very sore, O Lord,] neither remember iniquity for ever: behold, see, we beseech thee, we are all thy people.

Christus could not save them. This had seemed to her wild talk then——
A cold shudder ran through her—now did she begin to understand what
the monk had meant——

She bent over the bed again—drinking in the air that breathed from
the little child. Simon and Ramborg should not lose him. Even if 'twere
true that she had done this out of her need to set herself right in Simon's
eyes—to show him that she too was willing to do more than take gifts at
his hands; a need had been in her to dare all that she might requite
him——

Then again she knelt down and said over again and again as much as
she knew of the psalter——

That morning Simon went out and sowed winter rye on the new-
broken field, south in the wood. He had it in mind that he must make
as though it seemed to him fitting that the work on the farm should go
its wonted way. The serving-women had fallen into great wonderment
when he had come in to them in the night and said that Kristin would be
alone with the boy till she sent for them. He told Ramborg too, when
she awoke—Kristin had prayed that none should go near the women's
house to-day.

"Not you either?" she asked quickly, and Simon said no. 'Twas then
that he had gone out and fetched the seed-box.

But after the midday meal-time he stayed up at the manor—he had
no heart to go far from the houses. And he liked not the look in Ramborg's eyes. It came, a while after the midday rest: he was standing by
the corn-barn, and he saw his wife rush across the yard. He sprang
after—Ramborg flung herself at the door of the women's house and beat
upon it with her clenched fists, shrieking wildly to Kristin to open.

Simon put his arms about her, trying to soothe her—thereon she bent,
quick as lightning, and bit him on the hand; she seemed like some wild
beast in her rage:

"He is *my* child! What have you done with my son?"

"You know well your sister is doing naught but good to Andres"—
when he took hold of her again, she shrieked and struggled against him.

"Come now," said the man, in a voice of feigned harshness: "Ramborg—are you not ashamed, before our house-folk——"

But she went on screaming:

"He is mine, mine, I tell you—— You were not with us when I bore
him, Simon," she cried; "then we were not so dear to you——"

"You know well yourself what I had in hand in those days," answered
the man wearily. He dragged her away towards the hall by main
strength.

Thereafter he dared not leave her. In a while Ramborg grew quiet, and, when the evening was come, she gave in to him and let the women undress her.

Simon sat on by her side. His daughters were sleeping in their own bed; the serving-women he had sent out. Once, when he rose and went across the room, Ramborg asked from the bed—she was wide-awake by her voice—whither he was going.

"I had a mind to lie down a little by you," he answered after a moment. He took off his outer coat and shoes, and crept in between the skins and the woollen coverlid. Then he put an arm under his wife's neck: "I know well, my Ramborg, that this has been a long day and a heavy for you——"

"Your heart beats so hard, Simon," she said soon after.

"Ay, you may believe I am in dread for the boy, I too. But we must wait in patience till Kristin sends us word——"

He started up in the bed—lay propped on his elbow—looked up wildly into Kristin's white face—it was close above his own, and shone wet with tears in a glimmer of light; her hand was on his breast. For one moment he thought—this time 'twas not a dream only—— Simon threw himself back against the bed-head; with a stifled moan he hid his face on his arm. He felt sick, the heart in him hammered so wildly and so hard——

"Simon, wake up!" Kristin shook him again. "Andres is calling on his father; hear you not?—'twas the first word he spoke——" Her face shone with smiles, while the tears ran down it without cease.

Simon sat up, and passed his hand once and again across his face. Surely he had not said aught as she woke him, while yet amazed with sleep—— He looked up at Kristin—she was standing by the bed with a lantern in her hand.

Softly, not to wake Ramborg, he crept out with her. The qualmish sickness still weighed upon his breast. He felt as though something would break within him—why was he ever haunted by this hateful dream? He who, awake, strove and ever strove to drive all such thoughts from him. And then, when he lay sleeping, will-less and helpless, ever to dream this dream of the devil's own sending—even now, while she sat watching over his son that lay sick to death, to dream ike some monstrous wretch——

'Twas raining, and Kristin could not say rightly what time of night it might be. The boy had been half awake in the day, but he had not spoken. 'Twas not till on in the night that it had seemed to her he slept well and soundly—and she had dared to lie down a little and rest—with Andres in her arms, that she might feel if he moved. Then she had fallen asleep—

The boy looked a tiny, tiny thing, lying alone in the bed; woefully pale he was, but his eyes were clear and his face lit up with smiles when he saw his father. Simon went down on his knees by the bedside, but when he would have taken the little one to his breast, Kristin caught him by the arm:

"Nay, nay, Simon, he is all a-sweat, and 'tis cold here——" She pulled the bed-clothes closer about Andres. "Rather lay yourself in by his side —then will I send hither a woman to watch. I go now to the hall to lie down by Ramborg——"

Simon crept in under the covering. There was a warm hollow where she had lain, a faint, sweet scent of her hair on the pillow. Simon moaned very softly once—then he drew his little son in to him and pressed his face against the soft, damp child-head. He was so small now, he was well-nigh nothing to hold in one's arms, was Andres, but he lay there happily enough, saying a little word ever and again.

Then he took to fumbling and groping in the opening of his father's shirt, put his little clammy hand in on the man's breast, and pulled out the amulet:

"The cock," he said, well pleased; "here he is——"

The day Kristin stood ready to set forth for home, Simon came to her in the women's house and handed her a little wooden box:

"Methought maybe you would like to have this——"

Kristin knew by the wood-carving that 'twas her father's work. Within there lay, wrapped in a bit of glove leather, a small, small golden clasp, set with five emeralds. She knew it at once—Lavrans had used to wear it in his wristband at especial times, when he would go richly clad.

She thanked Simon, but then she blushed blood-red. It had come upon her of a sudden that she had surely never seen her father wear this trinket after she had come home from the cloister in Oslo.

"When gave father this to you——?" She repented her of the question as soon as asked.

"I got it for a parting gift, once when I was riding from the manor——"

"This seems to me to be all too great a gift," she said low, with eyes cast down.

Simon laughed a little as he answered:

"You will have need of many such, Kristin—when the time comes for you to send forth all your sons with bridal gifts——

Kristin looked at him and said:

"You know well, Simon—I deem that the things that have come to you from him—you know that I hold you as dear as though you were his own son——"

"Do you so——?" He touched her cheek lightly with the back of his hand, stroking it downwards, and smiled, a strange little smile, while he spoke as to a child:

"Ay, ay, Kristin, I have marked it——"

IV

S O M E W H A T later in the autumn, Simon Andressön had an errand that took him to his brother's house at Dyfrin. While he was there, a wooer made suit to him for his daughter Arngjerd.

The matter was not concluded, and Simon was somewhat restless and troubled in mind as he rode northward. Maybe he should have struck the bargain, for then the child would have been well settled and he himself quit of all fear for her future lot. Maybe Gyrd and Helga were right —'twas witless in him not to seize the chance, when he got such an offer for this daughter of his—— Eiken was a greater manor than Formo, and Aasmund owned outright more than the third part; he had never thought of wooing for his son a maid of Arngjerd's condition, low-born and kinless on the mother's side, had it not been that Simon held three hides of the manor's land in pledge. They had had to borrow moneys both from the nuns of Oslo and from Dyfrin, when Grunde Aasmundssön had to pay forfeit for manslaughter the second time. Grunde was wild and ungoverned when in drink—yet was he in all other ways an upright and well-natured fellow, said Gyrd, and 'twas sure he would let himself be guided by a clear-witted and kindly woman such as was Arngjerd——

But the thing was, that Grunde was not many years younger than Simon himself. And Arngjerd was young. And naught would serve the folk at Eiken but to have the wedding this coming spring——

A sore remembrance clung to Simon—he thought not on it when he could forbear. But now, since the matter of Arngjerd's wedding had been stirred, 'twas ever thrusting up its head. An unglad man had he been that first morning when he woke at Ramborg's side. He had been, for sure, no more flustered and wanton when he went to bed than a bridegroom should be—albeit to see Kristin amid the brideswomen had made him strange and wild of mood—and Erlend, his new brother-in-law, among the men who brought him up to the loft. And yet when he awoke the next morning and lay looking at the bride that still slept beside him, he had known a sore and bitter shame deep down in his heart—'twas as though he had mishandled some young child——

——Though all the time he knew he might have spared himself that sorrow.

She had laughed when she opened her great eyes.

"Now you are *mine*, Simon"—she pressed her hands on his breast. "My father is your father, and my sister your sister"—and he had grown clammy with fear, for he thought: what if she had felt the heart in his bosom start at her words?

Else was he well content with his marriage—to that he held firmly. His wife was rich, come of high kindred, young and fresh, fair and kindly. She had borne him a daughter and a son—and on that a man sets much price, when he has known what 'tis to have wealth and be without children to hold his estate together when their parents are gone. Two children—and their welfare was assured—and he was rich enough besides to make a good match for Arngjerd——

One other son he would fain have had—ay, 'twould be no grief to him if one, ay or two more children came to Formo. But he saw Ramborg was best pleased to escape those troubles. So 'twas somewhat to the good, that too. For he could not deny it : it made much for comfort in the house when Ramborg was in humour. He could have wished her, indeed, a more even temper. He knew not always how he stood with his wife. And 'twould not have been amiss had things been something better ordered within-doors at his home. But no man can hope that all his measures shall brim over, as the byword has it—— Simon said thus to himself again and again, as he rode homewards——

Now was Ramborg to go to Kruke the week before Clement's Mass*
—it ever livened her up to get from home awhile——

Yet God knew how things were to go there—this time. 'Twas her eighth child that Sigrid went with now. And he had been frighted when he looked in on his sister but now, on the way down—she looked not as though she had the strength for much more——

He had bestowed four thick wax tapers to set before the old picture of Mary Virgin at Eyabu—'twas of a rare wonder-working virtue, folk said —and vowed goodly gifts, if Sigrid came through this with life and health. For how 'twould fare with Geirmund and all the children if their mother died and left them—nay, that was hard to say——

And they lived in good accord, Sigrid and Geirmund. Never had she heard an ungentle word from the man, she said ; never had he left aught undone he deemed would pleasure her. When he saw that Sigrid was pining for the child she had had in her youth by Gjavvald Arnessön, he had had Simon fetch the boy, so that his mother might have him by her for a while. But sorrow and hope deceived were all that Sigrid had reaped from the meeting with that spoiled young spark. Thereafter

* 23rd November.

Sigrid Andresdatter had clung to her husband and the children she had
had by him, as a poor sick sinner to priest and sacrament.

In a fashion she seemed now well content. And this Simon could understand—few men were so good to be with as Geirmund. So tunable
was his speech that, talked he but of the hoof-bound horse they had
passed off on him, 'twas well-nigh like listening to harp-playing.

Ugly and strange of face Geirmund Hersteinssön had ever been, but
at least he had been strong and comely in build of body and limbs; the
best of bowmen, a rare hunter, and ahead of most others in all sports.
But for these three years past he had been a cripple—ever since he came
crawling down the valley from a hunt, on his hands and one knee, dragging the other leg crushed behind him. Now could he not cross the floor
without a staff, nor come up on a horse, nor crawl, without help, round
his steep hill-side fields. Mischance was ever at his heels; the man was
full of strange ways, and little fitted to care for his farm or his own fortunes; 'twas easy for any that had the heart to fool him in his dealings.
But he was deft of hand, a skilful workman in wood and iron, and
shrewd and kind in speech. And when this man took a harp upon his
knee, he could make folk laugh or weep at will with his singing and
playing. Ay, 'twas most like hearkening to the knight that Geirmund
sang of, who played the leaves from off the lindens and the horns from
off the living beasts.

Then would they take up the burden and sing with their father, the
eldest children—and 'twas fairer to hear than all the bells a-ringing in
Bishop's Hamar. The youngest child but one, Inga, could but just walk
when she held to the bench; speak she could not yet, but she hummed
and sang the livelong day, and her tiny voice was fine and clear as a
little silver bell——

They dwelt huddled together in a little, black old hearth-room house,
husband and wife, children and serving-folk. The loft Geirmund had
talked of building all these years 'twas not like he would ever get put up
—hardly had he made shift to get a new barn built in place of the one
burnt two years agone. But none of their many children could the
parents bring themselves to part with. Simon had made offer, each
time he was at Kruke, to take some of them and give them nurture—
Geirmund and Sigrid thanked him, but said no——

None the less, maybe, 'twas she of all his brothers and sisters who had
come off best, thought Simon at times. True, Gyrd said Astrid was well
content with her new husband—they lived far south in Ryfylke, and
Simon had not seen them since they were wed. But Torgrim's sons
wrangled much with their step-father, Gyrd had said——

And Gudmund was marvellous glad and well-content—— But if this
were happiness for a man, Simon deemed 'twere no sin to thank God

their father had not lived to see it—— Hard upon Andres Darre's death, as soon as ever 'twas seemly, Gudmund had drunk the bride-ale with the widow his father would not hear of his mating with. The Dyfrin knight deemed that, if none too good fortune had come to Gyrd and Simon through the rich and comely maids of noble birth and unstained fame he had sought out for his two eldest sons, naught but sheer wretchedness could come of it for Gudmund if his father let him have his witless will. Tordis Bergsdatter was much older than Gudmund. She was indifferent well-to-do and had no children by her first husband. But since then she had had a daughter by one of the priests of Maria Church in Oslo, and folk said, moreover, that she had been over kind to other men besides—to Gudmund Darre among them, when first she came to know him. Ugly as a troll she was, and, for a woman, foulmouthed and rough of speech, deemed Simon—but she was quick and witty, of good understanding and well humoured—he himself would have liked Tordis well enough, he knew—if only she had not married into their kin. But Gudmund throve so, 'twas uncanny to look on him; he was near as fat and heavy now as Simon himself—and 'twas not Gudmund's nature so to be; in youth he had been slender and comely. He had grown so lazy and lumpish that Simon's hands itched to thrash the fellow, each time he saw him. A moonstruck calf had Gudmund been all his days, truth to tell—and that his children took their wits from their mother and their looks from him was, after all, a piece of luck in ill luck—— But Gudmund throve——

So there was no need for him to vex himself as he did for that brother's sake. And in a way 'twas needless too that he should grieve so for Gyrd—— Yet each time he went home to his father's manor and saw how things stood there, it jarred upon him so that 'twas with a right sore heart he rode away——

They prospered greatly—was not that brother-in-law of his brother, Ulf Sakseson, in the King's full grace and favour now?—and he drew Gyrd Andresson along with him into the ring of men who had most power and profit in the land. But Simon misliked the fellow—and he felt that Gyrd liked him not either. Unwillingly and ungladly Gyrd of Dyfrin went the way his wife and her brother would have him go—to win a little peace at home.

Helga Saksesdatter was a troll—— But most like 'twas still more those two sons of his that made Gyrd look so grief-worn nowadays. Sakse, the elder, was a good sixteen winters old by now—— And wellnigh every single night his body-servant had to drag the whelp to bed, dead drunk. He had drunk wits and health away already—like enough he would drink himself to death ere he won to a grown man's age. And 'twould scarce be a great loss—Sakse had got himself a bad name in the

country-side, young as he was, for an overweening churl. That was the
mother's darling; Gyrd loved the younger, Jon, the most: and 'twas
true he had much more of the turn of mind that might have made him
an honour to his kin, if only he had not been—ay, he was somewhat misshapen, high-shouldered, and wry-backed. And then he had some inside stomach evil—could brook no other meat than milk gruel and
bannocks——

In his loving-kindness for his own kin Simon Andressön had ever
found a kind of secret refuge when his own life seemed to him—ay, out
of gear, or whatever one might call it. If aught went awry with him, it
touched him much less nearly if he could call to mind his brothers' and
sisters' fortune and prosperity. Had things but been at Dyfrin as they
were in his father's time—when peace, content, and well-being ruled at
the manor—'twould have done much, Simon thought, to ease his hidden unrest. 'Twas as though his own life-roots were twined in with
those of his kindred, somewhere deep down in the darksome earth.
Every blow that struck one of them, every ill that sucked the marrow of
any, was felt by all——
With Gyrd and him assuredly it had been so—at least in old days. He
knew not so surely if Gyrd felt so now——
This eldest brother—and Sigrid—had been most dear to him of all.
He minded—when a growing lad: he would sit and gaze at his youngest
sister till he joyed in her so that he *must* do something to show it. So he
would begin nagging at her, tease and fret her, pluck at her plaits, and
pinch her arms, for it was as though he could show his love in no other
wise and not be ashamed. All this bickering between them had to be,
else had he been too shamefaced to give her all his hidden store of good
things, or to join the little maid in his games, when he built mills in the
beck, made houses for her, or cut willow whistles for the girls in spring-
time——
Like a burnt-in brand mark was his memory of the day when first he
knew the whole truth of her mischance. The winter through he had
watched Sigrid grieving well-nigh to death over her dead groom—but
more he saw not. Then came a Sunday towards the spring—he stood on
the balcony at Mandvik, vexed that the women were so late of coming—
out in the yard stood horses decked and saddled for church, and the men
had waited long. At length he grew wroth and went in to the women's
house. Sigrid still lay abed—wondering, he asked if she were sick. His
wife was sitting on the bed-edge—a tremor passed over her gentle, faded
face as she looked up: "Sick is she truly, the poor child—but yet more
afraid I trow—of you—and of all her kindred—how you will take
this——"

His sister shrieked aloud, and threw herself headlong over Halfrid's lap, clinging to her, twining her thin, bare arms about her brother's wife—— Her scream cut Simon so to the quick, it seemed his heart grew grey and bloodless. Her grief, her shame, so pierced him through that no feeling was left in him—and then came fear, and he grew wet with sweat—— Their father, what would he do with Sigrid now——

His dread was such that, as he struggled towards his home in Rauma-rike over roads deep in slush, the man with him, knowing naught of the matter, began at last to jest at his lighting down so often. For long now he had been a full-grown wedded man, yet fear so gripped him as he thought on the meeting with his father, that his bowels turned to water——

And his father had spoken scarce a word—— But he had sunk to-gether—as though lightning-struck. It befell yet, sometimes, that Si-mon, when dropping into sleep, would see it all again, and all at once start broad awake. His father, sitting swaying, swaying, his head bowed down upon his breast; Gyrd standing by, his hand upon the high-seat's arm, something paler than his wont, with downcast eyes——

"God be thanked that she was not here when this came out—— At least 'tis well she is with you and Halfrid——" Gyrd had said, when they two were left alone.

'Twas the one time Simon had heard Gyrd say such a word as might betoken that he set not his wife above all other women——

Yet seen it he had—how Gyrd seemed to wither and dwine from the day he was wed with Helga Saksesdatter.

That time they were betrothed—Gyrd's words were ever few—but each time he had seen his bride, Gyrd went about so shining fair that Simon was most strangely moved at sight of him. He had seen Helga long since, Gyrd let Simon understand, but never had speech with her, and never could he have deemed her kinsfolk would give to him a maid so rich and beautiful——

Gyrd Darre's wondrous comeliness in his youth Simon had felt to be, as 'twere, an honour to himself. He was fair with a winsomeness all his own—'twas as though all must see that in this fine and still young man there dwelt goodness, high-mindedness, a brave and noble heart. Then he was wed with Helga Saksesdatter—and then there seemed an end to him——

Silent he had always been—but the two brothers were ever together, and Simon was well able to talk for both. Simon was glib-tongued, passed for a youth of parts, and was hail-fellow-well-met with all—for drink and frolic, for hunting and racing, for all manner of youthful sport, Simon had friends in crowds, all alike dear and near to him. His eldest brother went with him—said little, but smiled his sweet and sober smile, and what few words he dropped seemed all the more weighty——

Dumb as a locked chest was Gyrd Andressön now——

The summer that Simon came home and told his father Kristin Lavransdatter and he of one accord were minded that the bargain concerning them should be undone—Simon knew then that Gyrd had guessed the most that lay behind: that Simon loved his bride; that some weighty cause had brought him to give up his right—and that the cause was such that Simon was heart-scalded within with grief and wrath. Very quietly, Gyrd had counselled his father to let the matter fall. But to Simon he breathed no word that hinted of his knowledge. And Simon felt, could he ever have loved his brother more than he had done all his days, 'twould have been now, for his silence——

Simon *would* be glad and blithe of mood as he rode northwards towards his home. Upon the way he made himself errands to his friends' homes along the Dale, to bear them his greetings and to drink himself merry—and his friends saddled their horses and bore him company to the next manor where their own cronies dwelt. 'Twas good and easy riding in this clear and frosty weather——

The last stretch he rode in the dusk. His ale-born mettle was gone out of him. His men were lusty and loud-voiced—but the master seemed to have run dry of laughter and jest—he must sure be weary.

And now he was home. Andres toddled after, wherever his father stood or went. Ulvhild hung about the saddle-bags—had he brought home any gifts for her? Arngjerd bore forth ale and food; his wife sat down beside him while he ate, chatted and asked of the tidings. When the children had gone to bed, Simon took Ramborg on his knee, while he gave her messages and told her of kin and friends.

'Twas a shameful thing and an unmanly, so he deemed, if he could not be content, so well off as he was in all ways——

The day after, Simon was sitting in the Sæmund's Hall when Arngjerd came in to him bearing meat. He thought 'twere well to speak with her of her suitor while they were alone, and so he told his daughter of his talk with the Eiken men-folk.

Oh, no, she is none too fair, thought the father—he looked up at the young girl as she stood before him. Squat and broad-built she was, with short, coarse-grained, pale face; her grey-yellow hair was bushy; down her back it hung in two big plaits, but straggled above her forehead and hung in tufts about her eyes, and she had a trick of brushing it back every moment.

"It must be as you will, father," she said quietly, when he was done speaking.

"Ay, you are a good child, I know; but what think you yourself of this?"

"Nay, I think nothing. You must judge for me, dear father."

"'Tis thus, Arngjerd—'twould please me well for you to go free for some years yet—from child-bearing and household cares and pains—all such things as fall to women's lot when first they wed. But I have thought that maybe you think long till you have a house of your own and can be your own mistress——?"

"I am in no haste," said the girl, smiling a little.

"You know that, were you to wed at Eiken, you would have your rich kinsfolk near by—bare is back without brother behind it"—he saw a little gleam in Arngjerd's eyes, and her sly smile. "I mean Gyrd, your uncle," he said quickly, somewhat put out.

"Ay, I deemed well you meant not my kinswoman, Helga——" and they both laughed.

Simon's heart grew warm—in thankfulness to God and Mary Virgin, and to Halfrid, who had brought him to own this daughter of his. When it chanced that they laughed together thus, he and Arngjerd, he needed not any other proof that she was his own.

He rose and dusted off some flour she had got on her sleeve: "And your wooer—what think you of the man?" he asked.

"Oh! I like him, the little I have seen of him—and 'tis well not to hearken to all that's said—— But you must judge for me in this, father——"

"Then shall it be as I have said. Aasmund and Grunde can wait a while—we shall see if they are still of the same mind when you are somewhat older—— For the rest, you know well, my daughter, you have freedom to choose yourself whom you shall wed, so far as you have wit to judge of your own good. And of wit you have no lack, Arngjerd——"

He put his arms around her. She blushed when her father kissed her —and Simon bethought him it must be many a long day since last he had done this. He was not, for the most part, a man who feared to fondle his wife in the light of day, or romp with his children. But 'twas ever as in play—and Arngjerd—— It came home to Simon of a sudden that here on Formo this young daughter was the only being he spoke with in earnest now and then——

He went over and pulled the stopping from out of the slit in the south wall. Through the little hole he gazed out over the Dale. There was a southerly draught in the air, and below, where the hills met and hemmed in the sight, big grey clouds were rolling up. When a beam of sunlight broke through, all colours shone out, rich and clear. The mild weather had licked away the pale grey rime—the plough-lands were brown, the fir woods blue-black—and farthest up, along the treeless hill-brows, clothed with moss and lichen, the light streamed yellow-gold.

Simon felt as though there were a marvellous virtue to be drawn from the autumn wind out there and the fitful brightness over the country-side. Should there come rain in plenty at All Hallows' Mass, the streams might well have water for the mills, at least till on near Yule: and 'twould be worth while sending men to the hills to gather moss. Such a dry autumn had it been—the Laagen ran shrunk and little 'twixt frets of yellow gravel and whitened stones.

Here, northward of the parish, 'twas only Jörundgaard and the priest's farm that had mill-houses on the river. He was loth to pray for leave to grind at Jörundgaard—were't but that the whole parish doubt-less went thither with their corn. For Sira Eirik took toll for grinding. And folk deemed, besides, he got to know too well what corn they had—he was so greedy for his tithes. But Lavrans had ever let folk grind at his mill without price, and Kristin would have things go on as in his time——

The slightest thought of her, and there came a sick, strained trem-bling round his heart——

'Twas the day before Simon's and Jude's Mass*; he had ever been wont to go to shrift that day. 'Twas to commune with himself, to fast and pray, that he was sitting here in the Sæmund's-hall to-day, whilst the house-carls threshed in the barn——

It took no long time to bring to mind his sins—he had sworn, told cock-and-bull tales to folk that asked of things that concerned them not; there was the reindeer he had shot long after he had seen by the sun that the sabbath was begun; and he had hunted a Sunday morning while folk down in the parish were at mass——

What had newly befallen whilst the boy lay sick he might not and he dared not name. But 'twas the first time in his life that, unwillingly, he kept secret a sin from his parish priest. He had thought much on it, and it weighed much on his heart. A deadly sin it must sure be—whether he had trafficked with sorcery, or as much as lured another on to do the like——

Neither could he find in his heart to repent it—when he thought that but for this his son had surely lain now in the earth. But he was all the time cast down and fearful—spying to see whether the child was changed at all since that night. He deemed not he could see aught——

He knew it happened with many kind of fowl and wild beasts—if hand of man had lain upon their eggs, or their young, the parents would

* 28th October.

have naught more to do with them, but turned from their offspring. A man, who had from God the light of reason, could not do the like—with him now things were rather so that, when he took his son to his arms, he felt scarce able to let the child out of his hands again, so fearful had he grown for Andres. But none the less he could understand how 'twas the heathenish, unthinking brutes took such a misliking for their own brood once they had been *touched*. He, too, felt as though his child had been in some way soiled——

Yet he repented not—wished not that the thing had not been done. But he would that it had been another than Kristin.—'Twas hard enough for him, at all rates, to have these folk living in the parish——

——Arngjerd came in—to ask after a key. Ramborg thought not she had had it back again since her husband had the use of it.

The housekeeping on this manor of his was growing worse and worse—— Simon remembered he had given the key back to his wife; 'twas before he set off southward, too—— "Ay, then I shall find it, surely," said Arngjerd.

She had such a good smile—and wise eyes—and she was none so ill-favoured either, thought her father. Her hair was goodly, and when she let it flow loose on holy-days and feast days, 'twas thick and bright.

Erlend's bastard daughter had been fair enough—and naught but mischance had come of that——

But Erlend had had that daughter by a fair and well-born woman. 'Twas like Erlend had never cared to cast his eyes on such an one as Arngjerd's mother. He had flung on his haughty way through the world—and, where he went, proud and comely ladies and maidens had stood arow, proffering him love and adventure——

His own one sin in that sort—his boyish pranks while in the King's household he counted not—a little more nicety about that sin had not been amiss, if indeed he must needs wrong his good and noble wife—— 'Twas not as if he had even looked much at the woman, Jorunn—he could not so much as bring to mind how 'twas he first came to make too free with the wench. He had been abroad at merry-makings that winter with friends and acquaintance, and when he came home to his wife's manor, there sat the wench to see to it that he came to bed without setting the place afire.

No more glorious than so had *that* adventure been.

——All the less had he deserved that the child should promise so fairly and bring him so much gladness—— But he ought not to harbour such thoughts now—he should be thinking on his confession——

As Simon took his way home from Romundgaard in the dusk, fine rain was falling. He went slantwise across the fields. In the last wan rays of daylight the stubble gleamed pale and wet. Over by the wall of the old bath-house something small and white lay shining on the slope. Simon went thither and looked. 'Twas the shards of the French bowl that was broken that day in the spring—the children had laid the table with them on a board set upon two stones. Simon reached out with his axe and tumbled the whole down the bank——

He was vexed with himself the next moment. But he cared not to have that evening called to his mind.

To make some little amends for keeping back a sin, he had spoken to Sira Eirik of those dreams. Ay, and because too he felt a need to ease his heart of *that* at least. He stood ready to go—when it came upon him of a sudden—he must speak of this thing. And this old, half-blind priest had been his ghostly father these twelve years and more——

So he went back and knelt again at Sira Eirik's knees.

The priest sat unmoving till Simon had said his say. Then he spoke—his mighty voice came aged and veiled now from out the everlasting twilight—Sin it was not. Each member of the Church militant must be proven in battle with the enemy; therefore did God suffer the devil to beset a man with manifold temptations. So long as a man threw not away his weapons—so long as he forsook not the standard of his Lord, nor, open-eyed and in privity with the foe, yielded to the visions that unclean spirit would beguile him with—so long such sinful promptings were not sin——

"Nay!" Simon was shamed by the sound of his own voice.

Yielded he *never* had. He was tortured, tortured, tortured by them. When he awoke, having dreamed these sinful dreams, he felt as though he himself had been abused the while he slept.

Two stranger horses stood tied to the fence when he came into the courtyard. They were Erlend Nikulaussön's Soten and Kristin's riding-horse. He shouted to the horse-boy—why had they not been stabled? The strangers had said there was no need, the fellow answered sulkily.

He was a lad who had but now taken service with Simon, since he had come home—he had served at Dyfrin before. There all things must go now as 'twere in knightly fashion; Helga had had her way in that. But if this lout of a Sigurd deemed, because he, Simon, chose rather to talk cheerly and jestingly with his folk, and would sometimes suffer a pert answer from a serving-man, that, here at Formo, anyone might answer the master back, the devil was in it—— Simon was starting to rate the fellow soundly—but he caught himself up; had he not even now come from shrift? Jon Daalk would have to take this new-comer in hand, and teach him that good country breeding was no more to be set at naught than the courtly ways of Dyfrin——

So he did but ask, mildly enough, if Sigurd had but just come out of the mountain this year, and bade him put the horses in. But he was vexed——

The first thing that met his eyes, as he stepped into the hall, was Erlend's laughing face—the light from the taper on the board fell straight upon him, where he sat on the bench, and warded off Ulvhild, who was kneeling beside him, seeking to scratch him, or somewhat of the kind—she was clawing with her hands at the man's face, laughing till she hiccoughed——

Erlend sprang up and would have put the child aside, but she clung to his coat-sleeve and hung on his arm, as he came across the floor straight and light-footed, to greet his brother-in-law. She kept on teasing about something: Erlend and Simon could scarce come to speech.

Her father bade her, somewhat harshly, to go with the serving-women out to the kitchen—they were just done setting the board. When the little maid answered him back, he grasped her by the arm and dragged her away from Erlend.

"There then——!" Erlend took a lump of resin from his mouth and stuffed it into the child's. "Take it then, Ulvhild, blossom-cheek!—that daughter of yours, brother-in-law," said he, laughing, as he looked after the child, "will scarce be so biddable as Arngjerd!"

Simon had not been able to refrain him from telling his wife how well Arngjerd took this matter of her wedding. But it had not been his intent that she should speak of it to the Jörundgaard folk. 'Twas unlike Ramborg too—he knew that she loved Erlend but little. He liked it not—liked not that Ramborg had talked of this matter, liked not that she was so unstable, nor that Ulvhild, young child as she was, seemed so fond on Erlend—like most of the tribe of women——

He went and welcomed Kristin; she sat in the corner by the fireplace, with Andres in her lap. The boy had grown right loving with his mother's sister, since she had nursed him in the autumn when he lay gathering strength after his sickness.

Simon saw they must have some errand to him, since Erlend had come thus. 'Twas not often he darkened the doors of Formo. Simon could not but own that Erlend bore himself well in a case that was none too easy—things having come to be as they were betwixt the brothers-in-law. Erlend held himself aloof from the other as much as he well could, but they met as often as was needful, that no talk of unfriendliness betwixt the kinsmen should get about in the country-side, and when they met, 'twas as the best of friends; Erlend was quiet, and held back somewhat when they were together, yet was his bearing free and un-abashed.

When the food had been cleared from off the board and ale set forth, Erlend spoke:

"Methinks you will wonder at my errand, Simon—we are here to bid you and Ramborg to a bride-ale feast with us——"

"Nay, sure, you jest? I knew not that you had folk of age to marry on your manor?"

"That is as a man takes it, brother-in-law. 'Tis Ulf Haldorssön——"

Simon smote his thighs:

"Nay, now shall I hear next that my plough-oxen are to calve at Yule!"

"Never call Ulf a plough-ox," said Erlend, laughing. "It seems the mischief is that the man has been all too forward——"

Simon whistled. Erlend laughed again, and said:

"Ay, you may believe I scarce could trust my own ears when they came in on us to-day, the Herbrandssöns from Medalheim, and made claim that Ulf should wed their sister."

"Herbrand Remba's——? But they are but young lads—their sister cannot be so old that Ulf——?"

"She has twenty winters to her score. And Ulf is nearer the fifties. Ay." Erlend had grown grave. "You understand, Simon—they must account this no great match for Jardtrud; but 'tis the better choice of two bad ones, for her to wed him. Though, 'tis true, Ulf is a knight's son and a well-to-do man—he has no need to seek his bread in another man's house. But he came with us, for that he would rather dwell with us, his kinsfolk, than live upon his own farm in Skaun—after what had come and gone——"

Erlend fell silent a little while. His face grew soft and winning. Then he spoke again:

"Now, we are minded, Kristin and I, to hold this wedding in every wise as though he were our brother. 'Tis our intent that Ulf and I shall ride south to Medalheim a-wooing, this coming week. For appearance' sake, you understand. And now I had thought to crave a boon of you, brother-in-law—— I know, Simon, that I owe you much already. But Ulf is but ill liked here in this country-side. And you stand so high with folk that few men are your fellows—while I myself——" he shrugged his shoulders and laughed a little. "Will you do us this friendship, Simon: to ride with us and be spokesman for Ulf?—he and I have been com-rades since ever we were boys," said Erlend, beseechingly.

"That will I, brother!" Simon had gone red in the face—at Erlend's open-hearted speech he felt himself grow strangely abashed and pitiful. "All I can do to do honour to Ulf Haldorssön, that will I gladly do."

Kristin was still sitting over in the corner with Andres—the boy had set his heart on having his aunt undress him. Now she came forward into the light—the child sat half-naked on her arm, clasping her round the neck.

"This is kindly done of you, Simon!" said she, low, holding out her hand. "For this we thank you, all of us——"

Simon held her hand a moment, loosely:

"Nay, Kristin—— I ever liked him, Ulf—be sure, I do this gladly ——" He reached up to take his son, but Andres feigned coyness, and kicked at his father with his little naked feet, laughing and clinging to the woman.

Simon listened to the two while he sat talking with Erlend of Ulf's money affairs. The boy was in a fit of laughter all the time—she knew so many little chants and nursery jingles; and she laughed along with him, cooingly soft and gentle, deep down in her throat. Once, when he glanced their way, she had twisted her fingers into a kind of winding stairs, and Andres' fingers were folk that walked up them. At last she got him to his cradle, and set herself down by Ramborg. The sisters chatted together, whispering——

'Twas true enough, he thought, when he had lain down that evening —he had liked Ulf Haldorssön always. And since that winter in Oslo, when, together, they had striven to help Kristin, he had felt, in a fashion, knit to the man in a bond of fellowship. Naught else ever crossed his mind than that Ulf was his equal—a great man's son; and that he had no lawful footing amid his father's kin, being gotten in whoredom, made Simon yet more heedful in his dealings with Ulf— somewhere deep down in his own heart there dwelt ever a prayer for Arngjerd's welfare. Else was this none too seemly a matter for a man to be mixed with—an ageing man and a young girl like this.—Ay, well, if Jardtrud Herbrandsdatter had tripped when she was at the Thing last summer, it touched not him—he was no king to these folks, and Ulf was a near kinsman to his brother-in-law.

Unasked, Ramborg had proffered to help Kristin and to wait at the wedding-feast. He deemed this kindly done of her. When aught of weight was toward, Ramborg ever showed what manner of folk she came of. Yes, truly! Ramborg was kind——

v

T H E day after Katrine's Mass * Erlend Nikulaussön held his kinsman's wedding with great state and pride. Many good folk were come to-

* 25th November.

gether—Simon Darre had cared for that; he and his wife had many
friends in the parishes all about. Both the priests from Olav's Church
were there, and Sira Eirik blessed the house and bed—this was counted
an honour, for Sira Eirik said mass now on high holy-days only, and
rendered ghostly service to some few folk who had been his penitents
these many years. Simon Darre read out the deed concerning Ulf's
extra-gift and morning-gift to the bride; Erlend spoke right lovingly
to his kinsman over the board; Ramborg Lavransdatter, along with her
sister, played hostess at the feasting and helped to undress the bride
in the loft.

Yet was it no rightly merry bridal. The bride was of an old and
honoured yeoman stock here in the Dale; her kin and neighbours could
in no wise deem she had made a fitting match, since she must put up
with a stranger to the country-side, and one who served in another
man's house, albeit a kinsman's. Neither Ulf's birth—son of a rich
man and a knight by his serving-wench—nor his kinship with Erlend
Nikulaussön, did the Herbrandssöns seem to count for any great
honour——

Nor seemed it that the bride herself was over well pleased with what
she had made of things. Kristin seemed much disheartened when she
spoke to Simon of it—he had an errand to Jörundgaard a few weeks
after the wedding. Jardtrud was plaguing her man to move to his
estate in Skaun—she had said in Kristin's hearing, weeping bitterly, she
deemed it the worst that could befall, that her child should be pointed
at for a serving-man's son. To that Ulf had answered naught. The
newly-married folk dwelt in the house that had been called the steward's
house ever since Jon Einarssön abode there, before Lavrans bought
the whole of Laugarbru and moved him thither. But this name was not
to Jardtrud's liking. And she was wroth because she must keep her
cows in Kristin's byre—she feared, belike, that folk might think she was
Kristin's handmaid. The mistress deemed this was but reason—she
must have a byre built for the steward's house, if so be Ulf did not flit
to Skaun with his wife. And maybe that would be the best—he was not
so young but that he must find it hard to change his way of life; maybe
'twould come easier to him in a new place——

In this Simon thought she might well be right. And Ulf was ill liked
in the country-side. He hid not his scorn of the Dale and all its ways.
Good, hard-working husbandman as he was, there were many things
on this side of the land that he had no skill of—he reared more cattle
in the autumn than he could feed through the winter—and when the
beasts fell dead, or when, on towards spring, he had, after all, to kill
off part of the half-starved brutes, he grew angered, and would blame
it on his being unused to the cottar ways of this country-side, where,

as early as Paul's Mass,* folk must begin stripping bark to feed to their beasts.

Another thing was this: in the Trondheim country the custom 'twixt landlord and tenant had come to be that the landlord took for rent such goods as most he needed, hay, hides, meal, butter, or wool, even though at lease time they had agreed for some especial ware, or a money rent. And, furthermore, 'twas the landlord or his bailiffs that fixed the worth of rent-goods, as betwixt ware and ware, much as seemed good to them. But when Ulf came on Kristin's leaseholders with claims like these, folk called it high-handed and grossly unlawful—as, truly, it was—and the tenants made complaint to the mistress. She set Ulf right, soon as she heard of the matter, but Simon knew well that folks blamed not only Ulf, but also Kristin Lavransdatter. He had striven to make it clear, wherever this matter came up, that the mistress had not known aught of Ulf's demands, and that in the country the man came from these were warranted by use and wont. But Simon feared this had availed but little—though none gainsaid him to his face.

So he scarce knew whether to wish that Ulf would stay with her or go. How things would speed with her without this stout and faithful helper he could not think. Erlend was most unfit to take the guidance of the farm, and their sons were all too young. But Ulf had set the parish against her more than enough already—and now, on top of all, he had done wrong to a young maid of well-respected and well-to-do kindred here in the Dale. And yet, God knew, Kristin must toil hard enough even as things were——

Otherwise, too, the Jörundgaard folks were ill placed here. Erlend himself, 'twas sure, was no better liked than Ulf. If Erlend's head man and kinsman set folks on edge with his overweening ways, the master's easy-going, somewhat lazy bearing was yet more galling. For sure, it never crossed Erlend Nikulaussön's mind that he set folks against him—he seemed not to think but that, rich or poor, he was what he ever had been, and never dreamed that for *that* any man could call him haughty. He had plotted to raise rebellion against his King—he, Magnus' kinsman and vassal, and sworn to his service; and these same plans he had brought to naught by his own witless folly—and yet it seemed no thought ever came to him that in the eyes of any, by reason of these things, he might be brand-marked with the name of nithing. Simon could not mark, indeed, that Erlend thought much at all——

He was not easy to make out: when one sat talking with him, he was far from lacking wit, so Simon thought; but 'twas as though it never came to his mind to take to himself the wise and worthy things he often said. 'Twas no wise possible to bear in mind that this man

* 15th January.

would soon be old—might have had well-grown children's children
this long time past. When one marked him nearly, 'twas plain to be
seen that his face was furrowed and his hair sprinkled with grey—and
yet he and Nikulaus together were more like two brothers than father
and son. He was straight and slender, as when first Simon saw him,
his voice as young and full of tone. He went about among folk free and
self-assured as ever, with that somewhat of lazy grace in his bearing——
With strangers he had ever kept himself somewhat quiet and retired
—had let others seek him, rather than sought himself for company,
whether in fortune or mischance. But that none now sought his company Erlend seemed not to mark. And the whole band of esquires and
great yeomen up and down the Dale, close allied by marriage and by
fellowship as they were, waxed wroth over this haughty Trondheim
chieftain, cast into their midst by mischance, who yet reckoned himself
all too high in birth and in *kurteisi* to seek their company.

But in truth what most of all had made bad blood for Erlend Nikulaussön, was that he had dragged down the men of Sundbu with him into
ill-fortune. Guttorm and Borgar Trondssön were under ban of outlawry in Norway, and their shares of the great Gjesling estates, as also
their half part of the udal goods, were forfeit to the Crown. Ivar of
Sundbu had had to buy grace of King Magnus. When now the King
gave the forfeit estates—not without a price, folk said—to Sir Sigurd
Erlendssön Eldjarn, Ivar, and Haavard, the youngest of the Trondssöns, who had not been privy to his brothers' treason, sold their shares
of the Vaage estates to Sir Sigurd, who was cousin to them and to the
Lavransdatters: his mother, Gudrun Ivarsdatter, was sister to Trond
Gjesling and to Ragnfrid of Jörundgaard. Ivar Gjesling moved to
Ringheim at Toten, an estate he had with his wife; 'twas like his
children would find a home there, where were their mother's kin and
udal lands. Haavard still owned much land, but it lay for the most in
Valdres, and now, by marriage, great estates in the Borgesyssel had
come to him. But to the men of Vaage and the northern Dalemen it
seemed a most grievous mischance that the offspring of the old barons
had been parted from Sundbu, where their fathers had lived and ruled
the country-side time out of memory.

——For a short time Sundbu had been in the hands of King Haakon
Haakonssön's faithful baron, Erlend Eldjarn of Godaland in Agder—
the Gjeslings had never been warm friends of King Sverre and his
line, and they had joined with the Duke Skule when he raised revolt
against King Haakon. But Ivar the young had gotten Sundbu back
by barter of lands with Erlend Eldjarn, and had wed his eldest daughter
Gudrun, to him. Ivar's son, Trond, had done his kin no honour in
any wise, but his four sons were comely men, well liked and bold,

and folk took it much to heart that they had lost their father's
seat.

And ere yet Ivar had left the Dale, a mischance befell which woke
yet more grief and wrath amongst the people over the Gjeslings' evil
fate. Guttorm was unwed, but, when Borgar fled, his young wife was
left behind at Sundbu. Dagny Bjarnesdatter had ever been somewhat
weak of wits, and had ever plainly shown that she loved her husband
beyond all measure—— Borgar Trondssön was a comely youth, though
something loose-lived. The winter after he had fled the land, Dagny
fell into a lead in the ice on Vaage lake. Mishap, 'twas called, but folk
knew well that grief and longing had robbed Dagny of the little wit
she ever had, and men pitied with all their hearts the simple, sweet,
fair young woman who had met such an ill death. Thereafter folks'
wrath rose higher yet—against Erlend Nikulaussön, who had brought
all this ill-fortune upon the best folk in the parish. And now, too, 'twas
in all mouths how he had behaved him in the days when he was to wed
Lavrans Lagmandssön's daughter—ay, and she too was a Gjesling,
on the mother's side——

The new master of Sundbu was ill liked, though, for that matter,
none had aught to say against Sigurd himself. But he was a stranger
from Egde, and his father, Erlend Eldjarn, had made foes of every soul
in the country-side who had dealings with him. Kristin and Ramborg
had never met this cousin of theirs. Simon had known Sir Sigurd in
Raumarike—he was near of kin to the Haftorssöns, and they were near
kinsmen of Gurd Darre's wife. But, so tangled as these things were
now, Simon made shift to meet Sir Sigurd as little as might be. He
had no heart now to go to Sundbu; the Trondssöns had been his dear
friends; Ramborg and Ivar's and Borgar's wives had been wont,
each year, to change visits. Sir Sigurd Erlendssön, too, was much older
than Simon Andressön—a man nigh upon the sixties.

Therefore did it seem to Simon Darre, so tangled had all things grown
through Erlend and Kristin's coming to dwell at Jörundgaard, that,
even though their steward's marriage could not be deemed in itself
any great matter, yet 'twas enough to make the coil still worse. 'Twas
not his wont at other times to trouble his young wife with the matter,
if he were hard-set or crossed. But now he could not forbear to speak
somewhat with Ramborg of these things. And 'twas both a wonder and
a joy to him to see how understandingly she spoke of the matter, and
with what a good will she sought to do all she could to help.

She was with her sister at Jörundgaard much more often than had
been her wont, and she quite cast off her sullen bearing toward Erlend;
on Yule-day, when they met upon the church-green after mass, Ram-

borg kissed, not Kristin only, but her brother-in-law too. And ever before she had scoffed sourly at these outlandish tricks of his—at his using to kiss his mother-in-law in greeting and the like.

It flashed through Simon, when he saw Ramborg lay her hands about Erlend's neck—then he might do the like by his wife's sister. But yet —he felt he could not. Besides, he had never taken up this fashion of kissing women of his kin—his mother and his sisters had so laughed at him, if he offered to try it with them at his home-comings when he was a page in the body-guard.

At the Yule-tide feast Ramborg set Ulf Haldorssön's young wife in a high and honourable seat, and showed both to him and to her all the honour befitting a bride and bridegroom. And she betook her to Jörundgaard and was with Jardtrud when she bore her child.

This came to pass a month after Yule—two months before the time —and the boy was still-born. Jardtrud now fretted bitterly—could she have thought that 'twould go thus, she would never have wedded Ulf. But 'twas done now and could not be helped.

What Ulf Haldorssön thought of the whole matter, none could tell— he said naught.

The week before mid-Lent, Erlend Nikulaussön and Simon Andressön rode together southward to Kvam. Some years before he died, Lavrans, along with two other farmers, had bought a small farm in that parish ; the udalmen were now minded to buy it again, but 'twas not wholly clear how the law stood in the matter in that country-side, nor how far the kinsmen of the sellers had claimed their rights in lawful wise. After Lavrans' death, when his estate was parted among his heirs, this farm, and certain other Hall holdings, the title whereto might give cause for suits at law, were left undivided, and the sisters shared between them the revenues therefrom. Therefore it was that both of Lavrans' sons-in-law came now to the meeting in their wives' behalf.

Folks were come together in good number, and, since the tenant's wife and children lay sick in the house, the men were fain to hold their tryst in an old shed that stood in the farm-place. It was tumbledown and leaky, and so folk kept on their fur cloaks. Each man had his weapons lying close by him, and his sword in his belt—no one had a mind to stay here longer than was needful. But a bite of meat they must have ere they parted; so toward nones, when the business had been brought to an end, each man took his wallets, and sat and ate, with the sacks by him on the bench, or before him on the ground— board there was none in the shed.

In behalf of the parish priest of Kvam, his son, Holmgeir Moisessön, had come to tryst. He was a loose-tongued and trustless young man, that few folk liked. But his father was much beloved, and his mother had been of a good kindred; and, besides, Holmgeir was a big, strong fellow, and fiery and swift to fly up at folk; wherefore no one cared to fall out with the priest's son—many, too, deemed him sharp and witty of speech.

Simon knew him but little, and had no liking for his looks—he had a long and narrow, palely freckled face, with short upper-lip, so that the great yellow front teeth peeped out like a rat's. But Sira Moises had been a good friend of Lavrans, and the son, until his father had owned him at law, had for a while been nurtured at Jörundgaard, half as servant and half as foster-son. Therefore had Simon ever been wont to meet Holmgeir Moisessön in friendly wise.

He had rolled a wood-block forward to the hearth, and sat sticking bits of his victuals—roasted thrush and shreds of bacon—on his dagger and heating them at the fire. He had been sick, and had had to get fourteen days' indulgence, he told the others, who sat munching bread and hard-frozen fish, while the savoury smell of Holmgeir's food rose to their nostrils.

Simon was out of sorts—not outright ill-humoured, but somewhat dull and flat. 'Twas no easy matter to make head or tail of the case, and the letters left by his father-in-law were in no wise clear; yet, when he rode from home, he had deemed, none the less, that he had come to a right understanding of them—having compared them with other letters. But when here, at the tryst, he came to hear the testimony of the witnesses and saw the letters that were put in by others, he felt that his view of the matter could not be upheld. Yet for that matter none of the other men were better able to set things straight—even the Warden's sheriff, who was there too, was quite at sea. Some had begun to say that belike the case must go before the Thing—when, of a sudden, Erlend spoke up and prayed that he might see the letters.

Hitherto he had sat and listened, much as though he had no part in the matter. Now 'twas as if he waked up. He read carefully through all the papers, some of them more than once. And thereupon he made plain the whole case, shortly and clearly—the law-books read so and so, and thus were they most commonly understood; the unclear and clumsy wording of the letters must mean either this or that; were the matter to go before a Thing, judgment would fall either thus or thus. Thereafter he put forward a settlement which might well content the udalmen, and yet was not over unfavourable to the present owners.

He stood while he spoke, his left hand resting lightly on his sword-hilt, and holding the bundle of letters carelessly in his right. He bore him as though 'twere he that held the reins in the meeting—but Simon saw that he thought not of this himself. 'Twas thus he had been wont to stand and speak when he held the Warden's Thing in his county —when he turned to one of the others and asked whether 'twere not so, whether they understood what he put forward, he spoke as though he questioned witnesses—not uncourteously, but none the less as though 'twere his part to ask and the others' to answer him. When he was done speaking, he handed the letters to the sheriff, as though the man had been his servant, and sat him down again; and, while the others spoke together, and Simon too had his say to the company, Erlend listened indeed, yet in such wise as though he himself had had no concern in the case. He gave short, clear, enlightening answers when any spoke to him—all the while busy scraping with his finger-nails some grease spots that had come upon the bosom of his coat, settling his belt, drawing his gloves through his hands, and seeming to wait, something impatiently, the ending of the debate.

The others fell in with the settlement Erlend had laid before them, and 'twas one that gave Simon no great cause for miscontent; he could scarce have won aught more in a suit at law.

But he was out of heart. He deemed himself 'twas childish beyond measure that he should be vexed for that his brother-in-law had understood the case, and he himself had not. It was but reason that Erlend should have more skill in making plain the words of the law and clearing up the drift of unclear letters, since it had been the man's office to make inquiry and guide folk aright in disputed causes. But it had come upon Simon quite unlooked-for: the evening before, at Jörundgaard, when he spoke with him and Kristin of this meeting, Erlend had said no word of what he thought—'twas like he had listened with but half an ear. Ay, 'twas clear that Erlend must be better read in the law than plain farmers—but 'twas as though the law touched not himself, as he sat there guiding the others with careless friendliness—there came to Simon a dim feeling that in one way or another Erlend had never set aught by the law, as a rule to his own life——

And 'twas so strange, besides, that he could stand up thus, quite unabashed. He must know that this turned the minds of all to think who and what he had been, and what his state now was. Simon felt that the others sat and thought upon it—some grew wroth, doubtless, at this man who never list to heed what folk deemed of him. But no one said aught. And when the blue-frozen clerk, that was with the Warden's sheriff, sat him down and took the writing-board upon his knees, he kept all the time asking of Erlend, and Erlend spelt out for him what to write, playing the while with some straws he had picked from off the floor, twining them round his long, brown fingers and plaiting them to a ring. When the clerk was done, he reached forth the parchment to

Erlend; and he cast the straw ring on the fire, took the deed, and read it half aloud:

"To all men to whose ears or sight this deed may come, send Simon Andressön of Formo, Erlend Nikulaussön of Jörundgaard, Vidar Steinssön of Klaufastad, Ingemund and Toralde Björnssöns, Björn Ingemundssön of Lundar, Alf Einarssön, Holmgeir Moisessön, God's greetings and their own—— Have you the wax ready?" he asked the clerk, who stood blowing upon his frozen fingers. "Be it known unto you that in the year from our Lord's birth one thousand three hundred and eight-and-thirty, on the Friday before mid-Lent Sunday, we, the aforesaid, met at Granheim in the church parish of Kvam—— . . .

"——We can take the chest, Alf, that stands in the outhouse, and use it for a board." He turned to the sheriff, giving back the deed to the writer.

Simon remembered how Erlend had been whilst he lived and moved among his fellows in the north. Self-assured and bold enough, nothing lacking in that regard—reckless and wanton of tongue—yet ever with somewhat flattering in his ways that was his own; he was in no wise careless what they thought of him, those whom he counted as his fellows and kinsmen. Nay, for he had set much store by the winning of a good report among them.

With a strangely vehement bitterness, Simon felt himself of a sudden one with these farmers of the Dale—whom Erlend held in so low esteem that he cared not to wonder what they thought of him. 'Twas for Erlend's sake he had become one of them—'twas for his sake that he had bidden farewell to the company of rich men and nobles. 'Twas well enough to be the wealthy farmer at Formo—ay, but he could not forget that he had turned his back upon his fellows, his kinsmen and the friends of his youth, because he had gone round amongst them on such a beggar's errand that he could not bear to meet them again—could scarce bear to think on it. For this brother-in-law of his he had as good as defied his King and stepped out of the ranks of guardsmen. To Erlend he had laid himself bare in such wise that the thought of it was more bitter to him than death. And Erlend bore himself to him as though he had understood naught and remembered naught. It recked not this fellow overmuch that he had maimed another man's life——

Just then Erlend spoke to him:

"We must see and be on our way, Simon, if we are to win home to-night—I go now to see to the horses——" Simon looked up, with a strange, sick distaste, at the other's tall, comely form. Under the hood of his cloak Erlend wore a small, black silk cap, lying close around his head and tied beneath his chin—the narrow, dark face, with the great light-blue eyes deep in the shadow of the brows, looked, within it, yet more young and fine.——"And buckle up my wallet the while," said he from the door, as he went out.

The other men had gone on talking of the case. 'Twas strange enough, none the less, said some, that Lavrans should have ordered this matter with so little forethought; the man was wont else to know what he did—he was more skilled than any in the Dale in all that concerned the buying and selling of land.

"Likely 'tis my father who is to blame for this," said Holmgeir Prestesön. "He said himself this morning—had he listened to Lavrans that time, all had been straight and clear. But you know how 'twas with Lavrans—with priests he was ever biddable and meek as a lamb——"

For all that, Lavrans of Jörundgaard was wont to know what was for his own good, said someone.

"Ay, maybe he thought he did so when he hearkened to the priests' counsel," said Holmgeir, laughing; "'tis the part of wisdom, sometimes, even in worldly things—so long as one squints not at the same morsel the Church has set its eyes on——"

Marvellous pious had Lavrans been, for sure, deemed Vidar—he had never spared either goods or cattle when 'twas for the Church or the poor.

"No," said Holmgeir, musingly. "Ay, had I been so rich a man, I too might have been minded to spend somewhat for my soul's peace. But I had not been fain to strew out my goods with both hands, as he did, and go about besides with red eyes and white cheeks each time I had been to the priest and shrived me of my sins—and Lavrans went to shrift each month, he did——"

"Tears of repentance are the Holy Ghost's fair gifts of grace, Holmgeir," said old Ingemund Björnssön; "blessed is he who can weep for his sins in this earthly home; much the easier doth he enter in unto the next——"

"Ay, then must Lavrans be in heaven long ere now," said the other. "So he fasted and mortified his flesh—Good Friday he locked him in the storehouse loft and lashed him with a scourge, I have heard tell——"

"Hold your tongue," said Simon Andressön, trembling with fury; he was blood-red in the face. Whether 'twere true, what Holmgeir said, he knew not. But when he was setting in order his father-in-law's private chests, at the bottom of the book-chest he had found a long, narrow, little wooden box, and in it lay such a scourge as in the cloisters they call a "discipline"; the plaited leather thongs were darkly flecked: it might be with blood. Simon had burned it—with a kind of sorrowful awe: he felt he had come upon something in the other's life which Lavrans had not meant that living soul should know of.

"——Howsoever it be, he talked not of it, I trow, to his serving-lads," said Simon, when he could trust himself to speak.

"Nay, like enough 'tis but a tale that folk made up," answered Holmgeir, mildly. "I trow well he had no such sins to atone for that he should need——" the man smirked a little—"had I lived as virtuous and Christian a life as Lavrans Björgulfssön—and had been wedded to that unglad woman, Regnfrid Ivarsdatter—I had rather wept for the sins I had *not* wrought——"

Simon sprang up and struck Holmgeir hard on the mouth, so that the fellow tumbled backward towards the hearth-place. The dagger fell from his grasp—next moment he clutched it up and rushed upon the other. Simon warded off with the arm his cloak was over, gripped Holmgeir by the wrist, and tried to wrest the dagger from him—while the priest's son struck him blow after blow in the face. Now Simon got a grip round both the other's arms, but on that the youth fixed his teeth in the man's hand.

"Would you bite, dog——?" Simon let go, sprang back a few steps, and tore his sword from its sheath. He thrust at Holmgeir—the young man's body bent backwards, a couple of inches of steel in his breast. Then at once Holmgeir's body sank from off the sword-point and fell heavily, half over the hearth-fire.

Simon threw down his sword and stooped to lift Holmgeir from out the fire—then he saw, just above his head, Vidar's axe lifted for a blow. He ducked down and to the side, caught up his sword again, and was but just in time to strike aside Alf Einarssön the sheriff's blade—whirled round on guard once more against Vidar's axe—when with the corner of his eye he caught a glimpse, behind him, of the Björnssöns and Björn of Lunde thrusting at him with their spears from the far side of the hearth. On this, he drove Alf before him against the further wall, but marked that now Vidar came at him from behind (Vidar had dragged Holmgeir out of the fire; they were cousins, those two) and the carles of Lunde were closing on him round the hearth. He was hemmed in and uncovered on all aides—and amidst it all, with more than enough to do to guard his life, he felt a vague, unhappy wonder that all men's hands should be against him——

——The next instant Erlend's sword flashed between the Lunde men and him. Toralde reeled aside and away, crumpled up against the wall. Quick as lightning Erlend shifted his sword to his left hand and struck Alf's weapon from his grasp, so that it flew clanging across the floor, while at the same time, with his right, he clutched Björn's spear-shaft and bent it down——

——"Get you out," he said to Simon, under his breath, as he guarded his brother-in-law against Vidar. Simon ground his teeth, and rushed inwards to meet Björn and Ingemund. Erlend was at his side, shouting, through the trampling and the clash of arms: "Come out, hear you not—blockhead? Get you towards the door—we must run for it!"

When he saw Erlend meant they should both get out, he drew backwards, fighting, towards the door. They ran through the outer room, and stood fast in the courtyard—Simon a step or two farther from the house, Erlend right in front of the doorway, with his sword half lifted, facing the men who now came crowding after.

For a moment Simon was near blinded—the winter day without was so dazzling bright and clear—under the blue sky the white dome of the fell-top shone golden in the last sunshine; the woods stood smothered with snow and rime. All over the fields was a sparkling and glittering as of gems——

He heard Erlend say:

"'Twill not better this mischance that more men be slain. Let us come back to our wits, good men, and have no more bloodshed. 'Tis ill enough as it is for my brother-in-law to have been a man's bane——"

Simon went forward to Erlend's side.

"Sackless have you slain my cousin, Simon Andressön," said Vidar of Klaufastad—he stood foremost in the doorway.

"Wholly sackless he fell not, I trow. But you know well, Vidar, I shall not shun the reckoning—shall make good the mischief I have wrought you. You all know where you can find me at home——"

Erlend spoke some words more with the farmers: "Alf—how fared it with him——?" He went in with the men.

Simon was left behind, struck strangely speechless. Erlend came out in a little while: "Let us ride now," said he, and went down towards the stable.

"Is he dead?" asked Simon.

"Ay. And Alf and Toralde and Vidar all have wounds—but naught grievous, I trow. He has singed off his back hair, Holmgeir." Erlend had spoken most soberly—now, suddenly, he burst into a laugh: "*Now* is there a rare stink of roast thrush in there, trust me! What the devil— how was't possible you could fall so by the ears in so short a space?" he asked, in great amaze.

A half-grown boy stood holding their horses—neither of the brothers-in-law had brought his henchman with him on this journey.

Both still bore their swords in their hands. Erlend took up a wisp of hay and dried the blood from his. Simon did the like—when he had got off the most of it, he thrust the sword back into its sheath. Erlend scoured his with careful pains, and, at the end, furbished it with the skirt of his cloak. Then he made some little playful passes in the air before him—smiling the while, fleetingly, as at a memory—threw the sword high into the air, caught it again by the hilt, and stuck it into the scabbard.

"Your wounds—we must go into the house, and I will bind them——" Simon said 'twas nothing:

"You are bleeding, too, Erlend!"

"For me there's no fear. My flesh heals up so well. Fat folk ever heal slower, I have marked. And now, in this cold—we have far to ride——"

Erlend got grease and cloths from the tenant on the farm, and dressed the other's wounds with care—they were two flesh-wounds close together in the left breast; they bled much at first, but grievous they were not. Erlend had gotten a scratch from Björn's spear-point on the outer thigh—it must be irksome to ride with, Simon said, but his brother-in-law laughed: it had scarce pierced his leathern hose. He plastered a little grease upon it and bound it well about, against the frost.

It was biting cold. Before they were come down from the hillock where the farm stood, rime began to gather on the horses, and the fur edging on the men's hoods grew white.

"Hoo, hoo!" Erlend shivered. "Would we were home! We must turn in at the farm down here that you may give yourself out the slayer——"

"Is it needful?" asked Simon. "I spoke, you wot, with Vidar and the——"

"'Twere best that you did it," said Erlend. "That you told the tidings here yourself. Let them not have aught they can say against you——"

The sun was behind the ridges now, the evening a pale grey-blue, but still light. They rode along a beck, under birch trees yet more shaggy with rime than the woods around: there was a tang of raw frost fog in the air down here, fit to choke the breath in a man's throat. Erlend grumbled impatiently at the long cold they had had, and at the cold ride that lay before them.

"You have not got your face frost-bit, think you, brother-in-law——?" He peered uneasily in under Simon's hood. Simon chafed his face—frost-bitten 'twas not, but he was somewhat pale as he rode. It set him ill, for his big, fat face was weather-bitten and red-besprinkled, and the paleness spread over it in grey patches and made his hue seem as 'twere unclean.

"Saw you ever a man pitchfork dung with his sword?" said Erlend—he burst out laughing at the thought of it, leaned forward in his saddle and aped the motions "—like yonder Alf—a rare fellow for a sheriff, that! You should have seen Ulf at sword-play, Simon—Jesus Maria!"

Play—ay, now, indeed, he had seen Erlend Nikulaussön at that play. Again and again he saw himself and those men, in the mellay there by the hearth, like peasants hewing wood or pitching hay—Erlend's slender, flashing figure amidst them, his lightning glances, his sure wrist, while he sported with them, swift-thinking, skilled of fence——

'Twas twenty years and more since the time he himself had been accounted one of the first in skill of arms amongst the youth of the bodyguard—when they practised them on the play-green. And from that time on he had had but little use of an esquire's swordcraft.

And here he rode now, sick at heart for that he had slain a man—saw ever Holmgeir's corpse pitch from off his sword down into the fire; had his short, hoarse death-cry in his ears, and saw, again and again, glimpses of the short, furious fight that followed. Heart-sore was he, downcast and mazed—they had turned on him in a single instant to slay him, all those men he had sat with, feeling he belonged to their fellowship—and *Erlend* had come to his rescue——

A coward he had never deemed himself to be. He had hunted down six bears in the years he had dwelt at Formo—and twice he had risked his life as recklessly as well could be. With a slender fir-stem between him and a mad, wounded she-bear, without other weapon than his spear-head and a scant handbreadth of shaft—the peril of the game had not ruffled his sureness of thought and deed and sense. Now, down there in the hut—he knew not whether 'twas fearful he had been—but he had been mazed, his wits had failed him——

And when he sat at home, after that bear-hunt, with his clothes huddled on him as they best would hang, with his arm in a sling, burning with fever, his shoulder stiff and torn, he had felt naught but an overweening joy—things might have gone worse—how, he thought not on overmuch. But now he must think and think, endlessly, how all would have ended had Erlend not come so timely to his help. He had been—not afraid, surely, but strangely dashed. It was the look on the other men's faces—and Holmgeir's dying carcass——

Manslayer he had never been before——

——That Swedish trooper he had cut down—— 'Twas the year King Haakon carried war into Sweden to avenge the dukes' murder. He had been sent out to scout—three men sent with him, and he to be the leader —full blithe he was and proud. Simon remembered that his sword had stuck fast in the trooper's steel head-piece, so that he must twist and wrench it loose; there was a notch in the edge when he looked on it in the morning. He had never thought on that deed with aught but content—there were eight of the Swedes, too—he had got at least a taste of war; that fell not to the lot of all men who marched with the guard that year—— When daylight came, he saw that blood and brains had spurted out over his coat of mail—he had striven to seem lowly and not puffed up while he washed it off——

But 'twas no help to think on that poor devil of a trooper now. No, yonder time was not like this. He could not rid him of a gnawing sorrow for Holmgeir Moissessön.

And this too, that now he owed his life to Erlend. He knew not yet how much that might bring with it. But he felt as though all things must be changed now that he and Erlend were quits——

——On that score they were quits now, ay——

The brothers-in-law had ridden with scarce a word. Once Erlend said:

"Ay, 'twas foolish of you, too, Simon, that you bethought you not to make for the door at the first——

"How so?" asked Simon, something shortly. "Because you were without——?"

"Nay——" there was a little laugh in Erlend's voice. "Ay, that too—though I thought not on that. But out of that narrow door, see you they could not have come at you more than one at a time—— And besides, 'tis wonder often to see how quick folks come to their wits again once they get out beneath open sky. Much do I marvel now that no more than one man was slain."

Once and again he asked after Simon's wounds. The other said he felt them not much—though the truth was they burned sorely enough.

They came to Formo late at night, and Erlend turned in there with his brother-in-law. He had counselled him to write to the Warden, betimes in the morning, of what had befallen, so as to have order taken for a grace-deed* as soon as might be. Erlend might as well make up the letter for Simon that night—doubtless the wounds in his breast would hinder his writing: "And to-morrow you must lie quiet in your bed, I trow, for like enough you will have some touch of wound-fever——"

Ramborg and Arngjerd were sitting up waiting. Because of the cold, they had crept up on the bench against the warm fire-place wall, and had drawn up their feet beneath them—a draught-board lay between them—they looked like two children.

Simon had scarce got a few words said of what had befallen ere his young wife flew to him and flung her arms about his neck. She drew his face down to hers, pressed her cheek to his—and she wrung Erlend's hands so that he said, laughing, he had never deemed Ramborg had such strength of fingers——

Naught would serve but that her husband must sleep in there that night, and she herself sit up by him. She begged this, almost in tears—but on this Erlend proffered to stay there and lie by Simon, if she would send a man north to Jörundgaard with a message—'twas late after all

* See Note I.

for him to ride home: "and 'twere pity Kristin should sit up so late in this cold—she, too, waits for me always herself; good wives are you Lavransdatters——"

While the men ate and drank, Ramborg sat nestled close to her husband. Simon patted her arm and hand now and again—he was much moved, but a little put out as well, at her showing so much love and fearfulness. Being that 'twas now Lent, Simon was sleeping alone in the Sæmunds hall, and when the men went over there, Ramborg went with them and set a great kettle with honey-ale by the stone hearth-brim warm.

The Sæmunds hall was a little, ancient hearth-room house, warm and wind-tight—the timber was so massy that there were but four logs in the wall. 'Twas cold there now, but Simon threw a mighty armful of pine roots upon the fire and hunted his dog up on to the bed—it could lie there and warm it up for them. They drew the block-chair and the settle right up to the hearth and made themselves snug, for they were chilled through and through from their journey, and their meal in the great hall had but half thawed them.

Erlend wrote the letter for Simon. Then they set about loosing their clothes—as Simon's wounds began to bleed again if he moved his arms much, his brother-in-law helped him to get his doublet over his head and his boots from off his feet. Erlend himself halted on his wounded leg a little—'twas stiff and tender from the ride, he said, but naught to matter. And they settled them down by the fire again, half undressed— 'twas so good and warm here now, and a plenty of beer in the kettle yet.

"You take this over-hardly, brother-in-law, I see well," said Erlend once. They had been sitting dozing, gazing into the fire. "He was none so great a loss, this Holmgeir——"

"'Twill not seem so to Sira Moises," said Simon, low. "He is an old man and a good priest——"

Erlend nodded gravely.

"'Tis a grievous thing to have made an enemy of such a man. And you know well I often have errands in that parish——"

"Oh!—but, when all is said, the like may hap so easily—to any one of us. Like enough they will doom you to pay ten or twelve marks in gold for weregild. Ay, and you know too Bishop Halvard is a stern lord, when he is to shrive a man of a deed of blood—and the boy's father is one of his priests. But you will come off not much the worse from both reckonings——"

Simon said naught. Erlend went on again:

"I shall have to make amends for wounding, I trow"—he smiled to himself—"and I hold no more of Norway's ground for my own than that farm in Dovre——"

"How great a farm *is* Haugen?" asked Simon.

"I mind not rightly—it stands written in the deed. But the folks who farm the land pay only some hay for rent. None will dwell on it—the houses are nigh in ruins, they tell me—you know folk say Aashild and Sir Björn walk there in death——

——"But at the least I wot well that for this day's work I shall have much thanks of my wife. Kristin loves you, Simon, as though you were her own brother."

Simon's smile could scarce be marked, where he sat in shadow. He had thrust the block-chair back a little and screened his eyes with his hand from the heat of the blaze. But Erlend joyed in the fire like a cat—he sat close in to the hearth, leaning into a corner of the settle, with one arm over the back, and his wounded leg stretched out over the other arm-rest.

"Ay, she spoke so fairly of it here, one day in autumn," said Simon in a while; 'twas well-nigh as though his voice had a mocking sound. "She showed here last autumn, when our son was sick, that she is a faithful sister;" he spoke gravely now—but then again came the little tone of mocking. "Now, Erlend, have we kept faith one with another, even as we swore that time we laid our hands together in Lavrans's and vowed to stand by each other like brothers——"

"Ay," said Erlend, simply. "I am glad of this day's work; I too, brother Simon." For a time they both sat silent. Then Erlend, as though provingly, stretched out a hand towards the other. Simon took it; they crushed each other's fingers hard, let go, and shrank back shamefacedly, each into his seat.

At length Erlend broke the silence. He had sat long with his chin in his hand, staring into the hearth-fire, where now only one little flame and another flickered, flared up, flapped a little, and played along the charred sticks that snapped and fell to pieces with small brittle sighs. Soon naught would be left of the blaze but black charcoal and embers.

Erlend said very low:

"So high-heartedly have you borne you towards me, Simon Darre, that I deem few men could be your like. I—I have not forgotten——"

"Be still!—you know not, Erlend—— God in heaven alone knows," he whispered, in fear and distress; "—all that harbours in a man's mind——"

"It is so," said Erlend, as low and earnestly. "We need, all of us, I trow—that He judge us with His mercy——"

"——But man must judge man by his *deeds*. And I—I——God reward you, brother-in-law!"

After that they sat in dead silence—dared not to move lest they be put to shame.

Till, of a sudden, Erlend let his hand fall upon his knee—a fiery blue ray flashed from the stone of the ring he bore on his right forefinger. Simon knew he had had it of Kristin when he came out from his prison-cell.

"But you must mind, Simon," said he softly, "there goes an old word: Many a man wins what is meant for another, but another's lot none may win."

Simon lifted his head with a sudden start. Slowly he grew blood-red in the face—the veins in his temples stood out like dark, twisted cords.

Erlend glanced at the other—and withdrew his eyes swiftly. Then he too reddened—a strangely fine and girlish flush spreading under his dark skin. He sat still, shy and abashed, with mouth a little open, like a child.

Simon rose vehemently and went over to the bed:

"You had liefer lie outermost, I trow"; he tried to speak evenly and calmly, but his voice shook.

"Nay—be it as you will," said Erlend, haltingly. He rose up to his feet as in a maze. "The fire?" he asked. "Shall I rake it under——?" he began to shovel ashes over.

"Enough now—come and lie down," said Simon, as before. His heart beat so, he could scarce speak.

In the dark, Erlend crept, silent as a shadow, in among the skins at the outer edge, and lay down, still as a beast of the forest. To Simon it seemed that to have that other by him in his bed must stifle him.

VI

EVERY year, in Easter-week, Simon Andressön held an ale-feast for the folk from all the parish. They came to Formo the third day after the mass and tarried there till Thursday.

Kristin had never had much delight in these feastings. When mirth and merry-making were afoot, both Simon and Ramborg seemed to deem the more bustle and uproar there was at the feast the better was it. Simon ever prayed the guests to bring their own children, and their serving-folk with their children, as many as might be away from home. The first day things went quietly and peacefully; the great folk and the elders led the talk, while the youth listened and ate and drank, and the small children were for the most in another house. But on the second the host went about from early morning and egged on the young and unstaid folk and children to drink and make merry, and 'twas not long then, for the most part, till the mirth grew so wild and wanton that wives and young maids shrank into the corners and stood there in groups, tittering, ready to run out; while many of the most worshipful housewives gathered in Ramborg's ladies' house, whither already the mothers had carried off the smaller children out of the hurly-burly in the great hall.

But this year Easter had brought wondrous fair spring weather. On the Wednesday, from early morn 'twas so warm and sunny that, the morning meal scarce over, all the company swarmed out into the court-yard. Instead of racketing and raising riot, the young folks were soon busy playing ball, shooting at a mark, or hauling on the rope; then began the game of stag, and dancing on the log; after that they got Geirmund and Kruke to pluck his harp and sing—and thereon all, both young and old, were soon footing it in the dance. The snow still lay low on the fields, but the alder woods were brown with blossoms, and the sun shone warm and fair on every bare hill-side; when folks came out after the supper, there was such singing of birds everywhere—and they built a bonfire on the field beyond the smithy and sang and danced till far into the night. Next morning the guests lay long abed; and thus they broke up and took their leaves later than was their use. The folk from Jörundgaard were wont to be the last to leave—and now Simon prevailed on Erlend and Kristin to tarry over the next day—the Kruke folk were to stay the week out at Formo.

Simon had gone up to the highway with the last flock of guests. The evening sun shone so fair over his lands, lying spread out on the hill-slopes; he was warm and of good cheer with the drink and all the junketing, and as he went down between the fences, home to the quiet and easy fellowship that follows when, after a great banquet, a little ring of near kinsfolk are left together, he felt himself gladder and more light of heart than he had been for long.

Down on the fields by the smithy they had set the bonfire a-going again—Erlend's sons, Sigrid's eldest children, Jon Daalk's sons, and his own daughters. Simon hung over the fence awhile, watching them. Ulvhild's holy-day frock flared scarlet in the sun—she ran about dragging branches to the fire—and there she lay her length on the ground! Her father shouted to them, laughing, but they did not hear——

In the courtyard sat two wenches minding the smallest children—they sat close by the bower wall sunning themselves; over their heads the evening light burned like melted gold upon the small glass pane. Simon took little Inga Geirmundsdatter, heaved her high into the air, and set her upon his arm: "Can you sing to-day for your uncle, Inga winsome may—?"; and at that her brother and Andres set upon him, and would be thrown high on loft, they too——

Whistling, he climbed the stairway to the upper hall. The sun shone in so bravely—they had set the door wide. The folk within sat in goodly quiet. Up at the end of the board Erlend and Geirmund bent them over the harp, putting new strings to it; they had the meadhorn beside them on the board. Sigrid lay upon the bed, giving her youngest son the breast; Kristin and Ramborg sat by her; a silver mug stood on the foot-board between the sisters.

Simon filled his own gilded beaker with wine, went to the bed, and drank to Sigrid:

"All folks here have the wherewithal to slake their thirsts, I see, save you, my sister!"

Laughing, she raised herself on her elbow and took the beaker. The little child, disquieted at his meal, burst into a wrathful howl.

Simon sat down on the bench, still whistling softly and hearkening to the others with half an ear. Sigrid and Kristin gossiped of their children; Ramborg sat silent, toying with a little windmill of Andres's. The men by the board fingered the harp-strings to try them—Erlend sang a stave very softly; Geirmund picked out the air on the harp and sang the verse after him—they had such tuneful voices, both of them——

A little after, Simon went out on the balcony, stood leaning against the carven pillar, and gazed around. From the byre came the everlasting hungry bellowing. If this weather would but hold a while, maybe the spring dearth would not last so long this year.

'Twas Kristin who came. He needed not to turn—he knew her light tread. She stepped out and stood by his side in the evening sunlight.

So fair and fine, that she had never seemed to him so fair. And all at once he felt as though, in some wise, he were lifted up, as though he floated in this sunlight—he drew a long breath: suddenly it came upon him—'twas good, 'twas good to live. A rich and golden happiness flooded all his being——

She was his own sweet love—and all the heavy, bitter thoughts he had thought were but as half-forgotten follies. Poor, poor love of mine—could I but do you aught of good. Could you but be glad once more—gladly would I lay down my life, if that might help you——

O ay! for well he saw her lovesome face was worn and aged. Fine, small wrinkles had gathered beneath her eyes, her skin had lost its pure shining—had grown coarser far and sunburned, and she was pale beneath the brown. But to him for sure she would be ever alike fair; for her great grey eyes and her fine, still mouth, and her little round chin—her restful, tempered bearing, too, were the fairest things he knew on earth.

And 'twas good too—once more to see her clad as beseemed a highborn lady—— The thin little silken kerchief but half hid the masses of her yellow-brown hair—the plaits were caught up, so that they peeped forth above her ears—there were streaks of grey in her hair now, but 'twas no matter. And she bore a stately, blue outer robe of velvet, edged with ermine—it was cut so deeply at the bosom, and the arm-slits were so long, that over breast and shoulders it showed no more than the breast-straps of a horse's gear—'twas brave to look on. Underneath, there clung a somewhat, yellow as sand, an under-robe that lay smooth to the body, stood high around her throat and ran down to the wrists. 'Twas buttoned with many small gilded buttons, and they touched him to the heart—God forgive him, all these little gilt buttons gladdened him like the sight of a troop of angels.

He stood, feeling his own heart's strong, quiet beat. Something had slipped from him—ay, like fetters. Evil, hateful dreams—they were but shadows of the night, and now he saw his love for her by light of day, in full sunshine.

"You look at me so strangely, Simon—why smile you so?——"

The man laughed, low and joyously, but did not answer. Out before them lay the Dale, filled with the evening sun's golden glow; flocks of birds twittered and chirruped shrilly in the borders of the woods—then from somewhere deep in the forest a thrush's full, clear song ran out. And here she stood, warmed by the sun, shining in her festal pride—escaped from out the dark, cold house and the coarse, heavy garments reeking of sweat and toil—— Kristin mine, 'twas good to see you thus again——

He took her hand, that lay before him on the railing—lifted it up toward his face: "This ring you bear upon your finger is a fair one!" He turned the finger-ring a little, and laid her hand down again. The hand was chafed and reddened now, and he knew not how he could ever do enough to make it amends—so fair had it been, her long, slender hand——

"'Tis Arngjerd and Gaute," said Kristin. "Those two are quarrelling again——"

From below the loft-balcony came the voices, high and angry. Now the maid broke in with a cry of rage:

"——Ay, mind me of that, you!—meseems 'tis more honour to be called bastard daughter to my father than to be true-born son to yours!"

Kristin turned sharp about and ran down the stairway. Simon, following after, heard the sound of two or three buffets on a cheek. He saw her standing under the balcony holding her son by the shoulder.

The two children stood looking down, red-faced, silent and sullen.

"I see well you know how to behave you to your hosts—you do us honour, forsooth, your father and me——"

Gaute gazed down on the ground. Low and wrathfully he answered his mother:

"She said somewhat—I will not say it again——"

Simon took his daughter by the chin, forced her to look up at him.

Arngjerd grew redder and redder, and dropped her eyelids under her father's look.

"Ay"—she broke away from him—"I minded Gaute that his father was judged nithing and traitor to his King—but first he had called you, father—you, said he, you were the traitor, and you had Erlend to thank that you sat here rich and scatheless, on your own manor——"

"I had deemed you were a grown maid now—would you let you be egged on by a child's chatter, to forget both manners and the dues of kin?"—he pushed the girl from him in wrath, turned to Gaute, and asked, most soberly:

"How mean you, friend Gaute, that I have betrayed your father? I have felt before this that you were wroth with me—now must you say what the cause may be?"

"That know you well!"

Simon shook his head. And then the boy cried out, flaming with fury:

"The letter they broke my father on the rack for, to make him tell who hung their seals below it—*I* saw it. 'Twas I who went off with it and burnt it——"

"Be still!" Erlend burst in amongst them. His face was white to the very lips, his eyes burned.

"Nay, Erlend—'twere best, now, we came at the truth of this. Was my name in that letter then?"

"Be still!" In furious rage his father seized Gaute by the breast and shoulder. "I trusted you—you, my son! If I killed you, 'twere but your due——"

Kristin sprang forward; Simon too. The boy broke loose and clung to his mother. Quite beside himself with passion, he shouted at furious speed, while he hid himself behind the woman's arm:

"I looked on the seals before I burned it—father! I deemed the day might come when I could serve you thereby——"

"God's curse upon you——!" There broke from Erlend's frame a short, dry sob.

Simon, too, had grown pale, and then flushed dark red, with shame for the other. He dared not look towards where Erlend stood—the sight of the man's humiliation seemed to choke him.

Kristin stood as though spellbound—still with her arms about her son to guard him. But, within her brain, thought fitted into thought with lightning speed:

Erlend had had Simon's privy seal in his ward a short time that spring —the brothers-in-law were selling Lavrans's warehouse on Veöy to the Holm cloister-brothers. Erlend had said himself that it might well be this was unlawful, but 'twas like none would question it. He had shown her the seal and said that Simon might well have got him one more fairly graven—all three brothers had had their seals graven with their father's arms, only the legends were diverse. But Gyrd's was graven much finer, said Erlend——

——Gyrd Darre—Erlend had brought her greetings from him, both the last times he came from the south country—— She remembered she had marvelled that Erlend should visit Gyrd at Dyfrin—they had seen each other but the once, at Ramborg's wedding—— Ulf Sakseson was Gyrd Darre's brother-in-law; Ulf had been in the plot——

"You saw wrong, Gaute," said Simon, low and firmly.

"Simon!' Blindly Kristin grasped her husband's hand. "Remember —there are other men besides you who bear that device on their seal——"

"Be still! Would you too——" Erlend tore himself from his wife with a tortured cry and rushed across the courtyard towards the stable. Simon sprang after him:

"Erlend—was it my brother——?"

"And send for the lads—come you after me," cried Erlend back to his wife.

Simon caught him up again in the stable door, seized him by the arm:

"Erlend—was it Gyrd——?"

Erlend answered not—tried to wrench himself free. His face was set and drawn and white as death.

"Erlend—answer me—was my brother with you in the plot?"

"Maybe you would measure swords with me too——" Erlend snarled out the words, and Simon, as they wrestled, felt the other's whole body tremble.

"That you know I will not." Simon loosed his hold and staggered backwards against the door-jamb. "Erlend—for the love of God, that died for us—say if it was so!"

Erlend led Soten out, forcing Simon aside from the doorway. A too forward house-carl brought saddle and bridle; Simon took them and sent the man away; Erlend took them from Simon.

"Erlend—sure you can tell it *now!*—to *me!*" He knew not himself why he should beg thus, as though he were begging for his life. "Erlend —answer me—by Christ's wound-marks, I conjure you—tell me, man!"

"You can go on thinking what you thought," said Erlend, in a low biting voice.

"Erlend—I thought—naught——"

"I *know* what you thought." Erlend swung himself into the saddle. Simon caught the horse by the head-stall; it reared and flung about wildly.

"Let go—or I ride you down," said Erlend.

"Then will I ask Gyrd—no later than to-morrow will I ride south
—by God, Erlend, you *shall* tell me——"

"Ay, you will get an answer from *him*, I doubt not," said Erlend
scornfully—he spurred the stallion, and Simon must needs leap aside.
The other galloped from the manor——

Half-way up the courtyard, Simon met Kristin; she had her cloak
on. Gaute walked by her side, carrying the wallet with their clothes.
Ramborg was with her sister.

The boy glanced up an instant, fearful and at a loss. Then he looked
away. But Kristin fixed her great eyes full upon him—they were dark
with sorrow and anger:

"Could you believe this thing of Erlend—that he could betray you
so?"

"I believe naught," said Simon hotly. "I believed 'twas foolish
babble of that young scamp there——"

"Nay, Simon—I will not have you go with me," said Kristin, low.

He saw that she was unspeakably hurt and sorrowful.

In the evening, when he was left alone with his wife in the great hall—
they were putting off their clothes, and their daughters were asleep
already in the other bed—all at once Ramborg asked:

"Knew you naught of this, Simon?"

"No——? Knew *you* aught?" he asked, anxiously.

Ramborg came across and stood just within the light of the taper on
the board. She was half undressed—in shift and laced bodice; her hair
hung loose in tresses about her face.

"Knew?—I had my thoughts. Helga was so strange"—her face
twisted into a kind of smile, and she seemed as she were cold. "She
spoke of how now there would be other times in Norway. The great
nobles"—Ramborg smiled a wry, fluttering smile—"were to come to
their rights here as in other lands. Knights—and barons—they would
be called once more——

"——Afterward, when I saw you take up their cause so hotly—you
were from home almost all the year—you could not find time to come
north to me at Ringheim, when I was to bear your child in a strange
man's house—afterwards, I thought maybe you knew—there was
question of others than Erlend——"

"Ho! Knights and barons!" Simon laughed, short and angrily.

"Was't for Kristin's sake alone you did it?"

He saw her face was pale as it were bit with frost; 'twas impossible to
pretend he did not understand her meaning. Desperately and defiantly
he burst out:

"Ay!"

Then he bethought him—why, she was mad—and he himself was mad. Erlend was mad—all the world had lost their wits that day. But now there must be an end to it.

"I did it for your sister's sake, ay," said he, soberly, "and for the children's sake, who had no man nearer of blood or of kin than I to take their part. And for Erlend's sake, since we were to be true brothers one to the other.—And now begin not you to bear you witlessly—for of that have I seen more than enough in this house to-day——" He flamed up, and flung the shoe he had taken off against the wall.

Ramborg went and took it up—looked at the log where it had struck: "'Tis shame that Torbjörg could not think of it herself—to wash the soot off in here for the banquet—I forgot to tell her of it." She wiped the shoe—'twas of Simon's best pair, with long toes and red heels—then took up the other and laid the pair in his clothes-chest. But he marked that her hands shook sorely while she was about it.

On that, he went and took her to his arms. She twined her slender limbs vehemently about her husband, while she shook with strangled weeping, and whispered, on his bosom, that she was so weary——

The seventh day thereafter Simon and his henchman were riding north from Dyfrin through Kvam. They struggled forward against a storm of great, clinging snow-flakes. Towards midday they came to the little farm by the highway where there was a tavern.

The woman came out and begged Simon to step into their house— only small folk were sent to the rest-house. She shook his wet outer garments and hung them to dry on the cross-beam by the hearth, while she talked away: Such a filthy weather—'twas pity of the horses—and he must have had to ride the whole way round—belike there was no riding over Mjös now?

"Oh, yes, if a man be tired enough of his life——"

The woman, and the children standing beside her, laughed with a good will. The bigger ones made themselves errands into the room with firewood and beer; the little ones bunched them together away by the door. Often they got pennies from Master Simon of Formo when he stopped there, and if he had with him something good for his children from Hamar market, they were like enough to get a taste. But to-day it seemed he list not to look at them.

He sat on the bench, bent forward, with his hands hanging out over his knees, staring into the hearth-fire, and answering a word now and again to the woman's flood of talk. Then she let fall that Erlend Nikulaussön was at Granheim to-day—'twas to-day that the Udalmen should pay the handsel money to the wilom owners. Should she send one of the children to his brother-in-law and tell him, so that they might ride home together?

No, said Simon. She might give him a little food, and after that he would lie down and sleep a while.

——Erlend he would meet soon enough. What he meant to say he would say in Gaute's hearing. But he had liefer not speak of the thing more than once.

His man, Sigurd, had settled down in the kitchen-house while the woman was cooking the food. Ay, a toilsome journey—and, besides, the master had been like an angry bull nigh the whole way. Simon Andressön was wont to hearken gladly enough to all the news of his home parish that his men could pick up, when they had been at Dyfrin. He had most often one or more Raumerike men eating his bread: folk came and sought service with him when he was at Dyfrin, for he was known for a kindly man and an open-handed, merry-hearted and not wont to be too high and mighty with his men. But "hold your tongue" was wellnigh the softest answer he, Sigurd, had had of his master that journey.

Moreover, it seemed he had quite fallen out with his brothers—he had not even slept overnight at Dyfrin; they had taken lodging on a leasehold farm near by in the parish. Sir Gyrd—ay, for, she must know, the King had made his master's brother a knight at Yule-tide—Sir Gyrd had come out into the yard and prayed Simon, right fairly, to stay— Simon had scarce answered his brother. And they had roared and bellowed and shouted, the gentry in the high-loft hall—yonder Sir Ulf Sakseson and Gudmund Andressön had been at the manor—enough fairly to fright folk. God only knew what they had fallen so by the ears about——

Simon came past the kitchen-house door, stood a moment, and glared in. Sigurd said, quickly, he was getting an awl and a buckle to put the saddle-gear to rights that was broke that morning.

"Have they such-like things in the kitchen on this farm——?" Simon flung back at him, and went his way. Sigurd shook his head, and nodded to the woman, when he was out of sight.

Simon thrust the platter from him and sat on at the board. He was so weary he could scarce bring himself to rise. But after a while he went and threw himself upon the bed in his boots and spurs—but bethought him then 'twere pity, too, of the bed: it was clean and good for such a humble house. He sat up and pulled off his foot-gear. Stiff and weary as he was, he sure should be able to sleep now—and he was wet through and shivering with cold, though his face burned after the long ride against the storm.

He crept in under the bed-spread, turned and tossed about the pillows

—they smelt so strangely of fish. Then he lay still, half raised upon his elbow.

His thoughts began to go round again in a ring. He had thought and thought these days, as a beast tramps round in a tether-rope.

——Even if Erling Vidkunssön had known it might cost Gyrd and Gudmund Darre life and goods if Erlend Nikulaussön let himself be driven to speak—ay, that made it none the worse that he had gone all lengths to win the Bjarkö knight's help. Rather the contrary—surely a man owed it to his brothers to stand by them, to the death if need be. Yet would he be fain to know if indeed Erling had known it. Simon weighed the chances for and against. Quite without knowledge that a rising was a-brewing he sure could not have been. But *what* Erling knew——? Gyrd and Ulf, at least, seemed not to know if the man had knowledge that they were in it. But Simon minded that Erling had named the Haftorssöns, had counselled him to seek help there, for 'twas rather their friends who had need to be afraid—— The Haftorssöns were cousins of Ulf Saksesön and Helga. The nose is near to the eyes——!

But even if Erling Vidkunssön had believed that Simon was thinking of his own brothers too, what he had done was none the worse, surely, for *that*. And Erling might well have seen, too, that he knew naught of his brothers' peril. Besides, had he not said himself—he minded, he had said it to Stig—he believed not that they could wring speech from Erlend.

Nevertheless, they might well have need to fear Erlend's tongue. Having held his peace in despite of bonds and torture, he was the very man to betray himself after by a slip of the tongue. 'Twould be like him—— And yet—that, he felt, was the one thing he could be sure Erlend would not do. He was dumb as a stone each time the talk turned that way, for very fear he might be drawn on to say too much. Simon saw that such was Erlend's fevered, well-nigh childish dread of breaking his troth—childish, for, that 'twas himself that had betrayed the whole emprise to his paramour, Erlend, it seemed clear, deemed not such a stain on his honour as he need regard. Such a thing, he seemed to hold, might happen to the best. So long as he held his tongue himself, he counted his shield untarnished and his troth unbroken—and Simon had seen well that Erlend was tender of his honour, so far as he understood what good fame and honour were. Had he not gone clean beside himself with despair and wrath at but the thought that any of his fellow-plotters should be bewrayed— (now, so long after, and in such wise that 'twas not possible it could matter aught to the men he had shielded with his life—and his honour and his wealth)—by the words of his child spoken to him who was nearest of kin to these same men——?

——He would order it so that, if things went awry, he would pay the price for them all—this Erlend had sworn upon the crucifix before all who joined with him in this emprise. But that grown men in their right minds could put their trust in such an oath!—for 'twas clear the issue rested not with Erlend. Now that he knew all about the plot Simon deemed 'twas the most witless folly he had heard on. Erlend had been willing to be torn limb from limb that he might keep the letter of his oath. And all the while the secret lay in a ten-year-old boy's hands— Erlend had himself seen to that. Nor seemed it to be his fault, either, that Sunniva Olavsdatter knew no more than she did know—— Could anyone make such a fellow out?——

So, if he had for a moment thought—ay, what Erlend and his wife deemed he had thought—God knows, that thought lay close enough to hand when Gaute came out with this tale of having seen his seal below the treasonous letter. And they two might have remembered he knew one thing and another of Erlend Nikulaussön that gave him less ground than most men to believe at all times the best of that gallant. But 'twas like they had forgotten long ago how once he had come upon them and seen into the depths of their shamelessness——

So 'twas with little reason he lay there, ashamed as a beaten dog for that he had done Erlend wrong in his thoughts. God knew, 'twas not that he gladly deemed ill of his brother-in-law—naught but unhappiness had he felt at the thought. But he knew himself 'twas a witless, foolish misthought—he would have seen straightway, even without Kristin's words, that so it could not be. Well-nigh as soon as the thought came to him—that Erlend might have misused his seal—he had felt: nay, Erlend could never have done the like. Never in his life had Erlend done a dishonourable deed that had aught of forethought in it—or aught of sense——

Simon flung himself about in the bed and groaned. They had driven him half-crazy himself with all this foolishness. It hurt him so to think that Gaute had gone for years believing this of him—yet 'twas against reason to take it so hardly. Even though he were fond of the boy, fond of all Kristin's sons—they were scarce more than children after all; did he need to care so much what they deemed of him?

And why should such boiling wrath come on him when he thought on the men who had laid their hands on Erlend's sword-hilt and sworn to follow their chieftain? If so be they were such sheep as to let themselves be dazzled by Erlend's glib tongue and his hardihood, and to deem that man had the stuff of a chieftain in him—then 'twas no more than was to be looked for that they should behave them like frighted sheep once the whole plan went awry. He still felt giddy when he thought on what he had heard at Dyfrin but now—so many men had been willing to sell the peace of the land and their own welfare into Erlend's hands—and

Haftor Olafssön, and Borgar Trondssön——! And not *one* had had the manfulness to step forth and crave of the King that Erlend be granted an honourable atonement and safety for his udal lands. They were so many that, had they but stood together, it had been no hard matter to force their will through. It seemed that amongst the gentry of Norway there was less of man's wit and of manhood than he had deemed——

Angry, too, he was that he himself had been altogether left out of these counsels. Not that they could have got *him* to join with them in such a senseless complot. But because both Erlend and Gyrd had gone behind his back and kept him in the dark—— Was he not every whit as much a noble as any of the rest, and did he not count more than a little in the country-side where folk knew him——?

In a fashion he owned that Gyrd was right. So as Erlend had made wreck of his leadership, the man could not crave, with reason, that his fellows in the plot should come forth and own themselves leagued with him. Simon knew that, had he found Gyrd alone, he had not come to part from his brothers in this wise. But there lay yonder Sir Ulf, with his long legs stretched out before him, discoursing on Erlend's lack of wit—now, after the fray! And then Gudmund chimed in. Neither Gyrd nor he himself had ever before suffered their youngest brother to gainsay them in aught. But since he had wedded with the priest's leman—his own leman thereafter—the boy had grown so puffed up and self-glorious —as Simon sat there he soon grew wild at the very sight of him—he prated so pertly, and his round, red face looked so like a child's back-side, that Simon's hands itched to smack it—— In the end he had scarce known himself what he said to the three men.

——So now 'twas come to a breach betwixt him and his brothers. He felt as though he must bleed to death when he thought on it—as though bonds of flesh and blood had been torn asunder. It had made him poor. Bare is brotherless back——

But whether 'twere so or so, in the midst of their angry broil he had understood, of a sudden—he himself knew not how—that Gyrd's numbed, half-hearted bearing came not alone from his sore need of a little peace at home. He had seen in a flash that Gyrd loved Helga still; 'twas this that made his brother seem so fettered and strengthless. And strangely, he understood not how, this roused him to fury against —ay, against the whole of life.

——Simon hid his face in his hands. Ay, this it was to have been good, dutiful sons. It had come easy to both Gyrd and himself to feel love for the brides their father came and said he had chosen for them. The old man had spoken to them one evening right goodly words of counsel—so that at length they sat there, quite shamefaced, the two of them—of marriage, and friendship and faith 'twixt honourable, clean-living wedded folk; ay, and last of all their father had even talked of prayer and intercession and masses. 'Twas pity their father had not vouchsafed them counsel how to forget as well—when friendship is shattered, and honour dead, and faithfulness a sin and a secret, shameful torture, and the bond has left naught behind it save a bleeding sore that never can be healed——

After Erlend was set free, a kind of peace had fallen upon himsel.—if but because a man cannot go on suffering such pain as he had suffered that time in Oslo. Either somewhat happens—or it grows better of itself.

Glad he had not been when she moved in to Jörundgaard with her husband and all their children, and he had to meet them, and keep up friendship with them and the dues of kin. But he comforted himself—so much worse had it been when he had to dwell with her so as a man cannot bear to live with a woman he loves, if she be not his wife nor his blood kin. And what had befallen betwixt Erlend and himself that night they made festival for his brother-in-law's deliverance from prison—he made light of that: Erlend, like enough, had not understood more than half, and 'twas like he thought little on the matter. Erlend had such a rare gift for forgetting. And he himself had his manor, and his wife, who was dear to him, and his children.

He had found peace, after a fashion. 'Twas not his fault that he loved his wife's sister. She had been his betrothed maid once—'twas not he who had broken his troth to her. When first he set his heart on Kristin Lavransdatter, 'twas but his duty, for then he deemed she was to be his wife. That 'twas her sister he got—that was Ramborg's doing—and her father's. Lavrans, wise man though he was, had never bethought him to ask whether Simon had forgotten. Howbeit he knew, not even Lavrans would he have suffered to ask *that*.

He was no good hand at forgetting. 'Twas not his doing that it was so. And he had never said *one* word that should have been left unsaid. He could not help it if the devil tempted him with dreams and promptings that did wrong to the bond of blood—of his own free will he had never given himself up to sinful thoughts of love. And in *deeds* he had been as a trusty brother to her and hers. That he knew himself.

At length he had come to be not ill content with his lot.

So long as he knew 'twas he who had served those two yonder—Kristin and the man she had cast him off for—— They had ever been forced to take succour at his hands.

Now 'twas so no longer. Kristin had staked her life and her soul's heal to save his son's life. 'Twas as though all the old wounds had burst open since he had let this be.

And since then it had come to pass that he owed Erlend his life.

——And then, in return, he had wronged him—not with his will, in his thoughts only—but yet——!

"——*et dimitte nobis debita nostra, sicut et nos dimittimus debitoribus nostris.*" 'Twas strange that the Lord had not taught us also to pray: "*sicut et nos dimittimus creditoribus nostris.*" He knew not whether it were good Latin—he had never been strong in that tongue. But he knew he could ever bring himself to forgive his debtors fairly enough. To him it seemed much harder to forgive one who had laid a load of debt upon *his* shoulders——

And now that they could call themselves quits—he and those two— he felt every ancient grudge that he had trampled underfoot these many years sprout up and quicken——

No longer could he thrust Erlend aside in his thoughts—for a witless babbler, who could neither see, nor learn, nor think, nor bear aught in mind. The other weighed now upon his spirit, just because none could know *what* Erlend saw and thought and remembered—there was no counting on him.

"Many a man wins what is meant for another, but another's lot none may win."

'Twas a true word.

He had loved his young bride. Had he got her, for sure he had been a well-contented man; most like they had come to live well to-gether. And she would have been still as she was when first they met: gentle and pure, shrewd, so that a man might take counsel of her even in greater matters; something wilful in small things, but yielding in the main, used as she was, when in her father's hands, to let herself be led and helped and guarded.—But then this man got a hold on her —one not fit to guide himself, who never had guarded aught. He had ravaged her sweet maidenliness, broken her proud calm, torn asunder her woman's soul, and forced her to stretch to the uttermost all her powers. *She* had had to stand up for her lover, as a little bird guards its nest, with throbbing body and shrilling cries, when any draws near to its home. Her sweet, slender body had seemed to him made to be lifted aloft in a man's arms and shielded lovingly—he had seen it strained with wild resolve, the while her heart beat within her with fear and courage and lust of battle; and she fought for husband and children, as even a dove will grow fierce and fearless when she has young.

Had it been he who was her husband—had she lived fifteen winters through in the shelter of his honest good-will—full well he knew for him too she would have stood up, if aught of mischance had come his way. With wisdom and firm will would she have stood by his side. But never would he have come to see the stony face she turned on him that night in Oslo, as she sat and told him she had been to that house and looked around within it. Never would he have heard her cry out his name in a voice of such wild despair and woe. And 'twas not the pure and honourable love of his youth that had answered in his heart. The wild craving that rose and cried out in answer to her wildness—never had he learned that aught such could harbour in his soul, had it gone with him and her as their fathers planned——

Her face as she went past him out into the night to find help for his child—she had never dared to tread that road, had she not been Erlend's wife, and long used to go on undaunted, even though her heart might shake with dread. The smile on her tear-stained face when she woke him and said the boy was calling for his father—so piercing sweet can none smile who knows not what it is to lose a fight and what to win it——

'Twas Erlend's wife he loved—as now he loved her. But then must his love be sin, and so belike there was no help for it—he must needs be unhappy—— For he was so unhappy that at times he felt naught but a great wonder—that 'twas he who had come to this pass, and who could see no way out of his unhappiness.

——When, treading underfoot his own honour and all gentle breeding, he had reminded Erling Vidkunssön of things no man of honour would have whispered that he knew aught of—he had done it, not for brothers or kinsmen, but *only* for her. Only for her sake had he brought himself to beg of the other man as the lazars beg at church doors in the great towns, showing their loathly sores——

He had thought—some time she shall know of it. Not all, not how deeply he had abased himself. But when they both were come to be old folk, he had thought he would say to Kristin thus: I helped you as best I might, for I minded how dear I loved you that time you were my promised bride.

One thing there was he dared not to turn his thoughts upon. Had Erlend said aught to Kristin?—Ay, he had thought, some time she should hear it from his own mouth:—I have never forgot that I loved you when we were young. But if so it were that she knew, and that 'twas from her husband she had learned it—nay, then he deemed he could bear no more——

To her alone he had meant to say it—some time, long hence. When he thought on that hour when he himself had bewrayed it—of Erlend's stumbling upon the thing he had deemed hidden in his most secret heart! And Ramborg knew it—though how she had seen it he could not understand——

His own wife—and *her* husband—they knew it——

Simon cried out, a wild and choking cry, as he flung himself suddenly on his other side in the bed——

——God help him! 'Twas his turn now to lie, stripped naked, outraged, bleeding from torture wounds and quivering with shame——

The woman set the door ajar; from the bed Simon's hot, dry, glittering eyes met hers: "Did you not get to sleep?—Erlend Nikulaussön rode by even now, with other two—belike 'twas two of his sons that rode with him." Simon muttered some kind of answer, angry and unmeaning.

He would let them get well ahead. But else 'twould soon be time he too was thinking of the homeward road——

——As soon as he was come into the hall and had taken off his outer gear, Andres would seize his fur cap and put it on his own head. Whilst the boy sat astride the bench and rode to his uncle at Dyfrin, the big cap would slip down, now upon the little nose and now back over his bonny bright locks—— But it helped him not much to try to think on such things—God knew when the boy was like to go a-visiting to his uncle at Dyfrin now——

And, instead, came the memory of that other son of his—Halfrid's child. Erling—'twas not so oft that he thought on him. A little ashy-blue child body—the days that Erling lived he had scarce seen him—he had to sit by the dying mother. Had the child lived, or had it lived longer than its mother—then had Mandvik been his own. And then like enough he had sought a new mate there, in the south country. Only now and again would he have come to his estate here, north in the Dale. And so, maybe, he would have—not *forgotten* Kristin—she had led him too wondrous a dance for that ever to be—— The devil —a man might, sure, have leave to remember, as an adventure, that he had been fain to fetch his bride, a high-born maid, bred up in chaste and Christian ways, home from a bordel and another man's bed. But then, maybe, he had not gone on so remembering her that it racked him and took all relish from whatsoever else of good life held for him——

Erling—he would have been fourteen winters old by now. When in due time Andres drew so near to man's estate, he himself would be old and laid aside——

Oh, ay, Halfrid—you were not over happy with me. Maybe 'tis not so undeserved that things have gone with me as they have——

And then, for sure, Erlend Nikulaussön had had to pay for his folly with his life; and Kristin had been sitting now at Jörundgaard, a widow——

And he himself going about, maybe, rueing that he was a wedded man! There was naught so witless but that he could believe it of himself now——

The gale had died down, but big, wet flakes of spring snow still fell, as Simon rode from the tavern yard. And, now, towards evening, the birds were beginning to pipe and trill in the woody thickets, in despite of the falling snow.

As a cut in the skin bursts open again at a hasty movement, a chance memory gave him pain—— Not many days ago, at his Easter feast, they—a whole troop of them—had stood without, basking in the mid-day sun. High above them, in a birch-tree, sat a robin, piping out into the warm, blue air. Geirmund came round the house corner, limping, dragging himself along on his staff, with one hand on his eldest son's shoulder. He looked up, stopped, and mimicked the bird. The boy, too, pursed his mouth and whistled. They could copy well-nigh every bird note. Kristin stood a little way off, amidst of some other women. Her smile was so fair as she listened——

Towards sunset the clouds thinned out in the west—rolled in golden drifts along the white fell-sides, filled glens and little dales with thick grey mist. The river had a dull gleam, as of brass—it rushed and eddied, wide and dark, round the stones in its course, and on each stone lay a little white cushion of new-fallen snow.

The wearied horses made but slow going over the heavy roads. It was milk-white night, with a full moon peering out through driving haze and clouds, when Simon rode down the steep banks of the Ula. When he was come over the bridge and out upon the flat fir tree heath, where the road ran in winter, the horses made better speed—they knew they were nearing their stalls. Simon patted Digerbein's wet, steaming neck. He was glad, at all rates, that this journey was near an end. Ramborg, belike, was asleep long ere now.

Where the road makes a sharp turn to leave the woods, there stood a little house. He was right upon it, when he grew ware that some men on horseback had drawn rein before the door. He heard Erlend's voice cry:

"Then 'tis sure you will come the first day after holy-day—I may tell my wife so——?"

Simon shouted a greeting. 'Twould seem too out of the way not to stay and ride on in their company; but he bade Sigurd go on ahead. Then he rode up to the others: they were Naakkve and Gaute. Erlend came forth from the house door at the same moment.

He greeted them again—the three gave back his greeting somewhat

uneasily. He could see their faces but dimly in the glimmering light
—it seemed to Simon they looked at him doubtfully—seemed at once
curious and resentful. So he said straight out:

"I come from Dyfrin, brother-in-law."

"Ay, I heard tell you were gone south." Erlend stood with his
hand on the saddle-bow, looking down. "You have ridden hard,
'twould seem," he added, as if to break an irksome silence.

"Nay, stay a little," said Simon to the youths, as they made to ride
on. "You, too, must hearken to this. 'Twas my brother's seal you
saw on the letter, Gaute. And I wot it must seem to you they kept their
troth but ill with your father, he and the other knights who set their
seals to that letter to Prince Haakon your father was to bear to
Denmark——"

The boys looked down in silence. Erlend spoke:

" One thing, I trow, you thought not on, Simon, when you rode
to tryst with your brother. Dearly bought I safety for Gyrd and those
others—with all I owned, save the name of a trusty man that held
to his word. Now Gyrd Darre deems, for sure, not even that name
is left to me——"

Simon bowed his head, abashed. Of that he had not thought.

"Why said you not this to me, Erlend, when I told you I would ride
to Dyfrin——?"

"You must sure have seen yourself I was so mad with rage, when
I rode from your manor, there was neither thought nor counsel in
me——"

"I was scarce in my full wits either, Erlend——"

"No, but meseems you might have had time to bethink you on
yonder long road. Nor could I well have prayed you give up your
intent to question your brother, without bewraying things I had sworn
a dear oath to keep hidden——"

Simon said naught for a little—at first it seemed to him the other
was in the right of it. But then it struck him—nay, now was Erlend
wrong-headed as could be. Should he have sat still and suffered
Kristin and the boys to think such evil of him? He asked this something hotly.

"I have never breathed a word of this, kinsman, either to mother or
to my brothers," said Gaute, turning his comely, bright face to Simon.

"Ay, but none the less they learnt of it in the end," answered he,
stubbornly. "I trow, after all that befell yonder day at my house,
great need there was that we should clear the matter. And I see not
how it could come upon your father so unawares—much more than a
child you are not yet, my Gaute, and right young were you when you
were made a sharer in these—secret counsels."

"My own son I sure might well deem I could trust," cried Erlend hotly. "And choice I had none, when I must save the letter. 'Twas either give it to Gaute or let the Warden find it——"

It seemed to Simon bootless to speak more of the matter. But he could not refrain him from saying:

"Little did I like it when I learned what the boy had gone about believing of me these four years. I have ever set much by you, Gaute."

The boy urged his horse forward a few paces; he held out his hand, and Simon saw his face grew darker, as though he flushed:

"You must forgive me, Simon!"

Simon gripped the boy's hand. At times Gaute's face could be so like his mother's father's that it moved Simon strangely. He was something bow-legged and low of stature when afoot, but he was a rarely good rider, and on horseback he was as fair a sprig of young manhood as could gladden a father's eyes.

Now they rode northwards, all four, the boys ahead. When they were out of ear-shot, Simon said:

"Understand you, Erlend—I trow you cannot rightly blame me for seeking out my brother and praying him to tell me truth about this matter. But I wot you had cause for anger against me, you and Kristin. For as soon as these"—he groped for words—"these strange tidings came out—what Gaute said of my seal—I cannot deny I thought— I understand your believing that I thought what I should have had wit to know was unthinkable. So I say not but you have reason to be wroth——" he said again.

The horses plashed through the snow-slush. 'Twas a little while till Erlend answered, and then his voice sounded most meek and mild:

"I know not, after all, what else you could have thought. 'Twas sure the easiest thing to think——"

"Ah no, I should have known well 'twas impossible," Simon broke in, sorely. A little after he asked:

"Did you deem that I knew of this—of my brother? That 'twas for their sake I tried to help you?"

"Nay," said Erlend, wonderingly. "I knew for sure that you could not know it. That I had said naught, I knew. And that your brother had not let slip aught, that I deemed I could be full sure of." He laughed a little. Then he grew grave. "I know well," said he, softly, "you did it for our father-in-law's sake—and because you are good——"

Simon rode on for a time, and said no word.

"You were bitter wroth, I can conceive?" he asked in a little.

"Oh!—— When I got time to bethink me—I see not that there was any other meaning you could put on it——"

"And Kristin?" asked Simon, still lower.

"Ay, she——!" Erlend laughed as before. "You know well she brooks not that any point a finger at me—save her own self. She deems, I trow, she can see to that well enough herself. 'Tis the same with our children. God have mercy on me if I but speak a word of blame to them! But, trust me, I set her right——"

"You did that——?"

"Ay—when time and season serve I surely shall make her understand. You know well Kristin is such an one that, when she has bethought her, she will remember you have shown us such trusty friendship that——"

Simon felt his heart quiver with a tingling wrath. He felt 'twas more than he could bear—the other seemed to think that now they might cast this matter quite from their thoughts. His face, in the pale moonlight, showed utterly at peace. Simon's voice shook with the hurry of his spirits as he spoke again:

"Forgive me, Erlend, I understand not how I could believe——"

"You hear," the other broke in, a little impatiently, "that I understand. Methinks it had been hard for you to believe otherwise——"

"Would to God those two witless young ones had never spoken," said Simon, vehemently.

"Ay—— Gaute has never had such a beating in his life before—— And to think it all came of bickering over their far-off forbears—Reidar Birkebein and King Skule and Bishop Nikolas." Erlend shook his head. "But come, brother-in-law, think no more on it—'twere best we forget all this soon as we can——"

"I *cannot!*"

"Nay, Simon!" This came by way of protest, gentle and wondering. "'Tis not worth taking so hardly——!"

"I *cannot*, hear you! I am not so good a man as you!"

Erlend looked at him in a maze:

"Now know I not what you mean."

"I am not so good a man as you! I cannot forgive so easily them that I have wronged."

"I know not what you mean," said the other, as before.

"I mean——" Simon's face was drawn and marred with pain and passion; he spoke low, as though he crushed down a longing to cry aloud. "I mean—— I have heard you speak fair words of Sigurd, the Lagmand at Steigen, the old man whose wife you stole from him. I have seen and known that you loved Lavrans with all a son's love. And never have I marked that you bore me grudge for that you—lured me from my promised maid—— I am not so high-minded as you deem, Erlend—I am not so high-minded as you—I—*I* bear a grudge to the man whom *I* have wronged——"

His cheeks palely flecked with passion, he stared into the other's eyes. Erlend had listened to him with mouth half open.

"This had I never dreamed on till this hour! Do you *hate* me, Simon?" he whispered, astounded.

"Seems it not to you that I have cause——?"

Without knowing it, both men had stayed their horses. They sat gazing into each other's faces: Simon's little eyes glittered like steel. In the hazy-white light of the night he saw that Erlend's thin features worked, as though something stirred within him—an awakening—— He looked up from under half-closed eyelids, biting his quivering under-lip.

"I cannot bear to meet you any more!"

"Man!—'Tis twenty years agone," Erlend burst out, in amaze.

"Ay. Deem you not that—she—is worth remembering for twenty years?"

Erlend drew himself upright in his saddle—met Simon's gaze, full and steadfastly. The moonlight kindled a blue-green spark within his great light eyes.

"Yes. God—God bless her!"

So he sat for a moment. Then he set spurs to his horse and dashed forward along the miry track, splashing the water high behind him. Simon held Digerbein back—he was well-nigh thrown, so suddenly did he rein in the horse. He tarried there, on the edge of the woods, struggling with the impatient beast, for so long as he could hear the hoof-strokes in the slush.

Remorse had rushed over him in the moment he had said it. Remorse, and shame—as though he had struck the most defenceless of creatures—a child—or a fine and gentle, reasonless beast—in senseless wrath. His hate seemed like a shivered lance—he himself seemed shivered by the clash with this man's witless simplicity—so little understanding had this bird of ill omen, Erlend Nikulaussön, 'twas as though he must be held both helpless and innocent——

He cursed and swore under his breath as he rode on. Innocent— the fellow was long past two score years—'twas high time he learnt to suffer being spoken to, man to man. If Simon had wounded himself —ay, devil take him if 'twas not a cheap price to pay if he had but got a blow home on Erlend for once.

Now was he riding home to her—"God bless her," he mocked wryly. And then there would be an end to all this struggling for brotherly love—'twixt those two there, and him and his. He need nevermore meet with Kristin Lavransdatter——

——The thought took away his breath—— Yet, devil take it! why not——? "If thine eye offend thee, pluck it out," said the priests.

'Twas for this mostly, he told himself, that he had done this thing—to escape this make-believe of brother and sister's love with Kristin—he could bear it no more——

One only wish he had now—that Ramborg might not wake when he came home.

But when he rode down between the fences, he saw a dark form in a cloak standing under the aspen trees. Her head-linen showed white.

She had been waiting there, she said, ever since Sigurd came home. The serving-women were abed, and Ramborg herself ladled out the porridge from the pot which stood against the fire to keep warm, set bacon and bread on the board, and fetched fresh-drawn ale.

"Will you not to bed now, Ramborg?" asked the man, while he ate.

Ramborg answered not. She went over to her loom and began to thread the little many-coloured balls in and out of the warp. She had set up a tapestry before Yule, but she was not come far with it yet.

"Erlend rode northwards, a while ago," she said; as she stood with her back to him. "I deemed, from what Sigurd said, you were coming with him?"

"No—it fell not out so——"

"Erlend longed more for home and bed than you?" She laughed a little. As she got no answer, she said again: "He, I trow, ever longs to come home to Kristin, when he has had an errand from home——"

Simon kept silence for a good while ere he answered: "Erlend and I parted not as friends." Ramborg turned sharp round—he told her, then, what he had heard at Dyfrin, and of the first part of his talk with Erlend and his sons.

"Methinks 'tis scarce reason to fall at odds over this—when you have been able to keep friends till now."

"Maybe—yet so it fell out. But 'twere too long to tell the whole tale to-night."

Ramborg turned to her loom, and busied herself with the work again.

"Simon," she asked, all at once, "mind you a saga Sira Eirik read to us once upon a time—out of the Bible—of a young maid named Abishag the Shunammite?"

"No."

"What time King David grew old, and his strength and manhood began to fail," began the wife, but Simon broke in:

"My Ramborg, the night is too far spent; 'tis no time to begin telling sagas now.—And I mind, too, now, how 'twas with her you named——"

Ramborg beat the weft up with the reed; she held her peace for a little. Then she spoke again:

"Mind you that saga, then, that my father could tell—of Tristan the comely, and Isolde the fair, and Isolde the dark?"

"Ay, that one I mind." Simon pushed the dish from him, rubbed the back of his hand across his mouth, and stood up. He came over to the fire-place; with one foot up on the edge, elbow on knee and chin in hand, he stood looking into the fire that was burning itself out in the stone-built cavern. From the corner by the loom came Ramborg's voice, quavering and ready to break:

"I thought always, when I heard those sagas, that such men as King David and Sir Tristan—it seemed foolish—and cruel—that they loved not the young brides who brought them their maidenhood and their hearts' love in all gentleness and seemly purity, more than suchlike women as the Lady Bath-sheba or younger Isolde the fair, who had made waste of themselves in other men's arms. Methought had I been a man, I had not been so prideless—or so heartless"—she stopped, overcome. "Meseemed 'twas the hardest of fates—the lot they had; Abishag and that poor Isolde of Bretland——" She turned, vehemently, came across the room, and stood before her husband.

"What ails you, Ramborg?" Simon spoke low and with an ill grace. "I know not what you mean by this——"

"Yes, you know," said she, vehemently. "You yourself are like yonder Tristan——"

"That can I scarce trow," he tried to laugh, "that I am like—Tristan the fair—— And the two women you named—if I mind me aright, they lived and died spotless maids, untouched of their husbands——" He looked over at his wife: her little, three-cornered face was white, and she bit her lips.

Simon put his foot to the ground, stood upright, and laid both hands upon her shoulders:

"My Ramborg, have we not had two children, you and I?" he said softly.

She answered not.

"I have striven to show you I was thankful to you for that gift. I deemed myself—I have tried to be a good husband to you——"

She still said naught, and, letting fall his hands, he went and sat him down upon the bench. Ramborg followed, stood before him, looking down upon her husband: the broad thighs, in wet, muddied breeches, the unwieldy body, the heavy, red-brown face. She pursed up her lips in distaste:

"Ill-favoured, too, have you grown with the years, Simon."

"Ay, I have never deemed myself aught of a comely man," he said, soberly.

"And am I not young and fair——" She set her on his lap; the tears started from her eyes, as she clasped his head in both her hands: "Simon—look on me—wherefore can you not repay me for this?—never have I wished that any should have me save you—methought, even from the time I was a little maid, my husband should be such an one as you were—— Mind you how you led us both by the hand, Ulvhild and me—? you were to go with father to the west paddock to look upon his foals—you bore her over the beck, and father would have taken me up, but I screamed out that you must bear me too. Mind you?"

Simon nodded. He remembered well he had been much taken up with Ulvhild, the lovely crippled child had seemed to him so pitiful. Of the youngest he had had no memory, save that one there was younger than Ulvhild.

"You had the goodliest hair——" She ran her fingers through the thick-waved, light-brown forelock that hung somewhat down over her husband's brow. "Not one grey hair have you yet in your head—— Erlend's hair will soon be as much white as black.—And I liked so well that there came those deep dimples in your cheeks when you smiled—and that you were so merry of speech——"

"Ay, like enough I was something better-favoured then than I am now——"

"No," she whispered vehemently—"not when you look kindly on me—— Mind you the first time I slept in your arms?

"——I lay abed, crying with the toothache—father and mother had gone asleep; 'twas dark in the loft-room, but you came over to the bench where we lay, Ulvhild and I, and asked why I wept. You bade me to be quiet and not wake the others, and then you took me up into your arms, and then you lit the taper and cut a splint and pricked around the bad tooth till blood came. Then you said a blessing over the splint, and then I was soon well again, and I got leave to sleep in your bed and you held me in your arm——"

Simon laid his hand upon her head and pressed it in to his shoulder. Now she spoke of it, he remembered: 'twas that time he was at Jörundgaard and had told Lavrans that the bond 'twixt him and Kristin had best be loosed again. He had slept little that night—and now he remembered that he had got up once and done somewhat to help little Ramborg, who lay whimpering with the toothache——

"Have I so borne me to you at any time, my Ramborg—that you deem you have a right to say I love you not——?"

"Simon—seems it not to you that I deserve you should love me more than Kristin? Wicked and false she was to you—I have followed you about like a little lap-dog all these years——"

Simon lifted her gently down from his lap, stood up, and took her hands in his:

"Speak no more of your sister now, Ramborg—in that wise. I wonder if you understand yourself what you say. Think you not that I fear God—can you believe of me that I could be so dreadless of shame and the worst of sins, or that I should not remember my children and all my kin and friends? I am your husband, Ramborg—forget it not, and speak not so to me——"

"I know you have not broken God's law, or cast away faith and honour——"

"Never have I spoken one word to your sister or touched her with my hand in other wise than I can answer for on the judgment-day— God and Saint Simon, the apostle, are my witness——"

Ramborg nodded silently.

"Think you your sister would have met me as she has done all these years, if she thought as you do, that I loved her with sinful lust? Nay, then you know not Kristin."

"Oh, she has never so much as thought whether any other man save Erlend bears love to her. It scarce comes to her mind that we others are flesh and blood——"

"Ay, belike you speak truly there, Ramborg," said Simon calmly. "But then sure you can understand for yourself how witless 'tis for you to plague me with jealousy."

Ramborg drew away her hands.

"I meant it not so either, Simon. But never have you cared for me as you cared for her. She is for ever in your thought even yet—of me you think but seldom, when you see me not."

"'Tis not my doing, Ramborg, that a man's heart is so made that what is writ thereon when 'tis young and fresh stands more deeply graven than all the runes cut afterward——"

"Have you never heard the word that says: a man's heart is the first thing that quickens in his mother's womb, and the last thing in him to die?" said Ramborg, softly.

"Nay—— Is there a word that says the like——? Ay, and it may well be true, too." He stroked her white cheek lightly. "But if we are to sleep this night, we must to bed now," he said, wearily.

Ramborg slept after a while, and Simon stole his arm from under her neck, moved him gently towards the outer bed-edge and drew the fur coverlid right up under his chin. His shirt, at the shoulder, was wet through with her tears. He was bitterly heart-sore for his wife—

and he understood too, with a new desperation, that he could no longer make shift to live with her by taking her as though she were a blind, unlessoned child. Now must he make up his mind that Ramborg was a grown woman.

The window-pane was grey already with dawn—the May night was nigh its end. He was deathly weary—and to-morrow was mass-day. Go to church to-morrow he would not—though sure enough he had great need of it. He had promised Lavrans once, never would he miss a mass without full good cause—but, he thought bitterly, it had not helped him overmuch that he had kept his word all these years. To-morrow he would not ride to mass——

Part Two

DEBTORS

K R I S T I N learned but in part what had befallen 'twixt Erlend and Simon. Her husband told her and Björgulf what Simon had said of his journey to Dyfrin, and that, afterwards, they had changed high words, and in the end had parted unfriends. "More I cannot tell you of this matter."

Erlend was a little pale, his face set and resolved. She had seen it thus some few times before, in the years she had been wedded to him. And she knew 'twas a sign that these were matters he would say no more on.

She had never liked it when Erlend had met her questions with this look. God knew she craved not to be held for more than a simple woman; she had liefer had to answer for naught but her children and her housekeeping. But she had been driven to put her hand to so much that seemed to her fitter for a man to deal with—and Erlend, 'twas clear, had deemed it fitting that he should let such things rest upon her shoulders. And thus it beseemed him ill to carry things so high and answer so curtly, when she sought to know the rights of doings of his own which touched the welfare of them all.

She took this unfriendship 'twixt Erlend and Simon Darre hardly. Ramborg was her only sister. And when she thought on it, that now Simon would come among them no more, she understood fully, for the first time, how fond she had come to be of this man and how much of thanks she owed him—in the troublous lot that was hers she had had a sure stay in his trusty friendship.

And she knew now that, all over the country-side, the folk would have a new titbit of gossip—that yonder Jörundgaard people had broken with Simon of Formo too. Simon and Ramborg were liked and held in esteem by every soul. And for the most part she herself, her husband, and her sons were looked on with distrust and mis-liking—that she had known for long. Now would they be left quite unfriended——

Kristin felt as though she must sink into the ground with sorrow and shame the first Sunday when she came on to the church-green and saw Simon standing there, a little way off, in a cluster of yeomen. He bowed his head in greeting to her and hers, but 'twas the first time he came not forward to shake hands and chat with them.

But Ramborg went up to her sister and took her hand:

"'Tis ill, sister, that our husbands have fallen out—but I see not that you and I need fall out for that——" She raised herself upon her toes

* For explanation of the title of Part II, see Note 2.

and kissed Kristin, so that the folk in the churchyard could see it. But Kristin knew not how it was—she seemed to feel within her that, none the less, Ramborg was not greatly grieved. Never had she brought herself to like Erlend—God knew whether she had not set her husband against him, knowingly or unknowingly——

Yet thereafter Ramborg ever came and greeted her sister when they met at the church. Ulvhild called out aloud to know wherefore her aunt came not south to them any more; then she ran across to Erlend, and clung about him and his eldest sons. Arngjerd, standing quietly by her step-mother's side, took Kristin by the hand and looked troubled. Simon and Erlend and his sons held aloof from each other most diligently.

Kristin missed her sister's children sorely too. She had grown fond of the two young maids. And one day, when Ramborg had brought her son to mass, and Kristin, after worship, was kissing Andres, she fell a-weeping. This weak, sickly boy had grown so dear to her—and she could not but feel, now that she had no truly little children any more, 'twas in a way a comfort to her to care for this little sister's-son at Formo and spoil him, when his parents brought him with them to Jörundgaard.

From Gaute she heard somewhat more of the matter, for he told her the words that had fallen between Erlend and Simon that night they met by Skindfeld-Gudrun's cottage. The more she pondered these things, the more it seemed to her that Erlend was the most at fault. She had been wroth with Simon—so much he should sure have known of Erlend as to know that he could not have thus basely played his brother false howsoever strange the things he might do through thoughtlessness or hot temper—and when he saw what he had brought to pass, he bore himself often most like a shy stallion that has broken loose, and goes wild with fright at what he drags behind him.

But that Erlend never could understand that, sometimes, other men must needs cross him, to guard their own welfare against the mischief he had such a rare gift for making! And that then he cared not what he said, or how he bore himself! She remembered those days when she herself yet was young and tender—time after time she had felt as though he were trampling on her heart with his reckless doings. His own brother he had cut him off from—even before Gunnulf went into the cloister, he had drawn away from them, and she had known that Erlend was to blame—so often he had given offence to his pious and worthy brother, though never had Gunnulf done Erlend aught but good, that she wist of. And now he had thrust Simon from him, and when she would have known what 'twas that had brought unfriendship between him and their only friend, he but put on a lofty mien and answered that he might not tell her——

To Naakkve he had said more, she saw well.

The mother waxed sore and uneasy in mind when she marked that Erlend and their eldest son grew silent, or turned their talk to some other matter, so soon as she came near them—and this befell not seldom.

Both Gaute and Lavrans and Munan held closer to their mother than Nikulaus ever had done, and she had talked more with them than with him. Nevertheless it ever seemed to her that, of all the children, her first-born stood, in a way, closest to her heart. And since she was come to dwell on Jörundgaard again, the memories of the time when she bore this son under her heart, and of his birth, had grown strangely living and near. For she was made aware in many ways that, here in Sil, folks had not forgotten the sin of her youth. 'Twas almost as though they accounted her to have smirched the honour of the whole country-side of her birth when she, the daughter of the man all here looked up to as their head, had gone astray. They had not forgiven that, nor yet that she and Erlend had added insult to his shame and sorrow when they fooled him into giving away an erring maid with the most stately bridal that had been held in man's memory here in the northern Dale.

Kristin could not tell if Erlend knew that now folk were raking these old tales up again. But if know it he did, 'twas like he cared naught for the matter. He accounted her countrymen of the Dale naught but wadmal-farmers and village hinds, one and all—and he taught her sons to think the like. It seared her soul to know that these men and women, who had thought much of her and wished her so well in those days when they called her Lavrans Björgulfsön's winsome daughter, and the Rose of the Dale, now held Erlend Nikulaussön and his wife in scorn and judged them hardly. She besought not these folk, she wept not for that she was become a stranger amongst them. But it hurt her sorely. And it seemed to her that even the headlong hill-sides about the Dale, that had sheltered and guarded her childhood, now looked down upon her and her home in other guise—with darkling menace and hard, stony-grey will to cow her spirit.

Once she had wept bitterly—Erlend had known of it, and he had not long had patience with her then. When he learned that she had gone lonely through those many months with his child a heavy weight beneath her sad, fearful heart, he had not taken her into his arms and comforted her with gentleness and loving words. Angered and shame-struck had he been when he saw that now 'twould come to light how unworthily he had dealt with Lavrans—but he had not thought how much worse it needs must be for her, the day when she should stand shamed before her proud and loving father.

Nor had Erlend greeted his son with overmuch joy when, at last, she had borne this child forth to life and the light. In that hour, when she was delivered from her endless agony of soul and terror and torment, and saw the ugly, shapeless burthen of her sin take life under the priest's powerful prayers, and change to the loveliest child, whole and without blemish—in that moment it had seemed as though her heart melted with humble gladness, and that even the hot, defiant blood of her body turned to white, sweet, innocent milk. Ay, with God's help he may grow human in time, said Erlend, as she lay there in bed and would have had him rejoice with her over this costly treasure, that she could scarce suffer from out her arms long enough to let the woman tend the child. Yet his children by Eline Ormsdatter he loved; that she had both seen and known. But when she bore Naakkve to his father and would have laid him in the man's arms, Erlend had pulled a wry face and asked what should he do with this brat who leaked both top and bottom. For long had Erlend looked askance at his eldest true-born son —could not forget that Naakkve had come into the world at an unto-ward time—though yet the boy was so fair and winsome and likely a child that any father might well rejoice who saw such a son growing up to fill his place.

And Naakkve had loved his father so that 'twas marvel to see it—even from the time when he was a tiny babe. He had beamed like the sun over the whole of his little comely face if his father took him between his knees for a moment and said but two words to him, or if the man let him hold his hand crossing the courtyard. Staunchly had Naakkve striven to win his father's favour in those days when Erlend liked all his other children better than this one. Björgulf had been his father's favourite while the boys were small. Then would Erlend sometimes take his little sons with him up to the knights' armoury, when he had an errand thither—all the armour and weapons not in daily use at Husaby were kept there. While the father talked and jested with Björgulf, Naakkve would sit still as a mouse on a chest—panting for very joy that he had leave to be there.

But as time went on, and, by reason of his bad sight, Björgulf could not, so well as his brothers, go abroad with Erlend, and as the boy himself grew more withdrawn and silent when with his father, all this was changed. 'Twas now well-nigh as though Erlend were a little shy of this son. Kristin wondered at times whether Björgulf blamed his father in his heart because he had wasted all their substance and had dragged down his sons' fortunes with him in his downfall—and whether Erlend knew or guessed this. Howsoever it might be, it seemed as though Björgulf alone, of all Erlend's sons, looked not up to him with blind love and with unbounded pride in calling him father.

One day the two smallest boys had marked that their father was reading the psalter in the morning and keeping fast on bread and water. They asked why he did thus—for 'twas no fast-day. Erlend answered 'twas for his sins. Kristin knew that these days of fasting were a part of the penance laid upon Erlend for his adultery with Sunniva Olavsdatter, and that the eldest sons at least knew of this. Naakkve and Gaute seemed to think naught of it, but it chanced that she looked just then at Björgulf: the boy sat there blinking near-sightedly down into his meat-bowl and smiling to himself—so had Kristin seen Gunnulf smile one time and another when Erlend got on the high horse. The mother liked not the sight——

Now 'twas Naakkve whom Erlend would ever have by him. And the lad lived as though all the roots of his being were knit to his father. Naakkve served his father as a young page his lord and chieftain: he would have none but himself care for his father's horse, and keep his riding-gear and arms in good order; he buckled the spurs on Erlend's feet, and bore hat and cloak to him when he would go forth. He filled his father's beaker and carved for him at board, where he sat on the bench to the right of Erlend's seat. Erlend laughed a little at the lad's *kurteisi*, but he liked it well, and more and more he made Naakkve all his own.

Kristin saw that now he had quite forgot how she had striven and prayed to win from him a little fatherly love for this child. And Naakkve had forgot the time when he was young and little, and 'twas to her he came to seek comfort for all ills, and counsel in all his troubles. To his mother he had ever been a loving son, and this he was still in a fashion, but she felt that the older the boy grew the farther he drifted from her and all her concerns. Of all she had upon her hands Naakkve took no thought at all. He was never loth to do her will when she set him to any task, but he was strangely wooden-handed and clumsy at all that might be called farm work—he did it lifelessly and listlessly, and never could bring aught to an end. He was not unlike his dead half-brother, Orm Erlendssön, in many ways, his mother thought—was like him, too, in looks. But Naakkve was strong and sound, lusty in the dance and in all sports, a good marksman with the bow, and passably skilled, too, in the use of other weapons, a good rider and a ski-runner of the best. Kristin spoke of this one day with Ulf Haldorssön, Naakkve's foster-father. Ulf said:

"None has lost more through Erlend's folly than this lad. Better stuff than Naakkve for a knight and a great noble grows not in Norway in these days."

But his mother saw that Naakkve never thought of all he had been bereft of by his father's fault.

At this time there was again great unrest in Norway, and rumours flew northward over the parishes of the Dale, some likely enough and some wholly unbelievable. The great lords south and west in the realm and throughout the Uplands were so miscontent with King Magnus' rule—'twas said they had openly threatened to take to arms, to rouse the commons, and bring Sir Magnus Eirikssön to govern after their will and counsel, or else take for king his mother's sister's son, the young Jon Haftorssön of Sudrheim—his mother, the Lady Agnes, was daughter to King Haakon Haalegg, of blessed memory. Of Jon himself but little was heard, but 'twas said his brother, Sigurd, was the head and front of the whole emprise, and Bjarne, Erling Vidkunssön's young son, was of their counsels—folk told how Sigurd had sworn, if Jon became king, he should take one of Bjarne's sisters to his queen, for the maidens at Giske, too, were of the race of the old Norse kings. Sir Ivar Ogmundssön, who before had been King Magnus' stoutest stay, 'twas said had now gone over to the party of these young nobles, and many others of the land's richest and best-born men as well—of Erling Vidkunssön himself and the Bishop of Björgvin, folk said that they were pushing behind.

Kristin hearkened but little to these rumours; bitterly she thought: they were but small folk now, the matters of the realm touched them not. Yet, in the autumn gone by, she had spoken somewhat of them with Simon Andressön, and she knew, too, that he had talked of them with Erlend. But she had seen that Simon was not fain to talk of these things—in part, maybe, because he liked not that his brothers should mix themselves in such perilous doings; and Gyrd at least, she knew, was led by the nose by his wife's kinsfolk. But he was fearful too that talk of suchlike things might discomfort Erlend, since he was born to sit among the men who met in counsel for Norway's realm, and now mischance had barred him out from the fellowship of his peers.

But Kristin knew that Erlend spoke of these things with his sons. And one day she heard Naakkve say:

"But should these lords make good their right against King Magnus, they could not be so base, father, for sure, as not to take up your cause and force the King to mend the wrong he did you."

Erlend laughed; but his son went on:

"You first showed these lords the way, and brought to men's minds that 'twas not the wont of Norway's chiefs of old to sit still and brook oppression by their kings. It cost you your udal lands and fiefs—the men who had leagued them with you came off without a scratch—you alone paid for them all——"

"Ay, then have they the better reason to forget me, I trow," said Erlend laughing. "And Husaby hath the archbishopric got in pledge. I trow the lords of the council will scarce pester King Magnus, poor moneyless wretch, to redeem it——"

"The King is your kinsman, and so is Sigurd Haftorssön and most of these men," answered Naakkve vehemently. "How, without shame, can they forsake that man of all Norway's nobles who bore his shield with honour to the northern Marches, and purged Finland and the Gandvik coast of the King's foes and God's—caitiffs would they be——"

Erlend whistled.

"Son—one thing can I tell you. I know not how the Haftorssöns' emprise will fare, but I wager my neck they will not dare show Sir Magnus a naked Norse sword. Talk and bargaining I trow there will be, but not a bolt shot. And these gentry will never put on harness in my cause, for they know me, and know well that I am not so qualmish at sight of cold steel as be some others——

"——Kinsmen, say you—ay, they are your third cousins, both Magnus and the Haftorssöns. I remember them from the time I served in King Haakon's court—'twas well for your kinswoman, the Lady Agnes, that she was daughter of the King—else had she, belike, been fain to go upon the wharves and gut fish, if some such lady as your mother had not hired her to help in the byre out of pious charity. More times than one have I dried these Haftorssöns about the snout, when they were to be brought before their mother's father, and they came running into the hall as snotty-nosed as they crept off their mother's lap—and if I caught them a buffet, in cousinly kindness, to teach them somewhat of manners, they shrieked like stuck pigs. I hear it said these oafs of Sudrheim have been made men of at last. But to look for a kinsman's help from that side—as well shear the sow for wool——"

Afterwards Kristin said to Erlend:

"Naakkve is so young, dear my husband—deem you not 'tis unwise to talk so freely with him on such matters?"

"And you are so mild of speech, dear my wife," said Erlend, smiling, "that I see well you would take me to task—— When I was of Naakkve's age, I fared north to Vargöy the first time. Had Lady Ingebjörg been loyal and true to me," he burst out hotly, "then had I sent her Naakkve and Gaute to serve her—yonder in Denmark 'tis like there had been advancement for two mettlesome blades with warm blood in their veins——"

"I thought not," said Kristin, bitterly, "the time I bore you these children, that our sons should seek their bread in a foreign land."

"You know I thought not so either," said Erlend. "But man proposeth, and God disposeth——"

So Kristin said to herself, 'twas not alone that it hurt her heart to mark that Erlend, and her sons, now they were growing up, bore them as though their affairs were beyond a woman's kenning. She was afraid, too, of Erlend's reckless tongue—never did he call to mind that his sons were little more than children.

This, too, there was, that, young as the sons were—Nikulaus was now seventeen winters old, Björgulf would be sixteen, and Gaute fifteen at harvest-time—these three already had a way with women that made their mother uneasy.

True it was, naught had befallen that she could point to. They did not run after women-folk; they were never gross of tongue or foul-mouthed, and liked it little when the serving-carls offered to crack ribald jests or bring lewd tales to the manor. But Erlend, too, in such matters had ever borne him right seemly and modestly—she had seen him abashed at talk that made both her father and Simon laugh heartily. But at such times she had felt, dimly, that the others laughed as peasants laugh at tales of the devil's dull-wittedness—while learned men, who know better his wicked wiles, care little for such jesting.

And Erlend, too, might have claimed to be guiltless of the sin of running after women—only folk who knew not the man could think him loose, in the way of luring women to him and leading them astray of set purpose. She never denied to herself that Erlend had had his will with her without use of love-philtres, without force or guile. And as for the two wedded women he had sinned with, she was sure that 'twas not Erlend had been the tempter. But, when light women met him halfway with bold and luring laughter, she had seen that he grew curious as a young kid—a drift of secret, heedless lightness would seem to breathe from the whole man.

And, with dread, she deemed she saw the Erlendssöns were like to their father in this—they ever forgot to think, before doing aught, of the judgment of other folk—though afterward they took to heart keenly what was said. And, when women met them with smiles and oncoming, they grew not abashed or shy and sullen, like most lads of their age —they smiled back, chatted, and bore them as easily and freely as had they been to the King's court and learned a courtier's ways. Kristin grew fearful lest they should be drawn into trouble through sheer simplicity—to their mother, rich housewives and their daughters, as well as poor serving-women, seemed all too forthcoming in their bearing towards these fair youths.—— But they would grow hot with wrath, like other young men, if afterward any rallied them about a woman. Frida

Styrkaarsdatter in especial did this often—she was a fool in grain, old as she was, not many years younger than the mistress herself; and she had had two bastard children—for the last she had even been hard put to it to find a father. But Kristin had held a shielding hand over the poor creature; because she had fostered Björgulf and Skule with care and love, the mistress was long-suffering with the woman—though it vexed her that the old creature should ever prate to the boys of young maids.

Kristin thought now, 'twere best if she could get her sons wedded at a young age. But she knew 'twould not be easy—the men whose daughters might be equal matches for Naakkve and Björgulf in birth and blood would deem that her sons were not rich enough. And the King's enmity, and the judgment their father had brought down upon himself, would stand in the way if the lads should try to better their lot in the service of great lords. With bitterness she thought of the times when Erlend and Erling Vidkunssön had talked of a match 'twixt Nikulaus and one of the High Steward's daughters.

She knew, indeed, of one growing maid and another amongst the dales that would be a fitting match—rich and of good kindred, though their forbears, for the space of some lives back, had held themselves without the service of the court, and stayed at home in their own country. But she could not brook the thought that she and Erlend might get no for an answer if they made suit to these great landowners. Here Simon Darre might have been the best of spokesmen—and now had Erlend bereft them of this helper.

To the service of the Church she deemed none of her sons had a bent —unless 'twere Gaute or Lavrans. But Lavrans was still so young. And of all her sons Gaute was the only one whose help on the farm was of some avail to her.

Storm and snow had wrought havoc with the fences this year, and the snow-fall in the days about spring Holy Cross Mass* had hindered the work, so that the folk were hard driven to get through in time. Therefore, one day, Kristin sent off Naakkve and Björgulf to mend the fencing round a field that lay up nigh to the highway.

In the afternoon their mother went up to see how it fared with the lads at this unwonted work. Björgulf was working on the farm-road fence—she stopped a while and spoke with him. Then she went on northward. Soon she caught sight of Naakkve leaning over the fence talking with a woman on horseback who had stopped at the road's edge close by the paling. He fondled the horse, then he caught the girl by the ankle, and presently he moved his hand a little upward, as though heedlessly.

* 3rd May.

The young maid saw the lady first; she reddened and said somewhat to Naakkve. He drew away his hand quickly, and looked something dashed. The girl would have ridden on, but Kristin called out a greeting; afterwards she spoke a little with the maid, and asked after her kinswoman—the girl was sister's daughter to the mistress of Ulvsvoldene, and lately come a-visiting there. Kristin made as though she had seen naught, and talked a little with Naakkve of the fencing after the maid was gone.

Not long after, it chanced that Kristin was at Ulvsvoldene for the space of two weeks; the woman there was in the straw, and, after the child was born, lay gravely sick; Kristin was there as her neighbour, and one who was deemed the most skilled leech-woman in the parish. In this time Naakkve came often over with messages and errands to his mother, and this girl, Eyvor Haakonsdatter, found means always to meet him and talk with him. Kristin liked this little—she had no liking for the maid, nor could she see that Eyvor was fair, as she heard most men deemed. She was glad, the day she learned that Eyvor was gone home again to Raumsdal.

Yet she deemed not that Naakkve had cared aught for Eyvor; the more so when she heard Frida prating of the daughter of the house at Loptsgaard, Aasta Audunsdatter, and teasing Naakkve about her.

Kristin was in the brew-house one day, boiling a juniper brew, and she heard Frida's tongue busy again with this. Naakkve was with Gaute and his father without in the back courtyard; they were at work on a boat they meant to have for the fishing on the lake up in the fells— Erlend was a not unskilful boat-builder. Naakkve waxed wroth, but now Gaute joined in the teasing—Aasta would be a fitting match, he said——

"Ask for her yourself, if you deem so," said his brother, hotly.

"Nay, I will have none of her," answered Gaute, "for I have heard that red hair and fir woods thrive on barren ground—but I wot well you have a leaning to red hair——"

"Ay, but that word holds not for women neither, my son," said Erlend, laughing. "Red-haired wives are wont to be white and soft of flesh——"

Frida laughed noisily, but Kristin grew angry; this seemed to her unseemly talk before such young boys. She remembered, too, that Sunniva Olavsdatter had had red hair, though her friends had called it golden. Then Gaute said:

"Be glad that I said not: I durst not, for fear of sin. On Whitsunday watch-night you sat with Aasta in the tithe-barn all the time we danced on the church-green—so sure you must like her——"

Naakkve would have flown at his brother—but just then Kristin came out. When Gaute was gone, the mother asked her other son:

"What was this that Gaute said of you and Aasta Audunsdatter?"

"Methinks, mother, that naught was said you did not hear," answered the boy—he reddened and frowned angrily.

Kristin said vexedly:

"'Tis an ill thing that you young folks cannot keep a watch-night but you must dance and frolic about between the services. 'Twas not our use when I was a maid——"

"You have said yourself, mother, that when you were young, my grandfather would often sing for them, when folk danced upon the church-green——"

"Ay, but they were not such songs, and 'twas not such wild dancing," said his mother, "and we young folks kept us in seemly wise each by our parents—we went not off in pairs to sit in barns——"

Naakkve seemed ready to make a wrathful answer, when Kristin chanced to look over at Erlend. He was smiling stealthily, while he looked with one eye along the plank he was trimming with his axe. Angry and grieved, she went back into the brew-house again.

——But she thought not a little on what she had heard. Aasta Audunsdatter was none so bad a match—there was wealth at Lopts-gaard and three daughters only, but no son, and Ingebjörg, Aasta's mother, came of most worthy kindred.

That they at Jörundgaard should some day call Audun Torbergssön kinsman by marriage she had never thought. But he had had a stroke in the winter, and folk deemed not that he would live long—— And the girl was well mannered and winsome in her ways, and notable in the house, by what Kristin had heard. If Naakkve truly liked the maid, 'twere not wise to set oneself against this match. They must wait two years yet with the wedding—so young as both Aasta and Naakkve were —but she would gladly make Aasta welcome then as her son's wife.

But one fair day, in the middle of the summer, Sira Solmund's sister came in to Kristin to borrow somewhat. The women were standing out-side before the storehouses saying farewell, when the priest's sister said: Nay, but Eyvor Haakonsdatter! Her father had driven her from his house, for she was with child—so now had she come back for shelter to Ulvsvoldene.

Naakkve had been an errand up in the storehouse loft—he stopped short on the lowest step. When his mother caught sight of his face, such a sickness came on her, she felt as her legs would scarce bear her up. The boy was red to the roots of his hair as he went past towards the dwelling-house.

But she saw soon from the other's gossip that things must have been so with Eyvor long ere she first came to the parish that spring. My poor, harmless boy, thought Kristin with a lightened sigh—he is shamed now because he had thought well of the girl.

A few nights later Kristin lay in her bed alone, for Erlend was gone from home a-fishing. She knew not but that both Naakkve and Gaute were with him. But she was waked by Naakkve's touching her and whispering that he must speak with her. He crept up and sat him down on the bed by the footboard:

"Mother—I have been over and spoken with that poor woman, Eyvor, this night—I knew that they lied about her—I was so sure, I had gladly taken a red-hot iron in my hand to prove she lied, yonder magpie from Romundgaard——"

His mother lay still and waited. Naakkve strove to speak steadily, but all the time his voice kept shifting up and down with the hurry of his spirits:

"She was on her way to matins the day after Yule—she went alone, and the road from their farm lies, a long stretch, through forest. There she met two men—'twas yet dark, she knows not who they were; maybe outlawed robbers from the fells——At last she could keep them off no longer, poor weak young thing. To none durst she make her moan—when her mother and father saw her mischance, they dragged her by her hair and drove her from home with blows and curses. She wept so, mother, when she told me all this, 'twould have melted the very stones in the hill-sides." Naakkve stopped speaking suddenly and drew a long breath.

Kristin spoke of how it seemed to her a sore mischance that these villains had escaped. She hoped that God's justice would overtake them, and bring them to their due reward on the gallows-tree.

Thereupon Naakkve began to talk of Eyvor's father, how rich he was, and kin to one worthy family and another. The child Eyvor would send away to be fostered in another parish. Gudmund Darre's wife had had a bastard by a priest—and there sat Sigrid Andresdatter at Kruke, a good and honoured woman—— A man must be both hard of heart and unjust to deem Eyvor an outcast, for that, sorely against her will, it had been her lot to suffer shameful mischance—she might well be fit, none the less, to be wife to a man that held honour dear——

Kristin pitied the girl and cursed the ravishers—and, in her heart, thanked and praised fortune that not for three years yet would Naakkve be of age. Gently she prayed him to bethink him that now must he walk most heedfully, not seek Eyvor in her bower late of an evening, as he had done this night, nor show himself at Ulvsvoldene save when he had an errand to the folk of the house, else he might, all unwittingly, bring it about that folk should spread abroad yet uglier gossip of the luckless young child. Ay, 'twas well enough to say that they who doubted Eyvor's word, and believed not she had come to harm blamelessly would find his arm no nerveless one—nevertheless, 'twould be an evil thing for the poor girl if there were more talk——

Three weeks later, Eyvor's father came and fetched his daughter home to her betrothal and wedding. 'Twas a good farmer's son of her own parish that was the man; at first the parents on both sides had been against the match, because they were at odds about some farm lands. In the last winter the men had made friends again, and the two young folk were to have been betrothed, but then, suddenly, Eyvor would not —she had set her fancy on another man. But, afterwards, she saw it might well be something late to throw away her first lover. None the less she went to be with her mother's sister in Sil, deeming, belike, that here she would find help to hide her trouble, for now she was set upon having this new man. But when Hillebjörg at Ulvsvoldene saw how it was with the girl, she sent her back to her parents. That her father had flown in a fury and had beaten his daughter once and again, and that she had fled hither once more, was true enough. But now had he come to an accord with the first suitor—and now Eyvor must put up with him, little as she might like it.

Kristin saw that Naakkve took this hardly. For many days he went about scarce speaking a word, and his mother had such pity of him she scarce dared look his way—for if he met his mother's eye, he turned so red and looked so abashed that it cut Kristin to the heart.

When the serving-folk at Jörundgaard would have gossipped of these doings, the mistress bade them, sharply, to hold their tongues—she would not have that dirty matter or that wretched woman named in her house. Frida marvelled greatly: had she not many and many a time heard Kristin Lavransdatter judge mildly and help with boun- teous hands a maid who had fallen into such mischance—Frida herself had twice found safe shelter in her mistress's pity. But in the little she said of Eyvor Haakonsdatter she spoke as ill of her as any woman can of another.

Erlend laughed when she told him how sadly Naakkve had been fooled—'twas one evening when she sat out on the green spinning, and her husband came and stretched himself on the grass at her side.

"No great harm has been done, I trow," said the father; "rather seems it to me that the boy has learned a man's lesson at a cheap rate: put not your trust in women——"

"Say you so?" asked his wife; her voice shook with smothered anger.

"Ay——" Erlend smiled. "See, of you I believed, the time I met you first, you were so gentle a maid, you could scarce find in your heart to bite a slice of cheese—— Yielding as a silk ribbon and mild as any dove —but therein you fooled me finely, Kristin——"

"How think you 'twould have gone with us all," said she, "had I been so soft and gentle?"

"Nay——" Erlend took her hands, so that she was fain to stop her work; he smiled up at her, shining with gladness. Then he laid his head in her lap. "Nay, I knew not, my sweet one, *how* good was the luck God gave me when he led you into my path—Kristin!"

But, because she must ever and at all times keep herself in check, to hide her despair at Erlend's eternal heedlessness, it would chance at times that her temper took the upper hand when she must correct her sons: she grew heavy of hand and hot of speech. 'Twas oftenest Ivar and Skule that bore the brunt.

They were at the worst age now, in their thirteenth year, and so wild and self-willed that Kristin, at her wits' ends, thought many a time, was there any mother in Norway who had the rearing of two such ruffians. Comely they were, like all her children, with black, silky-soft ringletted hair, blue eyes beneath black brows, and narrow, fine-cut faces. They were tall for their age beyond the common, but narrow-shouldered still, with long, lean limbs—their joints stood out like the knots of a corn-stalk. They were so like that none outside their home knew them one from the other, and throughout the parish folk named them the Jörund-gaard dirksmen—and 'twas not meant as a title of honour. Simon had first given them this nickname in jest, for that Erlend had made them each the gift of a dirk, and these small swords they never laid from them, save when they were in church. Kristin liked it little that they had got the dirks, and yet less that they ever went about with axes, spears, or bows; she feared that these hot-headed boys might bring some mischief on themselves with such-like things. But Erlend said, curtly, they were so old now 'twas time they used them to bear arms.

She lived in one unending terror for these her twin sons. When she knew not whither they were gone, the mother wrung her hands in secret, and besought Mary Virgin and St. Olav to lead them home again, alive and unscathed. They climbed the fell-sides through rifts and up the face of headlong cliffs where none before had gone; they robbed eagles' nests, and came home with ugly, yellow-eyed, hissing fledgelings within the bosoms of their coats; they scrambled among the slate rocks along the Laagen, northward in the gorge, where the river dashes from fall to fall; once Ivar had been dragged by his stirrup and half killed—he was trying to ride a half-broken young stallion that the boys had got a saddle on, God only knows how. Errandless, for naught but prying's sake, they had ventured into the Finn's hut in the Toldstad woods—from their father they had learned some words of the Lapps' tongue, and when they greeted the old Finn witch-wife with these, she had feasted them on meat and drink, and they had stuffed them full to bursting, and that on a fast-day. And Kristin had ever held so strictly to it that when the grown folk fasted, the children must content them with little food and such-like things as they had no mind to—for to this had she been used by her parents when she was little. This time, for once in a way, Erlend, too, was stern with his sons, took and burnt the sweetmeats the Finn wife had given them to take with them, whilst he strictly forbade them ever again to go even to the edge of the forest where the Finns were. But, none the less, it tickled him to hear of the boys' adventure; and after, he would often tell Ivar and Skule tales of his doings and travels in the north, and of what he had seen there of these folks' ways, and he talked to the boys in this ugly heathenish speech of theirs.

For the rest, Erlend scarce ever chid his children, and turned it aside in jest when Kristin bewailed the twins' ways. At home on the manor they did endless mischief, though they could be useful too, when they must—unhandy, like Naakkve, they were not. But time and again, when their mother had set them some work and came to see how it fared, the tools would be lying there, and the boys standing watching their father, while he showed them how seamen made knots and such-like——

Lavrans Björgulfsön had often been wont, when he made a cross with tar over the byre door, or on suchlike places, to paint a little with the brush round about—paint a ring outside or draw a stroke over each cross-arm. One day the twins bethought themselves to make a target of one of these old cross-marks. Kristin was beside herself with despair and wrath at such Jewish doings, but Erlend took the children's part—they were so young, one could not look that they should think on the holiness of the cross each time they saw it tarred over a byre-door or on a cow's back. Let the boys go up to the cross on the church-green, kneel before it and kiss it, and say five paternosters and fifteen aves—no need to drag Sira Solmund to the manor for this. But this time Björgulf and Naakkve stood by their mother; the priest was fetched, and he sprinkled holy water on the wall and corrected the two young sinners most sternly.

——They gave Kristin's bulls and he-goats the heads of snakes to eat, to send them horn-mad. They teased Munan because he clung still to his mother's skirts, and Gaute too—he was the one they were oftenest at odds with—for the most part the Erlendssöns held together in the goodliest brotherhood. But now and again, when they got past bearing, Gaute would give them a drubbing. To chide them in words was like talking to a wall—and, if their mother grew hot with them, they would stand, their bodies stiff, their fists clenched, scowling at her with glittering eyes from under wrinkled brows, red as fire with fury. Kristin thought on what Gunnulf had told of Erlend—he had cast his knife at his father, and lifted his hand against him more times than one while he was yet a child. So she thrashed the twins, and thrashed hard, for she thought with terror: what would come of these children of hers if they were not tamed betimes.

Simon Darre was the only one who could do aught with these two madcaps—they loved their uncle, and ever grew meek and towardly when he talked to them good humouredly and quietly. But, now that they saw him no more, their mother could not see that they missed him. Sadly Kristin thought: the heart of a child is fickle.

And secretly, in her heart, the mother knew that, in spite of all, 'twas of these two sons she was well-nigh proudest. Could she but break this ill-omened defiance and wildness, it seemed to her none of the brothers promised a fairer manhood than these two. They had good health and were strong and sound of body, were fearless, truthful, generous, kindly to all poor folk, and more times than one had they shown a readiness and swiftness in counsel that far outwent, she thought, what one could look for from such young lads.

One evening in the hay harvest Kristin had been kept late in the kitchen-house, when Munan came rushing in, shouting that the old goat-shed was afire. There were no men at home or near by—some were at the smithy hammering their scythes sharp; some had gone north to the bridge, where the young folk were wont to gather on summer evenings. The mistress caught up a pair of buckets and ran, calling to her serving-women to follow after.

The goat-shed was a little old house with a roof going right down to the ground, and stood in the narrow way between the court-yard and the farm-yard, against the middle of the main stable wall and with other houses built close to it on either side. Kristin ran into the hearth-room penthouse and caught up a broad-axe and a fire-hook, but when she came round the corner of the stable, she saw no fire, but only a thick cloud of smoke pouring forth from a hole in the goat-shed roof. Ivar sat up on the roof-ridge hacking down at the roof, Skule and Lavrans were within the house tearing down burning flakes from the roofing, and trampling and stamping out the fire. Now came running Erlend, Ulf, and the men who had been at the smithy—Munan had run on thither and given warning—and now the fire was soon put out. But the worst mischance might well have befallen—the evening was still and sultry, but with a puff of wind from south ever and anon, and had the fire once been let blaze up in the goat-shed, most like all the houses round about the north end of the yard, the stables, the store-houses, and the dwelling-houses themselves, had been swept away.

Ivar and Skule had been up on the stable roof—they had trapped a hawk and had gone up to hang it from the gable cross—when they smelt burning, and saw smoke coming from the roof below them. Straightway they leaped down on the roof, and, with the small axes they had in their hands, began to hack away the smouldering turf, while they sent off Lavrans and Munan, who were playing near by, the one for hooks and the other to their mother. By good fortune the laths and rafters of the roof were too rotten to burn freely; but 'twas clear this time the twins had saved their mother's manor, by setting to work straightway to tear down the burning roof and wasting no time in running first for grown folks' help.

'Twas not easy to understand how the fire had arisen, if 'twere not in this wise, that Gaute, an hour before, had passed by that way with embers for the smithy, and he owned that the fire-pan had not been covered—so, belike, a spark had flown on to the tinder-dry turf roof.

But of that less was said than of the twins' and Lavrans's readiness— at the fire-watch that Ulf set, and wherein the whole household kept him company late into the night, while Kristin had strong ale and mead borne out to them. All three boys had burns on hands and feet—their foot-gear was so scorched it broke in bits. Young Lavrans was but nine years old, so 'twas hard for him to bear the pain with patience for long, but at the first he was the proudest of all, going about with bound-up hands and hearing all the manor-folk praise him.

That night, when they had gone to rest, Erlend pressed his wife in to him.

"Kristin mine, Kristin mine—be not so careful and troubled about your children—see you not, dear one, what metal our sons are made of? You bear you ever towards these two mettlesome lads as though you looked that their path must lie 'twixt gallows and block. Methinks now you should joy in your reward for all you have borne of pangs and pains and toils, in those years you went ever with a child beneath your belt and a child at your breast and a child upon your arm—naught would you speak of then but the little bratlings, and now, when they have grown to wit and manhood, you go about amongst them as though you were both deaf and dumb, scarce paying heed enough to answer if they speak to you. God help me, 'twould seem as though you loved them less, now you have not the cares of their childhood to plague you, and our fair, well-grown sons are a joy and a blessing to you——"

Kristin did not trust herself to answer a word.

But she lay there and could not fall asleep. And towards morning she climbed over the sleeping man quietly, went on bare feet over to the peep-hole, and opened it.

The sky was cloudy grey and the air cool—far to the south, where the hills drew together and closed the Dale, a rain-shower was sweeping over the uplands. The mistress stood a while looking out—'twas ever hot and close here in the new storehouse loft, where they slept in summer. On the breath of dampness that was in the air, the scent of hay was borne in to her, so strong and sweet. A bird here and there, out in the summer night, twittered a little in its sleep.

Kristin found her fire-steel and lit a stump of candle. She crept over to where Ivar and Skule slept on their bench bed—let the light shine upon them and felt their cheeks with the back of her hand—sure enough they had a little fever. Softly she said an Ave Maria, and made the sign of the cross over the two. Gallows and block—that Erlend could make a jest of such things—he who himself had been so near——

Lavrans moaned and murmured in his sleep. The mother stood a little, bent over the two youngest, who had their couch on a small bench cot behind the foot-board of their parents' bed. Lavrans was hot and flushed, and tossed about, but did not wake when she touched him.

Gaute lay with his milk-white arms behind his neck, in among his long flaxen-yellow hair—the bed-clothes he had thrown clean off him. Such hot blood had he, that he would ever sleep naked; and he was shining white of skin—the sun-burnt hue on face, neck, and hands stood out sharply. His mother drew the covering up above his waist.

——'Twas hard for her to be vexed at Gaute—he was so like her father. She had said but little to him of the mischance he so nearly had brought upon them all. So clear-headed and thoughtful was this boy, she deemed full surely he would take it to heart of his own accord and not forget it.

Naakkve and Björgulf had the second of the two beds in the loft. For a long time the mother stood and let the light shine upon the two sleeping youths. Black down already shadowed their childishly soft red mouths. Naakkve's foot stuck out from under the coverlid—narrow, high of instep, deep-arched in the sole—and not over clean. And yet it seemed to the mother 'twas not long since this man's foot was so little 'twas quite hidden in her closed hand, and she had pressed it in under her breast and lifted it to her mouth, gently biting each single little round toe-bud, for they were as pink and sweet as the flower-bells on a bilberry bush.

——It might well be that she was not thankful enough for the portion and the lot God had granted her. The memory of the time before Naakkve was born, and of the visions of horror she had writhed under—might shoot at times hot as fire through her mind: *she* had been delivered, as when one awakes from dream horrors and the crushing weight of nightmare to the blessed light of day.——But other women had wakened to find the day's misery worse than the worst they had dreamed. Even now, when she saw a cripple or a misshapen creature, Kristin would grow heartsick with the memory of her own fear for her unborn child. Then would she humble herself with burning ardour before God and Holy Olav; she would throw herself into good works; she would strive to wring tears of true repentance from her eyes the while she prayed. Yet ever did she feel within her heart this unyielding discontent, and the warm glow faded, and the tears of penitence sank back into her soul as water oozes away in sand. Then she comforted herself: 'twas that she had not that gift of holiness she had one time hoped was her heritage from her father. She was hard and sinful, but like enough she was no worse than most folk, and like most folk she must lay her account with suffering, in her second home, the fervent fires that were needful to melt and cleanse her heart.

Yet, between-whiles, she longed to be another. When she looked upon the seven fair sons who sat at her board; when, on mass-day mornings, she walked up towards the church, while the bells rang out and called so sweetly to gladness and God's peace, and saw the flock of tall, well-clad young lads, her sons, go up the slope before her. She knew of no other woman who had borne so many children and never had to know what 'twas to lose one—and all were fair and healthful, without blemish in body or mind—Björgulf alone was something near-sighted. She longed to be able to forget her cares altogether, to grow gentle and thankful, to love God and fear him, as her father had done—she remembered her father had said that he who with contrite heart minds him of his sins, and bows him before the Lord's cross, never needs to bend his neck beneath this world's mischance or wrong.

Kristin blew out the light, snuffed the wick, and put the stump in its place up under the topmost wall-log. She went to the peep-hole again —already 'twas light as day without, but grey and dead—upon the lower house-roofs that she looked over, the scant, sun-burnt grass shook gently in a breath of wind; a little whispering sound ran through the leaves of the birch trees that showed over against her above the hall-house roof.

She looked at her hands, clasping the peep-hole frame. They were rough and toil-worn, her arms right up to the elbows were brown, and the muscles swollen, hard as wood. While she was still young, the children had sucked blood and milk from her till all trace of a maiden's smooth, fresh roundness had been worn from her body. Now each day's toil took away something of what was left of the comeliness that had marked her out as daughter and wife and mother of men of noble blood—the narrow white hands; the soft fair-skinned arms; the clear and tender hue of face that she had shielded from the sun so heedfully with a kerchief, and tended with cunningly brewed washes. Long ere now she had grown careless whether the sun beat straight upon her sweat-stained face and burnt it brown as any poor peasant wife's.

Her hair was all that was left to her of her maiden beauty. 'Twas thick and brown as ever, seldom though she found time to wash and tend it. The heavy, tangled plait that hung down her back had not been undone these three days.

Kristin flung it forward over her shoulder, unplaited the hair, and shook it out—it still wrapped her about like a cloak and reached below her knee. She took a comb from out her case, and, shivering a little now and again, as she sat there in her bare shift beneath the little window that stood open to the morning chill, she combed out the tangled masses heedfully.

When she had smoothed her hair and plaited it again in a firm and heavy rope, 'twas as though she felt a little better. Then she lifted Munan, sound asleep, carefully in her arms, laid him down next the wall in the great bed, and herself slipped between him and the sleeping man. She took her youngest into her arms, laid his head to rest against her shoulder, and then she fell asleep——

She overslept next morning; when she awoke, Erlend and the lads were up. "I trow verily you suck your mother still, when no one sees," said Erlend, when he saw that Munan lay by his mother. Angered at this, the boy ran out and crept over the head-piece of one of the beams which bore the balcony—he would fain show his manhood. "Jump!" shouted Naakkve from the courtyard below; he caught his little brother in his arms, turned him upside down and flung him to Björgulf—his two grown brothers tumbled him about till he laughed and screamed.

But next day, when Munan stood weeping because a bow-string had caught his fingers in its rebound, the twins took and wrapped him up in a coverlid, bore him thus up to his mother's bed, and stuffed into his mouth a lump of bread so huge the boy was well-nigh choked.

II

ERLEND's house-priest at Husaby had taught the three eldest sons their books. They were not over-diligent scholars, but they were apt to learn, all three, and their mother, who herself had been brought up so learnedly, watched over them, so that they learned not so very little.

And the year Björgulf and Nikulaus were at Tautra cloister with Sira Eiliv, they had sucked—so said the priest—at the breasts of Lady Knowledge with fiery zeal. The teacher there was an aged monk who, busy as a bee, had gathered learning his whole life long from all the books he could come by, Latin or Norse. Sira Eiliv was himself a lover of wisdom, but, in the years at Husaby, he had had little chance to follow his bent towards book-lore. For him the fellowship with Lector Aslak was like sæter-pasture to starved cattle. And the two young boys, who, among the monks, clung to their home-priest, followed, open-mouthed, the two men's learned talk. And brother Aslak and Sira Eiliv found delight in feeding the two young minds with the most delicious honey from the cloister's bookshelves, whereto brother Aslak himself had added many copies and excerpts from the choicest books. Soon the boys became so skilled that the monk had rarely need to speak to them in the Norse tongue, and, when their parents came to fetch them, they both could answer the priest in Latin, glibly and without many slips.

This learning the brothers had kept up since. There were many books at Jörundgaard—Lavrans had owned five; of these, 'twas true, two had gone to Ramborg at the parting of the estate, but she had never had a mind to learn to read, and Simon was not so skilled in letters that he cared to read for pleasure's sake, though he could both make out a letter and print one himself well enough. Therefore he had prayed Kristin to keep the books until his children grew bigger. Three books, which had belonged to his parents, Erlend gave to Kristin some little time after they were wed, and yet another book she had got in gift from Gunnulf Nikulaussön; he himself had had the matter of it brought together and written down for his brother's wife out of books on Holy Olav and his miracles, some other sagas of the saints, and the writing the Franciscans in Oslo had sent to the Pope concerning brother Edvin Rikardssön, praying that he might be canonized. And, last of all, Naakkve had got a prayer-book of Sira Eiliv when they parted. So Naakkve read much to his brother—he read easily and well, with somewhat of a singing voice, just as brother Aslak had taught him; but he liked best the Latin books —his own prayer-book and one that had been Lavrans Björgulfsön's. Yet most of all he prized a great book, of a passing fair script, that had come down an heirloom in his kin from their renowned forefather, Bishop Nikulaus Arnessön himself.

Kristin would fain have got some learning for her younger sons, too, as was but fitting for men of their birth. But 'twas not easy to see how this could be: Sira Eirik was all too old, and Sira Solmund could but read from the books he used at mass; and many things in what he read he understood not well himself. Lavrans would now and again of an evening find pleasure in sitting by Naakkve and letting his brother teach him the letters on the wax tablet—but the other three had no mind at all to win such knowledge. One day Kristin took a Norse book and bade

Gaute see if he remembered aught of what he had learned in his child-hood of Sira Eiliv; but Gaute could not contrive to spell out three words, and when he came upon the first sign standing for several letters, he shut the book up, laughing, and said he liked not to play that game.

Now, 'twas for this reason that Sira Solmund, one evening in the late summer, came and prayed Nikulaus to come home with him. An out-land knight, who was come from the Olav's Mass at Nidaros, had bor-rowed a house at Romundgaard, but neither he nor his esquires and servants had the Norse tongue; the guide who had brought them hither understood but a word or two of their prate; Sira Eirik lay sick—could not Naakkve come and speak with the knight in Latin?

Naakkve seemed nowise ill pleased to be sent for thus to interpret, but he made as though 'twas nothing, and went with the priest. He came home very late in the night, in high feather and not a little drunken—'twas wine he had been given; the stranger knight had store of it with him, and had set it flowing, for the priest and the deacon and Naakkve too, something too freely. He was named somewhat like Sir Allan or Allart of Bekelar; he was from Flanders, and was on pilgrimage to the holy places round about the north countries. He was friendly beyond measure, the talking had gone smoothly.—And then Naakkve brought forth his message. The knight was bound hence to Oslo, and thereafter to places of pilgrimage in Denmark and Germany, and he was bent on having Nikulaus ride with him and be his interpreter, at least while yet he was here in Norway. And besides, he had dropped a hint that if the young man would follow him out into the world, Sir Allart was the man to make his fortune—it seemed as though, in the land he came from, golden spurs and neck-chains, heavy money-purses and goodly weapons did but lie waiting for such a man as young Nikulaus Erlendssön to come and pick them up. Naakkve had answered that he was yet under age, and must have his father's leave—but Sir Allart had pressed a gift upon him none the less; 'twould in no wise bind him, he had said, plainly—a half-length, plum-coloured silken jerkin with silver bells on the sleeve-flaps.

Erlend listened to him, all but silent, with a strangely high-wrought look. When Naakkve was done speaking, he sent Gaute for the casket with his writing-gear, and straightway set about inditing a letter in Latin—Björgulf had to help him, for Naakkve was in no case to be of much use, and his father sent him to bed. In the letter 'twas written that Erlend bade the knight to his home next day after prime, that they might talk of Sir Allart's proffer to take the well-born young man Niku-laus Erlendssön into his service as his esquire. He begged the knight to forgive that he sent back the proffered gift, with the prayer that Sir Allart would have it in his keeping until Nikulaus, with his father's allowance, had taken oath in the service of the stranger, in accordance with the use prevailing among the knighthood of all lands.

Erlend dropped a little wax at the bottom of the letter and pressed his small seal—that on his ring—lightly down on it. Then, forthwith, he sent a serving-man to Romundgaard with the letter and the silken jerkin.

"Husband—surely you cannot think to send your young son out into foreign lands with an unknown man and an outlander," said Kristin, trembling.

"We must see——" Erlend smiled so strangely. "——But I deem not that 'tis like to be," said he, when he saw her disquietude; he smiled something more broadly, and stroked her cheek.

At Erlend's bidding, Kristin had strewn the floor of the upper hall with juniper and flowers, spread the best cushions on the benches, and set the board with a linen cloth, and good meat in trenchers of fine wood, and drink in the rare, silver-mounted drinking-horns that the manor had in heritage from Lavrans. Erlend had shaven himself with care, curled his hair, and clad himself in a black, richly broidered, long coat of foreign cloth. He went to the gate of the manor to meet the guest, and when they came across the court-yard together, Kristin could not but deem her husband looked far more like one of those knights of Valland of whom the sagas tell, than did the fat, fair stranger in gay and motley garments of sarsenet and velvet. She stood upon the balcony of the upper hall, bravely decked and adorned with a silken coif; the Fleming kissed her hand when she bade him *Bien venu,* and more words passed not between her and him in the hours he was with them. She did not understand aught of the men's parleyings; neither did Sira Solmund, who was with his guest. But the priest said to the mistress that hereby he had surely made Nikulaus' fortune. She answered neither yea nor nay.

Erlend had a little French, and spoke glibly such German as hireling soldiers use, and the talk changed betwixt him and the stranger knight went smoothly and in courtly wise. But Kristin marked that the Fleming seemed not over well pleased as it went on, although this he strove to hide. His sons Erlend had bidden wait over in the new store-house loft, till he sent them word to come up hither—but no message was sent for them.

Erlend and the mistress went with the knight and the priest to the gate. When the guests were lost to sight among the fields, Erlend turned to Kristin and said, with a smile that she misliked:

"With yonder fellow would I not send Naakkve from home as far as to Breiden even——"

Ulf Haldorssön came up to them. He and Erlend spoke somewhat that Kristin could not hear, but Ulf swore fiercely and spat. Erlend laughed and patted the man's shoulder:

"Ay, had I been such a stay-at-home as the good farmers here—but I have seen so much, I promise you 'tis not I will sell my fair young falcons from out my hands and into the devil's—— Sira Solmund had not understood aught, the holy calf's-head——"

Kristin stood with hanging arms; the colour came and went in her face. Horror and shame took hold on her, so that she felt sick; her legs seemed to fail her. Sure enough, she had known that such things were—as of somewhat immeasurably far off—but that this unnamable thing dared thrust itself forward right to her very threshold—— 'Twas as the last billow that must needs overset her storm-tossed, over-laden boat. Holy Mary, must she go in dread of *such* things too for her sons——?

Erlend said, with the same ill-favoured smile:

"I thought my own thoughts, yester-eve already—Sir Allart seemed to me something too *kurteis*, by what Naakkve told. I wot well 'tis no knightly use anywhere in the world to greet a lad one would take in service with a kiss on the mouth, nor to give him costly gifts ere ever he has made proof of his worth——"

Trembling from head to foot, Kristin said:

"Why bade you me strew my floor with roses and spread my board with linen cloths for such a ——?" She spoke the worst of words.

Erlend knit his brows. He had picked up a stone—keeping an eye on Munan's red cat, which was stealing flat on its belly, through the long grass under the house wall, towards the chickens by the stable door. Whiz—he flung the stone; the cat was round the corner in a flash, and the bevy of hens flounced hither and thither. He turned to his wife:

"——Methought I might as well *see* the man; had he been a trustworthy fellow, then—and to see him I must needs show him courtesy—*I* am not Sir Allart's confessor. And you heard, belike, he is bound for Oslo." Erlend laughed again. "Now, like enough, some of my true friends and dear whilom kinsmen may hear tell that we sit not here at Jörundgaard either lousing our rags and eating herring and oat-meal bannock——"

Björgulf had the headache and lay abed when Kristin came up into the loft at supper-time; and Naakkve said somewhat of not going over to the hall to supper.

"Methinks you are dull this evening, son," said his mother to him.

"Nay, how can you think so, mother?"—Naakkve smiled scornfully. "That I seem to be a bigger fool than other men, and 'tis easier to throw dust in my eyes, is naught to mope for, sure——"

"Take comfort," said his father, when they sat at the board, and

Naakkve was still more silent than his wont. "You will come out into the world yet to try your fortune——"

"It depends, father," answered Naakkve, low, as if he meant Erlend alone to hear, "on whether Björgulf can bear me company." Then he laughed quietly. "But say to Ivar and Skule what you have said to me—'tis their one longing, I trow, to grow up and be of an age to fare forth——"

Kristin stood up, and drew on a hooded cloak. She thought to go north to the old beggar-man in Ingebjörg's cottage, she told them. The twins proffered to go along and carry the sack for her, but she would liefer go alone.

The evenings were somewhat dark already, and north of the church the road ran through woods and under the shadow of Hammer-hill. Here, cold gusts ever blew from out the gorge, and the river's roar seemed to bring with it a breath of damp. Swarms of great white moths hovered and flickered under the trees—sometimes they swept right against the woman; it seemed as, in the dusk, the palely shining linen about her head and breast lured them. She beat at them with her hands as she hastened upward, slipping on the smooth pine-needle carpet and stumbling on the writhen roots that wound across the path she followed.

——There was a dream that had haunted Kristin for many a year. The first time she had dreamed it was the night before Gaute was born, but even now it would chance that she waked all a-sweat, with her heart hammering as if 'twould beat itself in sunder in her breast, and knew that she had dreamed the selfsame dream.

She saw a flowery lawn—a steep hill-side, deep in pine forest that hemmed in the greensward on three sides, thick and murky; at the foot of the slope a little tarn mirrored the dark woods and the green, spangled clearing. The sun was behind the trees—from the very top of the hill-side the last golden light of evening sifted in long rays through the firs, and in the depths of the tarn shining sunset clouds swam amidst the water-lily leaves.

In the midst of the slope, standing deep in the scree of campions and buttercups and foamy clouds of the green-white angelica, she saw her child. Naakkve it must have been, the first time she dreamed it—she had but the two then, and Björgulf yet lay in his cradle. Afterwards she never knew surely which of her children it might be—the little round sunburnt face under the round-cropped yellow-brown hair seemed to her now like one, now like another, but ever the child was two to three years old, and clad in just such a little dark-yellow coat as she was used to sew for her little boys' everyday wear—of homespun wool, dyed with litmus and edged with red binding.

She herself, it seemed to her at times, was on the farther side of the tarn. Or she was not at the place at all, but yet she saw all that befell——

She saw her little son move hither and thither, and turn his face as he plucked the flowers. And a dull fear pressed heavy on her heart, a foreboding of an evil thing to come; yet first there came ever with this dream a mighty aching sweetness, as she gazed at the fair child there in the meadow.

Then she grows ware that from out the dark up in the forest fringe there parts itself a shaggy, living bulk. It moves without a sound; two tiny wicked eyes glare out. Right out on to the upper meadow comes the bear, stands and sways its head and shoulders, sniffing downwards. Then it springs. Kristin had never seen a living bear, but she knows they spring not thus; this is no right bear. This moves like a cat—now it turns grey—like a grey, shaggy giant-cat it leaps, with long lithe bounds, down the grassy slope.

The mother watches with the anguish of death upon her—and she cannot come where the little one is to save him; she cannot warn him with a sound. Then the child grows ware that *something* is there; it turns half round and looks over its shoulder. With a dreadful, little low cry of fear it tries to run down the slope, lifting its legs, as little children do, high in the long grass, and the mother hears clearly the little sounds of the sappy stalks breaking as the child pushes its way through the tangled growth of flowers. Then it stumbles on something in the grass, falls headlong, and next moment the monster is on top of it, with arched back and head thrust deep between its fore-paws. Then she wakes——

——And each time she lay awake for hours before it availed aught to try to calm herself—by thinking 'twas but a dream! Her smallest child, that lay betwixt her and the wall, she would draw close in to her—would think of how, had it been real, she might have done this or that—frightened the monster with shrieks or with a staff—and at her belt there hung ever the long keen knife——

No sooner had she talked herself into quietness in this wise, than 'twould break over her anew, the unbearable agony, as, in her dream, she stood strengthless, and saw her little one's poor, vain efforts to flee from the deadly swift and strong and cruel beast. She felt as though the blood boiled and surged within her, as though her body swelled and her heart must burst, since it could not contain such a wave of blood——

The cottage called Ingebjörg's cot lay up on Hammer-hill, a little below the highway, which here pressed up the height. It had stood empty many a year, and the ground was leased to a man who had got leave to clear a place and build close by. An old beggar-man, left behind from a gang of mumpers, had now got leave to creep in there. When she had heard of it, Kristin had sent up meat and clothes and healing simples, but she herself had till now had no time to go thither.

'Twould soon be all over with the poor man, she saw. She gave her sack to the beggar-woman who had stayed behind with him, did the little she now could to ease him, and, when she learned that they had sent for the priest, she washed his face, hands, and feet, that they might be clean, and ready for his last anointing.

'Twas thick with smoke in the little hovel, and there was a horribly sickly, foul stench. When two of the settler's women-folk came in, Kristin prayed them send to Jörundgaard for all they might need, then said farewell and went. A strange, sick fear of meeting the priest with the Lord's body had come upon her, and she turned aside into the first by-path she came to.

That 'twas naught but a cattle-path she soon saw; she found herself plunged in trackless wilderness. Fallen trees with their high, tangled masses of roots were fearsome to look on; she must creep over them, when she could not find a way round. Flakes of moss slipped from under her feet when she had to scramble down amongst great stones. Cobwebs clung to her face, and branches struck her and took hold on her clothes. When she must pass over a trickling beck, or came to a low swampy opening in the forest, 'twas nigh impossible to find a place where she could slip through the thick, wet scrub of leafy bushes. And the loathly white moths were everywhere thick under the trees in the dark, swarming up in great clouds from off the heather tufts where she trod.

But at length she came out on the low hills down towards the Laagen. Here the fir wood was scant and sparse, for here the trees must send their roots twisting far over the barren rock, and the forest floor was little else but dry, grey-white reindeer-moss that crackled beneath her feet—amid it stray tufts of heather stood out black. The smell of the pine-needles was hotter and dryer and sharper than higher up—hereabout the forest ever showed scorched and yellow needles from right early in the spring. The white moths still kept after her——

The thunder of the river drew her downward. She went right out on the edge and looked down. Deep down below the water shimmered white, where it boiled, thundering, over the slaty rocks from pool to pool.

The changeless roar of the falls went quivering through her overwrought body and soul. It minded and minded her of somewhat—of a time endlessly long since—even then she had known that she could not bear the lot she had chosen for herself. She had laid open her shielded, tender girlhood's life to ravaging, fleshly love—in dread, in dread, in dread had she lived ever since, a bondswoman from the first hour of motherhood. To the world she had given herself up in her youth, and the more she struggled and fluttered in the world's snare, the more straitly she found herself bound and prisoned by the world. Her sons she strove to guard, with vainly flapping wings tied down by worldly cares. Her dread, her unspeakable weakness, she had striven to hide from all men, had gone forward with a straight back and a calm face, held her peace, and fought to safeguard her children's welfare in every wise she could——

But ever with that hidden, breathless fear—if they fare ill, 'twere more than I can bear. And the deeps of her heart made moan at the memory of her father and mother. Even as they had walked, laden with fear and care for their children, day after day forward unto death, they had had strength to bear their burden; and 'twas not that they loved their children less, but that they loved them with a better love——

And was she now to see her strife end thus?—Had she but reared a brood of restless eyases, who lay in her nest impatiently waiting the hour when their wings would bear them out over the farthest blue fells——? And their father clapped his hands together and laughed—fly, fly, my young birds——

Bloody fibres from her heart's roots would they drag with them when they took flight, and they would know naught of it. And she would be left behind to sit alone; and all the heart-strings which once had bound her to this old home of hers she herself had torn asunder long ago—— Surely 'twould be such a life as is neither life nor death.

She turned, and half ran, with stumbling steps, up over the pale, sere carpet of reindeer-moss, her cloak gathered tightly about her, for 'twas so uncanny when it caught in the bushes. At last she came out upon the small hay-fields a little north of the gild-shelter and the church. As she went slantwise across the field she was ware of someone standing in the road. He called: "Is it you, Kristin?"—she knew 'twas her husband.

"You were long away," said Erlend. "'Tis deep night already, Kristin. I began to grow afraid."

"Were you afraid for me?" Her voice came from her harder and haughtier than she would have had it.

"Not so much afraid either. But it came to my mind that I had best come and meet you."

They scarce spoke a word as they went southward. All was still when they came into the courtyard. Some of the horses they had at home shambled along under the house walls, grazing, but all the folk were abed.

Erlend went straight to the storehouse loft, but Kristin turned her steps to the kitchen-house. "I must look for somewhat," she answered to her husband's question.

He stood hanging over the balcony waiting for his wife—and then he saw her come out from the kitchen-house with a lighted pine-root torch in her hand, and go over to the hearth-room house. The man waited a while—then he ran down and went in after her.

She had lit a candle and set it on the board. Erlend felt a strange chill of fear go through him as he saw her standing there by the lone taper in the empty house—there was naught in the room but the fixed furnishings, and in the candlelight the worn wood glistened, stripped and bare. The hearth was cold and clean swept, save for the pine-root brand, which lay there where it had been thrown, yet glowing. They were not wont to use this room, Erlend and Kristin; it might well be half a year since fire had been kindled there. The air was strangely close; the many blended, living odours left by man's abidings, his comings and goings, were lacking, and smoke-vent and door had not been opened in all that time—so the place smelt of wool and hides; some rolled-up skins and sacks, which Kristin had taken out from the wares in the store, were piled up in the empty bed that had been Lavrans' and Ragnfrid's.

Strewn on the top of the board lay a many small skeins—sewing thread and yarn for mending with, both linen and wool, which Kristin had set apart when she was dyeing. She stood fingering them and setting them in order.

Erlend sat him down in the high-seat at the board end. The room seemed strangely wide and empty about the slender man, as it gaped there, stripped of cushions and hangings. The two warriors of St. Olav with cross-marked helms and shields, that Lavrans had carven for high-seat posts, scowled, grim and moody, out from under Erlend's narrow brown hands. No man could carve out leafage and beasts fairlier than Lavrans, but with men's semblances he had never been over happy.

For long the two kept so still that not a sound was to be heard, save the dull thuds on the sward without, where the horses wandered in the summer night.

"Are you not for bed soon, Kristin?" he asked, at length.

"Are not you?"

"I thought to wait for you," said the man.

"I have no mind to go up yet—I cannot sleep——"

"What is't then that lies so heavy on your mind, Kristin, that you deem you will not sleep?" he asked after a little.

Kristin drew her upright. She stood with a skein of heather-green wool in her hands; she pulled at it and twisted it between her fingers.

"What was it you spoke with Naakkve to-day——" She swallowed once or twice, she was so dry in the throat. "Some plan—'twould not do for him he seemed to think—but you talked of how Ivar and Skule——"

"Oh—that!" Erlend smiled a little. "I but said to the lad—*I* have a kinsman by marriage, too, now that I bethink me.—Though Gerlak, I trow, will scarce be so ready to kiss my hands and take from me cloak and sword as before he was. But he has ships on the sea—and rich kinsmen, both at Bremen and at Lynn. And sure the man must understand that it behoves him to help his wife's brothers—*I* spared not my goods and gear when I was a rich man and gave my daughter to Gerlak Tiedekenssön to wife."

Kristin said naught. At last Erlend said, somewhat hotly:

"Jesus, Kristin, stand not so, staring as you were made of stone——"

"Little thought I, the time we first came together, that our children should need to wander the world around, begging their bread in strangers' houses——"

"Nay, devil fetch me if I meant that they should beg! But should they have, all seven of them, to wring their bread from your farms here, 'twill be but peasant's fare, my Kristin—and I trow my sons are little fit for that. Bully-boys they seem like to be, Ivar and Skule—and out in the world is there both wheaten bread and cake for the man who will carve out his meat with his sword."

"Hirelings and vassals would you have your sons to be——?"

"Hire I took myself, in the days when I was young and followed Count Jacob. God be gracious to him, say I—I learned somewhat then that a man gets not the knowledge of at home in this land of ours—here, either he sits peacocking in his high-seat with silver belt about his belly, swilling himself full with ale, or he walks behind his plough smelling to the rumps of his jades. 'Twas a hearty life I lived in the Count's service—I say it, even though I had got that block fast to my leg while yet I was of Naakkve's age.—At least I had some joy of my youth——"

"Be still!" Kristin's eyes seemed to grow black. "Would you not deem it the deadliest harm if your sons were ensnared in such sin and mischance——?"

"Ay, God defend them from the like of that—but 'twere not needful either that they should copy all their father's follies. A man *can*, sure, take service with a noble, Kristin, without such hangers-on to clog him——"

"'He who draws the sword shall perish by the sword,' so stands it written, Erlend!"

"Ay, I have heard it, my dear one. Yet did the most of both your forefathers and mine make a good and Christian end in their beds, with the last anointing and all ghostly comfort. You need but call to mind your own father—he had shown in his youth that he was a man that could wield the sword——"

"'Twas in war, Erlend, at the bidding of the King they had gone to help to guard our homes and hearths, that my father and the others took up arms. Yet father himself said 'twas not God's will with us that we should bear arms—christened, Christian men—one against the other——"

"Nay, that know I. But the world is what it is, since ever Adam and Eve ate of the tree—and that was fore my time; 'tis not my blame that we are born with sin within us——"

"Shameful is your talk——!"

Erlend broke in, vehemently:

"Kristin—you know it well—never was I slow to repent and make amends for my sins as well as might be. No godly man am I, 'tis true. I saw too much when I was child and youth—— My father was such a dear friend of the great lords of the chapter—they came and went in his house like grey swine; Lord Eiliv, when he was priest, and Sir Sigvat Lande and all their following; and little else came with them but wrangling and jars—hard-hearted and unmerciful they showed them to their own archbishop—no more holy and peace-loving than so were they, they who each day held in their hands the holiest of holy things and lifted God Himself aloft in the bread and wine——"

"'Tis not for us to judge the priests—father ever said 'twas our duty to bow down before their priesthood and obey them, but that their natural man lies under the judgment of Almighty God alone——"

"A—ay." Erlend lingered a little on the word. "So I know he said, and you have said it too, ere now. I wot well you are more godly in such-like things than I can ever be—yet, Kristin, 'tis hard for me to see how it should be a right reading of God's word to go on, as your way is, ever storing up wrath and never forgetting. A long memory he too had, Lavrans—oh, no! I say naught of your father but that he was pious and nobly good, and that are you too, I wot—but often when you speak so soft and sweet, as your mouth were filled with honey, I fear me you are thinking most upon old wrongs, and God may judge whether your heart is full as pious as your mouth——"

Of a sudden she dropped down, lay over the board with her face hidden on her arms, and wept aloud. Erlend sprang up—she lay weeping, with hoarse, racking sobs that shook her frame. Erlend laid his arm on her shoulders.

"Kristin, what is it——? What is't?" he said again, sitting down on the bench by her and trying to lift her head. "Kristin—nay, weep not so—methinks you have lost your wits——"

"I am frighted!" She sat up, clenched her hands in her lap. "I am

so frighted; Mary, gentle lady mine, help us all—I am so frighted—
what will become of all my sons——?"

"Ay, Kristin mine—but you must use you to the thought—you *cannot* hide them longer beneath your skirts—soon will they be grown men,
all our sons. And you are like the bitch still——" He sat with one leg
over the other, his hands folded over his knee, looking down somewhat
wearily at his wife—"you snap blindly both at friend and foe, when 'tis
aught that touches your children."

She got up sharply, and stood a moment dumb, wringing her hands.
Then she began to walk swiftly up and down the room. She said
naught, and Erlend sat silent, looking at her.

"Skule——" She stopped before the man. "A luckless name you
gave your son. But you would have it—you *willed* that the duke should
live again in the child——"

"'Tis a good name enough, Kristin. Luckless—there is ill luck of
many kinds. Well I remembered, when I named my son after my
father's mother's father, that fortune betrayed him, but, none the less,
king he was, with better right than the comb-maker's seed*——"

"You were proud enough, you and Munan Baardssön, that you were
of King Haakon Haalegg's near kindred——"

"Ay, for you know that my father's aunt, Margaret Skulesdatter,
brought kingly blood into Sverre's stock——"

For a long time man and wife stood and gazed into each other's eyes.

"Ay, I know what you are thinking on, my fair lady wife." Erlend
went and sat him down again in the high-seat. With his hands resting
on the two warrior-heads he leaned forward a little; he smiled a cold
and galling smile. "But you see, Kristin mine—me it has not broken,
that I am become now a poor and friendless man. 'Tis well you should
know it—I am not afraid that with me my father's line has fallen for all
time from might and honour. I too was betrayed by fortune—but had
my plan but sped, then had I and my sons now sat in the seats on the
King's right hand, that we, his near kinsmen, are born to. For me the
game is up now, mayhap—but I can see it on my sons, Kristin—they
will win back the place that befits their birth. You need not to grieve
so for them, and strive not so to bind them fast here in this nook-shotten
dale of yours—let them prove them freely, and you will see maybe, ere
you die, they will have won firm footing again on their father's rightful
heritage——"

"Oh, you can talk!" Hot, bitter tears of wrath were pricking in the
woman's eyes, but she forced them back and laughed, with mouth
twisted awry:

"Methinks you are yet more childish than the lads, Erlend! You can

* See Note 3.

sit and talk thus—and no longer ago than to-day Naakkve had well-nigh come to such fortune as a Christian man's mouth dare not name —had not God preserved us——"

"Ay, but this time 'twas I that had the luck to be God's instrument" —Erlend shrugged his shoulders. But then he said most earnestly:

"Such things—you need not to fear, my Kristin—is't this that has clean scared the wits from you, poor soul?" He looked down, and said almost shamefacedly: "You must mind, Kristin—your father of happy memory prayed for our children, as he prayed for all of us, early and late. And I deem, most sure and firmly, it avails for deliverance from much—from the worst things of all—so good a man's intercession——"
She saw the man cross his breast with his thumb as though by stealth.

But, so beside herself was she, it but embittered her the more:

"So—you comfort you with the thought, Erlend, as you sit there in my father's high-seat, that your sons shall be saved by his prayers, even as they are fed by his lands——"

Erlend grew pale:

"Mean you, Kristin—that I am unworthy to sit in Lavrans Björgulf-sön's high-seat——"

His wife's lips moved, but could bring forth no sound. Erlend rose and stood moveless:

"Mean you this—for then say I, as sure as God is above us both—I will sit there never more.

"Answer," said he again, as she stood speechless. A long tremor shook the woman's body.

"He was—a better master—he who—sat there before you"—she could scarce get the words out so as to be heard.

"Heed your tongue now, Kristin!" Swiftly Erlend strode a step or two nearer. She stood upright with a start:

"Ay, strike me—I have borne that too ere now; I can bear it again."

"Strike you—I thought not on it." He stood with his hand resting on the board; again they gazed at one another, and again his face had that strange far-off calm which she had seen on it at some rare times. Now it drove her to distraction. She knew 'twas she was in the right—Erlend's talk was witless, reckless; but that face of his made her feel as though all the wrong was hers.

She looked at him, and, sick with dread herself at what she said, she spoke:

"I fear me 'twill not be in *my* sons that your line will flourish again in the Trondheim country——"

Erlend flushed blood-red:

"You could not forbear to mind me of Sunniva Olavsdatter, I see——"

"'Twas not I who named her, but you."

Erlend reddened yet more deeply.

"Have you never thought, Kristin—that *you* were not wholly without blame in that—mischance——

"Mind you that night in Nidaros—I came and stood before your bed. Most humble was I, and sorrowful for that I had offended against you, my wife—I came to beg of you—to forgive me my wrong. Your answer was to bid me go and lay me where I had lain the night before——"

"Could I know that you had lain by your kinsman's wife——?"

Erlend stood a little. He grew pale, and again red. Then he turned and went from the room without a word.

The wife did not stir—long she stood moveless, her clenched hands pressed up beneath her chin, staring into the light.

Then she raised her head with a jerk—drew a long breath. Some time he must endure to hear it——

Then she grew ware of the sound of a horse's hoofs in the courtyard —heard by its gait that 'twas a horse being led by a house-carl. She stole to the door and out into the penthouse, stood behind the doorpost, and peered out.

Already the night was growing grey with dawn. Out in the court-yard stood Erlend and Ulf Haldorssön. Erlend held his horse, and she saw that it was saddled and the man clad for riding. The two spoke together for a while, but she could not catch one word. Then Erlend swung himself into the saddle and began to ride at a foot-pace north-ward to the manor-gate; he looked not back, but seemed to talk with Ulf, who walked by the horse's side.

When they were gone from sight up towards the road, she crept out, hastened as noiselessly as she could up to the gate, stood there and listened—she heard now that Erlend had started Soten at a trot up on the highway.

A little while after, Ulf came back. He stopped short when he caught sight of the woman there at the gate. For a while they stood looking at each other in the grey twilight. Ulf's feet in his shoes were bare, and he had but a linen shirt beneath his cloak.

"What is this?" asked the mistress wildly.

"You must sure know—I know not."

"Whither rode he?" said she again.

"To Haugen." Ulf stood a little. "Erlend came in and waked me— he said he would ride thither to-night—and he seemed in haste; there were some things he prayed me to see and have brought up after him."

Kristin was silent for a space.

"He was angry, then?"

"He was quiet." In a little Ulf said, low: "I am afeared, Kristin—I marvel if you have not said what you had better have left unsaid."

"For once, surely, Erlend might endure to be talked to as he were a grown man," said the wife, vehemently.

They went slowly downward. Ulf turned towards his own house, and at that she came after him.

"Ulf, kinsman," she prayed him, fearfully, "in old days 'twas you who told me, late and soon, that, for my sons' sakes I must harden my heart and speak to Erlend."

"Ay—I have grown wiser with the years, Kristin, and that have you not," he answered as before.

"You give me fair comfort, in sooth," said she, bitterly.

He laid a hand heavily upon the woman's shoulder, but at first he said naught. They stood there—'twas so still that they both heard the endless roar of the river, that other times came not to their ears. Out on the farms around the cocks were crowing, and, from the stable, Kristin's farm-cock sent forth a ringing answer.

"Ay—I have had to learn and deal heedfully with comfort, Kristin —heavily has that ware been drawn on these many years—we must go sparingly with it now, for we know not how long yet it will need to last——"

She shook herself free from his hand; with teeth set hard into her lower lip, she turned her face aside—then she fled downward, back to the hearth-room house.

The morning was biting cold; she wrapped her cloak close about her, and pulled the hood down over her head. Crouched together, with her dew-wet shoes drawn up beneath her skirt and her arms crossed upon her knees, she sat on the edge of the cold hearth, brooding. Now and again her face quivered, but she did not weep.

She must have slept—she started up with aching back, stiff-limbed and frozen to the marrow. The door stood ajar—she saw that out in the courtyard the sun was shining.

Kristin went out into the penthouse—the sun was high already, from down in the home pasture she heard the bell on the horse that had gone lame. She looked across at the new storehouse. And then she was ware that little Munan was standing up on the balcony peeping out through the railing arches.

Her sons—it flashed through her. What had they thought, when they awoke and saw their parents' bed unslept in?

She ran across the courtyard and up to the child—Munan had naught on but his shirt. As soon as his mother came to him, he thrust his hand in hers, as if he were afraid.

Within the loft none of the lads was yet full clad—none had waked them, she saw. All looked up quickly at their mother, and then down again. She took Munan's hose and would have helped him to draw them on.

"Whither is father gone?" asked Lavrans, wonderingly.

"Your father rode north to Haugen at early dawn," she answered. She marked that the big ones hearkened, and she said: "You know he has long said he must go up some time and see how it fares with his farm."

The two little ones looked up into their mother's face with wide-open, wondering eyes, but the five older brothers hid their gaze from her as they went out of the loft.

III

T H E days went by. At first Kristin felt no fear: she cared not to ponder what Erlend might mean by these doings—running off from home in sudden wrath at dead of night—or how long he was minded to sit up north there on his hill farm and punish her with his absence. She was bitterly wroth with her husband, angered all the more for that she denied not to herself that she too was in the wrong, and had spoken words that she wished from her heart could be unsaid.

Sure enough, she had been in the wrong many a time, and had often, in wrath, said hateful and unseemly things to her husband. But what hurt her most bitterly was that Erlend could never offer to forget and to forgive, except she first humbled her and begged it of him meekly. 'Twas not so often either, thought she, that she had done amiss—could he not understand, 'twas oftenest when she was wearied and worn with cares and fears that she had striven to bear in silence?—'twas then she most readily lost the mastery of herself. She deemed that Erlend might have remembered that, beside all the disquietude for their sons' future that she had borne these many, many days, twice this summer she had gone through a time of deadly fear for Naakkve. Her eyes had been opened now to see that, after the young mother's pains and travail are over, there come for the ageing mother fears and woe of a new kind.— His careless talk of having no fear for the fortunes of their sons had goaded her till she was like a wild mother-bear—or like a bitch with whelps; she cared not if Erlend likened her to a bitch in all that touched her children. For them would she be watchful and unsleeping as a mother-bitch, so long as life abode in her.

And if, for such a cause, he could forget that she had stood by him in every time of need, with all her powers; that, in despite of her anger, she had been both just and forgiving, when he struck her, and when he was false to her with the hateful, wanton Lensvik woman; then he must even forget. Even now, when she thought on it, she could not feel so much wrath and bitterness against Erlend for this, the worst of his offences against her—when she turned on him with reproaches for *that*, 'twas because she knew that he repented it himself, that in this he saw and felt he had done evil. But never had she been so wroth with Erlend —neither was she now—that the memory of his blow and of his faithlessness, with all it brought with it, did not trouble her, most of all, for the man's own sake—she felt ever that in these outbursts of his ungoverned spirit he had sinned against himself and his soul's welfare far more than against her.

What went on rankling in her spirit were all the little wounds he had dealt her with his unkind heedlessness, his childish lack of patience— even with his wild and thoughtless way of loving, when at times he showed that, despite of all, he loved her. 'Twas all the years when she was young and soft of soul, and had felt that both health and courage must fall short—cumbered as she was with all those helpless little children—if the father, the husband, would not show that he had strength and loving-kindness wherewith to guard her and the little sons upon her knees. It had been such a torment to feel herself weak of body, simple and unlessoned in mind, and not dare trust securely in her husband's strength and wisdom—'twas as though she had got heart-wounds then that would never heal again. Even the sweet delight that 'twas to lift up her suckling, set its lovesome mouth to her breast, and feel the little warm, soft body upon her arm, had been made bitter by fear and fret— so small, so defenceless you are, and all too oft your father forgets that his first thought should be to make you secure.

And now, when her little children's bones were set and their heads had hardened, but they yet lacked somewhat of a grown man's wit— now he lured them from her. They melted away from her, the whole flock, husband and sons, in that strange, boyish light-mindedness that she thought she had seen glimpses of in all the men she had met, and where a sad, careful woman can never follow.

So, for her own part, 'twas but sorrow and anger she felt when she thought on Erlend. But she grew fearful when she wondered what her sons were thinking.

Ulf had been up to Dovre with two pack-horses, to bear to Erlend the things he had asked should be sent after him—clothes, weapons in plenty; all his four bows, sacks full of arrow-heads and cross-bow bolts, and three of the dogs. Munan and Lavrans wept bitterly when Ulf took the little smooth-haired bitch with silky soft, hanging earlaps—she was a fine, outlandish beast that Erlend had had of the Abbot at Holm. That their father owned such a rare dog seemed, more than aught else, to raise him above all other men in the eyes of the two little ones. And then their father had promised them that, when the bitch had pups again, they should each choose him one from out the litter.

When Ulf Haldorssön came back, Kristin asked if Erlend had said when he thought to turn him home again.

"No," said Ulf. "It looks as though he had a mind to bide on there."

Of his own accord Ulf said but little more of his journey to Haugen. And Kristin was loath to ask.

In autumn, when they flitted in from the new storehouse, the eldest sons said they would like, this winter, to sleep above stairs in the upper hall-room. Kristin gave them leave, and thus she was left to sleep with the two youngest in the great hall below. The first evening she said that Lavrans too might lie in the bed with her now.

The boy lay blissfully rolling about and boring himself down into the bedding. The children were used to have their couch made up on the bench, on leathern sacks filled with straw, and to have fur skins to wrap them in. But in the bed there were blue bolster mattresses to lie upon, and fine coverlids beside the furs—and the parents had fine white linen covers on their pillows.

"'Twill be but till father comes home that I may lie here," asked Lavrans; "then, belike, we must go back to the bench again, mother?"

"Then you may sleep in Naakkve's and Björgulf's bed," answered his mother; "if the lads change not their minds and move down again, once the weather grows cold." Upstairs, too, there was a small masoned fireplace, but it gave out more smoke than heat, and the wind and weather were felt much more in the upper story.

As the autumn drew to an end, a vague fear came creeping over Kristin; it waxed from day to day, and the strain made life heavy to bear. No one seemed to hear word or whisper of Erlend.

In the long, black autumn nights she lay awake, heard the two little boys' even breathing, listened to the march of the storm about the house corners, and thought on Erlend. Had it only not been on that farm that he was——

She had liked it ill when the cousins had fallen to talking of Haugen —Munan Baardssön was with them at their lodging one of the last evenings ere they were to set forth from Oslo. At that time Munan was sole owner of this little farm—it had come to him from his mother. He and Erlend had been making merry, and both were not a little drunken, and while she sat chafing that they must needs bring up that unchancy place in their talk, things fell out so that Munan gave Erlend the farm— so should he be not wholly landless in Norway's land. The thing was settled amid jest and laughter—even those rumours that folk could not dwell there because 'twas haunted they made sport of. The terror that had taken hold on Munan Baardssön when his mother and her husband came to their miserable end up there, seemed by this time in some measure to have worn off the knight.

And, sure enough, he made over Haugen to Erlend by lawful deed. Kristin could not hide how hateful 'twas to her that her husband should own that uncanny place. But Erlend had turned it off with a jest:

"'Tis little like that either you or I will ever set foot in the houses up there—if they yet stand and are not quite in ruin. And I trow Moster Aashild and Sir Björn will not bring us home the rents themselves. So it sure can matter naught to us if 'tis true, as folk say, that they walk there——"

As the year waned, and Kristin's thoughts ran ever on how it might fare with Erlend north on Haugen, she grew so tongue-tied that she scarce spoke a word to her children or to the serving-folk, unless she must answer their questions—and they grew loath to speak to the mistress save when they needs must, for she made them short and impatient answers when they broke in upon and troubled her uneasy, overwrought brooding. She herself was so little ware of this that, when at last she marked that the two youngest children had stopped asking after their father or speaking of him to her, she sighed and thought: children forget apace—for she knew not how often she had frighted them from her with impatient answers, and bidden them be still and not plague her.

With the older sons she spoke scarce at all.

As long as the dry frost lasted she still could answer stranger-folk, who came to the manor and asked for the master, that he lay out in the fells trying his luck in hunting. Then there came a heavy snow-fall, both in the parish and in the hills, the first week in Advent.

Early in the morning of St. Lucia's Eve,* while 'twas yet pitch-dark without, and the stars showed clear, Kristin came from the byre. Then she saw, by the light of a pine-torch stuck into a heap of snow, that three of her sons stood without the house-door with ski in their hands, binding them on their feet—and a little way off stood Gaute's gelding with wicker snow-shoes on its feet and a pack-saddle on its back. She guessed whither they were bound; and she dared say naught more than to ask, when she saw that one of the lads was Björgulf—the two others were Naakkve and Gaute:

"Would you go out to-day on ski, Björgulf?—'tis like 'twill be bright weather, son!"

"As you see, mother."

"Maybe you will be home ere midday, then?" she asked, somewhat at

* 13th December.

a loss. Björgulf was ill at ski-running; the glare from the snow soon hurt his eyes, and he kept him mostly within-doors in winter-time. But Naakkve answered that they might be gone some days.

Kristin was left at home, uneasy and fearful. The twins were surly and sour—she saw that they had been fain to go too, but that their grown-up brothers would not let them.

Early on the fifth day, at breakfast time, the three came back. They had set out at cockcrow for Björgulf's sake, said Naakkve—that they might be home ere the sun got up. Those two went straightway up to the upper hall—Björgulf seemed like to drop with weariness—but Gaute bore the sacks and the pack-saddle into the room. He had with him two goodly little whelps for Lavrans and Munan—at the sight the little boys forgot all questions and all cares. Gaute seemed to be troubled, but strove to hide it:

"——And this," said he, drawing it out of a sack, "this father bade me give to you."

'Twas fourteen ermine skins, passing fair. His mother took them, with somewhat of an ill grace—she could not find a word to say in answer. There was all too much that she would fain have asked; she was afraid she might lose the mastery of herself if she gave her heart the smallest vent—and Gaute was so young. She brought out naught but:

"They are white already, I see—ay, we are far on in the winter half-year now——"

When Naakkve came down, and he and Gaute set them down to the porridge dish, Kristin said hastily to Frida that she herself would bear his food up to Björgulf in the loft. It had come to her all at once that with the silent boy, who she guessed was far riper in mind than his brothers, she could mayhap talk of this matter.

He had lain down on the bed, and held a linen cloth over his eyes. His mother hung a kettle of water on the pot-hook in the fire-place, and, while Björgulf lay propped on his elbow and ate, she brewed a wash of dried eyebright and celandine.

Kristin took from him the empty porridge bowl, bathed his red and swollen eyes with the wash and laid damped linen cloths upon them; and then, at length, she took courage to ask:

"Said he naught, your father, of when he thought to come home to us?"

"No."

"You are ever chary of your words, Björgulf," said his mother in a little while.

"It seems to run in the breed, my mother."—He said, a little after: "We met Simon and his men near by, north of the gorge—with loaded sleighs, driving northwards."

"Did you speak with them?" asked the woman.

"No——" He laughed as before. "It seems to run like a sickness through our kindred—friendship thrives not among us."

"Mean you to blame me for that?" his mother flashed out. "One moment you complain that we hold our peace too much—and then you say we cannot keep friendship——"

Björgulf only laughed again. Then he raised him on his elbow, as though he were hearkening to his mother's breathing:

"In God's name, mother, do not fall a-weeping now—— I am down-hearted and weary—so unused am I to go on ski—and take no account of what I say: I know full well that you are no contentious woman."

Kristin went forth from the loft soon after. For now she dared not, for aught in the world, ask this son what the young ones thought of these matters.

So she lay, night after night, when the lads had gone up to the loft—waking and listening: did they talk together when they were alone up there? she wondered. There was a thumping of boots thrown on the floor, a clatter of knife-belts falling down—she heard their voices, but could make out no words—their tongues all went at once; their voices rose—it seemed to be half quarrel, half jesting. One of the twins cried out aloud—then someone was dragged over the floor, so that dust showered from the planks above her down into the room—the balcony door flew open with a crash—something fell heavily on the balcony floor, and then Ivar and Skule's voices threatening and clamouring out there, while they beat on the door—then she caught Gaute's voice, high and laughing. He stood within the door, she could hear—'twas clear he and the twins had fallen out again, and the end had been that Gaute had thrown them out. Lastly she heard Naakkve's grown man's voice —he was making peace; the two came in. Yet a while the noise of talk and laughter came down to her, then the sounds of their getting into bed. Silence fell at last. In a little she heard an even drone, with still-ness ever and anon—a drone like far-off thunder, away in the hills.

The mother smiled in the dark. Gaute snored when he was wearied out. So, too, had her father done. 'Twas strange, this matter of likeness —the sons who took after Erlend in outward looks were like him too in that they slept as noiselessly as birds. And while she lay thinking on all the little marks of kinship one can find so strangely, lifetime after life-time, in the offspring of a stock, she could not forbear to smile to herself as she lay there. The torturing strain in the mother's mind slackened for a time, and drowsiness came and tangled all the threads of her thought, while she sank away, first into blissful ease and then into forgetfulness.

——They were young, she comforted herself—— 'Twas like they took it not so hardly——

But one day, when the new year was begun, Sira Solmund, the chaplain, came to Kristin at Jörundgaard. It was the first time he had come thither unbidden, and Kristin gave him fair welcome, though her mind foreboded evil straightway. As she had thought, so it proved—he deemed 'twas his duty to find out if she and her husband had wilfully and in ungodly wise severed their fellowship, and, if so it were, which of the pair bore the blame for this breach of God's law.

Kristin felt herself that she grew shifty-eyed and over glib of tongue, and that she used too many words, as she set forth to the priest how Erlend deemed he must look after his estate north in Dovre; it had lain quite uncared for these many years; the houses, for sure, were well-nigh fallen to ruin—with the many children they had, 'twas needful they see to their welfare—and much more to the like purpose. She glossed the matter in so many words that even Sira Solmund, no sharp-sighted man, must needs mark that she felt herself unsure—and now she talked and talked of how eager a hunter Erlend was, as the priest well knew. She brought out and showed him the ermine skins she had had from her husband—in her confusion she had given them to the priest almost ere she herself knew of it, ere she could bethink her——

She fretted when Sira Solmund was gone—Erlend might have known that, when he stayed from home in this wise, a priest such as they had now would surely take in his head to come and pry out whether aught were amiss——

Sira Solmund was a paltry little man to look on; 'twas not easy to guess his age, but folk deemed he was near about forty winters by now. He was not over bright-witted, and of a certainty he had no learning to spare; but he was an honest, pious, well-living priest. An oldish sister of his, a childless widow and a parlous tale-bearer, cared for his small household.

He would fain have shown himself a zealous servant of the Church, but 'twas mostly on small matters and small folk that he fastened—he was fearful of spirit and shy of grappling with the big landowners or taking up ticklish questions; but if once he had done so, he was apt to grow passing stubborn and hot-headed.

For all this, he was well enough liked by his parishioners. For one thing, folk held him in esteem for his quiet, seemly way of life; for another, he was not near so greedy of money or so stiff in matters that touched the Church's rights or folks' duties as had been Sira Eirik. Like enough this came in the main from his lacking altogether the old priest's boldness.

But Sira Eirik was loved and honoured by every man and every child
in the parishes round about. Folk had often taken it amiss in the old
days, when the priest had striven, with unseemly greed, to enrich and
make secure the children he had had unlawfully by his serving-wench;
and when he first came to dwell in the parish the people of Sil could ill
brook his masterful sternness toward all who transgressed the least of the
Church's laws. A warrior had he been before he took the priestly vows,
and he had followed the sea-rover earl, Sir Alf of Tornberg, in his
youth; 'twas easy to mark it in his ways.

But even then the parish folk had been proud of their priest, for he
was far above most priests of the country parishes in learning, wisdom,
strength of body, and chieftainly bearing, and he had the noblest singing-voice. And with the years, and under the heavy trials that God
seemed to have laid upon this His servant by reason of his youthful
untowardliness, Sira Eirik Kaaressön had so grown in wisdom, piety,
and righteousness that his name was now known and honoured over the
whole bishopric. When he journeyed to the synod at Hamar town, he
was honoured as a father by all the other priests, and 'twas said that
Bishop Halvard would gladly have preferred him to a church which
carried with it noble rank and a seat in the cathedral chapter. But
'twas said Sira Eirik had begged he might be left where he was—he had
pleaded his age, and that his sight had been dim these many years
past.

In Sil there stood by the highway, a little south of Formo, the fair
cross of potstone which Sira Eirik had set up at his own cost, where a
stone-slip from the mountain-side had taken from him both his young,
hopeful sons forty years agone. Even now the older folk of the parish
passed it not by without stopping to say Paternosters and Aves for Alf's
and Kaare's souls.

His daughter the priest had wedded from his manor with a fair dowry
of goods and cattle; he gave her to a comely and well-born farmer's son
from Viken; none thought other than that Jon Fis was a good young
fellow. Six years after, she came home to her father, starved, broken,
ragged and lousy, with a child by each hand and one beneath her belt.
The folk who had lived in Sil in those days knew well, though they never
spoke of it: the children's father had been hanged for a thief in Oslo.
The Jonssöns turned out but ill—and now they were dead, all three.

Even while his issue were yet alive, it had been Sira Eirik's zealous
care to deck and do honour to his church with gifts. Now 'twould be it,
belike, that would get the greater part of his wealth and his costly books.
The new church of Saint Olav and St. Thomas in Sil was much greater
and statelier than the old one that burned down, and Sira Eirik had bestowed upon it many noble and costly adornments. He went each day

to church for prayer and meditation, but for the folks he now said mass on the high holy-days only.

'Twas Sira Solmund, too, who now carried on most of the duties of the priestly office. But when folk had a heavy grief to bear, or were vexed at soul by great troubles or the stings of conscience, they rather sought the old parish priest, and all deemed that, from a communing with Sira Eirik, they ever brought comfort home with them.

And so, one evening on towards spring, Kristin Lavransdatter went to Romundgaard and knocked upon the door of Sira Eirik's house. But she knew not herself rightly how she should set forth what she had to say; so, when she had made her offering, she sat talking of this and that. At length the old man said, something impatiently:

"Have you come in but to greet me, Kristin, and see how I fare? 'Tis kindly done of you, if so—but methinks you have somewhat else upon your heart, and if so it be, speak of it now, and waste not time with empty talk——"

Kristin laid her hands together in her lap and looked down:

"It mislikes me much, Sira Eirik, that my husband bides on up yonder at Haugen."

"I trow the way is not so long," said the priest, "but that you can get you up thither easily enough, to speak with him and beg him to return home soon. So much there cannot be for him to see to, up on that little one-man's croft, that he need tarry there longer."

"I am afraid, when I think of him dwelling there alone these winter nights," said the wife, shuddering.

"Erlend Nikulaussön is sure old enough and bold enough to look to himself."

"Sira Eirik—you know all that befell up there once upon a time," whispered Kristin, so low as scarce to be heard.

The priest turned his dim old eyes towards her—once they had been coal-black, bright, and keen. He said naught.

"You have heard, belike, what folk say," she said as low as before. "That—the dead—walk there."

"Mean you you dare not seek him out for that—or are you feared that the drows will break your husband's neck? If so be they have not done it yet, Kristin, 'tis like they will let him be hereafter also"—the priest laughed harshly. "'Tis folly, naught but heathenish, superstitious prate, the most of the tales folks spread about of drows and of dead men that walk. There are stern door-keepers, I fear me, where Sir Björn and Lady Aashild are."

"Sira Eirik," she whispered, trembling, "deem you then there is no salvation for those two poor souls——?"

"God forbid that I should be so overbold, to judge of the bounds of His mercy. But scarce can I deem those two can have been able to quit their score so soon—not yet have all the tablets been shown forth on which they two carved their witness—her children that she forsook; you two that were prentices in the wise lady's school. If I deemed it could help, so that somewhat of the ill she did might be righted, then—but since Erlend tarries on there, 'tis like God deems not it would avail aught if his mother's sister should show her and warn him. For this we know, by God's mercy and Our Lady's pity and the prayers of the Church, it may befall that a poor soul have leave to come back to this earthly home out of the fires of purgatory, if his sin be such that it can be made good by the help of living men and his time of torture shortened thereby—as 'twas with the unhappy soul who had shifted the boundary between Hov and Jarpstad, and the farmer in Musudal with the false letters concerning the mill-race. But no soul can come out from purgatory fire except it have such a lawful errand—'tis trumpery else, the most of what folk prate of drows and ghosts; or 'tis the devil's juggleries, that melt away like smoke when you ward you with the sign of the cross and the Lord's name——"

"But the blessèd who are with God, Sira Eirik?" she asked again, low.

"The holy ones with Him you wot well He can send on His errands with good gifts and messages from Paradise."

"I told you once that I had seen Brother Edvin Rikardssön," she said as before.

"Ay, either 'twas a dream—and it might have been sent by God or by your guardian angel—or else the monk is a holy saint."

Kristin whispered, trembling:

"My father—— Sira Eirik, I have prayed so much that it might be granted me to see his face but once. I long to see him so unspeakably, Sira Eirik—and maybe I might understand by his mien what he would that I should do. Could I but once have counsel of my father, then——"

She had to bite her lips and, with the fall of her coif, brush away the tears that would out.

The priest shook his head.

"Pray you for his soul, Kristin—though I well believe that Lavrans, and your mother with him, are now long since comforted, in the house of them whose comfort they sought in all their sorrows while they lived here on earth. And true and sure it is that Lavrans holds you fast in his love in that place too—but your prayers and masses for his soul's peace bind you and us all to him—— Ay, the way of it, 'tis one of the secret things which are hard to understand—but doubt not that this way is better than that he should be disquieted in his peace that he might come hither and show himself to you——"

Kristin was forced to sit awhile, ere she grew so far mistress of herself that she dared speak. But then she told the priest all that had befallen betwixt her and Erlend that night in the hearth-room house, saying over every word that was spoken, as near as she remembered it.

The priest sat long silent when she had done speaking. Then she smote her hands together vehemently:

"Sira Eirik! Deem you that most of the wrong was with me? Deem you that *so* much of the wrong was with me that 'tis no sin of Erlend to have fled from me and all our sons in this wise? Think you 'tis just for him to crave that I should seek him out, kneel before him, and eat my words that I spoke amiss?—I know without that he will not come home to us!"

"Think you you need to call Lavrans back from his other home to ask his counsel in this matter?" The priest rose, and laid his hand upon the woman's shoulder: "The first time I saw you, Kristin, you were a tender little maid—Lavrans took you between his knees, laid your little hands cross-wise on your breast, and bade you say Paternoster to me—clearly and sweetly could you say it, though you understood not one word—afterward you learned the meaning of every prayer in our tongue—maybe you have forgotten it now——?

"Have you forgotten that your father taught you and did honour to you and loved you—he did honour to this man you are now so afeared to humble yourself before—or have you forgotten how fair he made the feast in honour of you two? And how you rode from his manor like two thieves—stealing away with you Lavrans Björgulfsön's worship and honour?"

Sobbing, Kristin hid her face in her hands.

"Can you remember yet, Kristin—did he crave of you two that you fall down on your knees before him, ere he deemed he could raise you up again into his fatherly love? Think you 'twere all too hard a morsel for your pride if you must bow yourself now before a man whom you have wronged, maybe, less than you sinned against your father——?"

"Jesus!" Kristin wept most piteously. "Jesus—have mercy——"

"You remember yet His name, I hear," said the priest, "the name of Him your father strove to follow as a disciple and to serve as a faithful knight." He touched the little crucifix which hung above them. "Sinless, God's Son died upon the cross to atone for our transgressions against Himself——

"Go home now, Kristin, and think over this that I have said to you," said Sira Eirik, when her weeping was a little allayed.

But in these same days southerly storms set in; gales, sleet, and rain in torrents—at times it so raged that folk found it hard to cross over their own courtyards without risk of being blown clean over the house-tops, as one might almost think. None could travel by the parish roads. The spring floods came down so sudden and furious that folk fled from the farms most in danger. Kristin shifted most of her goods up into the new storehouse loft, and she got leave to put the cattle in Sira Eirik's spring byre—the Jörundgaard spring byre lay on the further side of the river. 'Twas cruelly toilsome work in the rough weather—all through the paddocks the snow lay soft as melting butter—and the beasts were poor and weak; it had been a hard winter. Two of the best young steers broke a leg as they walked—they snapped like brittle stalks.

The day they shifted the cattle, Simon Darre, with four of his house-carls, appeared of a sudden, half-way. They set themselves to help. Amidst the wind and rain and all the press and bustle, with cows that had to be held up and sheep and lambs that must be borne, there was no making oneself heard, nor leisure for the kinsfolk to talk. But when they were come in to Jörundgaard in the evening, and Kristin had got Simon and his men seated in the hall—all who had been at work that day stood much in need of a draught of warm ale—Simon was able to have some speech with her. He begged her to come to Formo with the women and children, and he and two of his men would stay here with Ulf and the lads. Kristin thanked him, but said she would stay on her manor; Lavrans and Munan were at Ulvsvoldene already, and Jard-trud had sought refuge at Sira Solmund's—she had come to be such good friends with the priest's sister. Simon said:

"Folks deem it strange, Kristin, that you two sisters never meet to-gether. Ramborg will be ill content if I turn me home without you."

"I know well that it looks strange," said the woman, "but 'twould seem yet stranger, methinks, were I to go a-visiting my sister now, when the master of this house is from home—and folk know that you and he are unfriends."

On this, Simon said no more, and soon after he and his men took their leave.

Rogation week came in with a fearful storm, and by Tuesday news went round among the farms in the north of the parish that now had the flood swept away the bridge up in the gorge, which folk must cross when they were bound for the Hövring sæters. They began to fear for the great bridge south by the church. 'Twas built most strongly, of the stoutest timbers, and arched high in the middle, propped below with great tree-trunks set deep in the river-bed; but now the water swept over the bridge-ends, where they joined the banks, and the bridge-arch was packed and choked with all manner of driftage whirled down the stream from the north. The Laagen had flooded the low fields on both banks now, and at one place on the Jörundgaard lands, where was a hollow in the meadows, the water ran inwards, like a bay, almost up to the houses—and the roof of the smithy and the tops of the trees showed above it like small islands. The out-barn on the holm was gone down-stream already.

From the farms on the east side of the river but few men had come to church. They were fearful that the bridge might go in church-time, and cut them off from their homes. But up on the other bank, on the hill-side under the Laugarbru barn, where there was a little shelter from the storm, might be espied, between the snow flurries, a black clump of people. The word went round that Sira Eirik had said he would bear the cross over the bridge and set it on the eastern bank, even if none dared follow him.

A snow squall swept straight in the men's faces as the procession stepped out from the church. The snow drove through the air in slant-ing streaks—of the country-side but glimpses could be seen—now and again a cantlet of the blackening lake where the meadows had been; cloud-scud sweeping across the screes and the tongues of forest on the hill-sides; glimpses high up of fell-tops against the high-piled clouds. The air was loaded with a mingled roar—the river's drone, rising and falling; the rushing noise of the woods; the howling of the wind—and ever and again there was a dull booming echo of the raging of the storm among the mountains, and the thunder of slides of new snow.

The tapers were blown out as soon as they were borne from out the church cloister-way. This day grown young men had donned the choir-boys' white surplices—the wind tore at them; they walked, a whole cluster of them, holding the banner, with hands grasping the cloth that the wind might not tear it in shreds, while the procession, with bodies bent forward, clove its way against the wind across the hill-side. But over the raging of the storm rose, now and then, a few notes of Sira Eirik's ringing voice, as he fought his way forward, singing:

*Venite: revertamur ad Dominum; quia ipse cepit et sanabit nos: percutiet, et curabit nos, et vivemus in conspectu ejus. Sciemus sequemurque, ut cognoscamus Dominum. Alleluia.**

Kristin stopped, she and all the other women, when the procession came to the place where the water had overflowed the road, but the white-clad young men, the deacons, and the priests, were up on the bridge already, and well-nigh all the men followed after—the water reached to their knees.

The bridge trembled and shook, and now the women were ware that

* Come, and let us return unto the Lord: for he hath torn, and he will heal us; he hath smitten, and he will bind us up. . . . And we shall live in his sight. Then shall we know, if we follow on to know the Lord. . . . Hosea vi. 1-3.

from up stream a whole house was coming driving down upon the bridge. Round and round it was spun by the stream as it bore downwards; it was rent half in twain and the logs were spread asunder, but yet it hung together. The wife from Ulvsvoldene clung close to Kristin Lavransdatter and wailed aloud—her husband's two half-grown brothers were amongst the choir-lads. Kristin cried silently upon the Virgin Mary, and strained her eyes towards the crowd on the middle of the bridge, where she could make out Naakkve's white-clad form among the men holding the flag. Through all the hubbub the women deemed they still could hear tones of Sira Eirik's chant.

He halted on the crown of the bridge, and lifted the cross high as the house struck. The bridge tottered and groaned—to the folk on both banks it seemed as though it settled somewhat towards the south. Then the procession went on, was lost from sight behind the bridge's arching back—came into sight upon the other shore. The wrecked house had tangled itself in the mass of other driftage clinging to the lower timbers of the roadway.

Then, sudden as a heavenly sign, silvery light dropped through the wind-driven cloud masses—a faint gleam, as of molten lead, was spread over the swollen river, far and wide. Mists and clouds burst asunder— the sun broke through, and when the procession came back across the bridge again, its beams sparkled on the cross; on the priest's wet, white alb the crossed stripes of the stole shone a wondrous purple-blue. Golden and glittering wet the Dale lay, as in the bottom of a cave of blue darkness, for, smitten down by the sun's rays, the storm-clouds clung high up round the brows of the fells and made the uplands black —between the heights the mists were fleeing, and the great mountain-dome above Formo rose up from the blackness, blinding white with new-fallen snow.

She had seen Naakkve go by. The dripping wet vestments clung about the boys, while they sang with might and main, out into the sun-shine:

Salvator mundi, salva nos omnes. Kyrie, eleison; Christe, eleison; Christe, audi nos——*

The priests, the cross, had gone by; the crowd of farmers followed, heavy in their soaking clothes; but they looked about them with wondering, shining faces at the parting storm, as they joined in the pealing supplication—*Kyrie eleison!*

Then she saw—she believed not her eyes, 'twas she now who must cling to her neighbour-woman for support. 'Twas surely Erlend who walked there in the procession; he was clad in a dripping-wet, reindeer-

* Saviour of the world, save us all. Lord, have mercy; Christ, have mercy; Christ, hear us.

skin coat with the hood over his head—but it was he; with half-open mouth, he cried *Kyrie eleison* like the rest—now he looked straight at her as he went by—she could not read the look on his face aright; there was somewhat—like the shadow of a smile upon it——

Together with the other women she followed the procession up over the church-green, chanting loud with the others in unison with the young lads who sang the litany. She was ware of naught but the wild hammering of her own heart.

During the Mass she had a glimpse of him one only time. She dared not stand in her wonted place—hid herself in the gloom in the northern aisle.

Soon as the service was at an end she hasted out. She fled from her serving-women who had been in the church. Outside, the whole valley was steaming in the sun. Kristin ran home, heedless of the bottomless mire of the way.

She spread her board, and set the brimming mead-horn before the master's high-seat, before she gave herself time to change her wet clothes for her holy-day wear—the dark-blue broidered dress, the silver belt, the buckled shoes, and the coif with the blue borders. Then she fell on her knees in the closet. She could not think, she could find no words of her own, as she so fain would—over again and over again, she said Ave Maria—Blessed Lady mine, dear Lord, Son of the Virgin—Thou knowest what I would say——

Time dragged slowly by. From her maids she heard that the men had gone to the bridge again—they were plying axes and hooks to loosen the mass of wreckage that had stuck fast—striving to save the bridge. The priests had gone thither too, when they had laid aside their vestments.

It was long past midday when the men came in. Her sons, Ulf Haldorssön and the three house-carls, an old man and two small parish boys who were kept on the manor.

Naakkve had already set him down in his place, the right of the master's high-seat. Suddenly he rose, left his place, and made for the door.

Kristin called him by name, half aloud.

On that he came back, and sat him down again. The colour came and went in the young face; he kept his eyes cast down, and ever and anon would set his teeth in his under-lip. His mother saw he was hard put to it to keep the mastery over himself—yet he won through the trial.

And at last the meal was at an end. The sons on the inner bench rose, came round the end of the board where was the empty high-seat, settled their belts a little, as of wont, after they had stuck their knives back into the sheaths, and went out.

When they were all gone, Kristin followed. The sun shone warm, and runnels were pouring from every roof. There was not a soul in the courtyard save Ulf—he stood on the stone slab outside his own house door.

A strangely helpless look came to his face as the mistress came towards him. He said no word—she asked, low:

"Spoke you with him?"

"Not many words. Naakkve and he talked together, I saw——"

A little after, he spoke again:

"He was somewhat fearful—for all of you—when there came down such a flood. So the thought took him to come home-about and see how things were going. Naakkve told him how you had done——

"I know not where he had heard it—that you had given away the skins he sent you by Gaute in the autumn. He was angered at that. And so, too, when he found you had slipped straight home after Mass—he had thought you would have stayed and spoken with him——"

Kristin said naught; she turned and went in.

This summer there were endless broils and bickerings betwixt Ulf Haldorssön and his wife. Ulf's half-brother's son, Haldor Jonssön, had come to his kinsman in the spring and brought his wife with him; he had wedded the year before. Now 'twas meant that Haldor should take on lease the farm Ulf owned in Skaun, and flit thither on term-day; but Jardtrud was wroth, for she deemed Ulf had given his brother's son over-good terms, and she saw that the men had in mind that, in one way or another, things should be so ordered that the heritage of the farm be assured to Haldor.

Haldor had been Kristin's page-boy at Husaby, and she had much liking for the young man; his wife, too, a quiet, winsome young woman, she liked well. A little after midsummer the two young folk had a son born to them, and Kristin lent her the weaving-house, where the mistresses of the manor had themselves been wont to lie when they bore children—but Jardtrud took it ill that Kristin waited on the lying-in woman as the chief of the midwives—though Jardtrud herself was young and most unskilled, and could neither help a woman in child-birth nor care for a new-born babe.

Kristin was godmother to the boy, and Ulf gave the christening feast; but Jardtrud deemed that he spent too much on it, and that the gifts he laid in the cradle and on the mother's bed were by far too great. To stop her mouth a little, Ulf gave his wife, before all men's faces, divers costly things from among his chattels: a gilt cross and chain, a fur-lined cloak with a great silver clasp, a finger-ring of gold, and a brooch. But she saw that he would not give her a single rood of the land he owned, beyond what was her extra-gift when he wedded her—all his land was to go to his half-brothers and sisters, if he himself had no children. And now Jardtrud bemoaned herself that her child had been still-born, and that it looked not as though she should have more children—she was soon a laughing-stock among all the neighbours, for talking of this to everyone.

By reason of these bickerings Ulf had to pray Kristin to let Haldor and Audhild dwell in the hearth-room house when the young wife had held her churching. Kristin agreed gladly. She held aloof from Haldor, for it brought back to her so much that was sore to think on when she talked with him that had attended her in those old days. But much talk fell between her and the wife, for Audhild was bent on helping Kristin in every wise she could. And in the end of summer the child fell sorely sick; and on that Kristin took it in hand and tended it for the young, unlessoned mother.

When, in autumn, the two young folk forth set northwards, she missed them, but most of all the little baby boy. Foolish as she herself knew it was, yet she had not been able, these last years, to rid her of a kind of sorrow because, all at once, she seemed to have grown barren—though she was no old woman, not yet forty years.

It had helped her to keep her mind from grievous thoughts that she had the young, childish wife and the little babe to help and tend. And, heavy as she deemed it to see that Ulf Haldorssön had not had better fortune in his marriage, yet had the happenings in the steward's house helped to take her thoughts away from other things.

For, after the fashion Erlend had borne him on Rogation day, she dared scarce think how it all would end. That he had come down to the parish and to the church, before all folks' eyes, and then had made off north again without greeting his wife with so much as one word, seemed to her so cruel that she deemed now at last she no longer cared what he might do——

With Simon Andressön she had not changed a word since that day of the spring flood when he came to help her. At the church she greeted him, and most often spoke a few words with her sister. What they thought of her affairs, and of Erlend's betaking him up to Dovre, she knew not.

But the Sunday before St. Bartholomew Mass* Sir Gyrd of Dyfrin came with the Formo folks to church. Simon looked wondrous glad as he went in to Mass by his brother's side. And, after the service, Ramborg came over to Kristin, and whispered eagerly that she was with child again and looked to be brought to bed at Maria Mass, in the spring:

"Kristin, sister, can you not come home and drink with us this day?"

* 24th August.

Kristin shook her head sorrowfully, patted the young wife's pale cheek, and prayed that God might turn this to joy and blessing for the parents. But go to Formo she could not, she said.

After the breach with his brother-in-law, Simon had forced himself to believe that 'twas best so. He was so placed that he needed not to ask what folk judged of his doings in all things; he had helped Erlend and Kristin in their greatest need, and as for the stay he could be to them here in the parish, 'twas not so much worth that, to yield it them, he should make such a tangled web of his own life.

But when he heard that Erlend was gone from the parish, 'twas no longer possible for Simon to uphold the heavy, stubborn calm he had striven to feel. In vain he told himself that none, sure, knew rightly what was at the bottom of Erlend's long tarrying from home—folks prated so much and knew so little. And howsoever it might be, he could not mix himself in the matter. Yet was his mind never at rest. At times he pondered whether he should not seek out Erlend at Haugen, and eat the words he had said when they parted—thereafter he might see whether he could not find some way to set things right between his brother-in-law and his wife's sister. But he came no further than to think on it.

He believed not, indeed, anyone could mark on him that he was so uneasy in mind. He lived as he was wont, worked his farm and cared for his estates, was merry and drank man.ully with his boon companions, lay out in the fells a-hunting when he had time, spoiled his children when he was at home, and never did an unkind word fall 'twixt him and his wife. To the folk on the manor it must rather seem as if the love between him and Ramborg were greater than ever before, since his wife was much more quiet and even in her bearing, and no longer fell into those fits of whimsy and childish anger over trifling matters. But in secret Simon felt himself shy and unsure in his dealings with her—no longer could he bring himself to take her as though she too were still half a child, to be teased and spoiled. He knew not now how he should behave him towards her.

And so he knew not, either, how he should take it, when one evening she said to him that now was she with child again.

"You are not over-glad of it, belike," he said at length, stroking her hand.

"But *you* are glad, I trow?" Ramborg nestled close to him, half laughing, half crying, and he laughed somewhat shamefacedly as he took her in his arms.

"This time I will be good and quiet, Simon, and not moan and wail as before. But you must *stay* with me—hear you?—if all your brothers-in-law and your brothers were in bonds and being led arow to the gallows, you must not forsake me!"

Simon laughed sadly:

"Whither should I go, my Ramborg——? 'Tis not like that Geirmund, poor cripple, will broil himself in any great matter—and you know well he is the only man now, of my blood or kin, that I am not at odds with——"

"Oh!——" Ramborg laughed, too, through her tears. "Those quarrels will last no longer than till they need a helping hand and you deem you can give it. I know you well now, my husband——"

'Twas fourteen days later that, all unlooked for, Gyrd Andressön came to the manor. The Dyfrin knight had but one henchman attending him.

Few words passed between the brothers at their meeting. Sir Gyrd said somewhat of how he had not seen his sister and brother-in-law at Kruke these many years, and how the thought had come to him that he might journey up hither and give them greeting; and, once he was in the Dale, Sigrid thought surely he ought to visit at Formo too, "and I thought, brother, 'twas like you were not *so* wroth with me but that you would give me and my man food and shelter till to-morrow."

"You may believe that," said Simon—he stood looking down, flushed dark red in the face. "It was—kindly done of you, Gyrd, to come to me."

The brothers strolled out together after they had eaten. The corn was beginning to yellow here on the sunny slopes down towards the river. 'Twas most goodly weather—the Laagen shone gently enough now, in little white gleams down among the alder woods. Great white clouds sailed over the summer sky—sunshine filled the great bowl of the Dale, and the fell right over against them lay all soft blue and green in the haze of the heat and the drifting shadows of the clouds.

From within the paddock behind them came the thudding of horses' hoofs on the dry ground—the herd came trotting through the alder bush. Simon leaned over the fence: "Coltie—coltie—— He begins to grow old now, Bronsvein?" said he, as Gyrd's horse put his head over the paling and nosed at his master's shoulder.

"Eighteen winters"—Gyrd fondled the horse. "Methought, kinsman —this matter—'twere all too ill a thing if it should part the friendship betwixt you and me," he said—and looked not at his brother.

"It has grieved me every day," answered Simon, low. "And I thank you for your coming, Gyrd."

They went farther along the fence: Gyrd first, Simon tramping after. At last they sat them down on the edge of a little stony stretch of burned-up yellow sward. There was a sweet, strong scent from the small hay-cocks that lay here and there amid the stone heaps, where the sickles had scraped together a little short, flowery hay. Gyrd told of the parley between King Magnus and the Haftorssöns and their following. After a while Simon asked:

"Deem you 'tis not to be thought of that any of those kinsmen of Erlend Nikulaussön should try to win him a full pardon and bring him back to the King's favour?"

"*I* cannot do much," said Gyrd Darre. "And they have no love for him, Simon, they that might perchance have the power. Ay, I have little mind to speak of that *now*—— Methought he seemed a bold, win-ning fellow; but he showed up ill in that emprise of his; so deem the others. But I would liefer not talk of this now—I know well this brother-in-law of yours is so dear to you——"

Simon sat gazing out at the silvery gleams in the tree-tops on the slope below, and at the glittering sheen of the river. Wonderingly he thought —ay, in a way 'twas true too, what Gyrd said.

"Howbeit, in these days we are unfriends, Erlend and I," said he. "'Tis a good while since we spoke together."

"——Meseems you have grown passing quarrelsome with the years, Simon," said Gyrd, laughing a little.

"Have you never thought," he asked a little after, "to leave these dales? We kinsmen might be of more help one to the other if we dwelt more near together."

"Can you think of such a thing——? Formo is my udal heri-tage——"

"Aasmund of Eiken owns his part of that manor by right of udal. And I know he is not unwilling to change udal against udal—'tis still in his thoughts that he might get your Arngjerd for Grunde according to the terms he proffered——"

Simon shook his head.

"Our father's mother's kin have had their seat on Formo manor ever since this land was heathen. And 'tis here I have ever meant that Andres shall dwell after me. I trow you have lost your wits, brother— should I part me from Formo?"

"Nay, 'tis but reason, what you say." Gyrd grew somewhat red. "I thought but that—maybe—in Raumarike you have most of your kins-folk—and the friends of your youth—that perchance you might think that there you would thrive more happily."

"I thrive *here*," Simon, too, was grown red. "Here is the place where I can set the boy in a safe seat." He looked at Gyrd, and his brother's fine-cut, lined face took on somewhat of a bashful look. Gyrd's hair was well-nigh white now, but he was as slender and lithe of body as ever.

He moved a little uneasily—some stones slipped from the heap he leaned on and rolled down the slope into the corn.

"Would you rake the whole scree down on my fields?" asked Simon, laughing, with a feigned gruffness. Gyrd sprang up, light and nimble, and held out a hand to his brother, who had a heavier weight to move.

Simon kept his brother's hand in his for a moment after he had got to his feet. Then he laid his own hand upon his brother's shoulder. On that Gyrd did the like; with their hands lying lightly on each other's shoulders the brothers went slowly up over the hill-side towards the manor.

They sat together over in the Sæmund's hall in the evening—Simon was to sleep with his brother. They had said their evening prayers, but they felt they must empty the ale-bowl before they went to rest.

"*Benedictus tu in muliebris—mulieribus*—mind you?" laughed Simon all at once.

"Ay—it cost me a basted back many a time or ever Sira Magnus got my grandmother's false doctrine out of my head."—Gyrd smiled at the memory. "Hard-handed as the devil he was, too. Mind you, brother, once as he sat scratching his legs and had lifted the skirt of his habit —you whispered to me that, had you been so crook-legged as Magnus Ketilssön, you, too, had been a priest and gone ever in a long gown——?"

Simon smiled—it seemed to him he *saw* all at once his brother's boyish face, bursting with choked laughter for all its piteous rueful eyes: they were yet young boys then, and Sira Magnus *was* sorely hard of hand when he set to correcting them——

Over-bright Gyrd had not been when they were children. Ay, and 'twas not because he was an over and above wise man that he loved Gyrd now. But he grew warm with thankfulness and tenderness towards his brother as he sat here—for every day of their brotherhood, well-nigh forty years now—for Gyrd, even as he was, the most guileless, the most true-hearted of men.

And so this, that he had won back his brother Gyrd, seemed to Simon much as though he had at the least got a fast foothold with one foot. And for long now his life had been so woefully warped and tangled.

He felt a warm glow each time he thought on Gyrd, who had come to him to make good again the breach he himself had made, when he rode from his brother's manor in anger and with unseemly words. His heart overflowed with thankfulness—he had others to thank besides Gyrd.

A man like Lavrans, now—how *he* would have taken such a happening he knew well enough. He could follow his father-in-law as far as he was worthy to follow—with almsgiving and the like. Such things as a broken and contrite heart and adoration of the Lord's wounds were beyond him, unless he stared his eyes out at the crucifix—and that was not what Lavrans had meant. Tears of repentance he could not weep— he deemed not he had wept more than maybe two or three times since he had left childhood behind, and not then when he had the most need to have done so—those times when he had fallen into great transgression —with Arngjerd's mother, while he was a wedded man, and then that man-slaying a year back. And yet he had repented sorely—it seemed to him he repented his sins heartily at all times, confessed them fully, and made full amends according to the priest's behest. He said his prayers ever with diligence, took heed to give the right tithes and abundant alms—most of all to the honour of St. Simon the Apostle, St. Olav, St. Michael and Mary Virgin. Otherwise he rested content with what Sira Eirik said, that in the cross alone was salvation, and how else a man should meet and fight the enemy was in God's hand, not his.

But now he felt himself drawn to show, with somewhat more fervency, his deep thankfulness to all the holy ones. He had been born on the birthday of Mary Virgin, so his mother had said—it came to his mind that he would fain pay the Lord's mother his homage by a prayer he was not wont to say daily. He had had written down a goodly prayer, the time he was at the King's court, and now he sought out the little scroll.

He feared, indeed, now he thought of it, 'twas more to please King Haakon than for the sake of God and Mary, that he had got him, while he was with the body-guard, some such little rolls with prayers, and learnt them. All the young men did it, for 'twas the King's wont to question his pages on what they knew of such profitable lore, when he lay abed of nights and could not sleep.

Oh, ay—'twas long ago now. The King's bedchamber in the stone hall of the royal castle at Oslo. On the little board by the bed stood a single taper burning—its gleam fell upon the fine-cut, wan, and aged face that lay propped upon the red silk pillows. When the priest had ended his reading aloud and was gone, the King himself often took the book, and lay reading with the heavy tome leaned against his drawn-up knees. On two footstools, away by the great stone-walled chimney, sat the pages—he himself kept watch nigh always along with Gunstein Ingasön. 'Twas pleasant in the chamber—the fire burned clear and hot and gave out no smoke, the room seemed so warm and pleasant with its cross-vaulted ceiling and walls ever hung with tapestry. But they grew sleepy sitting so—first hearing the priest read and afterwards waiting for the King to fall asleep; 'twas scarce ever much before midnight. When he slept, they had leave to take turns at watching, and to rest between-whiles on the bench 'twixt the chimney and the door of the Council Hall. So they sat, longing for him to fall asleep, and swallowing down their yawns.

It might happen that the King would fall into talk with them—not often—but when he did he was marvellous kindly and winning. Or he would read aloud from a book a wise saw, or some few staves of verse that he thought might profit the young men or be wholesome for them to hear.

One night he was waked himself by King Haakon calling him—'twas pitch dark; the taper was burned out. Miserably shamed, he made shift to blow the embers alive again, and lit a new candle. The King lay smiling slyly:

"Doth this Gunstein ever snore so fearfully?"

"Ay, my lord!"

"You share his bed in the hostel too, I trow? Methinks 'twere but reason you should crave to be given for a while a bedfellow that makes less hubbub in his sleeping."

"I thank my good lord—but it matters naught to me, Lord King."

"But you must needs wake, Simon, when this thunder-peal breaks loose right by your ear—is't not so?"

"Ay, your Grace, but I have but to give him a jog and turn him over somewhat."

The King laughed.

"I marvel if you young men understand that such a stomach to sleep is a great gift from God. When you are come to my years, friend Simon, mayhap then you will remember these my words——"

'Twas endlessly far away—and yet clear; but it seemed not as if it could be the man sitting here that had been the young page——

One day when Advent was beginning, and Kristin was well-nigh alone at the manor—her sons were carting home firewood and moss—she wondered to see Simon Darre come riding into the courtyard. His errand was to bid her and her sons to a feast at Formo at Yule.

"Sure you must know, Simon, that we cannot do as you would," she said soberly. "Friends we can be, as much as ever, in our hearts, you and Ramborg and I—but you know well that it rests not always with us to do as we would."

"You cannot mean that you will go so far in this as not to come to your only sister's help when she is to lie in the straw?"

Kristin prayed that all might go well, and end in joy for them both, "but I cannot say for sure if I can come."

"All folk will deem it passing strange," said Simon vehemently. "You have the name of being the best of midwives—and she is your sister—and you two are mistresses of the two greatest manors in this northern country-side."

"Not a few children have been born into the world on the great manors here these last years, and I not even prayed to come. No longer is it so, Simon, that 'tis not reckoned that all is done fittingly in the lying-in room if the mistress of Jörundgaard be not there." She saw that he grew much disheartened at her words, and she went on: "Greet Ramborg, and say I will go to her and help her when the time comes— but to your Yule-tide feast I cannot come, Simon."

But on the eighth day of Yule she met Simon coming to Mass without Ramborg. No, all was well with her, he said; but 'twas well for her to rest and gather strength, for to-morrow he was faring south to Dyfrin with her and the children—the roads were so good for sleigh travel; and since Gyrd had begged them to come, and Ramborg had such a mind to it, why——

IV

T H E day after Paul's Mass* Simon Darre rode north over Mjös, with two henchmen in his company. It was set in hard frost, but he deemed he could not stay from home longer; the sledges with the women-folk must come later, as soon as the cold was somewhat bated.

At Hamar he met a friend, Vigleik Paalssön of Fagaberg, and they rode on together. When they were come to Little Hamar they rested a while at a farm where was an ale-tap. While they were sitting at their drink, some drunken fur-hawkers in the room fell foul of each other and came to blows; at last Simon got up, thrust in between, and parted them, but so doing he got a knife-cut in the right forearm. 'Twas little more than a scratch, and he took no heed of it, but the woman of the house made him suffer her to bind a cloth about it.

He rode home with Vigleik, and slept the night at his house. The men shared a bed, and on towards morning Simon was wakened by reason of the other crying out aloud in his sleep. Vigleik called out his name more times than one; so Simon waked him up and asked what was amiss with him.

Vigleik could not remember his dream rightly. "But an ugly dream it was, and you were in it. One thing I mind—Simon Reidarssön stood here in the room and bade you go with him—I saw him so plain I could have told the freckles on his face."

"That dream I would you could sell me," said Simon, half in jest and half in earnest. Simon Reidarssön was his father's brother's son, and they had been good friends in their youth; the cousin had died when he was thirteen or thereabout.

* 15th January.

In the morning, when the men were sitting down to break their fast, Vigleik saw that Simon had left the right sleeve of his jerkin unbuttoned at the wrist. The flesh was red and swollen all down the back of the hand. He spoke of it, but Simon laughed. And when, a little later, his friend begged him to stay there some days—to wait for his wife there—Vigleik could not forget his dream—Simon Andressön answered something peevishly: "Sure, you dreamed not aught so ill about me, Vigleik, as that I kept my bed for a louse-bite——?"

About sunset Simon and his men rode down to Losna lake. It had been the fairest day; now the high blue and white fells were grown golden and pink in the evening light, but the rime-laden thickets along the river stood all shaggy grey in the shadow. The men had rarely good horses, and they had a brisk ride before them over the long lake—small bits of icy flew out tinkling and clinking from under the horses' hoofs. A biting wind blew hard against them; Simon was bitter cold—but soon after strange, qualmish surges of heat ran through him, despite the cold —then ice waves that seemed to pierce right to the marrow of his spine. At times he felt his tongue swell and grow strangely thick far back in his throat. Ere yet they had got over the lake, he had to stop and pray one of his men to help him fasten up his cloak, for a sling for his right arm.

The men had heard Vigleik Paalssön talk of his dream; now they would have had their master show them the wound. But Simon said 'twas naught—it smarted a little: "——Belike I must content me to be left-handed some few days."

But as the evening wore on—the moon had risen and they were riding high up on the ridges north of the lake—Simon felt himself that his arm might likely be troublesome after all. It ached right up in the arm-pit; the jolting on the horse's back tormented him sorely— the blood throbbed and throbbed in the ailing limb. And his head throbbed and ached from the nape upwards. He grew hot and cold by turns.

The winter road went high up the hill-side here, in parts through forest, in parts over white farm-lands. Simon saw it all—the full moon sailed silver bright in the pale blue heavens; it had driven all the stars far from its path; only one or two great ones dared to show their face away far off in the sky. The white fields glittered and sparkled; the shadows fell short and sharp upon the snow—within the woods the light lay vaguely in splashes and stripes between the snow-laden firs. Simon saw all this——

——But at the same time he saw most plain, in sunshine of early spring, a field of tufted, ashy-brown grass. Some stunted firs had pushed up here and there in the outskirts; they shone like green velvet in the sun. He knew it again; 'twas the home-paddock at Dyfrin. The stems of the alder trees in the woods beyond the field stood glossy grey as in spring, and their tops brown with blossom—behind lay the long low Raumarike ridges, shining blue, still flecked with snow. They were on their way down to the alder thicket, Simon Reidarssön and he; they had fishing-tackle and pike-spears—they were bound for the lake lying there dark grey with rotten ice, to fish in the open water at the lake end.—His dead cousin walked by his side: he saw his playmate's curly hair bush-ing out from underneath his cap, reddish of hue in the spring sunlight; he could count each freckle in the boy's face. The other Simon stuck out his under-lip a little and blew—ph, ph, when he deemed his namesake's talk foolish. They hopped across the water-rills, sprang from tuft to tuft over the oozing snow-water in the grass-land. There was a mossy growth at the bottom—it frothed and mantled a lovely green, down below the water.

Though his senses had not left him—though he saw all the time the bridle-path uphill and downhill, through forest, over white farmlands in glittering moonshine—saw the sleeping, clustered houses under snow-buried roofs cast shadows across the fields, saw the mist-belt over the river in the bottom of the dale—and knew that 'twas Jon who rode just behind him and spurred up alongside when they came out on open clearings—yet he found himself more than once calling the man Simon. He knew 'twas wrong, but he could not help doing it, though he saw that his men grew afraid.

"We must see and come as far as the monks' at Roaldstad to-night, men," he said, once when his head grew clearer.

The serving-men pleaded with him—they should rather see and get within doors as soon as might be; they named the nearest priest's house. But the master would have his way.

"'Twill be hard for the horses, Simon——" The two henchmen glanced at each other.

But Simon laughed a little. They must abide it for once in a way. He thought on the weary miles. The pain drove through his whole body with each jolt in the saddle. But home he must and would. For now he knew that he was fey——

And though in the winter night he froze to the marrow and burned by turns, yet all the time he felt the mild spring sun in the grazing-paddock at home, and the dead boy and he went on and on towards the alder brake.

For brief moments the vision melted away, and his head grew clear—only that it ached fearfully. He prayed one of the men to cut open his sleeve over the aching arm. He went white, and the sweat trickled down over his face, as Jon Daalk warily ripped open his jerkin and shirt from wristband to shoulder, while he himself stayed the swollen limb with his left hand. That eased it for a while.

Thereafter the men fell a-talking—at Roaldstad they must see and have word sent south to Dyfrin. But Simon would hear naught of it. He would not disquiet his wife with such a message, when, belike, 'twas not needful—a sledge journey in such bitter cold was not good. Mayhap when he was come home to Formo; they would see. He tried to smile at Sigurd to hearten the lad—he looked awestruck and forlorn.

"But you must send for Kristin at Jörungaard, soon as we come home —she is so good a leech-woman." He felt his tongue thick and hard as wood as he said it.

Kiss me, Kristin, my promised maid! First she would think 'twas wandering talk. No, Kristin. Then would she marvel.

Erlend had seen it. Ramborg had seen it. But Kristin—she sat there full of her cares and her wrath—so vexed and so bitter as she was with yonder man Erlend—yet for others than him she had no thought even now. You never set so much by me, Kristin, my beloved, as to think if 'twere a heavy lot, to be brother to her who once was promised me to wife——

——In sooth he himself had not known it, that time he parted from her outside the cloister gate in Oslo—that he would go on ever thinking of her thus; that in the end 'twould seem to him naught he had got in life since then could make up fully for what then he had lost. For the maid that was sealed to me in my youth.

She should hear it before he died. One kiss should she give him——
——I am he who loved you, and who loves you still——

These words had he heard once, and he had never been able to forget them. They were from Mary Virgin's miracle book; 'twas a tale of a nun who fled away from her convent with a knight. Mary Virgin— in the end she saved these two, and forgave them in despite of their sin. If 'twere sin for him to say it to his wife's sister ere he died, then God's mother must win his forgiveness too for this—— 'Twas not so oft that he had troubled her by craving aught——

——I believed it not myself, that time—that never again should I be rightly glad or merry——

"Nay, Simon, 'twere all too heavy for Sokka, should she bear us both —so far as she has had to fare this night," he said to him who had got up behind him on his horse, and held him up. "Ay—I see 'tis you, Sigurd, but I deemed you were another——"

Towards morning they had come as far as the pilgrims' hostel, and the two monks, who were charged with the care of the place, took the sick man in hand. But when, under their tending, he had grown somewhat better and his fever wanderings were abated, naught would serve Simon but they must lend him a sledge to drive on farther north.

The going was good, and they changed horses by the way, journeyed all the night, and came to Formo next morning at daybreak. Simon had lain and dozed under the many coverings that had been spread over him. They weighed upon him so—sometimes he felt as he were lying crushed beneath huge rock slabs—and his head ached so. Between-whiles he seemed as 'twere to lose himself. Then the pains began to rage again within him—'twas as though his body boiled and boiled up, grew monstrously huge, and was like to burst in bits. His arm throbbed and throbbed——

He tried to get from the sledge and walk in on his feet—with his good arm over Jon's shoulder; Sigurd came behind to hold him up. Simon was ware that the men's faces were grey and drawn with weariness—for two whole nights on end had they sat in their saddles. He would have said somewhat to them of this, but his tongue obeyed him not. He stumbled over the threshold and fell forward into the room—with a roar of pain, as his shapeless, swollen arm struck against something. The sweat streamed from him, as he strove to choke down the groans that were wrung from him while he was unclothed and helped to bed.

Not long after, he saw that Kristin Lavransdatter stood over by the fire-place, pounding somewhat in a wooden bowl with a pestle. The sound tramped so through his head! She poured somewhat from a little pot into a beaker, and dropped drops into it from a glass flask that she took from her case—emptied the pounded stuff from the bowl into the pot and set it on the fire. How still and deft in all her ways——!

Now she came over to the bed with the beaker in her hand. She walked so lightly. She was straight and fair as the maid had been, this slender housewife with the thin, grave face under the linen coif. It hurt him, for the back of his neck was swollen too, when she passed one arm under his head and lifted him somewhat. She propped his head against her breast while she held the beaker to his mouth with her left hand.

Simon smiled a little, and when, warily, she let his head sink back upon the pillows, he caught her hand in his whole one. 'Twas not soft or white any more, the fine, long, narrow woman's hand.

"These fingers of yours are ill at sewing silk now, I trow," said Simon. "But good and light are they—and blessedly cold is your hand, Kristin!" He laid it on his brow. Kristin stood thus till she felt the palm of her hand grow warm; then she took it away and pressed her other hand gently upon his burning brow—close under the roots of the hair.

"You have an ugly arm, Simon," she said. "But with God's help I trust all will go well."

"I fear me, Kristin, me you cannot heal, skilful leech as you are," said Simon. But he looked almost cheerly. The drink was beginning to work; he felt the pains much less. But his eyes felt so strange—as though he could not guide them—it seemed to him he must be lying there with his eyes squinting one to either side.

"'Twill go with me as 'tis doomed to go, I trow," he said as before.

Kristin went back to her pots—smeared a paste upon linen cloths, came back and swathed the hot bandages around his arm from the finger-tips right round behind his back and over his breast, where the swelling spread from his arm-pit in red stripes. It hurt sorely at first, but soon it brought a little ease. She wrapped woollen over all and laid soft down cushions under the arm. Simon asked what 'twas she had upon the bandages.

"Oh, 'tis divers simples—salsify and swallow-wort for the most," said Kristin. "Had it but been summer, I could have gathered it fresh from my herb-garden. But I had a plenty—thanks to God—this winter I have had no need of it till now."

"What was it you told once of swallow-wort—you had heard it of the abbess when you were in the cloister—of the name——?"

"Mean you that in all tongues it has a name that means swallow-blossom—all the way from the sea of Greece hither to the northern lands?"

"Ay—for in all lands it springs into bloom when the swallows wake from their winter sleep." Simon shut his lips a little closer. By then he would have lain long in the earth——

"I would have my resting-place at the church here," said he, " if it so befall that I die now, Kristin. Now am I so rich a man that Andres, belike, will sit here in Formo a man of some power in time to come. I wonder much if 'twill be a son that Ramborg will bear in spring after I am gone—— I had been fain to live so long that I had seen two sons in my house——"

Kristin said she had sent word south to Dyfrin of his having fallen so sick. Gaute—that very morning he had set forth.

"You sent not the child to ride that road alone?" asked Simon, in alarm.

She had had none at hand that she deemed could keep pace with Gaute on Rauden, answered she. Simon said 'twas like to be a hard road for Ramborg—and if only she did not journey more hastily than was fit for her. "But my children, sure enough, I would fain see again——"

A while after, he began again to speak of his children. He talked of Arngjerd—of whether he had done wrong not to fall in with that proffer from the folk at Eiken. But the man seemed to him full old—and he had been fearful, for that Grunde had the name of being somewhat ungoverned when he was in drink. Arngjerd—her in especial he would fain have seen settled in full security. Now 'twould be for Gyrd and Gudmund to find a husband for her. "Tell my brothers, Kristin,—I sent them greetings and prayed that they would look well before them in this matter. Would you take her away with you to Jörundgaard for a while, I would be thankful to you, where I lie. And should Ramborg wed again ere Arngjerd is cared for, then must you take her to you, Kristin. Nay, you must not deem aught else than that Ramborg has been good to her at all times—but were she to have both step-mother and step-father, I fear me she might be looked on more as a serving-wench than as—you mind, I was wed with Halfrid when I became her father——"

Kristin laid her hand gently on Simon's, and gave her promise that she would do for the maid all that lay in her power. She remembered all she had seen—things were hard for the children that had a man of worship for father, and they born out of wedlock. Orm and Margret, Ulf Haldorssön—— She stroked and stroked Simon's hand.

"But 'tis not so sure, either, that you will die this time, brother-in-law," she said, smiling a little. Even yet, at times, there would pass as 'twere a shadow of the young maid's sweet, gentle smile over the thin, stern face of the woman. Thou sweet, young Kristin——!

Simon's fever was not so high this evening, and the pains were less, he said. When Kristin changed the bandages on his arm, 'twas not so swollen; the flesh was softer, the marks of her fingers stayed a while when she pressed it warily.

Kristin sent the serving-folk to bed. Jon Daalk, whom naught would serve but that he should watch over his master, she let lie down over on the bench. The box bench with the carven back she had drawn up before the bed, and she sat there, leaning in a corner. Simon dozed and slept—once, when he woke, he saw that she had got herself a spindle. She sat so straight; she had stuck the staff with the tuft of wool under her left arm, her fingers twisted the yarn, the staff sank and sank alongside her long, slender lap—then she wound up the thread, twisted again, the staff sank and sank—he drowsed off with watching it——

When he waked again, towards morning, she still sat there as before, spinning. The light from the taper she had placed so that the bed-hanging shaded him fell straight upon her face. It was so pale and still; the full, soft mouth had grown thin-lipped and firmly shut; she sat with downcast eyes, spinning. She could not see that he lay awake, gazing at her from the shelter of the bed-tent. She seemed so deathly sad, that

Simon felt as though his heart bled within him as he lay there and gazed at her.

She rose, went over and saw to the fire. So noiselessly! When she came back she peered in behind the bed-tent—met his open eyes looking from the dark.

"How is't with you now, Simon?" she asked, softly.

"Well—'tis with me now."

But he deemed he felt now a tenderness up under his left arm, too—and under his chin when he moved his head. Oh, no, 'twas naught but fancy, belike——

——Ah, sure it was she would never deem she had lost aught when she cast away his love—so far as that went, he might well tell her of it. 'Twas impossible *that* should make her more heavy-hearted. He *would* tell her, before he died—*once* only: I have loved you all these years——

The fever waxed again. And there *was* pain in the left arm——

"You must try if you can sleep again, Simon. Maybe you will mend now quickly," she said, low.

"I have slept much to-night——" He began speaking of his children again—the three he had and loved so dearly—and the one unborn. Then silence fell upon him—the pains took him again so sorely. "Lie down a little now, Kristin. Jon can sit up a while, I trow, if you deem 'tis needful that one keep watch."

In the morning, when she loosed the bandages, Simon looked up calmly into her despairing face: "Ah, no, Kristin, there was over-much foulness and poisonous stuff in the arm already—and freezing cold had I been too—ere I came into your hands. 'Tis as I said—me you cannot heal. Be not so sorrowful for this, Kristin."

"You should not have journeyed all that long way," she said, in a weak voice.

"No man outlives his fated day," answered Simon, as before. "I was set on getting home, you see—— There is one thing and another to speak about—how things shall be ordered when I am gone."

He laughed a little:

"All fires burn out at last."

Kristin looked at him with tear-bright eyes. He had ever had a by-word in his mouth. She looked down at his red-flecked face. The heavy cheeks, the folds below the chin, seemed as 'twere sunken—lay in deep layers. His eyes looked both dull and glittering—then again they cleared and thought came back to them; he looked up at her with the steadfast, searching look which most oft had been in his small, sharp, steel-grey eyes.

When broad daylight came in the room, Kristin saw that Simon's face was grown thin about the nose—a strip of white ran down on either side to the corners of his mouth.

She went over to the little glass pane, stood there, and swallowed down her tears. The thick coating of rime on the window glittered and shone a golden green. Without must still be such fair winter weather as had been all the week——

——'Twas the mark of death, she knew——

She came back, and passed her hand in under the coverlid—he was swollen around the ankles, and up along the legs.

"Would you—would you that we should send for Sira Eirik now?" she said softly.

"Ay, to-night," answered Simon.

He must speak of it *before* he confessed and took the sacrament. Afterward he must try and turn his thoughts another way.

"Strange it is that 'tis like to be you that will lay out my body," said Simon. "—And a fair corpse I fear me I shall not be."

Kristin choked down a sob. She went away and made ready a cooling draught again. But Simon said:

"I like not these drinks of yours, Kristin—a man's thoughts grow so unclear after them."

Yet, after a while, he begged that she would give him a little. "But put not overmuch in it of the drowsy stuff. I must speak with you of a matter."

He drank, and lay waiting for the pains to abate so much that he could talk with her clearly and calmly.

"Would you not that we should fetch Sira Eirik—that he might speak such words as would bring you solace at this pass?"

"Yes, soon. But there is somewhat I must get said to you first."

He lay a little. Then he said:

"Say to Erlend Nikulaussön, that the words I spoke when last we parted, those words have I repented each day since. Unmanly and little-minded did I show me to my brother-in-law that night—— Greet him and say—pray him to forgive it me."

Kristin sat with bowed head—Simon saw she flushed blood-red to the very brows.

"You will bear this message to your husband?" he asked.

She nodded a little. Then Simon said again:

"If Erlend come not to my grave-ale, then must you seek him out, Kristin, and tell him this."

Kristin sat silent, with face dark flushed.

"You will not deny me this that I beg of you, now that I am to die?" asked Simon Andressön.

"No," whispered the woman, "I will—do it——"

"'Tis ill for your sons, Kristin, that there is unfriendliness 'twixt their father and mother," Simon began again. "I marvel if you have seen how much it troubles them. Hard is it for the brave lads to know that their parents are the common talk of the parish."

Kristin answered, in a low, hard voice:

"Erlend forsook our sons—not I. First my sons lost their foothold in the country-side where they were born to rank and udal lands. If now they must suffer that their home here in the Dale, my home, is matter of parish talk—'tis not I that have wrought it."

Simon lay for a little in silence. Then he said:

"I have not forgot it, Kristin—much rightful cause have you to plain —ill has Erlend ordered things for his own. But you should remember— had this his plan gone forward, his sons' lot were now secure, and he himself had stood amid the mightiest knights of this realm. Traitor is he called who fails in such a venture—but if he wins, folk talk far otherwise. Half Norway thought with Erlend then—that we were ill served with sharing a king with the Swedes, and that in Knut Porse's son we might look to find other metal than in this weakling—could we have got Prince Haakon hither to us in his tender years. Many stood behind Erlend then and pulled the rope with him—they dropped it and crept to shelter when the matter came to light—so did my brothers and many others whom folk call now good knights and esquires-at-arms. Erlend alone went down—— And in that pinch, Kristin, your husband showed him a bold and manful fellow—howsoever he may have borne him before and since——"

Kristin sat quiet, trembling.

"I hold, Kristin, if 'tis by reason of this matter you have spoken to your husband bitter words, then must you eat them again. Surely you can bring you to do that, Kristin—once on a time you held to Erlend fast enough—would not hear a true word said of his dealings with you, when he had done such deeds as I could never have deemed an honest man, not to say a high-born knight and a *kurteis* gentleman-at-arms— mind you where I came upon you two in Oslo? *That* you could forgive Erlend, both then and since——"

Kristin answered low:

"I had cast in my lot with his then—what would have become of me afterwards, had I parted my life from Erlend's?"

"Look on me, Kristin," said Simon Darre, "and answer me true. Had I held your father fast to the word he had given—chosen to take you, even as you were—had I said to you that never should you be minded of your shame by me, but that loose you I would not—what had you then done?"

"I know not."

Simon laughed a hard laugh:

"Had I forced you to drink the bride-ale with me—I trow, you had scarce taken me to your arms willingly, Kristin, my fair one——"

Her face was white now. She sat looking down, answering naught. He laughed as before:

"I trow you had scarce welcomed me kindly, when I mounted the wedding-bed beside you——"

"Methinks I had taken a knife with me to bed," she said in a half-choked whisper.

"I hear you know the ballad of Knut of Borg"—Simon smiled grimly. "That such a thing has happed 'twixt living folk I have never heard. But God knows whether *you* had not done it!"

A little after he spoke again:

"'Tis unheard of, too, among Christian men, for lawfully wedded folk to part them of their own wills, as you have done—without lawful cause and the bishop's leave. Are you not ashamed, you two—? You trod all underfoot and braved all that you might come together; that time Erlend was in peril of life, you thought of naught but of saving him, and he thought more on you than on his seven sons and his name and his goods. But so soon as you can possess each other in peace and safety, then you throw seemliness and peace to the winds—wrangling and miscontent were betwixt you at Husaby, too; that saw I myself, Kristin——

——"I tell you, for your sons' sakes, you must seek atonement with your husband. If you be least in the wrong, then belike 'tis the easier too for you to proffer Erlend your hand," said he, more gently.

"——'Tis easier for you than for Erlend Nikulaussön, sitting up there at Haugen in poverty," said Simon again.

"'Tis not easy for me," she whispered. "Meseems I have shown that, for my children, I can do a little.—I have striven and striven for them——"

"It is so," said Simon. Then he asked: "Mind you the day we met on the road by Nidaros? You sat in the grass giving Naakkve suck——"

Kristin nodded.

"Could you have done for the child at your breast what my sister did for her son—given him from you to those better able to care for him?"

Kristin shook her head.

"But pray his father to forget what you may have said to him in anger —think you not you could do that for him and six fair sons besides—say to your man, 'tis needful for the young lads' sakes that he come home to them and to his manor——?"

"I will do as you would have me, Simon," said Kristin, low. "Hard are the words you have spoken to me," she said a little after. "Before

now, too, you have chidden me more harshly than any other lay-
man——"

"Ay, but now can I promise you 'twill be the last time"—his voice
took on the teasing, mirthful ring of old days. "Nay, weep not so, Kristin—but remember, sister mine, this have you promised to a dying
man." Once more the old, wicked gleam came to his eyes:

"You know well, Kristin—before now I have had cause to know you
were not one to put full trust on!"

"Be still now, dear one," he begged a little later; he had lain listening
to her broken, sore weeping. "Be sure I remember that you were to us a
good and faithful sister. We were friends at the last in spite of all, my
Kristin——"

Towards evening he prayed that they would fetch the priest to him.
Sira Eirik came, shrived him, and gave him the last oil and viaticum.
He took leave of his serving-folk and of the Erlendssöns, the five who
were at home—Naakkve, Kristin had sent to Kruke—— Simon had
begged to see Kristin's children that he might say farewell to them.

This night, too, Kristin watched over the dying man. Towards morning she fell asleep for a moment. She was wakened by a strange sound—
Simon lay moaning a little, softly. It shook her fearfully, when she
heard it—that *he* should bemoan himself, quietly and bitterly, like a
poor, forsaken child, now when, belike, he thought that none would
hear it. She bent down and kissed him many times upon the face. A
sickening, deathly smell came already from his breath and his body.
But, as the day grew light, she saw that his eyes were alive and clear and
steadfast as ever.

He suffered fearful pain, she saw, when Jon and Sigurd lifted him in a
sheet while she put his bed aright and made it as soft and easy as she
could. Food he had taken none for a whole day and night, but he had a
great thirst.

When she had settled him aright, he begged that she would make the
sign of the cross over him: "I cannot move the left arm either now."

——But when we cross ourselves, or mark with the cross anything that
we would guard, then shall we bear in mind why the cross was made
holy and what it means, and remember that 'twas by the pains and
death of the Lord that this sign came to honour and power——

Simon remembered, this had he heard one read aloud. Sure enough
he had been little wont to think much when he crossed his breast, or set
the cross upon his houses and his goods.—He felt him unready and ill
beseen to fare forth from this earthly home—he must comfort himself by
thinking that he had made him ready with shrift as well as could be in
the time, and that he had been given the last offices. Ramborg—but she
was so young, maybe she would live much happier with another man.

His children, God must take them in His ward—and Gyrd would care
for their welfare faithfully and wisely. And for the rest he must put his
trust in God, who judges a man, not according to his worth, but of His
own grace——

On in the day came Sigrid Andresdatter and Geirmund of Kruke.
Thereupon Simon would have it that Kristin must go out and rest, so
long she had watched and tended him now. "And soon 'twill be irksome to be near me," said he, smiling a little. At that, for a moment, she
broke into loud sobs—then she bent down and kissed again the poor
body that was already to decay.

Thereafter Simon lay still. The fever and the pains were now less
sore. He lay thinking, sure now it could not be long before he was set
free.

He marvelled himself that he had spoken to Kristin as he had done.
'Twas not this that he had meant to say to her. But he had not been
able to speak otherwise. At times he was well-nigh vexed about it.

But now the poison must have worked inward to his heart. A man's
heart is the first thing to quicken in his mother's womb, and the last to
grow still in him. But in him now it sure must soon come to rest.

In the evening he lay wandering. More than once he groaned aloud,
so that 'twas fearsome to hear it. But at other times he lay laughing
softly, and speaking his own name, as Kristin thought—but Sigrid, who
sat bent over him, whispered to her, she deemed he was talking of a boy,
their cousin, with whom he had been good friends in childhood. Towards midnight he grew still and seemed to sleep. Then Sigrid prevailed with Kristin to lie down a little upon the other bed in the room.

She was awaked by a noise in the room—'twas a little before dawn—
and then she heard that the death-throes had begun. Simon was past
speech, but he knew her yet; she could see it by his eyes. Then it
seemed as though a spring snapped within them—they turned up under
the eyelids. But yet a while he lay, the rattle in his throat, still living.
The priest was come, he read the prayers for the dying; the two women
sat by the bed, and the whole household were come into the room. At
last, a while before midday, he drew his last breath.

The day after, Gyrd Darre came riding in to the Formo courtyard.
He had broken down a horse on the way. Down by Breidin he had
heard of his brother's death, so that he was calm enough at first. But
when his sister threw herself weeping into his arms, he pressed her to
him, and he too wept like a child.

Ramborg Lavransdatter, he told them, lay at Dyfrin with a new-born
son. When Gaute Erlendssön came with the message, she had shrieked
aloud straightway that she knew 'twould be Simon's death. Then she

had fallen upon the floor in a fit. The child had come six weeks before its time, but they hoped 'twould live.

A goodly grave-ale was held for Simon Andressön, and he was buried close up to the choir by the Olav's Church. The parish folk were well pleased that he had chosen his resting-place there. The old Formo stock, that died out on the spear side with Simon Sæmundssön, had been a mighty and a gallant line; Astrid Simonsdatter wed richly; her sons bore the knightly name and sat in the King's council, but came home but seldom to their mother's udal lands. When, therefore, her grandson took up his abode upon the manor, folk deemed 'twas well-nigh as though the old race was set in their seat again; soon they forgot to account Simon Andressön a stranger, and they sorrowed much that he must die so young; for at his death he was but two-and-forty winters old.

v

W E E K after week went by, and Kristin made ready in her heart to bear to Erlend the dead man's message. Do it she would for sure—but she deemed it a hard matter. And meanwhile there was so much that must be done at home upon the manor. From day to day she put herself off with fresh pleas for delay——

At Whitsuntide Ramborg Lavransdatter came back to Formo. The children she had left behind at Dyfrin. They were well, she answered, when Kristin asked after them. The two young maids had wept bitterly and sorrowed over their father. Andres was too young to understand. The youngest, Simon Simonssön, throve well, and there was good hope that in time he would grow big and strong.

Ramborg came once or twice to the church, and to her husband's grave; else she stirred not from her home. But Kristin went south to her often as she could. She wished now from her heart that she had known more of her young sister. The widow looked most childlike in her weeds —frail and undergrown her body seemed in the heavy, dark-blue habit; the little, three-cornered face showed sallow and thin among the linen bands, under the black woollen veil falling in stiff folds from the crown of her head almost to the hem of her skirt. And she had dark rings under her big eyes, where the pupils ever gazed out now, wide and coal-black.

At the hay harvest there came a week when Kristin could not go to see her sister. From her hay-making folk she heard there was a guest with Ramborg at Formo—Jammælt Halvardssön. Kristin remembered that Simon had spoken of this man; he owned a great manor not far from Dyfrin, and he and Simon had been friends from childhood up.

A week on in the harvesting it set in rain; and Kristin rode down the

Dale to her sister. Kristin sat talking of the untoward weather and of the hay, and asked how things went here on Formo—when Ramborg said of a sudden:

"'Twill be for Jon now to see to all that—I am faring south a few days hence, Kristin."

"Ay, poor soul, you long for your children, I can well believe," said Kristin.

Ramborg rose and walked to and fro in the room.

"You shall hear somewhat that will make you wonder," the young woman said in a little. "Soon will you and your sons be bidden to a betrothal-ale at Dyfrin. I gave Jammælt my yea ere he went from here, and Gyrd will hold my betrothal feast."

Kristin sat dumb. Her sister stood, black-eyed and pale, gazing fixedly at her. At length the elder said:

"I see, then, not for long will Simon have left you widowed—— I had deemed you grieved for him so sorely.—But 'tis true you are your own mistress now——"

Ramborg made no answer; then, in a little, Kristin asked:

"Gyrd Darre knows that you are minded to wed again so soon?"

"Ay." Ramborg walked to and fro again. "Helga counsels it—Jammælt is rich." She laughed. "And Gyrd is so clear-sighted a man, I trow he has seen long since how wretchedly we lived together, Simon and I."

"What is't you say?" cried Kristin—— "None else knew, for sure, that you lived unhappily together," she said a little after. "I wot not that any has seen other than friendship and goodwill betwixt you. Simon gave you your way in all things, gave you all your heart desired, ever kept your youth in mind and was heedful that you should have joy of it, and be spared all toil and trouble. His children he loved, and showed you day by day his thankfulness for that you bore him those two——"

Ramborg smiled scornfully.

Kristin answered vehemently:

"Ay, if so it be that you have aught of reason to say you lived ill together, then for sure 'tis not Simon that bears the blame——"

"No," said Ramborg. "I will take the blame—if you dare not."

Kristin sat in amaze.

"I trow you know not yourself what you say, sister," said she at length.

"Yes, in sooth," answered Ramborg. "But full well I trow that you know it not. So little have you thought on Simon that I well believe 'tis news for you. You counted him good enough to turn to when there was need of a helper that had gladly borne red-hot iron for your sake—but never did you fling so much thought Simon Andressön's way as to ask how much it cost him—— I was left free to joy in my youth, ay—blithely and gently Simon lifted me into the saddle and sent me forth from him a-visiting and junketing; even as blithely and gently he welcomed me again when I came home—he patted me as he patted his dog and his horse—he felt no lack of me, wheresoever I went——"

Kristin had risen—she stood by the board moveless. Ramborg wrung her hands so that the joints cracked, going and coming, going and coming through the room:

"Jammælt——" she said, something more calmly. "I have known for long what *he* thought of me. I saw it even while his wife still lived. Not that he knows that he has bewrayed him in word or deed—believe not that! He grieved so himself over Simon—came to me time and again and would have comforted me—'tis true! 'Twas Helga who said to us both she deemed that now it were fitting if we——

"——And I wot not what I should wait for. Never shall I be more comforted or less than now I am—— Now I have a mind to try how 'tis to live with a man who has kept silence and has thought on *me* for long, long years. I know all too well how 'tis to live with one who keeps silence and is ever thinking on another——"

Kristin stood as before. Ramborg stopped before her, with flashing eyes:

"You know 'tis true, what I have said!"

Kristin went forth from the room, quietly, with bowed head. While she stood in the rain in the courtyard waiting for the serving-man to lead forth her horse, Ramborg came to the door of the hall—she gazed at her elder sister with black, hostile eyes.

'Twas not till the next day that Kristin called to mind what she had promised Simon if Ramborg should wed again. So she rode to Formo once more. This seemed to her no easy thing to do. And the worst was that she knew she could not say aught that would be a help or comfort to her young sister. To her this match with Jammælt of Ælin seemed rashly made—with Ramborg in the mind she now was in. But Kristin saw 'twould be of no avail for her to gainsay it.

Ramborg was sullen and peevish and would scarce answer the other. She would in no wise consent that her step-daughter should come to Jörundgaard. "Nor methinks are things so ordered at your manor that 'twere wise to send a young maid thither." Kristin answered mildly that herein Ramborg might mayhap be right. But she had given Simon her word to make this proffer——

"Ay, and if so be Simon, in his fever-wanderings, understood not that 'twas an affront to me to ask you this, you, at least, must know that 'tis an affront to tell me of it," answered Ramborg; and Kristin was fain to turn her home from her fruitless errand.

Next morning promised fair weather. But when her sons came in to the morning meal, Kristin said they must get in the hay without her; she was setting forth on a journey, and mayhap she would be gone some days.

"I think to go north to Dovre to seek out your father," said she. "'Tis in my mind to pray him to forget the troubles that have been between us—to ask when he will come home to us."

The sons flushed red; they scarce dared look up, but she marked well how glad they were. She drew Munan to her and bent her face over him:

"You scarce remember your father, I trow, little one?"

The boy nodded, dumbly, with shining eyes. One after another the other sons looked over at their mother: she was younger of face and fairer than they had seen her for many years.

She came out into the courtyard a little after, clad for the journey in her church-going clothes: a black woollen habit broidered with blue and silver about the neck and sleeves, and black, sleeveless, hooded cloak, since 'twas high summer. Naakkve and Gaute had saddled her horse and their own; they would go with their mother. She said naught against it. But she spoke little with her sons as they rode north across the gorge and up into Dovre. For the most she was silent and lost in thought, and if she talked with the young lads, 'twas of other things than of her errand.

When they were come so far that they could see up the hill-side and had sight of the house roofs of Haugen against the sky, she bade the lads turn back.

"You can understand well that your father and I may have much to say one to the other that we can best speak of alone."

The brothers nodded; they bade their mother farewell and turned their horses homewards.

The wind from the mountains swept, cool and fresh, against her hot cheeks as she came up over the last rise. The sun shone golden upon the small grey houses, casting long shadows across the courtyard. The corn up here would soon be earing—it showed fairly upon the small plots, shimmering and swaying in the wind. On all the stone heaps and over the hillocks tall waving willow-herb blossomed red, and in between were little haycocks. But on the farm was no living thing to be seen—not even a dog came forth to give warning.

Kristin unsaddled her horse and led it to the water-trough. She had

no mind to turn it loose up here—so she took it into the stable. The sun
shone in through a great hole in the roof—roof-turves hung down in
tatters from the beams. And there was no sign that any horse had stood
there for many a long day. Kristin saw to her beast, and betook her out
into the courtyard again.

She looked into the byre. It was dark and empty—she knew by the
smell that it must have stood long deserted.

Some skins of beasts were stretched upon the house wall to dry—a
swarm of blue-flies flew up, buzzing, as she drew near. At the north end
of the house earth had been heaped up and turf spread over it so that the
house timbers were quite hidden. He had done it for warmth, belike——

She looked for naught else but that the house would be lockfast, but
the door flew open when she laid hand upon the latch. Erlend had not
even barred his house.

An air noisome past bearing met her when she stepped in—the strong,
rank smell of skins and of the stable. The first feeling that rushed over
her as she stood within his house was heart-breaking remorse and pity.
This dwelling seemed to her most like a bear's winter lair——

O ay, ay, ay, Simon—you were right!

Small the room was, but 'twas choicely wrought and had once been
fine. The fire-place had even a masoned chimney above it, so that it
should not smoke out into the room, like the fire-places in the hall-house
at home. But when she would have opened the damper to clear the
foul air a little, she saw the pipe had been blocked with slabs of stone.
The glass pane in the window to the penthouse was broken, and had
been stopped up with cloths. The whole room was floored with wood,
but so thick with dirt was the floor that the planks could scarce be seen.
Not a cushion was there upon the benches, but weapons, furs, and old
clothes lay strewn about; the filthy board was littered with orts of food.
And flies buzzed high and low.

She started—stood trembling—breathless, with thumping heart. In
the farther bed—in yonder bed where *it* had lain when last she was
here—lay somewhat covered with a wadmal cloth. She knew not herself
what she thought——

Then she set her teeth, forced herself to go across and lift the cloth.
'Twas but Erlend's coat of mail, his helm and shield. They lay covered
up upon the bare bed-boards.

She looked towards the other bed. 'Twas there they had found Björn
and Aashild. 'Twas there Erlend slept now—— Belike she herself would
lie there this night——

But what must it have been for him to dwell in this house, to sleep
here——? Again all else that she felt was drowned in pity. She went
over to the bed—she saw it had not been made for many days. The hay

under the sheet of hide had been lain upon till 'twas hard as stone. There was nothing in the bed save some sheep-skins, and a pair of wadmal-covered pillows, so foul that they stank. Dust and trash showered from the bed-gear when she handled it. Erlend's resting-place was no whit better than a horse-boy's in a stable.

Erlend, who could never have bravery enough about him; Erlend, who would don a silken skirt, velvet and fine furs, on the least pretext—who chafed because she suffered his children to go clad in home-spun wadmal on workdays, and never could abide that she herself should suckle them and take a hand herself with her serving-women in the housework—like a cottar's wife, he said——

Jesus—and 'twas he himself that had brought things to this——

——No, I will not say a word—I will take back all that I have said, Simon. You were right—he shall not bide on here, the father of my sons. I will proffer him my hand and my mouth and pray him for forgiveness——

'Tis not easy, Simon. But you were right—— She remembered the sharp grey eyes—their look, steadfast as ever, well-nigh to the end. From out the poor body, already beginning to waste away, there shone through his eyes his pure and shining spirit, until his soul was taken home like a blade withdrawn. She knew 'twas as Ramborg had said. He had loved her all these years.

No day had gone by in these months since his death but she must think on him, and now it seemed to her that she had known it all ere ever Ramborg spoke. She had been driven in this time to turn over again every memory she had of him for as long as she had known Simon Darre. All these years she had borne within her false memories of him who had been her hand-fasted man; she had tampered with these memories as a bad ruler tampers with money, mixing base metal with the silver. When he set her free and took upon himself the blame for the breach of troth-plight—she had told herself, and believed, that Simon Andressön turned from her with scorn in the moment he knew of her dishonour. She had forgotten that when he freed her, that day in the nun's garden—then for sure he thought not aught else of her but that she was unstained and pure. But even then he was willing to bear the shame of her changefulness and revolt—craved only that her father should know 'twas not he who had willed the breach——

And *this*, too, she knew now: when he had learned the worst, and had stood up to save for her a semblance of honour in the world's eyes—had she been able to turn to him then, Simon would have taken her even then at the church door to be his wife, and he would have striven so to live with her that she should never have felt he had kept the memory of her shame.

And none the less she knew: never could she have loved him. Never could she have loved Simon Andressön—— Yet—all that Erlend was not and that she had raged to find he was not, Simon was. But then must she herself be a pitiable woman, to murmur at her lot——

Simon had given, with a measureless bounty, to her he loved. And she had deemed surely that she too did the like——

But when she took gifts at his hands, unthinking and unthankful, he had but smiled. She understood now that often when they were together he had been heavy of heart. She knew now that behind that strangely steadfast mien he had hidden sorrow—then, flinging out a few jesting words, he would thrust all aside, and stand ready once more to guard, to help, and to give——

She herself had raged, had stored up and brooded over every hurt—when she reached forth her gifts and Erlend saw them not——

Here, in this room, she had stood and spoken such brave words: "I went astray of my own will—never will I cast blame on Erlend, should the path lead o'er the cliff edge." She had said it to the woman she drove to death to make way for her love.

Kristin moaned aloud, clasped her hands before her breast, and stood, rocking. Ay—she had said so proudly, she would cast no blame on Erlend Nikulaussön if he grew weary of her, betrayed her, forsook her even——

Ay—and if Erlend had done *that*—it seemed to her she could have stood to her word. If he had betrayed her once for all—and there had been an end. But he had not betrayed her—only failed her, failed her, and made her live ever fearful and unsure—no, never had he played her false, but never had he sustained her—and she could see no end to it: here she stood now, come to beg him to turn back to her, to fill her cup each day to the brim with unsureness and disquiet, with vain expectancy, with longings and fears, and hope that broke in sunder——

And it seemed to her she was worn out by him now. She had not the youth and courage to live with him any more—and belike she would never grow so old that Erlend could not play upon her fondness. Never so young that she could live with him in gladness, never so old that she could bear with him in patience. A little, weak woman was she grown—belike had ever been. Simon was in the right——

Simon—and father. They had been constant ever in one in faithful love to her, for all she had trodden them down for the sake of this man she herself could bear with now no longer—

Oh, Simon, I know well, never have you wished for vengeance on me at any time. But I marvel, Simon, if, where you lie, you know not that now you are well avenged——

Nay, she must busy herself with somewhat, else she could not bear it. She set the bed in order; sought for a mop and a broom, but it seemed no such thing was in the house. She looked into the closet—now she saw whence came the smell of the stable. Erlend had made his horse's stall in there. But here the floor was swept and clean. The saddle and the gear that hung upon the wall were well kept and greased; their rents were mended.

Pity again drove all other thoughts away. Had he brought Soten in there because he could not bear to be all alone in the house——?

Kristin heard steps in the penthouse. She stepped over to the glass pane—'twas thick with dust and cobweb, but she thought she could dimly see a woman. She pulled out the cloth and peeped. Out there a woman was sitting down a milk-can and a small cheese. She was oldish, lame, ugly, and poorly clad. Kristin scarce knew herself how much freer she drew breath.

She set the room in order as best she could. She found the writing that Björn Gunnarssön had carved upon a log of the long wall—it was in Latin, and she could not read it all, but he named himself both *dominus* and *miles*, and she made out the name of his fathers' seat in Elvesyssel that he had lost for Aashild Gautesdatter's sake. Amidst the fine carvings on the high-seat was his shield, bearing its device of the unicorn and the lily-star leaves.

A while after Kristin thought she heard a horse somewhere without. She went to the outer room and peered forth.

Down from the wooded slope above the farm-stead came a tall black horse harnessed to a load of firewood. Erlend walked by its side, driving. One dog sat atop of the wood; some others ran about the sleigh.

Soten, the Castilian, strained at his collar and dragged the wood-sleigh forward over the courtyard sward. One of the dogs dashed down the slope barking—— Erlend, who had begun to unharness, marked now by the flurry among the dogs that something must be afoot. He took the wood-axe from the load and walked toward the dwelling-house——

Kristin fled in again, dropping the latch behind her. She shrank in to the wall of the fire-place, and stood trembling and waiting.

Erlend strode in, with the wood-axe in his hand and the dogs tumbling over the threshold before and after him. They found the stranger forthwith, and greeted her with a storm of barking——

The first she saw was the wave of young, red blood that rushed over his face—the fluttering quiver about his fine, weak mouth, the great eyes deep in the shadow of the brows——

The sight of him took away her breath. She saw, indeed, the old growth of stubble upon his lower face, she saw that his unkempt hair was iron-grey—but the colour came and went in his cheeks in hasty pulses, as when they were young—he was so young and so comely, 'twas as though naught had availed to quell him——

He was miserably clad—his blue shirt dirty and ragged; over it he wore a leathern jerkin, scarred and rubbed and rent at the lace-holes, but fitting closely and pliant to the body's strong and gracious motions. His tight leathern breeches had a rent over the one knee, and the seam behind the other leg was burst. Yet never, more than now, had he seemed the son of chiefs and nobles. So fairly and easily he bore his tall slim form, with the broad shoulders somewhat stooped, the long, fine limbs—he stood there, resting a little on one foot, one hand laid on the belt about his slender waist, the other, with the axe in it, hanging at his side.

He had called the dogs back to him—stood looking at her—went red and pale and said no word. For a good while they both stood dumb. At last the man spoke, in a voice that wavered a little:

"Are you come hither, Kristin?"

"I was fain to see how it fared with you," answered she.

"Ay, you have seen it, then." He cast a glance about the room. "You see things are passably well with me here—'tis good you chanced on a day when my house is trim and in order——" He grew ware of the shadow of a smile upon her face. "——Or maybe 'tis you who set it in order," said he, laughing low.

Erlend laid aside the axe and sat him down on the outer bench, with his back leaned against the board. Of a sudden he grew grave:

"You stand there so—is aught amiss at home—at Jörundgaard, I mean—with the lads?"

"No." Now was her time to bring out what she had to say: "Our sons are thriving and doing well. But they long so for you, Erlend. This was my errand—I came hither, husband, to beg you to come home to us. We miss you, all of us——" She cast down her eyes.

"You look well, none the less, Kristin——" Erlend looked at her with a little smile.

Red, as though he had struck her, Kristin stood:

"'Tis not for that——"

"Nay, I know 'tis not because you deem you too young and fresh to live as a widow woman," Erlend went on, when she stopped short. "I trow but little good would come of it should I come back home, Kristin," said he, more soberly. "In your hands all goes well on Jörund-gaard, that know I—you have fortune with you in your doings. And I am well content with the life I live here."

"'Tis not well for the boys—that we should be at odds," she answered in a low voice.

"Oh——" Erlend lingered on the word. "They are so young, I can scarce believe they take it so to heart that they will not forget it when they leave their childhood behind. I care not if I tell you," he said with a little smile, "I meet them now and again——"

She knew it—but she felt as though it humbled her, and felt as 'twere so he had meant it—he had deemed she knew it not. The sons had never known that she knew. But she answered gravely:

"Then you know also that much on Jörundgaard is not as it should be——"

"We never talk of such-like things," said he, smiling as before. "We go a-hunting together—but you must be hungry and thirsty"—he leapt up. "And you are standing too—nay, set you up in the high-seat, Kristin—ay, do so, sweetheart! You shall have it to yourself——"

He fetched in the milk and the cheese, and brought out bread, butter, and dried meat. Kristin was hungry and yet more thirsty; but she found it hard to swallow down the food. Erlend ate hastily and slovenly, as had always been his wont when he was not with strangers—but he was soon done.

He talked of himself the while. The folk down the hill here tilled his land and brought him milk and a little food—for the most part he lay out on the fells hunting game and fishing. Howsoever, he said on a sudden, he had thoughts now of faring from the land. Seeking service with some outland chieftain——

"Oh, no, Erlend!"

He looked at her quickly and searchingly. But she said no more. It began to grow dusk in the room—her face and head-linen shone palely against the dark wall. Erlend rose and made a fire in the fire-place. Then he sat him down aslant on the outer bench, turned towards her; the red glare from the fire flickered over his form.

But that he could even think of such a thing! He was nigh as old as had been her father when he died. And yet 'twas believable enough that he would do it one day—run after some such whimsy, off to seek for new adventures——

"Deem you 'tis not enough," said the wife vehemently, "'tis not enough that you have forsaken the parish and your sons and me—would you flee the land from us now?"

"Had I known your thoughts of me, Kristin," said Erlend gravely, "then had I gone forth from *your* manor long ago. But I understand now that you have had to bear *much* from me——"

"You know full well, Erlend—you say *my* manor, but you have a husband's right over all that is mine." She heard herself how faint of voice she grew.

"Ay," answered Erlend. "But I know myself I was an ill husband of my own good." He was silent a while. "Naakkve—I mind the time he was unborn—you spoke of him that you bore beneath your girdle, that was to mount into my high-seat after me. I see now, Kristin—'twas hard for you—best let things be as they are. And I thrive full well in this life——"

Kristin looked around her in the darkening room, shuddering—the shadows filled every corner now, and the fire-light danced——

"I understand not," she said, nigh sinking with heaviness, "that you can abide this house. Naught have you to do, none to bear you company—at the least you might get you a house-carl, I trow——"

"You mean that I should work the farm myself——?" Erlend laughed. "O no, Kristin, sure you must know how little fit I am to play the farmer. I cannot sit quiet——"

"Quiet—— Here surely you sit quiet enough—the long winter through——"

Erlend smiled to himself, his eyes far off and strange:

"Ay, when 'tis in that way—— When I need not to think of aught but what runs in my head—can go and come as I like—— And you know well—it has ever been so with me, that when there's naught to wake for, I can sleep—I sleep like a bear in its winter lair when 'tis not weather for the fells——"

"Are you never afraid to be alone here?" whispered Kristin.

At first he looked at her as though he understood not. Then he laughed:

"Because folks say 'tis haunted? Never have I marked aught. Sometimes I had been fain that my kinsman Björn *would* visit me. Mind you that he said once he deemed I would ill abide to feel the knife-edge at my throat. I could e'en have a mind to answer the knight now that I was not greatly feared when I had the rope about my neck——"

A long shudder passed through the woman's body. She sat there dumb.

Erlend rose.

"I trow 'tis time we went to rest now, Kristin."

Stiff and cold, she watched Erlend take the covering that lay over his armour, spread it on the bed, and turn it down over the dirty pillows. "'Tis the best I have," said he.

"Erlend!" She clasped her hands beneath her breast. She sought for something she might say to gain a little time yet—she was so afraid. Then she remembered the errand she was to fulfil:

"Erlend—I was given a message to bear to you. Simon prayed me, when he lay dying, that I would greet you from him and say he had repented him each day of the words he said to you when last you parted. Unmanly he called them himself—and he begged that you would forgive him for them."

"Simon." Erlend stood holding the bedpost with one hand, gazing down at the floor. "He is the man I am least fain to be remembered of."

"I know not what has been between you," said Kristin. Strangely heartless these words of Erlend's seemed to her. "But 'twere strange and unlike Simon if it were as he said, that he had shown him little-minded in his dealings with you. If so it be—I trow the blame was not all his."

Erlend shook his head: "He stood by me like a brother when my need was greatest," he said low. "And I took help and friendship at his hands, and I knew not that all the time he could scarce endure me——

"——Methinks it must have been easier to live in the old world, when two such fellows as he and I met together hand to hand—met on a holm and put it to the trial of arms which should win the fair-haired maid—"

He took an old cloak from the bench and flung it over his arm:

"Maybe you would have the dogs beside you to-night?"

Kristin had risen:

"Whither go you, Erlend?"

"Out to the barn to lie there——"

"No——!" Erlend stopped—he stood there, straight and slender and young in the dim red light of the waning embers. "I dare not lie alone here in this house—I dare not——"

"Dare you lie in my arms then?" She half saw his smile through the dusk, and drooped beneath it. "Are you not afraid I should crush you to death, Kristin——?"

"Would that you might——!" She sank into his arms.

When she awoke, she saw by the pane of glass that it must be day without. Something lay crushingly heavy on her breast—Erlend slept with his head upon her shoulder; he had laid one arm over her and his hand was around her left arm.

She looked at the man's iron-grey hair. She saw her own small, shrunken breasts—above and below them the high-arched curves of her ribs showed under the thin covering of flesh. A kind of terror came over her, while memory after memory arose from this night. In this house— they two, young no longer—— Disquiet and shame took hold on her when she saw the livid patches upon her work-worn, mother's arms, on her shrunken bosom. Wildly she caught at the coverlid and would have covered herself——

Erlend awoke, started up on his elbow, stared into her face—his eyes were coal-black from sleep:

"Methought——" He threw himself down beside her again; a deep wild tremor went through her whole being at the rejoicing and the fear in his voice. "——Methought I had dreamed again——"

She pressed her open lips upon his mouth and twined her arms about his neck. Never, never had it been so blessed——

Late in the afternoon, when the sunshine was yellow already and the shadows lay long over the green courtyard, they set out down to the beck to fetch water. Erlend bore the two great pails. Kristin walked by his side, slender, straight, and lissom. Her head-linen had slipped down, and lay around her shoulders; her hair shone bare and brown in the sunlight. She felt it herself, when she shut her eyes and lifted her face against the light—she had grown red in the cheeks; the lines of her face had softened. Each time she glanced at him, she sank her gaze, overcome—when she saw in Erlend's face how young she was.

Erlend bethought him that he would bathe. While he went a little farther down, Kristin sat on the greensward, leaning her back against a stone. The fell beck trilled and gurgled her into a doze—now and then, when the midges and gnats touched her skin, she opened her eyes a little and brushed them off. Down among the sallows around about the pool she caught a glimpse of Erlend's white body—he stood with a foot upon a stone, rubbing himself with wisps of grass. She closed her eyes again and smiled, in happy weariness. She was strengthless as ever against him——

The man came and flung himself on the grass before her—with dripping hair, the chill of the water upon his red mouth when he pressed it into the palm of her hand. He had shaved and found a better shirt—but this one even was none too brave. Laughing, he took hold on it up under the arm-pits, where it was tattered:

" You might as lief have brought me a shirt when you did come north here at the last."

"I shall set about sewing and hemming a shirt for you soon as I come home, Erlend," she answered smiling, and passed her hand across his brow. He grasped it:

"Never shall you go from here again, my Kristin——"

The woman did but smile and answered naught. Erlend dragged himself a little way, as he lay on his belly. Under the bushes in the damp shade grew a cluster of small, white starry flowers. The flower-leaves were veined with blue like a woman's breast; in the midst of each blossom was a little, blue-brown boss. Erlend plucked them one and all:

"You that have lore of such things, Kristin, I trow you know a name for these?"

"'Tis Friggja-grass*—nay, Erlend——" She flushed and put away his hand as he would have stuffed the blooms into her bosom.

Erlend laughed and lightly bit the white petals one by one. Then he laid all the blossoms in her open hand and closed up her fingers over them:

"Do you mind when we walked in the garden of the Hofvin Spital— you gave me a rose?"

Kristin shook her head slowly, smiling a little:

"No. But you took a rose from out my hand."

"And you suffered me to take it. And 'twas so you suffered me to take you, Kristin—as meek and gentle as a rose—afterwards you pricked me sometimes till the blood came, my sweet." He threw himself forward into her lap and laid his arms about her waist: "Last night, Kristin— 'twas of no avail—you did not get off by sitting meekly waiting——"

Kristin bent her head and hid her face against his shoulder.

On the fourth day they had taken harbour in the birch wood among the hillocks above the farm. For on that day the tenant was carrying the hay. And, without having spoken of it, Kristin and Erlend were at one that none need know she was with him. He went down to the houses once or twice to fetch food and drink, but she sat on in the heather up among the stunted birches. From where they sat they could see the man and woman toiling home, bearing the loads of hay upon their backs.

"Mind you," asked Erlend, "that time you promised me that, when I ended as a crofter away among the fells, then would you come and keep house for me? You will keep two cows here belike, and a few sheep and goats——?"

Kristin laughed low, playing with his hair.

"What think you our sons would say, Erlend—if their mother fled the parish and forsook them in that wise——?"

"I trow they would be fain enough to be their own masters on Jörund-gaard," said Erlend, laughing. "They are old enough for it. You wot well Gaute is a full good farmer, young as he is. And Naakkve is well-nigh a man."

"O no." The mother laughed quietly. "'Tis true he thinks so himself—ay, they think so, all five, I trow—but the lad lacks somewhat yet of a man's wit——"

"If 'tis after his father he takes, maybe 'twill come to him late or

* See Note 4.

never," answered Erlend. He smiled slyly: "You deem you can still hide your children behind your skirts, Kristin—— Naakkve had a son fathered on him up here this summer—you know not that, I trow——?"

"No——!" Kristin sat there red and aghast.

"Ay, 'twas still-born—and I trow the boy will think twice ere he come thither any more—'twas the widow of Paal's son, here at Haugsbrekken; she said 'twas his, and sackless, I trow, he was not, howsoever the matter stood. Ay, such old folk are we now, you and I——"

"Can you talk so, when your son has brought on him trouble and shame?" It cut her to the heart that the man could talk so lightly—and that it seemed to be a jest in his eyes that she had known naught of this.

"Ay, what would you have me say?" asked Erlend as before. "The lad is eighteen winters old. You see yourself now, it avails not much for you to go about keeping watch on your sons as though they were children. When you come up hither to me, we must see to getting him wed——"

"Think you 'twill be a light thing for us to find Naakkve an equal match——? No, husband, after this methinks you must come home with me and help to guide the lads."

Erlend raised himself sharply on his elbow:

"That will I not do, Kristin. A stranger in your country I am and ever will be—no man there minds aught of me but that I was doomed a traitor to king and country. Thought you never in those years I lived on Jörundgaard that I lived ill at ease—at home in Skaun I was wont to count for something more 'mongst folk. Even at that time—in my youth—when the tale of my evil life was buzzed abroad, when I lay under the Church's ban—none the less was I Erlend Nikulaussön of Husaby! Then came the time, Kristin—I had the fortune to show the folk yonder, north of the fells, that wholly unworthy of my forefathers I was not—— No, I tell you! Here, on this little croft, I am a free man —none gape after my doings or talk behind my back. Hearken to me, Kristin, my only love—stay with me! Never shall you have cause to repent it. Here is better dwelling than was at Husaby on any day. I wot not how it is, Kristin—I was never glad or light of heart there, not when I was a child, and never since. 'Twas hell while I had Eline with me, and never were you and I glad at heart together there—— Yet God the Almighty knows I have loved you each day and each hour I have known you. Bewitched, I trow, the manor was—mother was wrung to death there, and my father was ever an unglad man. Here 'tis good to be, Kristin—if only you will be with me. Kristin—as true God died for us upon the cross, I hold you as dear to-day as that night you slept beneath my cloak—the night after Margaret's Mass—and I sat and looked on you, pure and fresh and young and untouched blossom that you were."

Kristin answered low:

"Mind you, Erlend, too, you prayed that night that I should never have to weep a tear for your sake——"

"Ay—and God and all the saints in heaven know that I meant it! 'Tis true it fell out otherwise—maybe it had to—belike it ever so befalls while we dwell in this earthly home. But I loved you when I wrought you evil and when I wrought you good. Bide here, Kristin——"

"Have you never thought on this," she asked, gently as before, "that it might well make your son's lot hard to have their father talked of so as you say? Flee to the hills from the parish talk, they cannot, all the seven——"

Erlend looked down:

"They are young," said he, "comely and gallant lads—— They will make a way for themselves yet—— We, Kristin, we have not so many years before us, ere we grow old and grey—will you waste the time while yet you are fair and fresh and fit to joy in life? Kristin——?"

She cast down her eyes before the giddy gleam in his. In a little while she said:

"Have you forgot, Erlend, that two of our sons are little children yet? What deem you I were worth if I forsook Lavrans and Munan——"

"You must bring them up hither, then—if Lavrans would not rather bide with his brothers. So little a boy he is not neither.—Is Munan comely as ever?" the father asked, smiling.

"Ay," said the mother, "he is a fair child."

Thereafter they sat long silent. And when again they spoke, it was of other things.

She woke in the grey of dawn next morning, as she had waked each morning up here—lay and heard the horses stamping without the house wall. She had Erlend's head fast in her arms. The other mornings when she awoke in this grey and early hour she had been gripped by the same fear and shame as on the first—she had striven to stifle them. Were they not a wedded pair at odds who had now made up their quarrel? Could aught better befall the children than that their father and mother should make friends again?

But this morning she lay striving to remember her sons. For 'twas as though a spell was on her—and straight from the wood at Gerdarud, where first he had taken her to his arms, Erlend had borne her with him hither. They were so young—it could not be true that already she had borne this man seven sons, that she was mother to tall, grown men—— It seemed as though she must have lain here in his arms and but dreamed of the long years they had lived as man and wife at Husaby—— All his reckless words lured her and echoed in her—giddy with fear, she felt as though Erlend had swept from off her the seven-fold burden of her charge—thus must it be with a young mare when she stands unsaddled upon the sæter pasture-ground—pack and saddle and head-gear are gone from her; against her blow the winds and the airs of the uplands; she is set free to graze the tender mountain grass, free to run far as she will over all the upland wastes.

And at the same time she longed already, sweetly and yearningly, right willing to bear a new burden. Already she yearned with a little tender dizziness towards him who should abide next to her heart for nine long months. She had known full surely from the first morning she awoke up here in Erlend's arms. Along with the hard, dry, scorching fever in her mind, barrenness had passed away from her. She bore Erlend's child in her womb, and, with a strangely tender impatience, her soul stretched forward towards the hour when it should be brought forth to day.

Those great sons of mine have no need of me, she thought. To them I seem but doting and troublesome. We shall but stand in their way, the little one and I. No, I cannot part from here—we must bide here with Erlend. I cannot go——

Yet, none the less, as they sat together at their morning meal, she let fall that she must get her home now to her children.

'Twas of Lavrans and Munan she thought. They were so old now, that she was abashed when she thought of them dwelling up here with Erlend and her, and mayhap looking with wondering eyes at their father and mother, grown so young again. But do without her those two could not.

Erlend sat gazing at her while she spoke of her journey home. At last he spoke with a flitting smile.

"Ay—if so be you will, you must even go!"

He made ready to bear her company on her way. And he rode with her right down through the gorge into Sil, until he caught a glimpse of the church roof over the pine-tops. Then he bade her farewell. At the last he was still smiling, a roguishly secure smile.

"Ay, you know well, Kristin—whether you come by night or by day—whether I wait for you short or long—I shall welcome you as you were the Queen of Heaven come down to my croft from the skies——"

She laughed:

"Ay, with such great matters *I* dare not meddle. But I trow you know now, love, that great will be the joy in your house the day the master comes home to his own."

He shook his head, laughing a little. Smiling, they made their farewells; smiling, Erlend leaned over, as they sat a-horseback side by side, and kissed her many, many times, and between the kisses he looked at her with his laughing eyes:

"We must see, then," he said at last, " which of us two is the more stubborn, my sweet Kristin. This will not be our last meeting—that know we well, both you and I!"

As she rode by the church a little shudder ran through her. 'Twas as though she were coming home from the Mountain King's Hall; as though Erlend were the Mountain King himself, and could not pass the church and the cross on the green.

She drew rein—was well-nigh minded to turn about and ride after him——

Then she looked out over the green grassy slopes, down upon her own fair manor with meadows and tilled fields, and the river sweeping in shining loops down through the Dale. The mountains rose in a warm blue haze—the heavens were full of bellying summer clouds. 'Twas madness. There, at home with their sons, was his place. He was no knight of faerie—but a Christian man, full as he was of mad-brained moods and thoughtless whims; her wedded husband, with whom she had borne both good and ill—dear, dear, sorely as he had tormented her with his wayward fancies. She must bear with him; since she could not live without him, she must strive on and suffer dread and insecurity as best she might. Long, she deemed, it would not be till he came after—now that again they had been together.

VI

To her sons she said, their father must take order with one thing and another at Haugen ere he came home. Most like he would come down in early autumn.

At home she went about the manor, young, rosy-cheeked, her face soft and gentle, quicker at all her work—yet she made not such good speed as when she worked in her wonted quiet and ordered fashion. She took not her sons to task sharply, as had been her wont, when they did amiss or she had cause for miscontent with them. Now she spoke to them jestingly, or let it pass without saying aught.

Lavrans was now for sleeping in the loft with his big brothers.

"Ay, maybe we must reckon you among the grown lads now, my son." She ran her fingers through the boy's thick, yellow-brown hair, and drew him to her—he was as high already as her mid-breast. "And you, Munan, will you let your mother count you for a child a little while longer?"—Of an evening when the boy had gone to rest in the hall, he still liked that his mother should sit her down on the bedside and fondle him a little; he lay with his head in her lap, and prattled in more childish fashion than he would in the day, when his brothers could hear him. The two talked of the time when father would come home.

Then he would move over to the wall, and his mother would draw the covers over him. Kristin lit the candle, took her sons' garments that were to mend, and set herself to sew.

She unclasped the brooch over her bosom, and felt with her hand about her breasts. They were round and firm as a quite young woman's. She pushed her sleeve right up to the shoulder, and looked on her naked arm in the light. It was grown whiter and fuller. Then she rose and walked—felt how softly she trod in the supple within-door shoes—passed her hand down over her slim hips: no longer were they sharp and hard as a man's. The blood flowed through her body as in spring-time the sap flows in the trees. 'Twas youth burgeoning within her.

She was busy with Frida in the brew-house, pouring warm water upon the grain for the Yule malt. Frida had forgot to see to it in time; it had been suffered to go bone dry while yet swelling. But Kristin did not chide the woman—with a half-smile she listened to the other excusing herself. For the first time it had befallen that Kristin had forgot to look to it herself.

By Yule-tide she would have Erlend at home with her. When she sent him these tidings, he would come home at once, for sure. So mad the man could not be as not to give way now—he must see 'twas not possible she could go up to Haugen, far from all folk, when she bore another life with her. But she would tarry a little yet before she sent him this message—though 'twas sure enough—maybe even till she had felt it quicken—— The second autumn they dwelt on Jörundgaard she had had to go out of the way, as folk say. She had taken comfort quickly enough then. She was not afraid that 'twould fall out so this time—it *could* not be. Nevertheless——

She felt as though she must bend all her being to the shielding of this tiny, tender life that she bore beneath her heart—as one bends one's hands to guard a little, new-lit flame——

One day late in autumn Ivar and Skule came and said they were for riding up to their father—'twas rare and fine now in the fells; they would ask leave to go a-hunting with him, now 'twas clear black frost.

Naakkve and Björgulf were sitting at the chess-board; they stopped and listened.

"I know not," said Kristin. She had not thought on it before—whom she should send with the tidings. She looked at her two half-grown sons.

Foolish, she herself deemed it, but to tell them she could not bring herself. She might say they must take Lavrans with them, and tell him to speak with his father alone. He was so young he would not wonder. And yet——

"You wot well your father is coming hither soon," she said. "Like enough you would but be in his way. Soon, too, I shall have a message to send him myself."

The twins grumbled. Naakkve looked up from the chess-board and said shortly: "Do as our mother bids, boys."

When Yule was nigh she sent Naakkve north to Erlend. "——You must tell him, son, I begin now to long sore for his coming—and, so, I trow, do all of you!" She spoke not of the new reason there was now—'twas most like, she deemed, that the grown lad had seen it for himself; he should judge himself whether he would tell his father of it.

Naakkve came back—he had not found his father. Erlend was gone to Raumsdal; he had had word, it seemed, that his daughter and her husband were now to flit to Björgvin, and that Margret was wishful to meet her father at Veöy.

'Twas but reason, this—Kristin lay awake of nights—now and again she would stroke Munan's face as he slept there by her side. It grieved her that Erlend came not for Yule. But 'twas but reason that he would fain see his daughter when the chance offered. She wiped away the tears as they stole down her cheek. She wept so easily again now, even as when she was young.

Just after Yule-tide Sira Eirik died. Kristin had been to him at Romundgaard more than once in the autumn while he lay bedridden; and she was at his grave-ale. Else she never came out among folks now. She deemed it great loss that their old parish priest was gone.

At the grave-ale she heard that someone had met Erlend north at Lesja; he was on his way home then. So he would soon come, for sure——

In the days that followed, sitting on the bench under the little window, with her hand-mirror, that she had sought out, in her hand, she would breathe on it, and rub it bright, and scan her face in it.

She had been sunburned as a cottar's wife these last years, but all trace of that was gone now. Her skin was white, with round, clear red roses on her cheeks like some painted picture. So fair of face she had not been since she was a young maid—— Kristin sat and held her breath with wondering joy.

So, at length, they would have the daughter Erlend had wished so much—if it fell out as the wise women say. Magnhild. They must break with the custom this time and give the first daughter her father's mother's name——

There hovered before her some memory of a fairy-tale she had once heard told. Of seven sons who were outlawed and hunted into the wilds for a little unborn sister's sake. Then she laughed at herself—how she had come to think on it she understood not——

Out from her sewing-chair she took the shirt of finest white linen that she sewed upon when she was alone. She pulled out threads of the linen and sewed birds and beasts on a glassy drawn-work ground—'twas many and many a day since she had done such fine work.—Oh, would that Erlend might come *now*—while as yet this had but made her fair, young and straight, rosy and blooming——

When Gregory's Mass * was but just gone by, the weather grew so fair 'twas right spring-like. The snow was melting—it shone like silver; already there were brown patches on the slopes that took the sun; a blue haze lay upon the mountains.

Gaute stood in the courtyard one day mending a broken sledge. Naakkve stood leaning against the wood-shed wall watching his brother at his work, when Kristin came from the kitchen-house bearing in both arms a great trough of new-baked brown bread.

Gaute looked up at his mother. Then he laid axe and auger down upon the sledge, ran after her, and took the trough; he bore it over to the storehouse.

Kristin had stopped still; her cheeks were red. When Gaute came back, she went over to her sons:

"You must ride up to your father one of these days, I trow—say that now is there great need of him here at home, to take the care of things from off my shoulders. I can do so little now—and 'twill be in the very midst of the spring work, too, that I shall have to lie in——"

The young lads listened to her; they too flushed, but she saw they were full glad at heart. Naakkve said, with a show of carelessness:

"'Twere as well we rode to-day—towards nones—what think you, brother?"

It was but the next day at noon when Kristin heard horsemen in the courtyard. She went out—'twas Naakkve and Gaute—they were alone. They stood by their horses, looked down, and said naught.

"What answered your father?" asked the mother.

Gaute stood leaning on his spear—he still looked on the ground. On that Naakkve spoke:

"Father bade us say to you that he had looked each day, all winter,

* 12th March.

that you should come up to him. And he said you would be no less welcome than when last you went to visit him."

The colour came and went in Kristin's face:

"Said you not then to your father—that things stood thus with me—that 'twill not be long ere I shall have a child again——?"

Gaute answered without looking up:

"It seemed as though father deemed *that* no reason—thought not that because of that you should not be able to remove to Haugen."

Kristin stood a little silent:

"What *said* he?" she asked, in a low harsh voice.

Naakkve would have spoken. Gaute lifted his hand a little, and looked up quickly, beseechingly, at his brother. But the eldest son spoke out his message:

"Father bade us say this: you knew when the child was begot how rich a man he was. And if he be not grown richer since, neither is he grown poorer."

Kristin turned away from her sons and went slowly towards the hall-house. Heavily and wearily she sat her down on the bench under the little window, from which the spring sun had melted the ice and rime already.

——It *was* so. 'Twas she had prayed to be suffered to lie in his arms —first. But 'twas not well done of him to mind her of that now. She deemed 'twas not well done of Erlend to send her this answer by their sons——

The spring weather held. There came a week's south wind, with rain —the river rose, waxed great and loud. Down the hill-sides the waters gushed noisily; there were sounds of snow-slides from the mountain valleys. Then came sunshine again.

Kristin stood without, behind the house, in the grey-blue evening. The thicket below the field was full of the singing of birds. Gaute and the twins were gone up to the sæter—they were after black-cock. Even down to the manor the drumming of the game-birds came from all the hill-sides in the mornings.

She pressed her clenched hands beneath her bosom. 'Twas but a short time now—she must bear it with patience to the end. Often, doubtless, she had been wayward and hard to live with, she too—— Ill-judging in her endless carefulness for the children—ill-timed, as Erlend had said. It seemed to her, none the less, that now he was hard. But now the time would soon be here when he *must* come to her—that he too knew, for sure.

Sunshine and showers followed one another. One afternoon her sons called to her. They were standing without in the courtyard, all seven, with the whole household. Right across the Dale stretched three rain-bows; the innermost rested a foot upon the Formo houses; 'twas quite unbroken, and the colours shone strong and bright; the two outer ones were fainter and faded away above——

Even while they stood gazing at this strange and lovely sign, the air grew grey and dark. From the south a snow-squall came sweeping. It snowed till in a little while all the world was white.

Kristin sat in the evening and told Munan of King Snow and his fair white daughter—Mjöll* was her name—and of King Harold Luva,† who was fostered by Giant Dovre. She felt a pang of sorrow when she remembered 'twas years now since she had sat thus and told tales to her children—'twas pity of Lavrans and Munan that she had given them so little of this joy. And now they would soon be great boys. While the others were small, at home at Husaby, she had sat telling them fairy-tales of an evening—so often, so often.

She saw that the grown sons sat listening—she flushed red and stopped short. Munan begged her to tell more. Naakkve rose and drew near:

"Mind you, mother, Torstein Uksafot‡ and the trolls of Höiland's forest?—tell us that one!"

While she told the tale, her mind went back. They lay resting in the birch grove down by the river, having a bite of food, her father and his harvest-folk, men and women. Her father lay upon his belly; she sat astride the small of his back, kicking his sides with her heels—'twas a hot day, and she had got leave to go barefoot, as did the grown women. Her father reeled off the tale of the kindred of the Höiland trolls: Jernskjold§ had Skjoldvor; their daughters were Skjolddis and Skjold-gjerd, that Torstein Uksafot slew. Skjoldgjerd had been wed to Skjold-ketil; their sons were Skjoldbjörn and Skjoldhedin and Valskjold, who owned Skjoldskjessa; they begot Skjoldulf and Skjoldorm; Skjoldulf got Skjoldkatla, and begot on her Skjold and Skjoldketil——

Nay, he had named that name already, cried Kolbjörn laughing. For Lavrans had boasted that he could teach them two dozen troll names, but he had not even filled the first full dozen. Lavrans laughed too: "Ay, but sure you know the trolls, too, call their children for their fathers that are gone!" But the work-folk would not let it pass; they doomed him to pay them a drink of mead as fine. Ay, then, said the master, they must have it—to-night, when they came home. But the folk would have it now, at once—and at length Tordis was sent up for the mead.

They stood up in a ring, and the great horn went the round. Then

---

* Mjöll = Powdery snow.   † Luv = Snow-cap; e.g. on trees.
‡ = Ox-foot.   § = Iron-shield.

they took their scythes and rakes and went to the meadows again. Kristin was sent home with the empty horn. She held it before her in both hands as she ran barefoot in the sunshine on the green path up towards the manor. Between-whiles she stopped, when a drop of mead had gathered in the toe of the horn—then she tilted it over her little face and licked the gilded edge within and without, and then her fingers to catch the sweetness.

Kristin Lavransdatter sat still, gazing before her. Father! She remembered a shiver passing over his face, a whitening, as the wooded hill-sides grow white when a storm-gust turns the leaves upon the trees —a clang of cold, harsh scorn in his voice, a gleam in his grey eyes like the flash of a half-drawn sword. A moment, then it passed away—in merry, kindly jest while he was young; oftener and oftener, as he grew older, in a gentleness quiet and something sad. In her father's soul there had dwelt somewhat else besides that deep, tender sweetness. She had learned, with the years, to understand it—her father's wondrous gentleness came not therefrom that he saw not clear enough the faults and the vileness of mankind, but that he was ever searching his own heart before his God and bruising it with repentance for his own sins.

No, father, I will not be impatient. Much have I sinned against my husband, I too——

On the eve of Cross-Mass* day, Kristin sat at the board with the house-folk, and seemed not other than her wont. But when her sons had gone up to rest in the upper hall, she called Ulf Haldorssön softly to her. She asked him to go down to Isrid at the farm, and pray her to come up to the mistress in the old weaving-house.

Ulf said: "You must send word to Ranveig of Ulvsvolden and to Haldis, the priest's sister, Kristin—and most fitting 'twere if you could send to fetch Astrid and Ingebjörg of Loptsgaard to take the charge of the room——"

"There is no time," said Kristin. "I felt the first pains already before nones. Do as I say, Ulf—I will have none but my own women and Isrid with me."

"Kristin," said Ulf gravely, "see you not that much evil talk may come of it, if you should creep into hiding this night——"

Kristin let her arms fall heavily across the board. She shut her eyes.

"Then they must talk who will! I *cannot* bear to see these strange women around me to-night——"

Next morning the big sons sat silent—with eyes cast down; while

* 3rd May.

Munan prattled and prattled of the little brother he had seen in his mother's arms down in the weaving-house. At last Björgulf said he had best talk no more now of *that*.

Kristin did naught but lie and listen—it seemed to her she never slept so sound that she was not listening, and waiting.

She rose from her bed the eighth day, but the women about her knew 'twas not well with her. She shivered and felt waves of heat; one day the milk would stream from her breasts so that her clothes were wet through; the next day she would not have enough to give the child its fill. But she would not lie down again. She would not let the child out of her arms—she never laid it in the cradle; of nights she had it with her in the bed; in the day she went about bearing it in her arms, sat with it by the hearth, sat with it on her bed, listened and waited, and gazed on it; yet for hours she seemed neither to see it nor to hear its wailing. Then she would seem to wake—she took up the boy, walked and walked the floor with him; with her cheek bent down to his she crooned and crooned to him low and softly; then sat her down and held him to her breast; sat gazing on him as before, her face set as stone——

When the boy was near six weeks old—and the mother had not yet been over the weaving-house threshold—Ulf Haldorssön and Skule came in thither one day. They were clad for the road.

"Ay, now are we riding north to Haugen, Kristin," said Ulf. "There must be an end to these matters now——"

Kristin sat silent and stiff, with the boy at her breast. At first she seemed not to understand. All at once she started up, flushed blood-red in the face:

"Do as you will. If you long to go back to your right master, I will not hinder you. 'Twere best you took your wage—then you will not need to seek us down here again."

Ulf half uttered a savage oath. Then he looked at the woman standing there with the little child clutched to her breast. He pressed his lips together and held his peace.

But Skule took a step forward:

"Yes, mother mine—I ride now up to father—if so be you forget that Ulf has been foster-father to all us brothers, you must mind at least that me you cannot bid and forbid as though I were a serving-wench or a sucking child——"

"Can I not?" His mother struck him on the ear, so that the boy staggered: "Methinks I shall bid and you shall all do my bidding so long as I feed and clothe you—— Get you out!" she shrieked, stamping with her foot.

Skule was wild with rage. But Ulf said below his breath:

"'Tis better so, boy—better that she be wild and headstrong than to see her sitting staring as though she had grieved her wits away——"

Gunhild, the house-wench, came running after them. They were to come at once down to the weaving-house to the mistress—she would speak with them and with all her sons. Curtly and harshly Kristin bade Ulf ride down to Breidin and talk with a man who had hired two cows of her; the twins he should take with him, and they need not come home before the morrow. Naakkve and Gaute she sent up to the sæter—she bade them go up the Illmand dale, and see how it stood with the horse-shelter there—and on the way up they were to look in on the tar-burner, Björn, Isrid's son, and pray him to come to the manor that evening. 'Twas of no avail that they tried to make excuse, saying that the morrow was Mass-day——

Next morning, when the bells began to ring, the mistress set forth from Jörundgaard, followed by Björn, and by Isrid, who bore the child. She had given them good and seemly clothes—but Kristin herself was so decked out with gold for her churching that all might see she was the mistress and the other two her servants.

Proud and defiant, she faced the wonderment and ill-will that she felt look out on her from the eyes of the folk on the church-green. Oh, ay, another kind of churching had been hers ere now—with the highest ladies in her train. Sira Solmund looked at her with ungentle eyes, when she stood before the church door with the taper in her hand—but he gave her entrance in the wonted way.

Isrid was nigh to her second childhood now, and understood but little; Björn was a strange, tongue-tied man, who never troubled his head with other folks' affairs. These two were godmother and godfather.

Isrid named the child's name to the priest. He started—he faltered a moment—then he gave it out so that it rang down the nave to all the folks:

"Erlend—in the name of the Father, the Son, and the Holy Ghost——"

A shock seemed to run through the whole congregation. And Kristin felt a wild, revengeful joy.

The child had seemed strong enough when 'twas born. But even from the first week Kristin had seemed to know it would not thrive as it should with her. She herself had felt at the moment of her delivery—as though her heart fell to pieces now like a burnt-out cinder. And when Isrid showed her the new-born boy, she misdoubted that the spark of life had but a slender hold on this child. But she drove the thought from her—for untold times ere now she had felt as her heart were broken within her. And the child was big enough and looked not weakly——

But her disquiet for the boy grew from day to day. He was peevish and had but little stomach for food—she might sit trying for a long while ere she could bring him to take the breast. And when at last she had coaxed him to suck, he would fall asleep well-nigh at once.—She could not see that he grew——

In unspeakable fear and torment of heart, she seemed to mark that, from the day he had been christened and had got his father's name, little Erlend faded more and more.

None, no, none of her children had she loved as she loved this little child of sorrow. None had she conceived in such sweet, wild joy; none had she borne within her with such happy hope. Her thoughts went again over the past nine months; at the end there had been naught for her but to fight with all her might to hold fast to hope and faith. She *could* not lose this child—and she could not save it——

Almighty God, Queen of Mercy, Holy Olav—she felt herself this time it availed not that she threw herself down and begged for the life of the child——

Forgive us our trespasses, as we forgive them that trespass against us——

She went to church each Mass-day as she was wont to do. She kissed the doorpost, sprinkled herself with holy water, bent her knee before the ancient crucifix above the choir arch. The Saviour looked down, sorrowful and gentle, in the anguish of death. Christ died to save His murderers. Holy Olav stands before His face, in everlasting supplication for the folk that drove him into outlawry and slew him——

As we forgive them that trespass against us.

Blessed Mary—my child dies! Know you not, Kristin, rather had I borne His cross and suffered His death than have stood under my Son's cross and seen Him die—— But, since I knew that this must be, for the salvation of sinners, I gave consent in my heart—I gave consent when my Son prayed: Father, forgive them, for they know not what they do——

——As we forgive them that trespass against us——

The cry of your heart is no prayer until you have said your Paternoster without guile——

Forgive us our trespasses—— Mind you how oft your trespasses were forgiven.—Behold, yonder, your sons among the men. Behold him who stands foremost, the chief of this fair troop of youths. The fruit of your sin—for nigh twenty years have you seen God add to his comeliness, his understanding, and his manhood. Behold His mercy—where is your mercy towards your youngest son at home——?

Remember you your father; remember you Simon Darre——

——But in the depths of her heart she felt not that she had forgiven

Erlend. She could not, for she would not. She clung to her cup of love, would not let it go, even now when it held naught but the last bitter dregs. In the hour when she could forgive Erlend, could even think of him without this gnawing bitterness—then would all that had been between them be at an end.

'Twas thus she stood throughout the Mass, knowing that it profited her nothing. She tried to pray: Holy Olav, help me; work a miracle in my heart, that I may say my prayer without deceit or guile—may think of Erlend with god-fearing peace in my soul. But she knew she wished not herself that this prayer be heard. And so she felt 'twas of no avail when she prayed that she might have grace to keep the child. Young Erlend was lent her of God—on one condition only might she have leave to keep him, and that condition she would not fulfil. And to Saint Olav it availed not to lie——

So she sat over the sick child. Her tears flowed without ceasing; she wept without a sound, and without moving a muscle of her face; her whole face was grey and hard as stone; only little by little her eyes and her eyelids grew red as blood. If someone came in to her, she dried her face in haste and sat dumb and stark.

——Yet but little was needed to thaw her. If it chanced that one of the big sons came in, cast a look on the little child, and said a gentle, pitying word to it, the mother could scarce refrain her from sobbing aloud. Could she have spoken with her grown-up sons of her fears for the little one, she knew her heart would sure be melted. But they were grown shy of her now. Since the day they came home and heard what name she had given their youngest brother, the lads seemed to have drawn yet closer together, and stood, as it were, so far away from her. But one day, as Naakkve stood looking at the child, he said:

"Mother, give me leave—let me seek out father and tell him how it is with this boy——"

"Naught will avail now any more," answered the mother, hopelessly.

Munan understood it not. He brought his playthings to his little brother, was overjoyed when he had leave to hold him and deemed that he had got the child to smile. Munan talked of the time when father would come home, and wondered how he would like this new son. Kristin sat silent and grey of face, letting the boy's prattle cut her to the heart.

The babe was thin now, and wrinkled as an old man; his eyes were over large and bright. Yet had he begun to smile at his mother— she moaned softly when she saw it. Kristin fondled the small thin limbs, took his feet into her hand—never would this child lie clutching in wonder at the strange, sweet, pinky things dancing in the air above him, which he knew not were his own feet. Never would these little feet tread the earth.

When she had sat through all the weary week's workdays to the end, watching the dying child, she would think, while she dressed for church-going—nay, now was she humble enough for sure. She had forgiven Erlend—she cared about him no more; if only she might have leave to keep her sweetest, her most dearest treasure, gladly would she forgive the man.

But when before the cross she whispered out the Paternoster and came to the words: "*sicut et nos dimittimus debitoribus nostris*," then felt she her heart harden like a hand that clenches for a blow. No!

Hopeless and soul-sick, she wept, for *will* it she could not.

And so died Erlend Erlendssön, the day before Mary Magdalene's Feast,* something less than three months old.

VII

THIS autumn Bishop Halvard came on visitation north through the Dale. To Sil he came the day before Matthew's Mass.† 'Twas more than two years since the bishop had been so far north, so there were many children to be confirmed this time. Munan Erlendssön was amongst them; he was now eight years old.

Kristin prayed Ulf Haldorssön to take the boy up for the laying on of hands—not a friend had she now in her home parish of whom she would ask this. Ulf seemed glad when she spoke to him of it. When the bells rang for Mass, then, these three, Kristin, Ulf, and the boy, went up churchward. The other sons had been at early Mass, all but Lavrans, who lay abed with fever; to this Mass they had no mind to go, the throng in the church would be so great.

As they passed by the steward's house, Kristin saw that many strange horses stood tied outside the fence. A little up the road they were overtaken by Jardtrud, who came riding with a great following and passed them by. Ulf made as if he saw not his wife and her kinsfolk.

Kristin knew for sure that Ulf had not set foot inside his own threshold since just after the new year. 'Twas said that, at that time, things had gone even worse than their wont betwixt him and his wife; and thereafter he had shifted his clothes-chest and his weapons up into the upper-hall, and abode there with the lads. Once, early in spring, Kristin had said to him 'twas an ill thing that he and his wife were so sorely at odds—on that he had looked at her, and laughed in such wise that she said no more.

* 22nd July.   † 21st September.

'Twas sunshine and fair weather. Away over the Dale the air lay blue between the fells. The yellow leafage of the birch-clad slopes was beginning to grow thin, and in the parish most of the corn was cut, but here and there by the farms a pael barley-field still waved, and the aftermath stood green and dew-wet on the meadows. There were many folk at the church, and much nickering and neighing of stallions, for the church stables were full, and many had been fain to bind their steeds without.

A kind of smothered, hostile air ran through the throng, whithersoever Kristin and her companions went. A young fellow slapped his thigh and laughed, but was sharply hushed by elder folk. Kristin walked, with measured pace and head held high, over the green into the churchyard. She tarried first for a while by the child's grave, and then by Simon Andressön's. A flat grey slab of stone was laid upon it—thereon was graven the likeness of a man, in visored helm and coat of scale-armour, resting his hands upon his great three-cornered shield with its device. About the stone's rim stood carven:

In pace. Simon Armiger. Proles Dom. Andreæ Filii Gudmundi Militis Pater Noster.

Ulf stood without the south door; he had put off his sword in the cloister-way.

Then came Jardtrud into the churchyard with four men in her company—they were her two brothers and two old farmers; one was Kolbein Jonssön, that had been arms-bearer to Lavrans Björgulfsön for many years. They went towards the priest's door, south of the choir.

Ulf Haldorssön sprang down and set himself in their way. Kristin heard quick hot speech from where they stood. Ulf would have hindered his wife and her following from going farther. Folk in the churchyard drew near; Kristin, too, went over thither. Then Ulf sprang upon the stone base that bore the cloister arches, bent in through an arch, and seized the first axe he could lay hands on; and when one of Jardtrud's brothers would have pulled him down, Ulf leapt forward and flung up the axe. The blow struck his brother-in-law on the shoulder, and now folk ran up and laid hands on Ulf. He struggled to tear himself free— Kristin saw that his face was darkly flushed, writhen, and desperate.

Then came Sira Solmund and a clerk of the bishop's train to the priest's door. They spoke a few words with the farmers. Straightway three jackmen, who bore the bishop's white shield on their livery, took Ulf in charge and led him forth from the graveyard; but his wife and her following went into the church after the two priests.

Kristin stepped forward to the knot of farmers:

"What is it?" she asked sharply. "Wherefore took you Ulf in charge?"

"You saw, I trow, that he smote a man in the churchyard," answered one as sharply. All the folk drew away from her, so that she was left standing alone with her boy by the church door.

Kristin deemed she understood—Ulf's wife would make complaint of him before the bishop. And by forgetting himself and breaking the churchyard peace he had got him into ill case. When a stranger reading-deacon came to the door and looked out, she went forward to him, named her name, and asked that she might be brought before the bishop.

Within the church all its treasures were set forth, but the candles on the altar were not yet lit. A little sunlight came in through the small round windows high up, and streamed down amongst the dark-brown pillars. A part of the congregation was already come into the nave, and had sat them down on the bench that ran along the wall. In the choir before the bishop's throne stood a little knot of folk, Jardtrud Herbrandsdatter and her two brothers—Geirulv with his arm bound up—Kolbein Jonssön, Sigurd Geitung, and Tore Borghildssön. Behind and round about the carven chair stood two young priests from Hamar, some other men of the bishop's following, and Sira Solmund.

All these stared hard when the mistress of Jörundgaard stepped forward and made low obeisance before the bishop.

Sir Halvard was a tall, stout man of exceeding venerable mien. Beneath his red silk cap his hair shone snow-white on the temples, and his plump oval face glowed large and red; he had a strong, crooked nose, and a heavy chin; and his mouth, narrow as a slit, and all but lipless, ran straight across his face, on which closely shaven stubble showed greyish-white—but the bushy eyebrows, over his sparkling coal-black eyes, were still dark.

"God be with you, Kristin Lavransdatter," said Sir Halvard. He looked ponderingly at the woman from under his heavy brows. One of the old man's large, white hands clasped the gold cross on his breast; in the other, resting on the lap of his dark violet robe, he held a wax tablet.

"What moves you to seek me here, Mistress Kristin?" asked the bishop again. "Deem you not 'twere more fitting that you tarried till after noon, and came to me at Romundgaard to say what lies upon your heart?"

"Jardtrud Herbrandsdatter has sought you here, reverend father," answered Kristin. "Now hath Ulf Haldorssön been with my husband these five-and-thirty years; he was ever our true friend and helper and good kinsman—methought, perchance, I might help him in some wise——"

Jardtrud gave a low cry of scorn or rage—all the others stared at Kristin, the parish folk with bitter looks, the bishop's train keenly and curiously. Sir Halvard looked about him sternly; then he said to Kristin:

"Stands it so that you would essay to make Ulf Haldorssön's defence? You know, mayhap," he said quickly, raising a hand, as she would have answered, "none has the right to call on you to speak in this matter—saving your husband—if your own conscience drive you not thereto. Bethink you first——"

"I thought most of this, Lord Bishop, that Ulf had let anger carry him away and laid hand on his weapon at the church door—and whether I might help him at all by standing bail. Or else," she brought out painfully, "full sure I am my husband will do all he can in this matter to help his friend and kinsman——"

The bishop turned impatiently to the bystanders, who all seemed much wrought up:

"The woman need not tarry here. Her spokesmen may have leave to wait out in the nave—go down thither all of you, while I speak with the lady—and send the folk outside for a while—and Jardtrud Herbrandsdatter with them."

One of the young priests had been busy laying out the bishop's vestments. Now, with heedful care, he laid the mitre with its golden cross down on the outspread folds of the cope, and went down and spoke a little with the folk in the nave. The others followed him down thither The congregation went out, and with them Jardtrud, and the sacristan barred the doors.

"You spake of your husband," said the bishop, looking at her as before. "Is it sooth that last summer you sought atonement with him?"

"Ay, my lord."

"But you came not to an accord?"

"My lord—forgive me if I say it—but of my husband I have made no plaint. I sought you that I might speak of Ulf Haldorssön's matter——"

"Knew your husband of this—that you were with child?" asked Sir Halvard; he seemed to be wroth at her demurring thus.

"Ay, my lord," she said, very low.

"And how took Erlend Nikulaussön that tidings?" asked the bishop. Kristin stood with downcast eyes, twisting between her fingers the fall of her linen coif.

"He would not be reconciled with you when he heard it?"

"My lord, forgive me——" Kristin was grown very red. "Whether my lord Erlend have been thus or thus towards me—if it can help Ulf's cause aught that he come hither, I wot well that Erlend will hasten hither to him."

The bishop knit his brows, as he looked upon her:

"Mean you, out of friendship for this man Ulf—or, since the matter is now come to light—will Erlend now, after all, own the child you bore last spring?"

Kristin lifted her head—she gazed at the bishop with wide-open eyes and lips half parted. 'Twas as though now, little by little, the meaning of his words were coming home to her. Sir Halvard looked on her gravely:

"True it is, woman, that none but your spouse has the right to charge you with this offence. But you understand, belike, that both he and you were guilty of great sin if he took on himself the fatherhood of another's child to shield Ulf. Far better for you all, if you have sinned, that the sin be confessed and atoned for."

The colour came and went in Kristin's face:

"Has any said that 'twas not my husband—'twas not his child——?"

The bishop asked slowly:

"Would you, Kristin, I should believe you have not even known what folk say of you and your steward——?"

"I have not." She drew herself up—stood with her head thrown back a little, white of face under her flowing head-linen. "Now do I pray you, my reverend lord and father—if any have defamed me behind my back, that you charge them to make it good before my face!"

"No name has been named," answered the bishop. "'Tis against the law. But Jardtrud Herbrandsdatter has craved leave to part her from her husband and betake her home with her kinsmen, laying to his charge that he has lived with another woman, a wedded wife, and begotten a child with her."

For a while both were silent. Then Kristin spoke again:

"My lord—I pray you, do me so much grace, and demand of these men that they say in my hearing—that *I* am that woman."

Bishop Halvard looked at the lady sharply and searchingly. Then he beckoned—the men in the nave came up and stood about his chair. Sir Halvard spoke:

"You good men of Sil have come to me at an unbefitting time, and laid before me a complaint which rightly should first have come before my deputy. I fell in with this but now, for that I knew you can scarce have full skill in the law. But here is this woman, Mistress Kristin Lavransdatter of Jörundgaard, come to me with a strange prayer—she prays me to ask you if you dare to say to her, face to face, that word has gone about the parish that her husband, Erlend Nikulaussön, was not father to the child she bore in spring?"

Sira Solmund answered:

"It has been said in every manor and every cot in this our parish, that the child was begotten in whoredom and in incest 'twixt the mistress and her steward. And to us it seems not to be believed that the woman herself should not know such was the rumour."

The bishop would have spoken, but Kristin said, loud and firmly: "So help me God Almighty, Mary Maid, and Saint Olav, and Saint Thomas Archbishop—I have never known that this lie was told of us."

"'Tis not easy then to understand—wherefore deemed you then that you need hide so heedfully that you went with child," asked the priest. "You hid yourself from all folk, and scarce came forth from your house the winter through."

"'Tis long since I had friends amongst the people of this parish— little company have I kept with folk hereabout in these last years. Though I knew not, as now it seems, that all were my foes. But I came to church each Mass-day," said the woman.

"Ay—and you wrapped you in thick cloaks, and clothed you so that none might see you grew big beneath your belt——"

"So does every woman—she would fain look seemly when among folk," answered Kristin curtly.

The priest spoke again:

"Had it been your husband's child, as you say—I trow that then you had not tended it so ill that you wrought its death with your ill guidance."

One of the young Hamar priests stepped forth and put his arm about Kristin quickly. A moment after, she stood as before, pale and straight —she thanked the priest with a reverence.

Sira Solmund went on vehemently:

"The serving-women at Jörundgaard said it—my sister, who comes about the manor, saw it too—the woman went there, and the milk was spurting from her breasts so that her clothing was wet through—yet every woman that saw the boy's body can bear witness he died of hunger——"

Bishop Halvard struck out sidewise with his hand:

"Enough, Sira Solmund. We must keep to the matter before us, and that is whether Jardtrud Herbrandsdatter had naught else to go upon, when she made plaint against her husband, than that she had heard tales which the mistress here says are lies—and whether Kristin can prove these untrue.—None says, I trow, that she has laid hands upon her child——"

But Kristin stood pale and said no word.

The bishop turned to the parish priest:

"But you, Sira Solmund, 'twas your bounden duty to speak with the woman here and let her know what folks were saying. Did you this?"

The priest turned red:

"I have prayed from my heart for this woman, that she might of her own accord turn from her stiff-neckedness, repent her, and do penance. —My friend her father was not," said the priest vehemently. "But yet I know, too, that Lavrans of Jörundgaard was a righteous man and strong in the faith. True it is he had been worthy a better child—but this daughter of his has heaped on him shame upon shame. Scarce was she grown maid when, by her wantonness, she brought two good lads of the parish here to their death. Then she broke her faith and troth with a bold and gallant esquire that her father had chosen to be her husband, gained her end in dishonourable wise, and got this man, who you, my lord, know well was doomed outlaw and traitor. But methought at last, for sure, her heart must be softened, when she saw that she dwelt here hated and scorned and of the worst repute, she and all hers, at Jörundgaard—where her father and Ragnfrid Ivarsdatter lived with all men's love and reverence——

"But 'twas too much when she came hither at this time with her son to confirmation—and that man was to lead the boy before you whom all the parish know she had lived with in twofold adultery and incest——"

The bishop made a sign to the other to be silent:

"How near of kin to your husband is Ulf Haldorssön?" he said to Kristin.

"Ulf's true father was Sir Baard Peterssön of Hestnæs. He was brother, by the same mother, of Gaute Erlendssön of Skogheim, Erlend Nikulaussön's mother's father."

Sir Halvard turned to Sira Solmund impatiently:

"Incest 'tis not—her mother-in-law and Ulf are cousins—'tis breach of kinship's dues and grievous sin, if it be true—no need to make it worse."

"Ulf Haldorssön is godfather to this woman's eldest son," said Sira Solmund.

The bishop looked at her, and Kristin answered:

"Ay, my lord."

Sir Halvard sat a while in silence.

"God help you, Kristin Lavransdatter," he said sorrowfully. "I knew your father of old—I was his guest at Jörundgaard in my youth. I mind you well when you were a fair and sinless child. Had Lavrans Björgulfsön lived, then had this not befallen. Think on your father, Kristin—for his sake you must cast off this shameful charge, and clear you, if you can——"

Like a lightning-flash it came to her—she knew the bishop again. A winter's day at the sunset hour—a rearing, red young stallion in the courtyard, and a priest with a black ring of hair round his fiery red face; hanging to the halter-rope, spattered with foam, striving to master the unruly beast and mount him barebacked. Clusters of drunken, laughing Yule-guests hovering about, her father among them, red of face from drink and cold, shouting, dizzily merry——

She turned to Kolbein Jonssön:

"Kolbein! You that have known me from my cradle up—you that knew me and my sisters in our father and mother's home—I know you so loved my father that—— Kolbein—believe *you* this of me?"

Farmer Kolbein looked on her, hard and sorrowful of face:

"We loved your father, say you—— Ay, all we house-carls of his, poor serving-men and common folk who loved Lavrans of Jörundgaard and deemed him such an one as God would have a chieftain to be——

"Ask not us, Kristin Lavransdatter, who saw how your father loved you, and how you rewarded his love—ask not us what we deem is too evil for you to do!"

Kristin bowed her head upon her breast. The bishop could draw from her no further word—she answered his questions no longer.

Then Sir Halvard rose. By the side of the high altar was a little door that led to the closed-in cloister-way behind the apse. A part of this served as sacristy, and in part had been pierced some small openings, through which the leprous might receive the host when they stood without there and heard Mass apart from the rest of the congregation. But now, for many years, none in the parish had been sick of leprosy.

"Mayhap 'twere best you waited out there, Kristin, till the folk are come in to the service. I will speak with you afterwards—but now must you go home to your own place."

Kristin curtsied before the bishop.

"I would liefer go home straightway, reverend sir, if so be you give me leave."

"As you will, Kristin Lavransdatter. God be your shield, mistress— if you be guiltless, be sure they will work your assoilment, God Himself and His blood-witnesses who are this church's lords, Saint Olav and Saint Thomas, who died for righteousness' sake."

Kristin curtsied again before the bishop. Then she went through the priest's door out into the churchyard.

A little stripling in a new red habit stood there all alone, stiff and straight. For a moment Munan turned his pale child's-face up towards his mother; his eyes were big and frightened.

Her sons—she had not thought of them before. As in a flash she saw her troop of boys—as they had stood on the outskirts of her life this last year, thronging together like a herd of horses in a thunderstorm, at gaze, affrighted—far off from her, while she struggled in the last death-throes of her love. What had they seen, what had they thought, what had they suffered, while she tossed and writhed in her madness——? What would become of them now——?

She held Munan's little rough fist in her hand. The child stared straight out before him—his mouth quivered a little, but he held himself upright.

Hand in hand with her son, Kristin Lavransdatter went across the graveyard, out on to the church-green. She thought of her sons, and it seemed as though she must wholly break and sink to the earth. The throng of folk was drawing towards the church doors, while in the belfry all the bells were ringing.

She had heard a saga once of a slain man that could not fall to earth for the many spears stuck fast in him. She, as she walked there, could not drop down for all the eyes that stabbed her through.

The mother and the child came in to the upper hall. The sons stood in a cluster round Björgulf, who sat at the board. Naakkve's head towered high above his brothers', where he stood with one hand on the half-blind boy's shoulder. Kristin saw her first-born's narrow, dark, blue-eyed face, the soft, dark down about his red mouth.

"You know it?" she asked calmly, as she came forward towards the group of lads.

"Ay." Naakkve answered for them all. "Gunhild was at the church."

Kristin stood a little. The lads had turned again to their eldest brother, until the mother spoke:

"Have any of you known that such things were whispered in the parish—of Ulf and me?"

At that Ivar Erlendssön turned to her suddenly:

"Think you, mother, that, had we known, you had heard no tidings of *our* doings? 'Tis not *I* who had sat still and let my mother be miscalled for an adulteress—not if I knew 'twas true she *were* one!"

Kristin said sorrowfully:

"I marvel now, my sons, what you have thought of all this that has befallen in this last year."

The lads stood silent. Then Björgulf lifted his face, and looked up at his mother with his ailing eyes:

"Jesus Christus, mother—what should we think—this year—and all the years that went before? Trow you 'twas easy for us to know what we should think?"

Naakkve said:

"O ay, mother—it may be I should have spoken to you—but you bore you in such wise that we could not. And when you had our youngest brother christened as though you would give out our father for a dead man——" He broke off with a vehement gesture.

Björgulf spoke again:

"Of naught did you think, father and you, but of this strife of yours—— No thought had you that we were growing to manhood the while. Never did you take heed who might come between your weapons and be dealt bleeding wounds——"

He had sprung up. Naakkve laid a hand upon his shoulder. Kristin saw 'twas true—these two were grown men. It seemed as though she stood naked before them, as though she herself had stripped her shamelessly before her children——

'Twas this they had seen, more than aught else, in their upgrowing—that their father and mother had come to be old folk—and the heats of youth pitiably misbecame them—and yet they had not been able to grow old in honour and reverence——

Then the child's voice cut through the silence. Munan broke out into wild lamentation:

"Mother—are they coming to take you to prison, mother? Are they coming now to take mother away from us——?"

He flung his arms about her, and pressed his face up under her bosom. Kristin drew him to her, sank down upon the bench, and gathered the little weeping boy into her arms; she tried to soothe him:

"Little son, little son, weep not so——"

"None can take our mother from us." Gaute went and laid hold of his little brother. "Weep not so—they cannot harm her. Now must you be still, Munan—you sure must know, boy, we shall guard our mother!"

Kristin sat with the child crushed close to her—'twas as though the little one had saved her by his tears.

Then Lavrans said—he sat up with the flush of fever on his cheeks: "Ay—what will you do, brothers?"

"When Mass is sung to an end," said Naakkve, "we will go to the parsonage and proffer bail for our foster-father. That is the first thing we shall do—think you not so, good fellows?"

Björgulf, Gaute, Ivar, and Skule answered ay. Kristin said:

"Ulf has borne arms against a man in the churchyard. And somewhat must I do to free him and myself of these slanders. These are such grave matters, my sons, meseems you young lads must take counsel of someone how to deal with them."

"Whom think you we should pray for counsel?" asked Naakkve, with a touch of scorn.

"Sir Sigurd of Sundbu is my mother's sister's son," answered his mother, faltering a little.

"Since he has not bethought him of it ere now," said the young man as before, "methinks 'tis not like that we Erlendssöns will go a-begging to him now that a pinch has come. What say you, brothers? If we be not of full age, yet are we of age to bear arms, the five of us——"

"Boys," said Kristin. "In this matter you will make no speed with arms."

"You must leave us to judge, mother," answered Naakkve curtly. "But now, mother, 'twere well you let us have some food. And seat you in your wonted place—for the house-folk's sake," said he, as one giving command.

'Twas but little she could eat. She sat, thinking—she dared not ask if now they would send after their father. And she thought—in what wise would this matter go forward? She knew but little of the law in such things—maybe she must clear herself of the slander by oath with compurgators.* If so it were, 'twould most like be at the head church at Ullinsyn in Vaagaa—— There she had kin on her mother's side well-nigh on every great manor. And if her oath fell to the ground —and she should stand before their eyes unable to free herself of this shameful charge! Bring shame upon her father—— He had been a stranger here in the Dale. He had been able to make good his place; him all had honoured. Those times when Lavrans Björgulfsön took up a cause at Thing or moot, he had ever had a full following. But she knew her shame would strike back at him. She saw now, all at once, how lonely her father had stood—in spite of all, alone and a stranger amid the folk here, when time after time she loaded him, with a burthen of shame and sorrow and ill repute.

She had not thought she could feel the like of this any more—again and again it had seemed to her that her heart must break into bleeding shards—and now once more 'twas as though it were bursting.

Gaute went out upon the balcony and looked northwards:

"The folk are coming out now from the church," said he. "Shall we tarry till they have gone a little on their way?"

"No," answered Naakkve. "They may as lief see that the Erlends-söns are out. We must busk us now, boys. 'Twere well you took your morions on."

Only Naakkve owned right harness. His coat of mail he left, but set his helm on, and took shield and sword and a long halberd. Björgulf and Gaute put on the old iron casques the boys wore when they practised them in sword-play, but Ivar and Skule were fain to rest content with small steel caps, such as the yeoman levies still used. Their mother looked on. She felt a strange tightening in her breast:

"Meseems 'tis ill bethought, my sons, to arm yourselves thus to go

* See Note 5.

to the priest's manor," said she, uneasily. "Take heed you forget not
the holy-day peace and the bishop's reverence."

Naakkve answered:

"There is dearth of honour here on Jörundgaard now, mother—we
must buy it at what price we may."

"Not you, Björgulf," begged the mother, fearfully, for the weak-
sighted boy had taken up a great battle-axe. "Remember, son, you
can see but little!"

"Oh, as far as this reaches, I still can see," answered Björgulf,
weighing the axe in his hand.

Gaute went over to young Lavrans' bed and took down his grandfather's great battle sword, which the boy would ever have hanging on
the wall above his couch. He drew it from its sheath and looked on it:

"You must lend me your sword, kinsman—I deem that our grandsire
would like full well that it should go with us on this journey."

Kristin wrung her hands where she sat. It seemed as though she must
cry out—in agony and utmost horror, urged too by a power stronger
than agony or horror—as she had cried out when she gave these men
birth. Wounds and wounds and wounds without number had been
dealt her throughout her life, but now she knew they were all healed
over—the scars were tender as raw flesh—but bleed to death she knew
she could not—never had she been more alive than now——

Blossom and leaf were worn from off her, but her branches were not
lopped, and felled she was not. For the first time since she had borne
Erlend Nikulaussön's child, she forgot the father quite and saw naught
but his sons——

But the sons looked not at their mother, sitting white, with fixed,
wide eyes. Munan still lay across her lap—he had not unclasped her
all this time. The five lads went forth from the loft.

Kristin stood up and stepped out upon the balcony. Now they came
forth from behind the storehouses and, one behind the other, went up
the path to Romundgaard between the pale, waving barley-fields. The
morions and steel caps gleamed dully, but the sunlight glittered on
Naakkve's glaive and on the twins' spear-heads. She stood there looking
after the five young men. She was mother to them all——

Within the room she sank down before the chest, below where Mary
Virgin's picture hung. Her sobs and weeping seemed to tear her in
sunder. Munan, sobbing too, nestled close to his mother; Lavrans
sprang from his bed and cast himself down on his knees at her other
side. She flung her arms about her two youngest sons——

Since the little one died—she had thought: what was there to pray
for? Hard, cold, heavy as stone, she had felt her falling towards hell's
gaping jaws. But now prayer burst from her lips resistlessly—with-

out her conscious will her soul poured itself out to Mary, maid and mother, Queen of heaven and earth, cries of dread, of praise, of thanksgiving—Mary, Mary, I own so much, still have I endless treasures that may be reft from me.—Mother of Mercy, take them in thy ward——!

There were many folk in the courtyard at Romundgaard. When the Erlendssöns came in, some yeomen asked what they would.

"Of you we would naught—as yet," said Naakkve, with a galling smile. "We have an errand to the bishop to-day, Magnus. Afterward, mayhap, we brothers may deem we have somewhat to say to you folks too. But to-day you need not fear us."

There arose some cries and commotion. Sira Solmund came out and would have bidden the lads begone from there; but now some farmers spoke up: the boys should have leave, they said, to make inquiry concerning this charge against their mother. The bishop's servants came out and said to the Erlendssöns: they must go now; folk here were sitting down to meat, and none had time now to listen to them. But this the farmers liked not.

"What is this, good folk?" asked a loud voice above them. No one had marked that Sir Halvard himself was come out on the loft balcony. There he stood now in his violet robe, the red silk cap upon his white hair, tall, broadly built, chieftain-like. "Who are these young men?"

He was answered that these were Kristin of Jörundgaard's sons.

"Are you the eldest?" asked the bishop of Naakkve. "Then will I speak with you. These others must bide here in the courtyard the while."

Naakkve went up the stairs of the upper hall and followed the bishop into the room. Sir Halvard sat him down in the high-seat and looked at the young man, who stood before him leaning on the great halberd.

"What is your name?"

"Nikulaus Erlendssön, my lord."

"Think you 'tis needful to be so well armed, Nikulaus Erlendssön," said the other, smiling a little, "when you go to have speech with your bishop?"

Nikulaus flushed deep. He went over to the corner, laid aside his weapons and head-piece, and came back. He stood up before the bishop, his bared head bowed, one hand clasped about the other wrist, with an easy, yet seemly and reverent, bearing.

Sir Halvard thought: this young man had not lacked teaching in *kurteisi* and mannerly bearing. 'Twas true he could not have been so young a child when his father fell from wealth and honourable estate—he remembered, for sure, the time he was heir to Husaby. A comely fellow he was, too—'twas great pity of him, the bishop thought.

"Were they your brothers, all those who were in your company? How many are you Erlendssöns?"

"We are seven, my lord, living."

——So many young lives entangled in this broil. Unwittingly the bishop heaved a sigh.

"Be seated, Nikulaus—you would speak with me, belike, of these rumours that have gone abroad about your mother and her steward?"

"Thanks, reverend sir, I would liefer stand before you."

The bishop gazed thoughtfully at the young man. Then he said, slowly:

"The thing stands thus, Nikulaus; methinks 'tis hard to believe that this that is said of Kristin Lavransdatter can be true. And right to impeach her of adultery has none save her husband. But there is, besides, the kinship 'twixt your father and this Ulf, and this, too, that he is your godfather—— And Jardtrud has made her plaint in such wise that it must be read as importing your mother's dishonour.—Wot you if 'tis as she says, that her husband has beat her often, and that he has shunned her bed close on a year?"

"Ulf and Jardtrud lived not well together—our foster-father was not young when he wed, and something harsh and hasty he can be. Towards us brothers and to our father and mother he has ever been the most trusty friend and kinsman. 'Twas the first prayer I had thought to lay before you, dear my lord: that if 'twere in any wise possible, you would be pleased to let Ulf go free against bail."

"You are not of age yet?" asked the bishop.

"No, my lord. But our mother is willing to proffer whatever bail you may demand."

The bishop shook his head.

"My father will be of the same mind, that know I full surely. 'Tis my intent now to ride from here straightway up to him, and make known what has here befallen. If, then, you would grant him a hearing to-morrow——"

The bishop put his hand about his chin, and sat, rubbing his thumb softly over the stiff hairs with a little rasping noise.

"Be seated, Nikulaus," he said; "we can talk the better so." Naakkve bowed in thanks and sat him down. "——But it is true then that Ulf has denied to live with his wife?" he asked, as though he had just bethought himself of this again.

"Ay, my lord. So far as my knowledge goes——" A smile crossed the bishop's face, and at that the young man smiled a little too. "Ulf has slept in the loft with us brothers since Yule that is overpast."

The bishop sat silent for a while again: "And his food—where got he his food?"

"He had his wife give him his victuals out, when he had to go to the forest or the like." Naakkve faltered a little. "There was some trouble in the matter—mother deemed 'twere best he had his board with us again, as he had had before he wed. Ulf would not have this, for he said there would be so much talk if now they changed the bargain he and father struck, about the goods he was to have from the manor for his dwelling when he set up house—and he deemed it not just that mother should take him to board again without abatement of those supplies. But mother had her way—Ulf had his food with us—and the rest was to be settled hereafter."

"Hm. Your mother has else the name of one that looks narrowly to her goods, and is a most notable and thrifty housewife——"

"Not with food," said Naakkve eagerly. "To that every soul can bear witness, every carl and every woman that has served on our manor—with food is mother the most free-handed woman. In that way she is no otherwise now than when we were rich folk—never gladder than when she can set on her board some dainty dish—and she purveys such full measure that each serving-man and woman, down to the swineherd and the bedesfolk, get their share of the good things."

"Hm." The bishop sat in thought. "You said you were minded to fetch your father?"

"Ay, my lord. Surely aught else were against reason?" The bishop made no answer, and Naakkve went on: "We spoke with father in the winter, my brother Gaute and I—we told him, too, these tidings, that our mother was with child. But we saw no sign and we heard no word from his mouth which we could take to mean he doubted mother was true to him as gold, or that he marvelled. But father has never felt at ease in Sil; he was minded to dwell on his own farm in Dovre, and mother was there a while last summer. He was wroth because she would not bide there and keep his house—his will was that she should let Gaute and me have the care of Jörundgaard, and should move herself to Haugen——"

Bishop Halvard rubbed and rubbed his chin and gazed at the young man.

——What kind of man soever Erlend Nikulaussön might be—so base he could scarce be as to have charged his wife with whoredom before their young sons.

Though much seemed to tell against Kristin Lavransdatter—nevertheless he believed not the charge. He deemed he had seen that she spoke truth when she denied knowing that she was suspect with Ulf Haldorssön. Yet he remembered this woman had been weak before when fleshly lusts had lured—with ugly tricks had they forced Lavrans'

consent from him, she and this man with whom she lived now at
strife——

When the matter of the child's death came up, he saw at once that
conscience smote her. But even if she had been neglectful of her child,
she could not for that be haled before an earthly court. For that she
must atone to God according to her father confessor's bidding. And
the child *might* be the husband's none the less, even though she had
tended it but ill. Glad she could scarce have been to have a babe on
her hands again, well on in years as she was, forsaken of her husband,
with seven sons already to nurture, with narrower means by far than
they were born to. 'Twould be against reason to look that she should
love that child overmuch.

He believed not she was an unfaithful wife. Though God alone knew
what things he had heard and seen in the two score years he had been
priest and heard confession. But he believed her——

But Erlend Nikulaussön's doings in this matter he could not understand save in one way. He had not come near his wife while she was
with child, nor when the child was born, nor when it died. *He* must
needs believe that he was not the father——

Now 'twas to be thought on how the man would act. Whether, notwithstanding, he would stand forth and shield his wife for their seven
sons' sake—'twere thus a man of honour would bear him. Or would
he, now these tales were noised abroad, make plaint against her. From
what the bishop had heard of Erlend of Husaby, he deemed he could
not be sure the man might not do this.

"Who are your mother's nearest kin by blood and marriage?" he
asked again.

"Jammælt Halvardssön of Ælin is wed with her sister, widow of
Simon Darre of Formo. Then has she two cousins on the father's side,
Ketil Aasmundssön of Skog and his sister Ragna, wife to Sigurd Kyrning. Ivar Gjesling of Ringheim and his brother Haavard Trondssön
are her mother's brother's sons. But they all dwell far away——"

"But Sir Sigurd Eldjarn of Sundbu—your mother and he are sisters'
children. In such a cause the knight must stand forth and defend his
kinswoman, Nikulaus! You must ride thither to him even now—to-day
—and bring him word of this, friend!"

Hesitating a little, Naakkve answered:

"Reverend sir—there has been little fellowship 'twixt him and us.
And I believe not, my lord, 'twould vantage my mother's cause if that
man stood forth in her defence. Erlend Eldjarn's house are little liked
in this country-side. Naught harmed my father more in folk's esteem
than this, that the Gjeslings had bound them to him in that emprise
that cost us Husaby, and whereby they lost Sundbu."

"Ay, Erlend Eldjarn"; the bishop laughed a little. "Ay, he had the knack of falling at odds with folk—he quarrelled with all his brothers-in-law here in the north. Your mother's father, that was a godly man, and not afraid to bend if peace and concord 'twixt kinsmen could thereby be furthered—he fared no better than the rest; he and Erlend Eldjarn came to be the bitterest unfriends."

"Ay"; Naakkve began to laugh a little. "And 'twas not over any such great matters either—two sheets with fringes and a blue-bordered towel; 'twas valued at two marks in money, the whole matter. But mother's mother had been so urgent that her husband must get just these very things at the parting of the heritage, and Gudrun Ivarsdatter had spoken of them to her man also. In the end Erlend took them and hid them in his travelling bags, but Lavrans took them out again—he deemed he had most right to them, for 'twas Ragnfrid who had worked these things when she was a young maid at home on Sundbu. But when Erlend grew ware of this, he struck grandfather in the face, and then my grandfather laid hold on him and threw him three times and shook him like a pelt. After that they never changed a word again— and 'twas all for the sake of these trumpery rags—mother has them at home in her chest——"

The bishop laughed heartily. He knew this tale full well already— it had made much merriment for folks in its day—of how the husbands of Ivar's daughters were so zealous to please their wives. But he had gained his end—the young man's face had melted into a smile; the watchful, fearful look was driven for a while from the comely, blue-grey eyes. Then Sir Halvard laughed yet louder:

"Ay, but, Nikulaus, they spoke together once again, and I stood by. 'Twas in Oslo, at the Yule-tide feasting, the year before the Queen, the Lady Eufemia, died. Our lord, King Haakon of blessed memory, spoke with Lavrans—he had come south to greet his master and lay before him his faithful service—the King spoke of how 'twas unchristian and churl-like, this enmity 'twixt the husbands of two sisters. Lavrans went over to where Erlend stood with some gentlemen of the guard, prayed him lovingly to forgive his over-hastiness, and proffered to send the things to Lady Gudrun with loving greetings from her brother and sister. Erlend answered: he would make up the quarrel if Lavrans would own, before the men who stood there, that he had borne him like a thief and a robber at the parting of their father-in-law's goods. Lavrans turned upon his heel and walked away—and *that*, I trow, was the last time Ivar Gjesling's sons-in-law met on earth," the bishop ended, laughing.

"But hearken to me now, Nikulaus Erlendssön," he said, folding his hands together. "I know not if 'tis wise to make such haste to bring your father down hither—or to set this Ulf Haldorssön free. Clear herself your mother *must*, meseems—seeing how loud has been the talk of her having done amiss. But, as matters now stand, think you 'twill be easy for Kristin to find the matrons who will join with her in making oath?"

Nikulaus looked up at the bishop—his eyes grew doubtful and afraid.

"Wait but a few days, Nikulaus! Your father and Ulf are men from outland parishes and little liked—Kristin and Jardtrud are both from the Dale here—but Jardtrud, you wot, is from far farther south, and your mother is one of these folks' own. And I have marked well that Lavrans Björgulfsön is not forgotten of the people. Well-nigh it seems as though they had meant to chasten her because they deemed she had been a bad daughter—but I can tell already that many see they served the father but ill by raising such a cry against his child—they are vexed and repentant, and soon they will wish for naught so much as that Kristin may be able to clear herself. And, mayhap, 'twill be little enough that Jardtrud has to show, when we come to look into her wallet. Another matter would it be if her husband were to go about, chafing the folk and setting them against him——"

"My lord," said Naakkve, looking up at the bishop: "forgive me that I say it, but 'tis little to my mind—that we should do naught for our foster-father, and that we should not fetch my father to stand at this time by mother's side——"

"Nevertheless I pray you, my son," said Bishop Halvard, "to take my counsel. Press not on over-hastily by bringing Erlend Nikulaussön hither. Meanwhile will I have a letter written to Sir Sigurd of Sundbu, praying him to come forthwith and meet me—what is this?" He stood up and went out on the balcony.

Their backs against the storehouse wall, Gaute and Björgulf Erlendssöns stood, holding off a knot of the bishop's men, who made at them with uplifted weapons. Björgulf felled a man to the earth with a blow of his axe at the moment the bishop and Naakkve came out. Gaute was parrying blows with his sword. Some farmers held Ivar and Skule fast, while others led away a wounded man. Sira Solmund stood a little way off, bleeding from mouth and nose.

"Hold there," cried Sir Halvard. "Down with your arms, you Erlendssöns——" He went down into the courtyard, and up to the young men, who had obeyed straightway. "What is this?"

Sira Solmund came forward, bent him before the bishop, and said: "Thus it is, reverend father; Gaute Erlendssön has broken the holy-day peace, and smitten me, his parish priest, even as you see!"

At the same moment one of the elder farmers stepped forth, made obeisance to the bishop, and spoke:

"Reverend sir, the boy was sorely wrought on. The priest there spoke of his mother in such wise, that one could scarce look that Gaute should brook his words tamely."

"Hold your peace, Sira—I cannot hearken to more than one of you at a time," said Sir Halvard impatiently. "Speak, Olav Trondssön."

Olav Trondssön spoke:

"The priest sought to stir up the Erlendssöns, but Björgulf and Gaute answered him back, soberly enough. Gaute said, too, what we all know is true, that Kristin lived with her husband at Dovre a while last summer, and 'twas then he was smithied—the poor little soul there is all this stir about. But at that the priest says, since folk on Jörundgaard have ever been so book-learned—'twas like she knew the saga of King David and Lady Bath-sheba—but Erlend Nikulaussön had mayhap been as sleepy-headed as the knight Urias."

The bishop's face flushed as purple as his own robe; his black eyes flashed. He looked at Sira Solmund for a space. But 'twas not to him he spoke:

"You know, I trow, Gaute Erlendssön, that by this deed you have brought on you the Church's ban?" he said. Then he bade that the Erlendssöns be carried home to Jörundgaard; two of his henchmen, and four farmers whom the bishop chose as men of worth and of a good wit, he sent with them to keep guard on them.

"You must go with them too, Nikulaus," he said to Naakkve, "and keep you quiet. Your brothers have done their mother no good service, but I see well that they were sore provoked."

In his heart the Hamar bishop scarce deemed that Kristin's sons had harmed her cause. He had seen that already there were many who had other thoughts of the mistress of Jörundgaard than had been theirs that morning, when she had made the cup to overflow by coming to the church with Ulf Haldorssön to be sponsor for her son. One of these was Kolbein Jonssön—and him, therefore, Sir Halvard set over the guard.

Naakkve went the first into the upper hall, where Kristin was sitting on the edge of Lavrans' bed, with Munan on her lap. He told her what had befallen, but laid much weight thereon that the bishop held her to be guiltless, and thought, too, that the younger brothers had been sorely baited ere they broke the peace. He counselled his mother not to go herself and seek speech of the bishop.

The four brothers were led in now. Their mother gazed at them; she was pale and strange-eyed. In the midst of her deep despair and dread, her heart seemed to swell again to bursting. Yet she spoke calmly to Gaute:

"Ill have you borne you, son, in this matter—and 'twas little honour for Lavrans Björgulfsön's sword that you should draw it against a herd of tale-mongering boors——"

"Faith, I drew it first against the bishop's jackmen," said Gaute, angrily. "But true it is, 'twas small honour for our grandfather that we should need to take up arms in such a cause——"

Kristin looked at her son. Then she had perforce to turn her head away. Sorely as his words hurt her, she could not but smile—'twas as when a child bites with its milk-teeth into its mother's nipple, she thought.

"Mother," said Naakkve, "methinks 'twere best you went now, and took Munan with you.—You must not leave him alone at all, till things are better with him," he said low. "Keep him within the house, so he see not that his brothers are in durance."

Kristin stood up:

"My sons—if you deem not that I am unworthy, I would pray you kiss me ere I go from here."

Naakkve, Björgulf, Ivar, and Skule went one by one and kissed her. The outlaw gazed sorrowfully upon his mother—when she held out her hand to him, he took up a fold of her sleeve and kissed it. All these five, save Gaute, were taller now than she, Kristin saw. She tarried a little, setting Lavrans' bed in order, and then went out with Munan.

There were four loft-houses on Jörundgaard: the great hall; the new storehouse, that had been the summer dwelling in Kristin's childhood, before Lavrans built the great house; the old storehouse; and the salt-store—it had a loft where the women servants slept in summer.

Kristin went up to the new storehouse loft with Munan; they two had slept there since the little child's death. There she was pacing the floor to and fro, when Frida and Gunhild came with the evening porridge. Kristin bade Frida see to it that the watch were served with ale and meat. The woman answered she had done so already—at Naakkve's behest—but the men had said they would take naught at the mistress's hands, since they were at her manor on such an errand. They had gotten meat and drink from elsewhere.

"Nevertheless, see to it that an ale-keg is borne in to them," said Kristin.

Gunhild, the young serving-wench, was all red-eyed with weeping:

"There are none of us, your house-folk, that believe this of you, Kristin Lavransdatter, trust me—we ever said we knew for sure 'twas all lies."

"You have heard this talk then," said the mistress. "Better had it been had you told me of it——"

"We dared not, for fear of Ulf," said Frida, and Gunhild went on, weeping:

"He forced us to hold our peace with his threats—often I thought I should have told you, and begged you to be more wary—when you stayed behind talking with Ulf far into the night."

"Ulf—he knew of it too, then?" asked Kristin, low.

"Jardtrud has long been throwing it in his teeth—'twas ever for that he beat her, I trow. And one night this last Yule-tide, about the time you began to grow big—we sat drinking with them over at the steward's house—Solveig and Öivind were there, and some folk from south in the parish—Jardtrud said to him then that 'twas his doing. Ulf struck her with his belt so that the buckle drew blood. But thereafter Jardtrud went about saying that Ulf had not spoken one word in denial——"

"And afterward there was talk of this in the parish?" asked the mistress.

"Ay. But we house-folk of yours have ever stood out against it," said Gunhild, tearfully.

To quiet Munan, Kristin was forced to lay her down with the child and take him in her arms; but she put not off her clothing, and no sleep came to her that night.

Meanwhile in the upper-hall young Lavrans had arisen and donned his clothes. And later, towards evening, when Naakkve had gone down to help with the cattle, the boy went forth and down to the stable. He saddled the red gelding that Gaute owned; 'twas the best horse there, next to the stallion, and that he ventured not to back.

Some of the men on guard at the manor came out and asked the boy whither he would go.

"I wot not that *I* am a prisoner," answered young Lavrans. "But I care not if I let you know it—you cannot hinder me from riding to Sundbu to fetch the knight hither to stand by his kinswoman——"

"'Twill soon be dark, boy," said Kolbein Jonssön. "This child cannot be suffered to ride the Vaage Gorge by night. We must speak with his mother."

"No, do not so," said Lavrans. His mouth trembled a little. "I ride on such an errand that I put my trust in God and Mary Virgin—they will watch over my goings, if mother be guiltless. And else, naught matters——" He broke off, for he was nigh to tears.

The men stood silent for a little. Kolbein gazed at the comely, fair-haired child:

"Ride then—and God be with you, Lavrans Erlendssön," said he, and would have helped the boy into the saddle.

But Lavrans led forth the horse, so that the men must needs give way. At the great stone near the manor gate he climbed up and threw himself on Rauden's back, then galloped westward on the road to Vaagaa.

VIII

L a v r a n s had ridden his horse into a lather of sweat when he came to the spot whence he knew there went a path up through the screes and among the cliffs that everywhere rise sheerly on the north side of Silsaa dale. He must be up on the uplands, he knew, ere it grew dark. He was not at home in these falls between Vaagaa, Sil, and Dovre; but the gelding had been here to grass one summer, and had borne Gaute to Haugen many a time, though 'twas by other paths. Young Lavrans lay forward along the horse's neck and patted him:

"You must find your way to Haugen, Raud, my son. You must bear me up to father to-night; ay, good nag!"

Scarce was he come up on to the brow of the fell and could sit in the saddle again, when darkness came hastily on. He rode on through a shallow marshy glen, betwixt low crags in endless line against a sky that grew ever darker. There were birch brakes on the dale-sides, and the tree-stems shone white; time and again wet leaf clusters brushed against the horse's chest and the boy's face. Stones loosened underfoot and went rolling down into the beck in the dale-bottom—then the horse's hoofs would plash in deep mire. Rauden picked out his way in the dark, up and down the slopes, so that the gurgle of the beck now sounded near and loud, now dwindled away. Once some beast yelped, away in the night, but Lavrans knew not what it was—and the soughing and singing of the wind rose and fell.

The child held his spear along above the horse's neck so that the point stood out twixt the beast's ears. 'Twas the very haunt of bears, this dale. He wondered when it would end. Very softly he began to croon out into the dark: "*Kyrie, eleison, Christeleison, Kyrieleison, Christeleison——*"

Rauden plashed through a shallow place in a mountain stream. The star-strewn skies grew wider about him—the hill-tops stood farther off against the gloom, and the wind sang with another note in the open spaces. The boy let the horse go as it list, and hummed all he could call to mind of the hymn, *Jesus Redemptor omnium—Tu lumen et splendor patris*—and ever and anon *Kyrie eleison*. He was riding now almost due south, he could see by the stars; but he dared not do aught but trust to the horse and let it follow its own counsel. Now they were riding over rocky slabs, where the reindeer-moss beneath him showed palely upon the stones. Rauden stood a little, panting, and peered into the night. Lavrans saw that the sky in the east grew lighter; clouds were lifting yonder, silver-edged beneath. The horse went on again, straight now towards the rising moon. There must be an hour yet till midnight or thereabouts, by the boy's reckoning.

When the moon shot up clear of the far-off hills, and her light shone in on the new snow on peaks and domes, and whitened the mist wreaths drifting by cleft and hill-top, then Lavrans knew where he was come to in the fells. He was upon the marish grounds below the Blaahöer.

Soon after, he found a path that led down into the upland dale. And three hours later Rauden limped into the moon-blanched court-yard at Haugen.

When Erlend opened the door, the boy sank forward swooning on the penthouse floor.

Some while after, Lavrans woke in bed, under filthy, sour-smelling fur coverings. Light came from a pine-root brand stuck in a crack of the wall near by. His father stood over him, damping his face with somewhat; his father was but half clad, and the boy saw by the flickering light that his hair was wholly grey.

"Mother——" said young Lavrans, looking up.

Erlend turned, so that his son could not see his face. "Ay," he said in a little, so low he could scarce be heard. "Is your mother—has she —is your mother—sick?"

"You must come home straightway, father, and save her—they are laying the worst of things to her charge—they have prisoned Ulf and her and my brothers, father!"

Erlend felt the boy's hot face and hands; the fever had mounted again. "What is't you say——?" But Lavrans sat up and told clearly enough of all that had befallen at home the day before. His father listened in silence, but a little on in the boy's tale he began to finish his dressing; he drew on his boots and buckled spurs on them. Then he fetched some milk and food and brought them to the child.

"But you cannot bide alone in the house here, my son—I must take you to Aslaug at Brekken here hard by, ere I ride downward."

"Father——" Lavrans caught him by the arm; "no—I must go with you home——"

"You are sick, little son," said Erlend; and never before in the boy's memory had he heard such a tender tone in his father's voice.

"Nay, father—indeed, indeed I would go home with you to mother —I would home to my mother——" He wept now like a little child.

"But Rauden is lame, boy——" Erlend took his son on his lap, but he could not stay the child's weeping. "And you so weary—— Well, well," he said at length, "Soten can bear us both, belike——"

"You must mind, if you can," he said—when he had led the Castilian

out, put Rauden in his place, and cared for him—"to see that someone comes north hither to look to your horse—and my gear——"

"Will you stay at home now, father?" asked Lavrans joyfully.

Erlend gazed out before him.

"I know not—but 'tis in my mind that hither I shall come no
more."

"Should you not be better armed, father?" asked the boy again, for
Erlend, beside his sword, had taken but a small light axe, and he was
making to leave the house. "Will you not take your shield at least?"

Erlend looked upon his shield. The oxhide was so scarred and torn
that the red lion on the white field was all but blotted out. He laid it
down again and spread the covering over it.

"I am armed well enough to drive a herd of peasants from my
manor," he said. He went out, locked the house door, mounted his
horse, and helped the boy up behind him.

The sky clouded up more and more; when they were come a little
down the hill-side, where the woods grew thick, they rode in darkness.
Erlend marked that his son was so weary he could scarce keep himself
from falling off; and on that he made Lavrans sit before him and put
his arm about the lad. The young fair-haired boyish head against his
breast—Lavrans was of all the children the likest to his mother. Erlend
kissed the crown of his head as he drew the hood around it.

"Did she sorrow much, your mother, when the little child died in
summer?" he asked once, very low.

Young Lavrans answered:

"She wept not after he was dead. But she went up to the graveyard gate each night—— Gaute and Naakkve used to follow when she
went out, but they dared not speak to her, nor durst they let mother
see they watched her——"

A little after, Erlend said:

"She wept not—— I mind me, the time your mother was young,
she wept as easily as the dew drops from the willow twigs by the beck.
She was so mild and soft, Kristin, when she was amidst those she
deemed wished her well. Afterward she had to learn to be harder—
and most often, I trow, 'twas my doing."

"Gunhild and Frida say that all the time our youngest brother
lived, she wept each hour and each moment, when she thought that
none could see it."

"God help me," said Erlend, softly. "I have been an unwise man."

They were riding now in the dale-bottom, with the cold draught
from the river at their backs. Erlend wrapped his cloak about the
boy as closely as he could. Lavrans, as he dozed and was near dropping off to sleep, marked that his father's body smelt like a poor man's.

Dimly he remembered from his early childhood, while they were yet at Husaby, when his father came from the bath-house of a Saturday, he was wont to have some little balls that he held within his hand. They smelt so daintily, and their fine, sweet scent hung about the palms of his hands and in his clothes all the holy-day.

Erlend rode at an even quick pace; here, down on the flats, it was quite dark. Without thinking on it, he knew at each moment where he was—he knew, by the changing tone of the river's roar, where the Laagen ran in rapids and where in headlong falls. Now the path led over flat rocks, where the sparks flew from under the horse's hoofs; now Soten picked his way surely and easily mid twisted fir roots, where the road passed through thick forest; now there came sucking, sobbing sounds, as he rode over spongy green slopes, where some rill from the mountains trickled. He would be home by break of day—and that would fit in pat——

——All the time there ran in his mind that far-away night of frost and pale-blue moonlight when he had driven a sledge down through this dale—Björn Gunnarssön sat behind, holding a dead woman in his arms. But the memory was faint and far off, and far off and unreal was all this that the child had told—this that they said had happed down in the parish, and the crazy tales about Kristin—— 'Twas as though he could not get all this into his head. When he got home, there would be time enough, belike, to think what he should do. Naught was real save the strain and the fear—soon, now, he would meet Kristin.

He had waited and watched for her so. And never had he doubted but she would come at last—until he heard what name she had given the child——

In the grey dawn, folk who had been hearing one of the Hamar priests say early Mass came forth from the church. Those who came first saw Erlend Nikulaussön ride by towards his home, and told the others. There was some uneasiness and much talk; folk drew slowly down and stood in clusters where the way to Jörundgaard left the highway.

Erlend rode into the courtyard as the waning moon was sinking down between a cloud rim and the mountain crest, pale in the breaking day.

Without the steward's house stood a knot of folk—Jardtrud's kinsfolk and her friends who had been with her for the night. And at the sound of hoof-falls in the courtyard came out the men who had been on guard in the room below the upper hall.

Erlend drew up his horse. He looked out over the farmers' heads and spoke, loud and scornfully:

"Is a feast towards on my manor—and I know not of it—or where-fore are all you good folks gathered here in the morning so early?"

Dark and angry looks met him from every side. Erlend sat tall and slim on the long-legged, outlandish stallion. Soten had had a cropped mane, but now it was ragged and unclipped; the horse was ill groomed, and its head showed grey hairs, but there was a dangerous glitter in the beast's eyes, and it stamped and fidgeted restlessly, laid back its ears, and tossed its fine, small head so that the foam flakes bespattered its chest and shoulders and the rider on its back. The riding-gear had once been red, and the saddle stamped with gold; now it was worn and broken and patched. And the man was clothed much like a beggar; the hair that surged out from under a coarse black woollen hat was a whitish-grey, a grey stubble grew upon the pale, lined, big-nosed face. But he sat erect, and he smiled haughtily down at the crowd of peasants; young he looked, in despite of all, and like a chieftain—and hate rose hot against this stranger man at halt there, bearing his head high and unabashed—after all the sorrow and shame and misery he had brought down upon them that these peasant folk deemed their own chiefs.

Yet he spoke soberly enough, the farmer who answered Erlend first:

"I see you have found your son, Erlend—so methinks you know we are not gathered here for feasting—and strange it is that you would jest with such a matter."

Erlend looked down at the child, who was still asleep—his voice grew softer:

"The boy is sick, as you may see. The tidings he brought me from the parish here seemed so unbelievable, almost I thought he spoke in fever wanderings——

"——Some at least of what he told is empty talk, I see——" Erlend looked toward the stable door with a puckered brow. Ulf Haldorssön and a couple of men, a brother-in-law of his amongst them, were leading out some horses.

Ulf let go his horse and went up to his master quickly:

"Are you come at last, Erlend?—and there is the boy—praised be Christ and Mary Virgin! His mother knows not he has been gone. We were setting forth to seek for him—the bishop set me free upon my oath, when he heard the child had ridden alone to Vaagaa—how is't with Lavrans?" he asked, fearfully.

"Nay, God be praised that you have found the boy," said Jardtrud, weeping; she was come out into the courtyard.

"Is't you that are there, Jardtrud?" said Erlend. "'Tis the first thing I must see to, I trow, that you get you gone from my manor, you and your tribe. This slanderous hussy will we send packing first of all—and after, they that have lied about my wife shall have their deserts, one and all——"

"So it cannot be, Erlend," said Ulf Haldorssön. "Jardtrud is my wedded wife. I trow that she and I have little mind to hold together, but from my house she goes not ere I have made over to her brothers all her goods, her dowry and her extra-gift and morning-gift——"

"Is it I who am master on this manor?" asked Erlend, furiously.

"That you must ask of Kristin Lavransdatter," said Ulf. "Here she comes."

The mistress was standing up on the new storehouse balcony. Now she came slowly down the steps. Unwittingly she drew her coif forward over her head—it had slipped back—and smoothed the church-going dress that she had worn since the day before. But her face was set hard as stone.

Erlend rode to meet her, foot by foot—bending forward a little he gazed fearfully, despairingly, into his wife's grey, lifeless face.

"Kristin," he begged, "my Kristin—I am come home to you."

She seemed neither to hear nor see. Then Lavrans, who had sat in his father's arms and waked up little by little, slid down to the ground. As he touched the sward with his feet, the boy sank down and lay in a heap.

A quiver passed over the mother's face. She bowed her down and lifted the great boy up in her arms, laid his head close against her neck, as though he had been a little child—but his long legs hung limply down in front of her.

"Kristin, my dearest love," begged Erlend desperately, "oh, Kristin, I know 'tis all too late that I am come to you——"

Again a quiver ran across the woman's face:

"Too late 'tis not," she said in a low, hard voice. She gazed down at her son lying swooning in her arms. "Our last child lies in the earth already—and now 'tis Lavrans. On Gaute is the Church's ban—and our other sons—we too still have much that can be brought to ruin, Erlend!"

She turned away from him, and began to cross the courtyard with the child. Erlend rode after, keeping by her side:

"Kristin—Jesus, what shall I do for you?—Kristin, would you not, then, that I should bide here with you now——?"

"No longer need I now that you should do aught for me," said the wife, as before. "Me you cannot help, whether you abide here or make your bed in Laagen——"

Erlend's sons were come out upon the balcony of the upper hall; Gaute ran down now, sprang towards his mother, and would have stayed her.

"Mother," he prayed her. Then she looked at him, and he stood still, helpless.

By the foot of the hall stairs stood some peasants.

"Make room, men," said the mistress, and would have passed with her burden.

Soten tossed his head and danced restively; Erlend wheeled him half round, and Kolbein Jonssön caught hold of the bridle. Kristin had not rightly seen what was afoot—now she turned somewhat and said over her shoulder:

"Let the horse go, Kolbein—if he would ride forth, even let him ride——"

Kolbein took faster hold and answered:

"Understand you not, Kristin, that 'tis time the master stayed at home on the farm? *You* at least ought to understand it," he said to Erlend.

But Erlend struck the other over the hand, and drove the stallion on so that the old man reeled. A couple of men sprang forward. Erlend shouted:

"Away with you! Naught have you to do with my affairs and my wife's—and I am no master of a farm; never will I be bound to any stead like a steer in its stall. If I own not the manor here, at least the manor owns not me——!"

Kristin turned full round upon the man and shrieked:

"Ay, ride! Ride, ride to the devil, whither you have driven me and flung all you have ever owned or laid your hands on——"

What now befell came so swiftly that none rightly saw or could have hindered it. Tore Borghildssön and another farmer caught the woman by the arms:

"Kristin, speak not so to your husband now——"

Erlend rode at them:

"Would you dare lay hands upon my wife——?" He swung his axe and smote at Tore Borghildssön. The blow fell betwixt his shoulder-blades, and the man dropped. Erlend lifted the axe anew, but at the moment he rose in his stirrups, a man thrust a spear into his side—it pierced his groin. 'Twas Tore Borghildssön's son that did it.

Soten reared and struck out with his forefeet. Erlend pressed his knees into the horse's sides, bending forward somewhat, while he wound the reins about his left hand and again raised the axe. But at once almost he lost one of his stirrups, and down his left thigh blood ran in streams. Some arrows and javelins whizzed across the courtyard— Ulf and Erlend's sons ran into the crowd with uplifted axes and drawn swords—then a man stabbed the stallion under Erlend, and it fell forward on its knees, neighing wildly and shrilly, so that the horses answered from their stalls.

Erlend stood up, astride the beast. He clutched Björgulf's shoulder and stepped clear of the horse. Gaute came up and grasped his father under the other arm.

"Kill him," said he, pointing to the horse; it had fallen over now on its side, and lay with outstretched neck, frothing blood at the mouth and kicking with its mighty hoofs. Ulf Haldorssön did it.

The farmers had drawn aside. Two men bore Tore Borghildssön towards the steward's house, and one of the bishop's men led off his comrade, who was wounded.

Kristin had put down Lavrans, who had come to himself now; they stood, clinging fast to one another. She did not seem to understand what had befallen—the thing indeed had come about too quickly.

The sons would have led their father to the hall-house, but Erlend said:

"I will not thither—I will not die there, where Lavrans died——"

Kristin ran forward and flung her arms about her husband's neck. Her frozen mask broke up before a rush of weeping, as ice is splintered under the dint of a stone: "Erlend, Erlend!"

Erlend bowed his head so that his cheek brushed hers—he stood thus a moment.

"Help me up to the old storehouse, boys," he said. "I would liefest lie there——"

In haste the mother and the sons made ready the bed in the old storehouse loft, and put off Erlend's clothes. Kristin bound up his wounds. The blood welled in gushes from the spear-thrust in his groin, and he had got an arrow-wound low on the side of the left breast; but that bled not much.

Erlend passed his hand over his wife's head:

"Me you cannot heal, I trow, my Kristin——"

She looked up in despair—a deep shudder ran through all her frame. She remembered, Simon, too, had said this—and it seemed to her a forewarning of the worst, that Erlend should now say these same words.

He lay in the bed, propped up high with pillows and cushions, and with the left leg bent up to stop the bleeding from the groin wound. Kristin sat bending over him, and he took her hand:

"Mind you the first night we slept together in this bed, my sweet——? I knew not that even then you bore a secret sorrow that I had wrought you. And 'twas not the first sorrow, either, you had had to bear for my sake, Kristin——"

She took his hand in both of hers. Its skin was cracked, and 'twas ingrained black about the narrow, scored nails and in the creases of each joint of the long fingers. Kristin lifted it to her breast and to her lips; her tears streamed down upon it.

"So hot as your lips are!" said Erlend in a low voice. "I waited and I waited for you—— I thought so long—— At last I thought *I* would give way—come down hither to you—but then I heard—— Methought, when I heard that he was dead, 'twas too late, belike, for me to come to you——"

Kristin answered, sobbing:

"I looked for you still, Erlend. I thought, for sure, some time you must come to the boy's grave."

"You had scarce greeted me then as your friend, I trow," said Erlend. "And God knows you had no cause either.—So sweet and lovely as you were, my Kristin," he whispered, and closed his eyes.

She sobbed, low and piteously.

"Now is there nothing left," said the man, as before, "save that we try to forgive one another like Christian wedded folk—if you can——"

"Erlend, Erlend——" She bent down over him and kissed the white face. "You must not speak so much, my Erlend——"

"Rather must I make haste and say what I have to say," answered the man. "Where is Naakkve?" he asked uneasily.

They answered that yestereve, when Naakkve heard that his young brother had taken the road for Sundbu, he had ridden after as fast as horse could bear him. He would be clean beside himself, for sure, since he had not found the child. Erlend sighed and moved his hands restlessly on the coverlid.

The six sons came forward to his bed.

"Ay, by you I have not done well, my sons," said their father. He coughed a strange, guarded cough—a bloody froth came oozing over his lips. Kristin wiped it away with her coif. Erlend lay quiet a little:

"You must forgive it me now, if you deem you can. Never forget, good lads, that your mother has striven for you each day of all the years she and I were together—there never was ill blood between us but what I wrought, by thinking too little on your welfare—but *she* loved you more than her own life——"

"We shall not forget," answered Gaute, weeping, "that you, father, seemed to us all our days the most manful of men and the foremost of chieftains. Proud we were to be called your sons, no less when fortune forsook you than in your days of power."

"You speak so, knowing no better," answered Erlend; he laughed a little broken, coughing laugh. "And give not your mother the sorrow to see you follow in my footsteps—enough affliction has she had to suffer since she got me——"

"Erlend, Erlend," sobbed Kristin.

The sons kissed their father on hand and cheek; weeping they went away and sat them down by the wall. Gaute put his arm about Munan and drew the child to him; the twins sat hand in hand. Erlend laid his hand in Kristin's again. His was cold; and she drew the coverlids over him right to his chin, but sat clasping his hand in hers beneath the coverings.

"Erlend," said she, weeping. "God have mercy on us—we must fetch a priest now to you——"

"Ay," said Erlend, weakly. "Someone must ride up to Dovre, and fetch Sira Guttorm, my parish priest——"

"Erlend—he will not come in time," she said, in dismay.

"Yes," said Erlend, vehemently. "If so be God will be gracious to me—for the last office I will not take from this priest that spread lying tales of you——"

"Erlend—for Jesus' sake—you must not talk so——"

Ulf Haldorssön stepped forward, and leaned over the dying man; "I, Erlend, will ride to Dovre——"

"Mind you, Ulf," said Erlend—his voice began now to grow weak and unclear—"the time we set forth from Hestnæs, you and I——" He laughed a little. "Ay, I promised then to stand by you all our days as your trusty kinsman—— God mend us all, friend Ulf— oftenest 'twas you and not I—of us two—that showed a kinsman's faith and truth—— I must—thank you then—kinsman."

Ulf bowed down and kissed the other's bloody lips:

"Thanks to *you*, Erlend Nikulaussön——"

He lit a candle, set it near the dying man's couch, and went his way.

Erlend's eyes had fallen shut again. Kristin sat staring at his white face—she passed her hand over it now and again. She deemed she saw that he began to sink towards death.

"Erlend," she begged, softly. "For Jesus' sake—let us fetch Sira Solmund to you. God is God, whatever priest may bear him to us——"

"No!" The man sat up in bed, so that the coverings slid down from his naked, yellow body. The bandages over his breast and belly were stained anew in bright red patches by the fresh blood that welled forth. "A sinful man I am—God in His mercy grant me what forgiveness He will; but I feel——" He fell back on the pillows—whispered so that he could scarce be heard: "not long enough shall I live to grow— so old—and so meek—that I can suffer—stay quiet in one room with him that lied of you——"

"Erlend, Erlend—think on your soul!"

The man shook his head as it lay on the pillows. His eyelids had drooped close again.

"Erlend!" She clasped her hands; she cried aloud in utmost need. "Erlend—see you not that, so as you had borne towards me, this *must* needs be said!"

Erlend opened his great eyes. His lips were leaden—but a shadow of his young smile flitted over the sunken face:

"Kiss me, Kristin," he whispered. There was somewhat like a shade of laughter in his voice. "There has been too much else 'twixt you and me, I trow—beside Christendom and wedlock—for us easily—to forgive each other—as Christian man and wife——"

She called and called his name after him; but he lay with shut eyes, his face wan as new-cloven wood under his grey hair. A little blood oozed from the corners of his mouth; she wiped it away, whispering imploring words to him—when she moved she felt her clothing clinging cold and wet from the blood she had got upon her when she led him in and laid him in the bed. Now and again there was a gurgling sound in Erlend's breast, and he seemed to draw breath painfully—but he heard no more, and most like felt nothing, as he sank steadily and surely towards the sleep of death.

The hall door was opened suddenly; Naakkve rushed in, flung himself down before the bed, and grasped his father's hand, calling on his name.

Behind him came a tall and heavy man in a travelling-cloak. He bowed him before Kristin:

"Had I known, my kinswoman, that you stood in need of your kinsmen's help——" He broke off when he saw that the man was dying, crossed himself, and moved away to the farthest corner of the room. In a low voice the knight of Sundbu began to say the prayers for the dying—but Kristin seemed not even to have marked Sir Sigurd's coming.

Naakkve was upon his knees, bent over the bed:

"Father! Father! Know you not me, father?" He laid his face on the hand that Kristin sat holding; the youth's tears and kisses rained upon both his parents' hands.

Kristin thrust her son's head a little aside—as though half awaked:

"You trouble us," she said impatiently; "get you away from here——"

Naakkve rose upon his knees:

"Go——? But, mother?"

"Ay—set you down by your brothers yonder——"

Naakkve lifted his young face—wet with tears and drawn with sorrow —but his mother's eyes saw naught. Then he went over to the bench where his six brothers sat already. Kristin marked it not—she did but

stare, with wild eyes, at Erlend's face, that now shone snow-white in
the light of the taper.

A little after, the door was opened again. With candles and the
ringing of a silver bell, deacons and a priest came with Sir Halvard,
the bishop, into the hall. Ulf Haldorssön came in last. Erlend's sons
and Sir Sigurd rose, and fell to their knees before the Lord's body.
But Kristin only lifted her head a little—turned for a moment her tear-
blind, unseeing eyes towards the comers. Then she laid her down again,
as she had lain, stretched forward over Erlend's corpse

Part Three

THE CROSS

A l l fires burn out at last.

There came a time when these words of Simon Darre's rang again in Kristin's heart.

It was the summer of the fourth year after Erlend Nikulaussön's death, and of her flock of sons only Gaute and Lavrans were left with their mother at Jörundgaard.

Two years before, the old smithy had burned down, and Gaute had built a new one north of the manor up by the high-road. The old smithy had lain south of the houses, down towards the river, in a hollow between Jörundsbarrow and some mighty heaps of stones that they said had been cleared from off the fields in ancient days. Well-nigh every year at flood-time the water had come right up to the smithy.

Now naught was left to mark the spot but the heavy, fire-cracked slabs of stone that showed where the door had been, and the masoned fire-place. Fine, soft, pale-green grass sprouted up now from the black, charcoal-covered ground.

Kristin Lavransdatter had a plot of flax this year close to the old smithy-ground; Gaute would have corn now on the fields nearer the manor, where the mistresses of Jörundgaard time out of mind had been wont to sow flax and raise onions. And Kristin often had errands that took her that way besides looking to her flax. On Thursday evenings she bore her gift of ale and meat to the Old Man of the barrow; on bright summer eves the lonely hearth in the meadow would look then like some age-old heathen altar, glimmering there amidst the grass, greyish-white and streaked with soot. On scorching, hot summer days she would go with her basket to the stone heaps at noontide, to pluck raspberries, or gather the willow-herb leaves that are so good for brewing cooling drinks against the fever-sickness.

The last notes of the church bells' midday greeting to God's mother died away in the light-drenched air between the mountains. The country-side seemed to lay itself to rest under the flooding white sunshine. Since dewy dawn the song of the scythes in the flowery meadows, the ring of whetstones on iron, and voices calling, had sounded from the farms far and near. Now all sounds of toil were hushed; the midday rest sank over all. Kristin sat on the stone heap, listening. Only the rush of the river could be heard now, and the faint rustling of the leaves in the grove; the thin buzz and muted hum of flies and gnats above the meadow; the clink of a lonely cow-bell somewhere far away. A bird winged its way, swift and silent, along the edge of the alder wicket; a bird rose from the meadow tussocks and flew with a shrill thitter to light on a thistle-stalk.

But the drifting blue shadows along the hill-side, the fair-weather clouds that piled up over the edge of the fells and melted in the blue summer sky, the glitter of the Laagen's water between the tree-trunks, the white gleam of the sunlight on all the leaf-trees—these things she was ware of as the voice of the stillness, heard by an inner ear rather than as seen by the eye. With her coif drawn over her brow to ward off the sun, Kristin sat listening to the play of light and of shadows over the Dale.

——All fires burn out at last——

In the alder wood along the marshy river-bank, pools of water glittered in the darkness between the thick-growing sallows. Sedge grew there and tufts of cotton-grass, and thick as a carpet the marsh cinquefoil covered the ground with its grey-green, five-fingered leaves and redbrown blossoms. Kristin had plucked a heavy bunch of them. Often had she wondered whether this herb might not have in it some useful virtue; she had dried it and seethed it and added it to ale and mead. But it seemed to stand in no stead. Yet could Kristin never forbear to go out into the marsh and wet her shoes to gather it.

Now she stripped all the leaves from the stems and wove a wreath of the dark flower-heads. They were like both red wine and brown mead in hue; they were moist, as with honey, at the base of the red bunches of filaments. Sometimes Kristin would weave a wreath for the picture of Mary Virgin in the upper hall—such was their wont in southern lands, she had heard from priests who had been there.

Else had she none now to make wreaths for. Here in the Dale 'twas not the young men's use to deck themselves with wreaths when they went to dance on the green. In the Trondheim country, the men who came home from serving in the body-guard had brought the custom with them to some places. The mother thought this thick, dark-red wreath had gone passing well with Gaute's light-hued face and flaxen-yellow hair—or with Lavrans' nut-brown mane.

——'Twas an endless age since the time when she was wont to walk with all her little sons and their foster-mothers in the pasture above Husaby, those long, fair summer days. Then she and Frida could not make wreaths fast enough for all the impatient little ones. She remembered when she had Lavrans at her breast still, and Ivar and Skule had deemed the suckling child too should have a wreath—but it must be of quite little flowers, said the four-year-olds——

Now she had only grown-up children.

Young Lavrans was fifteen winters old; he should not be counted as

full-grown yet, maybe. But, as time went on, the mother had grown
ware that this son stood farthest from her of all her children. He did
not hold himself aloof from her of set purpose, as Björgulf had done; he
was not self-wrapped, nor seemed he close-lipped like the blind boy——
But 'twas like he was yet more silent than he by nature—only none had
marked it when all the brothers were at home: he was bright and fresh,
and seemed ever glad and well-humoured, and all were fond of the
winsome child, and never gave it a thought that Lavrans well-nigh
always went alone and spoke but little.

He was held to be the fairest of all Kristin of Jörundgaard's fair sons.
Their mother always deemed the one that at the moment she thought
on to be perhaps the fairest, but she felt, she too, how Lavrans Erlendssön seemed to give out brightness. His light-brown hair and apple-fresh
cheeks seemed, as 'twere, gilded, full-filled with sunshine; his great
dark-grey eyes, too, seemed sown full of yellow sparks—he was much
like what she herself had been in her youth, with her bright skin hue
veiled, as it were, with sun-browning. And he was big and strong for
his age, stout and handy at all work he was put to, biddable with his
mother and elder brothers, cheerful, kind, and friendly. But withal
there was this strange aloofness about the boy.

On winter evenings, when the household gathered in the weaving-
house and passed the time with jest and gossip, while each one had his
work to keep him busy, Lavrans would sit as in a dream. Many a
summer evening, when the day's work on the manor was done, Kristin
would go out and set her down by this boy, where he lay on the green,
chewing resin or rolling a sprig of sorrel in the corner of his mouth.
She marked his eyes as she talked with him—'twas as though he fetched
his thoughts home from afar off. Then he would smile up into his
mother's face, answer her clearly and with understanding; often would
they two sit out on the bank for hours in close and easy talk. But no
sooner did she rise to go in than 'twould seem as though Lavrans let
his thoughts wander far afield again.

And 'twas impossible for her to make out what it was the boy thought
so deeply on. He was good enough at sports and with his weapons—
yet he was much less keenly set on such things than had been her other
sons, and he never went off alone a-hunting, though he was glad when
Gaute took him out along with him. So far, at any rate, he did not
seem to mark that women looked upon his fair youth with kind eyes.
He had no mind at all to book-learning, and to all the talk of his elder
brothers' purpose to go into a cloister the youngest seemed to pay little
heed. Kristin could not mark that the lad looked for any other lot
than to stay here at home all his days, helping Gaute with the farming,
even as now he did——

Sometimes Kristin deemed that these strange, absent ways of Lavrans's put her in mind somewhat of his father—but Erlend's soft, drowsy ways had often given place to wild wantonness; and Lavrans lacked altogether his father's hasty, vehement moods. Erlend had never been *so* far away from what went on about him——

Lavrans was the youngest now. Soon now 'twould be a long time that Munan had slept in the graveyard beside his father and his little brother. He died early in spring the year after Erlend was slain.

The widow had gone about after her husband's death as though she neither heard nor saw. More than pain and sorrow, she felt a numbing chill, a dull nervelessness in body and soul, as if she herself were still bleeding to death from his death-wounds.

The whole of her life had lain within his arms, since that thunder-fraught midday hour in the out-barn at Skog, when for the first time she gave herself to Erlend Nikulaussön. Then was she so young and so unweeting, and knew so little what she did, that she strove to hide that she was near weeping because he wrought her pain, while she smiled because she deemed she gave her lover the most precious gift. And whether, after all, it had been a good gift or no—at least she had given him herself, wholly and for ever. Her maidenhood, which God in His mercy had adorned with comeliness and health, when he caused her to be born to a safe and honourable lot, and which her parents had guarded with most loving strictness all the years she was in their care —with both hands she had given all to Erlend, and thereafter she had lived but in his arms.

How often, in the years that followed, had she suffered his caresses, hard and cold with anger, dutifully yielded to her husband's will, while she felt as though she must perish, worn out with weariness. She had thought with a kind of wrathful joy, when she looked on Erlend's fair face and sound and comely body: *that* could no longer blind her to the man's faults. Ay, he was young and fair as ever; he could still over-power her with his caresses, fiery as when she too was young. But *she* was aged, she thought—and with the thought came a kind of passion of victorious pride. Easy to keep their youth for them who will never learn a lesson, who list not to fit themselves to the fate life brings them, nor to strive to master fate by man's will.

But even when she met his kisses with hard, locked lips, and turned with all her being from him to the fight for her sons' future, she knew dimly 'twas with the fire this man had once for all kindled in her blood that she threw herself into the work. The years had chilled her, so she deemed, for she no longer grew hot when Erlend's eyes had that old gleam, and his voice that deep note which had made her sink down, will-less and strengthless with happiness, when first she knew him. But as then she had longed to drown the heaviness and heart-ache of separation in her meetings with Erlend, so afterwards she longed, dully yet feverishly, after a goal which would be reached when, one day, a white-haired old woman, she saw her sons' lot settled and secure. Then 'twas for Erlend's sons that she suffered the old dread of the uncertainty that lay before them. She was tormented still by a craving like hunger and burning thirst—she must see her sons thrive and flourish.

And as at first she had given herself wholly to Erlend, so, afterwards, she gave herself wholly to the world that had sprung up around their wedded life—flung herself in the breach to answer every call that must be met, threw herself into every work that must be done to safeguard Erlend's and his children's welfare. She half understood herself that she lived ever with Erlend; when she sat at Husaby pondering with their priest over the papers in her husband's chest; when she talked with his tenants and working-folk; busied herself with her serving-wenches in storehouse and kitchen; sat up in the horse-paddock with the foster-mothers keeping watch on her children on fair summer days. It seemed to herself as though 'twas against Erlend she turned her wrath when aught went wrong in the house and when the children crossed their mother's will; 'twas to him her heart-felt joy went forth when they got the hay in dry in summer, or did well with the corn in autumn, when her calves throve, and when she heard her boys shout and laugh in the courtyard. The thought that she was his glowed hidden in her heart when she laid aside, full finished, the last of the holy-day garments for the seven sons, and stood joyful, looking at the pile of goodly, well-wrought work done by her own hands through the winter. It was of *him* she was sick and weary when, of a spring evening, she went home from the river with her women—and they had washed wool from the last shearing, boiled the water in a cauldron by the strand, rinsed the wool in the stream—and the mistress herself felt as though her back were broken across, and was coal-black with wool dirt high up her arms, and the smell of sheep and greasy filth had soaked into her clothes till it seemed three baths would not make her body clean again.

And now that he was gone, 'twas as though the widow could see no meaning any more in her life's restless busyness. *He* had been cut down, and so she must die, like a tree whose roots are severed. The young suckers that had shot up around her lap must grow now from their own roots. They were old enough for each of them to take order for his own lot. The thought flitted through Kristin's mind—if she had but understood this before, that time when Erlend said it! Shadow-like pictures of a life with Erlend up on his mountain croft drifted across her mind—they two, grown young again, the little child beside them.

But 'twas not that she repented or grieved for what might have been. She herself could not have parted her life from her sons' lives—now death would part them soon, for without Erlend she had not strength to live. All that had befallen, and all that was yet to befall, was their doom—all things fall out as they are doomed to fall.

She grew grey of hair and skin, scarce cared to keep her trim or put her clothes on rightly. Of nights she lay and thought of her life with Erlend; in the day she went about as in a dream, never spoke with any till spoken to, seemed not even to hear when her little sons spoke to her. The watchful and hard-working housewife set her hand to no work. Love had underlain all her strivings with earthly things.—Erlend had given her little thanks for it; 'twas not so that he listed to be loved. But she could do no otherwise; it was her nature to love with much toil and care.

At this time she seemed to be slipping down towards the trance of death. Then came a sickness that ran through all the parish, and laid her sons upon a sick-bed—and the mother awoke once more.

The sickness was more perilous for grown folk than for children. On Ivar it took such a hold that none looked that he should live. The young lad had a giant's strength in his fever fits; he roared, and struggled to get up and seize his weapons—his father's death seemed to run in his mind. 'Twas all Naakkve and Björgulf could do to hold him down by main force. Then Björgulf was laid low. Lavrans lay with his face so swollen with the breaking sores it scarce seemed his own—his eyes glittered dully through two small slits—seemed as though they must burn out in the glowing fever.

Their mother watched over these three in the loft. Naakkve and Gaute had had the sickness as small children, and Skule was much less sick than his brothers; Frida looked to him and Munan down below in the hall. None deemed that Munan was in any peril; but he had never been strong, and one evening, when they all believed he was near well, of a sudden he went off into a swoon. There was scarce time for Frida to warn his mother—Kristin ran down, and, a moment after, Munan breathed his last in her arms.

The child's death awoke her to a new, wide-eyed despair. Her wild sorrow for the suckling that died at its mother's breast had been, as it were, tinged red by the memory of all her slain dreams of happiness. The very storm in her heart had borne Kristin up in those days. And the fearful strain that had ended but when she saw her husband slain before her eyes, left behind it such a weariness of soul that Kristin herself deemed for sure she would soon die of grief for Erlend. But this surety had dulled the edge of sorrow. She had lived, feeling dusk and shadows thicken round her, while she waited for the door to be opened for her too——

But over Munan's little corpse the mother stood grey and wide awakened. The fair, sweet little boy had been her youngest child for so many years, the last little one that she still dared fondle and laugh at, when she should have been stern and grave and have corrected her son for his small misdeeds and giddinesses. And he had been so loving and so fond of his mother. It seemed to cut into her very flesh—so bound was she still to life; 'twas not so easy as she had thought for a woman to die, when she has poured her life's blood into so many new young hearts.

In cold, steadfast despair she passed to and fro betwixt the child that lay on the dead-straw and her sick sons. Munan lay in the old store-house, where first the little babe and then the father had lain—three corpses in her home in less than one year. With a heart withered with dread, but stark and dumb, she waited for the next to die—she waited as for a relentless fate. She had never set store enough by the gift she had got when God granted her so many children. And the worst was that *understood* it she had in a fashion. But she had thought more on the troubles, the pangs, the fears and struggles—though she had learned over again and over again, through what she missed each time a child grew too great for her arms, through the delight each time a fresh one lay upon her bosom—that the joy was unspeakably greater than the labour and the pain. She had murmured because the children's father was so trustless a man, with little forethought for the line that should come after him. She forgot always that he had been no other, that time she broke God's law and trod her own kin beneath her feet to come to him.

Now he had been torn from her side. And now she looked to see her sons die, one by one. Perchance 'twas her lot to be left a childless mother at the last.

——There were so many things that before she had seen indeed, but not thought of much, what time she saw the whole world through the mist of her own love and Erlend's. She had seen, truly, that to Naakkve 'twas an earnest matter that he was the first-born and that 'twas his to be the head and leader of the band of brothers. She had seen, too, that he loved Munan dearly. Yet she was shaken, as by something unlooked for, when she saw his vehement sorrow at the youngest brother's death.

But the other sons grew well again, though but slowly. On Easter Sunday she was able to take to church four sons; but Björgulf lay abed still, and Ivar was too weak to come without the house. Lavrans had grown much in height while he lay on his sick-bed, and in other ways, too, 'twas as though this half-year's happenings had advanced him far beyond his age.

And so it seemed to Kristin that she was an old woman now. A woman must be held young, she deemed, so long as she had little children sleeping in her arms at night, playing about their mother in the day-time, and needing her care day and night. When her little ones have grown too great for this, a mother is an old woman.

Her new brother-in-law, Jammælt Halvardssön, spoke to her of the Erlendssöns' tender age, and of how she herself was but little over forty years; she would soon feel, mayhap, that she must wed again; she needed a husband to help her with the care of the estate and the nurture of the younger sons. He named more than one good man who he deemed might be a fitting match for Kristin—she must visit their home at Ælin in the fall, and he would see to it that she met them, and thereafter they could talk more nearly of this matter.

Kristin smiled wanly. Ay—she *was* no more than forty years of age. Had she heard of another woman that had been widowed with a flock of growing children, she had said as Jammælt said—she must wed again, seek the stay of a new husband; she might even have more children by him.—But she herself would not——

'Twas when the Easter holy-days were just gone by that Jammælt of Ælin came to Jörundgaard, and Kristin met her sister's new husband for the second time. They had gone neither to the betrothal at Dyfrin nor to the bride-ale at Ælin, she and her sons. The two feasts had been held with but short space between, that spring when she was heavy with her last child. As soon as Jammælt had heard of the slaying of Erlend Nikulaussön, he had hasted to Sil; with rede and deed he helped his wife's sister and sister's sons, ordered, as well as he might all that must be done after the master's death, and took upon him the conduct of the charge against the man-slayers, since none of the Erlendssöns was yet of age. But at that time Kristin knew naught of what went on around her. Even the judgment on Gudmund Toressön, who was found to be Erlend's slayer, seemed to stir her little.

This time she spoke more with her brother-in-law, and he seemed to her a man to be liked. Young he was not—he and Simon Darre were of an age—a quiet and steady man, tall and big, of darker hue than common, comely of face, but somewhat stooped. He and Gaute were good friends at once. Naakkve and Björgulf, since their father's death, had held themselves yet closer together and apart from all the rest. But Ivar and Skule told their mother they liked Jammælt well—"Yet to us it seems, none the less, that Ramborg might well have done so much honour to Simon as to bide a widow something longer—this new husband of hers is noways the like of Simon." Kristin marked that these two madcaps of hers still remembered Simon Andressön: by him they had let them be guided, whether with sharp words or with kindly jest, though they would not suffer a word of correction from their own father and mother without their eyes flashing and their hands clenching with rage.

While Jammælt was at Jörundgaard, Munan Baardssön too came hither to visit Kristin. Not much was left now of Sir Dance Munan. He had been wide of girth and portly in the old days, and he had borne his heavy body not without grace, so that he looked taller and more stately than he was. Now the gout had crooked him, and the skin hung loosely on his shrunken frame; he looked most like a little hobgoblin, wholly bald but for a scant fringe of limp white tufts about his nape. Once a strong, blue-black beard had darkened his smooth, plump cheeks and chin, but now grey stubble grew rankly in all the flabby folds of his chin and neck, whither his razor found it hard to make its way. He was grown blear-eyed, drivelled a little—and was much plagued with a weak stomach.

With him he had his son Inge, whom folk called Fluga, after the mother; he was an oldish man already. The father had helped this son forward in the world right well; made a rich match for him, and got Bishop Halvard to lend Inge his countenance—Munan's wife Katrin had been the bishop's cousin, and therefore was Sir Halvard fain to help Inge to wealth, so that he should not trespass on the heritage of Lady Katrin's children. The bishop held the Hedemarken wardenship in fief, and he had made Inge Munanssön his deputy, so that he now owned no little land in Skaun and Ridabu. His mother too had bought her a manor in those parts; she was a most pious woman now, and did much good, and she had vowed to live a life of chastity till her death. "Ay, and she is none so old or so failing either," said Sir Munan, testily, when he saw Kristin smile. He would have been fain, indeed, to have so ordered things that Brynhild should come to him and keep house for him at his manor near Hamar, but that she would not do.

He had so little joy of his old days, Sir Munan complained. His children were so quarrelsome—the children of the same mother were at odds one with another, and fought and wrangled with their half-brothers and sisters. The worst was the youngest daughter; her he had got with a paramour while he was a wedded man, so that he could leave her no heritage, and therefore she plundered her father of all she could lay hands on while yet he lived. She was a widow, and had sat her down at Skogheim, the manor that was Sir Munan's proper seat; neither her father nor her brothers and sisters could shift her there-from. Munan was sore afraid of her, but when he tried to scape and live with any of his other children, he was plagued there, too, with plaints of the others' greed and dishonest dealings. He was happiest with the youngest of his true-born daughters, who was a nun at Gimsöy; he liked well to be in the hostel there for a while; at such times he strove much to make his soul with penance and prayers under his daughter's guidance, but he could not put up with the life there for long at a time. Kristin was not sure that Brynhild's sons were much kinder towards their father than the other children, but this Munan Baardssön would not own; he loved them best of all his offspring.

But miserable as this kinsman of hers now was, 'twas while he was with her that Kristin's stony sorrow first seemed to melt a little. Sir Munan talked of Erlend early and late—when he was not groaning over his own trials, he was ever speaking of his dead cousin and boasting of Erlend's deeds—but most of all of his reckless youth: Erlend's wild pranks when first he was let loose into the world, away from his home at Husaby—where Lady Magnhild evermore gloomed at his father and the father gloomed at his eldest son—and from Hestnæs and his grave, pious foster-father, Sir Baard. Sir Munan's prate might have seemed strange comfort for Erlend's sorrowing widow. But in his own way the knight had loved his young kinsman, and had ever deemed that Erlend outshone all other men in comeliness and manhood—ay, and in understanding as well, said Munan eagerly, only that he list not to use it. And though Kristin deemed full surely that 'twas not for Erlend's good that he had come out and into the King's guard when but sixteen, with this cousin of his for guide and teacher, she yet was fain to smile sorrowfully and tenderly when Munan Baardssön talked on and on, while the spittle ran out of the corners of his mouth and the tears oozed from his old, red-rimmed eyes—of Erlend's flashing joyous spirit in his boyish years, ere unhappy chance had led him astray after Eline Ormsdatter and scorched him for his lifetime.

Jammælt Halvardssön, sitting in earnest talk with Gaute and Naakkve, looked across at his sister-in-law wonderingly. She had sat her down on the cross wall-bench with this unsavoury old man and Ulf Haldorssön—Ulf seemed to Jammælt to look somewhat moodily, but she smiled as she chatted with them and filled their beakers—he had not seen her smile before, but it became her well, and her little, low laughter was like a quite young maid's.

Jammælt spoke once of how 'twas not possible all these six brothers could stay at home, living on their mother's manor. None could look that any rich man of equal birth would give kinswoman of his to Nikulaus if his five brothers were to dwell with him, and maybe draw their livelihood from the manor when they wed. And they ought to look about for a wife for the young man now—he was twenty winters old already and seemed to be of a lusty habit. Therefore Jammælt was minded to take Ivar and Skule with him when he journeyed south again; doubtless he would find a way to their advancement. When Erlend Nikulaussön had met his end in such hapless wise, it had plainly appeared that the great nobles of the land now bethought them once more that the slain man had been one of their own peers, marked out by birth and blood to take his place among the foremost, of a winning nature, high-minded in many ways, in war a hardy and valiant chieftain—though fortune had not been with him. The men who had taken part in slaying the master on his own manor were dealt with most sternly. And Jammælt could tell of many who had asked him of Erlend's sons. The men of Sudrheim he had met at Yule, and they had let fall that these young lads were their own kin; Sir Jon had bidden him greet them, and say he would welcome Erlend Nikulaussön's sons as a kinsman and gladly keep any of them that would join his household. Jon Haftorssön was now to be wed with the Lady Elin, Erling Vidkunssön's eldest daughter, and the young bride had asked if the youths were like their father: she well remembered that Erlend had visited them in Björgvin when she was a child, and that he seemed to her the comeliest of all men. And her brother, Bjarne Erlingssön, had said that all he could do for Erlend Nikulaussön's sons, that would he do with all his heart.

Kristin sat gazing at her twin sons while Jammælt talked. They grew more and more like their father: silky fine, soot-black hair clung close and smooth to their heads, but curled a little in their forelocks and down over their slim brown necks. They had narrow faces with high-bridged, outstanding noses, and fine small mouths with a knot of muscles at each corner. But they had shorter and broader chins and darker eyes than Erlend. And it was this most of all, his wife now thought, that had made Erlend so wondrous fair, that when his eyes looked up, light-blue and clear, out of that lean, dark face under the coal-black hair, they took one so unawares.

But there was a gleam of steel-blue in the young lads' eyes now as Skule answered his uncle (he was wont to be spokesman for the two):

"We thank you for this your good and kindly proffer, kinsman. But we have spoken already with Sir Munan and with Inge, and taken counsel of our eldest brother—and the upshot is that we have come to an accord with Inge and his father. These men are our near kindred on our father's side—and we are to bear Inge company when he rides south, and are minded to bide at his manor this summer, and for some further time——"

The boys came down to their mother in the hall that evening when she had gone to rest:

"Ay, we deem most like you understand this, mother," said Ivar.

"We will not claim kindred and beg for help and friendship from the men who sat dumb and looked on while our father suffered wrong," added Skule.

The mother nodded.

She deemed her sons did right. Jammælt was a prudent and right-minded man, she saw, and his proffer had been well meant—but she was well pleased that the lads were true to their father. Yet had she never thought of old that the day would come when her sons would serve Brynhild Fluga's son.

The twins set forth with Inge Fluga as soon as Ivar was strong enough to ride. The manor grew passing still when they were gone. The mother remembered—last year about this time she lay in the weaving-room with a new-born babe—it seemed to her like a dream. So short a time was it since she had felt her young, with her mind stirred and shaken by a young woman's cares and yearnings, by hope and hate and love.—Now was her flock shrunken to four sons, and in her mind naught stirred, save disquietude for the grown young men. In this stillness which fell upon Jörundgaard after the going of the twins, her smouldering fear for Björgulf broke out into flame.

On the guests' coming, he and Naakkve had moved down to the old hearth-room house. He rose from his bed in the daytime, but he had not yet been without the door. With deepest dread Kristin marked that Björgulf sat ever in the same spot, never crossed the floor, and scarce moved at all when she was in beside him. She knew that his eyes were grown worse in this last sickness. Naakkve was most still and silent—but so he had been ever since his father's death, and he seemed to hold aloof from his mother all that he could.

At length one day she took heart of grace and questioned the eldest how it stood now with Björgulf's sight. For long Naakkve turned off her questions. But at last she called on her son to tell his mother the truth.

Naakkve said:

"Strong light he can still see dimly——" As he said it the young man grew deadly pale, turned sharply, and went from the room.

Late in the day, when the mother had wept her so weary that she deemed now she might trust herself to speak calmly with her son, she went over to the old house.

Björgulf lay upon the bed. Soon as she came and sat her down by him on the bed's edge, she could see by his face that he knew she had spoken with Naakkve:

"Mother. You must not weep, mother," he prayed, affrighted.

She would fain have cast herself down over her son, taken him in her arms, wept over him, and wailed his hard lot. But she did but steal her hand into his under the coverlid:

"Greatly does God try your manhood, my son," she said, hoarsely.

The look on Björgulf's face changed, grew firm and steadfast. But it was a little while ere he could speak:

"I have known for long, mother, that I was chosen out to suffer this. Already that time we were at Tautra—brother Aslak spoke to me of this, and said that, should it go thus with me, then——

"——As our Lord Jesus was tempted in the wilderness, said he—— He said the true wilderness for a Christian man's soul was when sight and sense were barred—then followed he the Lord's footsteps out into the wilderness, even though his body were amidst his brethren and his kinsmen. He read of these things from the books of Saint Bernard. And if a soul but understand that him hath God chosen in especial for such a hard trial of manhood, then he need not fear that he cannot abide it. God knows my soul better than the soul knows itself——"

He went on speaking to his mother after this fashion, comforting her, with wisdom and strength of soul which seemed far beyond his years.

In the evening Naakkve came to Kristin and begged that he might speak with her alone. Thereupon he said that 'twas his intent and Björgulf's to enter a godly brotherhood and take the vows as monks at Tautra.

Kristin stood struck dumb, but Naakkve went on, calmly. They would wait till Gaute was of age and could see to their mother's and their younger brothers' affairs. They would go into the convent with goods in such measure as befitted the sons of Erlend Nikulaussön of Husaby, but they would have an eye also to their brothers' welfare. From their father the Erlendssöns had naught in heritage worth the speaking of, but the three who were born ere Gunnulf Nikulaussön went into the cloister owned some parcels of farms north of the fells— he had given gifts to his nephews when he made division of his wealth, though most of what he gave not to the Church and godly works he made over to his brother. And, said Naakkve, if he and Björgulf claimed not their full share of the heritage, 'twould be a help to Gaute too, who was now to be the head of the house and carry it onward, that they two should die to the world.

Kristin felt as though a blow had stunned her. Never had she dreamed that Naakkve would think of a monk's life. But she spoke naught against it—she was so overcome. And she dared not try to turn her son's mind from so fair and so profitable a purpose.

"Even while we were boys, dwelling together in the cloister there in the north, we two promised each other we would never part our company," said Naakkve.

His mother nodded; she knew it. But she had deemed 'twas so meant, that Björgulf should go on living with Naakkve, even when the eldest brother wed.

It seemed to Kristin well-nigh a miracle that Björgulf, so young as he was, could bear his ill-fortune so manfully. The times she spoke with him of it, throughout the spring, she heard naught from his lips but brave and god-fearing words. 'Twas scarce to be understood, it seemed to her—but it must surely be that he had known for many years already what would come of his dim-sightedness, and so, belike, he had been arming his soul with patience ever since the time he dwelt amongst the monks——

But, since this was so, she could not but think how hard and heavy had been the lot of this luckless child of hers—and how little she had understood, standing by with mind filled full of her own concerns. And now Kristin Lavransdatter would steal, each moment she was alone, to kneel down before the likeness of Mary Virgin at home in the loft, and before her altar northward in the church as oft as it was opened. Grieving from the bottom of her heart, and with humble tears, she prayed the Redeemer's gentle mother to be to Björgulf in a mother's stead, and make good to him all that his mother in the flesh had left undone.

One summer night Kristin lay awake. Naakkve and Björgulf had gone back to the upper hall, but Gaute lay below with Lavrans, for the elder brothers had a mind to practise them in watching and praying, Naakkve had said. She was about to drop asleep at last, when she was roused by a noise of one moving stealthily up in the loft balcony. There were footfalls on the stairs—she knew the blind man's tread.

'Twas but that he had some errand, she thought—yet she got up and felt for her clothes. Then she heard the door above thrown open —someone cleared the steps in two or three bounds.

The mother ran to the outer room and threw open the door. The mist lay so thick without that the storehouses across the courtyard were but dimly seen. Up by the manor gate Björgulf was fighting furiously to free him from his brother's hold:

"Will you lose aught," cried the blind man, "if you be quit of me? —then were you free of all your vows—and had no need to die to this earthly home——"

What Naakkve answered, Kristin could not hear. She ran out barefoot into the dripping wet grass. Björgulf had wrenched him free now —then he dropped, as though felled by a blow, down over the great stone, and beat upon it with his clenched fists.

Naakkve saw his mother, and came hastily some few steps towards her:
"Go in, mother—I can deal best with this alone—you *shall* go in, I say," he whispered urgently, then turned and stood again bowed over his brother.

The mother stood watching a little way off. The sward was soaking with wet; it dripped from all the roofs, and drops trickled from every leaf—it had rained all the day, but now the clouds were sunken low, in a thick, white fog. When after a while her sons came down the path—Naakkve had hold of Björgulf beneath the arm and led him thus—Kristin shrank back within the outer-room door.

She saw that Björgulf's face was bleeding; belike he had struck it against the stone. Unwittingly, Kristin thrust her hand within her mouth and bit into her own flesh.

On the stairs Björgulf tried once again to tear himself from Naakkve—he stumbled against the wall, crying:
"I curse, I curse the day that I was born——!"

When she had heard Naakkve bar the door of the loft behind them, their mother stole up after them and stood in the balcony without. Long she heard Björgulf's voice from within—he raged, shrieked, and cursed—one or two of his wild words she could make out. Between-whiles she heard that Naakkve spoke to him, but his voice came to her as a muffled murmur only. At length Björgulf fell into a loud and heart-rending sobbing.

The mother stood, shivering with cold and grief. She had on her but a cloak flung over her shift; she stood there so long that her loose-flowing hair was wetted by the raw night air. At last silence fell within the loft.

When she was come into the room below, she went to the bed where Gaute and Lavrans slept. They had heard naught. While her tears ran down, she put out her hand in the dark, felt the two warm faces, and listened to the boys' healthy breathing. It seemed to her that now were these two all she had left of her riches.

Shuddering with cold, she crept up into her own bed. One of the dogs that lay over by Gaute's bed pattered across the floor, jumped up beside her, and curled him up upon her feet. He was wont to do this of nights, and she scarce had the heart to drive him away, though he was heavy and weighed upon her legs so that they grew numb; but Erlend had owned the dog, and 'twas his favourite, a coal-black, ragged old bear-hound. To-night Kristin deemed 'twas good that it should lie there and thaw her frozen feet.

——She saw naught of Naakkve the next morning till the morning meal. Then he came in and sat him down in the high-seat; this place had been his since his father died.

He said not a word throughout the meal, and there were black rings about his eyes. His mother followed when he went out again.

"How is't with Björgulf now?" she asked, in a low voice.

Naakkve shunned her look, but he answered, as low, that Björgulf slept now.

"Has—has he been thus before?" she whispered, fearfully.

Naakkve nodded, turned from her, and went up to his brother again.

Naakkve watched over Björgulf late and early, and kept his mother from him all he could. But Kristin knew that the two young men had many a heavy hour together.

'Twas Nikulaus Erlendssön who should have been master at Jörundgaard now, but he could find no time to pay the least heed to the farming. It seemed too that, like his father, he had small mind to the work and small skill in it. So Kristin and Gaute had the whole charge upon their shoulders—for this summer Ulf Haldorssön, too, forsook her.

After the hapless doings that ended with Erlend Nikulaussön's slaying, Ulf's wife had gone home with her brother. Ulf stayed on at Jörundgaard—he said he would show folk he would not be driven out by lies and gossip. But he hinted, none the less, that here his time was well-nigh spent; he thought maybe he would betake him north of the fells to his own farm in Skaun, when so much time had gone by that none might say he had fled from the slanders.

But then the bishop's deputy began to bring in question whether Ulf Haldorssön had put away his wife unlawfully. On this Ulf made ready to depart, fetched Jardtrud, and was now to set forth for the north ere the autumn storms made the roads across the mountains over toilsome. To Gaute he said that he would join company with his half-sister's husband, that was an armourer in Nidaros; his brother's son would still work his Skjoldvirkstad farm for him, and he would send Jardtrud to dwell there.

On the last night Kristin drank to Ulf from the silver-gilt beaker her father had had in heritage from his father's father, Sir Ketil the Swede. She prayed that he would take the beaker and keep it in memory of her; thereafter she set a gold ring that had been Erlend's upon his finger, and bade him wear it for his kinsman's sake.

Ulf kissed her in thanks: "'Tis one of the dues of kin," said he, laughing. "You thought not, Kristin, for sure—when first we were acquaint, and I was the serving-man that came to fetch you and bring you to my master—that we should part in this wise?"

Kristin flushed crimson, for he was smiling at her with his old mocking smile—yet she deemed she saw in his eyes that he was sad. So she said:

"None the less, Ulf, I trow you think long till you are back in the

Trondheim country, you who were born and bred there in the north. I long for the fjord there many a time, I who lived there but those few years." Ulf laughed as before; and then she said, low: "If, in my youth, I affronted you at any time by haughtiness or—I knew not then that you were near kinsmen, you and Erlend—you must forgive it me now!"

"Nay—and 'twas not Erlend who would not own the kinship. But I was so high and mighty when I was young—since my father had cast me out from among my kindred, beg me a place I would not——" He rose hastily, and went over to where Björgulf sat on the bench: "Understand you, Björgulf, my fosterling—your father—and Gunnulf—they showed me the hearts of kinsmen from the time when first we met as lads—far otherwise than my brothers and sisters at Hestnæs. Afterward —never did I put me forward as Erlend's kinsman unless I saw that thereby I could the better serve him—and his wife—and you, my foster-sons. Understand you?" he said, vehemently; and laid his hand over Björgulf's face, hiding the sightless eyes.

"I understand." Björgulf's answer came half smothered through the other's fingers; he nodded behind Ulf's hand.

"We understand, foster-father"; Nikulaus laid his hand heavily on Ulf's shoulder, and Gaute drew closer to the group.

A strange feeling came to Kristin—'twas as though they would speak of things she had no knowledge of. Then she too went forward to the men, saying:

"Trust me, Ulf, kinsman, all of us understand—other friend so trusty as you not Erlend nor any of us ever had. God bless you!"

The next day Ulf Haldorssön set forth for the north.

As the winter went on, Björgulf grew more at peace, so far as Kristin could see. He came again to the household meals and went to Mass with the folk, and he took in willing and friendly wise at Kristin's hand the help and service she was so fain to render to him.

And as the time went by, and Kristin never heard her sons say aught more of the cloister, she felt herself how unspeakably loath she was to give up her eldest son to the convent life.

She could not but see that for Björgulf the cloister would for sure be the best. But she knew not how she could endure to lose Naakkve in this wise. It must be, after all, that the first-born was in a way knit to the mother's heart yet more closely than were the other sons.

Nor could she see that Naakkve was fitted to be a monk. True enough, he had a passing good head for the arts of learning and a love for godly exercises; yet, all the same, he seemed not to his mother to be truly devout of mind. He showed no zeal in attendance at his parish church, missing the services often on slender grounds, and she knew that neither he nor Björgulf made to their parish priest aught but the common confession of sins. The new priest, Sira Dag Rolfssön, was a son of Rolf of Blakarsarv, who had been wed with Ragnfrid Ivars-datter's cousin, and he came much to his kinswoman's manor; he was a young man of about thirty years, learned and a good clerk; but the two eldest sons met him with coldness. Howbeit with Gaute he was good friends straightway.

Gaute was the only one of the Erlendssöns who had made friends amongst the folk of Sil. But yet none of the others had kept himself so much a stranger in the parish as had Nikulaus. He never mixed with the other youths—if so be he went where the youth were met for dance or trysting, he would stand most often aside at the border of the green, and look on—with the mien of one who deemed himself too good to take part. But should the whim take him, he would join in the game unbidden—from vainglory folk said, to show off his powers: he was lusty, strong, and nimble, easily egged on to fight—and after he had set down two or three of the most renowned fighters of the parish, folk thought it best to put up with his manners. And if so were that he had a mind to dance with a maid, he paid no heed either to brothers or kinsmen, but danced with the girl and after sat alone with her—and never did it befall that a woman said no when Nikulaus Erlendssön proffered her his company. He was none the better liked for this.

Since his brother was grown quite blind, Naakkve seldom left him, but, if it chanced that he went out of an evening, he bore him no other-wise than he had ever done. He had given up too, for the most part, his long hunting-trips, but none the less this same autumn he had bought of the Warden a most costly white falcon, and he was zealous as ever to practise him in archery and sports. Björgulf had taught him-self to play chess in despite of his blindness, and the brothers often spent whole days over the chess-board; they were both most eager players.

At this time Kristin heard that folk were talking of Naakkve and a young maid, Tordis Gunnarsdatter of Skjenne. The next year the girl lay up at the sæter the summer through; and Naakkve more than once was away from home by night. Kristin came to know that he had been with Tordis.

The mother's heart trembled, and turned hither and thither like an aspen-leaf on its stalk. Tordis was of an old and honourable kin—she herself was a good, innocent child; 'twas impossible that Naakkve could have the heart to wrong her. If the two young folk forgot them-selves, then must he make this girl his wife. Sick with dread and shame of her own thoughts, Kristin yet knew in her heart that 'twould surely not grieve her overmuch if so it turned out. But two years agone she

would have heard naught of it—that Tordis Gunnarsdatter should be
mistress of Jörundgaard after her. The maid's father's father was still
living, and dwelt on the manor with four married sons; she herself had
many brothers and sisters; she would be a poorly dowered bride. And
each woman of that kindred had ever one witless child at the least.
The mountain-people either changed the children or cast a spell on
them—in despite of all they could do to guard the lying-in women and
make them safe, neither baptism nor exorcism seemed to avail aught.
There were two old men now at Skjenne whom Sira Eirik had adjudged
to be changelings; two deaf-and-dumb children—and Tordis's eldest
brother the wood-elf had bewitched when he was in his seventeenth
year. Otherwise the Skjenne kindred were a goodly tribe; they had
luck with their cattle, and they throve in all their doings; but there
were so many of them 'twas impossible they should lay up riches.

——God alone might know whether Naakkve could draw back from
his purpose without sin, if he had vowed him already to Mary Virgin's
service. But she knew that a man must ever prove him for a year as
novice in the cloister ere he took the vows—he could draw back even
then, if he felt he was not called to serve God in this wise. And she had
heard how that a count's lady of Valland, who was mother to the great
doctor in religion and preaching friar, Sir Thomas Aquinas, had shut
her son in with a fair and wanton woman, to shake his purpose when he
was minded to forsake the world. Kristin deemed 'twas the foulest deed
she had heard on—and yet this woman died at peace with God. So
belike it could not be so fearful a sin in her, if she thought now that she
would welcome Tordis of Skjenne with open arms as her son's wife.

In the autumn Jammælt Halvardssön came to Formo, and from him
they learned the truth of the rumours of great tidings that had spread
up through the Dale before his coming. With consent of the foremost
fathers of the Church, and the knights and esquires of the Council of
Norway's realm, Sir Magnus Eirikssön had resolved to part his kingdoms 'twixt the two sons he had got by his queen, the Lady Blanche.
At the Diet at Varberg he had bestowed on the younger, Prince
Haakon, the name of King in Norway; the chiefs of the realm, both
clerks and laymen, had sworn upon the Lord's body to hold and guard
the land for him. 'Twas said he was a fair and likely child of three
years old, and was to be nurtured here in Norway, with four of the best
Norse dames for foster-mothers, and two Church and two lay lords for
foster-fathers, when King Magnus and Queen Blanche were in Sweden.
Sir Erling Vidkunssön and the bishops of Björgvin and Oslo, 'twas said,
had thought out this choice of king, and Bjarne Erlingssön had furthered
the matter most with King Magnus; for of all men in Norway's land he
beloved Bjarne st. And all men deemed 'twould be of great gain to

Norway's might and welfare, that now we should have a king again who made his home amongst us and would guard our laws and rights and the land's weal, instead of wasting his time and strength and the realm's wealth on emprises in other lands.

Kristin had heard of the choice of king, even as she had heard of the feuds with the German merchants in Björgvin and of the King's wars in Sweden and Denmark. But the tidings had touched her little— 'twas like the echoes of thunder-claps amidst the mountains when the storm passes over far-off country-sides. Her sons, she knew, had talked among them of these things. But by Jammælt's tale Erlend's sons were vehemently stirred. Björgulf sat with his forehead on his hand, hiding his blind eyes; Gaute listened with lips a little open, his hand clutching his dagger's hilt; Lavrans breathed quick and heavily, and kept ever looking from his aunt's husband over at Naakkve in the high-seat. The eldest son was pale of face and his eyes glowed.

"It has been the lot of many a man," said Naakkve, "that they who stood against him most stiffly in life went forward to victory on the road he showed them—when they had first laid him out as food for worms. When once his mouth is filled with mould, lesser men than he are fain enough to own his words true."

"Ay, maybe so, kinsman," said Jammælt, soothingly, "there is truth in what you say; your father, first of all men, thought of this way out of the slough—to put two brothers on the thrones here and in Sweden. A deep-thinking, wise and great-hearted knight was Erlend Nikulaussön, I wot. But be wary in your speech, Nikulaus; I trow well you would not have such words go abroad from you as might work harm to Skule——"

"Skule asked not my leave for this he has done," said Naakkve sharply.

"Nay, he remembered not, belike, that you are come of age now," answered Jammælt, as before, "and I thought not on it either—so 'twas with my consent and goodwill that he laid his hand on Bjarne's sword and swore——"

"I trow he remembered it—but the cub knew full well I had never given consent. And the Giske men stood in need, no doubt, of this salve for a pricking conscience——"

—Skule Erlendssön had taken service with Bjarne Erlingssön as his sworn follower. He had met the young noble at Yule-tide when a-visiting his mother's sister at Ælin, and Bjarne had made it clear to the boy that it was most through Sir Erling's pleadings and his own that Erlend's life had been pardoned—without their backing 'twas impossible Simon Andressön's errand to King Magnus could have sped.— Ivar was still with Inge Fluga.

Kristin knew that what Bjarne Erlingssön had said was not wholly untrue—it fitted in well enough with Simon's own tale of his journey to Tunsberg. Nevertheless she had all these years thought with great bitterness of Erling Vidkunssön; it seemed to her he must needs have had the power to help her husband to win better terms had he had the will. Bjarne, belike, counted for little at that time, being but a boy. Howsoever it was, she liked not over well that Skule had bound him to this man—and it took her breath strangely that the twins took their own way, and had ventured them out into the wide world thus—they seemed to her still but children——

After this visit of Jammælt's, the unrest in her spirit waxed so great that she could scarce bear to think. If 'twere as the men thought, that 'twould further so much the well-being and safety of the people of the land that this tiny boy in Tunsberg castle should now be called King of Norway, then this great gain for the folk might have been won nigh ten years agone had Erlend not—— No! She would not think of *that*, when she thought of the dead. But she could not help herself, were it but because she knew that in the sons' eyes their father stood out glorious and perfect, the foremost of warriors and chieftains, without spot or blemish. And she herself, indeed, had thought all these years that Erlend had been betrayed by his fellows and his rich kinsmen; her husband had suffered great wrong—but Naakkve overshot the mark when he said *they* had laid him out to be food for worms. She, too, 'twas sure, bore her own heavy share of the blame—but most of all 'twas Erlend's own folly and his ungoverned self-will that had brought him to his hapless end.

Nay, but—none the less 'twas bitter to her that Skule should now be Bjarne Erlingssön's man.

Should she never see the day when she would be set free from the endless torture of unrest and dread——?" O Jesus, remembering the care and sorrow Thy blessed mother suffered for Thy sake, have mercy upon me, a mother, and comfort me——!

Even for Gaute she had fears. There was the stuff in the boy for a husbandman of the best, but he was so headlong in his eagerness to set the fortunes of the house on their feet again. Naakkve gave him a free hand—and Gaute had so many irons in the fire. Along with some other men in the parish he had now taken up the old iron blast-furnaces in the fells. And he sold away too much; sold not only of what came in as rent in kind, but of the stuff from the home farm too. Kristin had all her days been used to see storehouses and ware-rooms on her manor full to overflowing, and she was more than a little wroth when Gaute turned up his nose at rank butter, and made a mock of the ten-year-old bacon she had hanging. She had need to feel that on her manor there should never be lack of food; that no poor folk need be turned away unholpen from her door, if black dearth should come again to the country-side. And there should be naught lacking when days of bride-ales and child-ales and feasting came again to the old manor.

Her high-flown hopes for her sons shrank and dwindled. She would be content if they would come to rest here in her parish. She could exchange and bring together her estates so that three of them might be settled on their own farms. And Jörundgaard, with the part of Laugarbru that lay this side the river, would suffice to keep three free-holders. If their lot were not that of great esquires—yet, at the least, poor folk they would not be. And here in the Dale was peace—all this unrest among the chieftains of the land was little heard of and little heeded here. Even if this might be deemed an abatement of the power and worship of the kindred—yet 'twas in God's power to lead those who came after on to greater things if He saw 'twould be for their good. But belike 'twas vain for her to hope she should see them gathered about her in this wise—they would scarce come to rest so easily, these sons of hers who had Erlend Nikulaussön for father.

It was at this time that her soul was wont to find peace and solace if she let her thoughts run on the two little children she had laid to rest up in the graveyard.

Each day in these years she had thought of them—wondered, when she saw children as old as they growing and thriving, what hers would have been like now——

When now she went about her daily tasks, deft and diligent as ever, but withdrawn and full of thought, the dead children were ever with her; in her dreams they grew and throve, and their natures were in every wise just as she would have had them: Munan was as faithful to his kinsmen as Naakkve, while in his ways with his mother he was merry and frank as Gaute—but, unlike him, never affrighted her with doubtful plans; he was gentle and thoughtful as Lavrans, but all the strange thoughts that Munan pondered he talked of freely with his mother. In mother-wit he was Björgulf's like, but no mischance dark-ened his road through life, and thus his wisdom was untouched by bitterness; he was self-assured, strong and bold as the twins, but not so unruly and self-willed——

And all the sweet, joyous memories of her children's lovesomeness when they were little, these she called up again when she thought of little Erlend. He stood upon her lap to be dressed; she held her hands about his fat naked form, and with tiny hands and upturned face and all his precious body he strained upward towards her face and her caresses. She taught him to walk—she had laid a folded cloth across his breast and up below his arm-pits—in this harness he hung, heavy as a sack, working away so blunderingly and drolly with his feet, laughing himself till he twisted him about like a little worm. She bore him with her on her arm out into the farm-yard to the calves and lambs; he screamed with joy at the sow with all her piglets, threw back his head and gaped at the doves up on the stable loft. He ran beside her in the tall grass by the stone heaps, cried out for each berry he saw, and ate them from out her hand so eagerly that her palm was all wet from his little greedy mouth.

All the joys she had had of her children she called to mind and lived over again in this dream-life with these two little ones, and all the sorrows she forgot——

Spring was come for the third time since Erlend was laid in his grave. Kristin heard no more of Tordis and Naakkve. But neither did she hear aught of the cloister. And her hopes grew—she could not help herself: she was so loath to give up her eldest son to the monkish life.

Just before John's Mass* Ivar Erlendssön came home to Jörund-gaard. The twins had been sixteen-year-old, growing lads when they set forth from home. Ivar was a grown man now, near eighteen years old, and his mother deemed he had grown so fair and manly she could not look her fill on him.

His mother bore his breakfast up to Ivar the first morning, while he lay abed. Wheaten honey-bread, bannocks, and ale that she had drawn from the last barrel of the Yule-tide brew. She sat upon the bed's edge while he ate and drank, smiled at all he said, stood up and looked at his clothes, turned and felt each garment, rummaged in his travelling-bag, weighed his new silver buckle in her narrow, red-brown hand, drew his dagger from its sheath, praised it and all his gear. Then she sat her down again upon the bed, looked on her son, and listened with a smile in her eyes and about her lips to all the young man's tales.

Then Ivar said:

"'Twere best, mother mine, I should tell you what errand has brought me hither—I am come to get me Naakkve's assent to my marriage."

Astounded, Kristin smote her hands together:

"Ivar mine! And you so young—sure you have not been playing any foolish pranks?"

Ivar prayed his mother to hearken. 'Twas a youngish widow, Signe Gamalsdatter of Rognheim in Fauskar. The manor was worth six score silver marks, and the most of it her own; she had it in heritage from her only child. But she had been drawn into a lawsuit with her husband's kin, and Inge Fluga had sought all manner of unlawful gain for

* 24th June.

himself, if he was to help the widow to her rights. Ivar had grown angry, and had taken the woman's part and gone with her to the bishop himself, for Sir Halvard had shown Ivar fatherly goodwill at all times when he had met with him. Inge Munansson's doings in his warden-ship would ill bear to be looked into sharply—but he had known how to keep friendship with the great people in the parishes, and to frighten the common folk into a mouse-hole—and in throwing dust in the bishop's eyes he had shown great skill; 'twas like too that, for Munan's sake, Sir Halvard was not minded to be over strict. But now things looked none too well for Inge—and so the second-cousins had parted in most unfriendly wise when Ivar took his horse and rode from Inge Fluga's manor. But then it had come to his mind that he might go south and greet the folks at Rognheim ere he left that country-side. That was at Easter-tide, and he had been with Signe since—helped her on her manor in the spring—and now they had agreed together that he should wed her. *She* deemed not that Ivar Erlendssön was too young to be her husband and take her welfare in charge. And he was in favour with the bishop, as he had said—sure enough he was too young and untaught as yet for Sir Halvard to entrust him with any office, but Ivar had good hopes that he would make his way, if he wed at Rogn-heim.

Kristin sat playing with the bunch of keys in her lap. This, sure enough, was sage and sober talk. And well she deemed that Inge Fluga deserved naught better. But she wondered much what the poor old man, Munan Baardssön, would say to this.

Of the bride she learned that Signe was thirty winters old, and of poor and humble stock, but her first husband had prospered, so that now she was in good estate; and she was herself an honourable, kindly, and notable woman.

Nikulaus and Gaute went south with Ivar to see the widow, but Kristin stayed behind to be with Björgulf. When her sons came home, Naakkve brought the tidings to his mother that Ivar was now betrothed to Signe Gamalsdatter. The wedding was to be held at Rognheim in the autumn.

Not long after his home-coming, Naakkve came in to his mother one evening when she sat sewing in the weaving-house. He barred the door within. He said then to his mother that now Gaute was twenty, and Ivar, too, by reason of his marriage, was become his own master, 'twas his and Björgulf's intent to journey north this next autumn and pray to be received as novices into the cloister. Kristin said not much in answer, and what more was said was but of the ordering of the portion that the two eldest sons must now be given from the estate.

But a few days later men came to Jörundgaard to bid them to a feast—Aasmund of Skjenne was to hold his granddaughter Tordis's betrothal-ale with a worthy yeoman's son of Dovre.

Naakkve came in to his mother in the weaving-house that night too, and again he barred the door behind him. He set him down on the edge of the hearth-place, and sat raking with a stick in the embers— Kristin had made a little fire, for the nights were cold that summer.

"Naught but feasting and revelling, mother mine," he said, laughing a little. "Betrothal feast at Rognheim and betrothal feast at Skjenne, and then 'twill be Ivar's wedding—but when Tordis rides to church to her bridal, I shall not be of the company, I trow—I shall have donned the cloister garb by then——"

Kristin answered not for a while. But then she said, without looking up from her seam—'twas a wedding-coat for Ivar:

"Many had deemed, I trow, that 'twould be a grief to Tordis Gunnarsdatter if you turned monk."

"I had deemed so once myself," said Naakkve.

Kristin let the sewing sink upon her lap. She looked at her son—his face was set and calm. And he was so fair—his dark hair, combed back from his white forehead, clustered so softly behind his ears and over the slender brown pillar of his neck. His features were shapelier than his father's—his face was broader and firmer, the nose not so big and the mouth not so small; his clear blue eyes lay fairly set beneath the straight, black eyebrows—and yet he did not *seem* so comely as Erlend had been. 'Twas his father's animal-like suppleness and grace, the breath of never-fading youth about him, that Naakkve lacked.

The mother took up her work again, but she did not sew. After a little she said, while she looked down and smoothed in an edge of the cloth with her needle:

"Bear in mind, Naakkve, yet have I said no single word against your godly purpose. I dare not be so bold. But you are young—and you, who are much more learned than I, wot well—somewhere in the scriptures 'tis written: Ill beseems it a man to turn and look back over his shoulder when once he has set his hand to the plough."

Not a muscle of her son's face moved.

"I know that for long have you two had this in your thoughts," his mother went on. "Ever since you were children. You understood not then, yourselves, what you would forgo. Now you are come to man's estate—think you not 'twere fit you should prove you a little longer— whether or not you have the call? *You* are born to be the master of this manor and the head of your house——"

"You make bold to counsel me now?" Naakkve drew breath heavily once or twice. He rose—of a sudden he took hold on his bosom, tore apart his coat and shirt, so that the mother looked upon his naked breast, where the birth-mark, the five small blood-red, fiery flecks, shone amidst the black, curling down:

"You thought, maybe, I was too young to understand what you sighed out with tears and moans as you kissed me here when I was a little child—— I understood it not then, but the words you spoke I never could forget——

"Mother, mother—have you forgot that father died the most miser-able of deaths, unshriven and unhouseled?—And *you* dare to gainsay our purpose?

"——Methinks we brothers know well what we turn us from—— Meseems 'tis none so great a loss if I lose this manor and cut me off from wedlock—and such peace and joy as you and my father had together all the years I can remember——"

Kristin let fall her sewing. All her life with Erlend—the evil and the good—the rich wealth of memories came over her in a flood. *So* little, then, did this child know what he was forgoing. With all his boyish battles, his venturesome deeds, his playing at love and gallantry—naught else was he but an innocent child.

Naakkve saw the tears come into his mother's eyes; he cried aloud:

"*Quid mihi et tibi est, mulier**——?" Kristin started in dread, but her son spoke on in a vehement tumult of mind: "God said not these words, I trow, for that He contemned his mother—— But He corrected even her, the pure pearl without spot or blemish, when she would have counselled Him how He should use the power He had got from His Father in heaven and not from His mother in the flesh.—Mother, you must not counsel me in this matter—dare not to do it——"

Kristin bent her head upon her breast.

A little after Naakkve said, very low:

"Have you forgot, mother, that you drove me from you——?" He stopped, as though he could not trust his own voice. But then he went on again: "I would have knelt by you at my father's death-bed—but you bade me begone—— Think you not my heart has been wrung in my bosom as often as I thought on it——?"

Kristin whispered, so low 'twas scarce to be heard:

"Is it therefore you have been so—cold—towards me all these years, since I have been widowed?"

The son was silent.

"I begin to understand—you have never forgiven me this, Naak-kve——"

Naakkve looked down, aside.

* "Woman, what have I to do with thee?"—John ii 4.

"Sometimes—I have forgiven you, mother," he said, in a faint voice.

"Often was it not, I trow—Naakkve, Naakkve," she cried in bitter moan, "—think you my love for Björgulf was less than yours—am I not his mother—am I not mother to you both? Cruel were you when you ever barred the door 'twixt him and me——!"

Naakkve's pale face grew yet whiter:

"Ay, mother, I barred the door against you.—Cruel, say you——? Jesus comfort you, you know not——" His voice died away in a whisper, as though the boy's strength were ebbed away: "Methought you should not—you at least we must spare——"

He turned sharp about, went to the door, and unbarred it. But then he stood there unmoving, with his back to Kristin. At length she called him softly by his name. On that he came back, and stood before her with bowed head:

"Mother—— I know well this is not—easy—for you——"

She laid her hands upon his shoulders. He hid his face from her sight, but he bowed down his head and kissed one of her wrists. Kristin remembered that his father had done this once—when, she could not recall——

She stroked his sleeve, and on that he lifted his hand and patted her on the cheek. Afterwards they sat them down, and sat in silence a little.

"Mother," said Naakkve, in a while, in a steady, even voice. "Have you still the cross that was my brother Orm's?"

"Ay," said Kristin; "he told them to pray me never to part from it."

"I trow that, had Orm known of this, he had given consent that I should heir it of him. Now shall I, too, have neither kin nor heritage——"

Kristin drew forth from under her shift the little silver cross. Naakkve took it from her hand; 'twas warm yet from his mother's breast. Reverently he kissed the reliquary in the midst of the cross, clipped the thin chain about his neck, and thrust the trinket in under his clothing.

"Have you memory of your brother Orm?" asked his mother.

"I know not. At times it seems—but mayhap 'tis but that you spoke so much of him when I was little——"

Naakkve sat on there a little while before his mother. Then he stood up:

"Good-night, mother!"

"God bless you, Naakkve; good-night!"

He went. Kristin folded up Ivar's bridal coat, laid it with her sewing-gear, and quenched the fire.

"God bless you, God bless you, Naakkve mine——" Then she blew out the candle and left the old house.

It chanced, a little while after, that Kristin met Tordis at a manor in the outskirts of the parish. There was sickness amongst the manor-folk and they had not got in their hay; so the brothers and sisters of Olav's Gild* went thither to lend them a hand with the work. In the evening Kristin bore the girl company part of her way home. She walked slowly, as one well on in years, chatting with the girl; and before long she had led the talk in such wise that Tordis of her own accord had told Naakkve's mother all that had been 'twixt him and her.

Ay, she had been wont to meet him in their home paddock, and last summer, when she lay at the sæter, he had been with her more times than one of nights. But he had never offered to be overbold with her. She knew well what folk said of Naakkve in general—to her he had never done wrong, either in word or in deed. But he had lain by her side upon the bed-covers once or twice, and they had talked together—— Once she had asked him if 'twere his purpose to ask for her in marriage; and he had answered that he could not; he had vowed him to the service of Mary Virgin. He said the same this last spring one time they spoke together. And so she would no longer set her against her grandfather's and her father's wills.

"It must needs have brought down evil upon you both, had he broken his vow and you defied your kinsfolk," said Kristin. She stood leaning upon her rake, looking on the young maid—a gentle, round, and comely face this child had, and the fairest bright hair in a heavy plait. "God will surely grant you happiness withal, my Tordis—he seems a gallant, good lad, your betrothed."

"Ay, I like Haavard well," said the girl—and then burst into bitter weeping.

Kristin comforted her with such words as were fitting in the mouth of an old and a staid woman. Her own heart ached with yearning— she had so gladly called this good, fresh child her daughter.

After Ivar's wedding she stayed a while at Rognheim. Signe Gamals-datter was not fair, and she looked worn and old, but she was gentle and winning. She seemed to cherish a heart-felt love for her young husband, and she welcomed his mother and brothers as though she deemed they stood so far above her 'twas not possible she should honour and serve them enough. For Kristin 'twas a quite new thing that any should put themselves about to guess her wishes and care for her heed-fully. Not even while she was the rich lady of Husaby, with a host of

* See *The Bridal Wreath* (*The Garland*), Note 17, Peasant or Farmers' Guilds.

serving-folk to do her bidding, had any served her as though they took
thought for the mistress's ease and well-being. She had never spared
herself when all work for the good of the whole household was on her
shoulders, and none else had ever bethought them that she should be
spared. So Signe's ready thoughtfulness for her mother-in-law's well-
being all the time she was at Rognheim did Kristin's heart good; she
soon grew to love Signe so well that, well-nigh as earnestly as she
prayed God to bless Ivar's wedded life, she prayed also that Signe
might never have cause to repent that she had given herself and all she
had to so young a husband.

And so, just after Michael's Mass,* Naakkve and Björgulf journeyed
northward to the Trondheim country. All that she had heard of them
since was that they were come to Nidaros in good case, and that they
had been received as novices into the brotherhood at Tautra.

Soon now would Kristin have dwelt a year on Jörundgaard with but
two of her sons to bear her company. But she herself wondered—that
'twas but a year. For that day in autumn of last year when she had been
as far as Dovre with the two, and came riding by the church and looked
down upon the lower slopes, lying sheeted in cold mist so that she could
not make out the houses on her own manor—she had thought that so
much they feel, who ride towards their home knowing that the houses
lie there burned to ashes and cold charred wood——
——Now, when she turned homewards by the old path past the
smithy garth—this year 'twas all but overgrown, and tufts of yellow bedstraw, bluebells and vetch swept over it from the edges of the rank hay-
field—almost it seemed to her that what she saw was a picture of her
own life: the weather-beaten, sooty old hearth-place, that never again
would have fire kindled upon it. The ground about it was strewn thick
with powdered charcoal, but soft, short, glossy grass was springing up
over all the plot where the fire had raged. And from the cracks of the
old fireplace bloomed the long, pink tassels of the willow-herb, which
sows itself in all places.

II

I T would befall at times, when Kristin was gone to rest already, that
she would be awaked by folk coming riding into the courtyard. Someone would thunder at the loft door—she would hear Gaute meet his
guests with a loud, gay greeting. Serving-folk must up and out. There
was a clatter and tramping in the room above—Kristin could make out
Ingrid's voice raised in chiding. Ay, she was a good child, that young

* 29th September.

serving-wench; she would put up with no forwardness from any man. A roar of laughter from young throats greeted her sharp, ready answers. Frida squealed—poor thing, she would never grow wiser; not many years younger than Kristin herself—and yet the mistress had to keep a watchful eye on her——

Then Kristin would turn in her bed and sleep again.

Gaute would be up next morning at cock-crow as was his wont—he slept no longer of a morning for having sat up drinking ale at night. But his guests would not show themselves till the hour of the morning meal. Then they would stay at the manor the day through—sometimes they had a bargain to strike, and sometimes 'twas but a friendly visit. Gaute ever kept open house.

Kristin took heed that everything of the best was set before Gaute's friends. She knew not herself that she went about smiling quietly, as she heard once more the sounds of youth and joyous life on her father's manor. But she spoke little with the young men and saw but little of them. Enough for her to see that Gaute was happy and a man of many friends.

Gaute Erlendssön was as well liked by the small folk as amongst the rich landowners. Although the doom passed on Erlend's slayers had borne most hardly upon their kinsmen, so that there were farms and kindred whose folk were still most loath to meet with any of the Erlendssöns, yet Gaute himself had not a foe.

Sir Sigurd of Sundbu had conceived the greatest fondness for his young kinsman. This cousin of hers, whom Kristin had never met before fate led him to Erlend Nikulaussön's death-bed, had shown him at that time the most faithful kinsman to her. He had stayed at Jörundgaard till nigh to Yule-tide, and done all he could to help the widow and the fatherless young lads. The Erlendssöns showed their thankfulness fairly and courteously, but only Gaute made close friends with him, and he had been much at Sundbu since that time.

When this daughter's son of Ivar Gjesling died, the manor would pass wholly away out of the Gjesling house—he was childless, and the Haftorssöns were his nearest heirs. Sir Sigurd was somewhat of an old man already, and had had a heavy lot to bear—his young wife had gone from her wits at her first child-bearing. He had now dwelt with this mad wife nigh on forty years, but still almost daily he went to visit her and see how things were with her—she lived in one of the best houses on Sundbu, and had certain serving-women who did naught but tend her. "Know you me to-day, Gyrid?" her husband was wont to ask. Sometimes she made no answer, but at other times she would say: "I know you well—you are Ysaias the soothsayer that dwells at Brotveit, northward, under the Brotveit hill." She sat ever with a spindle in her hands

—when she was at her best she would spin a fine and even thread, but when 'twas ill with her, she would pluck her own spinning to pieces and strew the wool that her handmaidens had carded over the whole room. After Gaute had told Kristin of this, she ever welcomed her cousin with heart-felt friendliness, if it chanced that he came to the manor. But she would not consent to go herself to his manor—there she had not been since the day she stood, a bride, in the Sundbu church.

Gaute Erlendssön was much lower of stature than Kristin's other sons. Beside his tall mother and long-limbed brothers he looked somewhat short, but he was of a good middle height. Altogether Gaute seemed to bulk more largely in every way, now that the two eldest brothers, and the twins, who came next him in age, were gone—amongst them he had been quiet in his bearing. All through the country-side folk deemed him a most sightly man—and he was comely of face too. With his flaxen-yellow hair and his big grey eyes, well set beneath his brows, his oval, somewhat full face, fresh-hued skin and well-shaped mouth, he was much like his mother's father. His head was fairly set upon his shoulders, and his well-formed, large hands were strong beyond the common. But he was somewhat too short in the lower body, and his legs were much bowed. For this reason he went ever in long garments, save when, for his work's sake, he must needs wear a short coat—though just at this time 'twas growing more and more the use for men who would go fine and courtly clad to have their garments of state cut shorter than before. The country farmers saw this fashion on the great folk who journeyed through the Dale. But when Gaute Erlendssön came to church or to banquet in his long, green, broidered holy-day habit, with silver belt about his slim waist and great miniver-lined cape thrown back upon his shoulders, the parish folk would follow the young master of Jörund-gaard with glad and friendly eyes. In his hand Gaute bore ever a fair silver-mounted axe that Lavrans Björgulfsön had owned in heritage from his father-in-law, Ivar Gjesling—and folk deemed it right good to see Gaute Erlendssön following in his forefather's footsteps, and, young as he was, keeping to good old country ways, both in dress, in manner of life, and in bearing.

And on horseback Gaute was the comeliest man any could wish to see. He was a most venturous rider, and folk in the parish boasted there was never a horse in Norway's land that their Gaute could not tame and ride. When he was in Björgvin a year agone, 'twas said, he had mastered a young stallion that no man before him had been able to back—under Gaute's handling it grew so gentle that he rode it bare-backed, with a maiden's hair-riband for bridle. But when Kristin questioned her son about this matter, he only laughed and would not speak of it.

That Gaute was light in his dealings with women Kristin knew, and she misliked it much, but she thought 'twas most because women met the comely young man all too kindly, and Gaute was open-hearted and forthcoming. For the most 'twas doubtless sport and jesting—he took not such things hardly, nor kept them hidden, as Naakkve had done. He came himself and told his mother when he had got a child with a young girl over at Sundbu—that was now two years gone by. With the mother he had dealt open-handedly, giving her, for her rank, a fitting maintenance, so Kristin heard from Sir Sigurd; and the child Gaute would have home with him when 'twas weaned from the breast. It seemed he was most fond of his little daughter; he went to see her always when he was in Vaagaa—she was the fairest of children, said Gaute proudly, and he had had her christened Magnhild. Kristin too deemed that, since so it was that the boy had done amiss, 'twere best he should bring his child home and be a good father to her. She herself as nowise loath to have little Magnhild brought thither. But the child died when a year old. Gaute grieved much when he heard of it; and Kristin felt 'twas a sore thing that she had never had a sight of her son's little daughter.

It had ever been most hard for Kristin to chide Gaute. He had been so sickly when he was little, and after, too, he had kept by his mother's side more than the other children. And then he was like her father. And he had been so steady and trusty as a child—grave and like a grown-up man, he had gone about with her and done her many a well-meant hand's turn, such as he deemed in his childish simplicity must be of the greatest help to his mother. No, never had she had the heart to be hard with Gaute—and if he did wrong out of heedlessness or because at his age he knew no better, he needed naught but some gentle words of guidance; so sober and clear-witted was the boy.

When Gaute was two years old, their house priest at Husaby, who had more than common skill in little children's ails, counselled that he should again be given woman's milk, since other means had availed nothing. The twins were then new born, and Frida, who fostered Skule, had much more milk than the little child could drink. But the wench held the poor little being in dread—Gaute was an ill-favoured child, with his great head and his thin and wizen body, and he could neither talk nor stand upon his legs—so she was afeared he might be a change-ling, though the child had been sound and comely until the sickness took hold on it at ten months old. Howbeit Frida would nowise put Gaute to her breast; so there was naught to do but for Kristin herself to take him; and he sucked his mother's milk till he was four winters old.

Afterwards Frida could never take to Gaute; she had ever snapped at him, as much as she dared for fear of his mother. Frida sat next to the mistress now on the women's bench, and bore the keys when Kristin was from home. She said to the master and mistress whatever came into her head. Kristin bore with the woman and smiled at her ways, though she was often irked by her too—yet she sought ever to put matters to rights and smooth them over, when Frida had done aught foolish or had let her tongue wag too rudely. Frida took it greatly amiss that Gaute sat in the high-seat now, and was to be the master of the manor. Naught would bring her to account him for aught more than a witless youth; she boasted of his brothers, though most of Björgulf and Skule, whom she had nursed; and she scoffed at Gaute's short stature and crooked legs. Gaute took it in good part:

"Ay, be sure, Frida, had I had you to suck, I had been as good a giant as any brother of them all. But *I* had to be content with my mother's breast——" He smiled at Kristin.

Often mother and son would stroll out together of an evening. In many places the paths across the fields were so narrow that Kristin must follow after Gaute. He walked in front with his long-handled axe, so masterfully—his mother could not but smile behind his back. She felt a mischievous, youthful fancy to run at him from behind, clasp him to her, laugh and toy with Gaute as she had done when he was a child.

Sometimes they went right down to the washing-place by the river-side, and sat listening to the rushing sound of the stream as it hurried by, bright and swift in the twilight. Most often they spoke but little. But it might happen that Gaute would ask his mother of old times in this country-side and about her own kin. Kristin told of what she had heard and seen in her childhood. Of his father and the years at Husaby no word ever passed between them.

"Nay, mother, you are sitting there shivering, I trow," said Gaute; "—'tis cold this evening."

"Oh, ay—and I am stiff with sitting on this stone." Kristin got up too. "I am growing to be an old woman, my Gaute!"

On the way up she stayed herself with a hand on his shoulder.

Lavrans was sleeping like a stone in his bed. Kristin lit the little train-oil lamp—she had a mind to sit a little and solace her with the calm in her own soul. And there was ever enough she could busy her fingers with. From overhead came clattering noises—then she heard Gaute climb into his bed up there. The mother straightened her back a moment—smiling a little at the lamp's small flame. Her lips moved; she made the sign of the cross upon her face and breast in the air before her. Then she took up her seam again.

Björn, the old hound, got up and shook himself, stretched him flat upon his fore-paws with a yawn. Then he padded across the floor to his mistress. She patted him, and straightway he put his fore-paws up on her lap—when she spoke to him pettingly, he set to licking her face and hands, thumping the floor with his tail. Then Björn slunk back again—turned his head and looked at the woman; evil conscience looked out from his beady eyes and the whole of his rough, shaggy body, to the uttermost tip of his tail. Kristin smiled quietly and made as though she saw not—then the dog jumped up on her bed and curled himself up by the foot-board.

After a while she blew out the lamp, snuffed the wick, and dropped the snuff down into the oil. From without, through the little window-pane, the twilight of the summer night showed dimly. Kristin said over the last prayers for the day, undressed quietly, and crept into bed. She settled the pillows snugly about her breast and shoulders, and the old hound nestled in to her back. Soon after she fell asleep.

Bishop Halvard had made Sira Dag his steward in the parish, and from him Gaute had bought the bishop's tithes for the next three years. He bought hides and food stuffs in the parish too, and in winter, when the sleighing was good, he sent the wares to Raumsdal, and on to Björgvin in the spring by ship. Kristin liked not over well these dealings of her son's—she herself had ever sold at Hamar, for so both her father and Simon Andresön had done. But Gaute had joined with his brother-in-law, Gerlak Paus, in a kind of trading fellowship—and Gerlak was a stirring trader, and was near of kin to many of the richest German merchants in Björgvin.

Erlend's daughter Margret and her husband had come to Jörund-gaard the summer after her father's death; they made great offerings to the church for his soul's weal. When Margret was a young maid at home at Husaby there had been scant friendship 'twixt her and her step-mother, and she had cared but little then about her small half-brothers. Now she was thirty years old, and had had no children of her marriage; she showed her comely grown-up brothers now much sisterly love, and 'twas she who brought about the understanding 'twixt her husband and Gaute.

Margret was fair still, but she was grown so big and stout that Kristin deemed she had never seen so huge a woman. But all the more room was there for silver plates upon her belt, and a brooch as big as a small hand-shield adorned most fitly the space betwixt her broad breasts. Her mighty body was ever adorned, like an altar, with the most costly stuffs and fairly gilt metal—Gerlak Tiedekenssön seemed to prize his wife exceeding highly.

The year before, Gaute had visited his sister and brother-in-law in Björgvin at the time of the spring meetings, and in the autumn he crossed the fells with a drove of horses which he sold there. That journey brought him so much gain that Gaute swore he would do the like again next autumn. Kristin thought 'twas well to let him have his way in this. Belike he had somewhat of his father's thirst for travel in his blood—he would settle down when he grew older. When his mother saw that he was impatient to get away, she herself hastened his going—the year before he had had to make his way home over the fells after the winter storms had set in.

So he set forth one fair morning of sunshine, just after Bartholomew's Mass.* 'Tis the time for killing goats—and the whole manor smelt of boiled goats' flesh. The folk had eaten their fill and were happy; all summer long they had not tasted fresh meat save on the highest holy-days, but now for many days they had had the savoury meat and rich, fatty broth both at the morning and the evening meal. Kristin was tired, but in good spirits, after the first great slaughtering and sausage-making of the year, as she stood up on the highway and waved the fall of her coif after Gaute and his train. 'Twas brave to look on—fine horses, blithe young men who rode with shining weapons and jingling harness; the high bridge, when they came on to it, resounded with the hoof-beats. Gaute turned in his saddle and waved back with his hat, and Kristin waved again with a dizzy little cry of gladness and pride.

Soon after winter-night,† rain and sleet set in on the lowlands, storm and snow on the fells. Kristin was somewhat uneasy for Gaute, who had not yet come back. But, truth to tell, she was never so fearful for him as she had been for the others—she had faith in this son's fortune.

A week later Kristin was coming from the byre late in the evening, when she was ware of some horsemen up by the manor gate. The mist billowed like white smoke in front of the lanthorn she bore—she went upward in the rain to meet the troop of dark-clad men in furs: was it not Gaute?—'twas not like that strangers would come so late——

Then she saw that the first rider was Sir Sigurd of Sundbu—he lighted down from his horse with somewhat of an old man's stiffness.

"Ay—I bring you tidings of Gaute, Kristin," said the knight, when they had greeted one another. "He came to Sundbu yesterday——"

'Twas so dark where they stood that she could not make out his look. But his voice was so strange. And, as he went towards the door of the hall-house, he bade his henchmen follow Kristin's stable-boy to the men's lodging. She grew fearful as he said no more, but she asked calmly enough when they stood alone together in the room:

"What manner of tidings are they, then, kinsman? Is he sick, since he came not home with you?"

* 24th August   † 14th October.

"No, Gaute is as well as e'er I saw him. But his company was weary——"

He blew the froth off the bowl of ale that Kristin handed him, drank and praised the ale.

"A good regale for him that bears good tidings," said the mistress, smiling.

"Ay, let us hear what you will say when you have heard my news to an end," he said, most ruefully. "He came not alone this time, your son——"

Kristin stood waiting.

"He has with him—ay, 'tis the daughter of Helge of Hovland—it seems he has taken this—this maid—taken her from her father by the strong hand——"

Kristin still said naught. But she sat her down on the bench in front of him. Her mouth was pinched, with close-pressed lips.

"Gaute begged me to come hither—he feared, I trow, you would be ill pleased at this. He bade me tell you this—and now have I done it," Sir Sigurd ended, weakly.

"You must tell me all that you know of this matter, Sigurd," Kristin prayed, calmly.

Sir Sigurd did so—in a rambling, unclear fashion, with much beating about the bush. 'Twas clear he was himself much dismayed at Gaute's deed. But thus much Kristin made out from his tale: Gaute must have met the maid last year at Björgvin. Jofrid was her name—oh, no, she was not betrothed to any. But Gaute had seen, belike, 'twould be of no avail for him to speak of the maid to her kinsmen—Helge of Hovland was passing rich, of the house that bore the name Duk and had their estates mostly in Voss. So the devil had tempted the two young folk—— Sir Sigurd wriggled in his clothes and scratched his head, as though he were lousy all over.

So in summer—when Kristin believed that Gaute was at Sundbu and was out a-hunting with Sir Sigurd after the two big bears among the sæter hills—he had crossed the mountains to Sogn—she was there with a wedded sister; Helge had three daughters and no son. Sigurd groaned miserably—ay, he had promised Gaute then to say naught of it. 'Tis true he had known the boy was after a maid—but how could he dream that 'twas aught so witless Gaute had in mind——

"Ay, 'tis like he will have to pay dear for this, my son," said Kristin. Her face was set and calm.

Sigurd said the winter was setting in now in earnest—the roads would be scarce passable. And when the Hovland men got time to think over the matter, they would maybe deem—'twere best Gaute were given Jofrid with her kinsmen's consent—since she was his already.

"But if they deem *not* so—if they crave vengeance for the rape of their woman?"

Sir Sigurd twisted and scratched worse than ever:

"'Tis a felony,* belike," he said, low. "I know not to a nicety——"

Kristin was silent. So Sir Sigurd went on, in a pleading voice:

"He said, did Gaute, that he was well assured you would give them a loving welcome. He said for sure you were not so old that you had forgotten—ay, he meant, you understand, that you got the husband you had set your heart on."

Kristin nodded.

"She is the fairest child I have seen in all my days, Kristin," said Sigurd warmly; his eyes grew wet. "'Tis an ill thing that the devil's lure has led Gaute astray into this misdoing—but I trow you will welcome these two poor children in friendly wise?"

Kristin nodded again.

The country lay soaking wet, wan and black under drenching rain-showers, when Gaute rode into the courtyard next day about the time of nones.

Kristin felt a cold sweat damp her brow as she leaned forward under the door lintel to look—there stood Gaute lifting a woman in a dark, hooded cloak from off her horse. She was small of stature, reaching barely to the man's shoulder. Gaute would have taken her hand and led her forward—but she pushed him aside and went alone to meet Kristin. Gaute set to greeting the house-carls and giving orders to the men who had been with him. When he looked again towards the two before the house door, Kristin stood holding the stranger girl by both hands. Gaute sprang towards them with a glad greeting on his lips. In the outer room Sir Sigurd took him by the shoulder, and patted him right fatherly, puffing and panting now the strain was at an end.

Kristin had been taken unawares when the girl lifted a face so white and so lovely under the dripping hood of her cloak—and she was so young, and small as a very child. When the stranger said:

"I look not that you should welcome me, Gaute's mother—but now are all doors but this barred against me. If you will but suffer me here in your manor, mistress, I shall not forget that I am come hither without goods and without honour, with naught but goodwill to serve you and Gaute, my master——"

——Then had Kristin taken both the girl's hands ere she herself knew of it:

"God forgive my son the wrong he has done you, my fair child—come in, Jofrid—God help you both, as sure as I will help you all I can!"

* *Ubotamaal,* an offence that cannot be atoned by payment of fine and compensation.

Truly she felt, the moment after, that maybe she had been somewhat over warm in her greeting to this woman she did not know. But now had Jofrid laid aside her outer garments. Her heavy winter dress of sea-blue, homespun wadmal was dripping wet round the bottom, and on the shoulders, where the rain had soaked clean through her cloak. And there was a sad, gentle loftiness about this childlike girl—she bore her little dusky head graciously, bent a little forward, and two thick, coal-black plaits hung down below her waist. Kristin took Jofrid lovingly by the hand and led her to the warmest place on the bench by the fireplace wall: "You must be cold?"

Gaute came forward and took his mother vehemently to his arms: "Mother—things must go as they are doomed to go—saw you ever so fair a maid as my Jofrid? I had to have her, whatever it might cost me —and you will be good to her, my dearest mother——"

Lovely was Jofrid Helgesdatter—Kristin could not take her eyes off her. She was short in stature, broad across the shoulders and the hips, but round and fairly fashioned. And her skin showed so soft and clear that she was fair in despite of her dead-white hue. Short and broad were the features of her face, but the cheeks and the wide, strong arch of the chin made it, too, comely, and she had a wide, thin-lipped and bright red mouth with small, even teeth like a child's milk-teeth. And when she lifted her heavy eyelids, her clear, grey-green eyes were like shining stars under her long black lashes.—Black hair, light eyes— Kristin had deemed these the fairest of all, ever since first she saw Erlend—most of her own fair sons had them——

Kristin set Jofrid in a place on the women's bench by her own side. She sat dainty and bashful amid the strange house-folk, ate little, and blushed brightly each time that Gaute drank to her during the meal.

His face shone with pride and feverish happiness as he sat there in his high-seat. In honour of her son's home-coming Kristin had spread a cloth upon the board and set forth two wax candles in candlesticks of gilded copper. Gaute and Sir Sigurd drank to each other without cease, and the old knight grew more and more wrought up, laid his arm round Gaute's shoulder, and vowed to plead his cause with his rich kinsmen, ay, with King Magnus himself—'twould go hard but he would bring Gaute at one with the maid's affronted kinsfolk. Sigurd Eldjarn himself had not an enemy—'twas his father's shrewish temper and his own mis-hap in marriage that had made him so lonely.

At the last Gaute sprang up with the horn in his hand. How proper a man he is, thought Kristin—and how like to father! 'Twas thus her father had been at the beginning of a drinking bout—aglow with joy of life, erect and hearty——

"Now has it so befallen with me and this woman, Jofrid Helgesdatter, that this day we are drinking our home-coming-ale, and have yet to drink our bride-ale hereafter, if God will grant us such good fortune. You, Sigurd, we thank for kinsmanly faithfulness, and you, mother, that you have welcomed us as I looked you would, out of your true, motherly heart—for we brothers oft-times said amongst us, you seemed to us to be the most great-minded of women and the kindest of mothers. Therefore do I beg that you will honour us yet further, and yourself make our bridal bed so fair and stately that I may pray Jofrid without shame to sleep therein with me, and that you will yourself lead Jofrid to the loft, so that she may come to bed in as seemly wise as may be, seeing she has no mother living nor kinswomen here——"

Sir Sigurd was well on in drink now; he broke into a laugh:

"——But you slept together in the loft at my house—I knew no better, I deemed you two had lain in *one* bed before too——"

Gaute tossed his golden mane loftily:

"Ay, kinsman—but this is the first night Jofrid will sleep in my arms here in her own manor—if God so will.

"——But you good folk I pray to drink and be merry to-night—now you have seen her who shall be my wife, and mistress of Jörundgaard— she and no other woman, I swear it by God our Lord and my Christian faith. I look to you to honour her, all of you, both men and women, and I look that you, my men, will help me to hold her and guard her as befits men of mettle."

Amid the shouting and uproar that followed Gaute's speech, Kristin slipped from the board and whispered to Ingrid to come with her up to the loft.

Lavrans Björgulfsön's stately upper hall had fared ill in the years the Erlendssöns were housed there. Kristin had had no mind to throw away aught else than the most needful and the coarsest of bed-gear and loose furnishings on the reckless lads, and she seldom had the hall cleaned out, for 'twas not worth the pains. Gaute and his friends brought in dirt and litter as fast as she had got it swept out. There was a clinging smell as of men-folk who had come in and flung themselves down upon the beds, wet and sweat-drenched and dirty from the forest or the farm; a smell of the stable and of leathern clothes and wet hounds.

Now, hastily, Kristin and the serving-woman swept the room and set it to rights as best they could. And the mistress brought in fine bed-gear, coverlids and pillows; burned juniper to rid the smell, and set the silvern beaker with the last drop of wine she had in the house, wheaten cakes, and a wax taper in a metal candlestick on a little board, and moved it close to the bed. 'Twas as fine here now as she could make it at such short warning.

On the boarded wall by the closet weapons were hanging—Erlend's heavy, two-handed battle-sword and the smaller sword he was wont to wear, broad-axes, and fire-wood axes—and Björgulf's and Naakkve's light hand-axes hung there still. There, too, were two small axes which the boys seldom used, for that they deemed them too light—but with them had her father trimmed and fashioned all kinds of carpentry so featly and surely that 'twas only for finishing he needed to go over the work with gouge and knife. Kristin bore the axes into the closet and laid them in Erlend's chest, where were his bloody shirt and the axe he had in his hand when he got his death-wound.

When Gaute, laughing, bade Lavrans to light the bride up to the loft, the boy was both shamefaced and proud. Kristin saw that Lavrans understood well enough that his brother's lawless wedding was a perilous game, but he was dizzied and wrought up by these strange happenings—and he gazed with sparkling eyes at Gaute and his fair bride.

On the stairs to the loft the candle blew out. Jofrid said to Kristin:

"Gaute should not have craved this of you, even though he was drunken—go no farther with me, mistress. Fear not that I shall forget I am an erring woman, broken away from my kinsfolk's word."

"Too good to serve you I am not," said Kristin, "until my son has made amends for his sin against you, and you can call me mother-in-law with right. Sit you down, that I may comb out your hair—passing fair it is, child, your hair——"

But when the household had gone to rest, and Kristin lay in her bed, she felt again somewhat of disquiet—unwittingly she had been drawn on to say more to this Jofrid than she was sure she meant—yet. But the girl was so young—and she showed so clearly she did not crave to be judged as better than she was—a child who had fled away from honour and duty.

So *this* was how it looked—when folk had their bridal-ride and home-faring come before the wedding. Kristin sighed—once she too had been willing to venture this for Erlend—but she knew not whether she had dared, if his mother had been dwelling at Husaby. No, no, she would not make things worse for the child up there——

Sir Sigurd was still staggering about the hall—he was to sleep with Lavrans—talking, somewhat mistily but with the heartiest goodwill, of the two young folk—he would spare naught that might help them to a good ending of this perilous venture——

The day after, Jofrid showed Gaute's mother what she had brought with her to the manor—two leathern sacks of clothes; in a little casket of walrus ivory she had her trinkets. As if she had read Kristin's thoughts, Jofrid said that all these things were her own—she had got them either as gifts or in heritage, for the most from her mother; she had taken naught that was her father's.

Kristin sat sorrowful, her cheek upon her hand. That night, long ages ago, when she herself gathered together her precious things in a casket that she might steal from home—most of what *she* had laid together were gifts from the father and mother she had beshamed in secret and was planning to grieve and dishonour in full light of day——

——But if these were Jofrid's own possessions, and her heritage, in trinkets alone, from her mother, she must come from a most wealthy home. Kristin would reckon the gear she saw here to be worth more than thirty marks pure silver—the scarlet dress alone, with white fur and silver clasps and the silk-lined cape that belonged thereto, had cost ten to twelve marks at the least. If the maid's father would come to an accord with Gaute 'twould be good and well—but by no reckoning could he be accounted an even match for this woman. And should Helge press the matter home against Gaute as hardly as he had the right and the power to do, then did things look black indeed.

"This ring," said Jofrid, "my mother wore alway—if you will take it, mistress, at my hands, then shall I know you judge me not so hardly as a good and high-born lady well might."

"Nay, then 'twere likest I should strive to stand to you in a mother's stead," said Kristin smiling, and slipped the ring upon her finger. It was a little silver ring set with a fair white agate, and Kristin thought the child must hold it dear above its worth since it minded her of her mother. "Methinks 'tis but reason I should give you a gift in return." —She fetched her casket, and brought forth the gold ring set with sapphires. "This ring his father laid upon my bed when I had brought Gaute into the world."

Jofrid took the ring and kissed her hand: "But I had thought to beg another gift in return from you—mother——" She smiled so winningly. "Be not afraid that Gaute has brought home a slothful and handless woman. But I have no fitting workaday dress. Give me an old one of yours, and grudge me not the right to help you; mayhap then you will soon like me better than I can look you should now——"

But now 'twas for Kristin to show the young girl what she had in her chests, and Jofrid praised all Kristin's goodly handiwork so understandingly that the elder woman gave her one thing and another—two linen sheets with knotted silk fringes, a blue-hemmed towel, a twilled coverlid, and last of all the long tapestry with the hawking picture on it: "Loth would I be that these things should leave this manor—and by God's and Our Lady's help this house will some day be yours." Then 'twas as well they should go across to the storehouses—they spent many hours together there, and the time passed happily.

Kristin would have given Jofrid her green wadmal dress with the inwoven black spots—but Jofrid deemed it all too good for a working

dress. Poor soul, doubtless she was striving to please her husband's
mother, thought Kristin, hiding a smile. At last they found an old
brown kirtle which Jofrid thought would do, if she cut it short below
and put patches under the arms and on the elbows. Naught would
serve but she must straightway borrow a pair of scissors and sewing-
gear, and set her down to sew. Thereon Kristin, too, took up some
work, and thus the two women were sitting when Gaute and Sir Sigurd
came in for the evening meal.

III

KRISTIN avowed with all her heart that Jofrid was a woman who
had good use of her hands. *If* all went well, then Gaute had been
fortunate—he would have a wife who was as hard-working and diligent
as she was rich and fair. She herself could scarce have found a more
notable woman to step into her shoes at Jörundgaard—not if she had
searched all Norway through. So she said one day—and afterwards
she scarce knew how it was that the words had fallen from her lips—
that the day Jofrid Helgesdatter became Gaute's wedded wife, she would
make over her keys to the young woman and move into the old hall
with Lavrans.

Afterwards, indeed, she thought it had been well if she had weighed
the matter more nicely ere she spoke of it. Often already she had been
over-hasty when she spoke to Jofrid——

But one thing was that Jofrid was ailing. Kristin had seen it, well-
nigh as soon as the young girl came to the manor. And Kristin remembered that first winter when she dwelt at Husaby—*she* was a
wedded woman, her husband and her father were bound together in
law, howsoever things might go with their friendship when the wrong
done came to light. Yet had she suffered sore remorse and shame,
had been bitter against Erlend in her heart—and she had been full
nineteen winters old; Jofrid was but a bare seventeen. And here was
she now, carried off by force and rightless by law, far from her home
among strangers, with Gaute's child under her heart. In her heart
Kristin denied not that Jofrid seemed much more strong and stout-
hearted than she herself had been.

But then Jofrid had not profaned the cloister's holiness, nor broken
troth and handfasting, nor lied and deceived and stolen her parents'
honour behind their backs. Even though these two young folks in their
rashness had sinned against the law of the land, against duty and all
seemliness—yet *so* sore a conscience they needed not to have. Kristin
prayed instantly for a good issue to Gaute's deed of madness—and she
comforted her with the thought that 'twas impossible God's justice

could deal out to Gaute and Jofrid a harder lot than had fallen to her and Erlend—and *they* had been wedded; *their* child of sin was born to be lawful partaker in all his kindred's heritage.

Since neither Gaute nor Jofrid spoke of the matter, Kristin would not bring it forward, albeit she longed to speak to the unlessoned young girl: Jofrid ought to save her strength now, lie long in the morning and rest instead of being up and about the first of all on the manor—for Kristin marked that the girl had set her heart on being up before her mother-in-law, and doing more than she did. But Jofrid was not one to whom Kristin could proffer help or pity. She could but quietly take the heaviest work off her hands, and, for the rest, treat her, both when alone and before the house-folk, as though she were by lawful right the young mistress of the manor.

Frida was furious that she must give up her place next to the mistress to Gaute's—she used an ugly word of Jofrid, one day she and Kristin were in the kitchen-house together. For once Kristin struck her serving-woman:

"——Fair words to come from your mouth, old jade that you are and mad after men!"

Frida wiped away the blood from her nose and mouth:

"Should you be no better, great men's daughters like you and this Jofrid, than cottar's children——? You know that a bride-bed with silken sheets awaits you surely enough—*you* must be mad after men and shameless to boot when you cannot wait, but must make off to the woods with young blades and get you road-side brats—fie upon such doings, say I!"

"Be still now—go out and wash you—you are bleeding down into the dough," said the mistress, quietly enough.

In the doorway Frida and Jofrid met. Kristin saw by the young girl's face that she must have heard the words that had passed.

"The poor wretch chatters like the fool she is. I cannot drive her away—she has nowhere to turn her to." Jofrid smiled mockingly, and on that Kristin went on: "She fostered two of my sons."

"Gaute she did not foster," answered Jofrid. "Of that she is never tired of minding both him and me. Can you not have her wed?" she asked sharply.

Kristin could not but laugh.

"Think you I have not tried? But it never went further, when once the man had speech with the bride-to-be——"

Should she seize the chance, Kristin thought, and speak with Jofrid now—let her understand that from her she need look for naught but motherly goodwill? But Jofrid looked so cold and angered——

But yet 'twas plainly to be seen now on Jofrid that she bore another life within her. One day, soon after, she was to clean the feathers for new bolsters. Kristin counselled her to bind somewhat over her hair to keep the down from flying into it. Jofrid tied a linen cloth about her head:

"It becomes me better now, too, than a bare head, I trow," she said, laughing a little.

"That may well be," said Kristin, shortly.

She could not understand that, as things stood with her, Jofrid would jest about it.

Some days after, Kristin came out to the kitchen-house, and saw Jofrid standing there cleaning some black game—already blood had spurted up over her arms. In horror, Kristin pulled her aside:

"Child, you must not touch blood *now*—know you not so much as that even——?"

"Oh, deem you then that 'tis true, all such-like things that women say?" asked Jofrid, doubtingly.

Then Kristin told of the fire-marks that Naakkve had on his breast. Of set purpose she told the tale so that Jofrid might understand she was yet unwed when she watched the church burning.

"You had not thought such things of me, I trow?" she asked, in a low voice.

"Yes, Gaute told me it all—your father had promised you to Simon Andressön, but you ran from home with Erlend Nikulaussön to his mother's sister, and so Lavrans was forced to give consent——"

"Just so 'twas not—we ran not from home. Simon freed me so soon as he knew I loved Erlend better, and on that father gave consent—unwillingly, but he laid my hand in Erlend's—I was his handfasted maid for a year—— Deem you that this was worse?" she asked, for Jofrid was grown burning red and looked at the other aghast.

The girl scraped some blood and fibre from her white arm with the knife.

"Ay," she said, low, but right firmly. "Never had I cast away good name and honour needlessly.—Ay, I shall tell Gaute naught of this," she said quickly. "He believes his father carried you off by force because he could not win you by fair suit——"

Most like she was right, thought Kristin.

As time wore on and Kristin thought and thought upon the matter, it seemed to her 'twere the most honourable way for Gaute to send a word to Helge at Hovland; put his case into his hands and make suit to be given Jofrid to wife on such terms as Helge thought fit to grant them. But when she spoke of this to Gaute, he looked ill pleased and tried to turn the matter aside. At length he asked hotly whether his mother could send a letter over the mountains in winter-time? No, but Sira Dag could doubtless get a letter sent to Nes, and from there along the coast, said his mother; the priests could ever have letters sent forward, even in winter-time. Gaute said 'twould be too costly.

"Then 'twill not be your wife that will bear you a child this spring," said his mother angrily.

"In no case can the matter be set in order so hastily," said Gaute. Kristin marked that he was bitterly wroth.

An ugly, dark fear took hold on the mother as time went on. She could not but see that Gaute's first glowing joy in Jofrid was quite gone; he went about sullen and moody. From the first this matter of Gaute's bride-rape had looked so ill as might be—but his mother deemed 'twould be far worse if the man should now show him affrighted at what he had done. If the two young folk repented their sin, 'twere good and well—but there was an ugly look about it, as though there were here more of unmanly fear of the man he had wronged than of godfearing penitence. Gaute, this one of her sons that she had ever trusted most—it could not be true, as folk had said, that he was untrusty and light with women, that already he was weary of Jofrid, now that his bride was faded and dull, and the time drew near when he must answer to her kinsfolk for his lawless deed.

She made excuse for her son—if *she* could let herself be led astray so easily, she who never had aught before her eyes in her girlhood but the virtuous ways of righteous folk—— Her sons had known from childhood that their own mother had done amiss, that their father in his youth had children by another man's wife, and had sinned with a married woman when they were already great lads. Ulf Haldorssön, their foster-father, Frida's loose talk—oh, strange it was not if these young men were weak in such things—— Wed Jofrid Gaute must, if he could win her kinsfolk's consent—and be thankful—but 'twere pity of the maid if she should see now that Gaute took her because he needs must, against his will.

One day in the fast-time, Kristin and Jofrid were at work making ready the food-wallets for the wood-cutters. They beat the dried fish thin and flat, pressed butter into boxes, filled wooden bottles with beer and milk. Kristin saw that it irked Jofrid sorely now to stand thus on her feet the whole time, but Jofrid did but grow angry when Kristin prayed her to sit down and rest. To please her a little it came into Kristin's mind to ask of that story of the stallion that folk said Gaute had broken in with a maiden's hair-ribbon for bridle: "'Twas yours belike?"

"No," said Jofrid angrily, flushing a deep red. But then her mood changed:

"'Twas Aasa's—my sister's," she said, laughing. "'Twas her Gaute courted first; but when I came home, he knew not which of us he liked the best. But 'twas Aasa he had looked to find at Dagrun's house last summer when he came down to Sogn. And he grew wroth when I teased him about her—swore before God and all men that he was not such an one as would be overbold with good men's daughters—there had been naught more 'twixt Aasa and him, said he, but that he could sleep in my arms that night without sin. I took him at his word——" She laughed again. When she saw Kristin's face, she nodded defiantly.

"Ay, 'twas my will to have Gaute for my husband, and trust me, mother, I shall get him. Things fall out most often so that I get my will——"

Kristin woke in pitch darkness. The cold bit her cheeks and nose —when she drew the skins more closely about her, she felt they were rimy with her breath. It must be well on towards morning—but she shivered at the thought of rising to look at the stars. She curled herself up under the furs to keep warm a little longer. Of a sudden she remembered her dream.

She thought she lay in bed down in the little hall at Husaby and had even now borne a child. It lay in her arms, wrapped in a lamb's skin which had slipped up and twisted about the little dark-red body— its tiny hands it held clenched over its face; the knees were drawn up against its body and the feet crossed—now and again it moved a little. It crossed not her mind to wonder that the boy was not swaddled, and that there were no women in the room with them. The warmth of her own body still enwrapped the child as it lay there close to her; through her arms she still felt it to the very roots of her heart each time the child moved. Weariness and pain lay heavy upon her yet, like a darkness that begins to pass away, while she lay looking on her son, and feeling joy and love of him grow unceasingly, as the dawn-rim brightens along a mountain ridge——

But at the same time as she lay there in the bed, she was standing without too by the house wall. Beneath her lay the country-side shining in the morning sun. 'Twas early morning of a day between winter and spring—she drank in the sharp, fresh air—the wind was icy cold, but in it was a smack of the far-off sea and of melting snow; the ridges right across the dale lay in the morning sun, with snowless patches around the farms, and the crusted snow shone silvery white in all the clearings amid the dark-green woods. The sky seemed freshly swept, clear yellow and pale blue, with some few dark, wind-driven cloud-wisps swimming over it—but 'twas cold; where she stood the snow-drift was stone-hard still from the night's frost, and between the houses lay cold shadow, for the sun stood just above the eastern ridge behind the manor. And right in front of her, where the shadow ended, the morning wind moved the wan, last-year's grass; it waved and shone, though steely-bright ice clumps still bound its roots.

Ah!—ah! The moan burst from her breast against her will. Lavrans she had with her still—she heard the boy's even breathing from the other bed. And Gaute—he lay there in the loft, with his paramour. The mother sighed again, moved restlessly, and Erlend's old dog on the bed-spread shifted itself closer against her up-drawn legs.

Now she heard that Jofrid was afoot in the loft, walking about the floor. Kristin crept out swiftly, thrust her feet into her shaggy fur shoes, and threw on her wadmal dress and fur coat. In the dark she groped her way to the fireplace, squatted down, and blew and raked in the ashes; but there kindled no least spark—the embers had died out in the night.

She drew out the flint and steel from her belt-pouch, but the tinder must have got wet—'twas frozen. At last she gave up the struggle, took the fire-pan and went up to borrow live embers from Jofrid.

A good fire was burning in the little fireplace of the loft, casting its shine out into the room. In the flickering light Jofrid sat sewing the copper buckle more firmly upon Gaute's reindeer coat. Over in the twilight of the bed she could make out the man's naked breast and shoulders—Gaute slept without a shirt even in the bitterest cold. He was sitting up—he had had his morning bait in bed.

Jofrid rose, heavy and matronly—would not mother have a draught of ale? She had warmed up Gaute's morning drink. And mother must take this can to Lavrans—he was to go with Gaute to the timber-felling to-day. 'Twould be cold for the men——

Kristin pursed up her lips and misliking, as she stood in her own room again making up the fire. Jofrid's housewifely busyness, Gaute lying there openly having his woman wait on him—the paramour's thoughtful care for her unrightful brother-in-law—it all seemed to her so immodest and disgustful——

Lavrans stayed behind out in the woods, but Gaute came home to the evening meal, tired and hungry. So the women sat on for a little after the serving-folk had gone out, to keep the master company while he drank.

Kristin saw that 'twas not well with Jofrid this evening. Of a sudden the girl let her sewing sink upon her lap, and twinges of pain passed over her face.

"Are you in pain, Jofrid?" asked Kristin, low.

"Oh, ay, a little—in the feet and legs," answered the girl. She had worked all day long, as was her wont—would hear naught of sparing herself. Now she had got a stitch, and her legs were swollen up.

All at once little tears started out from beneath her lashes. Kristin had never seen a woman weep so strangely—she sat there without a sound, her teeth set hard; and round, bright tears—to Kristin they looked *hard* as pearls—rolled down her marred, brown-flecked face. She seemed angered that she had been forced to give way—unwillingly she let Kristin help her over to the bed.

Gaute came after them:

"Are you in pain, my Jofrid?" he asked, in a chapfallen fashion. He was red as fire in the face from the cold, and he looked on miserably while his mother made Jofrid easy on the bed, drew off her shoes and her hose, and began to tend the swollen feet and legs. "Are you in pain, my Jofrid?" he went on asking.

"Ay," said Jofrid, in a low voice, with smothered rage. "Think you, if I were not, I would bemoan me like this?"

"Are you in pain, my Jofrid——?" he began again.

"Sure you can see it—stand not there gaping like an oaf, boy!" Kristin turned on her son, her eyes flashing. The dull coil in her mind —dread for what might come of it all, impatience at having to suffer the young folks' lawless life here at her manor, gnawing doubts of her son's manhood—burst out in furious wrath: "Are you such a fool, you deem she can be *well*, perchance?—she sees you are not man enough to dare cross the fells, because, forsooth, 'tis blowing and snowing—— You know well that soon she must down upon her knees, this poor little thing, and writhe in the worst of torments—and her child shall be called bastard because you dare not face her father—you sit warming the bench in the hall, and dare not so much as lift a finger to safeguard the wife you have and the child that is coming to you—— *Your* father was not so fearful of my father that he dared not go to have speech with him, nor so afraid of cold that he durst not fare on ski over the fells in winter-time. Fie upon you, Gaute—and woe is me that I must live to call craven one of the sons Erlend begot with me!"

Gaute took the block-chair in both hands, dashed it on the floor, ran to the board, and swept off all that stood upon it. Then he rushed out of the door, with a parting kick to the block-chair—they heard him run cursing up the loft stairs.

"Nay, mother—now have you been over hard with Gaute——" Jofrid raised her on her elbow. "You cannot look with reason that he should peril his life on the fells in winter—to find my father and be told whether he must wed his dishonoured bride with the shift he carried me off in for portion, or flee the land, an outlaw——"

The waves of anger still ran high in Kristin's heart. She answered proudly:

"Nevertheless I scarce believe that *my* son can think so!"

"No," said Jofrid, "—had he not had me to think *for* him——" When she saw Kristin's face, she went on, in a voice that bubbled with laughter:

"Dear mother—hard enough have I had to fight to hold Gaute back —I will not have him do yet more follies for my sake, and part our children from the wealth I can look to have in heritage from my kinsmen, if Gaute can come to such accord with them as will be best and most honourable for us all——"

"What mean you by this?" asked Kristin.

"I mean that if my kinsfolk come in search of Gaute, Sir Sigurd will meet them in such wise that they will see Gaute lacks not kinsmen to back him. He will have to make full amends, but thereafter 'twill be for my father to handfast me to Gaute so that I shall again have right to share with my sisters what he leaves behind——"

"So you yourself must share the blame," asked Kristin, "when your child comes into the world and you still unwed?"

"Since I could flee from home with Gaute, why—— None will believe, now, I trow, that he has laid a drawn sword between us in bed of nights——"

"Has he never at all made suit for you to your kinsfolk?" asked Kristin.

"No; we knew 'twould be in vain, even had Gaute been a much richer man than he is." Jofrid broke into laughter again. "See you, mother, father deems himself the shrewdest of all men at a horse-bargain. But 'twould take a man far more wide-awake than my father to get the better of Gaute Erlendssön in an exchange of horses——"

Kristin could not forbear smiling—unglad though she was at heart.

"I know not the law so nicely in such matters," she said gravely, "but I misdoubt me much, Jofrid, 'twill not be easy for Gaute to come to such an accord as you will call good. Should Gaute be doomed outlaw—and your father take you home with him, and let you feel his wrath—or should he require that you go into a cloister and atone your sins——"

"Send me to a cloister he cannot, without giving such rich gifts with me that 'twere a cheaper bargain and more honourable to make accord with Gaute and take amends from him; see you, so could he wed me off and not need to lay out aught in goods and gear. And methinks, for all the love he bears Olav, my sister's husband, he would be loath that I should not share with my sisters in the heritage. Besides, then my kinsfolk would have this child of mine on their hands too. And I trow that father will bethink him twice ere he tries taking me home to Hovland with a bastard child—to make me feel his wrath—he knows *me*——

"——I know not so much of the law, either; but I know father and I know Gaute. And now so much time has gone by, that this matter can scarce go forward before I am lightened and grown sound again; and then, mother, you shall not see me weep! Oh, no, sure I am Gaute will win for us such an accord as——

"Nay, mother—Gaute, who is come of nobles and kings—and you who are kin to the best houses in the land—if so be you have had to brook seeing your sons sunk down from the place they were born to stand in, yet shall you see your offspring rise in the world again in Gaute's children and mine——"

Kristin sat silent. 'Twas not unlike, indeed, that things might go as Jofrid wished—she saw that she had had no need to grieve so much for the girl. She had grown thin of face now—her cheeks' soft rounding was quite worn away, and all the more clearly could it be seen how large and strong was her lower jaw.

Jofrid yawned, dragged her up into a sitting posture, and looked round for her foot-gear. Kristin helped her to draw them on. Jofrid thanked her:

"And vex not Gaute any more now, mother. He takes it not lightly himself that we cannot be wed before—but I will not have my child made poor before even 'tis born——"

Fourteen days after, Jofrid bore a son, a great and comely boy. Gaute sent word to Sundbu that same day; and Sir Sigurd came at once to Jörundgaard and held Erlend Gautessön at his christening. But, glad as was Kristin Lavransdatter of her son's son, it vexed her none the less that Erlend's name should be renewed for the first time in a base-born child.

"Your father dared more to win his son his rights," said she to Gaute one evening, as he sat down in the weaving-house watching her make the boy ready for the night. Jofrid was sleeping sweetly already in the bed by the wall. "He loved not old Sir Nikulaus over much, yet would he never have honoured his father so little as give his name to a son not born in wedlock."

"No—Orm—'twas after his mother's father, was't not?" asked Gaute. "—Ay, ay, mother, maybe this was no seemly speech of a son. But I trow you can understand that all we brothers marked well, what time our father lived, you deemed not then he could be a pattern for us in all things—but now you speak of him late and early as he had been a holy saint—almost. You wot well that we know he was not that. Proud should we all be if any day we should grow to our father's stature—ay, or to his shoulder—we mind ever that he was a chieftain, and a man outdoing all men in all such gifts as adorn a man—but you cannot make us believe he was the meekest and most virtuous of swains in a lady's bower, or the doughtiest of husbandmen——

"——Yet need none wish aught better for you, my Erlend, than that you may grow to be his like!" He took up the child, who was now swathed up for the night, and thrust his chin down on to the little red face in the bright woollen swaddling-cloth: "This well-gifted and hope-ful youth, Erlend Gautessön, of Jörundgaard—you must tell your grandmother *you* are not afraid your father will fail you——" He made the sign of the cross over the child and laid it back in.Kristin's lap, went over to the bed, and gazed on the slumbering young mother:

"'Tis as well with my Jofrid as can be, say you? She looks pale—but I trow you understand such things best—God's peace and sound sleep to all in this house!"

A month after the boy's birth Gaute held a great christening-ale, and to it his kinsmen gathered from far and near. Kristin guessed that Gaute had trysted them hither to take counsel with them in this pass—'twas spring now, and he might soon look to hear news of Jofrid's kin.

Kristin had the joy of seeing Ivar and Skule at home together. And hither came too her cousins: Sigurd Kyrning, who was wed with her father's brother's daughter from Skog, Ivar Gjesling of Ringheim and Haavard Trondssön. She had not seen the Trondssöns since Erlend had drawn the men of Sundbu along with him into mischance. They were of middle age now: they had ever been careless and light-headed, but high-minded and gallant; and they were little changed—they met both the Erlendssöns and their cousin, Sir Sigurd, who stood in their shoes at Sundbu, with the free and open bearing befitting kinsmen. Ale and mead now ran in rivers in honour of little Erlend; Gaute and Jofrid gave their guests as free and unabashed a welcome as had they been lawfully wed and the King himself had made their marriage—all was mirth, and none seemed to call to mind that the two young folks' honour and welfare were still at hazard. But Kristin learned that Jofrid had not forgotten it:

"The more freely and boldly they meet my father, the easier will he yield him," said she. "And Olav Piper could never hide that he loves full well to sit on the same bench with men of the old houses."

The only one that seemed not wholly happy in this gathering of kinsmen was Sir Jammælt Halvardssön. King Magnus had dubbed him knight this last Yule; Ramborg Lavransdatter now bore the name of lady.

This time Sir Jammælt had his eldest step-son, Andres Simonssön, with him. Kristin had begged this of him, when last Jammælt was north, for she had heard a waif word that the boy was strange. A great dread had fallen on her—could it be that he had taken hurt in soul and body from those dealings of hers with him when he was a child? But his step-father said no, the boy was sound and strong, good as gold—and maybe his wits were better than most folks'—'twas but that he saw visions: he would seem rapt at times, and afterwards would do often the strangest things—even as 'twas last year. He had taken his silver spoon one day—'twas the very one he had from Kristin as a birth-gift—and a shirt-pin that his father left him—and then he went forth from the manor and down to a bridge that is over the river on the highway near Ælin. There he sat waiting for many hours—at last there came over the bridge three beggars, an old man and a young woman, with a suckling-child. Andres goes up to them, gives them the trinkets, and begs leave to bear the child for the woman. At home they were beside themselves with fear, when Andres came not to the midday meal nor yet to supper—they went out and searched the country-side, and at length Jammælt got word that Andres had been seen far north in the neighbouring parish in company with some folk called Krepp and Kraaka; he was carrying their little one. When next day Jammælt got hold of the boy at last, he said, after much asking, that he had heard a voice the last Sunday during Mass, while he stood looking at the picture painted on the panel before the altar. 'Twas God's mother and Saint Joseph journeying with the child to the land of Egypt, and he had wished he had lived in those days, for then would he have prayed that he might have leave to go with them and bear the child for Mary Virgin. Then had he heard a voice, the gentlest and sweetest in all the world, and it promised to show him a sign if he would go to the Bjerkheim bridge on a certain day——

Else was Andres loath to speak of his visions—for their parish priest said they were likely part feigning and part brain-sick wanderings; and he frightened his mother well-nigh from her wits with his strange ways. But he talked much with an old serving-maid, a rarely pious woman, and with a preaching brother who was wont to wander through the parish at Lent and Advent. 'Twas like enough the boy would choose the spiritual life—and so, maybe, 'twould be Simon Simonssön who in time to come would settle down as master at Formo. He was a healthy and a lively child, most like to his father, and Ramborg's darling.

Ramborg and Jammælt had as yet had no children together. Kristin had heard, from folk who had seen her at Raumarike, that Ramborg was grown passing fat and sluggish. She went a-visiting among the richest and mightiest folk in the south-land, but north to her home country she would never come, and Kristin had not seen her only sister since that day of their parting at Formo. But Kristin deemed she could see that Ramborg still nursed the old grudge against her. She lived happily with Jammælt, and he cared for his step-children's welfare with love and forethought. He had taken order that the eldest son of the man who would be his chief heir if he died childless should wed Ulvhild Simonsdatter; thus, at the worst, Simon Darre's daughter would have the good of his estates after him. Arngjerd had been wedded with Grunde of Eiken the year after her father's death; Gyrd Darre and Jammælt had made her as rich a portion as they knew Simon meant to give this child of his, and she was happy, Jammælt said—Grunde let himself be guided in all things by his wife, and they had three fair children already.

Kristin was strangely moved when she saw Simon and Ramborg's eldest son once more. *He* was Lavrans Björgulfsön's living likeness— much more even than Gaute. And in these last years Kristin had had to give up her belief that Gaute was so like her father in his frame of mind.

Andres Darre was now in his twelfth year, tall and slender, fair-haired and comely, and somewhat quiet in bearing; though he seemed healthy and happy of mood, had good strength of body, and a good stomach to his food, save that he would eat no flesh. Somewhat there was that marked him out from other boys, but Kristin could not say *what* it was, though she watched him narrowly. Andres was soon good friends with his mother's sister, but he never let fall aught of his visions, and fell not into any raptures while he was in Sil.

The four Erlendssöns seemed to take pleasure in being together in their mother's manor, but Kristin got but little speech with her sons. When they talked among themselves, she felt that their lives and their concerns were slipping now beyond her range of sight—the two who had come from without had parted them from their home already, and the two who dwelt on the manor would soon, for sure, be taking its governance out of her hands. The meeting fell in the middle of the spring dearth, and she saw now that Gaute must have made ready for it by saving fodder in winter more than was common, and he had borrowed fodder from Sir Sigurd too—but all this he had ordered without taking counsel with her. And all the parleyings about Gaute's affair went on, as 'twere, over her head, even though she sat in the room with the men.

So 'twas little marvel to her when one day Ivar came and said that Lavrans would keep him company when he went back to Rognheim.

Howbeit one day Ivar Erlendssön said to his mother that he deemed 'twere well she should come to him at Rognheim when once Gaute was wedded:

"Signe were a more towardly daughter-in-law to bide in a house with, I trow—and easy for you sure it cannot be to give up the reins here, where you have been wont to rule." For the rest, 'twas plain he liked Jofrid, he and all the other men. Only Sir Jammælt seemed to look upon her somewhat coolly.

Kristin sat with her little grandson in her lap, and thought, easy 'twould scarce be for her either at the one or the other place. 'Twas a hard matter, growing old. So lately, it seemed, 'twas she herself who was the young woman—then it was about her fate that the men's strife and counsels tossed. Now she had drifted into a backwater. And not long ago her own sons had been even as this one here. She bethought her of her dream of the new-born babe—— At this time the thought of her own mother rose often in her mind—her mother that she could not remember as other than an ageing, heavy-hearted woman. Yet she had been young, she too, when she lay and warmed her baby girl with her body's warmth; her mother too had been marked in youth, body and soul, by the bearing and nourishing of children; and she had thought perchance no more than Kristin herself, when she sat with that sweet young life at her breast, that so long as they two lived each single day would lead the child farther and farther from her arms.

"When you yourself had borne a child, Kristin, methought you would understand," her mother had said once. Now she understood that her mother's heart had been scored deep with memories of her daughter, memories of thoughts for her child from the time it was unborn and from all the years a child remembers nothing of, memories of fear and hope and dreams which children never know have been dreamed for them, until their own time comes to fear and hope and dream in secret——

At length the gathering of kinsmen broke up, so far as that some took up their abode with Jammælt at Formo, and some went with Sigurd over to Vaagaa. But at last one day two of Gaute's tenants from south in the Dale came galloping in to the manor with tidings: the Warden was on his way north to seek out Gaute at his home, and the maid's father and kinsmen were in his train. Young Lavrans ran straightway to the stable—— Next evening it looked as though an army was gathered at Jörundgaard: all Gaute's kinsmen were there with their armed followers, and his friends in the parish had come to tryst too.

Then came Helge of Hovland with a great following to crave his right against the ravisher. Kristin caught a glimpse of Helge Duk, as he rode into the courtyard alongside of Sir Paal Sörkvessön, the Warden himself. Jofrid's father was an oldish, tall and bent-backed man of a sickly look—when he lighted from his horse 'twas seen one leg was shorter than the other. The sister's husband, Olav Piper, was short, broad, and thick-set, red of skin and hair.

Gaute went forward to meet them; he bore him gallantly, with head held high—and behind him he had the whole array of kinsmen and friends; they stood in a half-circle before the upper-hall steps, in the midst the two elder men of knightly rank, Sir Sigurd and Sir Jammælt. Kristin and Jofrid watched the meeting from the shed of the weaving-house, but they could not hear the words that fell.

The men went up into the loft, and the two women turned in to the weaving-house. They could not speak. Kristin sat by the hearth-place; Jofrid walked the floor, bearing her child in her arms. Some time went by thus—then Jofrid wrapped a coverlid about the boy and went out with him. An hour after, Jammælt Halvardssön came in to his sister-in-law as she sat there alone, and told her the outcome.

Gaute had proffered to Helge Duk sixteen marks in gold in amends for Jofrid's honour and for carrying her off by the strong hand—'twas the same as Helge's brother had got for his son's life. And he stood ready to espouse Jofrid at her father's hands, making her a fitting morning-gift and extra-gift; but on his part Helge should accord him and his daughter his full forgiveness, so that she should have a like portion with her sisters, and share with them in the heritage. Sir Sigurd, on behalf of Gaute's kin, stood surety that he would keep his bond. Helge Duk seemed willing to fall in with the proffer straightway; but his son-in-law, Olav Piper, and Nerid Kaaressön, who was Aasa's betrothed, spoke against it, and said that Gaute must be the most brazen of all men, to presume to fix terms himself for his wedding with a maid he had dishonoured while she was in her brother-in-law's manor, and thereafter borne away by force—or to crave that she should share in her sisters' heritage.

'Twas easy to see, said Jammælt, that Gaute himself liked but little this haggling over the price he should pay for wedding a well-born maid, whom he had led astray and who had now borne him a son. But 'twas easy to see, too, he had been made to learn both the lessons and the sermon by heart, so that he needed not to read them from a book.

While yet they were in the midst of the parleyings, and friends on

both sides were seeking to bring them to accord, Jofrid came in with
the child in her arms. At that her father broke down, and could not
keep back his tears. So 'twas settled as she had wished.

That Gaute could never have paid such amends was clear; but
Jofrid's portion was so fixed that the one quit the other. Thus, in very
deed, the outcome of the bargain was that Gaute took Jofrid, and got
little more with her than what she had in her wallets when she came to
the manor, while for her extra-gift and morning-gift he gave her by
deed the most of what he owned, his brothers consenting thereto. But
some day great riches would come to him through Jofrid—if, indeed,
the marriage were not childless, said Ivar Gjesling laughing—all the
men joined in the laugh; but Kristin flushed red, for Jammælt sat
listening to all the gross jests that now flew about.

The next day Gaute Erlendssön handfasted Jofrid Helgesdatter, and
forthwith she held her churching, with as much honour as she had been
a wife—Sira Dag said she had a right to this now. Then she journeyed
with the child to Sundbu and abode in Sir Sigurd's ward until the
wedding.

That day month, just after John's Mass,* the bridal was held; 'twas
a brave and a stately one. The morning after, with great solemnity,
Kristin Lavransdatter made over her keys to her son, and Gaute
fastened the bunch to his wife's girdle.

Thereafter Sir Sigurd Eldjarn gave a great banquet at Sundbu, and
thereat he and his cousins, the former owners of Sundbu, solemnly
swore friendship and confirmed the oath with their hands and seals.
With a bounteous hand, Sir Sigurd made gifts from the treasures that
were at his manor, both to the Gjeslings and to all the guests according
to the nearness of their kinship and friendship—drinking-horns, table-
plate, trinklets, weapons, fur robes, and horses. And thus all folk
deemed that Gaute Erlendssön had brought this matter of his bride-
theft to a most honourable issue.

IV

O N E summer morning the year after, Kristin was in the penthouse
in front of the old hearth-room house, setting in order some gear in the
chests that stood there. A noise came to her ears of horses being led out,
and she went and looked forth between the small pillars of the penthouse. One of the house-carls was leading out two horses, and Gaute
came forth from the stable doorway; the child Erlend was sitting astride
his father's shoulder. The bright little face looked out above the man's
yellow hair, and Gaute held the boy's little hands in his great brown

* 24th June.

one up under his chin. He handed the child to a maid who came across the yard, and mounted his horse. But when Erlend screamed and reached up after his father, Gaute took him again and set him on the saddle-bow before him. At that moment Jofrid came from the hall.

"Would you take Erlend with you—whither are you riding?"

Gaute made answer he was bound for the mill—the river was like to carry it away, "—and Erlend has a mind to go along with father, he says."

"Are you out of your wits——?" She caught the boy quickly to her arms, and Gaute laughed loud:

"I believe verily you deemed I meant to take him with me!"

"Ay——" His wife laughed too: "You drag the poor thing about with you everywhere—I well believe you would do as the lynx does—eat the little one up ere you let any other get him——"

She waved with one of the child's hands to Gaute as he rode from the manor. Then she set the boy down on the sward, crouched over him a moment, and talked to him a little, and then ran across to the new storehouse and up to the loft.

Kristin stood still, watching her grandson—the morning sun shone so fair on the little red-clad child. Young Erlend toddled round in rings, gazing down into the grass. Now he grew ware of a heap of chips, and straightway set to work, painfully heaving them about. Kristin laughed.

He was fifteen months old, but forward for his age, his parents thought, for he both walked and ran, and could say two or three words to boot. Now he steered his way straight for the little water-gutter that ran across the bottom of the courtyard and swelled to a purling beck when rain had fallen in the fells. Kristin ran out and took him up in her arms:

"Mustn't—mother will be angry if you wet you——"

The boy pouted—pondering belike if he should cry because he was kept from paddling in the beck, or if he should give in—to get wet was the deadly sin for him—Jofrid was all too strict with him in such-like things. But he looked so sage—laughingly Kristin kissed the boy, set him down, and got her back to the penthouse. But her work went but slowly—for the most part she stood looking out on the courtyard.

The morning sun shone so soft and fair on the three storehouses over against her—'twas as though Kristin had not seen them rightly for a long time past—how brave the houses were, with their loft-balconies adorned with pillars and rich carving. The gilded vane on the gable cross of the new storehouse glittered against the blue haze that hung over the fell behind. This year, after the wet early summer, the grass on the roofs was so fresh and green.

Kristin sighed a little, looked once more on little Erlend, and turned to her chests again.

All at once there came from without a child's wailing cry—she flung down all she had in her hands and rushed out. Erlend stood shrieking, looking from his finger to a half-dead wasp lying on the grass, and back again. When his grandmother lifted him up with pitying words, he shrieked still louder, and when, with yet more sounds of pity and compassion, she bound wet earth in a cold green leaf upon the sting, his wailing grew fearful to hear.

Lulling and caressing him, she bore him into her room, and he shrieked as though his last hour were come—and stopped short in the midst of a yell: he knew the box and the horn-spoon which his grandmother took from the door lintel. Kristin dipped bits of soft bannock in honey and fed him with them, while she went on petting him, rubbing her cheek against his neck, where the fair hair was still short and crinkled from the days when he had lain still in his cradle and worn it away on the pillow. And Erlend had forgotten his woes now—he turned his face up to the woman and offered to pat and kiss her with sticky hands and mouth.

In the midst of these doings, Jofrid stood in the door:

"Have you brought him in?—surely 'twas not needful, mother—I was but up in the loft."

Kristin told of the mischance that had befallen Erlend: "Heard you not how he shrieked?"

Jofrid thanked her mother-in-law, "—but now we will not trouble you longer——" She took the child, that now reached out to its mother and was fain to go to her, and went her way.

Kristin put away the honey-box. Then she sat on, her hands in her lap: the chests in the penthouse might wait till Ingrid came in.

It had been meant that she should have Frida Styrkaarsdatter to wait on her when she moved over into the old hall. But then Frida was wedded off to one of the jackmen who had come over with Helge Duk— a lad that might have been her son.

"'Tis the use in our quarter of the land that our underlings hearken to their masters when they counsel them for their good," said Jofrid, when Kristin marvelled that this match was come about.

"And in this country-side," said Kristin, "the common folk are unused to obey us further than 'tis reason they should, or to hearken to our counsel except 'tis for their good as fully as for ours. 'Tis good counsel I give you, Jofrid, when I pray you to bear this in mind."

"'Tis as mother says, Jofrid," said Gaute—but passing meekly.

——Even before he was wed with her, Kristin had seen that Gaute

was most loath to cross Jofrid. And he was grown to be a most compliant husband.

The mother-in-law denied not that in many things Gaute might do
well to give ear to his wife—she was shrewd, notable, and hard-working
far beyond the common. And *she* was no more wanton than Kristin
herself had been. She too had trodden underfoot her duty as a daughter
and sold her honour, because she could not win the man she had set her
heart on at a cheaper rate; but once she had won her will, she was the
most faithful and modest of wives. Kristin knew that Jofrid loved her
husband passing well—that she was proud of his good looks and of his
noble birth; her sisters were richly wed, but their husbands were best
seen at night when no moon was shining, and of their forefathers the
less said the better, Jofrid let fall scornfully. She was jealous of her husband's welfare and his honour, as she understood them, and at home
she spoiled him all she could—but if Gaute ventured to be of another
mind than his wife in the least of trifles, Jofrid would first agree in such
a fashion that Gaute faltered straightway—and then she would set to
work and talk him round.

But Gaute throve and was content. None could doubt that the two
young folks lived well together. Gaute was happy with his wife, and
both were marvellous proud of their son, and loved him beyond all
measure.

So now everything might have been for the best. If only Jofrid
Helgesdatter had not been—ay, she was niggardly; Kristin could not
call it aught else. Had she not been so, 'twould have vexed Kristin less
that her son's wife was so set on her own will.

The very first autumn, when she was but newly wedded and come to
be the mistress, Kristin had seen at the harvest-time that the work-folk
were ill content—though they scarce said a word. But the old mistress
marked it none the less.

It might have happed in Kristin's time, too, that the folk had to eat
herring that had gone musty, bacon as yellow and high-smelling as fir-
root splints, and tainted meat. But then all had known that the mistress
would surely make up for it with some extra good titbit at another time,
milk-porridge or fresh cheese, and good ale out of season. And when
food came round that had got a bad taste and must be eaten up, all
knew 'twas but the overflow, as it were, of Kristin's bursting storehouses
—and when folk were in sore need, then the abundance of the Jörundgaard storehouses was a blessing to the whole parish. Already folk felt
less sure that Jofrid would prove open-handed in dealing out help in
food, when the common folk felt the pinch of dearth.

This it was that vexed the mother-in-law—for it seemed to minish the
honour of the manor, and of its master.

That even in this one year she herself had been made to feel that her daughter-in-law favoured her own part unduly was a thing that touched her less nearly. It had shown already at Bartholomew's Mass,* when she had been given two of the slaughtered goats instead of the four she should have had. True, the glutton had made havoc among the small stock in the fells that summer—still Kristin deemed it shameful to take count of two goats on so great a manor; but she held her peace. And 'twas the same with all her dues from the manor—autumn slaughtering, corn and flour, fodder for her four cows and two saddle-horses—she was ever given short measure or poor wares. She marked that Gaute misliked this and was ashamed—but he dared not do aught for fear of his wife, and so he made as if he saw it not.

Gaute was as open-handed as were all Erlend Nikulaussön's sons. In his brothers the mother had called it wastefulness. But Gaute was a worker, and content with little for himself—had he but the best of horses and hounds and some good hawks, he cared not, for the rest, to live in other wise than the small farmers of the Dale. But, if folk came to the manor, he was a free-handed host to guests of every kind, and bountiful to beggars—and therein he was a house-master after his mother's heart; 'twas thus she deemed great folk should live who dwelt upon their udal lands in their own country-side, making their goods yield increase, wasting naught uselessly, but neither sparing aught when love of God and of His poor, or care for the honour of the house, required that they should give from their store.

She saw now that Jofrid set most by Gaute's rich friends and kinsmen of worship. Howbeit in this matter Gaute seemed least willing to be guided by his wife—he tried to hold fast to the old comrades of his youth —brother tipplers, Jofrid called them; and indeed Kristin learnt now that Gaute had been somewhat wilder than she knew of. But those friends came not unbidden to his manor after he was become a wedded man. And so far 'twas sure no poor man had been sent away empty by Gaute. But he gave much smaller gifts when Jofrid was looking on. Behind her back he would give more, as 'twere by stealth. But 'twas not much that could happen behind Jofrid's back.

And Kristin saw that Jofrid was jealous of her. His mother had had Gaute's friendship and trust so wholly and fully all these years, since he was her poor sick child that was able neither to live nor die. Now she marked that Jofrid liked it not if Gaute sat him down by his mother, asked her counsel, or got her to tell stories as in the old days. If the man forgot the time, and lingered a little by her down in the old hall, 'twould not be long ere Jofrid found an errand thither——

* 24th August.

And she would grow jealous if her mother-in-law made too much of little Erlend.

——Out in the yard there grew in the short, trodden grass certain herbs with coarse, dark, leathery leaves. But now, in the sunny days of midsummer, there sprang a little stalk, with clear, pale-blue flowerets, up from the middle of each flattened whorl. To Kristin it seemed that the old outer leaves, scarred as they were by every foot of man or beast that had trampled them, must love the sweet bright flowering heart-shoot even as she loved her son's son.

He seemed to her to be life of her life and flesh of her flesh, as surely as her own children, but yet more sweetly. When she had a chance to hold him in her lap, and saw that the boy's mother watched the two jealously the while, took him away as soon as for shame's sake she might, laid him, secure in her ownership, to her breast, and pressed him to her greedily—then it dawned on Kristin Lavransdatter as never before that the preachers of God's word were right. The life of the body was tainted with unrest beyond all cure; in the world where men mixed, begot new generations, were driven together by fleshly love, and loved their own flesh, there came heart-ache and broken hopes, as surely as rime comes in autumn; both life and death sundered friends at last, as surely as winter parts the tree from its leaves.

Now it befell one evening, fourteen days before Olav's Mass,* that a band of mumpers came to Jörundgaard, and prayed the loan of a house for the night. Kristin was standing on the balcony of the old storehouse —it was to be at her disposal now—she heard Jofrid come out and answer the beggars: food they should have, but she could not give them shelter: "We ourselves are many, and we have our mother-in-law living on the manor—she has the half of the houses——"

Wrath flamed up in the one-time lady of the manor—never had it happed before that wayfarers had been denied a night's shelter at Jörundgaard—and the sun was already touching the western ridges. She ran down and went across to Jofrid and the beggars:

"They can have lodging in my house, Jofrid, and, being there, 'twill be well I should give them their meat too. Never before on this manor have we denied a fellow-Christian shelter, when he asked it in God's name."

"Do as you think fit, mother," answered Jofrid, fiery red in the face.

When Kristin had looked more nearly at the beggars, she well-nigh repented her proffer—'twas not quite without reason that the young wife was loath to have these folk on the manor overnight. Gaute and the house-folk were away on the far meadows up by the Sil water, and

* 29th July.

would not be home at even; Jofrid was alone at home, with the parish
bedes-folk, an old couple and two children, and Kristin and her servant
in the old hall. And many and strange as were the kinds of folk Kristin
was used to see in wandering bands of beggars, she liked the looks of
these but ill. Four were big and strong young men—three of them red-
haired, with small wild eyes. These seemed to be brothers; but the
fourth, who had had both his nostrils slit and wanted his ears, spoke a
broken tongue, as though he were an outlander. Besides these these
were two old folks—a little crooked fellow, yellowish-green in face, hair,
and beard from dirt and age, with belly swollen as from some ailment—
he went on crutches—and an old woman, her neck and hands covered
with sores, and her head-cloth reeking with blood and matter. Kristin
shuddered at the thought that this creature might have come near to
Erlend. But, none the less, 'twas well for these wretched old folk that
the band should not need to wander about the Hammer-fells that night.

But the beggars behaved them peaceably enough. Once the earless
one tried to catch a hold of Ingrid as she was setting food on the board;
but Björn straightway bristled up and growled. For the rest they
seemed out of heart and weary—they had suffered much ill and got but
little gain, they answered to the mistress's questioning—'twould be
better at Nidaros maybe. The woman was pleased when Kristin gave
her a goat's horn full of good grease made of purest lamb's fat and little
children's water—but she would not have it when Kristin offered to
steep her head-clout in warm water and to give her a clean linen cloth—
the cloth, indeed, she took.

All the same, Kristin had Ingrid, the young serving-maid, sleep innermost in her bed. Once or twice during the night Björn growled, but
else all was still. A little after midnight the dog ran to the door and gave
a couple of short barks—Kristin heard hoof-beats in the courtyard, and
knew that 'twas Gaute coming home. She guessed that Jofrid had sent
word to him.

Kristin filled the beggars' wallets well the next morning; and they
were gone but a little way beyond the manor gate when she saw Jofrid
and Gaute making for her house.

Kristin sat her down and took up her spindle. She greeted her children fairly when they came in, and asked Gaute about the hay. Jofrid
sniffed—the guests had left a fusty smell behind them. But her mother-
in-law made as if she marked naught. Gaute shifted about uneasily and
seemed to find it hard to bring out his errand. On that Jofrid took the
word from him:

"There is one matter, mother, that I deem 'twere best we spoke of
now. I see well you think that I am more saving than you deem befits
the mistress of Jörundgaard. I know that you think this, and you deem

that I minish Gaute's honour thereby. Now I will not say aught of how I was afraid last night to take in this band, seeing that I was alone on the manor with my baby child and a few old parish folk, for I saw you understood it, so soon as you had come to sight of your guests. But I have marked before, too, that you deem I am a niggard with food and ungentle to the poor.

"I am not so, mother; but Jörundgaard is no longer the seat of a king's man and a rich man, as it was in your father's and mother's time. A rich man's child were you; you went about amongst rich and mighty kinsfolk; you were wedded richly, and your husband lifted you up to yet greater power and station than you were brought up to. None can look that you should fully understand in your old age how far otherwise it is with Gaute, who has lost his father's heritage, and who must share the half of your father's riches with many brothers. But *I* dare nowise forget that I brought little more to his estate than the child I bore beneath my heart, and a heavy burden of amends for my love to pay—seeing that I was party to the wrong he wrought my kin. Time may make that good—but 'tis my duty to pray God to grant my father long life. We are young folk, Gaute and I, we know not how many children 'twill be our lot to have—— You *must* believe, mother-in-law, I have no other thought in all I do but for the good of my husband and our children——"

"I believe it, Jofrid." Kristin looked gravely into her daughter-in-law's flushed face. "And never have I meddled with your householding, nor denied that you are a notable woman and a good and faithful wife to my son. But you must let me deal with my own as I am used to do. As you say, I am an old woman, and no longer apt to learn new ways."

The young folk understood that the mother had naught more to say to them, and soon after took their leave.

As ever, Kristin felt she must own that Jofrid was right—at first. But when she bethought her, it seemed to her—no, right she was not, after all; 'twas against reason to liken Gaute's alms with her father's. Gifts for the soul's peace of the poor and strangers dying in the parish; dowry gifts to fatherless maids; ale-feasts on the holy-days of her father's best-loved saints; doles to sick folk and sinners journeying to seek Saint Olav—even had Gaute been much richer than he was, none had looked that he should put himself to such costs; Gaute thought no more of his Maker than he needs must. He was free-handed and good-hearted; but Kristin had seen that her father held the poor he helped in reverence, because Jesus had chosen a poor man's lot when He came in the flesh. And her father had loved hard work and deemed that all handicraft was honoured, since that God's mother, Mary, chose to be a working-woman who spun to win bread for herself and hers, though she was a daughter of rich folk and came of the kindred of the kings and high-priests of the Jewish land.

Two days after, early in the morning, while Jofrid was still going about half clad and Gaute lay abed, Kristin came in to them. She had on a kirtle and cloak of grey wadmal, wore a wide-brimmed, black felt hat above her coif, and strong shoes upon her feet. Gaute flushed deeply when he saw his mother in this garb. Kristin said she was minded to go afoot to Nidaros to Saint Olav's feast, and she prayed her son to see to her affairs the while.

Gaute strove eagerly to shake her purpose—he would have had her at least borrow horses and groom from him and take her serving-maid with her—but, as was most like, coming from a man lying in his naked bed before his mother's eyes, his words carried little weight. So abashed was he, that in pity Kristin bethought her to say she had had a dream. "I think long, too, till I see your brothers again——" but at that she had to turn her away; she had not yet dared to confess to her own heart how she yearned and feared to meet her two eldest sons again.

Gaute was set on bearing his mother company the first part of her way. While he dressed himself and had a bite of food, Kristin sat laughing and playing with little Erlend—he crowed, and chirped, new wakened and in a twitter with morning life. She kissed Jofrid at parting, and this she had never done before. In the courtyard all the household was gathered—Ingrid had spread the tidings that mistress Kristin was going on pilgrimage to Nidaros.

Kristin took the heavy, iron-shod staff in her hand, and, as she would not ride, Gaute laid her double wallets across his horse and drove it on before him.

Up on the church-green Kristin turned about and looked down upon her manor—so fair it lay in the dewy, sun-bright morning. The river shone white. The house-folk stood there yet—she could make out Jofrid's light dress and coif, and the child, a patch of red, upon her arm. Gaute saw his mother's face grow pale with the fullness of her heart.

The road bore upwards through the woods under the shadow of Hammer-fell. Kristin walked as lightly as a young maid. She and her son spoke not much together. And when they had walked for two hours, they came where the way bears off over Rostkampen, and the whole Dovre country-side lies spread before one northward. Then Kristin said Gaute must go no farther with her; but she would sit a while and rest before going on.

Down beneath them lay the Dale, with the river's greenish-white riband wandering through it, and the farms like small green patches on the forest-covered slopes. But higher up the upland mosses arched, brownish or yellow with lichen, inward towards the grey screes and the bare heights flecked with snow-drifts. Cloud shadows drifted over the Dale and the uplands, but northward all was clear among the fells; the heaped-up hills had flung off their cloaks of mist, and shone blue, one behind the other. And Kristin's yearning moved with the cloud-flocks northward on the long road that lay before her, hurried over the Dale, in among the great mountains that blocked the way, and along the steep tracks across the uplands. A few days more, and she would be wending her way downward through Trondheim's rich, green dales, following the river's windings towards the great fiord. She shuddered at the memory of the well-known places by the sea, where she and youth had gone about together. Erlend's fair form moved before her sight, with changing looks and bearing, swift, unclear, as though she saw him mirrored in running water. Last of all she would come forth on Feginsbrekka, by the marble cross—and there would lie the town by the river mouth, between the blue fiord and the green ridge of Strind, and on the river bank the mighty, shining church with dizzy towers and golden vanes, the evening sunlight burning on the rose midway on its breast. And far up the fiord, under Frosta's blue hills, lay Tautra, low and black like a whale's back, the church tower standing up like the steering-fin. Oh, my Björgulf; oh, Naakkve——

But when she looked back over her shoulder, she could still see a little of the home fell below Hövringen. It lay in shadow, but her well-used eye could see where the sæter path went through the woods. She knew the grey mountain-tops that rose above the cloak of forest—they ringed about the Sil dwellers' old sæter fields.

From the hills above came stray notes of a cow horn—a few clear high tones, that died away and came again—it sounded like children practising them in blowing. Far off tinkling of bells—and the muffled roar of the river, and the deep sighs of the forest in the still, warm day. Kristin's heart trembled with unrest in the stillness. She was drawn as with home-sickness onward, as with home-sickness backward to the parish and the manor. Visions swarmed before her sight—pictures of daily life: she saw herself running with the goats on the path through the sparse woods south of their sæter—a cow had got mired in the bog —the sun shone brightly; when she stood a moment and listened, she felt her own sweat bite into her skin. She saw the courtyard at home in a flurry of snow—a grey day of storm, darkening into a wild winter night—— She was all but blown back into the outer room when she opened the door, the storm took her breath away; but there they loomed up, two shapeless bundles of men in snow-smothered fur coats:

Ivar and Skule had come home. Their ski sank deep into the big drift that ever heaped itself together right across the yard when 'twas blowing from the north-west. On such days there were always deep drifts in two places in the courtyard—and all at once 'twas as though she must think with love and longing of these two snowdrifts that she and all folk on the manor had cursed each winter—'twas as if she were doomed never to see them more.

It seemed as if these yearnings burst her heart in sunder—they ran hither and thither like streams of blood, seeking out ways to all places in the wide-stretched land where she had lived, to all the sons she had wandering in the world, to all her dead beneath the moulds—— She wondered—could it be that she was fey? She had never felt the like of this before——

Then she saw that Gaute was sitting staring at her. And she smiled quickly, as if in excuse—'twas time they should say farewell, and she go on her way.

Gaute called to his horse, that had wandered forward grazing along the green track. He ran after it and brought it back, and they said farewell. Kristin had her wallets over her shoulder already, and her son had set his foot in the stirrup—then he turned and took a step forward:

"Mother!" For a moment she looked deep into his beshamed, helpless eyes. "You have not—you have not been over well content this last year, I trow—mother, Jofrid means well, she holds you in great reverence—but mayhap even so I should have said more to her, of what manner of woman you are and ever were——"

"How come you to have such thoughts, my Gaute?" His mother spoke gently and wonderingly. "I know well myself that I am no longer young, and old folk, they say, are hard to please, but so old I am not yet that I have not wit to know your worth, yours and your wife's. An ill thing would I count it were Jofrid to deem it had been all vain and thankless toil, all she has done to spare me from work and care. Think not so of me, I pray you, my son, as to deem I set not all due store by your wife's worth and your faithful, duteous love—if so be I have not shown it as much as you could with reason look for, you must even bear with me, remembering that 'tis the way of old folk——"

Gaute stared at his mother, open-mouthed—"Mother——" Then he burst into tears, and leaned against his horse, shaking with sobs.

But Kristin kept a firm hold on herself; her voice bewrayed naught but wonder and motherly kindness.

"My Gaute, you are young in years, and true it is that you were my pet lamb, as your father was wont to say. But none the less you must not take this parting thus, son, now you are a man grown and the

master of a house. If I were bound for Rome or Jerusalem, then indeed
—but on this journey I shall scarce meet with such great perils—I shall
find folk to bear me company, you know, for sure when I come to
Toftar, if not before. For each morning at this season pilgrim troops
set out from thence——"

"Mother, mother—forgive it us! so as we took all power and all rule
out of your hands, thrusting you aside——"

Kristin shook her head with a little smile: "I fear me you children
must deem me a woman over fond to rule——"

Gaute turned him to her: she took his hand in one of hers and laid
her other hand on his shoulder, while she begged him once more to
believe she was not unthankful to him or Jofrid, and prayed that God
be with him. Then she turned him round towards his horse, and
laughingly smote him between the shoulders for good luck.

She stood looking after him, till he sank from sight below the brow
of the hill. So comely as he was on the big, dark-grey horse.

She felt her mood a strange one—all things without her came so
sharply to her sense: the sun-steeped air, the warm breath of the pine
wood, the twitter of tiny birds in the grass. Yet at the same time, looking within herself, she saw pictures like the visions that high fever bring-
—within her was an empty house, wholly soundless, dark, and breathing desolation. The vision changed—a strand at ebb, the tide far withdrawn from it; pale, worn stones; heaps of dark, lifeless tangle; all
kinds of driftage——

Then she settled her bag more easily on her shoulder, grasped her
staff, and set forth on her way down into the Dale.—If 'twere not fated
that she should come hither any more, then 'twas God's will—useless
to be afraid. And most like 'twas but that she was growing old——
She crossed herself and went her way with firmer step—willing all the
same to get down to the hill-slopes where the road ran among the
farms.

Only from one short stretch on the highway could one see the houses
at Haugen, high on the topmost mountain ridge. Her heart set to
throbbing at the thought.

As she had thought, she met with pilgrims not a few when she came
to Toftar late in the day. Next morning they made a little troop as
they set off up the fells in company.

A priest, with his servant, and two women, his mother and sister,
were on horseback and soon were far ahead of those on foot. Kristin
felt a pang in her heart as she looked after the second woman, who
rode between her two children.

In Kristin's company there were two oldish yeomen from a little farm here on Dovre. Then there were two younger men from Oslo, craftsmen of the city, and a farmer with his daughter and her husband; quite young people, these two; they were journeying with the young folks' child, a little maid, a year and a half old maybe, and had a horse they rode by turns. These three were from a parish far south in the land, Andabu by name—Kristin knew not where it was. That first evening Kristin begged to look at the child, for it cried and whimpered without cease—it looked wretchedly, with a great, hairless head and small, slack-jointed body; it could neither speak nor sit upright yet. The mother seemed ashamed of it—and when next morning Kristin proffered to bear her daughter a while for her, she was left with it on her hands—the mother pushed on far in front; she seemed to be a cuckoo mother. But they were over young, both she and her husband, scarce eighteen years old, and she might well be weary of bearing a heavy child that was ever puling and weeping. The grandfather was an ugly, sulky, cross-grained man; but 'twas he who had been set on journeying to Nidaros with his daughter's daughter, so he seemed to have some kindness for her. Kristin walked beside him and the two Franciscan monks at the tail of the troop—and it vexed her soul that the man from Andabu never thought to lend the monks his horse a while—all could see that the younger monk was grievously sick.

The elder, Brother Arngrim, was a round little man, with a round, red, freckled face, lively brown eyes, and a foxy-red ring of hair about his pate. He talked endlessly, most of the poverty they lived in, the barefoot monks of Skidan—the order had but newly got a house in that town, but they were so parlous poor they were scarce able to keep going the services, and the church they had been minded to build would never come to aught for sure. He laid the blame on the rich nuns of Gimsöy, who pursued the poor begging friars with envy and spite, and now had a suit at law against them; with glib-tongued relish he told all kinds of evil tales about them. Kristin misliked to hear the monk talk in this fashion, and his tales of how 'twas said their abbess had been chosen uncanonically, and how the nuns missed the offices in slothful slumber and were given to tattling and to unchaste talk over the board in the refectory, seemed to her little to be trusted—ay, of one sister he said right out that folk deemed she had not kept her vows of chastity. But she saw that Brother Arngrim was otherwise a good-hearted and kindly man. He bore the sick child long stretches when he saw that Kristin's arms were weary, and, when it screamed too grievously, he would set off at a run over the upland, with his gown kilted high, so that the juniper flogged his black, hairy legs and the mire splashed up from the bog holes, while he shouted and bawled to the mother that now she must bide for them, for the child was thirsty. Then he trotted back to the sick man, Brother Torgils; to him he was the tenderest and most loving of fathers.

With the sick monk 'twas impossible to come to Hjerdkinn that night; but the two Dovre men knew of a stone hut by a tarn a little southward in the waste, and the pilgrims made towards it. The evening was grown cold by now. The ground by the edge of the water was swampy, and white mist rose from the marsh, so that the birch trees dripped with wet. A thin sliver of moon hung over the mountain-tops in the west, its pale yellow scarce showing in the yellow evening sky. More and more often Brother Torgils was forced to stand still; he coughed so sorely 'twas pitiful to hear. Brother Arngrim held him up in these bouts, and after wiped his face and mouth, then with a shake of the head showed Kristin his hand—'twas bloody with the sick man's spittle.

They found the hut, but it had fallen into ruin. So they sought out a sheltered spot and made them a bonfire. But the poor folk from the south had not thought that night on the fells would be so icy cold. Kristin took from her sack the cloak that Gaute had forced upon her because 'twas so passing light and warm—of fine boughten cloth, lined with beaver fur. When she wrapped Brother Torgils in it, he whispered —he was so hoarse he could scarce speak—that he would be fain to have the child lie in it with him. So they put the child in with him; it whimpered and wailed, and the monk coughed; but between-whiles both of them got some sleep.

Part of the night Kristin kept watch with one of the Dovre men and Brother Arngrim, looking to the fire. The pale yellow light drew round to the northern sky—the tarn lay at their side white and still; fish rose and made rings upon the water—but under the hill on the farther side the water mirrored black darkness. Once an uncanny barking screech came to their ears from over there—the monk started and gripped the other two hard by the arms. Kristin and the farmer deemed 'twas some beast—then they heard a stone roll, as if someone was walking on the hill-side screes, and another cry like a gruff voice of a man. The monk began to pray aloud—she caught the words: "*Jesus Christus, Soter*," and "*vicit leo de tribu Juda*"*—then they heard a door shut to, away under the mountain.

The faint grey dawn began to show, the scree across the lake and the clumps of birch came into sight—then the other Dovre man and the man from Oslo took their place. The last thing Kristin thought, ere she fell asleep, close in to the fire, was that, should they make such short marches—and give an alms to the beggar monks she must when they parted—'twas like she would have to beg her meat at the farms when they came down into Gauldal.

* Jesus Christ, the Saviour.—The lion of the tribe of Judah has conquered.

The sun was well up already, and the morning wind was darkening the lake in little squalls, when the frozen pilgrims gathered about Brother Arngrim while he said the morning prayers. Brother Torgils sat crouched together, with chattering teeth, striving to keep back his cough as he mumbled the words over after him. When she looked at the monks' ashen-grey gowns with the sun shining on them, Kristin called to mind that she had dreamed of Brother Edvin—she could not remember her dream, but she kneeled and kissed the monks' hands and prayed for their blessing on the company.

The sight of the beaver-skin cloak had shown the other pilgrims that Kristin was not come of small folk. And when she chanced to say that she had journeyed twice before by the king's highway over the Dovre-fjeld, she became a sort of guide and leader to the band. The Dovre men had never been farther north than to Hjerdkinn, and the folk from Viken were, of course, quite strange here.

They came to Hjerdkinn before the hour of vespers, and, after the service in the chapel, Kristin went out into the hills alone. She would fain have found again the path she had followed with her father, and the spot by the beck where she had sat with him. These she could not find, but she deemed she had found the hillock she had clambered up that she might gaze after him as he rode away from her. So she thought —but the little stony ridges along the pathway here were much alike.

She knelt amid the bearberry vines at the top of the knoll. The summer evening was growing dusk—the birch-tree slopes on the hill-sides, the grey screes, and the brown stretches of marshland melted together, but, above the wide-stretched mountain waste, the evening sky arched its clear, fathomless bowl. All the pools shone whitely, and the heavenly brightness was given back, broken and more faint, from the little mountain beck that hurried, chafing restlessly over stones, to flow out between pale gravel banks into a little moorland tarn.

Again there came upon her that strange, feverish inner vision—the stream seemed to show her a picture of her own being; thus had she hurried restlessly through the waste of these earthly years, foamed up in turbulent chafing at every stone in her path—'twas but weakly and fitfully and palely that the everlasting light could mirror itself in her life.—But it dawned upon the mother dimly, that in anguish, and care, and love—each time the fruit of sin ripened into sorrow—it had been granted to her earth-bound, wilful soul to catch a reflection of the heavenly light.

Hail, all hail, Mary, rich in mercy! Blessed art thou among women, and blessed the fruit of thy womb, Jesus, who gave His sweat and blood for our sake——

While she said over the five Aves in memory of the redemption's mysteries of pain, she felt 'twas through her sorrows only that she dared seek shelter under the cloak of God's mother. Her sorrow for the children she had lost, her heavier sorrows for each stroke of fate that fell upon her sons and that she could not ward from them. Mary, the perfect in purity, in meekness, in obedience to the Father's will, had sorrowed the most of all mothers, and her mercy would see and understand the pale and weak reflection from a sinful woman's heart, that had burned with hot and ravaging fleshly love and with all the sins that fleshly love brings with it—untowardness and defiance, a stony, unforgiving spirit, stubbornness, and pride—yet was a mother's heart in despite of all.

Kristin hid her face in her hands. For a moment it seemed to her more than she could bear, that she was parted now from them all— from all her sons.

Then she said over the last Paternoster. She thought of her parting from her father on this spot all those long years agone, of her parting from Gaute but two days back. In childlike thoughtlessness her sons had offended against her—yet she knew that, even had they offended against her as she against her father—wilfully and in sin—it could never have changed her heart toward them. 'Twas easy to forgive one's children——

Gloria Patri et Filio et Spiritu Sancto—she said the words, and kissed the cross her father had given her, humbly thankful to feel that, despite of all, despite of her ungoverned spirit, yet had it been granted to her restless heart to catch a faint gleam of the love she had seen mirrored in her father's soul, clear and still, even as the brightness of the sky was thrown back now by the great still moorland tarn.

Next day the weather was so grey and windy and cold, with mist and rain-storms, that Kristin deemed she scarce dared go on with the sick child and Brother Torgils. But the monk himself was the most eager —she saw he was fearful he might die ere he came to Nidaros. So they took their way across the upland; but the fog was so thick at times that Kristin dared not venture down over the headlong tracks, with cliffs both above and below, that she remembered led down to the pilgrims' shelter in Drivdal. So they built a fire when they were come to the top of the glen and rested there for the night. After evening prayer Brother Arngrim told them a goodly saga of a ship in peril of the sea that was saved by an abbess's prayers to Mary Virgin; the morning star came out over the sea at her command.

The monk seemed to have taken a liking to Kristin. While she sat by the blaze, lulling and hushing the child that the others might get to sleep, he edged close to her and began to tell about himself in a whisper. He was a poor fisher's son, and when he was fourteen years old, he lost his father and brother at sea one winter night, but was saved himself by another boat. He had deemed this a sign and token, and besides he had grown afeared of the sea; and thus the thought came to him that he should turn monk. But for three years more he had had to tarry at home with his mother, and they toiled and starved, and he was ever afeared when in a boat—but then his sister was wed, and her husband took over the house and the share in the boat, and he could betake him to the Minorites of Tunsberg. There they had mocked at him at first for his low birth—but the guardian was kind and stood his friend. And, since Brother Torgils Olavssön was come into the brotherhood, all the monks had grown much more pious and peaceable, for he was passing pious and meek, though he was the best born of them all, of a rich yeoman kindred away in Slagn—and his mother and sisters were most bounteous to the cloister. But since they were come to Skidan, and since Brother Torgils was fallen sick, all things were grown much harder again. Brother Arngrim gave Kristin to understand that he marvelled Christ and Mary would make the path so stony for their poor brethren's feet.

"They chose poverty themselves, while they lived on earth," said Kristin.

"'Tis easy for you to say such things, rich woman as you doubtless are," said the monk angrily. "I warrant you have never proved what it is to go fasting——" and Kristin must even avow that so it was——

When they were come down among the tilled lands, and fared through Updal and Soknadal, Brother Torgils got now a ride and now a drive for stretches of the way; but he grew weaker and weaker, and Kristin's company was ever changing, for folk parted from them and went forward, and new pilgrims came up with them. When they came to Staurin, none of them who had crossed the mountains with her were left in her company, saving the two monks. And in the morning Brother Arngrim came to her weeping, and said that Brother Torgils had had a sore blood-spitting in the night; he could go no farther—now, belike, they would come to Nidaros too late, and would miss the festival.

Kristin thanked the brothers for their company, and for ghostly guidance and help on the journey. Brother Arngrim seemed to be astonished at the richness of her farewell gifts, for his face lighted up— ay, she must have a gift in return from him, he said; he drew forth from his wallet a case with some letters in it. On them was written a goodly prayer with all God's names at the end thereof; an open place was left in the scroll wherein to print the name of the supplicant.

Kristin told herself that 'twas not like the monk should know aught of her, with whom she had been wed, or her husband's fate, even if she gave her father's name. Yet did she pray him to write only: "Kristin, widow."

Down through Gauldal she took the paths on the outskirts of the parishes, for she thought that if she met folk from the great manors it might well befall that one or other would know the sometime mistress of Husaby again, and she was loath to be known, though she scarce knew why. The next day she climbed by the forest tracks up over the ridge to the little church on Vatsfjeld, that was sacred to John the Baptist—but the folk thereabout called it Saint Edvin's.

The chapel stood in an opening in the thick woods; it and the knoll behind were mirrored in a pond that fed the healing spring. A wooden cross stood by the beck, and round about lay crutches and staves, and on the bushes near by hung tatters from old bandages.

About the church was a little fenced-in plot, but the gate was fast shut. Kristin kneeled down without, and thought of the time she had sat within there with Gaute on her lap. Then she was clad in silks, one of the company of bravely clad great folks, men and women, from the country-side all around. Sira Eiliv stood close by, holding Naakkve and Björgulf firmly; in the throng without were her serving-maids and henchmen. Then had it been the burden of her burning prayer, that might this poor, unhappy child but be made whole in body and in wits, she would crave for naught more—not even to be freed herself of the sore hurt in her back that had plagued her since ever the twins were born.

She thought of Gaute, sitting his great iron-grey, a brave and goodly horseman. And she herself—not many women of her age, nigh to half a hundred years, were blessed with such health; she had marked it well on her journey across the mountains. Lord, give me but this and this and this—then will I thank Thee and crave no more than this and this and this——

Never, it seemed to her, had she prayed to God for aught else than that He might grant her her own will. And she had got always what she wished—most. And now she sat here with a bruised spirit—not because she had sinned against God, but because she was miscontent that it had been granted her to follow the devices of her own heart to the journey's end.

She had not come to God with her garland, nor with her sins and her sorrows—not so long as the world still held a drop of sweetness to mix in her cup. But she came now, now she had learned that the world is like a tavern—where he who has naught more to spend from is cast out at the door.

She felt no joy in her resolve—but it seemed to Kristin that 'twas not she herself who had resolved. The poor beggars who came in to her house had come to bid her go forth. Another will than her own had set her in the company of the poor and sick, and bidden her go with them, away from the home where she had been the mistress and had ruled as the mother of men. And if now she obeyed the call without too ill a grace, she knew 'twas because she saw that Gaute would thrive the better when she was gone from the manor. She had bent fate to her will, she had had the lot of her own choice—but her sons she could not fashion after her will; they were as God had fashioned them, and their natures drove them on; striving with them she must be worsted. Gaute was a good farmer, a good husband and faithful father, a doughty man, and as honourable as most folk—but the stuff for a chieftain he was not, nor was he of a mood to long for what she had coveted for him. But he loved her enough to be troubled, when he knew she looked for more from him than he could give. Therefore was she now minded to beg for harbour and sanctuary; though 'twas bitter to her pride to come in such utter poverty that she could bring no offerings in her hands.

But she knew that she was called to come. The fir woods on the knoll stood drinking in the sunlight that sifted through them, and sighing so gently; the little church lay there shut and silent, breathing forth a smell of tar. Yearningly Kristin thought of the dead monk who had taken her hand and led her into the radiance of God's enfolding love when she was an innocent child; had put forth a hand time after time to lead her home from the paths of transgression, both while he lived on earth and since—— And of a sudden she remembered as clear as day what she had dreamed of him that night upon the fell:

She had dreamed that she stood in the sunshine in the courtyard of some great manor, and Brother Edvin came towards her from the hall-house door. His hands were full of bread, and, when he came to her, he broke off a great piece and gave it her—she understood that she had had to do as she had thought, beg for alms when she came down into the parishes; but in some way or other she had joined company with Brother Edvin, and they two were faring on together, begging—— But at the same time she knew that the dream had a two-fold meaning: the manor was not only a great manor, but it seemed to her to betoken a holy place, and Brother Edvin was one of the household there; and the bread which he brought and gave to her was not the simple bannock it looked like—it betokened the host, *panis angelorum*, and she took the bread of the angels at his hands. And now she gave her promise to Brother Edvin's keeping.

v

S o at last she was at her journey's end. Kristin Lavransdatter sat resting on a haycock by the wayside below Sionsborg. There was sunshine and a blowing wind; the part of the meadow that was not yet mown waved red and silky bright with seeding grass. Nowhere but in the Trondheim country were the meadows red like this. Below the slope she could see a glimpse of the fjord, dark blue and flecked with foam; fresh white sea spray dashed up against the bluffs, as far as she could see along the strand below the forest-clad Byness.

Kristin drew a deep breath. After all, 'twas good to be here again; good, though 'twas strange as well to know that she should never go from here any more. The grey-clad sisters out at Rein followed the same rule, Saint Bernard's rule, as the brothers at Tautra. When she rose at cock-crow and went to the church, she would know that now Naakkve and Björgulf too were going to their places in the monks' choir. Thus, after all, she would come to live out her old age with certain of her sons—although not in the fashion she had thought.

She drew off her shoes and stockings and washed her feet in the beck. Into Nidaros she would walk barefoot.

Behind her on the path up the castle hill some boys were playing noisily—they were hard at work below the barbican, trying to find a way into the tumble-down work. When they grew ware of her, they fell to calling down foul words at her, laughing and hooting the while. She made as if she did not hear, till a little imp—eight years old the boy might have been—came rolling down the steep sward and almost bumped into her, shrieking out some ugly words he had picked up in wantonness from the older boys. Kristin turned towards him and said smiling:

"No need to shriek so to let me know you for a troll imp, for I see you have the rolling-breeches* on you——"

When the boys marked that the woman answered, they came bounding down, the whole pack. But they fell silent and abashed when they saw 'twas an ageing woman in pilgrim's garb, and that she chid them not for their bad words, but sat looking at them with great, clear, calm eyes and a stealthy little smile on her lips. She had a lean, round face with broad forehead and small rounded chin; she was sunburnt and much wrinkled under the eyes, but after all she looked not so exceeding old.

So the boldest of the boys took to talking and asking questions to hide the sheepishness of the troop. Kristin felt she could have laughed—these

* See Note 6.

boys seemed so like her own rascals, the twins, when they were small, though she prayed to God that *hers* had never been so foul-mouthed. These seemed to be children of common folk in the town.

And when the moment came that she had longed for all through her journey, when she stood below the cross on Feginsbrekka and looked down on Nidaros, it came not so that she could collect her thoughts for prayer or meditation. All the bells of the town burst forth at that moment to ring to Vespers, and the boys all talked together, wanting to point out all that was before her——

Tautra she could not see, for a squall of wind, with mist and scudding showers, was sweeping over the fjord beneath Frosta.

In the midst of the flock of boys she took the steep path that led down the Steinberg heights—and now cow-bells clinked and herdsmen whooped around them—the cows were bound homewards from the town pastures. At the gate in the town wall across the Nidareid, Kristin and her young attendants had to wait while the cattle were driven through —herdsmen hallooed, shouted, and cursed, oxen butted, cows were crowded and crushed together, and the boys named the owners of this bull or that as they passed. And when they were through the port and were passing towards the town lanes, Kristin had more than enough ado to pick her way with her naked feet amid the cow-dung on the poached-up track.

Some of the boys followed her unbidden even into Christ's Church. And as she stood in the dim forest of pillars and gazed towards the lights and the gilding of the choir, the boys plucked ever at the stranger-woman's gown, and would fain have shown her all such things as most draw children's eyes—from the patches of coloured sunlight falling through the rose-window among the arches, and the tombstones on the floor, to the canopies of costly stuffs above the altars. Kristin was given no peace to collect her thoughts—but each word the boys said wakened the dull yearning in her heart—for her sons first and foremost, but for the manor too, the houses, the outhouses, the cattle—for the toil and the sway of motherhood.

She had still that loathness to be known again of any who had been her friends or Erlend's in days gone by. They were wont ever to be in their town houses at festival tide and to have guests living with them— she shrank at the thought of meeting a company of them. Ulf Haldorssön she must seek out, for, as her bailiff, he had charge of the shares she still had in some farms north of the fells and meant now to give in payment for her commons in the Rein cloister. But 'twas like he would have with him now his kinsfolk from the farm at Skaun; so she must wait. But she had heard that a man who had served among Erlend's men-at-arms in the days he was Warden had his dwelling in a small yard out on

Bratören; he worked with the dolphin- and porpoise-fishers on the fjord, and kept a lodging for seafarers.

When she came thither she was told that all the houses were overfull already; but then came the man himself, Aamunde, and knew her straightway. 'Twas strange to hear him cry out her old name:

"Now I ween—is't not Erlend Nikulaussön's lady of Husaby—all hail, Kristin—how can it be that you are come hither to my house?"

He was full glad that she would be content with such shelter as he could give her for the night, and he promised he would sail her out to Tautra himself, the day after the festival.

Till far on in the night she sat out in the courtyard talking with their one-time house-carl, and it moved her deeply when she marked that they that had been Erlend's men still loved their young chieftain's memory and held it in high honour—again and again Aamunde spoke of him as "young." From Ulf Haldorssön they knew of his hapless death, and Aamunde said, never did he meet any of his old fellows of Husaby days but they drank to the memory of their gallant master—and twice some of them had put their money together and had masses said for him on his death-day. Aamunde asked much after Erlend's sons, and Kristin too asked of old acquaintance. 'Twas midnight ere she got to bed by the side of Aamunde's wife—naught would serve him at first but that they both should give up their bed to her, and at last she was fain to accept with thanks of his proffer that at least she should take his place.

Next day was Olav's Wake. From early morning Kristin walked about the shore by the river mouth, looking at the bustle on the wharves. Her heart beat faster when she saw the Lord Abbot of Tautra step ashore—but the monks who were with him were all elder men.

Long ere nones folk were streaming towards Christ's Church, bearing or holding up their sick and cripples, so that they might come near the shrine when it was borne out in procession next day after High Mass.

As Kristin came up through the booths set up by the fence round the churchyard—they sold, for the most, meat, and drink, wax-candles, and mats woven of rush or birch twigs to lay beneath one on the church floor —she stumbled upon the folk from Andabu, and Kristin took the child while the young wife got herself a draught of ale. At that moment came the procession of English pilgrims with songs and banners and lighted tapers; in the press and crush, as they made their way through the throng of folk by the booths, she lost the Andabu folk and could not find them again.

For long she wandered hither and thither on the outskirts of the crowd, lulling the shrieking child. When she laid its face against her neck and would have comforted it with caresses, it mouthed about and sucked at her skin; she saw that it was athirst, and she knew not what to do. It seemed vain to seek for the mother; she must go down into the streets and ask where she could get it milk. But when she came out on to Upper Langstræte and would have gone northward, there was again a great press of folk—from the south came a train of knights, and at the same time the men-at-arms from the palace marched into the space betwixt the church and the Crossed-friars' House. Kristin was thrust aside into the nearest lane; but here, too, folk were hurrying to the church ahorse and afoot, and the press grew so great that at length she had to take refuge up on a stone dyke.

The air above her was full of the noise of bells—the cathedral chimes ringing out *nona hora*. The child stopped shrieking at the sound—it looked up at the sky, and a gleam of understanding showed in its dull eyes—it smiled a little. Touched with pity, the mother of other children bent and kissed the poor little creature. Then she saw that she was sitting on the stone wall around the garden of the Nikulaus house, their old town mansion.

——Well should she know the stone-built chimney rising through the turf roof—the back of their hall-house. Close by her stood the houses of the spital whose right to share the garden with them had roused Erlend's wrath.

She pressed the stranger-woman's child to her breast, kissed it and kissed it. Then someone touched her knee——

——A monk in the white gown and black cowl of the preaching brothers. She looked down into a pale yellow, furrowed, old man's face —a long, narrow, in-fallen mouth, two deeply sunken, amber eyes.

"Can it be—is it you yourself, Kristin Lavransdatter?" The monk laid his crossed arms upon the dyke and buried his face in them. "Are you here?"

"Gunnulf!" At that he moved his head so that it touched her knee where she sat: "Deem you 'tis so strange that I am here——?" Then she called to mind that she was sitting on the garden wall of this house that had been his first and her own afterwards, and thought, 'twas strange indeed.

"But what child is this you have on your knee—sure, this cannot be Gaute's son?"

"No——" At the thought of little Erlend's healthy, sweet face, and strong, well-made body, she pressed the poor little stranger-child to her, overcome with pity: "'Tis the child of a woman that crossed the fells along with me."

——But then there dawned upon her what Andres Simonssön had seen in his childish wisdom. Filled with reverence, she gazed on the pitiful creature that lay upon her lap.

But now it wept again, and before aught else she had to ask the monk if he could tell her where she could get milk for the child. Gunnulf led her eastward round the church to the House of the Preaching Friars, and got her a bowl of milk. While Kristin was feeding her foster-child, they talked together, but their talk went but haltingly.

"So long a time has gone by, and so much has befallen since last we met," she said sorrowfully. "And heavy to bear for you, too, the tidings must have been—the tidings of your brother?"

"God be merciful to his poor soul," whispered brother Gunnulf in a shaken voice.

Only when she asked about her sons at Tautra did Gunnulf speak something more freely. With great gladness had the convent welcomed these two novices, come of the best kindreds in the land. Nikulaus seemed to have such excellent gifts of mind and made such strides in learning and godliness that the abbot must needs call to mind his noble forefather, the Church's well-gifted champion, Bishop Nikulaus Arnesson. That was in the first days. But a while after the brothers had taken the cowl, Nikulaus had misbehaved him grievously, and had wrought much trouble in the cloister. Gunnulf knew not the causes of the trouble fully—*one* was that Abbot Johannes would not suffer that young brothers should be ordained priests before they were full thirty years old, and he would not depart from this rule for Nikulaus' behoof. And as the reverend father deemed that Nikulaus read and pondered more than sorted with his measure of spiritual ripeness, and that he was breaking down his health with pious exercises, he thought fit to send him to one of the cloister's cattle-farms on Inderö, to work there, under some of the elder monks, at the planting of an apple orchard. Then, 'twas said, Nikulaus had broken out into flat disobedience to the abbot's behests, had charged his brethren with having wasted the cloister's goods in high living, with sluggishness in the worship of God, and with looseness in their talk. The matter, said Gunnulf, was kept, for the most part, within the convent walls, as was but reason; but 'twas said, too, that he had defied the brother whom the abbot appointed to chasten him. For some time he had lain in the penitentiary cell, Gunnulf knew, but since then he had humbled him, when the abbot threatened to part him from Brother Björgulf, and to send one of them to Munkabu—'twas like it had been the blind brother that egged him on. But on this threat Nikulaus had grown meek and contrite.

"'Tis their father's nature that is in them," said Gunnulf bitterly. "None could look that my brother's sons should find it easy to learn obedience, or that they should show steadfastness in the godly life——"

"'Tis as like to be their heritage from their mother," answered Kristin, sorrowfully. "Disobedience was the chief of my sins, Gunnulf—and

I too was unsteadfast. All the days of my life have I longed both to go the right way and to follow my own wildered paths as well——"

"Erlend's wildered paths, mean you?" said the monk, darkly. "'Twas not once only that my brother lured you astray, Kristin; I trow he lured you astray each day you lived with him. Such forgetfulness he wrought in you that you remembered not, when you thought thoughts you yourself blushed at, that you could not hide the thoughts of your heart from an all-knowing God——"

Kristin gazed before her.

"Now I know not, Gunnulf, if you are right in this—I wot not that I have forgotten at any time that God saw into my heart—all the greater, belike, is my sin. And, moreover, 'tis not so, as you deem perchance, that I had most need to blush for my immodest wantonness and for my weakness—rather must I feel shame that my thoughts of my husband were many a time more bitter than the poison of serpents. But like enough it must needs have come to this—'twas you who once said to me, that they who have loved one another with the fieriest desire come in the end to be as two vipers biting each other's tails.

"But it has been my comfort in these years, Gunnulf, as often as I thought how 'twas Erlend's lot to go before God's judgment-seat unhouseled and unholpen, struck down with wrath in his heart and blood upon his hands—that *he* did not grow to be—what you said, and what I became. He bore in mind anger, and wrong done him, as little as he bore aught else in mind—Gunnulf, he was so fair and he looked so peaceful when I had laid his body out—I wot that the all-knowing God knows that Erlend never bore a grudge to any man, for any cause——"

The brother gazed at her with wide-opened eyes. Then he nodded.

After a while the monk asked:

"Know you that Eiliv Serkssön is priest and counsellor to the nuns out at Rein?"

"No?" said Kristin, beaming with gladness.

"I deemed 'twas therefore you had chosen to enter there," said Gunnulf. Soon after, he said that he must go back to his cloister.

The first nocturn was begun already when Kristin came into the church. In the nave and about all the altars there was a throng of folk, but one of the vergers, who saw that she bore a most sickly child in her arms, pushed her forward through the press till she came right in front among the many cripples and sick folk in sorest need, who were gathered in the middle of the church under the great dome and in full view of the choir.

Many hundred lights burned in the church—the church servants took the pilgrims' tapers and fixed them upon the little hillock-shaped towers

studded with spikes, which were set up all down the nave and aisles.
As the light of day died out behind the many-coloured panes of glass,
the church grew warm with the smell of the burning wax, and ere long
it was filled, too, with the sour stench from the rags of the sick folk and
the poor.

When the song of the choir soared under the vaulting, and the organ
pealed, and the noise of flutes, drums, and stringed instruments resounded, Kristin understood why it might be that the church was called
a ship—in the mighty house of stone all these folk seemed to be on board
a vessel, and the singing was like the noise of the sea whereon it was
upborne. Ever and anon it came to rest, as when the billows are stilled,
and a single man's voice bore the lesson out over the listening throng.

The close-packed faces grew paler and more weary as the wake-night
wore on. Scarce one went out between the services, not at least of those
who had places midway of the church. Between the nocturns they dozed
or prayed. The child slept well-nigh the whole night—once or twice
Kristin had to lull it a little, or give it milk from a wooden flask that
Gunnulf had got in for her from the cloister.

The meeting with Erlend's brother had stirred her strangely—the
more so that every step of the road hither had brought her nearer and
nearer home to the memory of the dead man. She had *thought* little on
him in these last years, while her work for her growing sons gave her little
time for memory of her own fate—none the less the thought of him had
been ever, as it were, close behind her, only that she had not had the time
to turn her towards it. Now she seemed to see her soul as it had been in
these years; it had lived as folk live on a manor through the busy
summer half-year, when they move out of the great hall and bide in the
storehouse loft. All day long they go to and fro past the winter hall,
never thinking of going in thither, though they have but to lay their
hand on a latch and push open a door. And when at last some day they
have an errand thither, the house has grown strange and almost solemn,
because of the air of loneliness and quiet that has come to it——

But while she was speaking with him who was the last living witness
of the interplay 'twixt seed-time and harvest in her life with the dead
man, it seemed to her that she had come to look out over her life in a
new way: as when a man comes up on a height above his native place
where he has never climbed before, and looks down from it into his own
dale. He knows each farm and fence, each thicket, the gully of each
beck; but he seems to see for the first time how these things all lie on
the face of the land. And seeing things in this new way, she had found
all at once words that swept away both her bitterness against Erlend
and her terrors for his soul, borne off by sudden death. Ill-will he had
never borne to any; she saw it now, and God had seen it always.

So at last she was come so far that she deemed she could look on her own life as from the uppermost step of a glen. Now did her road lead down into the darkling valley, but ere she took that road she had been given grace to understand that, in the loneliness of the cloister and at the gates of death, there waited for her one who had ever beheld the life of mankind as men's parishes look, seen from the mountain brow. He had seen the sin and sorrow, the love and hate, in the hearts of men, as one sees the rich manors and the humble cots, the teeming cornfields and the abandoned wastes, all borne on the bosom of the same country-side. And he had descended; his feet had trodden the peopled lands, and stood in palaces and in huts; he had gathered up the sorrows and the sins of rich and poor, and lifted them aloft with him upon a cross. Not my happiness and my pride, but my sin and my sorrow, O my sweet Lord—— She looked up where the crucifix stood, uplifted high over the triumphal arch.

——While the morning sun lit up the high-set coloured panes deep among the pillars of the choir, and a glory, as of red and brown and green and blue gems, dimmed the light from the tapers on the altar and from the golden shrine behind, Kristin listened to the last vigil—the matins. She knew that the lessons in this service told of God's healing miracles through the power vouchsafed to his faithful knight King Olav Haraldssön. She lifted the sick stranger-child up towards the choir, and prayed for it.

But she was so icy chill from her long vigil in the cold of the church that her teeth chattered; and she felt faint from fasting. The smell of the many folk, and the sickening fumes of the sick and the beggars, mingled with the smoke of the wax-candles and sank down in a heavy, strangely greasy and clammy cloud upon the people kneeling on the stone floor, cold in the cold morning. But a fat, kind, cheerful country-woman who had sat dozing a little against the foot of the pillar just be-hind them, with a bearskin below her and another over her lame legs, awoke now and drew Kristin's weary head down upon her wide lap: "Rest a little now, sister—you have need of it, I trow——"

Kristin slept in the strange woman's lap, and dreamed:

She stepped over the threshold of the old hearth-room house at home. She was young and unwed, for she saw her own uncovered thick brown plaits hanging forward over her shoulders. She was in company with Erlend, for he was even now drawing him upright, after going through the doorway before her.

By the hearth her father was sitting, binding arrow-heads on the shafts—he had his lap full of bunches of sinew string, and on either side of him on the bench lay piles of arrow-heads and sharpened shafts. Just as they stepped in, he bent him forward over the heap of embers and made to take up the little three-legged metal cup that he ever used to melt resin in. But swiftly he caught back his hand, shook it in the air, and then he stuck his burnt finger-tips into his mouth and sucked them, while he turned his head towards her and Erlend, and looked up at them with a wrinkled brow and a smile about his lips——

Then she awoke, her face wet with tears.

She kneeled through the High Mass, when the Archbishop himself served the holy rite before the high altar. The clouds of incense rolled though the echoing church, where many-coloured sunlight was mingled now with the wax tapers' shining; the fresh, spicy scent of the frankincense spread abroad and overcame the smell of poverty and sickness. With a heart that seemed bursting with ruth for the flock of the infirm and the needy in whose midst God had set her, she prayed in a rush of sisterly tenderness for all who were poor as she, and who suffered as she herself had suffered——

——"I will arise and go to my father——"

VI

THE convent stood on a rising ground near the fjord, so that, with most winds, the roll of the surf on the beach drowned the soughing of the pinewoods that covered great part of the ridge's slopes, north and west, and hid the sea from sight.

Kristin had seen the church tower above the trees when she sailed by with Erlend, but the pilgrimage out to the nunnery that his forefather had founded, which Erlend had sometimes said they must make, had never come about. She had never landed at Rein Cloister before she came to make it her abiding-place.

She had thought that the life here would be like that she knew at the nunneries in Oslo or at Bakke, but here much was otherwise than there, and 'twas far more quiet. Here the sisters were truly dead to the world. Lady Ragnhild, the abbess, made it her boast that 'twas five years since she had been in to the market town, and as long since some of her nuns had set foot outside the bounds of the cloister.

There were no children here to be nurtured, and, at the time Kristin came to Rein, there were no novices either; so long was it since any young maid had sought to be taken into the sisterhood, that 'twas six winters already since the last, Sister Borghild Marcellina, had taken the veil. Youngest in age was Sister Turid, but she had been sent hither in her seventh year by her father's father, who was priest of Clement's Church, an exceeding strict and earnest man, and the child had had a shrivelled hand from birth and was besides something of a cripple, so she had donned the habit as soon as she reached the age for it. Now she was thirty years old, and sadly frail, but she had a lovesome face, and from the first day she came to the cloister Kristin took great joy in serving her, for she deemed that Sister Turid minded her of her own little sister Ulvhild, who died so young.

Sira Eiliv said that low birth should assuredly not stand in the way of any maids who were minded to come hither to serve God. Nevertheless, so it had been that, ever since the convent had been set up, few but the daughters or widows of mighty and high-born men of the Trondheim country entered there. But during the evil and restless days that had been in the realm since King Haakon Haalegg, of blessed memory, died, piety seemed to have fallen away greatly amongst the great nobles —now 'twas the daughters of townsmen and well-to-do farmers for the most part who turned their thoughts to a convent life. And they betook them rather to Bakke, where many of them had been nurtured in godliness and womanly handicrafts, and where the sisters for the most were come of homely people—there, too, the rule was not so strict, and the cloister lay not so far removed from the highway.

Howbeit, 'twas not often that Kristin had the chance to speak with Sira Eiliv, and she soon saw that the priest's duties and his footing in the cloister were both toilsome and ticklish. Though Rein was a rich cloister and the sisterhood scarce numbered half as many nuns as the foundation might well have fed, yet its money affairs were in great disorder, and it was hard put to it to meet its outgoings. The last three abbesses had been more pious than worldly-wise; none the less they and their convent had fought, with tooth and claw, to make good their freedom from the Archbishop's obedience—so far did they go in this that they would not even take counsel proffered in fatherly goodwill. And the brethren of their order from Tautra and Munkabu, chosen to be priests of the convent church, had ever been old men, that no colour might be given to evil speaking, and their guidance of the cloister's worldly weal had been none too skilful. When King Skule built the fair stone church and gave his udal manor to the cloister, the houses were first built of wood; and they had burnt down thirty winters agone. Lady Audhild, who was abbess then, began the building of them up again in stone; much was done in her time for the betterment of the church, and the goodly convent hall was built. She had journeyed also to the general chapter at the mother house of the order, Tart* in Burgundy, and from that journey she had brought back the noble ivory tower that stood in the choir near the high altar—a fitting tabernacle for God's body, the church's greatest adornment and the nuns' pride and darling treasure. Lady Audhild left behind her the fairest renown for piety and worth, but her unskilful conduct of the building works, and her unwise dealings

* See Note 7.

with the convent lands, had wrought mischief to the cloister's welfare and the later abbesses had not had the skill to repair the ill.

How it had come about that Sira Eiliv was sent thither as priest and counsellor, Kristin never learned; but so much she understood, that from the first the abbess and the sisters had met him, as a secular, with misliking and mistrust; and so 'twas Sira Eiliv's task at Rein to be the nuns' priest and spiritual guide, to set the husbandry of the estates on its feet again, and bring order into the convent's money affairs, while deferring to the abbess's overheadship, the sister's right of self-governance, and the right of the abbot of Tautra to oversee all, and keeping friends with the other priest at the church, a monk from Tautra.   His age and his name for unstained purity of walk and conversation, humble fear of God, and skill both of the canon law and of the law of the land, stood him in good stead, but he had to walk most warily in all his goings.   Together with the other priest and the church servants, he dwelt in a little house lying north-east from the cloister. 'Twas there, too, that the monks lodged who came out from Tautra on divers occasions.   Kristin knew that, if she lived so long, some time, when Nikulaus had come to be ordained priest, she should hear her eldest son say Mass in the convent church.

Kristin Lavransdatter had been received at first as a commoner.* But after she had taken a vow of chastity and obedience to the abbess and the sisterhood, before Lady Ragnhild and the sisters, in presence of Sira Eiliv and two monks from Tautra, and, in token that she forwent all rights over worldly goods, had put her seal into Sira Eiliv's hands to be broken in pieces, she was given leave to wear a garb like to the sisters', but without the scapular; a grey-white woollen robe, white head-linen and black veil. The intent was that, after some time had gone by, she should seek to be received into the sisterhood as a professed nun.

But 'twas still a hard matter for her not to think overmuch on what had been. To read aloud during meal-times in the refectory, Sira Eiliv had written out in the Norse tongue a book of the life of Christ, made by the general of the Minorites, the most learned and godly doctor Bonaventura.   And while Kristin listened to it, and her eyes filled with tears as she thought how blessed they must be who could love Christ and His mother, pains and afflictions, poverty and humility, in such wise as was there written—yet all the time she could not but remember the day at Husaby when Gunnulf and Sira Eiliv had shown her the Latin book from which this was taken. 'Twas a thick little book, written upon parchment so thin and shining white that she had never believed calf-skin could be wrought so fine; and there were the fairest pictures and

* See *The Bridal Wreath* (*The Garland*), Note 13.

capital letters in it, the colours glowing like jewels against the gold. And while she looked, Gunnulf spoke laughingly, and Sira Eiliv gave assent with his quiet smile—of how the buying of this book left them so penniless, they had to sell their clothes and get them meat along with the alms-folk in a cloister, till they came to know that some Norse churchmen were come to Paris, and made shift to raise a loan from them.

When, after matins, the sisters went back to the dormitory, Kristin would tarry behind in the church. On summer mornings 'twas sweet and delightsome to her there—but in winter it was bitterly cold, and she was fearful in the dark among all the tombstones, even though she kept her eyes bent fixedly on the little lamp that burned always before the ivory tower with the host in it. But, winter or summer, while she tarried in her corner of the nuns' choir, she thought of how Naakkve and Björgulf were now watching and praying for their father's soul; and that 'twas Nikulaus who had begged her to join with them in these prayers and penitential psalms each morning after matins.

Ever, ever she saw before her those two, as she had seen them that grey day of rain she went out to the monks' cloister: when Nikulaus stood before her in the parlour of a sudden, marvellous tall and strange in the grey-white monk's habit, with his hands thrust under the scapular, her son, and yet so changed. 'Twas most of all his likeness to his father that moved her so deeply—'twas as though she saw Erlend in monk's garb.

Whilst they sat talking together, and he had her tell him of all tha had befallen at the manor since he took his way from home, she was waiting, waiting. At length she asked fearfully if Björgulf would not come soon.

"I know not, mother," answered her son. A little after he said: "For Björgulf it has been a hard struggle to bow beneath his cross and serve God—— And it seemed to affright him when he heard that you were here—lest too many thoughts should be called up again——"

Thereafter she sat on, deathly sad, gazing at Nikulaus while he talked. He was much sunburned in the face, and his hands were worn with toil —he said, with a little smile, now had he had to learn after all how to guide a plough and work with scythe and sickle. In the hostel that night she could not sleep, and she hasted to the church when the bell rang to matins. But the monks stood so that there were but few whose faces she could see, and her sons were not amongst these.

But next day she walked in the garden with a lay brother who worked there, and he showed her the many rare plants and trees it was renowned for. While they so walked, the clouds broke, the sun came forth, and with it the scent of celery and onion and thyme, and the clumps of yellow lilies and blue columbines that decked the corners of the beds glittered with great raindrops. And then came her sons; they came forth, both of them, from the little arched door of the stone house. And Kristin deemed that she had a foretaste of the joy of Paradise when she saw the two tall brothers in light-hued raiment come down towards her on the path beneath the apple trees.

Yet they spoke not much together; Björgulf was silent well-nigh all the time. He had become a giant in frame, now he was full-grown. And it seemed as though in the long time they had been sundered her sight had grown keener—now, for the first time, she understood to the full what the battle was that this son of hers had fought, that doubtless he was still fighting, while he grew so great and strong of limb, while his inward sight waxed keen, and he felt his eyesight grow dim——

Once he asked after his foster-mother, Frida Styrkaarsdatter. Kristin told him that she was wed.

"God bless her," said the monk. "She was a good woman—to me she was a good and faithful foster-mother."

"Ay, methinks almost she was more a mother to you than was I," said Kristin, sadly. "Little must you have marked of the mother's heart in me, when you were tried so sorely in your youth."

Björgulf answered low:

"I thank God, none the less, that the enemy was never suffered to bow me to such unmanliness as to try the mother's heart in you—though I felt it, of a truth—but I saw that you bore too heavy a burden already —and after God 'twas Nikulaus here who saved me, those times I was like to fall into the Tempter's power——"

No more was said of this, nor of whether they were happy in the cloister, nor of how 'twas said they had done amiss and brought disgrace upon themselves. But it seemed to give them great joy when they heard 'twas their mother's purpose to take the veil in Rein convent.

When, after this hour of prayer, Kristin went back through the dormitory and saw the sisters sleeping two and two on sacks of straw in the beds, clad in the habits which they never put off, she thought how much unlike she must be to these women, who from their youth up had done naught but serve their Maker. The world was a master whom 'twas not easy to fly, when once one had yielded to its dominion. Ay, and in sooth she had not fled the world—she had been cast out, as a hard master drives a worn-out servant from his door—and now she had been taken in here, as a merciful lord takes in an old serving-maid and of his mercy gives her a little work, while he shelters and feeds the worn-out, friendless old creature——

From the nuns' sleeping-house a covered way led to the weaving-house. There Kristin now sat alone, and spun. The nuns of Rein were famed for their linen, and those days in summer and autumn, when all the sisters and lay sisters went to work in the flax-fields, were like feast days in the cloister; but most of all the day the plants were pulled. The nuns were busied in most of their working-hours with making ready the flax, spinning the thread, weaving the linen, and making vestments from it. Here were none who copied or adorned books, as the sisters in Oslo under Lady Groa Guttormsdatter had done with such great skill, nor did they practise much the craft of broidering with silk and gold thread.

In a while she would hear with joy the sounds of the wakening farmyard. The lay sisters went to the kitchen-house to make ready the food for the serving-folk; the nuns touched not meat nor drink till after the Mass of the day, saving when they were sick. When the bell rang for primes, Kristin went to the sick-ward, if any lay there, to take the place of Sister Agata or of whichever other nun was there. Sister Turid, poor soul, lay there often.

Soon, now, she might begin to look forward to the morning meal, which followed after the third hour of prayer and the Mass for the cloister's serving-folk. Each day alike Kristin took joy in this comely and solemn repast. The refectory was timber-built, but a fair hall notwithstanding, and there all the women in the cloister ate together—the nuns at the upper board, where the abbess sat in the high-seat, and where the three old dames who were commoners like herself had also seats—and the lay sisters further down. When the prayer was ended, the meat and drink borne in, and all sat eating and drinking in silence, with still, seemly behaviour, while often one of the sisters read aloud from a book, Kristin would think that, could folk in the world without but take their meals in such goodly wise, they might well come to see more clearly that food and drink are gifts from God, and they would begrudge them less to their fellow-Christians, and think less on scraping together for their own and their children's behoof. But she herself had felt quite otherwise, when she spread her board for a flock of wild, riotous men, amid laughter and uproar, while the dogs snuffed about beneath the board, or thrust up their noses and got a meat bone or a thwack, as the mood of the boys might chance to be.

Travellers seldom came hither. At times a vessel with folk from the nobles' seats around would put in when sailing down or up the fjord, and men and their wives, with children and young folk, would go up to Rein to greet a kinswoman among the sisters. Then there were the bailiffs from the cloister's farms and fisheries, and a messenger from Tautra now and then. At the feast-tides that were kept with greatest state—Mary Virgin's Mass days, Corpus Christi, and the day of Saint

Andrew the Apostle—folk sought the nuns' church from the parishes on both sides the fjord, but otherwise 'twas but those of the cloister's tenants and work-folk who dwelt nearest that came thither to the Masses. They took up but little room in the great church.

Then there were the poor—the alms-folk who had their doles of ale and meat at fixed times under rich folk's testaments, in requital of yearly masses for the donors' souls—and who, besides, drifted up to Rein wellnigh daily, sat by the kitchen-house wall and ate, and when the nuns came out into the courtyard made up to them to talk of their sorrows and troubles. Sick folks, cripples, and lepers wandered out and in—there were many here who suffered from leprosy, but 'twas ever so in the sea parishes, said Lady Ragnhild. Tenants came to crave abatements in their rents or grace time for their payments, and these had ever much to tell of hardships and adversity. The more wretched and hapless these folk were, the more open and unashamed they were in telling the sisters of their condition, though most often they blamed others for their ill-fortune, and had pious words ever on their lips. 'Twas not strange that the nuns' talk at recreation and in the weaving-house ran much on these folks' lives—nay, Sister Turid avowed to Kristin that when the nuns met in convent to take counsel together concerning bargains and the like, the talk would often wander, and turn to gossip about the folk who were mixed in the matters in hand. Kristin marked, by what the sisters said, that they knew little of what they talked of, save what they had heard from the folks themselves or from the lay servants who had been out into the parish. They were passing easy of belief, whether their underlings praised themselves or spoke ill of their neighbours—and she thought with anger of all the times she had heard godless lay folk, ay, even a beggar monk like Brother Arngrim, cry down the nunneries for dens of scandal, and tax the sisters with greedy swallowing of waif rumours and immodest gossip. The very folk who came hither and dinned Lady Ragnhild's ears, or any of the sisters' they could get speech of, full of idle talk, would be the first to blame the nuns for talking among themselves of the tidings that reached them from the world they had renounced. It seemed to her 'twas the same with the talk of the convent ladies' luxurious living—it came from folk's mouths who had many a time had both morning bite and breakfast at the sisters' hands, while these servants of God watched, prayed and laboured fasting, ere they all met for their first solemn meal in the refectory.

So Kristin served the nuns with loving reverence in the time that must go by before she might make profession. A good nun she could never be, she thought; she had scattered abroad all too much what gift she might have had for meditation and piety—but she would be as meek and as steadfast as God would give her grace to be. 'Twas now well on in the summer of the year 1349; she had dwelt in the Rein convent two years, and ere Yule-tide came she was to take the veil. And the glad tidings came to her that, for her dedication, both her sons would come out thither in Abbot Johannes' train. Brother Björgulf had said, when he heard of his mother's purpose:

"Now is my dream like to come true—I have dreamed twice this year that before Yule we should both see her—though *wholly* as it appeared in my dream it cannot be, for in my dream I *saw* her."

Brother Nikulaus, too, had been overjoyed. But at the same time she heard other tidings of him that were not so good. He had sorely mishandled certain farmers up the fjord near Steinker—they were at odds with the cloister over some fishing-rights, and when the monks came upon them one night while they were busy breaking up the cloister's salmon weir, brother Nikulaus had hurt one man grievously and flung another into the river and therewithal had sinned heinously in the matter of cursing and swearing.

VII

A FEW days after, Kristin went to the fir woods with some of the nuns and lay sisters, to gather moss for green dye. This moss is somewhat hard to come by, growing most on wind-fallen trees and dry branches. So the women soon scattered through the woods, and lost one another from sight in the fog.

For some days now this unwonted weather had held—windless, with a thick mist, that showed a strange leaden blue out over the sea and away against the hill-sides, when now and again it thinned so much that the eye caught glimpses of the country round. Between-whiles it thickened to a drizzling rain; then again it lightened so much that a whitish patch showed where the sun hung amid the towering mists. But there brooded ever a strange, heavy warmth, as of a bath-house, that was unwonted down here by the fjord, in especial at this time of the year— 'twas two days before Nativitas Mariæ*—so that all folk talked of the weather and marvelled what it might betoken.

Kristin sweated in the lifeless, damp heat, and the thought of this tidings that she had heard of Naakkve weighed upon her breast. She was come down to the skirts of the wood, to the log fence by the path up from the sea, and, as she stood there scraping moss from the fence, Sira Eiliv came riding homewards through the fog. He stopped his horse and said some words of the weather, and so they fell in talk. Then she asked the priest if he knew aught of this matter of Naakkve—though she

* 8th September.

knew 'twas in vain, for Sira Eiliv ever made as though he had no knowledge of the inside affairs of the Tautra cloister.

"I trow, Kristin, you need have no fear that 'twill hinder his coming hither in the winter, this mischance," said the priest. "'Tis that you feared, belike?"

"'Tis more than that, Sira Eiliv. I fear me Naakkve never was meant to be a monk."

"Think you that you dare judge of such things?" asked the priest, bending his brows. He lighted down from his horse, bound it to a fence log, and leaned over the fence, gazing fixedly and searchingly at the woman. Kristin said:

"I fear 'tis hard for Naakkve to bow beneath the rule of the order—and he was so young when he withdrew him from the world, he knew not what he forwent, and knew not his own mind. All that befell in his young days—the loss of his father's heritage, the sight of the discord 'twixt his father and mother, that ended in Erlend's death—so wrought in him that he lost all heart to live in the world. But I could never mark that it made him godly——"

"You could not?—It may well have been as hard for Nikulaus as for many another good monk to bow him beneath the order's rule; hot of mood is he, and a young man—too young, maybe, to have understood, ere he turned his back on the world, that the world is as hard a taskmaster as any other lord, and in the end a tyrant without mercy. Of that, I ween, you yourself can judge, sister——

"And if so it be that Naakkve entered into the cloister more for his brother's sake than from love for his Maker—none the less I believe not that God will let it go unrequited that he took up the cross for his brother's sake. God's mother Mary, whom I know that Naakkve honoured and loved from his boyhood up, will surely show him clearly one day, that her son came hither to this earthly home to be his brother and bear the cross for him——

"——Nay——" The horse whinnied, with its nose against the priest's breast; he caressed it, while he said, half to himself: "From his childhood up my Nikulaus had a wondrous gift of loving and of suffering—I deem that he should be right well fitted for a monk.

"But you, Kristin," he said, turning to the woman, "you should have seen so much now, methinks, that you might trust in God Almighty with a surer trust. Have you not yet understood that He bears up every soul so long as the soul lets not go its hold on Him? Think you, woman, child that you still are in your old age, that 'tis God punishing the sin, when you must reap sorrow and humiliation because you followed your lusts and your overweening pride over paths that God has forbidden His children to tread? Would you say that *you* had punished your children if they scalded their hands when they took up the boiling kettle you had forbidden them to touch, or if the slippery ice broke under them that you had warned them not to go upon? Have you not understood, when the brittle ice broke beneath you—that you were drawn under each time you let go God's hand, and you were saved from out the deep each time you called on Him? Was not the love that bound you and your father in the flesh together, even when you defied him and set your wilfulness against his will, was it not a comfort and a solace none the less when you had to reap the fruits of your disobedience to him?

"Have you not understood yet, sister, that God has helped you each time you prayed, though you prayed half-heartedly and with feigning, and helped you much beyond what you prayed for? You loved God as you loved your father, not so hotly as you loved your own will, yet none the less so that you ever sorrowed much when you forsook Him—and therefore His mercy towards you suffered good to grow, amidst the evil harvest you must needs reap from the seed of your stubborn will——

"Your sons—two of them He took to Himself while they were innocent little children; for them you need never fear. And the others have turned out well—even if they have not turned out as *you* would have had them. Doubtless Lavrans deemed the like of you——

"And your husband, Kristin—God be merciful to his soul—I wot you have blamed him in your heart early and late for his reckless unwisdom. Yet meseems it had been much harder for a proud woman to remember that Erlend Nikulaussön led you with him through shame and deceit and blood-guiltiness, if you had seen but *once* that the man could do aught with cold contrivance. And almost I believe, too, 'twas because you were steadfast in anger and hardness as in love, that you were able to hold Erlend fast so long as you both lived—with him 'twas out of sight, out of mind, with all things else but you. God help Erlend; I fear me he never had the wit to know true repentance for his sins—yet did your husband repent and sorrow truly for his deeds wherein he sinned against you. That lesson, we may dare to trust, has profited Erlend now that he is dead."

Kristin stood still and silent; neither did Sira Eiliv say any more. He loosed the reins, gave her a "Peace be with you," mounted his horse, and rode away.

When, a little after, she came back to the cloister, Sister Ingrid met her at the door with word that one of her sons was come to greet her—Skule he called himself; he was at the parlour gateway.

He was sitting talking with his boat-folk—he sprang up when his mother came to the door. Ah, she knew her own by the quick nimbleness—the small head, borne high above broad shoulders, the long-limbed, slender form. Beaming with joy she went towards him—but she stopped suddenly and caught her breath at the sight of his face—oh, who had done this to her fair son——?

His upper-lip showed as though kneaded out thin—a blow must have crushed it, and afterwards it had grown together flat and long and misshapen, barred with a network of white scars; it had left his mouth twisted awry, fixed in what seemed a sneering grimace—and the bone of his nose had been broken and had set again crooked. He lisped a little when he spoke—he wanted one front tooth, and another was blueblack and dead.

Skule reddened under his mother's gaze: "I trow you know me not, mother?" He laughed a little, and passed a finger over his lip—'twas not sure whether he pointed to his blemish, or whether 'twas but a chance movement.

"So long parted, I trow, we have not been, my son, that your mother should not know you again," Kristin answered calmly, with an untroubled smile.

Skule Erlendssön was come two days before with a light sloop from Björgvin, with letters from Bjarne Erlingssön for the Archbishop and the Treasurer of Nidaros. Later in the day, mother and son walked in the garden beneath the ash trees, and, now that they were alone, he gave his mother the news of his brothers:

Lavrans was in Iceland still.—His mother knew not even that he had gone thither! Ay, said Skule, he had met his youngest brother in Oslo the winter before at the gathering of the nobles; he was with Jammælt Halvardssön. But, as she knew, the boy had ever had a longing to come abroad and look about him in the world, and so he took service with the Bishop of Skaalholt and sailed away——

Ay, he himself had gone in Sir Bjarne's train to Sweden, and thereafter to the war in Russia. His mother shook her head gently—she had known naught of *that* either! Skule had liked the life, he said, laughing —it had given him his chance to greet the old friends his father spoke so much of—Karelians, Ingrians, Russians. No, that brave scar of honour was not won in war—he laughed a little—ay, 'twas in a fight; the fellow that gave it him would never have need now to beg his bread. More of it, or of the war, Skule seemed to have little mind to tell. Now he was captain of Sir Bjarne's horsemen at Björgvin, and the knight had promised to get back for him some of the manors his father had owned in Orkladal, that were now under the Crown—but Kristin saw that Skule's great, steel-grey eyes took on a strange, dark look as he said this.

"You deem you cannot put much faith in such a promise?" asked his mother.

"No, no." Skule shook his head. "The deeds are even now being drawn. Sir Bjarne has kept all he promised when I took service with him—calls me kinsman and friend. Almost I have the like place in his household that Ulf had at home with us"—he laughed; and the laugh became his marred face ill.

But he was the comeliest of men in bodily form, now that he was full-grown—he wore garments of a new-fashioned cut, tight hose and a small close-fitting *kothardi* that barely reached to the middle of his thigh and was buttoned with small brass buttons all down the front—it showed up in well-nigh unseemly wise his body's supple strength. He looked as though he went about in his undergarments, thought the mother. But his forehead and his comely eyes were not changed.

"You look as though something were weighing on you, Skule," the mother ventured.

"No, no, no." 'Twas but the weather, he said, shaking himself. There was a strange red-brown glow in the fog as the hidden sun went down. The church stood out above the garden tree-tops, strange and dark, melting into the dull red mist. They had had to row the whole fjord, from the very mouth, 'twas so calm, said Skule. Then again he shifted a little in his clothes, and began to speak once more of his brothers.

He had been an errand south in the land for Sir Bjarne this spring, so he could give her fresh tidings of Ivar and Gaute, for he had ridden up overland and made his way across the fells from Vaagaa home to the west country. All was well with Ivar; they had two little sons at Rogn-heim, Erlend and Gamal, comely children. "But at Jörundgaard I chanced upon a christening-ale—and Jofrid and Gaute deemed, as you were dead to the world now, they might name the little maid after you; Jofrid is so proud that you are her mother-in-law—ay, you laugh, but, now that you are not to dwell under one roof, be sure Jofrid knows well it has a brave sound when she talks of 'my mother-in-law, Kristin Lav-ransdatter.' But I gave Kristin Gautesdatter my best finger-ring, for she has such winsome eyes; almost I deem she will be like you——"

Kristin smiled sadly:

"Soon will you bring me to think, my Skule, that my sons deem me as great and good as old folk are wont to be, once they are beneath the sod."

"Speak not so, mother," said the man, with a strange vehemence. Then he laughed a little: "You wot well that all we brothers, ever since we were breeched, deemed you were the bravest and most high-minded of women—though you clinched us full tightly under your wings many a time, and we flapped back, maybe, somewhat hard again ere we scaped from the nest——

"——But it has proved, sure enough, that you were right in deeming

Gaute the one of us brothers that was born to be a chieftain," said he, laughing loud.

"No need to mock me for that now, Skule," said Kristin—and Skule saw that his mother flushed with a young, tender red. At that he laughed all the more:

"'Tis true, my mother—Gaute Erlendssön of Jörundgaard is grown a mighty man in the northern dales. This theft of his bride brought him such renown"—Skule laughed loudly, with the laughter that so ill became his ravaged mouth. "They sing a ballad of it; ay, they sing now that he took the maid with iron and with steel, and he fought her kinsmen three livelong days on the mountain—and the feast that Sir Sigurd held at Sundbu, and whereat he made peace betwixt the kinsmen with silver and with gold, for that too Gaute gets all the honour in the ballad —and it seems to make no matter that 'tis all a lie; Gaute rules the whole parish and somewhat beyond—and Jofrid rules Gaute——"

Kristin shook her head, with her little sad smile. But she grew young of face as she gazed on Skule. Now seemed it to her that *he* was most like his father—after all, the young warrior with the ravaged face had the most of Erlend's gallant mettle—and that he had so early had to take his fate into his own hands had given him a cool firmness of spirit that filled his mother's heart with a strange security. With Sira Eiliv's words of the day before in mind, she saw all at once—fearful as she had been for her headstrong sons, and hard as she had often laid hand upon them by reason of her dread—yet had she been much less content with her children had they been meek and unmanly.

Then she asked again and again of her grandson, little Erlend—but him had Skule given small heed to, it seemed—ay, he was strong and comely, and was wont to have his way at all times.

The uncanny glow in the fog, as of clotted blood, faded away; the dark was falling. The church's bells began to ring; Kristin and her son rose. Then Skule took her hand:

"Mother," he said in a low voice. "Mind you that I once lifted my hand against you? I threw a bat at you in anger, and it struck you on the brow—mind you of it? Mother, while we two are all alone, tell me that you have forgiven me!"

Kristin drew a long breath—ay, she remembered. She had bidden the twins go on an errand up to the sæter—but when she came out into the courtyard the horse was there, grazing, with the pack-saddle on its back, and her sons running about and playing at ball. When she chid them angrily for this, Skule flung the bat from him in a towering rage —— But she remembered best what came after—— How, as she went about after, one eye quite closed by the swelling of the lid—the brothers looked at her and at Skule, and shrank from him as though he were a leper—though Naakkve had beaten him mercilessly first. And Skule wandered away, and sat boiling with defiance and shame under a hard, scornful mien. But when in the evening she was standing putting off her clothes in the dark, he stole up to her—said nothing, but took her hand and kissed it. And, when she touched his shoulder, he cast his arms about her neck and pressed his cheek to hers—his was cool and soft and still a little rounded; she felt 'twas a child's cheek still—he was but a child, after all, this headstrong, fiery youth——

"That have I, Skule—so fully, that God alone knows, for I cannot tell you, how fully I have forgiven it you, my son!"

A moment she stood with her hand on his shoulder. Then he grasped her wrists, gripped them so tight that she winced with pain—and the next moment he flung his arms about her with the same passionate, fearful, bashful tenderness as that other time.

"My son—what ails you?" whispered the mother, in fear.

She felt in the dark that the man shook his head. Then he let her go, and together they went upward to the church.

During the Mass Kristin called to mind that she had forgotten to bring in blind Lady Aasa's cloak, from where they had sat together on the bench outside the priest's door that morning. After the service she went round to fetch it.

Under the archway stood Sira Eiliv, lanthorn in hand, and Skule "He died as we came alongside the wharf," she heard Skule say, in a strangely wild, despairing voice.

"Who?"

Both men started violently when they saw her.

"One of my ship-folk," said Skule, low.

Kristin looked from one to the other. At the sight of their blank, strained faces in the lanthorn's glimmer she broke unwittingly into a little cry of fear. The priest set his teeth in his under-lip—she saw that his chin quivered a little.

"'Twere best, my son, you should tell your mother. Better that we all make us ready to bear it, if 'tis God's will this folk too shall be awaked by so hard a——" But Skule uttered a kind of groan and said no word; and on that the priest spoke: "Pestilence has come to Björgvin, Kristin—— The great and deathly sickness that we have heard say is laying waste the lands in the world around——"

"The black death——?" whispered Kristin.

"It boots not to try to tell you how things were in Björgvin when I sailed from there," said Skule. "None can think it that has not seen it. At first Sir Bjarne took the hardest measures to quench the fire where it broke out, away in the houses around Jons cloister; he would have cut off the whole Nordnes from the town with a chain of his men-at-arms, though the monks of the Michael cloister threatened him with the Church's ban—— There came an English ship that had the pest aboard, and he would not suffer them to unload the lading or to leave the ship; every man on the sloop died, and then he had her scuttled. But some of the wares had already been brought to land, and some of the burghers smuggled more ashore one night—and the friars of the Jons church stood to it that the dying must have ghostly comfort—— Then folk began to die throughout all the town, so 'twas bootless, we saw—— Now is there not a living soul in the city save the bearers of the dead—all flee the town that can, but the pest goes with them——"

"O Jesus Christus!"

"Mother—mind you the last time 'twas lemming-year at home in Sil? The throngs that rolled along all the roads and paths—mind you how they lay and died in every bush, and rotted, and poisoned every runnel with stench and festering foulness——?" He clenched his fists; his mother shuddered:

"Lord, have mercy on us all—— Praise be to God and Mary Virgin that you were sent hither even now, my Skule——"

The man ground his teeth together in the dark:

"So said we too, my men and I, the morning we hoisted sail and stood down Vaagen out to sea. When we were come north to Moldö Sound, the first fell sick. We bound stones to his feet and a cross upon his breast when he was dead, vowed a mass for his soul when we came to Nidaros, and cast his body into the sea—God forgive us. We put in to shore with the next two and got them help for their souls, and Christian burial—for 'tis bootless to flee from fate. The fourth died as we pulled into the river, and the fifth last night——"

"Is it needful that you go back to the town?" asked his mother a little later. "Can you not bide here?"

Skule shook his head, with a joyless laugh:

"——Oh, soon, methinks, 'twill matter naught where one is. Useless to be afeared—a man in dread is half dead. But would that I were as old as you are, mother!"

"None knows what they are spared who die young," said his mother, low.

"Be still, mother! Think on the time when you yourself were three-and-twenty winters old—would you have missed the years you have lived since then——?"

Fourteen days later Kristin saw for the first time one sick of the plague. Rumour that the pest was raging in Nidaros and spreading through the country-side had come to Rissa—how, 'twas not easy to

understand, for folk kept their houses, and every man fled to the woods
or thickets if he saw an unknown wayfarer on the road; none would
open his door to stranger-folk.

But one morning two fishers came up to the cloister bearing a man
between them in a sail; when at daybreak they came down to their
boat, they had found a strange bark at the wharf, and in its bottom lay
this man, senseless—he had found strength to make his boat fast, but
not to get out of it to land. The man had been born in a house owned
by the cloister, but his kindred had all left the country-side.

The dying man lay on the wet sail in the midst of the grass-grown
courtyard; the fishermen stood afar off talking with Sira Eiliv. The
lay sisters and serving-women had fled into the houses, but the nuns
stood in a cluster at the door of the convent hall—a throng of startled,
trembling, despairing old women.

Then Lady Ragnhild stepped forth. She was a little, thin old woman,
with a broad, flat face and a little round, red nose like a button; her
great, light-brown eyes were red-rimmed, and always watered a little.
"*In nomine patris et filii et spiritus sancti*," she said in a clear voice, then
gulped once. "Bear him into the guest-house——"

And Sister Agata, the eldest of the nuns, elbowed her way through
the throng and, unbidden, went with the abbess and the men who bore
the sick man.

Kristin went in thither late at night with a remedy she had made
ready in the pantry, and Sister Agata asked if she durst bide there and
tend the fire.

She deemed herself she should have been hardened—well used as she
was to births and deaths, she had seen worse sights than this—she strove
to think of all the worst that she had seen—— The plague-stricken
man sat upright, for he was like to choke with the bloody spittle that
he brought up at each coughing-fit—Sister Agata had slung him up in
a band passed across his lean, yellow, red-haired chest, and his head
hung forward; his face was leaden grey-blue, and fit on fit of shivering
shook him. But Sister Agata sat calmly saying over her prayers, and,
when the cough took him, she rose, put one arm about his head, and
held a cup below his mouth. The sick man roared loud in his agony,
rolled his eyes fearfully, and at length thrust a black tongue far out of
his gullet, while his lamentable cries died away in pitiful groaning.
The nun emptied out the cup into the fire—and while Kristin threw on
more juniper, and the wet branches first filled the room with a stinging,
yellow smoke, and then burst hissing into flame, she saw Sister Agata
settle the cushions and pillows under the sick man's back and arm-pits,
wipe his face and cracked brown lips with vinegar-water, and draw the
fouled coverlid up about his body. 'Twould soon be over and done.

she said to Kristin—he was cold already; at first he had been hot as fire—but Sira Eiliv had prepared him already for his going. Then she sat her down beside him, thrust the calamus root into its place in her cheek with her tongue, and fell again to prayer.

Kristin strove to overcome the fearful horror that she felt. She had seen folk die a harder death—— But 'twas in vain—this was the plague, a chastisement from the Lord for all mankind's secret hardness of heart, of which He alone had knowledge. She felt as if she were rocked giddily on a sea, where all the bitter and angry thoughts she had ever thought towered up like one huge wave amid a thousand, and broke in helpless woe and lamentation. Lord, help us, for we perish——

Sira Eiliv came in late in the night. He chid Sister Agata sharply that she had not followed his counsel to bind a linen cloth dipped in vinegar over her mouth and nose. She mumbled testily that 'twas of no avail—but both she and Kristin had now to do as he bade them.

The priest's quietude and steadfastness put some measure of courage into Kristin—or awoke a feeling of shame—she ventured out of the juniper smoke and began to help Sister Agata. A choking stench came from the sick man, that the smoke availed not to deaden—filth, blood, sour sweat, and a noisome smell from his throat. She thought of Skule's words about the lemming swarm; once more there came upon her the awful longing to fly, though she knew there was no place whither one could flee from this. But when once she had taken heart of grace and touched the dying man, the worst was over; and she helped as well as she might until he had breathed his last. He was black in the face already when he died.

The nuns walked in procession, with the holy relics, crosses, and burning tapers, round the church and the cloister hill, and all in the parish who could walk or crawl went with them. But, not many days after, a woman died near by at Strömmen—and then the deadly sickness broke out at a stroke on every hand throughout the country-side.

Death and horror and direst need seemed to bear away the land and its folk into a timeless world—'twas not more than a few weeks that were gone by, if one were to reckon the days, and already it seemed as if the world that had been, ere pestilence and death stalked naked through the land, was fading from folk's memories, as a sea-coast sinks when one stands out to sea before a rushing wind. 'Twas as though no human soul could keep in memory that once life and the daily round of work had seemed sure and near, death far away—or had the power to conceive that so it would be again—if so be all men did not die. But "Belike, we shall all die," said the men who came to the cloister with their motherless little ones; some said it with dull, hard faces, some with weeping and lamentations; they said it when they fetched a priest to the dying, they said it when they bore the corpses to the parish church down the hill and to the graveyard by the cloister chapel. Often the bearers themselves must dig the grave—Sira Eiliv had set the lay serving-men—such as were left—to work at saving and garnering the corn from the cloister's fields; and wheresoever he went in the parish he admonished the folk to get their crops housed, and to help one another to care for the cattle, that so they might not perish in the dearth the plague was like to leave behind when it had spent its rage.

The nuns in the cloister met the visitation at first with a kind of bewildered calm. They settled them down for good in the convent hall, kept a fire blazing night and day in the great masoned fireplace, slept there, and there took their food. Sira Eiliv counselled that great fires should be kept up in the courts and in all the houses where there were fireplaces; but the sisters were afraid of fire—they had heard so many tales from the oldest sisters of the burning of the convent thirty years before. Meal-times and working-hours were kept no longer, and the divers offices of the sisters could not be kept apart, by reason of the many children who came from without, praying for food and help. Sick folk were brought in—these for the most were well-to-do folk who could pay for a grave-stead in the cloister and for masses for their souls, or the poorest and loneliest of the poor who could get no help at home. Those of a middle station lay and died in their own houses. On some manors every human being died. But amid all this the nuns had as yet made shift to keep up the hours of prayer.

The first of the nuns who fell sick was Sister Inga, a woman of Kristin's age, near fifty years; but none the less was she so afeared of death that 'twas horrible to see and hear her. The shivering fit came upon her in the church during Mass, and she crept on hands and knees, shaking and with chattering teeth, praying and beseeching God and Mary Virgin for her life—— Before long she lay in a burning fever, groaning, and sweating blood from all her body. Kristin's heart shuddered within her—doubtless she, too, would be as wretchedly afraid as this when her time came. 'Twas not alone that death was sure—'twas the awful horror that clung about death from pestilence.

Then Lady Ragnhild herself fell sick. Kristin had wondered a little that this woman had been chosen to an abbess's high office—she was a quiet, somewhat peevish old woman, unlearned, and, it seemed, lacking any great gifts of the spirit—but, when death laid his hand upon her, she showed she was in truth a bride of Christ. Her the sickness smote with boils—she would not suffer even her spiritual daughters to bare her old body, but under one of her arms the swelling grew at last as big as an apple, and under her chin too boils broke out and waxed huge

THE CROSS

...black; she suffered unbearable pains ...but... as oft as her mind was clear, ...ching to God for forgiveness ...rds for her cloister and ...the salvation of all ...ept, when he ... his un-

at. Lady Ragnhild had many ... keeping and prayed Him to take the nuns into His ward—and then at last the boils on her body began to burst. But this proved a turning towards life, not death—and after, too, folk deemed they saw that those whom the sickness smote with boils were sometimes healed, but those to whom it came with a bloody vomit, died everyone.

It seemed as though the nuns took new courage from the abbess's steadfastness, and from the having seen one stricken with the pest who yet did not die. They had now to milk and tend the byres themselves, to make ready their own food, and themselves fetch home juniper and fresh pine branches to burn for cleansing smoke—each one had to do what came to her hand. They cared for the sick as best they could, and doled out remedies—theriac and calamus root had given out; they dealt round ginger, pepper, saffron and vinegar to ward off the poison; and milk and meat—the bread gave out and they baked at night—the spices gave out, and folk must needs chew juniper-berries and pine-needles against the infection. One by one the sisters drooped and died; passing-bells rang from the cloister church and the parish church early and late in the heavy air; for the strange, uncanny mist still lay upon the land; there seemed to be a secret privity 'twixt the fog and the deadly sickness. Sometimes it turned to a frosty fog and sifted down in small ice-needles and a half-frozen drizzle, and the land grew white with rime—then came mild weather and mist again. Folk deemed it a sign of evil omen that the sea-fowl, that else were wont to flock in thousands along the creek that runs inland from the fjord and lies like a river between the low stretches of meadow, but widens to a salt-water lake north of Rein cloister—that they suddenly vanished, and in their stead came ravens in countless numbers—on every stone by the water-side the black birds sat amidst the fog, making their hideous croaking; while flocks of crows, so huge that none before had seen the like, settled on all the woods and groves, and flew with ugly screechings over the stricken land.

Now and again Kristin thought of her own—the sons who were scattered so far and wide, the grandchildren she should never see—little Erlend's golden head wavered before her sight. But they were grown to seem far off, ...on, and she would scarce remember to ... how things were with them at home; she would ... and lead them to the shelter of the chapter-hall, or some other place where a fire was burning, then stow them away in a bed in the dormitory.

She marked, with a kind of wonder, that in this time of calamity, when more than ever there was need that all should be vigilant in prayer, she scarce ever found time to meditate or to pray. She would fling her down in the church before the tabernacle when she found a vacant moment, but naught came of it but wordless sighs, and Paternosters and Aves uttered by rote. She herself knew not that the nunlike ways and bearing she had fallen into in these two years were dropping from her more and more, and that she was growing ever liker to the housewife of the old days—as the flock of nuns dwindled, the round of cloister duties fell into disarray, and the abbess still lay abed, weak and with half-palsied tongue—and the work grew more and more for the few that were left to do it.

One day she learned by chance that Skule was still in Nidaros—his ship-folk were dead or fled away, and he had not been able to get new folk. He was whole yet, but he had plunged into wild living, as had many young men in this desperate pass. For him who was afraid, death was sure, they said, and so they deadened thought with drink and riot, gambled and danced and wantoned with women. Even honourable burghers' wives and young maids of the best kindreds ran from their homes in this evil time; in company with the women of the bordels they caroused in the inns and taverns amongst the wildered men. God forgive them, thought the mother—but 'twas as though her heart were too weary to sorrow much for these things.

But in the country-side too, for sure, there was enough of sin and distraction. They heard little of it at the cloister, for there they had no time for much talk. But Sira Eiliv, who went about everywhere, without rest or respite, to the sick and dying, said one day to Kristin that the folk's souls stood in yet direr need than their bodies.

There came an evening when they were sitting round the chimney-place in the convent hall—the little flock of folk that were left alive in Rein cloister. Four nuns and two lay sisters, an old stable-man and a half-grown boy, two bedeswomen and some children, huddled together

THE CROSS 911

round the fire. On the high-seat bench, where a great crucifix gleamed in the dusk on the light-hued wall, lay the abbess, and Sister Kristin and Sister Turid sat at her hands and feet.

It was nine days since the last death among the sisters, and five days since any had died in the cloister or the nearer houses. The pestilence seemed to be lessening throughout the parish, too, said Sira Eiliv. And for the first time for near three months something like a gleam of peace and hope and comfort fell upon the silent and weary folk that sat together there. Old Sister Torunn Marta let her rosary sink upon her lap, and took the hand of the little girl who stood at her knee:

"What can it be she means? Ay, child, now seems it as we should see that never for long does God's mother, Mary, turn away her loving-kindness from her children."

"Nay, 'tis not Mary Virgin, Sister Torunn, 'tis Hel.* She will go from out this parish, with both rake and broom, when they offer up a man 'without blemish at the graveyard gate—to-morrow she'll be far away——"

"What means she?" asked the nun again, uneasily. "Fie upon you, Magnhild; what ugly heathenish talk is this? 'Twere fit you should taste the birch——"

"Tell us what it is, Magnhild—have no fear"—Sister Kristin was standing behind them; she asked the question breathlessly. She had remembered—she had heard in her youth from Lady Aashild—of dreadful, unnamably sinful devices that the devil tempts desperate men to practise——

The children had been down in the grove by the parish church in the falling dusk, and some of the boys had strayed through the wood to a turf hut that stood there, and had eavesdropped and heard some men in it laying plans. It seemed from what they heard that these men had laid hold on a little boy, Tore, the son of Steinunn, that lived by the strand, and to-night they were to offer him up to the pest-ogress, Hel. The children talked eagerly, proud that the grown-up folk were paying heed to what they said. They seemed not to think of pitying the hapless Tore—maybe because he was somewhat of an outcast. He wandered about the parish begging, but never came to the cloister, and if Sira Eiliv or any sent by the abbess sought out his mother, she ran away, or she kept a stubborn silence, whether they spoke lovingly or harshly to her. She had lived in the stews of Nidaros for ten years, but then a sickness took hold on her, and left her of so ill a favour that at last she could not win her livelihood so as she had used her to do; so she had forsaken the town for the Rein parish, and now dwelt in a hut down by the strand. It still befell at times that a chance beggar or some such

* See Note 8.

stroller would take lodging with her for a while. Who was father to her boy she herself knew not.

"We must go thither," said Kristin. "Here we cannot sit, I trow, while christened souls sell themselves to the devil at our very doors."

The nuns whimpered in fear. These were the worst men in the parish; rough, ungodly fellows; and uttermost need and despair must have turned them now into very devils. Had Sira Eiliv only been at home, they moaned. In this time of trial the priest had so won their trust, that they deemed he could do all things——

Kristin wrung her hands:

"Even if I must go alone—my mother, have I your leave to go thither?"

The abbess gripped her by the arm so hard that she cried out. The old, tongue-tied woman got upon her feet; by signs she made them understand that they should dress her to go out, and called for her golden cross, the badge of her office, and her staff. Then she took Kristin by the arm—for she was the youngest and strongest of the women. All the nuns stood up and followed.

Through the door of the little room 'twixt the chapter-hall and the choir of the church they went forth into the raw, cold winter night. Lady Ragnhild's teeth began to chatter and her whole frame to shiver— she still sweated without cease by reason of her sickness, and the pest-boil sores were not fully healed, so that it must have wrought her great agony to walk. But she muttered angrily and shook her head when the sisters prayed her to turn, clung the harder to Kristin's arm, and plodded, shaking with cold, on before them through the garden. As their eyes grew used to the darkness, the women made out the dim sheen of the withered leaves strewn on the path beneath their feet, and the faint light from the clouded sky above the naked tree-tops. Cold water-drops dripped from the branches, and puffs of wind went by with a faint soughing sound. The roll of the waves on the strand behind the high ground came to them in dull, heavy sighs.

At the bottom of the garden was a little wicket—the sisters shuddered when the bolt, fast rusted in its socket, shrieked as Kristin withdrew it by main force. Then they crept onward through the grove down towards the parish church. Now they could see dimly the black-tarred mass, darker against the darkness; and against the opening in the clouds above the low hills beyond the lake they saw the roof-top, and the ridge turret with its beasts' heads and cross over all.

Ay—there were folk in the graveyard—they felt rather than saw or heard it. And now a faint gleam of light was to be seen low down, as of a lanthorn set upon the ground. Close by it the darkness seemed moving.

The nuns pressed together, moaning almost soundlessly amid whispered prayers, went a few steps, halted and listened, and went on again. They were well-nigh come to the graveyard gate. Then they heard from out of the dark a thin child-voice crying:

"Oh, oh, my bannock; you've thrown dirt on it!"

Kristin let go the abbess's arm, and ran forward through the churchyard gate. She pushed aside some dark shapes of men's backs, stumbled over heaps of upturned earth, and then was at the edge of the open grave. She went down on her knees, bent over, and lifted up the little boy who stood at the bottom, still whimpering because the dirt had spoiled the good bannock he had been given for staying quietly down there.

The men stood there frighted from their wits—ready to fly—some stamped about on the same spot—Kristin saw their feet in the light from the lanthorn on the ground. Then one, she made sure, would have sprung at her—at the same moment the grey-white nuns' dresses came into sight—and the knot of men hung wavering——

Kristin had the boy in her arms still; he was crying for his bannock; so she set him down, took the bread, and brushed it clean:

"There, eat it—your bannock is as good as ever now—— And now go home, you men"—the shaking of her voice forced her to stop a little. "Go home and thank God you were saved from the doing of a deed 'twere hard to atone." She was speaking now as a mistress speaks to her serving-folk, mildly, but as if it could not cross her mind that they would not obey. Unwittingly some of the men turned towards the gate.

Then one of them shrieked:

"Stay a little—see you not our lives at the least are forfeit—mayhap all we own—now that these full-fed monks' whores have stuck their noses into this! Never must they come away from here to spread the tidings of it——"

Not a man moved—but Sister Agnes broke into a shrill shriek, and cried in a wailing voice:

"O sweet Jesus, my bridegroom—I thank Thee that Thou sufferest Thy handmaidens to die for the glory of Thy name——!"

Lady Ragnhild pushed her roughly behind her, tottered forward, and took up the lanthorn from the ground—no one moved a hand to hinder her. When she lifted it up, the gold cross on her breast shone out. She stood propped on her staff, and slowly turned the light upon the ring about her, nodding a little at each man she looked on. Then she made a sign to Kristin to speak. Kristin said:

"Go home peaceably and quietly, dear brothers—be sure that the reverend mother and these good sisters will be as merciful as their duty to God and the honour of His Church will suffer. But stand aside now, that we may come forth with this child—and thereafter let each man go his way."

The men stood wavering. Then one shrieked out as though in direst need:

"Is't not better that *one* be offered up than that we should all perish——? This child here who is owned by none——"

"Christ owns him. 'Twere better we should perish one and all than to hurt one of His little ones——"

But the man who had spoken first shouted again:

"Hold your tongue—no more such-like words, or I cram them back down your throat with this"—he shook his knife in the air. "Go you home, go to your beds and pray your priest to comfort you, and say naught of this—or I tell you, in Satan's name, you shall learn 'twas the worst thing you ever did to put your fingers into our affairs——"

"You need not to cry so loud for him you named to hear you, Arntor —be sure he is not far from here," said Kristin calmly, and some of the men seemed affrighted, and pressed unwittingly nearer to the abbess, who stood holding the lanthorn. "The worst had been, both for us and for you, had we sat quiet at home while you went about to make you a dwelling-place in hottest hell."

But the man Arntor swore and raved. Kristin knew that he hated the nuns; for his father had been forced to pledge his farm to them when he had to pay amends for man-slaying and incest with his wife's cousin. Now he went on casting up at the sisters all the Enemy's most hateful lies, charging them with sins so black and unnatural that only the devil himself could prompt a man to think such thoughts.

The poor nuns bowed them terrified and weeping under the hail of his taunts, but they stood fast around their old mother, and she held the lanthorn high, throwing the light upon the man, and looking him calmly in the face while he raved.

But anger flamed up in Kristin like new-kindled fire:

"Silence! Have you lost your wits, or has God smitten you with blindness? Should we dare to murmur under His chastisement—we who have seen His consecrated brides go forth to meet the sword that has been drawn by reason of the world's sins? They watched and prayed while we sinned and each day forgot our Maker—shut them from the world within the citadel of prayer while we scoured the world around, driven by greed of great and small possessions, of our own lusts and our own wrath. But they came forth to us when the angel of death was sent out amongst us—gathered in the sick and the defenceless and the hungry—twelve of our sisters have died in this plague—that you all know—not one turned aside, and not one gave over praying for us all in sisterly love, till the tongue dried in their mouths and their life's blood ebbed away——"

"Bravely speak you of yourself and your like——"

"*I* am *your* like," she cried, beside herself with anger; "I am not one of these holy sisters—I am one of you——"

"You have grown full humble, woman," said Arntor, scornfully; "you are frighted, I mark well. A little more and you will be fain to call her—the mother to this boy—your like."

"That must God judge—He died both for her and for me, and He knows us both.—Where is she—Steinunn?"

"Go down to her hut; you will find her there sure enough," answered Arntor.

"Ay, truly someone must send word to the poor woman that we have her boy," said Kristin to the nuns. "We must go out to her to-morrow."

Arntor gave a jeering laugh, but another man cried, uneasily:

"No, no—— She is dead," he said to Kristin. "'Tis fourteen days since Bjarne left her and barred the door. She lay in the death-throes then——"

"She lay in——" Kristin gazed at the men, horror-struck. "Was there none to fetch a priest to her——? Is the—body—lying there—and no one has had so much compassion on her as to bring her to hallowed ground—and her child you would have——?"

At the sight of the woman's horror, 'twas as though the men went clean beside themselves with fear and shame; all were shouting at once; a voice louder than all the rest rang out:

"Fetch her yourself, sister!"

"Ay! Which of you will go with me?"

None answered. Arntor cried:

"You will have to go alone, I trow."

"To-morrow—as soon as 'tis light—we will fetch her, Arntor—1 myself will buy her a resting-place and masses for her soul——"

"Go thither now, go to-night—then will I believe you nuns are choke-full of holiness and pureness——"

Arntor had stuck his head forward close to hers. Kristin drove her clenched fist into his face, with a single loud sob of rage and horror——

Lady Ragnhild went forward and placed herself at Kristin's side; she strove to bring forth some words. The nuns cried out that to-morrow the dead woman should be brought to her grave. But the devil seemed to have turned Arntor's brain; he went on shrieking:

"Go now—then will we believe on God's mercy——"

Kristin drew herself up, white and stiff:

"I will go."

She lifted the child and gave it into Sister Torunn's arms, pushed the men aside, and ran quickly, stumbling over grass tussocks and heaps of earth, towards the gate, while the nuns followed wailing, and Sister Agnes cried out that she would go with her. The abbess shook her clenched hands towards Kristin, beckoning her to stop; but she seemed quite beside herself and gave no heed——

Suddenly there was a great commotion in the dark over by the grave-yard gate—next moment Sira Eiliv's voice asked: who was holding Thing here. He came forward into the glimmer of the lanthorn—they saw that he bore an axe in his hand. The nuns flocked around him; the men made shift to steal away in the dark, but in the gateway they were met by a man bearing a drawn sword in his hand. There was some turmoil and the clash of arms, and Sira Eiliv shouted towards the gate: woe to any who broke the churchyard peace. Kristin heard one say 'twas the strong smith from Credo Lane—the moment after, a tall, broad-shouldered, white-haired man appeared at her side—'twas Ulf Haldorssön.

The priest handed him the axe—he had borrowed it from Ulf—and took the boy Tore from the nun, while he said:

"'Tis past midnight already—none the less 'twere best you all came with me to the church; I must get to the bottom of these doings this very night."

None had any thought but to obey. But, when they were come out on to the road, one of the light-grey women's forms stepped aside from the throng and turned off by the path through the wood. The priest called out, bidding her come on with the others. Kristin's voice answered from the darkness—she was some way along the track already:

"I cannot come, Sira Eiliv, till I have kept my promise——"

The priest and some others sprang after her. She was standing leaning against the fence when Sira Eiliv came up with her. He held up the lanthorn—she was fearfully white of face, but, when he looked into her eyes, he saw that she was not gone mad, as at first he had feared.

"Come home, Kristin," he said. "To-morrow we will go thither with you, some men—I myself will go with you——"

"I have given my word. I cannot go home, Sira Eiliv, till I have done that which I vowed to do."

The priest stood silent a little. Then he said in a low voice:

"Mayhap you are right. Go then, sister, in God's name."

Like a shadow, Kristin melted away into the darkness, which swallowed up her grey form.

When Ulf Haldorssön came up by her side, she said—she spoke by snatches, vehemently: "Go back—I asked not you to come with me——"

Ulf laughed low:

"Kristin, my lady—you have not learnt yet, I see, that some things can be done without your asking or bidding—nor, though you have seen it many a time, I ween—that you cannot alway carry through alone all that you take upon you. But this burden of yours *I* will help you to carry."

The fir woods sighed above them, and the boom of the rollers away on the strand came stronger or more faint as the gusts of wind rose or died away. They walked in pitch darkness. After a while Ulf said:

"——I have borne you company before, Kristin, when you went out at night—methought 'twere but fitting I should go with you this time too——"

She breathed hard and heavily in the dark. Once she stumbled over somewhat, and Ulf caught her. After that he took her hand and led her. In a while the man heard that she was weeping as she went, and he asked her why she wept.

"I weep to think how good and faithful you have been to us, Ulf, all our days. What can I say——? I know well enough 'twas most for Erlend's sake, but almost I believe, kinsman—all our days you have judged of me more kindly than you had a right to, after what you first saw of my doings."

"I loved you, Kristin—no less than him." He was silent. Kristin felt that he was strongly stirred. Then he said:

"Therefore meseemed 'twas a hard errand when I sailed out hither to-day—I came to bring you such tidings as I myself deemed it hard to utter. God strengthen you, Kristin!"

"Is it Skule?" asked Kristin softly in a little. "Skule is dead?"

"No; Skule was well when I spoke with him yesterday—and now not many are dying in the town. But I had news from Tautra this morning——" He heard her sigh heavily once, but she said naught. A little after he said:

"'Tis ten days now since they died. There are but four brothers left alive in the cloister, and the island is all but swept clean of folk."

They were come now where the wood ended. Over the flat stretch of land in front the roaring of the sea and the wind came to meet them. One spot out in the dark shone white—the surf in a little bay, by a steep, light-hued sand-hill.

"She dwells there," said Kristin. Ulf felt that long, convulsive shudders went through her frame. He gripped her hand hard:

"You took this on yourself. Remember that, and lose not your wits now."

Kristin said, in a strangely thin, clear voice, that the blast caught and bore away:

"Now will Björgulf's dream come true—I trust in God's and Mary's grace."

Ulf tried to see her face—but 'twas too dark. They were walking on the strand—in some places 'twas so narrow under the bluffs that now and then a wave washed right up to their feet. They tramped forward over tangled heaps of seaweed and great stones. After a while they were ware of a dark hump in against the sandy bank.

"Stay here," said Ulf, shortly. He went forward and thrust against the door—then she heard him hew at the withy bands and thrust at the door again. Then she was ware that the door had fallen inwards, and he had gone in through the black hole.

'Twas not a night of heavy storm. But it was so dark that Kristin could see naught save the little flashes of foam that came and vanished the same instant on the lifting sea, and the shining of the waves breaking along the shores of the bay—and against the sand-dune she could make out that black hump. And it seemed to her that she was standing in a cavern of night, and that 'twas the forecourt of death. The roll of breaking waves and the hiss of their waters ebbing among the stones of the beach kept time with the blood-waves surging through her, though all the time 'twas as though her body must shiver in pieces, as a vessel of wood falls apart in staves—her breast ached as if something would burst it in sunder from within; her head felt hollow and empty and as 'twere rifted, and the unceasing wind wrapped her round and swept clean through her. She felt, with a strange listlessness, that she herself had surely caught the sickness now—but 'twas as though she looked that the darkness should be riven by a great light that would drown the roar of the sea with its thunder, and that in the horror of this she should perish. She drew up her hood, blown back from her head by the wind, wrapped the black nun's cloak close about her, and stood with her hands crossed beneath it—but it came not into her thought to pray; 'twas as though her soul had more than enough to do to work a way forth from its mansion trembling to its fall, and as though it tore at her breast with every breath.

She saw a light flare up within the hut. A little after, Ulf Haldorssön called out to her: "You must come hither and hold the light for me, Kristin"—he was standing in the doorway—as she came, he reached her a torch of some tarred wood.

A choking stench from the corpse met her, though the hut was so draughty and the door was gone. With staring eyes and mouth half open—and she felt her jaws and lips grow stiff the while and wooden—she looked round for the dead. But there was naught to see but a long bundle lying in the corner on the earthen floor, wrapped in Ulf's cloak.

He had torn loose some long planks from somewhere and laid the door upon them. Cursing his unhandy tools, he made notches and holes with his light axe and dagger, and strove to lash the door fast to the boards. Once or twice he looked up at her swiftly, and each time his dark, grey-bearded face grew more hard set.

"I marvel much how you had thought to get through this piece of work alone," he said as he wrought—then glanced up at her—but the stiff, death-like face in the red gleam of the tar brand was set and unmoved as ever—'twas the face of a dead woman or of one distraught. "Can you tell me that, Kristin?" he laughed harshly—but still 'twas of no avail. "Methinks now were the time for you to say a prayer."

Stiff and lifeless as ever, she began to speak:

"*Pater noster qui es in cælis. Adveniat regnum tuum Fiat voluntas tua sicut in cælo et in terra*——" Then she came to a stop.

Ulf looked at her. Then he took up the prayer:

"*Panem nostrum quotidianum da nobis hodie*——" Swiftly and firmly he said the Lord's prayer to the end, went over and made the sign of the cross over the bundle—swiftly and firmly he took it up and bore it to the bier that he had fashioned.

"Go you in front," he said. "Maybe 'tis somewhat heavier, but you will smell the stench less there. Throw away the torch—we can see more surely without it—and see you miss not your footing, Kristin—for I had liefer not have to take a hold of this poor body any more."

The struggling pain in her breast seemed to rise in revolt when she got the bier poles set upon her shoulders; her chest *would* not bear up the weight. But she set her teeth hard. So long as they went along the strand, where the wind blew strong, but little of the corpse smell came to her.

"Here I must draw it up first, I trow, and the bier after," said Ulf, when they were come to the steep slope they had climbed down.

"We can go a little farther on," said Kristin; "'tis there they come down with the seaweed sleighs—there 'tis not steep."

She spoke calmly, the man heard, and as in her right mind. And a fit of sweating and trembling took him, now it was over—he had deemed she must lose her wits that night.

They struggled forward along the sandy track that led across the flat towards the pine wood. The wind swept in freely here, but yet 'twas not as it had been down on the strand, and, as they drew farther and farther away from the roar of the beach, she felt it as a homefaring from the horror of utter darkness. Beside their path the ground showed lighter—'twas a cornfield that there had been none to reap. The scent of it, and the sight of the beaten-down straw, welcomed her home again —and her eyes filled with tears of sisterly pity—out of her own desolate terror and woe she was coming home to fellowship with the living and the dead.

At times, when the wind was right behind, the fearful carrion stench enwrapped her wholly, but yet 'twas not so awful as when she stood in the hut—for the night was full of fresh, wet, cold, cleansing streams of air.

And much stronger than the feeling that she bore a thing of dread upon the bier behind her, was the thought that Ulf Haldorssön was there, guarding her back against the black and living horror they were leaving behind—and whose roar sounded fainter and more faint.

When they were come to the edge of the fir woods they were ware of lights: "They are coming to meet us," said Ulf.

Soon after, they were met by a whole throng of men bearing pine-root torches, a couple of lanthorns and a bier covered with a pall—Sira Eiliv was with them, and Kristin saw with wonder that in the troop were many of the men who had been that same night in the churchyard, and that many of them were weeping. When they lifted the burthen from her shoulders she was like to fall. Sira Eiliv would have caught a hold of her, but she said quickly:

"Touch me not—come not near me—I have the pest myself; I feel it——"

But none the less Sira Eiliv stayed her up with a hand below her arm:

"Then be of good cheer, woman, remembering that our Lord has said: 'Inasmuch as ye have done it unto one of the least of these My brethren or sisters, ye have done it unto Me.' "

Kristin gazed at the priest. Then she looked across to where the men were shifting the body from the stretcher that Ulf had fashioned to the bier they had brought. Ulf's cloak slipped aside a little—the point of a worn-out shoe stuck out, dark wet in the light of the torches.

Kristin went across, kneeled between the poles of the bier, and kissed the shoe:

"God be gracious to you, sister—God give your soul joy in His light —God look in His mercy on us here in our darkness——"

Then it seemed to her as 'twere life itself that tore its way from out of her—a grinding, inconceivable pain, as though something within her, rooted fast in every outermost fibre of her limbs, were riven loose. All that was within her breast was torn out—she felt her throat full of it, her mouth filled with blood that tasted of salt and foul copper— next moment her whole dress in front was a glistening wet blackness— Jesus! is there so much blood in an old woman? she thought.

Ulf Haldorssön lifted her in his arms and bore her away.

At the gate of the cloister the nuns, bearing lighted candles, came to meet the train of men. Already Kristin scarce had her full senses, but she felt that she was half borne, half helped, through the door, and was ware of the whitewashed, vaulted room, filled with the flickering light of yellow candle flames and red pine torches, and of the tramp of feet rolling like a sea—but to the dying woman the light was like the shimmer of her own dying life-flame, and the footfalls on the flags as the rushing of the rivers of death rising up to meet her.

Then the candlelight spread out into a wider space—she was once again under the open, murky sky—in the courtyard—the flickering light played upon a grey stone wall with heavy buttresses and high, tall windows—the church. She was borne in someone's arms—'twas Ulf again—but now he seemed to take on for her the semblance of all who had ever borne her up. When she laid her arms about his neck and pressed her cheek against his stubbly throat, 'twas as though she were a child again with her father, but also as though she were clasping a child to her own bosom—— And behind his dark head there were red lights, and they seemed like the glow of the fire that nourishes all love.

——A little later she opened her eyes, and her mind was clear and calm. She was sitting, propped up, in a bed in the dormitory; a nun with a linen band over her lower face stood bending over her; she marked the smell of vinegar. 'Twas Sister Agnes, she knew by her eyes and the little red wart she had on her forehead. And now 'twas day—clear, grey light was sifting into the room from the little glass window. She had no great pain now—she was but wet through with sweat, woefully worn and weary, and her breast stung and smarted when she breathed. Greedily she drank down a soothing drink that Sister Agnes held to her mouth. But she was cold——

Kristin lay back on the pillows, and now she remembered all that had befallen the night before. The while dream fantasies were wholly gone —her wits must have wandered a little, she understood—but 'twas good that she had got this thing done, had saved the little boy, and hindered these poor folk from burdening their souls with such a hideous deed She knew she had need to be overjoyed—that *she* had been given grace to do this thing just before she was to die—and yet she could not rejoice as 'twas meet she should; 'twas more a quiet content she felt, as when she lay in her bed at home at Jörundgaard, tired out after a day's work well done. And she must thank Ulf too——

——She had spoken his name, and he must have been sitting hidden away by the door, and have heard her, for here he came across the room and stood before her bed. She reached out her hand to him, and he took and pressed it in a firm clasp.

Suddenly the dying woman grew restless; her hands fumbled under the folds of linen about her throat.

"What is it, Kristin?" asked Ulf.

"The cross," she whispered, and painfully drew forth her father's gilded cross. It had come to her mind that yesterday she had promised to make a gift for the soul's weal of that poor Steinunn. She had not remembered then that she had no possessions on earth any more. She owned naught that she could give, saving the cross she had had of her father—and then her bridal ring. She wore that on her finger still.

She drew it off and gazed at it. It lay heavy in her hand; 'twas pure gold, set with great red stones. Erlend—she thought—and it came upon her now 'twere liker she should give this away—she knew not wherefore, but it seemed that she ought. She shut her eyes in pain and held it out to Ulf:

"To whom would you give this?" he asked, low, and as she did not answer: "Mean you I should give it to Skule——?"

Kristin shook her head, her eyes tight closed.

"Steinunn—I promised—masses for her——"

She opened her eyes, and sought with them the ring where it lay in the smith's dusky palm. And her tears burst forth in a swift stream, for it seemed to her that never before had she understood to the full what it betokened. The life that ring had wed her to, that she had complained against, had murmured at, had raged at and defied—none the less she had loved it so, joyed in it so, both in good days and evil, that not one day had there been when 'twould not have seemed hard to give it back to God, nor one grief that she could have forgone without regret——

Ulf and the nun changed some words that she could not hear, and he went from the room. Kristin would have lifted her hand to dry her eyes, but she could not—the hand lay moveless on her breast. And now the pain within was sore; her hand felt so heavy, and it seemed as though the ring were on her finger still. Her head began to grow unclear again —she *must* see if 'twere true that the ring was gone, that she had not only dreamed she had given it away—— And now too she began to grow uncertain—all that had befallen last night: the child in the grave; the black sea with its swift little flashing waves; the corpse she had borne— she knew not whether she had dreamed it all or had been awake. And she had no strength to open her eyes.

"Sister," said the nun, "you must not sleep now—Ulf is gone to fetch a priest for you."

Kristin woke up fully again with a start, and fixed her eyes upon her hand. The gold ring was gone, that was sure enough—but there was a white, worn mark where it had been on her middle finger. It showed forth quite clearly on the rough brown flesh—like a scar of thin, white skin—she deemed she could make out two round spots on either side where the rubies had been, and somewhat like a little mark, an M, where the middle plate of gold had been pierced with the first letter of Mary Virgin's holy name.

And the last clear thought that formed in her brain was that she should die ere this mark had time to vanish—and she was glad. It seemed to her to be a mystery that she could not fathom, but which she knew most surely none the less, that God had held her fast in a covenant made for her without her knowledge by a love poured out upon her richly—and in despite of her self-will, in despite of her heavy, earthbound spirit, somewhat of this love had become *part* of her, had wrought in her like sunlight in the earth, had brought forth increase which not even the hottest flames of fleshly love nor its wildest bursts of wrath could lay waste wholly. A handmaiden of God had she been—a wayward, unruly servant, oftenest an eye-servant in her prayers and faithless in her heart, slothful and neglectful, impatient under correction, but little constant in her deeds—yet had he held her fast in his service, and under the glittering golden ring a mark had been set secretly upon her, showing that she was His handmaid, owned by the Lord and King who was now coming, borne by the priest's anointed hands, to give her freedom and salvation——

Soon after Sira Eiliv had given her the last oil and viaticum, Kristin Lavransdatter again lost the knowledge of all around. She lay in the sway of sore fits of blood-vomiting and burning fever, and the priest, who stayed by her, told the nuns that 'twas like to go quickly with her.

——Once or twice the dying woman came so far to herself that she knew this or the other face—Sira Eiliv's, the sister's—Lady Ragnhild herself was there once, and Ulf too she saw. She strove to show she knew them, and that she felt 'twas good they should be by her and wished her well. But to those who stood around it seemed as she were but fighting with her hands in the throes of death.

Once she saw Munan's face—her little son peeped in at her through a half-open door. Then he drew back his head, and the mother lay gazing at the door—if perchance the boy might peep out again. But instead came Lady Ragnhild and wiped her face with a wet cloth; and that too was good—— Then all things were lost in a dark red mist, and a roar, that first grew fearsomely; but then it died away little by little, and the red mist grew thinner and lighter, and at last 'twas like a fair morning mist ere the sun breaks through, and all sound ceased, and she knew that now she was dying——

Sira Eiliv and Ulf Haldorssön went out together from the room of death. In the doorway out to the cloister yard they stopped short——

Snow had fallen. None had marked it, of them who had sat by the woman while she fought with death. The while gleam from the steep church roof over against the two men was strangely dazzling; the tower shone white against the ash-grey sky. The snow lay so fine and white on all the window-mouldings, and all buttresses and jutting points, against the church's walls of grey hewn stone. And 'twas as though the two men lingered because they were loath to break with their footprints the thin coverlid of new-fallen snow.

They drank in the air. After the noisome smell that ever fills the sick-room of one pest-stricken, it tasted sweet—cool, and as it were a little thin and empty; but it seemed as though this snow-fall must have washed the air clean of all poison and pestilence—'twas as good as fresh spring water.

The bell in the tower began to ring again—the two looked up to where it swung behind the belfry bars. Small grains of snow loosened from the tower roof as it shook, rolled down, and grew to little balls—leaving spots where the black of the shingles showed through.

"This snow will scarce lie," said Ulf.

"No, 'twill melt, belike, before evening," answered the priest. There were pale golden rifts in the clouds, and a faint gleam of sunshine fell, as it were provingly, across the snow.

The men stood still. Then Ulf Haldorssön said low:

"I am thinking, Sira Eiliv—I will give some land to the church here —and a beaker of Lavrans Björgulfssön's that she gave me—to found a mass for her—and my foster-sons—and for him, Erlend, my kins-man——"

The priest answered as low, without looking at the man:

"——Meseems, too, you might think you had need to show your thankfulness to Him who led you hither yestereven—you may be well content, I trow, that 'twas granted you to help her through this night."

"Ay, 'twas that I thought of," said Ulf Haldorssön. Then he laughed a little: "And now could I well-nigh repent me, priest, that I have been so meek a man—towards her!"

"Bootless to waste time in such vain regrets," answered the priest.

"What mean you——?"

"I mean, 'tis but a man's sins that it boots him to repent," said the priest.

"Why so?"

"For that none is good saving God only. And we can do no good save of Him. So it boots not to repent a good deed, Ulf, for the good you have done cannot be undone; though all the hills should crash in ruin, yet would it stand——"

"Ay, ay. These be things I understand not, my Sira. I am weary——"

"Ay—and hungry too you may well be—you must come with me to the kitchen-house, Ulf," said the priest.

"Thanks, but I have no stomach to meat," said Ulf Haldorssön.

"None the less must you go with me and eat," said Sira Eiliv—he laid his hand on Ulf's sleeve and led him along with him. They went out in-to the courtyard and down towards the kitchen-house. Unwittingly, both men trod as lightly and charily as they could upon the new-fallen snow.

NOTES

NOTES

THE GARLAND

p.11 *1. The Garland*

THIS was the old Norwegian word (directly borrowed from the English) for the gilt circlet which it was the prerogative of maidens of gentle birth to wear, on state occasions, on their outspread hair. In the title of this book it connotes, besides that circlet, the wreath of golden flowers with which the Elf-maiden tempts Kristin (p.25), and also the bridal crown (p.233), which was an heirloom kept to be worn by brides during the wedding festivities.

p.13 *2. Jörundgaard, see Plan, p.929*

The houses of an old Norwegian manor-farm were generally grouped in two adjacent squares or oblongs around the "ind-tun" and the "ut-tun" (the "courtyard" and "farmyard" of this translation). The dwelling-houses and store-houses, etc., lay around the "ind-tun," and the farm-buildings (barns, cow-houses, goat and sheep-houses, etc.) round the "ut-tun." The stable divided the two yards, turning one gable to the "ind-tun" and the other to the "ut-tun." Small buildings of all kinds were erected whenever needed, and when a building, small or large, was no longer needed, it was usually suffered to fall to ruin by decay, unless its site happened to be needed for a new building. To this day the buildings on a big Gudbrandsdal farm may number thirty or forty—old grey wooden houses.

There were usually no fortifications round a mediæval manor, but the houses were joined together by wooden fences, pierced here and there by wicket-gates, and there was a larger gate closing the main entrance to the courtyard. The manor was approached by a so-called "street" (*gade*) leading up to it between fenced-in corn-fields.

The courtyard was of green sward, and the roofs of all houses were thatched with turf—fresh, green, and gay with flowers in wet summers, yellow and dry in dry years, which are common in Gudbrandsdal. All the houses were built of large logs of fir-wood.

928 NOTES

Every house originally contained only one single room (often with the addition of a loft-room in the case of the storehouses described below). Thus the usual word for room (*stue*) was also often used as meaning "house." By the time when this book opens, however, the original single large, log-built room had been supplemented by pent-houses (*svale*) made of "staves" (see Note 23), built around it on one, two, three, or all four sides, to shield the timbers of the main room from the weather and to keep out draughts. The penthouse was entered by a porch supported on wooden pillars and arches, and, along one side of the house, was usually divided by partitions into small rooms. One of these was the "outer room" (*forstue*), from which opened the main door of the living-room; others were closets (*kove* or *kleve*), used for the storage of chests, etc., or to hold a bed.

Cooking was done in a separate kitchen-house (*ildstue*), and there were also usually a brew-house (*bryghus*), a weaving-house (*vaevstue*) for the looms of the mistress and maids, as well as workshops—for all farming implements were made and repaired on the place. The smithy and the bath-house (for steam baths) were placed some distance off in the fields, on account of the danger of fire.

Across the courtyard from the main dwelling-houses was a row of storehouses (*bur;* in modern times usually built on pillars, for security from rats and mice, and hence called "stabbur")—log-houses, often two-storeyed. The ground-floor of a "bur" was for the storage of all kinds of produce—hides, butter, cheese and candles, loaves of bread, dried fish, salted meat, etc. A wealthy man, owning several farms besides his home farm, received his rents in kind, and the produce so received, as well as that of the home farm, was stored in these "bure." Hides, wool, fish, and other strong-smelling wares would be kept in one "bur," milk products, flour, and bread, etc., in another.

The most characteristic buildings of the older type were the hearth-room house (*aarestue*) and the storehouses (*bure*).

Page 930 shows a typical "aarestue," the old form of living-room. The two beds (built against the wall) were occupied, one by the master and mistress, often with one or more young children, the other by the elder children, or other members of the family. For those of the family for whom there was no room in the beds, sleeping-places were made up on the wall-benches. On the smaller farms the servants also lay on these benches; but on large places like Jörundgaard there were separate houses for the men-servants and the maids, and a

Plan of Jörundgaard

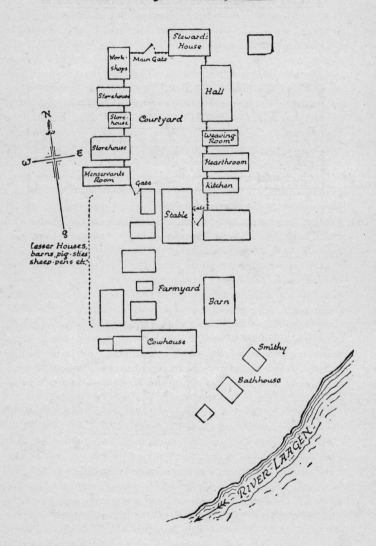

Plan of typical Hearthroom-house

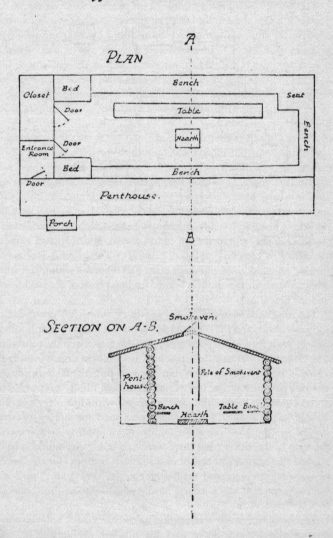

PLAN

A

Closet	Bed		Bench		Seat
	Door	Table			Bench
Entrance Room	Door	Hearth		
Door	Bed	Bench		
	Penthouse.			

Porch

B

SECTION ON A-B.

Smoke vent

Pent-house

Pole of Smokevent

Bench   Hearth   Table Bench

house for the bailiff and his wife (*raadmandsstue*), Jon and Tordis of this story.

The hearth (*aare*) in the middle of the hearth-room was the sacred centre of home and family life. The smoke escaped by a smoke-vent (*ljore*) in the ridge of the roof. A wooden frame, with a pane of bladder or horn in it, could be drawn across this vent, by means of a pole (*ljorestang*), which hung down into the room. As the smoke-vent had to lead into the open air, the hearth-house was necessarily originally a one-storeyed building. The hearth-room, being the warmest room, and therefore the one most used in winter, was sometimes called the winter-room.

The newer type of dwelling-house, such as the "hall" (*höienloftshus*) on Jörundgaard (see p.929), was built in two storeys, the difficulty as to heating being overcome, after a fashion, by the introduction of wall fireplaces in masonry (*murede ovne*) in both the ground-floor room and the loft-room. Such a fireplace was an erection of stone in clay, built into a corner of the room, opening to the room in an arch, with a flat or domed mantel. Usually, in country houses, such fireplaces had no sort of chimney, so that they of course smoked horribly, and came to be known as "smoke fireplaces" (*rökovne*). The ground-floor rooms of these new-fashioned buildings often had windows with glass panes, whereas the hearth-room was lighted exclusively from the smoke-vent and the door.

The upper storey of the "bur," known as "bursloft," protruded on the gable front, and the front portion formed a balcony (this, too, was called "svale"), with an open arcade looking down into the courtyard. The "bursloft" was usually reached by an outside staircase leading up into the balcony. The entire "bur" was (and is) the favourite architectural structure of the Norwegian farm, beautifully proportioned, of excellent workmanship, and adorned with fine carvings and wrought-iron locks. The "bursloft" was used for storing the best clothes and the jewellery of the family, spare bedding, weapons, and the arms of the master; but there were also beds in it, so that it could be used as a guest-chamber, or as a summer bedroom for the family, or for the daughters and maid-servants. As the whole "bur" was quite unheated, it was of course hardly possible to use the "bursloft" as a bedroom in the winter.

The space under the overhanging balcony (*bursvale*) is the favourite trysting-place of the lover and his mistress in Norwegian—and

Danish—ballads; and their conversation is often overheard by an eavesdropper in the dark balcony above.

The hall (*höienloftshus*) was built much on the same lines as the "bur" as to the overhanging upper storey, the balcony, and outside staircase; but was much larger, turned its side, instead of its gable, to the courtyard, and had its balcony (*svale* or *höeinloftsbro*) on the courtyard side. The large loft-room (the "upper hall" of this translation) was the state-room of the manor. The hall (*stue*) underneath was the new winter living-room of the master and his family, with its wall fireplace and window with glass panes.

p.13 *3. Lagmand*

The position and functions of the Swedish "Lagmand," with reference to the Assembly (Thing) of his province, seem to have been closely analogous to those of the Speaker of the early House of Commons in England. He was chosen by the people, presided over the meetings of the Thing, and when the King was present, it was the Lagmand's duty to communicate to him the resolutions of the Thing, and generally to represent the rights of the common people.

p.13 *4. King Haakon the Old*

King Haakon the Old is Haakon IV. (*Haakonssön*), the grandson of King Sverre and the hero of Ibsen's *The Pretenders*. The Kings of Norway during the period covered by this book, and that immediately preceding it, were:

Haakon IV   1217–1263
Magnus VI (Lagaböter)   1263–1280
Eirik   1280–1299
Haakon V   1299–1319
Magnus VII (Smek)   1319–1343

Magnus VII. was the grandson of Haakon V., being the son of Haakon's daughter Ingeborg (the Lady Ingebjörg of this book) by Duke Eirik of Sweden. He succeeded as a minor (see Part III., Chap. II.) to the thrones of Norway and Sweden. The complications arising from the vesting of the two crowns in one person form one of the springs of action in the second part of *Kristin Lavransdatter*, entitled *The Housewife (Husfruen)*.

p.15 *5. Domestic Arrangements of Priests*

For an explanation of Sira Eirik's domestic arrangements, see p.76.

"Sira" was the title (directly borrowed from the English) of parish priests.

p.20 *6. Peasant Guilds*

See Note 17.

pp.25, 26 *7. Elf-maiden or Dwarf Maiden*

For the many superstitions connected with the "mountain people" reference may be made to any of the collections of Norwegian Folk and Fairy Tales, of which the best known is the classical work of Asbjörnsen and Moe.

References to these superstitions occur on p.31 (where the Hamar Cathedral is likened, in Kristin's imagination, to the mountain folk's hall); p.51 (where Lady Aashild refers to the tales in which astute mortals get the better of the trolls or dwarfs); and p.176 (where the phrase translated "she goes around like one bewitched" is in the original "she goes about as if she were come out of the mountain").

p.37 *8. St. Sunniva and the Selje-men*

St. Sunniva was an Irish Princess who, to escape the unwelcome attentions of a heathen chief, fled across the sea, with a number of devoted followers, in a vessel without rudder, sail, or oars, and reached the Norwegian coast, where the party landed on the island of Selje. The refugees dwelt in caves of the hills, living on fish. The heathen inhabitants of the neighbouring mainland, missing from time to time some of their cattle left to graze on the islands off the coast, suspected that the strangers were responsible, and sent an armed party against them. On arrival, the party found that the caves occupied by the refugees had been blocked up and their occupants entombed by a great landslide.

Some time afterwards passers-by in boats noticed a strange light streaming from the spot where the strangers had been entombed. The matter reached the ears of the King, Olaf Tryggvesön (then engaged in his attempt to Christianize the land), and he proceeded to investigate, accompanied by a bishop. The caves were opened up, and, while the remains of Sunniva's companions showed their sanctity only by the emission of the supernatural light and of a sweet smell, the body of the Princess herself was found intact and uncorrupted. The King had a church built upon the spot and the body enshrined there. A hundred years later the body was removed to the Bergen Cathedral.

The Mass of the Selje-men was celebrated annually on the 8th July, in honour of Sunniva and her companions.

p.61 *9. Sewing-chair (Sömmestol)*

An arm-chair with a chest in the seat to hold the needle-work, sewing implements, etc.

p.84 *10. Birch-legs (Birkebeiner)*

The followers of King Sverre, so called because, in the many wanderings and privations in hills and wastes which eventually led that great adventurer to the throne, they covered their nakedness with garments of birch-bark. See Ibsen's *The Pretenders*.

p.89 *11. Hovedö*

The largest of the islands in the Christiania Fjord close to the town. Noted for the Cistercian monastery established there in the twelfth century by monks from Kirkstead in Lincolnshire. See p.108.

p.90 *12. Baron*

Lendermand in original. The lendermand was a high feudal dignitary holding a fief under the Crown in return for certain services to be rendered to the King in war and peace, which do not seem to have been prescribed generally, but were fixed separately in each particular case. Neither title nor fief was hereditary.

The title was changed to "Baron" by King Magnus Lagaböter, but continued to be personal, and not hereditary.

Haakon V., in pursuance of his policy of curbing the growth of the Norwegian aristocracy and preventing the formation of a feudal nobility on the European model, decreed (1308) that no more "barons" were to be made. The office and title thus became extinct.

p.92 *13. Commoners (Proventsfolk)*

The "proventsfolk" were what in modern times would be called boarders—laymen and women, chiefly elderly people, who were boarded and lodged by the convent on payment. Both monasteries and nunneries had such boarders, and as, in both cases, the boarders were of both sexes (in spite of the orders of the bishops to the contrary), they were lodged in houses outside the convent gates.

p.95 *14. Saint Days and Festivals*

As times and seasons are constantly marked in the text by Church festivals the dates of some of the less familiar of these may usefully be noted:

St. Gregory	13th February
St. Halvard	15th May
St. John	21st June
St. Lawrence (Lavrans)	10th August
St. Bartholomew	24th August
Birthday of the Virgin	8th September
Holy Cross Day (Elevation)	14th September
Michaelmas	29th September
St. Clement	23rd November

p.96 *15. Town "Dwelling-places" and "Yards"*

The word "gaard," which, when it refers to country-places, has been translated "manor" or "farm," was also used for the residences of families in towns and for the squares or yards occupied by merchants and shopkeepers. In the former case the word "dwelling-place" has been used, and in the latter the word "yard" (on the analogy of such places as Bell Yard or Tokenhouse Yard in London). In both cases the town "gaard" bore a general resemblance to the courtyard (*ind-tun*) part of a country "gaard," as described in Note 2; *i.e.* it consisted of a number of houses enclosing a square or oblong open space, the houses being connected by fences, and the entrance being through a gate.

Ordinarily several country families would share a town "gaard," each owning one or more of the houses.

Under regulations of King Haakon V. and his predecessors, each important trade was assigned its own "gaard," to which it was confined. Thus Mickle Yard (*Miklegaard*) was the quarter of the shoemakers and leather-merchants.

p.97 *16. Money*

What Lavrans gave Kristin as pocket-money was "a mark of silver in counted money." The following is a very brief and rough sketch of the somewhat confusing monetary arrangements of the period:

"A mark of pure silver" (*en mark brændt sölv*) was a *weight* of 215·8 grammes of silver, or rather less than $\frac{1}{2}$ lb. avoirdupois (227 grammes). The divisions of this weight were:

1 mark = 8 öre = 24 örtug = 240 penninger.

But the value of "a mark of silver in counted money" (*en mark sölv i tællede penger*) was only from $\frac{1}{3}$ to $\frac{1}{5}$ of that of a mark of pure silver.

Thus Kristin's pocket-money was equal in value to (say) $\frac{1}{3}$ of $\frac{1}{2}$, or $\frac{1}{6}$ lb. = $2\frac{1}{3}$ ounces of pure silver—the purchasing power of which was, of course, very greatly in excess of what it would be at the present day.

All sorts of foreign coins (including shillings and florins) were in circulation, being valued according to their weight and fineness.

On p.99 Kristin bargains with the Rostock men to pay them an "örtug," which, as shown above, was equal to 10 "penninger." We have rendered "örtug" by "silver ducat," a coin said to have had a value of about 3s. 4d., and "penning" by "silver penny," which we assume to have been worth about 4d.

On p.228 Erlend promises "four marks of silver (*fire mark sölv*) towards the rebuilding of the church. This was no doubt "pure silver," so that the contribution was equal in value to nearly 2 lb. avoirdupois of pure silver—a handsome offering, considering the high value of silver at the period.

p.106 *17. Peasant or Farmers' Guilds*

These included both freeholders and tenants, both men and women, and were associations for all kinds of mutual helpfulness and protection, ranging from insurance against fire (in times of peace—in wartime the functions of the guild were partially suspended) to the avenging of the deaths of members, and providing for the welfare of their souls by prayers and masses.

The guilds originated in heathen times, but were eagerly adopted and adapted by the Catholic Church. The various guilds were assigned patron Saints, and each held a great drinking festival on its Saint's day and the succeeding days. For these festivals somewhat elaborate regulations were laid down in the laws of the guilds, with a view to ensuring that they should be decorous and dignified functions. Thus quarrelling, foul language, and indecorous behaviour towards women were prohibited; no man was to become so drunk that he could not behave himself; no man was to bring his dogs or hawks into the hall; no child under three years old was to be admitted except in its mother's or foster-mother's charge; guild members were responsible for the behaviour of any outside guests they might introduce, etc.

The toasts usually included cups to the memory of the Saviour, the Virgin Mary, the Saints, and departed guild brothers and sisters.

p.118 *18. Mission to Vargöyhus*

Vargöyhus is now the little town of Vardö in the north-east of Finmark. The mission of Gissur Galle in 1310–1311 had for its object the regulation of the taxation taken from the Laplanders, and the erection or strengthening of a little fort on Vargöy (Wolf Island), which in the following centuries was the outpost of Norwegian power against Russian raids into Finmark.

p.126 *19. Barons and Wardens*

For Barons, see Note 12.

The word translated Wardens is in the original *sysselmænd*. The sysselmand was a high official in charge of a district, his duties being those of a chief administrator, military commander, and police officer. The appointment was made by the Crown from among gentlemen of distinction—at the period of this story a sysselmand would be usually, though not always, a knight. He had to maintain a certain number of armed men and subordinate officials. His remuneration varied in different cases—he might be paid directly by the Crown, or remunerated by a share in fines and fiefs.

p.200 20. The Sacred Blood at Schwerin

Some drops of blood from a bleeding Host preserved in a monastery at Schwerin were much venerated throughout the North, and were visited by many Scandinavian pilgrims.

p.206 21. Marriage Settlements

According to old Norwegian law and custom the normal marriage settlement was as follows:

The bride brought with her into the partnership her dowry (*hjemmefölge*); and the bridegroom was legally bound to transfer to her in addition an "extra-gift" (*tilgave*) which was fixed at one-third or one-half of the value of the dowry. The dowry and "extra-gift" together were generally calculated to be about one-third of the total joint estate.

This (dowry plus "extra-gift") was the wife's portion of the couple's joint possessions. If the marriage were childless, and the husband survived his wife, her family inherited it; if he died first, her family, in her name, had to see that the husband's heirs paid it over to the widow.

In the case of the wife's adultery, the husband kept the "extra-gift" in stewardship till her death; after which he was bound to pay it to her heirs.

In the case of the man's adultery (only with another man's wedded wife) his wife, if she chose to leave him, might claim that her portion be transferred to the stewardship of her kinsmen.

Husband and wife could not inherit from each other.

The "morning-gift" (*morgen-gave*) was a voluntary gift from the husband to his wife on the morning after marriage. It might often be much more valuable than the "extra-gift," the amount of which was fixed by law. But the bride's parents often let the bridegroom fix the intended "morning-gift" when the marriage-contract was made.

p.217 *22. Hatt*

Hatt was one of the incarnations of Odin.

p.224 *23. Stave-churches*

The mediæval "stav-kirker," the wooden churches of the inland districts of Norway, were built of "staves," very thick and heavy pieces of wood, something between a small plank and a small beam, cut out of the log, and hewn flat, by means of axes—the use of saws and planes being almost unknown. The roof was of tarred wooden shingles.

Norwegian Stave-church
Period 1150-1200.

To strengthen the building, and shield the walls against storms and rain, an open arcade or "cloister-way" (*svalgang*), with low arches opening outwards, ran all round the church, its roof of shingles being supported on the lower points of the roof construction of the aisles. It had small porches opposite the portals of the church. In this covered way men deposited their axes and swords before entering the church; penitents who had not received absolution must remain during the elevation of the Host in the mass, etc. It was also very much used as a meeting-place, for drawing up legal documents, for parish councils, arbitration meetings and the like.

The church had no tower, but a "ridge-turret"—a small turret on the ridge of the roof above the nave. This held the little bell. The great bells were in a separate belfry (stöpul) near the lych-gate.

Fine examples of mediæval "stave churches" still exist, or existed till recently, at Borgund, and at Hitterdal in Telemarken.

The words "stave" and "cloister-way" used in the text have been chosen as the least misleading renderings of the Norwegian "stav" and "svalgang." It should be borne in mind, however, that these "staves," though not unlike barrel staves in shape, were very much larger and thicker; and that the "cloister-way," instead of forming the *enceinte* of a courtyard, as a cloister usually does elsewhere, surrounded a solid building, and was open on its outer, not on its inner side.

p.228 *24. Land Measurement*

For "four marks of silver," see Note 16.

"Land to the value of sixty cows" is in the original "et markebol." Landed property in southern and central Norway was calculated in "öresbol" or "markebol" (one markebol = three öresbol). The "markebol" in Gudbrandsdal had a value varying from 16 to 20 silver marks, or from 40 to 60 cows, according to the quality of the land.

In western and northern Norway the unit of measurement was the "maanedsmatsbol," the literal meaning of which is: "as much land as will feed one man for one month."

p.234 *25. The Wedded Woman's Coif*

"Hustrulinet" in original. Only maidens wore their hair "down." For every woman who was not a maid, some kind of head-covering was obligatory. Wives tied up their hair and covered it with "hus-

trulinet"—the "long, snow-white, finely-pleated linen cloth" described on p.239. See also p.134.

p.247 *26. The Blood-eagle*

A method of execution (*riste blodörn paa ryggen*) practised in the Viking
age. The ribs were hewn from the backbone, and the lungs and heart
torn out through the wound. Sometimes a man would ask to be put
to death in this manner, to show his defiant spirit, and prove his
courage. So, at least, the sagas tell us.

NOTES

THE MISTRESS OF HUSABY

p.252 *1. Husaby (see Sketch Map)*

THE old manor of Husaby, comprising some thirty greater and smaller farms and homesteads, lies about twenty English miles southwest of Trondhjem (Nidaros). The head-quarter buildings are on a broad mountain slope above a little lake, about ten English miles from the nearest point on the Trondhjem Fjord (Birgsi), and between the great valleys of Guldal and Orkedal, which stretch southward up to the Dovrefjeld. The journey from Husaby to Nidaros would ordinarily be made by horse to Birgsi and thence by boat. The path followed by Kristin on her pilgrimage ran across the hills to the estuary of the Gula River, and thence across Bynes, the high promontory which shoots into the fjord between the Gula and Nid estuaries.

p.253 *2. Hall at Husaby (see Plan)*

The hall at Husaby was a large, ancient stone building, in the style of the Saga-times, when the chieftain and his house-carls dwelt and slept under one roof—the serving-women being quartered in a separate women's house (the "little hall" of this book).

Two rows of wooden pillars supported the roof. Between the line of pillars and the wall on each side was the sleeping-accommodation—two box-beds with doors at one end of the hall, and two broad fixed benches running the rest of the length of the wall. These benches were divided into sleeping-places for the warriors (originally called "rooms"), and were wide enough to admit of each man's keeping his belongings by him, while his weapons hung on the wall above him. As in the "hearth-room house" of the later mediæval manor, the room was heated from a hearth in the middle of the floor, and the only daylight came from the smoke-vent above this or from the door; but the hearth was much longer, and several fires were ordinarily kept burning on it, when artificial heat was required. On festival occasions long tables were set up—otherwise each man ate his meals sitting in his "room," with his porridge-bowl or his meat in his lap; or drank his beer sitting on the floor by the hearth.

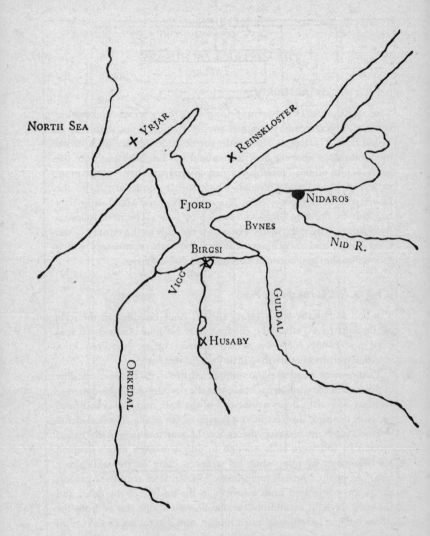

NORTH SEA

YRJAR

REINSKLOSTER

FJORD

NIDAROS

BYNES

NID R.

BIRGSI

VIGG

GULDAL

HUSABY

ORKEDAL

SKETCH MAP SHOWING HUSABY

E

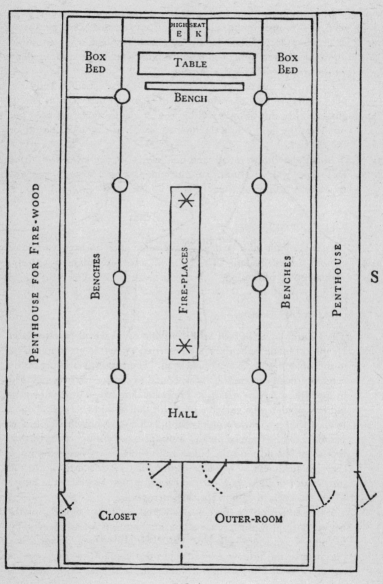

| HIGH | SEAT |
| E | K |

BOX BED

BOX BED

TABLE

BENCH

PENTHOUSE FOR FIRE-WOOD

BENCHES

BENCHES

PENTHOUSE

S

FIRE-PLACES

HALL

CLOSET

OUTER-ROOM

W

In later times, when a separate house was assigned to the serving-men, the "rooms" in the hall were left free to be used, when necessary, as sleeping-places for the family or guests. The high seat was moved up to the east end of the hall, and temporary tables were put up daily for the chief meal of the day (supper).

Later, yet further changes were, of course, made. Thus the plan shows the hall as arranged for the banquet described in Part I, chap. iii. By this time, it will be seen, a smaller table has been put up across the hall, before the high seat, with a loose outer bench for the servants.

Above the "outer room" and the "closet" at the lower end of the hall, there was, at Husaby, a loft-room (Margret's bower) reached by a ladder leading up from the hall.

p.299 *3. Gunnulf's Song*

Master Gunnulf must evidently have come upon an early version of the old English ballad, "The Falcon," and have adapted it freely, with an eye to edification.

p.300 *4. Lady Midwives*

The Church laws, as well as the custom, of mediæval Norway (and Denmark) made it the duty of all married women to act as midwives to the women of their neighbourhood. The housewives living in the neighbourhood (*grannekoner*) were bound to come, each accompanied by a serving-woman (*gridkone*). Professional midwives were unknown, but any woman who gained a name for skill in midwifery was bound to go wherever she was sent for within half a day's horseback journey. No fee could be claimed for this assistance, but custom required that the father should send the ladies and women away with gifts when they left his house. The value of the gifts was proportioned to the importance of the event—in the case of a first-born son the father would be expected to show special generosity.

When an heir to an estate was expected, the father should, months before, have prayed every neighbouring housewife of social standing to come to his wife's assistance. This was a matter of practical importance, as the ladies' evidence might be required to settle questions of inheritance. For instance, if the mother and child both died, the ladies could testify whether the child had been born alive and been christened, and whether it had died before or after its mother. In the former case the wife's family inherited her share of the joint estate; in the latter the husband inherited from the child. A conclave of *sages femmes* of quality would always be a guarantee as to the identity, etc. of an heir, if doubts of any kind arose.

Thus Erlend's failure to invite the ladies of the country-side to his wife's lying-in was a culpably rash, as well as a scandalous, omission.

p.335 5. *Trondhjem Cathedral*

In the steep sand-bank by the River Nid, where King Olav's body had lain buried the first winter after his death at the battle of Stiklestad (A.D. 1030), a spring welled up, the waters of which were credited with healing powers. On this site, first marked by a small chapel, a Bishop's Church, completed about the year 1057, was erected, in honour of Christ and St. Olav, the shrine containing the saint's remains being transferred to it from the wooden church in which his successors had lodged it.

In 1152 Norway was organised as an independent ecclesiastical province, and the Archbishopric of Nidaros created, by Cardinal Nicholas Breakspeare, afterwards Pope Hadrian IV. Shortly after, the building of the great Cathedral was begun, on the site of the existing Bishop's Church. "The man who had the most far-reaching influence on the work," says Professor Nordhagen, "was Eystein Erlandson, the imperious and highly gifted third Archbishop (1161–1188)." The work was begun in the Norman style, but, on returning from a three years' exile in England (1180–1183)—a result of his quarrel with the no less imperious and forceful King Sverre—Eystein brought with him the new ideas in architecture which had shortly before reached England and were even then being put into practice in the building of the choir of Canterbury Cathedral. Later, the work continued to be influenced by the contemporary developments of Gothic in England. Completed, in its first form, in the fourteenth century (about the period of this book), the Cathedral was the wonder of the North, and was sought by thousands of pilgrims, come to visit the shrine of the saint and the wonder-working well. The press was greatest at the time of the great Olav's Festival—the 29th July.

Feginsbrekka—"The Hill of Joy"—was the hill on the pilgrim's route from the top of which they first caught sight of the city and the Cathedral.

The first of numerous fires from which the Cathedral has suffered was that of 1328, referred to in this book. It was again swept by fire in 1432 and 1531, yet even as it stood half destroyed in 1567 it is described by a Norwegian writer of the period as "the crown, the flower and ornament of the kingdom." There were further visitations by fire in 1708 and 1719, so that in the eighteenth and nineteenth centuries its original glories were much obscured. Very elaborate schemes of restoration were put in hand towards the end of the nineteenth century, and have in great part been carried out; though the renovation of the west front remains to be completed.

p.345 6. Court of Six

Practically all nobles, and a great part of the landed gentry of Norway, were *hirdmænd* (in this book, translated "Guardsmen" or "King's-men"); that is to say, had at one time or another served in the King's household. Suits at law between such *hirdmænd* were referred, not to the ordinary *Things* (see Note 9), but to a special Court of Six (*seksmandsdom*), composed of six of the parties' fellow-*hirdmænd*.

p.345 7. Norway, 1319–1335

Magnus VII. (King of Norway 1319–1343) was the grandson of Haakon V., being the son of Haakon's daughter Ingeborg by Duke Eirik of Sweden. In 1318 Duke Eirik was murdered by his brother, King Birger. The party of the murdered Duke rose and drove away the King, making the baby prince Magnus King of Sweden in his place. The leader of their army was the gallant and handsome Danish knight, Knut Porse, who had been the Duke's loyal vassal.

Since Magnus was heir to the throne of Norway also, King Haakon on his death-bed foresaw a union of the two Crowns. He appointed eight Norwegian lords as a Council of State for the minor King, and made them swear solemnly to rule according to the laws of the country, and to keep out foreigners from all posts of influence, especially from the strongholds of the Crown. When, on the death of Haakon in 1319, Magnus became King of both countries, an agreement was entered into by the Councils of the two realms, providing for their independent relations and respective duties. The King's mother was given a very influential position in both countries.

She very soon began to abuse her power in favour of Knut Porse, and the attachment of the young widow to her champion became much talked of. Knut Porse's plan was to bring the then Danish province of Skaane (Scania in southern Sweden) by conquest under the Swedish Crown, and win a Dukedom for himself, so as to be in a position to marry the Lady Ingeborg. When, in 1321, King Magnus' little sister Eufemia was betrothed to a son of Duke Henry the Lion of Mecklenburg, in the presence of members of both the Swedish and Norwegian governments, a secret compact was made between the Duke and Sir Knut, by which the Duke pledged himself to furnish soldiers in support of the Skaane enterprise. Some Norwegian noblemen, among them Sir Munan Baardssön, who was an intimate friend of Sir Knut and Lady Ingeborg, attached their seals to this compact. And Lady Ingeborg, who had unlawfully carried the Great Seal out of Norway, tried by all means to raise funds for the war.

But in the summer of 1322 the Swedish lords met in parliament at Skara, and by a *coup d'etat* took all power out of the hands of the lady; and in February, 1323, the Norwegian nobles, under the leadership of Archbishop Eiliv, gathered at Oslo and followed the Swedish example. A young lord of the highest descent in the land and of great wealth, Sir Erling Vidkunssön, was made Regent of Norway, with the title of *Drotsete* (here translated High Steward), with the Council of nobles to assist him.

As a result of the union of the two Crowns, Norway had been dragged into the wars between Sweden and Russia, and for some years from 1323 onwards the Russians made a series of destructive raids on the coasts of Northern Norway, coming as far south as Haalogaland (the modern Nordland's Amt). Sir Erling took measures to defend the country, and achieved some success, but he wanted money badly, as Lady Ingeborg had left him an empty treasury. He sought assistance from the Bishops, as the Russians were accounted heretics or worse; the Archbishop stood by him, but Bishop Audfinn of Bergen refused help. In the years following, Erling had several quarrels with this Bishop, who was a staunch partisan of Lady Ingeborg. In particular the Bishop defended the lady's rights to some estates in his diocese, when, in 1326, she further enraged her native country by marrying Knut Porse, who, by one of the vicissitudes in the struggle between the Danish King, Christopher II., and his nobles, had now become a Danish Duke, Knut Porse, however, died in 1330, leaving his widow with two little sons, Haakon and Knut.

In 1326 peace was made between Norway and Russia, on terms not unfavourable to Norway.

In 1330 King Magnus, now sixteen years old, was declared to be of age, and Erling Vidkunssön resigned. King Magnus took up his stepfather's plan of winning Skaane, stayed on in Sweden, and made an old antagonist of Sir Erling's, Paal Baardsen, his Chancellor for Norway and bearer of the Great Seal. But when, in 1333, Paal was chosen Archbishop in succession to Archbishop Eiliv, Magnus failed to appoint a new Chancellor; and, as the King still stayed on in Sweden, always in want of money and demanding supplies, and leaving Norway without any lawful government, a party among the Norwegian nobles, headed by Erling Vidkunssön and the King's young cousins, Jon and Sigurd Haftorssön, rose against him. The matter was, however, settled the same year without bloodshed; the leaders of the revolt were forgiven, and kept their position and titles, King Magnus appointed Sir Ivar Ogmundssön *Drotsete* and Chancellor for Norway, the Council's powers were strengthened, and Norway once more had a working government. This seems to have been all that was aimed at by Erling Vidkunssön, whom history represents as an upright, honourable, brave and sensible man, though somewhat lacking in the vigour which achieves great things.

Erlend Nikulaussön's subsequent attempt to separate the Crowns of Norway and Sweden by placing Lady Ingeborg's son Haakon on the Norwegian throne has escaped the notice of history, which, however, records the wedding of King Magnus at Tunsberg in 1335 to the Countess Blanche of Namur.

p.349 *8. War Levies*

The word translated "levy" or "war levy" is in the original *leding*. All land-holders were bound to pay to the Crown an annual contribution (*leding*) towards the defence of the country. This was due in time of peace as well as in war-time; but they might be called on for additional voluntary assistance in emergencies.

Failure to pay the tax rendered the defaulter liable to fine. Lavrans undertakes to pay any fines that may be imposed on his tenants owing to their refusal to comply with the illegal demands made upon them under colour of the enforcement of the contribution.

p.361 9. *Things*

At the period of this book there were three classes of *Things* (popular assemblies):

I. The parish Thing (held ordinarily at regular intervals, but which could also be specially summoned) for the transaction of all sorts of local business. Appeals from its decisions could be taken to:

II. The county Thing (*Herreds*, or *Fylkesthing*), which was held in each *Fylke* (county) twice a year—in the middle of Lent, and three weeks after the return of the county representatives from the *Lagthing* (see below). These county assemblies were known as *sysselmandsthing*, as they were convened by the *sysselmand* (warden) of the county (see Note 12, *Wardens*). Lawsuits which were to be brought before a *Lagthing* must be announced at these county *Things*, and their sentences and decisions (arrived at by a jury, not by the *sysselmand*, who had no judicial functions) were appealable to the *Lagthing*.

III. The *Lagthing*. Norway was divided into four sections called *lagdömmer*, each of which had its annual *Lagthing*. These were known as *Frostathing*, *Gulathing*, *Eidsivathing and Borgarthing*, and, at the time of the story, all met on the same day, St. Botolph's day (17th June). The *Frostathing*, which represented the northern section of the country, met at Nidaros.

Each of the four *lagdömmer* was a complete legislative and judicial entity. The *Lagthing* was composed of representatives chosen by the *sysselmænd* from the members of the various county *Things*, and was attended by all the *sysselmænd* of the section, whose duty it was to follow the cases from their several counties, and to report the decisions and any new legislation, to the county *Things* summoned by them to meet three weeks after their return from the *Lagthing*.

The chairman of the *Lagthing* was known as the *Lagmand*. His functions corresponded roughly with those of the Speaker of the early House of Commons in England.

p.373 *10. Fourteenth-Century Rome*

Master Gunnulf had, of course, visited Rome during the so-called "Babylonian exile" of the Popes at Avignon, which began in 1305.

p.384 *11. Land Measurements*

The words here translated "half a hide" are in the original *to maaneds-matsbol*, meaning literally "two months'-meat's-area"—*i.e.* twice as much land as will feed one man for one month.

p.404 *12. Wardens*

The word translated "Warden" is in the original *sysselmand*. The *sysselmand* was a high official in charge of a district, roughly corresponding to a county in England, his duties being those of a chief administrator, military commander and chief police officer. The appointment was made by the Crown from among gentlemen of distinction—at the period of the story a *sysselmand* would be usually, though not always, a knight. He had to maintain a certain number of armed men and subordinate officials. His remuneration varied in different cases—he might be paid directly by the Crown or remunerated by a share in fines and fiefs.

Among other duties, the *sysselmand* had to hold each year in Lent a "wapinschaw" (*vaabenting*), at which he reviewed the weapons in the possession of the men of his district, to make sure that each man had the weapons he was bound by law to possess, according to his station. He had also to choose the delegates from his district to the annual *Lagthing* of his section of the country (see Note 9, *Things*), and to attend at the *Lagthing* to follow all cases relating to his district. Within three weeks from his return home he had to call a *sysselmands-thing* and there communicate to the people all decisions and sentences of the *Lagthing* affecting his district, all new laws passed, etc. He had to account for the fines and other dues of the crown to the Treasurer of his section of the country (see Note 15, *Treasurers*).

p.441 *13. Veöy*

A little island near Molde, where in the Middle Ages there was a small market town, with a couple of churches and a royal mansion.

p.473 *14. Grace to Criminals*

When a man had committed any offence punishable with outlawry (such as manslaughter or the abduction of a woman), he might, on making a payment to the Crown, be given leave to remain at his home under the protection of the law till his case was judged.

p.474 *15. Treasurers*

For purposes of financial administration, Norway was divided into four Treasury Districts (*fehirdsle*), each under a Treasurer (*fehirde*). The Treasurer of the district which had its head-quarters at Tunsberg was a sort of Minister of Finance, supervising the whole.

p.537 *16. Safe-Conduct*

As a *Hirdmand* (Guardsman—see Note 6), Erlend has the right to be tried by a court of his peers within the boundaries of the *lagdömme* (section—see note 9) where he is domiciled. Having appealed against the finding and sentence of the court on the ground of the illegality of its composition, and claimed a fresh trial, he is granted a safe-conduct in order that he may be taken outside the bounds of the *lagdömme* to be brought before the King. The effect of this is that, if he fails to make his peace with the King, he is entitled to be sent back in safety to his own *lagdömme*, there to be given a fresh trial or to suffer the execution of the sentence of the original court, according as his appeal is or is not admitted.

p.537 *17. Baagahus*

Now Baahus in Sweden, near Gothenburg. The boundary between Norway and Sweden at this time was the Göta River, and Baagahus was the Norwegian frontier town.

p.567 *18. Immunities of Freemen*

This passage, translated as literally as possible, would run: "why Erlend must not enjoy such personal immunities [*mandhelg*] as are the right of all men save thieves and nithings."

By the ancient laws every free man of Norway was guaranteed *mandhelg*—*i.e.* immunity from dishonouring bodily punishments and outrages against his person and honour. This involved, in Saga-times, his right to avenge himself and his kin.

NOTES

THE CROSS

p.643 *1. Grace-deed*

Simon, having committed an offence punishable with outlawry, has to obtain a grace-deed permitting him to remain at his home unmolested until his case is judged. See *The Mistress of Husaby*, Note 14.

p.675 *2. Debtors*

The word (*skyldnere* in the original) is, of course, used in the sense which it bears in the Lord's Prayer. In the text it has sometimes been necessary to render it by the equivalent phrase: "they that trespass against us."

p.706 *3. The Comb-maker's Seed*

King Sverre's putative father—the husband of his mother—was a comb-maker. He claimed to be an illegitimate son of King Sigurd Mund; but his opponents strenuously denied this.

p.759 *4. Friggja-grass*

Grass of Parnassus—*Parnassia palustris*. Popularly supposed to be an aphrodisiac, and hence named after the goddess of love.

p.784 *5. Oath with Compurgators*

The original has "*sættared eller tylvtared.*" In certain cases the accused might clear himself of a charge by taking oath to his innocence, along with five, or eleven, compurgators (*mededsmænd*). The oath with five compurgators was termed "*sættared,*" that with eleven, "*tylvtared.*" The compurgators swore, not to the facts of the case, but to their knowledge of the accused and their persuasion that he was telling the truth. According to Norse law, the compurgators in the case of a woman accused of an offence must be women.

p.883 *6. Rolling-breeches*

In the popular tales trolls are sometimes equipped with "rolling-breeches" (*trille-brok*)—breeches which enable them to lie down and roll rapidly after prey, or from their pursuers.

p.892 *7. Tart in Burgundy*

Now Tart l'Abbaye, in the Côte d'Or department, near Citeaux, the cradle of the Cistercian order. Tart was the mother house of all the Scandinavian Cistercian nunneries.

p.911 *8. Hel*

In Norse folk-lore the plague was personified as a hideous old woman carrying a rake and a broom. Where she used the rake, some part of the population survived; where she used the broom, she swept the country-side of every living soul. It would be natural, in the fourteenth century, for the popular imagination to identify her with Hel, the death goddess of the old mythology.

Knut Hamsun

The recent tremendous revival of interest in Knut Hamsun's work has its roots in his astonishingly contemporary qualities : a passionate concern with individual freedom, with the non-conforming outsider and the spiritual drop-out, combined with a wholly modern psychological awareness. Hamsun, like Hesse or Dostoievsky, is one of those writers who can create a new vision of the world for each new generation of readers.

'Hamsun has the qualities that belong to the very great, the completest omniscience about human nature' REBECCA WEST

Mysteries £1.25

'A gripping, haunting, tantalizing tale . . . the first of an exciting series' ARTHUR KOESTLER

'From the way I have marked up this new translation of the book it would seem as if I had never read it before : yet this must be the seventh or eighth time . . . it is closer to me than any other book I have read' HENRY MILLER

'This is no musuem piece redolent with the dust of literary respectability. It is as immediate and haunting as last night's dreams or nightmares' NEW YORK TIMES

Hunger £1

'The story of the semi-delirious "trip" of a young drop-out writer in search of his identity. It was published in 1890 . . . with a little scene-shifting, it could have been written today . . . he created a new style of writing . . . I wish you *bon appetit* with *Hunger*' ARTHUR KOESTLER

'What seems to us catastrophe his spirit experiences as a secret victory. *Hunger* is an amazing book' NEW STATESMAN

Knut Hamsun
Victoria 75p

'One of the great love stories of world literature' ARTHUR KOESTLER

No reader can fail to be spellbound by this beautiful and moving story of young love. The lovers are Johannes, the miller's son and Victoria, the daughter of the lord of the manor. Their moment of ecstasy is as transitory as their dreams. Yet, away from one another, they lead strangely incomplete lives. They resist what must in the end prove irresistible . . . for Victoria cannot live without Johannes.

'It triumphs as a sustained feat of shimmering lyricism'
NEW YORK TIMES

'One of the few books that actually produced tears dripping from cheek to chin' RACHEL BILLINGTON, COSMOPOLITAN

Bruno Schulz
The Street of Crocodiles £1.25

When Bruno Schulz was murdered by the Nazis in 1942 he had published only two works of fiction, *The Street of Crocodiles* being the first – a startling blend of the real and the fantastic in a collection of stories evoking the author's strange boyhood in a provincial Polish town and the characters – particularly his father: textile merchant and incorrigible fantasist – of the neighbourhood. This book brings to light a strange neglected genius.

'One of the great writers' JOHN UPDIKE

'A masterpiece of comic writing' V. S. PRITCHETT

'He wrote sometimes like Kafka, sometimes like Proust . . . reaching depths that neither of them reached' ISAAC BASHEVIS SINGER

Hermann Hesse
Autobiographical Writings £1.50

In this book, Hesse becomes his own biographer.
Rarely have biography and art been more fascinatingly interwoven.
Essential reading for all students and admirers of his work.

If The War Goes On . . . 80p

The faith in salvation via the 'Inward Way', so familiar to readers of
Hesse's fiction, is here expressed in his reflections on war and peace, on
politics and the individual.

Klingsor's Last Summer 90p

The work which Hesse called 'my revolutionary book'. Written in the same
period as SIDDHARTHA, these novellas describe a time of immense
emotional turmoil, of heightened pain, pleasure and perception in the lives
of three characters.

Knulp £1.25

The story of the loves and the wanderings of a vagabond whose role in
life is to bring 'a little nostalgia for freedom' into the lives of ordinary men.

Rosshalde 90p

The story of an artist's journey to self-discovery. By the Nobel Prizewinner
who is perhaps the most influential novelist of our time.

Hermann Hesse
Siddhartha £1.25

Siddhartha, son of a Brahmin, finds the Buddha but fails to find contentment as his disciple.

He takes the long and tortuous road in search of his destiny. It leads him through a season of passionate love in the arms of a beautiful courtesan, through the temptations of wealth and success, and through emotional conflict with his own son, before he reaches his final renunciation and ultimate self-knowledge.

This timeless story, the odyssey of a man in search of himself, is the perfect expression of Hesse's genius. Written in prose of biblical simplicity, *Siddhartha* is Hesse's great love story, a book that future generations may well call his masterpiece.

'A novel of great beauty . . . subtle distillation of wisdom, stylistic grace and symmetry of form' SUNDAY TIMES

Ian McEwan
The Cement Garden £1.25

'In many ways a shocking book, morbid, full of repellent imagery – and irresistibly readable . . . the effect achieved by McEwen's quiet, precise and sensuous touch is that of magic realism' NEW YORK REVIEW OF BOOKS

'A little masterpiece of appalling fascination' DAILY MAIL

'For a first novel, it is a darkly impressive piece of work . . . a touch of real fictional genius' THE TIMES

'Just about perfect' SPECTATOR

You can buy these and other Picador books from booksellers and newsagents; or direct from the following address:
Pan Books, Cavaye Place, London SW10 9PG
Send purchase price plus 20p for the first book and 10p for each additional book, to allow for postage and packing
Prices quoted are applicable in UK

While every effort is made to keep prices low, it is sometimes necessary to increase prices at short notice. Pan Books reserve the right to show on covers and charge new retail prices which may differ from those advertised in the text or elsewhere